D.H. Lawrence (1885-1930), dramatist and critic, was the son of a Nottinghamshire miner. Educated at University College, Nottingham, he was a schoolmaster before turning to writing as a profession. He and his wife, Frieda, lived mostly abroad in Italy, Australia and New Mexico. He died in Vence, near Nice. His most famous novels include *The Rainbow*, *Women in Love*, *Kangaroo*, and *Lady Chatterley's Lover*.

The Great Short Novels and Stories of
D.H. Lawrence

Robinson Publishing
London

Robinson Publishing
11 Shepherd House
5 Shepherd Street
London W1Y 7LD

Published by Robinson Publishing 1989

Cover: Portrait of a Girl by Albert Joseph Moore.
Reproduced courtesy of Fine Art Photographs.

ISBN 1 85487 007 6

Printed by Wm. Collins & Sons Ltd., Glasgow

10 9 8 7 6 5 4 3 2 1

CONTENTS

I

THEY had marched more than thirty kilometres since dawn, along the white, hot road where occasional thickets of trees threw a moment of shade, then out into the glare again. On either hand, the valley, wide and shallow, glittered with heat ; dark green patches of rye, pale young corn, fallow and meadow and black pine woods spread in a dull, hot diagram under a glistening sky. But right in front the mountains ranged across, pale blue and very still, snow gleaming gently out of the deep atmosphere. And towards the mountains, on and on, the regiment marched between the rye fields and the meadows, between the scraggy fruit trees set regularly on either side the high road. The burnished, dark green rye threw off a suffocating heat, the mountains drew gradually nearer and more distinct. While the feet of the soldiers grew hotter, sweat ran through their hair under their helmets, and their knapsacks could burn no more in contact with their shoulders, but seemed instead to give off a cold, prickly sensation.

He walked on and on in silence, staring at the mountains ahead, that rose sheer out of the land, and stood fold behind fold, half earth, half heaven, the heaven, the barrier with slits of soft snow, in the pale, bluish peaks.

He could now walk almost without pain. At the start, he had determined not to limp. It had made him sick to take the first steps, and during the first mile or so, he had compressed his breath, and the cold drops of sweat had stood on his forehead. But he had walked it off. What were they after all but bruises ! He had looked at them, as he was getting up : deep bruises on the backs of his thighs. And since he had made his first step in the morning, he had been conscious of them, till now he had a tight, hot place in his chest, with suppressing the pain, and holding himself in. There seemed no air when he breathed. But he walked almost lightly.

The Captain's hand had trembled at taking his coffee at dawn : his orderly saw it again. And he saw the fine figure of the Captain wheeling on horseback at the farm-house ahead, a handsome figure in pale blue uniform with facings of scarlet, and the metal gleaming on the black helmet and the sword-scabbard, and dark streaks of sweat coming on the silky bay horse. The orderly felt he was connected with that figure moving so suddenly on horseback : he followed it like a shadow, mute and inevitable and damned by it. And the officer was always aware of the tramp of the company behind, the march of his orderly among the men.

The Captain was a tall man of about forty, grey at the temples. He had a handsome, finely knit figure, and was one of the best horsemen in the West. His orderly, having to rub him down, admired the amazing riding-muscles of his loins.

For the rest, the orderly scarcely noticed the officer any more than he noticed himself. It was rarely he saw his master's face : he did not look at it. The Captain had reddish brown, stiff hair, that he wore short upon his skull. His moustache was also cut short and bristly over a full, brutal mouth. His face was rather rugged, the cheeks thin. Perhaps the man was the more handsome for the deep lines in his face, the irritable tension of his brow, which gave him the look of a man who fights with life. His fair eyebrows stood bushy over light blue eyes that were always flashing with cold fire.

He was a Prussian aristocrat, haughty and overbearing. But his mother had been a Polish Countess. Having made too many gambling debts when he was young, he had ruined his prospects in the Army, and remained an infantry captain. He had never married : his position did not allow of it, and no woman had ever moved him to it. His time he spent riding—occasionally he rode one of his own horses at the races—and at the officers' club. Now and then he took himself a mistress. But after such an event, he returned to duty with his brow still more tense, his eyes still more hostile and irritable. With the men, however, he was merely impersonal, though a devil when roused ; so that, on the whole, they feared him, but had no great aversion from him. They accepted him as the inevitable.

To his orderly he was at first cold and just and indifferent : he did not fuss over trifles. So that his servant knew practically nothing about him, except just what orders he would give, and how he wanted them obeyed. That was quite simple. Then the change gradually came.

The orderly was a youth of about twenty-two, of medium height, and well built. He had strong, heavy limbs, was swarthy, with a soft, black, young moustache. There was something altogether

warm and young about him. He had firmly marked eyebrows over
dark, expressionless eyes, that seemed never to have thought, only
to have received life direct through his senses, and acted straight
from instinct.

Gradually the officer had become aware of his servant's young,
vigorous, unconscious presence about him. He could not get away
from the sense of the youth's person, while he was in attendance.
It was like a warm flame upon the older man's tense, rigid body,
that had become almost unliving, fixed. There was something so
free and self-contained about him, and something in the young
fellow's movement, that made the officer aware of him. And this
irritated the Prussian. He did not choose to be touched into life
by his servant. He might easily have changed his man, but he did
not. He now very rarely looked direct at his orderly, but kept his
face averted, as if to avoid seeing him. And yet as the young soldier
moved unthinking about the apartment, the elder watched him,
and would notice the movement of his strong young shoulders
under the blue cloth, the bend of his neck. And it irritated him.
To see the soldier's young, brown, shapely peasant's hand grasp the
loaf or the wine-bottle sent a flash of hate or of anger through the
elder man's blood. It was not that the youth was clumsy : it
was rather the blind, instinctive sureness of movement of an un-
hampered young animal that irritated the officer to such a degree.

Once, when a bottle of wine had gone over, and the red gushed
out on to the tablecloth, the officer had started up with an oath,
and his eyes, bluey like fire, had held those of the confused youth for
a moment. It was a shock for the young soldier. He felt something
sink deeper, deeper into his soul, where nothing had ever gone
before. It left him rather blank and wondering. Some of his natural
completeness in himself was gone, a little uneasiness took its place.
And from that time an undiscovered feeling had held between the
two men.

Henceforward the orderly was afraid of really meeting his master.
His subconsciousness remembered those steely blue eyes and the
harsh brows, and did not intend to meet them again. So he always
stared past his master, and avoided him. Also, in a little anxiety,
he waited for the three months to have gone, when his time would be
up. He began to feel a constraint in the Captain's presence, and
the soldier even more than the officer wanted to be left alone, in his
neutrality as servant.

He had served the Captain for more than a year, and knew his
duty. This he performed easily, as if it were natural to him. The

officer and his commands he took for granted, as he took the sun and the rain, and he served as a matter of course. It did not implicate him personally.

But now if he were going to be forced into a personal interchange with his master he would be like a wild thing caught, he felt he must get away.

But the influence of the young soldier's being had penetrated through the officer's stiffened discipline, and perturbed the man in him. He, however, was a gentleman, with long, fine hands and cultivated movements, and was not going to allow such a thing as the stirring of his innate self. He was a man of passionate temper, who had always kept himself suppressed. Occasionally there had been a duel, an outburst before the soldiers. He knew himself to be always on the point of breaking out. But he kept himself hard to the idea of the Service. Whereas the young soldier seemed to live out his warm, full nature, to give it off in his very movements, which had a certain zest, such as wild animals have in free movement. And this irritated the officer more and more.

In spite of himself, the Captain could not regain his neutrality of feeling towards his orderly. Nor could he leave the man alone. In spite of himself, he watched him, gave him sharp orders, tried to take up as much of his time as possible. Sometimes he flew into a rage with the young soldier, and bullied him. Then the orderly shut himself off, as it were out of earshot, and waited, with sullen, flushed face, for the end of the noise. The words never pierced to his intelligence, he made himself, protectively, impervious to the feelings of his master.

He had a scar on his left thumb, a deep seam going across the knuckle. The officer had long suffered from it, and wanted to do something to it. Still it was there, ugly and brutal on the young, brown hand. At last the Captain's reserve gave way. One day, as the orderly was smoothing out the tablecloth, the officer pinned down his thumb with a pencil, asking :

" How did you come by that ? "

The young man winced and drew back at attention.

" A wood axe, Herr Hauptmann," he answered.

The officer waited for further explanation. None came. The orderly went about his duties. The elder man was sullenly angry. His servant avoided him. And the next day he had to use all his will-power to avoid seeing the scarred thumb. He wanted to get hold of it and—— A hot flame ran in his blood.

He knew his servant would soon be free, and would be glad. As yet, the soldier had held himself off from the elder man. The Captain grew madly irritable. He could not rest when the soldier was away, and when he was present, he glared at him with tormented eyes. He hated those fine, black brows over the unmeaning, dark eyes, he was infuriated by the free movement of the handsome limbs, which no military discipline could make stiff. And he became harsh and cruelly bullying, using contempt and satire. The young soldier only grew more mute and expressionless.

" What cattle were you bred by, that you can't keep straight eyes ? Look me in the eyes when I speak to you."

And the soldier turned his dark eyes to the other's face, but there was no sight in them : he stared with the slightest possible cast, holding back his sight, perceiving the blue of his master's eyes, but receiving no look from them. And the elder man went pale, and his reddish eyebrows twitched. He gave his order, barrenly.

Once he flung a heavy military glove into the young soldier's face. Then he had the satisfaction of seeing the black eyes flare up into his own, like a blaze when straw is thrown on a fire. And he had laughed with a little tremor and a sneer.

But there were only two months more. The youth instinctively tried to keep himself intact : he tried to serve the officer as if the latter were an abstract authority and not a man. All his instinct was to avoid personal contact, even definite hate. But in spite of himself the hate grew, responsive to the officer's passion. However, he put it in the background. When he had left the Army he could dare acknowledge it. By nature he was active, and had many friends. He thought what amazing good fellows they were. Bu without knowing it, he was alone. Now this solitariness was intensified. It would carry him through his term. But the officer seemed to be going irritably insane, and the youth was deeply frightened.

The soldier had a sweetheart, a girl from the mountains, independent and primitive. The two walked together, rather silently. He went with her, not to talk, but to have his arm round her, and for the physical contact. This eased him, made it easier for him to ignore the Captain ; for he could rest with her held fast against his chest. And she, in some unspoken fashion, was there for him. They loved each other.

The Captain perceived it, and was mad with irritation. He kept the young man engaged all the evenings long, and took pleasure in the dark look that came on his face. Occasionally, the eyes of the two men met, those of the younger sullen and dark, doggedly unalterable, those of the elder sneering with restless contempt.

The officer tried hard not to admit the passion that had got hold of him. He would not know that his feeling for his orderly was anything but that of a man incensed by his stupid, perverse servant. So, keeping quite justified and conventional in his consciousness, he let the other thing run on. His nerves, however, were suffering. At last he slung the end of a belt in his servant's face. When he saw the youth start back, the pain-tears in his eyes and the blood on his mouth, he had felt at once a thrill of deep pleasure and of shame.

But this, he acknowledged to himself, was a thing he had never done before. The fellow was too exasperating. His own nerves must be going to pieces. He went away for some days with a woman.

It was a mockery of pleasure. He simply did not want the woman. But he stayed on for his time. At the end of it, he came back in an agony of irritation, torment, and misery. He rode all the evening, then came straight in to supper. His orderly was out. The officer sat with his long, fine hands lying on the table, perfectly still, and all his blood seemed to be corroding.

At last his servant entered. He watched the strong, easy young figure, the fine eyebrows, the thick black hair. In a week's time the youth had got back his old well-being. The hands of the officer twitched and seemed to be full of mad flame. The young man stood at attention, unmoving, shut off.

The meal went in silence. But the orderly seemed eager. He made a clatter with the dishes.

" Are you in a hurry ? " asked the officer, watching the intent, warm face of his servant. The other did not reply.

" Will you answer my question ? " said the Captain.

" Yes, sir," replied the orderly, standing with his pile of deep Army plates. The Captain waited, looked at him, then asked again :

" Are you in a hurry ? "

" Yes, sir," came the answer, that sent a flash through the listener.

" For what ? "

" I was going out, sir."

" I want you this evening."

There was a moment's hesitation. The officer had a curious stiffness of countenance.

" Yes, sir," replied the servant, in his throat.

" I want you to-morrow evening also—in fact you may consider your evenings occupied, unless I give you leave."

The mouth with the young moustache set close.

" Yes, sir," answered the orderly, loosening his lips for a moment. He again turned to the door.

" And why have you a piece of pencil in your ear ? "

The orderly hesitated, then continued on his way without answering. He set the plates in a pile outside the door, took the stump of pencil from his ear, and put it in his pocket. He had been copying a verse for his sweetheart's birthday card. He returned to finish clearing the table. The officer's eyes were dancing, he had a little, eager smile.

" Why have you a piece of pencil in your ear ? " he asked.

The orderly took his hands full of dishes. His master was standing near the great green stove, a little smile on his face, his chin thrust forward. When the young soldier saw him his heart suddenly ran hot. He felt blind. Instead of answering, he turned dazedly to the door. As he was crouching to set down the dishes, he was pitched forward by a kick from behind. The pots went in a stream down the stairs, he clung to the pillar of the banisters. And as he was rising he was kicked heavily again and again, so that he clung sickly to the post for some moments. His master had gone swiftly into the room and closed the door. The maid-servant downstairs looked up the staircase and made a mocking face at the crockery disaster.

The officer's heart was plunging. He poured himself a glass of wine, part of which he spilled on the floor, and gulped the remainder, leaning against the cool, green stove. He heard his man collecting the dishes from the stairs. Pale, as if intoxicated, he waited. The servant entered again. The Captain's heart gave a pang, as of pleasure, seeing the young fellow bewildered and uncertain on his feet, with pain.

" Schöner ! " he said.

The soldier was a little slower in coming to attention.

" Yes, sir ! "

The youth stood before him, with pathetic young moustache, and fine eyebrows very distinct on his forehead of dark marble.

" I asked you a question."

" Yes, sir."

The officer's tone bit like acid.

" Why had you a pencil in your ear ? "

Again the servant's heart ran hot, and he could not breathe. With dark, strained eyes, he looked at the officer, as if fascinated. And he stood there sturdily planted, unconscious. The withering smile came into the Captain's eyes, and he lifted his foot.

" I—I forgot it—sir," panted the soldier, his dark eyes fixed on the other man's dancing blue ones.

" What was it doing there ? "

He saw the young man's breast heaving as he made an effort for words.

" I had been writing."

" Writing what ? "

Again the soldier looked him up and down. The officer could hear him panting. The smile came into the blue eyes. The soldier worked his dry throat, but could not speak. Suddenly the smile lit like a flame on the officer's face, and a kick came heavily against the orderly's thigh. The youth moved a pace sideways. His face went dead, with two black, staring eyes.

" Well ? " said the officer.

The orderly's mouth had gone dry, and his tongue rubbed in it as on dry brown-paper. He worked his throat. The officer raised his foot. The servant went stiff.

" Some poetry, sir," came the crackling, unrecognizable sound of his voice.

" Poetry, what poetry ? " asked the Captain, with a sickly smile.

Again there was the working in the throat. The Captain's heart had suddenly gone down heavily, and he stood sick and tired.

" For my girl, sir," he heard the dry, inhuman sound.

" Oh ! " he said, turning away. " Clear the table."

" Click ! " went the soldier's throat ; then again, " click ! " and then the half-articulate :

" Yes, sir."

The young soldier was gone, looking old, and walking heavily.

The officer, left alone, held himself rigid, to prevent himself from thinking. His instinct warned him that he must not think. Deep inside him was the intense gratification of his passion, still working powerfully. Then there was a counter-action, a horrible breaking down of something inside him, a whole agony of reaction. He stood there for an hour motionless, a chaos of sensations, but rigid with a will to keep blank his consciousness, to prevent his mind grasping. And he held himself so until the worst of the stress had passed, when he began to drink, drank himself to an intoxication, till he slept obliterated. When he woke in the morning he was shaken to the base of his nature. But he had fought off the realization of what he had done. He had prevented his mind from taking it in, had suppressed it along with his instincts, and the conscious man had nothing to do with it. He felt only as after a bout of intoxication, weak, but the affair itself all dim and not to be recovered. Of the drunkenness of his passion he successfully refused remembrance. And when his orderly appeared with coffee, the officer assumed the same self he had had the morning before. He refused the event of the past night—denied it had ever been—and was successful in his denial. He had not done any such thing—not he himself. Whatever there might be lay at the door of a stupid, insubordinate servant.

The orderly had gone about in a stupor all the evening. He drank some beer because he was parched, but not much, the alcohol made his feeling come back, and he could not bear it. He was dulled, as if nine-tenths of the ordinary man in him were inert. He crawled about disfigured. Still, when he thought of the kicks, he went sick, and when he thought of the threat of more kicking, in the room afterwards, his heart went hot and faint, and he panted, remembering the one that had come. He had been forced to say, " For my girl." He was much too done even to want to cry. His mouth hung slightly open, like an idiot's. He felt vacant, and wasted. So, he wandered at his work, painfully, and very slowly and clumsily, fumbling blindly with the brushes, and finding it difficult, when he sat down, to summon the energy to move again. His limbs, his jaw, were slack and nerveless. But he was very tired. He got to bed at last, and slept inert, relaxed, in a sleep that was rather stupor than slumber, a dead night of stupefaction shot through with gleams of anguish.

In the morning were the manœuvres. But he woke even before the bugle sounded. The painful ache in his chest, the dryness of his throat, the awful steady feeling of misery made his eyes come awake and dreary at once. He knew, without thinking, what had happened. And he knew that the day had come again, when he must go on with his round. The last bit of darkness was being pushed out of the room. He would have to move his inert body and go on. He was so young, and had known so little trouble, that he was bewildered. He only wished it would stay night, so that he could lie still, covered up by the darkness. And yet nothing would prevent the day from coming, nothing would save him from having to get up and saddle the Captain's horse, and make the Captain's coffee. It was there, inevitable. And then, he thought, it was impossible. Yet they would not leave him free. He must go and take the coffee to the Captain. He was too stunned to understand it. He only knew it was inevitable—inevitable, however long he lay inert.

At last, after heaving at himself, for he seemed to be a mass of inertia, he got up. But he had to force every one of his movements from behind, with his will. He felt lost, and dazed, and helpless. Then he clutched hold of the bed, the pain was so keen. And looking at his thighs he saw the darker bruises on his swarthy flesh, and he knew that if he pressed one of his fingers on one of the bruises, he should faint. But he did not want to faint—he did not want anybody to know. No one should ever know. It was between him and the Captain. There were only the two people in the world now—himself and the Captain.

Slowly, economically, he got dressed and forced himself to walk. Everything was obscure, except just what he had his hands on. But he managed to get through his work. The very pain revived his dull senses. The worst remained yet. He took the tray and went up to the Captain's room. The officer, pale and heavy, sat at the table. The orderly, as he saluted, felt himself put out of existence. He stood still for a moment submitting to his own nullification—then he gathered himself, seemed to regain himself, and then the Captain began to grow vague, unreal, and the younger soldier's heart beat up. He clung to this situation—that the Captain did not exist—so that he himself might live. But when he saw his officer's hand tremble as he took the coffee, he felt everything falling shattered. And he went away, feeling as if he himself were coming to pieces, disintegrated. And when the Captain was there on horseback, giving orders, while he himself stood, with rifle and knapsack, sick with pain, he felt as if he must shut his eyes—as if he must shut his eyes on everything. It was only the long agony of marching with a parched throat that filled him with one single, sleep-heavy intention : to save himself.

II

He was getting used even to his parched throat. That the snowy peaks were radiant among the sky, that the whity-green glacier-river twisted through its pale shoals, in the valley below, seemed almost supernatural. But he was going mad with fever and thirst. He plodded on uncomplaining. He did not want to speak, not to anybody. There were two gulls, like flakes of water and snow, over the river. The scent of green rye soaked in sunshine came like a sickness. And the march continued, monotonously, almost like a bad sleep.

At the next farm-house, which stood low and broad near the high road, tubs of water had been put out. The soldiers clustered round to drink. They took off their helmets, and the steam mounted from their wet hair. The Captain sat on horseback, watching. He needed to see his orderly. His helmet threw a dark shadow over his light, fierce eyes, but his moustache and mouth and chin were distinct in the sunshine. The orderly must move under the presence of the figure of the horseman. It was not that he was afraid, or cowed. It was as if he was disembowelled, made empty, like an empty shell. He felt himself as nothing, a shadow creeping under the sunshine. And, thirsty as he was, he could scarcely drink, feeling the Captain near him. He would not take off his helmet to wipe his wet hair. He wanted to stay in shadow, not to be forced into consciousness. Starting, he saw the light heel of the officer prick the belly of the horse ; the Captain cantered away, and he himself could relapse into vacancy.

Nothing, however, could give him back his living place in the hot, bright morning. He felt like a gap among it all. Whereas the Captain was prouder, overriding. A hot flash went through the young servant's body. The Captain was firmer and prouder with life, he himself was empty as a shadow. Again the flash went through him, dazing him out. But his heart ran a little firmer.

The company turned up the hill, to make a loop for the return. Below, from among the trees, the farm-bell clanged. He saw the labourers, mowing bare-foot at the thick grass, leave off their work and go downhill, their scythes hanging over their shoulders, like long, bright claws curving down behind them. They seemed like dream-people, as if they had no relation to himself. He felt as in a blackish dream : as if all the other things were there and had form, but he himself was only a consciousness, a gap that could think and perceive.

The soldiers were tramping silently up the glaring hill-side. Gradually his head began to revolve, slowly, rhythmically. Sometimes it was dark before his eyes, as if he saw this world through a smoked glass, frail shadows and unreal. It gave him a pain in his head to walk.

The air was too scented, it gave no breath. All the lush green-stuff seemed to be issuing its sap, till the air was deathly, sickly with the smell of greenness. There was the perfume of clover, like pure honey and bees. Then there grew a faint acrid tang—they were near the beeches ; and then a queer clattering noise, and a suffocating, hideous smell ; they were passing a flock of sheep, a shepherd in a black smock, holding his crook. Why should the sheep huddle together under this fierce sun ? He felt that the shepherd would not see him, though he could see the shepherd.

At last there was the halt. They stacked rifles in a conical stack, put down their kit in a scattered circle around it, and dispersed a little, sitting on a small knoll high on the hill-side. The chatter began. The soldiers were steaming with heat, but were lively. He sat still, seeing the blue mountains rising upon the land, twenty kilometres away. There was a blue fold in the ranges, then out of that, at the foot, the broad, pale bed of the river, stretches of whity-green water between pinkish-grey shoals among the dark pine woods. There it was, spread out a long way off. And it seemed to come downhill, the river. There was a raft being steered, a mile away. It was a strange country. Nearer, a red-roofed, broad farm with white base and square dots of windows crouched beside the wall of beech foliage on the wood's edge. There were long strips of rye and clover and pale green corn. And just at his feet, below the knoll, was a darkish bog, where globe flowers stood breathless still on their slim stalks. And some of the pale gold bubbles were burst, and a broken fragment hung in the air. He thought he was going to sleep.

Suddenly something moved into this coloured mirage before his eyes. The Captain, a small, light-blue and scarlet figure, was trotting evenly between the strips of corn, along the level brow of the hill. And the man making flag-signals was coming on. Proud and sure moved the horseman's figure, the quick, bright thing, in which was concentrated all the light of this morning, which for the rest lay a fragile, shining shadow. Submissive, apathetic, the young soldier sat and stared. But as the horse slowed to a walk, coming up the last steep path, the great flash flared over the body and soul of the orderly. He sat waiting. The back of his head felt as if it were weighted with a heavy piece of fire. He did not want to eat. His hands trembled slightly as he moved them. Meanwhile the officer on horseback was approaching slowly and proudly. The tension grew in the orderly's soul. Then again, seeing the Captain ease himself on the saddle, the flash blazed through him.

The Captain looked at the patch of light blue and scarlet, and dark heads, scattered closely on the hill-side. It pleased him. The command pleased him. And he was feeling proud. His orderly was among them in common subjection. The officer rose a little on his stirrups to look. The young soldier sat with averted, dumb face. The Captain relaxed on his seat. His slim-legged, beautiful horse, brown as a beech nut, walked proudly uphill. The Captain passed into the zone of the company's atmosphere : a hot smell of men, of sweat, of leather. He knew it very well. After a word with the lieutenant, he went a few paces higher, and sat there, a dominant figure, his sweat-marked horse swishing its tail, while he looked down on his men, on his orderly, a nonentity among the crowd.

The young soldier's heart was like fire in his chest, and he breathed with difficulty. The officer, looking downhill, saw three of the young soldiers, two pails of water between them, staggering across a sunny green field. A table had been set up under a tree, and there the slim lieutenant stood, importantly busy. Then the Captain summoned himself to an act of courage. He called his orderly.

The flame leapt into the young soldier's throat as he heard the command, and he rose blindly, stifled. He saluted, standing below the officer. He did not look up. But there was the flicker in the Captain's voice.

" Go to the inn and fetch me . . . " the officer gave his commands. " Quick ! " he added.

At the last word, the heart of the servant leapt with a flash, and he felt the strength come over his body. But he turned in mechanical obedience, and set off at a heavy run downhill, looking almost like a bear, his trousers bagging over his military boots. And the officer watched this blind, plunging run all the way.

But it was only the outside of the orderly's body that was obeying so humbly and mechanically. Inside had gradually accumulated a core into which all the energy of that young life was compact and concentrated. He executed his commission, and plodded quickly back uphill. There was a pain in his head as he walked that made him twist his features unknowingly. But hard there in the centre of his chest was himself, himself, firm, and not to be plucked to pieces.

The Captain had gone up into the wood. The orderly plodded through the hot, powerfully smelling zone of the company's atmosphere. He had a curious mass of energy inside him now. The Captain was less real than himself. He approached the green entrance to the wood. There, in the half-shade, he saw the horse standing, the sunshine and the flickering shadow of leaves dancing over his brown body. There was a clearing where timber had lately been felled. Here, in the gold-green shade beside the brilliant cup of sunshine, stood two figures, blue and pink, the bits of pink showing out plainly. The Captain was talking to his lieutenant.

The orderly stood on the edge of the bright clearing, where great trunks of trees, stripped and glistening, lay stretched like naked, brown-skinned bodies. Chips of wood littered the trampled floor, like splashed light, and the bases of the felled trees stood here and there, with their raw, level tops. Beyond was the brilliant, sunlit green of a beech.

" Then I will ride forward," the orderly heard his Captain say. The lieutenant saluted and strode away. He himself went forward. A hot flash passed through his belly, as he tramped towards his officer.

The Captain watched the rather heavy figure of the young soldier stumble forward, and his veins, too, ran hot. This was to be man to man between them. He yielded before the solid, stumbling figure with bent head. The orderly stooped and put the food on a level-sawn tree-base. The Captain watched the glistening, sun-inflamed, naked hands. He wanted to speak to the young soldier, but could not. The servant propped a bottle against his thigh, pressed open the cork, and poured out the beer into the mug. He kept his head bent. The Captain accepted the mug.

" Hot ! " he said, as if amiably.

The flame sprang out of the orderly's heart, nearly suffocating him.

" Yes, sir," he replied, between shut teeth.

And he heard the sound of the Captain's drinking, and he clenched his fists, such a strong torment came into his wrists. Then came the faint clang of the closing of the pot-lid. He looked up. The Captain was watching him. He glanced swiftly away. Then he saw the officer stoop and take a piece of bread from the tree-base. Again the flash of flame went through the young soldier, seeing the stiff body stoop beneath him, and his hands jerked. He looked away. He could feel the officer was nervous. The bread fell as it was being broken. The officer ate the other piece. The two men stood tense and still, the master laboriously chewing his bread, the servant staring with averted face, his fist clenched.

Then the young soldier started. The officer had pressed open the lid of the mug again. The orderly watched the lid of the mug, and the white hand that clenched the handle, as if he were fascinated. It was raised. The youth followed it with his eyes. And then he saw the thin, strong throat of the elder man moving up and down as he drank, the strong jaw working. And the instinct which had been jerking at the young man's wrists suddenly jerked free. He jumped, feeling as if it were rent in two by a strong flame.

The spur of the officer caught in a tree-root, he went down backwards with a crash, the middle of his back thudding sickeningly against a sharp-edged tree-base, the pot flying away. And in a second the orderly, with serious, earnest young face, and under-lip between his teeth, had got his knee in the officer's chest and was pressing the chin backward over the farther edge of the tree-stump, pressing, with all his heart behind in a passion of relief, the tension of his wrists exquisite with relief. And with the base of his palms he shoved at the chin, with all his might. And it was pleasant, too, to have that chin, that hard jaw already slightly rough with beard, in his hands. He did not relax one hair's breadth, but, all the force of all his blood exulting in his thrust, he shoved back the head of the other man, till there was a little " cluck " and a crunching sensation. Then he felt as if his head went to vapour. Heavy convulsions shook the body of the officer, frightening and horrifying the young soldier. Yet it pleased him, too, to repress them. It pleased him to keep his hands pressing back the chin, to feel the chest of the other man yield in expiration to the weight of his strong, young knees, to feel the hard twitchings of the prostrate body jerking his own whole frame, which was pressed down on it.

But it went still. He could look into the nostrils of the other man, the eyes he could scarcely see. How curiously the mouth was pushed out, exaggerating the full lips, and the moustache bristling up from them. Then, with a start, he noticed the nostrils gradually filled with blood. The red brimmed, hesitated, ran over, and went in a thin trickle down the face to the eyes.

It shocked and distressed him. Slowly, he got up. The body twitched and sprawled there, inert. He stood and looked at it in silence. It was a pity *it* was broken. It represented more than the thing which had kicked and bullied him. He was afraid to look at the eyes. They were hideous now, only the whites showing, and the blood running to them. The face of the orderly was drawn with horror at the sight. Well, it was so. In his heart he was satisfied. He had hated the face of the Captain. It was extinguished now. There was a heavy relief in the orderly's soul. That was as it should be. But he could not bear to see the long, military body lying broken over the tree-base, the fine fingers crisped. He wanted to hide it away.

Quickly, busily, he gathered it up and pushed it under the felled tree-trunks, which rested their beautiful, smooth length either end on logs. The face was horrible with blood. He covered it with the helmet. Then he pushed the limbs straight and decent, and brushed the dead leaves off the fine cloth of the uniform. So, it lay quite still in the shadow under there. A little strip of sunshine ran along the breast, from a chink between the logs. The orderly sat by it for a few moments. Here his own life also ended.

Then, through his daze, he heard the lieutenant, in a loud voice, explaining to the men outside the wood, that they were to suppose the bridge on the river below was held by the enemy. Now they were to march to the attack in such and such a manner. The lieutenant had no gift of expression. The orderly, listening from habit, got muddled. And when the lieutenant began it all again he ceased to hear.

He knew he must go. He stood up. It surprised him that the leaves were glittering in the sun, and the chips of wood reflecting white from the ground. For him a change had come over the world. But for the rest it had not—all seemed the same. Only he had left it. And he could not go back. It was his duty to return with the beer-pot and the bottle. He could not. He had left all that. The lieutenant was still hoarsely explaining. He must go, or they would overtake him. And he could not bear contact with any one now.

He drew his fingers over his eyes, trying to find out where he was. Then he turned away. He saw the horse standing in the path. He went up to it and mounted. It hurt him to sit in the saddle. The pain of keeping his seat occupied him as they cantered through the wood. He would not have minded anything, but he could not get away from the sense of being divided from the others. The path led out of the trees. On the edge of the wood he pulled up and stood watching. There in the spacious sunshine of the valley soldiers were moving in a little swarm. Every now and then, a man harrowing on a strip of fallow shouted to his oxen, at the turn. The village and the white-towered church was small in the sunshine. And he no longer belonged to it—he sat there, beyond, like a man outside in the dark. He had gone out from everyday life into the unknown and he could not, he even did not want to go back.

Turning from the sun-blazing valley, he rode deep into the wood. Tree-trunks, like people standing grey and still, took no notice as he went. A doe, herself a moving bit of sunshine and shadow, went running through the flecked shade. There were bright green rents in the foliage. Then it was all pine wood, dark and cool. And he was sick with pain, he had an intolerable great pulse in his head, and he was sick. He had never been ill in his life. He felt lost, quite dazed with all this.

Trying to get down from the horse, he fell, astonished at the pain and his lack of balance. The horse shifted uneasily. He jerked its bridle and sent it cantering jerkily away. It was his last connection with the rest of things.

But he only wanted to lie down and not be disturbed. Stumbling through the trees, he came on a quiet place where beeches and pine trees grew on a slope. Immediately he had lain down and closed his eyes, his consciousness went racing on without him. A big pulse of sickness beat in him as if it throbbed through the whole earth. He was burning with dry heat. But he was too busy, too tearingly active in the incoherent race of delirium to observe.

III

He came to with a start. His mouth was dry and hard, his heart beat heavily, but he had not the energy to get up. His heart beat heavily. Where was he?—the barracks—at home? There was something knocking. And, making an effort, he looked round—trees, and litter of greenery, and reddish, bright, still pieces of sunshine on the floor. He did not believe he was himself, he did not believe what he saw. Something was knocking. He made a struggle towards consciousness, but relapsed. Then he struggled again. And gradually his surroundings fell into relationship with himself. He knew, and a great pang of fear went through his heart. Somebody was knocking. He could see the heavy, black rags of a fir tree overhead. Then everything went black. Yet he did not believe he had closed his eyes. He had not. Out of the blackness sight slowly emerged again. And someone was knocking. Quickly, he saw the blood-disfigured face of his Captain, which he hated. And he held himself still with horror. Yet, deep inside him, he knew that it was so, the Captain should be dead. But the physical delirium got hold of him. Someone was knocking. He lay perfectly still, as if dead, with fear. And he went unconscious.

When he opened his eyes again he started, seeing something creeping swiftly up a tree-trunk. It was a little bird. And the bird was whistling overhead. Tap-tap-tap—it was the small, quick bird rapping the tree-trunk with its beak, as if its head were a little round hammer. He watched it curiously. It shifted sharply, in its creeping fashion. Then, like a mouse, it slid down the bare trunk. Its swift creeping sent a flash of revulsion through him. He raised his head. It felt a great weight. Then, the little bird ran out of the shadow across a still patch of sunshine, its little head bobbing swiftly, its white legs twinkling brightly for a moment. How neat it was in its build, so compact, with pieces of white on its wings. There were several of them. They were so pretty—but they crept like swift, erratic mice, running here and there among the beech-mast.

He lay down again exhausted, and his consciousness lapsed. He had a horror of the little creeping birds. All his blood seemed to be darting and creeping in his head. And yet he could not move.

He came to with a further ache of exhaustion. There was the pain in his head, and the horrible sickness, and his inability to move. He had never been ill in his life. He did not know where he was or what he was. Probably he had got sunstroke. Or what else?— he had silenced the Captain for ever—some time ago—oh, a long time ago. There had been blood on his face, and his eyes had turned upwards. It was all right, somehow. It was peace. But now he had got beyond himself. He had never been here before. Was it life, or not life? He was by himself. They were in a big, bright place, those others, and he was outside. The town, all the country, a big bright place of light : and he was outside, here, in the darkened open beyond, where each thing existed alone. But they would all have to come out there sometime, those others. Little, and left behind him, they all were. There had been father and mother and sweetheart. What did they all matter? This was the open land.

He sat up. Something scuffled. It was a little brown squirrel running in lovely undulating bounds over the floor, its red tail completing the undulation of its body—and then, as it sat up, furling and unfurling. He watched it, pleased. It ran on again, friskily, enjoying itself. It flew wildly at another squirrel, and they were chasing each other, and making little scolding, chattering noises. The soldier wanted to speak to them. But only a hoarse sound came out of his throat. The squirrels burst away—they flew up the trees. And then he saw the one peeping round at him, half-way up a tree-trunk. A start of fear went through him, though in so far as he was conscious, he was amused. It still stayed, its little keen face staring at him half way up the tree-trunk, its little ears pricked up, its clawey little hands clinging to the bark, its white breast reared. He started from it in panic.

Struggling to his feet, he lurched away. He went on walking, walking, looking for something—for a drink. His brain felt hot and inflamed for want of water. He stumbled on. Then he did not know anything. He went unconscious as he walked. Yet he stumbled on, his mouth open.

When, to his dumb wonder, he opened his eyes on the world again, he no longer tried to remember what it was. There was thick, golden light behind golden-green glitterings, and tall, grey-purple shafts, and darknesses further off, surrounding him, growing deeper. He was conscious of a sense of arrival. He was amid the reality, on the real, dark bottom. But there was the thirst burning in his brain. He felt lighter, not so heavy. He supposed it was newness. The air was muttering with thunder. He thought he was walking wonderfully swiftly and was coming straight to relief—or was it to water?

Suddenly he stood still with fear. There was a tremendous flare of gold, immense—just a few dark trunks like bars between him and it. All the young level wheat was burnished gold glaring on its silky green. A woman, full-skirted, a black cloth on her head for head-dress, was passing like a block of shadow through the glistening, green corn, into the full glare. There was a farm, too, pale blue in shadow, and the timber black. And there was a church spire, nearly fused away in the gold. The woman moved on, away from him. He had no language with which to speak to her. She was the bright, solid unreality. She would make a noise of words that would confuse him, and her eyes would look at him without seeing him. She was crossing there to the other side. He stood against a tree.

When at last he turned, looking down the long, bare grove whose flat bed was already filling dark, he saw the mountains in a wonder-light, not far away, and radiant. Behind the soft, grey ridge of the nearest range the further mountains stood golden and pale grey, the snow all radiant like pure, soft gold. So still, gleaming in the sky, fashioned pure out of the ore of the sky, they shone in their silence. He stood and looked at them, his face illuminated. And like the golden, lustrous gleaming of the snow he felt his own thirst bright in him. He stood and gazed, leaning against a tree. And then everything slid away into space.

During the night the lightning fluttered perpetually, making the whole sky white. He must have walked again. The world hung livid round him for moments, fields a level sheen of grey-green light, trees in dark bulk, and the range of clouds black across a white sky. Then the darkness fell like a shutter, and the night was whole. A faint flutter of a half-revealed world, that could not quite leap out of the darkness!—Then there again stood a sweep of pallor for the land, dark shapes looming, a range of clouds hanging overhead. The world was a ghostly shadow, thrown for a moment upon the pure darkness, which returned ever whole and complete.

And the mere delirium of sickness and fever went on inside him—his brain opening and shutting like the night—then sometimes convulsions of terror from something with great eyes that stared round a tree—then the long agony of the march, and the sun decomposing his blood—then the pang of hate for the Captain, followed by a pang of tenderness and ease. But everything was distorted, born of an ache and resolving into an ache.

In the morning he came definitely awake. Then his brain flamed with the sole horror of thirstiness ! The sun was on his face, the dew was steaming from his wet clothes. Like one possessed, he got up. There, straight in front of him, blue and cool and tender, the mountains ranged across the pale edge of the morning sky. He wanted them—he wanted them alone—he wanted to leave himself and be identified with them. They did not move, they were still and soft, with white, gentle markings of snow. He stood still, mad with suffering, his hands crisping and clutching. Then he was twisting in a paroxysm on the grass.

He lay still, in a kind of dream of anguish. His thirst seemed to have separated itself from him, and to stand apart, a single demand. Then the pain he felt was another single self. Then there was the clog of his body, another separate thing. He was divided among all kinds of separate beings. There was some strange, agonized connection between them, but they were drawing further apart. Then they would all split. The sun, drilling down on him, was drilling through the bond. Then they would all fall, fall through the everlasting lapse of space. Then again, his consciousness reasserted itself. He roused on to his elbow and stared at the gleaming mountains. There they ranked, all still and wonderful between earth and heaven. He stared till his eyes went black, and the mountains, as they stood in their beauty, so clean and cool, seemed to have it, that which was lost in him.

IV

When the soldiers found him, three hours later, he was lying with his face over his arm, his black hair giving off heat under the sun. But he was still alive. Seeing the open, black mouth the young soldiers dropped him in horror.

He died in the hospital at night, without having seen again.

The doctors saw the bruises on his legs, behind, and were silent.

The bodies of the two men lay together, side by side, in the mortuary, the one white and slender, but laid rigidly at rest, the other looking as if every moment it must rouse into life again, so young and unused, from a slumber.

THE THORN IN THE FLESH

I

A WIND was running, so that occasionally the poplars whitened as if a flame flew up them. The sky was broken and blue among moving clouds. Patches of sunshine lay on the level fields, and shadows on the rye and the vineyards. In the distance, very blue, the cathedral bristled against the sky, and the houses of the city of Metz clustered vaguely below, like a hill.

Among the fields by the lime trees stood the barracks, upon bare, dry ground, a collection of round-roofed huts of corrugated iron, where the soldiers' nasturtiums climbed brilliantly. There was a tract of vegetable garden at the side, with the soldiers' yellowish lettuces in rows, and at the back the big, hard drilling-yard surrounded by a wire fence.

At this time in the afternoon, the huts were deserted, all the beds pushed up, the soldiers were lounging about under the lime trees waiting for the call to drill. Bachmann sat on a bench in the shade that smelled sickly with blossom. Pale green, wrecked lime flowers were scattered on the ground. He was writing his weekly post card to his mother. He was a fair, long, limber youth, good-looking. He sat very still indeed, trying to write his post card. His blue uniform, sagging on him as he sat bent over the card, disfigured his youthful shape. His sunburnt hand waited motionless for the words to come. "Dear mother "—was all he had written. Then he scribbled mechanically : " Many thanks for your letter with what you sent. Everything is all right with me. We are just off to drill on the fortifications——" Here he broke off and sat suspended, oblivious of everything, held in some definite suspense. He looked again at the card. But he could write no more. Out of the knot of his consciousness no word would come. He signed himself, and looked up, as a man looks to see if any one has noticed him in his privacy.

There was a self-conscious strain in his blue eyes, and a pallor about his mouth, where the young, fair moustache glistened. He was almost girlish in his good looks and his grace. But he had something of military consciousness, as if he believed in the discipline for himself, and found satisfaction in delivering himself to his duty. There was also a trace of youthful swagger and dare-devilry about his mouth and his limber body, but this was in suppression now.

He put the post card in the pocket of his tunic, and went to join a group of his comrades who were lounging in the shade, laughing and talking grossly. To-day he was out of it. He only stood near to them for the warmth of the association. In his own consciousness something held him down.

Presently they were summoned to ranks. The sergeant came out to take command. He was a strongly built, rather heavy man of forty. His head was thrust forward, sunk a little between his powerful shoulders, and the strong jaw was pushed out aggressively. But the eyes were smouldering, the face hung slack and sodden with drink.

He gave his orders in brutal, barking shouts, and the little company moved forward, out of the wire-fenced yard to the open road, marching rhythmically, raising the dust. Bachmann, one of the inner file of four deep, marched in the airless ranks, half suffocated with heat and dust and enclosure. Through the moving of his comrades' bodies, he could see the small vines dusty by the roadside, the poppies among the tares fluttering and blown to pieces, the distant spaces of sky and fields all free with air and sunshine. But he was bound in a very dark enclosure of anxiety within himself.

He marched with his usual ease, being healthy and well adjusted. But his body went on by itself. His spirit was clenched apart. And ever the few soldiers drew nearer and nearer to the town, ever the consciousness of the youth became more gripped and separate, his body worked by a kind of mechanical intelligence, a mere presence of mind.

They diverged from the high road and passed in single file down a path among trees. All was silent and green and mysterious, with shadow of foliage and long, green, undisturbed grass. Then they came out in the sunshine on a moat of water, which wound silently between the long, flowery grass, at the foot of the earthworks, that rose in front in terraces walled smooth on the face, but all soft with long grass at the top. Marguerite daisies and lady's-slipper glimmered white and gold in the lush grass, preserved here in the intense peace of the fortifications. Thickets of trees stood round about. Occasionally a puff of mysterious wind made the flowers and the long grass that crested the earthworks above bow and shake as with signals of oncoming alarm.

The group of soldiers stood at the end of the moat, in their light blue and scarlet uniforms, very bright. The sergeant was giving them instructions, and his shout came sharp and alarming in the intense, untouched stillness of the place. They listened, finding it difficult to make the effort of understanding.

Then it was over, and the men were moving to make preparations. On the other side of the moat the ramparts rose smooth and clear in the sun, sloping slightly back. Along the summit grass grew and tall daisies stood ledged high, like magic, against the dark green of the tree-tops behind. The noise of the town, the running of tram-cars, was heard distinctly, but it seemed not to penetrate this still place.

The water of the moat was motionless. In silence the practice began. One of the soldiers took a scaling ladder, and passing along the narrow ledge at the foot of the earthworks, with the water of the moat just behind him, tried to get a fixture on the slightly sloping wall-face. There he stood, small and isolated, at the foot of the wall, trying to get his ladder settled. At last it held, and the clumsy, groping figure in the baggy blue uniform began to clamber up. The rest of the soldiers stood and watched. Occasionally the sergeant barked a command. Slowly the clumsy blue figure clambered higher up the wall-face. Bachmann stood with his bowels turned to water. The figure of the climbing soldier scrambled out on to the terrace up above, and moved, blue and distinct, among the bright green grass. The officer shouted from below. The soldier tramped along, fixed the ladder in another spot, and carefully lowered himself on to the rungs. Bachmann watched the blind foot groping in space for the ladder, and he felt the world fall away beneath him. The figure of the soldier clung cringing against the face of the wall, cleaving, groping downwards like some unsure insect working its way lower and lower, fearing every movement. At last, sweating and with a strained face, the figure had landed safely and turned to the group of soldiers. But still it had a stiffness and a blank, mechanical look, was something less than human.

Bachmann stood there heavy and condemned, waiting for his own turn and betrayal. Some of the men went up easily enough, and without fear. That only showed it could be done lightly, and made Bachmann's case more bitter. If only he could do it lightly, like that.

His turn came. He knew intuitively that nobody knew his condition. The officer just saw him as a mechanical thing. He tried to keep it up, to carry it through on the face of things. His inside gripped tight, as yet under control, he took the ladder and went along under the wall. He placed his ladder with quick success, and wild, quivering hope possessed him. Then blindly he began to climb. But the ladder was not very firm ; and at every hitch a great, sick, melting feeling took hold of him. He clung on fast. If only he could keep that grip on himself, he would get through. He knew this, in agony. What he could not understand was the blind gush of white-hot fear, that came with great force whenever the ladder swerved, and which almost melted his belly and all his joints, and left him powerless. If once it melted all his joints and his belly, he was done. He clung desperately to himself. He knew the fear, he knew what it did when it came, he knew he had only to keep a firm hold. He knew all this. Yet, when the ladder swerved and his foot missed, there was the great blast of fear blowing on his heart and bowels, and he was melting weaker and weaker, in a horror of fear and lack of control, melting to fall.

Yet he groped slowly higher and higher, always staring upwards with desperate face, and always conscious of the space below. But all of him, body and soul, was growing hot to fusion point. He would have to let go for very relief's sake. Suddenly his heart began to lurch. It gave a great, sickly swoop, rose, and again plunged in a swoop of horror. He lay against the wall inert as if dead, inert, at peace, save for one deep core of anxiety, which knew that it was *not* all over, that he was still high in space against the wall. But the chief effort of will was gone.

There came into his consciousness a small, foreign sensation. He woke up a little. What was it ? Then slowly it penetrated him. His water had run down his leg. He lay there, clinging, still with shame, half conscious of the echo of the sergeant's voice thundering from below. He waited, in depths of shame beginning to recover himself. He had been shamed so deeply. Then he could go on, for his fear for himself was conquered. His shame was known and published. He must go on.

Slowly he began to grope for the rung above, when a great shock shook through him. His wrists were grasped from above, he was being hauled out of himself up, up to the safe ground. Like a sack he was dragged over the edge of the earthworks by the large hands, and landed there on his knees, grovelling in the grass to recover command of himself, to rise up on his feet.

Shame, blind, deep shame and ignominy overthrew his spirit and left it writhing. He stood there shrunk over himself, trying to obliterate himself.

Then the presence of the officer who had hauled him up made

itself felt upon him. He heard the panting of the elder man, and then the voice came down on his veins like a fierce whip. He shrank in tension of shame.

" Put up your head—eyes front," shouted the enraged sergeant, and mechanically the soldier obeyed the command, forced to look into the eyes of the sergeant. The brutal, hanging face of the officer violated the youth. He hardened himself with all his might from seeing it. The tearing noise of the sergeant's voice continued to lacerate his body.

Suddenly he set back his head, rigid, and his heart leapt to burst. The face had suddenly thrust itself close, all distorted and showing the teeth, the eyes smouldering into him. The breath of the barking words was on his nose and mouth. He stepped aside in revulsion. With a scream the face was upon him again. He raised his arm, involuntarily, in self-defence. A shock of horror went through him, as he felt his forearm hit the face of the officer a brutal blow. The latter staggered, swerved back, and with a curious cry, reeled backwards over the ramparts, his hands clutching the air. There was a second of silence, then a crash to water.

Bachmann, rigid, looked out of his inner silence upon the scene. Soldiers were running.

" You'd better clear," said one young, excited voice to him. And with immediate instinctive decision he started to walk away from the spot. He went down the tree-hidden path to the high road where the trams ran to and from the town. In his heart was a sense of vindication, of escape. He was leaving it all, the military world, the shame. He was walking away from it.

Officers on horseback rode sauntering down the street, soldiers passed along the pavement. Coming to the bridge, Bachmann crossed over to the town that heaped before him, rising from the flat, picturesque French houses down below at the water's edge, up a jumble of roofs and chasms of streets, to the lovely dark cathedral with its myriad pinnacles making points at the sky.

He felt for the moment quite at peace, relieved from a great strain. So he turned along by the river to the public gardens. Beautiful were the heaped, purple lilac trees upon the green grass, and wonderful the walls of the horse-chestnut trees, lighted like an altar with white flowers on every ledge. Officers went by, elegant and all coloured, women and girls sauntered in the chequered shade. Beautiful it was, he walked in a vision, free.

II

But where was he going ? He began to come out of his trance of delight and liberty. Deep within him he felt the steady burning of shame in the flesh. As yet he could not bear to think of it. But there it was, submerged beneath his attention, the raw, steady-burning shame.

It behoved him to be intelligent. As yet he dared not remember what he had done. He only knew the need to get away, away from everything he had been in contact with.

But how ? A great pang of fear went through him. He could not bear his shamed flesh to be put again between the hands of authority. Already the hands had been laid upon him, brutally upon his nakedness, ripping open his shame and making him maimed, crippled in his own control.

Fear became an anguish. Almost blindly he was turning in the direction of the barracks. He could not take the responsibility of himself. He must give himself up to someone. Then his heart, obstinate in hope, became obsessed with the idea of his sweetheart. He would make himself her responsibility.

Blenching as he took courage, he mounted the small, quick-hurrying tram that ran out of the town in the direction of the barracks. He sat motionless and composed, static.

He got out at the terminus and went down the road. A wind was still running. He could hear the faint whisper of the rye, and the stronger swish as a sudden gust was upon it. No one was about. Feeling detached and impersonal, he went down a field-path between the low vines. Many little vine trees rose up in spires, holding out tender pink shoots, waving their tendrils. He saw them distinctly, and wondered over them. In a field a little way off, men and women were taking up the hay. The bullock-waggon stood by on the path, the men in their blue shirts, the women with white cloths over their heads carried hay in their arms to the cart, all brilliant and distinct upon the shorn, glowing green acres. He felt himself looking out of darkness on to the glamorous, brilliant beauty of the world around him, outside him.

The Baron's house, where Emilie was maidservant, stood square and mellow among trees and garden and fields. It was an old French grange. The barracks was quite near. Bachmann walked, drawn by a single purpose, towards the courtyard. He entered the spacious, shadowy, sun-swept place. The dog, seeing a soldier, only jumped and whined for greeting. The pump stood peacefully in a corner, under a lime tree, in the shade.

The kitchen door was open. He hesitated, then walked in, speaking shyly and smiling involuntarily. The two women started, but with pleasure. Emilie was preparing the tray for afternoon coffee. She stood beyond the table, drawn up, startled, and challenging, and glad. She had the proud, timid eyes of some wild animal, some proud animal. Her black hair was closely banded, her grey eyes watched steadily. She wore a peasant dress of blue cotton sprigged with little red roses, that buttoned tight over her strong maiden breasts.

At the table sat another young woman, the nursery governess, who was picking cherries from a huge heap, and dropping them into a bowl. She was young, pretty, freckled.

"Good day!" she said pleasantly. "The unexpected."

Emilie did not speak. The flush came in her dark cheek. She still stood watching, between fear and a desire to escape, and on the other hand joy that kept her in his presence.

"Yes," he said, bashful and strained, while the eyes of the two women were upon him. "I've got myself in a mess this time."

"What?" asked the nursery governess, dropping her hands in her lap. Emilie stood rigid.

Bachmann could not raise his head. He looked sideways at the glistening, ruddy cherries. He could not recover the normal world.

"I knocked Sergeant Huber over the fortifications down into the moat," he said. "It was accident—but——"

And he grasped at the cherries, and began to eat them, unknowing, hearing only Emilie's little exclamation.

"You knocked him over the fortifications!" echoed Fräulein Hesse in horror. "How?"

Spitting the cherry-stones into his hand, mechanically, absorbedly, he told them.

"Ach!" exclaimed Emilie sharply.

"And how did you get here?" asked Fräulein Hesse.

"I ran off," he said.

There was a dead silence. He stood, putting himself at the mercy of the women. There came a hissing from the stove, and a stronger smell of coffee. Emilie turned swiftly away. He saw her flat, straight back and her strong loins, as she bent over the stove.

"But what are you going to do?" said Fräulein Hesse, aghast.

"I don't know," he said, grasping at more cherries. He had come to an end.

"You'd better go to the barracks," she said. "We'll get the Herr Baron to come and see about it."

Emilie was swiftly and quietly preparing the tray. She picked it up, and stood with the glittering china and silver before her, impassive, waiting for his reply. Bachmann remained with his head dropped, pale and obstinate. He could not bear to go back.

"I'm going to try to get into France," he said.

"Yes, but they'll catch you," said Fräulein Hesse.

Emilie watched with steady, watchful grey eyes.

"I can have a try, if I could hide till to-night," he said.

Both women knew what he wanted. And they all knew it was no good. Emilie picked up the tray, and went out. Bachmann stood with his head dropped. Within himself he felt the dross of shame and incapacity.

"You'd never get away," said the governess.

"I can try," he said.

To-day he could not put himself between the hands of the military. Let them do as they liked with him to-morrow, if he escaped to-day.

They were silent. He ate cherries. The colour flushed bright into the cheek of the young governess.

Emilie returned to prepare another tray.

"He could hide in your room," the governess said to her.

The girl drew herself away. She could not bear the intrusion.

"That is all I can think of that is safe from the children," said Fräulein Hesse.

Emilie gave no answer. Bachmann stood waiting for the two women. Emilie did not want the close contact with him.

"You could sleep with me," Fräulein Hesse said to her.

Emilie lifted her eyes and looked at the young man, direct, clear, reserving herself.

"Do you want that?" she asked, her strong virginity proof against him.

"Yes—yes——" he said uncertainly, destroyed by shame.

She put back her head.

"Yes," she murmured to herself.

Quickly she filled the tray, and went out.

"But you can't walk over the frontier in a night," said Fräulein Hesse.

"I can cycle," he said.

Emilie returned, a restraint, a neutrality in her bearing.

"I'll see if it's all right," said the governess.

In a moment or two Bachmann was following Emilie through the square hall, where hung large maps on the walls. He noticed a child's blue coat with brass buttons on the peg, and it reminded him of Emilie walking holding the hand of the youngest child, whilst he watched, sitting under the lime tree. Already this was a long way off. That was a sort of freedom he had lost, changed for a new, immediate anxiety.

They went quickly, fearfully up the stairs and down a long corridor. Emilie opened her door, and he entered, ashamed, into her room.

" I must go down," she murmured, and she departed, closing the door softly.

It was a small, bare, neat room. There was a little dish for holy-water, a picture of the Sacred Heart, a crucifix, and a *prie-Dieu*. The small bed lay white and untouched, the wash-hand bowl of red earth stood on a bare table, there was a little mirror and a small chest of drawers. That was all.

Feeling safe, in sanctuary, he went to the window, looking over the courtyard at the shimmering, afternoon country. He was going to leave this land, this life. Already he was in the unknown.

He drew away into the room. The curious simplicity and severity of the little Roman Catholic bedroom was foreign but restoring to him. He looked at the crucifix. It was a long, lean, peasant Christ carved by a peasant in the Black Forest. For the first time in his life Bachmann saw the figure as a human thing. It represented a man hanging there in helpless torture. He stared at it, closely, as if for new knowledge.

Within his own flesh burned and smouldered the restless shame. He could not gather himself together. There was a gap in his soul. The shame within him seemed to displace his strength and his manhood.

He sat down on his chair. The shame, the roused feeling of exposure acted on his brain, made him heavy, unutterably heavy.

Mechanically, his wits all gone, he took off his boots, his belt, his tunic, put them aside, and lay down, heavy, and fell into a kind of drugged sleep.

Emilie came in a little while, and looked at him. But he was sunk in sleep. She saw him lying there inert, and terribly still, and she was afraid. His shirt was unfastened at the throat. She saw his pure white flesh, very clean and beautiful. And he slept inert. His legs, in the blue uniform trousers, his feet in the coarse stockings, lay foreign on her bed. She went away.

III

She was uneasy, perturbed to her last fibre. She wanted to remain clear, with no touch on her. A wild instinct made her shrink away from any hands which might be laid on her.

She was a foundling, probably of some gipsy race, brought up in a Roman Catholic Rescue Home. A naive, paganly religious being, she was attached to the Baroness, with whom she had served for seven years, since she was fourteen.

She came into contact with no one, unless it were with Ida Hesse, the governess. Ida was a calculating, good-natured, not very straightforward flirt. She was the daughter of a poor country doctor. Having gradually come into connection with Emilie, more an alliance than an attachment, she put no distinction of grade between the two of them. They worked together, sang together, walked together, and went together to the rooms of Franz Brand, Ida's sweetheart. There the three talked and laughed together, or the women listened to Franz, who was a forester, playing on his violin.

In all this alliance there was no personal intimacy between the young women. Emilie was naturally secluded in herself, of a reserved, native race. Ida used her as a kind of weight to balance her own flighty movement. But the quick, shifty governess, occupied always in her dealings with admirers, did all she could to move the violent nature of Emilie towards some connection with men.

But the dark girl, primitive yet sensitive to a high degree, was fiercely virgin. Her blood flamed with rage when the common soldiers made the long, sucking, kissing noise behind her as she passed. She hated them for their almost jeering offers. She was well protected by the Baroness.

And her contempt of the common men in general was ineffable. But she loved the Baroness, and she revered the Baron, and she was at her ease when she was doing something for the service of a gentleman. Her whole nature was at peace in the service of real masters or mistresses. For her, a gentleman had some mystic quality that left her free and proud in service. The common soldiers were brutes, merely nothing. Her desire was to serve.

She held herself aloof. When, on Sunday afternoon, she had looked through the windows of the Reichshalle in passing, and had seen the soldiers dancing with the common girls, a cold revulsion and anger had possessed her. She could not bear to see the soldiers taking off their belts and pulling open their tunics, dancing with their shirts showing through the open, sagging tunic, their movements gross, their faces transfigured and sweaty, their coarse hands holding their coarse girls under the arm-pits, drawing the female up to their breasts. She hated to see them clutched breast to breast, the legs of the men moving grossly in the dance.

At evening, when she had been in the garden, and heard on the other side of the hedge the sexual, inarticulate cries of the girls in the embraces of the soldiers, her anger had been too much for her, and she had cried, loud and cold :

" What are you doing there, in the hedge ? "

She would have had them whipped.

But Bachmann was not quite a common soldier. Fräulein Hesse had found out about him, and had drawn him and Emilie together. For he was a handsome, blond youth, erect and walking with a kind of pride, unconscious yet clear. Moreover, he came of a rich farming stock, rich for many generations. His father was dead, his mother controlled the moneys for the time being. But if Bachmann wanted a hundred pounds at any moment, he could have them. By trade he, with one of his brothers, was a waggon-builder. The family had the farming, smithy, and waggon-building of their village. They worked because that was the form of life they knew. If they had chosen, they could have lived independent upon their means.

In this way, he was a gentleman in sensibility, though his intellect was not developed. He could afford to pay freely for things. He had, moreover, his native, fine breeding. Emilie wavered uncertainly before him. So he became her sweetheart, and she hungered after him. But she was virgin, and shy, and needed to be in subjection, because she was primitive and had no grasp on civilized forms of living, nor on civilized purposes.

IV

At six o'clock came the inquiry of the soldiers : Had anything been seen of Bachmann ? Fräulein Hesse answered, pleased to be playing a rôle :

" No, I've not seen him since Sunday—have you, Emilie ? "

" No, I haven't seen him," said Emilie, and her awkwardness was construed as bashfulness. Ida Hesse, stimulated, asked questions, and played her part.

" But it hasn't killed Sergeant Huber ? " she cried in consternation.

" No. He fell into the water. But it gave him a bad shock, and smashed his foot on the side of the moat. He's in hospital. It's a bad look-out for Bachmann."

Emilie, implicated and captive, stood looking on. She was no longer free, working with all this regulated system which she could not understand and which was almost god-like to her. She was put out of her place. Bachmann was in her room, she was no longer the faithful in service serving with religious surety.

Her situation was intolerable to her. All evening long the burden was upon her, she could not live. The children must be fed and put to sleep. The Baron and Baroness were going out, she must give them light refreshment. The man-servant was coming in to supper after returning with the carriage. And all the while she had the insupportable feeling of being out of the order, self-responsible, bewildered. The control of her life should come from those above her, and she should move within that control. But now she was out of it, uncontrolled and troubled. More than that, the man, the lover, Bachmann, who was he, what was he? He alone of all men contained for her the unknown quantity which terrified her beyond her service. Oh, she had wanted him as a distant sweetheart, not close, like this, casting her out of her world.

When the Baron and Baroness had departed, and the young man-servant had gone out to enjoy himself, she went upstairs to Bachmann. He had wakened up, and sat dimly in the room. Out in the open he heard the soldiers, his comrades, singing the sentimental songs of the nightfall, the drone of the concertina rising in accompaniment.

"Wenn ich zu mei . . . nem Kinde geh' . . .
In seinem Au . . . g die Mutter seh' . . . ."

But he himself was removed from it now. Only the sentimental cry of young, unsatisfied desire in the soldiers' singing penetrated his blood and stirred him subtly. He let his head hang ; he had become gradually roused : and he waited in concentration, in another world.

The moment she entered the room where the man sat alone, waiting intensely, the thrill passed through her, she died in terror, and after the death, a great flame gushed up, obliterating her. He sat in trousers and shirt on the side of the bed. He looked up as she came in, and she shrank from his face. She could not bear it. Yet she entered near to him.

" Do you want anything to eat ? " she said.

" Yes," he answered, and as she stood in the twilight of the room with him, he could only hear his heart beat heavily. He saw her apron just level with his face. She stood silent, a little distance off, as if she would be there for ever. He suffered.

As if in a spell she waited, standing motionless and looming there, he sat rather crouching on the side of the bed. A second will in him was powerful and dominating. She drew gradually nearer to him, coming up slowly, as if unconscious. His heart beat up swiftly. He was going to move.

As she came quite close, almost invisibly he lifted his arms and put them round her waist, drawing her with his will and desire. He buried his face into her apron, into the terrible softness of her belly. And he was a flame of passion intense about her. He had forgotten. Shame and memory were gone in a whole, furious flame of passion.

She was quite helpless. Her hands leapt, fluttered, and closed over his head, pressing it deeper into her belly, vibrating as she did so. And his arms tightened on her, his hands spread over her loins, warm as flame on her loveliness. It was intense anguish of bliss for her, and she lost consciousness.

When she recovered, she lay translated in the peace of satisfaction. It was what she had had no inkling of, never known could be. She was strong with eternal gratitude. And he was there with her. Instinctively with an instinct of reverence and gratitude, her arms tightened in a little embrace upon him who held her thoroughly embraced.

And he was restored and completed, close to her. That little, twitching, momentary clasp of acknowledgment that she gave him in her satisfaction, roused his pride unconquerable. They loved each other, and all was whole. She loved him, he had taken her, she was given to him. It was right. He was given to her, and they were one, complete.

Warm, with a glow in their hearts and faces, they rose again, modest, but transfigured with happiness.

"I will get you something to eat," she said, and in joy and security of service again, she left him, making a curious little homage of departure. He sat on the side of the bed, escaped, liberated, wondering, and happy.

v

Soon she came again with the tray, followed by Fräulein Hesse. The two women watched him eat, watched the pride and wonder

of his being, as he sat there blond and naive again. Emilie felt rich
and complete. Ida was a lesser thing than herself.

"And what are you going to do?" asked Fräulein Hesse, jealous.

"I must get away," he said.

But words had no meaning for him. What did it matter? He
had the inner satisfaction and liberty.

"But you'll want a bicycle," said Ida Hesse.

"Yes," he said.

Emilie sat silent, removed and yet with him, connected with him
in passion. She looked from this talk of bicycles and escape.

They discussed plans. But in two of them was the one will, that
Bachmann should stay with Emilie. Ida Hesse was an outsider.

It was arranged, however, that Ida's lover should put out his
bicycle, leave it at the hut where he sometimes watched. Bachmann should fetch it in the night, and ride into France. The hearts
of all three beat hot in suspense, driven to thought. They sat in a
fire of agitation.

Then Bachmann would get away to America, and Emilie would
come and join him. They would be in a fine land then. The tale
burned up again.

Emilie and Ida had to go round to Franz Brand's lodging. They
departed with slight leave-taking. Bachmann sat in the dark, hearing the bugle for retreat sound out of the night. Then he remembered his post card to his mother. He slipped out after Emilie,
gave it her to post. His manner was careless and victorious, hers
shining and trustful. He slipped back to shelter.

There he sat on the side of the bed, thinking. Again he went
over the events of the afternoon, remembering his own anguish of
apprehension because he had known he could not climb the wall
without fainting with fear. Still, a flush of shame came alight in
him at the memory. But he said to himself: "What does it matter?
—I can't help it, well then I can't. If I go up a height, I get absolutely weak, and can't help myself." Again memory came over him,
and a gush of shame, like fire. But he sat and endured it. It had
to be endured, admitted, and accepted. "I'm not a coward, for
all that," he continued. "I'm not afraid of danger. If I'm made
that way, that heights melt me and make me let go my water"—
it was torture for him to pluck at this truth—"if I'm made like that,
I shall have to abide by it, that's all. It isn't all of me." He thought
of Emilie, and was satisfied. "What I am, I am; and let it be
enough," he thought.

Having accepted his own defect, he sat thinking, waiting for

Emilie, to tell her. She came at length, saying that Franz could not arrange about his bicycle this night. It was broken. Bachmann would have to stay over another day.

They were both happy. Emilie, confused before Ida, who was excited and prurient, came again to the young man. She was stiff and dignified with an agony of unusedness. But he took her between his hands, and uncovered her, and enjoyed almost like madness her helpless, virgin body that suffered so strongly, and that took its joy so deeply. While the moisture of torment and modesty was still in her eyes, she clasped him closer, and closer, to the victory and the deep satisfaction of both of them. And they slept together, he in repose still satisfied and peaceful, and she lying close in her static reality.

VI

In the morning, when the bugle sounded from the barracks they rose and looked out of the window. She loved his body that was proud and blond and able to take command. And he loved her body that was soft and eternal. They looked at the faint grey vapour of summer steaming off from the greenness and ripeness of the fields. There was no town anywhere, their look ended in the haze of the summer morning. Their bodies rested together, their minds tranquil. Then a little anxiety stirred in both of them from the sound of the bugle. She was called back to her old position, to realize the world of authority she did not understand but had wanted to serve. But this call died away again from her. She had all.

She went downstairs to her work, curiously changed. She was in a new world of her own, that she had never even imagined, and which was the land of promise for all that. In this she moved and had her being. And she extended it to her duties. She was curiously happy and absorbed. She had not to strive out of herself to do her work. The doing came from within her without call or command. It was a delicious outflow, like sunshine, the activity that flowed from her and put her tasks to rights.

.Bachmann sat busily thinking. He would have to get all his plans ready. He must write to his mother, and she must send him money to Paris. He would go to Paris, and from thence, quickly, to America. It had to be done. He must make all preparations. The dangerous part was the getting into France. He thrilled in anticipation. During the day he would need a time-table of the trains going to Paris—he would need to think. It gave him delicious pleasure, using all his wits. It seemed such an adventure.

This one day, and he would escape then into freedom. What an agony of need he had for absolute, imperious freedom. He had won to his own being, in himself and Emilie, he had drawn the stigma from his shame, he was beginning to be himself. And now he wanted madly to be free to go on. A home, his work, and absolute freedom to move and to be, in her, with her, this was his passionate desire. He thought in a kind of ecstasy, living an hour of painful intensity.

Suddenly he heard voices, and a tramping of feet. His heart gave a great leap, then went still. He was taken. He had known all along. A complete silence filled his body and soul, a silence like death, a suspension of life and sound. He stood motionless in the bedroom, in perfect suspension.

Emilie was busy passing swiftly about the kitchen preparing the children's breakfasts when she heard the tramp of feet and the voice of the Baron. The latter had come in from the garden, and was wearing an old green linen suit. He was a man of middle stature, quick, finely made, and of whimsical charm. His right hand had been shot in the Franco-Prussian war, and now, as always when he was much agitated, he shook it down at his side, as if it hurt. He was talking rapidly to a young, stiff Ober-leutnant. Two private soldiers stood bearishly in the doorway.

Emilie, shocked out of herself, stood pale and erect, recoiling.

"Yes, if you think so, we can look," the Baron was hastily and irascibly saying.

"Emilie," he said, turning to the girl, "did you put a post card to the mother of this Bachmann in the box last evening?"

Emilie stood erect and did not answer.

"Yes?" said the Baron sharply.

"Yes, Herr Baron," replied Emilie, neutral.

The Baron's wounded hand shook rapidly in exasperation. The lieutenant drew himself up still more stiffly. He was right.

"And do you know anything of the fellow?" asked the Baron, looking at her with his blazing, greyish-golden eyes. The girl looked back at him steadily, dumb, but her whole soul naked before him. For two seconds he looked at her in silence. Then in silence, ashamed and furious, he turned away.

"Go up!" he said, with his fierce, peremptory command, to the young officer.

The lieutenant gave his order, in military cold confidence, to the soldiers. They all tramped across the hall. Emilie stood motionless, her life suspended.

The Baron marched swiftly upstairs and down the corridor, the lieutenant and the common soldiers followed. The Baron flung open the door of Emilie's room, and looked at Bachmann, who stood watching, standing in shirt and trousers beside the bed, fronting the door. He was perfectly still. His eyes met the furious, blazing look of the Baron. The latter shook his wounded hand, and then went still. He looked into the eyes of the soldier, steadily. He saw the same naked soul exposed, as if he looked really into the *man*. And the man was helpless, the more helpless for his singular nakedness.

" Ha ! " he exclaimed impatiently, turning to the approaching lieutenant.

The latter appeared in the doorway. Quickly his eyes travelled over the bare-footed youth. He recognized him as his object. He gave the brief command to dress.

Bachmann turned round for his clothes. He was very still, silent in himself. He was in an abstract, motionless world. That the two gentlemen and the two soldiers stood watching him, he scarcely realized. They could not see him.

Soon he was ready. He stood at attention. But only the shell of his body was at attention. A curious silence, a blankness, like something eternal, possessed him. He remained true to himself.

The lieutenant gave the order to march. The little procession went down the stairs with careful, respectful tread, and passed through the hall to the kitchen. There Emilie stood with her face uplifted, motionless and expressionless. Bachmann did not look at her. They knew each other. They were themselves. Then the little file of men passed out into the courtyard.

The Baron stood in the doorway watching the four figures in uniform pass through the chequered shadow under the lime trees. Bachmann was walking neutralized, as if he were not there. The lieutenant went brittle and long, the two soldiers lumbered beside. They passed out into the sunny morning, growing smaller, going towards the barracks.

The Baron turned into the kitchen. Emilie was cutting bread.

" So he stayed the night here ? " he said.

The girl looked at him, scarcely seeing. She was too much herself. The Baron saw the dark, naked soul of her body in her unseeing eyes.

" What were you going to do ? " he asked.

" He was going to America," she replied, in a still voice.

" Pah ! You should have sent him straight back," fired the Baron.

Emilie stood at his bidding, untouched.

" He's done for now," he said.

But he could not bear the dark, deep nakedness of her eyes, that scarcely changed under this suffering.

" Nothing but a fool," he repeated, going away in agitation, and preparing himself for what he could do.

DAUGHTERS OF THE VICAR

I

MR. LINDLEY was first vicar of Aldecross. The cottages of this tiny hamlet had nestled in peace since their beginning, and the country folk had crossed the lanes and farm-lands, two or three miles, to the parish church at Greymeed, on the bright Sunday mornings.

But when the pits were sunk, blank rows of dwellings started up beside the high roads, and a new population, skimmed from the floating scum of workmen, was filled in, the cottages and the country people almost obliterated.

To suit the convenience of these new collier-inhabitants, a church must be built at Aldecross. There was not too much money. And so the little building crouched like a humped stone-and-mortar mouse, with two little turrets at the west corners for ears, in the fields near the cottages and the apple trees, as far as possible from the dwellings down the high road. It had an uncertain, timid look about it. And so they planted big-leaved ivy, to hide its shrinking newness. So that now the little church stands buried in its greenery, stranded and sleeping among the fields, while the brick houses elbow nearer and nearer, threatening to crush it down. It is already obsolete.

The Reverend Ernest Lindley, aged twenty-seven, and newly married, came from his curacy in Suffolk to take charge of his church. He was just an ordinary young man, who had been to Cambridge and taken orders. His wife was a self-assured young woman, daughter of a Cambridgeshire rector. Her father had spent the whole of his thousand a year, so that Mrs. Lindley had nothing of her own. Thus the young married people came to Aldecross to live on a stipend of about a hundred and twenty pounds, and to keep up a superior position.

They were not very well received by the new, raw, disaffected population of colliers. Being accustomed to farm labourers, Mr. Lindley had considered himself as belonging indisputably to the upper or ordering classes. He had to be humble to the ocunty

47

families, but still, he was of their kind, whilst the common people were something different. He had no doubts of himself.

He found, however, that the collier population refused to accept this arrangement. They had no use for him in their lives, and they told him so, callously. The women merely said, " they were throng," or else, " Oh, it's no good you coming here, we're Chapel." The men were quite good-humoured so long as he did not touch them too nigh, they were cheerfully contemptuous of him, with a preconceived contempt he was powerless against.

At last, passing from indignation to silent resentment, even, if he dared have acknowledged it, to conscious hatred of the majority of his flock, and unconscious hatred of himself, he confined his activities to a narrow round of cottages, and he had to submit. He had no particular character, having always depended on his position in society to give him position among men. Now he was so poor, he had no social standing even among the common vulgar tradespeople of the district, and he had not the nature nor the wish to make his society agreeable to them, nor the strength to impose himself where he would have liked to be recognized. He dragged on, pale and miserable and neutral.

At first his wife raged with mortification. She took on airs and used a high hand. But her income was too small, the wrestling with tradesmen's bills was too pitiful, she only met with general, callous ridicule when she tried to be impressive.

Wounded to the quick of her pride, she found herself isolated in an indifferent, callous population. She raged indoors and out. But soon she learned that she must pay too heavily for her outdoor rages, and then she only raged within the walls of the rectory. There her feeling was so strong that she frightened herself. She saw herself hating her husband, and she knew that, unless she were careful, she would smash her form of life and bring catastrophe upon him and upon herself. So in very fear she went quiet. She hid, bitter and beaten by fear, behind the only shelter she had in the world, her gloomy, poor parsonage.

Children were born one every year ; almost mechanically, she continued to perform her maternal duty, which was forced upon her. Gradually, broken by the suppressing of her violent anger and misery and disgust, she became an invalid and took to her couch.

The children grew up healthy, but unwarmed and rather rigid. Their father and mother educated them at home, made them very proud and very genteel, put them definitely and cruelly in the upper classes, apart from the vulgar around them. So they lived quite isolated. They were good-looking, and had that curiously clean, semi-transparent look of the genteel, isolated poor.

Gradually Mr. and Mrs. Lindley lost all hold on life, and spent their hours, weeks and years merely haggling to make ends meet, and bitterly repressing and pruning their children into gentility, urging them to ambition, weighting them with duty. On Sunday morning the whole family, except the mother, went down the lane to church, the long-legged girls in skimpy frocks, the boys in black coats and long, grey, unfitting trousers. They passed by their father's parishioners with mute, clear faces, childish mouths closed in pride that was like a doom to them, and childish eyes already unseeing. Miss Mary, the eldest, was the leader. She was a long, slim thing with a fine profile and a proud, pure look of submission to a high fate. Miss Louisa, the second, was short and plump and obstinate-looking. She had more enemies than ideals. She looked after the lesser children, Miss Mary after the elder. The collier children watched this pale, distinguished procession of the vicar's family pass mutely by, and they were impressed by the air of gentility and distance, they made mock of the trousers of the small sons, they felt inferior in themselves, and hate stirred their hearts.

In her time, Miss Mary received as governess a few little daughters of tradesmen ; Miss Louisa managed the house and went among her father's church-goers, giving lessons on the piano to the colliers' daughters at thirteen shillings for twenty-six lessons.

II

One winter morning, when his daughter Mary was about twenty years old, Mr. Lindley, a thin, unobtrusive figure in his black overcoat and his wideawake, went down into Aldecross with a packet of white papers under his arm. He was delivering the parish almanacs.

A rather pale, neutral man of middle age, he waited while the train thumped over the level-crossing, going up to the pit which rattled busily just along the line. A wooden-legged man hobbled to open the gate, Mr. Lindley passed on. Just at his left hand, below the road and the railway, was the red roof of a cottage, showing through the bare twigs of apple trees. Mr. Lindley passed round the low wall, and descended the worn steps that led from the highway down to the cottage which crouched darkly and quietly away below the rumble of passing trains and the clank of coal-carts, in a quiet little underworld of its own. Snowdrops with tight-shut buds were hanging very still under the bare currant bushes.

The clergyman was just going to knock when he heard a clinking noise, and turning saw through the open door of a black shed just behind him an elderly woman in a black lace cap stooping among reddish big cans, pouring a very bright liquid into a tundish. There was a smell of paraffin. The woman put down her can, took the tundish and laid it on a shelf, then rose with a tin bottle. Her eyes met those of the clergyman.

" Oh, is it you, Mr. Lin'ley ! " she said, in a complaining tone. " Go in."

The minister entered the house. In the hot kitchen sat a big, elderly man with a great grey beard, taking snuff. He grunted in a deep, muttering voice, telling the minister to sit down, and then took no more notice of him, but stared vacantly into the fire. Mr. Lindley waited.

The woman came in, the ribbons of her black lace cap, or bonnet, hanging on her shawl. She was of medium stature, everything about her was tidy. She went up a step out of the kitchen, carrying the paraffin tin. Feet were heard entering the room up the step. It was a little haberdashery shop, with parcels on the shelves of the walls, a big, old-fashioned sewing machine with tailor's work lying round it, in the open space. The woman went behind the counter, gave the child who had entered the paraffin bottle, and took from her a jug.

" My mother says shall yer put it down," said the child, and she was gone. The woman wrote in a book, then came into the kitchen with her jug. The husband, a very large man, rose and brought more coal to the already hot fire. He moved slowly and sluggishly. Already he was going dead ; being a tailor, his large form had become an encumbrance to him. In his youth he had been a great dancer and boxer. Now he was taciturn, and inert. The minister had nothing to say, so he sought for his phrases. But John Durant took no notice, existing silent and dull.

Mrs. Durant spread the cloth. Her husband poured himself beer into a mug, and began to smoke and drink.

" Shall you have some ? " he growled through his beard at the clergyman, looking slowly from the man to the jug, capable of this one idea.

" No, thank you," replied Mr. Lindley, though he would have liked some beer. He must set the example in a drinking parish.

" We need a drop to keep us going," said Mrs. Durant.

She had rather a complaining manner. The clergyman sat on uncomfortably while she laid the table for the half-past ten lunch. Her husband drew up to eat. She remained in her little round arm-chair by the fire.

She was a woman who would have liked to be easy in her life, but to whose lot had fallen a rough and turbulent family, and a slothful husband who did not care what became of himself or anybody. So, her rather good-looking square face was peevish, she had that air of having been compelled all her life to serve unwillingly, and to control where she did not want to control. There was about her, too, that masterful *aplomb* of a woman who has brought up and ruled her sons : but even them she had ruled unwillingly. She had enjoyed managing her little haberdashery shop, riding in the carrier's cart to Nottingham, going through the big warehouses to buy her goods. But the fret of managing her sons she did not like. Only she loved her youngest boy, because he was her last, and she saw herself free.

This was one of the houses the clergyman visited occasionally. Mrs. Durant, as part of her regulation, had brought up all her sons in the Church. Not that she had any religion. Only, it was what she was used to. Mr. Durant was without religion. He read the fervently evangelical *Life of John Wesley* with a curious pleasure, getting from it a satisfaction as from the warmth of the fire, or a glass of brandy. But he cared no more about John Wesley, in fact, than about John Milton, of whom he had never heard.

Mrs. Durant took her chair to the table.

" I don't feel like eating," she sighed.

" Why—aren't you well ? " asked the clergyman, patronizing.

" It isn't that," she sighed. She sat with shut, straight mouth. " I don't know what's going to become of us."

But the clergyman had ground himself down so long that he could not easily sympathize.

" Have you any trouble ? " he asked.

" Ay, have I any trouble ! " cried the elderly woman. " I shall end my days in the workhouse."

The minister waited unmoved. What could she know of poverty, in her little house of plenty !

" I hope not," he said.

" And the one lad as I wanted to keep by me——" she lamented.

The minister listened without sympathy, quite neutral.

" And the lad as would have been a support to my old age ! What is going to become of us ? " she said.

The clergyman, justly, did not believe in the cry of poverty, but wondered what had become of the son.

" Has anything happened to Alfred ? " he asked.

" We've got word he's gone for a Queen's sailor," she said sharply.

" He has joined the Navy ! " exclaimed Mr. Lindley. " I think he could scarcely have done better—to serve his Queen and country on the sea . . ."

" He is wanted to serve *me*," she cried. " And I wanted my lad at home."

Alfred was her baby, her last, whom she had allowed herself the luxury of spoiling.

" You will miss him," said Mr. Lindley, " that is certain. But this is no regrettable step for him to have taken—on the contrary."

" That's easy for you to say, Mr. Lindley," she replied tartly. " Do you think I want my lad climbing ropes at another man's bidding, like a monkey—— ? "

" There is no *dishonour*, surely, in serving in the Navy ? "

" Dishonour this dishonour that," cried the angry old woman. " He goes and makes a slave of himself, and he'll rue it."

Her angry, scornful impatience nettled the clergyman, and silenced him for some moments.

" I do not see," he retorted at last, white at the gills and inadequate, " that the Queen's service is any more to be called slavery than working in a mine."

" At home he was at home, and his own master. *I* know he'll find a difference."

" It may be the making of him," said the clergyman. " It will take him away from bad companionship and drink."

Some of the Durants' sons were notorious drinkers, and Alfred was not quite steady.

" And why indeed shouldn't he have his glass ? " cried the mother. " He picks no man's pocket to pay for it ! "

The clergyman stiffened at what he thought was an allusion to his own profession, and his unpaid bills.

" With all due consideration, I am glad to hear he has joined the Navy," he said.

" Me with my old age coming on, and his father working very little ! I'd thank you to be glad about something else besides that, Mr. Lindley."

The woman began to cry. Her husband, quite impassive, finished his lunch of meat-pie, and drank some beer. Then he turned to the fire, as if there were no one in the room but himself.

" I shall respect all men who serve God and their country on the sea, Mrs. Durant," said the clergyman stubbornly.

" That is very well, when they're not your sons who are doing the dirty work. It makes a difference," she replied tartly.

" I should be proud if one of my sons were to enter the Navy."

" Ay—well—we're not all of us made alike——"

The minister rose. He put down a large folded paper.

" I've brought the almanac," he said.

Mrs. Durant unfolded it.

" I do like a bit of colour in things," she said, petulantly.

The clergyman did not reply.

" There's that envelope for the organist's fund——" said the old woman, and rising, she took the thing from the mantelpiece, went into the shop, and returned sealing it up.

" Which is all I can afford," she said.

Mr. Lindley took his departure, in his pocket the envelope containing Mrs. Durant's offering for Miss Louisa's services. He went from door to door delivering the almanacs, in dull routine. Jaded with the monotony of the business, and with the repeated effort of greeting half-known people, he felt barren and rather irritable. At last he returned home.

In the dining-room was a small fire. Mrs. Lindley, growing very stout, lay on her couch. The vicar carved the cold mutton ; Miss Louisa, short and plump and rather flushed, came in from the kitchen ; Miss Mary, dark, with a beautiful white brow and grey eyes, served the vegetables ; the children chattered a little, but not exuberantly. The very air seemed starved.

" I went to the Durants," said the vicar, as he served out small portions of mutton ; " it appears Alfred has run away to join the Navy."

" Do him good," came the rough voice of the invalid.

Miss Louisa, attending to the youngest child, looked up in protest.

" Why has he done that ? " asked Mary's low, musical voice.

" He wanted some excitement, I suppose," said the vicar. " Shall we say grace ? "

The children were arranged, all bent their heads, grace was pronounced, at the last word every face was being raised to go on with the interesting subject.

" He's just done the right thing, for once," came the rather deep voice of the mother ; " save him from becoming a drunken sot, like the rest of them."

" They're not *all* drunken, mama," said Miss Louisa, stubbornly.

"It's no fault of their upbringing if they're not. Walter Durant is a standing disgrace."

"As I told Mrs. Durant," said the vicar, eating hungrily, "it is the best thing he could have done. It will take him away from temptation during the most dangerous years of his life—how old is he—nineteen?"

"Twenty," said Miss Louisa.

"Twenty!" repeated the vicar. "It will give him wholesome discipline and set before him some sort of standard of duty and honour—nothing could have been better for him. But——"

"We shall miss him from the choir," said Miss Louisa, as if taking opposite sides to her parents.

"That is as it may be," said the vicar. "I prefer to know he is safe in the Navy than running the risk of getting into bad ways here."

"Was he getting into bad ways?" asked the stubborn Miss Louisa.

"You know, Louisa, he wasn't quite what he used to be," said Miss Mary gently and steadily. Miss Louisa shut her rather heavy jaw sulkily. She wanted to deny it, but she knew it was true.

For her he had been a laughing, warm lad, with something kindly and something rich about him. He had made her feel warm. It seemed the days would be colder since he had gone.

"Quite the best thing he could do," said the mother with emphasis.

"I think so," said the vicar. "But his mother was almost abusive because I suggested it."

He spoke in an injured tone.

"What does she care for her children's welfare?" said the invalid. "Their wages is all her concern."

"I suppose she wanted him at home with her," said Miss Louisa.

"Yes, she did—at the expense of his learning to be a drunkard like the rest of them," retorted her mother.

"George Durant doesn't drink," defended her daughter.

"Because he got burned so badly when he was nineteen—in the pit—and that frightened him. The Navy is a better remedy than that, at least."

"Certainly," said the vicar. "Certainly."

And to this Miss Louisa agreed. Yet she could not but feel angry that he had gone away for so many years. She herself was only nineteen.

III

It happened when Miss Mary was twenty-three years old that Mr. Lindley was very ill. The family was exceedingly poor at the time, such a lot of money was needed, so little was forthcoming. Neither Miss Mary nor Miss Louisa had suitors. What chance had they? They met no eligible young men in Aldecross. And what they earned was a mere drop in a void. The girls' hearts were chilled and hardened with fear of this perpetual, cold penury, this narrow struggle, this horrible nothingness of their lives.

A clergyman had to be found for the church work. It so happened the son of an old friend of Mr. Lindley's was waiting three months before taking up his duties. He would come and officiate, for nothing. The young clergyman was keenly expected. He was not more than twenty-seven, a Master of Arts of Oxford, had written his thesis on Roman Law. He came of an old Cambridgeshire family, had some private means, was going to take a church in Northamptonshire with a good stipend, and was not married. Mrs. Lindley incurred new debts, and scarcely regretted her husband's illness.

But when Mr. Massy came there was a shock of disappointment in the house. They had expected a young man with a pipe and a deep voice, but with better manners than Sidney, the eldest of the Lindleys. There arrived instead a small, chétif man, scarcely larger than a boy of twelve, spectacled, timid in the extreme, without a word to utter at first ; yet with a certain inhuman self-sureness.

" What a little abortion ! " was Mrs. Lindley's exclamation to herself on first seeing him, in his buttoned-up clerical coat. And for the first time for many days she was profoundly thankful to God that all her children were decent specimens.

He had not normal powers of perception. They soon saw that he lacked the full range of human feelings, but had rather a strong, philosophical mind, from which he lived. His body was almost unthinkable, in intellect he was something definite. The conversation at once took a balanced, abstract tone when he participated. There was no spontaneous exclamation, no violent assertion or expression of personal conviction, but all cold, reasonable assertion. This was very hard on Mrs. Lindley. The little man would look at her, after one of her pronouncements, and then give, in his thin voice, his own calculated version, so that she felt as if she were tumbling into thin air through a hole in the flimsy floor on which their conversation stood. It was she who felt a fool. Soon she was reduced to a hardy silence.

Still, at the back of her mind, she remembered that he was an unattached gentleman, who would shortly have an income altogether of six or seven hundred a year. What did the man matter, if there were pecuniary ease ! The man was a trifle thrown in. After twenty-two years her sentimentality was ground away, and only the millstone of poverty mattered to her. So she supported the little man as a representative of a decent income.

His most irritating habit was that of a sneering little giggle, all on his own, which came when he perceived or related some illogical absurdity on the part of another person. It was the only form of humour he had. Stupidity in thinking seemed to him exquisitely funny. But any novel was unintelligibly meaningless and dull, and to an Irish sort of humour he listened curiously, examining it like mathematics, or else simply not hearing. In normal human relationship he was not there. Quite unable to take part in simple everyday talk, he padded silently round the house, or sat in the dining-room looking nervously from side to side, always apart in a cold, rarefied little world of his own. Sometimes he made an ironic remark, that did not seem humanly relevant, or he gave his little laugh, like a sneer. He had to defend himself and his own insufficiency. And he answered questions grudgingly, with a yes or no, because he did not see their import and was nervous. It seemed to Miss Louisa he scarcely distinguished one person from another, but that he liked to be near to her, or to Miss Mary, for some sort of contact which stimulated him unknown.

Apart from all this, he was the most admirable workman. He was unremittingly shy, but perfect in his sense of duty : as far as he could conceive Christianity, he was a perfect Christian. Nothing that he realized he could do for any one did he leave undone, although he was so incapable of coming into contact with another being that he could not proffer help. Now he attended assiduously to the sick man, investigated all the affairs of the parish or the church which Mr. Lindley had in control, straightened out accounts, made lists of the sick and needy, padded round with help and to see what he could do. He heard of Mrs. Lindley's anxiety about her sons, and began to investigate means of sending them to Cambridge. His kindness almost frightened Miss Mary. She honoured it so, and yet she shrank from it. For, in it all Mr. Massy seemed to have no sense of any person, any human being whom he was helping : he only realized a kind of mathematical working out, solving of given situations, a calculated well-doing. And it was as if he had accepted the Christian tenets as axioms. His religion consisted in what his scrupulous, abstract mind approved of.

Seeing his acts, Miss Mary must respect and honour him. In consequence she must serve him. To this she had to force herself, shuddering and yet desirous, but he did not perceive it. She accompanied him on his visiting in the parish, and whilst she was cold with admiration for him, often she was touched with pity for the little padding figure with bent shoulders, buttoned up to the chin in his overcoat. She was a handsome, calm girl, tall, with a beautiful repose. Her clothes were poor, and she wore a black silk scarf, having no furs. But she was a lady. As the people saw her walking down Aldecross beside Mr. Massy they said :

" My word, Miss Mary's got a catch. Did ever you see such a sickly little shrimp ! "

She knew they were talking so, and it made her heart grow hot against them, and she drew herself as it were protectively towards the little man beside her. At any rate, she could see and give honour to his genuine goodness.

He could not walk fast, or far.

" You have not been well ? " she asked, in her dignified way.

" I have an internal trouble."

He was not aware of her slight shudder. There was silence, whilst she bowed to recover her composure, to resume her gentle manner towards him.

He was fond of Miss Mary. She had made it a rule of hospitality that he should always be escorted by herself or by her sister on his visits in the parish, which were not many. But some mornings she was engaged. Then Miss Louisa took her place. It was no good Miss Louisa's trying to adopt to Mr. Massy an attitude of queenly service. She was unable to regard him save with aversion. When she saw him from behind, thin and bent-shouldered, looking like a sickly lad of thirteen, she disliked him exceedingly, and felt a desire to put him out of existence. And yet a deeper justice in Mary made Louisa humble before her sister.

They were going to see Mr. Durant, who was paralysed and not expected to live. Miss Louisa was crudely ashamed at being admitted to the cottage in company with the little clergyman.

Mrs. Durant was, however, much quieter in the face of her real trouble.

" How is Mr. Durant ? " asked Louisa.

" He is no different—and we don't expect him to be," was the reply. The little clergyman stood looking on.

They went upstairs. The three stood for some time looking at the bed, at the grey head of the old man on the pillow, the grey beard over the sheet. Miss Louisa was shocked and afraid.

" It is so dreadful," she said, with a shudder.

" It is how I always thought it would be," replied Mrs. Durant.

Then Miss Louisa was afraid of her. The two women were uneasy, waiting for Mr. Massy to say something. He stood, small and bent, too nervous to speak.

" Has he any understanding ? " he asked at length.

" Maybe," said Mrs. Durant. " Can you hear, John ? " she asked loudly. The dull blue eye of the inert man looked at her feebly.

" Yes, he understands," said Mrs. Durant to Mr. Massy. Except for the dull look in his eyes, the sick man lay as if dead. The three stood in silence. Miss Louisa was obstinate but heavy-hearted under the load of unlivingness. It was Mr. Massy who kept her there in discipline. His non-human will dominated them all.

Then they heard a sound below, a man's footsteps, and a man's voice called subduedly :

" Are you upstairs, mother ? "

Mrs. Durant started and moved to the door. But already a quick, firm step was running up the stairs.

" I'm a bit early, mother," a troubled voice said, and on the landing they saw the form of the sailor. His mother came and clung to him. She was suddenly aware that she needed something to hold on to. He put his arms round her, and bent over her, kissing her.

" He's not gone, mother ? " he asked anxiously, struggling to control his voice.

Miss Louisa looked away from the mother and son who stood together in the gloom on the landing. She could not bear it that she and Mr. Massy should be there. The latter stood nervously, as if ill at ease before the emotion that was running. He was a witness nervous, unwilling, but dispassionate. To Miss Louisa's hot heart it seemed all, all wrong that they should be there.

Mrs. Durant entered the bedroom, her face wet.

" There's Miss Louisa and the vicar," she said, out of voice and quavering.

Her son, red-faced and slender, drew himself up to salute. But Miss Louisa held out her hand. Then she saw his hazel eyes recognize her for a moment, and his small white teeth showed in a glimpse of the greeting she used to love. She was covered with confusion. He went round to the bed ; his boots clicked on the plaster floor, he bowed his head with dignity.

" How are you, dad ? " he said, laying his hand on the sheet, faltering. But the old man stared fixedly and unseeing. The son stood perfectly still for a few minutes, then slowly recoiled. Miss Louisa saw the fine outline of his breast, under the sailor's blue blouse, as his chest began to heave.

" He doesn't know me," he said, turning to his mother. He gradually went white.

" No, my boy ! " cried the mother, pitiful, lifting her face. And suddenly she put her face against his shoulder, he was stooping down to her, holding her against him, and she cried aloud for a moment or two. Miss Louisa saw his sides heaving, and heard the sharp hiss of his breath. She turned away, tears streaming down her face. The father lay inert upon the white bed, Mr. Massy looked queer and obliterated, so little now that the sailor with his sun-burned skin was in the room. He stood waiting. Miss Louisa wanted to die, she wanted to have done. She dared not turn round again to look.

" Shall I offer a prayer ? " came the frail voice of the clergyman, and all kneeled down.

Miss Louisa was frightened of the inert man upon the bed. Then she felt a flash of fear of Mr. Massy, hearing his thin, detached voice. And then, calmed, she looked up. On the far side of the bed were the heads of the mother and son, the one in the black lace cap, with the small white nape of the neck beneath, the other, with brown, sun-scorched hair too close and wiry to allow of a parting, and neck tanned firm, bowed as if unwillingly. The great grey beard of the old man did not move, the prayer continued. Mr. Massy prayed with a pure lucidity that they all might conform to the higher Will. He was like something that dominated the bowed heads, something dispassionate that governed them inexorably. Miss Louisa was afraid of him. And she was bound, during the course of the prayer, to have a little reverence for him. It was like a foretaste of inexorable, cold death, a taste of pure justice.

That evening she talked to Mary of the visit. Her heart, her veins were possessed by the thought of Alfred Durant as he held his mother in his arms ; then the break in his voice, as she remembered it again and again, was like a flame through her ; and she wanted to see his face more distinctly in her mind, ruddy with the sun, and his golden-brown eyes, kind and careless, strained now with a natural fear, the fine nose tanned hard by the sun, the mouth that could not help smiling at her. And it went through her with pride, to think of his figure, a straight, fine jet of life.

" He is a handsome lad," said she to Miss Mary, as if he had not been a year older than herself. Underneath was the deeper dread, almost hatred, of the inhuman being of Mr. Massy. She felt she must protect herself and Alfred from him.

" When I felt Mr. Massy there," she said, " I almost hated him. What right had he to be there ! "

" Surely he has all right," said Miss Mary after a pause. " He is *really* a Christian."

" He seems to me nearly an imbecile," said Miss Louisa.

Miss Mary, quiet and beautiful, was silent for a moment :

" Oh, no," she said. " Not *imbecile*——"

" Well then—he reminds me of a six months' child—or a five months' child—as if he didn't have time to get developed enough before he was born."

" Yes," said Miss Mary, slowly. " There is something lacking. But there is something wonderful in him : and he is really *good*——"

" Yes," said Miss Louisa, " it doesn't seem right that he should be. What right has *that* to be called goodness ! "

" But it *is* goodness," persisted Mary. Then she added, with a laugh : " And come, you wouldn't deny that as well."

There was a doggedness in her voice. She went about very quietly. In her soul, she knew what was going to happen. She knew that Mr. Massy was stronger than she, and that she must submit to what he was. Her physical self was prouder, stronger than he, her physical self disliked and despised him. But she was in the grip of his moral, mental being. And she felt the days allotted out to her. And her family watched.

IV

A few days after, old Mr. Durant died. Miss Louisa saw Alfred once more, but he was stiff before her now, treating her not like a person, but as if she were some sort of will in command and he a separate, distinct will waiting in front of her. She had never felt such utter steel-plate separation from any one. It puzzled her and frightened her. What had become of him ? And she hated the military discipline—she was antagonistic to it. Now he was not himself. He was the will which obeys set over against the will which commands. She hesitated over accepting this. He had put himself out of her range. He had ranked himself inferior, subordinate to her. And that was how he would get away from her, that was how he would avoid all connection with her : by fronting her impersonally from the opposite camp, by taking up the abstract position of an inferior.

She went brooding steadily and sullenly over this, brooding and brooding. Her fierce, obstinate heart could not give way. It clung to its own rights. Sometimes she dismissed him. Why should he, her inferior, trouble her ?

Then she relapsed to him, and almost hated him. It was his way of getting out of it. She felt the cowardice of it, his calmly placing her in a superior class, and placing himself inaccessibly apart, in an inferior, as if she, the sentient woman who was fond of him, did not count. But she was not going to submit. Dogged in her heart she held on to him.

v

In six months' time Miss Mary had married Mr. Massy. There had been no love-making, nobody had made any remark. But everybody was tense and callous with expectation. When one day Mr. Massy asked for Mary's hand, Mr. Lindley started and trembled from the thin, abstract voice of the little man. Mr. Massy was very nervous, but so curiously absolute.

" I shall be very glad," said the vicar, " but of course the decision lies with Mary herself." And his still feeble hand shook as he moved a Bible on his desk.

The small man, keeping fixedly to his idea, padded out of the room to find Miss Mary. He sat a long time by her, while she made some conversation, before he had readiness to speak. She was afraid of what was coming, and sat stiff in apprehension. She felt as if her body would rise and fling him aside. But her spirit quivered and waited. Almost in expectation she waited, almost wanting him. And then she knew he would speak.

" I have already asked Mr. Lindley," said the clergyman, while suddenly she looked with aversion at his little knees, " if he would consent to my proposal." He was aware of his own disadvantage, but his will was set.

She went cold as she sat, and impervious, almost as if she had become stone. He waited a moment nervously. He would not persuade her. He himself never even heard persuasion, but pursued his own course. He looked at her, sure of himself, unsure of her, and said :

" Will you become my wife, Mary ? "

Still her heart was hard and cold. She sat proudly.

" I should like to speak to mama first," she said.

"Very well,"replied Mr. Massy. And in a moment he padded away.

Mary went to her mother. She was cold and reserved.

" Mr. Massy has asked me to marry him, mama," she said. Mrs. Lindley went on staring at her book. She was cramped in her feeling.

" Well, and what did you say ? "

They were both keeping calm and cold.

" I said I would speak to you before answering him."

This was equivalent to a question. Mrs. Lindley did not want to reply to it. She shifted her heavy form irritably on the couch. Miss Mary sat calm and straight, with closed mouth.

" Your father thinks it would not be a bad match," said the mother, as if casually.

Nothing more was said. Everybody remained cold and shut-off. Miss Mary did not speak to Miss Louisa, the Reverend Ernest Lindley kept out of sight.

At evening Miss Mary accepted Mr. Massy.

" Yes, I will marry you," she said, with even a little movement of tenderness towards him. He was embarrassed, but satisfied. She could see him making some movement towards her, could feel the male in him, something cold and triumphant, asserting itself. She sat rigid, and waited.

When Miss Louisa knew, she was silent with bitter anger against everybody, even against Mary. She felt her faith wounded. Did the real things to her not matter after all ? She wanted to get away. She thought of Mr. Massy. He had some curious power, some unanswerable right. He was a will that they could not controvert. Suddenly a flush started in her. If he had come to her she would have flipped him out of the room. He was never going to touch *her*. And she was glad. She was glad that her blood would rise and exterminate the little man, if he came too near to her, no matter how her judgment was paralysed by him, no matter how he moved in abstract goodness. She thought she was perverse to be glad, but glad she was. " I would just flip him out of the room," she said, and she derived great satisfaction from the open statement. Nevertheless, perhaps she ought still to feel that Mary, on her plane, was a higher being than herself. But then Mary was Mary, and she was Louisa, and that also was inalterable.

Mary, in marrying him, tried to become a pure reason such as he was, without feeling or impulse. She shut herself up, she shut herself rigid against the agonies of shame and the terror of violation which came at first. She *would* not feel, and she *would* not feel. She was a pure will acquiescing to him. She elected a certain kind of fate. She would be good and purely just, she would live in a higher freedom than she had ever known, she would be free of mundane care, she was a pure will towards right. She had sold herself, but she had a new freedom. She had got rid of her body. She had sold a lower thing, her body, for a higher thing, her freedom from material things. She considered that she paid for all she got from her husband. So, in a kind of independence, she moved proud and free. She had paid with her body : that was henceforward out of consideration. She was glad to be rid of it. She had bought her position in the world—that henceforth was taken for granted. There remained only the direction of her activity towards charity and high-minded living.

She could scarcely bear other people to be present with her and her husband. Her private life was her shame. But then, she could keep it hidden. She lived almost isolated in the rectory of the tiny village miles from the railway. She suffered as if it were an insult to her own flesh, seeing the repulsion which some people felt for her husband, or the special manner they had of treating him, as if he were a " case." But most people were uneasy before him, which restored her pride.

If she had let herself, she would have hated him, hated his padding round the house, his thin voice devoid of human understanding, his bent little shoulders and rather incomplete face that reminded her of an abortion. But rigorously she kept to her position. She took care of him and was just to him. There was also a deep, craven fear of him, something slave-like.

There was not much fault to be found with his behaviour. He was scrupulously just and kind according to his lights. But the male in him was cold and self-complete, and utterly domineering. Weak, insufficient little thing as he was, she had not expected this of him. It was something in the bargain she had not understood. It made her hold her head, to keep still. She knew, vaguely, that she was murdering herself. After all, her body was not quite so easy to get rid of. And this manner of disposing of it—ah, sometimes she felt she must rise and bring about death, lift her hand for utter denial of everything, by a general destruction.

He was almost unaware of the conditions about him. He did not fuss in the domestic way, she did as she liked in the house. Indeed, she was a great deal free of him. He would sit obliterated for hours. He was kind, and almost anxiously considerate. But when he considered he was right, his will was just blindly male, like a cold machine. And on most points he was logically right, or he had with him the right of the creed they both accepted. It was so. There was nothing for her to go against.

Then she found herself with child, and felt for the first time horror, afraid before God and man. This also she had to go through —it was the right. When the child arrived, it was a bonny, healthy lad. Her heart hurt in her body, as she took the baby between her hands. The flesh that was trampled and silent in her must speak again in the boy. After all, she had to live—it was not so simple after all. Nothing was finished completely. She looked and looked at the baby, and almost hated it, and suffered an anguish of love for it. She hated it because it made her live again in the flesh, when she *could* not live in the flesh, she could not. She wanted to trample her flesh down, down, extinct, to live in the mind. And now there was this child. It was too cruel, too racking. For she must love the child. Her purpose was broken in two again. She had to become amorphous, purposeless, without real being. As a mother, she was a fragmentary, ignoble thing.

Mr. Massy, blind to everything else in the way of human feeling, became obsessed by the idea of his child. When it arrived, suddenly it filled the whole world of feeling for him. It was his obsession, his terror was for its safety and well-being. It was something new, as if he himself had been born a naked infant, conscious of his own exposure, and full of apprehension. He who had never been aware of any one else, all his life, now was aware of nothing but the child. Not that he ever played with it, or kissed it, or tended it. He did nothing for it. But it dominated him, it filled, and at the same time emptied his mind. The world was all baby for him.

This his wife must also bear, his question : " What is the reason that he cries ? "—his reminder, at the first sound : " Mary, that is the child,"—his restlessness if the feeding-time were five minutes past. She had bargained for this—now she must stand by her bargain.

VI

Miss Louisa, at home in the dingy vicarage, had suffered a great deal over her sister's wedding. Having once begun to cry out against it, during the engagement, she had been silenced by Mary's quiet : " I don't agree with you about him, Louisa, I *want* to marry him." Then Miss Louisa had been angry deep in her heart, and therefore silent. This dangerous state started the change in her. Her own revulsion made her recoil from the hitherto undoubted Mary.

" I'd beg the streets barefoot first," said Miss Louisa, thinking of Mr. Massy.

But evidently Mary could perform a different heroism. So she, Louisa the practical, suddenly felt that Mary, her ideal, was questionable after all. How could she be pure—one cannot be dirty in act and spiritual in being. Louisa distrusted Mary's high spirituality. It was no longer genuine for her. And if Mary were spiritual and misguided, why did not her father protect her ? Because of the money. He disliked the whole affair, but he backed away, because of the money. And the mother frankly did not care : her daughters could do as they liked. Her mother's pronouncement :

" Whatever happens to *him*, Mary is safe for life,"—so evidently and shallowly a calculation, incensed Louisa.

" I'd rather be safe in the workhouse," she cried.

" Your father will see to that," replied her mother brutally. This speech, in its indirectness, so injured Miss Louisa that she hated her mother deep, deep in her heart, and almost hated herself. It was a long time resolving itself out, this hate. But it worked and worked, and at last the young woman said :

" They are wrong—they are all wrong. They have ground out their souls for what isn't worth anything, and there isn't a grain of love in them anywhere. And I *will* have love. They want us to deny it. They've never found it, so they want to say it doesn't exist. But I *will* have it. I *will* love—it is my birthright. I will love the man I marry—that is all I care about."

So Miss Louisa stood isolated from everybody. She and Mary had parted over Mr. Massy. In Louisa's eyes, Mary was degraded, married to Mr. Massy. She could not bear to think of her lofty, spiritual sister degraded in the body like this. Mary was wrong, wrong, wrong : she was not superior, she was flawed, incomplete. The two sisters stood apart. They still loved each other, they would love each other as long as they lived. But they had parted ways. A new solitariness came over the obstinate Louisa, and her heavy jaw set stubbornly. She was going on her own way. But which way ? She was quite alone, with a blank world before her. How could she be said to have any way ? Yet she had her fixed will to love, to have the man she loved.

VII

When her boy was three years old, Mary had another baby, a girl. The three years had gone by monotonously. They might have been an eternity, they might have been brief as a sleep. She did not know. Only, there was always a weight on top of her, something that pressed down her life. The only thing that had happened was that Mr. Massy had had an operation. He was always exceedingly fragile. His wife had soon learned to attend to him mechanically, as part of her duty.

But this third year, after the baby girl had been born, Mary felt oppressed and depressed. Christmas drew near : the gloomy, unleavened Christmas of the rectory, where all the days were of the same dark fabric. And Mary was afraid. It was as if the darkness were coming upon her.

"Edward, I should like to go home for Christmas," she said, and a certain terror filled her as she spoke.

"But you can't leave baby," said her husband, blinking.

"We can all go."

He thought, and stared in his collective fashion.

"Why do you wish to go ? " he asked.

"Because I need a change. A change would do me good, and it would be good for the milk."

He heard the will in his wife's voice, and was at a loss. Her language was unintelligible to him. But somehow he felt that Mary was set upon it. And while she was breeding, either about to have a child, or nursing, he regarded her as a special sort of being.

"Wouldn't it hurt baby to take her by the train ? " he said.

"No," replied the mother, " why should it ? "

They went. When they were in the train it began to snow. From the window of his first-class carriage the little clergyman watched the big flakes sweep by, like a blind drawn across the country. He was obsessed by thought of the baby, and afraid of the draughts of the carriage.

"Sit right in the corner," he said to his wife, " and hold baby close back."

She moved at his bidding, and stared out of the window. His eternal presence was like an iron weight on her brain. But she was going partially to escape for a few days.

"Sit on the other side, Jack," said the father. " It is less draughty. Come to this window."

He watched the boy in anxiety. But his children were the

only beings in the world who took not the slightest notice of him.

"Look, mother, look!" cried the boy. "They fly right in my face"—he meant the snowflakes.

"Come into this corner," repeated his father, out of another world.

"He's jumped on this one's back, mother, an' they're riding to the bottom!" cried the boy, jumping with glee.

"Tell him to come on this side," the little man bade his wife.

"Jack, kneel on this cushion," said the mother, putting her white hand on the place.

The boy slid over in silence to the place she indicated, waited still for a moment, then almost deliberately, stridently cried:

"Look at all those in the corner, mother, making a heap," and he pointed to the cluster of snowflakes with finger pressed dramatically on the pane, and he turned to his mother a bit ostentatiously.

"All in a heap!" she said.

He had seen her face, and had her response, and he was somewhat assured. Vaguely uneasy, he was reassured if he could win her attention.

They arrived at the vicarage at half-past two, not having had lunch.

"How are you, Edward?" said Mr. Lindley, trying on his side to be fatherly. But he was always in a false position with his son-in-law, frustrated before him, therefore, as much as possible, he shut his eyes and ears to him. The vicar was looking thin and pale and ill-nourished. He had gone quite grey. He was, however, still haughty; but, since the growing-up of his children, it was a brittle haughtiness, that might break at any moment and leave the vicar only an impoverished, pitiable figure. Mrs. Lindley took all the notice of her daughter, and of the children. She ignored her son-in-law. Miss Louisa was clucking and laughing and rejoicing over the baby. Mr. Massy stood aside, a bent, persistent little figure.

"Oh a pretty!—a little pretty! oh a cold little pretty come in a railway-train!" Miss Louisa was cooing to the infant, crouching on the hearthrug, opening the white woollen wraps and exposing the child to the fireglow.

"Mary," said the little clergyman, "I think it would be better to give baby a warm bath; she may take a cold."

"I think it is not necessary," said the mother, coming and closing her hand judiciously over the rosy feet and hands of the mite. "She is not chilly."

"Not a bit," cried Miss Louisa. "She's not caught cold."

" I'll go and bring her flannels," said Mr. Massy, with one idea.

" I can bath her in the kitchen then," said Mary, in an altered, cold tone.

" You can't, the girl is scrubbing there," said Miss Louisa. " Besides, she doesn't want a bath at this time of day."

" She'd better have one," said Mary, quietly, out of submission. Miss Louisa's gorge rose, and she was silent. When the little man padded down with the flannels on his arm, Mrs. Lindley asked :

" Hadn't *you* better take a hot bath, Edward ? "

But the sarcasm was lost on the little clergyman. He was absorbed in the preparations round the baby.

The room was dull and threadbare, and the snow outside seemed fairy-like by comparison, so white on the lawn and tufted on the bushes. Indoors the heavy pictures hung obscurely on the walls, everything was dingy with gloom.

Except in the fireglow, where they had laid the bath on the hearth. Mrs. Massy, her black hair always smoothly coiled and queenly, kneeled by the bath, wearing a rubber apron, and holding the kicking child. Her husband stood holding the towels and the flannels to warm. Louisa, too cross to share in the joy of the baby's bath, was laying the table. The boy was hanging on the door-knob, wrestling with it to get out. His father looked round.

" Come away from the door, Jack," he said ineffectually. Jack tugged harder at the knob as if he did not hear. Mr. Massy blinked at him.

" He must come away from the door, Mary," he said. " There will be a draught if it is opened."

" Jack, come away from the door, dear," said the mother, dexterously turning the shiny wet baby on to her towelled knee. then glancing round : " Go and tell Auntie Louisa about the train."

Louisa, also afraid to open the door, was watching the scene on the hearth. Mr. Massy stood holding the baby's flannel, as if assisting at some ceremonial. If everybody had not been subduedly angry, it would have been ridiculous.

" I want to see out of the window," Jack said. His father turned hastily.

" Do *you* mind lifting him on to a chair, Louisa," said Mary hastily. The father was too delicate.

When the baby was flannelled, Mr. Massy went upstairs and returned with four pillows, which he set in the fender to warm. Then he stood watching the mother feed her child, obsessed by the idea of his infant.

Louisa went on with her preparations for the meal. She could not have told why she was so sullenly angry. Mrs. Lindley, as usual, lay silently watching.

Mary carried her child upstairs, followed by her husband with the pillows. After a while he came down again.

"What is Mary doing? Why doesn't she come down to eat?" asked Mrs. Lindley.

"She is staying with baby. The room is rather cold. I will ask the girl to put in a fire." He was going absorbedly to the door.

"But Mary has had nothing to eat. It is *she* who will catch cold," said the mother, exasperated.

Mr. Massy seemed as if he did not hear. Yet he looked at his mother-in-law, and answered :

"I will take her something."

He went out. Mrs. Lindley shifted on her couch with anger. Miss Louisa glowered. But no one said anything, because of the money that came to the vicarage from Mr. Massy.

Louisa went upstairs. Her sister was sitting by the bed, reading a scrap of paper.

"Won't you come down and eat?" the younger asked.

"In a moment or two," Mary replied, in a quiet, reserved voice, that forbade any one to approach her.

It was this that made Miss Louisa most furious. She went downstairs, and announced to her mother :

"I am going out. I may not be home to tea."

VIII

No one remarked on her exit. She put on her fur hat, that the village people knew so well, and the old Norfolk jacket. Louisa was short and plump and plain. She had her mother's heavy jaw, her father's proud brow, and her own grey, brooding eyes that were very beautiful when she smiled. It was true, as the people said, that she looked sulky. Her chief attraction was her glistening, heavy, deep-blonde hair, which shone and gleamed with a richness that was not entirely foreign to her.

"Where am I going?" she said to herself, when she got outside in the snow. She did not hesitate, however, but by mechanical walking found herself descending the hill towards Old Aldecross. In the valley that was black with trees, the colliery breathed in stertorous pants, sending out high conical columns of steam that remained upright, whiter than the snow on the hills, yet shadowy, in the dead air. Louisa would not acknowledge to herself whither she was making her way, till she came to the railway crossing. Then the bunches of snow in the twigs of the apple tree that leaned towards the fence told her she must go and see Mrs. Durant. The tree was in Mrs. Durant's garden.

Alfred was now at home again, living with his mother in the cottage below the road. From the highway hedge, by the railway crossing, the snowy garden sheered down steeply, like the side of a hole, then dropped straight in a wall. In this depth the house was snug, its chimney just level with the road. Miss Louisa descended the stone stairs, and stood below in the little backyard, in the dimness and the semi-secrecy. A big tree leaned overhead, above the paraffin hut. Louisa felt secure from all the world down there. She knocked at the open door, then looked round. The tongue of garden narrowing in from the quarry bed was white with snow : she thought of the thick fringes of snowdrops it would show beneath the currant bushes in a month's time. The ragged fringe of pinks hanging over the garden brim behind her was whitened now with snowflakes, that in summer held white blossom to Louisa's face. It was pleasant, she thought, to gather flowers that stooped to one's face from above.

She knocked again. Peeping in, she saw the scarlet glow of the kitchen, red firelight falling on the brick floor and on the bright chintz cushions. It was alive and bright as a peep-show. She crossed the scullery, where still an almanac hung. There was no one about. " Mrs. Durant," called Louisa softly, " Mrs. Durant."

She went up the brick step into the front room, that still had its little shop counter and its bundles of goods, and she called from the stair-foot. Then she knew Mrs. Durant was out.

She went into the yard, to follow the old woman's footsteps up the garden path.

She emerged from the bushes and raspberry canes. There was the whole quarry bed, a wide garden white and dimmed, brindled with dark bushes, lying half submerged. On the left, overhead, the little colliery train rumbled by. Right away at the back was a mass of trees.

Louisa followed the open path, looking from right to left, and then she gave a cry of concern. The old woman was sitting rocking slightly among the ragged snowy cabbages. Louisa ran to her, found her whimpering with little, involuntary cries.

" Whatever have you done ? " cried Louisa, kneeling in the snow.

" I've—I've—I was pulling a brussel-sprout stalk—and—oh-h !—

something tore inside me. I've had a pain," the old woman wept from shock and suffering, gasping between her whimpers,—" I've had a pain there—a long time—and now—oh—oh ! " She panted, pressed her hand on her side, leaned as if she would faint, looking yellow against the snow. Louisa supported her.

" Do you think you could walk now ? " she asked.

" Yes," gasped the old woman.

Louisa helped her to her feet.

" Get the cabbage—I want it for Alfred's dinner," panted Mrs. Durant. Louisa picked up the stalk of brussel-sprouts, and with difficulty got the old woman indoors. She gave her brandy, laid her on the couch, saying :

" I'm going to send for a doctor—wait just a minute."

The young woman ran up the steps to the public-house a few yards away. The landlady was astonished to see Miss Louisa.

" Will you send for a doctor at once to Mrs. Durant," she said, with some of her father in her commanding tone.

" Is something the matter ? " fluttered the landlady in concern.

Louisa, glancing out up the road, saw the grocer's cart driving to Eastwood. She ran and stopped the man, and told him.

Mrs. Durant lay on the sofa, her face turned away, when the young woman came back.

" Let me put you to bed," Louisa said. Mrs. Durant did not resist.

Louisa knew the ways of the working people. In the bottom drawer of the dresser she found dusters and flannels. With the old pit-flannel she snatched out the oven shelves, wrapped them up, and put them in the bed. From the son's bed she took a blanket, and, running down, set it before the fire. Having undressed the little old woman, Louisa carried her upstairs.

" You'll drop me, you'll drop me ! " cried Mrs. Durant.

Louisa did not answer, but bore her burden quickly. She could not light a fire, because there was no fire-place in the bedroom. And the floor was plaster. So she fetched the lamp, and stood it lighted in one corner.

" It will air the room," she said.

" Yes," moaned the old woman.

Louisa ran with more hot flannels, replacing those from the oven shelves. Then she made a bran-bag and laid it on the woman's side. There was a big lump on the side of the abdomen.

" I've felt it coming a long time," moaned the old lady, when the pain was easier, " but I've not said anything ; I didn't want to upset our Alfred."

Louisa did not see why " our Alfred " should be spared.

" What time is it ? " came the plaintive voice.

" A quarter to four."

" Oh ! " wailed the old lady, " he'll be here in half an hour, and no dinner ready for him."

" Let me do it ? " said Louisa, gently.

" There's that cabbage—and you'll find the meat in the pantry—and there's an apple pie you can hot up. But *don't you* do it—— ! "

" Who will, then ? " asked Louisa.

" I don't know," moaned the sick woman, unable to consider.

Louisa did it. The doctor came and gave serious examination. He looked very grave.

" What is it, doctor ? " asked the old lady, looking up at him with old, pathetic eyes in which already hope was dead.

" I think you've torn the skin in which a tumour hangs," he replied.

" Ay ! " she murmured, and she turned away.

" You see, she may die any minute—and it *may* be swaled away," said the old doctor to Louisa.

The young woman went upstairs again.

" He says the lump may be swaled away, and you may get quite well again," she said.

" Ay ! " murmured the old lady. It did not deceive her. Presently she asked :

" Is there a good fire ? "

" I think so," answered Louisa.

" He'll want a good fire," the mother said. Louisa attended to it.

Since the death of Durant, the widow had come to church occasionally, and Louisa had been friendly to her. In the girl's heart the purpose was fixed. No man had affected her as Alfred Durant had done, and to that she kept. In her heart, she adhered to him. A natural sympathy existed between her and his rather hard, materialistic mother.

Alfred was the most lovable of the old woman's sons. He had grown up like the rest, however, headstrong and blind to everything but his own will. Like the other boys, he had insisted on going into the pit as soon as he left school, because that was the only way speedily to become a man, level with all the other men. This was a great chagrin to his mother, who would have liked to have this last of her sons a gentleman.

But still he remained constant to her. His feeling for her was deep

and unexpressed. He noticed when she was tired, or when she had
a new cap. And he bought little things for her occasionally. She
was not wise enough to see how much he lived by her.

At the bottom he did not satisfy her, he did not seem manly
enough. He liked to read books occasionally, and better still he
liked to play the piccolo. It amused her to see his head nod over
the instrument as he made an effort to get the right note. It made
her fond of him, with tenderness, almost pity, but not with respect.
She wanted a man to be fixed, going his own way without knowledge of women. Whereas she knew Alfred depended on her. He
sang in the choir because he liked singing. In the summer he worked
in the garden, attended to the fowls and pigs. He kept pigeons.
He played on Saturday in the cricket or football team. But to her
he did not seem the man, the independent man her other boys had
been. He was her baby—and whilst she loved him for it, she was
a little bit contemptuous of him.

There grew up a little hostility between them. Then he began
to drink, as the others had done ; but not in their blind, oblivious
way. He was a little self-conscious over it. She saw this, and she
pitied it in him. She loved him most, but she was not satisfied
with him because he was not free of her. He could not quite go
his own way.

Then at twenty he ran away and served his time in the Navy.
This had made a man of him. He had hated it bitterly, the service,
the subordination. For years he fought with himself under the
military discipline, for his own self-respect, struggling through blind
anger and shame and a cramping sense of inferiority. Out of humiliation and self-hatred he rose into a sort of inner freedom. And his
love for his mother, whom he idealized, remained the fact of hope
and of belief.

He came home again, nearly thirty years old, but naïve and inex-
perienced as a boy, only with a silence about him that was new : a
sort of dumb humility before life, a fear of living. He was almost
quite chaste. A strong sensitiveness had kept him from women.
Sexual talk was all very well among men, but somehow it had no
application to living women. There were two things for him, the
idea of women, with which he sometimes debauched himself, and
real women, before whom he felt a deep uneasiness, and a need to
draw away. He shrank and defended himself from the approach
of any woman. And then he felt ashamed. In his innermost soul
he felt he was not a man, he was less than the normal man. In
Genoa he went with an under-officer to a drinking house where

the cheaper sort of girl came in to look for lovers. He sat there with his glass, the girls looked at him, but they never came to him. He knew that if they did come he could only pay for food and drink for them, because he felt a pity for them, and was anxious lest they lacked good necessities. He could not have gone with one of them ; he knew it, and was ashamed, looking with curious envy at the swaggering, easy-passionate Italian whose body went to a woman by instinctive impersonal attraction. They were men, he was not a man. He sat feeling short, feeling like a leper. And he went away imagining sexual scenes between himself and a woman, walking wrapt in this indulgence. But when the ready woman presented herself, the very fact that she was a palpable woman made it impossible for him to touch her. And this incapacity was like a core of rottenness in him.

So several times he went, drunk, with his companions, to the licensed prostitute houses abroad. But the sordid insignificance of the experience appalled him. It had not been anything really : it meant nothing. He felt as if he were, not physically, but spiritually impotent : not actually impotent, but intrinsically so.

He came home with this secret, never changing burden of his unknown, unbestowed self torturing him. His Navy training left him in perfect physical condition. He was sensible of, and proud of his body. He bathed and used dumb-bells, and kept himself fit. He played cricket and football. He read books and began to hold fixed ideas which he got from the Fabians. He played his piccolo, and was considered an expert. But at the bottom of his soul was always this canker of shame and incompleteness : he was miserable beneath all his healthy cheerfulness, he was uneasy and felt despicable among all his confidence and superiority of ideas. He would have changed with any mere brute, just to be free of himself, to be free of this shame of self-consciousness. He saw some collier lurching straight forward without misgiving, pursuing his own satisfactions, and he envied him. Anything, he would have given anything for this spontaneity and this blind stupidity which went to its own satisfaction direct.

IX

He was not unhappy in the pit. He was admired by the men, and well enough liked. It was only he himself who felt the difference between himself and the others. He seemed to hide his own stigma. But he was never sure that the others did not really despise him for a ninny, as being less a man than they were. Only he pretended to be more manly, and was surprised by the ease with which they were deceived. And, being naturally cheerful, he was happy at work. He was sure of himself there. Naked to the waist, hot and grimy with labour, they squatted on their heels for a few minutes and talked, seeing each other dimly by the light of the safety lamps, while the black coal rose jutting round them, and the props of wood stood like little pillars in the low, black, very dark temple. Then the pony came and the gang-lad with a message from Number 7, or with a bottle of water from the horse-trough or some news of the world above. The day passed pleasantly enough. There was an ease, a go-as-you-please about the day underground, a delightful camaraderie of men shut off alone from the rest of the world, in a dangerous place, and a variety of labour, holing, loading, timbering, and a glamour of mystery and adventure in the atmosphere, that made the pit not unattractive to him when he had again got over his anguish of desire for the open air and the sea.

This day there was much to do and Durant was not in humour to talk. He went on working in silence through the afternoon.

"Loose-all" came, and they tramped to the bottom. The white-washed underground office shone brightly. Men were putting out their lamps. They sat in dozens round the bottom of the shaft, down which black, heavy drops of water fell continuously into the sumph. The electric lights shone away down the main underground road.

"Is it raining?" asked Durant.

"Snowing," said an old man, and the younger was pleased. He liked to go up when it was snowing.

"It'll just come right for Christmas?" said the old man.

"Ay," replied Durant.

"A green Christmas, a fat churchyard," said the other sententiously.

Durant laughed, showing his small, rather pointed teeth.

The cage came down, a dozen men lined on. Durant noticed tufts of snow on the perforated, arched roof of the chain, and he was pleased. He wondered how it liked its excursion underground. But already it was getting soppy with black water.

He liked things about him. There was a little smile on his face. But underlying it was the curious consciousness he felt in himself.

The upper world came almost with a flash, because of the glimmer of snow. Hurrying along the bank, giving up his lamp at the office, he smiled to feel the open about him again, all glimmering round him with snow. The hills on either hand were pale blue in the dusk, and the hedges looked savage and dark. The snow was trampled between the railway lines. But far ahead, beyond the black figures of miners moving home, it became smooth again, spreading right up to the dark wall of the coppice.

To the west there was a pinkness, and a big star hovered half revealed. Below, the lights of the pit came out crisp and yellow among the darkness of the buildings, and the lights of Old Aldecross twinkled in rows down the bluish twilight.

Durant walked glad with life among the miners, who were all talking animatedly because of the snow. He liked their company, he liked the white dusky world. It gave him a little thrill to stop at the garden gate and see the light of home down below, shining on the silent blue snow.

x

By the big gate of the railway, in the fence, was a little gate, that he kept locked. As he unfastened it, he watched the kitchen light that shone on to the bushes and the snow outside. It was a candle burning till night set in, he thought to himself. He slid down the steep path to the level below. He liked making the first marks in the smooth snow. Then he came through the bushes to the house. The two women heard his heavy boots ring outside on the scraper, and his voice as he opened the door :

" How much worth of oil do you reckon to save by that candle, mother ? " He liked a good light from the lamp.

He had just put down his bottle and snap-bag and was hanging his coat behind the scullery door, when Miss Louisa came upon him. He was startled, but he smiled.

His eyes began to laugh—then his face went suddenly straight, and he was afraid.

" Your mother's had an accident," she said.

" How ? " he exclaimed.

" In the garden," she answered. He hesitated with his coat in his hands. Then he hung it up and turned to the kitchen.

" Is she in bed ? " he asked.

" Yes," said Miss Louisa, who found it hard to deceive him. He was silent. He went into the kitchen, sat down heavily in his father's old chair, and began to pull off his boots. His head was small, rather finely shapen. His brown hair, close and crisp, would look jolly whatever happened. He wore heavy, moleskin trousers that gave off the stale, exhausted scent of the pit. Having put on his slippers, he carried his boots into the scullery.

" What is it ? " he asked, afraid.

" Something internal," she replied.

He went upstairs. His mother kept herself calm for his coming. Louisa felt his tread shake the plaster floor of the bedroom above.

" What have you done ? " he asked.

" It's nothing, my lad," said the old woman, rather hard. " It's nothing. You needn't fret, my boy, it's nothing more the matter with me than I had yesterday, or last week. The doctor said I'd done nothing serious."

" What were you doing ? " asked her son.

" I was pulling up a cabbage, and I suppose I pulled too hard ; for, oh—there was such a pain——"

Her son looked at her quickly. She hardened herself.

" But who doesn't have a sudden pain sometimes, my boy? We all do."

" And what's it done ? "

" I don't know," she said, " but I don't suppose it's anything."

The big lamp in the corner was screened with a dark green screen, so that he could scarcely see her face. He was strung tight with apprehension and many emotions. Then his brow knitted.

" What did you go pulling your inside out at cabbages for," he asked, " and the ground frozen ? You'd go on dragging and dragging, if you killed yourself."

" Somebody's got to get them," she said.

" You needn't do yourself harm."

But they had reached futility.

Miss Louisa could hear plainly downstairs. Her heart sank. It seemed so hopeless between them.

" Are you sure it's nothing much, mother ? " he asked, appealing, after a little silence.

" Ay, it's nothing," said the old woman, rather bitter.

" I don't want you to—to—to be badly—you know."

" Go an' get your dinner," she said. She knew she was going to die : moreover, the pain was torture just then. " They're only cosseting me up a bit because I'm an old woman. Miss Louisa's *very* good—and she'll have got your dinner ready, so you'd better go and eat it."

He felt stupid and ashamed. His mother put him off. He had to turn away. The pain burned in his bowels. He went downstairs. The mother was glad he was gone, so that she could moan with pain.

He had resumed the old habit of eating before he washed himself. Miss Louisa served his dinner. It was strange and exciting to her.

She was strung up tense, trying to understand him and his mother. She watched him as he sat. He was turned away from his food, looking in the fire. Her soul watched him, trying to see what he was. His black face and arms were uncouth, he was foreign. His face was masked black with coal-dust. She could not see him, she could not know him. The brown eyebrows, the steady eyes, the coarse, small moustache above the closed mouth—these were the only familiar indications. What was he, as he sat there in his pit-dirt? She could not see him, and it hurt her.

She ran upstairs, presently coming down with the flannels and the bran-bag, to heat them, because the pain was on again.

He was half-way through his dinner. He put down the fork, suddenly nauseated.

"They will soothe the wrench," she said. He watched, useless and left out.

"Is she bad?" he asked.

"I think she is," she answered.

It was useless for him to stir or comment. Louisa was busy. She went upstairs. The poor old woman was in a white, cold sweat of pain. Louisa's face was sullen with suffering as she went about to relieve her. Then she sat and waited. The pain passed gradually, the old woman sank into a state of coma. Louisa still sat silent by the bed. She heard the sound of water downstairs. Then came the voice of the old mother, faint but unrelaxing:

"Alfred's washing himself—he'll want his back washing——"

Louisa listened anxiously, wondering what the sick woman wanted.

"He can't bear if his back isn't washed——" the old woman persisted, in a cruel attention to his needs. Louisa rose and wiped the sweat from the yellowish brow.

"I will go down," she said soothingly.

"If you would," murmured the sick woman.

Louisa waited a moment. Mrs. Durant closed her eyes, having discharged her duty. The young woman went downstairs. Herself, or the man, what did they matter? Only the suffering woman must be considered.

Alfred was kneeling on the hearthrug, stripped to the waist, washing himself in a large panchion of earthenware. He did so every evening, when he had eaten his dinner; his brothers had done so before him. But Miss Louisa was strange in the house.

He was mechanically rubbing the white lather on his head, with a repeated, unconscious movement, his hand every now and then passing over his neck. Louisa watched. She had to brace herself to this also. He bent his head into the water, washed it free of soap, and pressed the water out of his eyes.

"Your mother said you would want your back washing," she said.

Curious how it hurt her to take part in their fixed routine of life ! Louisa felt the almost repulsive intimacy being forced upon her. It was all so common, so like herding. She lost her own distinctness.

He ducked his face round, looking up at her in what was a very comical way. She had to harden herself.

"How funny he looks with his face upside down," she thought. After all, there was a difference between her and the common people. The water in which his arms were plunged was quite black, the soap-froth was darkish. She could scarcely conceive him as human. Mechanically, under the influence of habit, he groped in the black water, fished out soap and flannel, and handed them backward to Louisa. Then he remained rigid and submissive, his two arms thrust straight in the panchion, supporting the weight of his shoulders. His skin was beautifully white and unblemished, of an opaque, solid whiteness. Gradually Louisa saw it : this also was what he was. It fascinated her. Her feeling of separateness passed away : she ceased to draw back from contact with him and his mother. There was this living centre. Her heart ran hot. She had reached some goal in this beautiful, clear, male body. She loved him in a white, impersonal heat. But the sun-burnt, reddish neck and ears : they were more personal, more curious. A tenderness rose in her, she loved even his queer ears. A person—an intimate being he was to her. She put down the towel and went upstairs again, troubled in her heart. She had only seen one human being in her life—and that was Mary. All the rest were strangers. Now her soul was going to open, she was going to see another. She felt strange and pregnant.

"He'll be more comfortable," murmured the sick woman abstractedly, as Louisa entered the room. The latter did not answer. Her own heart was heavy with its own responsibility. Mrs. Durant lay silent awhile, then she murmured plaintively :

"You mustn't mind, Miss Louisa."

"Why should I ? " replied Louisa, deeply moved.

"It's what we're used to," said the old woman.

And Louisa felt herself excluded again from their life. She sat in pain, with the tears of disappointment distilling in her heart. Was that all ?

Alfred came upstairs. He was clean, and in his shirt-sleeves. He looked a workman now. Louisa felt that she and he were foreigners, moving in different lives. It dulled her again. Oh, if she could only find some fixed relations, something sure and abiding.

" How do you feel ? " he said to his mother.

" It's a bit better," she replied wearily, impersonally. This strange putting herself aside, this abstracting herself and answering him only what she thought good for him to hear, made the relations between mother and son poignant and cramping to Miss Louisa. It made the man so ineffectual, so nothing. Louisa groped as if she had lost him. The mother was real and positive—he was not very actual. It puzzled and chilled the young woman.

" I'd better fetch Mrs. Harrison ? " he said, waiting for his mother to decide.

" I suppose we shall have to have somebody," she replied.

Miss Louisa stood by, afraid to interfere in their business. They did not include her in their lives, they felt she had nothing to do with them, except as a help from outside. She was quite external to them. She felt hurt and powerless against this unconscious difference. But something patient and unyielding in her made her say :

" I will stay and do the nursing : you can't be left."

The other two were shy, and at a loss for an answer.

" We s'll manage to get somebody," said the old woman wearily. She did not care very much what happened, now.

" I will stay until to-morrow, in any case," said Louisa. " Then we can see."

" I'm sure you've no right to trouble yourself," moaned the old woman. But she must leave herself in my hands.

Miss Louisa felt glad that she was admitted, even in an official capacity. She wanted to share their lives. At home they would need her, now Mary had come. But they must manage without her.

" I must write a note to the vicarage," she said.

Alfred Durant looked at her inquiringly, for her service. He had always that intelligent readiness to serve, since he had been in the Navy. But there was a simple independence in his willingness, which she loved. She felt nevertheless it was hard to get at him. He was so deferential, quick to take the slightest suggestion of an order from her, implicitly, that she could not get at the man in him.

He looked at her very keenly. She noticed his eyes were golden brown, with a very small pupil, the kind of eyes that can see a long way off. He stood alert, at military attention. His face was still rather weather-reddened.

" Do you want pen and paper ? " he asked, with deferential suggestion to a superior, which was more difficult for her than reserve.

" Yes, please," she said.

He turned and went downstairs. He seemed to her so self-contained, so utterly sure in his movement. How was she to approach him ? For he would take not one step towards her. He would only put himself entirely and impersonally at her service, glad to serve her, but keeping himself quite removed from her. She could see he felt real joy in doing anything for her, but any recognition would confuse him and hurt him. Strange it was to her, to have a man going about the house in his shirt-sleeves, his waistcoat unbuttoned, his throat bare, waiting on her. He moved well, as if he had plenty of life to spare. She was attracted by his completeness. And yet, when all was ready, and there was nothing more for him to do, she quivered, meeting his questioning look.

As she sat writing, he placed another candle near her. The rather dense light fell in two places on the overfoldings of her hair till it glistened heavy and bright, like a dense golden plumage folded up. Then the nape of her neck was very white, with fine down and pointed wisps of gold. He watched it as it were a vision, losing himself. She was all that was beyond him, of revelation and exquisiteness. All that was ideal and beyond him, she was that—and he was lost to himself in looking at her. She had no connection with him. He did not approach her. She was there like a wonderful distance. But it was a treat, having her in the house. Even with this anguish for his mother tightening about him, he was sensible of the wonder of living this evening. The candles glistened on her hair, and seemed to fascinate him. He felt a little awe of her, and a sense of uplifting, that he and she and his mother should be together for a time, in the strange, unknown atmosphere. And, when he got out of the house, he was afraid. He saw the stars above ringing with fine brightness, the snow beneath just visible, and a new night was gathering round him. He was afraid almost with obliteration. What was this new night ringing about him, and what was he ? He could not recognize himself nor any of his surroundings. He was afraid to think of his mother. And yet his chest was conscious of her, and of what was happening to her. He could not escape from her, she carried him with her into an unformed, unknown chaos.

XI

He went up the road in an agony, not knowing what it was all about, but feeling as if a red-hot iron were gripped round his chest. Without thinking, he shook two or three tears on to the snow. Yet in his mind he did not believe his mother would die. He was in the grip of some greater consciousness. As he sat in the hall of the vicarage, waiting whilst Mary put things for Louisa into a bag, he wondered why he had been so upset. He felt abashed and humbled by the big house, he felt again as if he were one of the rank and file. When Miss Mary spoke to him, he almost saluted.

" An honest man," thought Mary. And the patronage was applied as salve to her own sickness. She had station, so she could patronize : it was almost all that was left to her. But she could not have lived without having a certain position. She could never have trusted herself outside a definite place, nor respected herself except as a woman of superior class.

As Alfred came to the latch-gate, he felt the grief at his heart again, and saw the new heavens. He stood a moment looking northward to the Plough climbing up the night, and at the far glimmer of snow in distant fields. Then his grief came on like physical pain. He held tight to the gate, biting his mouth, whispering " Mother ! " It was a fierce, cutting, physical pain of grief, that came on in bouts, as his mother's pain came on in bouts, and was so acute he could scarcely keep erect. He did not know where it came from, the pain, nor why. It had nothing to do with his thoughts. Almost it had nothing to do with him. Only it gripped him and he must submit. The whole tide of his soul, gathering in its unknown towards this expansion into death, carried him with it helplessly, all the fritter of his thought and consciousness caught up as nothing, the heave passing on towards its breaking, taking him further than he had ever been. When the young man had regained himself, he went indoors, and there he was almost gay. It seemed to excite him. He felt in high spirits : he made whimsical fun of things. He sat on one side of his mother's bed, Louisa on the other, and a certain gaiety seized them all. But the night and the dread was coming on.

Alfred kissed his mother and went to bed. When he was half undressed the knowledge of his mother came upon him, and the suffering seized him in its grip like two hands, in agony. He lay on the bed screwed up tight. It lasted so long, and exhausted him so much, that he fell asleep, without having the energy to get up and finish undressing. He awoke after midnight to find himself stone cold. He undressed and got into bed, and was soon asleep again.

At a quarter to six he woke, and instantly remembered. Having pulled on his trousers and lighted a candle, he went into his mother's room. He put his hand before the candle flame so that no light fell on the bed.

"Mother!" he whispered.

"Yes," was the reply.

There was a hesitation.

"Should I go to work?"

He waited, his heart was beating heavily.

"I think I'd go, my lad."

His heart went down in a kind of despair.

"You want me to?"

He let his hand down from the candle flame. The light fell on the bed. There he saw Louisa lying looking up at him. Her eyes were upon him. She quickly shut her eyes and half buried her face in the pillow, her back turned to him. He saw the rough hair like bright vapour about her round head, and the two plaits flung coiled among the bedclothes. It gave him a shock. He stood almost himself, determined. Louisa cowered down. He looked, and met his mother's eyes. Then he gave way again, and ceased to be sure, ceased to be himself.

"Yes, go to work, my boy," said the mother.

"All right," replied he, kissing her. His heart was down at despair, and bitter. He went away.

"Alfred!" cried his mother faintly.

He came back with beating heart.

"What, mother?"

"You'll always do what's right, Alfred?" the mother asked, beside herself in terror now he was leaving her. He was too terrified and bewildered to know what she meant.

"Yes," he said.

She turned her cheek to him. He kissed her, then went away, in bitter despair. He went to work.

XII

By midday his mother was dead. The word met him at the pit-mouth. As he had known, inwardly, it was not a shock to him, and yet he trembled. He went home quite calmly, feeling only heavy in his breathing.

Miss Louisa was still at the house. She had seen to everything possible. Very succinctly, she informed him of what he needed to know. But there was one point of anxiety for her.

" You *did* half expect it—it's not come as a blow to you ? " she asked, looking up at him. Her eyes were dark and calm and searching. She too felt lost. He was so dark and inchoate.

" I suppose—yes," he said stupidly. He looked aside, unable to endure her eyes on him.

" I could not bear to think you might not have guessed," she said.

He did not answer.

He felt it a great strain to have her near him at this time. He wanted to be alone. As soon as the relatives began to arrive, Louisa departed and came no more. While everything was arranging, and a crowd was in the house, whilst he had business to settle, he went well enough, with only those uncontrollable paroxysms of grief. For the rest, he was superficial. By himself, he endured the fierce, almost insane bursts of grief which passed again and left him calm, almost clear, just wondering. He had not known before that everything could break down, that he himself could break down, and all be a great chaos, very vast and wonderful. It seemed as if life in him had burst its bounds, and he was lost in a great, bewildering flood, immense and unpeopled. He himself was broken and spilled out amid it all. He could only breathe panting in silence. Then the anguish came on again.

When all the people had gone from the Quarry Cottage, leaving the young man alone with an elderly housekeeper, then the long trial began. The snow had thawed and frozen, a fresh fall had whitened the grey, this then began to thaw. The world was a place of loose grey slosh. Alfred had nothing to do in the evenings. He was a man whose life had been filled up with small activities. Without knowing it, he had been centralized, polarized in his mother. It was she who had kept him. Even now, when the old housekeeper had left him, he might still have gone on in his old way. But the force and balance of his life was lacking. He sat pretending to read, all the time holding his fists clenched, and holding himself in, enduring he did not know what. He walked the black and sodden miles of field-paths, till he was tired out : but all this was only running away from whence he must return. At work he was all right. If it had been summer he might have escaped by working in the garden till bedtime. But now, there was no escape, no relief, no help. He, perhaps, was made for action rather than for understanding ; for doing than for being. He was shocked out of his activities, like a swimmer who forgets to swim.

For a week, he had the force to endure this suffocation and struggle, then he began to get exhausted, and knew it must come out. The instinct of self-preservation became strongest. But there was the question : Where was he to go ? The public-house really meant nothing to him, it was no good going there. He began to think of emigration. In another country he would be all right. He wrote to the emigration offices.

On the Sunday after the funeral, when all the Durant people had attended church, Alfred had seen Miss Louisa, impassive and reserved, sitting with Miss Mary, who was proud and very distant, and with the other Lindleys, who were people removed. Alfred saw them as people remote. He did not think about it. They had nothing to do with his life. After service Louisa had come to him and shaken hands.

" My sister would like you to come to supper one evening, if you would be so good."

He looked at Miss Mary, who bowed. Out of kindness, Mary had proposed this to Louisa, disapproving of herself even as she did so. But she did not examine herself closely.

" Yes," said Durant awkwardly, " I'll come if you want me." But he vaguely felt that it was misplaced.

" You'll come to-morrow evening, then, about half-past six."

He went. Miss Louisa was very kind to him. There could be no music, because of the babies. He sat with his fists clenched on his thighs, very quiet and unmoved, lapsing, among all those people, into a kind of muse or daze. There was nothing between him and them. They knew it as well as he. But he remained very steady in himself, and the evening passed slowly. Mrs. Lindley called him " young man."

" Will you sit here, young man ? "

He sat there. One name was as good as another. What had they to do with him ?

Mr. Lindley kept a special tone for him, kind, indulgent, but patronizing. Durant took it all without criticism or offence, just submitting. But he did not want to eat—that troubled him, to have to eat in their presence. He knew he was out of place. But it was his duty to stay yet awhile. He answered precisely, in mono-syllables.

When he left he winced with confusion. He was glad it was

finished. He got away as quickly as possible. And he wanted still more intensely to go right away, to Canada.

Miss Louisa suffered in her soul, indignant with all of them, with him too, but quite unable to say why she was indignant.

XIII

Two evenings after, Louisa tapped at the door of the Quarry Cottage, at half-past six. He had finished dinner, the woman had washed up and gone away, but still he sat in his pit dirt. He was going later to the New Inn. He had begun to go there because he must go somewhere. The mere contact with other men was necessary to him, the noise, the warmth, the forgetful flight of the hours. But still he did not move. He sat alone in the empty house till it began to grow on him like something unnatural.

He was in his pit dirt when he opened the door.

"I have been wanting to call—I thought I would," she said, and she went to the sofa. He wondered why she wouldn't use his mother's round arm-chair. Yet something stirred in him, like anger, when the housekeeper placed herself in it.

"I ought to have been washed by now," he said, glancing at the clock, which was adorned with butterflies and cherries, and the name of "T. Brooks, Mansfield." He laid his black hands along his mottled dirty arms. Louisa looked at him. There was the reserve, and the simple neutrality towards her, which she dreaded in him. It made it impossible for her to approach him.

"I am afraid," she said, "that I wasn't kind in asking you to supper."

"I'm not used to it," he said, smiling with his mouth, showing the interspaced white teeth. His eyes, however, were steady and unseeing.

"It's not *that*," she said hastily. Her repose was exquisite and her dark grey eyes rich with understanding. He felt afraid of her as she sat there, as he began to grow conscious of her.

"How do you get on alone?" she asked.

He glanced away to the fire.

"Oh——" he answered, shifting uneasily, not finishing his answer.

Her face settled heavily.

"How close it is in this room. You have such immense fires. I will take off my coat," she said.

He watched her take off her hat and coat. She wore a cream

cashmir blouse embroidered with gold silk. It seemed to him a very fine garment, fitting her throat and wrists close. It gave him a feeling of pleasure and cleanness and relief from himself.

" What were you thinking about, that you didn't get washed ? " she asked, half intimately. He laughed, turning aside his head. The whites of his eyes showed very distinct in his black face.

" Oh," he said, " I couldn't tell you."

There was a pause.

" Are you going to keep this house on ? " she asked.

He stirred in his chair, under the question.

" I hardly know," he said. " I'm very likely going to Canada."

Her spirit became very quiet and attentive.

" What for ? " she asked.

Again he shifted restlessly on his seat.

" Well "—he said slowly—" to try the life."

" But which life ? "

" There's various things—farming or lumbering or mining. I don't mind much what it is."

" And is that what you want ? "

He did not think in these times, so he could not answer.

" I don't know," he said, " till I've tried."

She saw him drawing away from her for ever.

" Aren't you sorry to leave this house and garden ? " she asked.

" I don't know," he answered reluctantly. " I suppose our Fred would come in—that's what he's wanting."

" You don't want to settle down ? " she asked.

He was leaning forward on the arms of his chair. He turned to her. Her face was pale and set. It looked heavy and impassive, her hair shone richer as she grew white. She was to him something steady and immovable and eternal presented to him. His heart was hot in an anguish of suspense. Sharp twitches of fear and pain were in his limbs. He turned his whole body away from her. The silence was unendurable. He could not bear her to sit there any more. It made his heart go hot and stifled in his breast.

" Were you going out to-night ? " she asked.

" Only to the New Inn," he said.

Again there was silence.

She reached for her hat. Nothing else was suggested to her. She *had* to go. He sat waiting for her to be gone, for relief. And she knew that if she went out of that house as she was, she went out a failure. Yet she continued to pin on her hat ; in a moment she would have to go. Something was carrying her.

Then suddenly a sharp pang, like lightning, seared her from head to foot, and she was beyond herself.

" Do you want me to go ? " she asked, controlled, yet speaking out of a fiery anguish, as if the words were spoken from her without her intervention.

He went white under his dirt.

" Why ? " he asked, turning to her in fear, compelled.

" Do you want me to go ? " she repeated.

" Why ? " he asked again.

" Because I wanted to stay with you," she said, suffocated, with her lungs full of fire.

His face worked, he hung forward a little, suspended, staring straight into her eyes, in torment, in an agony of chaos, unable to collect himself. And as if turned to stone, she looked back into his eyes. Their souls were exposed bare for a few moments. It was agony. They could not bear it. He dropped his head, whilst his body jerked with little sharp twitchings.

She turned away for her coat. Her soul had gone dead in her. Her hands trembled, but she could not feel any more. She drew on her coat. There was a cruel suspense in the room. The moment had come for her to go. He lifted his head. His eyes were like agate, expressionless, save for the black points of torture. They held her, she had no will, no life any more. She felt broken.

" Don't you want me ? " she said helplessly.

A spasm of torture crossed his eyes, which held her fixed.

" I—I—— " he began, but he could not speak. Something drew him from his chair to her. She stood motionless, spellbound, like a creature given up as prey. He put his hand tentatively, uncertainly, on her arm. The expression of his face was strange and inhuman. She stood utterly motionless. Then clumsily he put his arms round her, and took her, cruelly, blindly, straining her till she nearly lost consciousness, till he himself had almost fallen.

Then, gradually, as he held her gripped, and his brain reeled round, and he felt himself falling, falling from himself, and whilst she, yielded up, swooned to a kind of death of herself, a moment of utter darkness came over him, and they began to wake up again as if from a long sleep. He was himself.

After a while his arms slackened, she loosened herself a little, and put her arms round him, as he held her. So they held each other close, and hid each against the other for assurance, helpless in speech. And it was ever her hands that trembled more closely upon him, drawing him nearer into her, with love.

And at last she drew back her face and looked up at him, her eyes wet, and shining with light. His heart, which saw, was silent with fear. He was with her. She saw his face all sombre and inscrutable, and he seemed eternal to her. And all the echo of pain came back into the rarity of bliss, and all her tears came up.

" I love you," she said, her lips drawn to sobbing. He put down his head against her, unable to hear her, unable to bear the sudden coming of the peace and passion that almost broke his heart. They stood together in silence whilst the thing moved away a little.

At last she wanted to see him. She looked up. His eyes were strange and glowing, with a tiny black pupil. Strange, they were, and powerful over her. And his mouth came to hers, and slowly her eyelids closed, as his mouth sought hers closer and closer, and took possession of her.

They were silent for a long time, too much mixed up with passion and grief and death to do anything but hold each other in pain and kiss with long, hurting kisses wherein fear was transfused into desire. At last she disengaged herself. He felt as if his heart were hurt, but glad, and he scarcely dared look at her.

" I'm glad," she said also.

He held her hands in passionate gratitude and desire. He had not yet the presence of mind to say anything. He was dazed with relief.

" I ought to go," she said.

He looked at her. He could not grasp the thought of her going, he knew he could never be separated from her any more. Yet he dared not assert himself. He held her hands tight.

" Your face is black," she said.

He laughed.

" Yours is a bit smudged," he said.

They were afraid of each other, afraid to talk. He could only keep her near to him. After a while she wanted to wash her face. He brought her some warm water, standing by and watching her. There was something he wanted to say, that he dared not. He watched her wiping her face, and making tidy her hair.

" They'll see your blouse is dirty," he said.

She looked at her sleeves and laughed for joy.

He was sharp with pride.

" What shall you do ? " he asked.

" How ? " she said.

He was awkward at a reply.

" About me," he said.

" What do you want me to do ? " she laughed.

He put his hand out slowly to her. What did it matter !

" But make yourself clean," she said.

XIV

As they went up the hill, the night seemed dense with the unknown. They kept close together, feeling as if the darkness were alive and full of knowledge, all around them. In silence they walked up the hill. At first the street lamps went their way. Several people passed them. He was more shy than she, and would have let her go had she loosened in the least. But she held firm.

Then they came into the true darkness, between the fields. They did not want to speak, feeling closer together in silence. So they arrived at the vicarage gate. They stood under the naked horse-chestnut tree.

" I wish you didn't have to go," he said.

She laughed a quick little laugh.

" Come to-morrow," she said, in a low tone, " and ask father."

She felt his hand close on hers.

She gave the same sorrowful little laugh of sympathy. Then she kissed him, sending him home.

At home, the old grief came on in another paroxysm, obliterating Louisa, obliterating even his mother for whom the stress was raging like a burst of fever in a wound. But something was sound in his heart.

XV

The next evening he dressed to go to the vicarage, feeling it was to be done, not imagining what it would be like. He would not take this seriously. He was sure of Louisa, and this marriage was like fate to him. It filled him also with a blessed feeling of fatality. He was not responsible, neither had her people anything really to do with it.

They ushered him into the little study, which was fireless. By and by the vicar came in. His voice was cold and hostile as he said :

" What can I do for you, young man ? "

He knew already, without asking.

Durant looked up at him, again like a sailor before a superior. He had the subordinate manner. Yet his spirit was clear.

" I wanted, Mr. Lindley——" he began respectfully, then all the colour suddenly left his face. It seemed now a violation to say what he had to say. What was he doing there? But he stood on, because it had to be done. He held firmly to his own independence and self-respect. He must not be indecisive. He must put himself aside: the matter was bigger than just his personal self. He must not feel. This was his highest duty.

" You wanted——" said the vicar.

Durant's mouth was dry, but he answered with steadiness:

" Miss Louisa—Louisa—promised to marry me——"

" You asked Miss Louisa if she would marry you—yes——" corrected the vicar. Durant reflected he had not asked her this:

" If she would marry me, sir. I hope you—don't mind."

He smiled. He was a good-looking man, and the vicar could not help seeing it.

" And my daughter was willing to marry you? " said Mr. Lindley.

" Yes," said Durant seriously. It was pain to him, nevertheless. He felt the natural hostility between himself and the elder man.

" Will you come this way? " said the vicar. He led into the dining-room, where were Mary, Louisa, and Mrs. Lindley. Mr. Massy sat in a corner with a lamp.

" This young man has come on your account, Louisa? " said Mr. Lindley.

" Yes," said Louisa, her eyes on Durant, who stood erect, in discipline. He dared not look at her, but he was aware of her.

" You don't want to marry a collier, you little fool," cried Mrs. Lindley harshly. She lay obese and helpless upon the couch, swathed in a loose dove-grey gown.

" Oh, hush, mother," cried Mary, with quiet intensity and pride.

" What means have you to support a wife? " demanded the vicar's wife roughly.

" I ! " Durant replied, starting. " I think I can earn enough."

" Well, and how much? " came the rough voice.

" Seven and six a day," replied the young man.

" And will it get to be any more? "

" I hope so."

" And are you going to live in that poky little house? "

" I think so," said Durant, " if it's all right."

He took small offence, only was upset, because they would not think him good enough. He knew that, in their sense, he was not.

" Then she's a fool, I tell you, if she marries you," cried the mother roughly, casting her decision.

"After all, mama, it is Louisa's affair," said Mary distinctly, "and we must remember——"

"As she makes her bed, she must lie—but she'll repent it," interrupted Mrs. Lindley.

"And after all," said Mr. Lindley, "Louisa cannot quite hold herself free to act entirely without consideration for her family."

"What do you want, papa?" asked Louisa sharply.

"I mean that if you marry this man, it will make my position very difficult for me, particularly if you stay in this parish. If you were moving quite away, it would be simpler. But living here in a collier's cottage, under my nose, as it were—it would be almost unseemly. I have my position to maintain, and a position which may not be taken lightly."

"Come over here, young man," cried the mother, in her rough voice, "and let us look at you."

Durant, flushing, went over and stood—not quite at attention, so that he did not know what to do with his hands. Miss Louisa was angry to see him standing there, obedient and acquiescent. He ought to show himself a man.

"Can't you take her away and live out of sight?" said the mother. "You'd both of you be better off."

"Yes, we can go away," he said.

"Do you want to?" asked Miss Mary clearly.

He faced round. Mary looked very stately and impressive. He flushed.

"I do if it's going to be a trouble to anybody," he said.

"For yourself, you would rather stay?" said Mary.

"It's my home," he said, "and that's the house I was born in."

"Then"—Mary turned clearly to her parents, "I really don't see how you can make the conditions, papa. He has his own rights, and if Louisa wants to marry him——"

"Louisa, Louisa!" cried the father impatiently. "I cannot understand why Louisa should not behave in the normal way. I cannot see why she should only think of herself, and leave her family out of count. The thing is enough in itself, and she ought to try to ameliorate it as much as possible. And if——"

"But I love the man, papa," said Louisa.

"And I hope you love your parents, and I hope you want to spare them as much of the—the loss of prestige, as possible."

"We *can* go away to live," said Louisa, her face breaking to tears. At last she was really hurt.

"Oh, yes, easily," Durant replied hastily, pale, distressed.

There was dead silence in the room.

" I think it would really be better," murmured the vicar, mollified.

" Very likely it would," said the rough-voiced invalid.

" Though I think we ought to apologize for asking such a thing," said Mary haughtily.

" No," said Durant. " It will be best all round." He was glad there was no more bother.

" And shall we put up the banns here or go to the registrar ? " he asked clearly, like a challenge.

" We will go to the registrar," replied Louisa decidedly.

Again there was a dead silence in the room.

" Well, if you will have your own way, you must go your own way," said the mother emphatically.

All the time Mr. Massy had sat obscure and unnoticed in a corner of the room. At this juncture he got up, saying :

" There is baby, Mary."

Mary rose and went out of the room, stately ; her little husband padded after her. Durant watched the fragile, small man go, wondering.

" And where," asked the vicar, almost genial, " do you think you will go when you are married ? "

Durant started.

" I was thinking of emigrating," he said.

" To Canada ? Or where ? "

" I think to Canada."

" Yes, that would be very good."

Again there was a pause.

" We shan't see much of you then, as a son-in-law," said the mother, roughly but amicably.

" Not much," he said.

Then he took his leave. Louisa went with him to the gate. She stood before him in distress.

" You won't mind them, will you ? " she said humbly.

" I don't mind them, if they don't mind me ! " he said. Then he stooped and kissed her.

" Let us be married soon," she murmured, in tears.

" All right," he said. " I'll go to-morrow to Barford."

BEAUVALE is, or was, the largest parish in England. It is thinly populated, only just netting the stragglers from shoals of houses in three large mining villages. For the rest, it holds a great tract of woodland, fragment of old Sherwood, a few hills of pasture and arable land, three collieries, and, finally, the ruins of a Cistercian abbey. These ruins lie in a still rich meadow at the foot of the last fall of woodland, through whose oaks shines a blue of hyacinths, like water, in May-time. Of the abbey, there remains only the east wall of the chancel standing, a wild thick mass of ivy weighting one shoulder, while pigeons perch in the tracery of the lofty window. This is the window in question.

The vicar of Beauvale is a bachelor of forty-two years. Quite early in life some illness caused a slight paralysis of his right side, so that he drags a little, and so that the right corner of his mouth is twisted up into his cheek with a constant grimace, unhidden by a heavy moustache. There is something pathetic about this twist on the vicar's countenance : his eyes are so shrewd and sad. It would be hard to get near to Mr. Colbran. Indeed, now, his soul has some of the twist of his face, so that, when he is not ironical, he is satiric. Yet a man of more complete tolerance and generosity scarcely exists. Let the boors mock him, he merely smiles on the other side, and there is no malice in his eyes, only a quiet expression of waiting till they have finished. His people do not like him, yet none could bring forth an accusation against him, save that " You never can tell when he's having you."

I dined the other evening with the vicar in his study. The room scandalizes the neighbourhood because of the statuary which adorns it : a Laocoön and other classic copies, with bronze and silver Italian Renaissance works. For the rest, it is all dark and tawny.

Mr. Colbran is an archæologist. · He does not take himself seriously, however, in his hobby, so that nobody knows the worth of his opinions on the subject.

" Here you are," he said to me after dinner, " I've found another paragraph for my great work."

" What's that ? " I asked.

"Haven't I told you I was compiling a Bible of the English people—the Bible of their hearts—their exclamations in presence of the unknown ? I've found a fragment at home, a jump at God from Beauvale."

" Where ? " I asked, startled.

The vicar closed his eyes whilst looking at me.

" Only on parchment," he said.

Then, slowly, he reached for a yellow book, and read, translating as he went :

" Then, while we chanted, came a crackling at the window, at the great east window, where hung our Lord on the Cross. It was a malicious coveitous Devil wrathed by us, rended the lovely image of the glasse. We saw the iron clutches of the fiend pick the window, and a face flaming red like fire in a basket did glower down on us. Our hearts melted away, our legs broke, we thought to die. The breath of the wretch filled the chapel.

" But our dear Saint, etc., etc., came hastening down heaven to defend us. The fiend began to groan and bray—he was daunted and beat off.

" When the sun uprose, and it was morning, some went out in dread upon the thin snow. There the figure of our Saint was broken and thrown down, whilst in the window was a wicked hole as from the Holy Wounds the Blessed Blood was run out at the touch of the Fiend, and on the snow was the Blood, sparkling like gold. Some gathered it up for the joy of this House. . . ."

" Interesting," I said. " Where's it from ? "

" Beauvale records—fifteenth century."

" Beauvale Abbey," I said ; " they were only very few, the monks. What frightened them, I wonder."

" I wonder," he repeated.

" Somebody climbed up," I supposed, " and attempted to get in."

" What ? " he exclaimed, smiling.

" Well, what do you think ? "

" Pretty much the same," he replied. " I glossed it out for my book."

" Your great work ? Tell me."

He put a shade over the lamp so that the room was almost in darkness.

" Am I more than a voice ? " he asked.

" I can see your hand," I replied. He moved entirely from the circle of light. Then his voice began, sing-song, sardonic :

" I was a serf at Rollestoun's, Newthorpe Manor, master of the stables I was. One day a horse bit me as I was grooming him. He was an old enemy of mine. I fetched him a blow across the nose. Then, when he got a chance, he lashed out at me and caught me a gash over the mouth. I snatched at a hatchet and cut his head. He yelled, fiend as he was, and strained for me with all his teeth bare. I brought him down.

" For killing him they flogged me till they thought I was dead. I was sturdy, because we horse-serfs got plenty to eat. I was sturdy, but they flogged me till I did not move. The next night I set fire to the stables, and the stables set fire to the house. I watched and saw the red flame rise and look out of the window, I saw the folk running, each for himself, master no more than one of a frightened party. It was freezing, but the heat made me sweat. I saw them all turn again to watch, all rimmed with red. They cried, all of them when the roof went in, when the sparks splashed up at rebound. They cried then like dogs at the bagpipes howling. Master cursed me, till I laughed as I lay under a bush quite near.

" As the fire went down I got frightened. I ran for the woods, with fire blazing in my eyes and crackling in my ears. For hours I was all fire. Then I went to sleep under the bracken. When I woke it was evening. I had no mantle, was frozen stiff. I was afraid to move, lest all the sores of my back should be broken like thin ice. I lay still until I could bear my hunger no longer. I moved then to get used to the pain of movement, when I began to hunt for food. There was nothing to be found but hips.

" After wandering about till I was faint I dropped again in the bracken. The boughs above me creaked with frost. I started and looked round. The branches were like hair among the starlight. My heart stood still. Again there was a creak, creak, and suddenly a whoop, that whistled in fading. I fell down in the bracken like dead wood. Yet, by the peculiar whistling sound at the end, I knew it was only the ice bending or tightening in the frost. I was in the woods above the lake, only two miles from the Manor. And yet, when the lake whooped hollowly again, I clutched the frozen soil, every one of my muscles as stiff as the stiff earth. So all the night long I dare not move my face, but pressed it flat down, and taut I lay as if pegged down and braced.

" When morning came still I did not move, I lay still in a dream. By afternoon my ache was such it enlivened me. I cried, rocking my breath in the ache of moving. Then again I became fierce. I beat my hands on the rough bark to hurt them, so that I should not ache so much. In such a rage I was I swung my limbs to torture till I fell sick with pain. Yet I fought the hurt, fought it and fought by twisting and flinging myself, until it was overcome. Then the evening began to draw on. All day the sun had not loosened the frost. I felt the sky chill again towards afternoon. Then I knew the night was coming, and, remembering the great space I had just come through, horrible so that it seemed to have made me another man, I fled across the wood.

"But in my running I came upon the oak where hanged five bodies. There they must hang, bar-stiff, night after night. It was a terror worse than any. Turning, blundering through the forest, I came out where the trees thinned, where only hawthorns, ragged and shaggy, went down to the lake's edge.

"The sky across was red, the ice on the water glistened as if it were warm. A few wild geese sat out like stones on the sheet of ice. I thought of Martha. She was the daughter of the miller at the upper end of the lake. Her hair was red like beech leaves in a wind. When I had gone often to the mill with the horses she had brought me food.

"'I thought,' said I to her, ''twas a squirrel sat on your shoulder. 'Tis your hair fallen loose.'

"'They call me the fox,' she said.

"'Would I were your dog,' said I. She would bring me bacon and good bread, when I called at the mill with the horses. The thought of cakes of bread and of bacon made me reel as if drunk. I had torn at the rabbit holes, I had chewed wood all day. In such a dimness was my head that I felt neither the soreness of my wounds nor the cuts of thorns on my knees, but stumbled towards the mill, almost past fear of man and death, panting with fear of the darkness that crept behind me from trunk to trunk.

"Coming to the gap in the wood, below which lay the pond, I heard no sound. Always I knew the place filled with the buzz of water, but now it was silent. In fear of this stillness I ran forward, forgetting myself, forgetting the frost. The wood seemed to pursue me. I fell, just in time, down by a shed wherein were housed the few wintry pigs. The miller came riding in on his horse, and the barking of dogs was for him. I heard him curse the day, curse his servant, curse me, whom he had been out to hunt, in his rage of wasted labour, curse all. As I lay I heard inside the shed a sucking. Then I knew that the sow was there, and that the most of her sucking pigs would be already killed for to-morrow's Christmas. The miller, from forethought to have young at that time, made profit by his sucking pigs that were sold for the mid-winter feast.

" When in a moment all was silent in the dusk, I broke the bar and came into the shed. The sow grunted, but did not come forth to discover me. By and by I crept in towards her warmth. She had but three young left, which now angered her, she being too full of milk. Every now and again she slashed at them and they squealed. Busy as she was with them, I in the darkness advanced towards her. I trembled so that scarce dared I trust myself near her, for long dared not put my naked face towards her. Shuddering with hunger and fear, I at last fed of her, guarding my face with my arm. Her own full young tumbled squealing against me, but she, feeling her ease, lay grunting. At last, I, too, lay drunk, swooning.

" I was roused by the shouting of the miller. He, angered by his daughter who wept, abused her, driving her from the house to feed the swine. She came, bowing under a yoke, to the door of the shed. Finding the pin broken she stood afraid, then, as the sow grunted, she came cautiously in. I took her with my arm, my hand over her mouth. As she struggled against my breast my heart began to beat loudly. At last she knew it was I. I clasped her. She hung in my arms, turning away her face, so that I kissed her throat. The tears blinded my eyes, I know not why, unless it were the hurt of my mouth, wounded by the horse, was keen.

" ' They will kill you,' she whispered.

" ' No,' I answered.

" And she wept softly. She took my head in her arms and kissed me, wetting me with her tears, brushing me with her keen hair, warming me through.

" ' I will not go away from here,' I said. ' Bring me a knife, and I will defend myself.'

" ' No,' she wept. ' Ah, no ! '

" When she went I lay down, pressing my chest where she had rested on the earth, lest being alone were worse emptiness than hunger.

" Later she came again. I saw her bend in the doorway, a lant-horn hanging in front. As she peered under the redness of her falling hair, I was afraid of her. But she came with food. We sat together in the dull light. Sometimes still I shivered and my throat would not swallow.

" ' If,' said I, ' I eat all this you have brought me, I shall sleep till somebody finds me.'

" Then she took away the rest of the meat.

" ' Why,' said I, ' should I not eat ? ' She looked at me in tears of fear.

" ' What ? ' I said, but still she had no answer. I kissed her, and the hurt of my wounded mouth angered me.

" ' Now there is my blood,' said I, ' on your mouth.' Wiping her smooth hand over her lips, she looked thereat, then at me.

" ' Leave me,' I said, ' I am tired.' She rose to leave me.

" ' But bring a knife,' I said. Then she held the lanthorn near my face, looking as at a picture.

" ' You look to me,' she said, ' like a stirk that is roped for the axe. Your eyes are dark, but they are wide open.'

" ' Then I will sleep,' said I, ' but will not wake too late.'

" ' Do not stay here,' she said.

" ' I will not sleep in the wood,' I answered, and it was my heart that spoke, ' for I am afraid. I had better be afraid of the voice of man and dogs, than the sounds in the woods. Bring me a knife, and in the morning I will go. Alone will I not go now.'

" ' The searchers will take you,' she said.

" ' Bring me a knife,' I answered.

" ' Ah, go,' she wept.

" ' Not now—I will not——'

" With that she lifted the lanthorn, lit up her own face and mine. Her blue eyes dried of tears. Then I took her to myself, knowing she was mine.

" ' I will come again,' she said.

" She went, and I folded my arms, lay down and slept.

" When I woke, she was rocking me wildly to rouse me.

" ' I dreamed,' said I, ' that a great heap, as if it were a hill, lay on me and above me.'

" She put a cloak over me, gave me a hunting-knife and a wallet of food, and other things I did not note. Then under her own cloak she hid the lanthorn.

" ' Let us go,' she said, and blindly I followed her.

" When I came out into the cold someone touched my face and my hair.

" ' Ha !' I cried, ' who now——?' Then she swiftly clung to me, hushed me.

" ' Someone has touched me,' I said aloud, still dazed with sleep.

" ' Oh hush !' she wept. ' 'Tis snowing.' The dogs within the house began to bark. She fled forward, I after her. Coming to the ford of the stream she ran swiftly over, but I broke through the ice. Then I knew where I was. Snowflakes, fine and rapid, were biting at my face. In the wood there was no wind nor snow.

" ' Listen,' said I to her, ' listen, for I am locked up with sleep.'

" ' I hear roaring overhead,' she answered. ' I hear in the trees like great bats squeaking.'

" ' Give me your hand,' said I.

" We heard many noises as we passed. Once as there uprose a whiteness before us, she cried aloud.

" ' Nay,' said I, ' do not untie thy hand from mine,' and soon we were crossing fallen snow. But ever and again she started back from fear.

" ' When you draw back my arm,' I said, angry, ' you loosen a weal on my shoulder.'

" Thereafter she ran by my side like a fawn beside its mother.

" ' We will cross the valley and gain the stream,' I said. ' That will lead us on its ice as on a path deep into the forest. There we can join the outlaws. The wolves are driven from this part. They have followed the driven deer.'

" We came directly on a large gleam that shaped itself up among flying grains of snow.

" ' Ah ! ' she cried, and she stood amazed.

" Then I thought we had gone through the bounds into faery realm, and I was no more a man. How did I know what eyes were gleaming at me between the snow, what cunning spirits in the draughts of air ? So I waited for what would happen, and I forgot her, that she was there. Only I could feel the spirits whirling and blowing about me.

" Whereupon she clung upon me, kissing me lavishly, and, were dogs or men or demons come upon us at that moment, she had let us be stricken down, nor heeded not. So we moved forward to the shadow that shone in colours upon the passing snow. We found ourselves under a door of light which shed its colours mixed with snow. This Martha had never seen, nor I, this door open for a red and brave issuing like fires. We wondered.

" ' It is faery,' she said, and after a while, ' Could one catch such—— Ah, no ! '

" Through the snow shone bunches of red and blue.

" ' Could one have such a little light like a red flower—only a little, like a rose-berry scarlet on one's breast !—then one were singled out as Our Lady.'

" I flung off my cloak and my burden to climb up the face of the shadow. Standing on rims of stone, then in pockets of snow, I reached upward. My hand was red and blue, but I could not take the stuff. Like colour of a moth's wing it was on my hand, it flew on the increasing snow. I stood higher on the head of a frozen

man, reached higher my hand. Then I felt the bright stuff cold.
I could not pluck it off. Down below she cried to me to come again
to her. I felt a rib that yielded, I struck at it with my knife. There
came a gap in the redness. Looking through, I saw below as it
were white stunted angels, with sad faces lifted in fear. Two faces
they had each, and round rings of hair. I was afraid. I grasped
the shining red, I pulled. Then the cold man under me sank, so
I fell as if broken on to the snow.

"Soon I was risen again, and we were running downwards
towards the stream. We felt ourselves eased when the smooth road
of ice was beneath us. For a while it was resting, to travel thus
evenly. But the wind blew round us, the snow hung upon us, we
leaned us this way and that, towards the storm. I drew her along,
for she came as a bird that stems lifting and swaying against the
wind. By and by the snow came smaller, there was no wind in the
wood. Then I felt nor labour, nor cold. Only I knew the darkness
drifted by on either side, that overhead was a lane of paleness where
a moon fled us before. Still, I can feel the moon fleeing from me,
can feel the trees passing round me in slow dizzy reel, can feel the
hurt of my shoulder and my straight arm torn with holding her. I
was following the moon and the stream, for I knew where the water
peeped from its burrow in the ground there were shelters of the
outlaw. But she fell, without sound or sign.

" I gathered her up and climbed the bank. There all round me
hissed the larchwood, dry beneath, and laced with its dry-fretted
cords. For a little way I carried her into the trees. Then I laid her
down till I cut flat hairy boughs. I put her in my bosom on this
dry bed, so we swooned together through the night. I laced her
round and covered her with myself, so she lay like a nut within its
shell.

"Again, when morning came, it was pain of cold that woke me.
I groaned, but my heart was warm as I saw the heap of red hair in
my arms. As I looked at her, her eyes opened into mine. She
smiled—from out of her smile came fear. As if in a trap she pressed
back her head.

" ' We have no flint,' said I.

" ' Yes—in the wallet, flint and steel and tinder box,' she answered.

" ' God yield you blessing,' I said.

" In a place a little open I kindled a fire of larch boughs. She
was afraid of me, hovering near, yet never crossing a space.

" ' Come,' said I, ' let us eat this food.'

" ' Your face,' she said, ' is smeared with blood.'

" I opened out my cloak.

" ' But come,' said I, ' you are frosted with cold.'

" I took a handful of snow in my hand, wiping my face with it, which then I dried on my cloak.

" ' My face is no longer painted with blood, you are no longer afraid of me. Come here then, sit by me while we eat.'

" But as I cut the cold bread for her, she clasped me suddenly, kissing me. She fell before me, clasped my knees to her breast, weeping. She laid her face down to my feet, so that her hair spread like a fire before me. I wondered at the woman. ' Nay,' I cried. At that she lifted her face to me from below. ' Nay,' I cried, feeling my tears fall. With her head on my breast, my own tears rose from their source, wetting my cheek and her hair, which was wet with the rain of my eyes.

" Then I remembered and took from my bosom the coloured light of that night before. I saw it was black and rough.

" ' Ah,' said I, ' this is magic.'

" ' The black stone ! ' she wondered.

" ' It is the red light of the night before,' I said.

" ' It is magic,' she answered.

" ' Shall I throw it ? ' said I, lifting the stone, ' shall I throw it away, for fear ? '

" ' It shines ! ' she cried, looking up, ' it shines like the eye of a creature at night, the eye of a wolf in the doorway.'

" ' 'Tis magic,' I said, ' let me throw it from us.' But nay, she held my arm.

" ' It is red and shining,' she cried.

" ' It is a bloodstone,' I answered. ' It will hurt us, we shall die in blood.'

" ' But give it to me,' she answered.

" ' It is red of blood,' I said.

" ' Ah, give it to me,' she called.

" ' It is my blood,' I said.

" ' Give it,' she commanded, low.

" ' It is my life-stone,' I said.

" ' Give it me,' she pleaded.

" ' I gave it her. She held it up, she smiled, she smiled in my face, lifting her arms to me. I took her with my mouth, her mouth, her white throat. Nor she ever shrank, but trembled with happiness.

" What woke us, when the woods were filling again with shadow, when the fire was out, when we opened our eyes and looked up as if drowned, into the light which stood bright and thick on the tree-tops, what woke us was the sound of wolves. . . ."

*   *   *   *   *

" Nay," said the vicar, suddenly rising, " they lived happily ever after."

" No," I said.

I

IT was a mile nearer through the wood. Mechanically, Syson turned up by the forge and lifted the field-gate. The blacksmith and his mate stood still, watching the trespasser. But Syson looked too much a gentleman to be accosted. They let him go on in silence across the small field to the wood.

There was not the least difference between this morning and those of the bright springs, six or eight years back. White and sandy-gold fowls still scratched round the gate, littering the earth and the field with feathers and scratched-up rubbish. Between the two thick holly bushes in the wood-hedge was the hidden gap, whose fence one climbed to get into the wood ; the bars were scored just the same by the keeper's boots. He was back in the eternal.

Syson was extraordinarily glad. Like an uneasy spirit he had returned to the country of his past, and he found it waiting for him, unaltered. The hazel still spread glad little hands downwards, the bluebells here were still wan and few, among the lush grass and in shade of the bushes.

The path through the wood, on the very brow of a slope, ran winding easily for a time. All around were twiggy oaks, just issuing their gold, and floor spaces diapered with woodruff, with patches of dog-mercury and tufts of hyacinth. Two fallen trees still lay across the track. Syson jolted down a steep, rough slope, and came again upon the open land, this time looking north as through a great window in the wood. He stayed to gaze over the level fields of the hill-top, at the village which strewed the bare upland as if it had tumbled off the passing waggons of industry, and been forsaken. There was a stiff, modern, grey little church, and blocks and rows of red dwellings lying at random ; at the back, the twinkling head-stocks of the pit, and the looming pit-hill. All was naked and out-of-doors, not a tree ! It was quite unaltered.

Syson turned, satisfied, to follow the path that sheered downhill into the wood. He was curiously elated, feeling himself back in an enduring vision. He started. A keeper was standing a few yards in front, barring the way.

"Where might you be going this road, sir?" asked the man. The tone of his question had a challenging twang. Syson looked at the fellow with an impersonal, observant gaze. It was a young man of four or five-and-twenty, ruddy and well favoured. His dark blue eyes now stared aggressively at the intruder. His black moustache, very thick, was cropped short over a small, rather soft mouth. In every other respect the fellow was manly and good-looking. He stood just above middle height; the strong forward thrust of his chest, and the perfect ease of his erect, self-sufficient body, gave one the feeling that he was taut with animal life, like the thick jet of a fountain balanced in itself. He stood with the butt of his gun on the ground, looking uncertainly and questioningly at Syson. The dark, restless eyes of the trespasser, examining the man and penetrating into him without heeding his office, troubled the keeper and made him flush.

"Where is Naylor? Have you got his job?" Syson asked.

"You're not from the House, are you?" inquired the keeper. It could not be, since every one was away.

"No, I'm not from the House," the other replied. It seemed to amuse him.

"Then might I ask where you were making for?" said the keeper, nettled.

"Where I am making for?" Syson repeated. "I am going to Willey-Water Farm."

"This isn't the road."

"I think so. Down this path, past the well, and out by the white gate."

"But that's not the public road."

"I suppose not. I used to come so often, in Naylor's time, I had forgotten. Where is he, by the way?"

"Crippled with rheumatism," the keeper answered reluctantly.

"Is he?" Syson exclaimed in pain.

"And who might you be?" asked the keeper, with a new intonation.

"John Adderley Syson; I used to live in Cordy Lane."

"Used to court Hilda Millership?"

Syson's eyes opened with a pained smile. He nodded. There was an awkward silence.

"And you—who are you?" asked Syson.

"Arthur Pilbeam—Naylor's my uncle," said the other.

"You live here in Nuttall?"

"I'm lodgin' at my uncle's—at Naylor's."

" I see ! "

" Did you say you was goin' down to Willey-Water ? " asked the keeper.

" Yes."

There was a pause of some moments, before the keeper blurted : " *I'm* courtin' Hilda Millership."

The young fellow looked at the intruder with a stubborn defiance, almost pathetic. Syson opened new eyes.

" Are you ? " he said, astonished. The keeper flushed dark.

" She and me are keeping company," he said.

" I didn't know ! " said Syson. The other man waited uncomfortably.

" What, is the thing settled ? " asked the intruder.

" How, settled ? " retorted the other sulkily.

" Are you going to get married soon, and all that ? "

The keeper stared in silence for some moments, impotent.

" I suppose so," he said, full of resentment.

" Ah ! " Syson watched closely.

" I'm married myself," he added, after a time.

" You are ? " said the other incredulously.

Syson laughed in his brilliant, unhappy way.

" This last fifteen months," he said.

The keeper gazed at him with wide, wondering eyes, apparently thinking back, and trying to make things out.

" Why, didn't you know ? " asked Syson.

" No, I didn't," said the other sulkily.

There was silence for a moment.

" Ah well ! " said Syson, " I will go on. I suppose I may." The keeper stood in silent opposition. The two men hesitated in the open, grassy space, set round with small sheaves of sturdy bluebells ; a little open platform on the brow of the hill. Syson took a few indecisive steps forward, then stopped.

" I say, how beautiful ! " he cried.

He had come in full view of the downslope. The wide path ran from his feet like a river, and it was full of bluebells, save for a green winding thread down the centre, where the keeper walked. Like a stream the path opened into azure shallows at the levels, and there were pools of bluebells, with still the green thread winding through, like a thin current of ice-water through blue lakes. And from under the twig-purple of the bushes swam the shadowed blue, as if the flowers lay in flood water over the woodland.

" Ah, isn't it lovely ! " Syson exclaimed ; this was his past, the country he had abandoned, and it hurt him to see it so beautiful. Wood-pigeons cooed overhead, and the air was full of the brightness of birds singing.

" If you're married, what do you keep writing to her for, and sending her poetry books and things ? " asked the keeper. Syson stared at him, taken aback and humiliated. Then he began to smile.

" Well," he said, " I did not know about you . . ."

Again the keeper flushed darkly.

" But if you are married——" he charged.

" I am," answered the other cynically.

Then, looking down the blue, beautiful path, Syson felt his own humiliation. " What right *have* I to hang on to her ? " he thought, bitterly self-contemptuous.

" She knows I'm married and all that," he said.

" But you keep sending her books," challenged the keeper.

Syson, silenced, looked at the other man quizzically, half pitying. Then he turned.

" Good day," he said, and was gone. Now, everything irritated him : the two sallows, one all gold and perfume and murmur, one silver-green and bristly, reminded him that here he had taught her about pollination. What a fool he was ! What god-forsaken folly it all was !

" Ah well," he said to himself ; " the poor devil seems to have a grudge against me. I'll do my best for him." He grinned to himself, in a very bad temper.

II

The farm was less than a hundred yards from the wood's edge. The wall of trees formed the fourth side to the open quadrangle. The house faced the wood. With tangled emotions, Syson noted the plum blossom falling on the profuse, coloured primroses, which he himself had brought here and set. How they had increased ! There were thick tufts of scarlet, and pink, and pale purple primroses under the plum trees. He saw somebody glance at him through the kitchen window, heard men's voices.

The door opened suddenly : very womanly she had grown ! He felt himself going pale.

" You ?—Addy ! " she exclaimed, and stood motionless.

" Who ? " called the farmer's voice. Men's low voices answered. Those low voices, curious and almost jeering, roused the tormented spirit in the visitor. Smiling brilliantly at her, he waited.

"Myself—why not?" he said.

The flush burned very deep on her cheek and throat.

"We are just finishing dinner," she said.

"Then I will stay outside." He made a motion to show that he would sit on the red earthenware pipkin that stood near the door among the daffodils, and contained the drinking water.

"Oh no, come in," she said hurriedly. He followed her. In the doorway, he glanced swiftly over the family, and bowed. Every one was confused. The farmer, his wife, and the four sons sat at the coarsely laid dinner-table, the men with arms bare to the elbows.

"I am sorry I come at lunch-time," said Syson.

"Hello, Addy!" said the farmer, assuming the old form of address, but his tone cold. "How are you?"

And he shook hands.

"Shall you have a bit?" he invited the young visitor, but taking for granted the offer would be refused. He assumed that Syson was become too refined to eat so roughly. The young man winced at the imputation.

"Have you had any dinner?" asked the daughter.

"No," replied Syson. "It is too early. I shall be back at half-past one."

"You call it lunch, don't you?" asked the eldest son, almost ironical. He had once been an intimate friend of this young man.

"We'll give Addy something when we've finished," said the mother, an invalid, deprecating.

"No—don't trouble. I don't want to give you any trouble," said Syson.

"You could allus live on fresh air an' scenery," laughed the youngest son, a lad of nineteen.

Syson went round the buildings, and into the orchard at the back of the house, where daffodils all along the hedgerow swung like yellow, ruffled birds on their perches. He loved the place extraordinarily, the hills ranging round, with bear-skin woods covering their giant shoulders, and small red farms like brooches clasping their garments ; the blue streak of water in the valley, the bareness of the home pasture, the sound of myriad-threaded bird-singing, which went mostly unheard. To his last day, he would dream of this place, when he felt the sun on his face, or saw the small handfuls of snow between the winter twigs, or smelt the coming of spring.

Hilda was very womanly. In her presence he felt constrained. She was twenty-nine, as he was, but she seemed to him much older. He felt foolish, almost unreal, beside her. She was so static. As he was fingering some shed plum blossom on a low bough, she came to the back door to shake the tablecloth. Fowls raced from the stack-yard, birds rustled from the trees. Her dark hair was gathered up in a coil like a crown on her head. She was very straight, distant in her bearing. As she folded the cloth, she looked away over the hills.

Presently Syson returned indoors. She had prepared eggs and curd cheese, stewed gooseberries and cream.

" Since you will dine to-night," she said, " I have only given you a light lunch."

" It is awfully nice," he said. " You keep a real idyllic atmos-phere—your belt of straw and ivy buds."

Still they hurt each other.

He was uneasy before her. Her brief, sure speech, her distant bearing, were unfamiliar to him. He admired again her grey-black eyebrows, and her lashes. Their eyes met. He saw, in the beautiful grey and black of her glance, tears and a strange light, and at the back of all, calm acceptance of herself, and triumph over him.

He felt himself shrinking. With an effort he kept up the ironic manner.

She sent him into the parlour while she washed the dishes. The long low room was refurnished from the Abbey sale, with chairs upholstered in claret-coloured rep, many years old, and an oval table of polished walnut, and another piano, handsome, though still antique. In spite of the strangeness, he was pleased. Opening a high cupboard let into the thickness of the wall, he found it full of his books, his old lesson-books, and volumes of verse he had sent her, English and German. The daffodils in the white window-bottoms shone across the room, he could almost feel their rays. The old glamour caught him again. His youthful water-colours on the wall no longer made him grin ; he remembered how fervently he had tried to paint for her, twelve years before.

She entered, wiping a dish, and he saw again the bright, kernel-white beauty of her arms.

" You are quite splendid here," he said, and their eyes met.

" Do you like it ? " she asked. It was the old, low, husky tone of intimacy. He felt a quick change beginning in his blood. It was the old, delicious sublimation, the thinning, almost the vaporizing of himself, as if his spirit were to be liberated.

" Aye," he nodded, smiling at her like a boy again. She bowed her head.

" This was the countess's chair," she said in low tones. " I found her scissors down here between the padding."

" Did you ? Where are they ? "

Quickly, with a lilt in her movement, she fetched her work-basket, and together they examined the long-shanked old scissors.

" What a ballad of dead ladies ! " he said, laughing, as he fitted his fingers into the round loops of the countess's scissors.

" I knew you could use them," she said, with certainty. He looked at his fingers, and at the scissors. She meant his fingers were fine enough for the small-looped scissors.

" That is something to be said for me," he laughed, putting the scissors aside. She turned to the window. He noticed the fine, fair down on her cheek and her upper lip, and her soft, white neck, like the throat of a nettle flower, and her fore-arms, bright as newly blanched kernels. He was looking at her with new eyes, and she was a different person to him. He did not know her. But he could regard her objectively now.

" Shall we go out awhile ? " she asked.

" Yes ! " he answered. But the predominant emotion, that troubled the excitement and perplexity of his heart, was fear, fear of that which he saw. There was about her the same manner, the same intonation in her voice, now as then, but she was not what he had known her to be. He knew quite well what she had been for him. And gradually he was realizing that she was something quite other, and always had been.

She put no covering on her head, merely took off her apron, saying, " We will go by the larches." As they passed the old orchard, she called him in to show him a blue-tit's nest in one of the apple trees, and a sycock's in the hedge. He rather wondered at her surety, at a certain hardness like arrogance hidden under her humility.

" Look at the apple buds," she said, and he then perceived myriads of little scarlet balls among the drooping boughs. Watching his face, her eyes went hard. She saw the scales were fallen from him, and at last he was going to see her as she was. It was the thing she had most dreaded in the past, and most needed, for her soul's sake. Now he was going to see her as she was. He would not love her, and he would know he never could have loved her. The old illusion gone, they were strangers, crude and entire. But he would give her her due—she would have her due from him.

She was brilliant as he had not known her. She showed him nests : a jenny wren's in a low bush.

" See this jinty's ! " she exclaimed.

He was surprised to hear her use the local name. She reached carefully through the thorns, and put her finger in the nest's round door.

" Five ! " she said. " Tiny little things."

She showed him nests of robins, and chaffinches, and linnets, and buntings ; of a wagtail beside the water.

" And if we go down, nearer the lake, I will show you a king-fisher's. . . ."

" Among the young fir trees," she said, " there's a throstle's or a blackie's on nearly every bough, every ledge. The first day, when I had seen them all, I felt as if I mustn't go in the wood. It seemed a city of birds : and in the morning, hearing them all, I thought of the noisy early markets. I was afraid to go in my own wood."

She was using the language they had both of them invented. Now it was all her own. He had done with it. She did not mind his silence, but was always dominant, letting him see her wood. As they came along a marshy path where forget-me-nots were opening in a rich blue drift : " We know all the birds, but there are many flowers we can't find out," she said. It was half an appeal to him, who had known the names of things.

She looked dreamily across to the open fields that slept in the sun.

" I have a lover as well, you know," she said, with assurance, yet dropping again almost into the intimate tone.

This woke in him the spirit to fight her.

" I think I met him. He is good-looking—also in Arcady."

Without answering, she turned into a dark path that led up-hill, where the trees and undergrowth were very thick.

" They did well," she said at length, " to have various altars to various gods, in old days."

" Ah yes ! " he agreed. " To whom is the new one ? "

" There are no old ones," she said. " I was always looking for this."

" And whose is it ? " he asked.

" I don't know," she said, looking full at him.

" I'm very glad, for your sake," he said, " that you are satisfied."

" Aye—but the man doesn't matter so much," she said. There was a pause.

" No ! " he exclaimed, astonished, yet recognizing her as her real self.

" It is one's self that matters," she said. " Whether one is being one's own self and serving one's own God."

There was silence, during which he pondered. The path was almost flowerless, gloomy. At the side, his heels sank into soft clay.

III

" I," she said, very slowly, " I was married the same night as you."

He looked at her.

" Not legally, of course," she replied. " But—actually."

" To the keeper ? " he said, not knowing what else to say.

She turned to him.

" You thought I could not ? " she said. But the flush was deep in her cheek and throat, for all her assurance.

Still he would not say anything.

" You see "—she was making an effort to explain—" *I* had to understand also."

" And what does it amount to, this *understanding ?* " he asked.

" A very great deal—does it not to you ? " she replied. " One is free."

" And you are not disappointed ? "

" Far from it ! " Her tone was deep and sincere.

" You love him ? "

" Yes, I love him."

" Good ! " he said.

This silenced her for a while.

" Here, among his things, I love him," she said.

His conceit would not let him be silent.

" It needs this setting ? " he asked.

" It does," she cried. " You were always making me to be not myself."

He laughed shortly.

" But is it a matter of surroundings ? " he said. He had considered her all spirit.

" I am like a plant," she replied. " I can only grow in my own soil."

They came to a place where the undergrowth shrank away, leaving a bare, brown space, pillared with the brick-red and purplish trunks of pine trees. On the fringe, hung the sombre green of elder trees, with flat flowers in bud, and below were bright, unfurling pennons of fern. In the midst of the bare space stood a keeper's log hut. Pheasant-coops were lying about, some occupied by a clucking hen, some empty.

Hilda walked over the brown pine-needles to the hut, took a key from among the eaves, and opened the door. It was a bare wooden place with a carpenter's bench and form, carpenter's tools, an axe, snares, traps, some skins pegged down, everything in order. Hilda closed the door. Syson examined the weird flat coats of wild animals, that were pegged down to be cured. She turned some knotch in the side wall, and disclosed a second, small apartment.

"How romantic!" said Syson.

"Yes. He is very curious—he has some of a wild animal's cunning—in a nice sense—and he is inventive, and thoughtful—but not beyond a certain point."

She pulled back a dark green curtain. The apartment was occupied almost entirely by a large couch of heather and bracken, on which was spread an ample rabbit-skin rug. On the floor were patchwork rugs of cat-skin, and a red calf-skin, while hanging from the wall were other furs. Hilda took down one, which she put on. It was a cloak of rabbit-skin and of white fur, with a hood, apparently of the skins of stoats. She laughed at Syson from out of this barbaric mantle, saying:

"What do you think of it?"

"Ah——! I congratulate you on your man," he replied.

"And look!" she said.

In a little jar on a shelf were some sprays, frail and white, of the first honeysuckle.

"They will scent the place at night," she said.

He looked round curiously.

"Where does he come short, then?" he asked. She gazed at him for a few moments. Then, turning aside:

"The stars aren't the same with him," she said. "You could make them flash and quiver, and the forget-me-nots come up at me like phosphorescence. You could make things *wonderful*. I have found it out—it is true. But I have them all for myself, now."

He laughed, saying:

"After all, stars and forget-me-nots are only luxuries. You ought to make poetry."

"Aye," she assented. "But I have them all now."

Again he laughed bitterly at her.

She turned swiftly. He was leaning against the small window of the tiny, obscure room, and was watching her, who stood in the doorway, still cloaked in her mantle. His cap was removed, so she saw his face and head distinctly in the dim room. His black, straight, glossy hair was brushed clean back from his brow. His black eyes were watching her, and his face, that was clear and cream, and perfectly smooth, was flickering.

"We are very different," she said bitterly.

Again he laughed.

" I see you disapprove of me," he said.

" I disapprove of what you have become," she said.

" You think we might "—he glanced at the hut—" have been like this—you and I ? "

She shook her head.

" You ! No ; never ! You plucked a thing and looked at it till you had found out all you wanted to know about it, then you threw it away," she said.

" Did I ? " he asked. " And could your way never have been my way ? I suppose not."

" Why should it ? " she said. " I am a separate being."

" But surely two people sometimes go the same way," he said.

" You took me away from myself," she said.

He knew he had mistaken her, had taken her for something she was not. That was his fault, not hers.

" And did you always know ? " he asked.

" No—you never let me know. You bullied me. I couldn't help myself. I was glad when you left me, really."

" I know you were," he said. But his face went paler, almost deathly luminous.

" Yet," he said, " it was you who sent me the way I have gone."

" I ! " she exclaimed, in pride.

" You *would* have me take the Grammar School scholarship— and you would have me foster poor little Botell's fervent attachment to me, till he couldn't live without me—and because Botell was rich and influential. You triumphed in the wine-merchant's offer to send me to Cambridge, to befriend his only child. You wanted me to rise in the world. And all the time you were sending me away from you—every new success of mine put a separation between us, and more for you than for me. You never wanted to come with me : you wanted just to send me to see what it was like. I believe you even wanted me to marry a lady. You wanted to triumph over society in me."

" And I am responsible," she said, with sarcasm.

" I distinguished myself to satisfy you," he replied.

" Ah ! " she cried, " you always wanted change, change, like a child."

" Very well ! And I am a success, and I know it, and I do some good work. But—I thought you were different. What right have you to a man ? "

"What do you want?" she said, looking at him with wide, fearful eyes.

He looked back at her, his eyes pointed, like weapons.

"Why, nothing," he laughed shortly.

There was a rattling at the outer latch, and the keeper entered. The woman glanced round, but remained standing, fur-cloaked, in the inner doorway. Syson did not move.

The other man entered, saw, and turned away without speaking. The two also were silent.

Pilbeam attended to his skins.

"I must go," said Syson.

"Yes," she replied.

"Then I give you 'To our vast and varying fortunes.'" He lifted his hand in pledge.

"'To our vast and varying fortunes,'" she answered gravely, and speaking in cold tones.

"Arthur!" she said.

The keeper pretended not to hear. Syson, watching keenly, began to smile. The woman drew herself up.

"Arthur!" she said again, with a curious upward inflection, which warned the two men that her soul was trembling on a dangerous crisis.

The keeper slowly put down his tool and came to her.

"Yes," he said.

"I wanted to introduce you," she said, trembling.

"I've met him a'ready," said the keeper.

"Have you? It is Addy, Mr. Syson, whom you know about.— This is Arthur, Mr. Pilbeam," she added, turning to Syson. The latter held out his hand to the keeper, and they shook hands in silence.

"I'm glad to have met you," said Syson. "We drop our correspondence, Hilda?"

"Why need we?" she asked.

The two men stood at a loss.

"*Is* there no need?" said Syson.

Still she was silent.

"It is as you will," she said.

They went all three together down the gloomy path.

"'Qu'il était bleu, le ciel, et grand l'espoir,'" quoted Syson, not knowing what to say.

"What do you mean?" she said. "Besides, *we* can't walk in *our* wild oats—we never sowed any."

Syson looked at her. He was startled to see his young love, his nun, his Botticelli angel, so revealed. It was he who had been the fool. He and she were more separate than any two strangers could be. She only wanted to keep up a correspondence with him—and he, of course, wanted it kept up, so that he could write to her, like Dante to some Beatrice who had never existed save in the man's own brain.

At the bottom of the path she left him. He went along with the keeper, towards the open, towards the gate that closed on the wood. The two men walked almost like friends. They did not broach the subject of their thoughts.

Instead of going straight to the high-road gate, Syson went along the wood's edge, where the brook spread out in a little bog, and under the alder trees, among the reeds, great yellow stools and bosses of marigolds shone. Threads of brown water trickled by, touched with gold from the flowers. Suddenly there was a blue flash in the air, as a kingfisher passed.

Syson was extraordinarily moved. He climbed the bank to the gorse bushes, whose sparks of blossom had not yet gathered into a flame. Lying on the dry brown turf, he discovered sprigs of tiny purple milkwort and pink spots of lousewort. What a wonderful world it was—marvellous, for ever new. He felt as if it were underground, like the fields of monotone hell, notwithstanding. Inside his breast was a pain like a wound. He remembered the poem of William Morris, where in the Chapel of Lyonesse a knight lay wounded, with the truncheon of a spear deep in his breast, lying always as dead, yet did not die, while day after day the coloured sunlight dipped from the painted window across the chancel, and passed away. He knew now it never had been true, that which was between him and her, not for a moment. The truth had stood apart all the time.

Syson turned over. The air was full of the sound of larks, as if the sunshine above were condensing and falling in a shower. Amid this bright sound, voices sounded small and distinct.

"But if he's married, an' quite willing to drop it off, what has ter against it?" said the man's voice.

"I don't want to talk about it now. I want to be alone."

Syson looked through the bushes. Hilda was standing in the wood, near the gate. The man was in the field, loitering by the hedge, and playing with the bees as they settled on the white bramble flowers.

There was silence for a while, in which Syson imagined her will among the brightness of the larks. Suddenly the keeper exclaimed "Ah!" and swore. He was gripping at the sleeve of his coat, near the shoulder. Then he pulled off his jacket, threw it on the ground, and absorbedly rolled up his shirt-sleeve right to the shoulder.

"Ah!" he said vindictively, as he picked out the bee and flung it away. He twisted his fine, bright arm, peering awkwardly over his shoulder.

"What is it?" asked Hilda.

"A bee—crawled up my sleeve," he answered.

"Come here to me," she said.

The keeper went to her, like a sulky boy. She took his arm in her hands.

"Here it is—and the sting left in—poor bee!"

She picked out the sting, put her mouth to his arm, and sucked away the drop of poison. As she looked at the red mark her mouth had made, and at his arm, she said, laughing:

"That is the reddest kiss you will ever have."

When Syson next looked up, at the sound of voices, he saw in the shadow the keeper with his mouth on the throat of his beloved, whose head was thrown back, and whose hair had fallen, so that one rough rope of dark brown hair hung across his bare arm.

"No," the woman answered. "I am not upset because he's gone. You won't understand. . . ."

Syson could not distinguish what the man said. Hilda replied, clear and distinct:

"You know I love you. He has gone quite out of my life—don't trouble about him. . . ." He kissed her, murmuring. She laughed hollowly.

"Yes," she said, indulgent. "We will be married, we will be married. But not just yet." He spoke to her again. Syson heard nothing for a time. Then she said:

"You must go home, now, dear—you will get no sleep."

Again was heard the murmur of the keeper's voice, troubled by fear and passion.

"But why should we be married at once?" she said. "What more would you have, by being married? It is most beautiful as it is."

At last he pulled on his coat and departed. She stood at the gate, not watching him, but looking over the sunny country.

When at last she had gone, Syson also departed, going back to town.

SECOND BEST

"OH, I'm tired!" Frances exclaimed petulantly, and in the same
instant she dropped down on the turf, near the hedge-bottom.
Anne stood a moment surprised, then, accustomed to the vagaries of
her beloved Frances, said:
"Well, and aren't you always likely to be tired, after travelling
that blessed long way from Liverpool yesterday.?" and she plumped
down beside her sister. Anne was a wise young body of fourteen,
very buxom, brimming with common sense. Frances was much
older, about twenty-three, and whimsical, spasmodic. She was the
beauty and the clever child of the family. She plucked the goose-
grass buttons from her dress in a nervous, desperate fashion. Her
beautiful profile, looped above with black hair, warm with the
dusky-and-scarlet complexion of a pear, was calm as a mask, her
thin brown hand plucked nervously.
"It's not the journey," she said, objecting to Anne's obtuseness.
Anne looked inquiringly at her darling. The young girl, in her
self-confident, practical way, proceeded to reckon up this whimsical
creature. But suddenly she found herself full in the eyes of Frances;
felt two dark, hectic eyes flaring challenge at her, and she shrank
away. Frances was peculiar for these great, exposed looks, which
disconcerted people by their violence and their suddenness.
"What's a matter, poor old duck?" asked Anne, as she folded
the slight, wilful form of her sister in her arms. Frances laughed
shakily, and nestled down for comfort on the budding breasts of the
strong girl.
"Oh, I'm only a bit tired," she murmured, on the point of tears.
"Well, of course you are, what do you expect?" soothed Anne.
It was a joke to Frances that Anne should play elder, almost mother
to her. But then, Anne was in her unvexed teens; men were like
big dogs to her: while Frances, at twenty-three, suffered a good
deal.
The country was intensely morning-still. On the common
everything shone beside its shadow, and the hill-side gave off heat in
silence. The brown turf seemed in a low state of combustion, the

leaves of the oaks were scorched brown. Among the blackish foliage in the distance shone the small red and orange of the village.

The willows in the brook-course at the foot of the common suddenly shook with a dazzling effect like diamonds. It was a puff of wind. Anne resumed her normal position. She spread her knees, and put in her lap a handful of hazel nuts, whity-green leafy things, whose one cheek was tanned between brown and pink. These she began to crack and eat. Frances, with bowed head, mused bitterly.

" Eh, you know Tom Smedley ? " began the young girl, as she pulled a tight kernel out of its shell.

" I suppose so," replied Frances sarcastically.

" Well, he gave me a wild rabbit what he'd caught, to keep with my tame one—and it's living."

" That's a good thing," said Frances, very detached and ironic.

" Well, it *is* ! He reckoned he'd take me to Ollerton Feast, but he never did. Look here, he took a servant from the rectory ; I saw him."

" So he ought," said Frances.

" No, he oughtn't ! And I told him so. And I told him I should tell you—an' I have done."

Click and snap went a nut between her teeth. She sorted out the kernel, and chewed complacently.

" It doesn't make much difference," said Frances.

" Well, 'appen it doesn't ; but I was mad with him all the same."

" Why ? "

" Because I was ; he's no right to go with a servant."

" He's a perfect right," persisted Frances, very just and cold.

" No, he hasn't, when he'd said he'd take me."

Frances burst into a laugh of amusement and relief.

" Oh, no ; I'd forgot that," she said, adding, " and what did he say when you promised to tell me ? "

" He laughed and said, ' She won't fret her fat over that.' "

" And she won't," sniffed Frances.

There was silence. The common, with its sere, blonde-headed thistles, its heaps of silent bramble, its brown-husked gorse in the glare of sunshine, seemed visionary. Across the brook began the immense pattern of agriculture, white chequering of barley stubble, brown squares of wheat, khaki patches of pasture, red stripes of fallow, with the woodland and the tiny village dark like ornaments, leading away to the distance, right to the hills, where the check-pattern grew smaller and smaller, till, in the blackish haze of heat, far off, only the tiny white squares of barley stubble showed distinct.

"Eh, I say, here's a rabbit hole!" cried Anne suddenly. "Should we watch if one comes out? You won't have to fidget, you know."

The two girls sat perfectly still. Frances watched certain objects in her surroundings: they had a peculiar, unfriendly look about them: the weight of greenish elderberries on their purpling stalks; the twinkling of the yellowing crab-apples that clustered high up in the hedge, against the sky: the exhausted, limp leaves of the prim-roses lying flat in the hedge-bottom: all looked strange to her. Then her eyes caught a movement. A mole was moving silently over the warm, red soil, nosing, shuffling hither and thither, flat, and dark as a shadow, shifting about, and as suddenly brisk, and as silent, like a very ghost of *joie de vivre*. Frances started, from habit was about to call on Anne to kill the little pest. But, to-day her lethargy of un-happiness was too much for her. She watched the little brute paddling, snuffing, touching things to discover them, running in blindness, delighted to ecstasy by the sunlight and the hot, strange things that caressed its belly and its nose. She felt a keen pity for the little creature.

"Eh, our Fran, look there! It's a mole."

Anne was on her feet, standing watching the dark, unconscious beast. Frances frowned with anxiety.

"It doesn't run off, does it?" said the young girl softly. Then she stealthily approached the creature. The mole paddled fumblingly away. In an instant Anne put her foot upon it, not too heavily. Frances could see the struggling, swimming movement of the little pink hands of the brute, the twisting and twitching of its pointed nose, as it wrestled under the sole of the boot.

"It *does* wriggle!" said the bonny girl, knitting her brows in a frown at the eerie sensation. Then she bent down to look at her trap. Frances could now see, beyond the edge of the boot-sole, the heaving of the velvet shoulders, the pitiful turning of the sightless face, the frantic rowing of the flat, pink hands.

"Kill the thing," she said, turning away her face.

"Oh—I'm not," laughed Anne, shrinking. "You can, if you like."

"I *don't* like," said Frances, with quiet intensity.

After several dabbing attempts, Anne succeeded in picking up the little animal by the scruff of its neck. It threw back its head, flung its long blind snout from side to side, the mouth open in a peculiar oblong, with tiny pinkish teeth at the edge. The blind, frantic mouth gaped and writhed. The body, heavy and clumsy, hung scarcely moving.

" Isn't it a snappy little thing," observed Anne, twisting to avoid the teeth.

" What are you going to do with it ? " asked Frances sharply.

" It's got to be killed—look at the damage they do. I s'll take it home and let dadda or somebody kill it. I'm not going to let it go."

She swaddled the creature clumsily in her pocket-handkerchief and sat down beside her sister. There was an interval of silence, during which Anne combated the efforts of the mole.

" You've not had much to say about Jimmy this time. Did you see him often in Liverpool ? " Anne asked suddenly.

" Once or twice," replied Frances, giving no sign of how the question troubled her.

" And aren't you sweet on him any more, then ? "

" I should think I'm not, seeing that he's engaged."

" Engaged ? Jimmy Barrass ! Well, of all things ! I never thought *he'd* get engaged."

" Why not, he's as much right as anybody else ? " snapped Frances.

Anne was fumbling with the mole.

" 'Appen so," she said at length ; " but I never thought Jimmy would, though."

" Why not ? " snapped Frances.

" *I* don't know—this blessed mole, it'll not keep still !—who's he got engaged to ? "

" How should I know ? "

" I thought you'd ask him ; you've known him long enough. I s'd think he thought he'd get engaged now he's a Doctor of Chemistry."

Frances laughed in spite of herself.

" What's that got to do with it ? " she asked.

" I'm sure it's got a lot. He'll want to feel *somebody* now, so he's got engaged. Hey, stop it ; go in ! "

But at this juncture the mole almost succeeded in wriggling clear. It wrestled and twisted frantically, waved its pointed blind head, its mouth standing open like a little shaft, its big, wrinkled hands spread out.

" Go in with you ! " urged Anne, poking the little creature with her forefinger, trying to get it back into the handkerchief. Suddenly the mouth turned like a spark on her finger.

" Oh ! " she cried, " he's bit me."

She dropped him to the floor. Dazed, the blind creature fumbled round. Frances felt like shrieking. She expected him to dart away in a flash, like a mouse, and there he remained groping ; she wanted to cry to him to be gone.   Anne, in a sudden decision of wrath, caught up her sister's walking-cane.   With one blow the mole was dead.   Frances was startled and shocked.   One moment the little wretch was fussing in the heat, and the next it lay like a little bag, inert and black—not a struggle, scarce a quiver.

"It is dead !" Frances said breathlessly.   Anne took her finger from her mouth, looked at the tiny pinpricks, and said :

"Yes, he is, and I'm glad.   They're vicious little nuisances, moles are."

With which her wrath vanished.   She picked up the dead animal.

"Hasn't it got a beautiful skin," she mused, stroking the fur with her forefinger, then with her cheek.

"Mind," said Frances sharply.   "You'll have the blood on your skirt !"

One ruby drop of blood hung on the small snout, ready to fall. Anne shook it off on to some harebells.   Frances suddenly became calm ; in that moment, grown-up.

"I suppose they have to be killed," she said, and a certain rather dreary indifference succeeded to her grief.   The twinkling crab-apples, the glitter of brilliant willows now seemed to her trifling, scarcely worth the notice.   Something had died in her, so that things lost their poignancy.   She was calm, indifference overlying her quiet sadness.   Rising, she walked down to the brook course.

"Here, wait for me," cried Anne, coming tumbling after.

Frances stood on the bridge, looking at the red mud trodden into pockets by the feet of cattle.   There was not a drain of water left, but everything smelled green, succulent.   Why did she care so little for Anne, who was so fond of her ? she asked herself.   Why did she care so little for any one ?   She did not know, but she felt a rather stubborn pride in her isolation and indifference.

They entered a field where stooks of barley stood in rows, the straight, blonde tresses of the corn streaming on to the ground.   The stubble was bleached by the intense summer, so that the expanse glared white.   The next field was sweet and soft with a second crop of seeds ; thin, straggling clover whose little pink knobs rested prettily in the dark green.   The scent was faint and sickly.   The girls came up in single file, Frances leading.

Near the gate a young man was mowing with the scythe some fodder for the afternoon feed of the cattle.   As he saw the girls he left off working and waited in an aimless kind of way.   Frances was dressed in white muslin, and she walked with dignity, detached and forgetful. Her lack of agitation, her simple, unheeding advance made him nervous. She had loved the far-off Jimmy for five years, having had in return his half-measures. This man only affected her slightly.

Tom was of medium stature, energetic in build. His smooth, fair-skinned face was burned red, not brown, by the sun, and this ruddiness enhanced his appearance of good humour and easiness. Being a year older than Frances, he would have courted her long ago had she been so inclined. As it was, he had gone his uneventful way amiably, chatting with many a girl, but remaining unattached, free of trouble for the most part. Only he knew he wanted a woman. He hitched his trousers just a trifle self-consciously as the girls approached. Frances was a rare, delicate kind of being, whom he realized with a queer and delicious stimulation in his veins. She gave him a slight sense of suffocation. Somehow, this morning, she affected him more than usual. She was dressed in white. He, however, being matter-of-fact in his mind, did not realize. His feeling had never become conscious, purposive.

Frances knew what she was about. Tom was ready to love her as soon as she would show him. Now that she could not have Jimmy, she did not poignantly care. Still, she would have something. If she could not have the best—Jimmy, whom she knew to be something of a snob—she would have the second best, Tom. She advanced rather indifferently.

" You are back, then ! " said Tom. She marked the touch of uncertainty in his voice.

" No," she laughed, " I'm still in Liverpool," and the undertone of intimacy made him burn.

" This isn't you, then ? " he asked.

Her heart leapt up in approval. She looked in his eyes, and for a second was with him.

" Why, what do you think ? " she laughed.

He lifted his hat from his head with a distracted little gesture. She liked him, his quaint ways, his humour, his ignorance, and his slow masculinity.

" Here, look here, Tom Smedley," broke in Anne.

" A moudiwarp ! Did you find it dead ? " he asked.

" No, it bit me," said Anne.

" Oh, aye ! An' that got your rag out, did it ? "

" No, it didn't ! " Anne scolded sharply. " Such language ! "

" Oh, what's up wi' it ? "

" I can't bear you to talk broad."

" Can't you ? "

He glanced at Frances.

" It isn't nice," Frances said. She did not care, really. The vulgar speech jarred on her as a rule ; Jimmy was a gentleman. But Tom's manner of speech did not matter to her.

" I like you to talk *nicely*," she added.

" Do you," he replied, tilting his hat, stirred.

" And generally you *do*, you know," she smiled.

" I s'll have to have a try," he said, rather tensely gallant.

" What ? " she asked brightly.

" To talk nice to you," he said. Frances coloured furiously, bent her head for a moment, then laughed gaily, as if she liked this clumsy hint.

" Eh now, you mind what you're saying," cried Anne, giving the young man an admonitory pat.

" You wouldn't have to give yon mole many knocks like that," he teased, relieved to get on safe ground, rubbing his arm.

" No indeed, it died in one blow," said Frances, with a flippancy that was hateful to her.

" You're not so good at knockin' 'em ? " he said, turning to her.

" I don't know, if I'm cross," she said decisively.

" No ? " he replied, with alert attentiveness.

" I could," she added, harder, " if it was necessary."

He was slow to feel her difference.

" And don't you consider it *is* necessary ? " he asked, with misgiving.

" W—ell—is it ? " she said, looking at him steadily, coldly.

" I reckon it is," he replied, looking away, but standing stubborn.

She laughed quickly.

" But it isn't necessary for *me*," she said, with slight contempt.

" Yes, that's quite true," he answered.

She laughed in a shaky fashion.

" *I know it is*," she said ; and there was an awkward pause.

" Why, would you *like* me to kill moles then ? " she asked tentatively, after a while.

" They do us a lot of damage," he said, standing firm on his own ground, angered.

" Well, I'll see the next time I come across one," she promised, defiantly. Their eyes met, and she sank before him, her pride troubled. He felt uneasy and triumphant and baffled, as if fate had gripped him. She smiled as she departed.

" Well," said Anne, as the sisters went through the wheat stubble ; " I don't know what you two's been jawing about, I'm sure."

" Don't you ? " laughed Frances significantly.

" No, I don't. But, at any rate, Tom Smedley's a good deal better to my thinking than Jimmy, so there—and nicer."

" Perhaps he is," said Frances coldly.

And the next day, after a secret, persistent hunt, she found another mole playing in the heat. She killed it, and in the evening, when Tom came to the gate to smoke his pipe after supper, she took him the dead creature.

" Here you are then ! " she said.

" Did you catch it ? " he replied, taking the velvet corpse into his fingers and examining it minutely. This was to hide his trepidation.

" Did you think I couldn't ? " she asked, her face very near his.

" Nay, I didn't know."

She laughed in his face, a strange little laugh that caught her breath, all agitation, and tears, and recklessness of desire. He looked frightened and upset. She put her hand to his arm.

" Shall you go out wi' me ? " he asked, in a difficult, troubled tone.

She turned her face away, with a shaky laugh. The blood came up in him, strong, overmastering. He resisted it. But it drove him down, and he was carried away. Seeing the winsome, frail nape of her neck, fierce love came upon him for her, and tenderness.

" We s'll 'ave to tell your mother," he said. And he stood, suffering, resisting his passion for her.

" Yes," she replied, in a dead voice. But there was a thrill of pleasure in this death.

A RATHER small young man sat by the window of a pretty seaside cottage trying to persuade himself that he was reading the newspaper. It was about half-past eight in the morning. Outside, the glory roses hung in the morning sunshine like little bowls of fire tipped up. The young man looked at the table, then at the clock, then at his own big silver watch. An expression of stiff endurance came on to his face. Then he rose and reflected on the oil-paintings that hung on the walls of the room, giving careful but hostile attention to "The Stag at Bay." He tried the lid of the piano, and found it locked. He caught sight of his own face in a little mirror, pulled his brown moustache, and an alert interest sprang into his eyes. He was not ill-favoured. He twisted his moustache. His figure was rather small, but alert and vigorous. As he turned from the mirror a look of self-commiseration mingled with his appreciation of his own physiognomy.

In a state of self-suppression, he went through into the garden. His jacket, however, did not look dejected. It was new, and had a smart and self-confident air, sitting upon a confident body. He contemplated the Tree of Heaven that flourished by the lawn, then sauntered on to the next plant. There was more promise in a crooked apple tree covered with brown-red fruit. Glancing round, he broke off an apple and, with his back to the house, took a clean, sharp bite. To his surprise the fruit was sweet. He took another. Then again he turned to survey the bedroom windows overlooking the garden. He started, seeing a woman's figure ; but it was only his wife. She was gazing across to the sea, apparently ignorant of him.

For a moment or two he looked at her, watching her. She was a good-looking woman, who seemed older than he, rather pale, but healthy, her face yearning. Her rich auburn hair was heaped in folds on her forehead. She looked apart from him and his world, gazing away to the sea. It irked her husband that she should continue abstracted and in ignorance of him ; he pulled poppy fruits and threw them at the window. She started, glanced at him with a wild smile, and looked away again. Then almost immediately she left the window. He went indoors to meet her. She had a fine carriage, very proud, and wore a dress of soft white muslin.

" I've been waiting long enough," he said.

" For me or for breakfast ? " she said lightly. " You know we said nine o'clock. I should have thought you could have slept after the journey."

" You know I'm always up at five, and I couldn't stop in bed after six. You might as well be in pit as in bed, on a morning like this."

" I shouldn't have thought the pit would occur to you, here."

She moved about examining the room, looking at the ornaments under glass covers. He, planted on the hearthrug, watched her rather uneasily, and grudgingly indulgent. She shrugged her shoulders at the apartment.

" Come," she said, taking his arm, " let us go into the garden till Mrs. Coates brings the tray."

" I hope she'll be quick," he said, pulling his moustache. She gave a short laugh, and leaned on his arm as they went. He had lighted a pipe.

Mrs. Coates entered the room as they went down the steps. The delightful, erect old lady hastened to the window for a good view of her visitors. Her china-blue eyes were bright as she watched the young couple go down the path, he walking in an easy, confident fashion, with his wife on his arm. The landlady began talking to herself in a soft, Yorkshire accent.

" Just of a height they are. She wouldn't ha' married a man less than herself in stature, I think, though he's not her equal otherwise." Here her granddaughter came in, setting a tray on the table. The girl went to the old woman's side.

" He's been eating the apples, gran'," she said.

" Has he, my pet ? Well, if he's happy, why not ? "

Outside, the young, well-favoured man listened with impatience to the chink of the teacups. At last, with a sigh of relief, the couple came in to breakfast. After he had eaten for some time, he rested a moment and said :

" Do you think it's any better place than Bridlington ? "

" I do," she said, " infinitely ! Besides, I am at home here—it's not like a strange sea-side place to me."

" How long were you here ? "

" Two years."

He ate reflectively.

" I should ha' thought you'd rather go to a fresh place," he said at length.

She sat very silent, and then, delicately, put out a feeler.

" Why ? " she said. " Do you think I shan't enjoy myself ? "

He laughed comfortably, putting the marmalade thick on his bread.

" I hope so," he said.

She again took no notice of him.

" But don't say anything about it in the village, Frank," she said casually. " Don't say who I am, or that I used to live here. There's nobody I want to meet, particularly, and we should never feel free if they knew me again."

" Why did you come, then ? "

" ' Why ? ' Can't you understand why ? "

" Not if you don't want to know anybody."

" I came to see the place, not the people."

He did not say any more.

" Women," she said, " are different from men. I don't know why I wanted to come—but I did."

She helped him to another cup of coffee, solicitously.

" Only," she resumed, " don't talk about me in the village." She laughed shakily. " I don't want my past brought up against me, you know."   And she moved the crumbs on the cloth with her finger-tip.

He looked at her as he drank his coffee ; he sucked his moustache, and putting down his cup, said phlegmatically :

" I'll bet you've had a lot of past."

She looked with a little guiltiness, that flattered him, down at the tablecloth.

" Well," she said, caressive, " you won't give me away, who I am, will you ? "

" No," he said, comforting, laughing, " I won't give you away." He was pleased.

She remained silent.   After a moment or two she lifted her head, saying :

" I've got to arrange with Mrs. Coates, and do various things. So you'd better go out by yourself this morning—and we'll be in to dinner at one."

" But you can't be arranging with Mrs. Coates all morning," he said.

" Oh, well—then I've some letters to write, and I must get that mark out of my skirt. I've got plenty of little things to do this morning. You'd better go out by yourself."

He perceived that she wanted to be rid of him, so that when she went upstairs, he took his hat and lounged out on to the cliffs, suppressedly angry.

Presently she too came out. She wore a hat with roses, and a long lace scarf hung over her white dress. Rather nervously, she put up her sunshade, and her face was half-hidden in its coloured shadow. She went along the narrow track of flag-stones that were worn hollow by the feet of the fishermen. She seemed to be avoiding her surroundings, as if she remained safe in the little obscurity of her parasol.

She passed the church, and went down the lane till she came to a high wall by the wayside. Under this she went slowly, stopping at length by an open doorway, which shone like a picture of light in the dark wall. There in the magic beyond the doorway, patterns of shadow lay on the sunny court, on the blue and white sea-pebbles of its paving, while a green lawn glowed beyond, where a bay tree glittered at the edges. She tiptoed nervously into the courtyard, glancing at the house that stood in shadow. The uncurtained windows looked black and soulless, the kitchen door stood open. Irresolutely she took a step forward, and again forward, leaning, yearning, towards the garden beyond.

She had almost gained the corner of the house when a heavy step came crunching through the trees. A gardener appeared before her. He held a wicker tray on which were rolling great, dark red gooseberries, overripe. He moved slowly.

" The garden isn't open to-day," he said quietly to the attractive woman, who was poised for retreat.

For a moment she was silent with surprise. How should it be public at all ?

" When is it open ? " she asked, quick-witted.

" The rector lets visitors in on Fridays and Tuesdays."

She stood still, reflecting. How strange to think of the rector opening his garden to the public !

" But everybody will be at church," she said coaxingly to the man. " There'll be nobody here, will there ? "

He moved, and the big gooseberries rolled.

" The rector lives at the new rectory," he said.

The two stood still. He did not like to ask her to go. At last she turned to him with a winning smile.

" Might I have *one* peep at the roses ? " she coaxed, with pretty wilfulness.

" I don't suppose it would matter," he said, moving aside ; " you won't stop long——"

She went forward, forgetting the gardener in a moment. Her face became strained, her movements eager. Glancing round, she saw all the windows giving on to the lawn were curtainless and dark. The house had a sterile appearance, as if it were still used, but not inhabited. A shadow seemed to go over her. She went across the lawn towards the garden, through an arch of crimson ramblers, a gate of colour. There beyond lay the soft blue sea within the bay, misty with morning, and the furthest headland of black rock jutting dimly out between blue and blue of the sky and water. Her face began to shine, transfigured with pain and joy. At her feet the garden fell steeply, all a confusion of flowers, and away below was the darkness of tree-tops covering the beck.

She turned to the garden that shone with sunny flowers around her. She knew the little corner where was the seat beneath the yew tree. Then there was the terrace where a great host of flowers shone, and from this, two paths went down, one at each side of the garden. She closed her sunshade and walked slowly among the many flowers. All round were rose bushes, big banks of roses, then roses hanging and tumbling from pillars, or roses balanced on the standard bushes. By the open earth were many other flowers. If she lifted her head, the sea was upraised beyond, and the Cape.

Slowly she went down one path, lingering, like one who has gone back into the past. Suddenly she was touching some heavy crimson roses that were soft as velvet, touching them thoughtfully, without knowing, as a mother sometimes fondles the hand of her child. She leaned slightly forward to catch the scent. Then she wandered on in abstraction. Sometimes a flame-coloured, scentless rose would hold her arrested. She stood gazing at it as if she could not understand it. Again the same softness of intimacy came over her, as she stood before a tumbling heap of pink petals. Then she wondered over the white rose, that was greenish, like ice, in the centre. So, slowly, like a white, pathetic butterfly, she drifted down the path, coming at last to a tiny terrace all full of roses. They seemed to fill the place, a sunny, gay throng. She was shy of them, they were so many and so bright. They seemed to be conversing and laughing. She felt herself in a strange crowd. It exhilarated her, carried her out of herself. She flushed with excitement. The air was pure scent.

Hastily, she went to a little seat among the white roses, and sat down. Her scarlet sunshade made a hard blot of colour. She sat quite still, feeling her own existence lapse. She was no more than a rose, a rose that could not quite come into blossom, but remained tense. A little fly dropped on her knee, on her white dress. She watched it, as if it had fallen on a rose. She was not herself.

Then she started cruelly as a shadow crossed her and a figure moved into her sight. It was a man who had come in slippers, unheard. He wore a linen coat. The morning was shattered, the spell vanished away. She was only afraid of being questioned. He came forward. She rose. Then, seeing him, the strength went from her and she sank on the seat again.

He was a young man, military in appearance, growing slightly stout. His black hair was brushed smooth and bright, his moustache was waxed. But there was something rambling in his gait. She looked up, blanched to the lips, and saw his eyes. They were black, and stared without seeing. They were not a man's eyes. He was coming towards her.

He stared at her fixedly, made an unconscious salute, and sat down beside her on the seat. He moved on the bench, shifted his feet, saying, in a gentlemanly, military voice :

" I don't disturb you—do I ? "

She was mute and helpless. He was scrupulously dressed in dark clothes and a linen coat. She could not move. Seeing his hands, with the ring she knew so well upon the little finger, she felt as if she were going dazed. The whole world was deranged. She sat unavailing. For his hands, her symbols of passionate love, filled her with horror as they rested now on his strong thighs.

" May I smoke ? " he asked intimately, almost secretly, his hand going to his pocket.

She could not answer, but it did not matter, he was in another world. She wondered, craving, if he recognized her—if he could recognize her. She sat pale with anguish. But she had to go through it.

" I haven't got any tobacco," he said thoughtfully.

But she paid no heed to his words, only she attended to him. Could he recognize her, or was it all gone ? She sat still in a frozen kind of suspense.

" I smoke John Cotton," he said, " and I must economize with it, it is expensive. You know, I'm not very well off while these lawsuits are going on."

" No," she said, and her heart was cold, her soul kept rigid.

He moved, made a loose salute, rose, and went away. She sat motionless. She could see his shape, the shape she had loved with all her passion : his compact, soldier's head, his fine figure now slackened. And it was not he. It only filled her with horror too difficult to know.

Suddenly he came again, his hand in his jacket pocket.

" Do you mind if I smoke ? " he said. " Perhaps I shall be able to see things more clearly."

He sat down beside her again, filling a pipe. She watched his hands with the fine strong fingers. They had always inclined to tremble slightly. It had surprised her, long ago, in such a healthy man. Now they moved inaccurately, and the tobacco hung raggedly out of the pipe.

" I have legal business to attend to. Legal affairs are always so uncertain. I tell my solicitor exactly, precisely what I want, but I can never get it done."

She sat and heard him talking. But it was not he. Yet those were the hands she had kissed, there were the glistening, strange black eyes that she had loved. Yet it was not he. She sat motionless with horror and silence. He dropped his tobacco pouch, and groped for it on the ground. Yet she must wait to see if he would recognize her. Why could she not go ! In a moment he rose.

" I must go at once," he said. " The owl is coming." Then he added confidentially : " His name isn't really the owl, but I call him that. I must go and see if he has come."

She rose too. He stood before her, uncertain. He was a handsome, soldierly fellow, and a lunatic. Her eyes searched him, and searched him, to see if he would recognize her, if she could discover him.

" You don't know me ? " she asked, from the terror of her soul, standing alone.

He looked back at her quizzically. She had to bear his eyes. They gleamed on her, but with no intelligence. He was drawing nearer to her.

" Yes, I do know you," he said, fixed, intent, but mad, drawing his face nearer hers. Her horror was too great. The powerful lunatic was coming too near to her.

A man approached, hastening.

" The garden isn't open this morning," he said.

The deranged man stopped and looked at him. The keeper went to the seat and picked up the tobacco pouch left lying there.

" Don't leave your tobacco, sir," he said, taking it to the gentleman in the linen coat.

" I was just asking this lady to stay to lunch," the latter said politely. " She is a friend of mine."

The woman turned and walked swiftly, blindly, between the sunny roses, out from the garden, past the house with the blank, dark windows, through the sea-pebbled courtyard to the street. Hastening and blind, she went forward without hesitating, not knowing whither. Directly she came to the house she went upstairs, took off her hat, and sat down on the bed. It was as if some membrane had been torn in two in her, so that she was not an entity that could think and feel. She sat staring across at the window, where an ivy spray waved slowly up and down in the sea wind. There was some of the uncanny luminousness of the sunlit sea in the air. She sat perfectly still, without any being. She only felt she might be sick, and it might be blood that was loose in her torn entrails. She sat perfectly still and passive.

After a time she heard the hard tread of her husband on the floor below, and, without herself changing, she registered his movement. She heard his rather disconsolate footsteps go out again, then his voice speaking, answering, growing cheery, and his solid tread drawing near.

He entered, ruddy, rather pleased, an air of complacency about his alert, sturdy figure. She moved stiffly. He faltered in his approach.

" What's the matter ? " he asked, a tinge of impatience in his voice. " Aren't you feeling well ? "

This was torture to her.

" Quite," she replied.

His brown eyes became puzzled and angry.

" What is the matter ? " he said.

" Nothing."

He took a few strides, and stood obstinately, looking out of the window.

" Have you run up against anybody ? " he asked.

" Nobody who knows me," she said.

His hands began to twitch. It exasperated him, that she was no more sensible of him than if he did not exist. Turning on her at length, driven, he asked :

" Something has upset you, hasn't it ? "

" No, why ? " she said, neutral. He did not exist for her, except as an irritant.

His anger rose, filling the veins in his throat.

" It seems like it," he said, making an effort not to show his anger, because there seemed no reason for it. He went away downstairs. She sat still on the bed, and with the residue of feeling left to her, she disliked him because he tormented her. The time went by. She could smell the dinner being served, the smoke of her husband's pipe from the garden. But she could not move. She had no being. There was a tinkle of the bell. She heard him come indoors. And

then he mounted the stairs again. At every step her heart grew tight
in her. He opened the door.

"Dinner is on the table," he said.

It was difficult for her to endure his presence, for he would interfere with her. She could not recover her life. She rose stiffly and
went down. She could neither eat nor talk during the meal. She
sat absent, torn, without any being of her own. He tried to go on as
if nothing were the matter. But at last he became silent with fury.
As soon as it was possible, she went upstairs again, and locked the
bedroom door. She must be alone. He went with his pipe into the
garden. All his suppressed anger against her who held herself
superior to him filled and blackened his heart. Though he had not
known it, yet he had never really won her, she had never loved
him. She had taken him on sufferance. This had foiled him. He
was only a labouring electrician in the mine, she was superior to
him. He had always given way to her. But all the while, the injury
and ignominy had been working in his soul because she did not hold
him seriously. And now all his rage came up against her.

He turned and went indoors. The third time, she heard him
mounting the stairs. Her heart stood still. He turned the catch
and pushed the door—it was locked. He tried it again, harder. Her
heart was standing still.

"Have you fastened the door?" he asked quietly, because of the
landlady.

"Yes. Wait a minute."

She rose and turned the lock, afraid he would burst it. She felt
hatred towards him, because he did not leave her free. He entered,
his pipe between his teeth, and she returned to her old position on the
bed. He closed the door and stood with his back to it.

"What's the matter?" he asked determinedly.

She was sick with him. She could not look at him.

"Can't you leave me alone?" she replied, averting her face from
him.

He looked at her quickly, fully, wincing with ignominy. Then he
seemed to consider for a moment.

"There's something up with you, isn't there?" he asked definitely.

"Yes," she said, "but that's no reason why you should torment
me."

"I don't torment you. What's the matter?"

"Why should you know?" she cried, in hate and desperation.

Something snapped. He started and caught his pipe as it fell
from his mouth. Then he pushed forward the bitten-off mouth-piece

with his tongue, took it from off his lips, and looked at it. Then he put out his pipe, and brushed the ash from his waistcoat. After which he raised his head.

" I want to know," he said. His face was greyish pale, and set uglily.

Neither looked at the other. She knew he was fired now. His heart was pounding heavily. She hated him, but she could not withstand him. Suddenly she lifted her head and turned on him.

" What right have you to know ? " she asked.

He looked at her. She felt a pang of surprise for his tortured eyes and his fixed face. But her heart hardened swiftly. She had never loved him. She did not love him now.

But suddenly she lifted her head again swiftly, like a thing that tries to get free. She wanted to be free of it. It was not him so much, but it, something she had put on herself, that bound her so horribly. And having put the bond on herself, it was hardest to take it off. But now she hated everything and felt destructive. He stood with his back to the door, fixed, as if he would oppose her eternally, till she was extinguished. She looked at him. Her eyes were cold and hostile. His workman's hands spread on the panels of the door behind him.

" You know I used to live here ? " she began, in a hard voice, as if wilfully to wound him. He braced himself against her, and nodded.

" Well, I was companion to Miss Birch of Torril Hall—she and the rector were friends, and Archie was the rector's son." There was a pause. He listened without knowing what was happening. He stared at his wife. She was squatted in her white dress on the bed, carefully folding and re-folding the hem of her skirt. Her voice was full of hostility.

" He was an officer—a sub-lieutenant—then he quarrelled with his colonel and came out of the army. At any rate "—she plucked at her skirt hem, her husband stood motionless, watching her movements which filled his veins with madness—" he was awfully fond of me, and I was of him—awfully."

" How old was he ? " asked the husband.

" When—when I first knew him ? Or when he went away ?——"

" When you first knew him."

" When I first knew him, he was twenty-six—now—he's thirty-one—nearly thirty-two—because I'm twenty-nine, and he is nearly three years older——"

She lifted her head and looked at the opposite wall.

" And what then ? " said her husband.

She hardened herself, and said callously :

" We were as good as engaged for nearly a year, though nobody knew—at least—they talked—but—it wasn't open.   Then he went away——"

" He chucked you ? " said the husband brutally, wanting to hurt her into contact with himself.   Her heart rose wildly with rage.   Then " Yes," she said, to anger him.   He shifted from one foot to the other, giving a " Ph ! " of rage.   There was silence for a time.

" Then," she resumed, her pain giving a mocking note to her words, " he suddenly went out to fight in Africa, and almost the very day I first met you, I heard from Miss Birch he'd got sunstroke— and two months after, that he was dead——"

" That was before you took on with me ? " said the husband.

There was no answer.   Neither spoke for a time.   He had not understood.   His eyes were contracted uglily.

" So you've been looking at your old courting places ! " he said. " That was what you wanted to go out by yourself for this morning."

Still she did not answer him anything.   He went away from the door to the window.   He stood with his hands behind him, his back to her.   She looked at him.   His hands seemed gross to her, the back of his head paltry.

At length, almost against his will, he turned round, asking :

" How long were you carrying on with him ? "

" What do you mean ? " she replied coldly.

" I mean how long were you carrying on with him ? "

She lifted her head, averting her face from him.   She refused to answer.   Then she said :

" I don't know what you mean, by carrying on.   I loved him from the first days I met him—two months after I went to stay with Miss Birch."

" And do you reckon he loved you ? " he jeered.

" I know he did."

" How do you know, if he'd have no more to do with you ? "

There was a long silence of hate and suffering.

" And how far did it go between you ? " he asked at length, in a frightened, stiff voice.

" I hate your not-straightforward questions," she cried, beside herself with his baiting.   " We loved each other, and we *were* lovers —we were.   I don't care what *you* think : what have you got to do with it ?   We were lovers before ever I knew you——"

" Lovers—lovers," he said, white with fury.   " You mean you had your fling with an army man, and then came to me to marry you when you'd done——"

She sat swallowing her bitterness. There was a long pause.

" Do you mean to say you used to go—the whole hogger ? " he asked, still incredulous.

" Why, what else do you think I mean ? " she cried brutally.

He shrank, and became white, impersonal. There was a long, paralysed silence. He seemed to have gone small.

" You never thought to tell me all this before I married you," he said, with bitter irony, at last.

" You never asked me," she replied.

" I never thought there was any need."

" Well, then, you *should* think."

He stood with expressionless, almost childlike set face, revolving many thoughts, whilst his heart was mad with anguish.

Suddenly she added :

" And I saw him to-day," she said.   " He is not dead, he's mad."

Her husband looked at her, startled.

" Mad ! " he said involuntarily.

" A lunatic," she said. It almost cost her her reason to utter the word. There was a pause.

" Did he know you ? " asked the husband, in a small voice.

" No," she said.

He stood and looked at her. At last he had learned the width of the breach between them. She still squatted on the bed. He could not go near her. It would be violation to each of them to be brought into contact with the other. The thing must work itself out. They were both shocked so much, they were impersonal, and no longer hated each other. After some minutes he left her and went out.

I

THROUGH the gloom of evening, and the flare of torches of the night before the fair, through the still fogs of the succeeding dawn came paddling the weary geese, lifting their poor feet that had been dipped in tar for shoes, and trailing them along the cobble-stones into the town. Last of all, in the afternoon, a country girl drove in her dozen birds, disconsolate because she was so late. She was a heavily built girl, fair, with regular features, and yet unprepossessing. She needed chiselling down, her contours were brutal. Perhaps it was weariness that hung her eyelids a little lower than was pleasant. When she spoke to her clumsily lagging birds it was in a snarling nasal tone. One of the silly things sat down in the gutter and refused to move. It looked very ridiculous, but also rather pitiful, squat there with its head up, refusing to be urged on by the ungentle toe of the girl. The latter swore heavily, then picked up the great complaining bird, and fronting her road stubbornly, drove on the lamentable eleven.

No one had noticed her. This afternoon the women were not sitting chatting on their doorsteps, seaming up the cotton hose, or swiftly passing through their fingers the piled white lace ; and in the high dark houses the song of the hosiery frames was hushed : " Shackety-boom, Shackety-shackety-boom, Z—zzz ! " As she dragged up Hollow Stone, people returning from the fair chaffed her and asked her what o'clock it was. She did not reply, her look was sullen. The Lace Market was quiet as the Sabbath : even the great brass plates on the doors were dull with neglect. There seemed an afternoon atmosphere of raw discontent. The girl stopped a moment before the dismal prospect of one of the great warehouses that had been gutted with fire. She looked at the lean, threatening walls, and watched her white flock waddling in reckless misery below, and she would have laughed out loud had the wall fallen flat upon them and relieved her of them. But the wall did not fall, so she crossed the road, and walking on the safe side, hurried after her charge. Her look was even more sullen. She remembered the state of trade—Trade, the invidious enemy ; Trade, which thrust out its hand and shut the factory doors, and pulled the stockingers off their seats, and left the web half-finished on the frame ; Trade, which mysteriously choked up the sources of the rivulets of wealth, and blacker and more secret than a pestilence, starved the town. Through this morose atmosphere of bad trade, in the afternoon of the first day of the fair, the girl strode down to the Poultry with eleven sound geese and one lame one to sell.

The Frenchmen were at the bottom of it ! So everybody said, though nobody quite knew how. At any rate, they had gone to war with the Prussians and got beaten, and trade was ruined in Nottingham !

A little fog rose up, and the twilight gathered around. Then they flared abroad their torches in the fair, insulting the night. The girl still sat in the Poultry, and her weary geese unsold on the stones, illuminated by the hissing lamp of a man who sold rabbits and pigeons and such-like assorted live-stock.

II

In another part of the town, near Sneinton Church, another girl came to the door to look at the night. She was tall and slender, dressed with the severe accuracy which marks the girl of superior culture. Her hair was arranged with simplicity about the long, pale, cleanly cut face. She leaned forward very slightly to glance down the street, listening. She very carefully preserved the appearance of having come quite casually to the door, yet she lingered and lingered and stood very still to listen when she heard a footstep, but when it proved to be only a common man, she drew herself up proudly and looked with a small smile over his head. He hesitated to glance into the open hall, lighted so spaciously with a scarlet-shaded lamp, and at the slim girl in brown silk lifted up before the light. But she, she looked over his head. He passed on.

Presently she started and hung in suspense. Somebody was crossing the road. She ran down the steps in a pretty welcome, not effuse, saying in quick but accurately articulated words : " Will ! I began to think you'd gone to the fair. I came out to listen to it. I felt almost sure you'd gone. You're coming in, aren't you ? " She waited a moment anxiously. " We expect you to dinner, you know," she added wistfully.

The man, who had a short face and spoke with his lip curling up on one side, in a drawling speech with ironically exaggerated intonation, replied after a short hesitation :

" I'm awfully sorry, I am, straight, Lois. It's a shame. I've got to go round to the biz. Man proposes—the devil disposes." He turned aside with irony in the darkness.

" But surely, Will ! " remonstrated the girl, keenly disappointed.

" Fact, Lois !—I feel wild about it myself. But I've got to go down to the works. They may be getting a bit warm down there, you know "—he jerked his head in the direction of the fair. " If the Lambs get frisky !—they're a bit off about the work, and they'd just be in their element if they could set a lighted match to something——"

" Will, you don't think—— ! " exclaimed the girl, laying her hand on his arm in the true fashion of romance, and looking up at him earnestly.

" Dad's not sure," he replied, looking down at her with gravity. They remained in this attitude for a moment, then he said :

" I might stop a bit. It's all right for an hour, I should think."

She looked at him earnestly, then said in tones of deep disappointment and of fortitude : " No, Will, you must go. You'd better go——"

" It's a shame ! " he murmured, standing a moment at a loose end. Then, glancing down the street to see he was alone, he put his arm round her waist and said in a difficult voice : " How goes it ? "

She let him keep her for a moment, then he kissed her as if afraid of what he was doing. They were both uncomfortable.

" Well—— ! " he said at length.

" Good night ! " she said, setting him free to go.

He hung a moment near her, as if ashamed. Then " Good night," he answered, and he broke away. She listened to his footsteps in the night, before composing herself to turn indoors.

" Helloa ! " said her father, glancing over his paper as she entered the dining-room. " What's up, then ? "

" Oh, nothing," she replied, in her calm tones. " Will won't be here to dinner to-night."

" What, gone to the fair ? "

" No."

" Oh ! What's got him then ? "

Lois looked at her father, and answered :

" He's gone down to the factory. They are afraid of the hands."

Her father looked at her closely.

" Oh, aye ! " he answered, undecided, and they sat down to dinner.

III

Lois retired very early. She had a fire in her bedroom. She drew the curtains and stood holding aside a heavy fold, looking out at the night. She could see only the nothingness of the fog ; not even the glare of the fair was evident, though the noise clamoured small in the distance. In front of everything she could see her own faint image. She crossed to the dressing-table, and there leaned her face to the mirror, and looked at herself. She looked a long time, then she rose, changed her dress for a dressing-jacket, and took up *Sesame and Lilies*.

Late in the night she was roused from sleep by a bustle in the house. She sat up and heard a hurrying to and fro and the sound of anxious voices. She put on her dressing-gown and went out to her mother's room. Seeing her mother at the head of the stairs, she said in her quick, clean voice :

" Mother, what is it ? "

" Oh, child, don't ask me ! Go to bed, dear, do ! I shall surely be worried out of my life."

" Mother, what is it ? " Lois was sharp and emphatic.

" I hope your father won't go. Now I do hope your father won't go. He's got a cold as it is."

" Mother, tell me what it is ? " Lois took her mother's arm.

" It's Selby's. I should have thought you would have heard the fire-engine, and Jack isn't in yet. I hope we're safe ! " Lois returned to her bedroom and dressed. She coiled her plaited hair, and having put on a cloak, left the house.

She hurried along under the fog-dripping trees towards the meaner part of the town. When she got near, she saw a glare in the fog, and closed her lips tight. She hastened on till she was in the crowd. With peaked, noble face she watched the fire. Then she looked a little wildly over the fire-reddened faces in the crowd, and catching sight of her father, hurried to him.

" Oh, Dadda—is he safe ? Is Will safe——? "

" Safe, aye, why not ? You've no business here. Here, here's Sampson, he'll take·you home. I've enough to bother me ; there's my own place to watch. Go home now, I can't do with you here."

" Have you seen Will ? " she asked.

" Go home—Sampson, just take Miss Lois home—now ! "

" You don't really know where he is—father ? "

" Go home now—I don't want you here——" her father ordered peremptorily.

The tears sprang to Lois' eyes. She looked at the fire and the tears were quickly dried by fear. The flames roared and struggled upward. The great wonder of the fire made her forget even her indignation at her father's light treatment of herself and of her lover. There was a crashing and bursting of timber, as the first floor fell in a mass into the blazing gulf, splashing the fire in all directions, to the terror of the crowd. She saw the steel of the machines growing white-hot and twisting like flaming letters. Piece after piece of the flooring gave way, and the machines dropped in red ruin as the wooden framework burned out. The air became unbreathable ; the fog was swallowed up ; sparks went rushing up as if they would burn the dark heavens ; sometimes cards of lace went whirling into the gulf of the sky, waving with wings of fire. It was dangerous to stand near this great cup of roaring destruction.

Sampson, the grey old manager of Buxton and Co.'s, led her away as soon as she would turn her face to listen to him. He was a stout, irritable man. He elbowed his way roughly through the crowd, and Lois followed him, her head high, her lips closed. He led her for some distance without speaking, then at last, unable to contain his garrulous irritability, he broke out :

" What do they expect ? What can they expect ? They can't expect to stand a bad time. They spring up like mushrooms as big as a house-side, but there's no stability in 'em. I remember William Selby when he'd run on my errands. Yes, there's some as can make much out of little, and there's some as can make much out of nothing, but they find it won't last. William Selby's sprung up in a day, and he'll vanish in a night. You can't trust to luck alone. Maybe he thinks it's a lucky thing this fire has come when things are looking black. But you can't get out of it as easy as that. There's been a few too many of 'em. No, indeed, a fire's the last thing I should hope to come to—the very last ! "

Lois hurried and hurried, so that she brought the old manager panting in distress up the steps of her home. She could not bear to hear him talking so. They could get no one to open the door for some time. When at last Lois ran upstairs, she found her mother dressed, but all unbuttoned again, lying back in the chair in her daughter's room, suffering from palpitation of the heart, with *Sesame and Lilies* crushed beneath her. Lois administered brandy, and her decisive words and movements helped largely to bring the good lady to a state of recovery sufficient to allow of her returning to her own bedroom.

Then Lois locked the door. She glanced at her fire-darkened

face, and taking the flattened Ruskin out of the chair, sat down and wept. After a while she calmed herself, rose, and sponged her face. Then once more on that fatal night she prepared for rest. Instead, however, of retiring, she pulled a silk quilt from her disordered bed and, wrapping it round her, sat miserably to think. It was two o'clock in the morning.

IV

The fire was sunk to cold ashes in the grate, and the grey morning was creeping through the half-opened curtains like a thing ashamed, when Lois awoke. It was painful to move her head : her neck was cramped. The girl awoke in full recollection. She sighed, roused herself and pulled the quilt closer about her. For a little while she sat and mused. A pale, tragic resignation fixed her face like a mask. She remembered her father's irritable answer to her question concerning her lover's safety—" Safe, aye—why not ? " She knew that he suspected the factory of having been purposely set on fire. But then, he had never liked Will. And yet—and yet—Lois' heart was heavy as lead. She felt her lover was guilty. And she felt she must hide her secret of his last communication to her. She saw herself being cross-examined—" When did you last see this man ? " But she would hide what he had said about watching at the works. How dreary it was—and how dreadful. Her life was ruined now, and nothing mattered any more. She must only behave with dignity, and submit to her own obliteration. For even if Will were never accused, she knew in her heart he was guilty. She knew it was over between them.

It was dawn among the yellow fog outside, and Lois, as she moved mechanically about her toilet, vaguely felt that all her days would arrive slowly struggling through a bleak fog. She felt an intense longing at this uncanny hour to slough the body's trammelled weariness and to issue at once into the new bright warmth of the far Dawn where a lover waited transfigured ; it is so easy and pleasant in imagination to step out of the chill grey dampness of another terrestrial daybreak, straight into the sunshine of the eternal morning? And who can escape his hour? So Lois performed the meaningless routine of her toilet, which at last she made meaningful when she took her black dress, and fastened a black jet brooch at her throat.

Then she went downstairs and found her father eating a mutton chop. She quickly approached and kissed him on the forehead.

Then she retreated to the other end of the table. Her father looked tired, even haggard.

" You are early," he said, after a while. Lois did not reply. Her father continued to eat for a few moments, then he said :

" Have a chop—here's one ! Ring for a hot plate. Eh, what ? Why not ? "

Lois was insulted, but she gave no sign. She sat down and took a cup of coffee, making no pretence to eat. Her father was absorbed, and had forgotten her.

" Our Jack's not come home yet," he said at last.

Lois stirred faintly. " Hasn't he ? " she said.

" No." There was silence for a time. Lois was frightened. Had something happened also to her brother ? This fear was closer and more irksome.

" Selby's was cleaned out, gutted. We had a near shave of it——"

" You have no loss, Dadda ? "

" Nothing to mention." After another silence, her father said :

" I'd rather be myself than William Selby. Of course it may merely be bad luck—you don't know. But whatever it was, I wouldn't like to add one to the list of fires just now. Selby was at the ' George ' when it broke out—I don't know where the lad was—— ! "

" Father," broke in Lois, " why do you talk like that ? Why do you talk as if Will had done it ? " She ended suddenly. Her father looked at her pale, mute face.

" I don't talk as if Will had done it," he said. " I don't even think it."

Feeling she was going to cry, Lois rose and left the room. Her father sighed, and leaning his elbows on his knees, whistled faintly into the fire. He was not thinking about her.

Lois went down to the kitchen and asked Lucy, the parlour-maid, to go out with her. She somehow shrank from going alone, lest people should stare at her overmuch : and she felt an overpowering impulse to go to the scene of the tragedy, to judge for herself.

The churches were chiming half-past eight when the young lady and the maid set off down the street. Nearer the fair, swarthy, thin-legged men were pushing barrels of water towards the market-place, and the gipsy women, with hard brows, and dressed in tight velvet bodices, hurried along the pavement with jugs of milk, and great brass water ewers and loaves and breakfast parcels. People were just getting up, and in the poorer streets was a continual splash of tea-leaves, flung out on to the cobble-stones. A teapot came crashing down from an upper story just behind Lois, and she, starting round and looking up, thought that the trembling, drink-bleared man at the upper window, who was stupidly staring after his pot, had had designs on her life ; and she went on her way shuddering at the grim tragedy of life.

In the dull October morning the ruined factory was black and ghastly. The window-frames were all jagged, and the walls stood gaunt. Inside was a tangle of twisted *débris*, the iron, in parts red with bright rust, looking still hot ; the charred wood was black and satiny ; from dishevelled heaps, sodden with water, a faint smoke rose dimly. Lois stood and looked. If he had done that ! He might even be dead there, burned to ash and lost for ever. It was almost soothing to feel so. He would be safe in the eternity which now she must hope in.

At her side the pretty, sympathetic maid chatted plaintively. Suddenly, from one of her lapses into silence, she exclaimed :

" Why if there isn't Mr. Jack ! "

Lois turned suddenly and saw her brother and her lover approaching her. Both looked soiled, untidy and wan. Will had a black eye, some ten hours old, well coloured. Lois turned very pale as they approached. They were looking gloomily at the factory, and for a moment did not notice the girls.

" I'll be jiggered if there ain't our Lois ! " exclaimed Jack, the reprobate, swearing under his breath.

" Oh, God ! " exclaimed the other in disgust.

" Jack, where have you been ? " said Lois sharply, in keen pain, not looking at her lover. Her sharp tone of suffering drove her lover to defend himself with an affectation of comic recklessness.

" In quod," replied her brother, smiling sicklily.

" Jack ! " cried his sister very sharply.

" Fact."

Will Selby shuffled on his feet and smiled, trying to turn away his face so that she should not see his black eye. She glanced at him. He felt her boundless anger and contempt, and with great courage he looked straight at her, smiling ironically. Unfortunately his smile would not go over his swollen eye, which remained grave and lurid.

" Do I look pretty ? " he inquired with a hateful twist of his lip.

" Very ! " she replied.

" I thought I did," he replied. And he turned to look at his father's ruined works, and he felt miserable and stubborn. The girl standing there so clean and out of it all ! Oh, God, he felt sick. He turned to go home.

The three went together, Lois silent in anger and resentment. Her brother was tired and overstrung, but not suppressed. He chattered on, blindly.

" It was a lark we had ! We met Bob Osborne and Freddy Mansell coming down Poultry. There was a girl with some geese. She looked a tanger sitting there, all like statues, her and the geese. It was Will who began it. He offered her threepence and asked her to begin the show. She called him a—she called him something, and then somebody poked an old gander to stir him up, and somebody squirted him in the eye. He upped and squawked and started off with his neck out. Laugh ! We nearly killed ourselves, keeping back those old birds with squirts and teasers. Oh, Lum ! Those old geese, oh, scrimmy, they didn't know where to turn, they fairly went off their dots, coming at us right an' left, and such a row—it was fun, you never knew ? Then the girl she got up and knocked somebody over the jaw, and we were right in for it. Well, in the end, Billy here got hold of her round the waist——"

" Oh, dry it up ! " exclaimed Will bitterly.

Jack looked at him, laughed mirthlessly, and continued : " An' we said we'd buy her birds. So we got hold of one goose apiece— an' they took some holding, I can tell you—and off we set round the fair, Billy leading with the girl. The bloomin' geese squawked an' pecked. Laugh—I thought I should a' died. Well, then we wanted the girl to have her birds back—and then she fired up. She got some other chaps on her side, and there was a proper old row. The girl went tooth and nail for Will there—she was dead set against him. She gave him a black eye, by gum, and we went at it, I can tell you. It was a free fight, a beauty, an' we got run in. I don't know what became of the girl."

Lois surveyed the two men. There was no glimmer of a smile on her face, though the maid behind her was sniggering. Will was very bitter. He glanced at his sweetheart and at the ruined factory.

" How's dad taken it ? " he asked, in a biting, almost humble tone.

" I don't know," she replied coldly. " Father's in an awful way. I believe everybody thinks you set the place on fire."

Lois drew herself up. She had delivered her blow. She drew herself up in cold condemnation and for a moment enjoyed her complete revenge. He was despicable, abject in his dishevelled, disfigured, unwashed condition.

" Aye, well, they made a mistake for once," he replied, with a curl of the lip.

Curiously enough, they walked side by side as if they belonged to each other. She was his conscience-keeper. She was far from forgiving him, but she was still further from letting him go. And he walked at her side like a boy who has to be punished before he can be exonerated. He submitted. But there was a genuine bitter contempt in the curl of his lip.

I

" I'm getting up, Teddilinks," said Mrs. Whiston, and she sprang out of bed briskly.

" What the Hanover's got you ? " asked Whiston.

" Nothing. Can't I get up ? " she replied animatedly.

It was about seven o'clock, scarcely light yet in the cold bedroom. Whiston lay still and looked at his wife. She was a pretty little thing, with her fleecy, short black hair all tousled. He watched her as she dressed quickly, flicking her small, delightful limbs, throwing her clothes about her. Her slovenliness and untidiness did not trouble him. When she picked up the edge of her petticoat, ripped off a torn string of white lace, and flung it on the dressing-table, her careless abandon made his spirit glow. She stood before the mirror and roughly scrambled together her profuse little mane of hair. He watched the quickness and softness of her young shoulders, calmly, like a husband, and appreciatively.

" Rise up," she cried, turning to him with a quick wave of her arm—" and shine forth."

They had been married two years. But still, when she had gone out of the room, he felt as if all his light and warmth were taken away, he became aware of the raw, cold morning. So he rose himself, wondering casually what had roused her so early. Usually she lay in bed as late as she could.

Whiston fastened a belt round his loins and went downstairs in shirt and trousers. He heard her singing in her snatchy fashion. The stairs creaked under his weight. He passed down the narrow little passage, which she called a hall, of the seven and sixpenny house which was his first home.

He was a shapely young fellow of about twenty-eight, sleepy now and easy with well-being. He heard the water drumming into the kettle, and she began to whistle. He loved the quick way she dodged the supper cups under the tap to wash them for breakfast. She looked an untidy minx, but she was quick and handy enough.

" Teddilinks," she cried.

" What ? "

" Light a fire, quick."

She wore an old, sack-like dressing-jacket of black silk pinned across her breast. But one of the sleeves, coming unfastened, showed some delightful pink upper-arm.

" Why don't you sew your sleeve up ? " he said, suffering from the sight of the exposed soft flesh.

" Where ? " she cried, peering round. " Nuisance," she said, seeing the gap, then with light fingers went on drying the cups.

The kitchen was of fair size, but gloomy. Whiston poked out the dead ashes.

Suddenly a thud was heard at the door down the passage.

" I'll go," cried Mrs. Whiston, and she was gone down the hall.

The postman was a ruddy-faced man who had been a soldier. He smiled broadly, handing her some packages.

" They've not forgot you," he said impudently.

" No—lucky for them," she said, with a toss of the head. But she was interested only in her envelopes this morning. The postman waited inquisitively, smiling in an ingratiating fashion. She slowly, abstractedly, as if she did not know any one was there, closed the door in his face, continuing to look at the addresses on her letters.

She tore open the thin envelope. There was a long, hideous, cartoon valentine. She smiled briefly and dropped it on the floor. Struggling with the string of a packet, she opened a white cardboard box, and there lay a white silk handkerchief packed neatly under the paper lace of the box, and her initial, worked in heliotrope, fully displayed. She smiled pleasantly, and gently put the box aside. The third envelope contained another white packet—apparently a cotton handkerchief neatly folded. She shook it out. It was a long white stocking, but there was a little weight in the toe. Quickly, she thrust down her arm, wriggling her fingers into the toe of the stocking, and brought out a small box. She peeped inside the box, then hastily opened a door on her left hand, and went into the little, cold sitting-room. She had her lower lip caught earnestly between her teeth.

With a little flash of triumph, she lifted a pair of pearl ear-rings from the small box, and she went to the mirror. There, earnestly, she began to hook them through her ears, looking at herself sideways in the glass. Curiously concentrated and intent she seemed as she fingered the lobes of her ears, her head bent on one side.

Then the pearl ear-rings dangled under her rosy, small ears. She shook her head sharply, to see the swing of the drops. They went chill against her neck, in little, sharp touches. Then she stood still to look at herself, bridling her head in the dignified fashion. Then she simpered at herself. Catching her own eye, she could not help winking at herself and laughing.

She turned to look at the box. There was a scrap of paper with this posy :

> " Pearls may be fair, but thou art fairer.
> Wear these for me, and I'll love the wearer."

She made a grimace and a grin. But she was drawn to the mirror again, to look at her ear-rings.

Whiston had made the fire burn, so he came to look for her. When she heard him, she started round quickly, guiltily. She was watching him with intent blue eyes when he appeared.

He did not see much, in his morning-drowsy warmth. He gave her, as ever, a feeling of warmth and slowness. His eyes were very blue, very kind, his manner simple.

" What ha' you got ? " he asked.

" Valentines," she said briskly, ostentatiously turning to show him the silk handkerchief. She thrust it under his nose. " Smell how good," she said.

" Who's that from ? " he replied, without smelling.

" It's a valentine," she cried. " How do I know who it's from ? "

" I'll bet you know," he said.

" Ted !—I don't ! " she cried, beginning to shake her head, then stopping because of the ear-rings.

He stood still a moment, displeased.

" They've no right to send you valentines, now," he said.

" Ted !—Why not ? You're not jealous, are you ? I haven't the least idea who it's from. Look—there's my initial "—she pointed with an emphatic finger at the heliotrope embroidery—

> " E for Elsie,
> Nice little gelsie,"

she sang.

" Get out," he said. " You know who it's from."

" Truth, I don't," she cried.

He looked round, and saw the white stocking lying on a chair.

" Is this another ? " he said.

" No, that's a sample," she said. " There's only a comic." And she fetched in the long cartoon.

He stretched it out and looked at it solemnly.

" Fools ! " he said, and went out of the room.

She flew upstairs and took off the ear-rings. When she returned, he was crouched before the fire blowing the coals. The skin of his face was flushed, and slightly pitted, as if he had had small-pox. But his neck was white and smooth and goodly. She hung her arms round his neck as he crouched there, and clung to him. He balanced on his toes.

"This fire's a slow-coach," he said.

"And who else is a slow-coach?" she said.

"One of us two, I know," he said, and he rose carefully. She remained clinging round his neck, so that she was lifted off her feet.

"Ha!—swing me," she cried.

He lowered his head, and she hung in the air, swinging from his neck, laughing. Then she slipped off.

"The kettle is singing," she sang, flying for the teapot. He bent down again to blow the fire. The veins in his neck stood out, his shirt collar seemed too tight.

> "Doctor Wyer,
> Blow the fire,
> Puff! puff! puff!"

she sang, laughing.

He smiled at her.

She was so glad because of her pearl ear-rings.

Over the breakfast she grew serious. He did not notice. She became portentous in her gravity. Almost it penetrated through his steady good-humour to irritate him.

"Teddy!" she said at last.

"What?" he asked.

"I told you a lie," she said, humbly tragic.

His soul stirred uneasily.

"Oh aye?" he said casually.

She was not satisfied. He ought to be more moved.

"Yes," she said.

He cut a piece of bread.

"Was it a good one?" he asked.

She was piqued. Then she considered—*was* it a good one? Then she laughed.

"No," she said, "it wasn't up to much."

"Ah!" he said easily, but with a steady strength of fondness for her in his tone. "Get it out then."

It became a little more difficult.

"You know that white stocking," she said earnestly. "I told you a lie. It wasn't a sample. It was a valentine."

A little frown came on his brow.

" Then what did you invent it as a sample for ? " he said. But he knew this weakness of hers. The touch of anger in his voice frightened her.

" I was afraid you'd be cross," she said pathetically.

" I'll bet you were vastly afraid," he said.

" I *was*, Teddy."

There was a pause. He was resolving one or two things in his mind.

" And who sent it ? " he asked.

" I can guess," she said, " though there wasn't a word with it— except——"

She ran to the sitting-room and returned with a slip of paper.

> " Pearls may be fair, but thou art fairer
>   Wear these for me, and I'll love the wearer."

He read it twice, then a dull red flush came on his face.

" And *who* do you guess it is ? " he asked, with a ringing of anger in his voice.

" I suspect it's Sam Adams," she said, with a little virtuous indignation.

Whiston was silent for a moment.

" Fool ! " he said. " An' what's it got to do with pearls ?—and how can he say ' wear these for me ' when there's only one ? He hasn't got the brain to invent a proper verse."

He screwed the slip of paper into a ball and flung it into the fire.

" I suppose he thinks it'll make a pair with the one last year," she said.

" Why, did he send one then ? "

" Yes. I thought you'd be wild if you knew."

His jaw set rather sullenly.

Presently he rose, and went to wash himself, rolling back his sleeves and pulling open his shirt at the breast. It was as if his fine, clear-cut temples and steady eyes were degraded by the lower, rather brutal part of his face. But she loved it. As she whisked about, clearing the table, she loved the way in which he stood washing himself. He was such a man. She liked to see his neck glistening with water as he swilled it. It amused her and pleased her and thrilled her. He was so sure, so permanent, he had her so utterly in his power. It gave her a delightful, mischievous sense of liberty. Within his grasp, she could dart about excitingly.

He turned round to her, his face red from the cold water, his eyes fresh and very blue.

" You haven't been seeing anything of him, have you ? " he asked roughly.

" Yes," she answered, after a moment, as if caught guilty. " He got into the tram with me, and he asked me to drink a coffee and a Benedictine in the Royal."

" You've got it off fine and glib," he said sullenly. " And did you ? "

" Yes," she replied, with the air of a traitor before the rack.

The blood came up into his neck and face, he stood motionless, dangerous.

" It was cold, and it was such fun to go into the Royal," she said.

" You'd go off with a nigger for a packet of chocolate," he said, in anger and contempt, and some bitterness. Queer how he drew away from her, cut her off from him.

" Ted—how beastly ! " she cried. " You know quite well——" She caught her lip, flushed, and the tears came to her eyes.

He turned away, to put on his necktie. She went about her work, making a queer pathetic little mouth, down which occasionally dripped a tear.

He was ready to go. With his hat jammed down on his head, and his overcoat buttoned up to his chin, he came to kiss her. He would be miserable all the day if he went without. She allowed herself to be kissed. Her cheek was wet under his lips, and his heart burned. She hurt him so deeply. And she felt aggrieved, and did not quite forgive him.

In a moment she went upstairs to her ear-rings. Sweet they looked nestling in the little drawer—sweet ! She examined them with voluptuous pleasure, she threaded them in her ears, she looked at herself, she posed and postured and smiled and looked sad and tragic and winning and appealing, all in turn before the mirror. And she was happy, and very pretty.

She wore her ear-rings all morning, in the house. She was self-conscious, and quite brilliantly winsome, when the baker came, wondering if he would notice. All the tradesmen left her door with a glow in them, feeling elated, and unconsciously favouring the delightful little creature, though there had been nothing to notice in her behaviour.

She was stimulated all the day. She did not think about her husband. He was the permanent basis from which she took these giddy little flights into nowhere. At night, like chickens and curses, she would come home to him, to roost.

Meanwhile Whiston, a traveller and confidential support of a small firm, hastened about his work, his heart all the while anxious for her, yearning for surety, and kept tense by not getting it.

II

She had been a warehouse girl in Adams's lace factory before she was married. Sam Adams was her employer. He was a bachelor of forty, growing stout, a man well dressed and florid, with a large brown moustache and thin hair. From the rest of his well-groomed, showy appearance, it was evident his baldness was a chagrin to him. He had a good presence, and some Irish blood in his veins.

His fondness for the girls, or the fondness of the girls for him, was notorious. And Elsie, quick, pretty, almost witty little thing—she *seemed* witty, although, when her sayings were repeated, they were entirely trivial—she had a great attraction for him. He would come into the warehouse dressed in a rather sporting reefer coat, of fawn colour, and trousers of fine black-and-white check, a cap with a big peak and scarlet carnation in his button-hole, to impress her. She was only half impressed. He was too loud for her good taste. Instinctively perceiving this, he sobered down to navy blue. Then a well-built man, florid, with large brown whiskers, smart navy blue suit, fashionable boots, and manly hat, he was the irreproachable. Elsie was impressed.

But meanwhile Whiston was courting her, and she made splendid little gestures, before her bedroom mirror, of the constant-and-true sort.

" True, true till death——"

That was her song. Whiston was made that way, so there was no need to take thought for him.

Every Christmas Sam Adams gave a party at his house, to which he invited his superior work-people—not factory hands and labourers but those above. He was a generous man in his way, with a real warm feeling for giving pleasure.

Two years ago Elsie had attended this Christmas-party for the last time. Whiston had accompanied her. At that time he worked for Sam Adams.

She had been very proud of herself, in her close-fitting, full-skirted dress of blue silk. Whiston called for her. Then she tripped beside him, holding her large cashmere shawl across her breast. He strode with long strides, his trousers handsomely strapped under his boots, and her silk shoes bulging the pockets of his full-skirted overcoat.

They passed through the park gates, and her spirits rose. Above them the Castle Rock loomed grandly in the night, the naked trees stood still and dark in the frost, along the boulevard.

They were rather late. Agitated with anticipation, in the cloak-room she gave up her shawl, donned her silk shoes, and looked at herself in the mirror. The loose bunches of curls on either side her face danced prettily, her mouth smiled.

She hung a moment in the door of the brilliantly lighted room. Many people were moving within the blaze of lamps, under the crystal chandeliers, the full skirts of the women balancing and floating, the side-whiskers and white cravats of the men bowing above. Then she entered the light.

In an instant Sam Adams was coming forward, lifting both his arms in boisterous welcome. There was a constant red laugh on his face.

" Come late, would you," he shouted, " like royalty."

He seized her hands and led her forward. He opened his mouth wide when he spoke, and the effect of the warm, dark opening behind the brown whiskers was disturbing. But she was floating into the throng on his arm. He was very gallant.

" Now then," he said, taking her card to write down the dances, " I've got *carte blanche*, haven't I ? "

" Mr. Whiston doesn't dance," she said.

" I am a lucky man ! " he said, scribbling his initials. " I was born with an *amourette* in my mouth."

He wrote on, quietly. She blushed and laughed, not knowing what it meant.

" Why, what is that ? " she said.

" It's you, even littler than you are, dressed in little wings," he said.

" I should have to be pretty small to get in your mouth," she said.

" You think you're too big, do you ! " he said easily.

He handed her her card, with a bow.

" Now I'm set up, my darling, for this evening," he said.

Then, quick, always at his ease, he looked over the room. She waited in front of him. He was ready. Catching the eye of the band, he nodded. In a moment, the music began. He seemed to relax, giving himself up.

" Now then, Elsie," he said, with a curious caress in his voice that seemed to lap the outside of her body in a warm glow, delicious. She gave herself to it. She liked it.

He was an excellent dancer. He seemed to draw her close in to him by some male warmth of attraction, so that she became all soft and pliant to him, flowing to his form, whilst he united her with him and they lapsed along in one movement. She was just carried in a kind of strong, warm flood, her feet moved of themselves, and only the music threw her away from him, threw her back to him, to his clasp, in his strong form moving against her, rhythmically, deliciously.

When it was over, he was pleased and his eyes had a curious gleam which thrilled her and yet had nothing to do with her. Yet it held her. He did not speak to her. He only looked straight into her eyes with a curious, gleaming look that disturbed her fearfully and deliciously. But also there was in his look some of the automatic irony of the *roué*. It left her partly cold. She was not carried away.

She went, driven by an opposite, heavier impulse, to Whiston. He stood looking gloomy, trying to admit that she had a perfect right to enjoy herself apart from him. He received her with rather grudging kindliness.

" Aren't you going to play whist ? " she asked.

" Aye," he said. " Directly."

" I do wish you could dance."

" Well, I can't," he said. " So you enjoy yourself."

" But I should enjoy it better if I could dance with you."

" Nay, you're all right," he said. " I'm not made that way."

" Then you ought to be ! " she cried.

" Well, it's my fault, not yours. You enjoy yourself," he bade her. Which she proceeded to do, a little bit irked.

She went with anticipation to the arms of Sam Adams, when the time came to dance with him. It *was* so gratifying, irrespective of the man. And she felt a little grudge against Whiston, soon forgotten when her host was holding her near to him, in a delicious embrace. And she watched his eyes, to meet the gleam in them, which gratified her.

She was getting warmed right through, the glow was penetrating into her, driving away everything else. Only in her heart was a little tightness, like conscience.

When she got a chance, she escaped from the dancing-room to the card-room. There, in a cloud of smoke, she found Whiston playing cribbage. Radiant, roused, animated, she came up to him and greeted him. She was too strong, too vibrant a note in the quiet room. He lifted his head, and a frown knitted his gloomy forehead.

" Are you playing cribbage ? Is it exciting ? How are you getting on ? " she chattered.

He looked at her. None of these questions needed answering, and he did not feel in touch with her. She turned to the cribbage-board

" Are you white or red ? " she asked.

" He's red," replied the partner.

" Then you're losing," she said, still to Whiston. And she lifted the red peg from the board. " One—two—three—four—five—six— seven—eight——Right up there you ought to jump——"

" Now put it back in its right place," said Whiston.

" Where was it ? " she asked gaily, knowing her transgression. He took the little red peg away from her and stuck it in its hole.

The cards were shuffled.

" What a shame you're losing ! " said Elsie.

" You'd better cut for him," said the partner.

She did so, hastily. The cards were dealt. She put her hand on his shoulder, looking at his cards.

" It's good," she cried, " isn't it ? "

He did not answer, but threw down two cards. It moved him more strongly than was comfortable, to have her hand on his shoulder, her curls dangling and touching his ears, whilst she was roused to another man. It made the blood flame over him.

At that moment Sam Adams appeared, florid and boisterous, intoxicated more with himself, with the dancing, than with wine. In his eye the curious, impersonal light gleamed.

" I thought I should find you here, Elsie," he cried boisterously, a disturbing, high note in his voice.

" What made you think so ? " she replied, the mischief rousing in her.

The florid, well-built man narrowed his eyes to a smile.

" I should never look for you among the ladies," he said, with a kind of intimate, animal call to her. He laughed, bowed, and offered her his arm.

" Madam, the music waits."

She went almost helplessly, carried along with him, unwilling, yet delighted.

That dance was an intoxication to her. After the first few steps, she felt herself slipping away from herself. She almost knew she was going, she did not even want to go. Yet she must have chosen to go. She lay in the arm of the steady, close man with whom she was dancing, and she seemed to swim away out of contact with the room, into him. She had passed into another, denser element of him, an essential privacy. The room was all vague around her, like an atmosphere, like under sea, with a flow of ghostly, dumb movements. But she herself was held real against her partner, and it seemed she was connected with him, as if the movements of his body and limbs were her own movements, yet not her own movements—and oh, delicious ! He also was given up, oblivious, concentrated, into the dance. His eye was unseeing. Only his large, voluptuous body gave off a subtle activity. His fingers seemed to search into her flesh. Every moment, and every moment, she felt she would give way utterly, and sink molten : the fusion point was coming when she would fuse down into perfect unconsciousness at his feet and knees. But he bore her round the room in the dance, and he seemed to sustain all her body with his limbs, his body, and his warmth seemed to come closer into her, nearer, till it would fuse right through her, and she would be as liquid to him, as an intoxication only.

It was exquisite. When it was over, she was dazed, and was scarcely breathing. She stood with him in the middle of the room as if she were alone in a remote place. He bent over her. She expected his lips on her bare shoulder, and waited. Yet they were not alone, they were not alone. It was cruel.

" 'Twas good, wasn't it, my darling ? " he said to her, low and delighted. There was a strange impersonality about his low, exultant call that appealed to her irresistibly. Yet why was she aware of some part shut off in her ? She pressed his arm, and he led her towards the door.

She was not aware of what she was doing, only a little grain of resistant trouble was in her. The man, possessed, yet with a superficial presence of mind, made way to the dining-room, as if to give her refreshment, cunningly working to his own escape with her. He was molten hot, filmed over with presence of mind, and bottomed with cold disbelief. In the dining-room was Whiston, carrying coffee to the plain, neglected ladies. Elsie saw him, but felt as if he could not see her. She was beyond his reach and ken. A sort of fusion existed between her and the large man at her side. She ate her custard, but an incomplete fusion all the while sustained and contained within the being of her employer.

But she was growing cooler. Whiston came up. She looked at him, and saw him with different eyes. She saw his slim, young man's figure real and enduring before her. That was he. But she was in the spell with the other man, fused with him, and she could not be taken away.

" Have you finished your cribbage ? " she asked, with hasty evasion of him.

" Yes," he replied. " Aren't you getting tired of dancing ? "

" Not a bit," she said.

" Not she," said Adams heartily. " No girl with any spirit gets

tired of dancing. Have something else, Elsie. Come—sherry. Have
a glass of sherry with us, Whiston."

Whilst they sipped the wine, Adams watched Whiston almost
cunningly, to find his advantage.

"We'd better be getting back—there's the music," he said. "See the
women get something to eat, Whiston, will you, there's a good chap."

And he began to draw away. Elsie was drifting helplessly with
him. But Whiston put himself beside them, and went along with
them. In silence they passed through to the dancing-room. There
Adams hesitated, and looked round the room. It was as if he could
not see.

A man came hurrying forward, claiming Elsie, and Adams went
to his other partner. Whiston stood watching during the dance.
She was conscious of him standing there observant of her, like a
ghost, or a judgment, or a guardian angel. She was also conscious,
much more intimately and impersonally, of the body of the other
man moving somewhere in the room. She still belonged to him,
but a feeling of distraction possessed her, and helplessness. Adams
danced on, adhering to Elsie, waiting his time, with the persistence
of cynicism.

The dance was over. Adams was detained. Elsie found herself
beside Whiston. There was something shapely about him as he sat,
about his knees and his distinct figure, that she clung to. It was as
if he had enduring form. She put her hand on his knee.

" Are you enjoying yourself ? " he asked.

" *Ever* so," she replied, with a fervent, yet detached tone.

" It's going on for one o'clock," he said.

" Is it ? " she answered. It meant nothing to her.

" Should we be going ? " he said.

She was silent. For the first time for an hour or more an inkling
of her normal consciousness returned. She resented it.

" What for ? " she said.

" I thought you might have had enough," he said.

A slight soberness came over her, an irritation at being frustrated
of her illusion.

" Why ? " she said.

" We've been here since nine," he said.

That was no answer, no reason. It conveyed nothing to her.
She sat detached from him. Across the room Sam Adams glanced
at her. She sat there exposed for him.

" You don't want to be too free with Sam Adams," said Whiston
cautiously, suffering. " You know what he is."

" How, free ? " she asked.

" Why—you don't want to have too much to do with him."

She sat silent. He was forcing her into consciousness of her position. But he could not get hold of her feelings, to change them. She had a curious, perverse desire that he should not.

" I like him," she said.

" What do you find to like in him ? " he said, with a hot heart.

" I don't know—but I like him," she said.

She was immutable. He sat feeling heavy and dulled with rage. He was not clear as to what he felt. He sat there unliving whilst she danced. And she, distracted, lost to herself between the opposing forces of the two men, drifted. Between the dances, Whiston kept near to her. She was scarcely conscious. She glanced repeatedly at her card, to see when she would dance again with Adams, half in desire, half in dread. Sometimes she met his steady, glaucous eye as she passed him in the dance. Sometimes she saw the steadiness of his flank as he danced. And it was always as if she rested on his arm, were borne along, upborne by him, away from herself. And always there was present the other's antagonism. She was divided.

The time came for her to dance with Adams. Oh, the delicious closing of contact with him, of his limbs touching her limbs, his arm supporting her. She seemed to resolve. Whiston had not made himself real to her. He was only a heavy place in her consciousness.

But she breathed heavily, beginning to suffer from the closeness of strain. She was nervous. Adams also was constrained. A tightness, a tension was coming over them all. And he was exasperated, feeling something counteracting physical magnetism, feeling a will stronger with her than his own, intervening in what was becoming a vital necessity to him.

Elsie was almost lost to her own control. As she went forward with him to take her place at the dance, she stooped for her pocket-handkerchief. The music sounded for quadrilles. Everybody was ready. Adams stood with his body near her, exerting his attraction over her. He was tense and fighting. She stooped for her pocket-handkerchief, and shook it as she rose. It shook out and fell from her hand. With agony, she saw she had taken a white stocking instead of a handkerchief. For a second it lay on the floor, a twist of white stocking. Then, in an instant, Adams picked it up, with a little, surprised laugh of triumph.

" That'll do for me," he whispered—seeming to take possession of her. And he stuffed the stocking in his trousers pocket, and quickly offered her his handkerchief.

The dance began. She felt weak and faint, as if her will were turned to water. A heavy sense of loss came over her. She could not help herself any more. But it was peace.

When the dance was over, Adams yielded her up. Whiston came to her.

" What was it as you dropped ? " Whiston asked.

" I thought it was my handkerchief—I'd taken a stocking by mistake," she said, detached and muted.

" And he's got it ? "

" Yes."

" What does he mean by that ? "

She lifted her shoulders.

" Are you going to let him keep it ? " he asked.

" I don't let him."

There was a long pause.

" Am I to go and have it out with him ? " he asked, his face flushed, his blue eyes going hard with opposition.

" No," she said, pale.

" Why ? "

" No—I don't want you to say anything about it."

He sat exasperated and nonplussed.

" You'll let him keep it, then ? " he asked.

She sat silent and made no form of answer.

" What do you mean by it ? " he said, dark with fury. And he started up.

" No ! " she cried. " Ted ! " And she caught hold of him, sharply detaining him.

It made him black with rage.

" Why ? " he said.

The something about her mouth was pitiful to him. He did not understand, but he felt she must have her reasons.

" Then I'm not stopping here," he said. " Are you coming with me ? "

She rose mutely, and they went out of the room. Adams had not noticed.

In a few moments they were in the street.

" What the hell do you mean ? " he said, in a black fury.

She went at his side, in silence, neutral.

" That great hog, an' all," he added.

Then they went a long time in silence through the frozen, deserted darkness of the town. She felt she could not go indoors. They were drawing near her house.

"I don't want to go home," she suddenly cried in distress and anguish. "I don't want to go home."

He looked at her.

"Why don't you?" he said.

"I don't want to go home," was all she could sob.

He heard somebody coming.

"Well, we can walk a bit farther," he said.

She was silent again. They passed out of the town into the fields. He held her by the arm—they could not speak.

"What's a-matter?" he asked at length, puzzled.

She began to cry again.

At last he took her in his arms, to soothe her. She sobbed by herself, almost unaware of him.

"Tell me what's a-matter, Elsie," he said. "Tell me what's a-matter—my dear—tell me, then——"

He kissed her wet face, and caressed her. She made no response. He was puzzled and tender and miserable.

At length she became quiet. Then he kissed her, and she put her arms round him, and clung to him very tight, as if for fear and anguish. He held her in his arms, wondering.

"Ted!" she whispered, frantic. "Ted!"

"What, my love?" he answered, becoming also afraid.

"Be good to me," she cried. "Don't be cruel to me."

"No, my pet," he said, amazed and grieved. "Why?"

"Oh, be good to me," she sobbed.

And he held her very safe, and his heart was white-hot with love for her. His mind was amazed. He could only hold her against his chest that was white-hot with love and belief in her. So she was restored at last.

III

She refused to go to her work at Adams's any more. Her father had to submit and she sent in her notice—she was not well. Sam Adams was ironical. But he had a curious patience. He did not fight.

In a few weeks, she and Whiston were married. She loved him with passion and worship, a fierce little abandon of love that moved him to the depths of his being, and gave him a permanent surety and sense of realness in himself. He did not trouble about himself any more: he felt he was fulfilled and now he had only the many things in the world to busy himself about. Whatever troubled him, at the bottom was surety. He had found himself in this love.

They spoke once or twice of the white stocking.

" Ah ! " Whiston exclaimed. " What does it matter ? "

He was impatient and angry, and could not bear to consider the matter. So it was left unresolved.

She was quite happy at first, carried away by her adoration of her husband. Then gradually she got used to him. He always was the ground of her happiness, but she got used to him, as to the air she breathed. He never got used to her in the same way.

Inside of marriage she found her liberty. She was rid of the responsibility of herself. Her husband must look after that. She was free to get what she could out of her time.

So that, when, after some months, she met Sam Adams, she was not quite as unkind to him as she might have been. With a young wife's new and exciting knowledge of men, she perceived he was in love with her, she knew he had always kept an unsatisfied desire for her. And, sportive, she could not help playing a little with this, though she cared not one jot for the man himself.

When Valentine's day came, which was near the first anniversary of her wedding day, there arrived a white stocking with a little amethyst brooch. Luckily Whiston did not see it, so she said nothing of it to him. She had not the faintest intention of having anything to do with Sam Adams, but once a little brooch was in her possession, it was hers, and she did not trouble her head for a moment how she had come by it. She kept it.

Now she had the pearl ear-rings. They were a more valuable and a more conspicuous present. She would have to ask her mother to give them to her, to explain their presence. She made a little plan in her head. And she was extraordinarily pleased. As for Sam Adams, even if he saw her wearing them, he would not give her away. What fun, if he saw her wearing his ear-rings ! She would pretend she had inherited them from her grandmother, her mother's mother. She laughed to herself as she went downtown in the afternoon, the pretty drops dangling in front of her curls. But she saw no one of importance.

Whiston came home tired and depressed. All day the male in him had been uneasy, and this had fatigued him. She was curiously against him, inclined, as she sometimes was nowadays, to make mock of him and jeer at him and cut him off. He did not understand this, and it angered him deeply. She was uneasy before him.

She knew he was in a state of suppressed irritation. The veins stood out on the backs of his hands, his brow was drawn stiffly. Yet she could not help goading him.

" What did you do wi' that white stocking ? " he asked, out of a gloomy silence, his voice strong and brutal.

" I put it in a drawer—why ? " she replied flippantly.

" Why didn't you put it on the fire-back ? " he said harshly. " What are you hoarding it up for ? "

" I'm not hoarding it up," she said. " I've got a pair."

He relapsed into gloomy silence. She, unable to move him, ran away upstairs, leaving him smoking by the fire. Again she tried on the ear-rings. Then another little inspiration came to her. She drew on the white stockings, both of them.

Presently she came down in them. Her husband still sat immovable and glowering by the fire.

" Look ! " she said. " They'll do beautifully."

And she picked up her skirts to her knees, and twisted round, looking at her pretty legs in the neat stockings.

He filled with unreasonable rage, and took the pipe from his mouth.

" Don't they look nice ? " she said. " One from last year and one from this, they just do. Save you buying a pair."

And she looked over her shoulders at her pretty calves, and at the dangling frills of her knickers.

" Put your skirts down and don't make a fool of yourself," he said.

" Why a fool of myself ? " she asked.

And she began to dance slowly round the room, kicking up her feet half reckless, half jeering, in a ballet-dancer's fashion. Almost fearfully, yet in defiance, she kicked up her legs at him, singing as she did so. She resented him.

" You little fool, ha' done with it," he said. " And you'll backfire them stockings, I'm telling you." He was angry. His face flushed dark, he kept his head bent. She ceased to dance.

" I shan't," she said. " They'll come in very useful."

He lifted his head and watched her, with lighted, dangerous eyes.

" You'll put 'em on the fire-back, I tell you," he said.

It was a war now. She bent forward, in a ballet-dancer's fashion, and put her tongue between her teeth.

" I shan't backfire them stockings," she sang, repeating his words, " I shan't, I shan't, I shan't."

And she danced round the room doing a high kick to the tune of her words. There was a real biting indifference in her behaviour.

" We'll see whether you will or not," he said, " trollops ! You'd like Sam Adams to know you was wearing 'em, wouldn't you? That's what would please you."

"Yes, I'd like him to see how nicely they fit me, he might give me some more then."

And she looked down at her pretty legs.

He knew somehow that she *would* like Sam Adams to see how pretty her legs looked in the white stockings. It made his anger go deep, almost to hatred.

"Yer nasty trolley," he cried. "Put yer petticoats down, and stop being so foul-minded."

"I'm not foul-minded," she said. "My legs are my own. And why shouldn't Sam Adams think they're nice?"

There was a pause. He watched her with eyes glittering to a point.

"Have you been havin' owt to do with him?" he asked.

"I've just spoken to him when I've seen him," she said. "He's not as bad as you would make out."

"Isn't he?" he cried, a certain wakefulness in his voice. "Them who has anything to do wi' him is too bad for me, I tell you."

"Why, what are you frightened of him for?" she mocked.

She was rousing all his uncontrollable anger. He sat glowering. Every one of her sentences stirred him up like a red-hot iron. Soon it would be too much. And she was afraid herself; but she was neither conquered nor convinced.

A curious little grin of hate came on his face. He had a long score against her.

"What am I frightened of him for?" he repeated automatically. "What am I frightened of him for? Why, for you, you stray-running little bitch."

She flushed. The insult went deep into her, right home.

"Well, if you're so dull——" she said, lowering her eyelids, and speaking coldly, haughtily.

"If I'm so dull I'll break your neck the first word you speak to him," he said, tense.

"Pf!" she sneered. "Do you think I'm frightened of you?" She spoke coldly, detached.

She was frightened, for all that, white round the mouth.

His heart was getting hotter.

"You *will* be frightened of me, the next time you have anything to do with him," he said.

"Do you think *you'd* ever be told—ha!"

Her jeering scorn made him go white-hot, molten. He knew he

was incoherent, scarcely responsible for what he might do. Slowly,
unseeing, he rose and went out of doors, stifled, moved to kill her.

He stood leaning against the garden fence, unable either to see or
hear. Below him, far off, fumed the lights of the town. He stood
still, unconscious with a black storm of rage, his face lifted to the
night.

Presently, still unconscious of what he was doing, he went indoors
again. She stood, a small, stubborn figure with tight-pressed lips
and big, sullen, childish eyes, watching him, white with fear. He
went heavily across the floor and dropped into his chair.

There was a silence.

" *You're* not going to tell me everything I shall do, and everything
I shan't," she broke out at last.

He lifted his head.

" I tell you *this*," he said, low and intense. " Have anything to
do with Sam Adams, and I'll break your neck."

She laughed, shrill and false.

" How I hate your word ' break your neck,' " she said, with a
grimace of the mouth. " It sounds so common and beastly. Can't
you say something else——"

There was a dead silence.

" And besides," she said, with a queer chirrup of mocking laughter,
" what do you know about anything ? He sent me an amethyst
brooch and a pair of pearl ear-rings."

" He what ? " said Whiston, in a suddenly normal voice. His
eyes were fixed on her.

" Sent me a pair of pearl ear-rings, and an amethyst brooch," she
repeated, mechanically, pale to the lips.

And her big, black, childish eyes watched him, fascinated, held in
her spell.

He seemed to thrust his face and his eyes forward at her, as he
rose slowly and came to her. She watched transfixed in terror. Her
throat made a small sound, as she tried to scream.

Then, quick as lightning, the back of his hand struck her with a
crash across the mouth, and she was flung black blinded against the
wall. The shock shook a queer sound out of her. And then she
saw him still coming on, his eyes holding her, his fist drawn back,
advancing slowly. At any instant the blow might crash into her.

Mad with terror, she raised her hands with a queer clawing
movement to cover her eyes and her temples, opening her mouth in
a dumb shriek. There was no sound. But the sight of her slowly
arrested him. He hung before her, looking at her fixedly, as she

stood crouched against the wall with open, bleeding mouth, and wide-staring eyes, and two hands clawing over her temples. And his lust to see her bleed, to break her and destroy her, rose from an old source against her. It carried him. He wanted satisfaction.

But he had seen her standing there, a piteous, horrified thing, and he turned his face aside in shame and nausea. He went and sat heavily in his chair, and a curious ease, almost like sleep, came over his brain.

She walked away from the wall towards the fire, dizzy, white to the lips, mechanically wiping her small, bleeding mouth. He sat motionless. Then, gradually, her breath began to hiss, she shook, and was sobbing silently, in grief for herself. Without looking, he saw. It made his mad desire to destroy her come back.

At length he lifted his head. His eyes were glowing again, fixed on her.

" And what did he give them you for ? " he asked, in a steady, unyielding voice.

Her crying dried up in a second. She also was tense.

" They came as valentines," she replied, still not subjugated, even if beaten.

" When, to-day ? "

" The pearl ear-rings to-day—the amethyst brooch last year."

" You've had it a year ? "

" Yes."

She felt that now nothing would prevent him if he rose to kill her. She could not prevent him any more. She was yielded up to him. They both trembled in the balance, unconscious.

" What have you had to do with him ? " he asked, in a barren voice.

" I've not had anything to do with him," she quavered.

" You just kept 'em because they were jewellery ? " he said.

A weariness came over him. What was the worth of speaking any more of it ? He did not care any more. He was dreary and sick.

She began to cry again, but he took no notice. She kept wiping her mouth on her handkerchief. He could see it, the blood-mark. It made him only more sick and tired of the responsibility of it, the violence, the shame.

When she began to move about again, he raised his head once more from his dead, motionless position.

" Where are the things ? " he said.

" They are upstairs," she quavered. She knew the passion had gone down in him.

" Bring them down," he said.

" I won't," she wept, with rage.   " You're not going to bully me and hit me like that on the mouth."

And she sobbed again.   He looked at her in contempt and compassion and in rising anger.

" Where are they ? " he said.

" They're in the little drawer under the looking-glass," she sobbed.

He went slowly upstairs, struck a match, and found the trinkets. He brought them downstairs in his hand.

" These ? " he said, looking at them as they lay in his palm.

She looked at them without answering.   She was not interested in them any more.

He looked at the little jewels.   They were pretty.

" It's none of their fault," he said to himself.

And he searched round slowly, persistently, for a box.   He tied the things up and addressed them to Sam Adams.   Then he went out in his slippers to post the little package.

When he came back she was still sitting crying.

" You'd better go to bed," he said.

She paid no attention.   He sat by the fire.   She still cried.

" I'm sleeping down here," he said.   " Go you to bed."

In a few moments she lifted her tear-stained, swollen face and looked at him with eyes all forlorn and pathetic.   A great flash of anguish went over his body.   He went over, slowly, and very gently took her in his hands.   She let herself be taken.   Then as she lay against his shoulder, she sobbed aloud :

" I never meant——"

" My love—my little love——" he cried, in anguish of spirit, holding her in his arms.

SHE was too good for him, everybody said. Yet still she did not regret marrying him. He had come courting her when he was only nine-teen, and she twenty. He was in build what they call a tight little fellow ; short, dark, with a warm colour, and that upright set of the head and chest, that flaunting way in movement recalling a mating bird, which denotes a body taut and compact with life. Being a good worker he had earned decent money in the mine, and having a good home had saved a little.

She was a cook at " Uplands," a tall, fair girl, very quiet. Having seen her walk down the street, Horsepool had followed her from a distance. He was taken with her, he did not drink, and he was not lazy. So, although he seemed a bit simple, without much intelligence, but having a sort of physical brightness, she considered, and accepted him.

When they were married they went to live in Scargill Street, in a highly respectable six-roomed house which they had furnished between them. The street was built up the side of a long, steep hill. It was narrow and rather tunnel-like. Nevertheless, the back looked out over the adjoining pasture, across a wide valley of fields and woods, in the bottom of which the mine lay snugly.

He made himself gaffer in his own house. She was unacquainted with a collier's mode of life. They were married on a Saturday. On the Sunday night he said :

" Set th' table for my breakfast, an' put my pit-things afront o' th' fire. I s'll be gettin' up at ha'ef pas' five. Tha nedna shift thysen not till when ter likes."

He showed her how to put a newspaper on the table for a cloth. When she demurred :

" I want none o' your white cloths i' th' mornin'. I like ter be able to slobber if I feel like it," he said.

He put before the fire his moleskin trousers, a clean singlet, or sleeveless vest of thick flannel, a pair of stockings and his pit boots, arranging them all to be warm and ready for morning.

" Now tha sees. That wants doin' ivery night."

Punctually at half-past five he left her, without any form of leave-taking, going downstairs in his shirt.

When he arrived home at four o'clock in the afternoon his dinner was ready to be dished up. She was startled when he came in, a short, sturdy figure, with a face indescribably black and streaked. She stood before the fire in her white blouse and white apron, a fair girl, the picture of beautiful cleanliness. He " clommaxed " in, in his heavy boots.

" Well, how 'as ter gone on ? " he asked.

" I was ready for you to come home," she replied tenderly. In his black face the whites of his brown eyes flashed at her.

" An' I wor ready for comin'," he said. He planked his tin bottle and snap-bag on the dresser, took off his coat and scarf and waist-coat, dragged his arm-chair nearer the fire and sat down.

" Let's ha'e a bit o' dinner, then—I'm about clammed," he said.

" Aren't you goin' to wash yourself first ? "

" What am I to wesh mysen for ? "

" Well, you can't eat your dinner——"

" Oh, strike a daisy, Missis ! Dunna I eat my snap i' th' pit wi'out weshin' ?—forced to."

She served the dinner and sat opposite him. His small bullet head was quite black, save for the whites of his eyes and his scarlet lips. It gave her a queer sensation to see him open his red mouth and bare his white teeth as he ate. His arms and hands were mottled black ; his bare, strong neck got a little fairer as it settled towards his shoulders, reassuring her. There was the faint indescribable odour of the pit in the room, an odour of damp, exhausted air.

" Why is your vest so black on the shoulders ? " she asked.

" My singlet ? That's wi' th' watter droppin' on us from th' roof. This is a dry un as I put on afore I come up. They ha'e gre't clothes-'osses, an' as we change us things, we put 'em on theer ter dry."

When he washed himself, kneeling on the hearth-rug stripped to the waist, she felt afraid of him again. He was so muscular, he seemed so intent on what he was doing, so intensely himself, like a vigorous animal. And as he stood wiping himself, with his naked breast towards her, she felt rather sick, seeing his thick arms bulge their muscles.

They were nevertheless very happy. He was at a great pitch of pride because of her. The men in the pit might chaff him, they might try to entice him away, but nothing could reduce his self-assured pride because of her, nothing could unsettle his almost infantile satisfaction. In the evening he sat in his arm-chair chattering to her, or listening as she read the newspaper to him. When it was fine, he would go into the street, squat on his heels as colliers do, with his back against the wall of his parlour, and call to the passers-by, in greeting, one after another. If no one were passing, he was content just to squat and smoke, having such a fund of sufficiency and satisfaction in his heart. He was well married.

They had not been wed a year when all Brent and Wellwood's men came out on strike. Willy was in the Union, so with a pinch they scrambled through. The furniture was not all paid for, and other debts were incurred. She worried and contrived, he left it to her. But he was a good husband ; he gave her all he had.

The men were out fifteen weeks. They had been back just over a year when Willy had an accident in the mine, tearing his bladder. At the pit head the doctor talked of the hospital. Losing his head entirely, the young collier raved like a madman, what with pain and fear of hospital.

" Tha s'lt go whoam, Willy, tha s'lt go whoam," the deputy said.

A lad warned the wife to have the bed ready. Without speaking or hesitating she prepared. But when the ambulance came, and she heard him shout with pain at being moved, she was afraid lest she should sink down. They carried him in.

" Yo' should 'a' had a bed i' th' parlour, Missis," said the deputy, " then we shouldna' ha' had to hawkse 'im upstairs, an' it 'ud 'a' saved your legs."

But it was too late now. They got him upstairs.

" They let me lie, Lucy," he was crying, " they let me lie two mortal hours on th' sleck afore they took me outer th' stall. Th' peen, Lucy, th' peen ; oh, Lucy, th' peen, th' peen ! "

" I know th' pain's bad, Willy, I know. But you must try an' bear it a bit."

" Tha manna carry on in that form, lad, thy missis'll niver be able ter stan' it," said the deputy.

" I canna 'elp it, it's th' peen, it's th' peen," he cried again. He had never been ill in his life. When he had smashed a finger he could look at the wound. But this pain came from inside, and terrified him. At last he was soothed and exhausted.

It was some time before she could undress him and wash him. He would let no other woman do for him, having that savage modesty usual in such men.

For six weeks he was in bed, suffering much pain. The doctors were not quite sure what was the matter with him, and scarcely knew what to do. He could eat, he did not lose flesh, nor strength, yet the pain continued, and he could hardly walk at all.

In the sixth week the men came out in the national strike. He would get up quite early in the morning and sit by the window. On Wednesday, the second week of the strike, he sat gazing out on the street as usual, a bullet-headed young man, still vigorous-looking, but with a peculiar expression of hunted fear in his face.

" Lucy," he called, " Lucy ! "

She, pale and worn, ran upstairs at his bidding.

" Gi'e me a han'kercher," he said.

" Why, you've got one," she replied, coming near.

" Tha nedna touch me," he cried. Feeling his pocket, he produced a white handkerchief.

" I non want a white un, gi'e me a red un," he said.

" An' if anybody comes to see you," she answered, giving him a red handkerchief.

" Besides," she continued, " you needn't ha' brought me upstairs for that."

" I b'lieve th' peen's commin' on again," he said, with a little horror in his voice.

" It isn't, you know it isn't," she replied. " The doctor says you imagine it's there when it isn't."

" Canna I feel what's inside me ? " he shouted.

" There's a traction-engine coming downhill," she said. " That'll scatter them.—I'll just go an' finish your pudding."

She left him. The traction-engine went by, shaking the houses. Then the street was quiet, save for the men. A gang of youths from fifteen to twenty-five years old were playing marbles in the middle of the road. Other little groups of men were playing on the pavement. The street was gloomy. Willy could hear the endless calling and shouting of men's voices.

" Tha'rt skinchin' ! "

" I arena ! "

" Come 'ere with that blood-alley."

" Swop us four for't."

" Shonna, gie's hold on't."

He wanted to be out, he wanted to be playing marbles. The pain had weakened his mind, so that he hardly knew any self-control.

Presently another gang of men lounged up the street. It was pay morning. The Union was paying the men in the Primitive Chapel. They were returning with their half-sovereigns.

" Sorry ! " bawled a voice. " Sorry ! "

The word is a form of address, corruption probably of " Sirrah."
Willy started almost out of his chair.

" Sorry ! " again bawled a great voice. " Art goin' wi' me to see
Notts play Villa ? "

Many of the marble players started up.

" What time is it ? There's no treens, we s'll ha'e ter walk."

The street was alive with men.

" Who's goin' ter Nottingham ter see th' match ? " shouted the
same big voice. A very large, tipsy man, with his cap over his eye,
was calling.

" Com' on—aye, com' on ! " came many voices. The street was
full of the shouting of men. They split up in excited cliques and
groups.

" Play up, Notts ! " the big man shouted.

" Plee up, Notts ! " shouted the youths and men. They were at
kindling pitch. It only needed a shout to rouse them. Of this the
careful authorities were aware.

" I'm goin', I'm goin' ! " shouted the sick man at his window.

Lucy came running upstairs.

" I'm goin' ter see Notts play Villa on th' Meadows ground," he
declared.

" You—*you* can't go. There are no trains. You can't walk nine
miles."

" I'm goin' ter see th' match," he declared, rising.

" You know you can't. Sit down now an' be quiet."

She put her hand on him. He shook it off.

" Leave me alone, leave me alone. It's thee as ma'es th' peen
come, it's thee. I'm goin' ter Nottingham to see th' football match."

" Sit down—folks'll hear you, and what will they think ? "

" Come off'n me. Com' off. It's her, it's her as does it. Com' off."

He seized hold of her. His little head was bristling with madness,
and he was strong as a lion.

" Oh, Willy ! " she cried.

" It's 'er, it's 'er. Kill her ! " he shouted, " kill her."

" Willy, folks'll hear you."

" Th' peen's commin' on again, I tell yer. I'll kill her for it."

He was completely out of his mind. She struggled with him to
prevent his going to the stairs. When she escaped from him, who
was shouting and raving, she beckoned to her neighbour, a girl of
twenty-four, who was cleaning the window across the road.

Ethel Mellor was the daughter of a well-to-do check-weighman.
She ran across in fear to Mrs. Horsepool. Hearing the man raving,

people were running out in the street and listening. Ethel hurried upstairs. Everything was clean and pretty in the young home.

Willy was staggering round the room, after the slowly retreating Lucy, shouting :

" Kill her ! Kill her ! "

" Mr. Horsepool ! " cried Ethel, leaning against the bed, white as the sheets, and trembling. " Whatever are you saying ? "

" I tell yer it's 'er fault as th' pain comes on—I tell yer it is ! Kill 'er—kill 'er ! "

" Kill Mrs. Horsepool ! " cried the trembling girl. " Why, you're ever so fond of her, you know you are."

" The peen—I ha'e such a lot o' peen—I want to kill 'er."

He was subsiding. When he sat down his wife collapsed in a chair, weeping noiselessly. The tears ran down Ethel's face. He sat staring out of the window ; then the old, hurt look came on his face.

" What 'ave I been sayin' ? " he asked, looking piteously at his wife.

" Why ! " said Ethel, " you've been carrying on something awful, saying, ' Kill her, kill her ! ' "

" Have I, Lucy ? " he faltered.

" You didn't know what you was saying," said his young wife gently but coldly.

His face puckered up. He bit his lip, then broke into tears, sobbing uncontrollably, with his face to the window.

There was no sound in the room but of three people crying bitterly, breath caught in sobs. Suddenly Lucy put away her tears and went over to him.

" You didn't know what you was sayin', Willy, I know you didn't. I knew you didn't, all the time. It doesn't matter, Willy. Only don't do it again."

In a little while, when they were calmer, she went downstairs with Ethel.

" See if anybody is looking in the street," she said.

Ethel went into the parlour and peeped through the curtains.

" Aye ! " she said. " You may back your life Lena an' Mrs. Severn'll be out gorping, and that clat-fartin' Mrs. Allsop."

" Oh, I hope they haven't heard anything ! If it gets about as he's out of his mind, they'll stop his compensation, I know they will."

" They'd never stop his compensation for *that*," protested Ethel.

" Well, they *have* been stopping some——"

" It'll not get about. I s'll tell nobody."

" Oh, but if it does, whatever shall we do ? . . ."

THE CHRISTENING

THE mistress of the British School stepped down from her school gate, and instead of turning to the left as usual, she turned to the right. Two women who were hastening home to scramble their husbands' dinners together—it was five minutes to four—stopped to look at her. They stood gazing after her for a moment ; then they glanced at each other with a woman's little grimace.

To be sure, the retreating figure was ridiculous : small and thin, with a black straw hat, and a rusty cashmere dress hanging full all round the skirt. For so small and frail and rusty a creature to sail with slow, deliberate stride was also absurd. Hilda Rowbotham was less than thirty, so it was not years that set the measure of her pace ; she had heart disease. Keeping her face, that was small with sickness, but not uncomely, firmly lifted and fronting ahead, the young woman sailed on past the market-place, like a black swan of mournful, disreputable plumage.

She turned into Berryman's, the baker's. The shop displayed bread and cakes, sacks of flour and oatmeal, flitches of bacon, hams, lard and sausages. The combination of scents was not unpleasing. Hilda Rowbotham stood for some minutes nervously tapping and pushing a large knife that lay on the counter, and looking at the tall, glittering brass scales. At last a morose man with sandy whiskers came down the step from the house-place.

" What is it ? " he asked, not apologizing for his delay.

" Will you give me six-pennyworth of assorted cakes and pastries— and put in some macaroons, please ? " she asked, in remarkably rapid and nervous speech. Her lips fluttered like two leaves in a wind, and her words crowded and rushed like a flock of sheep at a gate.

" We've got no macaroons," said the man churlishly.

He had evidently caught that word. He stood waiting.

" Then I can't have any, Mr. Berryman. Now I do feel disappointed. I like those macaroons, you know, and it's not often I treat myself. One gets so tired of trying to spoil oneself, don't you think ? It's less profitable even than trying to spoil somebody else."

She laughed a quick little nervous laugh, putting her hand to her face.

" Then what'll you have ? " asked the man, without the ghost of an answering smile. He evidently had not followed, so he looked more glum than ever.

" Oh, anything you've got," replied the schoolmistress, flushing slightly. The man moved slowly about, dropping the cakes from various dishes one by one into a paper bag.

" How's that sister o' yours getting on ? " he asked, as if he were talking to the flour scoop.

" Whom do you mean ? " snapped the schoolmistress.

" The youngest," answered the stooping, pale-faced man, with a note of sarcasm.

" Emma ! Oh, she's very well, thank you ! " The schoolmistress was very red, but she spoke with sharp, ironical defiance. The man grunted. Then he handed her the bag, and watched her out of the shop without bidding her " Good afternoon."

She had the whole length of the main street to traverse, a half-mile of slow-stepping torture, with shame flushing over her neck. But she carried her white bag with an appearance of steadfast unconcern. When she turned into the field she seemed to droop a little. The wide valley opened out from her, with the far woods withdrawing into twilight, and away in the centre the great pit streaming its white smoke and chuffing as the men were being turned up. A full, rose-coloured moon, like a flamingo flying low under the far, dusky east, drew out of the mist. It was beautiful, and it made her irritable sadness soften, diffuse.

Across the field, and she was at home. It was a new, substantial cottage, built with unstinted hand, such a house as an old miner could build himself out of his savings. In the rather small kitchen a woman of dark, saturnine complexion sat nursing a baby in a long white gown ; a young woman of heavy, brutal cast stood at the table, cutting bread and butter. She had a downcast, humble mien that sat unnaturally on her, and was strangely irritating. She did not look round when her sister entered. Hilda put down the bag of cakes and left the room, not having spoken to Emma, nor to the baby, nor to Mrs. Carlin, who had come in to help for the afternoon.

Almost immediately the father entered from the yard with a dust-pan full of coals. He was a large man, but he was going to pieces. As he passed through, he gripped the door with his free hand to steady himself, but turning, he lurched and swayed. He began putting the coals on the fire, piece by piece. One lump fell from his hand and smashed on the white hearth. Emma Rowbotham looked round, and began in a rough, loud voice of anger : " Look at you ! " Then she consciously moderated her tones. " I'll sweep it up in a minute—don't you bother ; you'll only be going head first into the fire."

Her father bent down nevertheless to clear up the mess he had made, saying, articulating his words loosely and slavering in his speech :

" The lousy bit of a thing, it slipped between my fingers like a fish."

As he spoke he went tilting toward the fire. The dark-browed woman cried out ; he put his hand on the hot stove to save himself ; Emma swung round and dragged him off.

" Didn't I tell you ! " she cried roughly. " Now, have you burnt yourself ? "

She held tight hold of the big man, and pushed him into his chair.

" What's the matter ? " cried a sharp voice from the other room. The speaker appeared, a hard well-favoured woman of twenty-eight. " Emma, don't speak like that to father." Then, in a tone not so cold, but just as sharp : " Now, father, what have you been doing ? "

Emma withdrew to her table sullenly.

" It's nöwt," said the old man, vainly protesting. " It's nöwt at a'. Get on wi' what you're doin'."

" I'm afraid 'e's burnt 'is 'and," said the black-browed woman, speaking of him with a kind of hard pity, as if he were a cumbersome child. Bertha took the old man's hand and looked at it, making a quick tut-tutting noise of impatience.

" Emma, get that zinc ointment—and some white rag," she commanded sharply. The younger sister put down her loaf with the knife in it, and went. To a sensitive observer, this obedience was more intolerable than the most hateful discord. The dark woman bent over the baby and made silent, gentle movements of motherliness to it. The little one smiled and moved on her lap. It continued to move and twist.

" I believe this child's hungry," she said. " How long is it since he had anything ? "

" Just afore dinner," said Emma dully.

" Good gracious ! " exclaimed Bertha. " You needn't starve the child now you've got it. Once every two hours it ought to be fed, as I've told you ; and now it's three. Take him, poor little mite— I'll cut the bread." She bent and looked at the bonny baby. She could not help herself : she smiled, and pressed its cheek with her finger, and nodded to it, making little noises. Then she turned and took the loaf from her sister. The woman rose and gave the child to its mother. Emma bent over the little sucking mite. She hated it when she looked at it, and saw it as a symbol, but when she felt it, her love was like fire in her blood.

" I should think 'e canna be comin'," said the father uneasily, looking up at the clock.

" Nonsense, father—the clock's fast ! It's but half-past four ! Don't fidget ! " Bertha continued to cut the bread and butter.

" Open a tin of pears," she said to the woman, in a much milder tone. Then she went into the next room. As soon as she was gone, the old man said again : " I should ha'e thought he'd 'a' been 'ere by now, if he means comin'."

Emma, engrossed, did not answer. The father had ceased to consider her, since she had become humbled.

" 'E'll come—'e'll come ! " assured the stranger.

A few minutes later Bertha hurried into the kitchen, taking off her apron. The dog barked furiously. She opened the door, com-manded the dog to silence, and said : " He will be quiet now, Mr. Kendal."

" Thank you," said a sonorous voice, and there was the sound of a bicycle being propped against a wall. A clergyman entered, a big-boned, thin, ugly man of nervous manner. He went straight to the father.

" Ah—how are you ? " he asked musically, peering down on the great frame of the miner, ruined by locomotor ataxy.

His voice was full of gentleness, but he seemed as if he could not see distinctly, could not get things clear.

" Have you hurt your hand ? " he said comfortingly, seeing the white rag.

" It wor nöwt but a pestered bit o' coal as dropped, an' I put my hand on th' hub. I thought tha worna commin'."

The familiar " tha," and the reproach, were unconscious retalia-tion on the old man's part. The minister smiled, half wistfully, half indulgently. He was full of vague tenderness. Then he turned to the young mother, who flushed sullenly because her dishonoured breast was uncovered.

" How are *you* ? " he asked, very softly and gently, as if she were ill and he were mindful of her.

" I'm all right," she replied, awkwardly taking his hand without rising, hiding her face and the anger that rose in her.

" Yes—yes "—he peered down at the baby, which sucked with distended mouth upon the firm breast. " Yes, yes." He seemed lost in a dim musing.

Coming to, he shook hands unseeingly with the woman.

Presently they all went into the next room, the minister hesitating to help his crippled old deacon.

" I can go by myself, thank yer," testily replied the father.

Soon all were seated. Everybody was separated in feeling and isolated at table. High tea was spread in the middle kitchen, a large, ugly room kept for special occasions.

Hilda appeared last, and the clumsy, raw-boned clergyman rose to meet her. He was afraid of this family, the well-to-do old collier, and the brutal, self-willed children. But Hilda was queen among them. She was the clever one, and had been to college. She felt responsible for the keeping up of a high standard of conduct in all the members of the family. There *was* a difference between the Rowbothams and the common collier folk. Woodbine Cottage was a superior house to most—and was built in pride by the old man. She, Hilda, was a college-trained schoolmistress ; she meant to keep up the prestige of her house in spite of blows.

She had put on a dress of green voile for this special occasion. But she was very thin ; her neck protruded painfully. The clergyman, however, greeted her almost with reverence, and, with some assumption of dignity, she sat down before the tray. At the far end of the table sat the broken, massive frame of her father. Next to him was the youngest daughter, nursing the restless baby. The minister sat between Hilda and Bertha, hulking his bony frame uncomfortably.

There was a great spread on the table, of tinned fruits and tinned salmon, ham and cakes. Miss Rowbotham kept a keen eye on everything : she felt the importance of the occasion. The young mother who had given rise to all this solemnity ate in sulky discomfort, snatching sullen little smiles at her child, smiles which came, in spite of her, when she felt its little limbs stirring vigorously on her lap. Bertha, sharp and abrupt, was chiefly concerned with the baby. She scorned her sister, and treated her like dirt. But the infant was a streak of light to her. Miss Rowbotham concerned herself with the function and the conversation. Her hands fluttered ; she talked in little volleys, exceedingly nervous. Toward the end of the meal, there came a pause. The old man wiped his mouth with his red handkerchief, then, his blue eyes going fixed and staring, he began to speak, in a loose, slobbering fashion, charging his words t the clergyman.

" Well, mester—we'n axed you to come here ter christen this childt, an' you'n come, an' I'm sure we're very thankful. I can't see lettin' the poor blessed childt miss baptizing, an' they aren't for goin' to church wi't——" He seemed to lapse into a muse. " So," he resumed, " we'n axed you to come here to do the job. I'm not sayin' as it's not 'ard on us, it is. I'm breakin' up, an' mother's gone. I don't like leavin' a girl o' mine in a situation like 'ers is, but what the Lord's done, He's done, an' it's no matter murmuring. . . . There's one thing to be thankful for, an' we *are* thankful for it : they never need know the want of bread."

Miss Rowbotham, the lady of the family, sat very stiff and pained during this discourse. She was sensitive to so many things that she was bewildered. She felt her young sister's shame, then a kind of swift protecting love for the baby, a feeling that included the mother; she was at a loss before her father's religious sentiment, and she felt and resented bitterly the mark upon the family, against which the common folk could lift their fingers. Still she winced from the sound of her father's words. It was a painful ordeal.

" It is hard for you," began the clergyman in his soft, lingering, unworldly voice. " It is hard for you to-day, but the Lord gives comfort in His time. A man child is born unto us, therefore let us rejoice and be glad. If sin has entered in among us, let us purify our hearts before the Lord. . . ."

He went on with his discourse. The young mother lifted the whimpering infant, till its face was hid in her loose hair. She was hurt, and a little glowering anger shone in her face. But nevertheless her fingers clasped the body of the child beautifully. She was stupefied with anger against this emotion let loose on her account.

Miss Bertha rose and went to the little kitchen, returning with water in a china bowl. She placed it there among the tea-things.

" Well, we're all ready," said the old man, and the clergyman began to read the service. Miss Bertha was godmother, the two men godfathers. The old man sat with bent head. The scene became impressive. At last Miss Bertha took the child and put it in the arms of the clergyman. He, big and ugly, shone with a kind of unreal love. He had never mixed with life, and women were all unliving, Biblical things to him. When he asked for the name, the old man lifted his head fiercely. " Joseph William, after me," he said, almost out of breath.

" Joseph William, I baptize thee . . ." resounded the strange, full, chanting voice of the clergyman. The baby was quite still.

" Let us pray ! " It came with relief to them all. They knelt before their chairs, all but the young mother, who bent and hid herself over her baby. The clergyman began his hesitating, struggling prayer.

Just then heavy footsteps were heard coming up the path, ceasing at the window. The young mother, glancing up, saw her brother, black in his pit dirt, grinning in through the panes. His red mouth curved in a sneer; his fair hair shone above his blackened skin. He caught the eye of his sister and grinned. Then his black face disappeared. He had gone on into the kitchen. The girl with the child sat still and anger filled her heart. She herself hated now the praying clergyman and the whole emotional business; she hated her brother bitterly. In anger and bondage she sat and listened.

Suddenly her father began to pray. His familiar, loud, rambling voice made her shut herself up and become even insentient. Folks said his mind was weakening. She believed it to be true, and kept herself always disconnected from him.

" We ask Thee, Lord," the old man cried, " to look after this childt. Fatherless he is. But what does the earthly father matter before Thee? The childt is Thine, he is Thy childt. Lord, what father has a man but Thee? Lord, when a man says he is a father, he is wrong from the first word. For Thou art the Father, Lord. Lord, take away from us the conceit that our children are ours. Lord, Thou art Father of this childt as is fatherless here. O God, Thou bring him up. For I have stood between Thee and my children; I've had *my* way with them, Lord; I've stood between Thee and my children; I've cut 'em off from Thee because they were mine. And they've grown twisted, because of me. Who is their father, Lord, but Thee? But I put myself in the way, they've been plants under a stone, because of me. Lord, if it hadn't been for me, they might ha' been trees in the sunshine. Let me own it, Lord, I've done 'em mischief. It would ha' been better if they'd never known no father. No man is a father, Lord: only Thou art. They can never grow beyond Thee, but I hampered them. Lift 'em up again, and undo what I've done to my children. And let this young childt be like a willow tree beside the waters, with no father but Thee, O God. Aye, an' I wish it had been so with my children, that they'd had no father but Thee. For I've been like a stone upon them, and they rise up and curse me in their wickedness. But let me go, an' lift Thou them up, Lord . . ."

The minister, unaware of the feelings of a father, knelt in trouble, hearing without understanding the special language of fatherhood. Miss Rowbotham alone felt and understood a little. Her heart began to flutter ; she was in pain. The two younger daughters kneeled unhearing, stiffened and impervious. Bertha was thinking of the baby ; and the young mother thought of the father of her child, whom she hated. There was a clatter outside in the scullery. There the youngest son made as much noise as he could, pouring out the water for his wash, muttering in deep anger :

" Blortin', slaverin' old fool ! "

And while the praying of his father continued, his heart was burning with rage. On the table was a paper bag. He picked it up and read, " John Berryman—Bread, Pastries, etc." Then he grinned with a grimace. The father of the baby was baker's man at Berryman's. The prayer went on in the middle kitchen. Laurie Rowbotham gathered together the mouth of the bag, inflated it, and burst it with his fist. There was a loud report. He grinned to himself. But he writhed at the same time with shame and fear of his father.

The father broke off from his prayer ; the party shuffled to their feet. The young mother went into the scullery.

" What art doin', fool ? " she said.

The collier youth tipped the baby under the chin, singing :

> " Pat-a-cake, pat-a-cake, baker's man,
> Bake me a cake as fast as you can. . . ."

The mother snatched the child away. " Shut thy mouth," she said, the colour coming into her cheek.

> " Prick it and stick it and mark it with P,
> And put it i' th' oven for baby an' me. . . ."

He grinned, showing a grimy, and jeering and unpleasant red mouth and white teeth.

" I s'll gi'e thee a dab ower th' mouth," said the mother of the baby grimly. He began to sing again, and she struck out at him.

" Now what's to do ? " said the father, staggering in.

The youth began to sing again. His sister stood sullen and furious.

" Why does *that* upset you ? " asked the eldest Miss Rowbotham, sharply, of Emma the mother. " Good gracious, it hasn't improved your temper."

Miss Bertha came in, and took the bonny baby.

The father sat big and unheeding in his chair, his eyes vacant, his physique wrecked. He let them do as they would, he fell to pieces. And yet some power, involuntary, like a curse, remained in him. The very ruin of him was like a lodestone that held them in its control. The wreck of him still dominated the house, in his dissolution even he compelled their being. They had never lived ; his life, his will had always been upon them and contained them. They were only half-individuals.

The day after the christening he staggered in at the doorway declaring, in a loud voice, with joy in life still : " The daisies light up the earth, they clap their hands in multitudes, in praise of the morning." And his daughters shrank, sullen.

I

The small locomotive engine, Number 4, came clanking, stumbling down from Selston with seven full waggons. It appeared round the corner with loud threats of speed, but the colt that it startled from among the gorse, which still flickered indistinctly in the raw afternoon, outdistanced it at a canter. A woman, walking up the railway line to Underwood, drew back into the hedge, held her basket aside, and watched the footplate of the engine advancing. The trucks thumped heavily past, one by one, with slow inevitable movement, as she stood insignificantly trapped between the jolting black waggons and the hedge ; then they curved away towards the coppice where the withered oak leaves dropped noiselessly, while the birds, pulling at the scarlet hips beside the track, made off into the dusk that had already crept into the spinney. In the open, the smoke from the engine sank and cleaved to the rough grass. The fields were dreary and forsaken, and in the marshy strip that led to the whimsey, a reedy pit-pond, the fowls had already abandoned their run among the alders, to roost in the tarred fowl-house. The pit-bank loomed up beyond the pond, flames like red sores licking its ashy sides, in the afternoon's stagnant light. Just beyond rose the tapering chimneys and the clumsy black headstocks of Brinsley Colliery. The two wheels were spinning fast up against the sky, and the winding-engine rapped out its little spasms. The miners were being turned up.

The engine whistled as it came into the wide bay of railway lines beside the colliery, where rows of trucks stood in harbour.

Miners, single, trailing and in groups, passed like shadows diverging home. At the edge of the ribbed level of sidings squat a low cottage, three steps down from the cinder track. A large bony vine clutched at the house, as if to claw down the tiled roof. Round the bricked yard grew a few wintry primroses. Beyond, the long garden sloped down to a bush-covered brook course. There were some twiggy apple trees, winter-crack trees, and ragged cabbages. Beside the path hung dishevelled pink chrysanthemums, like pink cloths hung on bushes. A woman came stooping out of the felt-covered fowl-house, half-way down the garden. She closed and padlocked the door, then drew herself erect, having brushed some bits from her white apron.

She was a tall woman of imperious mien, handsome, with definite black eyebrows. Her smooth black hair was parted exactly. For a few moments she stood steadily watching the miners as they passed along the railway : then she turned towards the brook course. Her face was calm and set, her mouth was closed with disillusionment. After a moment she called :

" John ! " There was no answer. She waited, and then said distinctly :

" Where are you ? "

" Here ! " replied a child's sulky voice from among the bushes. The woman looked piercingly through the dusk.

" Are you at that brook ? " she asked sternly.

For answer the child showed himself before the raspberry-canes that rose like whips. He was a small, sturdy boy of five. He stood quite still, defiantly.

" Oh ! " said the mother, conciliated. " I thought you were down at that wet brook—and you remember what I told you——"

The boy did not move or answer.

" Come, come on in," she said more gently, " it's getting dark. There's your grandfather's engine coming down the line ! "

The lad advanced slowly, with resentful, taciturn movement. He was dressed in trousers and waistcoat of cloth that was too thick and hard for the size of the garments. They were evidently cut down from a man's clothes.

As they went slowly towards the house he tore at the ragged wisps of chrysanthemums and dropped the petals in handfuls along the path.

" Don't do that—it does look nasty," said his mother. He refrained, and she, suddenly pitiful, broke off a twig with three or four wan flowers and held them against her face. When mother and son reached the yard her hand hesitated, and instead of laying the flower aside, she pushed it in her apron-band. The mother and son stood at the foot of the three steps looking across the bay of lines at the passing home of the miners. The trundle of the small train was imminent. Suddenly the engine loomed past the house and came to a stop opposite the gate.

The engine-driver, a short man with round grey beard, leaned out of the cab high above the woman.

" Have you got a cup of tea ? " he said in a cheery, hearty fashion. It was her father. She went in, saying she would mash. Directly, she returned.

" I didn't come to see you on Sunday," began the little grey-bearded man.

" I didn't expect you," said his daughter.

The engine-driver winced ; then, reassuming his cheery, airy manner, he said :

" Oh, have you heard then ? Well, and what do you think—— ? "

" I think it is soon enough," she replied.

At her brief censure the little man made an impatient gesture, and said coaxingly, yet with dangerous coldness :

" Well, what's a man to do ? It's no sort of life for a man of my years, to sit at my own hearth like a stranger. And if I'm going to marry again it may as well be soon as late—what does it matter to anybody ? "

The woman did not reply, but turned and went into the house. The man in the engine-cab stood assertive, till she returned with a cup of tea and a piece of bread and butter on a plate. She went up the steps and stood near the footplate of the hissing engine.

" You needn't 'a' brought me bread an' butter," said her father. " But a cup of tea "—he sipped appreciatively—" it's very nice." He sipped for a moment or two, then : " I hear as Walter's got another bout on," he said.

" When hasn't he ? " said the woman bitterly.

" I heered tell of him in the ' Lord Nelson ' braggin' as he was going to spend that b—— afore he went : half a sovereign that was."

" When ? " asked the woman.

" A' Sat'day night—I know that's true."

" Very likely," she laughed bitterly. " He gives me twenty-three shillings."

" Aye, it's a nice thing, when a man can do nothing with his money but make a beast of himself ! " said the grey-whiskered man. The woman turned her head away. Her father swallowed the last of his tea and handed her the cup.

" Aye," he sighed, wiping his mouth. " It's a settler, it is—— "

He put his hand on the lever. The little engine strained and groaned, and the train rumbled towards the crossing. The woman again looked across the metals. Darkness was settling over the spaces of the railway and trucks : the miners, in grey sombre groups, were still passing home. The winding-engine pulsed hurriedly, with brief pauses. Elizabeth Bates looked at the dreary flow of men, then she went indoors. Her husband did not come.

The kitchen was small and full of firelight ; red coals piled glowing up the chimney mouth. All the life of the room seemed in the white, warm hearth and the steel fender reflecting the red fire. The cloth was laid for tea ; cups glinted in the shadows. At the back, where the lowest stairs protruded into the room, the boy sat struggling with a knife and a piece of whitewood. He was almost hidden in the shadow. It was half-past four. They had but to await the father's coming to begin tea. As the mother watched her son's sullen little struggle with the wood, she saw herself in his silence and pertinacity ; she saw the father in her child's indifference to all but himself. She seemed to be occupied by her husband. He had probably gone past his home, slung past his own door, to drink before he came in, while his dinner spoiled and wasted in waiting. She glanced at the clock, then took the potatoes to strain them in the yard. The garden and fields beyond the brook were closed in uncertain darkness. When she rose with the saucepan, leaving the drain steaming into the night behind her, she saw the yellow lamps were lit along the high road that went up the hill away beyond the space of the railway lines and the field.

Then again she watched the men trooping home, fewer now and fewer.

Indoors the fire was sinking and the room was dark red. The woman put her saucepan on the hob, and set a batter pudding near the mouth of the oven. Then she stood unmoving. Directly, gratefully, came quick young steps to the door. Someone hung on the latch a moment, then a little girl entered and began pulling off her outdoor things, dragging a mass of curls, just ripening from gold to brown, over her eyes with her hat.

Her mother chid her for coming late from school, and said she would have to keep her at home the dark winter days.

" Why, mother, it's hardly a bit dark yet. The lamp's not lighted, and my father's not home."

" No, he isn't. But it's a quarter to five ! Did you see anything of him ? "

The child became serious. She looked at her mother with large, wistful blue eyes.

" No, mother, I've never seen him. Why ? Has he come up an' gone past, to Old Brinsley ? He hasn't, mother, 'cos I never saw him."

"He'd watch that," said the mother bitterly, "he'd take care as you didn't see him. But you may depend upon it, he's seated in the 'Prince o' Wales.' He wouldn't be this late."

The girl looked at her mother piteously.

"Let's have our teas, mother, should we?" said she.

The mother called John to table. She opened the door once more and looked out across the darkness of the lines. All was deserted: she could not hear the winding-engines.

"Perhaps," she said to herself, "he's stopped to get some ripping done."

They sat down to tea. John, at the end of the table near the door, was almost lost in the darkness. Their faces were hidden from each other. The girl crouched against the fender slowly moving a thick piece of bread before the fire. The lad, his face a dusky mark on the shadow, sat watching her who was transfigured in the red glow.

"I do think it's beautiful to look in the fire," said the child.

"Do you?" said her mother. "Why?"

"It's so red, and full of little caves—and it feels so nice, and you can fair smell it."

"It'll want mending directly," replied her mother, "and then if your father comes he'll carry on and say there never is a fire when a man comes home sweating from the pit. A public-house is always warm enough."

There was silence till the boy said complainingly: "Make haste, our Annie."

"Well, I am doing! I can't make the fire do it no faster, can I?"

"She keeps wafflin' it about so's to make 'er slow," grumbled the boy.

"Don't have such an evil imagination, child," replied the mother.

Soon the room was busy in the darkness with the crisp sound of crunching. The mother ate very little. She drank her tea determinedly, and sat thinking. When she rose her anger was evident in the stern unbending of her head. She looked at the pudding in the fender, and broke out:

"It is a scandalous thing as a man can't even come home to his dinner! If it's crozzled up to a cinder I don't see why I should care. Past his very door he goes to get to a public-house, and here I sit with his dinner waiting for him——"

She went out. As she dropped piece after piece of coal on the red fire, the shadows fell on the walls, till the room was almost in total darkness.

" I canna see," grumbled the invisible John. In spite of herself, the mother laughed.

" You know the way to your mouth," she said. She set the dust-pan outside the door. When she came again like a shadow on the hearth, the lad repeated, complaining sulkily :

" I canna see."

" Good gracious ! " cried the mother irritably, " you're as bad as your father if it's a bit dusk ! "

Nevertheless she took a paper spill from a sheaf on the mantelpiece and proceeded to light the lamp that hung from the ceiling in the middle of the room. As she reached up, her figure displayed itself just rounding with maternity.

" Oh, mother—— ! " exclaimed the girl.

" What ? " said the woman, suspended in the act of putting the lamp glass over the flame. The copper reflector shone handsomely on her, as she stood with uplifted arm, turning to face her daughter.

" You've got a flower in your apron ! " said the child, in a little rapture at this unusual event.

" Goodness me ! " exclaimed the woman, relieved. " One would think the house was afire." She replaced the glass and waited a moment before turning up the wick. A pale shadow was seen floating vaguely on the floor.

" Let me smell ! " said the child, still rapturously, coming forward and putting her face to her mother's waist.

" Go along, silly ! " said the mother, turning up the lamp. The light revealed their suspense so that the woman felt it almost unbearable. Annie was still bending at her waist. Irritably, the mother took the flowers out from her apron-band.

" Oh, mother—don't take them out ! " Annie cried, catching her hand and trying to replace the sprig.

" Such nonsense ! " said the mother, turning away. The child put the pale chrysanthemums to her lips, murmuring :

" Don't they smell beautiful ! "

Her mother gave a short laugh.

" No," she said, " not to me. It was chrysanthemums when I married him, and chrysanthemums when you were born, and the first time they ever brought him home drunk, he'd got brown chrysanthemums in his button-hole."

She looked at the children. Their eyes and their parted lips were wondering. The mother sat rocking in silence for some time. Then she looked at the clock.

" Twenty minutes to six ! " In a tone of fine bitter carelessness

she continued : " Eh, he'll not come now till they bring him.
There he'll stick ! But he needn't come rolling in here in his pit-
dirt, for *I* won't wash him. He can lie on the floor——Eh, what a
fool I've been, what a fool ! And this is what I came here for, to
this dirty hole, rats and all, for him to slink past his very door.
Twice last week—he's begun now——"

She silenced herself, and rose to clear the table.

While for an hour or more the children played, subduedly intent,
fertile of imagination, united in fear of the mother's wrath, and in
dread of their father's home-coming, Mrs. Bates sat in her rocking-
chair making a " singlet " of thick cream-coloured flannel, which
gave a dull wounded sound as she tore off the grey edge. She
worked at her sewing with energy, listening to the children, and her
anger wearied itself, lay down to rest, opening its eyes from time to
time and steadily watching, its ears raised to listen. Sometimes even
her anger quailed and shrank, and the mother suspended her sewing,
tracing the footsteps that thudded along the sleepers outside ; she
would lift her head sharply to bid the children " hush," but she
recovered herself in time, and the footsteps went past the gate,
and the children were not flung out of their play-world.

But at last Annie sighed, and gave in. She glanced at her waggon
of slippers, and loathed the game. She turned plaintively to her
mother.

" Mother ! "—but she was inarticulate.

John crept out like a frog from under the sofa. His mother
glanced up.

" Yes," she said, " just look at those shirt-sleeves ! "

The boy held them out to survey them, saying nothing. Then
somebody called in a hoarse voice away down the line, and suspense
bristled in the room, till two people had gone by outside, talking.

" It is time for bed," said the mother.

" My father hasn't come," wailed Annie plaintively. But her
mother was primed with courage.

" Never mind. They'll bring him when he does come—like a log."
She meant there would be no scene. " And he may sleep on the
floor till he wakes himself. I know he'll not go to work to-morrow
after this ! "

The children had their hands and faces wiped with a flannel.
They were very quiet. When they had put on their nightdresses,
they said their prayers, the boy mumbling. The mother looked
down at them, at the brown silken bush of intertwining curls in the
nape of the girl's neck, at the little black head of the lad, and her

heart burst with anger at their father who caused all three such distress. The children hid their faces in her skirts for comfort.

When Mrs. Bates came down, the room was strangely empty, with a tension of expectancy. She took up her sewing and stitched for some time without raising her head. Meantime her anger was tinged with fear.

II

The clock struck eight and she rose suddenly, dropping her sewing on her chair. She went to the stairfoot door, opened it, listening. Then she went out, locking the door behind her.

Something scuffled in the yard, and she started, though she knew it was only the rats with which the place was overrun. The night was very dark. In the great bay of railway lines, bulked with trucks, there was no trace of light, only away back she could see a few yellow lamps at the pit-top, and the red smear of the burning pit-bank on the night. She hurried along the edge of the track, then, crossing the converging lines, came to the stile by the white gates, whence she emerged on the road. Then the fear which had led her shrank. People were walking up to New Brinsley ; she saw the lights in the houses ; twenty yards further on were the broad windows of the "Prince of Wales," very warm and bright, and the loud voices of men could be heard distinctly. What a fool she had been to imagine that anything had happened to him ! He was merely drinking over there at the "Prince of Wales." She faltered. She had never yet been to fetch him, and she never would go. So she continued her walk towards the long straggling line of houses, standing blank on the highway. She entered a passage between the dwellings.

" Mr. Rigley ?—Yes ! Did you want him ? No, he's not in at this minute."

The raw-boned woman leaned forward from her dark scullery and peered at the other, upon whom fell a dim light through the blind of the kitchen window.

" Is it Mrs. Bates ? " she asked in a tone tinged with respect.

" Yes. I wondered if your Master was at home. Mine hasn't come yet."

" 'Asn't 'e ! Oh, Jack's been 'ome an' 'ad 'is dinner an' gone out. 'E's just gone for 'alf an hour afore bedtime. Did you call at the ' Prince of Wales ' ? "

" No——"

" No, you didn't like—— ! It's not very nice." The other woman was indulgent. There was an awkward pause. " Jack never said nothink about—about your Mester," she said.

" No !—I expect he's stuck in there ! "

Elizabeth Bates said this bitterly, and with recklessness. She knew that the woman across the yard was standing at her door listening, but she did not care. As she turned :

" Stop a minute ! I'll just go an' ask Jack if 'e knows anythink," said Mrs. Rigley.

" Oh, no—I wouldn't like to put—— ! "

" Yes, I will, if you'll just step inside an' see as th' childer doesn't come downstairs and set theirselves afire."

Elizabeth Bates, murmuring a remonstrance, stepped inside. The other woman apologized for the state of the room.

The kitchen needed apology. There were little frocks and trousers and childish undergarments on the squab and on the floor, and a litter of playthings everywhere. On the black American cloth of the table were pieces of bread and cake, crusts, slops, and a teapot with cold tea.

" Eh, ours is just as bad," said Elizabeth Bates, looking at the woman, not at the house. Mrs. Rigley put a shawl over her head and hurried out, saying :

" I shanna be a minute."

The other sat, noting with faint disapproval the general untidiness of the room. Then she fell to counting the shoes of various sizes scattered over the floor. There were twelve. She sighed and said to herself, " No wonder ! "—glancing at the litter. There came the scratching of two pairs of feet on the yard, and the Rigleys entered. Elizabeth Bates rose. Rigley was a big man, with very large bones. His head looked particularly bony. Across his temple was a blue scar, caused by a wound got in the pit, a wound in which the coal-dust remained blue like tattooing.

" 'Asna 'e come whoam yit ? " asked the man, without any form of greeting, but with deference and sympathy. " I couldna say wheer he is—'e's non ower theer ! "—he jerked his head to signify the " Prince of Wales."

" 'E's 'appen gone up to th' ' Yew,' " said Mrs. Rigley.

There was another pause. Rigley had evidently something to get off his mind :

" Ah left 'im finishin' a stint," he began. " Loose-all 'ad bin gone about ten minutes when we com'n away, an' I shouted, ' Are ter comin', Walt ? ' an' 'e said, ' Go on, Ah shanna be but a'ef a minnit,' " so we com'n ter th' bottom, me an' Bowers, thinkin' as 'e wor just behint, an' 'ud come up i' th' next bantle——"

He stood perplexed, as if answering a charge of deserting his mate. Elizabeth Bates, now again certain of disaster, hastened to reassure him:

" I expect 'e's gone up to th' ' Yew Tree,' as you say. It's not the first time. I've fretted myself into a fever before now. He'll come home when they carry him."

" Ay, isn't it too bad ! " deplored the other woman.

" I'll just step up to Dick's an' see if 'e *is* theer," offered the man, afraid of appearing alarmed, afraid of taking liberties.

" Oh, I wouldn't think of bothering you that far," said Elizabeth Bates, with emphasis, but he knew she was glad of his offer.

As they stumbled up the entry, Elizabeth Bates heard Rigley's wife run across the yard and open her neighbour's door. At this, suddenly all the blood in her body seemed to switch away from her heart.

" Mind ! " warned Rigley. " Ah've said many a time as Ah'd fill up them ruts in this entry, sumb'dy 'll be breakin' their legs yit."

She recovered herself and walked quickly along with the miner.

" I don't like leaving the children in bed, and nobody in the house," she said.

" No, you dunna ! " he replied courteously. They were soon at the gate of the cottage.

" Well, I shanna be many minnits. Dunna you be frettin' now, 'e'll be all right," said the butty.

" Thank you very much, Mr. Rigley," she replied.

" You're welcome ! " he stammered, moving away. " I shanna be many minnits."

The house was quiet. Elizabeth Bates took off her hat and shawl, and rolled back the rug. When she had finished, she sat down. It was a few minutes past nine. She was startled by the rapid chuff of the winding-engine at the pit, and the sharp whirr of the brakes on the rope as it descended. Again she felt the painful sweep of her blood, and she put her hand to her side, saying aloud, " Good gracious !—it's only the nine o'clock deputy going down," rebuking herself.

She sat still, listening. Half an hour of this, and she was wearied out.

" What am I working myself up like this for ? " she said pitiably to herself, " I s'll only be doing myself some damage."

She took out her sewing again.

At a quarter to ten there were footsteps. One person ! She watched
for the door to open. It was an elderly woman, in a black bonnet
and a black woollen shawl—his mother. She was about sixty years
old, pale, with blue eyes, and her face all wrinkled and lamentable.
She shut the door and turned to her daughter-in-law peevishly.

" Eh, Lizzie, whatever shall we do, whatever shall we do ! " she
cried.

Elizabeth drew back a little, sharply.

" What is it, mother ? " she said.

The elder woman seated herself on the sofa.

" I don't know, child, I can't tell you ! "—she shook her head
slowly. Elizabeth sat watching her, anxious and vexed.

" I don't know," replied the grandmother, sighing very deeply.
" There's no end to my troubles, there isn't. The things I've gone
through, I'm sure it's enough——— ! " She wept without wiping her
eyes, the tears running.

" But, mother," interrupted Elizabeth, " what do you mean ?
What is it ? "

The grandmother slowly wiped her eyes. The fountains of her
tears were stopped by Elizabeth's directness. She wiped her eyes
slowly.

" Poor child ! Eh, you poor thing ! " she moaned. " I don't
know what we're going to do, I don't—and you as you are—it's a
thing, it is indeed ! "

Elizabeth waited.

" Is he dead ? " she asked, and at the words her heart swung
violently, though she felt a slight flush of shame at the ultimate
extravagance of the question. Her words sufficiently frightened the
old lady, almost brought her to herself.

" Don't say so, Elizabeth ! We'll hope it's not as bad as that ;
no, may the Lord spare us that, Elizabeth. Jack Rigley came just
as I was sittin' down to a glass afore going to bed, an' 'e said, ' 'Appen
you'll go down th' line, Mrs. Bates. Walt's had an accident. 'Appen
you'll go an' sit wi' 'er till we can get him home.' I hadn't time to
ask him a word afore he was gone. An' I put my bonnet on an' come
straight down, Lizzie. I thought to myself, ' Eh, that poor blessed
child, if anybody should come an' tell her of a sudden, there's no
knowin' what'll 'appen to 'er.' You mustn't let it upset you,
Lizzie—or you know what to expect. How long is it, six months—
or is it five, Lizzie ? Ay ! "—the old woman shook her head—" time
slips on, it slips on ! Ay ! "

Elizabeth's thoughts were busy elsewhere. If he was killed—

would she be able to manage on the little pension and what she could earn ?—she counted up rapidly. If he was hurt—they wouldn't take him to the hospital—how tiresome he would be to nurse !— but perhaps she'd be able to get him away from the drink and his hateful ways. She would—while he was ill. The tears offered to come to her eyes at the picture. But what sentimental luxury was this she was beginning ? She turned to consider the children. At any rate she was absolutely necessary for them. They were her business.

" Ay ! " repeated the old woman, " it seems but a week or two since he brought me his first wages. Ay—he was a good lad, Elizabeth, he was, in his way. I don't know why he got to be such a trouble, I don't. He was a happy lad at home, only full of spirits. But there's no mistake he's been a handful of trouble, he has ! I hope the Lord'll spare him to mend his ways. I hope so, I hope so. You've had a sight o' trouble with him, Elizabeth, you have indeed. But he was a jolly enough lad wi' me, he was, I can assure you. I don't know how it is. . . ."

The old woman continued to muse aloud, a monotonous irritating sound, while Elizabeth thought concentratedly, startled once, when she heard the winding-engine chuff quickly, and the brakes skirr with a shriek. Then she heard the engine more slowly, and the brakes made no sound. The old woman did not notice. Elizabeth waited in suspense. The mother-in-law talked, with lapses into silence.

" But he wasn't your son, Lizzie, an' it makes a difference. Whatever he was, I remember him when he was little, an' I learned to understand him and to make allowances. You've got to make allowances for them——"

It was half-past ten, and the old woman was saying : " But it's trouble from beginning to end ; you're never too old for trouble, never too old for that——" when the gate banged back, and there were heavy feet on the steps.

" I'll go, Lizzie, let me go," cried the old woman, rising. But Elizabeth was at the door. It was a man in pit-clothes.

" They're bringin' 'im, Missis," he said. Elizabeth's heart halted a moment. Then it surged on again, almost suffocating her.

" Is he—is it bad ? " she asked.

The man turned away, looking at the darkness :

" The doctor says 'e'd been dead hours. 'E saw im i' th' lamp-cabin."

The old woman, who stood just behind Elizabeth, dropped into a chair, and folded her hands, crying : " Oh, my boy, my boy ! "

" Hush ! " said Elizabeth, with a sharp twitch of a frown.   " Be still, mother, don't waken th' children : I wouldn't have them down for anything ! "

The old woman moaned softly, rocking herself.   The man was drawing away.   Elizabeth took a step forward.

" How was it ? " she asked.

" Well, I couldn't say for sure," the man replied, very ill at ease. " 'E wor finishin' a stint an' th' butties 'ad gone, an' a lot o' stuff come down atop 'n 'im."

" And crushed him ? " cried the widow, with a shudder.

" No," said the man, " it fell at th' back of 'im.   'E wor under th' face, an' it niver touched 'im.   It shut 'im in.   It seems 'e wor smothered."

Elizabeth shrank back.   She heard the old woman behind her cry :

" What ?—what did e' say it was ? "

The man replied, more loudly :   " 'E wor smothered ! "

Then the old woman wailed aloud, and this relieved Elizabeth.

" Oh, mother," she said, putting her hand on the old woman, " don't waken th' children, don't waken th' children."

She wept a little, unknowing, while the old mother rocked herself and moaned.   Elizabeth remembered that they were bringing him home, and she must be ready.   " They'll lay him in the parlour," she said to herself, standing a moment pale and perplexed.

Then she lighted a candle and went into the tiny room.   The air was cold and damp, but she could not make a fire, there was no fireplace.   She set down the candle and looked round.   The candle-light glittered on the lustre-glasses, on the two vases that held some of the pink chrysanthemums, and on the dark mahogany.   There was a cold, deathly smell of chrysanthemums in the room.   Elizabeth stood looking at the flowers.   She turned away, and calculated whether there would be room to lay him on the floor, between the couch and the chiffonier.   She pushed the chairs aside.   There would be room to lay him down and to step round him.   Then she fetched the old red tablecloth, and another old cloth, spreading them down to save her bit of carpet.   She shivered on leaving the parlour ; so, from the dresser-drawer she took a clean shirt and put it at the fire to air.   All the time her mother-in-law was rocking herself in the chair and moaning.

" You'll have to move from there, mother," said Elizabeth. " They'll be bringing him in.   Come in the rocker."

The old mother rose mechanically, and seated herself by the fire, continuing to lament. Elizabeth went into the pantry for another candle, and there, in the little penthouse under the naked tiles, she heard them coming. She stood still in the pantry doorway, listening. She heard them pass the end of the house, and come awkwardly down the three steps, a jumble of shuffling footsteps and muttering voices. The old woman was silent. The men were in the yard.

Then Elizabeth heard Matthews, the manager of the pit, say : " You go in first, Jim. Mind ! "

The door came open, and the two women saw a collier backing into the room, holding one end of a stretcher, on which they could see the nailed pit-boots of the dead man. The two carriers halted, the man at the head stooping to the lintel of the door.

" Wheer will you have him ? " asked the manager, a short, white-bearded man.

Elizabeth roused herself and came from the pantry carrying the unlighted candle.

" In the parlour," she said.

" In there, Jim ! " pointed the manager, and the carriers backed round into the tiny room. The coat with which they had covered the body fell off as they awkwardly turned through the two door-ways, and the women saw their man, naked to the waist, lying stripped for work. The old woman began to moan in a low voice of horror.

" Lay th' stretcher at th' side," snapped the manager, " an' put 'im on th' cloths. Mind now, mind ! Look you now—— ! "

One of the men had knocked off a vase of chrysanthemums. He stared awkwardly, then they set down the stretcher. Elizabeth did not look at her husband. As soon as she could get in the room, she went and picked up the broken vase and the flowers.

" Wait a minute ! " she said.

The three men waited in silence while she mopped up the water with a duster.

" Eh, what a job, what a job, to be sure ! " the manager was say-ing, rubbing his brow with trouble and perplexity. " Never knew such a thing in my life, never ! He'd no business to ha' been left. I never knew such a thing in my life ! Fell over him clean as a whistle, an' shut him in. Not four foot of space, there wasn't—yet it scarce bruised him."

He looked down at the dead man, lying prone, half naked, all grimed with coal-dust.

" ' 'Sphyxiated,' the doctor said. It *is* the most terrible job I've ever known. Seems as if it was done o' purpose. Clean over him, an' shut 'im in, like a mouse-trap "—he made a sharp, descending gesture with his hand.

The colliers standing by jerked aside their heads in hopeless comment.

The horror of the thing bristled upon them all.

Then they heard the girl's voice upstairs calling shrilly : " Mother, mother—who is it ? Mother, who is it ? "

Elizabeth hurried to the foot of the stairs and opened the door : " Go to sleep ! " she commanded sharply. " What are you shouting about ? Go to sleep at once—there's nothing——"

Then she began to mount the stairs. They could hear her on the boards, and on the plaster floor of the little bedroom. They could hear her distinctly :

" What's the matter now ?—what's the matter with you, silly thing ? "—her voice was much agitated, with an unreal gentleness.

" I thought it was some men come," said the plaintive voice of the child. " Has he come ? "

" Yes, they've brought him. There's nothing to make a fuss about. Go to sleep now, like a good child."

They could hear her voice in the bedroom, they waited whilst she covered the children under the bedclothes.

" Is he drunk ? " asked the girl, timidly, faintly.

" No ! No—he's not ! He—he's asleep."

" Is he asleep downstairs ? "

" Yes—and don't make a noise."

There was silence for a moment, then the men heard the frightened child again :

" What's that noise ? "

" It's nothing, I tell you, what are you bothering for ? "

The noise was the grandmother moaning. She was oblivious of everything, sitting on her chair rocking and moaning. The manager put his hand on her arm and bade her " Sh—sh ! ! "

The old woman opened her eyes and looked at him. She was shocked by this interruption, and seemed to wonder.

" What time is it ? "—the plaintive thin voice of the child, sinking back unhappily into sleep, asked this last question.

" Ten o'clock," answered the mother more softly. Then she must have bent down and kissed the children.

Matthews beckoned to the men to come away. They put on their caps and took up the stretcher. Stepping over the body, they tiptoed out of the house. None of them spoke till they were far from the wakeful children.

When Elizabeth came down she found her mother alone on the parlour floor, leaning over the dead man, the tears dropping on him. "We must lay him out," the wife said. She put on the kettle, then returning knelt at the feet, and began to unfasten the knotted leather laces. The room was clammy and dim with only one candle, so that she had to bend her face almost to the floor. At last she got off the heavy boots and put them away.

"You must help me now," she whispered to the old woman. Together they stripped the man.

When they arose, saw him lying in the naïve dignity of death, the women stood arrested in fear and respect. For a few moments they remained still, looking down, the old mother whimpering. Elizabeth felt countermanded. She saw him, how utterly inviolable he lay in himself. She had nothing to do with him. She could not accept it. Stooping, she laid her hand on him, in claim. He was still warm, for the mine was hot where he had died. His mother had his face between her hands, and was murmuring incoherently. The old tears fell in succession as drops from wet leaves ; the mother was not weeping, merely her tears flowed. Elizabeth embraced the body of her husband, with cheek and lips. She seemed to be listening, inquiring, trying to get some connection. But she could not. She was driven away. He was impregnable.

She rose, went into the kitchen, where she poured warm water into a bowl, brought soap and flannel and a soft towel.

"I must wash him," she said.

Then the old mother rose stiffly, and watched Elizabeth as she carefully washed his face, carefully brushing the big blond moustache from his mouth with the flannel. She was afraid with a bottomless fear, so she ministered to him. The old woman, jealous, said :

"Let me wipe him !"—and she kneeled on the other side drying slowly as Elizabeth washed, her big black bonnet sometimes brushing the dark head of her daughter-in-law. They worked thus in silence for a long time. They never forgot it was death, and the touch of the man's dead body gave them strange emotions, different in each of the women ; a great dread possessed them both, the mother felt the lie was given to her womb, she was denied ; the wife felt the utter isolation of the human soul, the child within her was a weight apart from her.

At last it was finished. He was a man of handsome body, and his face showed no traces of drink. He was blond, full-fleshed, with fine limbs. But he was dead.

"Bless him," whispered his mother, looking always at his face, and speaking out of sheer terror. " Dear lad—bless him ! " She spoke in a faint, sibilant ecstasy of fear and mother love.

Elizabeth sank down again to the floor, and put her face against his neck, and trembled and shuddered. But she had to draw away again. He was dead, and her living flesh had no place against his. A great dread and weariness held her : she was so unavailing. Her life was gone like this.

" White as milk he is, clear as a twelve-month baby, bless him, the darling ! " the old mother murmured to herself. " Not a mark on him, clear and clean and white, beautiful as ever a child was made," she murmured with pride. Elizabeth kept her face hidden.

" He went peaceful, Lizzie—peaceful as sleep. Isn't he beautiful, the lamb ? Ay—he must ha' made his peace, Lizzie. 'Appen he made it all right, Lizzie, shut in there. He'd have time. He wouldn't look like this if he hadn't made his peace. The lamb, the dear lamb. Eh, but he had a hearty laugh. I loved to hear it. He had the heartiest laugh, Lizzie, as a lad——"

Elizabeth looked up. The man's mouth was fallen back, slightly open under the cover of the moustache. The eyes, half shut, did not show glazed in the obscurity. Life with its smoky burning gone from him, had left him apart and utterly alien to her. And she knew what a stranger he was to her. In her womb was ice of fear, because of this separate stranger with whom she had been living as one flesh. Was this what it all meant—utter, intact separateness, obscured by heat of living ? In dread she turned her face away. The fact was too deadly. There had been nothing between them, and yet they had come together, exchanging their nakedness repeatedly. Each time he had taken her, they had been two isolated beings, far apart as now. He was no more responsible than she. The child was like ice in her womb. For as she looked at the dead man, her mind, cold and detached, said clearly : " Who am I ? What have I been doing ? I have been fighting a husband who did not exist. *He* existed all the time. What wrong have I done ? What was that I have been living with ? There lies the reality, this man." And her soul died in her for fear : she knew she had never seen him, he had never seen her, they had met in the dark and had fought in the dark, not knowing whom they met nor whom they fought. And now she saw, and turned silent in seeing. For she had been wrong. She had said he was something he was not ; she had felt familiar with him. Whereas he was apart all the while, living as she never lived, feeling as she never felt.

In fear and shame she looked at his naked body, that she had known falsely. And he was the father of her children. Her soul was torn from her body and stood apart. She looked at his naked body and was ashamed, as if she had denied it. After all, it was itself. It seemed awful to her. She looked at his face, and she turned her own face to the wall. For his look was other than hers, his way was not her way. She had denied him what he was—she saw it now. She had refused him as himself. And this had been her life, and his life. She was grateful to death, which restored the truth. And she knew she was not dead.

And all the while her heart was bursting with grief and pity for him. What had he suffered? What stretch of horror for this help-less man! She was rigid with agony. She had not been able to help him. He had been cruelly injured, this naked man, this other being, and she could make no reparation. There were the children —but the children belonged to life. This dead man had nothing to do with them. He and she were only channels through which life had flowed to issue in the children. She was a mother—but how awful she knew it now to have been a wife. And he, dead now, how awful he must have felt it to be a husband. She felt that in the next world he would be a stranger to her. If they met there, in the beyond, they would only be ashamed of what had been before. The children had come, for some mysterious reason, out of both of them. But the children did not unite them. Now he was dead, she knew how eternally he was apart from her, how eternally he had nothing more to do with her. She saw this episode of her life closed. They had denied each other in life. Now he had withdrawn. An anguish came over her. It was finished then : it had become hopeless between them long before he died. Yet he had been her husband. But how little !

" Have you got his shirt, 'Lizabeth ? "

Elizabeth turned without answering, though she strove to weep and behave as her mother-in-law expected. But she could not, she was silenced. She went into the kitchen and returned with the garment.

" It is aired," she said, grasping the cotton shirt here and there to try. She was almost ashamed to handle him ; what right had she or any one to lay hands on him ; but her touch was humble on his body. It was hard work to clothe him. He was so heavy and inert. A terrible dread gripped her all the while : that he could be so heavy and utterly inert, unresponsive, apart. The horror of the distance between them was almost too much for her—it was so infinite a gap she must look across.

At last it was finished. They covered him with a sheet and left him lying, with his face bound. And she fastened the door of the little parlour, lest the children should see what was lying there. Then, with peace sunk heavy on her heart, she went about making tidy the kitchen. She knew she submitted to life, which was her immediate master. But from death, her ultimate master, she winced with fear and shame.

HE was working on the edge of the common, beyond the small brook that ran in the dip at the bottom of the garden, carrying the garden path in continuation from the plank bridge on to the common. He had cut the rough turf and bracken, leaving the grey, dryish soil bare. But he was worried because he could not get the path straight, there was a pleat between his brows. He had set up his sticks, and taken the sights between the big pine trees, but for some reason everything seemed wrong. He looked again, straining his keen blue eyes, that had a touch of the Viking in them, through the shadowy pine trees as through a doorway, at the green-grassed garden-path rising from the shadow of alders by the log bridge up to the sunlit flowers. Tall white and purple columbines, and the butt-end of the old Hampshire cottage that crouched near the earth amid flowers, blossoming in the bit of shaggy wildness round about.

There was a sound of children's voices calling and talking : high, childish, girlish voices, slightly didactic and tinged with domineering : " If you don't come quick, nurse, I shall run out there to where there are snakes." And nobody had the sang-froid to reply : " Run then, little fool." It was always, " No, darling. Very well, darling. In a moment, darling. Darling, you *must* be patient."

His heart was hard with disillusion : a continual gnawing and resistance. But he worked on. What was there to do but submit !

The sunlight blazed down upon the earth, there was a vividness of flamy vegetation, of fierce seclusion amid the savage peace of the commons. Strange how the savage England lingers in patches : as here, amid these shaggy gorse commons, and marshy, snake-infested places near the foot of the south downs. The spirit of place lingering on primeval, as when the Saxons came, so long ago.

Ah, how he had loved it ! The green garden path, the tufts of flowers, purple and white columbines, and great oriental red poppies with their black chaps and mulleins tall and yellow : this flamy garden which had been a garden for a thousand years, scooped out in the little hollow among the snake-infested commons. He had made it flame with flowers, in a sun cup under its hedges and trees. So old, so old a place ! And yet he had re-created it.

The timbered cottage with its sloping, cloak-like roof was old and forgotten. It belonged to the old England of hamlets and yeomen. Lost all alone on the edge of the common, at the end of a wide, grassy, briar-entangled lane shaded with oak, it had never known the world of to-day. Not till Egbert came with his bride. And he had come to fill it with flowers.

The house was ancient and very uncomfortable. But he did not want to alter it. Ah, marvellous to sit there in the wide, black, time-old chimney, at night when the wind roared overhead, and the wood which he had chopped himself sputtered on the hearth ! Himself on one side the angle, and Winifred on the other.

Ah, how he had wanted her : Winifred ! She was young and beautiful and strong with life, like a flame in sunshine. She moved with a slow grace of energy like a blossoming, red-flowered bush in motion. She, too, seemed to come out of the old England, ruddy, strong, with a certain crude, passionate quiescence and a hawthorn robustness. And he, he was tall and slim and agile, like an English archer with his long supple legs and fine movements. Her hair was nut-brown and all in energic curls and tendrils. Her eyes were nut-brown, too, like a robin's for brightness. And he was white-skinned with fine, silky hair that had darkened from fair, and a slightly arched nose of an old country family. They were a beautiful couple.

The house was Winifred's. Her father was a man of energy, too. He had come from the north poor. Now he was moderately rich. He had bought this fair stretch of inexpensive land, down in Hampshire. Not far from the tiny church of the almost extinct hamlet stood his own house, a commodious old farm-house standing back from the road across a bare grassed yard. On one side of this quadrangle was the long, long barn or shed which he had made into a cottage for his youngest daughter Priscilla. One saw little blue-and-white check curtains at the long windows, and inside, overhead, the grand old timbers of the high-pitched shed. This was Prissy's house. Fifty yards away was the pretty little new cottage which he had built for his daughter Magdalen, with the vegetable garden stretching away to the oak copse. And then away beyond the lawns and rose-trees of the house-garden went the track across a shaggy, wild grass space, towards the ridge of tall black pines that grew on a dyke-bank, through the pines and above the sloping little bog, under the wide, desolate oak trees, till there was Winifred's cottage crouching unexpectedly in front, so much alone, and so primitive.

It was Winifred's own house, and the gardens and the bit of common and the boggy slope were hers : her tiny domain. She had married just at the time when her father had bought the estate, about ten years before the war, so she had been able to come to Egbert with this for a marriage portion. And who was more delighted, he or she, it would be hard to say. She was only twenty at the time, and he was only twenty-one. He had about a hundred and fifty pounds a year of his own—and nothing else but his very considerable personal attractions. He had no profession : he earned nothing. But he talked of literature and music, he had a passion for old folk-music, collecting folk-songs and folk-dances, studying the Morris-dance and the old customs. Of course, in time he would make money in these ways.

Meanwhile youth and health and passion and promise. Winifred's father was always generous : but still, he was a man from the north with a hard head and a hard skin too, having received a good many knocks. At home he kept the hard head out of sight, and played at poetry and romance with his literary wife and his sturdy, passionate girls. He was a man of courage, not given to complaining, bearing his burdens by himself. No, he did not let the world intrude far into his home. He had a delicate, sensitive wife whose poetry won some fame in the narrow world of letters. He himself, with his tough old barbarian fighting spirit, had an almost child-like delight in verse, in sweet poetry, and in the delightful game of a cultured home. His blood was strong even to coarseness. But that only made the home more vigorous, more robust and Christmassy. There was always a touch of Christmas about him, now he was well off. If there was poetry after dinner, there were also chocolates, and nuts, and good little out-of-the-way things to be munching.

Well then, into this family came Egbert. He was made of quite a different paste. The girls and the father were strong-limbed, thick-blooded people, true English, as holly-trees and hawthorn are English. Their culture was grafted on to them, as one might perhaps graft a common pink rose on to a thorn-stem. It flowered oddly enough, but it did not alter their blood.

And Egbert was a born rose. The age-long breeding had left him with a delightful spontaneous passion. He was not clever, nor even " literary." No, but the intonation of his voice, and the movement of his supple, handsome body, and the fine texture of his flesh and his hair, the slight arch of his nose, the quickness of his blue eyes would easily take the place of poetry. Winifred loved him, loved him, this southerner, as a higher being. A *higher* being, mind you. Not a deeper. And as for him, he loved her in passion with every fibre of him. She was the very warm stuff of life to him.

Wonderful then, those days at Crockham Cottage, the first days, all alone save for the woman who came to work in the mornings. Marvellous days, when she had all his tall, supple, fine-fleshed youth to herself, for herself, and he had her like a ruddy fire into which he could cast himself for rejuvenation. Ah, that it might never end, this passion, this marriage ! The flame of their two bodies burnt again into that old cottage, that was haunted already by so much bygone, physical desire. You could not be in the dark room for an hour without the influences coming over you. The hot blood-desire of bygone yeomen, there in this old den where they had lusted and bred for so many generations. The silent house, dark, with thick, timbered walls and the big black chimney-place, and the sense of secrecy. Dark, with low, little windows, sunk into the earth. Dark, like a lair where strong beasts had lurked and mated, lonely at night and lonely by day, left to themselves and their own intensity for so many generations. It seemed to cast a spell on the two young people. They became different. There was a curious secret glow about them, a certain slumbering flame hard to understand, that enveloped them both. They too felt that they did not belong to the London world any more. Crockham had changed their blood : the sense of the snakes that lived and slept even in their own garden, in the sun, so that he, going forward with the spade, would see a curious coiled brownish pile on the black soil, which suddenly would start up, hiss, and dazzle rapidly away, hissing. One day Winifred heard the strangest scream from the flower-bed under the low window of the living room : ah, the strangest scream, like the very soul of the dark past crying aloud. She ran out, and saw a long brown snake on the flower-bed, and in its flat mouth the one hind leg of a frog was striving to escape, and screaming its strange, tiny, bellowing scream. She looked at the snake, and from its sullen flat head it looked at her, obstinately. She gave a cry, and it released the frog and slid angrily away.

That was Crockham. The spear of modern invention had not passed through it, and it lay there secret, primitive, savage as when the Saxons first came. And Egbert and she were caught there, caught out of the world.

He was not idle, nor was she. There were plenty of things to be done, the house to be put into final repair after the workmen had gone, cushions and curtains to sew, the paths to make, the water to fetch and attend to, and then the slope of the deep-soiled, neglected garden to level, to terrace with little terraces and paths, and to fill with flowers. He worked away, in his shirt-sleeves, worked all day intermittently doing this thing and the other. And she, quiet and rich in herself, seeing him stooping and labouring away by himself, would come to help him, to be near him. He of course was an amateur—a born amateur. He worked so hard, and did so little, and nothing he ever did would hold together for long. If he terraced the garden, he held up the earth with a couple of long narrow planks that soon began to bend with the pressure from behind, and would not need many years to rot through and break and let the soil slither all down again in a heap towards the stream-bed. But there you are. He had not been brought up to come to grips with anything, and he thought it would do. Nay, he did not think there was anything else except little temporary contrivances possible, he who had such a passion for his old enduring cottage, and for the old enduring things of the bygone England. Curious that the sense of permanency in the past had such a hold over him, whilst in the present he was all amateurish and sketchy.

Winifred could not criticize him. Town-bred, everything seemed to her splendid, and the very digging and shovelling itself seemed romantic. But neither Egbert nor she yet realized the difference between work and romance.

Godfrey Marshall, her father, was at first perfectly pleased with the ménage down at Crockham Cottage. He thought Egbert was wonderful, the many things he accomplished, and he was gratified by the glow of physical passion between the two young people. To the man who in London still worked hard to keep steady his modest fortune, the thought of this young couple digging away and loving one another down at Crockham Cottage, buried deep among the commons and marshes, near the pale-showing bulk of the downs, was like a chapter of living romance. And they drew the sustenance for their fire of passion from him, from the old man. It was he who fed their flame. He triumphed secretly in the thought. And it was to her father that Winifred still turned, as the one source of all surety and life and support. She loved Egbert with passion. But behind her was the power of her father. It was the power of her father she referred to, whenever she needed to refer. It never occurred to her to refer to Egbert, if she were in difficulty or doubt. No, in all the *serious* matters she depended on her father.

For Egbert had no intention of coming to grips with life. He had no ambition whatsoever. He came from a decent family, from a pleasant country home, from delightful surroundings. He should, of course, have had a profession. He should have studied law or entered business in some way. But no—that fatal three pounds a week would keep him from starving as long as he lived, and he did not want to give himself into bondage. It was not that he was idle. He was always doing something, in his amateurish way. But he had no desire to give himself to the world, and still less had he any desire to fight his way in the world. No, no, the world wasn't worth it. He wanted to ignore it, to go his own way apart, like a casual pilgrim down the forsaken side-tracks. He loved his wife, his cottage and garden. He would make his life there, as a sort of epicurean hermit. He loved the past, the old music and dances and customs of old England. He would try and live in the spirit of these, not in the spirit of the world of business.

But often Winifred's father called her to London: for he loved to have his children round him. So Egbert and she must have a tiny flat in town, and the young couple must transfer themselves from time to time from the country to the city. In town Egbert had plenty of friends, of the same ineffectual sort as himself, tampering with the arts, literature, painting, sculpture, music. He was not bored.

Three pounds a week, however, would not pay for all this. Winifred's father paid. He liked paying. He made her only a very small allowance, but he often gave her ten pounds—or gave Egbert ten pounds. So they both looked on the old man as the mainstay. Egbert didn't mind being patronized and paid for. Only when he felt the family was a little *too* condescending, on account of money, he began to get huffy.

Then of course children came: a lovely little blonde daughter with a head of thistle-down. Everybody adored the child. It was the first exquisite blonde thing that had come into the family, a little mite with the white, slim, beautiful limbs of its father, and as it grew up the dancing, dainty movement of a wild little daisy-spirit. No wonder the Marshalls all loved the child: they called her Joyce. They themselves had their own grace, but it was slow, rather heavy. They had every one of them strong, heavy limbs and darkish skins, and they were short in stature. And now they had for one of their own this light little cowslip child. She was like a little poem in herself.

But nevertheless, she brought a new difficulty. Winifred must have a nurse for her. Yes, yes, there must be a nurse. It was the family decree. Who was to pay for the nurse? The grandfather— seeing the father himself earned no money. Yes, the grandfather would pay, as he had paid all the lying-in expenses. There came a slight sense of money-strain. Egbert was living on his father-in-law.

After the child was born, it was never quite the same between him and Winifred. The difference was at first hardly perceptible. But it was there. In the first place Winifred had a new centre of interest. She was not going to adore her child. But she had what the modern mother so often has in the place of spontaneous love : a profound sense of duty towards her child. Winifred appreciated her darling little girl, and felt a deep sense of duty towards her. Strange, that this sense of duty should go deeper than the love for her husband. But so it was. And so it often is. The responsibility of motherhood was the prime responsibility in Winifred's heart : the responsibility of wifehood came a long way second.

Her child seemed to link her up again in a circuit with her own family. Her father and mother, herself, and her child, that was the human trinity for her. Her husband——? Yes, she loved him still. But that was like play. She had an almost barbaric sense of duty and of family. Till she married, her first human duty had been towards her father : he was the pillar, the source of life, the everlasting support. Now another link was added to the chain of duty : her father, herself, and her child.

Egbert was out of it. Without anything happening, he was gradually, unconsciously excluded from the circle. His wife still loved him, physically. But, but—he was *almost* the unnecessary party in the affair. He could not complain of Winifred. She still did her duty towards him. She still had a physical passion for him, that physical passion on which he had put all his life and soul. But—but——

It was for a long while an ever-recurring *but*. And then, after the second child, another blonde, winsome touching little thing, not so proud and flame-like as Joyce—after Annabel came, then Egbert began truly to realize how it was. His wife still loved him. But—and now the but had grown enormous—her physical love for him was of secondary importance to her. It became ever less important. After all, she had had it, this physical passion, for two years now. It was not this that one lived from. No, no—something sterner, realer.

She began to resent her own passion for Egbert—just a little she began to despise it. For after all there he was, he was charming, he was lovable, he was terribly desirable. But—but—oh, the awful looming cloud of that *but !*—he did not stand firm in the landscape of her life like a tower of strength, like a great pillar of significance. No, he was like a cat one has about the house, which will one day disappear and leave no trace. He was like a flower in the garden, trembling in the wind of life, and then gone, leaving nothing to show. As an adjunct, as an accessory, he was perfect. Many a

woman would have adored to have him about her all her life, the
most beautiful and desirable of all her possessions. But Winifred
belonged to another school.

The years went by, and instead of coming more to grips with life,
he relaxed more. He was of a subtle, sensitive, passionate nature.
But he simply *would* not give himself to what Winifred called life,
Work. No, he would not go into the world and work for money.
No, he just would not. If Winifred liked to live beyond their small
income—well, it was her look-out.

And Winifred did not really want him to go out into the world to
work for money. Money became, alas, a word like a firebrand between them, setting them both aflame with anger. But that is
because we must talk in symbols. Winifred did not really care
about money. She did not care whether he earned or did not earn
anything. Only she knew she was dependent on her father for
three-fourths of the money spent for herself and her children, that
she let that be the *casus belli*, the drawn weapon between herself
and Egbert.

What did she want—what did she want? Her mother once said
to her, with that characteristic touch of irony : " Well, dear, if it is
your fate to consider the lilies, that toil not, neither do they spin, that
is one destiny among many others, and perhaps not so unpleasant
as most. Why do you take it amiss, my child ? "

The mother was subtler than her children, they very rarely knew
how to answer her. So Winifred was only more confused. It was
not a question of lilies. At least, if it were a question of lilies, then
her children were the little blossoms. They at least *grew*. Doesn't
Jesus say : " Consider the lilies *how they grow*." Good then, she had
her growing babies. But as for that other tall, handsome flower of
a father of theirs, he was full grown already, so she did not want to
spend her life considering him in the flower of his days.

No, it was not that he didn't earn money. It was not that he was
idle. He was *not* idle. He was always doing something, always
working away, down at Crockham, doing little jobs. But, oh dear,
the little jobs—the garden paths—the gorgeous flowers—the chairs
to mend, old chairs to mend !

It was that he stood for nothing. If he had done something un-
successfully, and *lost* what money they had ! If he had but striven
with something. Nay, even if he had been wicked, a waster, she
would have been more free. She would have had something to
resist, at least. A waster stands for something, really. He says :
" No, I will not aid and abet society in this business of increase and

hanging together, I will upset the apple-cart as much as I can, in my small way." Or else he says : " No, I will *not* bother about others. If I have lusts, they are my own, and I prefer them to other people's virtues." So, a waster, a scamp, takes a sort of stand. He exposes himself to opposition and final castigation : at any rate in story-books.

But Egbert ! What are you to do with a man like Egbert ? He had no vices. He was really kind, nay generous. And he was not weak. If he had been weak Winifred could have been kind to him. But he did not even give her that consolation. He was not weak, and he did not want her consolation or her kindness. No, thank you. He was of a fine passionate temper, and of a rarer steel than she. He knew it, and she knew it. Hence she was only the more baffled and maddened, poor thing. He, the higher, the finer, in his way the stronger, played with his garden, and his old folk-songs and Morris-dances, just played, and let her support the pillars of the future on her own heart.

And he began to get bitter, and a wicked look began to come on his face. He did not give in to her ; not he. There were seven devils inside his long, slim, white body. He was healthy, full of restrained life. Yes, even he himself had to lock up his own vivid life inside himself, now she would not take it from him. Or rather, now that she only took it occasionally. For she had to yield at times. She loved him so, she desired him so, he was so exquisite to her, the fine creature that he was, finer than herself. Yes, with a groan she had to give in to her own unquenched passion for him. And he came to her then—ah, terrible, ah, wonderful, sometimes she wondered how either of them could live after the terror of the passion that swept between them. It was to her as if pure lightning, flash after flash, went through every fibre of her, till extinction came.

But it is the fate of human beings to live on. And it is the fate of clouds that seem nothing but bits of vapour slowly to pile up, to pile up and fill the heavens and blacken the sun entirely.

So it was. The love came back, the lightning of passion flashed tremendously between them. And there was blue sky and gorgeous-ness for a little while. And then, as inevitably, as inevitably, slowly the clouds began to edge up again above the horizon, slowly, slowly to lurk about the heavens, throwing an occasional cold and hateful shadow : slowly, slowly to congregate, to fill the empyrean space.

And as the years passed, the lightning cleared the sky more and more rarely, less and less the blue showed. Gradually the grey lid sank down upon them, as if it would be permanent.

Why didn't Egbert do something, then? Why didn't he come to grips with life? Why wasn't he like Winifred's father, a pillar of society, even if a slender, exquisite column? Why didn't he go into harness of some sort? Why didn't he take *some* direction?

Well, you can bring an ass to the water, but you cannot make him drink. The world was the water and Egbert was the ass. And he wasn't having any. He couldn't: he just couldn't. Since necessity did not force him to work for his bread and butter, he would not work for work's sake. You can't make the columbine flowers nod in January, nor make the cuckoo sing in England at Christmas. Why? It isn't his season. He doesn't want to. Nay, he *can't* want to.

And there it was with Egbert. He couldn't link up with the world's work, because the basic desire was absent from him. Nay, at the bottom of him he had an even stronger desire: to hold aloof. To hold aloof. To do nobody any damage. But to hold aloof. It was not his season.

Perhaps he should not have married and had children. But you can't stop the waters flowing.

Which held true for Winifred, too. She was not made to endure aloof. Her family tree was a robust vegetation that had to be stirring and believing. In one direction or another her life *had* to go. In her own home she had known nothing of this diffidence which she found in Egbert, and which she could not understand, and which threw her into such dismay. What was she to do, what was she to do, in face of this terrible diffidence?

It was all so different in her own home. Her father may have had his own misgivings, but he kept them to himself. Perhaps he had no very profound belief in this world of ours, this society which we have elaborated with so much effort, only to find ourselves elaborated to death at last. But Godfrey Marshall was of tough, rough fibre, not without a vein of healthy cunning through it all. It was for him a question of winning through, and leaving the rest to heaven. Without having many illusions to grace him, he still *did* believe in heaven. In a dark and unquestioning way, he had a sort of faith: an acrid faith like the sap of some not-to-be-exterminated tree. Just a blind acrid faith as sap is blind and acrid, and yet pushes on in growth and in faith. Perhaps he was unscrupulous, but only as a striving tree is unscrupulous, pushing its single way in a jungle of others.

In the end, it is only this robust, sap-like faith which keeps man going. He may live on for many generations inside the shelter of the social establishment which he has erected for himself, as pear-trees and currant bushes would go on bearing fruit for many seasons, inside a walled garden, even if the race of man were suddenly exterminated. But bit by bit the wall-fruit-trees would gradually pull down the very walls that sustained them. Bit by bit every establishment collapses, unless it is renewed or restored by living hands, all the while.

Egbert could not bring himself to any more of this restoring or renewing business. He was not aware of the fact : but awareness doesn't help much, anyhow. He just couldn't. He had the stoic and epicurean quality of his old, fine breeding. His father-in-law, however, though he was not one bit more of a fool than Egbert, realized that since we are here we may as well live. And so he applied himself to his own tiny section of the social work, and to doing the best for his family, and to leaving the rest to the ultimate will of heaven. A certain robustness of blood made him able to go on. But sometimes even from him spurted a sudden gall of bitterness against the world and its make-up. And yet—he had his own will-to-succeed, and this carried him through. He refused to ask himself what the success would amount to. It amounted to the estate down in Hampshire, and his children lacking for nothing, and himself of some importance in the world : and *basta !*—Basta ! Basta !

Nevertheless do not let us imagine that he was a common pusher. He was not. He knew as well as Egbert what disillusion meant. Perhaps in his soul he had the same estimation of success. But he had a certain acrid courage, and a certain will-to-power. In his own small circle he would emanate power, the single power of his own blind self. With all his spoiling of his children, he was still the father of the old English type. He was too wise to make laws and to domineer in the abstract. But he had kept, and all honour to him, a certain primitive dominion over the souls of his children, the old, almost magic prestige of paternity. There it was, still burning in him, the old smoky torch of paternal godhead.

And in the sacred glare of this torch his children had been brought up. He had given the girls every liberty, at last. But he had never really let them go beyond his power. And they, venturing out into the hard white light of our fatherless world, learned to see with the eyes of the world. They learned to criticize their father, even, from some effulgence of worldly white light, to see him as inferior. But this was all very well in the head. The moment they forgot their tricks of criticism, the old red glow of his authority came over them again. He was not to be quenched.

Let the psycho-analyst talk about father complex. It is just a word invented. Here was a man who had kept alive the old red flame of fatherhood, fatherhood that had even the right to sacrifice the child to God, like Isaac. Fatherhood that had life-and-death authority over the children : a great natural power. And till his children could be brought under some other great authority as girls ; or could arrive at manhood and become themselves centres of the same power, continuing the same male mystery as men ; until such time, willy-nilly, Godfrey Marshall would keep his children.

It had seemed as if he might lose Winifred. Winifred had *adored* her husband, and looked up to him as to something wonderful. Perhaps she had expected in him another great authority, a male authority greater, finer than her father's. For having once known the glow of male power, she would not easily turn to the cold white light of feminine independence. She would hunger, hunger all her life for the warmth and shelter of true male strength.

And hunger she might, for Egbert's power lay in the abnegation of power. He was himself the living negative of power. Even of responsibility. For the negation of power at last means the negation of responsibility. As far as these things went, he would confine himself to himself. He would try to confine his own *influence* even to himself. He would try, as far as possible, to abstain from influencing his children by assuming any responsibility for them. " A little child shall lead them——" His child should lead, then. He would try not to make it go in any direction whatever. He would abstain from influencing it. Liberty !—

Poor Winifred was like a fish out of water in this liberty, gasping for the denser element which should contain her. Till her child came. And then she knew that she must be responsible for it, that she must have authority over it.

But here Egbert, silently and negatively, stepped in. Silently, negatively, but fatally he neutralized her authority over her children.

There was a third little girl born. And after this Winifred wanted no more children. Her soul was turning to salt.

So she had charge of the children, they were her responsibility. The money for them had come from her father. She would do her very best for them, and have command over their life and death. But no ! Egbert would not take the responsibility. He would not even provide the money. But he would not let her have her way. Her dark, silent, passionate authority he would not allow. It was a battle between them, the battle between liberty and the old blood-power. And of course he won. The little girls loved him and adored him. "Daddy! Daddy!" They could do as they liked with him. Their mother would have ruled them. She would have ruled them passionately, with indulgence, with the old dark magic of parental authority, something looming and unquestioned and, after all, divine: if we believe in divine authority. The Marshalls did, being Catholic.

And Egbert, he turned her old dark, Catholic blood-authority into a sort of tyranny. He would not leave her her children. He stole them from her, and yet without assuming responsibility for them. He stole them from her, in emotion and spirit, and left her only to command their behaviour. A thankless lot for a mother. And her children adored him, adored him, little knowing the empty bitterness they were preparing for themselves when they too grew up to have husbands : husbands such as Egbert, adorable and null.

Joyce, the eldest, was still his favourite. She was now a quicksilver little thing of six years old. Barbara, the youngest, was a toddler of two years. They spent most of their time down at Crockham, because he wanted to be there. And even Winifred loved the place really. But now, in her frustrated and blinded state, it was full of menace for her children. The adders, the poison-berries, the brook, the marsh, the water that might not be pure—one thing and another. From mother and nurse it was a guerilla gunfire of commands, and blithe, quicksilver disobedience from the three blonde, never-still little girls. Behind the girls was the father, against mother and nurse. And so it was.

"If you don't come quick, nurse, I shall run out there to where there are snakes."

"Joyce, you *must* be patient. I'm just changing Annabel."

There you are. There it was : always the same. Working away on the common across the brook he heard it. And he worked on, just the same.

Suddenly he heard a shriek, and he flung the spade from him and started for the bridge, looking up like a startled deer. Ah, there was Winifred—Joyce had hurt herself. He went on up the garden.

"What is it ? "

The child was still screaming—now it was—"Daddy! Daddy! Oh—oh, Daddy ! " And the mother was saying :

"Don't be frightened, darling. Let mother look."

But the child only cried :

"Oh, Daddy, Daddy, Daddy ! "

She was terrified by the sight of the blood running from her own knee. Winifred crouched down, with her child of six in her lap, to examine the knee. Egbert bent over also.

" Don't make such a noise, Joyce," he said irritably. " How did she do it ? "

" She fell on that sickle thing which you left lying about after cutting the grass," said Winifred, looking into his face with bitter accusation as he bent near.

He had taken his handkerchief and tied it round the knee. Then he lifted the still sobbing child in his arms, and carried her into the house and upstairs to her bed. In his arms she became quiet. But his heart was burning with pain and with guilt. He had left the sickle there lying on the edge of the grass, and so his first-born child whom he loved so dearly had come to hurt. But then it was an accident—it was an accident. Why should he feel guilty ? It would probably be nothing, better in two or three days. Why take it to heart, why worry ? He put it aside.

The child lay on the bed in her little summer frock, her face very white now after the shock. Nurse had come carrying the youngest child : and little Annabel stood holding her skirt. Winifred, terribly serious and wooden-seeming, was bending over the knee, from which she had taken his blood-soaked handkerchief. Egbert bent forward, too, keeping more sang-froid in his face than in his heart. Winifred went all of a lump of seriousness, so he had to keep some reserve. The child moaned and whimpered.

The knee was still bleeding profusely—it was a deep cut right in the joint.

" You'd better go for the doctor, Egbert," said Winifred bitterly.

" Oh, no ! Oh, no ! " cried Joyce in a panic.

" Joyce, my darling, don't cry ! " said Winifred, suddenly catching the little girl to her breast in a strange tragic anguish, the *Mater Dolorata*. Even the child was frightened into silence. Egbert looked at the tragic figure of his wife with the child at her breast, and turned away. Only Annabel started suddenly to cry : " Joycey, Joycey, don't have your leg bleeding ! "

Egbert rode four miles to the village for the doctor. He could not help feeling that Winifred was laying it on rather. Surely the knee itself wasn't hurt ! Surely not. It was only a surface cut.

The doctor was out. Egbert left the message and came cycling swiftly home, his heart pinched with anxiety. He dropped sweating off his bicycle and went into the house, looking rather small, like a man who is at fault. Winifred was upstairs sitting by Joyce, who was looking pale and important in bed, and was eating some tapioca pudding. The pale, small, scared face of his child went to Egbert's heart.

" Doctor Wing was out. He'll be here about half-past two," said Egbert.

" I don't want him to come," whimpered Joyce.

" Joyce, dear, you must be patient and quiet," said Winifred. " He won't hurt you. But he will tell us what to do to make your knee better quickly. That is why he must come."

Winifred always explained carefully to her little girls : and it always took the words off their lips for the moment.

" Does it bleed yet ? " said Egbert.

Winifred moved the bedclothes carefully aside.

" I think not," she said.

Egbert stooped also to look.

" No, it doesn't," he said. Then he stood up with a relieved look on his face. He turned to the child.

" Eat your pudding, Joyce," he said. " It won't be anything. You've only got to keep still for a few days."

" You haven't had your dinner, have you, Daddy ? "

" Not yet."

" Nurse will give it to you," said Winifred.

" You'll be all right, Joyce," he said, smiling to the child and pushing the blonde hair aside off her brow. She smiled back winsomely into his face.

He went downstairs and ate his meal alone. Nurse served him. She liked waiting on him. All women liked him and liked to do things for him.

The doctor came—a fat country practitioner, pleasant and kind.

" What, little girl, been tumbling down, have you ? There's a thing to be doing, for a smart little lady like you ! What ! And cutting your knee ! Tut-tut-tut ! That *wasn't* clever of you, now was it ? Never mind, never mind, soon be better. Let us look at it. Won't hurt you. Not the least in life. Bring a bowl with a little warm water, nurse. Soon have it all right again, soon have it all right."

Joyce smiled at him with a pale smile of faint superiority. This was *not* the way in which she was used to being talked to.

He bent down, carefully looking at the little, thin, wounded knee of the child. Egbert bent over him.

" Oh, dear, oh, dear ! Quite a deep little cut. Nasty little cut. Nasty little cut. But, never mind. Never mind, little lady. We'll soon have it better. Soon have it better, little lady. What's your name ? "

" My name is Joyce," said the child distinctly.

" Oh, really ! " he replied. " Oh, really ! Well, that's a fine name too, in my opinion. Joyce, eh?—And how old might Miss Joyce be? Can she tell me that?"

"I'm six," said the child, slightly amused and very condescending.

"Six! There now. Add up and count as far as six, can you? Well, that's a clever little girl, a clever little girl. And if she has to drink a spoonful of medicine, she won't make a murmur, I'll be bound. Not like *some* little girls. What? Eh?"

"I take it if mother wishes me to," said Joyce.

"Ah, there now! That's the style! That's what I like to hear from a little lady in bed because she's cut her knee. That's the style——"

The comfortable and prolix doctor dressed and bandaged the knee and recommended bed and a light diet for the little lady. He thought a week or a fortnight would put it right. No bones or ligatures damaged—fortunately. Only a flesh cut. He would come again in a day or two.

So Joyce was reassured and stayed in bed and had all her toys up. Her father often played with her. The doctor came the third day. He was fairly pleased with the knee. It was healing. It was healing—yes—yes. Let the child continue in bed. He came again after a day or two. Winifred was a trifle uneasy. The wound seemed to be healing on the top, but it hurt the child too much. It didn't look quite right. She said so to Egbert.

"Egbert, I'm sure Joyce's knee isn't healing properly."

"I think it is," he said. "I think it's all right."

"I'd rather Doctor Wing came again—I don't feel satisfied."

"Aren't you trying to imagine it worse than it really is?"

"You would say so, of course. But I shall write a post card to Doctor Wing now."

The doctor came next day. He examined the knee. Yes, there was inflammation. Yes, there *might* be a little septic poisoning—there might. There might. Was the child feverish?

So a fortnight passed by, and the child *was* feverish, and the knee was more inflamed and grew worse and was painful, painful. She cried in the night, and her mother had to sit up with her. Egbert still insisted it was nothing, really—it would pass. But in his heart he was anxious.

Winifred wrote again to her father. On Saturday the elderly man appeared. And no sooner did Winifred see the thick, rather short figure in its grey suit than a great yearning came over her.

"Father, I'm not satisfied with Joyce. I'm not satisfied with Doctor Wing."

"Well, Winnie, dear, if you're not satisfied we must have further advice, that is all."

The sturdy, powerful, elderly man went upstairs, his voice sounding rather grating through the house, as if it cut upon the tense atmosphere.

"How are you, Joyce, darling?" he said to the child. "Does your knee hurt you? Does it hurt you, dear?"

"It does sometimes." The child was shy of him, cold towards him.

"Well, dear, I'm sorry for that. I hope you try to bear it, and not trouble mother too much."

There was no answer. He looked at the knee. It was red and stiff.

"Of course," he said, "I think we must have another doctor's opinion. And if we're going to have it, we had better have it at once. Egbert, do you think you might cycle in to Bingham for Doctor Wayne? I found him *very* satisfactory for Winnie's mother."

"I can go if you think it necessary," said Egbert.

"Certainly I think it necessary. Even if there *is* nothing, we can have peace of mind. Certainly I think it necessary. I should like Doctor Wayne to come this evening if possible."

So Egbert set off on his bicycle through the wind, like a boy sent on an errand, leaving his father-in-law a pillar of assurance, with Winifred.

Doctor Wayne came, and looked grave. Yes, the knee was certainly taking the wrong way. The child might be lame for life.

Up went the fire of fear and anger in every heart. Doctor Wayne came again the next day for a proper examination. And, yes, the knee had really taken bad ways. It should be X-rayed. It was very important.

Godfrey Marshall walked up and down the lane with the doctor, beside the standing motor-car: up and down, up and down in one of those consultations of which he had had so many in his life.

As a result he came indoors to Winifred.

"Well, Winnie, dear, the best thing to do is to take Joyce up to London, to a nursing home where she can have proper treatment. Of course this knee has been allowed to go wrong. And apparently there is a risk that the child may even lose her leg. What do you think, dear? You agree to our taking her up to town and putting her under the best care?"

"Oh, father, you *know* I would do anything on earth for her."

"I know you would, Winnie darling. The pity is that there has been this unfortunate delay already. I can't think what Doctor Wing was doing. Apparently the child is in danger of losing her leg. Well then, if you will have everything ready, we will take her up to town to-morrow. I will order the large car from Denley's to be here at ten. Egbert, will you take a telegram at once to Doctor Jackson? It is a small nursing home for children and for surgical cases, not far from Baker Street. I'm sure Joyce will be all right there."

" Oh, father, can't I nurse her myself? "

" Well, darling, if she is to have proper treatment, she had best be in a home. The X-ray treatment, and the electric treatment, and whatever is necessary."

" It will cost a great deal——" said Winifred.

" We can't think of cost, if the child's leg is in danger—or even her life. No use speaking of cost," said the elder man impatiently.

And so it was. Poor Joyce, stretched out on a bed in the big closed motor-car—the mother sitting by her head, the grandfather in his short grey beard and a bowler hat, sitting by her feet, thick, and implacable in his responsibility—they rolled slowly away from Crockham, and from Egbert who stood there bareheaded and a little ignominious, left behind. He was to shut up the house and bring the rest of the family back to town, by train, the next day.

Followed a dark and bitter time. The poor child. The poor, poor child, how she suffered, an agony and a long crucifixion in that nursing home. It was a bitter six weeks which changed the soul of Winifred for ever. As she sat by the bed of her poor, tortured little child, tortured with the agony of the knee, and the still worse agony of these diabolic, but perhaps necessary modern treatments, she felt her heart killed and going cold in her breast. Her little Joyce, her frail, brave, wonderful, little Joyce, frail and small and pale as a white flower ! Ah, how had she, Winifred, dared to be so wicked, so wicked, so careless, so sensual.

" Let my heart die ! Let my woman's heart of flesh die ! Saviour, let my heart die. And save my child. Let my heart die from the world and from the flesh. Oh, destroy my heart that is so wayward. Let my heart of pride die. Let my heart die."

She prayed beside the bed of her child. And like the Mother with the seven swords in her breast, slowly her heart of pride and passion died in her breast, bleeding away. Slowly it died, bleeding away, and she turned to the Church for comfort, to Jesus, to the Mother of God, but most of all, to that great and enduring institution, the Roman Catholic Church. She withdrew into the shadow of the Church. She was a mother with three children. But in her soul she died, her heart of pride and passion and desire bled to death, her soul belonged to her Church, her body belonged to her duty as a mother.

Her duty as a wife did not enter. As a wife she had no sense of duty : only a certain bitterness towards the man with whom she had known such sensuality and distraction. She was purely the *Mater Dolorata*. To the man she was closed as a tomb.

Egbert came to see his child. But Winifred seemed to be always seated there, like the tomb of his manhood and his fatherhood. Poor Winifred : she was still young, still strong and ruddy and beautiful like a ruddy hard flower of the field. Strange—her ruddy, healthy face, so sombre, and her strong, heavy, full-blooded body, so still. She, a nun ! Never. And yet the gates of her heart and soul had shut in his face with a slow, resonant clang, shutting him out for ever. There was no need for her to go into a convent. Her will had done it.

And between this young mother and this young father lay the crippled child, like a bit of pale silk floss on the pillow, and a little white pain-quenched face. He could not bear it. He just could not bear it. He turned aside. There was nothing to do but to turn aside. He turned aside, and went hither and thither, desultory. He was still attractive and desirable. But there was a little frown between his brow as if he had been cleft there with a hatchet : cleft right in, for ever, and that was the stigma.

The child's leg was saved : but the knee was locked stiff. The fear now was lest the lower leg should wither, or cease to grow. There must be long-continued massage and treatment, daily treatment, even when the child left the nursing home. And the whole of the expense was borne by the grandfather.

Egbert now had no real home. Winifred with the children and nurse was tied to the little flat in London. He could not live there : he could not contain himself. The cottage was shut-up—or lent to friends. He went down sometimes to work in his garden and keep the place in order. Then with the empty house around him at night, all the empty rooms, he felt his heart go wicked. The sense of frustration and futility, like some slow, torpid snake, slowly bit right through his heart. Futility, futility, futility : the horrible marsh-poison went through his veins and killed him.

As he worked in the garden in the silence of day he would listen for a sound. No sound. No sound of Winifred from the dark inside of the cottage : no sound of children's voices from the air, from the common, from the near distance. No sound, nothing but the old dark marsh-venomous atmosphere of the place. So he worked spasmodically through the day, and at night made a fire and cooked some food alone.

He was alone. He himself cleaned the cottage and made his bed. But his mending he did not do. His shirts were slit on the shoulders, when he had been working, and the white flesh showed through. He would feel the air and the spots of rain on his exposed flesh. And he would look again across the common, where the dark, tufted gorse was dying to seed, and the bits of cat-heather were coming pink in tufts, like a sprinkling of sacrificial blood.

His heart went back to the savage old spirit of the place : the desire for old gods, old, lost passions, the passion of the cold-blooded, darting snakes that hissed and shot away from him, the mystery of blood-sacrifices, all the lost, intense sensations of the primeval people of the place, whose passions seethed in the air still, from those long days before the Romans came. The seethe of a lost, dark passion in the air. The presence of unseen snakes.

A queer, baffled, half-wicked look came on his face. He could not stay long at the cottage. Suddenly he must swing on to his bicycle and go—anywhere. Anywhere, away from the place. He would stay a few days with his mother in the old home. His mother adored him and grieved as a mother would. But the little, baffled, half-wicked smile curled on his face, and he swung away from his mother's solicitude as from everything else.

Always moving on—from place to place, friend to friend : and always swinging away from sympathy. As soon as sympathy, like a soft hand, was reached out to touch him, away he swerved, instinctively, as a harmless snake swerves and swerves and swerves away from an outstretched hand. Away he must go. And periodically he went back to Winifred.

He was terrible to her now, like a temptation. She had devoted herself to her children and her Church. Joyce was once more on her feet ; but, alas ! lame, with iron supports to her leg, and a little crutch. It was strange how she had grown into a long, pallid, wild little thing. Strange that the pain had not made her soft and docile, but had brought out a wild, almost mænad temper in the child. She was seven, and long and white and thin, but by no means subdued. Her blonde hair was darkening. She still had long sufferings to face, and, in her own childish consciousness, the stigma of her lameness to bear.

And she bore it. An almost mænad courage seemed to possess

her, as if she were a long, thin, young weapon of life. She acknowledged all her mother's care. She would stand by her mother for ever.
But some of her father's fine-tempered desperation flashed in her.

When Egbert saw his little girl limping horribly—not only limping
but lurching horribly in crippled, childish way, his heart again
hardened with chagrin, like steel that is tempered again. There
was a tacit understanding between him and his little girl : not
what we would call love, but a weapon-like kinship. There was a
tiny touch of irony in his manner towards her, contrasting sharply
with Winifred's heavy, unleavened solicitude and care. The child
flickered back to him with an answering little smile of irony and
recklessness : an odd flippancy which made Winifred only the more
sombre and earnest.

The Marshalls took endless thought and trouble for the child,
searching out every means to save her limb and her active freedom.
They spared no effort and no money, they spared no strength of
will. With all their slow, heavy power of will they willed that Joyce
should save her liberty of movement, should win back her wild, free
grace. Even if it took a long time to recover, it should be recovered.

So the situation stood. And Joyce submitted, week after week,
month after month, to the tyranny and pain of the treatment.
She acknowledged the honourable effort on her behalf. But her
flamy reckless spirit was her father's. It was he who had all the
glamour for her. He and she were like members of some forbidden
secret society who know one another but may not recognize one
another. Knowledge they had in common, the same secret of life,
the father and the child. But the child stayed in the camp of her
mother, honourably, and the father wandered outside like Ishmael,
only coming sometimes to sit in the home for an hour or two, an
evening or two beside the camp fire, like Ishmael, in a curious
silence and tension, with the mocking answer of the desert speaking
out of his silence, and annulling the whole convention of the domestic
home.

His presence was almost an anguish to Winifred. She prayed
against it. That little cleft between his brow, that flickering, wicked
little smile that seemed to haunt his face, and above all, the triumphant loneliness, the Ishmael quality. And then the erectness of his
supple body, like a symbol. The very way he stood, so quiet, so
insidious, like an erect, supple symbol of life, the living body, con-
fronting her downcast soul, was torture to her. He was like a supple
living idol moving before her eyes, and she felt if she watched him
she was damned.

And he came and made himself at home in her little home. When he was there, moving in his own quiet way, she felt as if the whole great law of sacrifice, by which she had elected to live, were annulled. He annulled by his very presence the laws of her life. And what did he substitute? Ah, against that question she hardened herself in recoil.

It was awful to her to have to have him about—moving about in his shirt-sleeves, speaking in his tenor, throaty voice to the children. Annabel simply adored him, and he teased the little girl. The baby, Barbara, was not sure of him. She had been born a stranger to him. But even the nurse, when she saw his white shoulder of flesh through the slits of his torn shirt, thought it a shame.

Winifred felt it was only another weapon of his against her.

" You have other shirts—why do you wear that old one that is all torn, Egbert ? " she said.

" I may as well wear it out," he said subtly.

He knew she would not offer to mend it for him. She *could* not. And no, she would not. Had she not her own gods to honour ? And could she betray them, submitting to his Baal and Ashtaroth ? And it was terrible to her, his unsheathed presence, that seemed to annul her and her faith, like another revelation. Like a gleaming idol evoked against her, a vivid life-idol that might triumph.

He came and he went—and she persisted. And then the great war broke out. He was a man who could not go to the dogs. He could not dissipate himself. He was pure-bred in his Englishness, and even when he would have liked to be vicious, he could not.

So when the war broke out his whole instinct was against it : against war. He had not the faintest desire to overcome any foreigners or to help in their death. He had no conception of Imperial England, and Rule Britannia was just a joke to him. He was a pure-blooded Englishman, perfect in his race, and when he was truly himself he could no more have been aggressive on the score of his Englishness than a rose can be aggressive on the score of its rosiness.

No, he had no desire to defy Germany and to exalt England. The distinction between German and English was not for him the distinction between good and bad. It was the distinction between blue water-flowers and red or white bush-blossoms : just difference. The difference between the wild boar and the wild bear. And a man was good or bad according to his nature, not according to his nationality.

Egbert was well-bred, and this was part of his natural understanding. It was merely unnatural to him to hate a nation *en bloc*. Certain individuals he disliked, and others he liked, and the mass he knew nothing about. Certain deeds he disliked, certain deeds seemed natural to him, and about most deeds he had no particular feeling.

He had, however, the one deepest pure-bred instinct. He recoiled inevitably from having his feelings dictated to him by the mass feeling. His feelings were his own, his understanding was his own, and he would never go back on either, willingly. Shall a man become inferior to his own true knowledge and self, just because the mob expects it of him?

What Egbert felt subtly and without question, his father-in-law felt also in a rough, more combative way. Different as the two men were, they were two real Englishmen, and their instincts were almost the same.

And Godfrey Marshall had the world to reckon with. There was German military aggression, and the English non-military idea of liberty and the "conquests of peace"—meaning industrialism. Even if the choice between militarism and industrialism were a choice of evils, the elderly man asserted his choice of the latter, perforce. He whose soul was quick with the instinct of power.

Egbert just refused to reckon with the world. He just refused even to decide between German militarism and British industrialism. He chose neither. As for atrocities, he despised the people who committed them, as inferior criminal types. There was nothing national about crime.

And yet, war! War! Just war! Not right or wrong, but just war itself. Should he join? Should he give himself over to war? The question was in his mind for some weeks. Not because he thought England was right and Germany wrong. Probably Germany was wrong, but he refused to make a choice. Not because he felt inspired. No. But just—war.

The deterrent was, the giving himself over into the power of other men, and into the power of the mob-spirit of a democratic army. Should he give himself over? Should he make over his own life and body to the control of something which he *knew* was inferior, in spirit, to his own self? Should he commit himself into the power of an inferior control? Should he? Should he betray himself?

He was going to put himself into the power of his inferiors, and he knew it. He was going to subjugate himself. He was going to be ordered about by petty *canaille* of non-commissioned officers—and even commissioned officers. He who was born and bred free. Should he do it?

He went to his wife, to speak to her.

" Shall I join up, Winifred ? "

She was silent. Her instinct also was dead against it. And yet a certain profound resentment made her answer :

" You have three children dependent on you. I don't know whether you have thought of that."

It was still only the third month of the war, and the old pre-war ideas were still alive.

" Of course. But it won't make much difference to them. I shall be earning a shilling a day, at least."

" You'd better speak to father, I think," she replied heavily.

Egbert went to his father-in-law. The elderly man's heart was full of resentment.

" I should say," he said rather sourly, " it is the best thing you could do."

Egbert went and joined up immediately, as a private soldier. He was drafted into the light artillery.

Winifred now had a new duty towards him : the duty of a wife towards a husband who is himself performing his duty towards the world. She loved him still. She would always love him, as far as earthly love went. But it was duty she now lived by. When he came back to her in khaki, a soldier, she submitted to him as a wife. It was her duty. But to his passion she could never again fully submit. Something prevented her, for ever : even her own deepest choice.

He went back again to camp. It did not suit him to be a modern soldier. In the thick, gritty, hideous khaki his subtle physique was extinguished as if he had been killed. In the ugly intimacy of the camp his thorough-bred sensibilities were just degraded. But he had chosen, so he accepted. An ugly little look came on to his face, of a man who has accepted his own degradation.

In the early spring Winifred went down to Crockham to be there when primroses were out, and the tassels hanging on the hazel-bushes. She felt something like a reconciliation towards Egbert, now he was a prisoner in camp most of his days. Joyce was wild with delight at seeing the garden and the common again, after the eight or nine months of London and misery. She was still lame. She still had the irons up her leg. But she lurched about with a wild, crippled agility.

Egbert came for a week-end, in his gritty, thick, sandpaper khaki and puttees and the hideous cap. Nay, he looked terrible. And on his face a slightly impure look, a little sore on his lip, as if he had eaten too much or drunk too much or let his blood become a little unclean. He was almost uglily healthy, with the camp life. It did not suit him.

Winifred waited for him in a little passion of duty and sacrifice, willing to serve the soldier, if not the man. It only made him feel a little more ugly inside. The week-end was torment to him : the memory of the camp, the knowledge of the life he led there ; even the sight of his own legs in that abhorrent khaki. He felt as if the hideous cloth went into his blood and made it gritty and dirty. Then Winifred so ready to serve the *soldier*, when she repudiated the man. And this made the grit worse between his teeth. And the children running around playing and calling in the rather mincing fashion of children who have nurses and governesses and literature in the family. And Joyce so lame ! It had all become unreal to him, after the camp. It only set his soul on edge. He left at dawn on the Monday morning, glad to get back to the realness and vulgarity of the camp.

Winifred would never meet him again at the cottage—only in London, where the world was with them. But sometimes he came alone to Crockham, perhaps when friends were staying there. And then he would work awhile in his garden. This summer still it would flame with blue anchusas and big red poppies, the mulleins would sway their soft, downy erections in the air : he loved mulleins : and the honeysuckle would stream out scent like memory, when the owl was whooing. Then he sat by the fire with the friends and with Winifred's sisters, and they sang the folk-songs. He put on thin civilian clothes and his charm and his beauty and the supple dominancy of his body glowed out again. But Winifred was not there.

At the end of the summer he went to Flanders, into action. He seemed already to have gone out of life, beyond the pale of life. He hardly remembered his life any more, being like a man who is going to take a jump from a height, and is only looking to where he must land.

He was twice slightly wounded, in two months. But not enough to put him off duty for more than a day or two. They were retiring again, holding the enemy back. He was in the rear—three machine-guns. The country was all pleasant, war had not yet trampled it. Only the air seemed shattered, and the land awaiting death. It was a small, unimportant action in which he was engaged.

The guns were stationed on a little bushy hillock just outside a village. But occasionally, it was difficult to say from which direction came the sharp crackle of rifle-fire, and beyond, the far-off thud of cannon. The afternoon was wintry and cold.

A lieutenant stood on a little iron platform at the top of the ladders, taking the sights and giving the aim, calling in a high, tense, mechanical voice. Out of the sky came the sharp cry of the directions, then the warning numbers, then " Fire ! " The shot went, the piston of the gun sprang back, there was a sharp explosion, and a very faint film of smoke in the air. Then the other two guns fired, and there was a lull. The officer was uncertain of the enemy's position. The thick clump of horse-chestnut trees below was without change. Only in the far distance the sound of heavy firing continued, so far off as to give a sense of peace.

The gorse bushes on either hand were dark, but a few sparks of flowers showed yellow. He noticed them almost unconsciously as he waited, in the lull. He was in his shirt-sleeves, and the air came chill on his arms. Again his shirt was slit on the shoulders, and the flesh showed through. He was dirty and unkempt. But his face was quiet. So many things go out of consciousness before we come to the end of consciousness.

Before him, below, was the highroad, running between high banks of grass and gorse. He saw the whitish, muddy tracks and deep scores in the road, where the part of the regiment had retired. Now all was still. Sounds that came, came from the outside. The place where he stood was still silent, chill, serene : the white church among the trees beyond seemed like a thought only.

He moved into a lightning-like mechanical response at the sharp cry from the officer overhead. Mechanism, the pure mechanical action of obedience at the guns. Pure mechanical action at the guns. It left the soul unburdened, brooding in dark nakedness. In the end, the soul is alone, brooding on the face of the uncreated flux, as a bird on a dark sea.

Nothing could be seen but the road, and a crucifix knocked slanting and the dark, autumnal fields and woods. There appeared three horsemen on a little eminence, very small, on the crest of a ploughed field. They were our own men. Of the enemy, nothing.

The lull continued. Then suddenly came sharp orders, and a new direction of the guns, and an intense, exciting activity. Yet at the centre the soul remained dark and aloof, alone.

But even so, it was the soul that heard the new sound : the new, deep " papp ! " of a gun that seemed to touch right upon the soul. He kept up the rapid activity at the machine-gun, sweating. But in his soul was the echo of the new, deep sound, deeper than life.

And in confirmation came the awful faint whistling of a shell, advancing almost suddenly into a piercing, tearing shriek that would tear through the membrane of life. He heard it in his ears, but he heard it also in his soul, in tension. There was relief when the thing had swung by and struck, away beyond. He heard the hoarseness of its explosion, and the voice of the soldier calling to the horses. But he did not turn round to look. He only noticed a twig of holly with red berries fall like a gift on to the road below.

Not this time, not this time. Whither thou goest I will go. Did he say it to the shell, or to whom? Whither thou goest I will go. Then, the faint whistling of another shell dawned, and his blood became small and still to receive it. It drew nearer, like some horrible blast of wind; his blood lost consciousness. But in the second of suspension he saw the heavy shell swoop to earth, into the rocky bushes on the right, and earth and stones poured up into the sky. It was as if he heard no sound. The earth and stones and fragments of bush fell to earth again, and there was the same unchanging peace. The Germans had got the aim.

Would they move now? Would they retire? Yes. The officer was giving the last lightning-rapid orders to fire before withdrawing. A shell passed unnoticed in the rapidity of action. And then, into the silence, into the suspense where the soul brooded, finally crashed a noise and a darkness and a moment's flaming agony and horror. Ah, he had seen the dark bird flying towards him, flying home this time. In one instant life and eternity went up in a conflagration of agony, then there was a weight of darkness.

When faintly something began to struggle in the darkness, a consciousness of himself, he was aware of a great load and a clanging sound. To have known the moment of death! And to be forced, before dying, to review it. So, fate, even in death.

There was a resounding of pain. It seemed to sound from the outside of his consciousness: like a loud bell clanging very near. Yet he knew it was himself. He must associate himself with it. After a lapse and a new effort, he identified a pain in his head, a large pain that clanged and resounded. So far he could identify himself with himself. Then there was a lapse.

After a time he seemed to wake up again, and waking, to know that he was at the front, and that he was killed. He did not open his eyes. Light was not yet his. The clanging pain in his head rang out the rest of his consciousness. So he lapsed away from consciousness, in unutterable sick abandon of life.

Bit by bit, like a doom, came the necessity to know. He was hit in the head. It was only a vague surmise at first. But in the swinging of the pendulum of pain, swinging ever nearer and nearer, to touch him into an agony of consciousness and a consciousness of agony, gradually the knowledge emerged—he must be hit in the head—hit on the left brow ; if so, there would be blood—was there blood ?—could he feel blood in his left eye ? Then the clanging seemed to burst the membrane of his brain, like death-madness.

Was there blood on his face ? Was hot blood flowing ? Or was it dry blood congealing down his cheek ? It took him hours even to ask the question : time being no more than an agony in darkness, without measurement.

A long time after he had opened his eyes he realized he was seeing something—something, something, but the effort to recall what was too great. No, no ; no recall !

Were they the stars in the dark sky ? Was it possible it was stars in the dark sky ? Stars ? The world ? Ah, no, he could not know it ! Stars and the world were gone for him, he closed his eyes. No stars, no sky, no world. No, no ! The thick darkness of blood alone. It should be one great lapse into the thick darkness of blood in agony.

Death, oh, death ! The world all blood, and the blood all writhing with death. The soul like the tiniest little light out on a dark sea, the sea of blood. And the light guttering, beating, pulsing in a windless storm, wishing it could go out, yet unable.

There had been life. There had been Winifred and his children. But the frail death-agony effort to catch at straws of memory, straws of life from the past, brought on too great a nausea. No, no ! No Winifred, no children. No world, no people. Better the agony of dissolution ahead than the nausea of the effort backwards. Better the terrible work should go forward, the dissolving into the black sea of death, in the extremity of dissolution, than that there should be any reaching back towards life. To forget ! To forget ! Utterly, utterly to forget, in the great forgetting of death. To break the core and the unit of life, and to lapse out on the great darkness. Only that. To break the clue, and mingle and commingle with the one darkness, without afterwards or forwards. Let the black sea of death itself solve the problem of futurity. Let the will of man break and give up.

What was that ? A light ! A terrible light ! Was it figures ? Was it legs of a horse colossal—colossal above him : huge, huge ?

The Germans heard a slight noise, and started. Then, in the glare of a light-bomb, by the side of the heap of earth thrown up by the shell, they saw the dead face.

THERE is in the Midlands a single-line tramway system which boldly leaves the county town and plunges off into the black, industrial country-side, up hill and down dale, through the long ugly villages of workmen's houses, over canals and railways, past churches perched high and nobly over the smoke and shadows, through stark, grimy cold little market-places, tilting away in a rush past cinemas and shops down to the hollow where the collieries are, then up again, past a little rural church, under the ash trees, on in a rush to the terminus, the last little ugly place of industry, the cold little town that shivers on the edge of the wild, gloomy country beyond. There the green and creamy coloured tram-car seems to pause and purr with curious satisfaction. But in a few minutes—the clock on the turret of the Co-operative Wholesale Society's shops gives the time—away it starts once more on the adventure. Again there are the reckless swoops downhill, bouncing the loops : again the chilly wait in the hill-top market-place : again the breathless slithering round the precipitous drop under the church : again the patient halts at the loops, waiting for the outcoming car : so on and on, for two long hours, till at last the city looms beyond the fat gas-works, the narrow factories draw near, we are in the sordid streets of the great town, once more we sidle to a standstill at our terminus, abashed by the great crimson and cream-coloured city cars, but still perky, jaunty, somewhat dare-devil, green as a jaunty sprig of parsley out of a black colliery garden.

To ride on these cars is always an adventure. Since we are in war-time, the drivers are men unfit for active service : cripples and hunchbacks. So they have the spirit of the devil in them. The ride becomes a steeplechase. Hurray ! we have leapt in a clear jump over the canal bridges—now for the four-lane corner. With a shriek and a trail of sparks we are clear again. To be sure, a tram often leaps the rails—but what matter ! It sits in a ditch till other trams come to haul it out. It is quite common for a car, packed with one solid mass of living people, to come to a dead halt in the midst of unbroken blackness, the heart of nowhere on a dark night, and for the driver and the girl conductor to call, " All get off—car's on fire ! " Instead, however, of rushing out in a panic, the passengers stolidly reply : " Get on—get on ! We're not coming out. We're stopping where we are. Push on, George." So till flames actually appear.

The reason for this reluctance to dismount is that the nights are howlingly cold, black, and windswept, and a car is a haven of refuge. From village to village the miners travel, for a change of cinema, of girl, of pub. The trams are desperately packed. Who is going to risk himself in the black gulf outside, to wait perhaps an hour for another tram, then to see the forlorn notice " Depot Only," because there is something wrong ! Or to greet a unit of three bright cars all so tight with people that they sail past with a howl of derision. Trams that pass in the night.

This, the most dangerous tram-service in England, as the authorities themselves declare, with pride, is entirely conducted by girls, and driven by rash young men, a little crippled, or by delicate young men, who creep forward in terror. The girls are fearless young hussies. In their ugly blue uniform, skirts up to their knees, shapeless old peaked caps on their heads, they have all the sang-froid of an old non-commissioned officer. With a tram packed with howling colliers, roaring hymns downstairs and a sort of antiphony of obscenities upstairs, the lasses are perfectly at their ease. They pounce on the youths who try to evade their ticket-machine. They push off the men at the end of their distance. They are not going to be done in the eye—not they. They fear nobody—and everybody fears them.

" Hello, Annie ! "

" Hello, Ted ! "

" Oh, mind my corn, Miss Stone. It's my belief you've got a heart of stone, for you've trod on it again."

" You should keep it in your pocket," replies Miss Stone, and she goes sturdily upstairs in her high boots.

" Tick ts, please."

She is peremptory, suspicious, and ready to hit first. She can hold her own against ten thousand. The step of that tram-car is her Thermopylæ.

Therefore, there is a certain wild romance aboard these cars— and in the sturdy bosom of Annie herself. The time for soft romance is in the morning, between ten o'clock and one, when things are rather slack : that is, except market-day and Saturday. Thus Annie has time to look about her. Then she often hops off her car

and into a shop where she has spied something, while the driver
chats in the main road. There is very good feeling between the girls
and the drivers. Are they not companions in peril, shipments
aboard this careering vessel of a tram-car, for ever rocking on the
waves of a stormy land.

Then, also, during the easy hours, the inspectors are most in
evidence. For some reason, everybody employed in this tram-service
is young : there are no grey heads. It would not do. Therefore
the inspectors are of the right age, and one, the chief, is also good-
looking. See him stand on a wet, gloomy morning, in his long oilskin, his peaked cap well down over his eyes, waiting to board a
car. His face is ruddy, his small brown moustache is weathered,
he has a faint impudent smile. Fairly tall and agile, even in his
waterproof, he springs aboard a car and greets Annie.

" Hello, Annie ! Keeping the wet out ? "

" Trying to."

There are only two people in the car. Inspecting is soon over.
Then for a long and impudent chat on the foot-board, a good, easy,
twelve-mile chat.

The inspector's name is John Thomas Raynor—always called
John Thomas, except sometimes, in malice, Coddy. His face sets
in fury when he is addressed, from a distance, with this abbreviation.
There is considerable scandal about John Thomas in half a dozen
villages. He flirts with the girl conductors in the morning, and
walks out with them in the dark night, when they leave their tram-
car at the depôt. Of course, the girls quit the service frequently.
Then he flirts and walks out with the new-comer : always providing
she is sufficiently attractive, and that she will consent to walk. It is
remarkable, however, that most of the girls are quite comely, they
are all young, and this roving life aboard the car gives them a
sailor's dash and recklessness. What matter how they behave when
the ship is in port ? To-morrow they will be aboard again.

Annie, however, was something of a Tartar, and her sharp tongue
had kept John Thomas at arm's length for many months. Perhaps,
therefore, she liked him all the more : for he always came up smiling,
with impudence. She watched him vanquish one girl, then another.
She could tell by the movement of his mouth and eyes, when he
flirted with her in the morning, that he had been walking out with
this lass, or the other, the night before. A fine cock-of-the-walk he
was. She could sum him up pretty well.

In this subtle antagonism they knew each other like old friends,
they were as shrewd with one another almost as man and wife. But

Annie had always kept him sufficiently at arm's length. Besides, she had a boy of her own.

The Statutes fair, however, came in November, at Bestwood. It happened that Annie had the Monday night off. It was a drizzling ugly night, yet she dressed herself up and went to the fair ground. She was alone, but she expected soon to find a pal of some sort.

The roundabouts were veering round and grinding out their music, the side-shows were making as much commotion as possible. In the coco-nut shies there were no coco-nuts, but artificial war-time substitutes, which the lads declared were fastened into the irons. There was a sad decline in brilliance and luxury. None the less, the ground was muddy as ever, there was the same crush, the press of faces lighted up by the flares and the electric lights, the same smell of naphtha and a few fried potatoes, and of electricity.

Who should be the first to greet Miss Annie on the show-ground but John Thomas. He had a black overcoat buttoned up to his chin, and a tweed cap pulled down over his brows, his face between was ruddy and smiling and handy as ever. She knew so well the way his mouth moved.

She was very glad to have a " boy." To be at the Statutes without a fellow was no fun. Instantly, like the gallant he was, he took her on the Dragons, grim-toothed, roundabout switchbacks. It was not nearly so exciting as a tram-car actually. But, then, to be seated in a shaking, green dragon, uplifted above the sea of bubble faces, careering in a rickety fashion in the lower heavens, whilst John Thomas leaned over her, his cigarette in his mouth, was after all the right style. She was a plump, quick, alive little creature. So she was quite excited and happy.

John Thomas made her stay on for the next round. And therefore she could hardly for shame repulse him when he put his arm round her and drew her a little nearer to him, in a very warm and cuddly manner. Besides, he was fairly discreet, he kept his movement as hidden as possible. She looked down, and saw that his red, clean hand was out of sight of the crowd. And they knew each other so well. So they warmed up to the fair.

After the dragons they went on the horses. John Thomas paid each time, so she could but be complaisant. He, of course, sat astride on the outer horse—named " Black Bess "—and she sat sideways, towards him, on the inner horse—named " Wildfire." But of course John Thomas was not going to sit discreetly on " Black Bess," holding the brass bar. Round they spun and heaved, in the light. And round he swung on his wooden steed, flinging one leg across her

mount, and perilously tipping up and down, across the space, half
lying back, laughing at her. He was perfectly happy ; she was afraid
her hat was on one side, but she was excited.

He threw quoits on a table, and won for her two large, pale blue
hat-pins. And then, hearing the noise of the cinemas, announcing
another performance, they climbed the boards and went in.

Of course, during these performances pitch darkness falls from
time to time, when the machine goes wrong. Then there is a wild
whooping, and a loud smacking of simulated kisses. In these
moments John Thomas drew Annie towards him. After all, he had
a wonderfully warm, cosy way of holding a girl with his arm, he
seemed to make such a nice fit. And, after all, it was pleasant to be
so held : so very comforting and cosy and nice. He leaned over her
and she felt his breath on her hair ; she knew he wanted to kiss her
on the lips. And, after all, he was so warm and she fitted in to him
so softly. After all, she wanted him to touch her lips.

But the light sprang up ; she also started electrically, and put
her hat straight. He left his arm lying nonchalantly behind her.
Well, it was fun, it was exciting to be at the Statutes with John
Thomas.

When the cinema was over they went for a walk across the dark,
damp fields. He had all the arts of love-making. He was especially
good at holding a girl, when he sat with her on a stile in the black,
drizzling darkness. He seemed to be holding her in space, against
his own warmth and gratification. And his kisses were soft and
slow and searching.

So Annie walked out with John Thomas, though she kept her own
boy dangling in the distance. Some of the tram-girls chose to be
huffy. But there, you must take things as you find them, in this life.

There was no mistake about it, Annie liked John Thomas a good
deal. She felt so rich and warm in herself whenever he was near.
And John Thomas really liked Annie, more than usual. The soft,
melting way in which she could flow into a fellow, as if she melted
into his very bones, was something rare and good. He fully appreciated this.

But with a developing acquaintance there began a developing
intimacy. Annie wanted to consider him a person, a man : she
wanted to take an intelligent interest in him, and to have an intelligent response. She did not want a mere nocturnal presence, which
was what he was so far. And she prided herself that he could not
leave her.

Here she made a mistake. John Thomas intended to remain a

nocturnal presence ; he had no idea of becoming an all-round individual to her. When she started to take an intelligent interest in him and his life and his character, he sheered off. He hated intelligent interest. And he knew that the only way to stop it was to avoid it. The possessive female was aroused in Annie. So he left her.

It is no use saying she was not surprised. She was at first startled, thrown out of her count. For she had been so *very* sure of holding him. For a while she was staggered, and everything became uncertain to her. Then she wept with fury, indignation, desolation, and misery. Then she had a spasm of despair. And then, when he came, still impudently, on to her car, still familiar, but letting her see by the movement of his head that he had gone away to somebody else for the time being, and was enjoying pastures new, then she determined to have her own back.

She had a very shrewd idea what girls John Thomas had taken out. She went to Nora Purdy. Nora was a tall, rather pale, but well-built girl, with beautiful yellow hair. She was rather secretive.

" Hey ! " said Annie, accosting her ; then softly, " Who's John Thomas on with now ? "

" I don't know," said Nora.

" Why, tha does," said Annie, ironically lapsing into dialect. " Tha knows as well as I do."

" Well, I do, then," said Nora. " It isn't me, so don't bother."

" It's Cissy Meakin, isn't it ? "

" It is, for all I know."

" Hasn't he got a face on him ! " said Annie. " I don't half like his cheek. I could knock him off the footboard when he comes round at me."

" He'll get dropped on one of these days," said Nora.

" Ay, he will, when somebody makes up their mind to drop it on him. I should like to see him taken down a peg or two, shouldn't you ? "

" I shouldn't mind," said Nora.

" You've got quite as much cause to as I have," said Annie. " But we'll drop on him one of these days, my girl. What ? Don't you want to ? "

" I don't mind," said Nora.

But as a matter of fact, Nora was much more vindictive than Annie.

One by one Annie went the round of the old flames. It so happened that Cissy Meakin left the tramway service in quite a short time. Her mother made her leave. Then John Thomas was on the qui vive. He cast his eyes over his old flock. And his eyes lighted on Annie. He thought she would be safe now. Besides, he liked her.

She arranged to walk home with him on Sunday night. It so happened that her car would be in the depôt at half-past nine : the last car would come in at 10.15. So John Thomas was to wait for her there.

At the depôt the girls had a little waiting-room of their own. It was quite rough, but cosy, with a fire and an oven and a mirror, and table and wooden chairs. The half-dozen girls who knew John Thomas only too well had arranged to take service this Sunday afternoon. So, as the cars began to come in, early, the girls dropped into the waiting-room. And instead of hurrying off home, they sat around the fire and had a cup of tea. Outside was the darkness and lawlessness of war-time.

John Thomas came on the car after Annie, at about a quarter to ten. He poked his head easily into the girls' waiting-room.

" Prayer-meeting ? " he asked.

" Ay," said Laura Sharp. " Ladies only."

" That's me ! " said John Thomas. It was one of his favourite exclamations.

" Shut the door, boy," said Muriel Baggaley.

" Oh which side of me ? " said John Thomas.

" Which tha likes," said Polly Birkin.

He had come in and closed the door behind him. The girls moved in their circle, to make a place for him near the fire. He took off his great-coat and pushed back his hat.

" Who handles the teapot ? " he said.

Nora Purdy silently poured him out a cup of tea.

" Want a bit o' my bread and drippin' ? " said Muriel Baggaley to him.

" Ay, give us a bit."

And he began to eat his piece of bread.

" There's no place like home, girls," he said.

They all looked at him as he uttered this piece of impudence. He seemed to be sunning himself in the presence of so many damsels.

" Especially if you're not afraid to go home in the dark," said Laura Sharp.

" Me ! By myself I am."

They sat till they heard the last tram come in. In a few minutes Emma Houselay entered.

" Come on, my old duck ! " cried Polly Birkin.

" It *is* perishing," said Emma, holding her fingers to the fire.

" But—I'm afraid to, go home in, the dark," sang Laura Sharp, the tune having got into her mind.

" Who're you going with to-night, John Thomas ? " asked Muriel Baggaley, coolly.

" To-night ? " said John Thomas.   " Oh, I'm going home by myself to-night—all on my lonely-o."

" That's me ! " said Nora Purdy, using his own ejaculation.

The girls laughed shrilly.

" Me as well, Nora," said John Thomas.

" Don't know what you mean," said Laura.

" Yes, I'm toddling," said he, rising and reaching for his overcoat.

" Nay," said Polly.   " We're all here waiting for you."

" We've got to be up in good time in the morning," he said, in the benevolent official manner.

They all laughed.

" Nay," said Muriel.   " Don't leave us all lonely, John Thomas. Take one ! "

" I'll take the lot, if you like," he responded gallantly.

" That you won't, either," said Muriel.   " Two's company ; seven's too much of a good thing."

" Nay—take one," said Laura.   " Fair and square, all above board and say which."

" Ay," cried Annie, speaking for the first time.   " Pick, John Thomas ; let's hear thee."

" Nay," he said.   " I'm going home quiet to-night. Feeling good, for once."

" Whereabouts ? " said Annie.   " Take a good 'un, then. But tha's got to take one of us ! "

" Nay, how can I take one," he said, laughing uneasily.   " I don't want to make enemies."

" You'd only make *one*," said Annie.

" The chosen *one*," added Laura.

" Oh, my ! Who said girls ! " exclaimed John Thomas, again turning, as if to escape.   " Well—good-night."

" Nay, you've got to make your pick," said Muriel.   " Turn your face to the wall, and say which one touches you. Go on—we shall only just touch your back—one of us.   Go on—turn your face to the wall, and don't look, and say which one touches you."

He was uneasy, mistrusting them.   Yet he had not the courage to break away.   They pushed him to a wall and stood him there with his face to it.   Behind his back they all grimaced, tittering.   He looked so comical.   He looked around uneasily.

" Go on ! " he cried.

" You're looking—you're looking ! " they shouted.

He turned his head away. And suddenly, with a movement like a swift cat, Annie went forward and fetched him a box on the side of the head that sent his cap flying and himself staggering. He started round.

But at Annie's signal they all flew at him, slapping him, pinching him, pulling his hair, though more in fun than in spite or anger. He, however, saw red. His blue eyes flamed with strange fear as well as fury, and he butted through the girls to the door. It was locked. He wrenched at it. Roused, alert, the girls stood round and looked at him. He faced them, at bay. At that moment they were rather horrifying to him, as they stood in their short uniforms. He was distinctly afraid.

" Come on, John Thomas ! Come on ! Choose ! " said Annie.

" What are you after ? Open the door," he said.

" We shan't—not till you've chosen ! " said Muriel.

" Chosen what ? " he said.

" Chosen the one you're going to marry," she replied.

He hesitated a moment.

" Open the blasted door," he said, " and get back to your senses." He spoke with official authority.

" You've got to choose ! " cried the girls.

" Come on ! " cried Annie, looking him in the eye. " Come on ! Come on ! "

He went forward, rather vaguely. She had taken off her belt, and swinging it, she fetched him a sharp blow over the head with the buckle end. He sprang and seized her. But immediately the other girls rushed upon him, pulling and tearing and beating him. Their blood was now thoroughly up. He was their sport now. They were going to have their own back, out of him. Strange, wild creatures, they hung on him and rushed at him to bear him down. His tunic was torn right up the back, Nora had hold at the back of his collar, and was actually strangling him. Luckily the button burst. He struggled in a wild frenzy of fury and terror, almost mad terror. His tunic was simply torn off his back, his shirt-sleeves were torn away, his arms were naked. The girls rushed at him, clenched their hands on him and pulled at him : or they rushed at him and pushed him, butted him with all their might : or they struck him wild blows. He ducked and cringed and struck sideways. They became more intense.

At last he was down. They rushed on him, kneeling on him. He had neither breath nor strength to move. His face was bleeding with a long scratch, his brow was bruised.

Annie knelt on him, the other girls knelt and hung on to him. Their faces were flushed, their hair wild, their eyes were all glittering strangely. He lay at last quite still, with face averted, as an animal lies when it is defeated and at the mercy of the captor. Sometimes his eye glanced back at the wild faces of the girls. His breast rose heavily, his wrists were torn.

" Now, then, my fellow ! " gasped Annie at length. " Now then —now—— "

At the sound of her terrifying, cold triumph, he suddenly started to struggle as an animal might, but the girls threw themselves upon him with unnatural strength and power, forcing him down.

" Yes—now, then ! " gasped Annie at length.

And there was a dead silence, in which the thud of heart-beating was to be heard. It was a suspense of pure silence in every soul.

" Now you know where you are," said Annie.

The sight of his white, bare arm maddened the girls. He lay in a kind of trance of fear and antagonism. They felt themselves filled with supernatural strength.

Suddenly Polly started to laugh—to giggle wildly—helplessly— and Emma and Muriel joined in. But Annie and Nora and Laura remained the same, tense, watchful, with gleaming eyes. He winced away from these eyes.

" Yes," said Annie, in a curious low tone, secret and deadly. " Yes! You've got it now. You know what you've done, don't you ? You know what you've done."

He made no sound nor sign, but lay with bright, averted eyes, and averted, bleeding face.

" You ought to be *killed*, that's what you ought," said Annie, tensely. " You ought to be *killed*." And there was a terrifying lust in her voice.

Polly was ceasing to laugh, and giving long-drawn Oh-h-hs and sighs as she came to herself.

" He's got to choose," she said vaguely.

" Oh, yes, he has," said Laura, with vindictive decision.

" Do you hear—do you hear ? " said Annie. And with a sharp movement, that made him wince, she turned his face to her.

" Do you hear ? " she repeated, shaking him.

But he was quite dumb. She fetched him a sharp slap on the face. He started, and his eyes widened. Then his face darkened with defiance, after all.

" Do you hear ? " she repeated.

He only looked at her with hostile eyes.

" Speak ! " she said, putting her face devilishly near his.

" What ? " he said, almost overcome.

" You've got to *choose !* " she cried, as if it were some terrible menace, and as if it hurt her that she could not exact more.

" What ? " he said, in fear.

" Choose your girl, Coddy. You've got to choose her now. And you'll get your neck broken if you play any more of your tricks, my boy. You're settled now."

There was a pause. Again he averted his face. He was cunning in his overthrow. He did not give in to them really—no, not if they tore him to bits.

" All right, then," he said, " I choose Annie." His voice was strange and full of malice. Annie let go of him as if he had been a hot coal.

" He's chosen Annie ! " said the girls in chorus.

" Me ! " cried Annie. She was still kneeling, but away from him. He was still lying prostrate, with averted face. The girls grouped uneasily around.

" Me ! " repeated Annie, with a terrible bitter accent.

Then she got up, drawing away from him with strange disgust and bitterness.

" I wouldn't touch him," she said.

But her face quivered with a kind of agony, she seemed as if she would fall. The other girls turned aside. He remained lying on the floor, with his torn clothes and bleeding, averted face.

" Oh, if he's chosen——" said Polly.

" I don't want him—he can choose again," said Annie, with the same rather bitter hopelessness.

" Get up," said Polly, lifting his shoulder. " Get up."

He rose slowly, a strange, ragged, dazed creature. The girls eyed him from a distance, curiously, furtively, dangerously.

" Who wants him ? " cried Laura, roughly.

" Nobody," they answered, with contempt. Yet each one of them waited for him to look at her, hoped he would look at her. All except Annie, and something was broken in her.

He, however, kept his face closed and averted from them all. There was a silence of the end. He picked up the torn pieces of his tunic, without knowing what to do with them. The girls stood about uneasily, flushed, panting, tidying their hair and their dress unconsciously, and watching him. He looked at none of them. He espied his cap in a corner, and went and picked it up. He put it on his head, and one of the girls burst into a shrill, hysteric laugh at the sight he presented. He, however, took no heed, but went straight to where his overcoat hung on a peg. The girls moved away from contact with him as if he had been an electric wire. He put on his coat and buttoned it down. Then he rolled his tunic-rags into a bundle, and stood before the locked door, dumbly.

" Open the door, somebody," said Laura.

" Annie's got the key," said one.

Annie silently offered the key to the girls. Nora unlocked the door.

" Tit for tat, old man," she said. " Show yourself a man, and don't bear a grudge."

But without a word or sign he had opened the door and gone, his face closed, his head dropped.

" That'll learn him," said Laura.

" Coddy ! " said Nora.

" Shut up, for God's sake ! " cried Annie fiercely, as if in torture.

" Well, I'm about ready to go, Polly. Look sharp ! " said Muriel.

The girls were all anxious to be off. They were tidying themselves hurriedly, with mute, stupefied faces.

ISABEL PERVIN was listening for two sounds—for the sound of wheels on the drive outside and for the noise of her husband's footsteps in the hall. Her dearest and oldest friend, a man who seemed almost indispensable to her living, would drive up in the rainy dusk of the closing November day. The trap had gone to fetch him from the station. And her husband, who had been blinded in Flanders, and who had a disfiguring mark on his brow, would be coming in from the outhouses.

He had been home for a year now. He was totally blind. Yet they had been very happy. The Grange was Maurice's own place. The back was a farmstead, and the Wernhams, who occupied the rear premises, acted as farmers. Isabel lived with her husband in the handsome rooms in front. She and he had been almost entirely alone together since he was wounded. They talked and sang and read together in a wonderful and unspeakable intimacy. Then she reviewed books for a Scottish newspaper, carrying on her old interest, and he occupied himself a good deal with the farm. Sightless, he could still discuss everything with Wernham, and he could also do a good deal of work about the place—menial work, it is true, but it gave him satisfaction. He milked the cows, carried in the pails, turned the separator, attended to the pigs and horses. Life was still very full and strangely serene for the blind man, peaceful with the almost incomprehensible peace of immediate contact in darkness. With his wife he had a whole world, rich and real and invisible.

They were newly and remotely happy. He did not even regret the loss of his sight in these times of dark, palpable joy. A certain exultance swelled his soul.

But as time wore on, sometimes the rich glamour would leave them. Sometimes, after months of this intensity, a sense of burden overcame Isabel, a weariness, a terrible *ennui*, in that silent house approached between a colonnade of tall-shafted pines. Then she felt she would go mad, for she could not bear it. And sometimes he had devastating fits of depression, which seemed to lay waste his whole being. It was worse than depression—a black misery, when his own life was a torture to him, and when his presence was unbearable to his wife. The dread went down to the roots of her soul as these black days recurred. In a kind of panic she tried to wrap herself up still further in her husband. She forced the old spontaneous cheerfulness and joy to continue. But the effort it cost her was almost too much. She knew she could not keep it up. She felt she would scream with the strain, and would give anything, anything, to escape. She longed to possess her husband utterly ; it gave her inordinate joy to have him entirely to herself. And yet, when again he was gone in a black and massive misery, she could not bear him, she could not bear herself ; she wished she could be snatched away off the earth altogether, anything rather than live at this cost.

Dazed, she schemed for a way out. She invited friends, she tried to give him some further connection with the outer world. But it was no good. After all their joy and suffering, after their dark, great year of blindness and solitude and unspeakable nearness, other people seemed to them both shallow, prattling, rather impertinent. Shallow prattle seemed presumptuous. He became impatient and irritated, she was wearied. And so they lapsed into their solitude again. For they preferred it.

But now, in a few weeks' time, her second baby would be born. The first had died, an infant, when her husband first went out to France. She looked with joy and relief to the coming of the second. It would be her salvation. But also she felt some anxiety. She was thirty years old, her husband was a year younger. They both wanted the child very much. Yet she could not help feeling afraid. She had her husband on her hands, a terrible joy to her, and a terrifying burden. The child would occupy her love and attention. And then, what of Maurice ? What would he do ? If only she could feel that he, too, would be at peace and happy when the child came ! She did so want to luxuriate in a rich, physical satisfaction of maternity. But the man, what would he do ? How could she provide for him, how avert those shattering black moods of his, which destroyed them both ?

She sighed with fear. But at this time Bertie Reid wrote to Isabel. He was her old friend, a second or third cousin, a Scotchman, as she was a Scotchwoman. They had been brought up near to one another, and all her life he had been her friend, like a brother, but better than her own brothers. She loved him—though not in the marrying sense. There was a sort of kinship between them, an affinity. They understood one another instinctively. But Isabel would never have thought of marrying Bertie. It would have seemed like marrying in her own family.

Bertie was a barrister and a man of letters, a Scotchman of the intellectual type, quick, ironical, sentimental, and on his knees before the woman he adored but did not want to marry. Maurice Pervin was different. He came òf a good old country family—the Grange was not a very great distance from Oxford. He was passionate, sensitive, perhaps over-sensitive, wincing—a big fellow with heavy limbs and a forehead that flushed painfully. For his mind was slow, as if drugged by the strong provincial blood that beat in his veins. He was very sensitive to his own mental slowness, his feelings being quick and acute. So that he was just the opposite to Bertie, whose mind was much quicker than his emotions, which were not so very fine.

From the first the two men did not like each other. Isabel felt that they *ought* to get on together. But they did not. She felt that if only each could have the clue to the other there would be such a rare understanding between them. It did not come off, however. Bertie adopted a slightly ironical attitude, very offensive to Maurice, who returned the Scotch irony with English resentment, a resentment which deepened sometimes into stupid hatred.

This was a little puzzling to Isabel. However, she accepted it in the course of things. Men were made freakish and unreasonable. Therefore, when Maurice was going out to France for the second time, she felt that, for her husband's sake, she must discontinue her friendship with Bertie. She wrote to the barrister to this effect. Bertram Reid simply replied that in this, as in all other matters, he must obey her wishes, if these were indeed her wishes.

For nearly two years nothing had passed between the two friends. Isabel rather gloried in the fact ; she had no compunction. She had one great article of faith, which was, that husband and wife should be so important to one another, that the rest of the world simply did not count. She and Maurice were husband and wife. They loved one another. They would have children. Then let everybody and everything else fade into insignificance outside this connubial felicity. She professed herself quite happy and ready to receive Maurice's friends. She was happy and ready : the happy wife, the ready woman in possession. Without knowing why, the friends retired abashed, and came no more. Maurice, of course, took as much satisfaction in this connubial absorption as Isabel did.

He shared in Isabel's literary activities, she cultivated a real interest in agriculture and cattle-raising. For she, being at heart perhaps an emotional enthusiast, always cultivated the practical side of life, and prided herself on her mastery of practical affairs.

Thus the husband and wife had spent the five years of their married life. The last had been one of blindness and unspeakable intimacy. And now Isabel felt a great indifference coming over her, a sort of lethargy. She wanted to be allowed to bear her child in peace, to nod by the fire and drift vaguely, physically, from day to day. Maurice was like an ominous thunder-cloud. She had to keep waking up to remember him.

When a little note came from Bertie, asking if he were to put up a tombstone to their dead friendship, and speaking of the real pain he felt on account of her husband's loss of sight, she felt a pang, a fluttering agitation of re-awakening. And she read the letter to Maurice.

" Ask him to come down," he said.

" Ask Bertie to come here ! " she re-echoed.

" Yes—if he wants to."

Isabel paused for a few moments.

" I know he wants to—he'd only be too glad," she replied. " But what about you, Maurice ? How would you like it ? "

" I should like it."

" Well—in that case——But I thought you didn't care for him——"

" Oh, I don't know. I might think differently of him now," the blind man replied. It was rather abstruse to Isabel.

" Well, dear," she said, " if you're quite sure——"

" I'm sure enough. Let him come," said Maurice.

So Bertie was coming, coming this evening, in the November rain and darkness. Isabel was agitated, racked with her old restlessness and indecision. She had always suffered from this pain of doubt, just an agonizing sense of uncertainty. It had begun to pass off, in the lethargy of maternity. Now it returned, and she resented it. She struggled as usual to maintain her calm, composed, friendly bearing, a sort of mask she wore over all her body.

A woman had lighted a tall lamp beside the table, and spread the cloth. The long dining-room was dim, with its elegant but rather severe pieces of old furniture. Only the round table glowed softly under the light. It had a rich, beautiful effect. The white cloth glistened and dropped its heavy, pointed lace corners almost to the carpet, the china was old and handsome, creamy-yellow, with a blotched pattern of harsh red and deep blue, the cups large and bell-shaped, the teapot gallant. Isabel looked at it with superficial appreciation.

Her nerves were hurting her. She looked automatically again

at the high, uncurtained windows. In the last dusk she could just perceive outside a huge fir-tree swaying its boughs : it was as if she thought it rather than saw it. The rain came flying on the window panes. Ah, why had she no peace ? These two men, why did they tear at her ? Why did they not come—why was there this suspense ?

She sat in a lassitude that was really suspense and irritation. Maurice, at least, might come in—there was nothing to keep him out. She rose to her feet. Catching sight of her reflection in a mirror, she glanced at herself with a slight smile of recognition, as if she were an old friend to herself. Her face was oval and calm, her nose a little arched. Her neck made a beautiful line down to her shoulder. With hair knotted loosely behind, she had something of a warm, maternal look. Thinking this of herself, she arched her eyebrows and her rather heavy eyelids, with a little flicker of a smile, and for a moment her grey eyes looked amused and wicked, a little sardonic, out of her transfigured Madonna face.

Then, resuming her air of womanly patience—she was really fatally self-determined—she went with a little jerk towards the door. Her eyes were slightly reddened.

She passed down the wide hall, and through a door at the end. Then she was in the farm premises. The scent of dairy, and of farm-kitchen, and of farm-yard and of leather almost overcame her : but particularly the scent of dairy. They had been scalding out the pans. The flagged passage in front of her was dark, puddled and wet. Light came out from the open kitchen door. She went forward and stood in the doorway. The farm-people were at tea, seated at a little distance from her, round a long, narrow table, in the centre of which stood a white lamp. Ruddy faces, ruddy hands holding food, red mouths working, heads bent over the tea-cups : men, land-girls, boys : it was tea-time, feeding-time. Some faces caught sight of her. Mrs. Wernham, going round behind the chairs with a large black teapot, halting slightly in her walk, was not aware of her for a moment. Then she turned suddenly.

" Oh, is it Madam ! " she exclaimed. " Come in, then, come in ! We're at tea." And she dragged forward a chair.

" No, I won't come in," said Isabel. " I'm afraid I interrupt your meal."

" No—no—not likely, Madam, not likely."

" Hasn't Mr. Pervin come in, do you know ? "

" I'm sure I couldn't say ! Missed him, have you, Madam ? "

" No, I only wanted him to come in," laughed Isabel, as if shyly.

" Wanted him, did ye ? Get up, boy—get up, now——"

Mrs. Wernham knocked one of the boys on the shoulder. He began to scrape to his feet, chewing largely.

" I believe he's in top stable," said another face from the table.

" Ah ! No, don't get up. I'm going myself," said Isabel.

" Don't you go out of a dirty night like this. Let the lad go. Get along wi' ye, boy," said Mrs. Wernham.

" No, no," said Isabel, with a decision that was always obeyed. " Go on with your tea, Tom. I'd like to go across to the stable, Mrs. Wernham."

" Did ever you hear tell ! " exclaimed the woman.

" Isn't the trap late ? " asked Isabel.

" Why, no," said Mrs. Wernham, peering into the distance at the tall, dim clock. " No, Madam—we can give it another quarter or twenty minutes yet, good—yes, every bit of a quarter."

" Ah ! It seems late when darkness falls so early," said Isabel.

" It do, that it do. Bother the days, that they draw in so," answered Mrs. Wernham. " Proper miserable ! "

" They are," said Isabel, withdrawing.

She pulled on her overshoes, wrapped a large tartan shawl around her, put on a man's felt hat, and ventured out along the causeways of the first yard. It was very dark. The wind was roaring in the great elms behind the outhouses. When she came to the second yard the darkness seemed deeper. She was unsure of her footing. She wished she had brought a lantern. Rain blew against her. Half she liked it, half she felt unwilling to battle.

She reached at last the just visible door of the stable. There was no sign of a light anywhere. Opening the upper half, she looked in : into a simple well of darkness. The smell of horses, and ammonia, and of warmth was startling to her, in that full night. She listened with all her ears, but could hear nothing save the night, and the stirring of a horse.

"Maurice ! " she called, softly and musically, though she was afraid. "Maurice—are you there ? "

Nothing came from the darkness. She knew the rain and wind blew in upon the horses, the hot animal life. Feeling it wrong, she entered the stable, and drew the lower half of the door shut, holding the upper part close. She did not stir, because she was aware of the presence of the dark hindquarters of the horses, though she could not see them, and she was afraid. Something wild stirred in her heart.

She listened intensely. Then she heard a small noise in the distance—far away, it seemed—the chink of a pan, and a man's voice speaking a brief word. It would be Maurice, in the other part of the stable. She stood motionless, waiting for him to come through the partition door. The horses were so terrifyingly near to her, in the invisible.

The loud jarring of the inner door-latch made her start ; the door was opened. She could hear and feel her husband entering and invisibly passing among the horses near to her, in darkness as they were, actively intermingled. The rather low sound of his voice as he spoke to the horses came velvety to her nerves. How near he was, and how invisible ! The darkness seemed to be in a strange swirl of violent life, just upon her. She turned giddy.

Her presence of mind made her call, quietly and musically :

" Maurice ! Maurice—dea-ar ! "

" Yes," he answered. " Isabel ? "

She saw nothing, and the sound of his voice seemed to touch her.

" Hello ! " she answered cheerfully, straining her eyes to see him. He was still busy, attending to the horses near her, but she saw only darkness. It made her almost desperate.

" Won't you come in, dear ? " she said.

" Yes, I'm coming. Just half a minute. *Stand over—now !* Trap's not come, has it ? "

" Not yet," said Isabel.

His voice was pleasant and ordinary, but it had a slight suggestion of the stable to her. She wished he would come away. While he was so utterly invisible she was afraid of him.

" How's the time ? " he asked.

" Not yet six," she replied. She disliked to answer into the dark. Presently he came very near to her, and she retreated out of doors.

" The weather blows in here," he said, coming steadily forward, feeling for the doors. She shrank away. At last she could dimly see him.

" Bertie won't have much of a drive," he said, as he closed the doors.

" He won't indeed ! " said Isabel calmly, watching the dark shape at the door.

" Give me your arm, dear," she said.

She pressed his arm close to her, as she went. But she longed to see him, to look at him. She was nervous. He walked erect, with face rather lifted, but with a curious tentative movement of his powerful, muscular legs. She could feel the clever, careful, strong contact of his feet with the earth, as she balanced against him. For a moment he was a tower of darkness to her, as if he rose out of the earth.

In the house-passage he wavered, and went cautiously, with a curious look of silence about him as he felt for the bench. Then he sat down heavily. He was a man with rather sloping shoulders, but with heavy limbs, powerful legs that seemed to know the earth. His head was small, usually carried high and light. As he bent down to unfasten his gaiters and boots he did not look blind. His hair was brown and crisp, his hands were large, reddish, intelligent, the veins stood out in the wrists ; and his thighs and knees seemed massive. When he stood up his face and neck were surcharged with blood, the veins stood out on his temples. She did not look at his blindness.

Isabel was always glad when they had passed through the dividing door into their own regions of repose and beauty. She was a little afraid of him, out there in the animal grossness of the back. His bearing also changed, as he smelt the familiar, indefinable odour that pervaded his wife's surroundings, a delicate, refined scent, very faintly spicy. Perhaps it came from the potpourri bowls.

He stood at the foot of the stairs, arrested, listening. She watched him, and her heart sickened. He seemed to be listening to fate.

" He's not here yet," he said. " I'll go up and change."

" Maurice," she said, " you're not wishing he wouldn't come, are you ? "

" I couldn't quite say," he answered. " I feel myself rather on the qui vive."

" I can see you are," she answered. And she reached up and kissed his cheek. She saw his mouth relax into a slow smile.

" What are you laughing at ? " she said roguishly.

" You consoling me," he answered.

" Nay," she answered. " Why should I console you ? You know we love each other—you know *how* married we are ! What does anything else matter ? "

" Nothing at all, my dear."

He felt for her face, and touched it, smiling.

" *You're* all right, aren't you ? " he asked, anxiously.

" I'm wonderfully all right, love," she answered. " It's you I am a little troubled about, at times."

" Why me ? " he said, touching her cheeks delicately with the tips of his fingers. The touch had an almost hypnotizing effect on her.

He went away upstairs. She saw him mount into the darkness, unseeing and unchanging. He did not know that the lamps on the upper corridor were unlighted. He went on into the darkenss with unchanging step. She heard him in the bathroom.

Pervin moved about almost unconsciously in his familiar surroundings, dark though everything was. He seemed to know the
presence of objects before he touched them. It was a pleasure to
him to rock thus through a world of things, carried on the flood in a
sort of blood-prescience. He did not think much or trouble much.
So long as he kept this sheer immediacy of blood-contact with the
substantial world he was happy, he wanted no intervention of visual
consciousness. In this state there was a certain rich positivity,
bordering sometimes on rapture. Life seemed to move in him like
a tide lapping, lapping, and advancing, enveloping all things
darkly. It was a pleasure to stretch forth the hand and meet the
unseen object, clasp it, and possess it in pure contact. He did not
try to remember, to visualize. He did not want to. The new way
of consciousness substituted itself in him.

The rich suffusion of this state generally kept him happy, reaching
its culmination in the consuming passion for his wife. But at times
the flow would seem to be checked and thrown back. Then it
would beat inside him like a tangled sea, and he was tortured in the
shattered chaos of his own blood. He grew to dread this arrest, this
throw-back, this chaos inside himself, when he seemed merely at
the mercy of his own powerful and conflicting elements. How to
get some measure of control or surety, this was the question. And
when the question rose maddening in him, he would clench his
fists as if he would *compel* the whole universe to submit to him. But
it was in vain. He could not even compel himself.

To-night, however, he was still serene, though little tremors of
unreasonable exasperation ran through him. He had to handle the
razor very carefully, as he shaved, for it was not at one with him, he
was afraid of it. His hearing also was too much sharpened. He
heard the woman lighting the lamps on the corridor, and attending
to the fire in the visitor's room. And then, as he went to his room he
heard the trap arrive. Then came Isabel's voice, lifted and calling,
like a bell ringing :

" Is it you, Bertie ? Have you come ? "

And a man's voice answered out of the wind :

" Hello, Isabel ! There you are."

" Have you had a miserable drive ? I'm so sorry we couldn't send
a closed carriage. I can't see you at all, you know."

" I'm coming. No, I liked the drive—it was like Perthshire.
Well, how are you ? You're looking fit as ever, as far as I can see."

" Oh, yes," said Isabel. " I'm wonderfully well. How are you ?
Rather thin, I think——"

" Worked to death—everybody's old cry. But I'm all right, Ciss.
How's Pervin ?—isn't he here ? "

" Oh, yes, he's upstairs changing. Yes, he's awfully well. Take
off your wet things ; I'll send them to be dried."

" And how are you both, in spirits ? He doesn't fret ? "

" No—no, not at all. No, on the contrary, really. We've been
wonderfully happy, incredibly. It's more than I can understand—
so wonderful : the nearness, and the peace——"

" Ah ! Well, that's awfully good news——"

They moved away. Pervin heard no more. But a childish sense
of desolation had come over him, as he heard their brisk voices.
He seemed shut out—like a child that is left out. He was aimless
and excluded, he did not know what to do with himself. The
helpless desolation came over him. He fumbled nervously as he
dressed himself, in a state almost of childishness. He disliked the
Scotch accent in Bertie's speech, and the slight response it found on
Isabel's tongue. He disliked the slight purr of complacency in the
Scottish speech. He disliked intensely the glib way in which Isabel
spoke of their happiness and nearness. It made him recoil. He was
fretful and beside himself like a child, he had almost a childish
nostalgia to be included in the life circle. And at the same time he
was a man, dark and powerful and infuriated by his own weakness.
By some fatal flaw, he could not be by himself, he had to depend on
the support of another. And this very dependence enraged him.
He hated Bertie Reid, and at the same time he knew the hatred was
nonsense, he knew it was the outcome of his own weakness.

He went downstairs. Isabel was alone in the dining-room.
She watched him enter, head erect, his feet tentative. He looked
so strong-blooded and healthy, and, at the same time, cancelled.
Cancelled—that was the word that flew across her mind. Perhaps
it was his scars suggested it.

" You heard Bertie come, Maurice ? " she said.

" Yes—isn't he here ? "

" He's in his room. He looks very thin and worn."

" I suppose he works himself to death."

A woman came in with a tray—and after a few minutes Bertie
came down. He was a little dark man, with a very big forehead,
thin, wispy hair, and sad, large eyes. His expression was inordin-
ately sad—almost funny. He had odd, short legs.

Isabel watched him hesitate under the door, and glance nervously
at her husband. Pervin heard him and turned.

" Here you are, now," said Isabel. " Come, let us eat."

Bertie went across to Maurice.

" How are you, Pervin ? " he said, as he advanced.

The blind man stuck his hand out into space, and Bertie took it.

" Very fit. Glad you've come," said Maurice.

Isabel glanced at them, and glanced away, as if she could not bear to see them.

" Come," she said. " Come to table. Aren't you both awfully hungry ? I am, tremendously."

" I'm afraid you waited for me," said Bertie, as they sat down.

Maurice had a curious monolithic way of sitting in a chair, erect and distant. Isabel's heart always beat when she caught sight of him thus.

" No," she replied to Bertie. " We're very little later than usual. We're having a sort of high tea, not dinner. Do you mind ? It gives us such a nice long evening, uninterrupted."

" I like it," said Bertie.

Maurice was feeling, with curious little movements, almost like a cat kneading her bed, for his place, his knife and fork, his napkin. He was getting the whole geography of his cover into his consciousness. He sat erect and inscrutable, remote-seeming. Bertie watched the static figure of the blind man, the delicate tactile discernment of the large, ruddy hands, and the curious mindless silence of the brow, above the scar. With difficulty he looked away, and without knowing what he did, picked up a little crystal bowl of violets from the table, and held them to his nose.

" They are sweet-scented," he said. " Where do they come from ? "

" From the garden—under the windows," said Isabel.

" So late in the year—and so fragrant ! Do you remember the violets under Aunt Bell's south wall ? "

The two friends looked at each other and exchanged a smile, Isabel's eyes lighting up.

" Don't I ? " she replied. " *Wasn't* she queer ! "

" A curious old girl," laughed Bertie. " There's a streak of freakishness in the family, Isabel."

" Ah—but not in you and me, Bertie," said Isabel. " Give them to Maurice, will you ? " she added, as Bertie was putting down the flowers. " Have you smelled the violets, dear ? Do !—they are so scented."

Maurice held out his hand, and Bertie placed the tiny bowl against his large, warm-looking fingers. Maurice's hand closed over the thin white fingers of the barrister. Bertie carefully extricated himself.

Then the two watched the blind man smelling the violets. He bent his head and seemed to be thinking. Isabel waited.

" Aren't they sweet, Maurice ? " she said at last, anxiously.

" Very," he said. And he held out the bowl. Bertie took it. Both he and Isabel were a little afraid, and deeply disturbed.

The meal continued. Isabel and Bertie chatted spasmodically. The blind man was silent. He touched his food repeatedly, with quick, delicate touches of his knife-point, then cut irregular bits. He could not bear to be helped. Both Isabel and Bertie suffered : Isabel wondered why. She did not suffer when she was alone with Maurice. Bertie made her conscious of a strangeness.

After the meal the three drew their chairs to the fire, and sat down to talk. The decanters were put on a table near at hand. Isabel knocked the logs on the fire, and clouds of brilliant sparks went up the chimney. Bertie noticed a slight weariness in her bearing.

" You will be glad when your child comes now, Isabel ? " he said.

She looked up to him with a quick wan smile.

" Yes, I shall be glad," she answered. " It begins to seem long. Yes, I shall be very glad. So will you, Maurice, won't you ? " she added.

" Yes, I shall," replied her husband.

" We are both looking forward so much to having it," she said.

" Yes, of course," said Bertie.

He was a bachelor, three or four years older than Isabel. He lived in beautiful rooms overlooking the river, guarded by a faithful Scottish manservant. And he had his friends among the fair sex— not lovers, friends. So long as he could avoid any danger of court- ship or marriage, he adored a few good women with constant and unfailing homage, and he was chivalrously fond of quite a number. But if they seemed to encroach on him, he withdrew and detested them.

Isabel knew him very well, knew his beautiful constancy, and kindness, also his incurable weakness, which made him unable ever to enter into close contact of any sort. He was ashamed of himself, because he could not marry, could not approach women physically. He wanted to do so. But he could not. At the centre of him he was afraid, helplessly and even brutally afraid. He had given up hope, had ceased to expect any more that he could escape his own weakness. Hence he was a brilliant and successful barrister, also *littérateur* of high repute, a rich man, and a great social success. At the centre he felt himself neuter, nothing.

Isabel knew him well. She despised him even while she admired him. She looked at his sad face, his little short legs, and felt contempt of him. She looked at his dark grey eyes, with their uncanny, almost childlike intuition, and she loved him. He understood amazingly—but she had no fear of his understanding. As a man she patronized him.

And she turned to the impassive, silent figure of her husband. He sat leaning back, with folded arms, and face a little uptilted. His knees were straight and massive. She sighed, picked up the poker, and again began to prod the fire, to rouse the clouds of soft, brilliant sparks.

"Isabel tells me," Bertie began suddenly, "that you have not suffered unbearably from the loss of sight."

Maurice straightened himself to attend, but kept his arms folded.

"No," he said, "not unbearably. Now and again one struggles against it, you know. But there are compensations."

"They say it is much worse to be stone deaf," said Isabel.

"I believe it is," said Bertie. "Are there compensations?" he added, to Maurice.

"Yes. You cease to bother about a great many things." Again Maurice stretched his figure, stretched the strong muscles of his back, and leaned backwards, with uplifted face.

"And that is a relief," said Bertie. "But what is there in place of the bothering? What replaces the activity?"

There was a pause. At length the blind man replied, as out of a negligent, unattentive thinking :

"Oh, I don't know. There's a good deal when you're not active."

"Is there?" said Bertie. "What, exactly? It always seems to me that when there is no thought and no action, there is nothing."

Again Maurice was slow in replying.

"There is something," he replied. "I couldn't tell you what it is."

And the talk lapsed once more, Isabel and Bertie chatting gossip and reminiscence, the blind man silent.

At length Maurice rose restlessly, a big, obtrusive figure. He felt tight and hampered. He wanted to go away.

"Do you mind," he said, "if I go and speak to Wernham?"

"No—go along, dear," said Isabel.

And he went out. A silence came over the two friends. At length Bertie said :

"Nevertheless, it is a great deprivation, Cissie."

"It is, Bertie. I know it is."

"Something lacking all the time," said Bertie.

" Yes, I know. And yet—and yet—Maurice is right. There is something else, something *there*, which you never knew was there, and which you can't express."

" What is there ? " asked Bertie.

" I don't know—it's awfully hard to define it—but something strong and immediate. There's something strange in Maurice's presence—indefinable—but I couldn't do without it. I agree that it seems to put one's mind to sleep. But when we're alone I miss nothing ; it seems awfully rich, almost splendid, you know."

" I'm afraid I don't follow," said Bertie.

They talked desultorily. The wind blew loudly outside, rain chattered on the window-panes, making a sharp, drum-sound, because of the closed, mellow-golden shutters inside. The logs burned slowly, with hot, almost invisible small flames. Bertie seemed uneasy, there were dark circles round his eyes. Isabel, rich with her approaching maternity, leaned looking into the fire. Her hair curled in odd, loose strands, very pleasing to the man. But she had a curious feeling of old woe in her heart, old, timeless night-woe.

" I suppose we're all deficient somewhere," said Bertie.

" I suppose so," said Isabel wearily.

" Damned, sooner or later."

" I don't know," she said, rousing herself. " I feel quite all right, you know. The child coming seems to make me indifferent to everything, just placid. I can't feel that there's anything to trouble about, you know."

" A good thing, I should say," he replied slowly.

" Well, there it is. I suppose it's just Nature, If only I felt I needn't trouble about Maurice, I should be perfectly content——"

" But you feel you must trouble about him ? "

" Well—I don't know——" She even resented this much effort.

The evening passed slowly. Isabel looked at the clock. " I say," she said. " It's nearly ten o'clock. Where can Maurice be ? I'm sure they're all in bed at the back. Excuse me a moment."

She went out, returning almost immediately.

" It's all shut up and in darkness," she said. " I wonder where he is. He must have gone out to the farm——"

Bertie looked at her.

" I suppose he'll come in," he said.

" I suppose so," she said. " But it's unusual for him to be out now."

" Would you like me to go out and see ? "

" Well—if you wouldn't mind. I'd go, but——" She did not want to make the physical effort.

Bertie put on an old overcoat and took a lantern. He went out from the side door. He shrank from the wet and roaring night. Such weather had a nervous effect on him : too much moisture everywhere made him feel almost imbecile. Unwilling, he went through it all. A dog barked violently at him. He peered in all the buildings. At last, as he opened the upper door of a sort of inter-mediate barn, he heard a grinding noise, and looking in, holding up his lantern, saw Maurice, in his shirt-sleeves, standing listening, holding the handle of a turnip-pulper. He had been pulping sweet roots, a pile of which lay dimly heaped in a corner behind him.

" That you, Wernham ? " said Maurice, listening.

" No, it's me," said Bertie.

A large, half-wild grey cat was rubbing at Maurice's leg. The blind man stooped to rub its sides. Bertie watched the scene, then unconsciously entered and shut the door behind him. He was in a high sort of barn-place, from which, right and left, ran off the corri-dors in front of the stalled cattle. He watched the slow, stooping motion of the other man, as he caressed the great cat.

Maurice straightened himself.

" You came to look for me ? " he said.

" Isabel was a little uneasy," said Bertie.

" I'll come in. I like messing about doing these jobs."

The cat had reared her sinister, feline length against his leg, clawing at his thigh affectionately. He lifted her claws out of his flesh.

" I hope I'm not in your way at all at the Grange here," said Bertie, rather shy and stiff.

" My way ? No, not a bit. I'm glad Isabel has somebody to talk to. I'm afraid it's I who am in the way. I know I'm not very lively company. Isabel's all right, don't you think ? She's not unhappy, is she ? "

" I don't think so."

" What does she say ? "

" She says she's very content—only a little troubled about you."

" Why me ? "

" Perhaps afraid that you might brood," said Bertie, cautiously.

" She needn't be afraid of that." He continued to caress the flattened grey head of the cat with his fingers. " What I am a bit afraid of," he resumed, " is that she'll find me a dead weight, always alone with me down here."

"I don't think you need think that," said Bertie, though this was what he feared himself.

"I don't know," said Maurice. "Sometimes I feel it isn't fair that she's saddled with me." Then he dropped his voice curiously. "I say," he asked, secretly struggling, "is my face much disfigured? Do you mind telling me?"

"There is the scar," said Bertie, wondering. "Yes, it is a disfigurement. But more pitiable than shocking."

"A pretty bad scar, though," said Maurice.

"Oh, yes."

There was a pause.

"Sometimes I feel I am horrible," said Maurice, in a low voice, talking as if to himself. And Bertie actually felt a quiver of horror.

"That's nonsense," he said.

Maurice again straightened himself, leaving the cat.

"There's no telling," he said. Then again, in an odd tone, he added: "I don't really know you, do I?"

"Probably not," said Bertie.

"Do you mind if I touch you?"

The lawyer shrank away instinctively. And yet, out of very philanthropy, he said, in a small voice: "Not at all."

But he suffered as the blind man stretched out a strong, naked hand to him. Maurice accidentally knocked off Bertie's hat.

"I thought you were taller," he said, starting. Then he laid his hand on Bertie Reid's head, closing the dome of the skull in a soft, firm grasp, gathering it, as it were; then, shifting his grasp and softly closing again, with a fine, close pressure, till he had covered the skull and the face of the smaller man, tracing the brows, and touching the full, closed eyes, touching the small nose and the nostrils, the rough, short moustache, the mouth, the rather strong chin. The hand of the blind man grasped the shoulder, the arm, the hand of the other man. He seemed to take him, in the soft, travelling grasp.

"You seem young," he said quietly, at last.

The lawyer stood almost annihilated, unable to answer.

"Your head seems tender, as if you were young," Maurice repeated. "So do your hands. Touch my eyes, will you?—touch my scar."

Now Bertie quivered with revulsion. Yet he was under the power of the blind man, as if hypnotized. He lifted his hand, and laid the fingers on the scar, on the scarred eyes. Maurice suddenly covered them with his own hand, pressed the fingers of the other man upon his disfigured eye-sockets, trembling in every fibre, and rocking slightly, slowly, from side to side. He remained thus for a minute or more, whilst Bertie stood as if in a swoon, unconscious, imprisoned.

Then suddenly Maurice removed the hand of the other man from his brow, and stood holding it in his own.

" Oh, my God," he said, " we shall know each other now, shan't we ? We shall know each other now."

Bertie could not answer. He gazed mute and terror-struck, overcome by his own weakness. He knew he could not answer. He had an unreasonable fear, lest the other man should suddenly destroy him. Whereas Maurice was actually filled with hot, poignant love, the passion of friendship. Perhaps it was this very passion of friendship which Bertie shrank from most.

" We're all right together now, aren't we ? " said Maurice. " It's all right now, as long as we live, so far as we're concerned ? "

" Yes," said Bertie, trying by any means to escape.

Maurice stood with head lifted, as if listening. The new delicate fulfilment of mortal friendship had come as a revelation and surprise to him, something exquisite and unhoped-for. He seemed to be listening to hear if it were real.

Then he turned for his coat.

" Come," he said, " we'll go to Isabel."

Bertie took the lantern and opened the door. The cat disappeared. The two men went in silence along the causeways. Isabel, as they came, thought their footsteps sounded strange. She looked up pathetically and anxiously for their entrance. There seemed a curious elation about Maurice. Bertie was haggard, with sunken eyes.

" What is it ? " she asked.

" We've become friends," said Maurice, standing with his feet apart, like a strange colossus.

" Friends ! " re-echoed Isabel. And she looked again at Bertie. He met her eyes with a furtive, haggard look ; his eyes were as if glazed with misery.

" I'm so glad," she said, in sheer perplexity.

" Yes," said Maurice.

He was indeed so glad. Isabel took his hand with both hers, and held it fast.

" You'll be happier now, dear," she said.

But she was watching Bertie. She knew that he had one desire— to escape from this intimacy, this friendship, which had been thrust upon him. He could not bear it that he had been touched by the blind man, his insane reserve broken in. He was like a mollusc whose shell is broken.

At first Joe thought the job O.K. He was loading hay on the trucks, along with Albert, the corporal. The two men were pleasantly billeted in a cottage not far from the station : they were their own masters, for Joe never thought of Albert as a master. And the little sidings of the tiny village station was as pleasant a place as you could wish for. On one side, beyond the line, stretched the woods : on the other, the near side, across a green smooth field red houses were dotted among flowering apple trees. The weather being sunny, work being easy, Albert, a real good pal, what life could be better ! After Flanders, it was heaven itself.

Albert, the corporal, was a clean-shaven, shrewd-looking fellow of about forty. He seemed to think his one aim in life was to be full of fun and nonsense. In repose, his face looked a little withered, old. He was a very good pal to Joe, steady, decent and grave under all his " mischief " ; for his mischief was only his laborious way of skirting his own ennui.

Joe was much younger than Albert—only twenty-three. He was a tallish, quiet youth, pleasant-looking. He was of a slightly better class than his corporal, more personable. Careful about his appearance, he shaved every day. " I haven't got much of a face," said Albert. "If I was to shave every day like you, Joe, I should have none."

There was plenty of life in the little goods-yard : three porter youths, a continual come and go of farm waggons bringing hay, waggons with timber from the woods, coal carts loading at the trucks. The black coal seemed to make the place sleepier, hotter. Round the big white gate the station-master's children played and his white chickens walked, whilst the station-master himself, a young man getting too fat, helped his wife to peg out the washing on the clothes line in the meadow.

The great boat-shaped waggons came up from Playcross with the hay. At first the farm-men waggoned it. On the third day one of the land-girls appeared with the first load, drawing to a standstill easily at the head of her two great horses. She was a buxom girl, young, in linen overalls and gaiters. Her face was ruddy, she had large blue eyes.

"Now that's the waggoner for us, boys," said the corporal loudly.

"Whoa!" she said to her horses; and then to the corporal: "Which boys do you mean?"

"We are the pick of the bunch. That's Joe, my pal. Don't you let on that my name's Albert," said the corporal to his private. "I'm the corporal."

"And I'm Miss Stokes," said the land-girl coolly, "if that's all the boys you are."

"You know you couldn't want more, Miss Stokes," said Albert, politely. Joe, who was bare-headed, whose grey flannel sleeves were rolled up to the elbow, and whose shirt was open at the breast, looked modestly aside as if he had no part in the affair.

"Are you on this job regular then?" said the corporal to Miss Stokes.

"I don't know for sure," she said, pushing a piece of hair under her hat, and attending to her splendid horses.

"Oh, make it a certainty," said Albert.

She did not reply. She turned and looked over the two men coolly. She was pretty, moderately blonde, with crisp hair, a good skin, and large blue eyes. She was strong, too, and the work went on leisurely and easily.

"Now!" said the corporal, stopping as usual to look round, "pleasant company makes work a pleasure—don't hurry it, boys." He stood on the truck surveying the world. That was one of his great and absorbing occupations: to stand and look out on things in general. Joe, also standing on the truck, also turned round to look what was to be seen. But he could not become blankly absorbed, as Albert could.

Miss Stokes watched the two men from under her broad felt hat. She had seen hundreds of Alberts, khaki soldiers standing in loose attitudes, absorbed in watching nothing in particular. She had seen also a good many Joes, quiet, good-looking young soldiers with half-averted faces. But there was something in the turn of Joe's head, and something in his quiet, tender-looking form, young and fresh—which attracted her eye. As she watched him closely from below, he turned as if he felt her, and his dark-blue eye met her straight, light-blue gaze. He faltered and turned aside again and looked as if he were going to fall off the truck. A slight flush mounted under the girl's full, ruddy face. She liked him.

Always, after this, when she came into the sidings with her team, it was Joe she looked for. She acknowledged to herself that she was sweet on him. But Albert did all the talking. He was so full of fun and nonsense. Joe was a very shy bird, very brief and remote in his answers. Miss Stokes was driven to indulge in repartee with Albert, but she fixed her magnetic attention on the younger fellow. Joe would talk with Albert, and laugh at his jokes. But Miss Stokes could get little out of him. She had to depend on her silent forces. They were more effective than might be imagined.

Suddenly, on Saturday afternoon, at about two o'clock, Joe received a bolt from the blue—a telegram : " Meet me Belbury Station 6.00 p.m. to-day. M. S." He knew at once who M. S. was. His heart melted, he felt weak as if he had had a blow.

" What's the trouble, boy ? " asked Albert anxiously.

" No—no trouble—it's to meet somebody." Joe lifted his dark, blue eyes in confusion towards his corporal.

" Meet somebody ! " repeated the corporal, watching his young pal with keen blue eyes. " It's all right, then ; nothing wrong ? "

" No—nothing wrong. I'm not going," said Joe.

Albert was old and shrewd enough to see that nothing more should be said before the housewife. He also saw that Joe did not want to take him into confidence. So he held his peace, though he was piqued.

The two soldiers went into town, smartened up. Albert knew a fair number of the boys round about ; there would be plenty of gossip in the market-place, plenty of lounging in groups on the Bath Road, watching the Saturday evening shoppers. Then a modest drink or two, and the movies. They passed an agreeable, casual, nothing-in-particular evening, with which Joe was quite satisfied. He thought of Belbury Station, and of M. S. waiting there. He had not the faintest intention of meeting her. And he had not the faintest intention of telling Albert.

And yet, when the two men were in their bedroom, half undressed, Joe suddenly held out the telegram to his corporal, saying : " What d'you think of that ? "

Albert was just unbuttoning his braces. He desisted, took the telegram form, and turned towards the candle to read it.

" *Meet me Belbury Station 6.00 p.m. to-day. M. S.*," he read, *sotto voce*. His face took on its fun-and-nonsense look.

" Who's M. S. ? " he asked, looking shrewdly at Joe.

" You know as well as I do," said Joe, non-committal.

" *M. S.*," repeated Albert. " Blamed if I know, boy. Is it a woman ? "

The conversation was carried on in tiny voices, for fear of disturbing the householders.

" I don't know," said Joe, turning. He looked full at Albert, the two men looked straight into each other's eyes. There was a lurking grin in each of them.

" Well, I'm—*blamed !* " said Albert at last, throwing the telegram down emphatically on the bed.

" Wha—at ? " said Joe, grinning rather sheepishly, his eyes clouded none the less.

Albert sat on the bed and proceeded to undress, nodding his head with mock gravity all the while. Joe watched him foolishly.

" What ? " he repeated faintly.

Albert looked up at him with a knowing look.

" If that isn't coming it quick, boy ! " he said. " What the blazes ! What ha' you bin doing ? "

" Nothing ! " said Joe.

Albert slowly shook his head as he sat on the side of the bed.

" Don't happen to me when *I've* bin doin' nothing," he said. And he proceeded to pull off his stockings.

Joe turned away, looking at himself in the mirror as he unbuttoned his tunic.

" You didn't want to keep the appointment ? " Albert asked, in a changed voice, from the bedside.

Joe did not answer for a moment. Then he said :

" I made no appointment."

" I'm not saying you did, boy. Don't be nasty about it. I mean you didn't want to answer the—unknown person's summons—shall I put it that way ? "

" No," said Joe.

" What was the deterring motive ? " asked Albert, who was now lying on his back in bed.

" Oh," said Joe, suddenly looking round rather haughtily. " I didn't want to." He had a well-balanced head, and could take on a sudden distant bearing.

" Didn't want to—didn't cotton on, like. Well—*they be artful, the women*——" he mimicked his landlord. " Come on into bed, boy. Don't loiter about as if you'd lost something."

Albert turned over, to sleep.

On Monday Miss Stokes turned up as usual, striding beside her team. Her " whoa ! " was resonant and challenging, she looked up at the truck as her steeds came to a standstill. Joe had turned aside, and had his face averted from her. She glanced him over— save for his slender succulent tenderness she would have despised him. She sized him up in a steady look. Then she turned to Albert,

who was looking down at her and smiling in his mischievous turn.
She knew his aspects by now. She looked straight back at him,
though her eyes were hot. He saluted her.

" Beautiful morning, Miss Stokes."

" Very ! " she replied.

" Handsome is as handsome looks," said Albert.

Which produced no response.

" Now, Joe, come on here," said the corporal. " Don't keep the
ladies waiting—it's the sign of a weak heart."

Joe turned, and the work began. Nothing more was said for the
time being. As the week went on all parties became more comfortable. Joe remained silent, averted, neutral, a little on his dignity.
Miss Stokes was off-hand and masterful. Albert was full of mischief.

The great theme was a circus, which was coming to the market-
town on the following Saturday.

" You'll go to the circus, Miss Stokes ? " said Albert.

" I may go. Are you going ? "

" Certainly. Give us the pleasure of escorting you."

" No, thanks."

" That's what I call a flat refusal—what, Joe ? You don't mean
that you have no liking for our company, Miss Stokes ? "

" Oh, I don't know," said Miss Stokes. " How many are there of
you ? "

" Only me and Joe."

" Oh, is that all ? " she said, satirically.

Albert was a little nonplussed.

" Isn't that enough for you ? " he asked.

" Too many by half," blurted out Joe, jeeringly, in a sudden fit of
uncouth rudeness that made both the others stare.

" Oh, I'll stand out of the way, boy, if that's it," said Albert to
Joe. Then he turned mischievously to Miss Stokes. " He wants to
know what M. stands for," he said, confidentially.

" Monkeys," she replied, turning to her horses.

" What's M. S. ? " said Albert.

" Monkey-nuts," she retorted, leading off her team.

Albert looked after her a little discomfited. Joe had flushed dark,
and cursed Albert in his heart.

On the Saturday afternoon the two soldiers took the train into
town. They would have to walk home. They had tea at six o'clock, and
lounged about till half-past seven. The circus was in a meadow near
the river—a great red-and-white striped tent. Caravans stood at the
side. A great crowd of people was gathered round the ticket-caravan.

Inside the tent the lamps were lighted, shining on a ring of faces, a great circular bank of faces.round the green grassy centre. Along with some comrades, the two soldiers packed themselves on a thin plank seat, rather high. They were delighted with the flaring lights, the wild effect. But the circus performance did not affect them deeply. They admired the lady in black velvet with rose-purple legs who leapt so neatly on to the galloping horse ; they watched the feats of strength, and laughed at the clown. But they felt a little patronizing, they missed the sensational drama of the cinema.

Half-way through the performance Joe was electrified to see the face of Miss Stokes not very far from him. There she was, in her khaki and her felt hat, as usual ; he pretended not to see her. She was laughing at the clown ; she also pretended not to see him. It was a blow to him, and it made him angry. He would not even mention it to Albert. Least said, soonest mended. He liked to believe she had not seen him. But he knew, fatally, that she had.

When they came out it was nearly eleven o'clock ; a lovely night, with a moon and tall, dark, noble trees : a magnificent May night. Joe and Albert laughed and chaffed with the boys. Joe looked round frequently to see if he were safe from Miss Stokes. It seemed so.

But there were six miles to walk home. At last the two soldiers set off, swinging their canes. The road was white between tall hedges, other stragglers were passing out of the town towards the villages ; the air was full of pleased excitement.

They were drawing near to the village when they saw a dark figure ahead. Joe's heart sank with pure fear. It was a figure wheeling a bicycle ; a land girl ; Miss Stokes. Albert was ready with his nonsense. Miss Stokes had a puncture.

" Let me wheel the rattler," said Albert.

" Thank you," said Miss Stokes. " You *are* kind."

" Oh, I'd be kinder than that, if you'd show me how," said Albert.

" Are you sure ? " said Miss Stokes.

"Doubt my words?" said Albert. "That's cruel of you, Miss Stokes."
Miss Stokes walked between them, close to Joe.

" Have you been to the circus ? " she asked him.

" Yes," he replied, mildly.

" Have *you* been ? " Albert asked her.

" Yes. I didn't see you," she replied.

" What !—you say so ! Didn't see us ! Didn't think us worth looking at," began Albert. " Aren't I as handsome as the clown, now ? And you didn't as much as glance in our direction ? I call it a downright oversight."

"I never *saw* you," reiterated Miss Stokes. "I didn't know you saw me."

"That makes it worse," said Albert.

The road passed through a belt of dark pine-wood. The village, and the branch road, was very near. Miss Stokes put out her fingers and felt for Joe's hand as it swung at his side. To say he was staggered is to put it mildly. Yet he allowed her softly to clasp his fingers for a few moments. But he was a mortified youth.

At the cross-road they stopped—Miss Stokes should turn off. She had another mile to go.

"You'll let us see you home," said Albert.

"Do me a kindness," she said. "Put my bike in your shed, and take it to Baker's on Monday, will you?"

"I'll sit up all night and mend it for you, if you like."

"No thanks. And Joe and I'll walk on."

"Oh—ho! Oh—ho!" sang Albert. "Joe! Joe! What do you say to that, now, boy? Aren't you in luck's way? And I get the bloomin' old bike for my pal. Consider it again, Miss Stokes."

Joe turned aside his face, and did not speak.

"Oh, well! I wheel the grid, do I? I leave you, boy——"

"I'm not keen on going any further," barked out Joe, in an uncouth voice. "She bain't my choice."

The girl stood silent, and watched the two men.

"There now!" said Albert. "Think o' that! If it was *me* now——" But he was uncomfortable. "Well, Miss Stokes, have me," he added.

Miss Stokes stood quite still, neither moved nor spoke. And so the three remained for some time at the lane end. At last Joe began kicking the ground—then he suddenly lifted his face. At that moment Miss Stokes was at his side. She put her arm delicately round his waist.

"Seems I'm the one extra, don't you think?" Albert inquired of the high bland moon.

Joe had dropped his head and did not answer. Miss Stokes stood with her arm lightly round his waist. Albert bowed, saluted, and bade good night. He walked away, leaving the two standing.

Miss Stokes put a light pressure on Joe's waist, and drew him down the road. They walked in silence. The night was full of scent—wild cherry, the first bluebells. Still they walked in silence. A nightingale was singing. They approached nearer and nearer, till they stood close by his dark bush. The powerful notes sounded from the cover, almost like flashes of light—then the interval of silence—then the moaning notes, almost like a dog faintly howling, followed by the long, rich trill, and flashing notes. Then a short silence again.

Miss Stokes turned at last to Joe. She looked up at him, and in the moonlight he saw her faintly smiling. He felt maddened, but helpless. Her arm was round his waist, she drew him closely to her with a soft pressure that made all his bones rotten.

Meanwhile Albert was waiting at home. He put on his overcoat, for the fire was out, and he had had malarial fever. He looked fitfully at the *Daily Mirror* and the *Daily Sketch*, but he saw nothing. It seemed a long time. He began to yawn widely, even to nod. At last Joe came in.

Albert looked at him keenly. The young man's brow was black, his face sullen.

" All right, boy ? " asked Albert.

Joe merely grunted for a reply. There was nothing more to be got out of him. So they went to bed.

Next day Joe was silent, sullen. Albert could make nothing of him. He proposed a walk after tea.

" I'm going somewhere," said Joe.

" Where—Monkey-nuts ? " asked the corporal. But Joe's brow only became darker.

So the days went by. Almost every evening Joe went off alone, returning late. He was sullen, taciturn and had a hang-dog look, a curious way of dropping his head and looking dangerously from under his brows. And he and Albert did not get on so well any more with one another. For all his fun and nonsense, Albert was really irritable, soon made angry. And Joe's stand-offish sulkiness and complete lack of confidence riled him, got on his nerves. His fun and nonsense took a biting, sarcastic turn, at which Joe's eyes glittered occasionally, though the young man turned unheeding aside. Then again Joe would be full of odd, whimsical fun, outshining Albert himself.

Miss Stokes still came to the station with the wain : Monkey-nuts, Albert called her, though not to her face. For she was very clear and good-looking, almost she seemed to gleam. And Albert was a tiny bit afraid of her. She very rarely addressed Joe whilst the hay-loading was going on, and that young man always turned his back to her. He seemed thinner, and his limber figure looked more slouching. But still it had the tender, attractive appearance, especially from behind. His tanned face, a little thinned and darkened, took a handsome, slightly sinister look.

" Come on, Joe ! " the corporal urged sharply one day. " What're you doing, boy ? Looking for beetles on the bank ? "

Joe turned round swiftly, almost menacing, to work.

" He's a different fellow these days, Miss Stokes," said Albert to the young woman. " What's got him ? Is it Monkey-nuts that don't suit him, do you think ? "

" Choked with chaff, more like," she retorted. " It's as bad as feeding a threshing machine, to have to listen to some folks."

" As bad as what ? " said Albert. " You don't mean *me*, do you, Miss Stokes ? "

" No," she cried. " I don't mean you."

Joe's face became dark red during these sallies, but he said nothing. He would eye the young woman curiously, as she swung so easily at the work, and he had some of the look of a dog which is going to bite.

Albert, with his nerves on edge, began to find the strain rather severe. The next Saturday evening, when Joe came in more black-browed than ever, he watched him, determined to have it out with him.

When the boy went upstairs to bed, the corporal followed him. He closed the door behind him carefully, sat on the bed and watched the younger man undressing. And for once he spoke in a natural voice, neither chaffing nor commanding.

" What's gone wrong, boy ? "

Joe stopped a moment as if he had been shot. Then he went on unwinding his puttees, and did not answer or look up.

" You can hear, can't you ? " said Albert, nettled.

" Yes, I can hear," said Joe, stooping over his puttees till his face was purple.

" Then why don't you answer ? "

Joe sat up. He gave a long, sideways look at the corporal. Then he lifted his eyes and stared at a crack in the ceiling.

The corporal watched these movements shrewdly.

" And *then* what ? " he asked, ironically.

Again Joe turned and stared him in the face. The corporal smiled very slightly, but kindly.

" There'll be murder done one of these days," said Joe, in a quiet, unimpassioned voice.

" So long as it's by daylight——" replied Albert. Then he went over, sat down by Joe, put his hand on his shoulder affectionately, and continued, " What is it, boy ? What's gone wrong ? You can trust me, can't you ? "

Joe turned and looked curiously at the face so near to his.

" It's nothing, that's all," he said laconically.

Albert frowned.

" Then who's going to be murdered ?—and who's going to do the murdering ?—me or you—which is it, boy ? " He smiled gently at the stupid youth, looking straight at him all the while, into his eyes. Gradually the stupid, hunted glowering look died out of Joe's eyes. He turned his head aside, gently, as one rousing from a spell.

" I don't want her," he said, with fierce resentment.

" Then you needn't have her," said Albert. " What do you go for, boy ? "

But it wasn't as simple as all that. Joe made no remark.

" She's a smart-looking girl. What's wrong with her, my boy ? I should have thought you were a lucky chap, myself."

" I don't want 'er," Joe barked, with ferocity and resentment.

" Then tell her so and have done," said Albert. He waited awhile. There was no response. " Why don't you ? " he added.

" Because I don't," confessed Joe, sulkily.

Albert pondered—rubbed his head.

" You're too soft-hearted, that's where it is, boy. You want your mettle dipping in cold water, to temper it. You're too soft-hearted——"

He laid his arm affectionately across the shoulders of the younger man. Joe seemed to yield a little towards him.

" When are you going to see her again ? " Albert asked. For a long time there was no answer.

" When is it, boy ? " persisted the softened voice of the corporal.

" To-morrow," confessed Joe.

" Then let me go," said Albert. " Let me go, will you ? "

The morrow was Sunday, a sunny day, but a cold evening. The sky was grey, the new foliage very green, but the air was chill and depressing. Albert walked briskly down the white road towards Beeley. He crossed a larch plantation, and followed a narrow by-road, where blue speedwell flowers fell from the banks into the dust. He walked swinging his cane, with mixed sensations. Then having gone a certain length, he turned and began to walk in the opposite direction.

So he saw a young woman approaching him. She was wearing a wide hat of grey straw, and a loose, swinging dress of nigger-grey velvet. She walked with slow inevitability. Albert faltered a little as he approached her. Then he saluted her, and his roguish, slightly withered skin flushed. She was staring straight into his face.

He fell in by her side, saying impudently :

" Not so nice for a walk as it was, is it ? "

She only stared at him. He looked back at her.

" You've seen me before, you know," he said, grinning slightly.
" Perhaps you never noticed me. Oh, I'm quite nice-looking, in a
quiet way, you know. What——? "

But Miss Stokes did not speak : she only stared with large, icy
blue eyes at him. He became self-conscious, lifted up his chin,
walked with his nose in the air, and whistled at random. So they
went down the quiet, deserted grey lane. He was whistling the air :
" I'm Gilbert, the filbert, the colonel of the nuts."

At last she found her voice :

" Where's Joe ? "

" He thought you'd like a change : they say variety's the salt of
life—that's why I'm mostly in pickle."

" Where is he ? "

" Am I my brother's keeper ? He's gone his own ways."

" Where ? "

" Nay, how am I to know ? Not so far but he'll be back for supper."

She stopped in the middle of the lane. He stopped facing her.

" Where's Joe ? " she asked.

He struck a careless attitude, looked down the road this way and
that, lifted his eyebrows, pushed his khaki cap on one side, and
answered :

" He is not conducting the service to-night : he asked me if I'd
officiate."

" Why hasn't he come ? "

" Didn't want to, I expect. *I* wanted to."

She stared him up and down, and he felt uncomfortable in his
spine, but maintained his air of nonchalance. Then she turned slowly
on her heel, and started to walk back. The corporal went at her side.

" You're not going back, are you ? " he pleaded. " Why, me and
you, we should get on like a house on fire."

She took no need, but walked on. He went uncomfortably at her
side, making his funny remarks from time to time. But she was as
if stone deaf. He glanced at her, and to his dismay saw the tears
running down her cheeks. He stopped suddenly, and pushed back
his cap.

" I say, you know——" he began.

But she was walking on like an automaton, and he had to hurry
after her.

She never spoke to him. At the gate of her farm she walked
straight in, as if he were not there. He watched her disappear.
Then he turned on his heel, cursing silently, puzzled, lifting off his
cap to scratch his head.

That night, when they were in bed, he remarked :

" Say, Joe, boy ; strikes me you're well off without Monkey-nuts. Gord love us, beans ain't in it."

So they slept in amity. But they waited with some anxiety for the morrow.

It was a cold morning, a grey sky shifting in a cold wind, and threatening rain. They watched the waggon come up the road and through the yard gates. Miss Stokes was with her team as usual ; her " Whoa ! " rang out like a war-whoop.

She faced up at the truck where the two men stood.

" Joe ! " she called, to the averted figure which stood up in the wind.

" What ? " he turned unwillingly.

She made a queer movement, lifting her head slightly in a sipping, half-inviting, half-commanding gesture. And Joe was crouching already to jump off the truck to obey her, when Albert put his hand on his shoulder.

" Half a minute, boy ! Where are you off ? Work's work, and nuts is nuts. You stop here."

Joe slowly straightened himself.

" Joe ? " came the woman's clear call from below.

Again Joe looked at her. But Albert's hand was on his shoulder, detaining him. He stood half averted, with his tail between his legs.

" Take your hand off him, you ! " said Miss Stokes.

" Yes, Major," retorted Albert satirically.

She stood and watched.

" Joe ! " Her voice rang for the third time.

Joe turned and looked at her, and a slow, jeering smile gathered on his face.

" Monkey-nuts ! " he replied, in a tone mocking her call.

She turned white—dead white. The men thought she would fall. Albert began yelling to the porters up the line to come and help with the load. He could yell like any non-commissioned officer upon occasion.

Some way or other the waggon was unloaded, the girl was gone. Joe and his corporal looked at one another and smiled slowly. But they had a weight on their minds, they were afraid.

They were reassured, however, when they found that Miss Stokes came no more with the hay. As far as they were concerned, she had vanished into oblivion. And Joe felt more relieved even than he had felt when he heard the firing cease, after the news had come that the armistice was signed.

THERE was thin, crisp snow on the ground, the sky was blue, the wind very cold, the air clear. Farmers were just turning out the cows for an hour or so in the midday, and the smell of cowsheds was unendurable as I entered Tible. I noticed the ash-twigs up in the sky were pale and luminous, passing into the blue. And then I saw the peacocks. There they were in the road before me, three of them, and tailless, brown, speckled birds, with dark-blue necks and ragged crests. They stepped archly over the filigree snow, and their bodies moved with slow motion, like small, light, flat-bottomed boats. I admired them, they were curious. Then a gust of wind caught them, heeled them over as if they were three frail boats, opening their feathers like ragged sails. They hopped and skipped with discomfort, to get out of the draught of the wind. And then, in the lee of the walls, they resumed their arch, wintry motion, light and unballasted now their tails were gone, indifferent. They were indifferent to my presence. I might have touched them. They turned off to the shelter of an open shed.

As I passed the end of the upper house, I saw a young woman just coming out of the back door. I had spoken to her in the summer. She recognized me at once, and waved to me. She was carrying a pail, wearing a white apron that was longer than her preposterously short skirt, and she had on the cotton bonnet. I took off my hat to her and was going on. But she put down her pail and darted with a swift, furtive movement after me.

" Do you mind waiting a minute ? " she said. " I'll be out in a minute."

She gave me a slight, odd smile, and ran back. Her face was long and sallow and her nose rather red. But her gloomy black eyes softened caressively to me for a moment, with that momentary humility which makes a man lord of the earth.

I stood in the road, looking at the fluffy, dark-red young cattle that mooed and seemed to bark at me. They seemed happy, frisky cattle, a little impudent, and either determined to go back into the warm shed, or determined not to go back. I could not decide which.

Presently the woman came forward again, her head rather ducked. But she looked up at me and smiled, with that odd, immediate intimacy, something witchlike and impossible.

" Sorry to keep you waiting," she said. " Shall we stand in this cart-shed—it will be more out of the wind."

So we stood among the shafts of the open cart-shed that faced the road. Then she looked down at the ground, a little sideways, and I noticed a small black frown on her brows. She seemed to brood for a moment. Then she looked straight into my eyes, so that I blinked and wanted to turn my face aside. She was searching me for something and her look was too near. The frown was still on her keen, sallow brow.

" Can you speak French ? " she asked me abruptly.

" More or less," I replied.

" I was supposed to learn it at school," she said. " But I don't know a word." She ducked her head and laughed, with a slightly ugly grimace and a rolling of her black eyes.

" No good keeping your mind full of scraps," I answered.

But she had turned aside her sallow, long face, and did not hear what I said. Suddenly again she looked at me. She was searching. And at the same time she smiled at me, and her eyes looked softly, darkly, with infinite trustful humility into mine. I was being cajoled.

" Would you mind reading a letter for me, in French," she said, her face immediately black and bitter-looking. She glanced at me, frowning.

" Not at all," I said.

" It's a letter to my husband," she said, still scrutinizing.

I looked at her, and didn't quite realize. She looked too far into me, my wits were gone. She glanced round. Then she looked at me shrewdly. She drew a letter from her pocket, and handed it to me. It was addressed from France to Lance-Corporal Goyte, at Tible. I took out the letter and began to read it, as mere words. " Mon cher Alfred "—it might have been a bit of a torn newspaper. So I followed the script : the trite phrases of a letter from a French-speaking girl to an English soldier. " I think of you always, always. Do you think sometimes of me ? " And then I vaguely realized that I was reading a man's private correspondence. And yet, how could one consider these trivial, facile French phrases private ! Nothing more trite and vulgar in the world, than such a love-letter—no newspaper more obvious.

Therefore I read with a callous heart the effusions of the Belgian damsel. But then I gathered my attention. For the letter went on,

"Notre cher petit bébé—our dear little baby was born a week ago. Almost I died, knowing you were far away, and perhaps forgetting the fruit of our perfect love. But the child comforted me. He has the smiling eyes and virile air of his English father. I pray to the Mother of Jesus to send me the dear father of my child, that I may see him with my child in his arms, and that we may be united in holy family love. Ah, my Alfred, can I tell you how I miss you, how I weep for you. My thoughts are with you always, I think of nothing but you, I live for nothing but you and our dear baby. If you do not come back to me soon, I shall die, and our child will die. But no, you cannot come back to me. But I can come to you, come to England with our child. If you do not wish to present me to your good mother and father, you can meet me in some town, some city, for I shall be so frightened to be alone in England with my child, and no one to take care of us. Yet I must come to you, I must bring my child, my little Alfred to his father, the big, beautiful Alfred that I love so much. Oh, write and tell me where I shall come. I have some money, I am not a penniless creature. I have money for myself and my dear baby——"

I read to the end. It was signed : "Your very happy and still more unhappy Elise." I suppose I must have been smiling.

"I can see it makes you laugh," said Mrs. Goyte, sardonically. I looked up at her.

"It's a love-letter, I know that," she said. "There's too many 'Alfreds' in it."

"One too many," I said.

"Oh, yes—— And what does she say—Eliza? We know her name's Eliza, that's another thing." She grimaced a little, looking up at me with a mocking laugh.

"Where did you get this letter?" I said.

"Postman gave it me last week."

"And is your husband at home?"

"I expect him home to-night. He's been wounded, you know, and we've been applying for him home. He was home about six weeks ago—he's been in Scotland since then. Oh, he was wounded in the leg. Yes, he's all right, a great strapping fellow. But he's lame, he limps a bit. He expects he'll get his discharge—but I don't think he will. We married? We've been married six years—and he joined up the first day of the war. Oh, he thought he'd like the life. He'd been through the South African War. No, he was sick of it, fed up. I'm living with his father and mother—I've no home of my own now. My people had a big farm—over a thousand acres—in Oxfordshire. Not like here—no. Oh, they're very good to me, his father and mother. Oh, yes, they couldn't be better. They think more of me than of their own daughters. But it's not like being in a place of your own, is it? You can't *really* do as you like. No, there's only me and his father and mother at home. Before the war? Oh, he was anything. He's had a good education—but he liked the farming better. Then he was a chauffeur. That's how he knew French. He was driving a gentleman in France for a long time——"

At this point the peacocks came round the corner on a puff of wind.

"Hello, Joey!" she called, and one of the birds came forward, on delicate legs. Its grey speckled back was very elegant, it rolled its full, dark blue neck as it moved to her. She crouched down. "Joey, dear," she said, in an odd, saturnine caressive voice, "you're bound to find me, aren't you?" She put her face forward, and the bird rolled his neck, almost touching her face with his beak, as if kissing her.

"He loves you," I said.

She twisted her face up at me with a laugh.

"Yes," she said, "he loves me, Joey does,"—then, to the bird—"and I love Joey, don't I. I *do* love Joey." And she smoothed his feathers for a moment. Then she rose, saying: "He's an affectionate bird."

I smiled at the roll of her "bir-rrd."

"Oh, yes, he is," she protested. "He came with me from my home seven years ago. Those others are his descendants—but they're not like Joey—*are they, dee-urr?*" Her voice rose at the end with a witch-like cry.

Then she forgot the birds in the cart-shed and turned to business again.

"Won't you read that letter?" she said. "Read it, so that I know what it says."

"It's rather behind his back," I said.

"Oh, never mind him," she cried. "He's been behind my back long enough—all these four years. If he never did no worse things behind my back than I do behind his, he wouldn't have cause to grumble. You read me what it says."

Now I felt a distinct reluctance to do as she bid, and yet I began—"My dear Alfred."

"I guessed that much," she said. "Eliza's dear Alfred." She laughed. "How do you say it in French? *Eliza?*"

I told her, and she repeated the name with great contempt—*Elise*.

" Go on," she said. " You're not reading."

So I began—" I have been thinking of you sometimes—have you been thinking of me ?——"

" Of several others as well, beside her, I'll wager," said Mrs. Goyte.

" Probably not," said I, and continued. " A dear little baby was born here a week ago. Ah, can I tell you my feelings when I take my darling little brother into my arms——"

" I'll bet it's *his*," cried Mrs. Goyte.

" No," I said. " It's her mother's."

" Don't you believe it," she cried. " It's a blind. You mark, it's her own right enough—and his."

" No," I said, " it's her mother's." " He has sweet smiling eyes, but not like your beautiful English eyes——"

She suddenly struck her hand on her skirt with a wild motion, and bent down, doubled with laughter. Then she rose and covered her face with her hand.

" I'm forced to laugh at the beautiful English eyes," she said.

" Aren't his eyes beautiful ? " I asked.

" Oh, yes—*very!* Go on !—*Joey, dear, dee-urr, Joey !* "—this to the peacock.

—" Er—We miss you very much. We all miss you. We wish you were here to see the darling baby. Ah, Alfred, how happy we were when you stayed with us. We all loved you so much. My mother will call the baby Alfred so that we shall never forget you——"

" Of course it's his right enough," cried Mrs. Goyte.

" No," I said. " It's the mother's." Er—" My mother is very well. My father came home yesterday—on leave. He is delighted with his son, my little brother, and wishes to have him named after you, because you were so good to us all in that terrible time, which I shall never forget. I must weep now when I think of it. Well, you are far away in England, and perhaps I shall never see you again. How did you find your dear mother and father ? I am so happy that your wound is better, and that you can nearly walk——"

" How did he find his dear *wife* ? " cried Mrs. Goyte. " He never told her he had one. Think of taking the poor girl in like that ! "

" We are so pleased when you write to us. Yet now you are in England you will forget the family you served so well——"

" A bit too well—eh, *Joey* ? " cried the wife.

" If it had not been for you we should not be alive now, to grieve and to rejoice in this life, that is so hard for us. But we have recovered some of our losses, and no longer feel the burden of poverty. The little Alfred is a great comfort to me. I hold him to my breast and think of the big, good Alfred, and I weep to think that those times of suffering were perhaps the times of a great happiness that is gone for ever."

" Oh, but isn't it a shame, to take a poor girl in like that ! " cried Mrs. Goyte. " Never to let on that he was married, and raise her hopes—I call it beastly, I do."

" You don't know," I said. " You know how anxious women are to fall in love, wife or no wife. How could he help it, if she was determined to fall in love with him ? "

" He could have helped it if he'd wanted."

" Well," I said, " we aren't all heroes."

" Oh, but that's different ! The big, good Alfred !—did ever you hear such tommy-rot in your life ! Go on—what does she say at the end ? "

" Er—We shall be pleased to hear of your life in England. We all send many kind regards to your good parents. I wish you all happiness for your future days. Your very affectionate and ever-grateful, Elise."

There was silence for a moment, during which Mrs. Goyte remained with her head dropped, sinister and abstracted. Suddenly she lifted her face, and her eyes flashed.

" Oh, but I call it beastly, I call it mean, to take a girl in like that."

" Nay," I said. " Probably he hasn't taken her in at all. Do you think those French girls are such poor innocent things ? I guess she's a great deal more downy than he."

" Oh, he's one of the biggest fools that ever walked," she cried.

" There you are ! " said I.

" But it's his child right enough," she said.

" I don't think so," said I.

" I'm sure of it."

" Oh, well," I said, " if you prefer to think that way."

" What other reason has she for writing like that——"

I went out into the road and looked at the cattle.

" Who is this driving the cows ? " I said. She too came out.

" It's the boy from the next farm," she said.

" Oh, well," said I, " those Belgian girls ! You never know where their letters will end. And, after all, it's his affair—you needn't bother."

" Oh— ! " she cried, with rough scorn—" it's not *me* that bothers.

But it's the nasty meanness of it—me writing him such loving letters "
—she put her hand before her face and laughed malevolently—" and
sending him parcels all the time. You bet he fed that gurrl on my
parcels—I know he did. It's just like him. I'll bet they laughed
together over my letters. I'll bet anything they did——"

" Nay," said I. " He'd burn your letters for fear they'd give him
away."

There was a black look on her yellow face. Suddenly a voice was
heard calling. She poked her head out of the shed, and answered
coolly :

" All right ! " Then turning to me : " That's his mother looking
after me."

She laughed into my face, witch-like, and we turned down the
road.

When I awoke, the morning after this episode, I found the house
darkened with deep, soft snow, which had blown against the large
west windows, covering them with a screen. I went outside, and
saw the valley all white and ghastly below me, the trees beneath
black and thin-looking like wire, the rock-faces dark between the
glistening shroud, and the sky above sombre, heavy, yellowish-dark,
much too heavy for this world below of hollow bluey whiteness
figured with black. I felt I was in a valley of the dead. And I
sensed I was a prisoner, for the snow was everywhere deep, and drifted
in places. So all the morning I remained indoors, looking up the
drive at the shrubs so heavily plumed with snow, at the gateposts
raised high with a foot or more of extra whiteness. Or I looked
down into the white-and-black valley that was utterly motionless
and beyond life, a hollow sarcophagus.

Nothing stirred the whole day—no plume fell off the shrubs, the
valley was as abstracted as a grove of death. I looked over at the
tiny, half-buried farms away on the bare uplands beyond the valley
hollow, and I thought of Tible in the snow, of the black witch-like
little Mrs. Goyte. And the snow seemed to lay me bare to influences
I wanted to escape.

In the faint glow of the half-clear light that came about four
o'clock in the afternoon, I was roused to see a motion in the snow
away below, near where the thorn-trees stood very black and dwarfed,
like a little savage group, in the dismal white. I watched closely.
Yes, there was a flapping and a struggle—a big bird, it must be,
labouring in the snow. I wondered. Our biggest birds, in the
valley, were the large hawks that often hung flickering opposite my
windows, level with me, but high above some prey on the steep

valley-side. This was much too big for a hawk—too big for any known bird. I searched in my mind for the largest English wild birds, geese, buzzards.

Still it laboured and strove, then was still, a dark spot, then struggled again. I went out of the house and down the steep slope, at risk of breaking my leg between the rocks. I knew the ground so well—and yet I got well shaken before I drew near the thorn-trees.

Yes, it was a bird. It was Joey. It was the grey-brown peacock with a blue neck. He was snow-wet and spent.

"Joey—Joey, de-urr !" I said, staggering unevenly towards him. He looked so pathetic, rowing and struggling in the snow, too spent to rise, his blue neck stretching out and lying sometimes on the snow, his eye closing and opening quickly, his crest all battered.

"Joey dee-urr !" I said caressingly to him. And at last he lay still, blinking, in the surged and furrowed snow, whilst I came near and touched him, stroked him, gathered him under my arm. He stretched his long, wetted neck away from me as I held him, none the less he was quiet in my arm, too tired, perhaps, to struggle. Still he held his poor, crested head away from me, and seemed sometimes to droop, to wilt, as if he might suddenly die.

He was not so heavy as I expected, yet it was a struggle to get up to the house with him again. We set him down, not too near the fire, and gently wiped him with cloths. He submitted, only now and then stretched his soft neck away from us, avoiding us helplessly. Then we set warm food by him. I *put* it to his beak, tried to make him eat. But he ignored it. He seemed to be ignorant of what we were doing, recoiled inside himself inexplicably. So we put him in a basket with cloths, and left him crouching oblivious. His food we put near him. The blinds were drawn, the house was warm, it was night. Sometimes he stirred, but mostly he huddled still, leaning his queer crested head on one side. He touched no food, and took no heed of sounds or movements. We talked of brandy or stimulants. But I realized we had best leave him alone.

In the night, however, we heard him thumping about. I got up anxiously with a candle. He had eaten some food, and scattered more, making a mess. And he was perched on the back of a heavy arm-chair. So I concluded he was recovered, or recovering.

The next day was clear, and the snow had frozen, so I decided to carry him back to Tible. He consented, after various flappings, to sit in a big fish-bag with his battered head peeping out with wild uneasiness. And so I set off with him, slithering down into the valley,

making good progress down in the pale shadow beside the rushing
waters, then climbing painfully up the arrested white valley-side,
plumed with clusters of young pine trees, into the paler white
radiance of the snowy, upper regions, where the wind cut fine.
Joey seemed to watch all the time with wide, anxious, unseeing eye,
brilliant and inscrutable. As I drew near to Tible township he
stirred violently in the bag, though I do not know if he had recognized the place. Then, as I came to the sheds, he looked sharply
from side to side, and stretched his neck out long. I was a little
afraid of him. He gave a loud, vehement yell, opening his sinister
beak, and I stood still, looking at him as he struggled in the bag,
shaken myself by his struggles, yet not thinking to release him.

Mrs. Goyte came darting past the end of the house, her head
sticking forward in sharp scrutiny. She saw me, and came forward.

" Have you got Joey ! " she cried sharply, as if I were a thief.

I opened the bag, and he flopped out, flapping as if he hated the
touch of the snow now. She gathered him up, and put her lips to
his beak. She was flushed and handsome, her eyes bright, her hair
slack, thick, but more witch-like than ever. She did not speak.

She had been followed by a grey-haired woman with a round,
rather sallow face and a slightly hostile bearing.

" Did you bring him with you, then ? " she asked sharply. I
answered that I had rescued him the previous evening.

From the background slowly approached a slender man with a
grey moustache and large patches on his trousers.

" You've got 'im back 'gain, ah see," he said to his daughter-in-
law. His wife explained how I had found Joey.

" Ah," went on the grey man. " It wor our Alfred scarred him
off, back your life. He must'a flyed ower t'valley. Tha ma' thank
thy stars as 'e wor fun, Maggie. 'E'd a bin froze. They a bit nesh,
you know," he concluded to me.

" They are," I answered. " This isn't their country."

" No, it isna," replied Mr. Goyte. He spoke very slowly and
deliberately, quietly, as if the soft pedal were always down in his
voice. He looked at his daughter-in-law as she crouched, flushed
and dark, before the peacock, which would lay its long blue neck
for a moment along her lap. In spite of his grey moustache and thin
grey hair, the elderly man had a face young and almost delicate, like
a young man's. His blue eyes twinkled with some inscrutable source
of pleasure, his skin was fine and tender, his nose delicately arched.
His grey hair being slightly ruffled, he had a debonair look, as of
a youth who is in love.

"We mun tell 'im it's come," he said slowly, and turning he called : "Alfred—Alfred ! Wheer's ter gotten to ? "

Then he turned again to the group.

"Get up then, Maggie, lass, get up wi' thee. Tha ma'es too much o' th' bod."

A young man approached, wearing rough khaki and knee-breeches. He was Danish-looking, broad at the loins.

"I's come back then," said the father to the son ; "leastwise, he's bin browt back, flyed ower the Griff Low."

The son looked at me. He had a devil-may-care bearing, his cap on one side, his hands stuck in the front pockets of his breeches. But he said nothing.

"Shall you come in a minute, Master," said the elderly woman, to me.

"Ay, come in an' ha'e a cup o' tea or summat. You'll do wi' summat, carrin' that bod. Come on, Maggie wench, let's go in."

So we went indoors, into the rather stuffy, overcrowded living room, that was too cosy, and too warm. The son followed last, standing in the doorway. The father talked to me. Maggie put out the tea-cups. The mother went into the dairy again.

"Tha'lt rouse thysen up a bit again, now, Maggie," the father-in-law said—and then to me : " 'ers not bin very bright sin' Alfred come whoam, an' the bod flyed awee. 'E come whoam a Wednesday night, Alfred did. But ay, you knowed, didna yer. Ay, 'e comed 'a Wednesday—an' I reckon there wor a bit of a to-do between 'em, worn't there, Maggie ? "

He twinkled maliciously to his daughter-in-law, who was flushed, brilliant and handsome.

"Oh, be quiet, Father. You're wound up, by the sound of you," she said to him, as if crossly. But she could never be cross with him.

" 'Ers got 'er colour back this mornin'," continued the father-in-law slowly. "It's bin heavy weather wi' 'er this last two days. Ay —'er's bin north-east sin 'er seed you a Wednesday."

"Father, do stop talking. You'd wear the leg off an iron pot. I can't think where you've found your tongue, all of a sudden," said Maggie, with caressive sharpness.

"Ah've found it wheer I lost it. Aren't goin' ter come in an' sit thee down, Alfred ? "

But Alfred turned and disappeared.

" 'E's got th' monkey on 'is back ower this letter job," said the father secretly to me. "Mother, 'er knows nowt about it. Lot o' tom-foolery, isn't it ? Ay ! What's good o'makkin' a peck o' trouble

over what's far enough off, an' ned niver come no nigher. No—
not a smite o' use. That's what I tell 'er. 'Er should ta'e no notice
on't. Ty, what can y' expect."

The mother came in again, and the talk became general. Maggie
flashed her eyes at me from time to time, complacent and satisfied,
moving among the men. I paid her little compliments, which she
did not seem to hear. She attended to me with a kind of sinister,
witch-like graciousness, her dark head ducked between her shoulders,
at once humble and powerful. She was happy as a child attending
to her father-in-law and to me. But there was something ominous
between her eyebrows, as if a dark moth were settled there—and
something ominous in her bent, hulking bearing.

She sat on a low stool by the fire, near her father-in-law. Her
head was dropped, she seemed in a state of abstraction. From time
to time she would suddenly recover, and look up at us, laughing and
chatting. Then she would forget again. Yet in her hulked black
forgetting she seemed very near to us.

The door having been opened, the peacock came slowly in,
prancing calmly. He went near to her and crouched down, coiling
his blue neck. She glanced at him, but almost as if she did not
observe him. The bird sat silent, seeming to sleep, and the woman
also sat hulked and silent, seemingly oblivious. Then once more
there was a heavy step, and Alfred entered. He looked at his wife,
and he looked at the peacock crouching by her. He stood large in
the doorway, his hands stuck in front of him, in his breeches pockets.
Nobody spoke. He turned on his heel and went out again.

I rose also to go. Maggie started as if coming to herself.

"Must you go?" she asked, rising and coming near to me,
standing in front of me, twisting her head sideways and looking up
at me. "Can't you stop a bit longer? We can all be cosy to-day,
there's nothing to do outdoors." And she laughed, showing her
teeth oddly. She had a long chin.

I said I must go. The peacock uncoiled and coiled again his long
blue neck, as he lay on the hearth. Maggie still stood close in front
of me, so that I was acutely aware of my waistcoat buttons.

"Oh, well," she said, "you'll come again, won't you? Do come
again."

I promised.

"Come to tea one day—yes, do!"

I promised—one day.

The moment I went out of her presence I ceased utterly to exist for her—as utterly as I ceased to exist for Joey. With her curious abstractedness she forgot me again immediately. I knew it as I left her. Yet she seemed almost in physical contact with me while I was with her.

The sky was all pallid again, yellowish. When I went out there was no sun ; the snow was blue and cold. I hurried away down the hill, musing on Maggie. The road made a loop down the sharp face of the slope. As I went crunching over the laborious snow I became aware of a figure striding down the steep scarp to intercept me. It was a man with his hands in front of him, half stuck in his breeches pockets, and his shoulders square—a real farmer of the hills ; Alfred, of course. He waited for me by the stone fence.

" Excuse me," he said as I came up.

I came to a halt in front of him and looked into his sullen blue eyes. He had a certain odd haughtiness on his brows. But his blue eyes stared insolently at me.

" Do you know anything about a letter—in French—that my wife opened—a letter of mine—— ? "

" Yes," said I. " She asked me to read it to her."

He looked square at me. He did not know exactly how to feel.

" What was there in it ? " he asked.

" Why ? " I said. " Don't you know ? "

" She makes out she's burnt it," he said.

" Without showing it you ? " I asked.

He nodded slightly. He seemed to be meditating as to what line of action he should take. He wanted to know the contents of the letter : he must know : and therefore he must ask me, for evidently his wife had taunted him. At the same time, no doubt, he would like to wreak untold vengeance on my unfortunate person. So he eyed me, and I eyed him, and neither of us spoke. He did not want to repeat his request to me. And yet I only looked at him, and considered.

Suddenly he threw back his head and glanced down the valley. Then he changed his position—he was a horse-soldier. Then he looked at me more confidentially.

" She burnt the blasted thing before I saw it," he said.

" Well," I answered slowly, " she doesn't know herself what was in it."

He continued to watch me narrowly. I grinned to myself.

" I didn't like to read her out what there was in it," I continued.

He suddenly flushed so that the veins in his neck stood out, and he stirred again uncomfortably.

" The Belgian girl said her baby had been born a week ago, and that they were going to call it Alfred," I told him.

He met my eyes. I was grinning. He began to grin, too.

" Good luck to her," he said.

" Best of luck," said I.

" And what did you tell *her* ? " he asked.

" That the baby belonged to the old mother—that it was brother to your girl, who was writing to you as a friend of the family."

He stood smiling, with the long, subtle malice of a farmer.

" And did she take it in ? " he asked.

" As much as she took anything else."

He stood grinning fixedly. Then he broke into a short laugh.

" Good for *her* ! " he exclaimed cryptically.

And then he laughed aloud once more, evidently feeling he had won a big move in his contest with his wife.

" What about the other woman ? " I asked.

" Who ? "

" Elise."

" Oh "—he shifted uneasily—" she was all right——"

" You'll be getting back to her," I said.

He looked at me. Then he made a grimace with his mouth.

" Not me," he said.   " Back your life it's a plant."

" You don't think the *cher petit bébé* is a little Alfred ? "

" It might be," he said.

" Only might ? "

" Yes—an' there's lots of mites in a pound of cheese." He laughed boisterously but uneasily.

" What did she say, exactly ? " he asked.

I began to repeat, as well as I could, the phrases of the letter :

" *Mon cher Alfred— Figure-toi comme je suis desolée*——"

He listened with some confusion. When I had finished all I could remember, he said :

" They know how to pitch you out a letter, those Belgian lasses."

" Practice," said I.

" They get plenty," he said.

There was a pause.

" Oh, well," he said.   " I've never got that letter, anyhow."

The wind blew fine and keen, in the sunshine, across the snow. I blew my nose and prepared to depart.

" And *she* doesn't know anything ? " he continued, jerking his head up the hill in the direction of Tible.

" She knows nothing but what I've said—that is, if she really burnt the letter."

" I believe she burnt it," he said, " for spite. She's a little devil, she is. But I shall have it out with her." His jaw was stubborn and sullen. Then suddenly he turned to me with a new note.

" Why ? " he said. " Why didn't you wring that b—— peacock's neck—that b—— Joey ? "

" Why ? " I said. " What for ? "

" I hate the brute," he said. " I had a shot at him——"

I laughed. He stood and mused.

" Poor little Elise," he murmured.

" Was she small—petite ? " I asked. He jerked up his head.

" No," he said. " Rather tall."

" Taller than your wife, I suppose."

Again he looked into my eyes. And then once more he went into a loud burst of laughter that made the still, snow-deserted valley clap again.

" God, it's a knock-out ! " he said, thoroughly amused. Then he stood at ease, one foot out, his hands in his breeches pockets, in front of him, his head thrown back, a handsome figure of a man.

" But I'll do that blasted Joey in——" he mused.

I ran down the hill, shouting with laughter.

THE Pottery House was a square, ugly, brick house girt in by the wall that enclosed the whole grounds of the pottery itself. To be sure, a privet hedge partly masked the house and its ground from the pottery-yard and works : but only partly. Through the hedge could be seen the desolate yard, and the many-windowed, factory-like pottery, over the hedge could be seen the chimneys and the out-houses. But inside the hedge, a pleasant garden and lawn sloped down to a willow pool, which had once supplied the works.

The Pottery itself was now closed, the great doors of the yard permanently shut. No more the great crates with yellow straw showing through stood in stacks by the packing shed. No more the drays drawn by great horses rolled down the hill with a high load. No more the pottery-lasses in their clay-coloured overalls, their faces and hair splashed with grey fine mud, shrieked and larked with the men. All that was over.

" We like it much better—oh, much better—quieter," said Matilda Rockley.

" Oh, yes," assented Emmie Rockley, her sister.

" I'm sure you do," agreed the visitor.

But whether the two Rockley girls really liked it better, or whether they only imagined they did, is a question. Certainly their lives were much more grey and dreary now that the grey clay had ceased to spatter its mud and silt its dust over the premises. They did not quite realize how they missed the shrieking, shouting lasses, whom they had known all their lives and disliked so much.

Matilda and Emmie were already old maids. In a thorough industrial district, it is not easy for the girls who have expectations above the common to find husbands. The ugly industrial town was full of men, young men who were ready to marry. But they were all colliers or pottery-hands, mere workmen. The Rockley girls would have about ten thousand pounds each when their father died : ten thousand pounds' worth of profitable house-property. It was not to be sneezed at : they felt so themselves, and refrained from sneezing away such a fortune on any mere member of the proletariat. Consequently, bank-clerks or nonconformist clergymen or even school-teachers having failed to come forward, Matilda had begun to give up all idea of ever leaving the Pottery House.

Matilda was a tall, thin, graceful, fair girl, with a rather large nose. She was the Mary to Emmie's Martha : that is, Matilda loved painting and music, and read a good many novels, whilst Emmie looked after the housekeeping. Emmie was shorter, plumper than her sister, and she had no accomplishments. She looked up to Matilda, whose mind was naturally refined and sensible.

In their quiet, melancholy way, the two girls were happy. Their mother was dead. Their father was ill also. He was an intelligent man who had had some education, but preferred to remain as if he were one with the rest of the working people. He had a passion for music and played the violin pretty well. But now he was getting old, he was very ill, dying of a kidney disease. He had been rather a heavy whisky-drinker.

This quiet household, with one servant-maid, lived on year after year in the Pottery House. Friends came in, the girls went out, the father drank himself more and more ill. Outside in the street there was a continual racket of the colliers and their dogs and children. But inside the pottery wall was a deserted quiet.

In all this ointment there was one little fly. Ted Rockley, the father of the girls, had had four daughters, and no son. As his girls grew, he felt angry at finding himself always in a household of women. He went off to London and adopted a boy out of a Charity Institution. Emmie was fourteen years old, and Matilda sixteen, when their father arrived home with his prodigy, the boy of six, Hadrian.

Hadrian was just an ordinary boy from a Charity Home, with ordinary brownish hair and ordinary bluish eyes and of ordinary rather Cockney speech. The Rockley girls—there were three at home at the time of his arrival—had resented his being sprung on them. He, with his watchful, charity-institution instinct, knew this at once. Though he was only six years old, Hadrian had a subtle, jeering look on his face when he regarded the three young women. They insisted he should address them as Cousin : Cousin Flora, Cousin Matilda, Cousin Emmie. He complied, but there seemed a mockery in his tone.

The girls, however, were kind-hearted by nature. Flora married and left home. Hadrian did very much as he pleased with Matilda and Emmie, though they had certain strictnesses. He grew up in the Pottery House and about the Pottery premises, went to an elementary school, and was invariably called Hadrian Rockley. He regarded Cousin Matilda and Cousin Emmie with a certain laconic indifference, was quiet and reticent in his ways. The girls called him sly, but that was unjust. He was merely cautious, and without frankness. His uncle, Ted Rockley, understood him tacitly, their natures were somewhat akin. Hadrian and the elderly man had a real but unemotional regard for one another.

When he was thirteen years old the boy was sent to a High School in the County town. He did not like it. His Cousin Matilda had longed to make a little gentleman of him, but he refused to be made. He would give a little contemptuous curve to his lip, and take on a shy, charity-boy grin, when refinement was thrust upon him. He played truant from the High School, sold his books, his cap with its badge, even his very scarf and pocket-handkerchief, to his school-fellows, and went raking off heaven knows where with the money. So he spent two very unsatisfactory years.

When he was fifteen he announced that he wanted to leave England to go to the Colonies. He had kept touch with the Home. The Rockleys knew that, when Hadrian made a declaration, in his quiet, half-jeering manner, it was worse than useless to oppose him. So at last the boy departed, going to Canada under the protection of the Institution to which he had belonged. He said good-bye to the Rockleys, without a word of thanks, and parted, it seemed, without a pang. Matilda and Emmie wept often to think of how he left them : even on their father's face a queer look came. But Hadrian wrote fairly regularly from Canada. He had entered some electricity works near Montreal, and was doing well.

At last, however, the war came. In his turn, Hadrian joined up and came to Europe. The Rockleys saw nothing of him. They lived on, just the same, in the Pottery House. Ted Rockley was dying of a sort of dropsy, and in his heart he wanted to see the boy. When the Armistice was signed, Hadrian had a long leave, and wrote that he was coming home to the Pottery House.

The girls were terribly fluttered. To tell the truth, they were a little afraid of Hadrian. Matilda, tall and thin, was frail in her health, both girls were worn with nursing their father. To have Hadrian, a young man of twenty-one, in the house with them, after he had left them so coldly five years before, was a trying circumstance.

They were in a flutter. Emmie persuaded her father to have his bed made finally in the morning-room downstairs, whilst his room upstairs was prepared for Hadrian. This was done, and preparations were going on for the arrival, when, at ten o'clock in the morning, the young man suddenly turned up, quite unexpectedly. Cousin Emmie, with her hair bobbed up in absurd little bobs round her forehead, was busily polishing the stair-rods, while Cousin Matilda was in the kitchen washing the drawing-room ornaments in a lather, her sleeves rolled back on her thin arms, and her head tied up oddly and coquettishly in a duster.

Cousin Matilda blushed deep with mortification when the self-possessed young man walked in with his kit-bag, and put his cap on the sewing machine. He was little and self-confident, with a curious neatness about him that still suggested the Charity Institution. His face was brown, he had a small moustache, he was vigorous enough in his smallness.

" *Well*, is it Hadrian ! " exclaimed Cousin Matilda, wringing the lather off her hand. " We didn't expect you till to-morrow."

" I got off Monday night," said Hadrian, glancing round the room.

" Fancy ! " said Cousin Matilda. Then, having dried her hands, she went forward, held out her hand, and said :

" How are you ? "

" Quite well, thank you," said Hadrian.

" You're quite a man," said Cousin Matilda.

Hadrian glanced at her. She did not look her best : so thin, so large-nosed, with that pink-and-white checked duster tied round her head. She felt her disadvantage. But she had had a good deal of suffering and sorrow, she did not mind any more.

The servant entered—one that did not know Hadrian.

" Come and see my father," said Cousin Matilda.

In the hall they roused Cousin Emmie like a partridge from cover. She was on the stairs pushing the bright stair-rods into place. Instinctively her hand went to the little knobs, her front hair bobbed on her forehead.

"Why !" she exclaimed, crossly. "What have you come to-day for?"

" I got off a day earlier," said Hadrian, and his man's voice so deep and unexpected was like a blow to Cousin Emmie.

"Well, you've caught us in the midst of it," she said, with resentment. Then all three went into the middle room.

Mr. Rockley was dressed—that is, he had on his trousers and socks —but he was resting on the bed, propped up just under the window, from whence he could see his beloved and resplendent garden, where tulips and apple-trees were ablaze. He did not look as ill as he was, for the water puffed him up, and his face kept its colour. His stomach was much swollen. He glanced round swiftly, turning his eyes without turning his head. He was the wreck of a handsome, well-built man.

Seeing Hadrian, a queer, unwilling smile went over his face. The young man greeted him sheepishly.

" You wouldn't make a life-guardsman," he said. " Do you want something to eat ? "

Hadrian looked round—as if for the meal.

" I don't mind," he said.

" What shall you have—egg and bacon ? " asked Emmie shortly.

" Yes, I don't mind," said Hadrian.

The sisters went down to the kitchen, and sent the servant to finish the stairs.

" Isn't he *altered ?* " said Matilda, *sotto voce*.

" Isn't he ! " said Cousin Emmie. " *What* a little man ! "

They both made a grimace, and laughed nervously.

" Get the frying-pan," said Emmie to Matilda.

" But he's as cocky as ever," said Matilda, narrowing her eyes and shaking her head knowingly, as she handed the frying-pan.

" Mannie ! " said Emmie sarcastically. Hadrian's new-fledged, cocksure manliness evidently found no favour in her eyes.

" Oh, he's not bad," said Matilda. " You don't want to be prejudiced against him."

" I'm not prejudiced against him, I think he's all right for looks," said Emmie, " but there's too much of the little mannie about him."

" Fancy catching us like this," said Matilda.

" They've no thought for anything," said Emmie with contempt. " You go up and get dressed, our Matilda. I don't care about him. I can see to things, and you can talk to him. I shan't."

" He'll talk to my father," said Matilda, meaningful.

" *Sly*—— *!* " exclaimed Emmie, with a grimace.

The sisters believed that Hadrian had come hoping to get something out of their father—hoping for a legacy. And they were not at all sure he would not get it.

Matilda went upstairs to change. She had thought it all out how she would receive Hadrian, and impress him. And he had caught her with her head tied up in a duster, and her thin arms in a basin of lather. But she did not care. She now dressed herself most scrupulously, carefully folded her long, beautiful, blonde hair, touched her pallor with a little rouge, and put her long string of exquisite crystal beads over her soft green dress. Now she looked elegant, like a heroine in a magazine illustration, and almost as unreal.

She found Hadrian and her father talking away. The young man was short of speech as a rule, but he could find his tongue with his " uncle." They were both sipping a glass of brandy, and smoking, and chatting like a pair of old cronies. Hadrian was telling about Canada. He was going back there when his leave was up.

"You wouldn't like to stop in England, then?" said Mr. Rockley.

"No, I wouldn't stop in England," said Hadrian.

"How's that? There's plenty of electricians here," said Mr. Rockley.

"Yes. But there's too much difference between the men and the employers over here—too much of that for me," said Hadrian.

The sick man looked at him narrowly, with oddly smiling eyes.

"That's it, is it?" he replied.

Matilda heard and understood. "So that's your big idea, is it, my little man," she said to herself. She had always said of Hadrian that he had no proper *respect* for anybody or anything, that he was sly and *common*. She went down to the kitchen for a *sotto voce* confab with Emmie.

"He thinks a rare lot of himself!" she whispered.

"He's somebody, he is!" said Emmie with contempt.

"He thinks there's too much difference between masters and men, over here," said Matilda.

"Is it any different in Canada?" asked Emmie.

"Oh, yes—democratic," replied Matilda. "He thinks they're all on a level over there."

"Ay, well he's over here now," said Emmie drily, "so he can keep his place."

As they talked they saw the young man sauntering down the garden, looking casually at the flowers. He had his hands in his pockets, and his soldier's cap neatly on his head. He looked quite at his ease, as if in possession. The two women, fluttered, watched him through the window.

"We know what he's come for," said Emmie, churlishly. Matilda looked a long time at the neat khaki figure. It had something of the charity-boy about it still; but now it was a man's figure, laconic, charged with plebeian energy. She thought of the derisive passion in his voice as he had declaimed against the propertied classes, to her father.

"You don't know, Emmie. Perhaps he's not come for that," she rebuked her sister. They were both thinking of the money.

They were still watching the young soldier. He stood away at the bottom of the garden, with his back to them, his hands in his pockets, looking into the water of the willow pond. Matilda's dark blue eyes had a strange, full look in them, the lids, with the faint blue veins showing, dropped rather low. She carried her head light and

high, but she had a look of pain.   The young man at the bottom
of the garden turned and looked up the path.   Perhaps he saw them
through the window.   Matilda moved into shadow.

That afternoon their father seemed weak and ill.   He was easily
exhausted.   The doctor came, and told Matilda that the sick man
might die suddenly at any moment—but then he might not.   They
must be prepared.

So the day passed, and the next.   Hadrian made himself at home.
He went about in the morning in his brownish jersey and his khaki
trousers, collarless, his bare neck showing.   He explored the pottery
premises, as if he had some secret purpose in so doing, he talked with
Mr. Rockley, when the sick man had strength.   The two girls were
always angry when the two men sat talking together like cronies.
Yet it was chiefly a kind of politics they talked.

On the second day after Hadrian's arrival, Matilda sat with her
father in the evening.   She was drawing a picture which she wanted
to copy.   It was very still, Hadrian was gone out somewhere, no
one knew where, and Emmie was busy.   Mr. Rockley reclined on his
bed, looking out in silence over his evening-sunny garden.

" If anything happens to me, Matilda," he said, " you won't sell
this house—you'll stop here——"

Matilda's eyes took their slightly haggard look as she stared at her
father.

" Well, we couldn't do anything else," she said.

" You don't know what you might do," he said.   " Everything is
left to you and Emmie, equally.   You do as you like with it—only
don't sell this house, don't part with it."

" No," she said.

" And give Hadrian my watch and chain, and a hundred pounds
out of what's in the bank—and help him if he ever wants helping.
I haven't put his name in the will."

" Your watch and chain, and a hundred pounds—yes.   But you'll
be here when he goes back to Canada, father."

" You never know what'll happen," said her father.

Matilda sat and watched him, with her full, haggard eyes, for a
long time, as if tranced.   She saw that he knew he must go soon—
she saw like a clairvoyant.

Later on she told Emmie what her father had said about the watch
and chain and the money.

" What right has _he_ "—_he_—meaning Hadrian—" to my father's
watch and chain—what has it to do with him ?   Let him have the
money, and get off," said Emmie.   She loved her father.

That night Matilda sat late in her room. Her heart was anxious and breaking, her mind seemed entranced. She was too much entranced even to weep, and all the time she thought of her father, only her father. At last she felt she must go to him.

It was near midnight. She went along the passage and to his room. There was a faint light from the moon outside. She listened at his door. Then she softly opened and entered. The room was faintly dark. She heard a movement on the bed.

" Are you asleep? " she said softly, advancing to the side of the bed.

" Are you asleep? " she repeated gently, as she stood at the side of the bed. And she reached her hand in the darkness to touch his forehead. Delicately, her fingers met the nose and the eyebrows, she laid her fine, delicate hand on his brow. It seemed fresh and smooth —very fresh and smooth. A sort of surprise stirred her, in her entranced state. But it could not waken her. Gently, she leaned over the bed and stirred her fingers over the low-growing hair on his brow.

" Can't you sleep to-night? " she said.

There was a quick stirring in the bed. " Yes, I can," a voice answered. It was Hadrian's voice. She started away. Instantly, she was wakened from her late-at-night trance. She remembered that her father was downstairs, that Hadrian had his room. She stood in the darkness as if stung.

" Is it you, Hadrian? " she said. " I thought it was my father." She was so startled, so shocked, that she could not move. The young man gave an uncomfortable laugh, and turned in his bed.

At last she got out of the room, When she was back in her own room, in the light, and her door was closed, she stood holding up her hand that had touched him, as if it were hurt. She was almost too shocked, she could not endure.

" Well," said her calm and weary mind, " it was only a mistake, why take any notice of it."

But she could not reason her feelings so easily. She suffered, feeling herself in a false position. Her right hand, which she had laid so gently on his face, on his fresh skin, ached now, as if it were really injured. She could not forgive Hadrian for the mistake : it made her dislike him deeply.

Hadrian too slept badly. He had been awakened by the opening of the door, and had not realized what the question meant. But the soft, straying tenderness of her hand on his face startled something out of his soul. He was a charity boy, aloof and more or less at bay. The fragile exquisiteness of her caress startled him most, revealed unknown things to him.

In the morning she could feel the consciousness in his eyes, when she came downstairs. She tried to bear herself as if nothing at all had happened, and she succeeded. She had the calm self-control, self-indifference, of one who has suffered and borne her suffering. She looked at him from her darkish, almost drugged blue eyes, she met the spark of consciousness in his eyes, and quenched it. And with her long, fine hand she put the sugar in his coffee.

But she could not control him as she thought she could. He had a keen memory stinging his mind, a new set of sensations working in his consciousness. Something new was alert in him. At the back of his reticent, guarded mind he kept his secret alive and vivid. She was at his mercy, for he was unscrupulous, his standard was not her standard.

He looked at her curiously. She was not beautiful, her nose was too large, her chin was too small, her neck was too thin. But her skin was clear and fine, she had a high-bred sensitiveness. This queer, brave, high-bred quality she shared with her father. The charity boy could see it in her tapering fingers, which were white and ringed. The same glamour that he knew in the elderly man he now saw in the woman. And he wanted to possess himself of it, he wanted to make himself master of it. As he went about through the old pottery-yard, his secretive mind schemed and worked. To be master of that strange soft delicacy such as he had felt in her hand upon his face—this was what he set himself towards. He was secretly plotting.

He watched Matilda as she went about, and she became aware of his attention, as of some shadow following her. But her pride made her ignore it. When he sauntered near her, his hands in his pockets, she received him with that same commonplace kindliness which mastered him more than any contempt. Her superior breeding seemed to control him. She made herself feel towards him exactly as she had always felt : he was a young boy who lived in the house with them, but was a stranger. Only, she dared not remember his face under her hand. When she remembered that, she was bewildered. Her hand had offended her, she wanted to cut it off. And she wanted, fiercely, to cut off the memory in him. She assumed she had done so.

One day, when he sat talking with his " uncle," he looked straight into the eyes of the sick man, and said :

" But I shouldn't like to live and die here in Rawsley."

" No—well—you needn't," said the sick man.

" Do you think Cousin Matilda likes it ? "

" I should think so."

" I don't call it much of a life," said the youth. " How much older is she than me, Uncle ? "

The sick man looked at the young soldier.

" A good bit," he said.

" Over thirty ? " said Hadrian.

" Well, not so much. She's thirty-two."

Hadrian considered a while.

" She doesn't look it," he said.

Again the sick father looked at him.

" Do you think she'd like to leave here ? " said Hadrian.

" Nay, I don't know," replied the father, restive.

Hadrian sat still, having his own thoughts. Then in a small, quiet voice, as if he were speaking from inside himself, he said :

" I'd marry her if you wanted me to."

The sick man raised his eyes suddenly, and stared. He stared for a long time. The youth looked inscrutably out of the window.

" *You !* " said the sick man, mocking, with some contempt. Hadrian turned and met his eyes. The two men had an inexplicable understanding.

" If you wasn't against it," said Hadrian.

" Nay," said the father, turning aside, " I don't think I'm against it. I've never thought of it. But—but Emmie's the youngest."

He had flushed, and looked suddenly more alive. Secretly he loved the boy.

" You might ask her," said Hadrian.

The elder man considered.

" Hadn't you better ask her yourself ? " he said.

" She'd take more notice of you," said Hadrian.

They were both silent. Then Emmie came in.

For two days Mr. Rockley was excited and thoughtful. Hadrian went about quietly, secretly, unquestioning. At last the father and daughter were alone together. It was very early morning, the father had been in much pain. As the pain abated, he lay still, thinking.

" Matilda ! " he said suddenly, looking at his daughter.

" Yes, I'm here," she said.

" Ay ! I want you to do something——"

She rose in anticipation.

" Nay, sit still. I want you to marry Hadrian——"

She thought he was raving. She rose, bewildered and frightened.

" Nay, sit you still, sit you still. You hear what I tell you."

" But you don't know what you're saying, father."

" Ay, I know well enough. I want you to marry Hadrian, I tell you."

She was dumbfounded. He was a man of few words.

" You'll do what I tell you," he said.

She looked at him slowly.

" What put such an idea in your mind ? " she said proudly.

" He did."

Matilda almost looked her father down, her pride was so offended.

" Why, it's disgraceful," she said.

" Why ? "

She watched him slowly.

" What do you ask me for ? " she said. " It's disgusting."

" The lad's sound enough," he replied, testily.

" You'd better tell him to clear out," she said, coldly.

He turned and looked out of the window. She sat flushed and erect for a long time. At length her father turned to her, looking really malevolent.

" If you won't," he said, " you're a fool, and I'll make you pay for your foolishness, do you see ? "

Suddenly a cold fear gripped her. She could not believe her senses. She was terrified and bewildered. She stared at her father, believing him to be delirious, or mad, or drunk. What could she do ?

" I tell you," he said. " I'll send for Whittle to-morrow if you don't. You shall neither of you have anything of mine."

Whittle was the solicitor. She understood her father well enough : he would send for his solicitor, and make a will leaving all his property to Hadrian : neither she nor Emmie should have anything. It was too much. She rose and went out of the room, up to her own room, where she locked herself in.

She did not come out for some hours. At last, late at night, she confided in Emmie.

" The sliving demon, he wants the money," said Emmie. " My father's out of his mind."

The thought that Hadrian merely wanted the money was another blow to Matilda. She did not love the impossible youth—but she had not yet learned to think of him as a thing of evil. He now became hideous to her mind.

Emmie had a little scene with her father next day.

" You don't mean what you said to our Matilda yesterday, do you, father ? " she asked aggressively.

" Yes," he replied.

" What, that you'll alter your will ? "

" Yes."

" You won't," said his angry daughter.

But he looked at her with a malevolent little smile.

" Annie ! " he shouted. " Annie ! "

He had still power to make his voice carry. The servant maid came in from the kitchen.

" Put your things on, and go down to Whittle's office, and say I want to see Mr. Whittle as soon as he can, and will he bring a will-form."

The sick man lay back a little—he could not lie down. His daughter sat as if she had been struck. Then she left the room.

Hadrian was pottering about in the garden. She went straight down to him.

" Here," she said. " You'd better get off. You'd better take your things and go from here, quick."

Hadrian looked slowly at the infuriated girl.

" Who says so ? " he asked.

" *We* say so—get off, you've done enough mischief and damage."

" Does Uncle say so ? "

" Yes, he does."

" I'll go and ask him."

But like a fury Emmie barred his way.

" No, you needn't. You needn't ask him nothing at all. We don't want you, so you can go."

" Uncle's boss here."

" A man that's dying, and you crawling round and working on him for his money !—you're not fit to live."

" Oh ! " he said. " Who says I'm working for his money ? "

" I say. But my father told our Matilda, and *she* knows what you are. *She* knows what you're after. So you might as well clear out, for all you'll get—guttersnipe ! "

He turned his back on her, to think. It had not occurred to him that they would think he was after the money. He *did* want the money—badly. He badly wanted to be an employer himself, not one of the employed. But he knew, in his subtle, calculating way, that it was not for money he wanted Matilda. He wanted both the money and Matilda. But he told himself the two desires were separate, not one. He could not do with Matilda, *without* the money. But he did not want her *for* the money.

When he got this clear in his mind, he sought for an opportunity to tell it her, lurking and watching. But she avoided him. In the evening the lawyer came. Mr. Rockley seemed to have a new access of strength—a will was drawn up, making the previous arrangements wholly conditional. The old will held good, if Matilda would consent to marry Hadrian. If she refused then at the end of six months the whole property passed to Hadrian.

Mr. Rockley told this to the young man, with malevolent satisfaction. He seemed to have a strange desire, quite unreasonable, for revenge upon the women who had surrounded him for so long, and served him so carefully.

" Tell her in front of me," said Hadrian.

So Mr. Rockley sent for his daughters.

At last they came, pale, mute, stubborn. Matilda seemed to have retired far off, Emmie seemed like a fighter ready to fight to the death. The sick man reclined on the bed, his eyes bright, his puffed hand trembling. But his face had again some of its old, bright handsomeness. Hadrian sat quiet, a little aside : the indomitable, dangerous charity boy.

" There's the will," said their father, pointing them to the paper.

The two women sat mute and immovable, they took no notice.

" Either you marry Hadrian, or he has everything," said the father with satisfaction.

" Then let him have everything," said Matilda coldly.

" He's not ! He's not ! " cried Emmie fiercely. " He's not going to have it. The guttersnipe ! "

An amused look came on her father's face.

" You hear that, Hadrian," he said.

" I didn't offer to marry Cousin Matilda for the money," said Hadrian, flushing and moving on his seat.

Matilda looked at him slowly, with her dark blue, drugged eyes. He seemed a strange little monster to her.

" Why, you liar, you know you did," cried Emmie.

The sick man laughed. Matilda continued to gaze strangely at the young man.

" She knows I didn't," said Hadrian.

He too had his courage, as a rat has indomitable courage in the end. Hadrian had some of the neatness, the reserve, the underground quality of the rat. But he had perhaps the ultimate courage, the most unquenchable courage of all.

Emmie looked at her sister.

" Oh, well," she said. " Matilda—don't you bother. Let him have everything, we can look after ourselves."

" I know he'll take everything," said Matilda, abstractedly.

Hadrian did not answer. He knew in fact that if Matilda refused him he would take everything, and go off with it.

" A clever little mannie——! " said Emmie, with a jeering grimace. The father laughed noiselessly to himself. But he was tired. . . .

" Go on, then," he said. " Go on, let me be quiet."

Emmie turned and looked at him.

" You deserve what you've got," she said to her father bluntly.

" Go on," he answered mildly. " Go on."

Another night passed—a night nurse sat up with Mr. Rockley. Another day came. Hadrian was there as ever, in his woollen jersey and coarse khaki trousers and bare neck. Matilda went about, frail and distant, Emmie black-browed in spite of her blondness. They were all quiet, for they did not intend the mystified servant to learn anything.

Mr. Rockley had very bad attacks of pain, he could not breathe. The end seemed near. They all went about quiet and stoical, all unyielding. Hadrian pondered within himself. If he did not marry Matilda he would go to Canada with twenty thousand pounds. This was itself a very satisfactory prospect. If Matilda consented he would have nothing—she would have her own money.

Emmie was the one to act. She went off in search of the solicitor and brought him home with her. There was an interview, and Whittle tried to frighten the youth into withdrawal—but without avail. The clergyman and relatives were summoned—but Hadrian stared at them and took no notice. It made him angry, however.

He wanted to catch Matilda alone. Many days went by, and he was not successful : she avoided him. At last, lurking, he surprised her one day as she came to pick gooseberries, and he cut off her retreat. He came to the point at once.

"You don't want me, then?" he said, in his subtle, insinuating voice.

" I don't want to speak to you," she said, averting her face.

" You put your hand on me, though," he said. " You shouldn't have done that, and then I should never have thought of it. You shouldn't have touched me."

" If you were anything decent, you'd know that was a mistake, and forget it," she said.

" I know it was a mistake—but I shan't forget it. If you wake a man up, he can't go to sleep again because he's told to."

" If you had any decent feeling in you, you'd have gone away," she replied.

" I didn't want to," he replied.

She looked away into the distance. At last she asked :

" What do you persecute me for, if it isn't for the money ? I'm old enough to be your mother. In a way I've been your mother."

" Doesn't matter," he said. " You've been no mother to me. Let us marry and go out to Canada—you might as well—you've touched me."

She was white and trembling. Suddenly she flushed with anger.

" It's so *indecent*," she said.

" How ? " he retorted. " You touched me."

But she walked away from him. She felt as if he had trapped her. He was angry and depressed, he felt again despised.

That same evening she went into her father's room.

" Yes," she said suddenly. " I'll marry him."

Her father looked up at her. He was in pain, and very ill.

" You like him now, do you ? " he said, with a faint smile.

She looked down into his face, and saw death not far off. She turned and went coldly out of the room.

The solicitor was sent for, preparations were hastily made. In all the interval Matilda did not speak to Hadrian, never answered him if he addressed her. He approached her in the morning.

" You've come round to it, then ? " he said, giving her a pleasant look from his twinkling, almost kindly eyes. She looked down at him and turned aside. She looked down on him both literally and figuratively. Still he persisted, and triumphed.

Emmie raved and wept, the secret flew abroad. But Matilda was silent and unmoved, Hadrian was quiet and satisfied, and nipped with fear also. But he held out against his fear. Mr. Rockley was very ill, but unchanged.

On the third day the marriage took place. Matilda and Hadrian drove straight home from the registrar, and went straight into the room of the dying man. His face lit up with a clear twinkling smile.

" Hadrian—you've got her ? " he said, a little hoarsely.

" Yes," said Hadrian, who was pale round the gills.

" Ay, my lad, I'm glad you're mine," replied the dying man. Then he turned his eyes closely on Matilda.

" Let's look at you, Matilda," he said. Then his voice went strange and unrecognizable. " Kiss me," he said.

She stooped and kissed him. She had never kissed him before, not since she was a tiny child. But she was quiet, very still.

" Kiss him," the dying man said.

Obediently, Matilda put forward her mouth and kissed the young husband.

" That's right ! That's right ! " murmured the dying man.

SAMSON AND DELILAH

A MAN got down from the motor-omnibus that runs from Penzance to St. Just-in-Penwith, and turned northwards, uphill towards the Polestar. It was only half-past six, but already the stars were out, a cold little wind was blowing from the sea, and the crystalline, three-pulse flash of the lighthouse below the cliffs beat rhythmically in the first darkness.

The man was alone. He went his way unhesitating, but looked from side to side with cautious curiosity. Tall, ruined power-houses of tin-mines loomed in the darkness from time to time, like remnants of some by-gone civilization. The lights of many miners' cottages scattered on the hilly darkness twinkled desolate in their disorder, yet twinkled with the lonely homeliness of the Celtic night.

He tramped steadily on, always watchful with curiosity. He was a tall, well-built man, apparently in the prime of life. His shoulders were square and rather stiff, he leaned forwards a little as he went, from the hips, like a man who must stoop to lower his height. But he did not stoop his shoulders : he bent his straight back from the hips.

Now and again short, stump, thick-legged figures of Cornish miners passed him, and he invariably gave them good night, as if to insist that he was on his own ground. He spoke with the West Cornish intonation. And as he went along the dreary road, looking now at the lights of the dwellings on land, now at the lights away to sea, vessels veering round in sight of the Longships Lighthouse, the whole of the Atlantic Ocean in darkness and space between him and America, he seemed a little excited and pleased with himself, watchful, thrilled, veering along in a sense of mastery and of power in conflict.

The houses began to close on the road, he was entering the straggling, formless, desolate mining village, that he knew of old. On the left was a little space set back from the road, and cosy lights of an inn. There it was. He peered up at the sign : " The Tinners' Rest." But he could not make out the name of the proprietor. He listened. There was excited talking and laughing, a woman's voice laughing shrilly among the men's.

Stooping a little, he entered the warmly-lit bar. The lamp was burning, a buxom woman rose from the white-scrubbed deal table where the black and white and red cards were scattered, and several men, miners, lifted their faces from the game.

The stranger went to the counter, averting his face. His cap was pulled down over his brow.

" Good evening ! " said the landlady, in her rather ingratiating voice.

" Good evening. A glass of ale."

" A glass of ale," repeated the landlady suavely. " Cold night— but bright."

" Yes," the man assented, laconically. Then he added, when nobody expected him to say any more : " Seasonable weather."

" Quite seasonable, quite," said the landlady. " Thank you."

The man lifted his glass straight to his lips, and emptied it. He put it down again on the zinc counter with a click.

" Let's have another," he said.

The woman drew the beer, and the man went away with his glass to the second table, near the fire. The woman, after a moment's hesitation, took her seat again at the table with the card-players. She had noticed the man : a big fine fellow, well dressed, a stranger.

But he spoke with that Cornish-Yankee accent she accepted as the natural twang among the miners.

The stranger put his foot on the fender and looked into the fire. He was handsome, well coloured, with well-drawn Cornish eyebrows, and the usual dark, bright, mindless Cornish eyes. He seemed abstracted in thought. Then he watched the card-party.

The woman was buxom and healthy, with dark hair and small, quick brown eyes. She was bursting with life and vigour, the energy she threw into the game of cards excited all the men, they shouted, and laughed, and the woman held her breast, shrieking with laughter.

" Oh, my, it'll be the death o' me," she panted. " Now, come on, Mr. Trevorrow, play fair. Play fair, I say, or I s'll put the cards down."

" Play fair ! Why, who's played unfair ? " ejaculated Mr. Trevor- row. " Do you mean t'accuse me, as I haven't played fair, Mrs. Nankervis ? "

" I do. I say it, and I mean it. Haven't you got the Queen of Spades ? Now, come on, no dodging round me. _I_ know you've got that Queen, as well as I know my name's Alice."

" Well—if your name's Alice, you'll have to have it——"

" Ay, now—what did I say ? Did ever you see such a man ? My

word, but your missus must be easy took in, by the looks of things."

And off she went into peals of laughter. She was interrupted by the entrance of four men in khaki, a short, stumpy sergeant of middle age, a young corporal, and two young privates. The woman leaned back in her chair.

" Oh, my ! " she cried. " If there isn't the boys back : looking perished, I believe——"

" Perished, Ma ! " exclaimed the sergeant. " Not yet."

" Near enough," said a young private, uncouthly.

The woman got up.

" I'm sure you are, my dears. You'll be wanting your suppers, I'll be bound."

" We could do with 'em."

" Let's have a wet first," said the sergeant.

The woman bustled about getting the drinks. The soldiers moved to the fire, spreading out their hands.

" Have your suppers in here, will you ? " she said. " Or in the kitchen ? "

" Let's have it here," said the sergeant. " More cosier—*if* you don't mind."

" You shall have it where you like, boys, where you like."

She disappeared. In a minute a girl of about sixteen came in. She was tall and fresh, with dark, young, expressionless eyes, and well-drawn brows, and the immature softness and mindlessness of the sensuous Celtic type.

" Ho, Maryann ! Evenin', Maryann ! How's Maryann, now ? " came the multiple greeting.

She replied to everybody in a soft voice, a strange, soft *aplomb* that was very attractive. And she moved round with rather mechanical, attractive movements, as if her thoughts were elsewhere. But she had always this dim far-awayness in her bearing : a sort of modesty. The strange man by the fire watched her curiously. There was an alert, inquisitive, mindless curiosity on his well-coloured face.

" I'll have a bit of supper with you, if I might," he said.

She looked at him, with her clear, unreasoning eyes, just like the eyes of some non-human creature.

" I'll ask mother," she said. Her voice was soft-breathing, gently singsong.

When she came in again :

" Yes," she said, almost whispering. " What will you have ? "

" What have you got ? " he said, looking up into her face.

" There's cold meat——"

" That's for me, then."

The stranger sat at the end of the table, and ate with the tired, quiet soldiers. Now, the landlady was interested in him. Her brow was knit rather tense, there was a look of panic in her large, healthy face, but her small brown eyes were fixed most dangerously. She was a big woman, but her eyes were small and tense. She drew near the stranger. She wore a rather loud-patterned flannelette blouse, and a dark skirt.

" What will you have to drink with your supper ? " she asked, and there was a new, dangerous note in her voice.

He moved uneasily.

" Oh, I'll go on with ale."

She drew him another glass. Then she sat down on the bench at the table with him and the soldiers, and fixed him with her attention.

" You've come from St. Just, have you ? " she said.

He looked at her with those clear, dark, inscrutable Cornish eyes, and answered at length :

" No, from Penzance."

" Penzance !—but you're not thinking of going back there to-night ? "

" No—no."

He still looked at her with those wide, clear eyes that seemed like very bright agate. Her anger began to rise. It was seen on her brow. Yet her voice was still suave and deprecating.

" I *thought* not—but you're not living in these parts, are you ? "

" No—no, I'm not living here." He was always slow in answering, as if something intervened between him and any outside question.

" Oh, I see," she said. " You've got relations down here."

Again he looked straight into her eyes, as if looking her into silence.

" Yes," he said.

He did not say any more. She rose with a flounce. The anger was tight on her brow. There was no more laughing and card-playing that evening, though she kept up her motherly, suave, good-humoured way with the men. But they knew her, they were all afraid of her.

The supper was finished, the table cleared, the stranger did not go. Two of the young soldiers went off to bed, with their cheery :

" Good night, Ma. Good night, Maryann."

The stranger talked a little to the sergeant about the war, which was in its first year, about the new army, a fragment of which was quartered in this district, about America.

The landlady darted looks at him from her small eyes, minute by minute the electric storm welled in her bosom, as still he did not go. She was quivering with suppressed, violent passion, something frightening and abnormal. She could not sit still for a moment. Her heavy form seemed to flash with sudden, involuntary movements as the minutes passed by, and still he sat there, and the tension on her heart grew unbearable. She watched the hands of the clock move on. Three of the soldiers had gone to bed, only the crop-headed, terrier-like old sergeant remained.

The landlady sat behind the bar fidgeting spasmodically with the newspaper. She looked again at the clock. At last it was five minutes to ten.

" Gentlemen—the enemy ! " she said, in her diminished, furious voice. " Time, please. Time, my dears. And good night all ! "

The men began to drop out, with a brief good night. It was a minute to ten. The landlady rose.

" Come," she said. " I'm shutting the door."

The last of the miners passed out. She stood, stout and menacing, holding the door. Still the stranger sat on by the fire, his black overcoat opened, smoking.

" We're closed now, sir," came the perilous, narrowed voice of the landlady.

The little, dog-like, hard-headed sergeant touched the arm of the stranger.

" Closing time," he said.

The stranger turned round in his seat, and his quick-moving, dark, jewel-like eyes went from the sergeant to the landlady.

" I'm stopping here to-night," he said, in his laconic Cornish-Yankee accent.

The landlady seemed to tower. Her eyes lifted strangely, frightening.

" Oh, indeed ! " she cried. " Oh, indeed ! And whose orders are those, may I ask ? "

He looked at her again.

" My orders," he said.

Involuntarily she shut the door, and advanced like a great, dangerous bird. Her voice rose, there was a touch of hoarseness in it.

" And what might *your* orders be, if you please ? " she cried. " Who might *you* be, to give orders, in the house ? "

He sat still, watching her.

" You know who I am," he said. " At least, I know who you are."

" Oh, do you ? Oh, do you ? And who am *I* then, if you'll be so good as to tell me ? "

He stared at her with his bright, dark eyes.

" You're my Missis, you are," he said. " And you know it, as well as I do."

She started as if something had exploded in her.

Her eyes lifted and flared madly.

" *Do* I know it, indeed ! " she cried. " I know no such thing ! I know no such thing ! Do you think a man's going to walk into this bar, and tell me off-hand I'm his Missis, and I'm going to believe him ? I say to you, whoever you may be, you're mistaken. I know myself for no Missis of yours, and I'll thank you to go out of this house, this minute, before I get those that will put you out."

The man rose to his feet, stretching his head towards her a little. He was a handsomely built Cornishman in the prime of life.

" What you say, eh ? You don't know me ? " he said, in his sing-song voice, emotionless, but rather smothered and pressing : it reminded one of the girl's. " I should know you anywhere, you see. I should ! I shouldn't have to look twice to know you, you see. You see, now, don't you ? "

The woman was baffled.

" So you may say," she replied, staccato. " So you may say. That's easy enough. My name's known, and respected, by most people for ten miles round. But I don't know *you*."

Her voice ran to sarcasm. " I can't say I know *you*. You're a *perfect* stranger to me, and I don't believe I've ever set eyes on you before to-night."

Her voice was very flexible and sarcastic.

" Yes, you have," replied the man, in his reasonable way. " Yes, you have. Your name's my name, and that girl Maryann is my girl ; she's my daughter. You're my Missis right enough. As sure as I'm Willie Nankervis."

He spoke as if it were an accepted fact. His face was handsome, with a strange, watchful alertness and a fundamental fixity of inten-tion that maddened her.

" You villain ! " she cried. " You villain, to come to this house and dare to speak to me. You villain, you downright rascal ! "

He looked at her.

" Ay," he said, unmoved. " All that." He was uneasy before her. Only he was not afraid of her. There was something impenetrable about him, like his eyes, which were as bright as agate.

She towered, and drew near to him menacingly.

"You're going out of this house, aren't you?" She stamped her foot in sudden madness. "*This minute!*"

He watched her. He knew she wanted to strike him.

"No," he said, with suppressed emphasis. "I've told you, I'm stopping here."

He was afraid of her personality, but it did not alter him. She wavered. Her small, tawny-brown eyes concentrated in a point of vivid, sightless fury, like a tiger's. The man was wincing, but he stood his ground. Then she bethought herself. She would gather her forces.

"We'll see whether you're stopping here," she said. And she turned, with a curious, frightening lifting of her eyes, and surged out of the room. The man, listening, heard her go upstairs, heard her tapping at a bedroom door, heard her saying: "Do you mind coming down a minute, boys? I want you. I'm in trouble."

The man in the bar took off his cap and his black overcoat, and threw them on the seat behind him. His black hair was short and touched with grey at the temples. He wore a well-cut, well-fitting suit of dark grey, American in style, and a turn-down collar. He looked well-to-do, a fine, solid figure of a man. The rather rigid look of the shoulders came from his having had his collar-bone twice broken in the mines.

The little terrier of a sergeant, in dirty khaki, looked at him furtively.

"She's your Missis?" he asked, jerking his head in the direction of the departed woman.

"Yes, she is," barked the man. "She's that, sure enough."

"Not seen her for a long time, haven't ye?"

"Sixteen years come March month."

"Hm!"

And the sergeant laconically resumed his smoking.

The landlady was coming back, followed by the three young soldiers, who entered rather sheepishly, in trousers and shirt and stocking-feet. The woman stood histrionically at the end of the bar, and exclaimed:

"That man refuses to leave the house, claims he's stopping the night here. You know very well I have no bed, don't you? And this house doesn't accommodate travellers. Yet he's going to stop in spite of all! But not while I've a drop of blood in my body, that I declare with my dying breath. And not if you men are worth the name of men, and will help a woman as has no one to help her."

Her eyes sparkled, her face was flushed pink. She was drawn up like an Amazon.

The young soldiers did not quite know what to do. They looked at the man, they looked at the sergeant, one of them looked down and fastened his braces on the second button.

" What say, sergeant ? " asked one whose face twinkled for a little devilment.

" Man says he's husband to Mrs. Nankervis," said the sergeant.

" He's no husband of mine. I declare I never set eyes on him before this night. It's a dirty trick, nothing else, it's a dirty trick."

" Why, you're a liar, saying you never set eyes on me before," barked the man near the hearth. " You're married to me, and that girl Maryann you had by me—well enough you know it."

The young soldier looked on in delight, the sergeant smoked imperturbed.

" Yes," sang the landlady, slowly shaking her head in supreme sarcasm, " it sounds very pretty, doesn't it ? But you see we don't believe a word of it, and *how* are you going to prove it ? " She smiled nastily.

The man watched in silence for a moment, then he said :

" It wants no proof."

" Oh, yes, but it does ! Oh, yes, but it does, sir, it wants a lot of proving ! " sang the lady's sarcasm. " We're not such gulls as all that, to swallow your words whole."

But he stood unmoved near the fire. She stood with one hand resting on the zinc-covered bar, the sergeant sat with legs crossed, smoking, on the seat half-way between them, the three young soldiers in their shirts and braces stood wavering in the gloom behind the bar. There was silence.

" Do you know anything of the whereabouts of your husband, Mrs. Nankervis ? Is he still living ? " asked the sergeant, in his judicious fashion.

Suddenly the landlady began to cry, great scalding tears, that left the young men aghast.

" I know nothing of him," she sobbed, feeling for her pocket handkerchief. " He left me when Maryann was a baby, went mining to America, and after about six months never wrote a line nor sent me a penny bit. I can't say whether he's alive or dead, the villain. All I've heard of him's to the bad—and I've heard nothing for years an' all, now." She sobbed violently.

The golden-skinned, handsome man near the fire watched her

as she wept. He was frightened, he was troubled, he was bewildered, but none of his emotions altered him underneath.

There was no sound in the room but the violent sobbing of the landlady. The men, one and all, were overcome.

"Don't you think as you'd better go, for to-night?" said the sergeant to the man, with sweet reasonableness. "You'd better leave it a bit, and arrange something between you. You can't have much claim on a woman, I should imagine, if it's how she says. And you've come down on her a bit too sudden-like."

The landlady sobbed heart-brokenly. The man watched her large breasts shaken. They seemed to cast a spell over his mind.

"How I've treated her, that's no matter," he replied. "I've come back, and I'm going to stop in my own home—for a bit, anyhow. There you've got it."

"A dirty action," said the sergeant, his face flushing dark. "A dirty action, to come, after deserting a woman for that number of years, and want to force yourself on her! A dirty action—as isn't allowed by the law."

The landlady wiped her eyes.

"Never you mind about law nor nothing," cried the man, in a strange, strong voice. "I'm not moving out of this public to-night."

The woman turned to the soldiers behind her, and said in a wheedling, sarcastic tone:

"Are we going to stand it, boys? Are we going to be done like this, Sergeant Thomas, by a scoundrel and a bully as has led a life beyond *mention* in those American mining-camps, and then wants to come back and make havoc of a poor woman's life and savings, after having left her with a baby in arms to struggle as best she might? It's a crying shame if nobody will stand up for me—a crying shame—— !"

The soldiers and the little sergeant were bristling. The woman stooped and rummaged under the counter for a minute. Then, unseen to the man away near the fire, she threw out a plaited grass rope, such as is used for binding bales, and left it lying near the feet of the young soldiers, in the gloom at the back of the bar.

Then she rose and fronted the situation.

"Come now," she said to the man, in a reasonable, coldly-coaxing tone, "put your coat on and leave us alone. Be a man, and not worse than a brute of a German. You can get a bed easy enough in St. Just, and if you've nothing to pay for it sergeant would lend you a couple of shillings, I'm sure he would."

All eyes were fixed on the man. He was looking down at the

woman like a creature spell-bound or possessed by some devil's own intention.

" I've got money of my own," he said. " Don't you be frightened for your money, I've plenty of that, for the time."

" Well, then," she coaxed, in a cold, almost sneering propitiation, " put your coat on and go where you're wanted—be a *man*, not a brute of a German."

She had drawn quite near to him, in her challenging coaxing intentness. He looked down at her with his bewitched face.

" No, I shan't," he said. " I shan't do no such thing. *You'll* put me up for to-night."

" Shall I ? " she cried. And suddenly she flung her arms round him, hung on to him with all her powerful weight, calling to the soldiers : " Get the rope, boys, and fasten him up. Alfred—John, quick now——"

The man reared, looked round with maddened eyes, and heaved his powerful body. But the woman was powerful also, and very heavy, and was clenched with the determination of death. Her face, with its exulting, horribly vindictive look, was turned up to him from his own breast ; he reached back his head frantically, to get away from it. Meanwhile the young soldiers, after having watched this frightful Laocoon swaying for a moment, stirred, and the malicious one darted swiftly with the rope. It was tangled a little.

" Give me the end here," cried the sergeant.

Meanwhile the big man heaved and struggled, swung the woman round against the seat and the table, in his convulsive effort to get free. But she pinned down his arms like a cuttlefish wreathed heavily upon him. And he heaved and swayed, and they crashed about the room, the soldiers hopping, the furniture bumping.

The young soldier had got the rope once round, the brisk sergeant helping him. The woman sank heavily lower, they got the rope round several times. In the struggle the victim fell over against the table. The ropes tightened till they cut his arms. The woman clung to his knees. Another soldier ran in a flash of genius, and fastened the strange man's feet with the pair of braces. Seats had crashed over, the table was thrown against the wall, but the man was bound, his arms pinned against his sides, his feet tied. He lay half-fallen, sunk against the table, still for a moment.

The woman rose, and sank, faint, on to the seat against the wall. Her breast heaved, she could not speak, she thought she was going to die. The bound man lay against the overturned table, his coat all twisted and pulled up beneath the ropes, leaving the loins exposed. The soldiers stood around, a little dazed, but excited with the row.

The man began to struggle again, heaving instinctively against the ropes, taking great, deep breaths. His face, with its golden skin, flushed dark and surcharged, he heaved again. The great veins in his neck stood out. But it was no good, he went relaxed. Then again, suddenly, he jerked his feet.

"Another pair of braces, William," cried the excited soldier. He threw himself on the legs of the bound man, and managed to fasten the knees. Then again there was stillness. They could hear the clock tick.

The woman looked at the prostrate figure, the strong, straight limbs, the strong back bound in subjection, the wide-eyed face that reminded her of a calf tied in a sack in a cart, only its head stretched dumbly backwards. And she triumphed.

The bound-up body began to struggle again. She watched fascinated the muscles working, the shoulders, the hips, the large, clean thighs. Even now he might break the ropes. She was afraid. But the lively young soldier sat on the shoulders of the bound man, and after a few perilous moments, there was stillness again.

"Now," said the judicious sergeant to the bound man, "if we untie you, will you promise to go off and make no more trouble?"

"You'll not untie him in here," cried the woman. "I wouldn't trust him as far as I could blow him."

There was silence.

"We might carry him outside, and undo him there," said the soldier. "Then we could get the policeman, if he made any more bother."

"Yes," said the sergeant. "We could do that." Then again, in an altered, almost severe tone, to the prisoner : "If we undo you outside, will you take your coat and go without creating any more disturbance?"

But the prisoner would not answer, he only lay with wide, dark, bright eyes, like a bound animal. There was a space of perplexed silence.

"Well, then, do as you say," said the woman irritably. "Carry him out amongst you, and let us shut up the house."

They did so. Picking up the bound man, the four soldiers staggered clumsily into the silent square in front of the inn, the woman following with the cap and the overcoat. The young soldiers quickly unfastened the braces from the prisoner's legs, and they hopped indoors. They were in their stocking-feet, and outside the stars flashed cold. They stood in the doorway watching. The man lay quite still on the cold ground.

" Now," said the sergeant, in a subdued voice, " I'll loosen the knot, and he can work himself free, if you go in, Missis."

She gave a last look at the dishevelled, bound man, as he sat on the ground. Then she went indoors, followed quickly by the sergeant. Then they were heard locking and barring the door.

The man seated on the ground outside worked and strained at the rope. But it was not so easy to undo himself even now. So, with hands bound, making an effort, he got on his feet, and went and worked the cord against the rough edge of an old wall. The rope, being of a kind of plaited grass, soon frayed and broke, and he freed himself. He had various contusions. His arms were hurt and bruised from the bonds. He rubbed them slowly. Then he pulled his clothes straight, stooped, put on his cap, struggled into his overcoat, and walked away.

The stars were very brilliant. Clear as crystal, the beam from the lighthouse under the cliffs struck rhythmically on the night. Dazed, the man walked along the road past the church-yard. Then he stood leaning up against a wall, for a long time.

He was roused because his feet were so cold. So he pulled himself together, and turned again in the silent night, back towards the inn.

The bar was in darkness. But there was a light in the kitchen. He hesitated. Then very quietly he tried the door.

He was surprised to find it open. He entered, and quietly closed it behind him. Then he went down the step past the bar-counter, and through to the lighted doorway of the kitchen. There sat his wife, planted in front of the range, where a furze fire was burning. She sat in a chair full in front of the range, her knees wide apart on the fender. She looked over her shoulder at him as he entered, but she did not speak. Then she stared in the fire again.

It was a small, narrow kitchen. He dropped his cap on the table that was covered with yellowish American cloth, and took a seat with his back to the wall, near the oven. His wife still sat with her knees apart, her feet on the steel fender and stared into the fire, motionless. Her skin was smooth and rosy in the firelight. Everything in the house was very clean and bright. The man sat silent, too, his head dropped. And thus they remained.

It was a question who would speak first. The woman leaned forward and poked the ends of the sticks in between the bars of the range. He lifted his head and looked at her.

" Others gone to bed, have they ? " he asked.

But she remained closed in silence.

" 'S a cold night, out," he said, as if to himself.

And he laid his large, yet well-shapen workman's hand on the top of the stove, that was polished black and smooth as velvet. She would not look at him, yet she glanced out of the corners of her eyes.

His eyes were fixed brightly on her, the pupils large and electric like those of a cat.

" I should have picked you out among thousands," he said. " Though you're bigger than I'd have believed. Fine flesh you've made."

She was silent for some time. Then she turned in her chair upon him.

" What do you think of yourself," she said, " coming back on me like this after over fifteen year ? You don't think I've not heard of you, neither, in Butte City and elsewhere ? "

He was watching her with his clear, translucent, unchallenged eyes.

" Yes," he said. " Chaps comes an' goes—I've heard tell of you from time to time."

She drew herself up.

" And what lies have you heard about *me* ? " she demanded superbly.

" I dunno as I've heard any lies at all—'cept as you was getting on very well, like."

His voice ran warily and detached. Her anger stirred again in her violently. But she subdued it, because of the danger there was in him, and more, perhaps, because of the beauty of his head and his level drawn brows, which she could not bear to forfeit.

" That's more than I can say of *you*," she said. " I've heard more harm than good about *you*."

" Ay, I dessay," he said, looking in the fire. It was a long time since he had seen the furze burning, he said to himself. There was a silence, during which she watched his face.

" Do you call yourself a *man* ? " she said, more in contemptuous reproach than in anger. " Leave a woman as you've left me, you don't care to what !—and then to turn up in *this* fashion, without a word to say for yourself."

He stirred in his chair, planted his feet apart, and resting his arms on his knees, looked steadily into the fire, without answering. So near to her was his head, and the close black hair, she could scarcely refrain from starting away, as if it would bite her.

" Do you call that the action of a *man* ? " she repeated.

" No," he said, reaching and poking the bits of wood into the fire with his fingers. " I didn't call it anything, as I know of. It's no good calling things by any names whatsoever, as I know of."

She watched him in his actions. There was a longer and longer pause between each speech, though neither knew it.

" I *wonder* what you think of yourself ! " she exclaimed, with vexed emphasis. " I *wonder* what sort of a fellow you take yourself to be ! " She was really perplexed as well as angry.

" Well," he said, lifting his head to look at her, " I guess I'll answer for my own faults, if everybody else'll answer for theirs."

Her heart beat fiery hot as he lifted his face to her. She breathed heavily, averting her face, almost losing her self-control.

" And what do you take *me* to be ? " she cried, in real helplessness.

His face was lifted watching her, watching her soft, averted face, and the softly heaving mass of her breasts.

" I take you," he said, with that laconic truthfulness which exercised such power over her, " to be the deuce of a fine woman— darn me if you're not as fine a built woman as I've seen, handsome with it as well. I shouldn't have expected you to put on such hand- some flesh : 'struth I shouldn't."

Her heart beat fiery hot, as he watched her with those bright agate eyes, fixedly.

" Been very handsome to *you*, for fifteen years, my sakes ! " she replied.

He made no answer to this, but sat with his bright, quick eyes upon her.

Then he rose. She started involuntarily. But he only said, in his laconic, measured way :

" It's warm in here now."

And he pulled off his overcoat, throwing it on the table. She sat as if slightly cowed, whilst he did so.

" Them ropes has given my arms something, by Ga–ard," he drawled, feeling his arms with his hands.

Still she sat in her chair before him, slightly cowed.

" You was sharp, wasn't you, to catch me like that, eh ? " he smiled slowly. " By Ga–ard, you had me fixed proper, proper you had. Darn me, you fixed me up proper—proper, you did."

He leaned forwards in his chair towards her.

" I don't think no worse of you for it, no, darned if I do. Fine pluck in a woman's what I admire. That I do, indeed."

She only gazed into the fire.

" We fet from the start, we did. And, my word, you begin again quick the minute you see me, you did. Darn me, you was too sharp for me. A darn fine woman, puts up a darn good fight. Darn me if I could find a woman in all the darn States as could get me down like that. Wonderful fine woman you be, truth to say, at this minute."

She only sat glowering into the fire.

" As grand a pluck as a man could wish to find in a woman, true as I'm here," he said, reaching forward his hand and tentatively touching her between her full, warm breasts, quietly.

She started, and seemed to shudder. But his hand insinuated itself between her breasts, as she continued to gaze in the fire.

" And don't you think I've come back here a-begging," he said. " I've more than *one* thousand pounds to my name, I have. And a bit of a fight for a how-de-do pleases me, that it do. But that doesn't mean as you're going to deny as you're my Missis . . ."

A young man came out of the Victoria station, looking undecidedly at the taxi-cabs, dark red and black, pressing against the curb under the glass roof. Several men in great-coats and brass buttons jerked themselves erect to catch his attention, at the same time keeping an eye on the other people as they filtered through the open doorways of the station. Berry, however, was occupied by one of the men, a big, burly fellow whose blue eyes glared back and whose red-brown moustache bristled in defiance.

" Do you *want* a cab, sir ? " the man asked, in a half-mocking, challenging voice.

Berry hesitated still.

" Are you Daniel Sutton ? " he asked.

" Yes," replied the other defiantly, with uneasy conscience.

" Then you are my uncle," said Berry.

They were alike in colouring, and somewhat in features, but the taxi driver was a powerful, well-fleshed man who glared at the world aggressively, being really on the defensive against his own heart. His nephew, of the same height, was thin, well-dressed, quiet and indifferent in his manner. And yet they were obviously kin.

" And who the devil are you ? " asked the taxi driver.

" I'm Daniel Berry," replied the nephew.

" Well, I'm damned—never saw you since you were a kid."

Rather awkwardly at this late hour the two shook hands. " How are you, lad ? "

" All right. I thought you were in Australia."

" Been back three months—bought a couple of these damned things "—he kicked the tyre of his taxi-cab in affectionate disgust. There was a moment's silence.

" Oh, but I'm going back out there. I can't stand this cankering, rotten-hearted hell of a country any more ; you want to come out to Sydney with me, lad. That's the place for you—beautiful place, oh, you could wish for nothing better. And money in it, too. How's your mother ? "

" She died at Christmas," said the young man.

" Dead ! What !—our Anna ! " The big man's eyes stared, and he recoiled in fear. " God, lad," he said, " that's three of 'em gone ! "

The two men looked away at the people passing along the pale grey pavements, under the wall of Trinity Church.

" Well, strike me lucky ! " said the taxi driver at last, out of breath. " She wor th' best o' th' bunch of 'em. I see nowt nor hear nowt from any of 'em—they're not worth it, I'll be damned if they are—our sermon-lapping Adela and Maud," he looked scornfully at his nephew. " But she was the best of 'em, our Anna was, that's a fact."

He was talking because he was afraid.

" An' after a hard life like she'd had. How old was she, lad ? "

" Fifty-five."

" Fifty-five . . ." He hesitated. Then, in a rather hushed voice, he asked the question that frightened him : " And what was it, then ? "

" Cancer."

" Cancer again, like Julia ! I never knew there was cancer in our family. Oh, my good God, our poor Anna, after the life she'd had ! What, lad, do you see any God at the back of that ? I'm damned if I do."

He was glaring, very blue-eyed and fierce, at his nephew. Berry lifted his shoulders slightly.

" God ? " went on the taxi driver, in a curious intense tone. " You've only to look at the folk in the street to know there's nothing keeps it going but gravitation. Look at 'em. Look at him ! " A mongrel-looking man was nosing past. " Wouldn't *he* murder you for your watch-chain, but that he's afraid of society ? He's got it *in* him. . . . Look at 'em."

Berry watched the townspeople go by, and, sensitively feeling his uncle's antipathy, it seemed he was watching a sort of *danse macabre* of ugly criminals.

" Did you ever see such a God-forsaken crew creeping about ! It gives you the very horrors to look at 'em. I sit in this damned car and watch 'em till, I can tell you, I feel like running the cab amuck among 'em, and running myself to kingdom come——"

Berry wondered at this outburst. He knew his uncle was the black sheep, the youngest, the darling of his mother's family. He knew him to be at outs with respectability, mixing with the looser, sporting type, all betting and drinking and showing dogs and birds, and racing. As a critic of life, however, he did not know him. But the young man felt curiously understanding. " He uses words like I do, he talks nearly as I talk, except that I shouldn't say those things. But I might feel like that, in myself, if I went a certain road."

" I've got to go to Watmore," he said. " Can you take me ? "

" When d'you want to go ? " asked the uncle fiercely.

" Now."

" Come on, then. What d'yer stand gassin' on th' causeway for ? "

The nephew took his seat beside the driver. The cab began to quiver, then it started forward with a whirr. The uncle, his hands and feet acting mechanically, kept his blue eyes fixed on the highroad into whose traffic the car was insinuating its way. Berry felt curiously as if he were sitting beside an older development of himself. His mind went back to his mother. She had been twenty years older than this brother of hers, whom she had loved so dearly. " He was one of the most affectionate little lads, and such a curly head ! I could never have believed he would grow into the great, coarse bully he is—for he's nothing else. My father made a god of him—well, it's a good thing his father is dead. He got in with that sporting gang, that's what did it. Things were made too easy for him, and so he thought of no one but himself, and this is the result."

Not that " Joky " Sutton was so very black a sheep. He had lived idly till he was eighteen, then had suddenly married a young, beautiful girl with clear brows and dark grey eyes, a factory girl. Having taken her to live with his parents he, lover of dogs and pigeons, went on to the staff of a sporting paper. But his wife was without uplift or warmth. Though they made money enough, their house was dark and cold and uninviting. He had two or three dogs, and the whole attic was turned into a great pigeon-house. He and his wife lived together roughly, with no warmth, no refinement, no touch of beauty anywhere, except that she was beautiful. He was a bluster-ing, impetuous man, she was rather cold in her soul, did not care about anything very much, was rather capable and close with money. And she had a common accent in her speech. He outdid her a thousand times in coarse language, and yet that cold twang in her voice tortured him with shame that he stamped down in bully-ing and in becoming more violent in his own speech.

Only his dogs adored him, and to them, and to his pigeons, he talked with rough, yet curiously tender caresses while they leaped and fluttered for joy.

After he and his wife had been married for seven years a little girl was born to them, then later, another. But the husband and wife drew no nearer together. She had an affection for her children almost like a cool governess. He had an emotional man's fear of sentiment, which helped to nip his wife from putting out any shoots. He treated his children roughly, and pretended to think it a good job when one was adopted by a well-to-do maternal aunt. But in his soul he hated his wife that she could give away one of his children. For after her cool fashion, she loved him. With a chaos of a man such as he, she had no chance of being anything but cold and hard, poor thing. For she did love him.

In the end he fell absurdly and violently in love with a rather sentimental young woman who read Browning. He made his wife an allowance and established a new ménage with the young lady, shortly after emigrating with her to Australia. Meanwhile his wife had gone to live with a publican, a widower, with whom she had had one of those curious, tacit understandings of which quiet women are capable, something like an arrangement for provision in the future.

This was as much as the nephew knew. He sat beside his uncle, wondering how things stood at the present. They raced lightly out past the cemetery and along the boulevard, then turned into the rather grimy country. The mud flew out on either side, there was a fine mist of rain which blew in their faces. Berry covered himself up.

In the lanes the high hedges shone black with rain. The silvery grey sky, faintly dappled, spread wide over the low, green land. The elder man glanced fiercely up the road, then turned his red face to his nephew.

" And how're you going on, lad ? " he said loudly. Berry noticed that his uncle was slightly uneasy of him. It made him also uncomfortable. The elder man had evidently something pressing on his soul.

" Who are you living with in town ? " asked the nephew. " Have you gone back to Aunt Maud ? "   .

" No," barked the uncle. " She wouldn't have me. I offered to —I wanted to—but she wouldn't."

" You're alone, then ? "

" No, I'm not alone."

He turned and glared with his fierce blue eyes at his nephew, but said no more for some time. The car ran on through the mud, under the wet wall of the park.

" That other devil tried to poison me," suddenly shouted the elder man. " The one I went to Australia with." At which, in spite of himself, the younger smiled in secret.

" How was that ? " he asked.

" Wanted to get rid of me.   She got in with another fellow on the ship. . . . By Jove, I was bad."

" Where—on the ship ? "

" No," bellowed the other.   " No.   That was in Wellington, New Zealand.   I was bad, and got lower an' lower—couldn't think what was up.   I could hardly crawl about.   As certain as I'm here, she was poisoning me, to get to th' other chap—I'm certain of it."

" And what did you do ? "

" I cleared out—went to Sydney——"

" And left her ? "

" Yes, I thought begod, I'd better clear out if I wanted to live."

" And you were all right in Sydney ? "

" Better in no time—I *know* she was putting poison in my coffee."

" Hm ! "

There was a glum silence.   The driver stared at the road ahead, fixedly, managing the car as if it were a live thing.   The nephew felt that his uncle was afraid, quite stupefied with fear, fear of life, of death, of himself.

" You're in rooms, then ? " asked the nephew.

" No, I'm in a house of my own," said the uncle defiantly, " wi' th' best little woman in th' Midlands.   She's a marvel.   Why don't you come an' see us ? "

" I will.   Who is she ? "

" Oh, she's a good girl—a beautiful little thing.   I was clean gone on her first time I saw her.   An' she was on me.   Her mother lives with us—respectable girl, none o' your . . ."

" And how old is she ? "

" How old is she ?   She's twenty-one."

" Poor thing."

" *She's* right enough."

" You'd marry her—getting a divorce——? "

" I shall marry her."

There was a little antagonism between the two men.

" Where's Aunt Maud ? " asked the younger.

" She's at the Railway Arms—we passed it, just against Rollin's Mill Crossing. . . .   They sent me a note this morning to go an' see her when I can spare time.   She's got consumption."

" Good Lord !   Are you going ? "

" Yes——"

But again Berry felt that his uncle was afraid.

The young man got through his commission in the village, had a drink with his uncle at the inn, and the two were returning home.

The elder man's subject of conversation was Australia. As they drew near the town they grew silent, thinking both of the public-house. At last they saw the gates of the railway crossing were closed before them.

" Shan't you call ? " asked Berry, jerking his head in the direction of the inn, which stood at the corner between two roads, its sign hanging under a bare horse-chestnut tree in front.

" I might as well. Come in an' have a drink," said the uncle.

It had been raining all the morning, so shallow pools of water lay about. A brewer's wagon, with wet barrels and warm-smelling horses, stood near the door of the inn. Everywhere seemed silent, but for the rattle of trains at the crossing. The two men went uneasily up the steps and into the bar. The place was paddled with wet feet, empty. As the barman was heard approaching, the uncle asked, his usual bluster slightly hushed by fear :

" What yer goin' ta have, lad ? Same as last time ? "

A man entered, evidently the proprietor. He was good-looking, with a long, heavy face and quick, dark eyes. His glance at Sutton was swift, a start, a recognition, and a withdrawal, into heavy neutrality.

" How are yer, Dan ? " he said, scarcely troubling to speak.

" Are yer, George ? " replied Sutton, hanging back. " My nephew, Dan Berry. Give us Red Seal, George."

The publican nodded to the younger man, and set the glasses on the bar. He pushed forward the two glasses, then leaned back in the dark corner behind the door, his arms folded, evidently preferring to get back from the watchful eyes of the nephew.

" —'s luck," said Sutton.

The publican nodded in acknowledgment. Sutton and his nephew drank.

" Why the hell don't you get that road mended in Cinder Hill—," said Sutton fiercely, pushing back his driver's cap and showing his short-cut, bristling hair.

" They can't find it in their hearts to pull it up," replied the publican, laconically.

" Find in their hearts ! They want settin' in barrows an' runnin' up an' down it till they cried for mercy."

Sutton put down his glass. The publican renewed it with a sure hand, at ease in whatsoever he did. Then he leaned back against the bar. He wore no coat. He stood with arms folded, his chin on his chest, his long moustache hanging. His back was round and slack, so that the lower part of his abdomen stuck forward, though he was not stout. His cheek was healthy, brown-red, and he was muscular. Yet there was about him this physical slackness, a reluctance in his slow, sure movements. His eyes were keen under his dark brows, but reluctant also, as if he were gloomily apathetic.

There was a halt. The publican evidently would say nothing. Berry looked at the mahogany bar-counter, slopped with beer, at the whisky-bottles on the shelves. Sutton, his cap pushed back, showing a white brow above a weather-reddened face, rubbed his cropped hair uneasily.

The publican glanced round suddenly. It seemed that only his dark eyes moved.

" Going up ? " he asked.

And something, perhaps his eyes, indicated the unseen bedchamber.

" Ay—that's what I came for," replied Sutton, shifting nervously from one foot to the other. " She's been asking for me ? "

" This morning," replied the publican, neutral.

Then he put up a flap of the bar, and turned away through the dark doorway behind. Sutton, pulling off his cap, showing a round, short-cropped head which now was ducked forward, followed after him, the buttons holding the strap of his great-coat behind glittering for a moment.

They climbed the dark stairs, the husband placing his feet carefully, because of his big boots. Then he followed down the passage, trying vaguely to keep a grip on his bowels, which seemed to be melting away, and definitely wishing for a neat brandy. The publican opened a door. Sutton, big and burly in his great-coat, went past him.

The bedroom seemed light and warm after the passage. There was a red eider-down on the bed. Then, making an effort, Sutton turned his eyes to see the sick woman. He met her eyes direct, dark, dilated. It was such a shock he almost started away. For a second he remained in torture, as if some invisible flame were playing on him to reduce his bones and fuse him down. Then he saw the sharp white edge of her jaw, and the black hair beside the hollow cheek. With a start he went towards the bed.

" Hello, Maud ! " he said. " Why, what ye been doin' ? "

The publican stood at the window with his back to the bed. The husband, like one condemned but on the point of starting away, stood by the bedside staring in horror at his wife, whose dilated grey eyes, nearly all black now, watched him wearily, as if she were looking at something a long way off.

Going exceedingly pale, he jerked up his head and stared at the wall over the pillows. There was a little coloured picture of a bird perched on a bell, and a nest among ivy leaves beneath. It appealed to him, made him wonder, roused a feeling of childish magic in him. They were wonderfully fresh, green ivy leaves, and nobody had seen the nest among them save him.

Then suddenly he looked down again at the face on the bed, to try and recognize it. He knew the white brow and the beautiful clear eyebrows. That was his wife, with whom he had passed his youth, flesh of his flesh, his, himself. Then those tired eyes, which met his again from a long way off, disturbed him until he did not know where he was. Only the sunken cheeks, and the mouth that seemed to protrude now were foreign to him, and filled him with horror. It seemed he lost his identity. He was the young husband of the woman with the clear brows ; he was the married man fighting with her whose eyes watched him, a little indifferently, from a long way off ; and he was a child in horror of that protruding mouth.

There came a crackling sound of her voice. He knew she had consumption of the throat, and braced himself hard to bear the noise.

" What was it, Maud ? " he asked in panic.

Then the broken, crackling voice came again. He was too terrified of the sound of it to hear what was said. There was a pause.

" You'll take Winnie ? " the publican's voice interpreted from the window.

" Don't you bother, Maud, I'll take her," he said, stupefying his mind so as not to understand.

He looked curiously round the room. It was not a bad bedroom, light and warm. There were many medicine bottles aggregated in a corner of the washstand—and a bottle of Three Star brandy, half-full. And there were also photographs of strange people on the chest of drawers. It was not a bad room.

Again he started as if he were shot. She was speaking. He bent down, but did not look at her.

" Be good to her," she whispered.

When he realized her meaning, that he should be good to their child when the mother was gone, a blade went through his flesh.

" I'll be good to her, Maud, don't you bother," he said, beginning to feel shaky.

He looked again at the picture of the bird. It perched cheerfully under a blue sky, with robust, jolly ivy leaves near. He was gathering his courage to depart. He looked down, but struggled hard not to take in the sight of his wife's face.

" I s'll come again, Maud," he said. " I hope you'll go on all right. Is there anything as you want ? "

There was an almost imperceptible shake of the head from the sick woman, making his heart melt swiftly again. Then, dragging his limbs, he got out of the room and down the stairs.

The landlord came after him.

" I'll let you know if anything happens," the publican said, still laconic, but with his eyes dark and swift.

" Ay, a' right," said Sutton blindly. He looked round for his cap, which he had all the time in his hand. Then he got out of doors.

In a moment the uncle and nephew were in the car jolting on the level crossing. The elder man seemed as if something tight in his brain made him open his eyes wide, and stare. He held the steering-wheel firmly. He knew he could steer accurately, to a hair's breadth. Glaring fixedly ahead, he let the car go, till it bounded over the uneven road. There were three coal-carts in a string. In an instant the car grazed past them, almost biting the kerb on the other side. Sutton aimed his car like a projectile, staring ahead. He did not want to know, to think, to realize, he wanted to be only the driver of that quick taxi.

The town drew near, suddenly. There were allotment-gardens, with dark-purple twiggy fruit-trees and wet alleys between the hedges. Then suddenly the streets of dwelling-houses whirled close, and the car was climbing the hill, with an angry whirr—up—up— till they rode out on to the crest and could see the tramcars, dark red and yellow, threading their way round the corner below, and all the traffic roaring between the shops.

" Got anywhere to go ? " asked Sutton of his nephew.

" I was going to see one or two people."

" Come an' have a bit o' dinner with us," said the other.

Berry knew that his uncle wanted to be distracted, so that he should not think nor realize. The big man was running hard away from the horror of realization.

" All right," Berry agreed.

The car went quickly through the town. It ran up a long street nearly into the country again. Then it pulled up at a house that stood alone, below the road.

" I s'll be back in ten minutes," said the uncle.

The car went on to the garage. Berry stood curiously at the top of the stone stairs that led from the highroad down to the level of the house, an old stone place. The garden was dilapidated. Broken fruit-trees leaned at a sharp angle down the steep bank. Right across the dim grey atmosphere, in a kind of valley on the edge of the town, new suburb-patches showed pinkish on the dark earth. It was a kind of unresolved borderland.

Berry went down the steps. Through the broken black fence of the orchard, long grass showed yellow. The place seemed deserted. He knocked, then knocked again. An elderly woman appeared. She looked like a housekeeper. At first she said suspiciously that Mr. Sutton was not in.

" My uncle just put me down. He'll be in in ten minutes," replied the visitor.

" Oh, are you the Mr. Berry who is related to him ? " exclaimed the elderly woman. " Come in—come in."

She was at once kindly and a little bit servile. The young man entered. It was an old house, rather dark, and sparsely furnished. The elderly woman sat nervously on the edge of one of the chairs in a drawing-room that looked as if it were furnished from dismal relics of dismal homes, and there was a little straggling attempt at conversation. Mrs. Greenwell was evidently a working-class woman unused to service or to any formality.

Presently she gathered up courage to invite her visitor into the dining-room. There from the table under the window rose a tall, slim girl with a cat in her arms. She was evidently a little more lady-like than was habitual to her, but she had a gentle, delicate, small nature. Her brown hair almost covered her ears, her dark lashes came down in shy awkwardness over her beautiful blue eyes. She shook hands in a frank way, yet she was shrinking. Evidently she was not sure how her position would affect her visitor. And yet she was assured in herself, shrinking and timid as she was.

" She must be a good deal in love with him," thought Berry.

Both women glanced shamefacedly at the roughly laid table. Evidently they ate in a rather rough and ready fashion.

Elaine—she had this poetic name—fingered her cat timidly, not knowing what to say or to do, unable even to ask her visitor to sit down. He noticed how her skirt hung almost flat on her hips. She was young, scarce developed, a long, slender thing. Her colouring was warm and exquisite.

The elder woman bustled out to the kitchen. Berry fondled the terrier dogs that had come curiously to his heels, and glanced out of the window at the wet, deserted orchard.

This room, too, was not well furnished, and rather dark. But there was a big red fire.

" He always has fox terriers," he said.

"Yes," she answered, showing her teeth in a smile.

"Do you like them, too?"

"Yes"—she glanced down at the dogs. "I like Tam better than Sally——"

Her speech always tailed off into an awkward silence.

"We've been to see Aunt Maud," said the nephew.

Her eyes, blue and scared and shrinking, met his.

"Dan had a letter," he explained. "She's very bad."

"Isn't it horrible!" she exclaimed, her face crumbling up with fear.

The old woman, evidently a hard-used, rather down-trodden workman's wife, came in with two soup plates. She glanced anxiously to see how her daughter was progressing with the visitor.

"Mother, Dan's been to see Maud," said Elaine, in a quiet voice full of fear and trouble.

The old woman looked up anxiously, in question.

"I think she wanted him to take the child. She's very bad, I believe," explained Berry.

"Oh, we should take Winnie!" cried Elaine. But both women seemed uncertain, wavering in their position. Already Berry could see that his uncle had bullied them, as he bullied everybody. But they were used to unpleasant men, and seemed to keep at a distance.

"Will you have some soup?" asked the mother, humbly.

She evidently did the work. The daughter was to be a lady, more or less, always dressed and nice for when Sutton came in.

They heard him heavily running down the steps outside. The dogs got up. Elaine seemed to forget the visitor. It was as if she came into life. Yet she was nervous and afraid. The mother stood as if ready to exculpate herself.

Sutton burst open the door. Big, blustering, wet in his immense grey coat, he came into the dining-room.

"Hello!" he said to his nephew, "making yourself at home?"

"Oh, yes," replied Berry.

"Hello, Jack," he said to the girl. "Got owt to grizzle about?"

"What for?" she asked, in a clear, half-challenging voice, that had that peculiar twang, almost petulant, so female and so attractive. Yet she was defiant like a boy.

"It's a wonder if you haven't," growled Sutton. And, with a really intimate movement, he stooped down and fondled his dogs, though paying no attention to them. Then he stood up, and remained with feet apart on the hearthrug, his head ducked forward, watching the girl. He seemed abstracted, as if he could only watch her. His great-coat hung open, so that she could see his figure, simple and human in the great husk of cloth. She stood nervously with her hands behind her, glancing at him, unable to see anything else. And he was scarcely conscious but of her. His eyes were still strained and staring, and as they followed the girl, when, long-limbed and languid, she moved away, it was as if he saw in her something impersonal, the female, not the woman.

" Had your dinner ? " he asked.

" We were just going to have it," she replied, with the same curious little vibration in her voice, like the twang of a string.

The mother entered, bringing a saucepan from which she ladled soup into three plates.

" Sit down, lad," said Sutton. " You sit down, Jack, an' give me mine here."

" Oh, aren't you coming to table ? " she complained.

" No, I tell you," he snarled, almost pretending to be disagreeable. But she was slightly afraid even of the pretence, which pleased and relieved him. He stood on the hearthrug eating his soup noisily.

" Aren't you going to take your coat off ? " she said. " It's filling the place full of steam."

He did not answer, but, with his head bent forward over the plate, he ate his soup hastily, to get it done with. When he put down his empty plate, she rose and went to him.

" Do take your coat off, Dan," she said, and she took hold of the breast of his coat, trying to push it back over his shoulder. But she could not. Only the stare in his eyes changed to a glare as her hand moved over his shoulder. He looked down into her eyes. She became pale, rather frightened-looking, and she turned her face away, and it was drawn slightly with love and fear and misery. She tried again to put off his coat, her thin wrists pulling at it. He stood solidly planted, and did not look at her, but stared straight in front. She was playing with passion, afraid of it, and really wretched because it left her, the person, out of count. Yet she continued. And there came into his bearing, into his eyes, the curious smile of passion, pushing away even the death-horror. It was life stronger than death in him. She stood close to his breast. Their eyes met, and she was carried away.

" Take your coat off, Dan," she said coaxingly, in a low tone meant for no one but him. And she slid her hands on his shoulder, and he yielded, so that the coat was pushed back. She had flushed, and her eyes had grown very bright. She got hold of the cuff of his coat. Gently, he eased himself, so that she drew it off.

Then he stood in a thin suit, which revealed his vigorous, almost mature form.

"What a weight!" she exclaimed, in a peculiar penetrating voice, as she went out hugging the overcoat. In a moment she came back.

He stood still in the same position, a frown over his fiercely staring eyes. The pain, the fear, the horror in his breast were all burning away in the new, fiercest flame of passion.

"Get your dinner," he said roughly to her.

"I've had all I want," she said. "You come an' have yours."

He looked at the table as if he found it difficult to see things.

"I want no more," he said.

She stood close to his chest. She wanted to touch him and to comfort him. There was something about him now that fascinated her. Berry felt slightly ashamed that she seemed to ignore the presence of others in the room.

The mother came in. She glanced at Sutton, standing planted on the hearthrug, his head ducked, the heavy frown hiding his face. There was a peculiar braced intensity about him that made the elder woman afraid. Suddenly he jerked his head round to his nephew.

"Get on wi' your dinner, lad," he said, and he went to the door. The dogs, which had continually lain down and got up again, uneasy, now rose and watched. The girl went after him, saying, clearly:

"What did you want, Dan?"

Her slim, quick figure was gone, the door was closed behind her.

There was silence. The mother, still more slave-like in her movement, sat down in a low chair. Berry drank some beer.

"That girl will leave him," he said to himself. "She'll hate him like poison. And serve him right. Then she'll go off with somebody else."

And she did.

" WELL, Mabel, and what are you going to do with yourself ? " asked Joe, with foolish flippancy. He felt quite safe himself. Without listening for an answer, he turned aside, worked a grain of tobacco to the tip of his tongue, and spat it out. He did not care about anything, since he felt safe himself.

The three brothers and the sister sat round the desolate breakfast table, attempting some sort of desultory consultation. The morning's post had given the final tap to the family fortunes, and all was over. The dreary dining-room itself, with its heavy mahogany furniture, looked as if it were waiting to be done away with.

But the consultation amounted to nothing. There was a strange air of ineffectuality about the three men, as they sprawled at table, smoking and reflecting vaguely on their own condition. The girl was alone, a rather short, sullen-looking young woman of twenty-seven. She did not share the same life as her brothers. She would have been good-looking, save for the impassive fixity of her face, " bull-dog," as her brothers called it.

There was a confused tramping of horses' feet outside. The three men all sprawled round in their chairs to watch. Beyond the dark holly-bushes that separated the strip of lawn from the highroad, they could see a cavalcade of shire horses swinging out of their own yard, being taken for exercise. This was the last time. These were the last horses that would go through their hands. The young men watched with critical, callous look. They were all frightened at the collapse of their lives, and the sense of disaster in which they were involved left them no inner freedom.

Yet they were three fine, well-set fellows enough. Joe, the eldest, was a man of thirty-three, broad and handsome in a hot, flushed way. His face was red, he twisted his black moustache over a thick finger, his eyes were shallow and restless. He had a sensual way of uncovering his teeth when he laughed, and his bearing was stupid, Now he watched the horses with a glazed look of helplessness in his eyes, a certain stupor of downfall.

The great draught-horses swung past. They were tied head to

tail, four of them, and they heaved along to where a lane branched off from the highroad, planting their great hoofs floutingly in the fine black mud, swinging their great rounded haunches sumptuously, and trotting a few sudden steps as they were led into the lane, round the corner. Every movement showed a massive, slumbrous strength, and a stupidity which held them in subjection. The groom at the head looked back, jerking the leading rope. And the cavalcade moved out of sight up the lane, the tail of the last horse, bobbed up tight and stiff, held out taut from the swinging great haunches as they rocked behind the hedges in a motion-like sleep.

Joe watched with glazed hopeless eyes. The horses were almost like his own body to him. He felt he was done for now. Luckily he was engaged to a woman as old as himself, and therefore her father, who was steward of a neighbouring estate, would provide him with a job. He would marry and go into harness. His life was over, he would be a subject animal now.

He turned uneasily aside, the retreating steps of the horses echoing in his ears. Then, with foolish restlessness, he reached for the scraps of bacon-rind from the plates, and making a faint whistling sound, flung them to the terrier that lay against the fender. He watched the dog swallow them, and waited till the creature looked into his eyes. Then a faint grin came on his face, and in a high, foolish voice he said:

" You won't get much more bacon, shall you, you little b—— ? "

The dog faintly and dismally wagged its tail, then lowered its haunches, circled round, and lay down again.

There was another helpless silence at the table. Joe sprawled uneasily in his seat, not willing to go till the family conclave was dissolved. Fred Henry, the second brother, was erect, clean-limbed, alert. He had watched the passing of the horses with more sang-froid. If he was an animal, like Joe, he was an animal which controls, not one which is controlled. He was master of any horse, and he carried himself with a well-tempered air of mastery. But he was not master of the situations of life. He pushed his coarse brown moustache upwards, off his lip, and glanced irritably at his sister, who sat impassive and inscrutable.

" You'll go and stop with Lucy for a bit, shan't you ? " he asked. The girl did not answer.

" I don't see what else you can do," persisted Fred Henry.

" Go as a skivvy," Joe interpolated laconically.

The girl did not move a muscle.

" If I was her, I should go in for training for a nurse," said

Malcolm, the youngest of them all. He was the baby of the family, a young man of twenty-two, with a fresh, jaunty *museau*.

But Mabel did not take any notice of him. They had talked at her and round her for so many years, that she hardly heard them at all.

The marble clock on the mantelpiece softly chimed the half-hour, the dog rose uneasily from the hearthrug and looked at the party at the breakfast table. But still they sat on in ineffectual conclave.

"Oh, all right," said Joe suddenly, apropos of nothing. "I'll get a move on."

He pushed back his chair, straddled his knees with a downward jerk, to get them free, in horsey fashion, and went to the fire. Still he did not go out of the room ; he was curious to know what the others would do or say. He began to charge his pipe, looking down at the dog and saying, in a high, affected voice :

"Going wi' me ? Going wi' me are ter ? Tha'rt goin' further than tha counts on just now, dost hear ? "

The dog faintly wagged its tail, the man stuck out his jaw and covered his pipe with his hands, and puffed intently, losing himself in the tobacco, looking down all the while at the dog with an absent brown eye. The dog looked up at him in mournful distrust. Joe stood with his knees stuck out, in real horsey fashion.

"Have you had a letter from Lucy ? " Fred Henry asked of his sister.

"Last week," came the neutral reply.

"And what does she say ? "

There was no answer.

"Does she *ask* you to go and stop there ? " persisted Fred Henry.

"She says I can if I like."

"Well, then, you'd better. Tell her you'll come on Monday."

This was received in silence.

"That's what you'll do then, is it ? " said Fred Henry, in some exasperation.

But she made no answer. There was a silence of futility and irritation in the room. Malcolm grinned fatuously.

"You'll have to make up your mind between now and next Wednesday," said Joe loudly, " or else find yourself lodgings on the kerbstone."

The face of the young woman darkened, but she sat on immutable.

"Here's Jack Fergusson ! " exclaimed Malcolm, who was looking aimlessly out of the window.

"Where ? " exclaimed Joe, loudly.

" Just gone past."

" Coming in ? "

Malcolm craned his neck to see the gate.

" Yes," he said.

There was a silence. Mabel sat on like one condemned, at the head of the table. Then a whistle was heard from the kitchen. The dog got up and barked sharply. Joe opened the door and shouted :

" Come on."

After a moment a young man entered. He was muffled up in overcoat and a purple woollen scarf, and his tweed cap, which he did not remove, was pulled down on his head. He was of medium height, his face was rather long and pale, his eyes looked tired.

" Hello, Jack ! Well, Jack ! " exclaimed Malcolm and Joe. Fred Henry merely said, " Jack."

" What's doing ? " asked the newcomer, evidently addressing Fred Henry.

" Same. We've got to be out by Wednesday.   Got a cold ? "

" I have—got it bad, too."

" Why don't you stop in ? "

" *Me* stop in ? When I can't stand on my legs, perhaps I shall have a chance."   The young man spoke huskily. He had a slight Scotch accent.

" It's a knock-out, isn't it," said Joe, boisterously, " if a doctor goes round croaking with a cold. Looks bad for the patients, doesn't it ? "

The young doctor looked at him slowly.

" Anything the matter with *you*, then ? " he asked sarcastically.

" Not as I know of. Damn your eyes, I hope not. Why ? "

" I thought you were very concerned about the patients, wondered if you might be one yourself."

" Damn it, no, I've never been patient to no flaming doctor, and hope I never shall be," returned Joe.

At this point Mabel rose from the table, and they all seemed to become aware of her existence. She began putting the dishes to-together. The young doctor looked at her, but did not address her. He had not greeted her. She went out of the room with the tray, her face impassive and unchanged.

" When are you off then, all of you ? " asked the doctor.

" I'm catching the eleven-forty," replied Malcolm. " Are you goin' down wi' th' trap, Joe ? "

" Yes, I've told you I'm going down wi' th' trap, haven't I ? "

" We'd better be getting her in then. So long, Jack, if I don't see you before I go," said Malcolm, shaking hands.

He went out, followed by Joe, who seemed to have his tail between his legs.

" Well, this is the devil's own," exclaimed the doctor, when he was left alone with Fred Henry. " Going before Wednesday, are you ? "

" That's the orders," replied the other.

" Where, to Northampton ? "

" That's it."

" The devil ! " exclaimed Fergusson, with quiet chagrin.

And there was silence between the two.

" All settled up, are you ? " asked Fergusson.

" About."

There was another pause.

" Well, I shall miss yer, Freddy, boy," said the young doctor.

" And I shall miss thee, Jack," returned the other.

" Miss you like hell," mused the doctor.

Fred Henry turned aside. There was nothing to say. Mabel came in again, to finish clearing the table.

" What are *you* going to do, then, Miss Pervin ? " asked Fergusson. " Going to your sister's, are you ? "

Mabel looked at him with her steady, dangerous eyes, that always made him uncomfortable, unsettling his superficial ease.

" No," she said.

" Well, what in the name of fortune *are* you going to do ? Say what you mean to do," cried Fred Henry, with futile intensity.

But she only averted her head, and continued her work. She folded the white table-cloth, and put on the chenille cloth.

" The sulkiest bitch that ever trod ! " muttered her brother.

But she finished her task with perfectly impassive face, the young doctor watching her interestedly all the while. Then she went out.

Fred Henry stared after her, clenching his lips, his blue eyes fixing in sharp antagonism, as he made a grimace of sour exasperation.

" You could bray her into bits, and that's all you'd get out of her," he said, in a small, narrowed tone.

The doctor smiled faintly.

" What's she *going* to do, then ? " he asked.

" Strike me if *I* know ! " returned the other.

There was a pause. Then the doctor stirred.

" I'll be seeing you to-night, shall I ? " he said to his friend.

" Ay—where's it to be ? Are we going over to Jessdale ? "

" I don't know. I've got such a cold on me. I'll come round to the Moon and Stars, anyway."

" Let Lizzie and May miss their night for once, eh ? "

" That's it—if I feel as I do now."

" All's one——"

The two young men went through the passage and down to the back door together. The house was large, but it was servantless now, and desolate. At the back was a small bricked house-yard, and beyond that a big square, gravelled fine and red, and having stables on two sides. Sloping, dank, winter-dark fields stretched away on the open sides.

But the stables were empty. Joseph Pervin, the father of the family, had been a man of no education, who had become a fairly large horse dealer. The stables had been full of horses, there was a great turmoil and come-and-go of horses and of dealers and grooms. Then the kitchen was full of servants. But of late things had declined. The old man had married a second time, to retrieve his fortunes. Now he was dead and everything was gone to the dogs, there was nothing but debt and threatening.

For months, Mabel had been servantless in the big house, keeping the home together in penury for her ineffectual brothers. She had kept house for ten years. But previously it was with unstinted means. Then, however brutal and coarse everything was, the sense of money had kept her proud, confident. The men might be foul-mouthed, the women in the kitchen might have bad reputations, her brothers might have illegitimate children. But so long as there was money, the girl felt herself established, and brutally proud, reserved.

No company came to the house, save dealers and coarse men. Mabel had no associates of her own sex, after her sister went away. But she did not mind. She went regularly to church, she attended to her father. And she lived in the memory of her mother, who had died when she was fourteen, and whom she had loved. She had loved her father, too, in a different way, depending upon him, and feeling secure in him, until at the age of fifty-four he married again. And then she had set hard against him. Now he had died and left them all hopelessly in debt.

She had suffered badly during the period of poverty. Nothing, however, could shake the curious sullen, animal pride that domin-ated each member of the family. Now, for Mabel, the end had come. Still she would not cast about her. She would follow her own way just the same. She would always hold the keys of her own situation.

Mindless and persistent, she endured from day to day. Why should she think? Why should she answer anybody? It was enough that this was the end, and there was no way out. She need not pass any more darkly along the main street of the small town, avoiding every eye. She need not demean herself any more, going into the shops and buying the cheapest food. This was at an end. She thought of nobody, not even of herself. Mindless and persistent, she seemed in a sort of ecstasy to be coming nearer to her fulfilment, her own glorification, approaching her dead mother, who was glorified.

In the afternoon she took a little bag, with shears and sponge and a small scrubbing brush, and went out. It was a grey, wintry day, with saddened, dark green fields and an atmosphere blackened by the smoke of foundries not far off. She went quickly, darkly along the causeway, heeding nobody, through the town to the churchyard.

There she always felt secure, as if no one could see her, although as a matter of fact she was exposed to the stare of every one who passed along under the churchyard wall. Nevertheless, once under the shadow of the great looming church, among the graves, she felt immune from the world, reserved within the thick churchyard wall as in another country.

Carefully she clipped the grass from the grave, and arranged the pinky white, small chrysanthemums in the tin cross. When this was done, she took an empty jar from a neighbouring grave, brought water, and carefully, most scrupulously sponged the marble head-stone and the coping-stone.

It gave her sincere satisfaction to do this. She felt in immediate contact with the world of her mother. She took minute pains, went through the park in a state bordering on pure happiness, as if in performing this task she came into a subtle, intimate connection with her mother. For the life she followed here in the world was far less real than the world of death she inherited from her mother.

The doctor's house was just by the church. Fergusson, being a mere hired assistant, was slave to the country-side. As he hurried now to attend to the outpatients in the surgery, glancing across the graveyard with his quick eye, he saw the girl at her task at the grave. She seemed so intent and remote, it was like looking into another world. Some mystical element was touched in him. He slowed down as he walked, watching her as if spell-bound.

She lifted her eyes, feeling him looking. Their eyes met. And each looked again at once, each feeling, in some way, found out by the other. He lifted his cap and passed on down the road. There remained distinct in his consciousness, like a vision, the memory of her face, lifted from the tombstone in the churchyard, and looking at him with slow, large, portentous eyes. It *was* portentous, her face. It seemed to mesmerize him. There was a heavy power in her eyes which laid hold of his whole being, as if he had drunk some powerful drug. He had been feeling weak and done before. Now the life came back into him, he felt delivered from his own fretted, daily self.

He finished his duties at the surgery as quickly as might be, hastily filling up the bottles of the waiting people with cheap drugs. Then, in perpetual haste, he set off again to visit several cases in another part of his round, before teatime. At all times he preferred to walk if he could, but particularly when he was not well. He fancied the motion restored him.

The afternoon was falling. It was grey, deadened, and wintry, with a slow, moist, heavy coldness sinking in and deadening all the faculties. But why should he think or notice ? He hastily climbed the hill and turned across the dark green fields, following the black cinder-track. In the distance, across a shallow dip in the country, the small town was clustered like smouldering ash, a tower, a spire, a heap of low, raw, extinct houses. And on the nearest fringe of the town, sloping into the dip, was Oldmeadow, the Pervins' house. He could see the stables and the outbuildings distinctly, as they lay towards him on the slope. Well, he would not go there many more times ! Another resource would be lost to him, another place gone : the only company he cared for in the alien, ugly little town he was losing. Nothing but work, drudgery, constant hastening from dwelling to dwelling among the colliers and the iron-workers. It wore him out, but at the same time he had a craving for it. It was a stimulant to him to be in the homes of the working people, moving as it were through the innermost body of their life. His nerves were excited and gratified. He could come so near, into the very lives of the rough, inarticulate, powerfully emotional men and women. He grumbled, he said he hated the hellish hole. But as a matter of fact it excited him, the contact with the rough, strongly-feeling people was a stimulant applied direct to his nerves.

Below Oldmeadow, in the green, shallow, soddened hollow of fields, lay a square, deep pond. Roving across the landscape, the doctor's quick eye detected a figure in black passing through the gate of the field, down towards the pond. He looked again. It would be Mabel Pervin. His mind suddenly became alive and attentive.

Why was she going down there ? He pulled up on the path on the slope above, and stood staring. He could just make sure of the small black figure moving in the hollow of the failing day. He seemed to see her in the midst of such obscurity, that he was like a clairvoyant, seeing rather with the mind's eye than with ordinary sight. Yet he could see her positively enough, whilst he kept his eye attentive. He felt, if he looked away from her, in the thick, ugly, falling dusk, he would lose her altogether.

He followed her minutely as she moved, direct and intent, like something transmitted rather than stirring in voluntary activity, straight down the field towards the pond. There she stood on the bank for a moment. She never raised her head. Then she waded slowly into the water.

He stood motionless as the small black figure walked slowly and deliberately towards the centre of the pond, very slowly, gradually moving deeper into the motionless water, and still moving forward as the water got up to her breast. Then he could see her no more in the dusk of the dead afternoon.

" There ! " he exclaimed. " Would you believe it ? "

And he hastened straight down, running over the wet, soddened fields, pushing through the hedges, down into the depression of callous wintry obscurity. It took him several minutes to come to the pond. He stood on the bank, breathing heavily. He could see nothing. His eyes seemed to penetrate the dead water. Yes, perhaps that was the dark shadow of her black clothing beneath the surface of the water.

He slowly ventured into the pond. The bottom was deep, soft clay, he sank in, and the water clasped dead cold round his legs. As he stirred he could smell the cold, rotten clay that fouled up into the water. It was objectionable in his lungs. Still, repelled and yet not heeding, he moved deeper into the pond. The cold water rose over his thighs, over his loins, upon his abdomen. The lower part of his body was all sunk in the hideous cold element. And the bottom was so deeply soft and uncertain, he was afraid of pitching with his mouth underneath. He could not swim, and was afraid.

He crouched a little, spreading his hands under the water and moving them round, trying to feel for her. The dead cold pond swayed upon his chest. He moved again, a little deeper, and again, with his hands underneath, he felt all around under the water. And he touched her clothing. But it evaded his fingers. He made a desperate effort to grasp it.

And so doing he lost his balance and went under, horribly, suffocating in the foul earthy water, struggling madly for a few moments. At last, after what seemed an eternity, he got his footing, rose again

into the air and looked around. He gasped, and knew he was in the
world. Then he looked at the water. She had risen near him. He
grasped her clothing, and drawing her nearer, turned to take his
way to land again.

He went very slowly, carefully, absorbed in the slow progress.
He rose higher, climbing out of the pond. The water was now only
about his legs ; he was thankful, full of relief to be out of the clutches
of the pond. He lifted her and staggered on to the bank, out of the
horror of wet, grey clay.

He laid her down on the bank. She was quite unconscious and
running with water. He made the water come from her mouth, he
worked to restore her. He did not have to work very long before he
could feel the breathing begin again in her ; she was breathing
naturally. He worked a little longer. He could feel her live
beneath his hands ; she was coming back. He wiped her face,
wrapped her in his overcoat, looked round into the dim, dark grey
world, then lifted her and staggered down the bank and across the
fields.

It seemed an unthinkably long way, and his burden so heavy he
felt he would never get to the house. But at last he was in the stable-
yard, and then in the house-yard. He opened the door and went into
the house. In the kitchen he laid her down on the hearthrug, and
called. The house was empty. But the fire was burning in the grate.

Then again he kneeled to attend to her. She was breathing
regularly, her eyes were wide open and as if conscious, but there
seemed something missing in her look. She was conscious in herself,
but unconscious of her surroundings.

He ran upstairs, took blankets from a bed, and put them before
the fire to warm. Then he removed her saturated, earthy-smelling
clothing, rubbed her dry with a towel, and wrapped her naked in
the blankets. Then he went into the dining-room, to look for spirits.
There was a little whisky. He drank a gulp himself, and put some
into her mouth.

The effect was instantaneous. She looked full into his face, as if
she had been seeing him for some time, and yet had only just become
conscious of him.

" Dr. Fergusson ? " she said.

" What ? " he answered.

He was divesting himself of his coat, intending to find some dry
clothing upstairs. He could not bear the smell of the dead, clayey
water, and he was mortally afraid for his own health.

" What did I do ? " she asked.

"Walked into the pond," he replied. He had begun to shudder like one sick, and could hardly attend to her. Her eyes remained full on him, he seemed to be going dark in his mind, looking back at her helplessly. The shuddering became quieter in him, his life came back in him, dark and unknowing, but strong again.

"Was I out of my mind?" she asked, while her eyes were fixed on him all the time.

"Maybe, for the moment," he replied. He felt quiet, because his strength had come back. The strange fretful strain had left him.

"Am I out of my mind now?" she asked.

"Are you?" he reflected a moment. "No," he answered truthfully, "I don't see that you are." He turned his face aside. He was afraid now, because he felt dazed, and felt dimly that her power was stronger than his, in this issue. And she continued to look at him fixedly all the time. "Can you tell me where I shall find some dry things to put on?" he asked.

"Did you dive into the pond for me?" she asked.

"No," he answered. "I walked in. But I went in overhead as well."

There was silence for a moment. He hesitated. He very much wanted to go upstairs to get into dry clothing. But there was another desire in him. And she seemed to hold him. His will seemed to have gone to sleep, and left him, standing there slack before her. But he felt warm inside himself. He did not shudder at all, though his clothes were sodden on him.

"Why did you?" she asked.

"Because I didn't want you to do such a foolish thing," he said.

"It wasn't foolish," she said, still gazing at him as she lay on the floor, with a sofa cushion under her head. "It was the right thing to do. *I* knew best, then."

"I'll go and shift these wet things," he said. But still he had not the power to move out of her presence, until she sent him. It was as if she had the life of his body in her hands, and he could not extricate himself. Or perhaps he did not want to.

Suddenly she sat up. Then she became aware of her own immediate condition. She felt the blankets about her, she knew her own limbs. For a moment it seemed as if her reason were going. She looked round, with wild eye, as if seeking something. He stood still with fear. She saw her clothing lying scattered.

"Who undressed me?" she asked, her eyes resting full and inevitable on his face.

"I did," he replied, "to bring you round."

For some moments she sat and gazed at him awfully, her lips parted.

" Do you love me, then ? " she asked.

He only stood and stared at her, fascinated. His soul seemed to melt.

She shuffled forward on her knees, and put her arms round him, round his legs, as he stood there, pressing her breasts against his knees and thighs, clutching him with strange, convulsive certainty, pressing his thighs against her, drawing him to her face, her throat, as she looked up at him with flaring, humble eyes of transfiguration, triumphant in first possession.

" You love me," she murmured, in strange transport, yearning and triumphant and confident. " You love me. I know you love me, I know."

And she was passionately kissing his knees, through the wet clothing, passionately and indiscriminately kissing his knees, his legs, as if unaware of everything.

He looked down at the tangled wet hair, the wild, bare, animal shoulders. He was amazed, bewildered, and afraid. He had never thought of loving her. He had never wanted to love her. When he rescued her and restored her, he was a doctor, and she was a patient. He had had no single personal thought of her. Nay, this introduction of the personal element was very distasteful to him, a violation of his professional honour. It was horrible to have her there embracing his knees. It was horrible. He revolted from it, violently. And yet—and yet—he had not the power to break away.

She looked at him again, with the same supplication of powerful love, and that same transcendent, frightening light of triumph. In view of the delicate flame which seemed to come from her face like a light, he was powerless. And yet he had never intended to love her. He had never intended. And something stubborn in him could not give way.

" You love me," she repeated, in a murmur of deep, rhapsodic assurance. " You love me."

Her hands were drawing him, drawing him down to her. He was afraid, even a little horrified. For he had, really, no intention of loving her. Yet her hands were drawing him towards her. He put out his hand quickly to steady himself, and grasped her bare shoulder. A flame seemed to burn the hand that grasped her soft shoulder. He had no intention of loving her : his whole will was against his yielding. It was horrible. And yet wonderful was the touch of her shoulders, beautiful the shining of her face. Was she perhaps mad ? He had a horror of yielding to her. Yet something in him ached also.

He had been staring away at the door, away from her. But his hand remained on her shoulder. She had gone suddenly very still. He looked down at her. Her eyes were now wide with fear, with doubt, the light was dying from her face, a shadow of terrible greyness was returning. He could not bear the touch of her eyes' question upon him, and the look of death behind the question.

With an inward groan he gave way, and let his heart yield towards her. A sudden gentle smile came on his face. And her eyes, which never left his face, slowly, slowly filled with tears. He watched the strange water rise in her eyes, like some slow fountain coming up. And his heart seemed to burn and melt away in his breast.

He could not bear to look at her any more. He dropped on his knees and caught her head with his arms and pressed her face against his throat. She was very still. His heart, which seemed to have broken, was burning with a kind of agony in his breast. And he felt her slow, hot tears wetting his throat. But he could not move.

He felt the hot tears wet his neck and the hollows of his neck, and he remained motionless, suspended through one of man's eternities. Only now it had become indispensable to him to have her face pressed close to him ; he could never let her go again. He could never let her head go away from the close clutch of his arm. He wanted to remain like that for ever, with his heart hurting him in a pain that was also life to him. Without knowing, he was looking down on her damp, soft brown hair.

Then, as it were suddenly, he smelt the horrid stagnant smell of that water. And at the same moment she drew away from him and looked at him. Her eyes were wistful and unfathomable. He was afraid of them, and he fell to kissing her, not knowing what he was doing. He wanted her eyes not to have that terrible, wistful, unfathomable look.

When she turned her face to him again, a faint delicate flush was glowing, and there was again dawning that terrible shining of joy in her eyes, which really terrified him, and yet which he now wanted to see, because he feared the look of doubt still more.

" You love me ? " she said, rather faltering.

" Yes." The word cost him a painful effort. Not because it wasn't true. But because it was too newly true, the *saying* seemed to tear open again his newly-torn heart. And he hardly wanted it to be true, even now.

She lifted her face to him, and he bent forward and kissed her on the mouth, gently, with the one kiss that is an eternal pledge. And as he kissed her his heart strained again in his breast. He never intended to love her. But now it was over. He had crossed over the gulf to her, and all that he had left behind had shrivelled and become void.

After the kiss, her eyes again slowly filled with tears. She sat still, away from him, with her face drooped aside, and her hands folded in her lap. The tears fell very slowly. There was complete silence. He too sat there motionless and silent on the hearthrug. The strange pain of his heart that was broken seemed to consume him. That he should love her? That this was love! That he should be ripped open in this way! Him, a doctor! How they would all jeer if they knew! It was agony to him to think they might know.

In the curious naked pain of the thought he looked again to her. She was sitting there drooped into a muse. He saw a tear fall, and his heart flared hot. He saw for the first time that one of her shoulders was quite uncovered, one arm bare, he could see one of her small breasts ; dimly, because it had become almost dark in the room.

" Why are you crying ? " he asked, in an altered voice.

She looked up at him, and behind her tears the consciousness of her situation for the first time brought a dark look of shame to her eyes.

" I'm not crying, really," she said, watching him half frightened.

He reached his hand, and softly closed it on her bare arm.

" I love you ! I love you ! " he said in a soft, low vibrating voice, unlike himself.

She shrank, and dropped her head. The soft, penetrating grip of his hand on her arm distressed her. She looked up at him.

" I want to go," she said. " I want to go and get you some dry things."

" Why ? " he said. " I'm all right."

" But I want to go," she said. " And I want you to change your things."

He released her arm, and she wrapped herself in the blanket, looking at him rather frightened. And still she did not rise.

" Kiss me," she said wistfully.

He kissed her, but briefly, half in anger.

Then, after a second, she rose nervously, all mixed up in the blanket. He watched her in her confusion, as she tried to extricate herself and wrap herself up so that she could walk. He watched her relentlessly, as she knew. And as she went, the blanket trailing, and as he saw a glimpse of her feet and her white leg, he tried to remember her as she was when he had wrapped her in the blanket. But then he didn't want to remember, because she had been nothing to him then, and his nature revolted from remembering her as she was when she was nothing to him.

A tumbling, muffled noise from within the dark house startled him. Then he heard her voice :—" There are clothes." He rose and went to the foot of the stairs, and gathered up the garments she had thrown down. Then he came back to the fire, to rub himself down and dress. He grinned at his own appearance when he had finished.

The fire was sinking, so he put on coal. The house was now quite dark, save for the light of a street-lamp that shone in faintly from beyond the holly trees. He lit the gas with matches he found on the mantelpiece. Then he emptied the pockets of his own clothes, and threw all his wet things in a heap into the scullery. After which he gathered up her sodden clothes, gently, and put them in a separate heap on the copper-top in the scullery.

It was six o'clock on the clock. His own watch had stopped. He ought to go back to the surgery. He waited, and still she did not come down. So he went to the foot of the stairs and called :

" I shall have to go."

Almost immediately he heard her coming down. She had on her best dress of black voile, and her hair was tidy, but still damp. She looked at him—and in spite of herself, smiled.

" I don't like you in those clothes," she said.

" Do I look a sight ? " he answered.

They were shy of one another.

" I'll make you some tea," she said.

" No, I must go."

" Must you ? " And she looked at him again with the wide, strained, doubtful eyes. And again, from the pain of his breast, he knew how he loved her. He went and bent to kiss her, gently, passionately, with his heart's painful kiss.

" And my hair smells so horrible," she murmured in distraction. " And I'm so awful, I'm so awful ! Oh, no, I'm too awful." And she broke into bitter, heart-broken sobbing. " You can't want to love me, I'm horrible."

" Don't be silly, don't be silly," he said, trying to comfort her, kissing her, holding her in his arms. " I want you, I want to marry you, we're going to be married, quickly, quickly—to-morrow if I can."

But she only sobbed terribly, and cried :

" I feel awful. I feel awful. I feel I'm horrible to you."

" No, I want you, I want you," was all he answered, blindly, with that terrible intonation which frightened her almost more than her horror lest he should *not* want her.

FLAME-LURID his face as he turned among the throng of flame-lit and dark faces upon the platform. In the light of the furnace she caught sight of his drifting countenance, like a piece of floating fire. And the nostalgia, the doom of home-coming went through her veins like a drug. His eternal face, flame-lit now ! The pulse and darkness of red fire from the furnace towers in the sky, lighting the desultory, industrial crowd on the wayside station, lit him and went out.

Of course he did not see her. Flame-lit and unseeing ! Always the same, with his meeting eyebrows, his common cap, and his red-and-black scarf knotted round his throat. Not even a collar to meet her ! The flames had sunk, there was shadow.

She opened the door of her grimy, branch-line carriage, and began to get down her bags. The porter was nowhere, of course, but there was Harry, obscure, on the outer edge of the little crowd, missing her, of course.

" Here ! Harry ! " she called, waving her umbrella in the twilight. He hurried forward.

" Tha's come, has ter ? " he said, in a sort of cheerful welcome. She got down, rather flustered, and gave him a peck of a kiss.

" Two suit-cases ! " she said.

Her soul groaned within her, as he clambered into the carriage after her bags. Up shot the fire in the twilight sky, from the great furnace behind the station. She felt the red flame go across her face. She had come back, she had come back for good. And her spirit groaned dismally. She doubted if she could bear it.

There, on the sordid little station under the furnaces, she stood, tall and distinguished, in her well-made coat and skirt and her broad grey velour hat. She held her umbrella, her bead chatelaine, and a little leather case in her grey-gloved hands, while Harry staggered out of the ugly little train with her bags.

" There's a trunk at the back," she said in her bright voice. But she was not feeling bright. The twin black cones of the iron foundry blasted their sky-high fires into the night. The whole scene was lurid. The train waited cheerfully. It would wait another ten minutes. She knew it. It was all so deadly familiar.

Let us confess it at once. She was a lady's maid, thirty years old, come back to marry her first-love, a foundry worker : after having kept him dangling, off and on, for a dozen years. Why had she come back? Did she love him? No. She didn't pretend to. She had loved her brilliant and ambitious cousin, who had jilted her, and who had died. She had had other affairs which had come to nothing. So here she was, come back suddenly to marry her first-love, who had waited—or remained single—all these years.

" Won't a porter carry those ? " she said, as Harry strode with his workman's stride down the platform towards the guard's van.

" I can manage," he said.

And with her umbrella, her chatelaine, and her little leather case, she followed him.

The trunk was there.

" We'll get Heather's green-grocer's cart to fetch it up," he said.

" Isn't there a cab ? " said Fanny, knowing dismally enough that there wasn't.

" I'll just put it aside o' the penny-in-the-slot, and Heather's green-grocers'll fetch it about half-past eight," he said.

He seized the box by its two handles and staggered with it across the level-crossing, bumping his legs against it as he waddled. Then he dropped it by the red sweetmeats machine.

" Will it be safe there ? " she said.

" Ay—safe as houses," he answered. He returned for the two bags. Thus laden, they started to plod up the hill, under the great long black building of the foundry. She walked beside him—workman of workmen he was, trudging with that luggage. The red lights flared over the deepening darkness. From the foundry came the horrible, slow clang, clang, clang of iron, a great noise, with an interval just long enough to make it unendurable.

Compare this with the arrival at Gloucester : the carriage for her mistress, the dog-cart for herself with the luggage ; the drive out past the river, the pleasant trees of the carriage-approach ; and herself sitting beside Arthur, everybody so polite to her.

She had come home—for good ! Her heart nearly stopped beating as she trudged up that hideous and interminable hill, beside the laden figure. What a come-down ! What a come-down ! She could not take it with her usual bright cheerfulness. She knew it all too well. It is easy to bear up against the unusual, but the deadly familiarity of an old stale past !

He dumped the bags down under a lamp-post, for a rest. There they stood, the two of them, in the lamp-light. Passers-by stared at her, and gave good night to Harry. Her they hardly knew, she had become a stranger.

" They're too heavy for you, let me carry one," she said.

" They begin to weigh a bit by the time you've gone a mile," he answered.

" Let me carry the little one," she insisted.

" Tha can ha'e it for a minute, if ter's a mind," he said, handing over the valise.

And thus they arrived in the streets of shops of the little ugly town on top of the hill. How everybody stared at her ; my word, how they stared ! And the cinema was just going in, and the queues were tailing down the road to the corner. And everybody took full stock of her. " Night, Harry ! " shouted the fellows, in an interested voice.

However, they arrived at her aunt's—a little sweet-shop in a side street. They " pinged " the door-bell, and her aunt came running forward out of the kitchen.

" There you are, child ! Dying for a cup of tea, I'm sure. How are you ? "

Fanny's aunt kissed her, and it was all Fanny could do to refrain from bursting into tears, she felt so low. Perhaps it was her tea she wanted.

"You've had a drag with that luggage," said Fanny's aunt to Harry.

" Ay—I'm not sorry to put it down," he said, looking at his hand which was crushed and cramped by the bag handle.

Then he departed to see about Heather's green-grocery cart.

When Fanny sat at tea, her aunt, a grey-haired, fair-faced little woman, looked at her with an admiring heart, feeling bitterly sore for her. For Fanny was beautiful : tall, erect, finely coloured, with her delicately arched nose, her rich brown hair, her large lustrous grey eyes. A passionate woman—a woman to be afraid of. So proud, so inwardly violent ! She came of a violent race.

It needed a woman to sympathize with her. Men had not the courage. Poor Fanny ! She was such a lady, and so straight and magnificent. And yet everything seemed to do her down. Every time she seemed to be doomed to humiliation and disappointment, this handsome, brilliantly sensitive woman, with her nervous, overwrought laugh.

" So you've really come back, child ? " said her aunt.

" I really have, Aunt," said Fanny.

" Poor Harry ! I'm not sure, you know, Fanny, that you're not taking a bit of an advantage of him."

"Oh, Aunt, he's waited so long, he may as well have what he's waited for." Fanny laughed grimly.

"Yes, child, he's waited so long, that I'm not sure it isn't a bit hard on him. You know, I *like* him, Fanny—though as you know quite well, I don't think he's good enough for you. And I think he thinks so himself, poor fellow."

"Don't you be so sure of that, Aunt. Harry is common, but he's not humble. He wouldn't think the Queen was any too good for him, if he'd a mind to her."

"Well—it's as well if he has a proper opinion of himself."

"It depends what you call proper," said Fanny. "But he's got his good points——"

"Oh, he's a nice fellow, and I like him, I do like him. Only, as I tell you, he's not good enough for you."

"I've made up my mind, Aunt," said Fanny, grimly.

"Yes," mused the aunt. "They say all things come to him who waits——"

"More than he's bargained for, eh, Aunt?" laughed Fanny rather bitterly.

The poor aunt, this bitterness grieved her for her niece.

They were interrupted by the ping of the shop-bell, and Harry's call of "Right!" But as he did not come in at once, Fanny, feeling solicitous for him presumably at the moment, rose and went into the shop. She saw a cart outside, and went to the door.

And the moment she stood in the doorway, she heard a woman's common vituperative voice crying from the darkness of the opposite side of the road:

"Tha'rt theer, are ter? I'll shame thee, Mester. I'll shame thee, see if I dunna."

Startled, Fanny stared across the darkness, and saw a woman in a black bonnet go under one of the lamps up the side street.

Harry and Bill Heather had dragged the trunk off the little dray, and she retreated before them as they came up the shop step with it.

"Wheer shalt ha'e it?" asked Harry.

"Best take it upstairs," said Fanny.

She went up first to light the gas.

When Heather had gone, and Harry was sitting down having tea and pork pie, Fanny asked:

"Who was that woman shouting?"

"Nay, I canna tell thee. To somebody, I s'd think," replied Harry. Fanny looked at him, but asked no more.

He was a fair haired fellow of thirty-two, with a fair moustache.

He was broad in his speech, and looked like a foundry-hand, which
he was. But women always liked him. There was something of a
mother's lad about him—something warm and playful and really
sensitive.

He had his attractions even for Fanny. What she rebelled against
so bitterly was that he had no sort of ambition. He was a moulder,
but of very commonplace skill. He was thirty-two years old, and
hadn't saved twenty pounds. She would have to provide the money
for the home. He didn't care. He just didn't care. He had no
initiative at all. He had no vices—no obvious ones. But he was just
indifferent, spending as he went, and not caring. Yet he did not
look happy. She remembered his face in the fire-glow : something
haunted, abstracted about it. As he sat there eating his pork pie,
bulging his cheek out, she felt he was like a doom to her. And she
raged against the doom of him. It wasn't that he was gross. His
way was common, almost on purpose. But he himself wasn't really
common. For instance, his food was not particularly important to
him, he was not greedy. He had a charm, too, particularly for
women, with his blondness and his sensitiveness and his way of
making a woman feel that she was a higher being. But Fanny knew
him, knew the peculiar obstinate limitedness of him, that would
nearly send her mad.

He stayed till about half-past nine. She went to the door with him.

" When are you coming up ? " he said, jerking his head in the
direction, presumably, of his own home.

" I'll come to-morrow afternoon," she said brightly. Between
Fanny and Mrs. Goodall, his mother, there was naturally no love lost.

Again she gave him an awkward little kiss, and said good night.

" You can't wonder, you know, child, if he doesn't seem so very
keen," said her aunt. " It's your own fault."

" Oh, Aunt, I couldn't stand him when he was keen. I can do
with him a lot better as he is."

The two women sat and talked far into the night. They understood each other. The aunt, too, had married as Fanny was marrying : a man who was no companion to her, a violent man, brother of
Fanny's father. He was dead, Fanny's father was dead.

Poor Aunt Lizzie, she cried woefully over her bright niece, when
she had gone to bed.

Fanny paid the promised visit to his people the next afternoon.
Mrs. Goodall was a large woman with smooth-parted hair, a common, obstinate woman, who had spoiled her four lads and her one
vixen of a married daughter. She was one of those old-fashioned

powerful natures that couldn't do with looks or education or any form of showing off. She fairly hated the sound of correct English. She *thee'd* and *tha'd* her prospective daughter-in-law, and said :

" I'm none as ormin' as I look, seest ta."

Fanny did not think her prospective mother-in-law looked at all orming, so the speech was unnecessary.

" I towd him mysen," said Mrs. Goodall, " 'Er's held back all this long, let 'er stop as 'er is. 'E'd none ha' had thee for *my* tellin'—tha hears. No, 'e's a fool, an' I know it. I says to him, ' Tha looks a man, doesn't ter, at thy age, goin' an' openin' to her when ter hears her scrat' at th' gate, after she's done gallivantin' round wherever she'd a mind. That looks rare an' soft.' But it's no use o' any talking : he answered that letter o' thine and made his own bad bargain."

But in spite of the old woman's anger, she was also flattered at Fanny's coming back to Harry. For Mrs. Goodall was impressed by Fanny—a woman of her own match. And more than this, everybody knew that Fanny's Aunt Kate had left her two hundred pounds : this apart from the girl's savings.

So there was high tea in Princes Street when Harry came home black from work, and a rather acrid odour of cordiality, the vixen Jinny darting in to say vulgar things. Of course Jinny lived in a house whose garden end joined the paternal garden. They were a clan who stuck together, these Goodalls.

It was arranged that Fanny should come to tea again on the Sunday, and the wedding was discussed. It should take place in a fortnight's time at Morley Chapel. Morley was a hamlet on the edge of the real country, and in its little Congregational Chapel Fanny and Harry had first met.

What a creature of habit he was ! He was still in the choir of Morley Chapel—not very regular. He belonged just because he had a tenor voice, and enjoyed singing. Indeed, his solos were only spoilt to local fame because when he sang he handled his aitches so hopelessly.

> " And I saw 'eaven hopened
> And be'old, a wite 'orse——"

This was one of Harry's classics, only surpassed by the fine outburst of his heaving :

> " Hangels—hever bright an' fair——"

It was a pity, but it was unalterable. He had a good voice, and he sang with a certain lacerating fire, but his pronunciation made it all funny. And *nothing* could alter him.

So he was never heard save at cheap concerts and in the little, poorer chapels. The others scoffed.

Now the month was September, and Sunday was Harvest Festival at Morley Chapel, and Harry was singing solos. So that Fanny was to go to afternoon service, and come home to a grand spread of Sunday tea with him. Poor Fanny! One of the most wonderful afternoons had been a Sunday afternoon service, with her cousin Luther at her side, Harvest Festival in Morley Chapel. Harry had sung solos then—ten years ago. She remembered his pale blue tie, and the purple asters and the great vegetable marrows in which he was framed, and her cousin Luther at her side, young, clever, come down from London, where he was getting on well, learning his Latin and his French and German so brilliantly.

However, once again it was Harvest Festival at Morley Chapel, and once again, as ten years before, a soft, exquisite September day, with the last roses pink in the cottage gardens, the last dahlias crimson, the last sunflowers yellow. And again the little old chapel was a bower, with its famous sheaves of corn and corn-plaited pillars, its great bunches of grapes, dangling like tassels from the pulpit corners, its marrows and potatoes and pears and apples and damsons, its purple asters and yellow Japanese sunflowers. Just as before, the red dahlias round the pillars were dropping, weak-headed among the oats. The place was crowded and hot, the plates of tomatoes seemed balanced perilous on the gallery front, the Rev. Enderby was weirder than ever to look at, so long and emaciated and hairless.

The Rev. Enderby, probably forewarned, came and shook hands with her and welcomed her, in his broad northern, melancholy sing-song before he mounted the pulpit. Fanny was handsome in a gauzy dress and a beautiful lace hat. Being a little late, she sat in a chair in the side-aisle wedged in, right in the front of the chapel. Harry was in the gallery above, and she could only see him from the eyes upwards. She noticed again how his eyebrows met, blond and not very marked, over his nose. He was attractive, too : physically lovable, very. If only—if only her *pride* had not suffered ! She felt he dragged her down.

> " Come, ye thankful people, come,
>   Raise the song of harvest-home. .
>   All is safley gathered in
>   Ere the winter storms begin——"

Even the hymn was a falsehood, as the season had been wet, and half the crops were still out, and in a poor way.

Poor Fanny ! She sang little, and looked beautiful through that inappropriate hymn. Above her stood Harry—mercifully in a dark suit and a dark tie, looking almost handsome. And his lacerating, pure tenor sounded well, when the words were drowned in the general commotion. Brilliant she looked, and brilliant she felt, for she was hot and angrily miserable and inflamed with a sort of fatal despair. Because there was about him a physical attraction which she really hated, but which she could not escape from. He was the first man who had ever kissed her. And his kisses, even while she rebelled from them, had lived in her blood and sent roots down into her soul. After all this time she had come back to them. And her soul groaned, for she felt dragged down, dragged down to earth, as a bird which some dog has got down in the dust. She knew her life would be unhappy. She knew that what she was doing was fatal. Yet it was her doom. She had to come back to him.

He had to sing two solos this afternoon : one before the " address " from the pulpit and one after. Fanny looked at him, and wondered he was not too shy to stand up there in front of all the people. But no, he was not shy. He had even a kind of assurance on his face as he looked down from the choir gallery at her : the assurance of a common man deliberately entrenched in his commonness. Oh, such a rage went through her veins as she saw the air of triumph, laconic, indifferent triumph which sat so obstinately and recklessly on his eyelids as he looked down at her. Ah, she despised him ! But there he stood up in that choir gallery like Balaam's ass in front of her, and she could not get beyond him. A certain winsomeness also about him. A certain physical winsomeness, and as if his flesh were new and lovely to touch. The thorn of desire rankled bitterly in her heart.

He, it goes without saying, sang like a canary this particular afternoon, with a certain defiant passion which pleasantly crisped the blood of the congregation. Fanny felt the crisp flames go through her veins as she listened. Even the curious loud-mouthed vernacular had a certain fascination. But, oh, also, it was so repugnant. He would triumph over her, obstinately he would drag her right back into the common people : a doom, a vulgar doom.

The second performance was an anthem, in which Harry sang the solo parts. It was clumsy, but beautiful, with lovely words.

> " They that sow in tears shall reap in joy,
>   He that goeth forth and weepeth, bearing precious seed
>   Shall doubtless come again with rejoicing, bringing his
>   sheaves with him——"

" Shall doubtless come, Shall doubtless come——" softly intoned the altos—" Bringing his she-e-eaves with him," the trebles flourished brightly, and then again began the half-wistful solo :

> " They that sow in tears shall reap in joy——"

Yes, it was effective and moving.

But at the moment when Harry's voice sank carelessly down to his close, and the choir, standing behind him, were opening their mouths for the final triumphant outburst, a shouting female voice rose up from the body of the congregation. The organ gave one startled trump, and went silent ; the choir stood transfixed.

" You look well standing there, singing in God's holy house," came the loud, angry female shout. Everybody turned electrified. A stoutish, red-faced woman in a black bonnet was standing up denouncing the soloist. Almost fainting with shock, the congregation realized it. " You look well, don't you, standing there singing solos in God's holy house, you, Goodall. But I said I'd shame you. You look well, bringing your young woman here with you, don't you ? I'll let her know who she's dealing with. A scamp as won't take the consequences of what he's done." The hard-faced, frenzied woman turned in the direction of Fanny. " That's what Harry Goodall is, if you want to know."

And she sat down again in her seat. Fanny, startled like all the rest, had turned to look. She had gone white, and then a burning red, under the attack. She knew the woman : a Mrs. Nixon, a devil of a woman, who beat her pathetic, drunken, red-nosed second husband, Bob, and her two lanky daughters, grown-up as they were. A notorious character. Fanny turned round again, and sat motionless as eternity in her seat.

There was a minute of perfect silence and suspense. The audience was open-mouthed and dumb ; the choir stood like Lot's wife ; and Harry, with his music-sheet, stood there uplifted, looking down with a dumb sort of indifference on Mrs. Nixon, his face naïve and faintly mocking. Mrs. Nixon sat defiant in her seat, braving them all.

Then a rustle, like a wood when the wind suddenly catches the leaves. And then the tall, weird minister got to his feet, and in his strong, bell-like, beautiful voice—the only beautiful thing about him—he said with infinite mournful pathos :

" Let us unite in singing the last hymn on the hymn-sheet ; the last hymn on the hymn-sheet, number eleven.

> ' Fair waved the golden corn,
>   In Canaan's pleasant land.' "

The organ tuned up promptly. During the hymn the offertory was taken. And after the hymn, the prayer.

Mr. Enderby came from Northumberland. Like Harry, he had never been able to conquer his accent, which was very broad. He was a little simple, one of God's fools, perhaps, an odd bachelor soul, emotional, ugly, but very gentle.

"And if, O our dear Lord, beloved Jesus, there should fall a shadow of sin upon our harvest, we leave it to Thee to judge, for Thou art judge. We lift our spirits and our sorrow, Jesus, to Thee, and our mouths are dumb. O Lord, keep us from froward speech, restrain us from foolish words and thoughts, we pray Thee, Lord Jesus, who knowest all and judgest all."

Thus the minister said in his sad, resonant voice, washed his hands before the Lord. Fanny bent forward open-eyed during the prayer. She could see the roundish head of Harry, also bent forward. His face was inscrutable and expressionless. The shock left her bewildered. Anger perhaps was her dominating emotion.

The audience began to rustle to its feet, to ooze slowly and excitedly out of the chapel, looking with wildly interested eyes at Fanny, at Mrs. Nixon, and at Harry. Mrs. Nixon, shortish, stood defiant in her pew, facing the aisle, as if announcing that, without rolling her sleeves up, she was ready for anybody. Fanny sat quite still. Luckily the people did not have to pass her. And Harry, with red ears, was making his way sheepishly out of the gallery. The loud noise of the organ covered all the downstairs commotion of exit.

The minister sat silent and inscrutable in his pulpit, rather like a death's-head, while the congregation filed out. When the last lingerers had unwillingly departed, craning their necks to stare at the still seated Fanny, he rose, stalked in his hooked fashion down the little country chapel and fastened the door. Then he returned and sat down by the silent young woman.

"This is most unfortunate, most unfortunate!" he moaned. "I am so sorry, I am so sorry, indeed, indeed, ah, indeed!" he sighed himself to a close.

"It's a sudden surprise, that's one thing," said Fanny brightly.

"Yes—yes—indeed. Yes, a surprise, yes. I don't know the woman, I don't know her."

"I know her," said Fanny. "She's a bad one."

"Well! Well!" said the minister. "I don't know her. I don't understand. I don't understand at all. But it is to be regretted, it is very much to be regretted. I am very sorry."

Fanny was watching the vestry door. The gallery stairs

communicated with the vestry, not with the body of the chapel. She knew the choir members had been peeping for information.

At last Harry came—rather sheepishly—with his hat in his hand.

" Well ! " said Fanny, rising to her feet.

" We've had a bit of an extra," said Harry.

" I should think so," said Fanny.

" A most unfortunate circumstance—a most *unfortunate* circumstance. Do you understand it, Harry ? I don't understand it at all."

" Ay, I understand it. The daughter's goin' to have a childt, an' 'er lays it on to me."

" And has she no occasion to ? " asked Fanny, rather censorious.

" It's no more mine than it is some other chap's," said Harry, looking aside.

There was a moment of pause.

" Which girl is it ? " asked Fanny.

" Annie—the young one——"

There followed another silence.

" I don't think I know them, do I ? " asked the minister.

" I shouldn't think so. Their name's Nixon—mother married old Bob for her second husband. She's a tanger, she's driven the gel to what she is. They live in Manners Road."

" Why, what's amiss with the girl ? " asked Fanny sharply. " She was all right when I knew her."

" Ay—she's all right. But she's always in an' out o' th' pubs, wi' th' fellows," said Harry.

" A nice thing ! " said Fanny.

Harry glanced towards the door. He wanted to get out.

" Most distressing, indeed ! " The minister slowly shook his head.

" What about to-night, Mr. Enderby ? " asked Harry, in rather a small voice. " Shall you want me ? "

Mr. Enderby looked up painedly, and put his hand to his brow. He studied Harry for some time, vacantly. There was the faintest sort of a resemblance between the two men.

" Yes," he said. " Yes, I think. I think we must take no notice and cause as little remark as possible."

Fanny hesitated. Then she said to Harry :

" But *will* you come ? "

He looked at her.

" Ay, I s'll come," he said.

Then he turned to Mr. Enderby.

" Well, good afternoon, Mr. Enderby," he said.

" Good afternoon, Harry, good afternoon," replied the mournful minister. Fanny followed Harry to the door, and for some time they walked in silence through the late afternoon.

" And it's yours as much as anybody else's ? " she said.

" Ay," he answered shortly.

And they went without another word, for the long mile or so, till they came to the corner of the street where Harry lived. Fanny hesitated. Should she go on to her aunt's ? Should she ? It would mean leaving all this, for ever. Harry stood silent.

Some obstinacy made her turn with him along the road to his own home. When they entered the house-place, the whole family was there, mother and father and Jinny, with Jinny's husband and children and Harry's two brothers.

" You've been having your ears warmed, they tell me," said Mrs. Goodall grimly.

" Who told thee ? " asked Harry shortly.

" Maggie and Luke's both been in."

" You look well, don't you ! " said interfering Jinny.

Harry went and hung his hat up, without replying.

" Come upstairs and take your hat off," said Mrs. Goodall to Fanny, almost kindly. It would have annoyed her very much if Fanny had dropped her son at this moment.

" What's 'er say, then? " asked the father secretly of Harry, jerking his head in the direction of the stairs whence Fanny had disappeared.

" Nowt yet," said Harry.

" Serve you right if she chucks you now," said Jinny. " I'll bet it's right about Annie Nixon an' you."

" Tha bets so much," said Harry.

" Yi—but you can't deny it," said Jinny.

" I can if I've a mind."

His father looked at him enquiringly.

" It's no more mine than it is Bill Bower's, or Ted Slaney's, or six or seven on 'em," said Harry to his father.

And the father nodded silently.

" That'll not get you out of it, in court," said Jinny.

Upstairs Fanny evaded all the thrusts made by his mother, and did not declare her hand. She tidied her hair, washed her hands, and put the tiniest bit of powder on her face, for coolness, there in front of Mrs. Goodall's indignant gaze. It was like a declaration of independence. But the old woman said nothing.

They came down to Sunday tea, with sardines and tinned salmon and tinned peaches, besides tarts and cakes. The chatter was general. It concerned the Nixon family and the scandal.

" Oh, she's a foul-mouthed woman," said Jinny of Mrs. Nixon.
" She may well talk about God's holy house, *she* had. It's first time
she's set foot in it, ever since she dropped off from being converted.
She's a devil and she always was one. Can't you remember how she
treated Bob's children, mother, when we lived down in the Buildings?
I can remember when I was a little girl she used to bathe them in
the yard, in the cold, so that they shouldn't splash the house. She'd
half kill them if they made a mark on the floor, and the language
she'd use! And one Saturday I can remember Garry, that was
Bob's own girl, she ran off when her stepmother was going to bathe
her—ran off without a rag of clothes on—can you remember, mother?
And she hid in Smedley's closes—it was the time of mowing-grass—
and nobody could find her. She hid out there all night, didn't
she, mother? Nobody could find her. My word, there was a talk.
They found her on Sunday morning——"

" Fred Coutts threatened to break every bone in the woman's
body, if she touched the children again," put in the father.

" Anyhow, they frightened her," said Jinny. " But she was nearly
as bad with her own two. And anybody can see that she's driven
old Bob till he's gone soft."

" Ah, soft as mush," said Jack Goodall. " 'E'd never addle a
week's wage, nor yet a day's, if th' chaps didn't make it up to him."

" My word, if he didn't bring her a week's wage, she'd pull his
head off," said Jinny.

" But a clean woman, and respectable, except for her foul mouth,"
said Mrs. Goodall. " Keeps to herself like a bull-dog. Never lets
anybody come near the house, and neighbours with nobody."

" Wanted it thrashed out of her," said Mr. Goodall, a silent, evasive
sort of man.

" Where Bob gets the money for his drink from is a mystery," said
Jinny.

" Chaps treats him," said Harry.

" Well, he's got the pair of frightenedest rabbit-eyes you'd wish to
see," said Jinny.

" Ay, with a drunken man's murder in them, *I* think," said Mrs.
Goodall.

So the talk went on after tea, till it was practically time to start
off to chapel again.

" You'll have to be getting ready, Fanny," said Mrs. Goodall.

" I'm not going to-night," said Fanny abruptly. And there was a sudden halt in the family. " I'll stop with *you* to-night, mother," she added.

" Best you had, my gel," said Mrs. Goodall, flattered and assured.

How many swords had Lady Beveridge in her pierced heart ! Yet there always seemed room for another. Since she had determined that her heart of pity and kindness should never die. If it had not been for this determination she herself might have died of sheer agony, in the years 1916 and 1917, when her boys were killed, and her brother, and death seemed to be mowing with wide swaths through her family. But let us forget.

Lady Beveridge loved humanity, and come what might, she would continue to love it. Nay, in the human sense, she would love her enemies. Not the criminals among the enemy, the men who committed atrocities. But the men who were enemies through no choice of their own. She would be swept into no general hate.

Somebody had called her the soul of England. It was not ill said, though she was half Irish. But of an old, aristocratic, loyal family famous for its brilliant men. And she, Lady Beveridge, had for years as much influence on the tone of English politics as any individual alive. The close friend of the real leaders in the House of Lords and in the Cabinet, she was content that the men should act, so long as they breathed from her as from the rose of life the pure fragrance of truth and genuine love. She had no misgiving regarding her own spirit.

She, she would never lower her delicate silken flag. For instance, throughout all the agony of the war she never forgot the enemy prisoners ; she was determined to do her best for them. During the first years she still had influence. But during the last years of the war power slipped out of the hands of her and her sort, and she found she could do nothing any more : almost nothing. Then it seemed as if the many swords had gone home into the heart of this little, unyielding Mater Dolorosa. The new generation jeered at her. She was a shabby, old-fashioned little aristocrat, and her drawing-room was out of date.

But we anticipate. The years 1916 and 1917 were the years when the old spirit died for ever in England. But Lady Beveridge struggled on. She was being beaten.

It was in the winter of 1917—or in the late autumn. She had been for a fortnight sick, stricken, paralysed by the fearful death of her youngest boy. She felt she *must* give in, and just die. And then she remembered how many others were lying in agony.

So she rose, trembling, frail, to pay a visit to the hospital where lay the enemy sick and wounded, near London. Countess Beveridge was still a privileged woman. Society was beginning to jeer at this little, worn bird of an out-of-date righteousness and æsthetic. But they dared not think ill of her.

She ordered the car and went alone. The Earl, her husband, had taken his gloom to Scotland. So, on a sunny, wan November morning, Lady Beveridge descended at the hospital, Hurst Place. The guard knew her, and saluted as she passed. Ah, she was used to such deep respect ! It was strange that she felt it so bitterly, when the respect became shallower. But she did. It was the beginning of the end to her.

The matron went with her into the ward. Alas, the beds were all full, and men were even lying on pallets on the floor. There was a desperate, crowded dreariness and helplessness in the place : as if nobody wanted to make a sound or utter a word. Many of the men were haggard and unshaven, one was delirious, and talking fitfully in the Saxon dialect. It went to Lady Beveridge's heart. She had been educated in Dresden, and had had many dear friendships in the city. Her children also had been educated there. She heard the Saxon dialect with pain.

She was a little, frail, bird-like woman, elegant, but with that touch of the blue-stocking of the 'nineties which was unmistakable. She fluttered delicately from bed to bed, speaking in perfect German, but with a thin, English intonation : and always asking if there was anything she could do. The men were mostly officers and gentlemen. They made little requests which she wrote down in a book. Her long, pale, rather worn face, and her nervous little gestures somehow inspired confidence.

One man lay quite still, with his eyes shut. He had a black beard. His face was rather small and sallow. He might be dead. Lady Beveridge looked at him earnestly, and fear came into her face.

" Why, Count Dionys ! " she said, fluttered. " Are you asleep ? "

It was Count Johann Dionys Psanek, a Bohemian. She had known him when he was a boy, and only in the spring of 1914 he and his wife had stayed with Lady Beveridge in her country house in Leicestershire.

His black eyes opened : large, black, unseeing eyes, with curved

black lashes. He was a small man, small as a boy, and his face too
was rather small. But all the lines were fine, as if they had been
fired with a keen male energy. Now the yellowish swarthy paste of
his flesh seemed dead, and the fine black brows seemed drawn on the
face of one dead. The eyes, however, were alive : but only just
alive, unseeing and unknowing.

" You know me, Count Dionys ? You know me, don't you ? "
said Lady Beveridge, bending forward over the bed.

There was no reply for some time. Then the black eyes gathered
a look of recognition, and there came the ghost of a polite smile.

" Lady Beveridge." The lips formed the words. There was
practically no sound.

" I am so glad you can recognize me. And I am so sorry you are
hurt. I am so sorry."

The black eyes watched her from that terrible remoteness of
death, without changing.

" There is nothing I can do for you ? Nothing at all ? " she said,
always speaking German.

And after a time, and from a distance, came the answer from his
eyes, a look of weariness, of refusal, and a wish to be left alone ; he
was unable to strain himself into consciousness. His eyelids dropped.

" I am so sorry," she said. " If ever there is anything I can do——"
The eyes opened again, looking at her. He seemed at last to hear,
and it was as if his eyes made the last weary gesture of a polite bow.
Then slowly his eyelids closed again.

Poor Lady Beveridge felt another sword-thrust of sorrow in her
heart, as she stood looking down at the motionless face, and at the
black fine beard. The black hairs came out of his skin thin and
fine, not very close together. A queer, dark aboriginal little face he
had, with a fine little nose : not an Aryan, surely. And he was going
to die.

He had a bullet through the upper part of his chest, and another
bullet had broken one of his ribs. He had been in hospital five days.

Lady Beveridge asked the matron to ring her up if anything
happened. Then she drove away, saddened. Instead of going to
Beveridge House, she went to her daughter's flat near the park—
near Hyde Park. Lady Daphne was poor. She had married a
commoner, son of one of the most famous politicians in England,
but a man with no money. And Earl Beveridge had wasted most
of the large fortune that had come to him, so that the daughter had
very little, comparatively.

Lady Beveridge suffered, going in the narrow doorway into the rather ugly flat. Lady Daphne was sitting by the electric fire in the small yellow drawing-room, talking to a visitor. She rose at once, seeing her little mother.

" Why, mother, ought you to be out ? I'm sure not."

" Yes, Daphne darling. Of course I ought to be out."

" How are you ? " The daughter's voice was slow and sonorous, protective, sad. Lady Daphne was tall, only twenty-five years old. She had been one of the beauties, when the war broke out, and her father had hoped she would make a splendid match. Truly, she had married fame : but without money. Now, sorrow, pain, thwarted passion had done her great damage. Her husband was missing in the East. Her baby had been born dead. Her two darling brothers were dead. And she was ill, always ill.

A tall, beautifully-built girl, she had the fine stature of her father. Her shoulders were still straight. But how thin her white throat ! She wore a simple black frock stitched with coloured wool round the top, and held in a loose coloured girdle : otherwise no ornaments. And her face was lovely, fair, with a soft exotic white complexion and delicate pink cheeks. Her hair was soft and heavy, of a lovely pallid gold colour, ash-blonde. Her hair, her complexion were so perfectly cared for as to be almost artificial, like a hot-house flower.

But alas, her beauty was a failure. She was threatened with phthisis, and was far too thin. Her eyes were the saddest part of her. They had slightly reddened rims, nerve-worn, with heavy, veined lids that seemed as if they did not want to keep up. The eyes themselves were large and of a beautiful green-blue colour. But they were dull, languid, almost glaucous.

Standing as she was, a tall, finely built girl, looking down with affectionate care on her mother, she filled the heart with ashes. The little pathetic mother, so wonderful in her way, was not really to be pitied for all her sorrow. Her life was in her sorrows, and her efforts on behalf of the sorrows of others. But Daphne was not born for grief and philanthropy. With her splendid frame, and her lovely, long, strong legs, she was Artemis or Atalanta rather than Daphne. There was a certain width of brow and even of chin that spoke a strong, reckless nature, and the curious, distraught slant of her eyes told of a wild energy dammed up inside her.

That was what ailed her : her own wild energy. She had it from her father, and from her father's desperate race. The earldom had begun with a riotous, dare-devil border soldier, and this was the blood that flowed on. And alas, what was to be done with it ?

Daphne had married an adorable husband : truly an adorable husband. Whereas she needed a dare-devil. But in her *mind* she hated all dare-devils : she had been brought up by her mother to admire only the good.

So, her reckless, anti-philanthropic passion could find no outlet—and *should* find no outlet, she thought. So her own blood turned against her, beat on her own nerves, and destroyed her. It was nothing but frustration and anger which made her ill, and made the doctors fear consumption. There it was, drawn on her rather wide mouth : frustration, anger, bitterness. There it was the same in the roll of her green-blue eyes, a slanting, averted look : the same anger furtively turning back on itself. This anger reddened her eyes and shattered her nerves. And yet, her whole will was fixed in her adoption of her mother's creed, and in condemnation of her hand-some, proud, brutal father, who had made so much misery in the family. Yes, her will was fixed in the determination that life should be gentle and good and benevolent. Whereas her blood was reck-less, the blood of dare-devils. Her will was the stronger of the two. But her blood had its revenge on her. So it is with strong natures to-day : shattered from the inside.

" You have no news, darling ? " asked the mother.

" No. My father-in-law had information that British prisoners had been brought into Hasrun, and that details would be forwarded by the Turks. And there was a rumour from some Arab prisoners that Basil was one of the British brought in wounded."

" When did you hear this ? "

" Primrose came in this morning."

" Then we can hope, dear."

" Yes."

Never was anything more dull and bitter than Daphne's affirma-tive of hope. Hope had become almost a curse to her. She wished there need be no such thing. Ha, the torment of hoping, and the *insult* to one's soul. Like the importunate widow dunning for her deserts. Why could it not all be just clean disaster, and have done with it ? This dilly-dallying with despair was worse than despair. She had hoped so much : ah, for her darling brothers she had hoped with such anguish. And the two she loved best were dead. So were most others she had hoped for, dead. Only this uncertainty about her husband still rankling.

" You feel better, dear ? " said the little, unquenched mother.

" Rather better," came the resentful answer.

" And your night ? "

" No better."

There was a pause.

" You are coming to lunch with me, Daphne darling ? "

" No, mother dear. I promised to lunch at the Howards' with Primrose. But I needn't go for a quarter of an hour. Do sit down."

Both women seated themselves near the electric fire. There was that bitter pause, neither knowing what to say. Then Daphne roused herself to look at her mother.

" Are you sure you were fit to go out ? " she said. " What took you out so suddenly ? "

" I went to Hurst Place, dear. I had the men on my mind, after the way the newspapers have been talking."

" Why ever do you read the newspapers ! " blurted Daphne, with a certain burning, acid anger. " Well," she said, more composed. " And do you feel better now you've been ? "

" So many people suffer besides ourselves, darling."

" I know they do. Makes it all the worse. It wouldn't matter if it were only just us. At least, it would matter, but one could bear it more easily. To be just one of a crowd all in the same state."

" And some even worse, dear."

" Oh quite ! And the worse it is for all, the worse it is for one."

" Is that so, darling ? Try not to see too darkly. I feel if I can give just a little bit of myself to help the others—you know—it alleviates me. I feel that what I can give to the men lying there, Daphne, I give to my own boys. I can only help them now through helping others. But I can still do that, Daphne, my girl."

And the mother put her little white hand into the long, white, cold hand of her daughter. Tears came to Daphne's eyes, and a fearful stony grimace to her mouth.

" It's so wonderful of you that you can feel like that," she said.

" But you feel the same, my love. I know you do."

" No, I don't. Every one I see suffering these same awful things, it makes me wish more for the end of the world. And I quite see that the world won't end——"

" But it will get better, dear. This time it's like a great sickness—like a terrible pneumonia tearing the breast of the world."

" Do you believe it will get better ? I don't."

" It will get better. Of course it will get better. It is perverse to think otherwise, Daphne. Remember what *has* been before, even in Europe. Ah, Daphne, we must take a bigger view."

" Yes, I suppose we must."

The daughter spoke rapidly, from the lips, in a resonant, monotonous tone. The mother spoke from the heart.

".And Daphne, I found an old friend among the men at Hurst Place."

" Who ? "

" Little Count Dionys Psanek. You remember him ? "

" Quite. What's wrong ? "

" Wounded rather badly—through the chest. So ill."

" Did you speak to him ? "

" Yes. I recognized him in spite of his beard."

" Beard ! "

" Yes—a black beard. I suppose he could not be shaven. It seems strange that he is still alive, poor man."

" Why strange ? He isn't old. How old is he ? "

" Between thirty and forty. But so ill, so wounded, Daphne. And so small. So small, so sallow—*smorto*, you know the Italian word. The way dark people look. There is something so distressing in it."

" Does he look *very* small now—uncanny ? " asked the daughter.

" No, not uncanny. Something of the terrible far-awayness of a child that is very ill and can't tell you what hurts it. Poor Count Dionys, Daphne. I didn't know, dear, that his eyes were so black, and his lashes so curved and long. I had never thought of him as beautiful."

" Nor I. Only a little comical. Such a dapper little man."

" Yes. And yet now, Daphne, there is something remote and in a sad way heroic in his dark face. Something primitive."

" What did he say to you ? "

" He couldn't speak to me. Only with his lips, just my name."

" So bad as that ? "

" Oh yes. They are afraid he will die."

" Poor Count Dionys. I liked him. He was a bit like a monkey, but he had his points. He gave me a thimble on my seventeenth birthday. Such an amusing thimble."

" I remember, dear."

" Unpleasant wife, though. Wonder if he minds dying far away from her. Wonder if she knows."

" I think not. They didn't even know his name properly. Only that he was a Colonel of such and such a regiment."

" Fourth Cavalry," said Daphne. " Poor Count Dionys. Such a lovely name, I always thought : Count Johann Dionys Psanek. Extraordinary dandy he was. And an amazingly good dancer, small, yet electric. Wonder if he minds dying ? "

" He was so full of life, in his own little animal way. They say small people are always conceited. But he doesn't look conceited now, dear. Something ages old in his face—and, yes, a certain beauty, Daphne."

" You mean long lashes."

" No. So still, so solitary—and ages old, in his race. I suppose he must belong to one of those curious little aboriginal races of Central Europe. I felt quite new beside him."

" How nice of you," said Daphne

Nevertheless, next day Daphne telephoned to Hurst Place to ask for news of him. He was about the same. She telephoned every day. Then she was told he was a little stronger. The day she received the message that her husband was wounded and a prisoner in Turkey, and that his wounds were healing, she forgot to telephone for news of the little enemy Count. And the following day she telephoned that she was coming to the hospital to see him.

He was awake, more restless, more in physical excitement. They could see the nausea of pain round his nose. His face seemed to Daphne curiously hidden behind the black beard, which nevertheless was thin, each hair coming thin and fine, singly, from the sallow, slightly translucent skin. In the same way his moustache made a thin black line round his mouth. His eyes were wide open, very black, and of no legible expression. He watched the two women coming down the crowded, dreary room, as if he did not see them. His eyes seemed too wide.

It was a cold day, and Daphne was huddled in a black sealskin coat with a skunk collar pulled up to her ears, and a dull gold cap with wings pulled down on her brow. Lady Beveridge wore her sable coat, and had that odd, untidy elegance which was natural to her rather like a ruffled chicken.

Daphne was upset by the hospital. She looked from right to left in spite of herself, and everything gave her a dull feeling of horror : the terror of these sick, wounded enemy men. She loomed tall and obtrusive in her furs by the bed, her little mother at her side.

" I hope you don't mind my coming ! " she said in German to the sick man. Her tongue felt rusty, speaking the language.

" Who is it then ? " he asked.

" It is my daughter, Lady Daphne. You remembered *me*, Lady Beveridge ! This is my daughter, whom you knew in Saxony. She was so sorry to hear you were wounded."

The black eyes rested on the little lady. Then they returned to the looming figure of Daphne. And a certain fear grew on the low sick brow. It was evident the presence loomed and frightened him. He turned his face aside. Daphne noticed how his fine black hair grew uncut over his small, animal ears.

"You don't remember me, Count Dionys?" she said dully.

"Yes," he said. But he kept his face averted.

She stood there feeling confused and miserable, as if she had made a *faux pas* in coming.

"Would you rather be left alone?" she said. "I'm sorry."

Her voice was monotonous. She felt suddenly stifled in her closed furs, and threw her coat open, showing her thin white throat and plain black slip dress on her flat breast. He turned again unwillingly to look at her. He looked at her as if she were some strange creature standing near him.

"Good-bye," she said. "Do get better."

She was looking at him with a queer, slanting, downward look of her heavy eyes, as she turned away. She was still a little red round the eyes, with nervous exhaustion.

"You are so tall," he said, still frightened.

"I was always tall," she replied, turning half to him again.

"And I, small," he said.

"I am so glad you are getting better," she said.

"I am not glad," he said.

"Why? I'm sure you are. Just as we are glad because we want you to get better."

"Thank you," he said. "I have wished to die."

"Don't do that, Count Dionys. Do get better," she said, in the rather deep, laconic manner of her girlhood. He looked at her with a farther look of recognition. But his short, rather pointed nose was lifted with the disgust and weariness of pain, his brows were tense. He watched her with that curious flame of suffering which is forced to give a little outside attention, but which speaks only to itself.

"Why did they not let me die?" he said. "I wanted death now."

"No," she said. "You mustn't. You must live. If we *can* live we must."

"I wanted death," he said.

"Ah well," she said, "even death we can't have when we want it, or when we think we want it."

"That is true," he said, watching her with the same wide black eyes. "Please to sit down. You are too tall as you stand."

It was evident he was a little frightened still by her looming, overhanging figure.

"I am sorry I am too tall," she said, taking a chair which a man-nurse had brought her. Lady Beveridge had gone away to speak with the men. Daphne sat down, not knowing what to say further. The pitch-black look in the Count's wide eyes puzzled her.

" Why do you come here ? Why does your lady mother come ? " he said.

" To see if we can do anything," she answered.

" When I am well, I will thank your ladyship."

" All right," she replied. " When you are well I will let my lord the Count thank me. Please do get well."

" We are enemies," he said.

" Who ? You and I and my mother ? "

" Are we not ? The most difficult thing is to be sure of anything. If they had let me die ! "

" That is at least ungrateful, Count Dionys."

" *Lady Daphne* ! Yes. *Lady Daphne* ! Beautiful, the name is. You are always called Lady Daphne ? I remember you were so bright a maiden."

" More or less," she said, answering his question.

" Ach ! We should all have new names now. I thought of a name for myself, but I have forgotten it. No longer Johann Dionys. That is shot away. I am Karl or Wilhelm or Ernst or Georg. Those are names I hate. Do you hate them ? "

" I don't like them—but I don't hate them. And you mustn't leave off being Count Johann Dionys. If you do I shall have to leave off being Daphne. I like your name so much."

" Lady Daphne ! Lady Daphne ! " he repeated. " Yes, it rings well, it sounds beautiful to me. I think I talk foolishly. I hear myself talking foolishly to you." He looked at her anxiously.

" Not at all," she said.

" Ach ! I have a head on my shoulders that is like a child's wind-mill, and I can't prevent its making foolish words. Please to go away, not to hear me. I can hear myself."

" Can't I do anything for you ? " she asked.

" No, no ! No, no ! If I could be buried deep, very deep down, where everything is forgotten ! But they draw me up, back to the surface. I would not mind if they buried me alive, if it were very deep, and dark, and the earth heavy above."

" Don't say that," she replied, rising.

" No, I am saying it when I don't wish to say it. Why am I here ? Why am I here ? Why have I survived into this ? Why can I not stop talking ? "

He turned his face aside. The black, fine, elfish hair was so long, and pushed up in tufts from the smooth brown nape of his neck. Daphne looked at him in sorrow. He could not turn his body. He could only move his head. And he lay with his face hard averted, the fine hair of his beard coming up strange from under his chin and from his throat, up to the socket of his ear. He lay quite still, in this position. And she turned away, looking for her mother. She had suddenly realized that the bonds, the connections between him and his life in the world had broken, and he lay there a bit of loose, palpitating humanity, shot away from the body of humanity.

It was ten days before she went to the hospital again. She had wanted never to go again, to forget him, as one tries to forget incurable things. But she could not forget him. He came again and again into her mind. She had to go back. She had heard that he was recovering very slowly.

He looked really better. His eyes were not so wide open, they had lost that black, inky exposure which had given him such an unnatural look, unpleasant. He watched her guardedly. She had taken off her furs, and wore only her dress and a dark, soft feather toque.

" How are you ? " she said, keeping her face averted, unwilling to meet his eyes.

" Thank you, I am better. The nights are not so long."

She shuddered, knowing what long nights meant. He saw the worn look in her face, too, the reddened rims of her eyes.

" Are you not well ? Have you some trouble ? " he asked her.

" No, no," she answered.

She had brought a handful of pinky, daisy-shaped flowers.

" Do you care for flowers ? " she asked.

He looked at them. Then he slowly shook his head.

" No," he said. " If I am on horseback, riding through the marshes or through the hills, I like to see them below me. But not here. Not now. Please do not bring flowers into this grave. Even in gardens, I do not like them. When they are upholstery to human life."

" I will take them away again," she said.

" Please do. Please give them to the nurse."

Daphne paused.

" Perhaps," she said, " you wish I would not come to disturb you."

He looked into her face.

" No," he said. " You are like a flower behind a rock, near an icy water. No, you do not live too much. I am afraid I cannot talk sensibly. I wish to hold my mouth shut. If I open it, I talk this absurdity. It escapes from my mouth."

" It is not so very absurd," she said.

But he was silent—looking away from her.

" I want you to tell me if there is really nothing I can do for you," she said.

" Nothing," he answered.

" If I can write any letter for you."

" None," he answered.

" But your wife and your two children. Do they know where you are ? "

" I should think not."

" And where are they ? "

" I do not know. Probably they are in Hungary."

" Not at your home ? "

" My castle was burnt down in a riot. My wife went to Hungary with the children. She has her relatives there. She went away from me. I wished it too. Alas, for her, I wished to be dead. Pardon me the personal tone."

Daphne looked down at him—the queer, obstinate little fellow.

" But you have somebody you wish to tell—somebody you want to hear from ? "

" Nobody. Nobody. I wish the bullet had gone through my heart. I wish to be dead. It is only I have a devil in my body that will not die."

She looked at him as he lay with closed, averted face.

" Surely it is not a devil which keeps you alive," she said. " It is something good."

" No, a devil," he said.

She sat looking at him with long, slow, wondering look.

" Must one hate a devil that makes one live ? " she asked.

He turned his eyes to her with a touch of a satiric smile.

" If one lives, no," he said.

She looked away from him the moment he looked at her. For her life she could not have met his dark eyes direct.

She left him, and he lay still. He neither read nor talked, throughout the long winter nights and the short winter days. He only lay for hours with black, open eyes, seeing everything around with a touch of disgust, and heeding nothing.

Daphne went to see him now and then. She never forgot him for long. He seemed to come into her mind suddenly, as if by sorcery.

One day he said to her :

" I see you are married. May I ask you who is your husband ? "

She told him. She had had a letter also from Basil. The Count smiled slowly.

" You can look forward," he said, " to a happy reunion, and new, lovely children, Lady Daphne. Is it not so ? "

" Yes, of course," she said.

" But you are ill," he said to her.

" Yes—rather ill."

" Of what ? "

" Oh ! " she answered fretfully, turning her face aside. " They talk about lungs." She hated speaking of it. " Why, how do you know I am ill ? " she added quickly.

Again he smiled slowly.

" I see it in your face, and hear it in your voice. One would say the Evil One had cast a spell on you."

" Oh no," she said hastily. " But do I look ill ? "

" Yes. You look as if something had struck you across the face, and you could not forget it."

" Nothing has," she said. " Unless it's the war."

" The war ! " he repeated.

" Oh well, don't let us talk of it," she said.

Another time he said to her :

" The year has turned—the sun must shine at last, even in England. I am afraid of getting well too soon. I am a prisoner, am I not ? But I wish the sun would shine. I wish the sun would shine on my face."

" You won't always be a prisoner. The war will end. And the sun *does* shine even in the winter in England," she said.

" I wish it would shine on my face," he said.

So that when in February there came a blue, bright morning, the morning that suggests yellow crocuses and the smell of a mezereon tree and the smell of damp, warm earth, Daphne hastily got a taxi and drove out to the hospital.

" You have come to put me in the sun," he said the moment he saw her.

" Yes, that's what I came for," she said.

She spoke to the matron, and had his bed carried out where there was a big window that came low. There he was put full in the sun. Turning, he could see the blue sky, and the twinkling tops of purplish, bare trees.

" The world ! The world ! " he murmured.

He lay with his eyes shut, and the sun on his swarthy, transparent, immobile face. The breath came and went through his nostrils invisibly. Daphne wondered how he could lie so still, how he could look so immobile. It was true as her mother had said : he looked as if he had been cast in the mould when the metal was white hot, all his lines were so clean. So small, he was, and in his way perfect.

Suddenly his dark eyes opened and caught her looking.

" The sun makes even anger open like a flower," he said.

" Whose anger ? " she said.

" I don't know. But I can make flowers, looking through my eyelashes. Do you know how ? "

" You mean rainbows ? "

" Yes, flowers."

And she saw him, with a curious smile on his lips, looking through his almost closed eyelids at the sun.

" The sun is neither English nor German nor Bohemian," he said. " I am a subject of the sun. I belong to the fire-worshippers."

" Do you ? " she replied.

" Yes, truly, by tradition." He looked at her smiling. " You stand there like a flower that will melt," he added.

She smiled slowly at him, with a slow, cautious look of her eyes as if she feared something.

" I am much more solid than you imagine," she said.

Still he watched her.

" One day," he said, " before I go, let me wrap your hair round my hands, will you ? " He lifted his thin, short dark hands. " Let me wrap your hair round my hands, like a bandage. They hurt me. I don't know what it is. I think it is all the gun explosions. But if you let me wrap your hair round my hands. You know, it is the hermetic gold—but so much of water in it, of the moon. That will soothe my hands. One day, will you ? "

" Let us wait till the day comes," she said.

" Yes," he answered, and was still again.

" It troubles me," he said after a while, " that I complain like a child, and ask for things. I feel I have lost my manhood for the time being. The continual explosions of guns and shells ! It seems to have driven my soul out of me like a bird frightened away at last. But it will come back, you know. And I am so grateful to you ; you are good to me when I am soulless, and you don't take advantage of me. Your soul is quiet and heroic."

" Don't," she said. " Don't talk ! "

The expression of shame and anguish and disgust crossed his face.

" It is because I can't help it," he said. " I have lost my soul, and I can't stop talking to you. I can't stop. But I don't talk to any one else. I try not to talk, but I can't prevent it. Do you draw the words out of me ? "

Her wide, green-blue eyes seemed like the heart of some curious, full-open flower, some Christmas rose with its petals of snow and flush. Her hair glinted heavy, like water-gold. She stood there passive and indomitable with the wide-eyed persistence of her wintry, blonde nature.

Another day when she came to see him he watched her for a time, then he said :

" Do they all tell you you are lovely, you are beautiful ? "

" Not quite all," she replied.

" But your husband ? "

" He has said so."

" Is he gentle ? Is he tender ? Is he a dear lover ? "

She turned her face aside, displeased.

" Yes," she replied curtly.

He did not answer. And when she looked again he was lying with his eyes shut, a faint smile seeming to curl round his short, transparent nose. She could faintly see the flesh through his beard, as water through reeds. His black hair was brushed smooth as glass, his black eyebrows glinted like a curve of black glass on the swarthy opalescence of his brow.

Suddenly he spoke, without opening his eyes.

" You have been very kind to me," he said.

" Have I ? Nothing to speak of."

He opened his eyes and looked at her.

" Everything finds its mate," he said. " The ermine and the pole-cat and the buzzard. One thinks so often that only the dove and the nightingale and the stag with his antlers have gentle mates. But the pole-cat and the ice-bears of the north have their mates. And a white she-bear lies with her cubs under a rock as a snake lies hidden, and the male-bear slowly swims back from the sea, like a clot of snow or a shadow of a white cloud passing on the speckled sea. I have seen her too, and I did not shoot her, nor him when he landed with fish in his mouth, wading wet and slow and yellow-white over the black stones."

" You have been in the North Sea ? "

" Yes. And with the Eskimo in Siberia, and across the Tundras. And a white sea-hawk makes a nest on a high stone, and sometimes looks out with her white head over the edge of the rocks. It is not only a world of men, Lady Daphne."

" Not by any means," said she.

" Else it were a sorry place."

" It is bad enough," said she.

"Foxes have their holes. They have even their mates, Lady Daphne, that they bark to and are answered. And an adder finds his female. Psanek means an outlaw; did you know?"

"I did not."

"Outlaws, and brigands, have often the finest woman-mates."

"They do," she said.

"I will be Psanek, Lady Daphne. I will not be Johann Dionys any more. I will be Psanek. The law has shot me through."

"You might be Psanek and Johann and Dionys as well," she said.

"With the sun on my face? Maybe," he said, looking to the sun.

There were some lovely days in the spring of 1918. In March the Count was able to get up. They dressed him in a simple, dark blue uniform. He was not very thin, only swarthy-transparent, now his beard was shaven and his hair was cut. His smallness made him noticeable, but he was masculine, perfect in his small stature. All the smiling dapperness that had made him seem like a monkey to Daphne when she was a girl had gone now. His eyes were dark and haughty; he seemed to keep inside his own reserves, speaking to nobody if he could help it, neither to the nurses nor the visitors nor to his fellow-prisoners, fellow-officers. He seemed to put a shadow between himself and them, and from across this shadow he looked with his dark, beautifully fringed eyes, as a proud little beast from the shadow of its lair. Only to Daphne he laughed and chatted.

She sat with him one day in March on the terrace of the hospital, on a morning when white clouds went endlessly and magnificently about a blue sky, and the sunshine felt warm after the blots of shadow.

"When you had a birthday, and you were seventeen, didn't I give you a thimble?" he asked her.

"Yes. I have it still."

"With a gold snake at the bottom, and a Mary-beetle of green stone at the top, to push the needle with."

"Yes."

"Do you ever use it?"

"No. I sew so rarely."

"Would it displease you to sew something for me?"

"You won't admire my stitches. What would you wish me to sew?"

"Sew me a shirt that I can wear. I have never before worn shirts from a shop, with a maker's name inside. It is very distasteful to me."

She looked at him—his haughty little brows.

"Shall I ask my maid to do it?" she said.

" Oh, please no ! Oh, please no, do not trouble. No, please, I would not want it unless you sewed it yourself, with the Psanek thimble."

She paused before she answered. Then came her slow :

" Why ? "

He turned and looked at her with dark, searching eyes.

" I have no reason," he said, rather haughtily.

She left the matter there. For two weeks she did not go to see him. Then suddenly one day she took the 'bus down Oxford Street and bought some fine white flannel. She decided he must wear flannel.

That afternoon she drove out to Hurst Place. She found him sitting on the terrace, looking across the garden at the red suburb of London smoking fumily in the near distance, interrupted by patches of uncovered ground and a flat, tin-roofed laundry.

" Will you give me measurements for your shirt ? " she said.

" The number of the neck-band of this English shirt is fifteen. If you ask the matron she will give you the measurement. It is a little too large, too long in the sleeves, you see," and he shook his shirt cuff over his wrist. " Also too long altogether."

" Mine will probably be unwearable when I've made them," said she.

" Oh no. Let your maid direct you. But please do not let her sew them."

" Will you tell me why you want me to do it ? "

" Because I am a prisoner, in other people's clothes, and I have nothing of my own. All the things I touch are distasteful to me. If your maid sews for me, it will still be the same. Only you might give me what I want, something that buttons round my throat and on my wrists."

" And in Germany—or in Austria ? "

" My mother sewed for me. And after her, my mother's sister, who was the head of my house."

" Not your wife ? "

" Naturally not. She would have been insulted. She was never more than a guest in my house. In my family there are old traditions—but with me they have come to an end. I had best try to revive them."

" Beginning with traditions of shirts ? "

" Yes. In our family the shirt should be made and washed by a woman of our own blood : but when we marry, by the wife. So when I married I had sixty shirts, and many other things—sewn by my mother and my aunt, all with my initial, and the ladybird, which is our crest."

" And where did they put the initial ? "

" Here ! " He put his finger on the back of his neck, on the swarthy, transparent skin. " I fancy I can feel the embroidered ladybird still. On our linen we had no crown : only the ladybird."

She was silent, thinking.

" You will forgive what I ask you ? " he said, " since I am a prisoner and can do no other, and since fate has made you so that you understand the world as I understand it. It is not really indelicate, what I ask you. There will be a ladybird on your finger when you sew, and those who wear the ladybird understand."

" I suppose," she mused, " it is as bad to have your bee in your shirt as in your bonnet."

He looked at her with round eyes.

" Don't you know what it is to have a bee in your bonnet ? " she said.

" No."

" To have a bee buzzing among your hair ! To be out of your wits," she smiled at him.

" So ! " he said. " Ah, the Psaneks have had a ladybird in their bonnets for many hundred years."

" Quite, quite mad," she said.

" It may be," he answered. " But with my wife I was quite sane for ten years. Now give me the madness of the ladybird. The world I was sane about has gone raving. The ladybird I was mad with is wise still."

" At least, when I sew the shirts, if I sew them," she said, " I shall have the ladybird at my finger's end."

" You want to laugh at me."

" But surely you know you are funny, with your family insect."

" My family insect ? Now you want to be rude to me."

" How many spots must it have ? "

" Seven."

" Three on each wing. And what do I do with the odd one ? "

" You put that one between its teeth, like the cake for Cerberus."

" I'll remember that."

When she brought the first shirt, she gave it to the matron. Then she found Count Dionys sitting on the terrace. It was a beautiful spring day. Near at hand were tall elm trees, and some rooks cawing.

" What a lovely day ! " she said. " Are you liking the world any better ? "

" The world ? " he said, looking up at her with the same old discontent and disgust on his fine, transparent nose.

" Yes," she replied, a shadow coming over her face.

" Is this the world—all those little red-brick boxes in rows, where couples of little people live, who decree my destiny ? "

" You don't like England ? "

" Ah, England ! Little houses like little boxes, each with its domestic Englishman and his domestic wife, each ruling the world because all are alike, so alike."

" But England isn't all houses."

" Fields then ! Little fields with innumerable hedges. Like a net with an irregular mesh, pinned down over this island and everything under the net. Ah, Lady Daphne, forgive me. I am ungrateful. I am so full of bile, of spleen, you say. My only wisdom is to keep my mouth shut."

" Why do you hate everything ? " she said, her own face going bitter.

" Not everything. If I were free ! If I were outside the law. Ah, Lady Daphne, how does one get outside the law ? "

" By going inside oneself," she said. " Not outside."

His face took on a greater expression of disgust.

" No, no. I am a man, I am a man, even if I am little. I am not a spirit, that coils itself inside a shell. In my soul is anger, anger, anger. Give me room for my anger. Give me room for that."

His black eyes looked keenly into hers. She rolled her eyes as if in a half-trance. And in a monotonous, tranced voice she said :

" Much better get over your anger. And *why* are you angry ? "

" There is no why. If it were love, you would not ask me, *why do you love ?* But it is anger, anger, anger. What else can I call it ? And there is no why."

Again he looked at her with his dark, sharp, questioning, tormented eyes.

" Can't you get rid of it ? " she said, looking aside.

" If a shell exploded and blew me into a thousand fragments," he said, " it would not destroy the anger that is in me. I know that. No, it will never dissipate. And to die is no release. The anger goes on gnashing and whimpering in death. Lady Daphne, Lady Daphne, we have used up all the love, and this is what is left."

" Perhaps *you* have used up all your love," she replied. " You are not everybody."

" I know it. I speak for me and you."

" Not for me," she said rapidly.

He did not answer, and they remained silent.

At length she turned her eyes slowly to him.

"Why do you say you speak for me?" she said, in an accusing tone.

"Pardon me. I was hasty."

But a faint touch of superciliousness in his tone showed he meant what he had said. She mused, her brow cold and stony.

"And why do you tell *me* about your anger?" she said. "Will that make it better?"

"Even the adder finds his mate. And she has as much poison in her mouth as he."

She gave a little sudden squirt of laughter.

"Awfully poetic thing to say about me," she said.

He smiled, but with the same corrosive quality.

"Ah," he said, "you are not a dove. You are a wild-cat with open eyes, half-dreaming on a bough, in a lonely place, as I have seen her. And I ask myself—What are her memories, then?"

"I wish I were a wild-cat," she said suddenly.

He eyed her shrewdly, and did not answer.

"You want more war?" she said to him bitterly.

"More trenches? More Big Berthas, more shells and poison-gas, more machine-drilled science-manœuvred so-called armies? Never. Never. I would rather work in a factory that makes boots and shoes. And I would rather deliberately starve to death than work in a factory that makes boots and shoes."

"Then what do you want?"

"I want my anger to have room to grow."

"How?"

"I do not know. That is why I sit still here, day after day. I wait."

"For your anger to have room to grow?"

"For that."

"Good-bye, Count Dionys."

"Good-bye, Lady Daphne."

She had determined never to go and see him again. She had no sign from him. Since she had begun the second shirt, she went on with it. And then she hurried to finish it, because she was starting a round of visits that would end in the summer sojourn in Scotland. She intended to post the shirt. But after all, she took it herself.

She found Count Dionys had been removed from Hurst Place to Voynich Hall, where other enemy officers were interned. The being thwarted made her more determined. She took the train next day to go to Voynich Hall.

When he came into the ante-room where he was to receive her, she felt at once the old influence of his silence and his subtle power. His face had still that swarthy-transparent look of one who is unhappy, but his bearing was proud and reserved. He kissed her hand politely, leaving her to speak.

" How are you ? " she said. " I didn't know you were here. I am going away for the summer."

" I wish you a pleasant time," he said. They were speaking English.

" I brought the other shirt," she said. " It is finished at last."

" That is a greater honour than I dared expect," he said.

. " I'm afraid it may be more honourable than useful. The other didn't fit, did it ? "

" Almost," he said. " It fitted the spirit, if not the flesh," he smiled.

" I'd rather it had been the reverse, for once," she said. " Sorry."

" I would not have it one stitch different."

" Can we sit in the garden ? "

" I think we may."

They sat on a bench. Other prisoners were playing croquet not far off. But these two were left comparatively alone.

" Do you like it better here ? " she said.

" I have nothing to complain of," he said.

" And the anger ? "

" It is doing well, I thank you," he smiled.

" You mean getting better ? "

" Making strong roots," he said, laughing.

" Ah, so long as it only makes roots ! " she said.

" And your ladyship, how is she ? "

" My ladyship is rather better," she replied.

" Much better, indeed," he said, looking into her face.

" Do you mean I *look* much better ? " she asked quickly.

" Very much. It is your beauty you think of. Well, your beauty is almost itself again."

" Thanks."

" You brood on your beauty as I on my anger. Ah, your ladyship, be wise, and make friends with your anger. That is the way to let your beauty blossom."

" I was not unfriends with you, was I ? " she said.

" With me ? " His face flickered with a laugh. " Am I your anger ? Your vicar in wrath ? So then, be friends with the angry me, your ladyship. I ask nothing better."

"What is the use," she said, "being friends with the *angry* you? I would much rather be friends with the happy you."

"That little animal is extinct," he laughed. "And I am glad of it."

"But what remains? Only the angry you? Then it is no use my trying to be friends."

"You remember, dear Lady Daphne, that the adder does not suck his poison all alone, and the pole-cat knows where to find his she-pole-cat. You remember that each one has his own dear mate," he laughed. "Dear, deadly mate."

"And what if I do remember those bits of natural history, Count Dionys?"

"The she-adder is dainty, delicate, and carries her poison lightly. The wild-cat has wonderful green eyes that she closes with memory like a screen. The ice-bear hides like a snake with her cubs, and her snarl is the strangest thing in the world."

"Have you ever heard me snarl?" she asked suddenly.

He only laughed, and looked away.

They were silent. And immediately the strange thrill of secrecy was between them. Something had gone beyond sadness into another secret, thrilling communion which she would never admit.

"What do you do all day here?" she asked.

"Play chess, play this foolish croquet, play billiards, and read, and wait, and remember."

"What do you wait for?"

"I don't know."

"And what do you remember?"

"Ah, that. Shall I tell you what amuses me? Shall I tell you a secret?"

"Please don't, if it's anything that matters."

"It matters to nobody but me. Will you hear it?"

"If it does not implicate me in any way."

"It does not. Well, I am a member of a certain old secret society—no, don't look at me, nothing frightening—only a society like the freemasons."

"And?"

"And—well, as you know, one is initiated into certain so-called secrets and rites. My family has always been initiated. So I am an initiate too. Does it interest you?"

"Why, of course."

"Well. I was always rather thrilled by these secrets. Or some of them. Some seemed to me far-fetched. The ones that thrilled me even never had any relation to actual life. When you knew me in Dresden and Prague, you would not have thought me a man invested with awful secret knowledge, now would you ? "

" Never."

" No. It was just a little exciting side-show. And I was a grimacing little society man. But now they become true. It becomes true."

" The secret knowledge ? "

" Yes."

" What, for instance ? "

" Take actual fire. It will bore you. Do you want to hear ? "

" Go on."

" This is what I was taught. The true fire is invisible. Flame, and the red fire we see burning, has its back to us. It is running away from us. Does that mean anything to you ? "

" Yes."

" Well then, the yellowness of sunshine—light itself—that is only the glancing aside of the real original fire. You know that is true. There would be no light if there was no refraction, no bits of dust and stuff to turn the dark fire into visibility. You know that's a fact. And that being so, even the sun is dark. It is only his jacket of dust that makes him visible. You know that too. And the true sunbeams coming towards us flow darkly, a moving darkness of the genuine fire. The sun is dark, the sunshine flowing to us is dark. And light is only the inside out of it all, the lining, and the yellow beams are only the turning away of the sun's directness that was coming to us. Does that interest you at all ? "

" Yes," she said dubiously.

" Well, we've got the world inside out. The true living world of fire is dark, throbbing, darker than blood. Our luminous world that we go by is only the reverse of this."

" Yes, I like that," she said.

" Well ! Now listen. The same with love. This white love that we have is the same. It is only the reverse, the whited sepulchre of the true love. True love is dark, a throbbing together in darkness, like the wild-cat in the night, when the green screen opens and her eyes are on the darkness."

" No, I don't see that," she said, in a slow, clanging voice.

" You, and your beauty—that is only the inside-out of you. The real you is the wild-cat invisible in the night, with red fire perhaps coming out if its wide, dark eyes. Your beauty is your whited sepulchre."

" You mean cosmetics," she said. " I've got none on to-day— not even powder."

He laughed.

" Very good," he said. " Consider me. I used to think myself small but handsome, and the ladies used to admire me moderately, never very much. A trim little fellow, you know. Well, that was just the inside-out of me. I am a black tom-cat howling in the night, and it is then that fire comes out of me. This me you look at is my whited sepulchre. What do you say ? "

She was looking into his eyes. She could see the darkness swaying in the depths. She perceived the invisible, cat-like fire stirring deep inside them, felt it coming towards her. She turned her face aside. Then he laughed, showing his strong white teeth, that seemed a little too large, rather dreadful.

She rose to go.

" Well," she said. " I shall have the summer in which to think about the world inside-out. Do write if there is anything to say. Write to Thoresway. Good-bye ! "

" Ah, your eyes ! " he said. " They are like jewels of stone."

Being away from the Count, she put him out of her mind. Only she was sorry for him a prisoner in that sickening Voynich Hall. But she did not write. Nor did he.

As a matter of fact her mind was now much more occupied with her husband. All arrangements were being made to effect his exchange. From month to month she looked for his return. And so she thought of him.

Whatever happened to her, she thought about it, thought and thought a great deal. The consciousness of her mind was like tablets of stone weighing her down. And whoever would make a new entry into her must break these tablets of stone piece by piece. So it was that in her own way she thought often enough of the Count's world inside-out. A curious latency stirred in her consciousness that was not yet an idea.

He said her eyes were like jewels of stone. What a horrid thing to say ! What did he want her eyes to be like ? He wanted them to dilate and become all black pupil, like a cat's at night. She shrank convulsively from the thought, and tightened her breast.

He said her beauty was her whited sepulchre. Even that, she knew what he meant. The invisibility of her he wanted to love. But ah, her pearl-like beauty was so dear to her, and it was so famous in the world.

He said her white love was like moonshine, harmful, the reverse of love. He meant Basil, of course. Basil always said she was the moon. But then Basil loved her for that. The ecstasy of it ! She shivered, thinking of her husband. But it had also made her nerve-worn, her husband's love. Ah, nerve-worn.

What then would the Count's love be like? Something so secret and different. She would not be lovely and a queen to him. He hated her loveliness. The wild-cat has its mate. The little wild-cat that he was. Ah!

She caught her breath, determined not to think. When she thought of Count Dionys she felt the world slipping away from her. She would sit in front of a mirror, looking at her wonderful cared-for face that had appeared in so many society magazines. She loved it so, it made her feel so vain. And she looked at her blue-green eyes—the eyes of the wild-cat on a bough. Yes, the lovely blue-green iris drawn tight like a screen. Supposing it should relax. Supposing it should unfold, and open out the dark depths, the dark, dilated pupil! Supposing it should?

Never! She always caught herself back. She felt she might be killed before she could give way to that relaxation that the Count wanted of her. She could not. She just could not. At the very thought of it some hypersensitive nerve started with a great twinge in her breast; she drew back, forced to keep her guard. Ah no, Monsieur le Comte, you shall never take her ladyship off her guard.

She disliked the thought of the Count. An impudent little fellow. An impertinent little fellow! A little madman, really. A little outsider. No, no. She would think of her husband: an adorable, tall, well-bred Englishman, so easy and simple, and with the amused look in his blue eyes. She thought of the cultured, casual trail of his voice. It set her nerves on fire. She thought of his strong, easy body—beautiful, white-fleshed, with the fine springing of warm-brown hair like tiny flames. He was the Dionysus, full of sap, milk and honey, and northern golden wine: he, her husband. Not that little unreal Count. Ah, she dreamed of her husband, of the love-days, and the honeymoon, the lovely, simple intimacy. Ah, the marvellous revelation of that intimacy, when he left himself to her so generously. Ah, she was his wife for this reason, that he had given himself to her so greatly, so generously. Like an ear of corn he was there for her gathering—her husband, her own, lovely, English husband. Ah, when would he come again, when would he come again!

She had letters from him—and how he loved her. Far away, his life was all hers. All hers, flowing to her as the beam flows from a white star right down to us, to our heart. Her lover, her husband.

He was now expecting to come home soon. It had all been arranged. "I hope you won't be disappointed in me when I do

get back," he wrote. "I am afraid I am no longer the plump
and well-looking young man I was. I've got a big scar at the side
of my mouth, and I'm as thin as a starved rabbit, and my hair's
going grey. Doesn't sound attractive, does it? And it isn't attractive. But once I can get out of this infernal place, and once I can be
with you again, I shall come in for my second blooming. The very
thought of being quietly in the same house with you, quiet and in
peace, makes me realize that if I've been through hell, I have known
heaven on earth and can hope to know it again. I am a miserable
brute to look at now. But I have faith in you. You will forgive my
appearance, and that alone will make me feel handsome."

She read this letter many times. She was not afraid of his scar or
his looks. She would love him all the more.

Since she had started making shirts—those two for the Count
had been an enormous labour, even though her maid had come to
her assistance forty times : but since she had started making shirts,
she thought she might continue. She had some good suitable silk :
her husband liked silk underwear.

But still she used the Count's thimble. It was gold outside and
silver inside, and was too heavy. A snake was coiled round the
base, and at the top, for pressing the needle, was inlet a semi-
translucent apple-green stone, perhaps jade, carved like a scarab,
with little dots. It was too heavy. But then she sewed so slowly.
And she liked to feel her hand heavy, weighted. And as she sewed
she thought about her husband, and she felt herself in love with
him. She thought of him, how beautiful he was, and how she would
love him now he was thin : she would love him all the more. She
would love to trace his bones, as if to trace his living skeleton. The
thought made her rest her hands in her lap, and drift into a muse.
Then she felt the weight of the thimble on her finger, and took it off,
and sat looking at the green stone. The ladybird. The ladybird.
And if only her husband would come soon, soon. It was wanting
him that made her so ill. Nothing but that. She had wanted him
so badly. She wanted now. Ah, if she could go to him now, and find
him, wherever he was, and see him and touch him and take all his love.

As she mused, she put the thimble down in front of her, took up a
little silver pencil from her work-basket, and on a bit of blue paper
that had been the band of a small skein of silk she wrote the lines of
the silly little song :

> "Wenn ich ein Vöglein wär'
> Und auch zwei Flüglein hätt'
> Flög' ich zu dir——"

That was all she could get on her bit of pale-blue paper.

> " If I were a little bird
> And had two little wings
> I'd fly to thee——"

Silly enough, in all conscience. But she did not translate it, so it did not seem quite so silly.

At that moment her maid announced Lady Bingham—her husband's sister. Daphne crumpled up the bit of paper in a flurry, and in another minute Primrose, his sister, came in. The newcomer was not a bit like a primrose, being long-faced and clever, smart, but not a bit elegant, in her new clothes.

" Daphne dear, what a domestic scene ! I suppose it's rehearsal. Well, you may as well rehearse, he's with Admiral Burns on the *Ariadne*. Father just heard from the Admiralty : quite fit. He'll be here in a day or two. Splendid, isn't it ? And the war is going to end. At least it seems like it. You'll be safe of your man now, dear. Thank heaven when it's all over. What are you sewing ? "

" A shirt," said Daphne.

" A shirt ! Why, how clever of you. I should never know which end to begin. Who showed you ? "

" Millicent."

" And how did *she* know ? She's no business to know how to sew shirts : nor cushions nor sheets either. Do let me look. Why, how perfectly marvellous you are !—every bit by hand, too. Basil isn't worth it, dear, really he isn't. Let him order his shirts in Oxford Street. Your business is to be beautiful, not to sew shirts. What a dear little pin-poppet, or rather needle-woman ! I say, a satire on us, that is. But what a darling, with mother-of-pearl wings to her skirts ! And darling little gold-eyed needles inside her. You screw her head off, and you find she's full of pins and needles. Woman for you ! Mother says won't you come to lunch to-morrow. And won't you come to Brassey's to tea with me at this minute. Do, there's a dear. I've got a taxi."

Daphne bundled her sewing loosely together.

When she tried to do a bit more, two days later, she could not find her thimble. She asked her maid, whom she could absolutely trust. The girl had not seen it. She searched everywhere. She asked her nurse—who was now her housekeeper—and footman. No, nobody had seen it. Daphne even asked her sister-in-law.

" Thimble, darling ? No, I don't remember a thimble. I remember a dear little needle lady, whom I thought such a precious satire on us women. I didn't notice a thimble."

Poor Daphne wandered about in a muse. She did not want to believe it lost. It had been like a talisman to her. She tried to forget it. Her husband was coming, quite soon, quite soon. But she could not raise herself to joy. She had lost her thimble. It was as if Count Dionys accused her in her sleep of something, she did not quite know what.

And though she did not really want to go to Voynich Hall, yet like a fatality she went, like one doomed. It was already late autumn, and some lovely days. This was the last of the lovely days. She was told that Count Dionys was in the small park, finding chestnuts. She went to look for him. Yes, there he was in his blue uniform stooping over the brilliant yellow leaves of the sweet chestnut tree, that lay around him like a fallen nimbus of glowing yellow, under his feet, as he kicked and rustled, looking for the chestnut burrs. And with his short, brown hands he was pulling out the small chestnuts and putting them in his pockets. But as she approached he peeled a nut to eat it. His teeth were white and powerful.

" You remind me of a squirrel laying in a winter store," said she.

" Ah, Lady Daphne—I was thinking, and did not hear you."

" I thought you were gathering chestnuts—even eating them."

" Also ! " he laughed. He had a dark, sudden charm when he laughed, showing his rather large white teeth. She was not quite sure whether she found him a little repulsive.

" Were you *really* thinking ? " she said, in her slow, resonant way.

" Very truly."

" And weren't you enjoying the chestnut a bit ? "

" Very much. Like sweet milk. Excellent, excellent." He had the fragments of the nut between his teeth, and bit them finely. " Will you take one, too." He held out the little, pointed brown nuts on the palm of his hand.

She looked at them doubtfully.

" Are they as tough as they always were ? " she said.

" No, they are fresh and good. Wait, I will peel one for you."

They strayed about through the thin clump of trees.

" You have had a pleasant summer ; you are strong ? "

" Almost *quite* strong," said she. " Lovely summer, thanks. I suppose it's no good asking you if you have been happy ? "

" Happy ? " He looked at her direct. His eyes were black, and seemed to examine her. She always felt he had a little contempt of her. " Oh, yes," he said, smiling. " I have been very happy."

" So glad."

They drifted a little further, and he picked up an apple-green chestnut burr out of the yellow-brown leaves, handling it with sensitive fingers that still suggested paws to her.

" How did you succeed in being happy ? " she said.

" How shall I tell you ? I felt that the same power which put up the mountains could pull them down again—no matter how long it took."

" And was that all ? "

" Was it not enough ? "

" I should say decidedly too little."

He laughed broadly, showing the strong, negroid teeth.

" You do not know all it means," he said.

" The thought that the mountains were going to be pulled down ? " she said. " It will be so long after my day."

" Ah, you are bored," he said. " But I—I found the God who pulls things down : especially the things that men have put up. Do they not say that life is a search after God, Lady Daphne ? I have found my God."

" The god of destruction," she said, blanching.

" Yes—not the devil of destruction, but the god of destruction. The blessed god of destruction. It is strange "—he stood before her, looking up at her—" but I have found my God. The god of anger, who throws down the steeples and the factory chimneys. Ah, Lady Daphne, he is a man's God, a man's God. I have found my God, Lady Daphne."

" Apparently. And how are you going to serve him ? "

A naïve glow transfigured his face.

" Oh, I will help. With my heart I will help while I can do nothing with my hands. I say to my heart : Beat, hammer, beat with little strokes. Beat, hammer of God, beat them down. Beat it all down."

Her brows knitted, her face took on a look of discontent.

" Beat what down ? " she asked harshly.

" The world, the world of man. Not the trees—these chestnuts for example "—he looked up at them, at the tufts and loose pinions of yellow—" not these—nor the chattering sorcerers, the squirrels— nor the hawk that comes. Not those."

" You mean beat England ? " she said.

" Ah, no. Ah, no. Not England any more than Germany— perhaps not as much. Not Europe any more than Asia."

" Just the end of the world ? "

" No, no. No, no. What grudge have I against a world where little chestnuts are so sweet as these ! Do you like yours ? Will you take another ? "

" No, thanks."

" What grudge have I against a world where even the hedges are full of berries, bunches of black berries that hang down, and red berries that thrust up. Never would I hate the world. But the world of man. Lady Daphne "—his voice sank to a whisper—" *I hate it.* Zzz ! " he hissed. " Strike, little heart ! Strike, strike, hit, smite ! Oh, Lady Daphne ! "—his eyes dilated with a ring of fire.

" What ? " she said, scared.

" I believe in the power of my red, dark heart. God has put the hammer in my breast—the little eternal hammer. Hit—hit—hit ! It hits on the world of man. It hits, it hits ! And it hears the thin sound of cracking. The thin sound of cracking. Hark ! "

He stood still and made her listen. It was late afternoon. The strange laugh of his face made the air seem dark to her. And she could easily have believed that she heard a faint, fine shivering, cracking, through the air, a delicate crackling noise.

" You hear it ? Yes ? Oh, may I live long ! May I live long, so that my hammer may strike and strike, and the cracks go deeper, deeper ! Ah, the world of man ! Ah, the joy, the passion in every heart-beat ! Strike home, strike true, strike sure. Strike to destroy it. Strike ! Strike ! To destroy the world of man. Ah, God. Ah, God, prisoner of peace. Do I not know you, Lady Daphne ? Do I not ? Do I not ? "

She was silent for some moments, looking away at the twinkling lights of a station beyond.

" Not the white plucked lily of your body. I have gathered no flower for my ostentatious life. But in the cold dark, your lily root, Lady Daphne. Ah, yes, you will know it all your life, that I know where your root lies buried, with its sad, sad quick of life. What does it matter ! "

They had walked slowly towards the house. She was silent. Then at last she said, in a peculiar voice :

" And you would never want to kiss me ? "

" Ah, no ! " he answered sharply.

She held out her hand.

" Good-bye, Count Dionys," she drawled, fashionably. He bowed over her hand, but did not kiss it.

" Good-bye, Lady Daphne."

She went away, with her brow set hard. And henceforth she thought only of her husband, of Basil. She made the Count die out of her. Basil was coming, he was near. He was coming back from the East, from war and death. Ah, he had been through awful fire of experience. He would be something new, something she did not know. He was something new, a stronger lover who had been through terrible fire, and had come out strange and new, like a god. Ah, new and terrible his love would be, pure and intensified by the awful fire of suffering. A new lover—a new bridegroom—a new, supernatural wedding-night. She shivered in anticipation, waiting for her husband. She hardly noticed the wild excitement of the Armistice. She was waiting for something more wonderful to her.

And yet the moment she heard his voice on the telephone, her heart contracted with fear. It was his well-known voice, deliberate, diffident, almost drawling, with the same subtle suggestion of deference, and the rather exaggerated Cambridge intonation, up and down. But there was a difference, a new icy note that went through her veins like death.

" Is that you, Daphne ? I shall be with you in half an hour. Is that all right for you ? Yes, I've just landed, and shall come straight to you ? Yes, a taxi. Shall I be too sudden for you, darling ? No ? Good, oh good ! Half an hour, then ! I say, Daphne ? There won't be any one else there, will there ? Quite alone ! Good ! I can ring up Dad afterwards. Yes, splendid, splendid. Sure you're all right, my darling ? I'm at death's door till I see you. Yes. Good-bye— half an hour. Good-bye."

When Daphne had hung up the receiver she sat down almost in a faint. What was it that so frightened her ? His terrible, terrible altered voice, like cold, blue steel. She had no time to think. She rang for her maid.

" Oh, my lady, it isn't bad news ? " cried Millicent, when she caught sight of her mistress white as death.

" No, good news. Major Apsley will be here in half an hour. Help me to dress. Ring to Murry's first to send in some roses, red ones, and some lilac-coloured iris—two dozen of each, at once."

Daphne went to her room. She didn't know what to wear, she didn't know how she wanted her hair dressed. She spoke hastily to her maid. She chose a violet coloured dress. She did not know what she was doing. In the middle of dressing the flowers came, and she left off to put them in the bowls. So that when she heard his voice in the hall, she was still standing in front of the mirror reddening her lips and wiping it away again.

" Major Apsley, my lady ! " murmured the maid, in excitement.

" Yes, I can hear. Go and tell him I shall be *one* minute."

Daphne's voice had become slow and sonorous, like bronze, as it always did when she was upset. Her face looked almost haggard, and in vain she dabbed with the rouge.

" How does he look ? " she asked curtly, when her maid came back.

" A long scar here," said the maid, and she drew her finger from the left hand corner of her mouth into her cheek, slanting downwards.

" Make him look very different ? " asked Daphne.

" Not so *very* different, my lady," said Millicent gently. " His eyes are the same, I think." The girl also was distressed.

" All right," said Daphne. She looked at herself, a long, last look as she turned away from the mirror. The sight of her own face made her feel almost sick. She had seen so much of herself. And yet even now she was fascinated by the heavy droop of her lilac-veined lids over her slow, strange, large, green-blue eyes. They *were* mysterious-looking. And she gave herself a long, sideways glance, curious and Chinese. How was it possible there was a touch of the Chinese in her face ?—she so purely an English blonde, an Aphrodite of the foam, as Basil had called her in poetry. Ah well ! She left off her thoughts and went through the hall to the drawing-room.

He was standing nervously in the middle of the room, in his uniform. She hardly glanced at his face—and saw only the scar.

" Hullo, Daphne," he said, in a voice full of the expected emotion. He stepped forward and took her in his arms, and kissed her forehead.

" So glad ! So glad it's happened at last," she said, hiding her tears.

" So glad what has happened, darling ? " he asked, in his deliberate manner.   •

" That you're back." Her voice had the bronze resonance, she spoke rather fast.

" Yes, I'm back, Daphne darling—as much of me as there is to bring back."

" Why ? " she said. " You've come back whole, surely ? " She was frightened.

" Yes, apparently I have. Apparently. But don't let's talk of that. Let's talk of you, darling. How are you ? Let me look at you. You are thinner, you are older. But you are more wonderful than ever. Far more wonderful."

" How ? " said she.

" I can't exactly say how. You were only a girl. Now you are a woman. I suppose it's all that's happened. But you are wonderful as a woman, Daphne darling—more wonderful than all that's happened. I couldn't have believed you'd be so wonderful. I'd forgotten—or else I'd never known. I say, I'm a lucky chap really. Here I am, alive and well, and I've got you for a wife. It's brought you out like a flower. I say, darling, there is more now that Venus of the foam—grander. How beautiful you are ! But you look like the beauty of all life—as if you were moon-mother of the world— Aphrodite. God is good to me after all, darling. I ought never to utter a single complaint. How lovely you are—how lovely you are, my darling ! I'd forgotten you—and I thought I knew you so well. Is it true that you belong to me ? Are you really mine ? "

They were seated on the yellow sofa. He was holding her hand, and his eyes were going up and down, from her face to her throat and her breast. The sound of his words, and the strong, cold desire in his voice excited her, pleased her, and made her heart freeze. She turned and looked into his light blue eyes. They had no longer the amused light, nor the young look. They burned with a hard, focused light, whitish.

" It's all right. You are mine, aren't you, Daphne darling ? " came his cultured, musical voice, that had always the well-bred twang of diffidence.

She looked back into his eyes.

" Yes, I am yours," she said, from the lips.

" Darling ! Darling ! " he murmured, kissing her hand.

Her heart beat suddenly so terribly, as if her breast would be ruptured, and she rose in one movement and went across the room. She leaned her hand on the mantelpiece and looked down at the electric fire. She could hear the faint, faint noise of it. There was silence for a few moments.

Then she turned and looked at him. He was watching her intently.

His face was gaunt, and there was a curious deathly sub-pallor, though his cheeks were not white. The scar ran livid from the side of his mouth. It was not so very big. But it seemed like a scar in him himself, in his brain as it were. In his eyes was that hard, white, focused light that fascinated her and was terrible to her. He was different. He was like death ; like risen death. She felt she dared not touch him. White death was still upon him. She could tell that he shrank with a kind of agony from contact. "Touch me not, I am not yet ascended unto the Father." Yet for contact he had come. Something, someone seemed to be looking over his shoulder. His own young ghost looking over his shoulder. Oh God ! She closed her eyes, seeming to swoon. He remained leaning forward on the sofa, watching her.

" Aren't you well, darling ? " he asked. There was a strange, incomprehensible coldness in his very fire. He did not move to come near her.

"Yes, I'm well. It is only that after all it is so sudden. Let me get used to you," she said, turning aside her face from him. She felt utterly like a victim of his white, awful face.

"I suppose I must be a bit of a shock to you," he said. "I hope you won't leave off loving me. It won't be that, will it?"

The strange coldness in his voice! And yet the white, uncanny fire.

"No, I shan't leave off loving you," she admitted, in a low tone, as if almost ashamed. She *dared* not have said otherwise. And the saying it made it true.

"Ah, if you're sure of that," he said. "I'm a pretty unlovely sight to behold, I know, with this wound-scar. But if you can forgive me, darling. Do you think you can?" There was something like compulsion in his tone.

She looked at him, and shivered slightly.

"I love you—more than before," she said hurriedly.

"Even the scar?" came his terrible voice, inquiring.

She glanced again, with that slow, Chinese side-look, and felt she would die.

"Yes," she said, looking away at nothingness. It was an awful moment to her. A little, slightly imbecile smile widened on her face.

He suddenly knelt at her feet, and kissed the toe of her slipper, and kissed the instep, and kissed the ankle in the thin, black stocking.

"I knew," he said in a muffled voice. "I knew you would make good. I knew if I had to kneel, it was before you. I knew you were divine, you were the one—Cybele—Isis. I knew I was your slave. I knew. It has all been just a long initiation. I had to learn how to worship you."

He kissed her feet again and again, without the slightest self-consciousness, or the slightest misgiving. Then he went back to the sofa, and sat there looking at her, saying:

"It isn't love, it is worship. Love between me and you will be a sacrament, Daphne. That's what I had to learn. You are beyond me. A mystery to me. My God, how great it all is. How marvellous!"

She stood with her hand on the mantelpiece, looking down and not answering. She was frightened—almost horrified: but she was thrilled deep down to her soul. She really felt she could glow white and fill the universe like the moon, like Astarte, like Isis, like Venus.

The grandeur of her own pale power. The man religiously worshipped her, not merely amorously. She was ready for him—for the sacrament of his supreme worship.

He sat on the sofa with his hands spread on the yellow brocade and pushing downwards behind him, down between the deep upholstery of the back and the seat. He had long, white hands with pale freckles. And his fingers touched something. With his long white fingers he groped and brought it out. It was the lost thimble. And inside it was the bit of screwed-up blue paper.

" I say, is that *your* thimble ? " he asked.

She started, and went hurriedly forward for it.

" Where was it ? " she said, agitated.

But he did not give it to her. He turned it round and pulled out the bit of blue paper. He saw the faint pencil marks on the screwed-up ball, and unrolled the band of paper, and slowly deciphered the verse.

> " Wenn ich ein Vöglein wär'
> Und auch zwei Flüglein hätt'
> Flög' ich zu dir——"

" How awfully touching that is," he said. " A Vöglein with two little Flüglein ! But what a precious darling child you are ! Whom did you want to fly to, if you were a Vöglein ? " He looked up at her with a curious smile.

" I can't remember," she said, turning aside her head.

" I hope it was to me," he said. " Anyhow I shall consider it was, and shall love you all the more for it. What a darling child ! A Vöglein if you please, with two little wings ! Why, how beautifully absurd of you, darling ! "

He folded the scrap of paper carefully, and put it in his pocketbook, keeping the thimble all the time between his knees.

" Tell me when you lost it, Daphne," he said, examining the bauble.

" About a month ago—or two months."

" About a month ago—or two months. And what were you sewing ? Do you mind if I ask ? I like to think of you then. I was still in that beastly El Hasrun. What were you sewing, darling, two months ago, when you lost your thimble ? "

" A shirt."

" I say, a shirt ! Whose shirt ? "

" Yours."

" There. Now we've run it to earth. Were you really sewing a shirt for me ! Is it finished ? Can I put it on at this minute ? "

" That one isn't finished, but the first one is."

" I say, darling, let me go and put it on. To think I should have it next my skin ! I shall feel you all round me, all over me. I say how marvellous that will be ! Won't you come."

" Won't you give me the thimble ? " she said.

" Yes, of course. What a noble thimble, too ! Who gave it you ? "

" Count Dionys Psanek."

" Who was he ? "

" A Bohemian Count, in Dresden. He once stayed with us in Thoresway—with a tall wife. Didn't you meet them ? "

" I don't think I did. I don't think I did. I don't remember. What was he like ? "

" A little man with black hair and a rather low, dark forehead—rather dressy."

" No, I don't remember him at all. So he gave it you. Well, I wonder where he is now ? Probably rotted, poor devil."

" No, he's interned in Voynich Hall. Mother and I have been to see him several times. He was awfully badly wounded."

" Poor little beggar ! In Voynich Hall ! I'll look at him before he goes. Odd thing, to give you a thimble. Odd gift ! You were a girl then, though. Do you think he had it made, or do you think he found it in a shop."

" I think it belonged to the family. The ladybird at the top is part of their crest—and the snake as well, I think."

" A ladybird ! Funny thing for a crest. Americans would call it a bug. I must look at him before he goes. And you were sewing a shirt for me ! And then you posted me this little letter into the sofa. Well, I'm awfully glad I received it, and that it didn't go astray in the post, like so many things. ' Wenn ich ein Vöglein wär '—you perfect child ! But that is the beauty of a woman like you : you are so superb and beyond worship, and then such an exquisite naïve child. Who could help worshipping you and loving you : immortal and mortal together. What, you want the thimble ? Here ! Wonderful, wonderful white fingers. Ah, darling, you are more goddess than child, you long, limber Isis with sacred hands. White, white, and immortal ! Don't tell me your hands could die, darling : your wonderful Proserpine fingers. They are immortal as February and snowdrops. If you lift your hands the spring comes. I *can't* help kneeling before you, darling. I am no more than a sacrifice to you, an offering. I *wish* I could die in giving myself to you, give you all my blood on your altar, for ever."

She looked at him with a long, slow look, as he turned his face to her. His face was white with ecstasy. And she was not afraid. Somewhere, saturnine, she knew it was absurd. But she chose not to know. A certain swoon-sleep was on her. With her slow, green-blue eyes she looked down on his ecstasied face, almost benign. But in her right hand unconsciously she held the thimble fast, she only gave him her left hand. He took her hand and rose to his feet in that curious priestly ecstasy which made him more than a man or a soldier, far, far more than a lover to her.

Nevertheless his home-coming made her begin to be ill again. Afterwards, after his love, she had to bear herself in torment. To her shame and her heaviness, she knew she was not strong enough, or pure enough, to bear this awful outpouring adoration-lust. It was not her fault she felt weak and fretful afterwards, as if she wanted to cry and be fretful and petulant, wanted someone to save her. She could not turn to Basil, her husband. After his ecstasy of adoration-lust for her, she recoiled from him. Alas, she was not the goddess, the superb person he named her. She was flawed with the fatal humility of her age. She could not harden her heart and burn her soul pure of this humility, this misgiving. She could not finally believe in her own woman-godhead—only in her own female mortality.

That fierce power of being alone, even with your lover, the fierce power of the woman in excelsis—alas, she could not keep it. She could rise to the height for the time, the incandescent, transcendent, moon-fierce womanhood. But alas, she could not stay intensified and resplendent in her white, womanly powers, her female mystery. She relaxed, she lost her glory, and became fretful. Fretful and ill and never to be soothed. And then naturally her man became ashy and somewhat acrid, while she ached with nerves, and could not eat.

Of course she began to dream, about Count Dionys : to yearn wistfully for him. And it was absolutely a fatal thought to her that he was going away. When she thought that—that he was leaving England soon—going away into the dark for ever—then the last spark seemed to die in her. She felt her soul perish, whilst she herself was worn and soulless like a prostitute. A prostitute goddess. And her husband, the gaunt, white, intensified priest of her, who never ceased from being before her like a lust.

"To-morrow," she said to him, gathering her last courage and looking at him with a side-look, " I want to go to Voynich Hall."

"What, to see Count Psanek? Oh, good ! Yes, very good ! I'll come along as well. I should like very much to see him. I suppose he'll be getting sent back before long."

It was a fortnight before Christmas, very dark weather. Her husband was in khaki. She wore her black furs, and a black lace veil over her face, so that she seemed mysterious. But she lifted the veil and looped it behind, so that it made a frame for her face. She looked very lovely like that—her face pure like the most white hellebore flower, touched with winter pink, amid the blackness of her drapery and furs. Only she was rather too much like the picture of a modern beauty : too much the actual thing. She had half an idea that Dionys would hate her for her effective loveliness. He would see it and hate it. The thought was like a bitter balm to her. For herself, she loved her loveliness almost with obsession.

The Count came cautiously forward, glancing from the lovely figure of Lady Daphne to the gaunt well-bred Major at her side. Daphne was so beautiful in her dark furs, the black lace of her veil thrown back over her close-fitting, dull-gold-threaded hat, and her face fair like a winter flower in a cranny of darkness. But on her face, that was smiling with a slow self-satisfaction of beauty and of knowledge that she was dangling the two men, and setting all the imprisoned officers wildly on the alert, the Count could read that acridity of dissatisfaction and of inefficiency. And he looked away to the livid scar on the Major's cheek.

" Count Dionys, I wanted to bring my husband to see you. May I introduce him to you. Major Apsley—Count Dionys Psanek."

The two men shook hands, rather stiffly.

" I can sympathize with you being fastened up in this place," said Basil in his slow, easy fashion. " I hated it, I assure you, out there in the East."

" But your conditions were much worse than mine," smiled the Count.

" Well, perhaps they were. But prison is prison, even if it were heaven itself."

" Lady Apsley has been the one angel of my heaven," smiled the Count.

" I'm afraid I was as inefficient as most angels," said she.

The small smile never left the Count's dark face. It was true as she said, he was low-browed, the black hair growing low on his brow, and his eyebrows making a thick bow above his dark eyes, which had again long black lashes. So that the upper part of his face seemed very dusky-black. His nose was small and somewhat translucent. There was a touch of mockery about him, which was intensified even by his small, energic stature. He was still carefully dressed in the dark blue uniform, whose shabbiness could not hinder the dark flame of life which seemed to glow through the cloth from his body. He was not thin—but still had a curious swarthy translucency of skin in his low-browed face.

" What would you have been more ? " he laughed, making equivocal dark eyes at her.

" Oh, of course, a delivering angel—a cinema heroine," she replied, closing her eyes and turning her face aside.

All the while the white-faced, tall Major watched the little man with a fixed, half-smiling scrutiny. The Count seemed not to notice. He turned to the Englishman.

" I am glad that I can congratulate you, Major Apsley, on your safe and happy return to your home."

" Thanks. I hope I may be able to congratulate you in the same way before long."

" Oh yes," said the Count. " Before long I shall be shipped back."

" Have you any news of your family ? " interrupted Daphne.

" No news," he replied briefly, with sudden gravity.

" It seems you'll find a fairish mess out in Austria," said Basil.

" Yes, probably. It is what we had to expect," replied the Count.

" Well, I don't know. Sometimes things do turn out for the best. I feel that's as good as true in my case," said the Major.

" Things have turned out for the best ? " said the Count, with an intonation of polite inquiry.

" Yes. Just for me personally, I mean—to put it quite selfishly. After all, what we've learned is that a man can only speak for himself. And I feel it's been dreadful, but it's not been lost. It was like an ordeal one had to go through," said Basil.

" You mean the war ? "

" The war and everything that went with it."

" And when you've been through the ordeal ? " politely inquired the Count.

" Why, you arrive at a higher state of consciousness, and therefore of life. And so, of course, at a higher plane of love. A surprisingly higher plane of love, that you had never suspected the existence of before."

The Count looked from Basil to Daphne, who was posing her head a little self-consciously.

" Then indeed the war has been a valuable thing," he said.

" Exactly ! " cried Basil. " I am another man."

" And Lady Daphne ? " queried the Count.

" Oh "—her husband faced round to her—" she is *absolutely* another woman—and *much* more wonderful, more marvellous."

The Count smiled and bowed slightly.

" When we knew her ten years ago, we should have said then that it was impossible," said he, " for her to be more wonderful."

" Oh quite ! " returned the husband.   " It always seems impossible.   And the impossible is always happening.   As a matter of fact, I think the war has opened another circle of life to us—a wider ring."

" It may be so," said the Count.

" You don't feel it so yourself ? "   The Major looked with his keen, white attention into the dark, low-browed face of the other man.   The Count looked smiling at Daphne.

" I am only a prisoner still, Major, therefore I feel my ring quite small."

" Yes, of course you do.   Of course.   Well, I do hope you won't be a prisoner much longer.   You must be dying to get back into your own country."

" Yes, I shall be glad to be free.   Also," he smiled, " I shall miss my prison and my visits from the angels."

Even Daphne could not be sure he was mocking her.   It was evident the visit was unpleasant to him.   She could see he did not like Basil.   Nay more, she could feel that the presence of her tall, gaunt, idealistic husband was hateful to the little swarthy man.   But he passed it all off in smiles and polite speeches.

On the other hand, Basil was as if fascinated by the Count.   He watched him absorbedly all the time, quite forgetting Daphne.   She knew this.   She knew that she was quite gone out of her husband's consciousness, like a lamp that has been carried away into another room.   There he stood completely in the dark, as far as she was concerned, and all his attention focused on the other man.   On his pale, gaunt face was a fixed smile of amused attention.

" But don't you get awfully bored," he said, " between the visits ? "

The Count looked up with an affectation of frankness.

" No, I do not," he said.   " I can brood, you see, on the things that come to pass."

" I think that's where the harm comes in," replied the Major.   " One sits and broods, and is cut off from everything, and one loses one's contact with reality.   That's the effect it had on me, being a prisoner."

" Contact with reality—what is that ? "

" Well—contact with anybody, really—or anything."

" Why must one have contact ? "

" Well, because one must," said Basil.

The Count smiled slowly.

" But I can sit and watch fate flowing, like black water, deep down in my own soul," he said. " I feel that there, in the dark of my own soul, things are happening."

" That may be. But whatever happens, it is only one thing, really. It is a contact between your own soul and the soul of one other being, or of many other beings. Nothing else can happen to man. That's how I figured it out for myself. I may be wrong. But that's how I figured it out, when I was wounded and a prisoner."

The Count's face had gone dark and serious.

" But is this contact an aim in itself ? " he asked.

" Well," said the Major—he had taken his degree in philosophy— " it seems to me it is. It results inevitably in some form of activity. But the cause and the origin and the life-impetus of all action, activity, whether constructive or destructive, seems to me to be in the dynamic contact between human beings. You bring to pass a certain dynamic contact between men, and you get war. Another sort of dynamic contact, and you get them all building a cathedral, as they did in the Middle Ages."

" But was not the war, or the cathedral, the real aim, and the emotional contact just the means ? " said the Count.

" I don't think so," said the Major, his curious white passion beginning to glow through his face. The three were seated in a little card-room, left alone by courtesy by the other men. Daphne was still draped in her dark, too-becoming drapery. But alas, she sat now ignored by both men. She might just as well have been an ugly little nobody, for all the notice that was taken of her. She sat in the window-seat of the dreary small room with a look of discontent on her exotic, rare face, that was like a delicate white and pink hot-house flower. From time to time she glanced with long, slow looks from man to man : from her husband, whose pallid, intense, white glowing face was pressed forward across the table, to the Count, who sat back in his chair, as if in opposition, and whose dark face seemed clubbed together in a dark, unwilling stare. Her husband was *quite* unaware of anything but his own white identity. But the Count still had a grain of secondary consciousness which hovered round and remained aware of the woman in the window-seat. The whole of his face, and his forward-looking attention was con-centrated on Basil. But somewhere at the back of him he kept track of Daphne. She sat uneasy, in discontent, as women always do sit when men are locked together in a combustion of words. At the same time, she followed the argument. It was curious that, while her sympathy at this moment was with the Count, it was her husband whose words she believed to be true. The contact, the emotional contact was the real thing, the so-called " aim " was only a by-product. Even wars and cathedrals, in her mind, were only by-products. The real thing was what the warriors and cathedral-builders had had in common, as a great uniting feeling : the thing they felt for one another, and for their women in particular, of course.

" There are a great many kinds of contact, nevertheless," said Dionys.

" Well, do you know," said the Major, " it seems to me there is really only one supreme contact, the contact of love. Mind you, the love may take on an infinite variety of forms. And in my opinion, no form of love is wrong, so long as it *is* love, and you yourself *honour* what you are doing. Love has an extraordinary variety of forms ! And that is all that there is in life, it seems to me. But I grant you, if you deny the *variety* of love you deny love altogether. If you try to specialize love into one set of accepted feelings, you wound the very soul of love. Love *must* be multiform, else it is just tyranny, just death."

" But why call it all *love ?* " said the Count.

" Because it seems to me it *is* love : the great power that draws human beings together, no matter what the result of the contact may be. Of course there is hate, but hate is only the recoil of love."

" Do you think the old Egypt was established on love ? " asked Dionys.

" Why, of course ! And perhaps the most multiform, the most comprehensive love that the world has seen. All that we suffer from now is that our way of love is narrow, exclusive, and therefore not love at all ; more like death and tyranny."

The Count slowly shook his head, smiling slowly and as if sadly.

" No," he said. " No. It is no good. You must use another word than love."

" I don't agree at all," said Basil.

" What word then ? " blurted Daphne.

The Count looked at her.

" Obedience, submission, faith, belief, responsibility, power," he said slowly, picking out the words slowly, as if searching for what he wanted, and never quite finding it. He looked with his quiet dark eyes into her eyes. It was curious, she disliked his words intensely, but she liked him. On the other hand, she believed absolutely what her husband said, yet her physical sympathy was against him.

" Do you agree, Daphne ? " asked Basil.

" Not a bit," she replied, with a heavy look at her husband.

" Nor I," said Basil. " It seems to me, if you love, there is no obedience nor submission, except to the soul of love. If you mean obedience, submission, and all the rest, to the soul of love itself, I quite agree. But if you mean obedience, submission of one person to another, and one man having power over others—I don't agree, and never shall. It seems to me just there where we have gone wrong. Kaiser Wilhelm II wanted power——"

" No, no," said the Count. " He was a mountebank. He had no conception of the sacredness of power."

" He proved himself very dangerous."

" Oh yes. But peace can be even more dangerous still."

" Tell me, then. Do you believe that you, as an aristocrat, should have feudal power over a few hundreds of other men, who happen to be born serfs, or not aristocrats ? "

" Not as a hereditary aristocrat, but as a *man* who is by nature an aristocrat," said the Count, " it is my sacred duty to hold the lives of other men in my hands, and to shape the issue. But I can never fulfil my destiny till men will willingly put their lives in my hands."

" You don't expect them to, do you ? " smiled Basil.

" At this moment, no."

" Or at any moment ! " The Major was sarcastic.

" At a certain moment the men who are really living will come beseeching to put their lives into the hands of the greater men among them, beseeching the greater men to take the sacred responsibility of power."

" Do you think so ? Perhaps you mean men will at last begin to choose leaders whom they will *love*," said Basil. " I wish they would."

" No, I mean that they will at last yield themselves before men who are greater than they : become vassals, by choice."

" Vassals ! " exclaimed Basil, smiling. " You are still in the feudal ages, Count."

" Vassals. Not to any hereditary aristocrat—Hohenzollern or Hapsburg or Psanek," smiled the Count. " But to the man whose soul is born single, able to be alone, to choose and to command. At last the masses will come to such men and say, ' You are greater than we. Be our lords. Take our life and our death in your hands, and dispose of us according to your will. Because we see a light in your face, and a burning on your mouth.' "

The Major smiled for many moments, really piqued and amused, watching the Count, who did not turn a hair.

"I say, you must be awfully naïve, Count, if you believe the modern masses are ever going to behave like that. I assure you, they never will."

"If they did," said the Count, "would you call it a new reign of love, or something else?"

"Well, of course, it would contain an element of love. There would have to be an element of love in their feeling for their leaders."

"Do you think so? I thought that love assumed an equality in difference. I thought that love gave to every man the right to judge the acts of other men—'This was not an act of love, therefore it was wrong.' Does not democracy, and love, give to every man this right?"

"Certainly," said Basil.

"Ah, but my chosen aristocrat would say to those who chose him: 'If you choose me, you give up forever your right to judge me. If you have truly chosen to follow me, you have thereby rejected all your right to criticize me. You can no longer either approve or disapprove of me. You have performed the sacred act of choice. Henceforth you can only obey.'"

"They wouldn't be able to help criticizing, for all that," said Daphne, blurting in her say.

He looked at her slowly, and for the first time in her life she was doubtful of what she was saying.

"The day of Judas," he said, "ends with the day of love."

Basil woke up from a sort of trance.

"I think, of course, Count," he said, "that it's an awfully amusing idea. A retrogression slap back to the Dark Ages."

"Not so," said the Count. "Men—the mass of men—were never before free to perform the sacred act of choice. To-day—soon—they may be free."

"Oh, I don't know. Many tribes chose their kings and chiefs."

"Men have never before been quite free to choose: and to know what they are doing."

"You mean they've only made themselves free in order voluntarily to saddle themselves with new lords and masters?"

"I do mean that."

"In short, life is just a vicious circle?"

"Not at all. An ever-widening circle, as you say. Always more wonderful."

"Well, it's all frightfully interesting and amusing—don't you think so, Daphne? By the way, Count, where would women be? Would they be allowed to criticize their husbands?"

"Only before marriage," smiled the Count. "Not after."

" Splendid ! " said Basil. " I'm all for that bit of your scheme, Count. I hope you're listening, Daphne."

" Oh, yes. But then I've only married *you*. I've got my right to criticize all the other men," she said, in a dull, angry voice.

" Exactly. Clever of you ! So the Count won't get off ! Well now, what do you think of the Count's aristocratic scheme for the future, Daphne ? Do you approve ? "

" Not at all. But then little men have always wanted power," she said, cruelly.

" Oh, big men as well, for that matter," said Basil, conciliatory.

" I have been told before," smiled the Count, "little men are always bossy. I am afraid I have offended Lady Daphne ? "

" No," she said. " Not really. I'm amused, really. But I always dislike any suggestion of bullying."

" Indeed, so do I," said he.

" The Count didn't mean bullying, Daphne," said Basil. " Come, there is really an allowable distinction between responsible power and bullying."

" When men put their heads together about it," said she.

She was haughty and angry, as if she were afraid of losing something. The Count smiled mischievously at her.

" You are offended, Lady Daphne ? But why ? You are safe from any spark of my dangerous and extensive authority."

Basil burst into a roar of laughter.

" It *is* rather funny, you to be talking of power and of not being criticized," he said. " But I should like to hear more : I would like to hear more."

As they drove home, he said to his wife :

" You know I like that little man. He's a quaint little bantam. And he sets one thinking."

Lady Daphne froze to four degrees below zero, under the north-wind of this statement, and not another word was to be thawed out of her.

Curiously enough, it was now Basil who was attracted by the Count and Daphne who was repelled. Not that she was so bound up in her husband. Not at all. She was feeling rather sore against men altogether. But as so often happens, in this life based on the wicked triangle, Basil could only follow his enthusiasm for the Count in his wife's presence. When the two men were alone together, they were awkward, resistant, they could hardly get out a dozen words to one another. When Daphne was there, however, to complete the circuit of the opposing currents, things went like a house on fire.

This, however, was not much consolation to Lady Daphne. Merely to sit as a passive medium between two men who are squibbing philosophical nonsense to one another : no, it was not good enough ! She almost hated the Count : low-browed little fellow, belonging to the race of prehistoric slaves. But her grudge against her white-faced, spiritually intense husband was sharp as vinegar. Let down : she was let down between the pair of them.

What next ? Well, what followed was entirely Basil's fault. The winter was passing : it was obvious the war was really over, that Germany was finished. The Hohenzollern had fizzled out like a very poor squib, the Hapsburg was popping feebly in obscurity, the Romanov was smudged out without a sputter. So much for imperial royalty. Henceforth democratic peace.

The Count, of course, would be shipped back now like returned goods that had no market any more. There was a world peace ahead. A week or two, and Voynich Hall would be empty.

Basil, however, could not let matters follow their simple course. He was awfully intrigued by the Count. He wanted to entertain him as a guest before he went. And Major Apsley could get anything in reason, at this moment. So he obtained permission for the poor little Count to stay a fortnight at Thoresway, before being shipped back to Austria. Earl Beveridge, whose soul was black as ink since the war, would never have allowed the little alien enemy to enter his house, had it not been for the hatred which had been aroused in him, during the last two years, by the degrading spectacle of the so-called patriots who had been howling their mongrel indecency in the public face. These mongrels had held the press and the British public in abeyance for almost two years. Their one aim was to degrade and humiliate anything that was proud or dignified remaining in England. It was almost the worst nightmare of all, this coming to the top of a lot of public filth which was determined to suffocate the souls of all dignified men.

Hence, the Earl, who never intended to be swamped by unclean scum, whatever else happened to him, stamped his heels in the ground and stood on his own feet. When Basil said to him, would he allow the Count to have a fortnight's decent peace in Thoresway before all was finished, Lord Beveridge gave a slow consent, scandal or no scandal. Indeed, it was really to defy scandal that he took such a step. For the thought of his dead boys was bitter to him : and the thought of England fallen under the paws of smelly mongrels was bitterer still.

Lord Beveridge was at Thoresway to receive the Count, who

arrived escorted by Basil. The English Earl was a big, handsome man, rather heavy, with a dark, sombre face that would have been haughty if haughtiness had not been made so ridiculous. He was a passionate man, with a passionate man's sensitiveness, generosity, and instinctive overbearing. But *his* dark passionate nature, and his violent sensitiveness had been subjected now to fifty-five years' subtle repression, condemnation, repudiation, till he had almost come to believe in his own wrongness. His little, frail wife, all love for humanity, she was the genuine article. Himself, he was labelled selfish, sensual, cruel, etc., etc. So by now he always seemed to be standing aside, in the shadow, letting himself be obliterated by the pallid rabble of the democratic hurry. That was the impression he gave, of a man standing back, half-shamed, half-haughty, semi-hidden in the dark background.

He was a little on the defensive as Basil came in with the Count.

" Ah—how do you do, Count Psanek ? " he said, striding largely forward and holding out his hand. Because he was the father of Daphne, the Count felt a certain tenderness for the taciturn Englishman.

" You do me too much honour, my lord, receiving me in your house," said the small Count proudly.

The Earl looked at him slowly, without speaking : seemed to look down on him, in every sense of the word.

" We are still men, Count. We are not beasts altogether."

" You wish to say that my countrymen are so very nearly beasts, Lord Beveridge ? " smiled the Count, curling his fine nose.

Again the Earl was slow in replying.

" You have a low opinion of my manners, Count Psanek."

" But perhaps a just appreciation of your meaning, Lord Beveridge," smiled the Count, with the same reckless little look of contempt on his nose.

Lord Beveridge flushed dark, with all his native anger offended.

" I am glad Count Psanek makes my own meaning clear to me," he said.

" I beg your pardon a thousand times, my lord, if I give offence in doing so," replied the Count.

The Earl went black, and felt a fool. He turned his back on the Count. And then he turned round again, offering his cigar-case.

" Will you smoke ? " he said. There was kindness in his tone.

" Thank you," said the Count, taking a cigar.

" I daresay," said Lord Beveridge, " that all men are beasts in some way. I am afraid I have fallen into the common habit of speaking by rote, and not what I really mean. Won't you take a seat ? "

" It is only as a prisoner that I have learned that I am *not* truly a beast. No, I am myself. I am not a beast," said the Count, seating himself.

The Earl eyed him curiously.

" Well," he said, smiling, " I suppose it is best to come to a decision about it."

" It is necessary, if one is to be safe from vulgarity."

The Earl felt a twinge of accusation. With his agate-brown, hard-looking eyes he watched the black-browed little Count.

" You are probably right," he said.

But he turned his face aside.

They were five people at dinner—Lady Beveridge was there as hostess.

" Ah, Count Dionys," she said with a sigh, " do you really feel that the war is over ? "

" Oh, yes," he replied quickly. " *This* war is over. The armies will go home. *Their* cannon will not sound any more. Never again like this."

" Ah, I hope so," she sighed.

" I am sure," he said.

" You think there'll be no more war ? " said Daphne.

For some reason she had made herself very fine, in her newest dress of silver and black and pink chenille, with bare shoulders, and her hair fashionably done. The Count in his shabby uniform turned to her. She was nervous, hurried. Her slim white arm was near him, with the bit of silver at the shoulder. Her skin was white like a hot-house flower. Her lips moved hurriedly.

" Such a war as this there will never be again," he said.

" What makes you so sure ? " she replied, glancing into his eyes.

" The machine of war has got out of our control. We shall never start it again, till it has fallen to pieces. We shall be afraid."

" Will everybody be afraid ? " said she, looking down and pressing back her chin.

" I think so."

" We will hope so," said Lady Beveridge.

" Do you mind if I ask you, Count," said Basil, " what you feel about the way the war has ended ? The way it has ended for *you*, I mean."

" You mean that Germany and Austria have lost the war ? It was bound to be. We have all lost the war. All Europe."

" I agree there," said Lord Beveridge.

" We've all lost the war ? " said Daphne, turning to look at him.

There was pain on his dark, low-browed face. He suffered having the sensitive woman beside him. Her skin had a hot-house delicacy that made his head go round. Her shoulders were broad, rather thin, but the skin was white and so sensitive, so hot-house delicate. It affected him like the perfume of some white, exotic flower. And she seemed to be sending her heart towards him. It was as if she wanted to press her breast to his. From the breast she loved him, and sent out love to him. And it made him unhappy ; he wanted to be quiet, and to keep his honour before these hosts.

He looked into her eyes, his own eyes dark with knowledge and pain. She, in her silence and her brief words seemed to be holding them all under her spell. She seemed to have cast a certain muteness on the table, in the midst of which she remained silently master, leaning forward to her plate, and silently mastering them all.

" Don't I think we've all lost the war ? " he replied, in answer to her question. " It was a war of suicide. Nobody could win it. It was suicide for all of us."

" Oh, I don't know," she replied. " What about America and Japan ? "

" They don't count. They only helped *us* to commit suicide. They did not enter vitally."

There was such a look of pain on his face, and such a sound of pain in his voice, that the other three closed their ears, shut off from attending. Only Daphne was making him speak. It was she who was drawing the soul out of him, trying to read the future in him as the augurs read the future in the quivering entrails of the sacrificed beast. She looked direct into his face, searching his soul.

" You think Europe has committed suicide ? " she said.

" Morally."

" Only morally ? " came her slow, bronze-like words, so fatal.

" That is enough," he smiled.

" Quite," she said, with a slow droop of her eyelids. Then she turned away her face. But he felt the heart strangling inside his breast. What was she doing now ? What was she thinking ? She filled him with uncertainty and with uncanny fear.

" At least," said Basil, " those infernal guns are quiet."

" For ever," said Dionys.

" I wish I could believe you, Count," said the Major.

The talk became more general—or more personal. Lady Beveridge asked Dionys about his wife and family. He knew nothing save that they had gone to Hungary in 1916, when his own house was burnt down. His wife might even have gone to Bulgaria with Prince Bogorik. He did not know.

"But your children, Count!" cried Lady Beveridge.

"I do not know. Probably in Hungary, with their grandmother. I will go when I get back."

"But have you never *written?*—never inquired?"

"I could not write. I shall know soon enough—everything."

"You have no son?"

"No. Two girls."

"Poor things!"

"Yes."

"I say, isn't it an odd thing to have a ladybird on your crest?" asked Basil, to cheer up the conversation.

"Why queer? Charlemagne had bees. And it is a Marienkäfer— a Mary-beetle. The beetle of Our Lady. I think it is quite a heraldic insect, Major," smiled the Count.

"You're proud of it?" said Daphne, suddenly turning to look at him again, with her slow, pregnant look.

"I am, you know. It has such a long genealogy—our spotted beetle. Much longer than the Psaneks. I think, you know, it is a descendant of the Egyptian scarabæus, which is a very mysterious emblem. So I connect myself with the Pharaohs: just through my ladybird."

"You feel your ladybird has crept through so many ages," she said.

"Imagine it!" he laughed.

"The scarab *is* a piquant insect," said Basil.

"Do you know Fabre?" put in Lord Beveridge. "He suggests that the beetle rolling a little ball of dung before him, in a dry old field, must have suggested to the Egyptians the First Principle that set the globe rolling. And so the scarab became the symbol of the creative principle—or something like that."

"That the earth is a tiny ball of dry dung is good," said Basil.

"Between the claws of a ladybird," added Daphne.

"That is what it is, to go back to one's origin," said Lady Beveridge.

"Perhaps they meant that it was the principle of decomposition which first set the ball rolling," said the Count.

"The ball would have to be *there* first," said Basil.

"Certainly. But it hadn't started to roll. Then the principle of decomposition started it." The Count smiled as if it were a joke.

"I am no Egyptologist," said Lady Beveridge, "so I can't judge."

The Earl and Countess Beveridge left next day. Count Dionys was left with the two young people in the house. It was a beautiful Elizabethan mansion, not very large, but with those magical rooms that are all a twinkle of small-paned windows, looking out from the dark panelled interior. The interior was cosy, panelled to the ceiling, and the ceiling moulded and touched with gold. And then the great square bow of the window with its little panes intervening like magic between oneself and the world outside, the crest in stained glass crowning its colour, the broad window-seat cushioned in faded green. Dionys wandered round the house like a little ghost, through the succession of small and large twinkling sitting-rooms and lounge rooms in front, down the long, wide corridor with the wide stair-head at each end, and up the narrow stairs to the bedrooms above, and on to the roof.

It was early spring, and he loved to sit on the leaded, pale-grey roof that had its queer seats and slopes, a little pale world in itself. Then to look down over the garden and the sloping lawn to the ponds massed round with trees, and away to the elms and furrows and hedges of the shires. On the left of the house was the farm-stead, with ricks and great-roofed barns and dark-red cattle. Away to the right, beyond the park, was a village among trees, and the spark of a grey church-spire.

He liked to be alone, feeling his soul heavy with its own fate. He would sit for hours watching the elm-trees standing in rows like giants, like warriors across the country. The Earl had told him that the Romans had brought these elms to Britain. And he seemed to see the spirit of the Romans in them still. Sitting there alone in the spring sunshine, in the solitude of the roof, he saw the glamour of this England of hedgerows and elm-trees, and the labourers with slow horses slowly drilling the sod, crossing the brown furrow : and the roofs of the village, with the church-steeple rising beside a big black yew-tree : and the chequer of fields away to the distance.

And the charm of the old manor around him, the garden with its grey stone walls and yew hedges—broad, broad yew hedges—and a peacock pausing to glitter and scream in the busy silence of an English spring, when celandines open their yellow under the hedges, and violets are in the secret, and by the broad paths of the garden polyanthus and crocuses vary the velvet and flame, and bits of yellow wallflower shake raggedly, with a wonderful triumphance, out of the cracks of the wall. There was a fold somewhere near, and he could hear the treble bleat of the growing lambs, and the deeper, contented baa-ing of the ewes.

This was Daphne's home, where she had been born. She loved it with an ache of affection. But now it was hard to forget her dead brothers. She wandered about in the sun, with two old dogs paddling after her. She talked with everybody—gardener, groom, stableman, with the farm-hands. That filled a large part of her life—straying round talking with the work-people. They were, of course, respectful to her—but not at all afraid of her. They knew she was poor, that she could not afford a car, nor anything. So they talked to her very freely : perhaps a little too freely. Yet she let it be. It was her one passion at Thoresway to hear the dependants talk and talk— about everything. The curious feeling of intimacy across a breach fascinated her. Their lives fascinated her : what they thought, what they *felt*. These, what they felt. That fascinated her. There was a gamekeeper she could have loved—an impudent, ruddy-faced, laughing, ingratiating fellow ; she could have loved him, if she had not been isolated beyond the breach of his birth, her culture, her consciousness. Her *consciousness* seemed to make a great gulf between her and the lower classes, the unconscious classes. She accepted it as her doom. She could never meet in real contact any one but a superconscious, finished being like herself : or like her husband. Her father had some of the unconscious blood-warmth of the lower classes. But he was like a man who is damned. And the Count, of course. The Count had something that was hot and invisible, a dark flame of life that might warm the cold white fire of her own blood. But——

They avoided each other. All three, they avoided one another. Basil, too, went off alone. Or he immersed himself in poetry. Sometimes he and the Count played billiards. Sometimes all three walked in the park. Often Basil and Daphne walked to the village, to post. But truly, they avoided one another, all three. The days slipped by.

At evening they sat together in the small west-room that had books and a piano and comfortable shabby furniture of faded rose-coloured tapestry : a shabby room. Sometimes Basil read aloud : sometimes the Count played the piano. And they talked. And Daphne stitch by stitch went on with a big embroidered bedspread, which she might finish if she lived long enough. But they always went to bed early. They were nearly always avoiding one another.

Dionys had a bedroom in the east bay—a long way from the rooms of the others. He had a habit, when he was quite alone, of singing, or rather crooning to himself the old songs of his childhood. It was only when he felt he was quite alone : when other people seemed to fade out of him, and all the world seemed to dissolve into darkness, and there was nothing but himself, his own soul, alive in the middle of his own small night, isolate for ever. Then, half unconscious, he would croon in a small, high-pitched, squeezed voice, a sort of high dream-voice, the songs of his childhood dialect. It was a curious noise : the sound of a man who is alone in his own blood : almost the sound of a man who is going to be executed.

Daphne heard the sound one night when she was going downstairs again with the corridor lantern, to find a book. She was a bad sleeper, and her nights were a torture to her. She too, like a neurotic, was nailed inside her own fretful self-consciousness. But she had a very keen ear. So she started as she heard the small, bat-like sound of the Count's singing to himself. She stood in the midst of the wide corridor, that was wide as a room, carpeted with a faded lavender-coloured carpet, with a piece of massive dark furniture at intervals by the wall, and an oak arm-chair and sometimes a faded, reddish oriental rug. The big horn lantern which stood at nights at the end of the corridor she held in her hand. The intense " peeping " sound of the Count, like a witchcraft, made her forget everything. She could not understand a word, of course. She could not understand the noise even. After listening for a long time, she went on downstairs. When she came back again he was still, and the light was gone from under his door.

After this, it became almost an obsession to her to listen for him. She waited with fretful impatience for ten o'clock, when she could retire. She waited more fretfully still for the maid to leave her, and for her husband to come and say good night. Basil had the room across the corridor. And then in resentful impatience she waited for the sounds of the house to become still. Then she opened her door to listen.

And far away, as if from far, far away in the unseen, like a ventriloquist sound or a bat's uncanny peeping, came the frail, almost inaudible sound of the Count's singing to himself before he went to bed. It *was* inaudible to any one but herself. But she, by concentration, seemed to hear supernaturally. She had a low arm-chair by the door, and there, wrapped in a huge old black silk shawl, she sat and listened. At first she could not hear. That is, she could hear the sound. But it was only a sound. And then, gradually, gradually she began to follow the thread of it. It was like a thread which she followed out of the world : out of the world. And as she went, slowly, by degrees, far, far away, down the thin thread of his singing, she knew peace—she knew forgetfulness. She could pass beyond the world, away beyond where her soul balanced like a bird on wings, and was perfected.

So it was, in her upper spirit. But underneath was a wild, wild yearning, actually to go, actually to be given. Actually to go, actually to die the death, actually to cross the border and be gone, to be gone. To be gone from this herself, from this Daphne, to be gone from father and mother, brothers and husband, and home and land and world : to be gone. To be gone to the call from the beyond : the call. It was the Count calling. He was calling her. She was sure he was calling her. Out of herself, out of her world, he was calling her.

Two nights she sat just inside her room, by the open door, and listened. Then when he finished she went to sleep, a queer, light, bewitched sleep. In the day she was bewitched. She felt strange and light, as if pressure had been removed from around her. Some pressure had been clamped round her all her life. She had never realized it till now ; now it was removed, and her feet felt so light, and her breathing delicate and exquisite. There had always been a pressure against her breathing. Now she breathed delicate and exquisite, so that it was a delight to breathe. Life came in exquisite breaths, quickly, as if it delighted to come to her.

The third night he was silent—though she waited and waited till the small hours of the morning. He was silent, he did not sing. And then she knew the terror and blackness of the feeling that he might never sing any more. She waited like one doomed, throughout the day. And when the night came she trembled. It was her greatest nervous terror, lest her spell should be broken, and she should be thrown back to what she was before.

Night came, and the kind of swoon upon her. Yes, and the call from the night. The call ! She rose helplessly and hurried down the corridor. The light was under his door. She sat down in the big oak arm-chair that stood near his door, and huddled herself tight in her black shawl. The corridor was dim with the big, star-studded, yellow lantern-light. Away down she could see the lamplight in her doorway ; she had left her door ajar.

But she saw nothing. Only she wrapped herself close in the black shawl, and listened to the sound from the room. It called. Oh, it called her ! Why could she not go ? Why could she not cross through the closed door.

Then the noise ceased. And then the light went out, under the door of his room. Must she go back? Must she go back? Oh, impossible. As impossible as that the moon should go back on her tracks, once she has risen. Daphne sat on, wrapped in her black shawl. If it must be so, she would sit on through eternity. Return she never could.

And then began the most terrible song of all. It began with a rather dreary, slow, horrible sound, like death. And then suddenly came a real call—fluty, and a kind of whistling and a strange whirr at the changes, most imperative, and utterly inhuman. Daphne rose to her feet. And at the same moment up rose the whistling throb of a summons out of the death moan.

Daphne tapped low and rapidly at the door. " Count ! Count ! " she whispered. The sound inside ceased. The door suddenly opened. The pale, obscure figure of Dionys.

" Lady Daphne ! " he said in astonishment, automatically standing aside.

" You called," she murmured rapidly, and she passed intent into his room.

" No, I did not call," he said gently, his hand on the door still.

" Shut the door," she said abruptly.

He did as he was bid. The room was in complete darkness. There was no moon outside. She could not see him.

" Where can I sit down ? ' she said abruptly.

" I will take you to the couch," he said, putting out his hand and touching her in the dark. She shuddered.

She found the couch and sat down. It was quite dark.

" What are you singing ? " she said rapidly.

"·I am so sorry. I did not think any one could hear."

" What was it you were singing ? "

" A song of my country."

" Had it any words ? "

" Yes, it is a woman who was a swan, and who loved a hunter by the marsh. So she became a woman and married him and had three children. Then in the night one night the king of the swans called to her to come back, or else he would die. So slowly she turned into a swan again, and slowly she opened her wide, wide wings, and left her husband and her children."

There was silence in the dark room. The Count had been really startled, startled out of his mood of the song into the day-mood of human convention. He was distressed and embarrassed by Daphne's presence in his dark room. She, however, sat on and did not make a sound. He, too, sat down in a chair by the window. It was everywhere dark. A wind was blowing in gusts outside. He could see nothing inside his room : only the faint, faint strip of light under the door. But he could feel her presence in the darkness. It was uncanny, to feel her near in the dark, and not to see any sign of her, not to hear any sound.

She had been wounded in her bewitched state by the contact with the every-day human being in him. But now she began to relapse into her spell, as she sat there in the dark. And he, too, in the silence, felt the world sinking away from him once more, leaving him once more alone on a darkened earth, with nothing between him and the infinite dark space. Except now her presence. Darkness answering to darkness, and deep answering to deep. An answer, near to him, and invisible.

But he did not know what to do. He sat still and silent as she was still and silent. The darkness inside the room seemed alive like blood. He had no power to move. The distance between them seemed absolute.

Then suddenly, without knowing, he ·went across in the dark, feeling for the end of the couch. And he sat beside her on the couch. But he did not touch her. Neither did she move. The darkness flowed about them thick like blood, and time seemed dissolved in it. They sat with the small, invisible distance between them, motionless, speechless, thoughtless.

Then suddenly he felt her finger-tips touch his arm, and a flame went over him that left him no more a man. He was something seated in flame, in flame unconscious, seated erect, like an Egyptian King-god in the statues. Her finger-tips slid down him, and she herself slid down in a strange silent rush, and he felt her face against his closed feet and ankles, her hands pressing his ankles. He felt her brow and hair against his ankles, her face against his feet, and there she clung in the dark, as if in space below him. He still sat erect and motionless. Then he bent forward and put his hand on her hair.

" Do you come to me ? " he murmured. " Do you come to me ? " The flame that enveloped him seemed to sway him silently.

" Do you really come to me ? " he repeated. " But we have no-where to go."

He felt his bare feet wet with her tears. Two things were struggling in him, the sense of eternal solitude, like space, and the rush of dark flame that would throw him out of his solitude towards her.

He was thinking too. He was thinking of the future. He had no future in the world : of that he was conscious. He had no future in this life. Even if he lived on, it would only be a kind of enduring. But he felt that in the after-life the inheritance was his. He felt the after-life belonged to him.

Future in the world he could not give her. Life in the world he had not to offer her. Better go on alone. Surely better go on alone.

But then the tears on his feet : and her face that would face him as he left her ! No, no. The next life was his. He was master of the after-life. Why fear for this life ? Why not take the soul she offered him ? Now and forever, for the life that would come when they both were dead. Take her into the underworld. Take her into the dark Hades with him, like Francesca and Paolo. And in hell hold her fast, queen of the underworld, himself master of the underworld. Master of the life to come. Father of the soul that would come after.

"Listen," he said to her softly. "Now you are mine. In the dark you are mine. And when you die you are mine. But in the day you are not mine, because I have no power in the day. In the night, in the dark, and in death, you are mine. And that is forever. No matter if I must leave you. I shall come again from time to time. In the dark you are mine. But in the day I cannot claim you. I have no power in the day, and no place. So remember. When the darkness comes, I shall always be in the darkness of you. And as long as I live, from time to time I shall come to find you, when I am able to, when I am not a prisoner. But I shall have to go away soon. So don't forget—you are the night-wife of the ladybird, while you live and even when you die."

Later, when he took her back to her room, he saw her door still ajar.

"You shouldn't leave a light in your room," he murmured.

In the morning there was a curious remote look about him. He was quieter than ever, and seemed very far away. Daphne slept late. She had a strange feeling as if she had slipped off all her cares. She did not care, she did not grieve, she did not fret any more. All that had left her. She felt she could sleep, sleep, sleep—for ever. Her face, too, was very still, with a delicate look of virginity that she had never had before. She had always been Aphrodite, the self-conscious one. And her eyes, the green-blue, had been like slow, living jewels, resistant. Now they had unfolded from the hard flower-bud, and had the wonder, and the stillness of a quiet night.

Basil noticed it at once.

"You're different, Daphne," he said. "What are you thinking about ? "

"I wasn't thinking," she said, looking at him with candour.

" What were you doing then ? "

" What does one do when one doesn't think ? Don't make me puzzle it out, Basil."

" Not a bit of it, if you don't want to."

But he was puzzled by her. The sting of his ecstatic love for her seemed to have left him. Yet he did not know what else to do but to make love to her. She went very pale. She submitted to him, bowing her head because she was his wife. But she looked at him with fear, with sorrow, with real suffering. He could feel the heaving of her breast, and knew she was weeping. But there were no tears on her face, she was only death-pale. Her eyes were shut.

" Are you in pain ? " he asked her.

" No, no ! " She opened her eyes, afraid lest she had disturbed him. She did not want to disturb him.

He was puzzled. His own ecstatic, deadly love for her had received a check. He was out of the reckoning.

He watched her when she was with the Count. Then she seemed so meek—so maidenly—so different from what he had known of her. She was so still, like a virgin girl. And it was this quiet, intact quality of virginity in her which puzzled him most, puzzled his emotions and his ideas. He became suddenly ashamed to make love to her. And because he was ashamed, he said to her as he stood in her room that night :

" Daphne, are you in love with the Count ? "

He was standing by the dressing-table, uneasy. She was seated in a low chair by the tiny dying wood fire. She looked up at him with wide, slow eyes. Without a word, with wide, soft, dilated eyes she watched him. What was it that made him feel all confused. He turned his face aside, away from her wide, soft eyes.

" Pardon me, dear. I didn't intend to ask such a question. Don't take any notice of it," he said. And he strode away and picked up a book. She lowered her head and gazed abstractedly into the fire, without a sound. Then he looked at her again, at her bright hair that the maid had plaited for the night. Her plait hung down over her soft pinkish wrap. His heart softened to her as he saw her sitting there. She seemed like his sister. The excitement of desire had left him, and now he seemed to see clear and feel true for the first time in his life. She was like a dear, dear sister to him. He felt that she was his blood-sister, nearer to him than he had imagined any woman could be. So near—so dear—and all the sex and the desire gone. He didn't want it—he hadn't wanted it. This new pure feeling was so much more wonderful.

He went to her side.

"Forgive me, darling," he said, "for having questioned you."

She looked up at him with the wide eyes, without a word. His face was good and beautiful. Tears came to her eyes.

"You have the right to question me," she said sadly.

"No," he said. "No, darling. I have no right to question you. Daphne! Daphne, darling! It shall be as *you* wish, between us. Shall it? Shall it be as you wish?"

"You are the husband, Basil," she said sadly.

"Yes, darling. But"—he went on his knees beside her—"perhaps, darling, something has changed in us. I feel as if I ought never to touch you again—as if I never *wanted* to touch you—in that way. I feel it was wrong, darling. Tell me what you think."

"Basil, don't be angry with me."

"It isn't anger; it's pure love, darling—it is."

"Let us not come any nearer to one another than this, Basil— physically—shall we?" she said. "And don't be angry with me, will you?"

"Why," he said. "I think myself the sexual part has been a mistake. I had rather love you—as I love now. I *know* that this is true love. The other was always a bit whipped up. I *know* I love you now, darling: now I'm free from that other. But what if it comes upon me, that other, Daphne?"

"I am always your wife," she said quietly. "I am always your wife. I want always to obey you, Basil: what you wish."

"Give me your hand, dear."

She gave him her hand. But the look in her eyes at the same time warned him and frightened him. He kissed her hand and left her.

It was to the Count she belonged. This had decided itself in her down to the depths of her soul. If she could not marry him and be his wife in the world, it had nevertheless happened to her for ever. She could no more question it. Question had gone out of her.

Strange how different she had become—a strange new quiescence. The last days were slipping past. He would be going away—Dionys: he with the still remote face, the man she belonged to in the dark and in the light, for ever. He would be going away. He said it must be so. And she acquiesced. The grief was deep, deep inside her. He must go away. Their lives could not be one life, in this world's day. Even in her anguish she knew it was so. She knew he was right. He was for her infallible. He spoke the deepest soul in her.

She never *saw* him, as a lover. When she saw him, he was the little officer, a prisoner, quiet, claiming nothing in all the world. And when she went to him as his lover, his wife, it was always dark. She only knew his voice and his contact in darkness. " My wife in darkness," he said to her. And in this too she believed him. She would not have contradicted him, no, not for anything on earth : lest, contradicting him she should lose the dark treasure of stillness and bliss which she kept in her breast even when her heart was wrung with the agony of knowing he must go.

No, she had found this wonderful thing after she had heard him singing : she had suddenly collapsed away from her old self into this darkness, this peace, this quiescence that was like a full dark river flowing eternally in her soul. She had gone to sleep from the *nuit blanche* of her days. And Basil, wonderful, had changed almost at once. She feared him, lest he might change back again. She would always have him to fear. But deep inside her she only feared for this love of hers for the Count : this dark, everlasting love that was like a full river flowing for ever inside her. Ah, let that not be broken.

She was so still inside her. She could sit so still, and feel the day slowly, richly changing to night. And she wanted nothing, she was short of nothing. If only Dionys need not go away ! If only he need not go away !

But he said to her, the last morning :

" Don't forget me. Always remember me. I leave my soul in your hands and your womb. Nothing can ever separate us, unless we betray one another. If you have to give yourself to your husband, do so, and obey him. If you are true to me, innerly, innerly true, he will not hurt us. He is generous, be generous to him. And never fail to believe in me. Because even on the other side of death I shall be watching for you. I shall be king in Hades when I am dead. And you will be at my side. You will never leave me any more, in the after-death. So don't be afraid in life. Don't be afraid. If you have to cry tears, cry them. But in your heart of hearts know that I shall come again, and that I have taken you for ever. And so, in your heart of hearts be still, be still, since you are the wife of the ladybird." He laughed as he left her, with his own beautiful, fearless laugh. But they were strange eyes that looked after him.

He went in the car with Basil back to Voynich Hall.

" I believe Daphne will miss you," said Basil.

The Count did not reply for some moments.

" Well, if she does," he said, " there will be no bitterness in it."

" Are you sure ? " smiled Basil.

" Why—if we are sure of anything," smiled the Count.

" She's changed, isn't she ? "

" Is she ? "

" Yes, she's quite changed since you came, Count."

" She does not seem to me so very different from the girl of seventeen whom I knew."

" No—perhaps not. I didn't know her then. But she's very different from the wife I have known."

" A regrettable difference ? "

" Well—no, not as far as she goes. She is much quieter inside herself. You know, Count, something of me died in the war. I feel it will take me an eternity to sit and think about it all."

" I hope you may think it out to your satisfaction, Major."

" Yes, I hope so too. But that is how it has left me—feeling as if I needed eternity now to brood about it all, you know. Without the need to act—or even to love, really. I suppose love is action."

" Intense action," said the Count.

" Quite so. I know really how I feel. I only ask of life to spare me from further effort of action of any sort—even love. And then to fulfil myself, brooding through eternity. Of course I don't mind *work*, mechanical action. That in itself is a form of inaction."

" A man can only be happy following his own inmost need," said the Count.

" Exactly ! " said Basil. " I will lay down the law for nobody, not even for myself. And live my day——"

" Then you will be happy in your own way. I find it so difficult to keep from laying the law down for myself," said the Count. " Only the thought of death and the after-life saves me from doing it any more."

" As the thought of eternity helps me," said Basil. " I suppose it amounts to the same thing."

THE two girls were usually known by their surnames, Banford and March. They had taken the farm together, intending to work it all by themselves : that is, they were going to rear chickens, make a living by poultry, and add to this by keeping a cow, and raising one or two young beasts. Unfortunately, things did not turn out well.

Banford was a small, thin, delicate thing with spectacles. She, however, was the principal investor, for March had little or no money. Banford's father, who was a tradesman in Islington, gave his daughter the start, for her health's sake, and because he loved her, and because it did not look as if she would marry. March was more robust. She had learned carpentry and joinery at the evening classes in Islington. She would be the man about the place. They had, moreover, Banford's old grandfather living with them at the start. He had been a farmer. But unfortunately the old man died after he had been at Bailey Farm for a year. Then the two girls were left alone.

They were neither of them young : that is, they were near thirty. But they certainly were not old. They set out quite gallantly with their enterprise. They had numbers of chickens, black Leghorns and white Leghorns, Plymouths and Wyandottes ; also some ducks ; also two heifers in the fields. One heifer, unfortunately, refused absolutely to stay in the Bailey Farm closes. No matter how March made up the fences, the heifer was out, wild in the woods, or trespassing on the neighbouring pasture, and March and Banford were away, flying after her, with more haste than success. So this heifer they sold in despair. Then, just before the other beast was expecting her first calf, the old man died, and the girls, afraid of the coming event, sold her in a panic, and limited their attentions to fowls and ducks.

In spite of a little chagrin, it was a relief to have no more cattle on hand. Life was not made merely to be slaved away. Both girls agreed in this. The fowls were quite enough trouble. March had set up her carpenter's bench at the end of the open shed. Here she worked, making coops and doors and other appurtenances. The

fowls were housed in the bigger building, which had served as barn
and cowshed in old days. They had a beautiful home, and should
have been perfectly content. Indeed, they looked well enough.
But the girls were disgusted at their tendency to strange illnesses,
at their exacting way of life, and at their refusal, obstinate refusal
to lay eggs.

March did most of the outdoor work. When she was out and
about, in her puttees and breeches, her belted coat and her loose
cap, she looked almost like some graceful, loose-balanced young
man, for her shoulders were straight, and her movements easy and
confident, even tinged with a little indifference, or irony. But her
face was not a man's face, ever. The wisps of her crisp dark hair
blew about her as she stooped, her eyes were big and wide and dark,
when she looked up again, strange, startled, shy and sardonic at
once. Her mouth, too, was almost pinched as if in pain and irony.
There was something odd and unexplained about her. She would
stand balanced on one hip, looking at the fowls pattering about in
the obnoxious fine mud of the sloping yard, and calling to her
favourite white hen, which came in answer to her name. But there
was an almost satirical flicker in March's big, dark eyes as she
looked at her three-toed flock pottering about under her gaze, and
the same slight dangerous satire in her voice as she spoke to the
favoured Patty, who pecked at March's boot by way of friendly
demonstration.

Fowls did not flourish at Bailey Farm, in spite of all that March
did for them. When she provided hot food for them in the morning,
according to rule, she noticed that it made them heavy and dozy for
hours. She expected to see them lean against the pillars of the shed
in their languid processes of digestion. And she knew quite well
that they ought to be busily scratching and foraging about, if they
were to come to any good. So she decided to give them their hot
food at night, and let them sleep on it. Which she did. But it
made no difference.

War conditions, again, were very unfavourable to poultry keeping. Food was scarce and bad. And when the Daylight Saving Bill
was passed, the fowls obstinately refused to go to bed as usual, about
nine o'clock in the summer-time. That was late enough, indeed, for
there was no peace till they were shut up and asleep. Now they
cheerfully walked around, without so much as glancing at the barn,
until ten o'clock or later. Both Banford and March disbelieved in
living for work alone. They wanted to read or take a cycle-ride in
the evening, or perhaps March wished to paint curvilinear swans on

porcelain, with green background, or else make a marvellous fire-screen by processes of elaborate cabinet work. For she was a creature of odd whims and unsatisfied tendencies. But from all these things she was prevented by the stupid fowls.

One evil there was greater than any other. Bailey Farm was a little homestead, with ancient wooden barn and low-gabled farm-house, lying just one field removed from the edge of the wood. Since the war the fox was a demon. He carried off the hens under the very noses of March and Banford. Banford would start and stare through her big spectacles with all her eyes, as another squawk and flutter took place at her heels. Too late ! Another white Leghorn gone. It was disheartening.

They did what they could to remedy it. When it became per-mitted to shoot foxes, they stood sentinel with their guns, the two of them, at the favoured hours. But it was no good. The fox was too quick for them. So another year passed, and another, and they were living on their losses, as Banford said. They let their farm-house one summer, and retired to live in a railway-carriage that was deposited as a sort of out-house in a corner of the field. This amused them, and helped their finances. None the less, things looked dark.

Although they were usually the best of friends, because Banford, though nervous and delicate, was a warm, generous soul, and March, though so odd and absent in herself, had a strange magna-nimity, yet, in the long solitude, they were apt to become a little irritable with one another, tired of one another. March had four-fifths of the work to do, and though she did not mind, there seemed no relief, and it made her eyes flash curiously sometimes. Then Banford, feeling more nerve-worn than ever, would become despon-dent, and March would speak sharply to her. They seemed to be losing ground, somehow, losing hope as the months went by. There alone in the fields by the wood, with the wide country stretching hollow and dim to the round hills of the White Horse, in the far distance, they seemed to have to live too much off themselves. There was nothing to keep them up—and no hope.

The fox really exasperated them both. As soon as they had let the fowls out, in the early summer mornings, they had to take their guns and keep guard : and then again, as soon as evening began to mellow, they must go once more. And he was so sly. He slid along in the deep grass ; he was difficult as a serpent to see. And he seemed to circumvent the girls deliberately. Once or twice March had caught sight of the white tip of his brush, or the ruddy shadow of him in the deep grass, and she had let fire at him. But he made no account of this.

One evening March was standing with her back to the sunset, her gun under her arm, her hair pushed under her cap. She was half watching, half musing. It was her constant state. Her eyes were keen and observant, but her inner mind took no notice of what she saw. She was always lapsing into this odd, rapt state, her mouth rather screwed up. It was a question whether she was there, actually conscious present, or not.

The trees on the wood-edge were a darkish, brownish green in the full light—for it was the end of August. Beyond, the naked, copper-like shafts and limbs of the pine-trees shone in the air. Nearer the rough grass, with its long brownish stalks all agleam, was full of light. The fowls were round about—the ducks were still swimming on the pond under the pine-trees. March looked at it all, saw it all, and did not see it. She heard Banford speaking to the fowls in the distance—and she did not hear. What was she thinking about? Heaven knows. Her consciousness was, as it were, held back.

She lowered her eyes, and suddenly saw the fox. He was looking up at her. His chin was pressed down, and his eyes were looking up. They met her eyes. And he knew her. She was spellbound—she knew he knew her. So he looked into her eyes, and her soul failed her. He knew her, he was not daunted.

She struggled, confusedly she came to herself, and saw him making off, with slow leaps over some fallen boughs, slow, impudent jumps. Then he glanced over his shoulder, and ran smoothly away. She saw his brush held smooth like a feather, she saw his white buttocks twinkle. And he was gone, softly, soft as the wind.

She put her gun to her shoulder, but even then pursed her mouth, knowing it was nonsense to pretend to fire. So she began to walk slowly after him, in the direction he had gone, slowly, pertinaciously. She expected to find him. In her heart she was determined to find him. What she would do when she saw him again she did not consider. But she was determined to find him. So she walked abstractedly about on the edge of the wood, with wide, vivid dark eyes, and a faint flush in her cheeks. She did not think. In strange mindlessness she walked hither and thither.

At last she became aware that Banford was calling her. She made an effort of attention, turned, and gave some sort of screaming call in answer. Then again she was striding off towards the homestead. The red sun was setting, the fowls were retiring towards their roost. She watched them, white creatures, black creatures, gathering to the barn. She watched them spellbound, without seeing them. But her automatic intelligence told her when it was time to shut the door.

She went indoors to supper, which Banford had set on the table. Banford chatted easily. March seemed to listen, in her distant, manly way. She answered a brief word now and then. But all the time she was as if spellbound. And as soon as supper was over, she rose again to go out, without saying why.

She took her gun again and went to look for the fox. For he had lifted his eyes upon her, and his knowing look seemed to have entered her brain. She did not so much think of him : she was possessed by him. She saw his dark, shrewd, unabashed eye looking into her, knowing her. She felt him invisibly master her spirit. She knew the way he lowered his chin as he looked up, she knew his muzzle, the golden brown, and the greyish white. And again, she saw him glance over his shoulder at her, half inviting, half contemptuous, and cunning. So she went, with her great startled eyes glowing, her gun under her arm, along the wood edge. Meanwhile the night fell, and a great moon rose above the pine-trees. And again Banford was calling.

So she went indoors. She was silent and busy. She examined her gun, and cleaned it, musing abstractedly by the lamp-light. Then she went out again, under the great moon, to see if everything was right. When she saw the dark crests of the pine-trees against the blood-red sky, again her heart beat to the fox, the fox. She wanted to follow him, with her gun.

It was some days before she mentioned the affair to Banford. Then suddenly one evening she said :

" The fox was right at my feet on Saturday night."

" Where ? " said Banford, her eyes opening behind her spectacles.

" When I stood just above the pond."

" Did you fire ? " cried Banford.

" No, I didn't."

" Why not ? "

" Why, I was too much surprised, I suppose."

It was the same old, slow, laconic way of speech March always had. Banford stared at her friend for a few moments.

" You saw him ? " she cried.

" Oh yes ! He was looking up at me, cool as anything."

" I tell you," cried Banford—" the cheek ! They're not afraid of us, Nellie."

" Oh no," said March.

" Pity you didn't get a shot at him," said Banford.

" Isn't it a pity ! I've been looking for him ever since. But I don't suppose he'll come so near again."

" I don't suppose he will," said Banford.

And she proceeded to forget about it, except that she was more indignant than ever at the impudence of the beggar. March also was not conscious that she thought of the fox. But whenever she fell into her half-musing, when she was half rapt and half intelligently aware of what passed under her vision, then it was the fox which somehow dominated her unconsciousness, possessed the blank half of her musing. And so it was for weeks, and months. No matter whether she had been climbing the trees for the apples, or beating down the last of the damsons, or whether she had been digging out the ditch from the duck-pond, or clearing out the barn, when she had finished, or when she straightened herself, and pushed the wisps of hair away again from her forehead, and pursed up her mouth again in an odd, screwed fashion, much too old for her years, there was sure to come over her mind the old spell of the fox, as it came when he was looking at her. It was as if she could smell him at these times. And it always recurred, at unexpected moments, just as she was going to sleep at night, or just as she was pouring the water into the teapot to make tea—it was the fox, it came over her like a spell.

So the months passed. She still looked for him unconsciously when she went towards the wood. He had become a settled effect in her spirit, a state permanently established, not continuous, but always recurring. She did not know what she felt or thought : only the state came over her, as when he looked at her.

The months passed, the dark evenings came, heavy, dark November, when March went about in high boots, ankle deep in mud, when the night began to fall at four o'clock, and the day never properly dawned. Both girls dreaded these times. They dreaded the almost continuous darkness that enveloped them on their desolate little farm near the wood. Banford was physically afraid. She was afraid of tramps, afraid lest someone should come prowling round. March was not so much afraid as uncomfortable, and disturbed. She felt discomfort and gloom in all her physique.

Usually the two girls had tea in the sitting-room. March lighted a fire at dusk, and put on the wood she had chopped and sawed during the day. Then the long evening was in front, dark, sodden, black outside, lonely and rather oppressive inside, a little dismal. March was content not to talk, but Banford could not keep still. Merely listening to the wind in the pines outside, or the drip of water, was too much for her.

One evening the girls had washed up the tea-things in the kitchen, and March had put on her house-shoes, and taken up a roll of crochet-work, which she worked at slowly from time to time. So she lapsed into silence. Banford stared at the red fire, which, being of wood, needed constant attention. She was afraid to begin to read too early, because her eyes would not bear any strain. So she sat staring at the fire, listening to the distant sounds, sound of cattle lowing, of a dull, heavy, moist wind, of the rattle of the evening train on the little railway not far off. She was almost fascinated by the red glow of the fire.

Suddenly both girls started, and lifted their heads. They heard a footstep—distinctly a footstep. Banford recoiled in fear. March stood listening. Then rapidly she approached the door that led into the kitchen. At the same time they heard the footsteps approach the back door. They waited a second. The back door opened softly. Banford gave a loud cry. A man's voice said softly :

" Hello ! "

March recoiled, and took a gun from a corner.

" What do you want ? " she cried, in a sharp voice.

Again the soft, softly vibrating man's voice said :

" Hello ! What's wrong ? "

" I shall shoot ! " cried March. " What do you want ? "

" Why, what's wrong ? What's wrong ? " came the soft, wondering, rather scared voice : and a young soldier, with his heavy kit on his back, advanced into the dim light.

" Why," he said, " who lives here then ? "

" We live here," said March. " What do you want ? "

" Oh ! " came the long, melodious, wonder-note from the young soldier. " Doesn't William Grenfel live here then ? "

" No—you know he doesn't."

" Do I ? Do I ? I don't, you see. He *did* live here, because he was my grandfather, and I lived here myself five years ago. What's become of him then ? "

The young man—or youth, for he would not be more than twenty —now advanced and stood in the inner doorway. March, already under the influence of his strange, soft, modulated voice, stared at him spellbound. He had a ruddy, roundish face, with fairish hair, rather long, flattened to his forehead with sweat. His eyes were blue, and very bright and sharp. On his cheeks, on the fresh ruddy skin were fine, fair hairs, like a down, but sharper. It gave him a slightly glistening look. Having his heavy sack on his shoulders, he stooped, thrusting his head forward. His hat was loose in one hand. He stared brightly, very keenly from girl to girl, particularly at March, who stood pale, with great dilated eyes, in her belted coat and puttees, her hair knotted in a big crisp knot behind. She still had the gun in her hand. Behind her, Banford, clinging to the sofa-arm, was shrinking away, with half-averted head.

" I thought my grandfather still lived here? I wonder if he's dead."

" We've been here for three years," said Banford, who was beginning to recover her wits, seeing something boyish in the round head with its rather long sweaty hair.

" Three years! You don't say so! And you don't know who was here before you?"

" I know it was an old man, who lived by himself."

" Ay! Yes, that's him! And what became of him then?"

" He died. I know he died."

" Ay! He's dead then!"

The youth stared at them without changing colour or expression. If he had any expression, besides a slight baffled look of wonder, it was one of sharp curiosity concerning the two girls ; sharp, impersonal curiosity, the curiosity of that round young head.

But to March he was the fox. Whether it was the thrusting forward of his head, or the glisten of fine whitish hairs on the ruddy cheek-bones, or the bright, keen eyes, that can never be said : but the boy was to her the fox, and she could not see him otherwise.

" How is it you didn't know if your grandfather was alive or dead?" asked Banford, recovering her natural sharpness.

" Ay, that's it," replied the softly-breathing youth. " You see I joined up in Canada, and I hadn't heard for three or four years. I ran away to Canada."

" And now have you just come from France?"

" Well—from Salonika really."

There was a pause, nobody knowing quite what to say.

" So you've nowhere to go now?" said Banford rather lamely.

" Oh, I know some people in the village. Anyhow, I can go to the Swan."

" You came on the train, I suppose. Would you like to sit down a bit?"

" Well—I don't mind."

He gave an odd little groan as he swung off his kit. Banford looked at March.

" Put the gun down," she said. " We'll make a cup of tea."

" Ay," said the youth. " We've seen enough of rifles."

He sat down rather tired on the sofa, leaning forward.

March recovered her presence of mind, and went into the kitchen. There she heard the soft young voice musing :

" Well, to think I should come back and find it like this ! " He did not seem sad, not at all—only rather interestedly surprised.

" And what a difference in the place, eh ? " he continued, looking round the room.

" You see a difference, do you ? " said Banford.

" Yes—don't I ! "

His eyes were unnaturally clear and bright, though it was the brightness of abundant health.

March was busy in the kitchen preparing another meal. It was about seven o'clock. All the time, while she was active, she was attending to the youth in the sitting-room, not so much listening to what he said as feeling the soft run of his voice. She primmed up her mouth tighter and tighter, puckering it as if it were sewed, in her effort to keep her will uppermost. Yet her large eyes dilated and glowed in spite of her ; she lost herself. Rapidly and carelessly she prepared the meal, cutting large chunks of bread and margarine— for there was no butter. She racked her brain to think of something else to put on the tray—she had only bread, margarine, and jam, and the larder was bare. Unable to conjure anything up, she went into the sitting-room with her tray.

She did not want to be noticed. Above all, she did not want him to look at her. But when she came in, and was busy setting the table just behind him, he pulled himself up from his sprawling, and turned and looked over his shoulder. She became pale and wan.

The youth watched her as she bent over the table, looked at her slim, well-shapen legs, at the belted coat dropping around her thighs, at the knot of dark hair, and his curiosity, vivid and widely alert, was again arrested by her.

The lamp was shaded with a dark-green shade, so that the light was thrown downwards and the upper half of the room was dim. His face moved bright under the light, but March loomed shadowy in the distance.

She turned round, but kept her eyes sideways, dropping and lifting her dark lashes. Her mouth unpuckered as she said to Banford :

" Will you pour out ? "

Then she went into the kitchen again.

" Have your tea where you are, will you ? " said Banford to the youth—" unless you'd rather come to the table."

" Well," said he, " I'm nice and comfortable here, aren't I ? I will have it here, if you don't mind."

"There's nothing but bread and jam," she said. And she put his plate on a stool by him. She was very happy now, waiting on him. For she loved company. And now she was no more afraid of him than if he were her own younger brother. He was such a boy.

"Nellie," she called. "I've poured you a cup out."

March appeared in the doorway, took her cup, and sat down in a corner, as far from the light as possible. She was very sensitive in her knees. Having no skirts to cover them, and being forced to sit with them boldly exposed, she suffered. She shrank and shrank, trying not to be seen. And the youth, sprawling low on the couch, glanced up at her, with long, steady, penetrating looks, till she was almost ready to disappear. Yet she held her cup balanced, she drank her tea, screwed up her mouth and held her head averted. Her desire to be invisible was so strong that it quite baffled the youth. He felt he could not see her distinctly. She seemed like a shadow within the shadow. And ever his eyes came back to her, searching, unremitting, with unconscious fixed attention.

Meanwhile he was talking softly and smoothly to Banford, who loved nothing so much as gossip, and who was full of perky interest, like a bird. Also he ate largely and quickly and voraciously, so that March had to cut more chunks of bread and margarine, for the roughness of which Banford apologized.

"Oh well," said March, suddenly speaking, "if there's no butter to put on it, it's no good trying to make dainty pieces."

Again the youth watched her, and he laughed, with a sudden, quick laugh, showing his teeth and wrinkling his nose.

"It isn't, is it," he answered, in his soft, near voice.

It appeared he was Cornish by birth and upbringing. When he was twelve years old he had come to Bailey Farm with his grandfather, with whom he had never agreed very well. So he had run away to Canada, and worked far away in the West. Now he was here—and that was the end of it.

He was very curious about the girls, to find out exactly what they were doing. His questions were those of a farm youth ; acute, practical, a little mocking. He was very much amused by their attitude to their losses : for they were amusing on the score of heifers and fowls.

"Oh well," broke in March, "we don't believe in living for nothing but work."

"Don't you ? " he answered. And again the quick young laugh came over his face. He kept his eyes steadily on the obscure woman in the corner.

" But what will you do when you've used up all your capital ? "
he said.

" Oh, I don't know," answered March laconically. " Hire ourselves out for land-workers, I suppose."

" Yes, but there won't be any demand for women land-workers
now the war's over," said the youth.

" Oh, we'll see. We shall hold on a bit longer yet," said March,
with a plangent, half-sad, half-ironical indifference.

" There wants a man about the place," said the youth softly.

Banford burst out laughing.

" Take care what you say," she interrupted. " We consider
ourselves quite efficient."

" Oh," came March's slow plangent voice, " it isn't a case of
efficiency, I'm afraid. If you're going to do farming you must be at
it from morning till night, and you might as well be a beast yourself."

" Yes, that's it," said the youth. " You aren't willing to put
yourselves into it."

" We aren't," said March, " and we know it."

" We want some of our time for ourselves," said Banford.

The youth threw himself back on the sofa, his face tight with
laughter, and laughed silently but thoroughly. The calm scorn of
the girls tickled him tremendously.

" Yes," he said, " but why did you begin then ? "

" Oh," said March, " we had a better opinion of the nature of
fowls then than we have now."

" Of Nature altogether, I'm afraid," said Banford. " Don't talk
to me about Nature."

Again the face of the youth tightened with delighted laughter.

" You haven't a very high opinion of fowls and cattle, haven't
you ? " he said.

" Oh no—quite a low one," said March.

He laughed out.

" Neither fowls nor heifers," said Banford, " nor goats nor the
weather."

The youth broke into a sharp yap of laughter, delighted. The
girls began to laugh too, March turning aside her face and wrinkling
her mouth in amusement.

" Oh, well," said Banford, " we don't mind, do we, Nellie ? "

" No," said March, " we don't mind."

The youth was very pleased. He had eaten and drunk his fill.
Banford began to question him. His name was Henry Grenfel—no,
he was not called Harry, always Henry. He continued to answer

with courteous simplicity, grave and charming. March, who was not included, cast long, slow glances at him from her recess, as he sat there on the sofa, his hands clasping his knees, his face under the lamp bright and alert, turned to Banford. She became almost peaceful at last. He was identified with the fox—and he was here in full presence. She need not go after him any more. There in the shadow of her corner she gave herself up to a warm, relaxed peace, almost like sleep, accepting the spell that was on her. But she wished to remain hidden. She was only fully at peace whilst he forgot her, talking to Banford. Hidden in the shadow of the corner, she need not any more be divided in herself, trying to keep up two planes of consciousness. She could at last lapse into the odour of the fox.

For the youth, sitting before the fire in his uniform, sent a faint but distinct odour into the room, indefinable, but something like a wild creature. March no longer tried to reserve herself from it. She was still and soft in her corner like a passive creature in its cave.

At last the talk dwindled. The youth relaxed his clasp of his knees, pulled himself together a little, and looked round. Again he became aware of the silent, half-invisible woman in the corner.

"Well," he said, unwillingly, "I suppose I'd better be going, or they'll be in bed at the Swan."

"I'm afraid they're in bed anyhow," said Banford. "They've all got this influenza."

"Have they!" he exclaimed. And he pondered. "Well," he continued, "I shall find a place somewhere."

"I'd say you could stay here, only——" Banford began.

He turned and watched her, holding his head forward.

"What?" he asked.

"Oh, well," she said, "propriety, I suppose." She was rather confused.

"It wouldn't be improper, would it?" he said, gently surprised.

"Not as far as we're concerned," said Banford.

"And not as far as *I'm* concerned," he said, with grave *naïveté*. "After all, it's my own home, in a way."

Banford smiled at this.

"It's what the village will have to say," she said.

There was a moment's blank pause.

"What do you say, Nellie?" asked Banford.

"I don't mind," said March, in her distinct tone. "The village doesn't matter to me, anyhow."

"No," said the youth, quick and soft. "Why should it? I mean, what should they say?"

" Oh, well," came March's plangent, laconic voice, " they'll easily find something to say. But it makes no difference what they say. We can look after ourselves."

" Of course you can," said the youth.

" Well, then, stop if you like," said Banford. " The spare room is quite ready."

His face shone with pleasure.

" If you're quite sure it isn't troubling you too much," he said, with that soft courtesy which distinguished him.

" Oh, it's no trouble," they both said.

He looked, smiled with delight, from one to another.

" It's awfully nice not to have to turn out again, isn't it ? " he said gratefully.

" I suppose it is," said Banford.

March disappeared to attend to the room. Banford was as pleased and thoughtful as if she had her own young brother home from France. It gave her just the same kind of gratification to attend on him, to get out the bath for him, and everything. Her natural warmth and kindliness had now an outlet. And the youth luxuriated in her sisterly attention. But it puzzled him slightly to know that March was silently working for him too. She was so curiously silent and obliterated. It seemed to him he had not really seen her. He felt he should not know her if he met her in the road.

That night March dreamed vividly. She dreamed she heard a singing outside which she could not understand, a singing that roamed round the house, in the fields, and in the darkness. It moved her so that she felt she must weep. She went out, and suddenly she knew it was the fox singing. He was very yellow and bright, like corn. She went nearer to him, but he ran away and ceased singing. He seemed near, and she wanted to touch him. She stretched out her hand, but suddenly he bit her wrist, and at the same instant, as she drew back, the fox, turning round to bound away, whisked his brush across her face, and it seemed his brush was on fire, for it seared and burned her mouth with a great pain. She awoke with the pain of it, and lay trembling as if she were really seared.

In the morning, however, she only remembered it as a distant memory. She arose and was busy preparing the house and attending to the fowls. Banford flew into the village on her bicycle to try and buy food. She was a hospitable soul. But alas, in the year 1918 there was not much food to buy. The youth came downstairs in his shirt-sleeves. He was young and fresh, but he walked with his head thrust forward, so that his shoulders seemed raised and rounded, as if he had a slight curvature of the spine. It must have been only a manner of bearing himself, for he was young and vigorous. He washed himself and went outside, whilst the women were preparing breakfast.

He saw everything, and examined everything. His curiosity was quick and insatiable. He compared the state of things with that which he remembered before, and cast over in his mind the effect of the changes. He watched the fowls and the ducks, to see their condition ; he noticed the flight of wood-pigeons overhead : they were very numerous ; he saw the few apples high up, which March had not been able to reach ; he remarked that they had borrowed a draw-pump, presumably to empty the big soft-water cistern which was on the north side of the house.

"It's a funny, dilapidated old place," he said to the girls as he sat at breakfast.

His eyes were wise and childish, with thinking about things. He did not say much, but ate largely. March kept her face averted. She, too, in the early morning could not be aware of him, though something about the glint of his khaki reminded her of the brilliance of her dream-fox.

During the day the girls went about their business. In the morning he attended to the guns, shot a rabbit and a wild duck that was flying high towards the wood. That was a great addition to the empty larder. The girls felt that already he had earned his keep. He said nothing about leaving, however. In the afternoon he went to the village. He came back at tea-time. He had the same alert, forward-reaching look on his roundish face. He hung his hat on a peg with a little swinging gesture. He was thinking about something.

"Well," he said to the girls, as he sat at table. "What am I going to do?"

"How do you mean—what are you going to do?" said Banford.

"Where am I going to find a place in the village to stay?" he said.

"I don't know," said Banford. "Where do you think of staying?"

"Well "—he hesitated—" at the Swan they've got this flu, and at the Plough and Harrow they've got the soldiers who are collecting the hay for the army : besides, in the private houses, there's ten men and a corporal altogether billeted in the village, they tell me. I'm not sure where I could get a bed."

He left the matter to them. He was rather calm about it. March sat with her elbows on the table, her two hands supporting her chin, looking at him unconsciously. Suddenly he lifted his clouded blue eyes, and unthinking looked straight into March's eyes. He was

startled as well as she. He, too, recoiled a little. March felt the
same sly, taunting, knowing spark leap out of his eyes, as he turned
his head aside, and fall into her soul, as it had fallen from the dark
eyes of the fox. She pursed her mouth as if in pain, as if asleep too.

"Well, I don't know," Banford was saying. She seemed reluctant,
as if she were afraid of being imposed upon. She looked at March.
But, with her weak, troubled sight, she only saw the usual semi-
abstraction on her friend's face. "Why don't you speak, Nellie?"
she said.

But March was wide-eyed and silent, and the youth, as if fascinated, was watching her without moving his eyes.

"Go on—answer something," said Banford. And March turned
her head slightly aside, as if coming to consciousness, or trying to
come to consciousness.

"What do you expect me to say?" she asked automatically.

"Say what you think," said Banford.

"It's all the same to me," said March.

And again there was silence. A pointed light seemed to be on the
boy's eyes, penetrating like a needle.

"So it is to me," said Banford. "You can stop on here if you like."

A smile like a cunning little flame came over his face, suddenly
and involuntarily. He dropped his head quickly to hide it, and
remained with his head dropped, his face hidden.

"You can stop on here if you like. You can please yourself,
Henry," Banford concluded.

Still he did not reply, but remained with his head dropped. Then
he lifted his face. It was bright with a curious light, as if exultant,
and his eyes were strangely clear as he watched March. She turned
her face aside, her mouth suffering as if wounded, and her consciousness dim.

Banford became a little puzzled. She watched the steady,
pellucid gaze of the youth's eyes as he looked at March, with the
invisible smile gleaming on his face. She did not know how he was
smiling, for no feature moved. It seemed only in the gleam, almost
the glitter of the fine hairs on his cheeks. Then he looked with quite
a changed look at Banford.

"I'm sure," he said in his soft, courteous voice, "you're awfully
good. You're too good. You don't want to be bothered with me,
I'm sure."

"Cut a bit of bread, Nellie," said Banford uneasily, adding : "It's
no bother, if you like to stay. It's like having my own brother here
for a few days. He's a boy like you are."

" That's awfully kind of you," the lad repeated. " I should like to stay ever so much, if you're sure I'm not a trouble to you."

" No, of course you're no trouble. I tell you, it's a pleasure to have somebody in the house besides ourselves," said warm-hearted Banford.

" But Miss March ? " he said in his soft voice, looking at her.

" Oh, it's quite all right as far as I'm concerned," said March vaguely.

His face beamed, and he almost rubbed his hands with pleasure.

" Well then," he said, " I should love it, if you'd let me pay my board and help with the work."

" You've no need to talk about board," said Banford.

One or two days went by, and the youth stayed on at the farm. Banford was quite charmed by him. He was so soft and courteous in speech, not wanting to say much himself, preferring to hear what she had to say, and to laugh in his quick, half-mocking way. He helped readily with the work—but not too much. He loved to be out alone with the gun in his hands, to watch, to see. For his sharp-eyed, impersonal curiosity was insatiable, and he was most free when he was quite alone, half-hidden, watching.

Particularly he watched March. She was a strange character to him. Her figure, like a graceful young man's, piqued him. Her dark eyes made something rise in his soul, with a curious elate excitement, when he looked into them, an excitement he was afraid to let be seen, it was so keen and secret. And then her odd, shrewd speech made him laugh outright. He felt he must go further, he was inevitably impelled. But he put away the thought of her and went off towards the wood's edge with the gun.

The dusk was falling as he came home, and with the dusk, a fine, late November rain. He saw the fire-light leaping in the window of the sitting-room, a leaping light in the little cluster of the dark buildings. And he thought to himself it would be a good thing to have this place for his own. And then the thought entered him shrewdly : why not marry March ? He stood still in the middle of the field for some moments, the dead rabbit hanging still in his hand, arrested by this thought. His mind waited in amazement—it seemed to calculate—and then he smiled curiously to himself in acquiescence. Why not ? Why not indeed ? It was a good idea. What if it was rather ridiculous ? What did it matter ? What if she was older than he ? It didn't matter. When he thought of her dark, startled, vulnerable eyes he smiled subtly to himself. He was older than she, really. He was master of her.

He scarcely admitted his intention even to himself. He kept it as
a secret even from himself. It was all too uncertain as yet. He
would have to see how things went. Yes, he would have to see how
things went. If he wasn't careful, she would just simply mock at the
idea. He knew, sly and subtle as he was, that if he went to her
plainly and said : " Miss March, I love you and want you to marry
me," her inevitable answer would be : " Get out. I don't want any
of that tomfoolery." This was her attitude to men and their " tomfoolery." If he was not careful, she would turn round on him with her
savage, sardonic ridicule, and dismiss him from the farm and from
her own mind for ever. He would have to go gently. He would
have to catch her as you catch a deer or a woodcock when you go out
shooting. It's no good walking out into the forest and saying to the
deer : " Please fall to my gun." No, it is a slow, subtle battle.
When you really go out to get a deer, you gather yourself together,
you coil yourself inside yourself, and you advance secretly, before
dawn, into the mountains. It is not so much what you do, when you
go out hunting, as how you feel. You have to be subtle and cunning
and absolutely fatally ready. It becomes like a fate. Your own fate
overtakes and determines the fate of the deer you are hunting.
First of all, even before you come in sight of your quarry, there is a
strange battle, like mesmerism. Your own soul, as a hunter, has
gone out to fasten on the soul of the deer, even before you see any
deer. And the soul of the deer fights to escape. Even before the deer
has any wind of you, it is so. It is a subtle, profound battle of wills
which takes place in the invisible. And it is a battle never finished
till your bullet goes home. When you are *really* worked up to the
true pitch, and you come at last into range, you don't then aim as
you do when you are firing at a bottle. It is your own *will* which
carries the bullet into the heart of your quarry. The bullet's flight
home is a sheer projection of your own fate into the fate of the deer.
It happens like a supreme wish, a supreme act of volition, not as a
dodge of cleverness.

He was a huntsman in spirit, not a farmer, and not a soldier stuck
in a regiment. And it was as a young hunter that he wanted to bring
down March as his quarry, to make her his wife. So he gathered
himself subtly together, seemed to withdraw into a kind of invisibility.
He was not quite sure how he would go on. And March was
suspicious as a hare. So he remained in appearance just the nice,
odd stranger-youth, staying for a fortnight on the place.

He had been sawing logs for the fire in the afternoon. Darkness
came very early. It was still a cold, raw mist. It was getting almost

too dark to see. A pile of short sawed logs lay beside the trestle. March came to carry them indoors, or into the shed, as he was busy sawing the last log. He was working in his shirt-sleeves, and did not notice her approach ; she came unwillingly, as if shy. He saw her stooping to the bright-ended logs, and he stopped sawing. A fire like lightning flew down his legs in the nerves.

" March ? " he said, in his quiet, young voice.

She looked up from the logs she was piling.

" Yes ! " she said.

He looked down on her in the dusk. He could see her not too distinctly.

" I wanted to ask you something," he said.

" Did you ? What was it ? " she said. Already the fright was in her voice. But she was too much mistress of herself.

" Why "—his voice seemed to draw out soft and subtle, it penetrated her nerves—" why, what do you think it is ? "

She stood up, placed her hands on her hips, and stood looking at him transfixed, without answering. Again he burned with a sudden power.

" Well," he said, and his voice was so soft it seemed rather like a subtle touch, like the merest touch of a cat's paw, a feeling rather than a sound. " Well—I wanted to ask you to marry me."

March felt rather than heard him. She was trying in vain to turn aside her face. A great relaxation seemed to have come over her. She stood silent, her head slightly on one side. He seemed to be bending towards her, invisibly smiling. It seemed to her fine sparks came out of him.

Then very suddenly she said :

" Don't try any of your tomfoolery on me."

A quiver went over his nerves. He had missed. He waited a moment to collect himself again. Then he said, putting all the strange softness into his voice, as if he were imperceptibly stroking her :

" Why, it's not tomfoolery. It's not tomfoolery. I mean it. I mean it. What makes you disbelieve me ? "

He sounded hurt. And his voice had such a curious power over her ; making her feel loose and relaxed. She struggled somewhere for her own power. She felt for a moment that she was lost—lost—lost. The word seemed to rock in her as if she were dying. Suddenly again she spoke.

" You don't know what you are talking about," she said, in a brief and transient stroke of scorn. " What nonsense ! I'm old enough to be your mother."

"Yes, I do know what I'm talking about. Yes, I do," he persisted softly, as if he were producing his voice in her blood. "I know quite well what I'm talking about. You're not old enough to be my mother. That isn't true. And what does it matter even if it was. You can marry me whatever age we are. What is age to me? And what is age to you! Age is nothing."

A swoon went over her as he concluded. He spoke rapidly—in the rapid Cornish fashion—and his voice seemed to sound in her somewhere where she was helpless against it. "Age is nothing!" The soft, heavy insistence of it made her sway dimly out there in the darkness. She could not answer.

A great exultance leaped like fire over his limbs. He felt he had won.

"I want to marry you, you see. Why shouldn't I?" he proceeded, soft and rapid. He waited for her to answer. In the dusk he saw her almost phosphorescent. Her eyelids were dropped, her face half-averted and unconscious. She seemed to be in his power. But he waited, watchful. He dared not yet touch her.

"Say then," he said, "say then you'll marry me. Say—say!" He was softly insistent.

"What?" she asked, faint, from a distance, like one in pain. His voice was now unthinkably near and soft. He drew very near to her. "Say yes."

"Oh, I can't," she wailed helplessly, half-articulate, as if semi-conscious, and as if in pain, like one who dies. "How can I?"

"You can," he said softly, laying his hand gently on her shoulder as she stood with her head averted and dropped, dazed. "You can. Yes, you can. What makes you say you can't? You can. You can." And with awful softness he bent forward and just touched her neck with his mouth and his chin.

"Don't!" she cried, with a faint mad cry like hysteria, starting away and facing round on him. "What do you mean?" But she had no breath to speak with. It was as if she was killed.

"I mean what I say," he persisted softly and cruelly. "I want you to marry me. I want you to marry me. You know that, now, don't you? You know that, now? Don't you? Don't you?"

"What?" she said.

"Know," he replied.

"Yes," she said. "I know you say so."

"And you know I mean it, don't you?"

"I know you say so."

"You believe me?" he said.

She was silent for some time. Then she pursed her lips.

"I don't know what I believe," she said.

"Are you out there?" came Banford's voice, calling from the house.

"Yes, we're bringing in the logs," he answered.

"I thought you'd gone lost," said Banford disconsolately. "Hurry up, do, and come and let's have tea. The kettle's boiling."

He stooped at once, to take an armful of little logs and carry them into the kitchen, where they were piled in a corner. March also helped, filling her arms and carrying the logs on her breast as if they were some heavy child. The night had fallen cold.

When the logs were all in, the two cleaned their boots noisily on the scraper outside, then rubbed them on the mat. March shut the door and took off her old felt hat—her farm-girl hat. Her thick, crisp black hair was loose, her face was pale and strained. She pushed back her hair vaguely, and washed her hands. Banford came hurrying into the dimly lighted kitchen, to take from the oven the scones she was keeping hot.

"Whatever have you been doing all this time?" she asked fretfully. "I thought you were never coming in. And it's ages since you stopped sawing. What were you doing out there?"

"Well," said Henry, "we had to stop that hole in the barn, to keep the rats out."

"Why, I could see you standing there in the shed. I could see your shirt-sleeves," challenged Banford.

"Yes, I was just putting the saw away."

They went in to tea. March was quite mute. Her face was pale and strained and vague. The youth, who always had the same ruddy, self-contained look on his face, as though he were keeping himself to himself, had come to tea in his shirt-sleeves as if he were at home. He bent over his plate as he ate his food.

"Aren't you cold?" said Banford spitefully. "In your shirt-sleeves."

He looked up at her, with his chin near his plate, and his eyes very clear, pellucid, and unwavering as he watched her.

"No, I'm not cold," he said with his usual soft courtesy. "It's much warmer in here than it is outside, you see."

"I hope it is," said Banford, feeling nettled by him. He had a strange suave assurance, and a wide-eyed bright look that got on her nerves this evening.

"But perhaps," he said softly and courteously, "you don't like me coming to tea without my coat. I forgot that."

"Oh, I don't mind," said Banford : although she *did*.

"I'll go and get it, shall I ? " he said.

March's dark eyes turned slowly down to him.

"No, don't you bother," she said in her queer, twanging tone "If you feel all right as you are, stop as you are." She spoke with a crude authority.

"Yes," said he, "I *feel* all right, if I'm not rude."

"It's usually considered rude," said Banford. "But we don't mind."

"Go along, 'considered rude,'" ejaculated March. "Who considers it rude ? "

"Why you do, Nellie, in anybody else," said Banford, bridling a little behind her spectacles, and feeling her food stick in her throat.

But March had again gone vague and unheeding, chewing her food as if she did not know she was eating at all. And the youth looked from one to another, with bright, watchful eyes.

Banford was offended. For all his suave courtesy and soft voice, the youth seemed to her impudent. She did not like to look at him. She did not like to meet his clear, watchful eyes, she did not like to see the strange glow in his face, his cheeks with their delicate fine hair, and his ruddy skin that was quite dull and yet which seemed to burn with a curious heat of life. It made her feel a little ill to look at him : the quality of his physical presence was too penetrating, too hot.

After tea the evening was very quiet. The youth rarely went into the village. As a rule he read : he was a great reader, in his own hours. That is, when he did begin, he read absorbedly. But he was not very eager to begin. Often he walked about the fields and along the hedges alone in the dark at night, prowling with a queer instinct for the night, and listening to the wild sounds.

To-night, however, he took a Captain Mayne Reid book from Banford's shelf and sat down with knees wide apart and immersed himself in his story. His brownish fair hair was long, and lay on his head like a thick cap, combed sideways. He was still in his shirt-sleeves, and bending forward under the lamp-light, with his knees stuck wide apart and the book in his hand and his whole figure absorbed in the rather strenuous business of reading, he gave Banford's sitting-room the look of a lumber-camp. She resented this. For on her sitting-room floor she had a red Turkey rug and dark stain round, the fire-place had fashionable green tiles, the piano stood open with the latest dance-music—she played quite well : and on the walls were March's hand-painted swans and water-lilies. Moreover, with the logs nicely, tremulously burning in the grate, the thick curtains drawn, the doors all shut, and the pine-trees hissing and shuddering in the wind outside, it was cosy, it was refined and nice. She resented the big, raw, long-legged youth sticking his khaki knees out and sitting there with his soldier's shirt-cuffs buttoned on his thick red wrists. From time to time he turned a page, and from time to time he gave a sharp look at the fire, settling the logs. Then he immersed himself again in the intense and isolated business of reading.

March, on the far side of the table, was spasmodically crocheting. Her mouth was pursed in an odd way, as when she had dreamed the fox's brush burned it, her beautiful, crisp black hair strayed in wisps. But her whole figure was absorbed in its bearing, as if she herself was miles away. In a sort of semi-dream she seemed to be hearing the fox singing round the house in the wind, singing wildly and sweetly and like a madness. With red but well-shaped hands she slowly crocheted the white cotton, very slowly, awkwardly.

Banford was also trying to read, sitting in her low chair. But between those two she felt fidgety. She kept moving and looking round and listening to the wind, and glancing secretly from one to the other of her companions. March, seated on a straight chair, with her knees in their close breeches crossed, and slowly, laboriously crocheting, was also a trial.

" Oh dear ! " said Banford. " My eyes are bad to-night." And she pressed her fingers on her eyes.

The youth looked up at her with his clear, bright look, but did not speak.

" Are they, Jill ? " said March absently.

Then the youth began to read again, and Banford perforce returned to her book. But she could not keep still. After a while she looked up at March, and a queer, almost malignant little smile was on her thin face.

" A penny for them, Nell," she said suddenly.

March looked round with big, startled black eyes, and went pale as if with terror. She had been listening to the fox singing so tenderly, so tenderly, as he wandered round the house.

" What ? " she said vaguely.

" A penny for them," said Banford sarcastically. " Or twopence, if they're as deep as all that."

The youth was watching with bright, clear eyes from beneath the lamp.

" Why," came March's vague voice, " what do you want to waste your money for ? "

" I thought it would be well spent," said Banford.

" I wasn't thinking of anything except the way the wind was blowing," said March.

" Oh dear," replied Banford, " I could have had as original thoughts as that myself. I'm afraid I *have* wasted my money this time."

" Well, you needn't pay," said March.

The youth suddenly laughed. Both women looked at him : March rather surprised-looking, as if she had hardly known he was there.

" Why, do you ever pay up on these occasions ? " he asked.

" Oh yes," said Banford. " We always do. I've sometimes had to pass a shilling a week to Nellie, in the winter-time. It costs much less in summer.

" What, paying for each other's thoughts ? " he laughed.

" Yes, when we've absolutely come to the end of everything else."

He laughed quickly, wrinkling his nose sharply like a puppy and laughing with quick pleasure, his eyes shining.

" It's the first time I ever heard of that," he said.

" I guess you'd hear of it often enough if you stayed a winter on Bailey Farm," said Banford lamentably.

" Do you get so tired, then ? " he asked.

" So bored," said Banford.

" Oh ! " he said gravely. " But why should you be bored ? "

" Who wouldn't be bored ? " said Banford.

" I'm sorry to hear that," he said gravely.

" You must be, if you were hoping to have a lively time here," said Banford.

He looked at her long and gravely.

" Well," he said, with his odd, young seriousness, " it's quite lively enough for me."

" I'm glad to hear it," said Banford.

And she returned to her book. In her thin, frail hair were already many threads of grey, though she was not yet thirty. The boy did not look down, but turned his eyes to March, who was sitting with pursed mouth laboriously crocheting, her eyes wide and absent. She had a warm, pale, fine skin, and a delicate nose. Her pursed mouth looked shrewish. But the shrewish look was contradicted by the curious lifted arch of her dark brows, and the wideness of her eyes ; a look of startled wonder and vagueness. She was listening again for the fox, who seemed to have wandered farther off into the night.

From under the edge of the lamp-light the boy sat with his face looking up, watching her silently, his eyes round and very clear and intent. Banford, biting her fingers irritably, was glancing at him under her hair. He sat there perfectly still, his ruddy face tilted up from the low level under the light, on the edge of the dimness, and watching with perfect abstract intentness. March suddenly lifted her great, dark eyes from her crocheting, and saw him. She started, giving a little exclamation.

"There he is!" she cried, involuntarily, as if terribly startled.

Banford looked around in amazement, sitting up straight.

"Whatever has got you, Nellie?" she cried.

But March, her face flushed a delicate rose colour, was looking away to the door.

"Nothing! Nothing!" she said crossly. "Can't one speak?"

"Yes, if you speak sensibly," said Banford. "Whatever did you mean?"

"I don't know what I meant," cried March testily.

"Oh, Nellie, I hope you aren't going jumpy and nervy. I feel I can't stand another *thing*! Whoever did you mean? Did you mean Henry?" cried poor, frightened Banford.

"Yes. I suppose so," said March laconically. She would never confess to the fox.

"Oh dear, my nerves are all gone for to-night," wailed Banford.

At nine o'clock March brought in a tray with bread and cheese and tea—Henry had confessed that he liked a cup of tea. Banford drank a glass of milk, and ate a little bread. And soon she said:

"I'm going to bed, Nellie. I'm all nerves to-night. Are you coming?"

"Yes, I'm coming the minute I've taken the tray away," said March.

"Don't be long then," said Banford fretfully. "Good night, Henry. You'll see the fire is safe, if you come up last, won't you?"

"Yes, Miss Banford, I'll see it's safe," he replied in his reassuring way.

March was lighting the candle to go to the kitchen. Banford took her candle and went upstairs. When March came back to the fire, she said to him:

"I suppose we can trust you to put out the fire and everything?" She stood there with her hand on her hip, and one knee loose, her head averted shyly, as if she could not look at him. He had his face lifted, watching her.

"Come and sit down a minute," he said softly.

" No, I'll be going. Jill will be waiting, and she'll get upset if I don't come."

" What made you jump like that this evening ? " he asked.

" When did I jump ? " she retorted, looking at him.

" Why, just now you did," he said. " When you cried out."

" Oh ! " she said. " Then ! Why, I thought you were the fox !" And her face screwed into a queer smile, half-ironic.

" The fox ! Why the fox ? " he asked softly.

" Why, one evening last summer when I was out with the gun I saw the fox in the grass nearly at my feet, looking straight up at me. I don't know—I suppose he made an impression on me." She turned aside her head again, and let one foot stray loose, self-consciously.

" And did you shoot him ? " asked the boy.

" No, he gave me such a start, staring straight at me as he did, and then stopping to look back at me over his shoulder with a laugh on his face."

" A laugh on his face ! " repeated Henry, also laughing. " He frightened you, did he ? "

" No, he didn't frighten me. He made an impression on me, that's all."

" And you thought I was the fox, did you ? " he laughed, with the same queer, quick little laugh, like a puppy wrinkling its nose.

" Yes, I did, for the moment," she said. " Perhaps he'd been in my mind without my knowing."

" Perhaps you think I've come to steal your chickens or some-thing," he said, with the same young laugh.

But she only looked at him with a wide, dark, vacant eye.

" It's the first time," he said, " that I've ever been taken for a fox. Won't you sit down for a minute ? " His voice was very soft and cajoling.

" No," she said. " Jill will be waiting." But still she did not go, but stood with one foot loose and her face turned aside, just outside the circle of light.

" But won't you answer my question ? " he said, lowering his voice still more.

" I don't know what question you mean."

" Yes, you do. Of course you do. I mean the question of you marrying me."

" No, I shan't answer that question," she said flatly.

" Won't you ? " The queer, young laugh came on his nose again.

" Is it because I'm like the fox? Is that why? " And still he laughed.

She turned and looked at him with a long, slow look.

" I wouldn't let that put you against me," he said. " Let me turn the lamp low, and come and sit down a minute."

He put his red hand under the glow of the lamp, and suddenly made the light very dim. March stood there in the dimness quite shadowy, but unmoving. He rose silently to his feet, on his long legs. And now his voice was extraordinarily soft and suggestive, hardly audible.

" You'll stay a moment," he said. " Just a moment." And he put his hand on her shoulder. She turned her face from him. " I'm sure you don't really think I'm like the fox," he said, with the same softness and with a suggestion of laughter in his tone, a subtle mockery. " Do you now? " And he drew her gently towards him and kissed her neck, softly. She winced and trembled and hung away. But his strong, young arm held her, and he kissed her softly again, still on the neck, for her face was averted.

" Won't you answer my question? Won't you now? " came his soft, lingering voice. He was trying to draw her near to kiss her face. And he kissed her cheek softly, near the ear.

At that moment Banford's voice was heard calling fretfully, crossly from upstairs.

" There's Jill ! " cried March, starting and drawing erect.

And as she did so, quick as lightning he kissed her on the mouth, with a quick brushing kiss. It seemed to burn through her every fibre. She gave a queer little cry.

" You will, won't you? You will? " he insisted softly.

" Nellie ! *Nellie !* Whatever are you so long for? " came Banford's faint cry from the outer darkness.

But he held her fast, and was murmuring with that intolerable softness and insistency :

" You will, won't you? Say yes ! Say yes ! "

March, who felt as if the fire had gone through her and scathed her, and as if she could do no more, murmured :

" Yes ! Yes ! Anything you like ! Anything you like ! Only let me go ! Only let me go ! Jill's calling."

" You know you've promised," he said insidiously.

" Yes ! Yes ! I do ! " Her voice suddenly rose into a shrill cry. " All right, Jill I'm coming."

Startled, he let her go, and she went straight upstairs.

In the morning at breakfast, after he had looked round the place and attended to the stock and thought to himself that one could live easily enough here, he said to Banford :

" Do you know what, Miss Banford ? "

" Well, what ? " said the good-natured, nervy Banford.

He looked at March, who was spreading jam on her bread.

" Shall I tell ? " he said to her.

She looked up at him, and a deep pink colour flushed over her face.

" Yes, if you mean Jill," she said. " I hope you won't go talking all over the village, that's all." And she swallowed her dry bread with difficulty.

" Whatever's coming ? " said Banford, looking up with wide, tired, slightly reddened eyes. She was a thin, frail little thing, and her hair, which was delicate and thin, was bobbed, so it hung softly by her worn face in its faded brown and grey.

" Why, what do you think ? " he said, smiling like one who has a secret.

" How do I know ! " said Banford.

" Can't you guess ? " he said, making bright eyes, and smiling, pleased with himself.

" I'm sure I can't. What's more, I'm not going to try."

" Nellie and I are going to be married."

Banford put down her knife out of her thin, delicate fingers, as if she would never take it up to eat any more. She stared with blank, reddened eyes.

" You what ? " she exclaimed.

" We're going to get married. Aren't we, Nellie ? " and he turned to March.

" You say so, anyway," said March laconically. But again she flushed with an agonized flush. She, too, could swallow no more.

Banford looked at her like a bird that has been shot : a poor, little sick bird. She gazed at her with all her wounded soul in her face, at the deep-flushed March.

" Never ! " she exclaimed, helpless.

" It's quite right," said the bright and gloating youth.

Banford turned aside her face, as if the sight of the food on the table made her sick. She sat like this for some moments, as if she were sick. Then, with one hand on the edge of the table, she rose to her feet.

" I'll *never* believe it, Nellie," she cried. " It's absolutely impossible ! "

Her plaintive, fretful voice had a thread of hot anger and despair.

" Why ? Why shouldn't you believe it ? " asked the youth, with all his soft, velvety impertinence in his voice.

Banford looked at him from her wide, vague eyes, as if he were some creature in a museum.

" Oh," she said languidly, " because she can never be such a fool. She can't lose her self-respect to such an extent." Her voice was cold and plaintive, drifting.

" In what way will she lose her self-respect ? " asked the boy.

Banford looked at him with vague fixity from behind her spectacles.

" If she hasn't lost it already," she said.

He became very red, vermilion, under the slow, vague stare from behind the spectacles.

" I don't see it at all," he said.

" Probably you don't. I shouldn't expect you would," said Banford, with that straying mild tone of remoteness which made her words even more insulting.

He sat stiff in his chair, staring with hot, blue eyes from his scarlet face. An ugly look had come on his brow.

" My word, she doesn't know what she's letting herself in for," said Banford, in her plaintive, drifting, insulting voice.

" What has it got to do with you, anyway ? " said the youth, in a temper.

" More than it has to do with you, probably," she replied, plaintive and venomous.

" Oh, has it ! I don't see that at all," he jerked out.

" No, you wouldn't," she answered, drifting.

" Anyhow," said March, pushing back her chair and rising uncouthly. " It's no good arguing about it." And she seized the bread and the teapot, and strode away to the kitchen.

Banford let her fingers stray across her brow and along her hair, like one bemused. Then she turned and went away upstairs.

Henry sat stiff and sulky in his chair, with his face and his eyes on fire. March came and went, clearing the table. But Henry sat on, stiff with temper. He took no notice of her. She had regained her composure and her soft, even, creamy complexion. But her mouth was pursed up. She glanced at him each time as she came to take things from the table, glanced from her large, curious eyes, more in curiosity than anything. Such a long, red-faced, sulky boy ! That was all he was. He seemed as remote from her as if his red face were a red chimney-pot on a cottage across the fields, and she looked at him just as objectively, as remotely.

At length he got up and stalked out into the fields with the gun. He came in only at dinner-time, with the devil still in his face, but his manners quite polite. Nobody said anything particular ; they sat each one at the sharp corner of a triangle, in obstinate remoteness. In the afternoon he went out again at once with the gun. He came in at nightfall with a rabbit and a pigeon. He stayed in all the evening, but hardly opened his mouth. He was in the devil of a temper, feeling he had been insulted.

Banford's eyes were red, she had evidently been crying. But her manner was more remote and supercilious than ever ; the way she turned her head if he spoke at all, as if he were some tramp or inferior intruder of that sort, made his blue eyes go almost black with rage. His face looked sulkier. But he never forgot his polite intonation, if he opened his mouth to speak.

March seemed to flourish in this atmosphere. She seemed to sit between the two antagonists with a little wicked smile on her face, enjoying herself. There was even a sort of complacency in the way she laboriously crocheted this evening.

When he was in bed, the youth could hear the two women talking and arguing in their room. He sat up in bed and strained his ears to hear what they said. But he could hear nothing, it was too far off. Yet he could hear the soft, plaintive drip of Banford's voice, and March's deeper note.

The night was quiet, frosty. Big stars were snapping outside, beyond the ridge-tops of the pine-trees. He listened and listened. In the distance he heard a fox yelping : and the dogs from the farms barking in answer. But it was not that he wanted to hear. It was what the two women were saying.

He got stealthily out of bed, and stood by his door. He could hear no more than before. Very, very carefully he began to lift the door latch. After quite a time he had his door open. Then he stepped stealthily out into the passage. The old oak planks were cold under his feet, and they creaked preposterously. He crept very, very gently up the one step, and along by the wall, till he stood outside their door. And there he held his breath and listened. Banford's voice :

" No, I simply couldn't stand it. I should be dead in a month. Which is just what he would be aiming at, of course. That would just be his game, to see me in the churchyard. No, Nellie, if you were to do such a thing as to marry him, you could never stop here. I couldn't, I couldn't live in the same house with him. Oh—h ! I feel quite sick with the smell of his clothes. And his red face simply turns me over. I can't eat my food when he's at the table. What a fool I was ever to let him stop. One ought *never* to try to do a kind action. It always flies back in your face like a boomerang."

" Well, he's only got two more days," said March.

" Yes, thank heaven. And when he's gone he'll never come in this house again. I feel so bad while he's here. And I know, I know he's only counting what he can get out of you. I *know* that's all it is. He's just a good-for-nothing, who doesn't want to work, and who thinks he'll live on us. But he won't live on me. If you're such a fool, then it's your own look-out. Mrs. Burgess knew him all the time he was here. And the old man could never get him to do any steady work. He was off with the gun on every occasion, just as he is now. Nothing but the gun ! Oh, I do hate it. You don't know what you're doing, Nellie, you don't. If you marry him he'll just make a fool of you. He'll go off and leave you stranded. I know he will, if he can't get Bailey Farm out of us—and he's not going to, while I live. While I live he's never going to set foot here. I know what it would be. He'd soon think he was master of both of us, as he thinks he's master of you already."

" But he isn't," said Nellie.

" He thinks he is, anyway. And that's what he wants : to come and be master here. Yes, imagine it ! That's what we've got the place together for, is it, to be bossed and bullied by a hateful red-faced boy, a beastly labourer. Oh, we *did* make a mistake when we let him stop. We ought never to have lowered ourselves. And I've had such a fight with all the people here, not to be pulled down to their level. No, he's not coming here. And then you see—if he can't have the place, he'll run off to Canada or somewhere again, as if he'd never known you. And here you'll be, absolutely ruined and made a fool of. I know I shall never have any peace of mind again."

" We'll tell him he can't come here. We'll tell him that," said March.

" Oh, don't you bother ; I'm going to tell him that, and other things as well, before he goes. He's not going to have all his own way while I've got the strength left to speak. Oh, Nellie, he'll despise you, he'll despise you, like the awful little beast he is, if you give way to him. I'd no more trust him than I'd trust a cat not to steal. He's deep, he's deep, and he's·bossy, and he's selfish through and through, as cold as ice. All he wants is to make use of you. And when you're no more use to him, then I pity you."

" I don't think he's as bad as all that," said March.

" No, because he's been playing up to you. But you'll find out, if you see much more of him. Oh, Nellie, I can't bear to think of it."

" Well, it won't hurt you, Jill, darling."

" Won't it ! Won't it ! I shall never know a moment's peace again while I live, nor a moment's happiness. No, Nellie——" and Banford began to weep bitterly.

The boy outside could hear the stifled sound of the woman's sobbing, and could hear March's soft, deep, tender voice comforting, with wonderful gentleness and tenderness, the weeping woman.

His eyes were so round and wide that he seemed to see the whole night, and his ears were almost jumping off his head. He was frozen stiff. He crept back to bed, but felt as if the top of his head were coming off. He could not sleep. He could not keep still. He rose, quietly dressed himself, and crept out on to the landing once more. The women were silent. He went softly downstairs and out to the kitchen.

Then he put on his boots and his overcoat, and took the gun. He did not think to go away from the farm. No, he only took the gun. As softly as possible he unfastened the door and went out into the frosty December night. The air was still, the stars bright, the pine-trees seemed to bristle audibly in the sky. He went stealthily away down a fence-side, looking for something to shoot. At the same time he remembered that he ought not to shoot and frighten the women.

So he prowled round the edge of the gorse cover, and through the grove of tall old hollies, to the woodside. There he skirted the fence, peering through the darkness with dilated eyes that seemed to be able to grow black and full of sight in the dark, like a cat's. An owl was slowly and mournfully whooing round a great oak-tree. He stepped stealthily with his gun, listening, listening, watching.

As he stood under the oaks of the wood-edge he heard the dogs from the neighbouring cottage up the hill yelling suddenly and startlingly, and the wakened dogs from the farms around barking answer. And suddenly, it seemed to him England was little and tight, he felt the landscape was constricted even in the dark, and that there were too many dogs in the night, making a noise like a fence of sound, like the network of English hedges netting the view. He felt the fox didn't have a chance. For it must be the fox that had started all this hullabaloo.

Why not watch for him, anyhow ! He would, no doubt, be coming sniffing round. The lad walked downhill to where the farmstead with its few pine-trees crouched blackly. In the angle of the long shed, in the black dark, he crouched down. He knew the fox would be coming. It seemed to him it would be the last of the foxes in this loudly barking, thick-voiced England, tight with innumerable little houses.

He sat a long time with his eyes fixed unchanging upon the open gateway, where a little light seemed to fall from the stars or from the horizon, who knows. He was sitting on a log in a dark corner with the gun across his knees. The pine-trees snapped. Once a chicken fell off its perch in the barn with a loud crawk and cackle and commotion that startled him, and he stood up, watching with all his eyes, thinking it might be a rat. But he *felt* it was nothing. So he sat down again with the gun on his knees and his hands tucked in to keep them warm, and his eyes fixed unblinking on the pale reach of the open gateway. He felt he could smell the hot, sickly, rich smell of live chickens on the cold air.

And then—a shadow. A sliding shadow in the gateway. He gathered all his vision into a concentrated spark, and saw the shadow of the fox, the fox creeping on his belly through the gate. There he went, on his belly like a snake. The boy smiled to himself and brought the gun to his shoulder. He knew quite well what would happen. He knew the fox would go to where the fowl-door was boarded up, and sniff there. He knew he would lie there for a minute, sniffing the fowls within. And then he would start again prowling under the edge of the old barn, waiting to get in.

The fowl-door was at the top of a slight incline. Soft, soft as a shadow the fox slid up this incline, and crouched with his nose to the boards. And at the same moment there was the awful crash of a gun reverberating between the old buildings, as if all the night had gone smash. But the boy watched keenly. He saw even the white belly of the fox as the beast beat his paws in death. So he went forward.

There was a commotion everywhere. The fowls were scuffling and crawking, the ducks were quark-quarking, the pony had stamped wildly to his feet. But the fox was on his side, struggling in his last tremors. The boy bent over him and smelt his foxy smell.

There was a sound of a window opening upstairs, then March's voice calling :

" Who is it ? "

" It's me," said Henry ; " I've shot the fox."

" Oh, goodness ! You nearly frightened us to death "

" Did I ? I'm awfully sorry."

" Whatever made you get up ? "

" I heard him about."

" And have you shot him ? "

"Yes, he's here," and the boy stood in the yard holding up the warm, dead brute. "You can't see, can you? Wait a minute." And he took his flashlight from his pocket, and flashed it on to the dead animal. He was holding it by the brush. March saw, in the middle of the darkness, just the reddish fleece and the white belly and the white underneath of the pointed chin, and the queer, dangling paws. She did not know what to say.

"He's a beauty," he said. "He will make you a lovely fur."

"You don't catch me wearing a fox fur," she replied.

"Oh!" he said. And he switched off the light.

"Well, I should think you'll come in and go to bed again now," she said.

"Probably I shall. What time is it?"

"What time is it, Jill?" called March's voice. It was a quarter to one.

That night March had another dream. She dreamed that Banford was dead, and that she, March, was sobbing her heart out. Then she had to put Banford into her coffin. And the coffin was the rough wood-box in which the bits of chopped wood were kept in the kitchen, by the fire. This was the coffin, and there was no other, and March was in agony and dazed bewilderment, looking for something to line the box with, something to make it soft with, something to cover up the poor, dead darling. Because she couldn't lay her in there just in her white, thin nightdress, in the horrible wood-box. So she hunted and hunted, and picked up thing after thing, and threw it aside in the agony of dream-frustration. And in her dream-despair all she could find that would do was a fox-skin. She knew that it wasn't right, that this was not what she should have. But it was all she could find. And so she folded the brush of the fox, and laid her darling Jill's head on this, and she brought round the skin of the fox and laid it on the top of the body, so that it seemed to make a whole ruddy, fiery coverlet, and she cried and cried, and woke to find the tears streaming down her face.

The first thing that both she and Banford did in the morning was to go out to see the fox. Henry had hung it up by the heels in the shed, with its poor brush falling backwards. It was a lovely dog-fox in its prime, with a handsome, thick, winter coat: a lovely golden-red colour, with grey as it passed to the belly, and belly all white, and a great full brush with a delicate black and grey and pure white tip.

"Poor brute!" said Banford. "If it wasn't such a thieving wretch, you'd feel sorry for it."

March said nothing, but stood with her foot trailing aside, one hip out ; her face was pale and her eyes big and black, watching the dead animal that was suspended upside down. White and soft as snow his belly : white and soft as snow. She passed her hand softly down it. And his wonderful black-glinted brush was full and frictional, wonderful. She passed her hand down this also, and quivered. Time after time, she took the full fur of that thick tail between her fingers, and passed her hand slowly downwards. Wonderful, sharp, thick, splendour of a tail. And he was dead ! She pursed her lips, and her eyes went black and vacant. Then she took the head in her hand.

Henry was sauntering up, so Banford walked rather pointedly away. March stood there bemused, with the head of the fox in her hand. She was wondering, wondering, wondering over his long fine muzzle. For some reason it reminded her of a spoon or a spatula. She felt she could not understand it. The beast was a strange beast to her, incomprehensible, out of her range. Wonderful silver whiskers he had, like ice-threads. And pricked ears with hair inside. But that long, long, slender spoon of a nose !—and the marvellous white teeth beneath ! It was to thrust forward and bite with, deep, deep into the living prey, to bite and bite the blood.

" He's a beauty, isn't he ? " said Henry, standing by.

" Oh yes, he's a fine big fox. I wonder how many chickens he's responsible for," she replied.

" A good many. Do you think he's the same one you saw in the summer ? "

" I should think very likely he is," she replied.

He watched her, but he could make nothing of her. Partly she was so shy and virgin, and partly she was so grim, matter-of-fact, shrewish. What she said seemed to him so different from the look of her big, queer, dark eyes.

" Are you going to skin him ? " she asked.

" Yes, when I've had breakfast, and got a board to peg him on."

" My word, what a strong smell he's got ! Pooo ! It'll take some washing off one's hands. I don't know why I was so silly as to handle him." And she looked at her right hand, that had passed down his belly and along his tail, and had even got a tiny streak of blood from one dark place in his fur.

" Have you seen the chickens when they smell him, how frightened they are ? " he said.

" Yes, aren't they ! "

" You must mind you don't get some of his fleas."

"Oh, fleas!" she replied, nonchalant.

Later in the day she saw the fox's skin nailed flat on a board, as if crucified. It gave her an uneasy feeling.

The boy was angry. He went about with his mouth shut, as if he had swallowed part of his chin. But in behaviour he was polite and affable. He did not say anything about his intention. And he left March alone.

That evening they sat in the dining-room. Banford wouldn't have him in her sitting-room any more. There was a very big log on the fire. And everybody was busy. Banford had letters to write, March was sewing a dress, and he was mending some little contrivance.

Banford stopped her letter-writing from time to time to look round and rest her eyes. The boy had his head down, his face hidden over his job.

"Let's see," said Banford. "What train do you go by, Henry?"

He looked up straight at her.

"The morning train. In the morning," he said.

"What, the eight-ten or the eleven-twenty?"

"The eleven-twenty, I suppose," he said.

"That is the day after to-morrow?" said Banford.

"Yes, the day after to-morrow."

"Mm!" murmured Banford, and she returned to her writing. But as she was licking her envelope, she asked:

"And what plans have you made for the future, if I may ask?"

"Plans?" he said, his face very bright and angry.

"I mean about you and Nellie, if you are going on with this business. When do you expect the wedding to come off?" She spoke in a jeering tone.

"Oh, the wedding!" he replied. "I don't know."

"Don't you know anything?" said Banford. "Are you going to clear out on Friday and leave things no more settled than they are?"

"Well, why shouldn't I? We can always write letters."

"Yes, of course you can. But I wanted to know because of this place. If Nellie is going to get married all of a sudden, I shall have to be looking round for a new partner."

"Couldn't she stay on here if she were married?" he said. He knew quite well what was coming.

"Oh," said Banford, "this is no place for a married couple. There's not enough work to keep a man going, for one thing. And there's no money to be made. It's quite useless your thinking of staying on here if you marry. Absolutely!"

"Yes, but I wasn't thinking of staying on here," he said.

"Well, that's what I want to know. And what about Nellie, then? How long is *she* going to be here with me, in that case."

The two antagonists looked at one another.

"That I can't say," he answered.

"Oh, go along," she cried petulantly. "You must have some idea what you are going to do, if you ask a woman to marry you. Unless it's all a hoax."

"Why should it be a hoax? I am going back to Canada."

"And taking her with you?"

"Yes, certainly."

"You hear that, Nellie?" said Banford.

March, who had had her head bent over her sewing, now looked up with a sharp, pink blush on her face, and a queer, sardonic laugh in her eyes and on her twisted mouth.

"That's the first time I've heard that I was going to Canada," she said.

"Well, you have to hear it for the first time, haven't you?" said the boy.

"Yes, I suppose I have," she said nonchalantly. And she went back to her sewing.

"You're quite ready, are you, to go to Canada? Are you, Nellie?" asked Banford.

March looked up again. She let her shoulders go slack, and let her hand that held the needle lie loose in her lap.

"It depends on *how* I'm going," she said. "I don't think I want to go jammed up in the steerage, as a soldier's wife. I'm afraid I'm not used to that way."

The boy watched her with bright eyes.

"Would you rather stay over here while I go first?" he asked.

"I would, if that's the only alternative," she replied.

"That's much the wisest. Don't make it any fixed engagement," said Banford. "Leave yourself free to go or not after he's got back and found you a place, Nellie. Anything else is madness, madness."

"Don't you think," said the youth, "we ought to get married before I go—and then go together, or separate, according to how it happens?"

"I think it's a terrible idea," cried Banford.

But the boy was watching March.

"What do you think?" he asked her.

She let her eyes stray vaguely into space.

"Well, I don't know," she said. "I shall have to think about it."

" Why ? " he asked, pertinently.

" Why ? "   She repeated his question in a mocking way, and
looked at him laughing, though her face was pink again.   " I should
think there's plenty of reasons why."

He watched her in silence.   She seemed to have escaped him.   She
had got into league with Banford against him.   There was again
the queer sardonic look about her ;   she would mock stoically at
everything he said or which life offered.

" Of course," he said, " I don't want to press you to do anything
you don't wish to do."

" I should think not, indeed," cried Banford indignantly.

At bedtime Banford said plaintively to March :

" You take my hot bottle up for me, Nellie, will you."

" Yes, I'll do it," said March, with the kind of willing unwilling-
ness she so often showed towards her beloved but uncertain Jill.

The two women went upstairs.   After a time March called from
the top of the stairs :   " Good night, Henry.   I shan't be coming
down.   You'll see to the lamp and the fire, won't you ? "

The next day Henry went about with the cloud on his brow and
his young cub's face shut up tight.   He was cogitating all the time.
He had wanted March to marry him and go back to Canada with
him.   And he had been sure she would do it.   Why he wanted her
he didn't know.   But he did want her.   He had set his mind on her.
And he was convulsed with a youth's fury at being thwarted.   To be
thwarted, to be thwarted !   It made him so furious inside that he
did not know what to do with himself.   But he kept himself in hand.
Because even now things might turn out differently.   She might
come over to him.   Of course she might.   It was her business to do so.

Things drew to a tension again towards evening.   He and Banford
had avoided each other all day.   In fact, Banford went in to the
little town by the 11.20 train.   It was market day.   She arrived back
on the 4.25.   Just as the night was falling Henry saw her little figure
in a dark-blue coat and a dark blue tam-o'-shanter hat crossing the
first meadow from the station.   He stood under one of the wild pear-
trees, with the old dead leaves round his feet.   And he watched the
little blue figure advancing persistently over the rough winter-
ragged meadow.   She had her arms full of parcels, and advanced
slowly, frail thing she was, but with that devilish little certainty which
he so detested in her.   He stood invisible under the pear-tree,
watching her every step.   And if looks could have affected her, she
would have felt a log of iron on each of her ankles as she made her
way forward.   " You're a nasty little thing, you are," he was saying

softly, across the distance. " You're a nasty little thing. I hope
you'll be paid back for all the harm you've done me for nothing. I
hope you will—you nasty little thing. I hope you'll have to pay for it.
You will, if wishes are anything. You nasty little creature that you are."

She was toiling slowly up the slope. But if she had been slipping
back at every step towards the Bottomless Pit, he would not have
gone to help her with her parcels. Aha, there went March, striding
with her long, land stride in her breeches and her short tunic !
Striding downhill at a great pace, and even running a few steps now
and then, in her great solicitude and desire to come to the rescue of
the little Banford. The boy watched her with rage in his heart. See
her leap a ditch, and run, run as if a house was on fire, just to get to
that creeping, dark little object down there ! So, the Banford just
stood still and waited. And March strode up and took *all* the parcels
except a bunch of yellow chrysanthemums. These the Banford still
carried—yellow chrysanthemums !

" Yes, you look well, don't you," he said softly into the dusk air.
" You look well, pottering up there with a bunch of flowers, you do.
I'd make you eat them for your tea, if you hug them so tight. And
I'd give them you for breakfast again, I would. I'd give you
flowers. Nothing but flowers."

He watched the progress of the two women. He could hear their
voices : March always outspoken and rather scolding in her tenderness, Banford murmuring rather vaguely. They were evidently good
friends. He could not hear what they said till they came to the
fence of the home meadow, which they must climb. Then he saw
March manfully climbing over the bars with all her packages in her
arms, and on the still air he heard Banford's fretful :

" Why don't you let me help you with the parcels ? " She had a
queer, plaintive hitch in her voice. Then came March's robust
and reckless :

" Oh, I can manage. Don't you bother about me. You've all
you can do to get yourself over."

" Yes, that's all very well," said Banford fretfully. " You say,
Don't you bother about me, and then all the while you feel injured
because nobody thinks of you."

" When do I feel injured ? " said March.

" Always. You always feel injured. Now you're feeling injured
because I won't have that boy to come and live on the farm."

" I'm not feeling injured at all," said March.

" I know you are. When he's gone you'll sulk over it. I know you
will."

" Shall I ? " said March. " We'll see."

" Yes, we *shall* see, unfortunately. I can't think how you can make yourself so cheap. I can't *imagine* how you can lower yourself like it."

" I haven't lowered myself," said March.

" I don't know what you call it, then. Letting a boy like that come so cheeky and impudent and make a mug of you. I don't know what you think of yourself. How much respect do you think he's going to have for you afterwards ? My word, I wouldn't be in your shoes, if you married him."

" Of course you wouldn't. My boots are a good bit too big for you, and not half dainty enough," said March, with rather a miss-fire sarcasm.

" I thought you had too much pride, really I did. A woman's got to hold herself high, especially with a youth like that. Why, he's impudent. Even the way he forced himself on us at the start."

" We asked him to stay," said March.

" Not till he'd almost forced us to. And then he's so cocky and self-assured. My word, he puts my back up. I simply can't imagine how you can let him treat you so cheaply."

" I don't let him treat me cheaply," said March. " Don't you worry yourself, nobody's going to treat me cheaply. And even you aren't, either." She had a tender defiance, and a certain fire in her voice.

" Yes, it's sure to come back to me," said Banford bitterly. " That's always the end of it. I believe you only do it to spite me."

They went now in silence up the steep, grassy slope and over the brow, through the gorse-bushes. On the other side of the hedge the boy followed in the dusk, at some little distance. Now and then, through the huge ancient hedge of hawthorn, risen into trees, he saw the two dark figures creeping up the hill. As he came to the top of the slope he saw the homestead dark in the twilight, with a huge old pear-tree leaning from the near gable, and a little yellow light twinkling in the small side windows of the kitchen. He heard the clink of the latch and saw the kitchen door open into light as the two women went indoors. So, they were at home.

And so !—this was what they thought of him. It was rather in his nature to be a listener, so he was not at all surprised whatever he heard. The things people said about him always missed him person-ally. He was only rather surprised at the women's way with one another. And he disliked the Banford with an acid dislike. And he felt drawn to the March again. He felt again irresistibly drawn to her. He felt there was a secret bond, a secret thread between him and her, something very exclusive, which shut out everybody else and made him and her possess each other in secret.

He hoped again that she would have him. He hoped with his blood suddenly firing up that she would agree to marry him quite quickly : at Christmas, very likely. Christmas was not far off. He wanted, whatever else happened, to snatch her into a hasty marriage and a consummation with him. Then for the future, they could arrange later. But he hoped it would happen as he wanted it. He hoped that to-night she would stay a little while with him, after Banford had gone upstairs. He hoped he could touch her soft, creamy cheek, her strange, frightened face. He hoped he could look into her dilated, frightened dark eyes, quite near. He hoped he might even put his hand on her bosom and feel her soft breasts under her tunic. His heart beat deep and powerful as he thought of that. He wanted very much to do so. He wanted to make sure of her soft woman's breasts under her tunic. She always kept the brown linen coat buttoned so close up to her throat. It seemed to him like some perilous secret, that her soft woman's breasts must be buttoned up in that uniform. It seemed to him, moreover, that they were so much softer, tenderer, more lovely and lovable, shut up in that tunic, than were the Banford's breasts, under her soft blouses and chiffon dresses. The Banford would have little iron breasts, he said to himself. For all her frailty and fretfulness and delicacy, she would have tiny iron breasts. But March, under her crude, fast, workman's tunic, would have soft, white breasts, white and unseen. So he told himself, and his blood burned.

When he went in to tea, he had a surprise. He appeared at the inner door, his face very ruddy and vivid and his blue eyes shining, dropping his head forward as he came in, in his usual way, and hesitating in the doorway to watch the inside of the room, keenly and cautiously, before he entered. He was wearing a long-sleeved waist-coat. His face seemed extraordinarily like a piece of the out-of-doors come indoors : as holly-berries do. In his second of pause in the doorway he took in the two women sitting at table, at opposite ends, saw them sharply. And to his amazement March was dressed in a dress of dull, green silk crape. His mouth came open in surprise. If she had suddenly grown a moustache he could not have been more surprised.

" Why," he said, " do you wear a dress, then ? "

She looked up, flushing a deep rose colour, and twisting her mouth with a smile, said :

"Of course I do. What else do you expect me to wear, but a dress?"

"A land-girl's uniform, of course," said he.

"Oh," she cried, nonchalant, "that's only for this dirty, mucky work about here."

"Isn't it your proper dress, then?" he said.

"No, not indoors it isn't," she said. But she was blushing all the time as she poured out his tea. He sat down in his chair at table, unable to take his eyes off her. Her dress was a perfectly simple slip of bluey-green crape, with a line of gold stitching round the top and round the sleeves, which came to the elbow. It was cut just plain and round at the top, and showed her white, soft throat. Her arms he knew, strong and firm muscled, for he had often seen her with her sleeves rolled up. But he looked her up and down, up and down.

Banford, at the other end of the table, said not a word, but piggled with the sardine on her plate. He had forgotten her existence. He just simply stared at March, while he ate his bread and margarine in huge mouthfuls, forgetting even his tea.

"Well, I never knew anything make such a difference!" he murmured, across his mouthfuls.

"Oh goodness!" cried March, blushing still more. "I might be a pink monkey!"

And she rose quickly to her feet and took the teapot to the fire, to the kettle. And as she crouched on the hearth with her green slip about her, the boy stared more wide-eyed than ever. Through the crape her woman's form seemed soft and womanly. And when she stood up and walked he saw her legs move soft within her modernly short skirt. She had on black silk stockings, and small patent shoes with little gold buckles.

No, she was another being. She was something quite different. Seeing her always in the hard-cloth breeches, wide on the hips, buttoned on the knee, strong as armour, and in the brown puttees and thick boots, it had never occurred to him that she had a woman's legs and feet. Now it came upon him. She had a woman's soft, skirted legs, and she was accessible. He blushed to the roots of his hair, shoved his nose in his tea-cup and drank his tea with a little noise that made Banford simply squirm: and strangely, suddenly he felt a man, no longer a youth. He felt a man, with all a man's grave weight of responsibility. A curious quietness and gravity came over his soul. He felt a man, quiet, with a little of the heaviness of male destiny upon him.

She was soft and accessible in her dress. The thought went home in him like an everlasting responsibility.

" Oh, for goodness' sake, say something, somebody," cried Banford fretfully. " It might be a funeral." The boy looked at her, and she could not bear his face.

"A funeral !" said March, with a twisted smile. "Why, that breaks my dream."

Suddenly she had thought of Banford in the wood-box for a coffin.

" What, have you been dreaming of a wedding ? " said Banford sarcastically.

" Must have been," said March.

" Whose wedding ? " asked the boy.

" I can't remember," said March.

She was shy and rather awkward that evening, in spite of the fact that, wearing a dress, her bearing was much more subdued than in her uniform. She felt unpeeled and rather exposed. She felt almost improper.

They talked desultorily about Henry's departure next morning, and made the trivial arrangement. But of the matter on their minds, none of them spoke. They were rather quiet and friendly this evening ; Banford had practically nothing to say. But inside herself she seemed still, perhaps kindly.

At nine o'clock March brought in the tray with the everlasting tea and a little cold meat which Banford had managed to procure. It was the last supper, so Banford did not want to be disagreeable. She felt a bit sorry for the boy, and felt she must be as nice as she could.

He wanted her to go to bed. She was usually the first. But she sat on in her chair under the lamp, glancing at her book now and then, and staring into the fire. A deep silence had come into the room. It was broken by March asking, in a rather small tone :

" What time is it, Jill ? "

" Five past ten," said Banford, looking at her wrist.

And then not a sound. The boy had looked up from the book he was holding between his knees. His rather wide, cat-shaped face had its obstinate look, his eyes were watchful.

" What about bed ? " said March at last.

" I'm ready when you are," said Banford.

" Oh, very well," said March. " I'll fill your bottle."

She was as good as her word. When the hot-water bottle was ready, she lit a candle and went upstairs with it. Banford remained in her chair, listening acutely. March came downstairs again.

" There you are, then," she said. " Are you going up ? "

" Yes, in a minute," said Banford. But the minute passed, and she sat on in her chair under the lamp.

Henry, whose eyes were shining like a cat's as he watched from under his brows, and whose face seemed wider, more chubbed and cat-like with unalterable obstinacy, now rose to his feet to try his throw.

" I think I'll go and look if I can see the she-fox," he said. " She may be creeping round. Won't you come as well for a minute, Nellie, and see if we see anything ? "

" Me ! " cried March, looking up with her startled, wondering face.

" Yes. Come on," he said. It was wonderful how soft and warm and coaxing his voice could be, how near. The very sound of it made Banford's blood boil. " Come on for a minute," he said, looking down into her uplifted, unsure face.

And she rose to her feet as if drawn up by his young, ruddy face that was looking down on her.

" I should think you're never going out at this time of night, Nellie ! " cried Banford.

" Yes, just for a minute," said the boy, looking round on her, and speaking with an odd, sharp yelp in his voice.

March looked from one to the other, as if confused, vague. Banford rose to her feet for battle.

" Why, it's ridiculous. It's bitter cold. You'll catch your death in that thin frock. And in those slippers. You're not going to do any such thing."

There was a moment's pause. Banford turtled up like a little fighting cock, facing March and the boy.

" Oh, I don't think you need worry yourself," he replied. " A moment under the stars won't do anybody any damage. I'll get the rug off the sofa in the dining-room. You're coming, Nellie."

His voice had so much anger and contempt and fury in it as he spoke to Banford : and as much tenderness and proud authority as he spoke to March, that the latter answered :

" Yes, I'm coming."

And she turned with him to the door.

Banford, standing there in the middle of the room, suddenly burst into a long wail and a spasm of sobs. She covered her face with her poor, thin hands, and her thin shoulders shook in an agony of weeping. March looked back from the door.

" Jill ! " she cried in a frantic tone, like someone just coming awake. And she seemed to start towards her darling.

But the boy had March's arm in his grip, and she could not move. She did not know why she could not move. It was as in a dream when the heart strains and the body cannot stir.

"Never mind," said the boy softly. "Let her cry. Let her cry. She will have to cry sooner or later. And the tears will relieve her feelings. They will do her good."

So he drew March slowly through the doorway. But her last look was back to the poor little figure which stood in the middle of the room with covered face and thin shoulders shaken with bitter weeping.

In the dining-room he picked up the rug and said :

"Wrap yourself up in this."

She obeyed—and they reached the kitchen door, he holding her soft and firm by the arm, though she did not know it. When she saw the night outside she started back.

"I must go back to Jill," she said. "I *must!* Oh yes, I must."

Her tone sounded final. The boy let go of her and she turned indoors. But he seized her again and arrested her.

"Wait a minute," he said. "Wait a minute. Even if you go, you're not going yet."

"Leave go ! Leave go ! " she cried. "My place is at Jill's side. Poor little thing, she's sobbing her heart out."

"Yes," said the boy bitterly. "And your heart too, and mine as well."

"Your heart ? " said March. He still gripped her and detained her.

"Isn't it as good as her heart ? " he said. "Or do you think it's not ? "

"Your heart ? " she said again, incredulous.

"Yes, mine ! Mine ! Do you think I haven't *got* a heart ? " And with his hot grasp he took her hand and pressed it under his left breast. "There's my heart," he said, "if you don't believe in it."

It was wonder which made her attend. And then she felt the deep, heavy, powerful stroke of his heart, terrible, like something from beyond. It was like something from beyond, something awful from outside, signalling to her. And the signal paralysed her. It beat upon her very soul, and made her helpless. She forgot Jill. She could not think of Jill any more. She could not think of her. That terrible signalling from outside !

The boy put his arm round her waist.

"Come with me," he said gently. "Come and let us say what we've got to say."

And he drew her outside, closed the door. And she went with him

darkly down the garden path. That he should have a beating heart !
And that he should have his arm round her, outside the blanket !
She was too confused to think who he was or what he was.

He took her to a dark corner of the shed, where there was a tool-
box with a lid, long and low.

" We'll sit here a minute," he said.

And obediently she sat down by his side.

" Give me your hand," he said.

She gave him both her hands, and he held them between his own.
He was young, and it made him tremble.

" You'll marry me. You'll marry me before I go back, won't
you ? " he pleaded.

" Why, aren't we both a pair of fools ? " she said.

He had put her in the corner, so that she should not look out and
see the lighted window of the house, across the dark yard and
garden. He tried to keep her all there inside the shed with him.

" In what way a pair of fools ? " he said. " If you go back to
Canada with me, I've got a job and a good wage waiting for me,
and it's a nice place, near the mountains. Why shouldn't you marry
me ? Why shouldn't we marry ? I should like to have you there
with me. I should like to feel I'd got somebody there, at the back
of me, all my life."

" You'd easily find somebody else who'd suit you better," she said.

" Yes, I might easily find another girl. I know I could. But not
one I really wanted. I've never met one I really wanted, for good.
You see, I'm thinking of all my life. If I marry, I want to feel it's
for all my life. Other girls : well, they're just girls, nice enough to
go a walk with now and then. Nice enough for a bit of play. But
when I think of my life, then I should be very sorry to have to marry
one of them, I should indeed."

" You mean they wouldn't make you a good wife."

" Yes, I mean that. But I don't mean they wouldn't do their duty
by me. I mean—I don't know what I mean. Only when I think
of my life, and of you, then the two things go together."

" And what if they didn't ? " she said, with her odd, sardonic
touch.

" Well, I think they would."

They sat for some time silent. He held her hands in his, but he
did not make love to her. Since he had realized that she was a
woman, and vulnerable, accessible, a certain heaviness had possessed
his soul. He did not want to make love to her. He shrank from any
such performance, almost with fear. She was a woman, and vulner-

able, accessible to him finally, and he held back from that which was ahead, almost with dread. It was a kind of darkness he knew he would enter finally, but of which he did not want as yet even to think. She was the woman, and he was responsible for the strange vulnerability he had suddenly realized in her.

" No," she said at last, " I'm a fool. I know I'm a fool."

" What for ? " he asked.

" To go on with this business."

" Do you mean me ? " he asked.

" No, I mean myself. I'm making a fool of myself, and a big one."

" Why, because you don't want to marry me, really ? "

" Oh, I don't know whether I'm against it, as a matter of fact. That's just it. I don't know."

He looked at her in the darkness, puzzled. He did not in the least know what she meant.

" And don't you know whether you like to sit here with me this minute, or not ? " he asked.

" No, I don't really. I don't know whether I wish I was somewhere else, or whether I like being here. I don't know, really."

" Do you wish you were with Miss Banford ? Do you wish you'd gone to bed with her ? " he asked, as a challenge.

She waited a long time before she answered :

" No," she said at last. " I don't wish that."

" And do you think you would spend all your life with her— when your hair goes white, and you are old ? " he said.

" No," she said, without much hesitation. " I don't see Jill and me two old women together."

" And don't you think, when I'm an old man and you're an old woman, we might be together still, as we are now ? " he said.

" Well, not as we are now," she replied. " But I could imagine— no, I can't. I can't imagine you an old man. Besides, it's dreadful !"

" What, to be an old man ? "

" Yes, of course."

" Not when the time comes," he said. " But it hasn't come. Only it will. And when it does, I should like to think you'd be there as well."

" Sort of old age pensions," she said drily.

Her kind of witless humour always startled him. He never knew what she meant. Probably she didn't quite know herself.

" No," he said, hurt.

" I don't know why you harp on old age," she said. " I'm not ninety."

" Did anybody ever say you were ? " he asked, offended.

They were silent for some time, pulling different ways in the silence.

" I don't want you to make fun of me," he said.

" Don't you ? " she replied, enigmatic.

" No, because just this minute I'm serious. And when I'm serious, I believe in not making fun of it."

" You mean nobody else must make fun of you," she replied.

" Yes, I mean that. And I mean I don't believe in making fun of it myself. When it comes over me so that I'm serious, then— there it is, I don't want it to be laughed at."

She was silent for some time. Then she said, in a vague, almost pained voice :

" No, I'm not laughing at you."

A hot wave rose in his heart.

" You believe me, do you ? " he asked.

" Yes, I believe you," she replied, with a twang of her old tired nonchalance, as if she gave in because she was tired. But he didn't care. His heart was hot and clamorous.

" So you agree to marry me before I go ?—perhaps at Christmas ? "

" Yes, I agree."

" There ! " he exclaimed. " That's settled it."

And he sat silent, unconscious, with all the blood burning in all his veins, like fire in all the branches and twigs of him. He only pressed her two hands to his chest, without knowing. When the curious passion began to die down, he seemed to come awake to the world.

" We'll go in, shall we ? " he said : as if he realized it was cold.

She rose without answering.

" Kiss me before we go, now you've said it," he said.

And he kissed her gently on the mouth, with a young, frightened kiss. It made her feel so young, too, and frightened, and wondering : and tired, tired, as if she were going to sleep.

They went indoors. And in the sitting-room, there, crouched by the fire like a queer little witch, was Banford. She looked round with reddened eyes as they entered, but did not rise. He thought she looked frightening, unnatural, crouching there and looking round at them. Evil he thought her look was, and he crossed his fingers.

Banford saw the ruddy, elate face of the youth : he seemed strangely tall and bright and looming. And March had a delicate look on her face ; she wanted to hide her face, to screen it, to let it not be seen.

"You've come at last," said Banford uglily.

"Yes, we've come," said he.

"You've been long enough for anything," she said.

"Yes, we have. We've settled it. We shall marry as soon as possible," he replied.

"Oh, you've settled it, have you! Well, I hope you won't live to repent it," said Banford.

"I hope so too," he replied.

"Are you going to bed *now*, Nellie?" said Banford.

"Yes, I'm going now."

"Then for goodness' sake come along."

March looked at the boy. He was glancing with his very bright eyes at her and at Banford. March looked at him wistfully. She wished she could stay with him. She wished she had married him already, and it was all over. For oh, she felt suddenly so safe with him. She felt so strangely safe and peaceful in his presence. If only she could sleep in his shelter, and not with Jill. She felt afraid of Jill. In her dim, tender state, it was agony to have to go with Jill and sleep with her. She wanted the boy to save her. She looked again at him.

And he, watching with bright eyes, divined something of what she felt. It puzzled and distressed him that she must go with Jill.

"I shan't forget what you've promised," he said, looking clear into her eyes, right into her eyes, so that he seemed to occupy all her self with his queer, bright look.

She smiled to him, faintly, gently. She felt safe again—safe with him.

But in spite of all the boy's precautions, he had a set-back. The morning he was leaving the farm he got March to accompany him to the market-town, about six miles away, where they went to the registrar and had their names stuck up as two people who were going to marry. He was to come at Christmas, and the wedding was to take place then. He hoped in the spring to be able to take March back to Canada with him, now the war was really over. Though he was so young, he had saved some money.

"You never have to be without *some* money at the back of you, if you can help it," he said.

So she saw him off in the train that was going West: his camp was on Salisbury Plain. And with big, dark eyes she watched him go, and it seemed as if everything real in life was retreating as the train retreated with his queer, chubby, ruddy face, that seemed so broad across the cheeks, and which never seemed to change its expression, save when a cloud of sulky anger hung on the brow, or the bright eyes fixed themselves in their stare. This was what happened now. He leaned there out of the carriage window as the train drew off, saying good-bye and staring back at her, but his face quite unchanged. There was no emotion on his face. Only his eyes tightened and became fixed and intent in their watching like a cat's when suddenly she sees something and stares. So the boy's eyes stared fixedly as the train drew away, and she was left feeling intensely forlorn. Failing his physical presence, she seemed to have nothing of him. And she had nothing of anything. Only his face was fixed in her mind : the full, ruddy, unchanging cheeks, and the straight snout of a nose, and the two eyes staring above. All she could remember was how he suddenly wrinkled his nose when he laughed, as a puppy does when he is playfully growling. But him, himself, and what he was—she knew nothing, she had nothing of him when he left her.

On the ninth day after he had left her he received this letter.

" DEAR HENRY,

I have been over it all again in my mind, this business of me and you, and it seems to me impossible. When you aren't there I see what I fool I am. When you are there you seem to blind me to things as they actually are. You make me see things all unreal, and I don't know what. Then when I am alone again with Jill I seem to come to my own senses and realize what a fool I am making of myself, and how I am treating you unfairly. Because it must be unfair to you for me to go on with this affair when I can't feel in my heart that I really love you. I know people talk a lot of stuff and nonsense about love, and I don't want to do that. I want to keep to plain facts and act in a sensible way. And that seems to me what I'm not doing. I don't see on what grounds I am going to marry you. I know I am not head over heels in love with you, as I have fancied myself to be with fellows when I was a young fool of a girl. You are an absolute stranger to me, and it seems to me you will always be one. So on what grounds am I going to marry you ? When I think of Jill, she is ten times more real to me. I know her and I'm awfully fond of her, and I hate myself for a beast if I ever hurt her little finger. We have a life together. And even if it can't last for ever, it is a life while it does last. And it might last as long as either of us lives. Who knows how long we've got to live ? She is a delicate little thing, perhaps nobody but me knows how delicate. And as for me, I feel I might fall down the well any day. What I don't seem to see at all is you. When I think of what I've been and what I've done with you, I'm afraid I am a few screws loose. I should be sorry to think that softening of the brain is setting in so soon, but that is what it seems like. You are such an absolute stranger, and so different from what I'm used to, and we don't seem to have a thing in common. As for love, the very word seems impossible. I know what love means even in Jill's case, and I know that in this affair with you it's an absolute impossibility. And then going to Canada. I'm sure I must have been clean off my chump when I promised such a thing. It makes me feel fairly frightened of myself. I feel I might do something really silly, that I wasn't responsible for—and end my days in a lunatic asylum. You may think that's all I'm fit for after the way I've gone on, but it isn't a very nice thought for me. Thank goodness Jill is here, and her being here makes me feel sane again, else I don't know what I might do ; I might have an accident with the gun one evening. I love Jill, and she makes me feel safe and sane, with her loving anger against me for being such a fool. Well, what I want to say is, won't you let us cry the whole thing off ? I can't marry you, and really, I won't do such a thing if it seems to me wrong. It is all a great mistake. I've made a complete fool of myself, and all I can do is to apologize to you and ask you please to forget it, and please to take no further notice of me. Your fox skin is nearly ready, and seems all right. I will post it to you if you will let me know if this address is still right, and if you will accept my apology for the awful and lunatic way I have behaved with you, and then let the matter rest.

Jill sends her kindest regards. Her mother and father are staying with us over Christmas.

Yours very sincerely,

ELLEN MARCH."

The boy read this letter in camp as he was cleaning his kit. He set his teeth, and for a moment went almost pale, yellow round the eyes with fury. He said nothing and saw nothing and felt nothing but a livid rage that was quite unreasoning. Balked ! Balked again ! Balked ! He wanted the woman, he had fixed like doom upon having her. He felt that was his doom, his destiny, and his reward, to have this woman. She was his heaven and hell on earth, and he would have none elsewhere. Sightless with rage and thwarted madness he got through the morning. Save that in his mind he was lurking and scheming towards an issue, he would have committed some insane act. Deep in himself he felt like roaring and howling and gnashing his teeth and breaking things. But he was too intelligent. He knew society was on top of him, and he must scheme. So with his teeth bitten together, and his nose curiously slightly lifted, like some creature that is vicious, and his eyes fixed and staring, he went through the morning's affairs drunk with anger and suppression. In his mind was one thing—Banford. He took no heed of all March's outpouring : none. One thorn rankled, stuck in his mind. Banford. In his mind, in his soul, in his whole being, one thorn rankling to insanity. And he would have to get it out. He would have to get the thorn of Banford out of his life, if he died for it.

With this one fixed idea in his mind, he went to ask for twenty-four hours' leave of absence. He knew it was not due to him. His consciousness was supernaturally keen. He knew where he must go—he must go to the captain. But how could he get at the captain ? In that great camp of wooden huts and tents he had no idea where his captain was.

But he went to the officers' canteen. There was his captain standing talking with three other officers. Henry stood in the doorway at attention.

" May I speak to Captain Berryman ? " The captain was Cornish like himself.

" What do you want ? " called the captain.

" May I speak to you, Captain ? "

" What do you want ? " replied the captain, not stirring from among his group of fellow-officers.

Henry watched his superior for a minute without speaking.

" You won't refuse me, sir, will you ? " he asked gravely.

" It depends what it is."

" Can I have twenty-four hours' leave ? "

" No, you've no business to ask."

" I know I haven't. But I must ask you."

" You've had your answer."

" Don't send me away, Captain."

There was something strange about the boy as he stood there so everlasting in the doorway. The Cornish captain felt the strangeness at once, and eyed him shrewdly.

" Why, what's afoot ? " he said, curious.

" I'm in trouble about something. I must go to Blewbury," said the boy.

" Blewbury, eh ? After the girls ? "

" Yes, it is a woman, Captain." And the boy, as he stood there with his head reaching forward a little, went suddenly terribly pale, or yellow, and his lips seemed to give off pain. The captain saw and paled a little also. He turned aside.

"Go on, then," he said. "But for God's sake don't cause any trouble of any sort."

"I won't, Captain, thank you."

He was gone. The captain, upset, took a gin and bitters. Henry managed to hire a bicycle. It was twelve o'clock when he left the camp. He had sixty miles of wet and muddy cross-roads to ride. But he was in the saddle and down the road without a thought of food.

At the farm, March was busy with a work she had had some time in hand. A bunch of Scotch fir-trees stood at the end of the open shed, on a little bank where ran the fence between two of the gorse-shaggy meadows. The furthest of these trees was dead—it had died in the summer, and stood with all its needles brown and sere in the air. It was not a very big tree. And it was absolutely dead. So March determined to have it, although they were not allowed to cut any of the timber. But it would make such splendid firing, in these days of scarce fuel.

She had been giving a few stealthy chops at the trunk for a week or more, every now and then hacking away for five minutes, low down, near the ground, so no one should notice. She had not tried the saw, it was such hard work, alone. Now the tree stood with a great yawning gap in his base, perched as it were on one sinew, and ready to fall. But he did not fall.

It was late in the damp December afternoon, with cold mists creeping out of the woods and up the hollows, and darkness waiting to sink in from above. There was a bit of yellowness where the sun was fading away beyond the low woods of the distance. March took her axe and went to the tree. The small thud-thud of her blows resounded rather ineffectual about the wintry homestead. Banford came out wearing her thick coat, but with no hat on her head, so that her thin, bobbed hair blew on the uneasy wind that sounded in the pines and in the wood.

"What I'm afraid of," said Banford, "is that it will fall on the shed and we sh'll have another job repairing that."

"Oh, I don't think so," said March, straightening herself, and wiping her arm over her hot brow. She was flushed red, her eyes were very wide-open and queer, her upper lip lifted away from her two white, front teeth with a curious, almost rabbit-look.

A little stout man in a black overcoat and a bowler hat came pottering across the yard. He had a pink face and a white beard and smallish, pale-blue eyes. He was not very old, but nervy, and he walked with little short steps.

"What do you think, father?" said Banford. "Don't you think it might hit the shed in falling?"

"Shed, no!" said the old man. "Can't hit the shed. Might as well say the fence."

"The fence doesn't matter," said March, in her high voice.

"Wrong as usual, am I!" said Banford, wiping her straying hair from her eyes.

The tree stood as it were on one spelch of itself, leaning, and creaking in the wind. It grew on the bank of a little dry ditch between the two meadows. On the top of the bank straggled one fence, running to the bushes uphill. Several trees clustered there in the corner of the field near the shed and near the gate which led into the yard. Towards this gate, horizontal across the weary meadows, came the grassy, rutted approach from the high road. There trailed another ricketty fence, long split poles joining the short, thick, wide-apart uprights. The three people stood at the back of the tree, in the corner of the shed meadow, just above the yard gate. The house, with its two gables and its porch, stood tidy in a little grassed garden across the yard. A little, stout, rosy-faced woman in a little red woollen shoulder shawl had come and taken her stand in the porch.

"Isn't it down yet?" she cried, in a high little voice.

"Just thinking about it," called her husband. His tone towards the two girls was always rather mocking and satirical. March did not want to go on with her hitting while he was there. As for him, he wouldn't lift a stick from the ground if he could help it, complaining, like his daughter, of rheumatics in his shoulder. So the three stood there a moment silent in the cold afternoon, in the bottom corner near the yard.

They heard the far-off taps of a gate, and craned to look. Away across, on the green horizontal approach, a figure was just swinging on to a bicycle again, and lurching up and down over the grass, approaching.

"Why, it's one of our boys—it's Jack," said the old man.

"Can't be," said Banford.

March craned her head to look. She alone recognized the khaki figure. She flushed, but said nothing.

"No, it isn't Jack, I don't think," said the old man, staring with little round blue eyes under his white lashes.

In another moment the bicycle lurched into sight, and the rider dropped off at the gate. It was Henry, his face wet and red and spotted with mud. He was altogether a muddy sight.

"Oh!" cried Banford, as if afraid. "Why, it's Henry!"

"What!" muttered the old man. He had a thick, rapid, muttering way of speaking, and was slightly deaf. "What? What? Who is it? Who is it, do you say? That young fellow? That young fellow of Nellie's? Oh! Oh!" And the satiric smile came on his pink face and white eyelashes.

Henry, pushing the wet hair off his steaming brow, had caught sight of them and heard what the old man said. His hot, young face seemed to flame in the cold light.

"Oh, are you all there!" he said, giving his sudden, puppy's little laugh. He was so hot and dazed with cycling he hardly knew where he was. He leaned the bicycle against the fence and climbed over into the corner on to the bank, without going into the yard.

"Well, I must say, we weren't expecting *you*," said Banford laconically.

"No, I suppose not," said he, looking at March.

She stood aside, slack, with one knee drooped and the axe resting its head loosely on the ground. Her eyes were wide and vacant, and her upper lip lifted from her teeth in that helpless, fascinated rabbit-look. The moment she saw his glowing, red face it was all over with her. She was as helpless as if she had been bound. The moment she saw the way his head seemed to reach forward.

"Well, who is it? Who is it, anyway?" asked the smiling, satiric old man in his muttering voice.

"Why, Mr. Grenfel, whom you've heard us tell about, father," said Banford coldly.

"Heard you tell about, I should think so. Heard of nothing else practically," muttered the elderly man, with his queer little jeering smile on his face. "How do you do," he added, suddenly reaching out his hand to Henry.

The boy shook hands just as startled. Then the two men fell apart.

"Cycled over from Salisbury Plain, have you?" asked the old man.

"Yes."

"Hm! Longish ride. How long d'it take you, eh? Some time, eh? Several hours, I suppose."

"About four."

"Eh? Four! Yes, I should have thought so. When are you going back, then?"

"I've got till to-morrow evening."

" Till to-morrow evening, eh? Yes. Hm! Girls weren't expecting you, were they? "

And the old man turned his pale-blue, round little eyes under their white lashes mockingly towards the girls. Henry also looked round. He had become a little awkward. He looked at March, who was still staring away into the distance as if to see where the cattle were. Her hand was on the pommel of the axe, whose head rested loosely on the ground.

" What were you doing there? " he asked in his soft, courteous voice. " Cutting a tree down? "

March seemed not to hear, as if in a trance.

" Yes," said Banford. " We've been at it for over a week."

" Oh! And have you done it all by yourselves then? "

" Nellie's done it all, I've done nothing," said Banford.

" Really! You must have worked quite hard," he said, addressing himself in a curious gentle tone direct to March. She did not answer, but remained half averted, staring away towards the woods above as if in a trance.

" *Nellie!* " cried Banford sharply. " Can't you answer? "

" What—me? " cried March, starting round, and looking from one to the other. " Did anyone speak to me? "

" Dreaming! " muttered the old man, turning aside to smile. " Must be in love, eh, dreaming in the day-time! "

" Did you say anything to me? " said March, looking at the boy as from a strange distance, her eyes wide and doubtful, her face delicately flushed.

" I said you must have worked hard at the tree," he replied courteously.

" Oh that! Bit by bit. I thought it would have come down by now."

" I'm thankful it hasn't come down in the night, to frighten us to death," said Banford.

" Let me just finish it for you, shall I? " said the boy.

March slanted the axe-shaft in his direction.

" Would you like to? " she said.

" Yes, if you wish it," he said.

" Oh, I'm thankful when the thing's down, that's all," she replied, nonchalant.

" Which way is it going to fall? " said Banford. " Will it hit the shed? "

" No, it won't hit the shed," he said. " I should think it will fall there—quite clear. Though it might gave a twist and catch the fence."

" Catch the fence ! " cried the old man. " What, catch the fence ! When it's leaning at that angle ? Why, it's further off than the shed. It won't catch the fence."

" No," said Henry, " I don't suppose it will. It has plenty of room to fall quite clear, and I suppose it will fall clear."

" Won't tumble backwards on top of *us*, will it ? " asked the old man, sarcastic.

" No, it won't do that," said Henry, taking off his short overcoat and his tunic. " Ducks ! Ducks ! Go back ! "

A line of four brown-speckled ducks led by a brown-and-green drake were stemming away downhill from the upper meadow, coming like boats running on a ruffled sea, cockling their way top speed downwards towards the fence and towards the little group of people, and cackling as excitedly as if they brought news of the Spanish Armada.

" Silly things ! Silly things ! " cried Banford, going forward to turn them off. But they came eagerly towards her, opening their yellow-green beaks and quacking as if they were so excited to say something.

" There's no food. There's nothing here. You must wait a bit," said Banford to them. " Go away. Go away. Go round to the yard."

They didn't go, so she climbed the fence to swerve them round under the gate and into the yard. So off they waggled in an excited string once more, wagging their rumps like the stems of little gondolas, ducking under the bar of the gate. Banford stood on the top of the bank, just over the fence, looking down on the other three.

Henry looked up at her, and met her queer, round-pupilled, weak eyes staring behind her spectacles. He was perfectly still. He looked away, up at the weak, leaning tree. And as he looked into the sky, like a huntsman who is watching a flying bird, he thought to himself : " If the tree falls in just such a way, and spins just so much as it falls, then the branch there will strike her exactly as she stands on top of that bank."

He looked at her again. She was wiping the hair from her brow again, with that perpetual gesture. In his heart he had decided her death. A terrible still force seemed in him, and a power that was just his. If he turned even a hair's breadth in the wrong direction, he would lose the power.

" Mind yourself, Miss Banford," he said. And his heart held perfectly still, in the terrible pure will that she should not move.

" Who, me, mind myself ? " she cried, her father's jeering tone in her voice. " Why, do you think you might hit me with the axe ? "

" No, it's just possible the tree might, though," he answered
soberly. But the tone of his voice seemed to her to imply that he
was only being falsely solicitous, and trying to make her move because
it was his will to move her.

" Absolutely impossible," she said.

He heard her. But he held himself icy still, lest he should lose
his power.

" No, it's just possible. You'd better come down this way."

" Oh, all right. Let us see some crack Canadian tree-felling,"
she retorted.

" Ready, then," he said, taking the axe, looking round to see he
was clear.

There was a moment of pure, motionless suspense, when the world
seemed to stand still. Then suddenly his form seemed to flash up
enormously tall and fearful, he gave two swift, flashing blows, in
immediate succession, the tree was severed, turning slowly, spinning
strangely in the air and coming down like a sudden darkness on the
earth. No one saw what was happening except himself. No one
heard the strange little cry which the Banford gave as the dark end
of the bough swooped down, down on her. No one saw her crouch
a little and receive the blow on the back of the neck. No one saw
her flung outwards and laid, a little twitching heap, at the foot of the
fence. No one except the boy. And he watched with intense bright
eyes, as he would watch a wild goose he had shot. Was it winged,
or dead ? Dead !

Immediately he gave a loud cry. Immediately March gave a wild
shriek that went far, far down the afternoon. And the father started
a strange bellowing sound.

The boy leapt the fence and ran to the figure. The back of the
neck and head was a mass of blood, of horror. He turned it over.
The body was quivering with little convulsions. But she was dead
really. He knew it, that it was so. He knew it in his soul and his
blood. The inner necessity of his life was fulfilling itself, it was he
who was to live. The thorn was drawn out of his bowels. So he
put her down gently. She was dead.

He stood up. March was standing there petrified and absolutely
motionless. Her face was dead white, her eyes big black pools. The
old man was scrambling horribly over the fence.

" I'm afraid it's killed her," said the boy.

The old man was making curious, blubbering noises as he huddled
over the fence. " What ! " cried March, starting electric.

" Yes, I'm afraid," repeated the boy.

March was coming forward. The boy was over the fence before she reached it.

" What do you say, killed her ? " she asked in a sharp voice.

" I'm afraid so," he answered softly.

She went still whiter, fearful. The two stood facing one another. Her black eyes gazed on him with the last look of resistance. And then in a last agonized failure she began to grizzle, to cry in a shivery little fashion of a child that doesn't want to cry, but which is beaten from within, and gives that little first shudder of sobbing which is not yet weeping, dry and fearful.

He had won. She stood there absolutely helpless, shuddering her dry sobs and her mouth trembling rapidly. And then, as in a child, with a little crash came the tears and the blind agony of sightless weeping. She sank down on the grass, and sat there with her hands on her breast and her face lifted in sightless, convulsed weeping. He stood above her, looking down on her, mute, pale, and everlasting seeming. He never moved, but looked down on her. And among all the torture of the scene, the torture of his own heart and bowels, he was glad, he had won.

After a long time he stooped to her and took her hands.

" Don't cry," he said softly. " Don't cry."

She looked up at him with tears running from her eyes, a senseless look of helplessness and submission. So she gazed on him as if sightless, yet looking up to him. She would never leave him again. He had won her. And he knew it and was glad, because he wanted her for his life. His life must have her. And now he had won her. It was what his life must have.

But if he had won her, he had not yet got her. They were married at Christmas as he had planned, and he got again ten days' leave. They went to Cornwall, to his own village, on the sea. He realized that it was awful for her to be at the farm any more.

But though she belonged to him, though she lived in his shadow, as if she could not be away from him, she was not happy. She did not want to leave him : and yet she did not feel free with him. Everything around her seemed to watch her, seemed to press on her. He had won her, he had her with him, she was his wife. And she—she belonged to him, she knew it. But she was not glad. And he was still foiled. He realized that though he was married to her and possessed her in every possible way, apparently, and though she *wanted* him to possess her, she wanted it, she wanted nothing else, now, still he did not quite succeed.

Something was missing. Instead of her soul swaying with new

life, it seemed to droop, to bleed, as if it were wounded. She would sit for a long time with her hand in his, looking away at the sea. And in her dark, vacant eyes was a sort of wound, and her face looked a little peaked. If he spoke to her, she would turn to him with a faint new smile, the strange, quivering little smile of a woman who has died in the old way of love, and can't quite rise to the new way. She still felt she ought to *do* something, to strain herself in some direction. And there was nothing to do, and no direction in which to strain herself. And she could not quite accept the submergence which his new love put upon her. If she was in love, she ought to exert herself, in some way, loving. She felt the weary need of our day to *exert* herself in love. But she knew that in fact she must no more exert herself in love. He would not have the love which exerted itself towards him. It made his brow go black. No, he wouldn't let her exert her love towards him. No, she had to be passive, to acquiesce, and to be submerged under the surface of love. She had to be like the seaweeds she saw as she peered down from the boat, swaying forever delicately under water, with all their delicate fibrils put tenderly out upon the flood, sensitive, utterly sensitive and receptive within the shadowy sea, and never, never rising and looking forth above water while they lived. Never. Never looking forth from the water until they died, only then washing, corpses, upon the surface. But while they lived, always submerged, always beneath the wave. Beneath the wave they might have powerful roots, stronger than iron ; they might be tenacious and dangerous in their soft waving within the flood. Beneath the water they might be stronger, more indestructible than resistant oak trees are on land. But it was always under-water, always under-water. And she, being a woman, must be like that.

And she had been so used to the very opposite. She had had to take all the thought for love and for life, and all the responsibility. Day after day she had been responsible for the coming day, for the coming year : for her dear Jill's health and happiness and well-being. Verily, in her own small way, she had felt herself responsible for the well-being of the world. And this had been her great stimu-lant, this grand feeling that, in her own small sphere, she was responsible for the well-being of the world.

And she had failed. She knew that, even in her small way, she had failed. She had failed to satisfy her own feeling of responsibility. It was so difficult. It seemed so grand and easy at first. And the more you tried, the more difficult it became. It had seemed so easy to make one beloved creature happy. And the more you tried, the worse the failure. It was terrible. She had been all her life reaching, reaching, and what she reached for seemed so near, until she had stretched to her utmost limit. And then it was always beyond her.

Always beyond her, vaguely, unrealizably beyond her, and she was left with nothingness at last. The life she reached for, the happiness she reached for, the well-being she reached for all slipped back, became unreal, the further she stretched her hand. She wanted some goal, some finality—and there was none. Always this ghastly reaching, reaching, striving for something that might be just beyond. Even to make Jill happy. She was glad Jill was dead. For she had realized that she could never make her happy. Jill would always be fretting herself thinner and thinner, weaker and weaker. Her pains grew worse instead of less. It would be so for ever. She was glad she was dead.

And if Jill had married a man it would have been just the same. The woman striving, striving to make the man happy, striving within her own limits for the well-being of her world. And always achieving failure. Little, foolish successes in money or in ambition. But at the very point where she most wanted success, in the anguished effort to make some one beloved human being happy and perfect, there the failure was almost catastrophic. You wanted to make your beloved happy, and his happiness seemed always achievable. If only you did just this, that, and the other. And you did this, that, and the other, in all good faith, and every time the failure became a little more ghastly. You could love yourself to ribbons, and strive and strain yourself to the bone, and things would go from bad to worse, bad to worse, as far as happiness went. The awful mistake of happiness.

Poor March, in her goodwill and her responsibility, she had strained herself till it seemed to her that the whole of life and everything was only a horrible abyss of nothingness. The more you reached after the fatal flower of happiness, which trembles so blue and lovely in a crevice just beyond your grasp, the more fearfully you become aware of the ghastly and awful gulf of the precipice below you, into which you will inevitably plunge, as into the bottomless pit, if you reach any further. You pluck flower after flower—it is never *the* flower. The flower itself—its calyx is a horrible gulf, it is the bottomless pit.

That is the whole history of the search for happiness, whether it be your own or somebody else's that you want to win. It ends, and it always ends, in the ghastly sense of the bottomless nothingness into which you will inevitably fall if you strain any further.

And women? What goal can any woman conceive, except happiness? Just happiness, for herself and the whole world. That, and nothing else. And so, she assumes the responsibility, and sets off towards her goal. She can see it there, at the foot of the rainbow. Or she can see it a little way beyond, in the blue distance. Not far, not far.

But the end of the rainbow is a bottomless gulf down which you can fall forever without arriving, and the blue distance is a void pit which can swallow you and all your efforts into its emptiness, and still be no emptier. You and all your efforts. So, the illusion of attainable happiness!

Poor March, she had set off so wonderfully towards the blue goal. And the further and further she had gone, the more fearful had become the realization of emptiness. An agony, an insanity at last.

She was glad it was over. She was glad to sit on the shore and look westwards over the sea, and know the great strain had ended. She would never strain for love and happiness any more. And Jill was safely dead. Poor Jill, poor Jill. It must be sweet to be dead.

For her own part, death was not her destiny. She would have to leave her destiny to the boy. But then, the boy. He wanted more than that. He wanted her to give herself without defences, to sink and become submerged in him. And she—she wanted to sit still, like a woman on the last milestone, and watch. She wanted to see, to know, to understand. She wanted to be alone : with him at her side.

And he! He did not want her to watch any more, to see any more, to understand any more. He wanted to veil her woman's spirit, as Orientals veil the woman's face. He wanted her to commit herself to him, and to put her independent spirit to sleep. He wanted to take away from her all her effort, all that seemed her very *raison d'être*. He wanted to make her submit, yield, blindly pass away out of all her strenuous consciousness. He wanted to take away her consciousness, and make her just his woman. Just his woman.

And she was so tired, so tired, like a child that wants to go to sleep, but which fights against sleep, as if sleep were death. She seemed to stretch her eyes wider in the obstinate effort and tension of keeping awake. She *would* keep awake. She *would* know. She *would* consider and judge and decide. She *would* have the reins of her own life between her own hands. She *would* be an independent woman, to the last. But she was so tired, so tired of everything. And sleep seemed near. And there was such rest in the boy.

Yet there, sitting in a niche of the high, wild cliffs of West Cornwall, looking over the westward sea, she stretched her eyes wider and wider. Away to the West, Canada, America. She *would* know and she *would* see what was ahead. And the boy, sitting beside her, staring down at the gulls, had a cloud between his brows and the strain of discontent in his eyes. He wanted her asleep, at peace in him. He wanted her at peace, asleep in him. And *there* she was, dying with the strain of her own wakefulness. Yet she would not sleep : no, never. Sometimes he thought bitterly that he ought to have left her. He ought never to have killed Banford. He should have left Banford and March to kill one another.

But that was only impatience : and he knew it. He was waiting, waiting to go west. He was aching almost in torment to leave England, to go west, to take March away. To leave this shore ! He believed that as they crossed the seas, as they left this England which he so hated, because in some way it seemed to have stung him with poison, she would go to sleep. She would close her eyes at last, and give in to him.

And then he would have her, and he would have his own life at last. He chafed, feeling he hadn't got his own life. He would never have it till she yielded and slept in him. Then he would have all his own life as a young man and a male, and she would have all her own life as a woman and a female. There would be no more of this awful straining. She would not be a man any more, an independent woman with a man's responsibility. Nay, even the responsibility for her own soul she would have to commit to him. He knew it was so, and obstinately held out against her, waiting for the surrender.

" You'll feel better when once we get over the seas to Canada over there," he said to her as they sat among the rocks on the cliff.

She looked away to the sea's horizon, as if it were not real. Then she looked round at him, with the strained, strange look of a child that is struggling against sleep.

" Shall I ? " she said.

" Yes," he answered quietly.

And her eyelids dropped with the slow motion, sleep weighing them unconscious. But she pulled them open again to say :

" Yes, I may. I can't tell. I can't tell what it will be like over there."

" If only we could go soon ! " he said, with pain in his voice.

" HANNELE ! "

  " Ja—a."

  " Wo bist du ? "

  " Hier."

  " Wo dann ? "

Hannele did not lift her head from her work. She sat in a low chair under a reading-lamp, a basket of coloured silk pieces beside her, and in her hands a doll, or mannikin, which she was dressing. She was doing something to the knee of the mannikin, so that the poor little gentleman flourished head downwards with arms wildly tossed out. And it was not at all seemly, because the doll was a Scotch soldier in tight-fitting tartan trews.

There was a tap at the door, and the same voice, a woman's, calling :

  " Hannele ? "

  " Ja—a ! "

  " Are you here ? Are you alone ? " asked the voice, in German.

  " Yes—come in."

Hannele did not sound very encouraging. She turned round her doll as the door opened, and straightened his coat. A dark-eyed young woman peeped in through the door, with a roguish coyness. She was dressed fashionably for the street, in a thick cape-wrap, and a little black hat pulled down to her ears.

  " Quite, quite alone ! " said the newcomer, in a tone of wonder. " Where is he, then ? "

  " That I don't know," said Hannele.

  " And you sit here alone, and wait for him ? But no ! That I call courage ! Aren't you afraid ? " Mitchka strolled across to her friend.

  " Why shall I be afraid ? " said Hannele curtly.

  " But no ! And what are you doing ? Another puppet ? He is a good one, though ! Ha—ha—ha ! *Him !* It is him ! No—no— that is too beautiful ! No—that is too beautiful, Hannele. It is him—exactly him. Only the trousers."

"He wears those trousers too," said Hannele, standing her doll on her knee. It was a perfect portrait of an officer of a Scottish regiment, slender, delicately made, with a slight, elegant stoop of the shoulders, and close-fitting tartan trousers. The face was beautifully modelled, and a wonderful portrait, dark-skinned, with a little, close-cut, dark moustache, and wide-open dark eyes, and that air of aloofness and perfect diffidence which marks an officer and a gentleman.

Mitchka bent forward, studying the doll. She was a handsome woman with a warm, dark golden skin and clear black eyebrows over her russet-brown eyes.

"No," she whispered to herself, as if awestruck. "That is him. That is him. Only not the trousers. Beautiful, though, the trousers. Has he really such beautiful fine legs?"

Hannele did not answer.

"Exactly him. Just as finished as he is. Just as complete. He is just like that : finished off. Has he seen it?"

"No," said Hannele.

"What will he say, then?" She started. Her quick ear had caught a sound on the stone stairs. A look of fear came to her face. She flew to the door and out of the room, closing the door to behind her.

"Who is it?" her voice was heard calling anxiously down the stairs.

The answer came in German. Mitchka immediately opened the door again and came back to join Hannele.

"Only Martin," she said.

She stood waiting. A man appeared in the doorway—erect, military.

"Ah! Countess Hannele," he said in his quick, precise way, as he stood on the threshold in the distance. "May one come in?"

"Yes, come in," said Hannele.

The man entered with a quick, military step, bowed, and kissed the hand of the woman who was sewing the doll. Then, much more intimately, he touched Mitchka's hand with his lips.

Mitchka meanwhile was glancing round the room. It was a very large attic, with the ceiling sloping and then bending in two handsome movements towards the walls. The light from the dark-shaded reading-lamp fell softly on the huge white-washed vaulting of the ceiling, on the various objects round the walls, and made a brilliant pool of colour where Hannele sat in her soft, red dress, with her basket of silks.

She was a fair woman with dark-blond hair and a beautiful fine skin. Her face seemed luminous, a certain quick gleam of life about it as she looked up at the man. He was handsome, clean-shaven, with very blue eyes strained a little too wide. One could see the war in his face.

Mitchka was wandering round the room, looking at everything, and saying : " Beautiful ! But beautiful ! Such good taste ! A man, and such good taste ! No, they don't need a woman. No, look here, Martin, the Captain Hepburn has arranged all this room himself. Here you have the man. Do you see ? So simple, yet so elegant. He needs no woman."

The room was really beautiful, spacious, pale, soft-lighted. It was heated by a large stove of dark-blue tiles, and had very little furniture save large peasant cupboards or presses of painted wood, and a huge writing table, on which were writing materials and some scientific apparatus and a cactus plant with fine scarlet blossoms. But it was a man's room. Tobacco and pipes were on a little tray, on the pegs in the distance hung military overcoats and belts, and two guns on a bracket. Then there were two telescopes, one mounted on a stand near a window. Various astronomical apparatus lay upon the table.

" And he reads the stars. Only think—he is an astronomer and reads the stars. Queer, queer people, the English ! "

" He is Scottish," said Hannele.

" Yes, Scottish," said Mitchka. " But, you know, I am afraid when I am with him. He is at a closed end. I don't know where I can get to with him. Are you afraid of him, too, Hannele ? Ach, like a closed road ! "

" Why should I be ? "

" Ah, you ! Perhaps you don't know when you should be afraid. But if he were to come and find us here ? No, no—let us go. Let us go, Martin. Come, let us go. I don't want the Captain Hepburn to come and find me in his room. Oh no ! " Mitchka was busily pushing Martin to the door, and he was laughing with the queer, mad laugh in his strained eyes. " Oh no ! I don't like. I don't like it," said Mitchka, trying her English now. She spoke a few sentences prettily. " Oh no, Sir Captain, I don't want that you come. I don't like it, to be here when you come. Oh no. Not at all. I go. I go, Hannele. I go, my Hannele. And you will really stay here and wait for him ? But when will he come ? You don't know ? Oh dear, I don't like it, I don't like it. I do not wait in the man's room. No, no—never—*jamais—jamais, voyez vous*. Ach, you poor Hannele !

And he has got wife and children in England? Nevair! No, nevair shall I wait for him."

She had bustlingly pushed Martin through the door, and settled her wrap and taken a mincing, elegant pose, ready for the street, and waved her hand and made wide, scared eyes at Hannele, and was gone. The Countess Hannele picked up the doll again and began to sew its shoe. What living she now had she earned making these puppets.

But she was restless. She pressed her arms into her lap, as if holding them bent had wearied her. Then she looked at the little clock on his writing table. It was long after dinner-time—why hadn't he come? She sighed rather exasperated. She was tired of her doll.

Putting aside her basket of silks, she went to one of the windows. Outside the stars seemed white, and very near. Below was the dark agglomeration of the roofs of houses, a fume of light came up from beneath the darkness of roofs, and a faint breakage of noise from the town far below. The room seemed high, remote, in the sky.

She went to the table and looked at his letter-clip with letters in it, and at his sealing-wax, and his stamp-box, touching things and moving them a little, just for the sake of the contrast, not really noticing what she touched. Then she took a pencil, and in stiff gothic characters began to write her name—Johanna zu Rassentlow—time after time her own name—and then once, bitterly, curiously, with a curious sharpening of her nose: Alexander Hepburn.

But she threw the pencil down, having no more interest in her writing. She wandered to where the large telescope stood near a further window, and stood for some minutes with her fingers on the barrel, where it was a little brighter from his touching it. Then she drifted restlessly back to her chair. She had picked up her puppet when she heard him on the stairs. She lifted her face and watched as he entered.

"Hello, you there!" he said quietly, as he closed the door behind him. She glanced at him swiftly, but did not move nor answer.

He took off his overcoat, with quick, quiet movements, and went to hang it up on the pegs. She heard his step, and looked again. He was like the doll, a tall, slender, well-bred man in uniform. When he turned, his dark eyes seemed very wide open. His black hair was growing grey at the temples—the first touch.

She was sewing her doll. Without saying anything, he wheeled round the chair from the writing table, so that he sat with his knees almost touching her. Then he crossed one leg over the other. He wore fine tartan socks. His ankles seemed slender and elegant, his brown shoes fitted as if they were part of him. For some moments he watched her as she sat sewing. The light fell on her soft, delicate hair, that was full of strands of gold and of tarnished gold and shadow. She did not look up.

In silence he held out his small, naked-looking brown hand for the doll. On his forearm were black hairs.

She glanced up at him. Curious how fresh and luminous her face looked in contrast to his.

" Do you want to see it ? " she asked, in natural English.

" Yes," he said.

She broke off her thread of cotton and handed him the puppet. He sat with one leg thrown over the other, holding the doll in one hand, and smiling inscrutably with his dark eyes. His hair, parted perfectly on one side, was jet black and glossy.

" You've got me," he said at last, in his amused, melodious voice.

" What ? " she said.

" You've got me," he repeated.

" I don't care," she said.

" What—— You don't care ? " His face broke into a smile. He had an odd way of answering, as if he were only half attending, as if he were thinking of something else.

" You are very late, aren't you ? " she ventured.

" Yes. I am rather late."

" Why are you ? "

" Well, as a matter of fact, I was talking with the Colonel."

" About me ? "

" Yes. It was about you."

She went pale as she sat looking up into his face. But it was impossible to tell whether there was distress on his dark brow or not.

" Anything nasty ? " she said.

" Well, yes. It was rather nasty. Not about you, I mean. But rather awkward for me."

She watched him. But still he said no more.

" What was it ? " she said.

" Oh, well—only what I expected. They seem to know rather too much about you—about you and me, I mean. Not that anybody cares one bit, you know, unofficially. The trouble is, they are apparently going to have to take official notice."

" Why ? "

" Oh, well—it appears my wife has been writing letters to the

Major-General. He is one of her family acquaintances—known her all his life. And I suppose she's been hearing rumours. In fact, I know she has. She said so in her letter to me."

" And what do you say to her then ? "

" Oh, I tell her I'm all right—not to worry."

" You don't expect *that* to stop her worrying, do you ? " she asked.

" Oh, I don't know. Why should she worry ? " he said.

" I think she might have some reason," said Hannele. " You've not seen her for a year. And if she adores you——"

" Oh, I don't think she adores me. I think she quite likes me."

" Do you think you matter as little as that to her ? "

" I don't see why not. Of course she likes to feel *safe* about me."

" But now she doesn't feel safe ? "

" No—exactly. Exactly. That's the point. That's where it is. The Colonel advises me to go home on leave."

He sat gazing with curious bright, dark, unseeing eyes at the doll which he held by one arm. It was an extraordinary likeness of himself, true even to the smooth parting of his hair and his peculiar way of fixing his dark eyes.

" For how long ? " she asked.

" I don't know. For a month," he replied, first vaguely, then definitely.

" For a month ! " She watched him, and seemed to see him fade from her eyes.

" And will you go ? " she asked.

" I don't know. I don't know." His head remained bent, he seemed to muse rather vaguely. " I don't know," he repeated. " I can't make up my mind what I shall do."

" Would you like to go ? " she asked.

He lifted his brows and looked at her. Her heart always melted in her when he looked straight at her with his black eyes, and that curious, bright unseeing look that was more like second sight than direct human vision. She never knew what he saw when he looked at her.

" No," he said simply. " I don't *want* to go. I don't think I've any desire at all to go to England."

" Why not ? " she asked.

" I can't say." Then again he looked at her, and a curious white light seemed to shine on his eyes, as he smiled slowly with his mouth, and said : " I suppose you ought to know, if anybody does."

A glad, half-frightened look came on her face.

" You mean you don't want to leave me ? " she asked, breathless.

" Yes. I suppose that's what I mean."

" But you aren't sure ? "

" Yes, I am, I'm quite sure," he said, and the curious smile lingered on his face, and the strange light shone in his eyes.

" That you don't want to leave me ? " she stammered, looking aside.

" Yes, I'm quite sure I don't want to leave you," he repeated. He had a curious, very melodious Scottish voice. But it was the incomprehensible smile on his face that convinced and frightened her. It was almost a gargoyle smile, a strange, lurking, changeless-seeming grin.

She was frightened, and turned aside her face. When she looked at him again, his face was like a mask, with strange, deep-graven lines and a glossy dark skin and a fixed look—as if carved half grotesque in some glossy stone. His black hair on his smooth, beautifully-shaped head seemed changeless.

" Are you rather tired ? " she asked him.

" Yes, I think I am." He looked at her with black, unseeing eyes, and a mask-like face. Then he glanced aside as if he heard something. Then he rose with his hand on his belt, saying : " I'll take off my belt, and change my coat, if you don't mind."

He walked across the room, unfastening his broad, brown belt. He was in well-fitting, well-cut khaki. He hung up his belt and came back to her wearing an old, light tunic, which he left unbuttoned. He carried his slippers in one hand. When he sat down to unfasten his shoes, she noticed again how black and hairy his forearm was, how naked his brown hand seemed. His hair was black and smooth and perfect on his head, like some close helmet, as he stooped down.

He put on his slippers, carried his shoes aside, and resumed his chair, stretching luxuriously.

" There," he said. " I feel better now." And he looked at her. " Well," he said, " and how are you ? "

" Me ? " she said. " Do I matter ? " She was rather bitter.

" Do you matter ? " he repeated, without noticing her bitterness. " Why, what a question ! Of course you are of the very highest importance. What ? Aren't you ? " And smiling his curious smile —it made her for a moment think of the fixed sadness of monkeys, of those Chinese carved soapstone apes. He put his hand under her chin, and gently drew his finger along her cheek. She flushed deeply.

" But I'm not as important as you, am I ? " she asked defiantly.

" As important as me ! Why, bless you, I'm not important a bit.

I'm not important a bit ! "—the odd, straying sound of his words mystified her. What did he really mean ?

" And I'm even less important than that," she said bitterly.

" Oh no, you're not. Oh no, you're not. You're very important. You're very important indeed, I assure you."

" And your wife ? "—the question came rebelliously. " Your wife ? Isn't she important ? "

" My wife ? My wife ? " he seemed to let the word stray out of him as if he did not quite know what it meant. " Why, yes, I suppose she is important in her own sphere."

" What sphere ? " blurted Hannele, with a laugh.

" Why, her own sphere, of course. Her own house, her own home, and her two children ; that's her sphere."

" And you ?—where do you come in ? "

" At present I don't come in," he said.

" But isn't that just the trouble," said Hannele. " If you have a wife and a home, it's your business to belong to it, isn't it ? "

" Yes, I suppose it is, if I want to," he replied.

" And you *do* want to ? " she challenged.

" No, I don't," he replied.

" Well, then ? " she said.

" Yes, quite," he answered. " I admit it's a dilemma."

" But what will you *do* ? " she insisted.

" Why, I don't know. I don't know yet. I haven't made up my mind what I'm going to do."

" Then you'd better begin to make it up," she said.

" Yes, I know that. I know that."

He rose, and began to walk uneasily up and down the room. But the same vacant darkness was on his brow. He had his hands in his pockets. Hannele sat feeling helpless. She couldn't help being in love with the man : with his hands, with his strange, fascinating physique, with his incalculable presence. She loved the way he put his feet down, she loved the way he moved his legs as he walked, she loved the mould of his loins, she loved the way he dropped his head a little, and the strange, dark vacancy of his brow, his not-thinking. But now his restlessness only made her unhappy. Nothing would come of it. Yet she had driven him to it.

He took his hands out of his pockets and returned to her like a piece of iron returning to a magnet. He sat down again in front of her and put his hands out to her, looking into her face.

" Give me your hands," he said softly, with that strange, mindless, soft, suggestive tone which left her powerless to disobey. " Give me your hands, and let me feel that we are together. Words mean so little. They mean nothing. And all that one thinks and plans doesn't amount to anything. Let me feel that we are together, and I don't care about all the rest."

He spoke in his slow, melodious way, and closed her hands in his. She struggled still for voice.

"But you'll *have* to care about it. You'll *have* to make up your mind. You'll just *have* to," she insisted.

"Yes, I suppose I shall. I suppose I shall. But now that we are together, I won't bother. Now that we are together, let us forget it."

"But when we *can't* forget it any more?"

"Well—then I don't know. But—to-night—it seems to me—we might just as well forget it."

The soft, melodious, straying sound of his voice made her feel helpless. She felt that he never answered her. Words of reply seemed to stray out of him, in the need to say *something*. But he himself never spoke. There he was, a continual blank silence in front of her.

She had a battle with herself. When he put his hand again on her cheek, softly, with the most extraordinary soft half-touch, as a kitten's paw sometimes touches one, like a fluff of living air, then, if it had not been for the magic of that almost indiscernible caress of his hand, she would have stiffened herself and drawn away and told him she could have nothing to do with him, while he was so half-hearted and unsatisfactory. She wanted to tell him these things. But when she began he answered invariably in the same soft, straying voice, that seemed to spin gossamer threads all over her, so that she could neither think nor act nor even feel distinctly. Her soul groaned rebelliously in her. And yet, when he put his hand softly under her chin, and lifted her face and smiled down on her with that gargoyle smile of his—she let him kiss her.

"What are you thinking about to-night?" he said. "What are you thinking about?"

"What did your Colonel say to you, exactly?" she replied, trying to harden her eyes.

"Oh, that!" he answered. "Never mind that. That is of no significance whatever."

"But what *is* of any significance?" she insisted. She almost hated him.

"What is of any significance? Well, nothing to me, outside of this room, at this minute. Nothing in time or space matters to me."

"Yes, *this minute*!" she repeated bitterly. "But then there's the future. *I've* got to live in the future."

" The future ! The future ! The future is used up every day.
The future to me is like a big tangle of black thread. Every morning
you begin to untangle one loose end—and that's your day. And every
evening you break off and throw away what you've untangled, and the
heap is so much less : just one thread less, one day less. That's all
the future matters to me."

" Then nothing matters to you. And I don't matter to you. As
you say, only an end of waste thread," she resisted him.

" No, there you're wrong. You aren't the future to me."

" What am I then ?—the past ? "

" No, not any of those things. You're nothing. As far as all that
goes, you're nothing."

" Thank you," she said sarcastically, " if I'm nothing."

But the very irrelevancy of the man overcame her. He kissed her
with half discernible, dim kisses, and touched her throat. And the
meaningless of him fascinated her and left her powerless. She could
ascribe no meaning to him, none whatever. And yet his mouth,
so strange in kissing, and his hairy forearms, and his slender, beautiful
breast with black hair—it was all like a mystery to her, as if one of the
men from Mars were loving her. And she was heavy and spell-
bound, and she loved the spell that bound her. But also she didn't
love it.

II

Countess zu Rassentlow had a studio in one of the main streets.
She was really a refugee. And nowadays you can be a grand-duke
and a pauper, if you are a refugee. But Hannele was not a pauper,
because she and her friend Mitchka had the studio where they made
these dolls, and beautiful cushions of embroidered coloured wools, and
such-like objects of feminine art. The dolls were quite famous, so
the two women did not starve.

Hannele did not work much in the studio. She preferred to be
alone in her own room, which was another fine attic, not quite so
large as the captain's, under the same roof. But often she went to
the studio in the afternoon, and if purchasers came, then they were
offered a cup of tea.

The Alexander doll was never intended for sale. What made
Hannele take it to the studio one afternoon, we do not know. But
she did so, and stood it on a little bureau. It was a wonderful little
portrait of an officer and gentleman, the physique modelled so that
it made you hold your breath.

" And *that*—that is genius ! " cried Mitchka. " That is a *chef*

d'œuvre ! That is my masterpiece, Hannele. That is really marvellous. And beautiful ! A beautiful man, what ! But no, that is *too*
real. I don't understand how you *dare*. I always thought you were
good, Hannele, so much better-natured than I am. But now you frighten
me. I am afraid you are wicked, do you know. It frightens me to think
that you are wicked. *Aber nein !* But you won't leave him there ? "

" Why not ? " said Hannele, satiric.

Mitchka made big dark eyes of wonder, reproach, and fear.

" But you *must* not," she said.

" Why not ? "

" No, that you *may* not do. You love the man."

" What then ? "

" You can't leave his puppet standing there."

" Why can't I ? "

" But you are really wicked. *Du bist wirklich bös.* Only think !
—and he is an English officer."

" He isn't sacrosanct even then."

" They will expel you from the town. They will deport you."

" Let them, then."

" But no ! What will you do ? That would be horrible if we had
to go to Berlin or to Munich and begin again. Here everything
has happened so well."

" I don't care," said Hannele.

Mitchka looked at her friend and said no more. But she was
angry. After some time she turned and uttered her ultimatum.

" When you are not there," she said, " I shall put the puppet
away in a drawer. I shall show it to nobody, nobody. And I must
tell you, it makes me afraid to see it there. It makes me afraid.
And you have no right to get me into trouble, do you see. It is not
I who look at the English officers. I don't like them, they are too
cold and finished off for me. I shall never bring trouble on *myself*
because of the English officers."

" Don't be afraid," said Hannele. " They won't trouble *you*.
They know everything we do, well enough. They have their spies
everywhere. Nothing will happen to you."

" But if they make you go away—and I am planted here with the
studio——"

It was no good, however ; Hannele was obstinate.

So, one sunny afternoon there was a ring at the door : a little
lady in white, with a wrinkled face that still had its prettiness.

" Good afternoon ! "—in rather lardy-dardy middle-class English.
" I wonder if I may see your things in your studio."

" Oh yes ! " said Mitchka. " Please to come in."

Entered the little lady in her finery and her crumpled prettiness. She would not be very old ; perhaps younger than fifty. And it was odd that her face had gone so crumpled, because her figure was very trim, her eyes were bright, and she had pretty teeth when she aughed. She was very fine in her clothes : a dress of thick knitted white silk, a large ermine scarf with the tails only at the ends, and a black hat over which dripped a trail of green feathers of the osprey sort. She wore rather a lot of jewellery, and two bangles tinkled over her white kid gloves as she put up her fingers to touch her hair, whilst she stood complacently and looked round.

" You've got a *charming* studio—*charming*—perfectly delightful ! I couldn't imagine anything more delightful."

Mitchka gave a slight ironic bow, and said, in her odd, plangent English :

" Oh yes. We like it very much also."

Hannele, who had dodged behind a screen, now came quickly forth.

" Oh, how do you do ! " smiled the elderly lady. " I heard there were two of you. Now which is which, if I may be so bold ? This " —and she gave a winsome smile and pointed a white kid finger at Mitchka—" is the—— ? "

" Annamaria von Prielau-Carolath," said Mitchka, slightly bowing.

" Oh ! "—and the white kid finger jerked away. " Then this——"

" Johanna zu Rassentlow," said Hannele, smiling.

" Ah, yes ! Countess von Rassentlow ! And this is Baroness von— von—but I shall never remember even if you tell me, for I'm awful at names. Anyhow, I shall call one *Countess* and the other *Baroness*. That will do, won't it, for poor me ! Now I should like awfully to see your things, if I may. I want to buy a little present to take back to England with me. I suppose I shan't have to pay the world in duty on things like these, shall I ? "

" Oh no," said Mitchka. " No duty. Toys, you know, they— there is—— " Her English stammered to an end, so she turned to Hannele.

" They don't charge duty on toys, and the embroideries they don't notice," said Hannele.

" Oh well. Then I'm all right," said the visitor. " I hope I can buy something really nice ! I see a perfectly lovely jumper over there, perfectly delightful. But a little too gay for me, I'm afraid.

I'm not quite so young as I was, alas." She smiled her winsome little smile, showing her pretty teeth, and the old pearls in her ears shook.

" I've heard so much about your dolls. I hear they're perfectly exquisite, quite works of art. May I see some, please."

" Oh yes," came Mitchka's invariable answer, this exclamation being the foundation stone of all her English.

There were never more than three or four dolls in stock. This time there were only two. The famous captain was hidden in his drawer.

" Perfectly beautiful ! Perfectly wonderful ! " murmured the little lady, in an artistic murmur. " I think they're perfectly delightful. It's wonderful of you, Countess, to make them. It is you who make them, is it not ? Or do you both do them together ? "

Hannele explained, and the inspection and the rhapsody went on together. But it was evident that the little lady was a cautious buyer. She went over the things very carefully, and thought more than twice. The dolls attracted her—but she thought them expensive, and hung fire.

" I do wish," she said wistfully, " there had been a larger selection of the dolls. I feel, you know, there might have been one which I *just loved*. Of course these are *darlings*—darlings they are : and worth every *penny*, considering the work there is in them. And the art, of course. But I have a feeling, don't you know how it is, that if there had been just one or two more, I should have found one which I *absolutely* couldn't live without. Don't you know how it is ? One is so foolish, of course. What does Goethe say—' Dort wo du nicht bist . . .' ? My German isn't even a beginning, so you must excuse it. But it means you always feel you would be happy somewhere else, and not just where you are. Isn't that it ? Ah well, it's so very often true—so very often. But not always, thank goodness." She smiled an odd little smile to herself, pursed her lips, and resumed : " Well now, that's how I feel about the dolls. If only there had been one or two more. Isn't there a single one ? "

She looked winsomely at Hannele.

" Yes," said Hannele, " there is one. But it is ordered. It isn't for sale."

" Oh, do you think I might see it ? I'm sure it's lovely. Oh, I'm dying to see it. You know what woman's curiosity is, don't you ? " —she laughed her tinkling little laugh. " Well, I'm afraid I'm all woman, unfortunately. One is so much harder if one has a touch of the man in one, don't you think, and more able to bear things. But I'm afraid I'm all woman." She sighed and became silent.

Hannele went quietly to the drawer and took out the captain. She handed him to the little woman. The latter looked frightened. Her eyes became round and childish, her face went yellowish. Her jewels tinkled nervously as she stammered :

" Now *that*—isn't that——" and she laughed a little, hysterical laugh.

She turned round, as if to escape.

" Do you mind if I sit down," she said. " I think the standing——" and she subsided into a chair. She kept her face averted. But she held the puppet fast, her small, white fingers with their heavy jewelled rings clasped round his waist.

" You know," rushed in Mitchka, who was terrified. " You know, that is a life-picture of one of the Englishmen, of a gentleman, you know. A life-picture, you know."

" A portrait," said Hannele brightly.

" Yes," murmured the visitor vaguely. " I'm sure it is. I'm sure it is a very clever portrait indeed."

She fumbled with a chain, and put up a small gold lorgnette before her eyes, as if to screen herself. And from behind the screen of her lorgnette she peered at the image in her hand.

" But," she said, " none of the English officers, or rather Scottish, wear the close-fitting tartan trews any more—except for fancy dress." Her voice was vague and distant.

" No, they don't now," said Hannele. " But that is the correct dress. I think they are so handsome, don't you ? "

" Well. I don't know. It depends "—and the little woman laughed shakily.

" Oh yes," said Hannele. " It needs well-shapen legs."

" Such as the original of your doll must have had—quite," said the lady.

" Oh yes," said Hannele. " I think his legs are very handsome."

" Quite ! " said the lady. " Judging from his portrait, as you call it. May I ask the name of the gentleman—if it is not too indiscreet ? "

" Captain Hepburn," said Hannele.

" Yes, of course it is. I knew him at once. I've known him for many years."

" Oh, please," broke in Mitchka. " Oh, please, do not tell him you have seen it ! Oh, please ! Please not to tell any one ! "

The visitor looked up with a grey little smile.

" But why not ? " she said. " Anyhow, I can't tell him at once, because I hear he is away at present. You don't happen to know when he will be back ? "

" I believe to-morrow," said Hannele.

" To-morrow ! "

" And please ! " pleaded Mitchka, who looked lovely in her pleading distress, " please not to tell anybody that you have seen it."

" Must I promise ? " smiled the little lady wanly. " Very well, then, I won't tell him I've seen it. And now I think I must be going. Yes, I'll just take the cushion cover, thank you. Tell me again how much it is, please."

That evening Hannele was restless. He had been away on some duty for three days. He was returning that night—should have been back in time for dinner. But he had not arrived, and his room was locked and dark. Hannele had heard the servant light the stove some hours ago. Now the room was locked and blank as it had been for three days.

Hannele was most uneasy because she seemed to have forgotten him in the three days whilst he had been away. He seemed to have quite disappeared out of her. She could hardly even remember him. He had become so insignificant to her she was dazed.

Now she wanted to see him again, to know if it was really so. She felt that he was coming. She felt that he was already putting out some influence towards her. But what ? And was he real ? Why had she made his doll ? Why had his doll been so important, if he was nothing ? Why had she shown it to that funny little woman this afternoon ? Why was she herself such a fool, getting herself into tangles in this place where it was so unpleasant to be entangled ? Why was she entangled, after all ? It was all so unreal. And particularly *he* was unreal : as unreal as a person in a dream, whom one has never heard of in actual life. In actual life, her own German friends were real. Martin was real ; German men were real to her. But this other, he was simply not there. He didn't really exist. He was a nullus, in reality. A nullus—and she had somehow got herself complicated with him.

Was it possible ? Was it possible she had been so closely entangled with an absolute nothing ? Now he was absent she couldn't even *imagine* him. He had gone out of her imagination, and even when she looked at his doll she saw nothing but a barren puppet. And yet for this dead puppet, she had been compromising herself, now, when it was so risky for her to be compromised.

Her own German friends—her own German men—they were men, they were real beings. But this English officer, he was neither fish, flesh, fowl, nor good red herring, as they say. He was just a hypothetical presence. She felt that if he never came back, she would be just as if she had read a rather peculiar but false story, a *tour de force* which works up one's imagination all falsely.

Nevertheless she was uneasy. She had a lurking suspicion that there might be something else. So she kept uneasily wandering out on to the landing, and listening, to hear if he might be coming.

Yes—there was a sound. Yes, there was his slow step on the stairs, and the slow, straying purr of his voice. And instantly she heard his voice she was afraid again. She knew there *was* something there. And instantly she felt the reality of his presence, she felt the unreality of her own German men-friends. The moment she heard the peculiar, slow melody of his foreign voice everything seemed to go changed in her, and Martin and Otto and Albrecht, her German friends, seemed to go pale and dim as if one could almost see through them, like unsubstantial things.

This was what she had to reckon with, this recoil from one to the other. When he was present, he seemed so terribly real. When he was absent he was completely vague, and her own men of her own race seemed so absolutely the only reality.

But he was talking. Who was he talking to? She heard the steps echo up the hollows of the stone staircase, slowly, as if wearily, and voices slowly, confusedly mingle. The slow, soft trail of his voice—and then the peculiar, quick tones—yes, of a woman. And not one of the maids, because they were speaking English. She listened hard. The quick, and yet slightly hushed, slightly sad-sounding voice of a woman who talks a good deal, as if talking to herself. Hannele's quick ears caught the sound of what she was saying: " Yes, I thought the Baroness a perfectly beautiful creature, perfectly lovely. But so extraordinarily like a Spaniard. Do you remember, Alec, at Malaga? I always thought they fascinated you then, with their mantillas. Perfectly lovely she would look in a mantilla. Only perhaps she is too open-hearted, too impulsive, poor thing. She lacks the Spanish reserve. Poor thing, I feel sorry for her. For them both, indeed. It must be very hard to have to do these things for a living, after you've been accustomed to be made much of for your own sake, and for your aristocratic title. It's very hard for them, poor things. Baroness, Countess, it sounds just a little ridiculous, when you're buying woollen embroideries from them. But I suppose, poor things, they can't help it. Better drop the titles altogether, I think——"

" Well, they do, if people will let them. Only English and American people find it so much easier to say Baroness or Countess than Fräulein von Prielau-Carolath, or whatever it is."

" They could say simply Fräulein, as we do to our governesses—or as we used to, when we *had* German governesses," came the voice of *her*.

" Yes, we *could*," said his voice.

" After all, what is the good, what is the good of titles if you have to sell dolls and woollen embroideries—not so very beautiful, either."

" Oh, quite ! Oh, quite ! I think titles are perhaps a mistake, anyhow. But they've always had them," came his slow, musical voice, with its sing-song note of hopeless indifference. He sounded rather like a man talking out of his sleep.

Hannele caught sight of the tail of blue-green crane feathers veering round a turn in the stairs away below, and she beat a hasty retreat.

III

There was a little platform out on the roof, where he used sometimes to stand his telescope and observe the stars or the moon : the moon when possible. It was not a very safe platform, just a little ledge of the roof, outside the window at the end of the top corridor : or rather, the top landing, for it was only the space between the attics. Hannele had the one attic-room at the back, he had the room we have seen, and a little bedroom which was really only a lumber-room. Before he came, Hannele had been alone under the roof. His rooms were then lumber-room and laundry-room, where the clothes were dried. But he had wanted to be high up, because of his stars, and this was the place that pleased him.

Hannele heard him quite late in the night, wandering about. She heard him also on the ledge outside. She could not sleep. He disturbed her. The moon was risen, large and bright in the sky. She heard the bells from the cathedral slowly strike two : two great drops of sound in the livid night. And again, from outside on the roof, she heard him clear his throat. Then a cat howled.

She rose, wrapped herself in a dark wrap, and went down the landing to the window at the end. The sky outside was full of moonlight. He was squatted like a great cat peering up his telescope, sitting on a stool, his knees wide apart. Quite motionless he sat in that attitude, like some leaden figure on the roof. The moonlight glistened with a gleam of plumbago on the great slope of black tiles. She stood still in the window, watching. And he remained fixed and motionless at the end of the telescope.

She tapped softly on the window-pane. He looked round, like

some tom-cat staring round with wide night-eyes. Then he reached down his hand and pulled the window open.

" Hello," he said quietly. " You not asleep ? "

" Aren't *you* tired ? " she replied, rather resentful.

" No, I was as wide awake as I could be. *Isn't* the moon fine to-night ! What ? Perfectly amazing. Wouldn't you like to come up and have a look at her ? "

" No, thank you," she said hastily, terrified at the thought.

He resumed his posture, peering up the telescope.

" Perfectly amazing," he said, murmuring. She waited for some time, bewitched likewise by the great October moon and the sky full of resplendent white-green light. It seemed like another sort of day-time. And there he straddled on the roof like some cat ! It was exactly like day in some other planet.

At length he turned round to her. His face glistened faintly, and his eyes were dilated like a cat's at night.

" You know I had a visitor ? " he said.

" Yes."

" My wife."

" Your *wife* ! "—she looked up really astonished. She had thought it might be an acquaintance—perhaps his aunt—or even an elder sister. " But she's years older than you," she added.

" Eight years," he said. " I'm forty-one."

There was a silence.

" Yes," he mused. " She arrived suddenly, by surprise, yesterday, and found me away. She's staying in the hotel in the Vier Jahreszeiten."

There was a pause.

" Aren't you going to stay with her ? " asked Hannele.

" Yes, I shall probably join her to-morrow."

There was a still longer pause.

" Why not to-night ? " asked Hannele.

" Oh, well—I put it off for to-night. It meant all the bother of my wife changing her room at the hotel—and it was late—and I was all mucky after travelling."

" But you'll go to-morrow ? "

" Yes, I shall go to-morrow. For a week or so. After that I'm not sure what will happen."

There was quite a long pause. He remained seated on his stool on the roof, looking with dilated, blank, black eyes at nothingness. She stood below in the open window-space, pondering.

" Do you want to go to her at the hotel ? " asked Hannele.

" Well, I don't, particularly. But I don't mind, really. We're very good friends. Why, we've been friends for eighteen years—we've been married seventeen. Oh, she's a nice little woman. I don't want to hurt her feelings. I wish her no harm, you know. On the contrary, I wish her all the good in the world."

He had no idea of the blank amazement in which Hannele listened to these stray remarks.

" But——" she stammered. " But doesn't she expect you to make *love* to her ? "

" Oh, yes, she expects that. You bet she does : woman-like."

" And you ? "—the question had a dangerous ring.

" Why, I don't mind, really, you know, if it's only for a short time. I'm used to her. I've always been fond of her, you know—and so if it gives her any pleasure—why, I like her to get what pleasure out of life she can."

" But *you*—you *yourself* ! Don't *you* feel anything ? " Hannele's amazement was reaching the point of incredulity. She began to feel that he was making it up. It was all so different from her own point of view. To sit there so quiet and to make such statements in all good faith : no, it was impossible.

" I don't consider I count," he said naïvely.

Hannele looked aside. If that wasn't lying, it was imbecility, or worse. She had for the moment nothing to say. She felt he was a sort of psychic phenomenon like a grasshopper or a tadpole or an ammonite. Not to be regarded from a human point of view. No, he just wasn't normal. And she had been fascinated by him ! It was only sheer, amazed curiosity that carried her on to her next question.

" But do you *never* count, then ? " she asked, and there was a touch of derision, of laughter in her tone. He took no offence.

" Well—very rarely," he said. " I count very rarely. That's how life appears to me. One matters so *very* little."

She felt quite dizzy with astonishment. And he called himself a man !

" But if you matter so very little, what do you do anything at all for ? " she asked.

" Oh, one has to. And then, why not ? Why not do things, even if oneself hardly matters. Look at the moon. It doesn't matter in the least to the moon whether I exist or whether I don't. So why should it matter to me ? "

After a blank pause of incredulity she said :

" I could die with laughter. It seems to me all so ridiculous—no, I can't believe it."

" Perhaps it is a point of view," he said.

There was a long and pregnant silence : we should not like to say pregnant with what.

" And so I don't mean anything to you at all ? " she said.

" I didn't say that," he replied.

" Nothing means anything to you," she challenged.

" I don't say that."

" Whether it's your wife—or me—or the moon—*toute la même chose.*"

" No—no—that's hardly the way to look at at."

She gazed at him in such utter amazement that she felt something would really explode in her if she heard another word. Was this a man ?—or what was it ! It was too much for her, that was all.

" Well, good-bye," she said. " I hope you will have a nice time at the Vier Jahreszeiten."

So she left him still sitting on the roof.

" I suppose," she said to herself, " that is love *à l'anglaise.* But it's more than I can swallow."

IV

" Won't you come and have tea with me—do ! Come right along now. Don't you find it bitterly cold ? Yes—well now—come in with me and we'll have a cup of nice, hot tea, in our little sitting-room. The weather changes so suddenly, and really, one needs a little reinforcement. But perhaps you don't take tea ? "

" Oh yes. I got so used to it in England," said Hannele.

" Did you now ! Well now, were you long in England ? "

" Oh yes——"

The two women had met in the Domplatz. Mrs. Hepburn was looking extraordinarily like one of Hannele's dolls, in a funny little cape of odd striped skins, and a little dark-green skirt, and a rather fuzzy sort of hat. Hannele looked almost huge beside her.

" But now you will come in and have tea, won't you ? Oh, please do. Never mind whether it's *de rigueur* or not. I *always* please myself *what* I do. I'm afraid my husband gets some shocks sometimes—but that we can't help. I won't have anybody laying down the law to me." She laughed her winsome little laugh. " So now come along in, and we'll see if there aren't hot scones as well. I love a hot scone for tea in cold weather. And I hope you do. That is, if there are any. We don't know yet." She tinkled her little laugh. " My husband may or may not be in. But that makes no difference to you and me, does it ? There, it's just striking half-past four. In

England we always have tea at half-past. My husband *adores* his tea. I don't suppose our man is five minutes off the half-past, ringing the gong for tea, not once in twelve months. My husband doesn't mind at all if dinner is a little late. But he gets quite—well, quite ' ratty ' if tea is late." She tinkled a laugh. " Though I shouldn't say that. He is the soul of kindness and patience. I don't think I've ever known him to do an unkind thing—or hardly say an unkind word. But I doubt if he will be in to-day."

He *was* in, however, standing with his feet apart and his hands in his trouser pockets in the little sitting-room upstairs in the hotel. He raised his eyebrows the smallest degree, seeing Hannele enter.

" Ah, Countess Hannele—my wife has brought you along ! Very nice, very nice ! Let me take your wrap. Oh, yes, certainly . . ."

" Have you rung for tea, dear ? " asked Mrs. Hepburn.

" Er—yes. I said as soon as you came in they were to bring it."

" Yes—well. Won't you ring again, dear, and say for *three*."

" Yes—certainly. Certainly."

He rang, and stood about with his hands in his pockets waiting for tea.

" Well now," said Mrs. Hepburn, as she lifted the teapot, and her bangles tinkled, and her huge rings of brilliants twinkled, and her big ear-rings of clustered seed-pearls bobbed against her rather withered cheek, " isn't it charming of Countess zu—Countess zu——"

" Rassentlow," said he. " I believe most people say Countess Hannele. I know we always do among ourselves. We say Countess Hannele's shop."

" Countess Hannele's shop ! Now, isn't that perfectly delightful : such a romance in the very sound of it. You take cream ? "

" Thank you," said Hannele.

The tea passed in a cloud of chatter, while Mrs. Hepburn manipulated the teapot, and lit the spirit-flame, and blew it out, and peeped into the steam of the teapot, and couldn't see whether there was any more tea or not—and—" At home I *know*—I was going to say to a teaspoonful—how much tea there is in the pot. But this teapot—I don't know what it's made of—it isn't silver, I know that—it is so heavy in itself, that it's deceived me several times already. And my husband is a greedy man, a greedy man—he likes at least three cups —and four if he can get them, or five ! Yes, dear, I've plenty of tea to-day. You shall have even five, if you don't mind the last two weak. Do let me fill your cup, Countess Hannele. I think it's a *charming* name."

"There's a play called *Hannele*, isn't there?" said he.

When he had had his five cups, and his wife had got her cigarette perched in the end of a long, long slim white holder, and was puffing like a little China-woman from the distance, there was a little lull.

"Alec, dear," said Mrs. Hepburn. "You won't forget to leave that message for me at Mrs. Rackham's. I'm so afraid it will be forgotten."

"No, dear, I won't forget. Er—would you like me to go round now?"

Hannele noticed how often he said "er," when he was beginning to speak to his wife. But they *were* such good friends, the two of them.

"Why if you *would*, dear, I should feel perfectly comfortable. But I don't want you to hurry one bit."

"Oh, I may as well go now."

And he went. Mrs. Hepburn detained her guest.

"He *is* so charming to me," said the little woman. "He's really wonderful. And he always has been the same—invariably. So that if he *did* make a little slip—well, you know, I don't have to take it so seriously."

"No," said Hannele, feeling as if her ears were stretching with astonishment.

"It's the war. It's just the war. It's had a terribly deteriorating effect on the men."

"In what way?" said Hannele.

"Why, morally. Really, there's hardly one man left the same as he was before the war. Terribly degenerated."

"Is that so?" said Hannele.

"It is indeed. Why, isn't it the same with the German men and officers?"

"Yes, I think so," said Hannele.

"And I'm sure so, from what I hear. But of course it is the women who are to blame in the first place. We poor women! We are a guilty race, I am afraid. But I never throw stones. I know what it is myself to have temptations. I have to flirt a little—and when I was younger—well, the men didn't escape me, I assure you. And I was *so* often scorched. But never *quite* singed. My husband never minded. He knew I was *really* safe. Oh yes, I have always been faithful to him. But still—I have been *very* near the flame." And she laughed her winsome little laugh.

Hannele put her fingers to her ears, to make sure they were not falling off.

"Of course during the war it was terrible. I know that in a

certain hospital it was quite impossible for a girl to stay on if she kept straight. The matrons and sisters just turned her out. They wouldn't have her unless she was one of themselves. And you know what that means. Quite like the convent in Balzac's story—you know which I mean, I'm sure." And the laugh tinkled gaily.

"But then, what can you expect, when there aren't enough men to go round ! Why, I had a friend in Ireland. She and her husband had been an ideal couple, an *ideal* couple. Real playmates. And you can't say more than that, can you ? Well, then, he became a major during the war. And she was so looking forward, poor thing, to the perfectly lovely times they would have together when he came home. She is like me, and is lucky enough to have a little income of her own—not a great fortune—but—well—— Well now, what was I going to say. Oh yes, she was looking forward to the perfectly lovely times they would have when he came home : building on her dreams, poor thing, as we unfortunate women always do. I suppose we shall never be cured of it." A little tinkling laugh. "Well now, not a bit of it. Not a bit of it." Mrs. Hepburn lifted her heavily-jewelled little hand in a motion of protest. It was curious, her hands were pretty and white, and her neck and breast, now she wore a little tea-gown, were also smooth and white and pretty, under the medley of twinkling little chains and coloured jewels. Why should her face have played her this nasty trick of going all crumpled ? However, it was so.

"Not one bit of it," reiterated the little lady. "He came home quite changed. She said she could hardly recognize him for the same man. Let me tell you one little incident. Just a trifle, but significant. He was coming home—this was some time after he was free from the army—he was coming home from London, and he told her to meet him at the boat : gave her the time and everything. Well, she went to the boat, poor thing, and he didn't come. She waited, and no word of explanation or anything. So she couldn't make up her mind whether to go next day and meet the boat again. However, she decided she wouldn't. So of course, on that boat he arrived. When he got home, he said to her, ' Why didn't you meet the boat ? ' ' Well,' she said, ' I went yesterday, and you didn't come.' ' Then why didn't you meet it again to-day ? ' Imagine it, the sauce ! And they had been real playmates. Heartbreaking, isn't it ? ' Well,' she said in self-defence, ' why didn't you come yesterday ? ' ' Oh,' he said, ' I met a woman in town whom I liked, and she asked me to spend the night with her, so I did.' Now what do you think of that ? Can you conceive of such a thing ? "

"Oh no," said Hannele. "I call that unnecessary brutality."

"Exactly! So terrible to say such a thing to her! The brutality of it! Well, that's how the world is to-day. I'm thankful my husband isn't that sort. I don't say he's perfect. But whatever else he did, he'd never be unkind, and he *couldn't* be brutal. He just couldn't. He'd never tell me a lie—I know *that*. But callous brutality, no, thank goodness, he hasn't a spark of it in him. I'm the wicked one, if either of us is wicked." The little laugh tinkled. "Oh! but he's been perfect to me, perfect. Hardly a cross word. Why, on our wedding night, he kneeled down in front of me and promised, with God's help, to make my life happy. And I must say, as far as possible, he's kept his word. It has been his one aim in life, to make my life happy."

The little lady looked away with a bright, musing look, towards the window. She was being a heroine in a romance. Hannele could see her being a heroine, playing the chief part in her own life-romance. It is such a feminine occupation, that no woman takes offence when she is made audience.

"I'm afraid I've more of the woman than the mother in my composition," resumed the little heroine. "I adore my two children. The boy is at Winchester, and my little girl is in a convent in Brittany. Oh, they are perfect darlings, both of them. But the man is first in my mind, I'm afraid. I fear I'm rather old-fashioned. But never mind. I can see the attractions in other men—can't I indeed! There was a perfectly exquisite creature—he was a very clever engineer—but much, much more than *that*. But never mind." The little heroine sniffed as if there were perfume in the air, folded her jewelled hands, and resumed: "However—I know what it is myself to flutter round the flame. You know I'm Irish myself, and we Irish can't help it. Oh, I wouldn't be English for anything. Just that little touch of imagination, you know . . ." The little laugh tinkled. "And that's what makes me able to sympathize with my husband even when, perhaps, I shouldn't. Why, when he was at home with me, he never gave a thought, not a thought to another woman. I must say, he used to make *me* feel a little guilty sometimes. But there! I don't think he ever thought of another woman as being flesh and blood, after he knew me. I could tell. Pleasant, courteous, charming—but other women were not flesh and blood to him, they were just people, callers—that kind of thing. It used to amaze me, when some perfectly lovely creature came, whom I should have been head over heels in love with in a minute—and he, he was charming, delightful; he could see her points, but she was no more to him than, let me say, a pot of carnations, or a beautiful old piece of punto di Milano. Not flesh and blood. Well, perhaps one can feel too safe. Perhaps one needs a tiny pinch of the salt of jealousy. I believe one does. And I have not had one jealous moment for seventeen years. So that, *really*, when I heard a whisper of something going on here, I felt almost pleased. I felt exonerated for my own little peccadilloes, for one thing. And I felt he was perhaps a little more human. Because, after all, it is nothing but human to fall in love, if you are alone for a long time and in the company of a beautiful woman—and if you're an attractive man yourself."

Hannele sat with her eyes propped open and her ears buttoned back with amazement, expecting the next revelations.

"Why, of course," she said, knowing she was expected to say something.

"Yes, of course," said Mrs. Hepburn, eyeing her sharply. "So I thought I'd better come and see how far things had gone. I had nothing but a hint to go on. I knew no name—nothing. I had just a hint that she was German, and a refugee aristocrat —and that he used to call at the studio." The little lady eyed Hannele sharply, and gave a breathless little laugh, clasping her hands nervously. Hannele sat absolutely blank : really dazed.

"Of course," resumed Mrs. Hepburn, "that was enough. That was quite a sufficient clue. I'm afraid my intentions when I called at the studio were not as pure as they might have been. I'm afraid I wanted to see something more than the dolls. But when you showed me *his* doll, then I knew. Of course there wasn't a shadow of doubt after that. And I saw at once that she loved him, poor thing. She was *so* agitated. And no idea who I was. And you were so unkind to show me the doll. Of course you had no idea who you were showing it to. But for her, poor thing, it was such a trial. I could see how she suffered. And I must say she's very lovely—she's very, very lovely, with her golden skin and her reddish amber eyes and her beautiful, beautiful carriage. And such a naïve, impulsive nature. Gives everything away in a minute. And then her deep voice— ' *Oh yes—Oh please !* '—such a child. And such an aristocrat, that lovely turn of her head, and her simple, elegant dress. Oh, she's very charming. And she's just the type I always knew would attract him, if he hadn't got me. I've thought about it many a time—many a time. When a woman is older than a man, she does think these things—especially if he has his attractive points too. And when I've dreamed of the woman he would love if he hadn't got me, it has always been a Spanish type. And the Baroness is extraordinarily Spanish in her appearance. She must have had some noble Spanish ancestor. Don't you think so?"

"Oh yes," said Hannele. "There were such a lot of Spaniards in Austria, too, with the various emperors."

"With Charles V, exactly. Exactly. That's how it must have been. And so she has all the Spanish beauty, and all the German feeling. Of course, for myself, I miss the *reserve*, the haughtiness. But she's very, very lovely, and I'm sure I could never *hate* her. I couldn't even if I tried. And I'm not going to try. But I think she's much too dangerous for my husband to see much of her. Don't you agree, now?"

"Oh, but really," stammered Hannele. "There's nothing in it, really."

"Well," said the little lady, cocking her head shrewdly aside, "I shouldn't like there to be any *more* in it."

And there was a moment's dead pause. Each woman was reflecting. Hannele wondered if the little lady was just fooling her.

"Anyhow," continued Mrs. Hepburn, "the spark is there, and I don't intend the fire to spread. I am going to be very, very careful, myself, not to fan the flames. The last thing I should think of would be to make my husband scenes. I believe it would be fatal."

"Yes," said Hannele, during the pause.

"I'm going very carefully. You think there isn't much in it— between him and the Baroness?"

"No—no—I'm sure there isn't," cried Hannele, with a full voice of conviction. She was almost indignant at being slighted so completely herself, in the little lady's suspicions.

"Hm!—mm!" hummed the little woman, sapiently nodding her head slowly up and down. "I'm not so sure! I'm not so sure that it hasn't gone pretty far."

"Oh *no*!" cried Hannele, in real irritation of protest.

"Well," said the other. "In any case, I don't intend it to go any further."

There was dead silence for some time.

"There's more in it than you say. There's more in it than you say," ruminated the little woman. "I know *him*, for one thing. I know he's got a cloud on his brow. And I know it hasn't left his brow for a single minute. And when I told him I had been to the studio, and showed him the cushion-cover, I knew he felt guilty. I am not so easily deceived. We Irish all have a touch of second sight, I believe. Of course I haven't challenged him. I haven't even

mentioned the doll. By the way, *who* ordered the doll? Do you
mind telling me?"

"No, it wasn't ordered," confessed Hannele.

"Ah—I thought not—I thought not!" said Mrs. Hepburn,
lifting her finger. "At least, I knew no outsider had ordered it. Of
course I knew." And she smiled to herself.

"So," she continued, "I had too much sense to say anything
about it. I don't believe in stripping wounds bare. I believe in
gently covering them and letting them heal. But I *did* say I
thought her a lovely creature." The little lady looked brightly at
Hannele.

"Yes," said Hannele.

"And he was very vague in his manner. 'Yes, not bad,' he said.
I thought to myself, Aha, my boy, you don't deceive me with your
not bad. She's very much more than not bad. I said so, too. I
wanted, of course, to let him know I had a suspicion."

"And do you think he knew?"

"Of course he did. Of course he did. 'She's much too dangerous,' I said, 'to be in a town where there are so many strange
men : married and unmarried.' And then he turned round to
me and gave himself away, oh, so plainly. 'Why?' he said. But
such a haughty, distant tone. I said to myself, 'It's time, my
dear boy, you were removed out of the danger-zone.' But I
answered him : 'Surely somebody is bound to fall in love with her.'
'Not at all,' he said, 'she keeps to her own countrymen.' 'You don't
tell *me*,' I answered him, 'with her pretty broken English ! It is a
wonder the two of them are allowed to stay in the town.' And then
again he rounded on me. 'Good gracious !' he said. 'Would you
have them turned out just because they're beautiful to look at, when
they have nowhere else to go, and they make their bit of a livelihood
here?' I assure you, he hasn't rounded on me in that overbearing
way, not once before, in all our married life. So I just said quietly :
'I should like to protect *our own men*.' And he didn't say anything
more. But he looked at me under his brows, and went out of the
room."

There was a silence. Hannele waited with her hands in her lap,
and Mrs. Hepburn mused, with her hands in *her* lap. Her face
looked yellow, and *very* wrinkled.

"Well now," she said, breaking again suddenly into life. "What
are we to do? I mean what is to be done? You are the Baroness'
nearest friend. And I wish her *no* harm, none whatever."

"What can we do?" said Hannele, in the pause.

" I have been urging my husband for some time to get his discharge from the army," said the little woman. " I know he could have it in three months' time. But like so many more men, he has no income of his own, and he doesn't want to feel dependent. Perfect nonsense ! So he says he wants to stay on in the army. I have never known him before go against my real wishes."

" But it *is* better for a man to be independent," said Hannele.

" I know it is. But it is also better for him to be *at home*. And I could get him a post in one of the observatories. He could do something in meteorological work."

Hannele refused to answer any more.

" Of course," said Mrs. Hepburn, " if he *does* stay on here, it would be much better if the Baroness left the town."

" I'm sure she will never leave of her own choice," said Hannele.

" I'm sure she won't either. But she might be made to see that it would be very much *wiser* of her to move of her own free will."

" Why ? " said Hannele.

" Why, because she might any time be removed by the British authorities."

" Why should she ? " said Hannele.

" I think the women who are a menace to our men should be removed."

" But she is *not* a menace to your men."

" Well, I have my own opinion on that point."

Which was a decided deadlock.

" I'm sure I've kept you an awful long time with my chatter," said Mrs. Hepburn. " But I did want to make everything as simple as possible. As I said before, I can't feel any ill-will against her. Yet I can't let things just go on. Heaven alone knows when they may end. Of course if I can persuade my husband to resign his commission and come back to England—anyhow, we will see. I'm sure I am the last person in the world to bear malice."

The tone in which she said it conveyed a dire threat.

Hannele rose from her chair.

" Oh, and one other thing," said her hostess, taking out a tiny lace handkerchief and touching her nose delicately with it. " Do you think "—dab—dab—" that I might have that *doll*—you know—— ? "

" That—— ? "

" Yes, of my husband "—the little lady rubbed her nose with her kerchief.

" The price is three guineas," said Hannele.

" Oh, indeed ! "—the tone was very cold. " I thought it was not for sale."

Hannele put on her wrap.

" You'll send it round—will you ?—if you will be so kind."

" I must ask my friend, first."

" Yes, of course. But I'm sure she will be so kind as to send it me. It is a little—er—indelicate, don't you think ! "

" No," said Hannele. " No more than a painted portrait."

" Don't you ? " said her hostess coldly. " Well, even a painted portrait I think I should like in my own possession. This *doll*——"

Hannele waited, but there was no conclusion.

" Anyhow," she said, " the price is three guineas : or the equivalent in marks."

" Very well," said the little lady, " you shall have your three guineas when I get the doll."

V

Hannele went her way pondering. A man never is quite such an abject specimen as his wife makes him look, talking about " my husband." Therefore, if any woman wishes to rescue her husband from the clutches of another female, let her only invite this female to tea and talk quite sincerely about " my husband, you know." Every man has made a ghastly fool of himself with a woman, at some time or other. No woman ever forgets. And most women will give the show away, with real pathos, to another woman. For instance, the picture of Alec at his wife's feet on his wedding night, vowing to devote himself to her lifelong happiness—this picture strayed across Hannele's mind time after time, whenever she thought of her dear captain. With disastrous consequences to the captain. Of course if he had been at her own feet, then Hannele would have thought it almost natural : almost a necessary part of the show of love. But at the feet of that other little woman ! And what was that other little woman wearing ? Her wedding night ! Hannele hoped before heaven it wasn't some awful little nighty of frail flowered silk. Imagine it, that little lady ! Perhaps in a chic little boudoir cap of punto di Milano, and this slip of frail flowered silk : and the man, perhaps, in his braces ! Oh, merciful heaven, save us from other people's indiscretions. No, let us be sure it was in proper evening dress—twenty years ago—very low cut, with a full skirt gathered behind and trailing a little, and a little feather-erection in her high-dressed hair, and all those jewels : pearls of course : and he in a dinner-jacket and a white waistcoat : probably in an hotel bedroom in Lugano, or Biarritz. And she? Was she standing with one small hand on his shoulder? Or was she seated on the couch in the bedroom? Oh, dreadful thought! And yet, it was almost inevitable, that scene. Hannele had never been married, but she had come quite near enough to the realization of the event to know that such a scene *was* practically inevitable. An indispensable part of any honeymoon. Him on his knees, with his heels up!

And how black and tidy his hair must have been then! And no grey at the temples at all. Such a good-looking bridegroom. Perhaps with a white rose in his button-hole still. And she could see him kneeling there, in his new black trousers, and a wing collar. And she could see his head bowed. And she could hear his plangent, musical voice saying: "With God's help, I will make your life happy. I will live for that and for nothing else." And then the little lady must have had tears in her eyes, and she must have said, rather superbly: "Thank you, dear. I'm perfectly sure of it."

Ach! Ach! Husbands should be left to their own wives: and wives should be left to their own husbands. And *no* stranger should ever be made a party to these terrible bits of connubial staging. Nay, thought Hannele, that scene was really true. It actually took place. And with the man of that scene I have been in love! With the devoted husband of that little lady. Oh God, oh God, how was it possible! Him on his knees, on his knees, with his heels up!

Am I a perfect fool? she thought to herself. Am I really just an idiot, gaping with love for him? How *could* I? How could I? The very way he says "Yes, dear!" to her! The way he does what she tells him! The way he fidgets about the room with his hands in his pockets! The way he goes off when she sends him away because she wants to talk to me. And he knows she wants to talk to me. And he knows what she *might* have to say to me. Yet he goes off on his errand without a question, like a servant. "I will do whatever you wish, darling." He must have said those words time after time, to the little lady. And fulfilled them, also. Performed all his pledges and his promises.

Ach! Ach! Hannele wrung her hands to think of *herself* being mixed up with him. And he had seemed to her so manly. He seemed to have so much silent male passion in him. And yet—the little lady! "My husband has *always* been *perfectly sweet* to me." Think of it! On his knees too. And his "Yes, dear! Certainly. Certainly." Not that he was afraid of the little lady. He was just committed to her, as he might have been committed to gaol, or committed to paradise.

Had she been dreaming, to be in love with him? Oh, she wished so much she had never been. She *wished* she had never given herself away. To him!—given herself away to him!—and so abjectly. Hung upon his words and his emotions, and looked up to him as if he were Cæsar. So he had seemed to her : like a mute Cæsar. Like Germanicus. Like—she did not know what.

How had it all happened? What had taken her in? Was it just his good looks? No, not really. Because they were the kind of staring good looks she didn't really care for. He must have had charm. He must have charm. Yes, he *had* charm. When it worked.

His charm had not worked on her now for some time—never since that evening after his wife's arrival. Since then he had seemed to her—rather awful. Rather awful—stupid—an ass—a limited, rather vulgar person. That was what he seemed to her when his charm wouldn't work. A limited, rather inferior person. And in a world of *Schiebers* and profiteers and vulgar, pretentious persons, this was the worst thing possible. A limited, inferior, slightly pretentious individual! The husband of the little lady! And oh heaven, she was so deeply implicated with him! He had not, however, spoken with her in private since his wife's arrival. Probably he would never speak with her in private again. She hoped to heaven, never again. The awful thing was the past, that which had been between him and her. She shuddered when she thought of it. The husband of the little lady!

But surely there was something to account for it! Charm, just charm. He had a charm. And then, oh heaven, when the charm left off working! It had left off so completely at this moment, in Hannele's case, that her very mouth tasted salt. What *did* it all amount to?

What was his charm, after all? How could it have affected her? She began to think of him again, at his best : his presence, when they were alone high up in that big, lonely attic near the stars. His room! The big white-washed walls, the first scent of tobacco, the silence, the sense of the stars being near, the telescopes, the cactus with fine scarlet flowers : and above all, the strange, remote, insidious silence of his presence, that was so congenial to her also. The curious way he had of turning his head to listen—to listen to what?—as if he heard something in the stars. The strange look, like destiny, in his wide-open, almost staring dark eyes. The beautiful lines of his brow, that seemed always to have a certain cloud on it. The slow elegance of his straight, beautiful legs as he walked, and the exquisiteness of his dark, slender chest! Ah, she could feel the charm mounting over her again. She could feel the snake biting her heart. She could feel the arrows of desire rankling.

But then—and she turned from her thoughts back to this last little tea-party in the Vier Jahreszeiten. She thought of his voice : " Yes, dear. Certainly. Certainly I will." And she thought of the stupid, inferior look on his face. And the something of a servant-like way in which he went out to do his wife's bidding.

And then the charm was gone again, as the glow of sunset goes off a burning city and leaves it a sordid industrial hole. So much for charm !

So much for charm. She had better have stuck to her own sort of men, Martin, for instance, who was a gentleman and a daring soldier, and a queer soul and pleasant to talk to. Only he hadn't any *magic*. Magic ? The very word made her writhe. Magic ? Swindle. Swindle, that was all it amounted to. Magic !

And yet—let us not be too hasty. If the magic had *really* been there, on those evenings in that great lofty attic. Had it ? Yes. Yes, she was bound to admit it. There had been magic. If there had been magic in his presence and in his contact, the husband of the little lady—— But the distaste was in her mouth again.

So she started afresh, trying to keep a tight hold on the tail of that all-too-evanescent magic of his. Dear, it slipped so quickly into disillusion. Nevertheless. If it had existed, it did exist. And if it did exist, it was worth having. You could call it an illusion if you liked. But an illusion which is a real experience is worth having. Perhaps this disillusion was a greater illusion than the illusion itself. Perhaps all this disillusion of the little lady and the husband of the little lady was falser than the illusion and magic of those few evenings. Perhaps the long disillusion of life was falser than the brief moments of real illusion. After all—the delicate darkness of his breast, the mystery that seemed to come with him as he trod slowly across the floor of his room, after changing his tunic—— Nay, nay, if she could keep the illusion of his charm, she would give all disillusion to the devils. Nay, only let her be under the spell of his charm. Only let the spell be upon her. It was all she yearned for. And the thing she had to fight was the vulgarity of disillusion. The vulgarity of the little lady, the vulgarity of the husband of the little lady, the vulgarity of his insincerity, his " Yes, dear. Certainly ! Certainly !" —this was what she had to fight. He *was* vulgar and horrible, then. But also, the queer figure that sat alone on the roof watching the stars ! The wonderful red flower of the cactus. The mystery that advanced with him as he came across the room after changing his tunic. The glamour and sadness of him, his silence, as he stooped unfastening his boots. And the strange gargoyle smile, fixed, when he caressed her with his hand under the chin ! Life is all a choice. And if she chose the glamour, the magic, the charm, the illusion, the spell ! Better death than that other, the husband of the little lady. When all was said and done, was he as much the husband of the little lady as he was that queer, delicate-breasted Cæsar of her own knowledge ? Which was he ?

No, she was *not* going to send her the doll. The little lady should never have the doll.

What a doll she would make herself ! Heavens, what a wizened jewel !

VI

Captain Hepburn still called occasionally at the house for his post. The maid always put his letters in a certain place in the hall, so that he should not have to climb the stairs.

Among his letters—that is to say, along with another letter, for his correspondence was very meagre—he one day found an envelope with a crest. Inside this envelope two letters.

" Dear Captain Hepburn,

I had the enclosed letter from Mrs. Hepburn. I don't intend her to have the doll which is your portrait, so I shall not answer this note. Also I don't see why she should try to turn us out of the town. She talked to me after tea that day, and it seems she believes that Mitchka is your lover. I didn't say anything at all—except that it wasn't true. But she needn't be afraid of me. I don't want you to trouble yourself. But you may as well *know* how things are.

                                              Johanna z. R."

The other letter was on his wife's well-known heavy paper, and in her well-known large, " aristocratic " hand.

" My dear Countess.

I wonder if there has been some mistake, or some misunderstanding. Four days ago you said you would send round that *doll* we spoke of, but I have seen no sign of it yet. I thought of calling at the studio, but did not wish to disturb the Baroness. I should be very much obliged if you could send the doll at once, as I do not feel easy while it is out of my possession. You may rely on having a cheque by return.

Our old family friend, Major-General Barlow, called on me

yesterday, and we had a most interesting conversation on our *Tommies*, and the protection of their morals here. It seems we have full power to send away any person or persons deemed undesirable, with twenty-four hours' notice to leave. But of course all this is done as quietly and with the intention of causing as little scandal as possible.

Please let me have the doll by to-morrow, and perhaps some hint as to your future intentions.

With very best wishes from one who only seeks to be your friend,

Yours very sincerely,

EVANGELINE HEPBURN."

VII

And then a dreadful thing happened : really a very dreadful thing. Hannele read of it in the evening newspaper of the town— the *Abendblatt*. Mitchka came rushing up with the paper at ten o'clock at night, just when Hannele was going to bed.

Mrs. Hepburn had fallen out of her bedroom window, from the third floor of the hotel, down on to the pavement below, and was killed. She was dressing for dinner. And apparently she had in the morning washed a certain little camisole, and put it on the window-sill to dry. She must have stood on a chair reaching for it, when she fell out of the window. Her husband, who was in the dressing-room, heard a queer little noise, a sort of choking cry and came into her room to see what it was. And she wasn't there. The window was open, and the chair by the window. He looked round, and thought she had left the room for a moment, so returned to his shaving. He was half shaved when one of the maids rushed in. When he looked out of the window down into the street he fainted, and would have fallen too if the maid had not pulled him in in time.

The very next day the captain came back to his attic. Hannele did not know, until quite late at night when he tapped on her door. She knew his soft tap immediately.

" Won't you come over for a chat ? " he said.

She paused for some moments before she answered. And then perhaps surprise made her agree : surprise and curiosity.

" Yes, in a minute," she said, closing her door in his face.

She found him sitting quite still, not even smoking, in his quiet attic. He did not rise, but just glanced round with a faint smile. And she thought his face seemed different, more flexible. But in the half-light she could not tell. She sat at some little distance from him.

" I suppose you've heard," he said.

"Yes."

After a long pause, he resumed :

"Yes. It seems an impossible thing to have happened. Yet it *has* happened."

Hannele's ears were sharp. But strain them as she might she could not catch the meaning of his voice.

"A terrible thing. A *very* terrible thing," she said.

"Yes."

"Do you think she fell quite accidentally ? " she said.

"Must have done. The maid was in just a minute before, and she seemed as happy as possible. I suppose reaching over that broad window-ledge, her brain must suddenly have turned. I can't imagine why she didn't call me. She could never bear even to look out of a high window. Turned her ill instantly if she saw a space below her. She used to say she couldn't really look at the moon, it made her feel as if she would fall down a dreadful height. She never dared do more than glance at it. She always had the feeling, I suppose, of the awful space beneath her, if she were on the moon."

Hannele was not listening to his words, but to his voice. There was something a little automatic in what he said. But then that is always so when people have had a shock.

"It must have been terrible for you too," she said.

"Ah, yes. At the time it was awful. Awful. I felt the smash right inside me, you know."

"Awful ! " she repeated.

"But now," he said, "I feel very strangely happy about it. I feel happy about it. I feel happy for her sake, if you can understand that. I feel she has got out of some great tension. I feel she's free now for the first time in her life. She was a gentle soul, and an original soul, but she was like a fairy who is condemned to live in houses and sit on furniture and all that, don't you know. It was never her nature."

"No ? " said Hannele, herself sitting in blank amazement.

"I always felt she was born in the wrong period—or on the wrong planet. Like some sort of delicate creature you take out of a tropical forest the moment it is born, and from the first moment teach it to perform tricks. You know what I mean. All her life she performed the tricks of life, clever little monkey she was at it too. Beat me into fits. But her own poor little soul, a sort of fairy soul, those queer Irish creatures, was cooped up inside her all her life, tombed in. There it was, tombed in, while she went through all the tricks of life that you have to go through if you are born to-day."

" But," stammered Hannele, " what would she have done if she *had* been free ? "

" Why, don't you see, there *is* nothing for her to do in the world to-day. Take her language, for instance. She never ought to have been speaking English. I don't know what language she ought to have spoken. Because if you take the Irish language, they only learn it back from English. They think in English, and just put Irish words on top. But English was never her language. It bubbled off her lips, so to speak. And she had no other language. Like a starling that you've made talk from the very beginning, and so it can only shout these talking noises, don't you know. It can't whistle its own whistling to save its life. Couldn't do it. It's lost it. All its own natural mode of expressing itself has collapsed, and it can only be artificial."

There was a long pause.

" Would she have been wonderful, then, if she had been able to talk in some unknown language ? " said Hannele jealously.

" I don't say she would have been wonderful. As a matter of fact we think a talking starling is much more wonderful than an ordinary starling. I don't myself, but most people do. And she would have been a sort of starling. And she would have had her own language and her own ways. As it was, poor thing, she was always arranging herself and fluttering and chattering inside a cage. And she never knew she was in the cage, any more than we know we are inside our own skins."

" But," said Hannele, with a touch of mockery, " how do you know you haven't made it all up—just to console yourself ? "

" Oh, I've thought it long ago," he said.

" Still," she blurted, " you may have invented it all—as a sort of consolation for—for—for your life."

" Yes, I may," he said. " But I don't think so. It was her eyes. Did you ever notice her eyes ? I often used to catch her eyes. And she'd be talking away, all the language bubbling off her lips. And her eyes were so clear and bright and different. Like a child's that is listening to something, and is going to be frightened. She was always listening—and waiting—for something else. I tell you what, she was exactly like that fairy in the Scotch song, who is in love with a mortal, and sits by the high road in terror waiting for him to come, and hearing the plovers and the curlews. Only nowadays motor lorries go along the moor roads, and the poor thing is struck unconscious, and carried into our world in a state of unconsciousness, and when she comes round, she tries to talk our language, and behave as we behave, and she can't remember anything else, so she goes on and on, till she falls with a crash, back to her own world."

Hannele was silent, and so was he.

" You loved her then ? " she said at length.

" Yes. But in this way. When I was a boy I caught a bird, a black-cap, and I put it in a cage. *And I loved that bird. I don't know why, but I loved it. I simply loved that bird. All the gorse, and the heather, and the rock, and the hot smell of yellow gorse-blossom, and the sky that seemed to have no end to it, when I was a boy, everything that I almost was *mad* with, as boys are, seemed to me to be in that little, fluttering black-cap. And it would peck its seed as if it didn't quite know what else to do ; and look round about, and begin to sing. But in quite a few days it turned its head aside and died. Yes, it died. I never had the feeling again that I got from that black-cap when I was a boy—not until I saw her. And then I felt it all again. I felt it all again. And it was the same feeling. I knew, quite soon I knew, that she would die. She would peck her seed and look round in the cage just the same. But she would die in the end. Only it would last much longer. But she would die in the cage, like the black-cap."

" But she loved the cage. She loved her clothes and her jewels. She must have loved her house and her furniture and all that with a perfect frenzy."

" She did. She did. But like a child with playthings. Only they were big, marvellous playthings to her. Oh, yes, she was never away from them. She never forgot her things—her trinkets and her furs and her furniture. She never got away from them for a minute. And everything in her mind was mixed up with them."

" Dreadful ! " said Hannele.

" Yes, it was dreadful," he answered.

" Dreadful," repeated Hannele.

" Yes, quite. Quite ! And it got worse. And her way of talking got worse. As if it bubbled off her lips. But her eyes never lost their brightness, they never lost that faery look. Only I used to see fear in them. Fear of everything—even all the things she surrounded herself with. Just like my black-cap used to look out of his cage—so bright and sharp, and yet as if he didn't know that it was just the cage that was between him and the outside. He thought it was inside himself, the barrier. He thought it was part of his own nature to be shut in. And she thought it was part of her own nature. And so they both died."

"What I can't see," said Hannele, "is what she would have done outside her cage. What other life could she have, except her *bibelots* and her furniture and her talk?"

"Why, none. There *is* no life outside for human beings."

"Then there's nothing," said Hannele.

"That's true. In a great measure, there's nothing."

"Thank you," said Hannele.

There was a long pause.

"And perhaps I was to blame. Perhaps I ought to have made some sort of a move. But I didn't know what to do. For my life, I didn't know what to do, except try to make her happy. She had enough money—and I didn't think it mattered if she shared it with me. I always had a garden—and the astronomy. It's been an immense relief to me watching the moon. It's been wonderful. Instead of looking inside the cage, as I did at my bird, or at her—I look right out—into freedom—into freedom."

"The moon, you mean?" said Hannele.

"Yes, the moon."

"And that's your freedom?"

"That's where I've found the greatest sense of freedom," he said.

"Well, I'm not going to be jealous of the moon," said Hannele at length.

"Why should you. It's not a thing to be jealous of."

In a little while, she bade him good-night, and left him.

VIII

The chief thing that the captain knew, at this juncture, was that a hatchet had gone through the ligatures and veins that connected him with the people of his affection, and that he was left with the bleeding ends of all his vital human relationships. Why it should be so he did not know. But then one never can know the whys and the wherefores of one's passional changes.

He only knew that it was so. The emotional flow between him and all the people he knew and cared for was broken, and for the time being he was conscious only of the cleavage. The cleavage that had occurred between him and his fellow-men, the cleft that was now between him and them. It was not the fault of anybody or anything. He could neither reproach himself nor them. What had happened had been preparing for a long time. Now suddenly the cleavage. There had been a long, slow weaning away : and now this sudden silent rupture.

What it amounted to principally was that he did not want even to see Hannele. He did not want to think of her even. But neither did he want to see anybody else, or to think of anybody else. He shrank with a feeling almost of disgust from his friends and acquaintances, and their expressions of sympathy. It affected him with instantaneous disgust, when anybody wanted to share emotions with him. He did not want to share emotions or feelings of any sort. He wanted to be by himself, essentially, even if he was moving about among other people.

So he went to England to settle his own affairs, and out of duty to see his children. He wished his children all the well in the world—everything except any emotional connection with himself. He decided to take his girl away from the convent at once, and to put her into a jolly English school. His boy was all right where he was.

The captain had now an income sufficient to give him his independence, but not sufficient to keep up his wife's house. So he prepared to sell the house and most of the things in it. He decided also to leave the army as soon as he could be free. And he thought he would wander about for a time, till he came upon something he wanted.

So the winter passed, without his going back to Germany. He was free of the army. He drifted along, settling his affairs. They were of no very great importance. And all the time he never wrote once to Hannele. He could not get over his disgust that people insisted on his sharing their emotions. He could not bear their emotions, neither their activities. Other people might have all the emotions and feelings and earnestnesses and busy activities they liked. Quite nice even that they had such a multifarious commotion for themselves. But the moment they approached him to spread their feelings over him or to entangle him in their activities a helpless disgust came up in him, and until he could get away he felt sick, even physically.

This was no state of mind for a lover. He could not even think of Hannele. Anybody else he felt he need not think about. He was deeply, profoundly thankful that his wife was dead. It was an end of pity now ; because, poor thing, she had escaped and gone her own way into the void, like a flown bird.

IX

Nevertheless, a man hasn't finished his life at forty. He may, however, have finished one great phase of his life.

And Alexander Hepburn was not the man to live alone. All our troubles, says somebody wise, come upon us because we cannot be alone. And that is all very well. We must all be *able* to be alone, otherwise we are just victims. But when we *are* able to be alone, then we realize that the only thing to do is to start a new relationship with another—or even the same—human being. That people should all be stuck up apart, like so many telegraph poles, is nonsense.

So with out dear captain. He had his convulsion into a sort of telegraph-pole isolation : which was absolutely necessary for him. But then he began to bud with a new yearning for—for what ? For love ?

It was a question he kept nicely putting to himself. And really, the nice young girls of eighteen or twenty attracted him very much : so fresh, so impulsive, and looking up to him as if he were something wonderful. If only he could have married two or three of them, instead of just one !

Love ! When a man has no particular ambition, his mind turns back perpetually, as a needle towards the pole. That tiresome word Love. It means so many things. It meant the feeling he had had for his wife. He had loved her. But he shuddered at the thought of having to go through such love again. It meant also the feeling he had for the awfully nice young things he met here and there : fresh, impulsive girls ready to give all their hearts away. Oh yes, he could fall in love with half a dozen of them. But he knew he'd better not.

At last he wrote to Hannele : and got no answer. So he wrote to Mitchka and still got no answer. So he wrote for information—and there was none forthcoming, except that the two women had gone to Munich.

For the time being he left it at that. To him, Hannele did not exactly represent rosy love. Rather a hard destiny. He did not adore her. He did not feel one bit of adoration for her. As a matter of fact, not all the beauties and virtues of woman put together with all the gold in the Indies would have tempted him into the business of adoration any more. He had gone on his knees once, vowing with faltering tones to try and make the adored one happy. And now— never again. Never.

The temptation this time was to be adored. One of those fresh young things would have adored him as if he were a god. And there was something *very* alluring about the thought. Very—very alluring. To be god-almighty in your own house, with a lovely young thing adoring you, and you giving off beams of bright effulgence like a

Gloria ! Who wouldn't be tempted : at the age of forty ? And this was why he dallied.

But in the end he suddenly took the train to Munich. And when he got there he found the town beastly uncomfortable, the Bavarians rude and disagreeable, and no sign of the missing females, not even in the Café Stephanie. He wandered round and round.

And then one day, oh heaven, he saw his doll in a shop window : a little art shop. He stood and stared quite spellbound.

" Well, if that isn't the devil," he said. " Seeing yourself in a shop-window ! "

He was so disgusted that he would not go into the shop.

Then, every day for a week did he walk down that little street and look at himself in the shop window. Yes, there he stood, with one hand in his pocket. And the figure had one hand in its pocket. There he stood, with his cap pulled rather low over his brow. And the figure had its cap pulled low over its brow. But thank goodness, his own cap now was a civilian tweed. But there he stood, his head rather forward, gazing with fixed dark eyes. And himself in little, that wretched figure, stood there with its head rather forward, staring with fixed dark eyes. It was such a real little *man* that it fairly staggered him. The oftener he saw it, the more it staggered him. And the more he hated it. Yet it fascinated him, and he came again to look.

And it was always there. A lonely little individual lounging there with one hand in its pocket, and nothing to do, among the bric-à-brac and the *bibelots*. Poor devil, stuck so incongruously in the world. And yet losing none of his masculinity.

A male little devil, for all his forlornness. But such an air of isolation, of not-belonging. Yet taut and male, in his tartan trews. And what a situation to be in—lounging with his back against a little Japanese lacquer cabinet, with a few old pots on his right hand and a tiresome brass ink-tray on his left, while pieces of not-very-nice filet lace hung their length up and down the background. Poor little devil : it was like a deliberate satire.

And then one day it was gone. There was the cabinet and the filet lace and the tiresome ink-stand tray : and the little gentleman wasn't there. The captain at once walked into the shop.

" Have you sold that doll—that unknown soldier ? " he added, without knowing quite what he was saying.

The doll was sold.

" Do you know who bought it ? "

The girl looked at him very coldly, and did not know.

"I once knew the lady who made it. In fact, the doll was *me*," he said.

The girl now looked at him with sudden interest.

"Don't you think it was like me?" he said.

"Perhaps"—she began to smile.

"It was me. And the lady who made it was a friend of mine. Do you know her name?"

"Yes."

"Gräfin zu Rassentlow," he cried, his eyes shining.

"Oh yes. But her dolls are famous."

"Do you know where she is? Is she in Munich?"

"That I don't now."

"Could you find out?"

"I don't know. I can ask."

"Or the Baroness von Prielau-Carolath."

"The Baroness is dead."

"Dead!"

"She was shot in a riot in Salzburg. They say a lover——"

"How do you know?"

"From the newspapers."

"Dead! Is it possible. Poor Hannele."

There was a pause.

"Well," he said, "if you would enquire about the address—I'll call again."

Then he turned back from the door.

"By the way, do you mind telling me how much you sold the doll for?"

The girl hesitated. She was by no means anxious to give away any of her trade details. But at length she answered reluctantly:

"Five hundred marks."

"So cheap," he said. "Good-day. Then I will call again."

x

Then again he got a trace. It was in the chit-chat column of the *Muenchener Neue Zeitung* : under Studio Comments. "Theodor Worpswede's latest picture is a still-life, containing an entertaining group of a doll, two sun-flowers in a glass jar, and a poached egg on toast. The contrast between the three substances is highly diverting and instructive, and this is perhaps one of the most interesting of Worpswede's works. The doll, by the way, is one of the creations of our fertile Countess Hannele. It is the figure of an English, or rather Scottish officer, in the famous tartan trousers which, clinging closely to the legs of the lively Gaul, so shocked the eminent Julius Cæsar and his cohorts. We, of course, are no longer shocked, but full of admiration for the creative genius of our dear Countess. The doll itself is a masterpiece, and has begotten another masterpiece in Theodor Worpswede's Still-life. We have heard, by the way, a rumour of Countess zu Rassentlow's engagement. Apparently the Herr Regierungsrat von Poldi, of that most beautiful of summer-resorts, Kaprun, in the Tyrol, is the fortunate man——"

XI

The captain bought the Still-life. This new version of himself along with the poached egg and the sun-flowers was rather frightening. So he packed up for Austria, for Kaprun, with his picture, and had a fight to get the beastly thing out of Germany, and another fight to get it into Austria. Fatigued and furious he arrived in Salzburg, seeing no beauty in anything. Next day he was in Kaprun.

It was an elegant and fashionable watering-place before the war : a lovely little lake in the midst of the Alps, an old Tyrolese town on the water-side, green slopes sheering up opposite, and away beyond, a glacier. It was still crowded and still elegant. But alas, with a broken, bankrupt, desperate elegance, and almost empty shops.

The captain felt rather dazed. He found himself in an hotel full of Jews of the wrong, rich sort, and wondered what next. The place was beautiful, but the life wasn't.

XII

The Herr Regierungsrat was not at first sight prepossessing. He was approaching fifty, and had gone stout and rather loose, as so many men of his class and race do. Then he wore one of those dreadful full-bottom coats, a kind of poor relation to our full-skirted frock-coat : it would best be described as a family coat. It flapped about him as he walked, and he looked at first glance lower middle-class.

But he wasn't. Of course, being in office in the collapsed Austria, he was a republican. But by nature he was a monarchist, nay, an imperialist, as every true Austrian is. And he was a true Austrian. And as such he was much finer and subtler than he looked. As one got used to him, his rather fat face, with its fine nose and slightly bitter, pursed mouth, came to have a resemblance to the busts of some of the late Roman emperors. And as one was with him, one came gradually to realize that out of all his baggy bourgeois appearance came something of a *grande geste*. He could not help it. There was something sweeping and careless about his soul : big, rather assertive, and ill-bred-seeming ; but in fact, not ill-bred at all, only a little bitter and a good deal indifferent to his surroundings. He looked at first sight so common and *parvenu*. And then one had to realize that he was a member of a big, old empire, fallen into a sort of epicureanism, and a little bitter. There was no littleness, no meanness, and no real coarseness. But he was a great talker, and relentless towards his audience.

Hannele was attracted to him by his talk. He began as soon as dinner appeared : and he went on, carrying the decanter and the wine-glass with him out on to the balcony of the villa, over the lake, on and on until midnight. The summer night was still and warm : the lake lay deep and full, and the old town twinkled away across. There was the faintest tang of snow in the air, from the great glacier-peaks that were hidden in the night opposite. Sometimes a boat with a lantern twanged a guitar. The clematis flowers were quite black, like leaves, dangling from the terrace.

It was so beautiful, there in the very heart of the Tyrol. The hotels glittered with lights : electric light was still cheap. There seemed a fulness and a loveliness in the night. And yet for some reason it was all terrible and devastating : the life-spirit seemed to be squirming, bleeding all the time.

And on and on talked the Herr Regierungsrat, with all the witty volubility of the more versatile Austrian. He was really very witty, very human, and with a touch of salty cynicism that reminded one of a real old Roman of the Empire. That subtle stoicism, that unsentimental epicureanism, that kind of reckless hopelessness, of course, fascinated the women. And particularly Hannele. He talked on and on—about his work before the war, when he held an important post and was one of the governing class—then about the war—then about the hopelessness of the present : and in it all there seemed a bigness, a carelessness based on indifference, and hopelessness that laughed at its very self. The real old Austria had always fascinated Hannele. As represented in the witty, bitter-indifferent Herr Regierungsrat it carried her away.

And he, of course, turned instinctively to her, talking in his rapid, ceaseless fashion, with a laugh and a pause to drink and a new start taken. She liked the sound of his Austrian speech : its racy carelessness, its salty indifference to standards of correctness. Oh yes, here was the *grande geste* still lingering.

He turned his large breast towards her, and made a quick gesture with his fat, well-shapen hand, blurted out another subtle, rough-seeming romance, pursed his mouth, and emptied his glass once more. Then he looked at his half-forgotten cigar and started again.

There was something almost boyish and impulsive about him : the way he turned to her, and the odd way he seemed to open his big breast to her. And again, he seemed almost eternal, sitting there in his chair with knees planted apart. It was as if he would never rise again, but would remain sitting for ever, and talking. He seemed as if he had no legs, save to sit with. As if to stand on his feet and walk would not be natural to him.

Yet he rose at last, and kissed her hand with the grand gesture that France or Germany have never acquired : carelessness, profound indifference to other people's standards, and then such a sudden stillness, as he bent and kissed her hand. Of course she felt a queen in exile.

And perhaps it is more dangerous to feel yourself a queen in exile than a queen *in situ*. She fell in love with him, with this large, stout, loose widower of fifty, with two children. He had no money except some Austrian money that was worth nothing outside Austria. He could not even go to Germany. There he was, fixed in this hollow in the middle of the Tyrol.

But he had an ambition still, old Roman of the decadence that he was. He had year by year and without making any fuss collected the material for a very minute and thorough history of his own district : the Chiemgau and the Pinzgau. Hannele found that his fund of information on this subject was inexhaustible, and his intelligence was so delicate, so human, and his scope seemed so wide, that she felt a touch of reverence for him. He wanted to write this history. And she wanted to help him.

For, of course, as things were he would never write it. He was Regierungsrat : that is, he was the petty local governor of his town and immediate district. The Amthaus was a great old building, and there young ladies in high heels flirted among masses of papers with bare-kneed young gentlemen in Tyrolese costume, and occasionally they parted, to take a pleasant, interesting attitude and write a word or two, after which they fluttered together for a little more interesting diversion. It was extraordinary how many finely built, handsome young people of an age fitted for nothing but love-affairs, ran the governmental business of this department. And the Herr Regierungsrat sailed in and out of the big, old room, his wide coat flying like wings and making the papers flutter, his rather wine-reddened, old-Roman face smiling with its bitter look. And of course it was a witticism he uttered first, even if Hungary was invading the frontier or cholera was in Vienna.

When he was on his legs, he walked nimbly, briskly, and his coat-bottoms always flew. So he waved through the town, greeting some-body at every few strides, and grinning, and yet with a certain haughty reserve. Oh yes, there was a certain salty *hauteur* about him which made the people trust him. And he spoke the vernacular so racily.

Hannele felt she would like to marry him. She would like to be near him. She would like him to write his history. She would like him to make her feel a queen in exile. No one had ever *quite* kissed her hand as he kissed it : with that sudden stillness and strange, chivalric abandon of himself. How he would abandon himself to her !—terribly—wonderfully—perhaps a little horribly. His wife, whom he had married late, had died after seven years of marriage. Hannele could understand that too. One or the other must die.

She became engaged. But something made her hesitate before marriage. Being in Austria was like being on a wrecked ship that *must* sink after a certain short length of time. And marrying the Herr Regierungsrat was like marrying the doomed captain of the doomed ship. The sense of fatality was part of the attraction.

And yet she hesitated. The summer weeks passed. The strangers flooded in and crowded the town, and ate up the food like locusts. People no longer counted the paper money, they weighed it by the kilogram. Peasants stored it in a corner of the meal-bin, and mice came and chewed holes in it. Nobody knew where the next lot of food was going to come from : yet it always came. And the lake teemed with bathers. When the captain arrived he looked with amazement on the crowds of strapping, powerful fellows who bathed all day long, magnificent blond flesh of men and women. No wonder the old Romans stood in astonishment before the huge blond limbs of the savage Germans.

Well, the life was like a madness. The hotels charged fifteen-hundred kronen a day : the women, old and young, paraded in the peasant-costume, in flowery cotton dresses with gaudy, expensive silk aprons : the men wore the Tyrolese costume, bare knees and little short jackets. And for the men, the correct thing was to have the leathern hose and the blue linen jacket as old as possible. If you had a hole in your leathern seat, so much the better.

Everything so physical. Such magnificent naked limbs and naked bodies, and in the streets, in the hotels, everywhere, bare, white arms

of women and bare, brown, powerful knees and thighs of men. The
sense of flesh everywhere, and the endless ache of flesh. Even in the
peasants who rowed across the lake, standing and rowing with a
slow, heavy, gondolier motion at the one curved oar, there was the
same endless ache of physical yearning.

XIII

It was August when Alexander met Hannele. She was walking
under a chintz parasol, wearing a dress of blue cotton with little red
roses, and a red silk apron. She had no hat, her arms were bare and
soft, and she had white stockings under her short dress. The Herr
Regierungsrat was at her side, large, nimble, and laughing with a
new witticism.

Alexander, in a light summer suit and Panama hat, was just
coming out of the bank, shoving twenty thousand kronen into his
pocket. He saw her coming across from the Amtsgericht, with the
Herr Regierungsrat at her side, across the space of sunshine. She
was laughing, and did not notice him.

She did not notice till he had taken off his hat and was saluting
her. Then what she saw was the black, smooth, shining head, and
she went pale. His black, smooth, close head—and all the blue
Austrian day seemed to shrivel before her eyes.

" How do you do, Countess ! I hoped I should meet you."

She heard his slow, sad-clanging, straying voice again, and she
pressed her hand with the umbrella stick against her breast. She
had forgotten it—forgotten his peculiar, slow voice. And now it
seemed like a noise that sounds in the silence of night. Ah, how
difficult it was, that suddenly the world could split under her eyes,
and show this darkness inside. She wished he had not come.

She presented him to the Herr Regierungsrat, who was stiff and
cold. She asked where the captain was staying. And then, not
knowing what else to say, she said :

" Won't you come to tea ? "

She was staying in a villa across the lake. Yes, he would come
to tea.

He went. He hired a boat and a man to row him across. It was
not far. There stood the villa, with its brown balconies one above
the other, the bright red geraniums and white geraniums twinkling
all round, the trees of purple clematis tumbling at one corner. All
the green window-doors were open : but nobody about. In the
little garden by the water's edge the rose-trees were tall and lank,

drawn up by the dark green trees of the background. A white table with chairs and garden seats stood under the shadow of a big willow tree, and a hammock with cushions swung just behind. But no one in sight. There was a little landing bridge on to the garden : and a fairly large boat-house at the garden end.

The captain was not sure that the boat-house belonged to the villa. Voices were shouting and laughing from the water's surface, bathers swimming. A tall, naked youth with a little red cap on his head and a tiny red loin-cloth round his slender young hips was standing on the steps of the boat-house calling to the three women who were swimming near. The dark-haired woman with the white cap swam up to the steps and caught the boy by the ankle. He cried and laughed and remonstrated, and poked her in the breast with his foot.

" Nein, nein, Hardu ! " she cried as he tickled her with his toe. " Hardu ! Hardu ! Hör' auf ! Leave off ! "—and she fell with a crash back into the water. The youth laughed a loud, deep laugh of a lad whose voice is newly broken.

" Was macht er dann ? " cried a voice from the waters. " What is he doing ? " It was a dark-skinned girl swimming swiftly, her big dark eyes watching amused from the water-surface.

" Jetzt Hardu hör' auf. Nein. Jetzt ruhig ! Now leave off ! Now be quiet." And the dark-haired woman was climbing out in the sunshine on to the pale, raw-wood steps of the boat-house, the water glistening on her dark-blue, stockinette, soft-moulded back and loins : while the boy, with his foot stretched out, was trying to push her back into the water. She clambered out, however, and sat on the steps in the sun, panting slightly. She was dark and attractive-looking, with a mature beautiful figure, and handsome, strong woman's legs.

In the garden appeared a black-and-white maid-servant with a tray.

" Kaffee, gnädige Frau ! "

The voice came so distinct over the water.

" Hannele ! Hannele ! Kaffee ! " called the woman on the steps of the bathing-house.

" Tante Hannele ! Kaffee ! " called the dark-eyed girl, turning round in the water, then swimming for home.

" Kaffee ! Kaffee ! " roard the youth, in anticipation.

" Ja—a ! Ich kom—mm," sang Hannele's voice from the water.

The dark-eyed girl, her hair tied up in a silk bandana, had reached the steps and was climbing out, a slim young fish in her close dark suit. The three stood clustered on the steps, the elder woman with one arm over the naked shoulders of the youth, the other arm over the shoulders of the girl. And all in chorus sang :

"Hannele ! Hannele ! Hannele ! Wir warten auf dich."

The boatman had left off rowing, and the boat was drifting slowly in. The family became quiet, because of the intrusion. The attractive-looking woman turned and picked up her blue bath-robe, of a mid-blue colour that became her. She swung it round her as if it were an opera cloak. The youth stared at the boat.

The captain was watching Hannele. With a white kerchief tied round her silky, brownish hair, she was swimming home. He saw her white shoulders, and her white, wavering legs below in the clear water. Round the boat fishes were suddenly jumping.

The three on the steps beyond stood silent, watching the intruding boat with resentment. The boatman twisted his head round and watched them. The captain, who was facing them, watched Hannele. She swam slowly and easily up, caught the rail of the steps and stooping forward, climbed slowly out of the water. Her legs were large and flashing white and looked rich, the rich, white thighs with the blue veins behind, and the full, rich softness of her sloping loins.

"Ach ! Schön ! 'S war schön ! Das Wasser ist gut," her voice was heard, half singing as she took her breath. "It was lovely."

"Heiss," said the woman above. "Zu warm. Too warm."

The youth made way for Hannele, who drew herself erect at the top of the steps, looking round, panting a little, and putting up her hands to the knot of her kerchief on her head. Her legs were magnificent and white.

"Kuck die Leut die da bleiben," said the woman in the blue wrap, in a low voice. "Look at the people stopping there."

"Ja !" said Hannele negligently. Then she looked. She started as if in fear, looked round, as if to run away, looked back again, and met the eyes of the captain, who took off his hat.

She cried, in a loud frightened voice :

"Oh, but—I thought it was *to-morrow* !"

"No—to-day," came the quiet voice of the captain over the water.

"*To-day !* Are you *sure* ?" she cried, calling to the boat.

"Quite sure. But we'll make it to-morrow if you like," he said.

"To-day ! To-day !" she repeated in bewilderment. "No ! Wait a minute," And she ran into the boat-house.

"Was ist es ?" asked the dark woman, following her. "What is it ?"

"A friend—a visitor—Captain Hepburn," came Hannele's voice.

The boatman now rowed slowly to the landing stage. The dark woman, huddled in her blue wrap as in an opera cloak, walked proudly and unconcernedly across the background of the garden, and up the steps to the first balcony. Hannele, her feet slip-slopping in loose slippers, clutching an old yellow wrap round her, came to the landing stage and shook hands.

"I am so sorry. It is so stupid of me. I was sure it was to-morrow," she said.

"No, it was to-day. But I wish for your sake it had been to-morrow," he replied.

"No. No. It doesn't matter. You won't mind waiting a minute, will you? You mustn't be angry with me for being so stupid."

So she went away, the heel-less slippers flipping up to her naked heels. Then the big-eyed, dusky girl stole into the house: and then the naked youth, who went with sang-froid. He would make a fine, handsome man: and he knew it.

XIV

Hepburn and Hannele were to make a small excursion to the glacier which stood there always in sight, coldly grinning in the sky. The weather had been very hot, but this morning there were loose clouds in the sky. The captain rowed over the lake soon after dawn. Hannele stepped into the little craft, and they pulled back to the town. There was a wind ruffling the water, so that the boat leaped and chuckled. The glacier, in a recess among the folded mountains, looked cold and angry. But morning was very sweet in the sky, and blowing very sweet with a faint scent of the second hay, from the low lands at the head of the lake. Beyond stood naked grey rock like a wall of mountains, pure rock, with faint thin slashes of snow. Yesterday it had rained on the lake. The sun was going to appear from behind the Breitsteinhorn, the sky with its clouds floating in blue light and yellow radiance was lovely and cheering again. But dark clouds seemed to spout up from the Pinzgau valley. And once across the lake, all was shadow, when the water no longer gave back the sky-morning.

The day was a feast day, a holiday. Already so early three young men from the mountains were bathing near the steps of the Badean-stalt. Handsome, physical fellows, with good limbs rolling and swaying in the early morning water. They seemed to enjoy it too. But to Hepburn it was always as if a dark wing were stretched in the sky, over these mountains, like a doom. And these three young, lusty naked men swimming and rolling in the shadow.

Hepburn's was the first boat stirring. He made fast in the hotel boat-house, and he and Hannele went into the little town. It was deep in shadow, though the light of the sky, curdled with cloud, was bright overhead. But dark and chill and heavy lay the shadow in the black-and-white town, like a sediment.

The shops were all shut, but peasants from the hills were already strolling about, in their holiday dress : the men in their short leather trousers, like football drawers, and bare brown knees, and great boots : their little grey jackets faced with green, and their green hats with the proud chamois-brush behind. They seemed to stray about like lost souls, and the proud chamois-brush behind their hats, this proud, cocky, perking-up tail, like a mountain-buck with his tail up, was belied by the lost-soul look of the men, as they loitered about with their hands shoved in the front pockets of their trousers. Some women also were creeping about : peasant women, in the funny little black hats that had thick gold under the brim and long black streamers of ribbon, broad, black, water-wave ribbon starting from a bow under the brim behind, and streaming right to the bottom of the skirt. These women, in their thick, dark dresses with tight bodices, and massive, heavy, full skirts, and bright or dark aprons, strode about with the heavy stride of the mountain women, the heavy, quick, forward-leaning motion. They were waiting for the town-day to begin.

Hepburn had a knapsack on his back, with food for the day. But bread was wanting. They found the door of the bakery open, and got a loaf : a long, hot loaf of pure white bread, beautiful sweet bread. It cost seventy kronen. To Hepburn it was always a mystery where this exquisite bread came from, in a lost land.

In the little square where the clock stood were bunches of people, and a big motor-omnibus, and a motor-car that would hold about eight people. Hepburn had paid his seven hundred kronen for the two tickets. Hannele tied up her head in a thin scarf, and put on her thick coat. She and Hepburn sat in front by the peaked driver. And at seven o'clock away went the car, swooping out of the town, past the handsome old Tyrolese Schloss, or manor, black-and-white, with its little black spires pricking up, past the station, and under the trees by the lake-side. The road was not good, but they ran at a great speed, out past the end of the lake, where the reeds grew, out into the open valley-mouth, where the mountains opened in two clefts. It was cold in the car. Hepburn buttoned himself up to the throat and pulled his hat down on his ears. Hannele's scarf fluttered. She sat without saying anything, erect, her face fine and keen, watching ahead. From the deep Pinzgau valley came the river roaring and raging, a glacier river of pale, seething ice-water. Over went the car, over the log bridge, darting towards the great slopes opposite. And then a sudden immense turn, a swerve under the height of the mountain-side, and again a darting lurch forward, under the pear-trees of the high-road, past the big old ruined castle that so magnificently watched the valley mouth, and the foaming river ; on, rushing under the huge roofs of the balconied peasant houses of a village, then swinging again to take another valley mouth, there where a little village clustered all black and white on a knoll, with a white church that had a black steeple, and a white castle with black spines, and clustering, ample black-and-white houses of the Tyrol. There is a grandeur even in the peasant houses, with their great wide passage halls where the swallows build, and where one could build a whole English cottage.

So the motor-car darted up this new, narrow, wilder, more sinister valley. A herd of almost wild young horses, handsome reddish things, burst around the car, and one great mare with full flanks went crashing up the road ahead, her heels flashing to the car, while her foal whinneyed and screamed from behind. But no, she could not turn from the road. On and on she crashed, forging ahead, the car behind her. And then at last she did swerve aside, among the thin alder trees by the wild river-bed.

" If it isn't a cow, it's a horse," said the driver, who was thin and weaselish and silent, with his ear-flaps over his ears.

But the great mare had shaken herself in a wild swerve, and screaming and whinneying was plunging back to her foal. Hannele had been frightened.

The car rushed on, through water-meadows, along a naked, white bit of mountain road. Ahead was a darkness of mountain front and pine trees. To the right was the stony, furious, lion-like river, tawny-coloured here, and the slope up beyond. But the road for the moment was swinging fairly level through the stunned water-meadows of the savage valley. There were gates to open, and Hepburn jumped down to open them, as if he were the foot-boy. The heavy Jews of the wrong sort, seated behind, of course did not stir.

At a house on a knoll the driver sounded his horn, and out rushed children crying " Papa ! Papa !" then a woman with a basket. A few brief words from the weaselish man, who smiled with warm, manly blue eyes at his children, then the car leaped forward. The whole bearing of the man was so different when he was looking at his own family. He could not even say thank-you when Hepburn opened the gates. He hated and even despised his human cargo of middle-class people. Deep, deep is class-hatred, and it begins to swallow all human feeling in its abyss. So, stiff, silent, thin, capable, and neuter towards his fares, sat the little driver with the flaps over his ears, and his thin nose cold.

The car swept round, suddenly, into the trees : and into the ravine. The river shouted at the bottom of a gulf. Bristling pine-trees stood around. The air was black and cold and forever sunless. The motor-car rushed on, in this blackness, under the rock-walls and the fir-trees.

Then it suddenly stopped. There was a huge motor-omnibus ahead, drab and enormous-looking. Tourists and trippers of last night coming back from the glacier. It stood like a great rock. And the smaller motor-car edged past, tilting into the rock-gutter under the face of stone.

So, after a while of this valley of the shadow of death, lurching in steep loops upwards, the motor-car scrambling wonderfully, struggling past trees and rock upwards, at last they came to the end. It was a huge inn or tourist-hotel of brown wood : and here the road ended in a little wide bay surrounded and overhung by trees. Beyond was a garage and a bridge over a roaring river : and always the overhung darkness of trees and the intolerable steep slopes immediately above.

Hannele left her big coat. The sky looked blue above the gloom. They set out across the hollow-sounding bridge, over the everlasting mad rush of ice-water, to the immediate upslope of the path, under dark trees. But a little old man in a sort of sentry-box wanted fifty or sixty kronen : apparently for the upkeep of the road, a sort of toll.

The other tourists were coming—some stopping to have a drink first. The second omnibus had not yet arrived. Hannele and Hepburn were the first two, treading slowly up that dark path, under the trees. The grasses hanging on the rock face were still dewy. There were a few wild raspberries, and a tiny tuft of bil-berries with black berries here and there, and a few tufts of unripe cranberries. The many hundreds of tourists who passed up and down did not leave much to pick. Some mountain hare-bells, like bells of blue water, hung coldly glistening in their darkness. Some-times the hairy mountain-bell, pale-blue and bristling, stood alone, curving his head right down, stiff and taut. There was an occasional big, moist, lolling daisy.

So the two climbed slowly up the steep ledge of a road. This valley was just a mountain cleft, cleft sheer in the hard, living rock, with black trees like hair flourishing in this secret, naked place of the earth. At the bottom of the open wedge forever roared the rampant, insatiable water. The sky from above was like a sharp wedge forcing its way into the earth's cleavage, and that eternal ferocious water was like the steel edge of the wedge, the terrible tip biting in into the rocks' intensity. Who could have thought that the soft sky of light, and the soft foam of water could thrust and penetrate into the dark, strong earth? But so it was. Hannele and Hepburn, toiling up the steep little ledge of a road that hung half-way down the gulf, looked back, time after time, back down upon the brown timbers and shingle roofs of the hotel, that now, away below, looked damp and wedged in like boulders. Then back at the next tourists struggling up. Then down at the water, that rushed like a beast of prey. And then, as they rose higher, they looked up also, at the livid great sides of rock, livid bare rock that sloped from the sky-ridge in a hideous sheer swerve downwards.

In his heart of hearts Hepburn hated it. He hated it, he loathed it, it seemed almost obscene, this livid, naked slide of rock, unthinkably huge and massive, sliding down to this gulf where bushes grew like hair in the darkness, and water roared. Above, there were thin slashes of snow.

So the two climbed slowly on, up the eternal side of that valley, sweating with the exertion. Sometimes the sun, now risen high, shone full on their side of the gulley. Tourists were trickling downhill too : two maidens with bare arms and bare heads and huge boots : men tourists with great knapsacks and edelweiss in their hats : giving Bergheil for a greeting. But the captain said Goodday. He refused this Bergheil business. People swarming touristy on these horrible mountains made him feel almost sick.

He and Hannele also were not in good company together. There was a sort of silent hostility between them. She hated the effort of climbing ; but the high air, the cold in the air, the savage cat-howling sound of the water, those awful flanks of livid rock, all this thrilled and excited her to another sort of savageness. And he, dark, rather slender and feline, with something of the physical suavity of a delicate-footed race, he hated beating his way up the rock, he hated the sound of the water, it frightened him, and the high air bit him in his chest, like a viper.

"Wonderful ! Wonderful ! " she cried, taking great breaths in her splendid chest.

"Yes. And horrible. Detestable," he said.

She turned with a flash, and the high strident sound of the mountain in her voice.

" If you don't like it," she said, rather jeering, " why ever did you come ? "

" I had to try," he said.

" And if you don't like it," she said, " why should you try to spoil it for me ? "

" I hate it," he answered.

They were climbing more into the height, more into the light, into the open, in the full sun. The valley-cleft was sinking below them. Opposite was only the sheer livid slide of the naked rock, tipping from the pure sky. At a certain angle they could see away beyond, the lake lying far off and small, the wall of those other rocks like a curtain of stone, dim and diminished to the horizon. And the sky with curdling clouds and blue sunshine intermittent.

" Wonderful, wonderful, to be high up," she said, breathing great breaths.

" Yes," he said. " It *is* wonderful. But very detestable. I want to live near the sea-level. I am no mountain-topper."

" Evidently not," she said.

" Bergheil ! " cried a youth with bare arms and bare chest, bare head, terrific fanged boots, a knapsack and an alpenstock, and all the bronzed wind and sun of the mountain snow in his skin and his faintly bleached hair. With his great heavy knapsack, his rumpled thick stockings, his ghastly fanged boots, Hepburn found him repulsive.

" Guten Tag," he answered coldly.

" Grüss Gott," said Hannele.

And the young Tannhäuser, the young Siegfried, this young Balder beautiful strode climbing down the rocks, marching and swinging with his alpenstock. And immediately after the youth came a maiden, with hair on the wind and her shirt-breast open, striding in corduroy breeches, rumpled worsted stockings, thick boots, a knapsack, and an alpenstock. She passed without greeting. And our pair stopped in angry silence and watched her dropping down the mountain-side.

xv

Ah, well, everything comes to an end, even the longest up-climb. So, after much sweat and effort and crossness, Hepburn and Hannele emerged on to the rounded bluff where the road wound out of that hideous great valley-cleft, into upper regions. So they emerged more on the level, out of the trees as out of something horrible, on to a naked, great bank of rock and grass.

" Thank the Lord ! " said Hannele.

So they trudged on round the bluff, and then in front of them saw what is always, always wonderful, one of those shallow upper valleys, naked, where the first waters are rocked. A flat, shallow, utterly desolate valley, wide as a wide bowl under the sky, with rock slopes and grey stone-slides and precipices all around, and the zig-zag of snow-stripes and ice-roots descending, and then rivers, streams and rivers rushing from many points downwards, down out of the ice-roots and the snow-dagger-points, waters rushing in newly-liberated frenzy downwards, down in waterfalls and cascades and threads, down into the wide, shallow bed of the valley, strewn with rocks and stones innumerable, and not a tree, not a visible bush.

Only, of course, two hotels or restaurant places. But these no more than low, sprawling, peasant-looking places lost among the stones, with stones on their roofs so that they seemed just a part of the valley bed. There was the valley, dotted with rock and rolled-down stone, and these two house-places, and woven with innumerable new waters, and one hoarse stone-tracked river in the desert, and the thin road-track winding along the desolate flat, past first one house, then the other, over one stream, then another, on to the far rock-face above which the glacier seemed to loll like some awful great tongue put out.

"Ah, it is wonderful ! " he said, as if to himself.

And she looked quickly at his face, saw the queer, blank, sphinx-look with which he gazed out beyond himself. His eyes were black and set, and he seemed so motionless, as if he were eternal, facing these upper facts.

She thrilled with triumph. She felt he was overcome.

" It *is* wonderful," she said.

" Wonderful. And for ever wonderful," he said.

" Ah, in *winter*——" she cried.

His face changed, and he looked at her.

" In winter you couldn't get up here," he said.

They went on. Up the slopes cattle were feeding : came that isolated tong-tong-tong of cowbells, dropping like the slow clink of ice on the arrested air. The sound always woke in him a primeval, almost hopeless melancholy. Always made him feel *navré*. He looked round. There was no tree, no bush, only great grey rocks and pale boulders scattered in place of trees and bushes. But yes, clinging on one side like a dark close beard were the alpenrose shrubs.

" In May," he said, " that side there must be all pink with alpen-roses."

" I *must* come. I *must* come ! " she cried.

There were tourists dotted along the road : and two tiny low carts drawn by silky, long-eared mules. These carts went right down to meet the motor-cars, and to bring up provisions for the Glacier Hotel : for there was still another big hotel ahead. Hepburn was happy in that upper valley, that first rocking cradle of early water. He liked to see the great fangs and slashes of ice and snow thrust down into the rock, as if the ice had bitten into the flesh of the earth. And from the fang-tips the hoarse water crying its birth-cry, rushing down.

By the turfy road and under the rocks were many flowers : wonderful hare-bells, big and cold and dark, almost black, and seeming like purple-dark ice : then little tufts of tiny pale-blue bells, as if some fairy frog had been blowing spume-bubbles out of the ice : then the bishop's-crozier of the stiff, bigger, hairy mountain-bell : then many stars of pale-lavender gentian, touched with earth-colour : and then monkshood, yellow, primrose yellow monkshood and sudden places full of dark monkshood. That dark-blue, black-blue, terrible colour of the strange rich monkshood made Hepburn look and look and look again. How did the ice come by that lustrous blue-purple intense darkness ? And by that royal poison—that laughing-snake gorgeousness of much monkshood?

XVI

By one of the loud streams, under a rock in the sun, with scented minty or thyme flowers near, they sat down to eat some lunch. It was about eleven o'clock. A thin bee went in and out the scented flowers and the eyebright. The water poured with all the lust and greed of unloosed water over the stones. He took a cupful for our Han-nele, bright and icy, and she mixed it with the red Hungarian wine.

Down the road strayed the tourists like pilgrims, and at the closed end of the valley they could be seen, quite tiny, climbing the cut-out road that went up like a stair-way. Just by their movement you perceived them. But on the valley-bed they went like rolling stones, little as stones. A very elegant mule came stepping by, following a middle-aged woman in tweeds and a tall, high-browed man in knickerbockers. The mule was drawing a very amusing little cart, a chair, rather like a round office-chair upholstered in red velvet, and mounted on two wheels. The red velvet had gone gold and orange and like fruit-juice, being old : really a lovely colour. And the muleteer, a little shabby creature, waddled beside excitedly.

"Ach," cried Hannele, "that looks almost like before the war : almost as peaceful."

"Except that the chair is too shabby, and that they all feel exceptional," he remarked.

There in that upper valley, there was no sense of peace. The rush of the waters seemed like weapons, and the tourists all seemed in a sort of frenzy, in a frenzy to be happy, or to be thrilled. It was a feeling that desolated the heart.

The two sat in the changing sunshine under their rock, with the mountain flowers scenting the snow-bitter air, and they ate their eggs and sausage and cheese, and drank the bright-red Hungarian wine. It seemed lovely : almost like before the war : almost the same feeling of eternal holiday, as if the world was made for man's everlasting holiday. But not quite. Never again quite the same. The world is not made for man's everlasting holiday.

As Alexander was putting the bread back into his shoulder-sack, he exclaimed :

"Oh, look here !"

She looked, and saw him drawing out a flat package wrapped in paper : evidently a.picture.

"A picture !" she cried.

He unwrapped the thing, and handed it to her. It was Theodor Worpswede's Still-leben : not very large, painted on a board.

Hannele looked at it, and went pale.

"It's *good*," she cried, in an equivocal tone.

"Quite good," he said.

"Especially the poached egg," she said.

"Yes, the poached egg is almost living."

"But where did you find it ?"

"Oh, I found it in the artist's studio." And he told her how he had traced her.

"How extraordinary !" she cried. "But why did you buy it ?"

"I don't quite know."

"Did you *like* it ?"

"No, not quite that."

"You could *never* hang it up."

"No, never," he said.

"But do you think it is good as a work of art ?"

"I think it is quite clever as a painting. I don't like the spirit of it, of course. I'm too catholic for that."

" No. No," she faltered. " It's rather horrid really. That's why I wonder why you bought it."

" Perhaps to prevent any one else's buying it," he said.

" Do you mind very much then ? " she asked.

" No, I don't mind very much. I didn't quite like it that you sold the doll," he said.

" I needed the money," she said quietly.

" Oh, quite."

There was a pause for some moments.

" I felt you'd sold *me*," she said, quiet and savage.

" When ? "

" When your wife appeared. And when you *disappeared*."

Again there was a pause : his pause this time.

" I did write to you," he said.

" When ? "

" Oh—March, I believe."

" Oh, yes. I had that letter." Her tone was just as quiet, and even savager.

So there was a pause that belonged to both of them. Then she rose.

" I want to be going," she said. " We shall never get to the glacier at this rate."

He packed up the picture, slung on his knapsack, and they set off. She stooped now and then to pick the starry, earth-lavender gentians from the road-side. As they passed the second of the valley hotels, they saw the man and wife sitting at a little table outside eating bread and cheese, while the mule-chair with its red velvet waited aside on the grass. They passed a whole grove of black-purple nightshade on the left, and some long, low cattle-huts which, with the stones on their roofs, looked as if they had grown up as stones grow in such places through the grass. In the wild, desert place some black pigs were snouting.

So they wound into the head of the valley, and saw the steep face ahead, and high up, like vapour or foam dripping from the fangs of a beast, waterfalls vapouring down from the deep fangs of ice. And there was one end of the glacier, like a great bluey-white fur just slipping over the slope of the rock.

As the valley closed in again the flowers were very lovely, especially the big, dark, icy bells, like hare-bells, that would sway so easily, but which hung dark and with that terrible motionlessness of upper mountain flowers. And the road turned to get on to the long slant in the cliff-face, where it climbed like a stair. Slowly, slowly the two climbed up. Now again they saw the valley below, behind. The mule-chair was coming, hastening, the lady seated tight facing backwards, as the chair faced, and wrapped in rugs. The tall, fair, middle-aged husband in knickerbockers strode just behind, bare-headed.

Alexander and Hannele climbed slowly, slowly up the slant, under the dripping rock-face where the white and veined flowers of the grass of Parnassus still rose straight and chilly in the shadow, like water which had taken on itself white flower-flesh. Above they saw the slipping edge of the glacier, like a terrible great paw, bluey. And from the skyline dark grey clouds were fuming up, fuming up as if breathed black and icily out from some ice-cauldron.

" It is going to rain," said Alexander.

" Not much," said Hannele shortly.

" I hope not," said he.

And still she would not hurry up that steep slant, but insisted on standing to look. So the dark, ice-black clouds fumed solid, and the rain began to fly on a cold wind. The mule-chair hastened past, the lady sitting comfortably with her back to the mule, a little pheasant-trimming in her tweed hat, while her Tannhäuser husband reached for his dark, cape-frilled mantle.

Alexander had his dust-coat, but Hannele had nothing but a light knitted jersey-coat, such as women wear indoors. Over the hollow crest above came the cold, steel rain. They pushed on up the slope. From behind came another mule, and a little old man hurrying, and a little cart like a hand-barrow, on which were hampers with cabbage and carrots and peas and joints of meat, for the hotel above.

" Wird es viel sein ? " asked Alexander of the little gnome. " Will it be much ? "

" Was meint der Herr ? " replied the other. " What does the gentleman say ? "

" Der Regen, wird es lang dauern ? Will the rain last long ? "

" Nein. Nein. Dies ist kein langer Regen."

So, with his mule which had to stand exactly at that spot to make droppings, the little man resumed his way, and Hannele and Alexander were the last on the slope. The air smelt steel-cold of rain, and of hot mule-droppings. Alexander watched the rain beat on the shoulders and on the blue skirt of Hannele.

" It is a pity you left your big coat down below," he said.

" What good is it saying so now ! " she replied, pale at the nose with anger.

" Quite," he said, as his eyes glowed and his brow blackened. " What good suggesting anything at any time, apparently ! "

She turned round on him in the rain, as they stood perched nearly at the summit of that slanting cliff-climb, with a glacier-paw hung almost invisible above, and waters gloating aloud in the gulf below.

She faced him, and he faced her.

" What have you ever suggested to me ? " she said, her face naked as the rain itself with an ice-bitter fury. " What have you ever suggested to me ? "

" When have you ever been open to suggestion ? " he said, his face dark and his eyes curiously glowing.

" I ? I ? Ha ! Haven't I waited for you to suggest something ? And all you can do is to come here with a picture to reproach me for having sold your doll. Ha ! I'm glad I sold it. A foolish barren effigy it was too, a foolish staring thing. What should I do but sell it. Why should I keep it, do you imagine ? "

" Why do you come here with me to-day, then ? "

" Why do I come here with you to-day ? " she replied. " I come to see the mountains, which are wonderful, and give me strength. And I come to see the glacier. Do you think I come here to see *you* ? Why should I ? You are always in some hotel or other away below."

" You came to see the glacier and the mountains *with* me," he replied.

" Did I ? Then I made a mistake. You can do nothing but find fault even with God's mountains."

A dark flame suddenly went over his face.

" Yes," he said, " I hate them, I hate them. I hate their snow and their affectations."

" *Affectation !* " she laughed. " Oh ! Even the mountains are affected for you, are they ? "

" Yes," he said. " Their loftiness and their uplift. I hate their uplift. I hate people prancing on mountain-tops and feeling exalted. I'd like to make them all stop up there, on their mountain-tops, and chew ice to fill their stomachs. I wouldn't let them down again, I wouldn't. I hate it all, I tell you ; I hate it."

She looked in wonder on his dark, glowing, ineffectual face. It seemed to her like a dark flame burning in the daylight and in the ice-rains : very ineffectual and unnecessary.

" You must be a little mad," she said superbly, " to talk like that about the mountains. They are so much bigger than you."

" No," he said. " No ! They are not."

" What ! " she laughed aloud. " The mountains are not bigger than you ? But you are extraordinary."

"They are not bigger than me," he cried. "Any more than you are bigger than me if you stand on a ladder. They are not bigger than me. They are less than me."

"Oh! Oh!" she cried in wonder and ridicule. "The mountains are less than you."

"Yes," he cried, "they are less."

He seemed suddenly to go silent and remote as she watched him. The speech had gone out of his face again, he seemed to be standing a long way off from her, beyond some border-line. And in the midst of her indignant amazement she watched him with wonder and a touch of fascination. To what country did he belong then—to what dark, different atmosphere?

"You must suffer from megalomania," she said. And she said what she felt.

But he only looked at her out of dark, dangerous, haughty eyes.

They went on their way in the rain in silence. He was filled with a passionate silence and imperiousness, a curious, dark, masterful force that supplanted thought in him. And she, who always pondered, went pondering : "Is he mad? What does he mean? Is he a madman? He wants to bully me. He wants to bully me into something. What does he want to bully me into? Does he want me to love him?"

At this final question she rested. She decided that what he wanted was that she should love him. And this thought flattered her vanity and her pride and appeased her wrath against him. She felt quite mollified towards him.

But what a way he went about it! He wanted her to love him. Of this she was sure. He had always wanted her to love him, even from the first. Only he had not made up his *mind* about it. He had not made up his mind. After his wife had died he had gone away to make up his mind. Now he had made it up. He wanted her to love him. And he was offended, mortally offended because she had sold his doll.

So, this was the conclusion to which Hannele came. And it pleased her, and it flattered her. And it made her feel quite warm towards him, as they walked in the rain. The rain, by the way, was abating. The spume over the hollow crest to which they were approaching was thinning considerably. They could again see the glacier-paw hanging out, a little beyond. The rain was going to pass. And they were not far now from the hotel, and the third level of Lammerboden.

He wanted her to love him. She felt again quite glowing and

triumphant inside herself, and did not care a bit about the rain on her shoulders. He wanted her to love him. Yes, that was how she had to put it. He didn't want to *love* her. No. He wanted *her* to love *him*.

But then, of course, woman-like, she took his love for granted. So many men had been so very ready to love her. And this one—to her amazement, to her indignation, and rather to her secret satisfaction—just blackly insisted that *she* must love *him*. Very well— she would give him a run for his money. That was it : he blackly insisted that *she* must love *him*. What he felt was not to be considered. *She* must love *him*. And be bullied into it. That was what it amounted to. In his silent, black, overbearing soul, he wanted to compel her, he wanted to have power over her. He wanted to make her love him so that he had power over her. He wanted to bully her, physically, sexually, and from the inside.

And she ! Well, she was just as confident that she was not going to be bullied. She would love him : probably she would : most probably she did already. But she was not going to be bullied by him in any way whatsoever. No, he must go down on his knees to her if he wanted her love. And then she would love him. Because she *did* love him. But a dark-eyed little master and bully she would never have.

And this was her triumphant conclusion. Meanwhile the rain had almost ceased, they had almost reached the rim of the upper level, towards which they were climbing, and he was walking in that silent diffidence which made her watch him because she was not sure what he was feeling, what he was thinking, or even what he was. He was a puzzle to her : eternally incomprehensible in his feelings and even his sayings. There seemed to her no logic and no reason in what he felt and said. She could never tell what his next mood would come out of. And this made her uneasy, made her watch him. And at the same time it piqued her attention. He had some of the fascination of the incomprehensible. And his curious inscrutable face—it wasn't really only a meaningless mask, because she had seen it half an hour ago melt with a quite incomprehensible and rather, to her mind, foolish passion. Strange, black, inconsequential passion. Asserting with that curious dark ferocity that he was bigger than the mountains. Madness ! Madness ! Megalomania.

But because he gave himself away, she forgave him and even liked him. And the strange passion of his, that gave out incomprehensible flashes, *was* rather fascinating to her. She felt just a tiny bit sorry for him. But she wasn't going to be bullied by him. She wasn't going to give in to him and his black passion. No, never. It must be love on equal terms, or nothing. For love on equal terms she was quite ready. She only waited for him to offer it.

XVII

In the hotel was a buzz of tourists. Alexander and Hannele sat in the restaurant drinking hot coffee and milk, and watching the maidens in cotton frocks and aprons and bare arms, and the fair youths with maidenly necks and huge voracious boots, and the many Jews of the wrong sort and the wrong shape. These Jews were all being very Austrian, in Tyrol costume that didn't sit on them, assuming the whole gesture and intonation of aristocratic Austria, so that you might think they *were* Austrian aristocrats, if you weren't properly listening, or if you didn't look twice. Certainly they were lords of the Alps, or at least lords of the Alpine hotels this summer, let prejudice be what it might. Jews of the wrong sort. And yet even they imparted a wholesome breath of sanity, disillusion, unsentimentality to the excited " Bergheil " atmosphere. Their dark-eyed, sardonic presence seemed to say to the maidenly-necked mountain youths : " Don't sprout wings of the spirit too much, my dears."

The rain had ceased. There was a wisp of sunshine from a grey sky. Alexander left the knapsack, and the two went out into the air. Before them lay the last level of the up-climb, the Lammerboden. It was a rather gruesome hollow between the peaks, a last shallow valley about a mile long. At the end the enormous static stream of the glacier poured in from the blunt mountain-top of ice. The ice was dull, sullen-coloured, melted on the surface by the very hot summer : and so it seemed a huge, arrested, sodden flood, ending in a wave-wall of stone-speckled ice upon the valley bed of rocky débris. A gruesome descent of stone and blocks of rock, the little valley bed, with a river raving through. On the left rose the grey rock, but the glacier was there, sending down great paws of ice. It was like some great, deep-furred ice-bear lying spread upon the top heights, and reaching down terrible paws of ice into the valley : like some immense sky-bear fishing in the earth's solid hollows from above. Hepburn it just filled with terror. Hannele too it scared, but it gave her a sense of ecstasy. Some of the immense, furrowed paws of ice held down between the rock were vivid blue in colour, but of a frightening, poisonous blue, like crystal copper-sulphate. Most of the ice was a sullen, semi-translucent greeny grey.

The two set off to walk through the massy, desolate stone-bed, under rocks and over waters, to the main glacier. The flowers were even more beautiful on this last reach. Particularly the dark hare-bells were large and almost black and ice-metallic : one could imagine they gave a dull ice-chink. And the grass of Parnassus stood erect, white-veined big cups held terribly naked and open to their ice-air.

From behind the great blunt summit of ice that blocked the distance at the end of the valley, a pale-grey, woolly mist or cloud was fusing up, exhaling huge, like some grey-dead aura into the sky, and covering the top of the glacier. All the way along the valley people were threading, strangely insignificant, among the grey dishevel of stone and rock, like insects. Hannele and Alexander went ahead quickly, along the tiring track.

" Are you glad now that you came ? " she said, looking at him triumphant.

" Very glad I came," he said. His eyes were dilated with excitement that was ordeal or mystic battle rather than the Bergheil ecstasy. The curious vibration of his excitement made the scene strange, rather horrible to her. She too shuddered. But it still seemed to her to hold the key to all glamour and ecstasy, the great silent, living glacier. It seemed to her like a grand beast.

As they came near they saw the wall of ice : the glacier end, thick crusted and speckled with stone and dirt débris. From underneath, secret in stones, water rushed out. When they came quite near, they saw the great monster was sweating all over, trickles and rivulets of sweat running down his sides of pure, slush-translucent ice. There it was, the glacier, ending abruptly in the wall of ice under which they stood. Near to, the ice was pure, but waterlogged, all the surface rather rotten from the hot summer. It was sullenly translucent, and of a watery, darkish bluey-green colour. But near the earth it became again bright coloured, gleams of green like jade, gleams of blue like thin, pale sapphire, in little caverns above the wet stones where the walls trickled forever.

Alexander wanted to climb on to the glacier. It was his one desire—to stand upon it. So under the pellucid wet wall they toiled among rocks upwards, to where the guide-track mounted the ice. Several other people were before them—mere day-tourists—and all uncertain about venturing any further. For the ice-slope rose steep and slithery, pure, sun-locked, sweating ice. Still, it was like a curved back. One could scramble on to it, and on up to the first level, like the flat on top of some huge paw.

There stood the little cluster of people, facing the uphill of sullen, pure, sodden-looking ice. They were all afraid : naturally. But being human, they all wanted to go beyond their fear. It was strange that the ice looked so pure, like flesh. Not bright, because the surface was soft like a soft, deep epidermis. But pure ice away down to immense depths.

Alexander, after some hesitation, began gingerly to try the ice. He was frightened of it. And he had no stick, and only smooth-soled boots. But he had a great desire to stand on the glacier. So, gingerly and shakily, he began to struggle a few steps up the pure slope. The ice was soft on the surface, he could kick his heel in it and get a little sideways grip. So, staggering and going sideways he got up a few yards, and was on the naked ice-slope.

Immediately the youths and the fat man below began to tackle it too : also two maidens. For some time, however, Alexander gingerly and scramblingly led the way. The slope of ice was steeper, and rounded, so that it was difficult to stand up in any way. Sometimes he slipped, and was clinging with burnt finger-ends to the soft ice-mass. Then he tried throwing his coat down, and getting a foot-hold on that. Then he went quite quickly by bending down and get-ting a little grip with his fingers, and going ridiculously as on four legs.

Hannele watched from below, and saw the ridiculous exhibition, and was frightened and amused, but more frightened. And she kept calling, to the great joy of the Austrians down below :

" Come back. Do come back."

But when he got on to his feet again he only waved his hand at her, half crossly, as she stood away down there in her blue frock. The other fellows with sticks and nail-boots had now taken heart and were scrambling like crabs past our hero, doing better than he.

He had come to a rift in the ice. He sat near the edge and looked down. Clean, pure ice, fused with pale colour, and fused into intense copper-sulphate blue away down in the crack. It was not like crystal, but fused as one fuses a borax bead under a blow-flame. And keenly, wickedly blue in the depths of the crack.

He looked upwards. He had not half mounted the slope. So on he went, upon the huge body of the soft-fleshed ice, slanting his way sometimes on all fours, sometimes using his coat, usually hitting-in with the side of his heel. Hannele down below was crying him to come back. But two other youths were now almost level with him.

So he struggled on till he was more or less over the brim. There he stood and looked at the ice. It came down from above in a great hollow world of ice. A world, a terrible place of hills and valleys and slopes, all motionless, all of ice. Away above the grey mist-cloud was looming bigger. And near at hand were long huge cracks, side by side, like gills in the ice. It would seem as if the ice breathed through these great ridged gills. One could look down into the series of gulfs, fearful depths, and the colour burning that acid, intense blue, intenser as the crack went deeper. And the crests of the open gills ridged and grouped pale blue above the crevices. It seemed as if the ice breathed there.

The wonder, the terror, and the bitterness of it. Never a warm leaf to unfold, never a gesture of life to give off. A world sufficient unto itself in lifelessness, all this ice.

He turned to go down, though the youths were passing beyond him. And seeing the naked translucent ice heaving downwards in a vicious curve, always the same dark translucency underfoot, he was afraid. If he slipped, he would certainly slither the whole way down, and break some of his bones. Even when he sat down, he had to cling with his finger-nails in the ice, because if he had started to slide he would have slid the whole way down on his trouser-seat, precipitously, and have landed heaven knows how.

Hannele was watching from below. And he was frightened, perched seated on the shoulder of ice and not knowing how to get off. Above he saw the great blue gills of ice ridging the air. Down below were two blue cracks—then the last wet level claws of ice upon the stones. And there stood Hannele and the three or four people who had got so far.

However, he found that by striking in his heels sideways with sufficient sharpness he could keep his footing, no matter how steep the slope. So he started to jerk his way zig-zag downwards.

As he descended, arrived a guide with a black beard and all the paraphernalia of ropes and pole and bristling boots. He and his gentleman began to strike their way up the ice. With those bristling nails like teeth in one's boots, it was quite easy : and a pole to press on to.

Hannele, who had got sick of waiting, and who was also frightened, had gone scuttling on the return journey. He hurried after her, thankful to be off the ice, but excited and gratified. Looking round, he saw the guide and the man on the ice watching the ice-world and the weather. Then they too turned to come down. The day wasn't safe.

XVIII

Pondering, rather thrilled, they threaded their way through the desert of rock and rushing water back to the hotel. The sun was shining warmly for a moment, and he felt happy, though his finger-ends were bleeding a little from the ice.

" But one day," said Hannele, " I should love to go with a guide right up, high, right into the glacier."

" No," said he. " I've been far enough. I prefer the world where cabbages will grow on the soil. Nothing grows on glaciers."

" They say there are glacier-fleas, which only live on glaciers," she said.

" Well, to me the ice didn't look good to eat, even for a flea."

" You never know," she laughed. " But you're glad you've been, aren't you ? "

" Very glad. Now I need never go again."

" But you *did* think it wonderful ? "

" Marvellous. And awful, to my mind."

XIX

They ate venison and spinach in the hotel, then set off down again. Both felt happier. She gathered some flowers, and put them in her handkerchief so they should not die. And again they sat by the stream, to drink a little wine.

But the fume of cloud was blowing up again, thick from behind the glacier. Hannele was uneasy. She wanted to get down. So they went fairly quickly. Many other tourists were hurrying downwards also. The rain began—a sharp handful of drops flung from beyond the glacier. So Hannele and he did not stay to rest, but dropped easily down the steep, dark valley towards the motor-car terminus.

There they had tea, rather tired but comfortably so. The big hotel restaurant was hideous, and seemed sordid. So in the gloom of a grey, early twilight they went out again and sat on a seat, watching the tourists and the trippers and the motor-car men. There were three Jews from Vienna : and the girl had a huge white woolly dog, as big as a calf, and white and woolly and silky and amiable as a toy. The men, of course, came patting it and admiring it, just as men always do, in life and in novels. And the girl, holding the leash, posed and leaned backwards in the attitude of heroines on novel-covers. She said the white cool monster was a Siberian steppe-dog. Alexander wondered what the steppes made of such a wuffer. And the three Jews pretended they were elegant Austrians out of popular romances.

" Do you think," said Alexander, "you will marry the Herr Regierungsrat ? "

She looked round, making wide eyes.

"It looks like it, doesn't it!" she said.

"Quite," he said.

Hannele watched the woolly white dog. So of course it came wagging its ever-amiable hindquarters towards her. She looked at it still, but did not touch it.

"What makes you ask such a question," she said.

"I can't say. But even so you haven't really answered. Do you really fully intend to marry the Herr Regierungsrat? Is that your final intention at this moment?"

She looked at him again.

"But before I answer," she said, "oughtn't I to know why you ask?"

"Probably you know already," he said.

"I assure you I don't."

He was silent for some moments. The huge, woolly dog stood in front of him and breathed enticingly, with its tongue out. He only looked at it blankly.

"Well," he said, "if you were not going to marry the Herr Regierungsrat, I should suggest that you marry me."

She stared away at the auto-garage, a very faint look of amusement, or pleasure, or ridicule on her face: or all three. And a certain shyness.

"But why?" she said.

"Why what?" he returned.

"Why should you suggest that I should marry you?"

"*Why?*" he replied, in his lingering tones. "*Why?* Well, for what purpose does a man usually ask a woman to marry him?"

"For what *purpose*!" she repeated, rather haughtily.

"For what reason, then!" he corrected.

She was silent for some moments. Her face was closed and a little numb-looking, her hands lay very still in her lap. She looked away from him, across the road.

"There is usually only one reason," she replied, in a rather small voice.

"Yes?" he replied curiously. "What would you say that was?"

She hesitated. Then she said, rather stiffly:

"Because he really loved her, I suppose. That seems to me the only excuse for a man asking a woman to marry him."

Followed a dead silence, which she did not intend to break. He knew he would have to answer, and for some reason he didn't want to say what was obviously the thing to say.

" Leaving aside the question of whether you love me or I love you——" he began.

" I certainly *won't* leave it aside," she said.

" And I certainly won't consider it," he said, just as obstinately.

She turned now and looked full at him, with amazement, ridicule, and anger in her face.

" I really think you must be mad," she said.

" I doubt if you do think that," he replied. " It is only a method of retaliation, that is. I think you understand my point very clearly."

" Your point ! " she cried. " Your point ! Oh, so you have a point in all this palavering ? "

" Quite ! " said he.

She was silent with indignation for some time. Then she said angrily :

" I assure you I do *not* see your point. I don't see any point at all. I see only impertinence."

" Very good," he replied. " The point is whether we marry on a basis of love."

" Indeed ! Marry ! We, marry ! I don't think that is by any means the point."

He took his knapsack from under the seat, between his feet. And from the knapsack he took the famous picture.

" When," he said, " we were supposed to be in love with one another, you made that doll of me, didn't you ? " And he sat looking at the odious picture.

" I never for one moment deluded myself that you *really* loved me," she said bitterly.

" Take the other point, whether *you* loved *me*, or not," said he.

" How could I love you, when I couldn't believe in your love for me ? " she cried.

He put the picture down between his knees again.

" All this about love," he said, " is very confusing, and very complicated."

" Very ! In *your* case. Love to me is simple enough," she said.

" Is it ? Is it ? And was it simple love which made you make that doll of me ? "

" Why shouldn't I make a doll of you ? Does it do you any harm ? And *weren't* you a doll, good heavens ! You *were* nothing but a doll. So what hurt does it do you ? "

" Yes, it does. It does me the greatest possible damage," he replied.

She turned on him with wide-open eyes of amazement and rage.

" Why ? Pray why ? Can you tell me why ? "

" Not quite, I can't," he replied, taking up the picture and holding it in front of him. She turned her face from it as a cat turns its nose away from a lighted cigarette. " But when I look at it—when I look at this—then I *know* that there's no love between you and me."

" Then why are you talking at me in this shameful way," she flashed at him, tears of anger and mortification rising to her eyes. " You want your little revenge on me, I suppose, because I made that doll of you."

" That may be so, in a small measure," he said.

" That is *all*. That is all and everything," she cried. " And that is all you came back to me for—for this petty revenge. Well, you've had it now. But please don't speak to me any more. I shall see if I can go home in the big omnibus."

She rose and walked away. He saw her hunting for the motor-bus conductor. He saw her penetrate into the yard of the garage. And he saw her emerge again, after a time, and take the path to the river. He sat on in front of the hotel. There was nothing else to do.

The tourists who had arrived in the big 'bus now began to collect. And soon the huge drab vehicle itself rolled up, and stood big as a house before the hotel door. The passengers began to scramble into their seats. The two men of the white dog were going : but the woman of the white dog, and the dog, were staying behind. Hepburn wondered if Hannele had managed to get herself transferred. He doubted it, because he knew the omnibus was crowded.

Moreover, he had her ticket.

The passengers were packed in. The conductor was collecting the tickets. And at last the great 'bus rolled away. The bay of the road-end seemed very empty. Even the woman with the white dog had gone. Soon the other car, the Luxus, so-called, must appear. Hepburn sat and waited. The evening was falling chilly, the trees looked gruesome.

At last Hannele sauntered up again, unwillingly.

" I think," she said, " you have my ticket."

" Yes, I have," he replied.

" Will you give it me, please ? "

He gave it to her. She lingered a moment. Then she walked away.

There was the sound of a motor-car. With a triumphant purr the Luxus came steering out of the garage yard, and drew up at the hotel door. Hannele came hastening also. She went straight to one of the hinder doors—she and Hepburn had their seats in front, beside the driver. She had her foot on the step of the back seat. And then

she was afraid. The little sharp-faced driver—there was no conductor—came round looking at the car. He looked at her with his
sharp, metallic eye of a mechanic.

" Are all the people going back who came ? " she asked, shrinking.

" Jawohl."

" It is full—this car ? "

" Jawohl."

" There's no other place ? "

" Nein."

Hannele shrank away. The driver was absolutely laconic.

Six of the passengers were here : four were already seated.
Hepburn sat still by the hotel door, Hannele lingered in the road by
the car, and the little driver, with a huge woollen muffler round his
throat, was running round and in and out looking for the two missing
passengers. Of course there were two missing passengers. No, he
could not find them. And off he trotted again, silently, like a weasel
after two rabbits. And at last, when everybody was getting cross,
he unearthed them and brought them scuttling to the car.

Now Hannele took her seat, and Hepburn beside her. The driver
snapped up the tickets and climbed in past them. With a vindictive
screech the car glided away down the ravine. Another beastly
trip was over, another infernal joyful holiday done with.

" I think," said Hepburn, " I may as well finish what I had to say."

" What ? " cried Hannele, fluttering in the wind of the rushing car.

" I may as well finish what I had to say," shouted he, his breath
blown away.

" Finish then," she screamed, the ends of her scarf flickering
behind her.

" When my wife died," he said loudly, " I knew I couldn't love
any more."

" Oh—h ! " she screamed ironically.

" In fact," he shouted, " I realised that, as far as I was concerned,
love was a mistake."

" *What* was a mistake ? " she screamed.

" Love," he bawled.

" Love ! " she screamed. " A mistake ? " Her tone was derisive.

" For me personally," he said, shouting.

" Oh, only for you personally," she cried, with a pouf of laughter.

The car gave a great swerve, and she fell on the driver. Then she
righted herself. It gave another swerve, and she fell on Alexander.
She righted herself angrily. And now they ran straight on : and it
seemed a little quieter.

" I realized," he said, " that I had always made a mistake, under-taking to love."

" It must have been an undertaking, for *you*," she cried.

" Yes, I'm afraid it was. I never really wanted it. But I thought I did. And that's where I made my mistake."

" Whom have you ever loved—even as an undertaking ? " she asked.

" To begin with, my mother : and that was a mistake. Then my sister : and that was a mistake. Then a girl I had known all my life : and that was a mistake. Then my wife : and that was my most terrible mistake. And then I began the mistake of loving you."

" Undertaking to love me, you mean," she said. " But then you never did properly undertake it. You never really *undertook* to love me."

" Not quite, did I ? " said he.

And she sat feeling angry that he had never made the under-taking.

" No," he continued. " Not quite. That is why I came back to you. I don't want to love you. I don't want marriage on a basis of love."

" On a basis of what, then ? "

" I think you know without my putting it into words," he said.

" Indeed, I assure you I don't. You are much too mysterious," she replied.

Talking in a swiftly-running motor-car is a nerve-wracking business. They both had a pause, to rest, and to wait for a quieter stretch of road.

" It isn't very easy to put it into words," he said. " But I tried marriage once on a basis of love, and I must say it was a ghastly affair in the long run. And I believe it would be so, for me, *whatever* woman I had."

" There must be something wrong with you, then," said she.

" As far as love goes. And yet I want marriage. I want marriage. I want a woman to honour and obey me."

" If you are quite reasonable and *very* sparing with your com-mands," said Hannele. "And very careful how you give your orders."

" In fact, I want a sort of patient Griselda. I want to be honoured and obeyed. I don't want love."

" How Griselda managed to honour that fool of a husband of hers, even if she obeyed him, is more than I can say," said Hannele. " I'd like to know what she *really* thought of him. Just what any woman thinks of a bullying fool of a husband."

" Well," said he, " that's no good to me."

They were silent now until the car stopped at the station. There they descended and walked on under the trees by the lake.

" Sit on a seat," he said, " and let us finish."

Hannele, who was really anxious to hear what he should say, and who, woman-like, was fascinated by a man when he began to give away his own inmost thoughts—no matter how much she might jeer afterwards—sat down by his side. It was a grey evening, just falling dark. Lights twinkled across the lake, the hotel over there threaded its strings of light. Some little boats came rowing quietly to shore. It was a grey, heavy evening, with that special sense of dreariness with which a public holiday usually winds up.

" Honour, and obedience : and the proper physical feelings," he said. " To me that is marriage. Nothing else."

" But what are the proper physical feelings but love ? " asked Hannele.

" No," he said. " A woman wants you to adore her, and be in love with her—and I shan't. I will not do it again, if I live a monk for the rest of my days. I will neither adore you nor be in love with you."

" You won't get a chance, thank you. And what do you call the proper physical feelings, if you are not in love ? I think you want something vile."

" If a woman honours me—absolutely from the bottom of her nature honours me—and obeys me because of that, I take it, my desire for her goes very much deeper than if I was in love with her, or if I adored her."

" It's the same thing. If you love, then everything is there—all the lot : your honour and obedience and everything. And if love isn't there, nothing is there," she said.

" That isn't true," he replied. " A woman may love you, she may adore you, but she'll neither honour you nor obey you. The most loving and adoring woman to-day could any minute start and make a doll of her husband—as you made of me."

" Oh, that eternal doll ! What makes it stick so in your mind ? "

" I don't know. But there it is. It wasn't malicious. It was flattering, if you like. But it just sticks in me like a thorn : like a thorn. And there it is, in the world, in Germany somewhere. And you can say what you like, but *any* woman, to-day, no matter *how* much she loves her man—she could start any minute and make a doll of him. And the doll would be her hero : and her hero would be no more than her doll. My wife might have done it. She did do it, in her mind. She had her doll of me right enough. Why, I heard her talk about me to other women. And her doll was a great deal sillier than the one you made. But it's all the same. If a woman loves you, she'll make a doll out of you. She'll never be satisfied till she's made your doll. And when she's got your doll, that's all she wants. And that's what love means. And so, I won't be loved. And I won't love. I won't have anybody loving me. It is an insult. I feel I've been insulted for forty years : by love, and the women who've loved me. I won't be loved. And I won't love. I'll be honoured and I'll be obeyed : or nothing."

" Then it'll most probably be nothing," said Hannele sarcastically. " For I assure you, I've nothing but love to offer."

" Then keep your love," said he.

She laughed shortly.

" And you ? " she cried. " You ! Even suppose you *were* honoured and obeyed. I suppose all you've got to do is to sit there like a sultan and sup it up."

" Oh no, I have many things to do. And woman or no woman, I'm going to start to do them."

" What, pray ? "

" Why, nothing very exciting. I'm going to East Africa to join a man who's breaking his neck to get his three thousand acres of land under control. And when I've done a few more experiments and observations, and got all the necessary facts, I'm going to do a book on the moon. Woman or no woman, I'm going to do that."

" And the woman—supposing you got the poor thing ? "

"Why, she'll come along with me, and we'll set ourselves up out there."

" And she'll do all the honouring and obeying and housekeeping incidentally, while you ride about in the day and stare at the moon in the night."

He did not answer. He was staring away across the lake.

" What will you do for the woman, poor thing, while she's racking herself to pieces honouring you and obeying you and doing frightful housekeeping in Africa : because I know it can be *awful* : awful."

" Well," he said slowly, " she'll be my wife, and I shall treat her as such. If the marriage service says love and cherish—well, in that sense I shall do so."

" Oh ! " cried Hannele. " What, *love* her ? Actually love the poor thing ? "

" Not in that sense of the word, no. I shan't adore her or be in love with her. But she'll be my wife, and I shall love and cherish her as such."

"Just because she's your wife. Not because she's herself. Ghastly fate for any miserable woman," said Hannele.

"I don't think so. I think it's her highest fate."

"To be your wife?"

"To be a wife—and to be loved and shielded as a wife—not as a flirting woman."

"To be loved and cherished just because you're his wife! No, thank you. All I can admire is the conceit and impudence of it."

"Very well, then—there it is," he said, rising.

She rose too, and then went on towards where the boat was tied.

As they were rowing in silence over the lake, he said:

"I shall leave to-morrow."

She made no answer. She sat and watched the lights of the villa draw near. And then she said:

"I'll come to Africa with you. But I won't promise to honour and obey you."

"I don't want you otherwise," he said, very quietly.

The boat was drifting to the little landing stage. Hannele's friends were hallooing to her from the balcony.

"Hallo!" she cried. "Ja. Da bin ich. Ja, 's war wunderschön."

Then to him she said:

"You'll come in?"

"No," he said, "I'll row straight back."

From the villa they were running down the steps to meet Hannele.

"But won't you have me even if I love you?" she asked him.

"You must promise the other," he said. "It comes in the marriage service."

"Hat's geregnet? Wie war das Wetter? Warst du auf dem Gletscher?" cried the voices from the garden.

"Nein—kein Regen. Wunderschön! Ja, er war ganz auf dem Gletscher," cried Hannele in reply. And to him, *sotto voce*:

"Don't be a solemn ass. Do come in."

"No," he said, "I don't want to come in."

"Do you want to go away to-morrow? Go if you *do*. But any-way, I won't say it *before* the marriage service. I needn't, need I?"

She stepped from the boat on to the plank.

"Oh," she said, turning round, "give me that picture, please, will you? I want to burn it."

He handed it to her.

"And come to-morrow, will you?" she said.

"Yes, in the morning."

He pulled back quickly into the darkness.

Lou Witt had had her own way so long, that by the age of twenty-five she didn't know where she was. Having one's own way landed one completely at sea.

To be sure for a while she had failed in her grand love affair with Rico. And then she had had something really to despair about. But even that had worked out as she wanted. Rico had come back to her, and was dutifully married to her. And now, when she was twenty-five and he was three months older, they were a charming married couple. He flirted with other women still, to be sure. He wouldn't be the handsome Rico if he didn't. But she had " got " him. Oh yes ! You had only to see the uneasy backward glance at her, from his big blue eyes : just like a horse that is edging away from its master : to know how completely he was mastered.

She, with her odd little *museau*, not exactly pretty, but very attractive ; and her quaint air of playing at being well-bred, in a sort of charade game ; and her queer familiarity with foreign cities and foreign languages ; and the lurking sense of being an outsider everywhere, like a sort of gipsy, who is at home anywhere and nowhere : all this made up her charm and her failure. She didn't quite belong.

Of course she was American : Lousiana family, moved down to Texas. And she was moderately rich, with no close relation except her mother. But she had been sent to school in France when she was twelve, and since she had finished school, she had drifted from Paris to Palermo, Biarritz to Vienna and back via Munich to London, then down again to Rome. Only fleeting trips to her America.

So what sort of American was she, after all ?

And what sort of European was she either ? She didn't " belong " anywhere. Perhaps most of all in Rome, among the artists and the Embassy people.

It was in Rome she had met Rico. He was an Australian, son of a government official in Melbourne, who had been made a baronet. So one day Rico would be Sir Henry, as he was the only son. Meanwhile he floated round Europe on a very small allowance—his father wasn't rich in capital—and was being an artist.

They met in Rome when they were twenty-two, and had a love affair in Capri. Rico was handsome, elegant, but mostly he had spots of paint on his trousers and he ruined a necktie pulling it off. He behaved in a most floridly elegant fashion, fascinating to the Italians. But at the same time he was canny and shrewd and sensible as any young poser could be and, on principle, good-hearted, anxious. He was anxious for his future, and anxious for his place in the world, he was poor, and suddenly wasteful in spite of all his tension of economy, and suddenly spiteful in spite of all his ingratiating efforts, and suddenly ungrateful in spite of all his burden of gratitude, and suddenly rude in spite of all his good manners, and suddenly detestable in spite of all his suave, courtier-like amiability.

He was fascinated by Lou's quaint aplomb, her experiences, her " knowledge," her *gamine* knowingness, her aloneness, her pretty clothes that were sometimes an utter failure, and her southern " drawl " that was sometimes so irritating. That sing-song which was so American. Yet she used no Americanisms at all, except when she lapsed into her odd spasms of acid irony, when she was very American indeed !

And she was fascinated by Rico. They played to each other like two butterflies at one flower. They pretended to be very poor in Rome—he *was* poor : and very rich in Naples. Everybody stared their eyes out at them. And they had that love affair in Capri.

But they reacted badly on each other's nerves. She became ill. Her mother appeared. He couldn't stand Mrs. Witt, and Mrs. Witt couldn't stand him. There was a terrible fortnight. Then Lou was popped into a convent nursing-home in Umbria, and Rico dashed off to Paris. Nothing would stop him. He must go back to Australia.

He went to Melbourne, and while there his father died, leaving him a baronet's title and an income still very moderate. Lou visited America once more, as the strangest of strange lands to her. She came away disheartened, panting for Europe, and, of course, doomed to meet Rico again.

They couldn't get away from one another, even though in the course of their rather restrained correspondence he informed her that he was " probably " marrying a very dear girl, friend of his childhood, only daughter of one of the oldest families in Victoria. Not saying much.

He didn't commit the probability, but reappeared in Paris, wanting to paint his head off, terribly inspired by Cezanne and by old Renoir. He dined at the Rotonde with Lou and Mrs. Witt, who, with her queer democratic New Orleans sort of conceit looked round the drinking-hall with savage contempt, and at Rico as part of the show. " Certainly," she said, " when these people here have got any money, they fall in love on a full stomach. And when they've got no money, they fall in love with a full pocket. I never was in a more disgusting place. They take their love like some people take after-dinner pills."

She would watch with her arching, full, strong grey eyes, sitting there erect and silent in her well-bought American clothes. And then she would deliver some such charge of grape-shot. Rico always writhed.

Mrs. Witt hated Paris : " this sordid, unlucky city," she called it. " Something unlucky is bound to happen to me in this sinister, unclean town," she said. " I feel *contagion* in the air of this place. For heaven's sake, Louise, let us go to Morocco or somewhere."

" No, mother dear, I can't now. Rico has proposed to me, and I have accepted him. Let us think about a wedding, shall we ? "

" There ! " said Mrs. Witt. " I said it was an unlucky city ! "

And the peculiar look of extreme New Orleans annoyance came round her sharp nose. But Lou and Rico were both twenty-four years old, and beyond management. And anyhow, Lou would be Lady Carrington. But Mrs. Witt was exasperated beyond exasperation. She would almost rather have preferred Lou to elope with one of the great, evil porters of Les Halles. Mrs. Witt was at the age when the malevolent male in man, the old Adam, begins to loom above all the social tailoring. And yet—and yet—it was better to have Lady Carrington for a daughter, seeing Lou was that sort.

There was a marriage, after which Mrs. Witt departed to America, Lou and Rico leased a little old house in Westminster, and began to settle into a certain layer of English society. Rico was becoming an almost fashionable portrait painter. At least, *he* was almost fashionable, whether his portraits were or not. And Lou too was almost fashionable : almost a hit. There was some flaw somewhere. In spite of their appearances, both Rico and she would never quite go down in any society. They were the drifting artist sort. Yet neither of them was content to be of the drifting artist sort. They wanted to fit in, to make good.

Hence the little house in Westminster, the portraits, the dinners, the friends, and the visits. Mrs. Witt came and sardonically established herself in a suite in a quiet but good-class hotel not far off. Being on the spot. And her terrible grey eyes with the touch of a leer looked on at the hollow mockery of things. As if *she* knew of anything better !

Lou and Rico had a curious exhausting effect on one another : neither knew why. They were fond of one another. Some inscrutable bond held them together. But it was a strange vibration of the nerves, rather than of the blood. A nervous attachment, rather than a sexual love. A curious tension of will, rather than a spontaneous passion. Each was curiously under the domination of the other. They were a pair—they had to be together. Yet quite soon they shrank from one another. This attachment of the will and the nerves was destructive. As soon as one felt strong, the other felt ill. As soon as the ill one recovered strength, down went the one who had been well.

And soon, tacitly, the marriage became more like a friendship, platonic. It was a marriage, but without sex. Sex was shattering and exhausting, they shrank from it, and became like brother and sister. But still they were husband and wife. And the lack of physical relation was a secret source of uneasiness and chagrin to both of them. They would neither of them accept it. Rico looked with contemplative, anxious eyes at other women.

Mrs. Witt kept track of everything, watching as it were from outside the fence, like a potent well-dressed demon, full of uncanny energy and a shattering sort of sense. She said little : but her small, occasionally biting remarks revealed her attitude of contempt for the *ménage*.

Rico entertained clever and well-known people. Mrs. Witt would appear, in her New York gowns and few good jewels. She was handsome, with her vigorous grey hair. But her heavy-lidded grey eyes were the despair of any hostess. They looked too many shattering things. And it was but too obvious that these clever, well-known English people got on her nerves terribly, with their finickiness and their fine-drawn discriminations. She wanted to put her foot through all these fine-drawn distinctions. She thought continually of the house of her girlhood, the plantation, the negroes, the planters : the sardonic grimness that underlay all the big, shiftless life. And she wanted to cleave with some of this grimness of the big, dangerous America, into the safe, finicky drawing-rooms of London. So naturally she was not popular.

But being a woman of energy, she had to do *something*. During the latter part of the war she had worked in the American Red Cross in France, nursing. She loved men—real men. But, on close contact, it was difficult to define what she meant by " real " men. She never met any.

Out of the débâcle of the war she had emerged with an odd piece of débris, in the shape of Geronimo Trujillo. He was an American, son of a Mexican father and a Navajo Indian mother, from Arizona. When you knew him well, you recognized the real half-breed, though at a glance he might pass as a sunburnt citizen of any nation, particularly of France. He looked like a certain sort of Frenchman, with his curiously-set dark eyes, his straight black hair, his thin black moustache, his rather long cheeks, and his almost slouching, diffident, sardonic bearing. Only when you knew him, and looked right into his eyes, you saw that unforgettable glint of the Indian.

He had been badly shell-shocked, and was for a time a wreck. Mrs. Witt, having nursed him into convalescence, asked him where he was going next. He didn't know. His father and mother were dead, and he had nothing to take him back to Phœnix, Arizona. Having had an education in one of the Indian high schools, the unhappy fellow had now no place in life at all. Another of the many misfits.

There was something of the Paris Apache in his appearance : but he was all the time withheld, and nervously shut inside himself. Mrs. Witt was intrigued by him.

" Very well, Phœnix," she said, refusing to adopt his Spanish name, " I'll see what I can do."

What she did was to get him a place on a sort of manor farm, with some acquaintances of hers. He was very good with horses, and had a curious success with turkeys and geese and fowls.

Some time after Lou's marriage, Mrs. Witt reappeared in London, from the country, with Phœnix in tow, and a couple of horses. She had decided that she would ride in the Park in the morning, and see the world that way. Phœnix was to be her groom.

So, to the great misgiving of Rico, behold Mrs. Witt in splendidly tailored habit and perfect boots, a smart black hat on her smart grey hair, riding a grey gelding as smart as she was, and looking down her conceited, inquisitive, scornful, aristocratic-democratic Lousiana nose at the people in Piccadilly, as she crossed to the Row, followed by the taciturn shadow of Phœnix, who sat on a chestnut with three white feet as if he had grown there.

Mrs. Witt, like many other people, always expected to find the real *beau monde* and the real *grand monde* somewhere or other. She didn't quite give in to what she saw in the Bois de Boulogne, or in Monte Carlo, or on the Pincio ; all a bit shoddy, and not very *beau* and not at all *grand*. There she was, with her grey eagle eye, her splendid complexion and her weapon-like health of a woman of fifty, dropping her eyelids a little, very slightly nervous, but completely prepared to despise the *monde* she was entering in Rotten Row.

In she sailed, and up and down that regatta-canal of horsemen and horsewomen under the trees of the Park. And yes, there were lovely girls with fair hair down their backs, on happy ponies. And awfully well-groomed papas, and tight mamas who looked as if they were going to pour tea between the ears of their horses and converse with banal skill, one eye on the teapot, one on the visitor with whom she was talking, and all the rest of her hostess' argus-eyes upon everybody in sight. That alert argus capability of the English matron was startling and a bit horrifying. Mrs. Witt would at once think of the old negro mammies, away in Lousiana. And her eyes became dagger-like as she watched the clipped, shorn, mincing young Englishmen. She refused to look at the prosperous Jews.

It was still the days before motor-cars were allowed in the Park, but Rico and Lou, sliding round Hyde Park Corner and up Park Lane in their car, would watch the steely horsewoman and the saturnine groom with a sort of dismay. Mrs. Witt seemed to be pointing a pistol at the bosom of every other horseman or horsewoman, and announcing : *Your virility or your life ! Your femininity or your life !* She didn't know herself what she really wanted them to be : but it was something as democratic as Abraham Lincoln and as aristocratic as a Russian Czar, as highbrow as Arthur Balfour, and as taciturn and unideal as Phœnix. Everything at once.

There was nothing for it : Lou had to buy herself a horse and ride at her mother's side, for very decency's sake. Mrs. Witt was *so* like a smooth, levelled, gunmetal pistol, Lou had to be a sort of sheath. And she really looked pretty, with her clusters of dark, curly, New Orleans hair, like grapes, and her quaint brown eyes that didn't quite match, and that looked a bit sleepy and vague, and at the same time quick as a squirrel's. She was slight and elegant, and a tiny bit rakish, and somebody suggested she might be on the movies.

Nevertheless, they were in the society columns next morning—*Two new and striking figures in the Row this morning were Lady Henry Carrington and her mother Mrs. Witt,* etc. And Mrs. Witt liked it, let her say what she might. So did Lou. Lou liked it immensely. She simply luxuriated in the sun of publicity.

" Rico dear, you must get a horse."

The tone was soft and southern and drawling, but the overtone had a decisive finality. In vain Rico squirmed—he had a way of writhing and squirming which perhaps he had caught at Oxford.

In vain he protested that he couldn't ride, and that he didn't care for riding. He got quite angry, and his handsome arched nose tilted and his upper lip lifted from his teeth, like a dog that is going to bite. Yet daren't quite bite.

And that was Rico. He daren't quite bite. Not that he was really afraid of the others. He was afraid of himself, once he let himself go. He might rip up in an eruption of life-long anger all this pretty-pretty picture of a charming young wife and a delightful little home and a fascinating success as a painter of fashionable, and at the same time " great " portraits : with colour, wonderful colour, and at the same time, form, marvellous form. He had composed this little *tableau vivant* with great effort. He didn't want to erupt like some suddenly wicked horse—Rico was really more like a horse than a dog, a horse that might go nasty any moment. For the time, he was good, very good, dangerously good.

" Why, Rico dear, I thought you used to ride so much, in Australia, when you were young ? Didn't you tell me all about it, hm ? "—and as she ended on that slow, singing *hm* ?, which acted on him like an irritant, and a drug, he knew he was beaten.

Lou kept the sorrel mare in a mews just behind the house in Westminster, and she was always slipping round to the stables. She had a funny little nostalgia for the place : something that really surprised her. She had never had the faintest notion that she cared for horses and stables and grooms. But she did. She was fascinated. Perhaps it was her childhood's Texas associations come back. Whatever it was, her life with Rico in the elegant little house, and all her social engagements seemed like a dream, the substantial reality of which was those mews in Westminster, her sorrel mare, the owner of the mews, Mr. Saintsbury, and the grooms he employed. Mr. Saintsbury was a horsey elderly man like an old maid, and he loved the sound of titles.

" Lady Carrington !—well I never ! You've come to us for a bit of company again, I see. I don't know whatever we shall do if you go away, we shall be that lonely ! " and he flashed his old-maid's smile at her. " No matter how grey the morning, your ladyship would make a beam of sunshine. Poppy is all right, I think . . ."

Poppy was the sorrel mare with the three white feet and the startled eye, and she was all right. And Mr. Saintsbury was smiling with his old-maid's mouth, and showing all his teeth.

" Come across with me, Lady Carrington, and look at a new horse just up from the country. I think he's worth a look, and I believe you have a moment to spare, your ladyship."

Her ladyship had too many moments to spare. She followed the sprightly, elderly, clean-shaven man across the yard to a loose-box, and waited while he opened the door.

In the inner dark she saw a handsome bay horse with his clean ears pricked like daggers from his naked head as he swung handsomely round to stare at the open doorway. He had big, black, brilliant eyes, with a sharp questioning glint, and that air of tense, alert quietness which betrays an animal that can be dangerous.

" Is he quiet ? " Lou asked.

" Why—yes—my lady ! He's quiet, with those that know how to handle him. *Cup ! my boy ! Cup my beauty ! Cup then ! St. Mawr !* "

Loquacious even with the animals, he went softly forward and laid his hand on the horse's shoulder, soft and quiet as a fly settling. Lou saw the brilliant skin of the horse crinkle a little in apprehensive anticipation, like the shadow of the descending hand on a bright red-gold liquid. But then the animal relaxed again.

" Quiet with those that know how to handle him, and a bit of a ruffian with those that don't. Isn't that the ticket, eh, St. Mawr ? "

" What is his name ? " Lou asked.

The man repeated it, with a slight Welsh twist—" He's from the Welsh borders, belonging to a Welsh gentleman, Mr. Griffith Edwards. But they're wanting to sell him."

" How old is he ? " asked Lou.

" About seven years—seven years and five months," said Mr. Saintsbury, dropping his voice as if it were a secret.

" Could one ride him in the Park ? "

" Well—yes ! I should say a gentleman who knew how to handle him could ride him very well and make a very handsome figure in the Park."

Lou at once decided that this handsome figure should be Rico's. For she was already half in love with St. Mawr. He was of such a lovely red-gold colour, and a dark, invisible fire seemed to come out of him. But in his big black eyes there was a lurking afterthought. Something told her that the horse was not quite happy : that somewhere deep in his animal consciousness lived a dangerous, half-revealed resentment, a diffused sense of hostility. She realized that he was sensitive, in spite of his flaming, healthy strength, and nervous with a touchy uneasiness that might make him vindictive.

" Has he got any tricks ? " she asked.

" Not that I know of, my lady : not tricks exactly. But he's one of these temperamental creatures, as they say. Though *I* say, every horse is temperamental, when you come down to it. But this one, it is as if he was a trifle raw somewhere. Touch this raw spot, and there's no answering for him."

"Where is he raw?" asked Lou, somewhat mystified. She thought he might really have some physical sore.

"Why, that's hard to say, my lady. If he was a human being, you'd say something had gone wrong in his life. But with a horse it's not that, exactly. A high-bred animal like St. Mawr needs understanding, and I don't know as anybody has quite got the hang of him. I confess I haven't myself. But I do realize that he is a special animal and needs a special sort of touch, and I'm willing he should have it, did I but know exactly what it is."

She looked at the glowing bay horse that stood there with his ears back, his face averted, but attending as if he were some lightning conductor. He was a stallion. When she realized this, she became more afraid of him.

"Why does Mr. Griffith Edwards want to sell him?" she asked.

"Well—my lady—they raised him for stud purposes—but he didn't answer. There are horses like that : don't seem to fancy the mares, for some reason. Well anyway, they couldn't keep him for the stud. And as you see, he's a powerful, beautiful hackney, clean as a whistle, and eaten up with his own power. But there's no putting him between the shafts. He won't stand it. He's a fine saddle-horse, beautiful action, and lovely to ride. But he's got to be handled, and there you are."

Lou felt there was something behind the man's reticence.

"Has he ever made a break?" she asked, apprehensive.

"Made a break?" replied the man. "Well, if I must admit it, he's had two accidents. Mr. Griffith Edwards' son rode him a bit wild, away there in the Forest of Deane, and the young fellow had his skull smashed in, against a low oak bough. Last autumn, that was. And some time back, he crushed a groom against the side of the stall —injured him fatally. But they were both accidents, my lady. Things will happen."

The man spoke in a melancholy, fatalistic way. The horse, with his ears laid back, seemed to be listening tensely, his face averted. He looked like something finely bred and passionate, that has been judged and condemned.

"May I say *how do you do?*" she said to the horse, drawing a little nearer in her white, summery dress, and lifting her hand that glittered with emeralds and diamonds.

He drifted away from her, as if some wind blew him. Then he ducked his head, and looked sideways at her, from his black, full eye.

" I think I'm all right," she said, edging nearer, while he watched her.

She laid her hand on his side, and gently stroked him. Then she stroked his shoulder, and then the hard, tense arch of his neck. And she was startled to feel the vivid heat of his life come through to her, through the lacquer of red-gold gloss. So slippery with vivid, hot life !

She paused, as if thinking, while her hand rested on the horse's sun-arched neck. Dimly, in her weary young-woman's soul, an ancient understanding seemed to flood in.

She wanted to buy St. Mawr.

" I think," she said to Saintsbury, " if I can, I will buy him."

The man looked at her long and shrewdly.

" Well, my lady," he said at last, " there shall be nothing kept from you. But what would your ladyship do with him, if I may make so bold ? "

" I don't know," she replied, vaguely. " I might take him to America."

The man paused once more, then said :

" They say it's been the making of some horses, to take them over the water, to Australia, or such places. It might repay you—you never know."

She wanted to buy St. Mawr. She wanted him to belong to her. For some reason the sight of him, his power, his alive, alert intensity, his unyieldingness, made her want to cry.

She never did cry : except sometimes with vexation, or to get her own way. As far as weeping went, her heart felt as dry as a Christmas walnut. What was the good of tears, anyhow ? You had to keep on holding on, in this life, never give way, and never give in. Tears only left one weakened and ragged.

But now, as if that mysterious fire of the horse's body had split some rock in her, she went home and hid herself in her room, and just cried. The wild, brilliant, alert ahead of St. Mawr seemed to look at her out of another world. It was as if she had had a vision, as if the walls of her own world had suddenly melted away, leaving her in a great darkness, in the midst of which the large, brilliant eyes of that horse looked at her with demonish question, while his naked ears stood up like daggers from the naked lines of his inhuman head, and his great body glowed red with power.

What was it ? Almost like a god looking at her terribly out of the everlasting dark, she had felt the eyes of that horse ; great, glowing, fearsome eyes, arched with a question, and containing a white blade of light like a threat. What was his non-human question, and his uncanny threat ? She didn't know. He was some splendid demon, and she must worship him.

She hid herself away from Rico. She could not bear the triviality and superficiality of her human relationships. Looming like some god out of the darkness was the head of that horse, with the wide, terrible, questioning eyes. And she felt that it forbade her to be her ordinary, commonplace self. It forbade her to be just Rico's wife, young Lady Carrington, and all that.

It haunted her, the horse. It had looked at her as she had never been looked at before : terrible, gleaming, questioning eyes arching out of darkness, and backed by all the fire of that great ruddy body. What did it mean, and what ban did it put upon her ? She felt it put a ban on her heart : wielded some uncanny authority over her, that she dared not, could not understand.

No matter where she was, what she was doing, at the back of her consciousness loomed a great, over-aweing figure out of a dark background : St. Mawr, looking at her without really seeing her, yet gleaming a question at her, from his wide terrible eyes, and gleaming a sort of menace, doom. Master of doom, he seemed to be !

" You are thinking about something, Lou dear ! " Rico said to her that evening.

He was so quick and sensitive to detect her moods—so exciting in this respect. And his big, slightly prominent blue eyes, with the whites a little bloodshot, glanced at her quickly, with searching, and anxiety, and a touch of fear, as if his conscience were always uneasy. He, too, was rather like a horse—but forever quivering with a sort of cold, dangerous mistrust, which he covered with anxious love.

At the middle of his eyes was a central powerlessness, that left him anxious. It used to touch her to pity, that central look of powerlessness in him. But now, since she had seen the full, dark, passionate blaze of power and of different life in the eyes of the thwarted horse, the anxious powerlessness of the man drove her mad. Rico was so handsome, and he was so self-controlled, he had a gallant sort of kindness and a real worldly shrewdness. One had to admire him : at least *she* had to.

But after all, and after all, it was a bluff, an attitude. He kept it all working in himself, deliberately. It was an attitude. She read psychologists who said that everything was an attitude. Even the best of everything. But now she realized that, with men and women, everything is an attitude only when something else is lacking. Something is lacking and they are thrown back on their own devices. That black fiery flow in the eyes of the horse was not "attitude." It was something much more terrifying, and real, the only thing that was real. Gushing from the darkness in menace and question, and blazing out in the splendid body of the horse.

"Was I thinking about something?" she replied, in her slow, amused, casual fashion. As if everything was so casual and easy to her. And so it was, from the hard, polished side of herself. But that wasn't the whole story.

"I think you were, Loulina. May we offer the penny?"

"Don't trouble," she said. "I was thinking, if I was thinking of anything, about a bay horse called St. Mawr." Her secret *almost* crept into her eyes.

"The name is awfully attractive," he said with a laugh.

"Not so attractive as the creature himself. I'm going to buy him."

"Not really!" he said. "But why?"

"He *is* so attractive. I'm going to buy him for you."

"For *me! Darling!* How you do take me for granted. He may not be in the least attractive to me. As you know, I have hardly any feeling for horses at all. Besides, how much does he cost?"

"That I don't know, Rico dear. But I'm sure you'll love him, for my sake." She felt, now, she was merely playing for her own ends.

"Lou dearest, *don't* spend a fortune on a horse for me, which I *don't* want. Honestly, I prefer a car."

"Won't you ride with me in the Park, Rico?"

"Honestly, dear Lou, I don't want to."

"Why not, dear boy? You'd look so beautiful. I wish you would. And anyhow, come with me to look at St. Mawr."

Rico was divided. He had a certain uneasy feeling about horses. At the same time, he *would* like to cut a handsome figure in the Park.

They went across to the mews. A little Welsh groom was watering the brilliant horse.

"Yes, dear, he certainly *is* beautiful : such a marvellous colour! Almost orange! But rather large, I should say, to ride in the Park."

"No, for you he's perfect. You are so tall."

"He'd be marvellous in a composition. That colour!"

And all Rico could do was to gaze with the artist's eye at the horse, with a glance at the groom.

"Don't you think the man is rather fascinating too?" he said, nursing his chin artistically and penetratingly.

The groom, Lewis, was a little, quick, rather bow-legged, loosely-built fellow of indeterminate age, with a mop of black hair and a little black beard. He was grooming the brilliant St. Mawr, out in the open. The horse was really glorious : like a marigold, with a pure golden sheen, a shimmer of green-gold lacquer, upon a burning red-orange. There on the shoulder you saw the yellow lacquer glisten. Lewis, a little scrub of a fellow, worked absorbedly, unheedingly at the horse, with an absorption that was almost ritualistic. He seemed the attendant shadow of the ruddy animal.

" He goes with the horse," said Lou. " If we buy St. Mawr we get the man thrown in."

" They'd be *so* amusing to paint : such an extraordinary contrast ! But darling, I *hope* you won't insist on buying the horse. It's so frightfully expensive."

" Mother will help me. You'd look so well on him, Rico."

" If ever I dared take the liberty of getting on his back—— ! "

" Why not ? " She went quickly across the cobbled yard.

" Good morning, Lewis. How is St. Mawr ? "

Lewis straightened himself and looked at her from under the falling mop of his black hair.

" All right," he said.

He peered straight at her from under his overhanging black hair. He had pale grey eyes, that looked phosphorescent, and suggested the eyes of a wild cat peering intent from under the darkness of some bush where it lies unseen. Lou, with her brown, unmatched, oddly perplexed eyes, felt herself found out. " He's a common little fellow," she thought to herself. " But he knows a woman and a horse, at sight." Aloud she said, in her southern drawl :

" How do you think he'd be with Sir Henry ? "

Lewis turned his remote, coldly watchful eyes on the young baronet. Rico was tall and handsome and balanced on his hips. His face was long and well-defined, and with the hair taken straight back from the brow. It seemed as well-made as his clothing, and as perpetually presentable. You could not imagine his face dirty, or scrubby and unshaven, or bearded, or even moustached. It was perfectly prepared for social purposes. If his head had been cut off, like John the Baptist's, it would have been a thing complete in itself, would not have missed the body in the least. The body was perfectly tailored. The head was one of the famous " talking heads " of modern youth, with eyebrows a trifle Mephistophelian, large blue eyes a trifle bold, and curved mouth thrilling to death to kiss.

Lewis, the groom, staring from between his bush of hair and his beard, watched like an animal from the underbrush. And Rico was still sufficiently a colonial to be uneasily aware of the underbrush, uneasy under the watchfulness of the pale grey eyes, and uneasy in that man-to-man exposure which is characteristic of the democratic colonies and of America. He knew he must ultimately be judged on his merits as a man, alone without a background : an ungarnished colonial.

This lack of background, this defenceless man-to-man business which left him at the mercy of every servant, was bad for his nerves. For he was *also* an artist. He bore up against it in a kind of desperation, and was easily moved to rancorous resentment. At the same time he was free of the Englishman's water-tight *suffisance*. He really was aware that he would have to hold his own all alone, thrown alone on his own defences in the universe. The extreme democracy of the Colonies had taught him this.

And this, the little aboriginal Lewis recognized in him. He recognized also Rico's curious hollow misgiving, fear of some deficiency in himself, beneath all his handsome, young-hero appearance.

" He'd be all right with anybody as would meet him half-way," said Lewis, in the quick Welsh manner of speech, impersonal.

" You hear, Rico ! " said Lou in her sing-song, turning to her husband.

" Perfectly, darling ! "

" Would you be willing to meet St. Mawr half-way, hm ? "

" All the way, darling ! Mahomet would go *all* the way to that mountain. Who would dare do otherwise ? "

He spoke with a laughing, yet piqued sarcasm.

" Why, I think St. Mawr would understand perfectly," she said in the soft voice of a woman haunted by love. And she went and laid her hand on the slippery, life-smooth shoulder of the horse. He, with his strange equine head lowered, its exquisite fine lines reaching a little snake-like forward, and his ears a little back, was watching her sideways, from the corner of his eye. He was in a state of absolute mistrust, like a cat crouching to spring.

" St. Mawr ! " she said. " St. Mawr ! What is the matter ? Surely you and I are all right ! "

And she spoke softly, dreamily stroked the animal's neck. She could feel a response gradually coming from him. But he would not lift up his head. And when Rico suddenly moved nearer, he sprang with a sudden jerk backwards, as if lightning exploded in his four hoofs.

The groom spoke a few low words in Welsh. Lou, frightened, stood with lifted hand arrested. She had been going to stroke him.

" Why did he do that," she said.

"They gave him a beating once or twice," said the groom in a neutral voice, "and he doesn't forget."

She could hear a neutral sort of judgment in Lewis' voice. And she thought of the "raw spot."

Not any raw spot at all. A battle between two worlds. She realized that St. Mawr drew his hot breaths in another world from Rico's, from our world. Perhaps the old Greek horses had lived in St. Mawr's world. And the old Greek heroes, even Hippolytus, had known it.

With their strangely naked equine heads, and something of a snake in their way of looking round, and lifting their sensitive, dangerous muzzles, they moved in a prehistoric twilight where all things loomed phantasmagoric, all on one plane, sudden presences suddenly jutting out of the matrix. It was another world, an older, heavily potent world. And in this world the horse was swift and fierce and supreme, undominated and unsurpassed. "Meet him half-way," Lewis said. But half-way across from our human world to that terrific equine twilight was not a small step. It was a step, she knew, that Rico could never take. She knew it. But she was prepared to sacrifice Rico.

St. Mawr was bought, and Lewis was hired along with him. At first, Lewis rode him behind Lou, in the Row, to get him going. He behaved perfectly.

Phœnix, the half Indian, was very jealous when he saw the black-bearded Welsh groom on St. Mawr.

"What horse you got there?" he asked, looking at the other man with the curious unseeing stare in his hard, Navajo eyes, in which the Indian glint moved like a spark upon a dark chaos. In Phœnix's high-boned face there was all the race-misery of the dispossessed Indian, with an added blankness left by shell-shock. But at the same time, there was that unyielding, save to death, which is characteristic of his tribe; his mother's tribe. Difficult to say what subtle thread bound him to the Navajo, and made his destiny a Red Man's destiny still.

They were a curious pair of grooms, following the correct, and yet extraordinary, pair of American mistresses. Mrs. Witt and Phœnix both rode with long stirrups and straight leg, sitting close to the saddle, without posting. Phœnix looked as if he and the horse were all one piece, he never seemed to rise in the saddle at all, neither trotting nor galloping, but sat like a man riding bareback. And all the time he stared around, at the riders in the Row, at the people grouped outside the rail, chatting, at the children walking with

their nurses, as if he were looking at a mirage, in whose actuality
he never believed for a moment. London was all a sort of dark
mirage to him. His wide, nervous-looking brown eyes with a smallish brown pupil, that showed the white all round, seemed to be
focussed on the far distance, as if he could not see things too near.
He was watching the pale deserts of Arizona shimmer with moving
light, the long mirage of a shallow lake ripple, the great pallid concave of earth and sky expanding with interchanged light. And a
horse-shape loom large and portentous in the mirage, like some
prehistoric beast.

That was real to him : the phantasm of Arizona. But this London
was something his eye passed over, as a false mirage.

He looked too smart in his well-tailored groom's clothes, so smart,
he might have been one of the satirized new-rich. Perhaps it was a
sort of half-breed physical assertion that came through his clothing,
the savage's physical assertion of himself. Anyhow, he looked
" common," rather horsey and loud.

Except his face. In the golden suavity of his high-boned Indian
face, that was hairless, with hardly any eyebrows, there was a blank,
lost look that was almost touching. The same startled blank look
was in his eyes. But in the smallish dark pupils the dagger-point
of light still gleamed unbroken.

He was a good groom, watchful, quick, and on the spot in an
instant if anything went wrong. He had a curious quiet power over
the horses, unemotional, unsympathetic, but silently potent. In the
same way, watching the traffic of Piccadilly with his blank, glinting
eye, he would calculate everything instinctively, as if it were an
enemy, and pilot Mrs. Witt by the strength of his silent will. He
threw around her the tense watchfulness of her own America,
and made her feel at home.

" Phœnix," she said, turning abruptly in her saddle as they
walked the horses past the sheltering policeman at Hyde Park
Corner, " I can't tell you how glad I am to have something a
hundred per cent American at the back of me, when I go through
these gates."

She looked at him from dangerous grey eyes as if she meant it
indeed, in vindictive earnest. A ghost of a smile went up to his
high cheek-bones, but he did not answer.

" Why, mother ? " said Lou, sing-song. " It feels to me so
friendly—— ! "

" Yes, Louise, it does. So friendly ! That's why I mistrust it so
entirely——"

And she set off at a canter up the Row, under the green trees, her face like the face of Medusa at fifty, a weapon in itself. She stared at everything and everybody, with that stare of cold dynamite waiting to explode them all. Lou posted trotting at her side, graceful and elegant, and faintly amused. Behind came Phœnix, like a shadow, with his yellowish, high-boned face still looking sick. And at his side, on the big brilliant bay horse, the smallish, black-bearded Welshman.

Between Phœnix and Lewis there was a latent, but unspoken and wary sympathy. Phœnix was terribly impressed by St. Mawr, he could not leave off staring at him. And Lewis rode the brilliant, handsome-moving stallion so very quietly, like an insinuation.

Of the two men, Lewis looked the darker, with his black beard coming up to his thick black eyebrows. He was swarthy, with a rather short nose, and the uncanny pale-grey eyes that watched everything and cared about nothing. He cared about nothing in the world, except at the present, St. Mawr. People did not matter to him. He rode his horse and watched the world from the vantage ground of St. Mawr, with a final indifference.

" You have been with that horse long ? " asked Phœnix.

" Since he was born."

Phœnix watched the action of St. Mawr as they went. The bay moved proud and springy, but with perfect good sense, among the stream of riders. It was a beautiful June morning, the leaves overhead were thick and green ; there came the first whiff of lime-tree scent. To Phœnix, however, the city was a sort of nightmare mirage, and to Lewis, it was a sort of prison. The presence of people he felt as a prison around him.

Mrs. Witt and Lou were turning, at the end of the Row, bowing to some acquaintances. The grooms pulled aside. Mrs. Witt looked at Lewis with a cold eye.

" It seems an extraordinary thing to me, Louise," she said, " to see a groom with a beard."

" It isn't usual, mother," said Lou. " Do you mind ? "

" Not at all. At least, I think I don't. I get very tired of modern barefaced young men, *very* ! The clean, pure boy, don't you know ! Doesn't it make you tired ? No, I think a groom with a beard is quite attractive."

She gazed into the crowd defiantly, perching her finely shod toe with warlike firmness on the stirrup-iron. Then suddenly she reined in, and turned her horse towards the grooms.

" Lewis ! " she said. " I want to ask you a question. Supposing, now, that Lady Carrington wanted you to shave off that beard, what should you say ? "

Lewis instinctively put up his hand to the said beard.

" They've wanted me to shave it off, Mam," he said. " But I've never done it."

" But why ? Tell me why ? "

" It's part of me, Mam."

Mrs. Witt pulled on again.

" Isn't that extraordinary, Louise ? " she said. " Don't you like the way he says *Mam* ? It sounds so impossible to me. Could any woman think of herself as Mam ? Never ! Since Queen Victoria. But, do you know it hadn't occurred to me that a man's beard was really part of him. It always seemed to me that men wore their beards, like they wear their neckties, for show. I shall always remember Lewis for saying his beard was part of him. Isn't it curious, the way he rides ? He seems to sink himself in the horse. When I speak to him, I'm not sure whether I'm speaking to a man or to a horse."

A few days later, Rico himself appeared on St. Mawr, for the morning ride. He rode self-consciously, as he did everything, and he was just a little nervous. But his mother-in-law was benevolent. She made him ride between her and Lou, like three ships slowly sailing abreast.

And that very day, who should come driving in an open carriage through the Park but the Queen Mother ! Dear old Queen Alexandra, there was a flutter everywhere. And she bowed expressly to Rico, mistaking him, no doubt, for somebody else.

" Do you know," said Rico as they sat at lunch, he and Lou and Mrs. Witt, in Mrs. Witt's sitting-room in the dark, quiet hotel in Mayfair ; " I really like riding St. Mawr *so* much. He really is a noble animal. If ever I am made a Lord—which heaven forbid !— I shall be Lord St. Mawr."

" You mean," said Mrs. Witt, " his real lordship would be the horse ? "

" Very possible, I admit," said Rico, with a curl of his long upper lip.

" Don't you think, mother," said Lou, " there *is* something quite noble about St. Mawr ? He strikes me as the first noble thing I have ever seen."

" Certainly I've not seen any *man* that could compare with him. Because these English noblemen—well ! I'd rather look at a negro Pullman-boy, if I was looking for what *I* call nobility."

Poor Rico was getting crosser and crosser. There was a devil in Mrs. Witt. She had a hard, bright devil inside her, that she seemed to be able to let loose at will.

She let it loose the next day, when Rico and Lou joined her in the Row. She was silent but deadly with the horses, balking them in every way. She suddenly crowded over against the rail, in front of St. Mawr, so that the stallion had to rear to pull himself up. Then, having a clear track, she suddenly set off at a gallop, like an explosion, and the stallion, all on edge, set off after her.

It seemed as if the whole Park, that morning, were in a state of nervous tension. Perhaps there was thunder in the air. But St. Mawr kept on dancing and pulling at the bit, and wheeling sideways up against the railing, to the terror of the children and the onlookers, who squealed and jumped back suddenly, sending the nerves of the stallion into a rush like rockets. He reared and fought as Rico pulled him round.

Then he went on : dancing, pulling, springily progressing sideways, possessed with all the demons of perversity. Poor Rico's face grew longer and angrier. A fury rose in him, which he could hardly control. He hated his horse, and viciously tried to force him to a quiet, straight trot. Up went St. Mawr on his hind legs, to the terror of the Row. He got the bit in his teeth, and began to fight.

But Phœnix, cleverly, was in front of him.

" You get off, Rico ! " called Mrs. Witt's voice, with all the calm of her wicked exultance.

And almost before he knew what he was doing, Rico had sprung lightly to the ground, and was hanging on to the bridle of the rearing stallion.

Phœnix also lightly jumped down, and ran to St. Mawr, handing his bridle to Rico. Then began a dancing and a splashing, a rearing and a plunging. St. Mawr was being wicked. But Phœnix, the indifference of conflict in his face, sat tight and immovable, without any emotion, only the heaviness of his impersonal will settling down like a weight, all the time, on the horse. There was, perhaps, a curious barbaric exultance in bare, dark will devoid of emotion or personal feeling.

So they had a little display in the Row for almost five minutes, the brilliant horse rearing and fighting. Rico, with a stiff long face, scrambled on to Phœnix's horse, and withdrew to a safe distance. Policemen came, and an officious mounted police rode up to save the situation. But it was obvious that Phœnix, detached and apparently unconcerned, but barbarically potent in his will, would bring the horse to order.

Which he did, and rode the creature home. Rico was requested not to ride St. Mawr in the Row any more, as the stallion was dangerous to public safety. The authorities knew all about him.

Where ended the first fiasco of St. Mawr.

" We didn't get on very well with his lordship this morning," said Mrs. Witt triumphantly.

" No, he didn't like his company *at all* ! " Rico snarled back.

He wanted Lou to sell the horse again.

" I doubt if any one would buy him, dear," she said. " He's a known character."

" Then make a gift of him—to your mother," said Rico with venom.

" Why to mother ? " asked Lou innocently.

" She might be able to cope with him—or he with her ! " The last phrase was deadly. Having delivered it, Rico departed.

Lou remained at a loss. She felt almost always a little bit dazed, as if she could not see clear nor feel clear. A curious deadness upon her, like the first touch of death. And through this cloud of numbness, or deadness, came all her muted experiences.

Why was it ? She did not know. But she felt that in some way it came from a battle of wills. Her mother, Rico, herself, it was always an unspoken, unconscious battle of wills, which was gradually numbing and paralysing her. She knew Rico meant nothing but kindness by her. She knew her mother only wanted to watch over her. Yet always there was this tension of will, that was so numbing. As if at the depths of him, Rico were always angry, though he seemed so " happy " on top. And Mrs. Witt was organically angry. So they were like a couple of bombs, timed to explode some day, but ticking on like two ordinary timepieces, in the meanwhile.

She had come definitely to realize this : that Rico's anger was wound up tight at the bottom of him, like a steel spring that kept his works going, while he himself was " charming," like a bomb-clock with Sèvres paintings or Dresden figures on the outside. But his very charm was a sort of anger, and his love was a destruction in itself. He just couldn't help it.

And she ? Perhaps she was a good deal the same herself. Wound up tight inside, and enjoying herself being " lovely." But wound up tight on some tension that, she realized now with wonder, was really a sort of anger. This, the mainspring that drove her on the round of " joys."

She used really to enjoy the tension, and the *élan* it gave her. While she knew nothing about it. So long as she felt it really was life and happiness, this *élan*, this tension and excitement of " enjoying oneself."

Now suddenly she doubted the whole show. She attributed to it the curious numbness that was overcoming her, as if she couldn't feel any more.

She wanted to come unwound. She wanted to escape this battle of wills.

Only St. Mawr gave her some hint of the possibility. He was so powerful, and so dangerous. But in his dark eye, that looked, with its cloudy brown pupil, a cloud within a dark fire, like a world beyond our world, there was a dark vitality glowing, and within the fire, another sort of wisdom. She felt sure of it : even when he put his ears back, and bared his teeth, and his great eyes came bolting out of his naked horse's head, and she saw demons upon demons in the chaos of his horrid eyes.

Why did he seem to her like some living background, into which she wanted to retreat ? When he reared his head and neighed from his deep chest, like deep wind-bells resounding, she seemed to hear the echoes of another darker, more spacious, more dangerous, more splendid world than ours, that was beyond her. And there she wanted to go.

She kept it utterly a secret, to herself. Because Rico would just have lifted his long upper lip, in his bare face, in a condescending sort of " understanding." And her mother would, as usual, have suspected her of side-stepping. People, all the people she knew, seemed so entirely contained within their cardboard lets-be-happy world. Their wills were fixed like machines on happiness, or fun, or the-best-ever. This ghastly cheery-o touch, that made all her blood go numb.

Since she had really seen St. Mawr looming fiery and terrible in an outer darkness, she could not believe the world she lived in. She could not believe it was actually happening, when she was dancing in the afternoon at Claridge's, or in the evening at the Carlton, sliding about with some suave young man who wasn't like a man at all to her. Or down in Sussex for the week-end with the Enderleys : the talk, the eating and drinking, the flirtation, the endless dancing : it all seemed far more bodiless and, in a strange way, wraith-like, than any fairy story. She seemed to be eating Barmecide food, that had been conjured up out of thin air, by the power of words. She seemed to be talking to handsome young barefaced unrealities, not men at all : as she slid about with them, in the perpetual dance, they too seemed to have been conjured up out of air, merely for this soaring, slithering dance-business. And she could not believe that, when the lights went out, they wouldn't melt back into thin air again, and complete nonentity. The strange nonentity of it all ! Everything just conjured up, and nothing real. " *Isn't this the best ever !* " they would beamingly assert, like the wraiths of enjoyment, without any genuine substance. And she would beam back : " *Lots of fun !* "

She was thankful the season was over, and everybody was leaving London. She and Rico were due to go to Scotland, but not till August. In the meantime they would go to her mother.

Mrs. Witt had taken a cottage in Shropshire, on the Welsh border, and had moved down there with Phœnix and her horses. The open, heather-and-bilberry-covered hills were splendid for riding.

Rico consented to spend the month in Shropshire, because for near neighbours Mrs. Witt had the Manbys, at Corrabach Hall. The Manbys were rich Australians returned to the old country and set up as squires, all in full blow. Rico had known them in Victoria : they were of good family : and the girls made a great fuss of him.

So down went Lou and Rico, Lewis, Poppy, and St. Mawr, to Shrewsbury, then out into the country. Mrs. Witt's " cottage " was a tall red-brick Georgian house looking straight on to the church-yard, and the dark, looming big church.

" I never knew what a comfort it would be," said Mrs. Witt, " to have grave-stones under my drawing-room windows, and funerals for lunch."

She really did take a strange pleasure in sitting in her panelled room, that was painted grey, and watching the Dean or one of the curates officiating at the graveside, among a group of Black Country mourners with black-bordered handkerchiefs luxuriantly in use.

" Mother ! " said Lou. " I think it's gruesome ! "

She had a room at the back, looking over the walled garden and the stables. Nevertheless there was the *boom ! boom !* of the passing-bell, and the chiming and pealing on Sundays. The shadow of the church, indeed ! A very audible shadow, making itself heard insistently.

The Dean was a big, burly, fat man with a pleasant manner. He was a gentleman, and a man of learning in his own line. But he let Mrs. Witt know that he looked down on her just a trifle—as a parvenu American, a Yankee—though she never was a Yankee : and at the same time he had a sincere respect for her, as a rich woman. Yes, a sincere respect for her, as a rich woman.

Lou knew that every Englishman, especially of the upper classes, has a wholesome respect for riches. But then, who hasn't?

The Dean was more *impressed* by Mrs. Witt than by little Lou. But to Lady Carrington he was charming : she was *almost* " one of us," you know. And he was very gracious to Rico : " your father's splendid colonial service."

Mrs. Witt had now a new pantomime to amuse her : the Georgian house, her own pew in church—it went with the old house : a village of thatched cottages—some of them with corrugated iron over the thatch : the cottage people, farm labourers and their families, with a few, very few, outsiders : the wicked little group of cottagers down at Mile End, famous for ill-living. The Mile-Enders were all Allisons and Jephsons, and in-bred, the Dean said : result of working through the centuries at the Quarry, and living isolated there at Mile End.

Isolated ! Imagine it ! A mile and a half from the railway station, ten miles from Shrewsbury. Mrs. Witt thought of Texas, and said :

" Yes, they are *very* isolated, away down there ! "

And the Dean never for a moment suspected sarcasm.

But there she had the whole thing staged complete for her : English village life. Even miners breaking in to shatter the rather stuffy, unwholesome harmony. All the men touched their caps to her, all the women did a bit of a reverence, the children stood aside for her, if she appeared in the street.

They were all poor again : the labourers could no longer afford even a glass of beer in the evenings, since the Glorious War.

" Now I think that *is* terrible," said Mrs. Witt. " Not to be able to get away from those stuffy, squalid, picturesque cottages for an hour in the evening, to drink a glass of beer."

" It's a pity, I do agree with you, Mrs. Witt. But Mr. Watson has organized a men's reading-room, where the men can smoke and play dominoes, and read if they wish."

" But that," said Mrs. Witt, " is not the same as that cosy parlour in the ' Moon and Stars.' "

" I quite agree," said the Dean. " It isn't."

Mrs. Witt marched to the landlord of the ' Moon and Stars,' and asked for a glass of cider.

" I want," she said, in her American accent, " these poor labourers to have their glass of beer in the evenings."

" They want it themselves," said Harvey.

" Then they must have it——"

The upshot was, she decided to supply one large barrel of beer per week and the landlord was to sell it to the labourers at a penny a glass.

" My own country has gone dry," she asserted. " But not because we can't *afford* it."

By the time Lou and Rico appeared, she was deep in. She actually interfered very little : the barrel of beer was her one public act. But she *did* know everybody by sight, already, and she *did* know everybody's circumstances. And she had attended one prayer-meeting, one mother's meeting, one sewing-bee, one " social," one Sunday School meeting, one Band of Hope meeting, and one Sunday School treat. She ignored the poky little Wesleyan and Baptist chapels, and was true-blue Episcopalian.

" How strange these picturesque old villages are, Louise ! " she said, with a duskiness around her sharp, well-bred nose. " How *easy* it all seems, all on a definite pattern. And how false ! And underneath, *how corrupt !* "

She gave that queer, triumphant leer from her grey eyes, and queer demonish wrinkles seemed to twitter on her face.

Lou shrank away. She was beginning to be afraid of her mother's insatiable curiosity, that always looked for the snake under the flowers. Or rather, for the maggots.

Always this same morbid interest in other people and their doings, their privacies, their dirty linen. Always this air of alertness for personal happenings, personalities, personalities, personalities. Always this subtle criticism and appraisal of other people, this analysis of other people's motives. If anatomy presupposes a corpse, then psychology presupposes a world of corpses. Personalities, which means personal criticism and analysis, presupposes a whole world-laboratory of human psyches waiting to be vivisected. If you cut a thing up, of course it will smell. Hence, nothing raises such an infernal stink, at last, as human psychology.

Mrs. Witt was a pure psychologist, a fiendish psychologist. And Rico, in his way, was a psychologist too. But he had a formula. " Let's *know* the worst, dear ! But let's look on the bright side, and believe the best."

" Isn't the Dean a priceless old darling ! " said Rico at breakfast.

And it had begun. Work had started in the psychic vivisection laboratory.

" Isn't he wonderful ! " said Lou vaguely.

" So delightfully worldly ! *Some of us are not born to make money, dear boy. Luckily for us, we can marry it.*"—Rico made a priceless face.

" Is Mrs. Vyner so rich ? " asked Lou.

" She is, quite a wealthy woman—in coal," replied Mrs. Witt. " But the Dean is surely worth his weight even in gold. And he's a massive figure. I can imagine there would be great satisfaction in having him for a husband."

" Why, mother ? " asked Lou.

" Oh, such a presence ! One of these old Englishmen, that nobody can put in their pocket. You can't imagine his wife asking him to thread her needle. Something after all so *robust !* So different from *young* Englishmen, who all seem to me like ladies, perfect ladies."

" *Somebody* has to keep up the tradition of the perfect lady," said Rico.

" I know it," said Mrs. Witt. " And if the women won't do it, the young gentlemen take on the burden. They bear it very well."

It was in full swing, the cut and thrust. And poor Lou, who had reached the point of stupefaction in the game, felt she did not know what to do with herself.

Rico and Mrs. Witt were deadly enemies, yet neither could keep clear of the other. It might have been they who were married to one another, their duel and their duet were so relentless.

But Rico immediately started the social round : first the Manbys : then motor twenty miles to luncheon at Lady Tewkesbury's : then young Mr. Burns came flying down in his aeroplane from Chester : then they must motor to the sea, to Sir Edward Edwards' place, where there was a moonlight bathing party. Everything intensely thrilling, and so innerly wearisome, Lou felt.

But back of it all was St. Mawr, looming like a bonfire in the dark. He really was a tiresome horse to own. He worried the mares, if they were in the same paddock with him, always driving them round. And with any other horse he just fought with definite intent to kill. So he had to stay alone.

" That St. Mawr, he's a bad horse," said Phœnix.

" Maybe ! " said Lewis.

" You don't like quiet horses ? " said Phœnix.

" Most horses *is* quiet," said Lewis. " St. Mawr, he's different."

" Why don't he never get any foals ? "

" Doesn't want to, I should think. Same as me."

" What good is a horse like that ? Better shoot him, before he kill somebody."

" What good'll they get, shooting St. Mawr ? " said Lewis.

" If he kills somebody ! " said Phœnix.

But there was no answer.

The two grooms both lived over the stables, and Lou, from her window, saw a good deal of them. They were two quiet men, yet she was very much aware of their presence, aware of Phœnix's rather high square shoulders and his fine, straight, vigorous black hair that tended to stand up assertively on his head, as he went quietly drifting about his various jobs. He was not lazy, but he did everything with a sort of diffidence, as if from a distance, and handled his horses carefully, cautiously, and cleverly, but without sympathy. He seemed to be holding something back, all the time, unconsciously, as if in his very being there was some secret. But it was a secret of *will*. His quiet, reluctant movements, as if he never really wanted to do anything ; his long flat-stepping stride ; the permanent challenge in his high cheek-bones, the Indian glint in his eyes, and his peculiar stare, watchful and yet unseeing, made him unpopular with the women servants.

Nevertheless, women had a certain fascination for him : he would stare at the pretty young maids with an intent blank stare, when they were not looking. Yet he was rather overbearing, domineering with them, and they resented him. It was evident to Lou that he looked upon himself as belonging to the master, not to the servant class. When he flirted with the maids, as he very often did, for he had a certain crude ostentatiousness, he seemed to let them feel that he despised them as inferiors, servants, while he admired their pretty charms, as fresh, country maids.

" I'm fair nervous of that Phœnix," said Fanny, the fair-haired maid. " He makes you feel what he'd do to you if he could."

" He'd better not try with me," said Mabel. " I'd scratch his cheeky eyes out. Cheek !—for it's nothing else ! He's nobody— Common as they're made ! "

" He makes you feel you was there for him to trample on," said Fanny.

" Mercy, you *are* soft ! If anybody's that it's him. Oh my, Fanny, you've no right to let a fellow make you feel like *that !* Make *them* feel that *they're* dirt, for you to trample on : which they are ! "

Fanny, however, being a shy little blonde thing, wasn't good at assuming the trampling rôle. She was definitely nervous of Phœnix. And he enjoyed it. An invisible smile seemed to creep up his cheek-bones, and the glint moved in his eyes as he teased her. He tormented her by his very presence, as he knew.

He would come silently up when she was busy, and stand behind her perfectly still, so that she was unaware of his presence. Then, silently, he would *make* her aware. Till she glanced nervously round, and with a scream, saw him.

One day Lou watched this little play. Fanny had been picking over a bowl of black currants, sitting on the bench under the maple tree in a corner of the yard. She didn't look round till she had picked up her bowl to go to the kitchen. Then there was a scream and a crash.

When Lou came out, Phœnix was crouching down silently gathering up the currants, which the little maid, scarlet and trembling, was collecting into another bowl. Phœnix seemed to be smiling down his back.

" Phœnix ! " said Lou. " I wish you wouldn't startle Fanny ! "

He looked up, and she saw the glint of ridicule in his eyes.

" Who, me ? " he said.

" Yes, you. You go up behind Fanny, to startle her. You're not to do it."

He slowly stood erect, and lapsed into his peculiar invisible silence. Only for a second his eyes glanced at Lou's, and then she saw the cold anger, the gleam of malevolence and contempt. He could not bear being commanded, or reprimanded, by a woman.

Yet it was even worse with a man.

" What's that, Lou ? " said Rico, appearing all handsome and in the picture, in white flannels with an apricot silk shirt.

" I'm telling Phœnix he's not to torment Fanny ! "

" Oh ! "—and Rico's voice immediately became his father's, the important government official's. " Certainly *not !* Most certainly *not !* " He looked at the scattered currants and the broken bowl. Fanny melted into tears. " This, I suppose, is some of the results ! Now look here, Phœnix, you're to leave the maids strictly alone. I shall ask them to report to me whenever, or *if* ever, you interfere with them. But I hope you *won't* interfere with them—in any way. You understand ? "

As Rico became more and more Sir Henry and the government official, Lou's bones melted more and more into discomfort. Phœnix stood in his peculiar silence, the invisible smile on his cheek-bones.

" You understand what I'm saying to you ? " Rico demanded, in intensified acid tones.

But Phœnix only stood there, as it were behind a cover of his own will, and looked back at Rico with a faint smile on his face and the glint moving in his eyes.

" Do you intend to answer ? " Rico's upper lip lifted nastily.

" Mrs. Witt is my boss," came from Phœnix.

The scarlet flew up Rico's throat and flushed his face, his eyes went glaucous. Then quickly his face turned yellow.

Lou looked at the two men : her husband, whose rages, over-controlled, were organically terrible : the half-breed, whose dark-coloured lips were widened in a faint smile of derision, but in whose eyes caution and hate were playing against one another. She realized that Phœnix would accept *her* reprimand, or her mother's, because he could despise the two of them as mere women. But Rico's bossiness aroused murder pure and simple.

She took her husband's arm.

" Come dear ! " she said, in her half-plaintive way. " I'm sure Phœnix understands. We all understand. Go to the kitchen, Fanny, never mind the currants. There are plenty more in the garden."

Rico was always thankful to be drawn quickly, submissively away from his own rage. He was afraid of it. He was afraid lest he should fly at the groom in some horrible fashion. The very thought horrified him. But in actuality he came very near to it.

He walked stiffly, feeling paralysed by his own fury. And those words, *Mrs. Witt is my boss*, were like hot acid in his brain. An insult !

" By the way, Belle-Mère ! " he said when they joined Mrs. Witt —she hated being called Belle-Mère, and once said : " If I'm the bell-mare, are you one of the colts ? " She also hated his voice of smothered fury—" I had to speak to Phœnix about persecuting the maids. He took the liberty of informing me that you were his boss, so perhaps you had better speak to him."

" I certainly will. I believe they're my maids, and nobody else's, so it's my duty to look after them. Who was he persecuting ? "

" I'm the responsible one, mother," said Lou——

Rico disappeared in a moment. He must get out : get away from the house. How ? Something was wrong with the car. Yet he must get away, away. He would go over to Corrabach. He would ride St. Mawr. He had been talking about the horse, and Flora Manby was dying to see him. She had said : " Oh, I can't *wait* to see that marvellous horse of yours."

He would ride him over. It was only seven miles. He found Lou's maid Elena, and sent her to tell Lewis. Meanwhile, to soothe himself, he dressed himself most carefully in white riding breeches and a shirt of purple silk crape, with a flowing black tie spotted red like a ladybird, and black riding boots. Then he took a *chic* little white hat with a black band.

St. Mawr was saddled and waiting, and Lewis had saddled a second horse.

"Thanks, Lewis, I'm going alone!" said Rico.

This was the first time he had ridden St. Mawr in the country, and he was nervous. But he was also in the hell of a smothered fury. All his careful dressing had not really soothed him. So his fury consumed his nervousness.

He mounted with a swing, blind and rough. St. Mawr reared.

"Stop that!" snarled Rico, and put him to the gate.

Once out in the village street, the horse went dancing, sideways. He insisted on dancing at the sidewalk, to the exaggerated terror of the children. Rico, exasperated, pulled him across. But no, he wouldn't go down the centre of the village street. He began dancing and edging on to the other sidewalk, so the foot-passengers fled into the shops in terror.

The devil was in him. He would turn down every turning where he was not meant to go. He reared with panic at a furniture van. He *insisted* on going down the wrong side of the road. Rico was riding him with a martingale, and he could see the rolling, bloodshot eye.

"Damn you, *go!*" said Rico, giving him a dig with the spurs.

And away they went, down the high road, in a thunderbolt. It was a hot day, with thunder threatening, so Rico was soon in a flame of heat. He held on tight, with fixed eyes, trying all the time to rein in the horse. What he really was afraid of was that the brute would shy suddenly, as he galloped. Watching for this, he didn't care when they sailed past the turning to Corrabach.

St. Mawr flew on, in a sort of *élan*. Marvellous the power and life in the creature. There was really a great joy in the motion. If only he wouldn't take the corners at a gallop, nearly swerving Rico off! Luckily the road was clear. To ride, to ride at this terrific gallop, on into eternity!

After several miles, the horse slowed down, and Rico managed to pull him into a lane that might lead to Corrabach. When all was said and done, it was a wonderful ride. St. Mawr could go like the wind, but with that luxurious heavy ripple of life which is like nothing else on earth. It seemed to carry one at once into another world, away from the life of the nerves.

So Rico arrived after all something of a conqueror at Corrabach. To be sure, he was perspiring, and so was his horse. But he was a hero from another, heroic world.

"Oh, such a hot ride!" he said, as he walked on to the lawn at Corrabach Hall. "Between the sun and the horse, really!—between two fires!"

"Don't you trouble, you're looking dandy, a bit hot and flushed like," said Flora Manby. "Let's go and see your horse."

And her exclamation was : "Oh, he's *lovely!* He's *fine!* I'd love to try him once——"

Rico decided to accept the invitation to stay overnight at Corrabach. Usually he was very careful, and refused to stay, unless Lou was with him. But they telephoned to the post-office at Chomesbury, would Mr. Jones please send a message to Lady Carrington that Sir Henry was staying the night at Corrabach Hall, but would be home next day. Mr. Jones received the request with unction, and said he would go over himself to give the message to Lady Carrington.

Lady Carrington was in the walled garden. The peculiarity of Mrs. Witt's house was that, for grounds proper, it had the church-yard.

"I never thought, Louise, that one day I should have an old English churchyard for my lawns and shrubbery and park, and funeral mourners for my herds of deer. It's curious. For the first time in my life a funeral has become a real thing to me. I feel I could write a book on them."

But Louise only felt intimidated.

At the back of the house was a flagged courtyard, with stables and a maple tree in a corner, and big doors opening on to the village street. But at the side was a walled garden, with fruit trees and currant bushes and a great bed of rhubarb, and some tufts of flowers, peonies, pink roses, sweet williams. Phœnix, who had a certain taste for gardening, would be out there thinning the carrots or tying up the lettuce. He was not lazy. Only he would not take work seriously, as a job. He would be quite amused tying up lettuces, and would tie up head after head, quite prettily. Then, becoming bored, he would abandon his task, light a cigarette, and go and stand on the threshold of the big doors, in full view of the street, watching, and yet completely indifferent.

After Rico's departure on St. Mawr, Lou went into the garden. And there she saw Phœnix working in the onion bed. He was bending over, in his own silence, busy with nimble, amused fingers among the grassy young onions. She thought he had not seen her, so she went down another path to where a swing bed hung under the apple trees. There she sat with a book and a bundle of magazines. But she did not read.

She was musing vaguely. Vaguely, she was glad that Rico was away for a while. Vaguely, she felt a sense of bitterness, of complete futility : the complete futility of her living. This left her drifting in a sea of utter chagrin. And Rico seemed to her the symbol of the futility. Vaguely, she was aware that something else existed, but she didn't know where it was or what it was.

In the distance she could see Phœnix's dark, rather tall-built head, with its black, fine, intensely-living hair tending to stand on end, like a brush with long, very fine black bristles. His hair, she thought, betrayed him as an animal of a different species. He was growing a little bored by weeding onions : that also she could tell. Soon he would want some other amusement.

Presently Lewis appeared. He was small, energetic, a little bit bow-legged, and he walked with a slight strut. He wore khaki riding-breeches, leather gaiters, and a blue shirt. And like Phœnix, he rarely had any cap or hat on his head. His thick black hair was parted at the side and brushed over heavily sideways, dropping on his forehead at the right. It was very long, a real mop, under which his eyebrows were dark and steady.

" Seen Lady Carrington ? " he asked of Phœnix.

" Yes, she's sitting on that swing over there—she's been there quite a while."

The wretch—he had seen her from the very first !

Lewis came striding over, looking towards her with his pale-grey eyes, from under his mop of hair.

" Mr. Jones from the post-office wants to see you, my lady, with a message from Sir Henry."

Instantly alarm took possession of Lou's soul.

" Oh ! Does he want to see me personally ? What message ? Is anything wrong ? " And her voice trailed out over the last word, with a sort of anxious nonchalance.

" I don't thing it's anything amiss," said Lewis reassuringly.

" Oh ! You don't ! " the relief came into her voice. Then she looked at Lewis with a slight, winning smile in her unmatched eyes. " I'm so afraid of St. Mawr, you know." Her voice was soft and cajoling. Phœnix was listening in the distance.

" St. Mawr's all right, if you don't do nothing to him," Lewis replied.

" I'm sure he is ! But how is one to know when one is doing something to him ? Tell Mr. Jones to come here, please," she concluded, on a changed tone.

Mr. Jones, a man of forty-five, thick set, with a fresh complexion and rather foolish brown eyes, and a big brown moustache, came prancing down the path, smiling rather fatuously, and doffing his straw hat with a gorgeous bow the moment he saw Lou sitting in her slim white frock on the coloured swing bed under the trees with their hard green apples.

" Good morning, Mr. Jones ! "

" Good morning, Lady Carrington. If I may say so, what a picture you make—a beautiful picture——"

He beamed under his big brown moustache like the greatest lady-killer.

" Do I ! Did Sir Henry say he was all right ? "

" He didn't *say* exactly, but I should expect he is all right——" and Mr. Jones delivered his message, in the mayonnaise of his own unction.

" Thank you so much, Mr. Jones. It's awfully good of you to come and tell me. Now I shan't worry about Sir Henry *at all*."

" It's a great pleasure to come and deliver a satisfactory message to Lady Carrington. But it won't be kind to Sir Henry if you don't worry about him *at all* in his absence. We all enjoy being worried about by those we love—so long as there is nothing to worry about of course ! "

" Quite ! " said Lou. " Now won't you take a glass of port and a biscuit, or a whisky and soda ? And thank you ever so much."

" Thank *you*, my lady. I might drink a whisky and soda, since you are so good."

And he beamed fatuously.

" Let Mr. Jones mix himself a whisky and soda, Lewis," said Lou.

" Heavens ! " she thought, as the postmaster retreated a little uncomfortably down the garden path, his bald spot passing in and out of the sun, under the trees : " How ridiculous everything is, how ridiculous, ridiculous ! " Yet she didn't really dislike Mr. Jones and his interlude.

Phœnix was melting away out of the garden. He had to follow the fun.

" Phœnix ! " Lou called. " Bring me a glass of water, will you ? Or send somebody with it."

He stood in the path looking round at her.

" All right ! " he said.

And he turned away again.

She did not like being alone in the garden. She liked to have the men working somewhere near. Curious how pleasant it was to sit there in the garden when Phœnix was about, or Lewis. It made her feel she could never be lonely or jumpy. But when Rico was there, she was all aching nerve.

Phœnix came back with a glass of water, lemon juice, sugar, and a small bottle of brandy. He knew Lou liked a spoonful of brandy in her iced lemonade.

" How thoughtful of you, Phœnix ! " she said. " Did Mr. Jones get his whisky ? "

" He was just getting it."

" That's right. By the way, Phœnix, I wish you wouldn't get mad if Sir Henry speaks to you. He is *really* so kind."

She looked up at the man. He stood there watching her in silence, the invisible smile on his face, and the inscrutable Indian glint moving in his eyes. What was he thinking ? There was something passive and almost submissive about him, but underneath this, an unyielding resistance and cruelty : yes, even cruelty. She felt that, on top, he was submissive and attentive, bringing her her lemonade as she liked it, without being told : thinking for her quite subtly. But underneath there was an unchanging hatred. He submitted circumstantially, he worked for a wage. And even circumstantially, he *liked* his mistress—*la patrona*—and her daughter. But much deeper than any circumstance or any circumstantial liking, was the categorical hatred upon which he was founded, and with which he was powerless. His liking for Lou and for Mrs. Witt, his serving them and working for a wage, was all side-tracking his own nature, which was grounded on hatred of their very existence. But what was he to do ? He had to live. Therefore he had to serve, to work for a wage, and even to be faithful.

And yet *their* existence made his own existence negative. If he was to exist, positively, they would have to cease to exist. At the same time, a fatal sort of tolerance made him serve these women, and go on serving.

" Sir Henry is *so* kind to everybody," Lou insisted.

The half-breed met her eyes, and smiled uncomfortably.

" Yes, he's a kind man," he replied, as if sincerely.

" Then why do you mind if he speaks to you ? "

" I don't mind," said Phœnix glibly.

" But you do. Or else you wouldn't make him so angry."

" Was he angry ? I don't know," said Phœnix.

" He was very angry. And you *do* know."

" No, I don't know if he's angry. I don't know," the fellow persisted. And there was a glib sort of satisfaction in his tone.

" That's awfully unkind of you, Phœnix," she said, growing offended in her turn.

" No, I don't know if he's angry. I don't want to make him angry. I don't know——"

He had taken on a tone of naïve ignorance, which at once gratified her pride as a woman, and deceived her.

" Well, you believe me when I tell you you *did* make him angry, don't you ? "

" Yes, I believe when you tell me."

" And you promise me, won't you, not to do it again ? It's *so* bad for him—so bad for his nerves and for his eyes. It makes them inflamed, and injures his eyesight. And you know, as an artist, it's terrible if anything happens to his eyesight——"

Phœnix was watching her closely, to take it in. He still was not good at understanding continuous, logical statement. Logical connection in speech seemed to stupefy him, make him stupid. He understood in disconnected assertions of fact. But he had gathered what she said. " He gets mad at you. When he gets mad, it hurts his eyes. His eyes hurt him. He can't see, because his eyes hurt him. He wants to paint a picture, he can't. He can't paint a picture, he can't see clear——"

Yes, he had understood. She saw he had understood. The bright glint of satisfaction moved in his eyes.

" So now promise me, won't you, you won't make him mad again : you won't make him angry ? "

" No, I won't make him angry. I don't do anything to make him angry," Phœnix answered, rather glibly.

" And you do understand, don't you ? You do know how kind he is : how he'd do a good turn to anybody ? "

" Yes, he's a kind man," said Phœnix.

" I'm so glad you realize. There, that's luncheon ! How nice it is to sit here in the garden, when everybody is nice to you ! No, I can carry the tray, don't you bother."

But he took the tray from her hand, and followed her to the house. And as he walked behind her, he watched the slim white nape of her neck, beneath the clustering of her bobbed hair, something as a stoat watches a rabbit he is following.

In the afternoon Lou retreated once more to her place in the garden. There she lay, sitting with a bunch of pillows behind her, neither reading nor working, just musing. She had learned the new joy : to do absolutely nothing, but to lie and let the sunshine filter through the leaves, to see the bunch of red-hot-poker flowers pierce scarlet into the afternoon, beside the comparative neutrality of some foxgloves. The mere colour of hard red, like the big Oriental poppies that had fallen, and these poker flowers, lingered in her consciousness like a communication.

Into this peaceful indolence, when even the big, dark-grey tower of the church beyond the wall and the yew-trees, was keeping its bells in silence, advanced Mrs. Witt, in a broad panama hat and a white dress.

" Don't you want to ride, or do something, Louise ? " she asked ominously.

" Don't you want to be peaceful, mother ? " retorted Louise.

" Yes—an *active* peace. I can't *believe* that my daughter can be content to lie on a hammock and do *nothing*, not even read or improve her mind, the greater part of the day."

" Well, your daughter *is* content to do that. It's her greatest pleasure."

" I know it. I can see it. And it surprises me *very* much. When I was your age, I was never still. I had so much *go*——"

> " ' Those maids, thank God,
>   Are 'neath the sod,
>   And all their generation.'

No ; but, mother, I only take life differently. Perhaps you used up that sort of *go*. I'm the harem type, mother : only I never want the men inside the lattice."

" Are you really my daughter ?   Well ! A woman never knows what will happen to her. I'm an *American* woman, and I suppose I've got to remain one, no matter where I am. What did you want, Lewis ? "

The groom had approached down the path.

" If I am to saddle Poppy ? " said Lewis.

" No, apparently *not !* " replied Mrs. Witt. " Your mistress prefers the hammock to the saddle."

" Thank you, Lewis. What mother says is true this afternoon, at least." And she gave him a peculiar little cross-eyed smile.

" Who," said Mrs. Witt to the man, " has been cutting at your hair ? "

There was a moment of silent resentment.

" I did it myself, Mam ! Sir Henry said it was too long."

" He certainly spoke the truth. But I believe there's a barber in the village on Saturdays—or you could ride over to Shrewsbury. Just turn round, and let me look at the back. Is it the money ? "

" No, Mam. I don't like these fellows touching my head."

He spoke coldly, with a certain hostile reserve that at once piqued Mrs. Witt.

" Don't you really ! " she said. " But it's quite *impossible* for you

to go about as you are. It gives you a half-witted appearance. Go
now into the yard, and get a chair and a dust-sheet. I'll cut your
hair."

The man hesitated, hostile.

" Don't be afraid, I know how it's done. I've cut the hair of
many a poor wounded boy in hospital : and shaved them too.
You've got such a touch, nurse ! Poor fellow, he was dying, though none
of us knew it. Those are the compliments I value, Louise. Get
that chair now, and a dust-sheet. I'll borrow your hair-scissors from
Elena, Louise."

Mrs. Witt, happily on the war-path, was herself again. She didn't
care for work, actual work. But she loved trimming. She loved
arranging unnatural and pretty salads, devising new and piquant-
looking ice-creams, having a turkey stuffed exactly as she knew a
stuffed turkey in Louisiana, with chestnuts and butter and stuff,
or showing a servant how to turn waffles on a waffle-iron, or to bake
a ham with brown sugar and cloves and a moistening of rum. She
liked pruning rose-trees, or beginning to cut a yew hedge into shape.
She liked ordering her own and Louise's shoes, with an exactitude
and a knowledge of shoe-making that sent the salesmen crazy. She
was a demon in shoes. Reappearing from America, she would
pounce on her daughter. " Louise, throw those shoes away. Give
them to one of the maids."—" But, mother, they are some of the
best French shoes. I like them."—" Throw them away. A shoe has
only two excuses for existing : perfect comfort or perfect appearance.
Those have neither. I have brought you some shoes."—Yes, she
had brought ten pairs of shoes from New York. She knew her
daughter's foot as she knew her own.

So now she was in her element, looming behind Lewis as he sat in
the middle of the yard swathed in a dust-sheet. She had on an
overall and a pair of wash-leather gloves, and she poised a pair of
long scissors like one of the Fates. In her big hat she looked curiously
young, but with the youth of a bygone generation. Her heavy-
lidded, laconic grey eyes were alert, studying the groom's black mop
of hair. Her eyebrows made thin, uptilting black arches on her
brow. Her fresh skin was slightly powdered, and she was really
handsome, in a bold, bygone, eighteenth-century style. Some of the
curious, adventurous stoicism of the eighteenth century : and then
a certain blatant American efficiency.

Lou, who had strayed into the yard to see, looked so much younger
and so many thousand of years older than her mother, as she stood
in her wisp-like diffidence, the clusters of grape-like bobbed hair

hanging beside her face, with its fresh colouring and its ancient weariness, her slightly squinting eyes, that were so disillusioned they were becoming faun-like.

" Not too short, mother, not too short ! " she remonstrated, as Mrs. Witt, with a terrific flourish of efficiency, darted at the man's black hair, and the thick flakes fell like black snow.

" Now, Louise, I'm right in this job, please don't interfere. Two things I hate to see : a man with his wool in his neck and ears : and a bare-faced young man who looks as if he'd bought his face as well as his hair from a men's beauty-specialist."

And efficiently she bent down, clip—clip—clipping, while Lewis sat utterly immobile, with sunken head, in a sort of despair.

Phœnix stood against the stable door, with his restless, eternal cigarette. And in the kitchen doorway the maids appeared and fled, appeared and fled in delight. The old gardener, a fixture who went with the house, creaked in and stood with his legs apart, silent in intense condemnation.

" First time I ever see such a thing ! " he muttered to himself, as he creaked on into the garden. He was a bad-tempered old soul, who thoroughly disapproved of the household, and would have given notice, but that he knew which side his bread was buttered : and there was butter unstinted on his bread, in Mrs. Witt's kitchen.

Mrs. Witt stood back to survey her handiwork, holding those terrifying shears with their beak erect. Lewis lifted his head and looked stealthily round, like a creature in a trap.

" Keep still ! " she said. " I haven't finished."

And she went for his front hair, with vigour, lifting up long layers and snipping off the ends artistically : till at last he sat with a black aureole upon the floor, and his ears standing out with curious new alertness from the sides of his clean-clipped head.

" Stand up," she said, " and let me look."

He stood up, looking absurdly young, with the hair all cut away from his neck and ears, left thick only on top. She surveyed her work with satisfaction.

" You look so much younger," she said : " you would be surprised. Sit down again."

She clipped the back of his neck with the shears, and then, with a very slight hesitation, she said :

" Now about the beard ! "

But the man rose suddenly from the chair, pulling the dust-cloth from his neck with desperation.

" No, I'll do that myself," he said, looking her in the eyes with a cold light in his pale-grey, uncanny eyes.

She hesitated in a kind of wonder at his queer male rebellion.

" Now, listen, I shall do it much better than you—and besides," she added hurriedly, snatching at the dust-cloth he was flinging on the chair—" I haven't quite finished round the ears."

" I think I shall do," he said, again looking her in the eyes, with a cold, white gleam of finality. " Thank you for what you've done."

And he walked away to the stable.

" You'd better sweep up here," Mrs. Witt called.

" Yes, Mam," he replied, looking round at her again with an odd resentment, but continuing to walk away.

" However ! " said Mrs. Witt. " I suppose he'll do."

And she divested herself of gloves and overall, and walked indoors to wash and to change. Lou went indoors too.

" It is extraordinary what hair that man has ! " said Mrs. Witt. " Did I tell you when I was in Paris, I saw a woman's face in the hotel that I thought I knew ? I couldn't place her, till she was coming towards me. *Aren't you Rachel Fannière ?* she said. *Aren't you Janette Leroy ?* We hadn't seen each other since we were girls of twelve and thirteen, at school in New Orleans. *Oh !* she said to me. *Is every illusion doomed to perish ? You had such wonderful golden curls ! All my life I've said, Oh, if only I had such lovely hair as Rachel Fannière ! I've seen those beautiful golden curls of yours all my life. And now I meet you, you're grey !* Wasn't that terrible, Louise ? Well, that man's hair made me think of it—so thick and curious. It's strange, what a difference there is in hair ; I suppose it's because he's just an animal—no mind ! There's nothing I admire in a man like a good *mind*. Your father was a very clever man, and all the men I've admired have been clever. But isn't it curious now, I've never cared much to touch their hair. How strange life is ! If it gives one thing, it takes away another. And even those poor boys in hospital : I have shaved them, or cut their hair, like a mother, never thinking anything of it. Lovely, intelligent, clean boys, most of them were. Yet it never did anything to me. I never knew before that something could happen to one from a person's *hair !* Like to Janette Leroy from my curls when I was a child. And now I'm grey, as she says. I wonder how old a man Lewis is, Louise ! Didn't he look absurdly young, with his ears pricking up ? "

" I think Rico said he was forty or forty-one."

" And never been married ? "

" No—not as far as I know."

" Isn't that curious now ! Just an animal, no mind ! A man
with no mind ! I've always thought that the *most* despicable thing.
Yet such wonderful hair to touch. Your Henry has quite a good
mind, yet I would simply shrink from touching his hair. I suppose
one likes stroking a cat's fur, just the same. Just the animal in man.
Curious that I never seem to have met it, Louise. Now I come to
think of it, he has the eyes of a human cat : a human tom-cat.
Would you call him stupid ? Yes, he's very stupid."

" No, mother, he's not stupid. He only doesn't care about most
things."

" Like an animal ! But what a strange look he has in his eyes !
A strange sort of intelligence ! And a confidence in himself. Isn't
that curious, Louise, in a man with as little mind as he has ? Do you
know, I should say he could see through a woman pretty well."

" Why, mother ! " said Lou impatiently. " I think one gets so
tired of your men with mind, as you call it. There are so many of
that sort of clever men. And there are lots of men who aren't very
clever, but are rather nice : and lots are stupid. It seems to me
there's something else besides mind and cleverness, or niceness or
cleanness. Perhaps it is the animal. Just think of St. Mawr ! I've
thought so much about him. We call him an animal, but we never
know what it means. He seems a far greater mystery to me than a
clever man. He's a horse. Why can't one say in the same way,
of a man : *He's a man ?* There seems no mystery in being a man.
But there's a terrible mystery in St. Mawr. "

Mrs. Witt watched her daugher quizzically.

" Louise," she said, " you won't tell me that the mere animal is
all that counts in a man. I will never believe it. Man is wonderful
because he is able to *think*."

" But is he ? " cried Lou, with sudden exasperation. " Their
thinking seems to me all so childish : like stringing the same beads
over and over again. Ah, men ! They and their thinking are all so
paltry. How can you be impressed ? "

Mrs. Witt raised her eyebrows sardonically.

" Perhaps I'm not—any more," she said with a grim smile.

" But," she added, " I still can't see that I am to be impressed by
the mere animal in man. The animals are the same as we are. It
seems to me they have the same feelings and wants as we have in a
commonplace way. The only difference is that they have no minds :
no human minds, at least. And no matter what you say, Louise,
lack of mind makes the commonplace."

Lou knitted her brows nervously.

"I suppose it does, mother. But men's minds *are* so common-place : look at Dean Vyner and his mind ! Or look at Arthur Balfour, as a shining example. Isn't *that* commonplace, that clever-ness ? I would hate St. Mawr to be spoilt by such a mind."

"Yes, Louise, so would I. Because the men you mention are really old women, knitting the same pattern over and over again. Nevertheless, I shall never alter my belief that real mind is all that matters in a man, and it's *that* that we women love."

"Yes, mother ! But what *is* real mind ? The old woman who knits the most complicated pattern ? Oh, I can hear all their needles clicking, the clever men ! As a matter of fact, mother, I believe Lewis has far more real mind that Dean Vyner or any of the clever ones. He has a good intuitive mind, he knows things without thinking them."

"That may be, Louise ! But he is a servant. He is *under*. A real man should never be under. And then you could never be intimate with a man like Lewis."

"I don't want intimacy, mother. I'm too tired of it all. I love St. Mawr because he isn't intimate. He stands where one can't get at him. And he burns with life. And where does his life come from, to him ? That's the mystery. That great burning life in him, which never is dead. Most men have a deadness in them, that frightens me so, because of my own deadness. Why can't men get their life straight, like St. Mawr, and then think ? Why can't they think quick, mother : quick as a woman : only farther than we do ? Why isn't men's thinking quick like fire, mother ? Why is it so slow, so dead, so deadly dull ? "

"I can't tell you, Louise. My own opinion of the men of to-day has grown very small. But I can live in spite of it."

"No, mother. We seem to be living off old fuel, like the camel when he lives off his hump. Life doesn't rush into us, as it does even into St. Mawr, and he's a dependent animal. I can't live, mother. I just can't."

"I don't see why not ? *I'm* full of life."

"I know you are, mother. But I'm not, and I'm your daughter.— And don't misunderstand me, mother. I don't want to be an animal like a horse or a cat or a lioness, though they all fascinate me, the way they get their life *straight*, not from a lot of old tanks, as we do. I don't admire the cave man, and that sort of thing. But think, mother, if we could get our lives straight from the source, as the animals do, and still be ourselves. You don't like men yourself. But you've no idea how men just tire me out : even the very thought of them. You say they are too animal. But they're not, mother. It's the animal in them has gone perverse, or cringing, or humble, or domesticated, like dogs. I don't know one single man who is a proud living animal. I know they've left off really thinking. But then men always do leave off really thinking, when the last bit of wild animal dies in them."

" Because we have minds——"

" We have no minds once we are tame, mother. Men are all women, knitting and crocheting words together."

" I can't altogether agree, you know, Louise."

" I know you don't. You like clever men. But clever men are mostly such unpleasant *animals*. As animals, so very unpleasant. And in men like Rico, the animal has gone queer and wrong. And in those nice clean boys you liked so much in the war, there is no wild animal left in them. They're all tame dogs, even when they're brave and well-bred. They're all tame dogs, mother, with human masters. There's no mystery in them."

" What do you want, Louise ? You *do* want the cave-man, who'll knock you on the head with a club."

" Don't be silly, mother. That's much more your subconscious line, you admirer of Mind. I don't consider the cave-man is a real human animal at all. He's a brute, a degenerate. A pure animal man would be as lovely as a deer or a leopard, burning like a flame fed straight from underneath. And he'd be part of the unseen, like a mouse is, even. And he'd never cease to wonder, he'd breathe silence and unseen wonder, as the partridges do, running in the stubble. He'd be all the animals in turn, instead of one, fixed, automatic thing, which he is now, grinding on the nerves. Ah no, mother, I want the wonder back again, or I shall die. I don't want to be like you, just criticizing and annihilating these dreary people, and enjoying it."

" My dear daughter, whatever else the human animal might be, he'd be a dangerous commodity."

" I wish he would, mother. I'm dying of these empty, dangerless men, who are only sentimental and spiteful."

" Nonsense, you're not dying."

" I am, mother. And I should be dead if there weren't St. Mawr and Phœnix and Lewis in the world."

" St. Mawr and Phœnix and Lewis ! I thought you said they were servants."

" That's the worst of it. If only they were masters ! If only there were some men with as much natural life as they have, and their brave, quick minds that commanded instead of serving ! "

"There are no such men," said Mrs. Witt, with a certain grim satisfaction.

"I know it. But I'm young, and I've got to live. And the thing that is offered me as life just starves me, starves me to death, mother. What am I to do? You enjoy shattering people like Dean Vyner. But I am young, I can't live that way."

"That may be."

It had long ago struck Lou how much more her mother realized and understood than ever Rico did. Rico was afraid, always afraid of realizing. Rico, with his good manners and his habitual kindness, and that peculiar imprisoned sneer of his.

He arrived home next morning on St. Mawr, rather flushed and gaudy, and over-kind, with an *empressé* anxiety about Lou's welfare which spoke too many volumes. Especially as he was accompanied by Flora Manby, and by Flora's sister Elsie, and Elsie's husband, Frederick Edwards. They all came on horseback.

"Such awful ages since I saw you!" said Flora to Lou. "Sorry if we burst in on you. We're only just saying *How do you do!* and going on to the inn. They've got rooms all ready for us there. We thought we'd stay just one night over here, and ride to-morrow to the Devil's Chair. Won't you come? Lots of fun! Isn't Mrs. Witt at home?"

Mrs. Witt was out for the moment. When she returned she had on her curious stiff face, yet she greeted the newcomers with a certain cordiality: she felt it would be diplomatic, no doubt.

"There *are* two rooms here," she said, "and if you care to poke into them, why we shall be *delighted* to have you. But I'll show them to you first, because they are poor, inconvenient rooms, with no running water and *miles* from the baths."

Flora and Elsie declared that they were "perfectly darling sweet rooms—not overcrowded."

"Well," said Mrs. Witt, "the conveniences certainly don't fill up much space. But if you like to take them for what they are——"

"Why, we feel absolutely overwhelmed, don't we, Elsie!—But we've no clothes——?"

Suddenly the silence had turned into a house-party. The Manby girls appeared to lunch in fine muslin dresses, bought in Paris, fresh as daisies. Women's clothing takes up so little space, especially in summer! Fred Edwards was one of those blond Englishmen with a little brush moustache and those strong blue eyes which were always attempting the sentimental, but which Lou, in her prejudice, considered cruel: upon what grounds she never analysed. However, he took a gallant tone with her at once, and she had to seem to simper. Rico, watching her, was so relieved when he saw the simper coming.

It had begun again, the whole clockwork of " lots of fun ! "

" Isn't Fred flirting perfectly outrageously with Lady Carrington ! She looks so *sweet* ! " cried Flora, over her coffee-cup. " Don't you mind, Harry ? "

They called Rico " Harry." His boy-name.

" Only a very little," said Harry. " *L'uomo é cacciatore.* "

" Oh, now, what does that mean ? " cried Flora, who always thrilled to Rico's bits of affectation.

" It means," said Mrs. Witt, leaning forward and speaking in her most suave voice, " that man is a hunter."

Even Flora shrank under the smooth acid of the irony.

" Oh, well now ! " she cried. " If he is, then what is woman ? "

" The hunted," said Mrs. Witt, in a still smoother acid.

" At least," said Rico, " she is always *game !* "

" Ah, is she though ! " came Fred's manly, well-bred tones. " I'm not so sure."

Mrs. Witt looked from one man to the other, as if she were dropping them down the bottomless pit.

Lou escaped to look at St. Mawr. He was still moist where the saddle had been. And he seemed a little bit extinguished, as if virtue had gone out of him.

But when he lifted his lovely naked head, like a bunch of flames, to see who it was had entered, she saw he was still himself. For ever sensitive and alert, his head lifted like the summit of a fountain. And within him the clean bones striking to the earth, his hoofs intervening between him and the ground like lesser jewels.

He knew her and did not resent her. But he took no notice of her. He would never " respond." At first she had resented it. Now she was glad. He would never be intimate, thank heaven.

She hid herself away till tea-time, but she could not hide from the sound of voices. Dinner was early, at seven. Dean Vyner came— Mrs. Vyner was an invalid—and also an artist who had a studio in the village and did etchings. He was a man of about thirty-eight, and poor, just beginning to accept himself as a failure, as far as making money goes. But he worked at his etchings and studied esoteric matters like astrology and alchemy. Rico patronized him, and was a little afraid of him. Lou could not quite make him out. After knocking about Paris and London and Munich, he was trying to become staid, and to persuade himself that English village life, with squire and dean in the background, humble artist in the middle, and labourer in the common foreground, was a genuine life. His self-persuasion was only moderately successful. This was betrayed by the curious arrest in his body : he seemed to have to force himself into movement : and by the curious duplicity in his yellow-grey, twinkling eyes, that twinkled and expanded like a goat's ; with mockery, irony, and frustration.

"Your face is curiously like Pan's," said Lou to him at dinner.

It was true, in a commonplace sense. He had the tilted eyebrows, the twinkling goaty look, and the pointed ears of a goat-Pan.

"People have said so," he replied. "But I'm afraid it's not the face of the Great God Pan. Isn't it rather the Great Goat Pan ! "

"I say, that's good ! " cried Rico. "The Great Goat Pan ! "

"I have always found it difficult," said the Dean, "to see the Great God Pan in that goat-legged old father of satyrs. He may have a good deal of influence—the world will always be full of goaty old satyrs. But we find them somewhat vulgar. The goaty old satyrs are too comprehensible to me to be venerable, and I fail to see a Great God in the father of them all."

"Your ears should be getting red," said Lou to Cartwright. She, too, had an odd squinting smile that suggested nymphs, so irresponsible and unbelieving.

"Oh no, nothing personal ! " cried the Dean.

"I am not sure," said Cartwright, with a small smile. "But don't you imagine Pan once *was* a great god, before the anthropomorphic Greeks turned him into half a man ? "

"Ah !—maybe. That is very possible. But—I have noticed the limitation in myself—my mind has no grasp whatsoever of Europe before the Greeks arose. Mr. Wells' Outline does not help me there, either," the Dean added with a smile.

"But what was Pan before he was a man with goat legs ? " asked Lou.

"Before he looked like me ? " said Cartwright, with a faint grin. "I should say he was the god that is hidden in everything. In those days you saw the thing, you never saw the god in it : I mean in the tree or the fountain or the animal. If you ever saw the god instead of the thing, you died. If you saw it with the naked eye, that is. But in the night you might see the god. And you knew it was there."

"The modern pantheist not only sees the god in everything, he takes photographs of it," said the Dean.

"Oh, and the divine pictures he paints ! " cried Rico.

"Quite ! " said Cartwright.

" But if they never *saw* the god in the thing, the old ones, how did they know he was there? How did they have any Pan at all?" said Lou.

" Pan was the hidden mystery—the hidden cause. That's how it was a Great God. Pan wasn't *he* at all : not even a great god. He was Pan. All : what you see when you see in full. In the daytime you see the thing. But if your third eye is open, which sees only the things that can't be seen, you may see Pan within the thing, hidden : you may see with your third eye, which is darkness."

" Do you think I might see Pan in a horse, for example? "

" Easily. In St. Mawr ! " Cartwright gave her a knowing look.

" But," said Mrs. Witt, " it would be difficult, I should say, to open the third eye and see Pan in a man."

" Probably," said Cartwright, smiling. " In man he is over-visible : the old satyr : the fallen Pan."

" Exactly ! " said Mrs. Witt. And she fell into a muse. " The fallen Pan ! " she re-echoed. " Wouldn't a man be wonderful in whom Pan hadn't fallen ! "

Over the coffee in the grey drawing-room she suddenly asked :

" Supposing, Mr. Cartwright, one *did* open the third eye and see Pan in an actual man—I wonder what it would be like? "

She half lowered her eyelids and tilted her face in a strange way, as if she were tasting something, and not quite sure.

" I wonder ! " he said, smiling his enigmatic smile. But she could see he did not understand.

" Louise ! " said Mrs. Witt at bedtime. " Come into my room for a moment, I want to ask you something."

" What is it, mother? "

" You, you *get* something from what Mr. Cartwright said about seeing Pan with the third eye? Seeing Pan in something? "

Mrs. Witt came rather close, and tilted her face with strange insinuating question at her daughter.

" I think I do, mother."

" In what? " The question came as a pistol-shot.

" I think, mother," said Lou reluctantly, " in St. Mawr."

" In a horse ! " Mrs. Witt contracted her eyes slightly. " Yes, I can see that. I know what you mean. It *is* in St. Mawr. It *is!* But in St. Mawr it makes me *afraid*——" she dragged out the word. Then she came a step closer. " But, Louise, did you ever see it in a man? "

" What, mother? "

" Pan. Did you ever see Pan in a man, as you see Pan in St. Mawr? "

Louise hesitated.

" No, mother, I don't think I did. When I look at men with my third eye, as you call it—I think I see—mostly—a sort of—pancake." She uttered the last word with a despairing grin, not knowing quite what to say.

" Oh, Louise, isn't that it ! Doesn't one always see a pancake ! Now listen, Louise. Have you ever been in love ? "

" Yes, as far as I understand it."

" Listen now. Did you ever see Pan in the man you loved ? Tell me if you did ? "

" As I see Pan in St. Mawr ?—no, mother." And suddenly her lips began to tremble and the tears came to her eyes.

" Listen, Louise. I've been in love innumerable times—and *really* in love twice. Twice !—yet for fifteen years I've left off wanting to have anything to do with a man, really. For fifteen years ! And why ? Do you know ? Because I couldn't see that peculiar hidden Pan in any of them. And I became that I needed to. I needed it. But it wasn't there. Not in any man. Even when I was in love with a man, it was for other things : because I *understood* him so well, or he understood me, or we had such sympathy. Never the hidden Pan. Do you understand what I mean ? Unfallen Pan ! "

" More or less, mother."

" But now my third eye is coming open, I believe. I am tired of all these men like breakfast cakes, with a teaspoonful of mind or a tea-spoonful of spirit in them, for baking powder. Isn't it extraordinary : that young man Cartwright talks about Pan, but he knows nothing of it all. He knows nothing of the unfallen Pan : only the fallen Pan with goat legs and a leer—and that sort of power, don't you know."

" But what do you know of the unfallen Pan, mother ? "

" Don't ask me, Louise ! I feel all of a tremble, as if I was just on the verge."

She flashed a little look of incipient triumph, and said good night.

An excursion on horseback had been arranged for the next day, to two old groups of rocks, called the Angel's Chair and the Devil's Chair, which crowned the moorlike hills looking into Wales, ten miles away. Everybody was going—they were to start early in the morning, and Lewis would be the guide, since no one exactly knew the way.

Lou got up soon after sunrise. There was a summer scent in the trees of early morning, and monkshood flowers stood up dark and tall, with shadows. She dressed in the green linen riding-skirt her maid had put ready for her, with a close bluish smock.

" Are you going out already, dear ? " called Rico from his room.
" Just to smell the roses before we start, Rico."

He appeared in the doorway in his yellow silk pyjamas. His large
blue eyes had that rolling irritable look and the slightly bloodshot
whites which made her want to escape.

" Booted and spurred !—the *energy* ! " he cried.

" It's a lovely day to ride," she said.

" A lovely day to do anything *except* ride ! " he said. " Why spoil
the day riding ! " A curious bitter-acid escaped into his tone. It
was evident he hated the excursion.

" Why, we needn't go if you don't want to, Rico."

" Oh, I'm sure I shall love it, once I get started. It's all this
business of *starting*, with horses and paraphernalia——"

Lou went into the yard. The horses were drinking at the trough
under the pump, their colours strong and rich in the shadow of the
tree.

" You're not coming with us, Phœnix ? " she said.

" Lewis, he's riding my horse."

She could tell Phœnix did not like being left behind.

By half-past seven everybody was ready. The sun was in the
yard, the horses were saddled. They came swishing their tails.
Lewis brought out St. Mawr from his separate box, speaking to him
very quietly in Welsh : a murmuring, soothing little speech. Lou,
alert, could see that he was uneasy.

" How is St. Mawr this morning ? " she asked.

" He's all right. He doesn't like so many people. He'll be all
right once he's started."

The strangers were in the saddle : they moved out to the deep
shade of the village road outside. Rico came to his horse to mount.
St. Mawr jumped away as if he had seen the devil.

" Steady, fool ! " cried Rico.

The bay stood with his four feet spread, his neck arched, his big
dark eye glancing sideways with that watchful, frightening look.

" You shouldn't be irritable with him, Rico ! " said Lou.
" Steady then, St. Mawr ! Be steady."

But a certain anger rose also in her. The creature was so big, so
brilliant, and so stupid, standing there with his hind legs spread,
ready to jump aside or to rear terrifically, and his great eye glancing
with a sort of suspicious frenzy. What was there to be suspicious of,
after all ? Rico would do him no harm.

" No one will harm you, St. Mawr," she reasoned, a bit
exasperated.

The groom was talking quietly, murmuringly, in Welsh. Rico was slowly advancing again, to put his foot in the stirrup. The stallion was watching from the corner of his eye, a strange glare of suspicious frenzy burning stupidly. Any moment his immense physical force might be let loose in a frenzy of panic—or malice. He was really very irritating.

" Probably he doesn't like that apricot shirt," said Mrs. Witt, " although it tones into him wonderfully well."

She pronounced it *ap*—ricot, and it irritated Rico terribly.

" Ought we to have *asked* him before we put it on ? " he flashed, his upper lip lifting venomously.

" I should say you should," replied Mrs. Witt coolly.

Rico turned with a sudden rush to the horse. Back went the great animal, with a sudden splashing crash of hoofs on the cobble-stones, and Lewis hanging on like a shadow. Up went the fore feet, showing the belly.

" The thing is accursed," said Rico, who had dropped the reins in sudden shock, and stood marooned. His rage overwhelmed him like a black flood.

" Nothing in the world is so irritating as a horse that is acting up," thought Lou.

" Say, Harry ! " called Flora from the road. " Come out here into the road to mount him."

Lewis looked at Rico and nodded. Then soothing the big, quiver-ing animal, he led him springily out to the road under the trees, where the three friends were waiting. Lou and her mother got quickly into the saddle to follow. And in another moment Rico was mounted and bouncing down the road in the wrong direction, Lewis following on the chestnut. It was some time before Rico could get St. Mawr round. Watching him from behind, those waiting could judge how the young Baronet hated it.

But at last they set off—Rico ahead, unevenly but quietly, with the two Manby girls, Lou following with the fair young man who had been in a cavalry regiment and who kept looking round for Mrs. Witt.

" Don't look round for me," she called. " I'm riding behind, out of the dust."

Just behind Mrs. Witt came Lewis. It was a whole cavalcade trotting in the morning sun past the cottages and the cottage gardens, round the field that was the recreation ground, into the deep hedges of the lane.

" Why is St. Mawr so bad at starting ? Can't you get him into better shape ? " she asked over her shoulder.

" Beg your pardon, Mam ! "

Lewis trotted a little nearer. She glanced over her shoulder at him, at his dark, unmoved face, his cool little figure.

" I think *Mam* is so ugly. Why not leave it out ! " she said. Then she repeated her question.

" St. Mawr doesn't trust anybody," Lewis replied.

" Not you ? "

" Yes, he trusts me—mostly."

" Then why not other people ? "

" They're different."

" All of them ? "

" About all of them."

" How are they different ? "

He looked at her with his remote, uncanny grey eyes.

" Different," he said, not knowing how else to put it.

They rode on slowly, up the steep rise of the wood, then down into a glade where ran a little railway built for hauling some mysterious mineral out of the hill, in war-time, and now already abandoned. Even on this countryside the dead hand of the war lay like a corpse decomposing.

They rode up again, past the foxgloves under the trees. Ahead the brilliant St. Mawr and the sorrel and grey horses were swimming like butterflies through the sea of bracken, glittering from sun to shade, shade to sun. Then once more they were on a crest, and through the thinning trees could see the slopes of the moors beyond the next dip.

Soon they were in the open, rolling hills, golden in the morning and empty save for a couple of distant bilberry-pickers, whitish figures pick—pick—picking with curious, rather disgusting assiduity. The horses were on an old trail which climbed through the pinky tips of heather and ling, across patches of green bilberry. Here and there were tufts of harebells blue as bubbles.

They were out, high on the hills. And there to west lay Wales, folded in crumpled folds, goldish in the morning light, with its moor-like slopes and patches of corn uncannily distinct. Between was a hollow, wide valley of summer haze, showing white farms among trees, and grey slate roofs.

" Ride beside me," she said to Lewis. " Nothing makes me want to go back to America like the old look of these little villages. You have never been to America ? "

" No, Mam."

" Don't you ever want to go ? "

" I wouldn't mind going."

" But you're not just crazy to go ? "

" No, Mam."

" Quite content as you are ? "

He looked at her, and his pale, remote eyes met hers.

" I don't fret myself," he replied.

" Not about anything at all—ever ? "

His eyes glanced ahead, at the other riders.

" No, Mam ! " he replied, without looking at her.

She rode a few moments in silence.

" What is that over there ? " she asked, pointing across the valley. " What is it called ? "

" Yon's Montgomery."

" Montgomery ! And is that *Wales*—— ? " she trailed the ending curiously.

" Yes, Mam."

" Where you come from ? "

" No, Mam ! I come from Merioneth."

" Not from Wales ? I thought you were Welsh ? "

" Yes, Mam. Merioneth *is* Wales."

" And you are Welsh ? "

" Yes, Mam."

" I had a Welsh grandmother. But I come from Louisiana, and when I go back home, the negroes still call me Miss Rachel. *Oh, my, it's little Miss Rachel come back home ! Why, ain't I mighty glad to see you—u, Miss Rachel !* That gives me such a strange feeling, you know."

The man glanced at her curiously, especially when she imitated the negroes.

" Do you feel strange when you go home ? " she asked.

" I was brought up by an aunt and uncle," he said. " I never want to see them."

" And you don't have any home ? "

" No, Mam."

" No wife nor anything ? "

" No, Mam."

" But what do you do with your life ? "

" I keep to myself."

" And care about nothing ? "

" I mind St. Mawr."

" But you've not always had St. Mawr—and you won't **always** have him. Were you in the war ? "

" Yes, Mam."

" At the front ? "

" Yes, Mam—but I was a groom."

" And you came out all right ? "

" I lost my little finger from a bullet."

He held up his small, dark left hand, from which the little finger was missing.

" And did you like the war—or didn't you ? "

" I didn't like it."

Again his pale grey eyes met hers, and they looked so non-human and uncommunicative, so without connection, and inaccessible, she was troubled.

" Tell me," she said. " Did you never want a wife and a home and children, like other men ? "

" No, Mam. I never wanted a home of my own."

" Nor a wife of your own ? "

" No, Mam."

" Nor children of your own ? "

" No, Mam."

She reined in her horse.

" Now wait a minute," she said. " Now tell me why."

His horse came to a standstill, and the two riders faced one another.

" Tell me why—I must know why you never wanted a wife and children and a home. I must know why you're not like other men."

" I never felt like it," he said. " I made my life with horses."

" Did you hate people very much ? Did you have a very unhappy time as a child ? "

" My aunt and uncle didn't like me, and I didn't like them."

" So you've never liked anybody ? "

" Maybe not," he said. " Not to get as far as marrying them."

She touched her horse and moved on.

" Isn't that curious ! " she said. " I've loved people, at various times. But I don't believe *I've* ever liked anybody, except a few of our negroes. I don't like Louise, though she's my daughter and I love her. But I don't really *like* her. I think you're the first person I've ever liked since I was on our plantation, and we had some *very fine* negroes. And I think that's very curious. Now I want to know if you like *me*."

She looked at him searchingly, but he did not answer.

" Tell me," she said. " I don't mind if you say no. But tell me if you like me. I feel I must know."

The flicker of a smile went over his face—a very rare thing with him.

"Maybe I do," he said. He was thinking that she put him on a level with a negro slave on a plantation : in his idea, negroes were still slaves. But he did not care where she put him.

"Well, I'm glad—I'm glad if you like me. Because you *don't* like most people, I know that."

They had passed the hollow where the old Aldecar Chapel hid in damp isolation, beside the ruined mill, over the stream that came down from the moors. Climbing the sharp slope, they saw the folded hills like great shut fingers, with steep, deep clefts between. On the near skyline was a bunch of rocks : and away to the right another bunch.

"Yon's the Angel's Chair," said Lewis, pointing to the nearer rocks. "And yon's the Devil's Chair, where we're going."

"Oh !" said Mrs. Witt. "And aren't we going to the Angel's Chair ? "

"No, Mam ! "

"Why not ? "

"There's nothing to see there. The other's higher, and bigger, and that's where folks mostly go."

"Is that so ! They give the Devil the higher seat in this country, do they ? I think they're right." And as she got no answer, she added : " You believe in the Devil, don't you ? "

"I never met him," he answered, evasively.

Ahead, they could see the other horses twinkling in a cavalcade up the slope, the black, the bay, the two greys, and the sorrel, sometimes bunching, sometimes straggling. At a gate all waited for Mrs. Witt. The fair young man fell in beside her, and talked hunting at her. He had hunted the fox over these hills, and was vigorously excited locating the spot where the hounds first gave cry, etc.

"Really !" said Mrs. Witt. " *Really !* Is that so ! "

If irony could have been condensed to prussic acid, the fair young man would have ended his life's history with his reminiscences.

They came at last, trotting in file along a narrow track between heather, along the saddle of a hill, to where the knot of pale granite suddenly cropped out. It was one of those places where the spirit of aboriginal England still lingers, the old savage England, whose last blood flows still in a few Englishmen, Welshmen, Cornishmen. The rocks, whitish with weather of all the ages, jutted against the blue August sky, heavy with age-moulded roundnesses.

Lewis stayed below with the horses, the party scrambled rather awkwardly, in their riding-boots, up the foot-worn boulders. At length they stood in the place called the Chair, looking west, west towards Wales, that rolled in golden folds upwards. It was neither impressive nor a very picturesque landscape : the hollow valley with farms, and then the rather bare upheaval of hills, slopes with corn and moor and pasture, rising like a barricade, seemingly high, slantingly. Yet it had a strange effect on the imagination.

" Oh mother," said Lou, " doesn't it make you feel old, old, older than anything ever was ? "

" It certainly does seem aged," said Mrs. Witt.

" It makes me want to die," said Lou. " I feel we've lasted almost too long."

" Don't say that, Lady Carrington. Why, you're a spring chicken yet : or shall I say an unopened rosebud," remarked the fair young man.

" No," said Lou. " All these millions of ancestors have used all the life up. We're not really alive, in the sense that they were alive."

" But who ? " said Rico. " Who are *they* ? "

" The people who lived on these hills, in the days gone by."

" But the same people still live on the hills, darling. It's just the same stock."

" No, Rico. That old fighting stock that worshipped devils among these stones—I'm sure they did——"

" But look here, do you mean they were any better than we are ? " asked the fair young man.

Lou looked at him quizzically.

" We don't exist," she said, squinting at him oddly.

" I jolly well know *I* do," said the fair young man.

" I consider these days are the best ever, especially for girls," said Flora Manby. " And anyhow they're our own days, so I don't jolly well see the use of crying them down."

They were all silent, with the last echoes of emphatic *joie de vivre* trumpeting on the air, across the hills of Wales.

" Spoken like a brick, Flora," said Rico. " Say it again, we may not have the Devil's Chair for a pulpit next time."

" I do," reiterated Flora. " I think this is the best age there ever was for a girl to have a good time in. I read all through H. G. Wells' history, and I shut it up and thanked my stars I live in nineteen-twenty odd, not in some other beastly date when a woman had to cringe before mouldy domineering men."

After this they turned to scramble to another part of the rocks, to the famous Needle's Eye.

" Thank you so much, I am really better without help," said Mrs.

Witt to the fair young man, as she slid downwards till a piece of grey silk stocking showed above her tall boot. But she got her toe in a safe place, and in a moment stood beside him, while he caught her arm protectingly. He might as well have caught the paw of a mountain lion protectingly.

" I should like *so* much to know," she said suavely, looking into his eyes with a demonish straight look, " what makes you so certain that you exist ? "

He looked back at her, and his jaunty blue eyes went baffled. Then a slow, hot, salmon-coloured flush stole over his face, and he turned abruptly round.

The Needle's Eye was a hole in the ancient grey rock, like a window, looking to England ; England at the moment in shadow. A stream wound and glinted in the flat shadow, and beyond that the flat, insignificant hills heaped in mounds of shade. Cloud was coming—the English side was in shadow. Wales was still in the sun, but the shadow was spreading. The day was going to disappoint them. Lou was a tiny bit chilled, already.

Luncheon was still several miles away. The party hastened down to the horses. Lou picked a few sprigs of ling, and some hare-bells, and some straggling yellow flowers : not because she wanted them, but to distract herself. The atmosphere of " enjoying ourselves " was becoming cruel to her : it sapped all the life out of her. " Oh, if only I needn't enjoy myself," she moaned inwardly. But the Manby girls were enjoying themselves so much. " I think it's frantically lovely up here," said the other one—not Flora—Elsie.

" It *is* beautiful, isn't it ! I'm *so* glad you like it," replied Rico. And he was really relieved and gratified, because the other one said she was enjoying it so frightfully. He dared not say to Lou, as he wanted to : " I'm afraid, Lou darling, you don't love it as much as we do." He was afraid of her answer : " No, dear, I don't love it at all ! I want to be away from these people."

Slightly piqued, he rode on with the Manby group, and Lou came behind with her mother. Cloud was covering the sky with grey. There was a cold wind. Everybody was anxious to get to the farm for luncheon, and be safely home before rain came.

They were riding along one of the narrow little foot-tracks, mere grooves of grass between heather and bright green bilberry. The blond young man was ahead, then his wife, then Flora, then Rico. Lou, from a little distance, watched the glossy, powerful haunches of St. Mawr swaying with life, always too much life, like a menace. The fair young man was whistling a new dance tune.

"That's an awfully attractive tune," Rico called. "Do whistle it again, Fred, I should like to memorize it."

Fred began to whistle it again.

At that moment St. Mawr exploded again, shied sideways as if a bomb had gone off, and kept backing through the heather.

"Fool!" cried Rico, thoroughly unnerved : he had been terribly sideways in the saddle, Lou had feared he was going to fall. But he got his seat, and pulled the reins viciously, to bring the horse to order, and put him on the track again. St. Mawr began to rear : his favourite trick. Rico got him forward a few yards, when up he went again.

"Fool!" yelled Rico, hanging in the air.

He pulled the horse over backwards on top of him.

Lou gave a loud, unnatural, horrible scream : she heard it herself, at the same time as she heard the crash of the falling horse. Then she saw a pale gold belly, and hoofs that worked and flashed in the air, and St. Mawr writhing, straining his head terrifically upwards, his great eyes starting from the naked lines of his nose. With a great neck arching cruelly from the ground, he was pulling frantically at the reins, which Rico still held tight. Yes, Rico, lying strangely sideways, his eyes also starting from his yellow-white face, among the heather, still clutched the reins.

Young Edwards was rushing forward, and circling round the writhing, immense horse, whose pale gold, inverted bulk seemed to fill the universe.

"Let him get up, Carrington! Let him get up!" he was yelling, darting warily near, to get the reins. Another spasmodic convulsion of the horse.

Horror! The young man reeled backwards with his face in his hands. He had got a kick in the face. Red blood running down his chin!

Lewis was there, on the ground, getting the reins out of Rico's hands. St. Mawr gave a great curve like a fish, spread his forefeet on the earth and reared his head, looking round in a ghastly fashion. His eyes were arched, his nostrils wide, his face ghastly in a sort of panic. He rested thus, seated with his fore-feet planted and his face in panic, almost like some terrible lizard, for several moments. Then he heaved sickeningly to his feet, and stood convulsed, trembling.

There lay Rico, crumpled and rather sideways, staring at the heavens from a yellow, dead-looking face. Lewis, glancing round in a sort of horror, looked in dread at St. Mawr again. Flora had been hovering. She now rushed screeching to the prostrate Rico.

"Harry! Harry! You're not dead! Oh, Harry! Harry! Harry!"

Lou had dismounted. She didn't know when. She stood a little way off, as if spellbound, while Flora cried *Harry! Harry! Harry!*

Suddenly Rico sat up.

"Where is the horse?" he said.

At the same time an added whiteness came on his face, and he bit his lip with pain, and he fell prostrate again in a faint. Flora rushed to put her arm round him.

Where was the horse? He had backed slowly away, in an agony of suspicion, while Lewis murmured to him in vain. His head was raised again, the eyes still starting from their sockets, and a terrible guilty, ghost-like look on his face. When Lewis drew a little nearer he twitched and shrank like a shaken steel spring, away—not to be touched. He seemed to be seeing legions of ghosts, down the dark avenues of all the centuries that have lapsed since the horse became subject to man.

And the other young man? He was still standing, at a little distance, with his face in his hands, motionless, the blood falling on his white shirt, and his wife at his side, pleading, distracted.

Mrs. Witt too was there, as if cast in steel, watching. She made no sound and did not move, only, from a fixed, impassive face, watched each thing.

"Do tell me what you think is the matter?" Lou pleaded, distracted, to Flora, who was supporting Rico and weeping torrents of unknown tears.

Then Mrs. Witt came forward and began in a very practical manner to unclose the shirt-neck and feel the young man's heart. Rico opened his eyes again, said "*Really!*" and closed his eyes once more.

"It's fainting!" said Mrs. Witt. "We have no brandy."

Lou, too weary to be able to feel anything, said :

"I'll go and get some."

She went to her alarmed horse, who stood among the others with her head down, in suspense. Almost unconsciously Lou mounted, set her face ahead, and was riding away.

Then Poppy shied too, with a sudden start, and Lou pulled up. "Why?" she said to her horse. "Why did you do that?"

She looked round, and saw in the heather a glimpse of yellow and black.

"A snake!" she said wonderingly.

And she looked closer.

It was a dead adder that had been drinking at a reedy pool in a
little depression just off the road, and had been killed with stones.
There it lay, also crumpled, its head crushed, its gold-and-yellow
back still glittering dully, and a bit of pale-blue belly showing, killed
that morning.

Lou rode on, her face set, towards the farm. An unspeakable
weariness had overcome her. She could not even suffer. Weariness
of spirit left her in a sort of apathy.

And she had a vision, a vision of evil. Or not strictly a vision.
She became aware of evil, evil, evil, rolling in great waves over the
earth. Always she had thought there was no such thing—only a
mere negation of good. Now, like an ocean to whose surface she
had risen, she saw the dark-grey waves of evil rearing in a great tide.

And it had swept mankind away without mankind's knowing. It
had caught up the nations as the rising ocean might lift the fishes,
and was sweeping them on in a great tide of evil. They did not
know. The people did not know. They did not even wish it. They
wanted to be good and to have everything joyful and enjoyable.
Everything joyful and enjoyable : for everybody. This was what
they wanted, if you asked them.

But at the same time, they had fallen under the spell of evil. It
was a soft, subtle thing, soft as water, and its motion was soft and
imperceptible, as the running of a tide is invisible to one who is out
on the ocean. And they were all out on the ocean, being borne
along in the current of the mysterious evil, creatures of the evil
principle, as fishes are creatures of the sea.

There was no relief. The whole world was enveloped in one great
flood. All the nations, the white, the brown, the black, the yellow,
all were immersed in the strange tide of evil that was subtly, irresistibly rising. No one, perhaps, deliberately wished it. Nearly
every individual wanted peace and a good time all round : everybody to have a good time.

But some strange thing had happened, and the vast, mysterious
force of positive evil was let loose. She felt that from the core of
Asia the evil welled up, as from some strange pole, and slowly was
drowning earth.

It was something horrifying, something you could not escape from.
It had come to her as in a vision, when she saw the pale gold belly
of the stallion upturned, the hoofs working wildly, the wicked curved
hams of the horse, and then the evil straining of that arched, fish-
like neck, with the dilated eyes of the head. Thrown backwards,
and working its hoofs in the air. Reversed, and purely evil.

She saw the same in people. They were thrown backwards, and writhing with evil. And the rider, crushed, was still reining them down.

What did it mean? Evil, evil, and a rapid return to the sordid chaos. Which was wrong, the horse or the rider? Or both?

She thought with horror of St. Mawr, and of the look on his face. But she thought with horror, a colder horror, of Rico's face as he snarled *Fool!* His fear, his impotence as a master, as a rider, his presumption. And she thought with horror of those other people, so glib, so glibly evil.

What did they want to do, those Manby girls? Undermine, undermine, undermine. They wanted to undermine Rico, just as that fair young man would have liked to undermine her. Believe in nothing, care about nothing: but keep the surface easy, and have a good time. *Let us undermine one another. There is nothing to believe in, so let us undermine everything. But look out! No scenes, no spoiling the game. Stick to the rules of the game. Be sporting, and don't do anything that would make a commotion. Keep the game going smooth and jolly, and bear your bit like a sport. Never, by any chance, injure your fellow man openly. But always injure him secretly. Make a fool of him, and undermine his nature. Break him up by undermining him, if you can. It's good sport.*

The evil! The mysterious potency of evil. She could see it all the time, in individuals, in society, in the press. There it was in socialism and bolshevism: the same evil. But bolshevism made a mess of the outside of life, so turn it down. Try fascism. Fascism would keep the surface of life intact, and carry on the undermining business all the better. All the better sport. Never draw blood. Keep the hæmorrhage internal, invisible.

And as soon as fascism makes a break—which it is bound to, because all evil works up to a break—then turn it down. With gusto, turn it down.

Mankind, like a horse, ridden by a stranger, smooth-faced, evil rider. Evil himself, smooth-faced and pseudo-handsome, riding mankind past the dead snake, to the last break.

Mankind no longer its own master. Ridden by this pseudo-handsome ghoul of outward loyalty, inward treachery, in a game of betrayal, betrayal, betrayal. The last of the gods of our era, Judas supreme!

People performing outward acts of loyalty, piety, self-sacrifice. But inwardly bent on undermining, betraying. Directing all their subtle evil will against any positive living thing. Masquerading as the ideal, in order to poison the real.

Creation destroys as it goes, throws down one tree for the rise of another. But ideal mankind would abolish death, multiply itself million upon million, rear up city upon city, save every parasite alive, until the accumulation of mere existence is swollen to a horror. But go on saving life, the ghastly salvation army of ideal mankind. At the same time secretly, viciously, potently undermine the natural creation, betray it with kiss after kiss, destroy it from the inside, till you have the swollen rottenness of our teeming existences. But keep the game going. Nobody's going to make another bad break, such as Germany and Russia made.

Two bad breaks the secret evil has made : in Germany and in Russia. Watch it ! Let evil keep a policeman's eye on evil ! The surface of life must remain unruptured. Production must be heaped upon production. And the natural creation must be betrayed by many more kisses, yet. Judas is the last God, and, by heaven, the most potent.

But even Judas made a break : hanged himself, and his bowels gushed out. Not long after his triumph.

Man must destroy as he goes, as trees fall for trees to rise. The accumulation of life and things means rottenness. Life must destroy life, in the unfolding of creation. We save up life at the expense of the unfolding, till all is full of rottenness. Then at last, we make a break.

What's to be done ? Generally speaking, nothing. The dead will have to bury their dead, while the earth stinks of corpses. The individual can but depart from the mass, and try to cleanse himself. Try to hold fast to the living thing, which destroys as it goes, but remains sweet. And in his soul fight, fight, fight to preserve that which is life in him from the ghastly kisses and poison-bites of the myriad evil ones. Retreat to the desert, and fight. But in his soul adhere to that which is life itself, creatively destroying as it goes : destroying the stiff old thing to let the new bud come through. The one passionate principle of creative being, which recognizes the natural good, and has a sword for the swarms of evil. Fights, fights, fights to protect itself. But with itself, is strong and at peace.

Lou came to the farm, and got brandy, and asked the men to come out to carry in the injured.

It turned out that the kick in the face had knocked a couple of young Edward's teeth out, and would disfigure him a little.

" To go through the war, and then get this ! " he mumbled, with a vindictive glance at St. Mawr.

And it turned out that Rico had two broken ribs and a crushed ankle. Poor Rico, he would limp for life.

" I want St. Mawr *shot!* " was almost his first word, when he was in bed at the farm and Lou was sitting beside him.

" What good would that do, dear ? " she said.

" The brute is evil. I want him *shot!* "

Rico could make the last word sound like the spitting of a bullet.

" Do you want to shoot him yourself ? "

" No. But I want to have him shot. I shall never be easy till I know he has a bullet through him. He's got a wicked character. I don't feel you are safe, with him down there. I shall get one of the Manby's gamekeepers to shoot him. You might tell Flora—or I'll tell her myself, when she comes."

" Don't talk about it now, dear. You've got a temperature."

Was it true St. Mawr was evil ? She would never forget him writhing and lunging on the ground, nor his awful face when he reared up. But then that noble look of his : surely he was not mean ? Whereas all evil had an inner meanness, mean ! Was he mean ! Was he meanly treacherous ? Did he know he could kill, and meanly wait his opportunity ?

She was afraid. And if this were true, then he *should* be shot. Perhaps he ought to be shot.

This thought haunted her. Was there something mean and treacherous in St. Mawr's spirit, the vulgar evil ? If so, then have him shot. At moments, an anger would rise in her, as she thought of his frenzied rearing, and his mad, hideous writhing on the ground, and in the heat of her anger she would want to hurry down to her mother's house and have the creature shot at once. It would be a satisfaction, and a vindication of human rights. Because after all, Rico was so considerate of the brutal horse. But not a spark of consideration did the stallion have for Rico. No, it was the slavish malevolence of a domesticated creature that kept cropping up in St. Mawr. The slave, taking his slavish vengeance, then dropping back into subservience.

All the slaves of this world, accumulating their preparations for slavish vengeance, and then, when they have taken it, ready to drop back into servility. Freedom ! Most slaves can't be freed, no matter how you let them loose. Like domestic animals, they are, in the long run, more afraid of freedom than of masters : and freed by some generous master, they will at last crawl back to some mean boss, who will have no scruples about kicking them. Because, for them, far better kicks and servility than the hard, lonely responsibility of real freedom.

The wild animal is at every moment intensely self-disciplined, poised in the tension of self-defence, self-preservation, and self-assertion. The moments of relaxation are rare and most carefully chosen. Even sleep is watchful, guarded, unrelaxing, the wild courage pitched one degree higher than the wild fear. Courage, the wild thing's courage to maintain itself alone and living in the midst of a diverse universe.

Did St. Mawr have this courage ?

And did Rico ?

Ah, Rico ! He was one of mankind's myriad conspirators, who conspire to live in absolute physical safety, whilst willing the minor disintegration of all positive living.

But St. Mawr ? Was it the natural wild thing in him which caused these disasters ? Or was it the slave, asserting himself for vengeance ?

If the latter, let him be shot. It would be a great satisfaction, to see him dead.

But if the former——

When she could leave Rico with the nurse, she motored down to her mother for a couple of days. Rico lay in bed at the farm.

Everything seemed curiously changed. There was a new silence about the place, a new coolness. Summer had passed with several thunderstorms, and the blue, cool touch of autumn was about the house. Dahlias and perennial yellow sunflowers were out, the yellow of ending summer, the red coals of early autumn. First mauve tips of Michaelmas daisies were showing. Something suddenly carried her away to the great bare spaces of Texas, the blue sky, the flat, burnt earth, the miles of sunflowers. Another sky, another silence, towards the setting sun.

And suddenly, she craved again for the more absolute silence of America. English stillness was so soft, like an inaudible murmur of voices, of presences. But the silence in the empty spaces of America was still unutterable, almost cruel.

St. Mawr was in a small field by himself : she could not bear that he should be always in stable. Slowly she went through the gate towards him. And he stood there looking at her, the bright bay creature.

She could tell he was feeling somewhat subdued, after his late escapade. He was aware of the general human condemnation : the human damning. But something obstinate and uncanny in him made him not relent.

" Hello ! St. Mawr ! " she said, as she drew near, and he stood watching her, his ears pricked, his big eyes glancing sideways at her.

But he moved away when she wanted to touch him.

"Don't trouble," she said. "I don't want to catch you or do anything to you."

He stood still, listening to the sound of her voice, and giving quick, small glances at her. His underlip trembled. But he did not blink. His eyes remained wide and unrelenting. There was a curious malicious obstinacy in him which roused her anger.

"I don't want to touch you," she said. "I only want to look at you, and even you can't prevent that."

She stood gazing hard at him, wanting to know, to settle the question of his meanness or his spirit. A thing with a brave spirit is not mean.

He was uneasy as she watched him. He pretended to hear something, the mares two fields away, and he lifted his head and neighed. She knew the powerful, splendid sound so well : like bells made of living membrane. And he looked so noble again, with his head tilted up, listening, and his male eyes looking proudly over the distance, eagerly.

But it was all a bluff.

He knew, and became silent again. And as he stood there a few yards away from her, his head lifted and wary, his body full of power and tension, his face slightly averted from her, she felt a great animal sadness come from him. A strange animal atmosphere of sadness, that was vague and disseminated through the air, and made her feel as though she breathed grief. She breathed it into her breast, as if it were a great sigh down the ages, that passed into her breast. And she felt a great woe : the woe of human unworthiness. The race of men judged in the consciousness of the animals they have subdued, and there found unworthy, ignoble.

Ignoble men, unworthy of the animals they have subjugated, bred the woe in the spirit of their creatures. St. Mawr, that bright horse, one of the kings of creation in the order below man, it had been a fulfilment for him to serve the brave, reckless, perhaps cruel men of the past, who had a flickering, rising flame of nobility in them. To serve that flame of mysterious further nobility. Nothing matters, but that strange flame, of inborn nobility that obliges men to be brave, and onward plunging. And the horse will bear him on.

But now where is the flame of dangerous, forward-pressing nobility in men ? Dead, dead, guttering out in a stink of self-sacrifice whose feeble light is a light of exhaustion and *laissez-faire*.

And the horse, is he to go on carrying man forward into this ?— this gutter ?

No ! Man wisely invents motor-cars and other machines, automobile and locomotive. The horse is superannuated, for man.

But alas, man is even more superannuated, for the horse.

Dimly in a woman's muse, Lou realized this, as she breathed the horse's sadness, his accumulated vague woe from the generations of latter-day ignobility. And a grief and a sympathy flooded her, for the horse. She realized now how his sadness recoiled into these frenzies of obstinacy and malevolence. Underneath it all was grief, an unconscious, vague, pervading animal grief, which perhaps only Lewis understood, because he felt the same. The grief of the generous creature which sees all ends turning to the morass of ignoble living.

She did not want to say any more to the horse : she did not want to look at him any more. The grief flooded her soul, that made her want to be alone. She knew now what it all amounted to. She knew that the horse, born to serve nobly, had waited in vain for some one noble to serve. His spirit knew that nobility had gone out of men. And this left him high and dry, in a sort of despair.

As she walked away from him, towards the gate, slowly he began to walk after her.

Phœnix came striding through the gate towards her.

" You not afraid of that horse ? " he asked sardonically, in his quiet, subtle voice.

" Not at the present moment," she replied, even more quietly, looking direct at him. She was not in any mood to be jeered at.

And instantly the sardonic grimace left his face, followed by the sudden blankness, and the look of race-misery in the keen eyes.

" Do you want me to be afraid ? " she said, continuing to the gate.

" No, I don't want it," he replied, dejected.

" Are you afraid of him yourself? " she said, glancing round. St. Mawr had stopped, seeing Phœnix, and had turned away again.

" I'm not afraid of no horses," said Phœnix.

Lou went on quietly. At the gate, she asked him :

" Don't you like St. Mawr, Phœnix ? "

" I like him. He's a very good horse."

" Even after what he's done to Sir Henry ? "

" That don't make no difference to him being a good horse."

" But suppose he'd done it to you ? "

" I don't care. I say it my own fault."

" Don't you think he is wicked ? "

" I don't think so. He don't kick anybody. He don't bite anybody. He don't pitch, he don't buck, he don't do nothing."

" He rears," said Lou.

" Well, what is rearing ! " said the man, with a slow, contemp-tuous smile.

" A good deal, when a horse falls back on you."

" That horse don't want to fall back on you, if you don't make him. If you know how to ride him. That horse want his own way some-time. If you don't let him, you got to fight him. Then look out ! "

" Look out he doesn't kill you, you mean ! "

" Look out you don't let him," said Phœnix, with his slow, grim, sardonic smile.

Lou watched the smooth, golden face with its thin line of mous-tache and its sad eyes with the glint in them. Cruel—there was some-thing cruel in him, right down in the abyss of him. But at the same time, there was an aloneness, and a grim little satisfaction in a fight, and the peculiar courage of an inherited despair. People who inherit despair may at last turn it into greater heroism. It was almost so with Phœnix. Three-quarters of his blood was probably Indian and the remaining quarter, that came through the Mexican father, had the Spanish-American despair to add to the Indian. It was almost complete enough to leave him free to be heroic.

" What are we going to do with him, though ? " she asked.

" Why don't you and Mrs. Witt go back to America—you never been west. You go west."

" Where, to California ? "

" No. To Arizona or New Mexico or Colorado or Wyoming, anywhere. Not to California."

Phœnix looked at her keenly, and she saw the desire dark in him. He wanted to go back. But he was afraid to go back alone, empty-handed, as it were. He had suffered too much, and in that country his sufferings would overcome him, unless he had some other back-ground. He had been too much in contact with the white world, and his own world was too dejected, in a sense, too hopeless for his own hopelessness. He needed an alien contact to give him relief.

But he wanted to go back. His necessity to go back was becoming too strong for him.

" What is it like in Arizona ? " she asked. " Isn't it all pale-coloured sand and alkali, and a few cactuses, and terribly hot and deathly ? "

" No ! " he cried. " I don't take you there. I take you to the mountains—trees——" he lifted up his hand and looked at the sky— " big trees—pine ! *Pino-real* and *pinovetes*, smell good. And then you come down, *piñon*, not very tall, and *cedro*, cedar, smell good in the fire. And then you see the desert, away below, go miles and

miles, and where the canyon go, the crack where it look red !
I know, I been there, working a cattle ranch."

He looked at her with a haunted glow in his dark eyes. The poor
fellow was suffering from nostalgia. And as he glowed at her in that
queer mystical way, she too seemed to see that country, with its
dark, heavy mountains holding in their lap the great stretches of
pale, creased, silent desert that still is virgin of idea, its word
unspoken.

Phœnix was watching her closely and subtly. He wanted something of her. He wanted it intensely, heavily, and he watched her
as if he could force her to give it him. He wanted her to take him
back to America, because, rudderless, he was afraid to go back
alone. He wanted her to take him back : avidly he wanted it. She
was to be the means to his end.

Why shouldn't he go back by himself ? Why should he crave for
her to go too ? Why should he want her there ?

There was no answer, except that he did.

"Why, Phœnix," she said. "I might possibly go back to
America. But you know, Sir Henry would never go there. He
doesn't like America, though he's never been. But I'm sure he'd
never go there to live."

"Let him stay here," said Phœnix abruptly, the sardonic look on
his face as he watched her face. "You come, and let him stay here."

"Ah, that's a whole story !" she said, and moved away.

As she went, he looked after her, standing silent and arrested and
watching as an Indian watches. It was not love. Personal love
counts so little when the greater griefs, the greater hopes, the great
despairs and the great resolutions come upon us.

She found Mrs. Witt rather more silent, more firmly closed within
herself, than usual. Her mouth was shut tight, her brows were
arched rather more imperiously than ever, she was revolving some
inward problem about which Lou was far too wise to inquire.

In the afternoon Dean Vyner and Mrs. Vyner came to call on
Lady Carrington.

"What bad luck this is, Lady Carrington !" said the Dean.
"Knocks Scotland on the head for you this year, I'm afraid. How
did you leave your husband ? "

"He seems to be doing as well as he could do !" said Lou.

"But how *very* unfortunate !" murmured the invalid Mrs.
Vyner. "Such a handsome young man, in the bloom of youth !
Does he suffer much pain ? "

"Chiefly his foot," said Lou.

"Oh, I *do* so hope they'll be able to restore the ankle. Oh, how dreadful to be lamed at his age!"

"The doctor doesn't know. There *may* be a limp," said Lou.

"That horse has certainly left his mark on two good-looking young fellows," said the Dean. "If you don't mind my saying so, Lady Carrington, I think he's a bad egg."

"Who, St. Mawr?" said Lou, in her American sing-song.

"Yes, Lady Carrington," murmured Mrs. Vyner, in her invalid's low tone. "Don't you think he ought to be put away? He seems to me the incarnation of cruelty. His neigh. It goes through me like knives. Cruel! Cruel! Oh, I think he should be put away."

"How put away?" murmured Lou, taking on an invalid's low tone herself.

"Shot, I suppose," said the Dean.

"It is quite painless. He'll know nothing," murmured Mrs. Vyner hastily. "And think of the harm he has done already! Horrible! Horrible!" she shuddered. "Poor Sir Henry lame for life, and Eddy Edwards disfigured. Besides all that has gone before. Ah no, such a creature ought not to live!"

"To live, and have a groom to look after him and feed him," said the Dean. "It's a bit thick, while he's smashing up the very people that give him bread—or oats, since he's a horse. But I suppose you'll be wanting to get rid of him?"

"Rico does," murmured Lou.

"Very naturally. So should I. A vicious horse is worse than a vicious man—except that you are free to put him six feet underground, and end his vice finally, by your own act."

"Do you think St. Mawr is vicious?" said Lou.

"Well, of course—if we're driven to definitions! I *know* he's dangerous."

"And do you think we ought to shoot everything that is dangerous?" asked Lou, her colour rising.

"But Lady Carrington, have you consulted your husband? Surely his wish should be law, in a matter of this sort! And on such an occasion! For *you*, who are a woman, it is enough that the horse is cruel, cruel, evil! I felt it long before anything happened. That evil male cruelty! Ah!" and she clasped her hands convulsively.

"I suppose," said Lou slowly, "that St. Mawr is really Rico's horse: I gave him to him, I suppose. But I don't believe I could let him shoot him, for all that."

"Ah, Lady Carrington," said the Dean breezily, "you can shift the responsibility. The horse is a public menace, put it at that. We can get an order to have him done away with, at the public expense. And among ourselves we can find some suitable compensation for you, as a mark of sympathy. Which, believe me, is very sincere ! One hates to have to destroy a fine-looking animal. But I would sacrifice a dozen rather than have our Rico limping."

" Yes, indeed," murmured Mrs. Vyner.

" Will you excuse me one moment, while I see about tea," said Lou, rising and leaving the room. Her colour was high, and there was a glint in her eye. These people almost roused her to hatred. Oh, these awful, house-bred, house-inbred human beings, how repulsive they were !

She hurried to her mother's dressing-room. Mrs. Witt was very carefully putting a touch of red on her lips.

" Mother, they want to shoot St. Mawr," she said.

" I know," said Mrs. Witt, as calmly as if Lou had said tea was ready.

" Well——" stammered Lou, rather put out. " Don't you think it cheek ? "

" It depends, I suppose, on the point of view," said Mrs. Witt dispassionately, looking closely at her lips. " I don't think the English climate agrees with me. I need something to stand up against, no matter whether it's great heat or great cold. This climate, like the food and the people, is most always lukewarm or tepid, one or the other. And the tepid and the lukewarm are not really my line." She spoke with a slow drawl.

" But they're in the drawing-room, mother, trying to force me to have St. Mawr killed."

" What about tea ? " said Mrs. Witt.

" I don't care," said Lou.

Mrs. Witt worked the bell-handle.

" I suppose, Louise," she said, in her most beaming eighteenth-century manner, " that these are your guests, so you will preside over the ceremony of pouring out."

" No, mother, you do it. I can't smile to-day."

" I can," said Mrs. Witt.

And she bowed her head slowly, with a faint, ceremoniously-effusive smile, as if handing a cup of tea.

Lou's face flickered to a smile.

" Then you pour out for them. You can stand them better than I can."

" Yes," said Mrs. Witt. " I saw Mrs. Vyner's hat coming across the churchyard. It looks so like a crumpled cup and saucer, that

I have been saying to myself ever since : *Dear Mrs. Vyner, can't I fill your cup !*—and then pouring tea into that hat. And I hear the Dean responding : *My head is covered with cream, my cup runneth over.* That is the way they make *me* feel."

They marched downstairs, and Mrs. Witt poured tea with that devastating correctness which made Mrs. Vyner, who was utterly impervious to sarcasm, pronounce her " indecipherably vulgar."

But the Dean was the old bull-dog, and he had set his teeth in a subject.

" I was talking to Lady Carrington about that stallion, Mrs. Witt."

" Did you say stallion ? " asked Mrs. Witt, with perfect neutrality.

" Why, yes, I presume that's what he is."

" I presume so," said Mrs. Witt colourlessly.

" I'm afraid Lady Carrington is a little sensitive on the wrong score," said the Dean.

" I beg your pardon," said Mrs. Witt, leaning forward in her most colourless polite manner. " You mean the stallion's score ? "

" Yes," said the Dean testily. " The horse St. Mawr."

" The stallion St. Mawr," echoed Mrs. Witt, with utmost mild vagueness. She completely ignored Mrs. Vyner, who felt plunged like a specimen into methylated spirit. There was a moment's full-stop.

" Yes ? " said Mrs. Witt naïvely.

" You agree that we can't have any more of these accidents to your young men ? " said the Dean rather hastily.

" I certainly do ! " Mrs. Witt spoke very slowly, and the Dean's lady began to look up. She might find a loop-hole through which to wriggle into the contest. " You know, Dean, that my son-in-law calls me, for preference, *belle mère* ! It sounds so awfully English when he says it ; I always see myself as an old grey mare with a bell round her neck, leading a bunch of horses." She smiled a prim little smile, *very* conversationally. " Well ! " and she pulled herself up from the aside. " Now as the bell-mare of the bunch of horses, I shall see to it that my son-in-law doesn't go too near that stallion again. That stallion won't stand mischief."

She spoke so earnestly that the Dean looked at her with round wide eyes, completely taken aback.

" We all know, Mrs. Witt, that the author of the mischief is St. Mawr himself," he said, in a loud tone.

" Really ! you think *that* ? " Her voice went up in American surprise. " Why, how *strange*—— ! " and she lingered over the last word.

" Strange, eh ?   After what's just happened ? " said the Dean,
with a deadly little smile.

" Why, yes !   Most strange !   I saw with my own eyes my son-
in-law pull that stallion over backwards, and hold him down with
the reins as tight as he could hold them ;   pull St. Mawr's head
backwards on to the ground, till the groom had to crawl up and force
the reins out of my son-in-law's hands.   Don't you think that was
mischievous on Sir Henry's part ? "

The Dean was growing purple.   He made an apoplectic movement with his hand.   Mrs. Vyner was turned to a seated pillar of
salt, strangely dressed up.

" Mrs. Witt, you are playing on words."

" No, Dean Vyner, I am not.   My son-in-law pulled that horse
over backwards and pinned him down with the reins."

" I am sorry for the horse," said the Dean, with heavy sarcasm.

" I am *very*," said Mrs. Witt, " sorry for that stallion : *very !* "

Here Mrs. Vyner rose as if a chair-spring had suddenly propelled
her to her feet.   She was streaky pink in the face.

" Mrs. Witt," she panted, " you misdirect your sympathies.
That poor young man—in the beauty of youth."

" Isn't he *beautiful*——" murmured Mrs. Witt, extravagantly in
sympathy.   " He's my daughter's husband ! "   And she looked at
the petrified Lou.

" Certainly ! " panted the Dean's wife.   " And you can defend
that—that——"

" That stallion," said Mrs. Witt.   " But you see, Mrs. Vyner," she
added, leaning forward female and confidential, " if the old grey
mare doesn't defend the stallion, who will ?   All the blooming young
ladies will defend my beautiful son-in-law.   You feel so *warmly* for
him yourself !   I'm an American woman, and I always have to
stand up for the accused.   And I stand up for that stallion.   I say
it is not right.   He was pulled over backwards and then pinned down
by my son-in-law—who may have meant to do it, or may not.   And
now people abuse him.   Just tell everybody, Mrs. Vyner and Dean
Vyner "—she looked round at the Dean—" that the *belle-mère's*
sympathies are with the stallion."

She looked from one to the other with a faint and gracious little
bow, her black eyebrows arching in her eighteenth-century face like
black rainbows, and her full, bold grey eyes absolutely incomprehensible.

" Well, it's a peculiar message to have to hand round, Mrs. Witt,"
the Dean began to boom, when she interrupted him by laying her

hand on his arm and leaning forward, looking up into his face like a clinging, pleading female :

"Oh, but *do* hand it, Dean, *do* hand it," she pleaded, gazing intently into his face.

He backed uncomfortably from that gaze.

"Since you wish it," he said, in a chest voice.

"I most certainly *do*——" she said, as if she were wishing the sweetest wish on earth. Then turning to Mrs. Vyner :

"Good-bye, Mrs. Vyner. We *do* appreciate your coming, my daughter and I."

"I came out of kindness——" said Mrs. Vyner.

"Oh, I know it, I know it," said Mrs. Witt. "Thank you *so* much. Good-bye ! Good-bye, Dean ! Who is taking the morning service on Sunday ? I hope it is you, because I want to come."

"It *is* me," said the Dean. "Good-bye ! Well, good-bye, Lady Carrington. I shall be going over to see your young man to-morrow, and will gladly take you or anything you have to send."

"Perhaps mother would like to go," said Lou, softly, plaintively.

"Well, we shall see," said the Dean. "Good-bye for the present ! "

Mother and daughter stood at the window watching the two cross the churchyard. Dean and wife knew it, but daren't look round, and daren't admit the fact to one another.

Lou was grinning with a complete grin that gave her an odd, dryad or faun look, intensified.

"It was almost as good as pouring tea into her hat," said Mrs. Witt serenely. "People like that tire me out. I shall take a glass of sherry."

"So will I, mother. It was even better than pouring tea in her hat. You meant, didn't you, if you poured tea in her hat, to put cream and sugar in first ? "

"I did," said Mrs. Witt.

But after the excitement of the encounter had passed away, Lou felt as if her life had passed away too. She went to bed, feeling she could stand no more.

In the morning she found her mother sitting at a window watching a funeral. It was raining heavily, so that some of the mourners even wore mackintosh coats. The funeral was in the poorer corner of the churchyard, where another new grave was covered with wreaths of sodden, shrivelling flowers. The yellowish coffin stood on the wet earth, in the rain : the curate held his hat, in a sort of permanent salute, above his head, like a little umbrella, as he hastened on with the service. The people seemed too wet to weep more wet.

It was a long coffin.

" Mother, do you really *like* watching ? " asked Lou irritably, as Mrs. Witt sat in complete absorption.

" I do, Louise, I really enjoy it."

" Enjoy, mother ! "   Lou was almost disgusted.

" I'll tell you why.   I imagine I'm the one in the coffin—this is a girl of eighteen, who died of consumption—and those are my relatives, and I'm watching them put me away.   And you know, Louise, I've come to the conclusion that hardly anybody in the world really lives, and so hardly anybody really dies.   They may well say *Oh Death, where is thy sting-a-ling-a-ling ?*   Even Death can't sting those that have never really lived.   I always used to want that—to die without death stinging me.   And I'm sure the girl in the coffin is saying to herself : *Fancy Aunt Emma putting on a drab slicker, and wearing it while they bury me.   Doesn't show much respect.   But then my mother's family always were common !*   I feel there should be a solemn burial of a roll of newspapers containing the account of the death and funeral, next week.   It would be just as serious : the grave of all the world's remarks——"

" I don't want to think about it, mother.   One ought to be able to laugh at it.   I want to laugh at it."

" Well, Louise, I think it's just as great a mistake to laugh at everything as to cry at everything.   Laughter's not the one panacea, either.   I should *really* like, before I do come to be buried in a box, to know where I am.   That young girl in that coffin never was anywhere—any more than the newspaper remarks on her death and burial.   And I begin to wonder if I've ever been anywhere.   I seem to have been a daily sequence of newspaper remarks, myself.   I'm sure I never really conceived you and gave you birth.   It all happened in newspaper notices.   It's a newspaper fact that you are my child, and that's about all there is to it."

Lou smiled as she listened.

" I always knew you were philosophic, mother.   But I never dreamed it would come to elegies in a country churchyard, written to your motherhood."

" *Exactly*, Louise !   Here I sit and sing the elegy to my own motherhood.   I never had any motherhood, except in newspaper fact.   I never was a wife, except in newspaper notices.   I never was a young girl, except in newspaper remarks.   Bury everything I ever said or that was said about me, and you've buried *me*.   But since Kind Words Can Never Die, I can't be buried, and death has no sting-a-ling-a-ling for *me !*   Now listen to me, Louise : I want death to be real to me—not as it was to that young girl. I *want* it to hurt me, Louise. If it hurts me enough, I shall know I was alive."

She set her face and gazed under half-dropped lids at the funeral, stoic, fate-like, and yet, for the first time, with a certain pure wistfulness of a young, virgin girl. This frightened Lou very much. She was so used to the matchless Amazon in her mother, that when she saw her sit there, still, wistful, virginal, tender as a girl who has never taken armour, wistful at the window that only looked on graves, a serious terror took hold of the young woman. The terror of *too late !*

Lou felt years, centuries older than her mother, at that moment, with the tiresome responsibility of youth to protect and guide their elders.

"What can we do about it, mother ? " she asked protectively.

"Do nothing, Louise. I'm not going to have anybody wisely steering my canoe, now I feel the rapids are near. I shall go with the river. Don't you pretend to do anything for me. I've done enough mischief myself, that way. I'm going down the stream, at last."

There was a pause.

"But in actuality, what ? " asked Lou, a little ironically.

"I don't quite know. Wait a while."

"Go back to America ? "

"That is possible."

"I may come too."

"I've always waited for you to go back of your own will."

Lou went away, wandering round the house. She was so unutterably tired of everything—weary of the house, the graveyard, weary of the thought of Rico. She would have to go back to him to-morrow, to nurse him. Poor old Rico, going on like an amiable machine from day to day. It wasn't his fault. But his life was a rattling nullity, and her life rattled in null correspondence. She had hardly strength enough to stop rattling and be still. Perhaps she had not strength enough.

She did not know. She felt so weak, that unless something carried her away she would go on rattling her bit in the great machine of human life, till she collapsed, and her rattle rattled itself out, and there was a sort of barren silence where the sound of her had been.

She wandered out in the rain, to the coach-house where Lewis and Phœnix were sitting facing one another, one on a bin, the other on the inner doorstep.

"Well," she said, smiling oddly. "What's to be done ? "

The two men stood up. Outside the rain fell steadily on the flag-stones of the yard, past the leaves of trees. Lou sat down on the little iron step of the dogcart.

" That's cold," said Phœnix. " You sit here." And he threw a yellow horse-blanket on the box where he had been sitting.

" I don't want to take your seat," she said.

" All right, you take it."

He moved across and sat gingerly on the shaft of the dogcart. Lou seated herself, and loosened her soft tartan shawl. Her face was pink and fresh, and her dark hair curled almost merrily in the damp. But under her eyes were the finger-prints of deadly weariness.

She looked up at the two men, again smiling in her odd fashion.

" What are we going to do ? " she asked.

They looked at her closely, seeking her meaning.

" What about ? " said Phœnix, a faint smile reflecting on his face, merely because she smiled.

" Oh, everything," she said, hugging her shawl again. " You know what they want ? They want to shoot St. Mawr."

The two men exchanged glances.

" Who want it ? " said Phœnix.

" Why—all our *friends !* " she made a little *moue*. " Dean Vyner does."

Again the men exchanged glances. There was a pause. Then Phœnix said, looking aside :

" The boss is selling him."

" Who ? "

" Sir Henry." The half-breed always spoke the title with difficulty, and with a sort of sneer. " He sell him to Miss Manby."

" How do you know ? "

" The man from Corrabach told me last night. Flora, she say it."

Lou's eyes met the sardonic, empty-seeing eyes of Phœnix direct. There was too much sarcastic understanding. She looked aside.

" What else did he say ? " she asked.

" I don't know," said Phœnix, evasively. " He say they cut him—else shoot him. Think they cut him—and if he die, he die."

Lou understood. He meant they would geld St. Mawr—at his age.

She looked at Lewis. He sat with his head down, so she could not see his face.

" Do you think it is true ? " she asked. " Lewis ? Do you think they would try to geld St. Mawr—to make him a gelding ? "

Lewis looked up at her. There was a faint deadly glimmer of contempt on his face.

" Very likely, Mam," he said.

She was afraid of his cold, uncanny pale eyes, with their uneasy grey dawn of contempt. These two men, with their silent, deadly inner purpose, were not like other men. They seemed like two silent enemies of all the other men she knew. Enemies in the great white camp, disguised as servants, waiting the incalculable opportunity. What the opportunity might be, none knew.

"Sir Henry hasn't mentioned anything to me about selling St. Mawr to Miss Manby," she said. .

The derisive flicker of a smile came on Phœnix's face.

"He sell him first, and tell you then," he said, with his deadly impassive manner.

"But do you really think so?" she asked.

It was extraordinary how much corrosive contempt Phœnix could convey, saying nothing. She felt it almost as an insult. Yet it was a relief to her.

"You know, I can't believe it. I can't believe Sir Henry would want to have St. Mawr mutilated. I believe he'd rather shoot him."

"You think so?" said Phœnix, with a faint grin.

Lou turned to Lewis.

"Lewis, will you tell me what you truly think?"

Lewis looked at her with a hard, straight, fearless British stare.

"That man Philips was in the 'Moon and Stars' last night. He said Miss Manby told him she was buying St. Mawr, and she asked him if he thought it would be safe to cut him, and make a horse of him. He said it would be better, take some of the nonsense out of him. He's no good for a sire, anyhow——"

Lewis dropped his head again, and tapped a tattoo with the toe of his rather small foot.

"And what do you think?" said Lou. It occurred to her how sensible and practical Miss Manby was, so much more so than the Dean.

Lewis looked up at her with his pale eyes.

"It won't have anything to do with me," he said. "I shan't go to Corrabach Hall."

"What will you do, then?"

Lewis did not answer. He looked at Phœnix.

"Maybe him and me go to America," said Phœnix, looking at the void.

"Can he get in?" said Lou.

"Yes, he can. I know how," said Phœnix.

"And the money?" she said.

"We got money."

There was a silence, after which she asked of Lewis :

" You'd leave St. Mawr to his fate ? "

" I can't help his fate," said Lewis. " There's too many people in the world for me to help anything."

" Poor St. Mawr ! "

She went indoors again, and up to her room : then higher, to the top rooms of the tall Georgian house. From one window she could see the fields in the rain. She could see St. Mawr himself, alone as usual, standing with his head up, looking across the fences. He was streaked dark with rain. Beautiful, with his poised head and massive neck, and his supple hindquarters. He was neighing to Poppy. Clear on the wet wind came the sound of his bell-like, stallion's calling, that Mrs. Vyner called cruel. It was a strange noise, with a splendour that belonged to another world-age. The mean cruelty of Mrs. Vyner's humanitarianism, the barren cruelty of Flora Manby, the eunuch cruelty of Rico. Our whole eunuch civilization, nasty-minded as eunuchs are, with their kind of sneaking, sterilizing cruelty.

Yet even she herself, seeing St. Mawr's conceited march along the fence, could not help addressing him :

" Yes, my boy ! If you knew what Miss Flora Manby was preparing for you ! *She'll* sharpen a knife that will settle you."

And Lou called her mother.

The two American women stood high at the window, overlooking the wet, close, hedged-and-fenced English landscape. Everything enclosed, enclosed, to stifling. The very apples on the trees looked so shut in, it was impossible to imagine any speck of " knowledge " lurking inside them. Good to eat, good to cook, good even for show. But the wild sap of untameable and inexhaustible knowledge —no ! Bred out of them. Geldings, even the apples.

Mrs. Witt listened to Lou's half-humorous statements.

" You must admit, mother, Flora is a sensible girl," she said.

" I admit it, Louise."

" She goes straight to the root of the matter."

" And eradicates the root. Wise girl ! And what is your answer?"

" I don't know, mother. What would you say ? "

" I know what *I* should say."

" Tell me."

" I should say : *Miss Manby, you may have my husband, but not my horse. My husband won't need emasculating, and my horse I won't have you meddle with. I'll preserve one last male thing in the museum of this world, if I can.*"

Lou listened, smiling faintly.

"That's what I will say," she replied at length. "The funny thing is, mother, they think all their men with their bare faces or their little quotation-marks moustaches *are* so tremendously male. That fox-hunting one !"

"I know it. Like little male motor-cars. Give him a little gas, and start him on the low gear, and away he goes : all his male gear rattling, like a cheap motor-car."

"I'm afraid I dislike men altogether, mother."

"You may, Louise. Think of Flora Manby, and how you love the fair sex."

"After all, St. Mawr is better. And I'm glad if he gives them a kick in the face."

"Ah, Louise !" Mrs. Witt suddenly clasped her hands with wicked passion. "*Ay, qué gozo !* as our Juan used to say, on your father's ranch in Texas." She gazed in a sort of wicked ecstasy out of the window.

They heard Lou's maid softly calling Lady Carrington from below. Lou went to the stairs.

"What is it ?"

"Lewis want to speak to you, my lady."

"Send him into the sitting-room."

The two women went down.

"What is it, Lewis ?" asked Lou.

"Am I to bring in St. Mawr, in case they send for him from Corrabach ?"

"No," said Lou swiftly.

"Wait a minute," put in Mrs. Witt. "What makes you think they will send for St. Mawr from Corrabach, Lewis ?" she asked, suave as a grey leopard cat.

"Miss Manby went up to Flints Farm with Dean Vyner this morning, and they've just come back. They stopped the car, and Miss Manby got out at the field gate, to look at St. Mawr. I'm thinking, if she made the bargain with Sir Henry, she'll be sending a man over this afternoon, and if I'd better brush St. Mawr down a bit, in case."

The man stood strangely still, and the words came like shadows of his real meaning. It was a challenge.

"I see," said Mrs. Witt slowly.

Lou's face darkened. She too saw.

"So that is her game," she said. "That is why they got me down here."

"Never mind, Louise," said Mrs. Witt. Then to Lewis : "Yes, please bring in St. Mawr. You wish it, don't you, Louise?"

"Yes," hesitated Lou. She saw by Mrs. Witt's closed face that a counter-move was prepared.

"And Lewis," said Mrs. Witt, "my daughter may wish you to ride St. Mawr this afternoon—not to Corrabach Hall."

"Very good, Mam."

Mrs. Witt sat silent for some time, after Lewis had gone, gathering inspiration from the wet, grisly grave-stones.

"Don't you think it's time we made a move, daughter?" she asked.

"Any move," said Lou desperately.

"Very well then. My dearest friends, and my *only* friends, in this country, are in Oxfordshire. I will set off to *ride* to Merriton this afternoon, and Lewis will ride with me on St. Mawr."

"But you can't ride to Merriton in an afternoon," said Lou.

"I know it. I shall ride across country. I shall *enjoy* it, Louise. Yes, I shall consider I am on my way back to America. I am most deadly tired of this country. From Merriton I shall make my arrangements to go to America, and take Lewis and Phœnix and St. Mawr along with me. I think they want to go. You will decide for yourself."

"Yes, I'll come too," said Lou casually.

"Very well. I'll start immediately after lunch, for I can't *breathe* in this place any longer. Where are Henry's automobile maps?"

Afternoon saw Mrs. Witt, in a large waterproof cape, mounted on her horse, Lewis, in another cape, mounted on St. Mawr, trotting through the rain, splashing in the puddles, moving slowly southwards. They took the open country, and would pass quite near to Flints Farm. But Mrs. Witt did not care. With great difficulty she had managed to fasten a small waterproof roll behind her, containing her night-things. She seemed to breathe the first breath of freedom.

And sure enough, an hour or so after Mrs. Witt's departure, arrived Flora Manby in a splashed up motor-car, accompanied by her sister, and bringing a groom and a saddle.

"Do you know, Harry sold me St. Mawr," she said. "I'm just wild to get that horse in hand."

"How?" said Lou.

"Oh, I don't know. There are ways. Do you mind if Philips rides him over now, to Corrabach? Oh, I forgot, Harry sent you a note."

"*Dearest Loulina : Have you been gone from here two days or two years. It seems the latter. You are terribly missed. Flora wanted so much to buy St. Mawr, to save us further trouble, that I have sold him to her. She is giving me what we paid ; rather, what you paid ; so of course, the money is yours. I am thankful we are rid of the animal, and that he falls into competent hands —I asked her please to remove him from your charge to-day. And I can't tell how much easier I am in my mind, to think of him gone. You are coming back to me to-morrow, aren't you ? I shall think of nothing else but you, till I see you. Arrivederci, darling dear ! R.*"

"I'm so sorry," said Lou. "Mother went on horseback to see some friends, and Lewis went with her on St. Mawr. He knows the road."

"She'll be back this evening ? " said Flora.

"I don't know. Mother is so uncertain. She may be away a day or two."

"Well, here's the cheque for St. Mawr."

"No, I won't take it now—no, thank you—not till mother comes back with the goods."

Flora was chagrined. The two women knew they hated one another. The visit was a brief one.

Mrs. Witt rode on in the rain, which abated as the afternoon wore down, and the evening came without rain, and with a suffusion of pale yellow light. All the time she had trotted in silence, with Lewis just behind her. And she scarcely saw the heather-covered hills with the deep clefts between them, nor the oak-woods, nor the lingering foxgloves, nor the earth at all. Inside herself she felt a profound repugnance for the English country : she preferred even the crudeness of Central Park in New York.

And she felt an almost savage desire to get away from Europe, from everything European. Now she was really *en route*, she cared not a straw for St. Mawr or for Lewis or anything. Something just writhed inside her, all the time, against Europe. That closeness, that sense of cohesion, that sense of being fused into a lump with all the rest—no matter how much distance you kept—this drove her mad. In America the cohesion was a matter of choice and will. But in Europe it was organic, like the helpless particles of one sprawling body. And the great body in a state of incipient decay.

She was a woman of fifty-one : and she seemed hardly to have lived a day. She looked behind her—the thin trees and swamps of Louisiana, the sultry, sub-tropical excitement of decaying New Orleans, the vast bare dryness of Texas, with mobs of cattle in an illumined dust ! The half-European thrills of New York ! The false stability of Boston ! A clever husband, who was a brilliant lawyer, but who was far more thrilled by his cattle ranch than by his law : and who drank heavily and died. The years of first widowhood in Boston, consoled by a self-satisfied sort of intellectual courtship from clever men. For curiously enough, while she wanted it, she had always been able to compel men to pay court to her. All kinds of men. Then a rather dashing time in New York—when she was in her early forties. Then the long *visual* philandering in Europe. She left off "loving," save through the eye, when she came to Europe. And when she made her trips to America, she found it was finished there also, her "loving."

What was the matter ? Examining herself, she had long ago decided that her nature was a destructive force. But then, she justified herself, she had only destroyed that which was destructible. If she could have found something indestructible, especially in men, though she would have fought against it, she would have been glad at last to be defeated by it.

That was the point. She really wanted to be defeated in her own eyes. And nobody had ever defeated her. Men were never really her match. A woman of terrible strong health, she felt even that in her strong limbs there was far more electric power than in the limbs of any man she had met. That curious fluid electric force, that could make any man kiss her hand, if she so willed it. A queen, as far as she wished. And not having been very clever at school, she always had the greatest respect for the mental powers. Her own were not mental powers. Rather electric, as of some strange physical dynamo within her. So she had been ready to bow before Mind.

But alas ! After a brief time, she had found Mind, at least the man who was supposed to have the mind, bowing before her. Her own peculiar dynamic force was stronger than the force of Mind. She could make Mind kiss her hand.

And not by any sensual tricks. She did not really care about sensualities, especially as a younger woman. Sex was a mere adjunct. She cared about the mysterious, intense, dynamic sympathy that could flow between her and some "live" man—a man who was highly conscious, a real live wire. That she cared about.

But she had never rested until she had made the man she admired —and admiration was the root of her attraction to any man—made him kiss her hand. In both senses, actual and metaphorical. Physical and metaphysical. Conquered his country.

She had always succeeded. And she believed that, if she cared, she always *would* succeed. In the world of living men. Because of the power that was in her, in her arms, in her strong, shapely, but terrible hands, in all the great dynamo of her body.

For this reason she had been so terribly contemptuous of Rico, and of Lou's infatuation. Ye gods ! What was Rico in the scale of men !

Perhaps she despised the younger generation too easily. Because she did not see its sources of power, she concluded it was powerless. Whereas perhaps the power of accommodating oneself to any circumstance and committing oneself to no circumstance is the last triumph of mankind.

Her generation had had its day. She had had her day. The world of her men had sunk into a sort of insignificance. And with a great contempt she despised the world that had come into place instead : the world of Rico and Flora Manby, the world represented, to her, by the Prince of Wales.

In such a world there was nothing even to conquer. It gave everything and gave nothing to everybody and anybody all the time. *Dio benedetto !* as Rico would say. A great complicated tangle of nonentities ravelled in nothingness. So it seemed to her.

Great God ! This was the generation she had helped to bring into the world.

She had had her day. And, as far as the mysterious battle of life went, she had won all the way. Just as Cleopatra, in the mysterious business of a woman's life, won all the way.

Though that bald tough Cæsar had drawn his iron from the fire without losing much of its temper. And he had gone his way. And Antony surely was splendid to die with.

In her life there had been no tough Cæsar to go his way in cold blood, away from her. Her men had gone from her like dogs on three legs, into the crowd. And certainly there was no gorgeous Antony to die for and with.

Almost she was tempted in her heart to cry : " Conquer me, oh God, before I die ! " But then she had a terrible contempt for the God that was supposed to rule this universe. She felt she could make *Him* kiss her hand. Here she was a woman of fifty-one, past the change of life. And her great dread was to die an empty, barren death. Oh, if only Death might open dark wings of mystery and consolation. To die an easy, barren death. To pass out as she had passed in, without mystery or the rustling of darkness ! That was her last, final, ashy dread.

" Old ! " she said to herself. " I am not *old !* I have lived many years, that is all. But I am as timeless as an hour-glass that turns morning and night, and spills the hours of sleep one way, the hours of consciousness the other way, without itself being affected. Nothing in all my life has ever truly affected me. I believe Cleopatra only tried the asp, as she tried her pearls in wine, to see if it would really, really have any effect on her. Nothing had ever really had any effect on her, neither Cæsar nor Antony nor any of them. Never once had she really been lost, lost to herself. Then try death, see if that trick would work. If she would lose herself to herself that way. Ah death—— ! "

But Mrs. Witt mistrusted death too. She felt she might pass out as a bed of asters passes out in autumn, to mere nothingness. And something in her longed to die, at least, *positively* : to be folded then at last into throbbing wings of mystery, like a hawk that goes to sleep. Not like a thing made into a parcel and put into the last rubbish-heap.

So she rode trotting across the hills, mile after mile, in silence. Avoiding the roads, avoiding everything, avoiding everybody, just trotting forwards, towards night.

And by nightfall they had travelled twenty-five miles. She had motored around this country, and knew the little towns and the inns. She knew where she would sleep.　　•

The morning came beautiful and sunny. A woman so strong in health, why should she ride with the fact of death before her eyes ? But she did.

Yet in sunny morning she must do something about it.

" Lewis ! " she said. " Come here and tell me something, please ! Tell me," she said, " do you believe in God ? "

" In God ! " he said, wondering. " I never think about it."

" But do you say your prayers ? "

" No, Mam ! "

" Why don't you ? "

He thought about it for some minutes.

" I don't like religion. My aunt and uncle were religious."

" You don't like religion," she repeated. " And you don't believe in God. Well then——"

" Nay ! " he hesitated. " I never said I didn't believe in God. Only I'm sure I'm not a Methodist. And I feel a fool in a proper church. And I feel a fool saying my prayers. And I feel a fool when ministers and parsons come getting at me. I never think about God, if folks don't try to make me." He had a small, sly smile, almost gay.

" And you don't like feeling a fool ? " She smiled rather patronisingly.

" No, Mam."

" Do I make you feel a fool ? " she asked, drily.

He looked at her without answering.

" Why don't you answer ? " she said, pressing.

" I think you'd like to make a fool of me sometimes," he said.

" Now ? " she pressed.

He looked at her with that slow, distant look.

" Maybe ! " he said, rather unconcernedly.

Curiously, she couldn't touch him. He always seemed to be watching her from a distance, as if from another country. Even if she made a fool of him, something in him would all the time be far away from her, not implicated.

She caught herself up in the personal game, and returned to her own isolated question. A vicious habit made her start the personal tricks. She didn't want to, really.

There was something about this little man—sometimes, to herself, she called him *Little Jack Horner, Sat in a Corner*—that irritated her and made her want to taunt him. His peculiar little inaccessibility, that was so tight and easy.

Then again, there was something, his way of looking at her as if he looked from out of another country, a country of which he was an inhabitant, and where she had never been : this touched her strangely. Perhaps behind this little man was the mystery. In spite of the fact that in actual life, in her world, he was only a groom, almost chétif, with his legs a little bit horsey and bowed ; and of no education, saying, *Yes Mam !* and *No Mam !* and accomplishing nothing, simply nothing at all on the face of the earth. Strictly a nonentity.

And yet, what made him perhaps the only real entity to her, his seeming to inhabit another world than hers ? A world dark and still, where language never ruffled the growing leaves, and seared their edges like a bad wind.

Was it an illusion, however ? Sometimes she thought it was. Just bunkum, which she had faked up, in order to have something to mystify about.

But then, when she saw Phœnix and Lewis silently together, she knew there *was* another communion, silent, excluding her. And sometimes when Lewis was alone with St. Mawr ; and once, when she saw him pick up a bird that had stunned itself against a wire : she had realized another world, silent, where each creature is alone in its own aura of silence, the mystery of power : as Lewis had power with St. Mawr, and even with Phœnix.

The visible world, and the invisible. Or rather, the audible and the inaudible. She had lived so long, and so completely, in the visible, audible world. She would not easily admit that other, inaudible. She always wanted to jeer, as she approached the brink of it.

Even now, she wanted to jeer at the little fellow, because of his holding himself inaccessible within the inaudible, silent world. And she knew he knew it.

" Did you never want to be rich, and be a gentleman, like Sir Henry ? " she asked.

" I would many times have liked to be rich. But I never exactly wanted to be a gentleman," he said.

" Why not ? "

" I can't exactly say. I should be uncomfortable if I was like they are."

" And are you comfortable now ? "

" When I'm let alone."

" And do they let you alone ? Does the world let you alone ? "

" No, they don't."

" Well then—— ! "

" I keep to myself all I can."

" And are you comfortable, as you call it, when you keep to yourself ? "

" Yes, I am."

" But when you keep to yourself, what do you keep to ? What precious treasure have you to keep to ? "

He looked, and saw she was jeering.

" None," he said. " I've got nothing of that sort."

She rode impatiently on ahead.

And the moment she had done so, she regretted it. She might put the little fellow, with contempt, out of her reckoning. But no, she would not do it.

She had put so much out of her reckoning : soon she would be left in an empty circle, with her empty self at the centre.

She reined in again.

" Lewis ! " she said. " I don't want you to take offence at anything I say."

" No, Mam."

" I don't want you to say just *No Mam !* all the time ! " she cried impulsively. " Promise me."

" Yes, Mam ! "

" But really ! Promise me you won't be offended at whatever I say."

" Yes, Mam ! "

She looked at him searchingly. To her surprise, she was almost
in tears. A woman of her years ! And with a servant !

But his face was blank and stony, with a stony, distant look of
pride that made him inaccessible to her emotions. He met her eyes
again : with that cold distant look, looking straight into her hot,
confused, pained self. So cold and as if merely refuting her. He
didn't believe her, nor trust her, nor like her even. She was an
attacking enemy to him. Only he stayed really far away from her,
looking down at her from a sort of distant hill where her weapons
could not reach : not quite.

And at the same time, it hurt him in a dumb, living way, that she
made these attacks on him. She could see the cloud of hurt in his
eyes, no matter how distantly he looked at her.

They bought food in a village shop, and sat under a tree near a
field where men were already cutting oats, in a warm valley. Lewis
had stabled the horses for a couple of hours, to feed and rest. But
he came to join her under the tree, to eat. He sat at a little distance
from her, with the bread and cheese in his small brown hands, eating
silently, and watching the harvesters. She was cross with him, and
therefore she was stingy, would give him nothing to eat but dry
bread and cheese. Herself, she was not hungry. So all the time he
kept his face a little averted from her. As a matter of fact, he kept
his whole being averted from her, away from her. He did not want
to touch her, nor to be touched by her. He kept his spirit there,
alert, on its guard, but out of contact. It was as if he had unconsciously accepted the battle, the old battle. He was her target, the
old object of her deadly weapons. But he refused to shoot back.
It was as if he caught all her missiles in full flight, before they touched
him, and silently threw them on the ground behind him. And in
some essential part of himself he ignored her, staying in another
world.

That other world ! Mere male armour of artificial impervious-
ness ! It angered her.

Yet she knew, by the way he watched the harvesters, and the
grasshoppers popping into notice, that it was another world. And
when a girl went by, carrying food to the field, it was at him she
glanced. And he gave that quick, animal little smile that came
from him unawares. Another world !

Yet also, there was a sort of meanness about him : a *suffisance !*
A keep-yourself-for-yourself, and don't give yourself away.

Well ! She rose impatiently.

It was hot in the afternoon, and she was rather tired. She went to the inn and slept, and did not start again till tea-time.

Then they had to ride rather late. The sun sank, among a smell of cornfields, clear and yellow-red behind motionless dark trees. Pale smoke rose from cottage chimneys. Not a cloud was in the sky, which held the upward-floating light like a bowl inverted on purpose. A new moon sparkled and was gone. It was beginning of night.

Away in the distance, they saw a curious pinkish glare of fire, probably furnaces. And Mrs. Witt thought she could detect the scent of furnace smoke, or factory smoke. But then she always said that of the English air : it was never quite free of the smell of smoke, coal-smoke.

They were riding slowly on a path through fields, down a long slope. Away below was a puther of lights. All the darkness seemed full of half-spent crossing lights, a curious uneasiness. High in the sky a star seemed to be walking. It was an aeroplane with a light. Its buzz rattled above. Not a space, not a speck of this country that wasn't humanized, occupied by the human claim. Not even the sky.

They descended slowly through a dark wood, which they had entered through a gate. Lewis was all the time dismounting and opening gates, letting her pass, shutting the gate and mounting again.

So, in a while she came to the edge of the wood's darkness, and saw the open pale concave of the world beyond. The darkness was never dark. It shook with the concussion of many invisible lights, lights of towns, villages, mines, factories, furnaces, squatting in the valleys and behind all the hills.

Yet, as Rachel Witt drew rein at the gate emerging from the wood, a very big, soft star fell in heaven, cleaving the hubbub of this human night with a gleam from the greater world.

" See, a star falling ! " said Lewis, as he opened the gate.

" I saw it," said Mrs. Witt, walking her horse past him.

There was a curious excitement of wonder, or magic, in the little man's voice. Even in this night something strange had stirred awake in him.

" You ask me about God," he said to her, walking his horse along-side in the shadow of the wood's edge, the darkness of the old Pan, that kept our artificially-lit world at bay. " I don't know about God. But when I see a star fall like that out of long-distance places in the sky : and the moon sinking, saying Good-bye ! Good-bye ! Good-bye ! and nobody listening : I think I hear something, though I wouldn't call it God."

" What then ? " said Rachel Witt.

" And you smell the smell of oak-leaves now," he said, " now the air is cold. They smell to me more alive than people. The trees hold their bodies hard and still, but they watch and listen with their leaves. And I think they say to me : *Is that you passing there, Morgan Lewis ? All right, you pass quickly, we shan't do anything to you. You are like a holly-bush.*"

" Yes," said Rachel Witt, drily. " *Why ?* "

" All the time, the trees grow, and listen. And if you cut a tree down without asking pardon, trees will hurt you some time in your life, in the night-time."

" I suppose," said Rachel Witt, " that's an old superstition."

" They say that ash-trees don't like people. When the other people were most in the country—I mean like what they call fairies, that have all gone now—they liked ash-trees best. And you know the little green things with little small nuts in them, that come flying down from ash-trees—*pigeons,* we call them—they're the seeds —the other people used to catch them and eat them before they fell to the ground. And that made the people so they could hear trees living and feeling things. But when all these people that there are now came to England, they liked the oak-trees best, because their pigs ate the acorns. So now you can tell the ash-trees are mad, they want to kill all these people. But the oak-trees are many more than the ash-trees."

" And do you eat the ash-tree seeds ? " she asked.

" I always ate them, when I was little. Then I wasn't frightened of ash-trees, like most of the others. And I wasn't frightened of the moon. If you didn't go near the fire all day, and if you didn't eat any cooked food nor anything that had been in the sun, but only things like turnips or radishes or pig-nuts, and then went without any clothes on, in the full moon, then you could see the people in the moon, and go with them. They never have fire, and they never speak, and their bodies are clear almost like jelly. They die in a minute if there's a bit of fire near them. But they know more than we. Because unless fire touches them, they never die. They see people live and they see people perish, and they say, people are only like twigs on a tree, you break them off the tree, and kindle fire with them. You made a fire of them, and they are gone, the fire is gone, everything is gone. But the people of the moon don't die, and fire is nothing to them. They look at it from the distance of the sky, and see it burning things up, people all appearing and disappearing like twigs that come in spring and you cut them in autumn and make a fire of them and they are gone. And they say : what do people matter ? If you want to matter, you must become a moon-boy. Then all your life, fire can't blind you and people can't hurt you. Because at full moon you can join the moon people, and go through the air and pass any cool places, pass through rocks and through the trunks of trees, and when you come to people lying warm in bed, you punish them."

" How ? "

" You sit on the pillow where they breathe, and you put a web across their mouth, so they can't breathe the fresh air that comes from the moon. So they go on breathing the same air again and again, and that makes them more and more stupefied. The sun gives out heat, but the moon gives out fresh air. That's what the moon people do : they wash the air clean with moonlight."

He was talking with a strange eager *naïveté* that amused Rachel Witt, and made her a little uncomfortable in her skin. Was he after all no more than a sort of imbecile ?

" Who told you all this stuff ? " she asked abruptly.

And, as abruptly, he pulled himself up.

" We used to say it, when we were children."

" But you don't believe it ? It *is* only childishness, after all."

He paused a moment or two.

" No," he said, in his ironical little day-voice. " I know I shan't make anything but a fool of myself, with that talk. But all sorts of things go through our heads, and some seem to linger, and some don't. But you asking me about God put it into my mind, I suppose. I don't know what sort of things I believe in : only I know it's not what the chapel-folks believe in. We none of us believe in them when it comes to earning a living, or, with you people, when it comes to spending your fortune. Then we know that bread costs money, and even your sleep you have to pay for. That's work. Or, with you people, it's just owning property and seeing you get your value for your money. But a man's mind is always full of things. And some people's minds, like my aunt and uncle, are full of religion and hell for everybody except themselves. And some people's minds are all money, money, money, and how to get hold of something they haven't got hold of yet. And some people, like you, are always curious about what everybody else in the world is after. And some people are all for enjoying themselves and being thought much of, and some, like Lady Carrington, don't know what to do with themselves. Myself, I don't want to have in my mind the things other people have in their minds. I'm one that likes my own things best.

And if, when I see a bright star fall, like to-night, I think to myself :
*There's movement in the sky. The world is going to change again. They're
throwing something to us from the distance, and we've got to have it, whether
we want it or not. To-morrow there will be a difference for everybody,
thrown out of the sky upon us, whether we want it or not :* then that's how
I want to think, so let me please myself."

" You know what a shooting star actually is, I suppose ?—and
that there are always many in August, because we pass through a
region of them ? "

" Yes, Mam, I've been told. But stones don't come at us from the
sky for nothing. Either it's like when a man tosses an apple to you
out of his orchard, as you go by. Or it's like when somebody shies
a stone at you, to cut your head open. You'll never make me believe
the sky is like an empty house with a slate falling from the roof.
The world has its own life, the sky has a life of its own, and never is
it like stones rolling down a rubbish heap and falling into a pond.
Many things twitch and twitter within the sky, and many things
happen beyond us. My own way of thinking is my own way."

" I never knew you talk so much."

" No, Mam. It's your asking me that about God. Or else it's the
night-time. I don't believe in God and being good and going to
Heaven. Neither do I worship idols, so I'm not a heathen as my
aunt called me. Never from a boy did I want to believe the things
they kept grinding in their guts at home, and at Sunday School,
and at school. A man's mind has to be full of something, so I keep
to what we used to think as lads. It's childish nonsense, I know it.
But it suits me. Better than other people's stuff. Your man Phœnix
is about the same, when he lets on. Anyhow, it's my own stuff, that
we believed as lads, and I like it better than other people's stuff.
You asking about God made me let on. But I would never belong
to any club, or trades' union, and God's the same to my
mind."

With this he gave a little kick to his horse, and St. Mawr went
dancing excitedly along the highway they now entered, leaving Mrs.
Witt to trot after as rapidly as she could.

When she came to the hotel, to which she had telegraphed for
rooms, Lewis disappeared, and she was left thinking hard.

It was not till they were twenty miles from Merriton, riding
through a slow morning mist, and she had a rather far-away, wistful
look on her face, unusual for her, that she turned to him in the saddle
and said :

" Now don't be surprised, Lewis, at what I am going to say. I am going to ask you, now, supposing I wanted to marry you, what should you say ? "

He looked at her quickly, and was at once on his guard.

" That you didn't mean it," he replied hastily.

" Yes "—she hesitated, and her face looked wistful and tired.— " Supposing I *did* mean it. Supposing I did *really*, from my heart, want to marry you and be a wife to you——" she looked away across the fields—" then what should you say ? "

Her voice sounded sad, a little broken.

" Why, Mam ! " he replied, knitting his brow and shaking his head a little. " I should say you didn't mean it, you know. Something would have come over you."

" But supposing I *wanted* something to come over me ? "

He shook his head.

" It would never do, Mam ! Some people's flesh and blood is kneaded like bread : and that's me. And some are rolled like fine pastry, like Lady Carrington. And some are mixed with gunpowder. They're like a cartridge you put in a gun, Mam."

She listened impatiently.

" Don't talk," she said, " about bread and cakes and pastry, it all means nothing. You used to answer short enough, *Yes Mam ! No Mam !* That will do now. Do you mean *Yes !* or *No ?* "

His eyes met hers. She was again hectoring.

" No, Mam ! " he said, quite neutral.

" Why ? "

As she waited for his answer, she saw the fountains of his loquacity dry up, his face go distant and mute again, as it always used to be, till these last two days, when it had had a funny touch of inconsequential merriness.

He looked steadily into her eyes, and his look was neutral, sombre, and hurt. He looked at her as if infinite seas, infinite spaces divided him and her. And his eyes seemed to put her away beyond some sort of fence. An anger, congealed cold like lava, set impassive against her and all her sort.

" No, Mam. I couldn't give my body to any woman who didn't respect it."

" But I do respect it, I do ! "—she flushed hot like a girl.

" No, Mam. Not as *I* mean it," he replied.

There was a touch of anger against her in his voice, and a distance of distaste.

" And how do *you* mean it ? " she replied, the full sarcasm coming back into her tones. She could see that, as a woman to touch and fondle he saw her as repellent : only repellent.

" I have to be a servant to women now," he said, " even to earn my wage. I could never touch with my body a woman whose servant I was."

" You're not my servant : my daughter pays your wages. And all that is beside the point, between a man and a woman."

" No woman who I touched with my body should ever speak to me as you speak to me, or think of me as you think of me," he said.

" But !——" she stammered. " I think of you—with love. And can you be so unkind as to notice the way I speak ? You know it's only my way."

" You, as a woman," he said, " you have no respect for a man."

" Respect ! Respect ! " she cried. " I'm likely to lose what respect I have left. I know I can *love* a man. But whether a man can love a woman——"

" No," said Lewis. " I never could, and I think I never shall. Because I don't want to. The thought of it makes me feel shame."

" What do you mean ? " she cried.

" Nothing in the world," he said, " would make me feel such shame as to have a woman shouting at me, or mocking at me, as I see women mocking and despising the men they marry. No woman shall touch my body, and mock me or despise me. No woman."

" But men must be mocked, or despised even, sometimes."

" No. Not this man. Not by the woman I touch with my body."

" Are you perfect ? "

" I don't know. But if I touch a woman with my body, it must put a lock on her, to respect what I will never have despised : never ! "

" What will you never have despised ? "

" My body ! And my touch upon the woman."

" Why insist so on your body ? " And she looked at him with a touch of contemptuous mockery, raillery.

He looked her in the eyes, steadily and coldly, putting her away from him, and himself far away from her.

" Do you expect that any woman will stay your humble slave, to-day ? " she asked cuttingly.

But he only watched her, coldly, distant, refusing any connection.

" Between men and women, it's a question of give and take. A man can't expect *always* to be humbly adored."

He watched her still, cold, rather pale, putting her far from him. Then he turned his horse and set off rapidly along the road, leaving her to follow.

She walked her horse and let him go, thinking to herself :

" There's a little bantam cock. And a groom ! Imagine it ! Thinking he can dictate to a woman ! "

She was in love with him. And he, in an odd way, was in love with her. She had known it by the odd, uncanny merriment in him, and his unexpected loquacity. But he would not have her come physically near him. Unapproachable there as a cactus, guarding his " body " from her contact. As if contact with her would be mortal insult and fatal injury to his marvellous " body."

What a little cock-sparrow !

Let him ride ahead. He would have to wait for her somewhere.

She found him at the entrance to the next village. His face was pallid and set. She could tell he felt he had been insulted, so he had congealed into stiff insentience.

" At the bottom of all men is the same," she said to herself : " an empty, male conceit of themselves."

She too rode up with a face like a mask, and straight on to the hotel.

" Can you serve dinner to myself and my servant ? " she asked at the inn : which, fortunately for her, accommodated motorists, otherwise they would have said *No !*

" I think," said Lewis as they came in sight of Merriton, " I'd better give Lady Carrington a week's notice."

A complete little stranger ! And an impudent one.

" Exactly as you please," she said.

She found several letters from her daughter at Marshal Place.

" Dear Mother : No sooner had you gone off than Flora appeared, not at all in the bud, but rather in full blow. She demanded her victim ; Shylock demanding the pound of flesh : and wanted to hand over the shekels.

" Joyfully I refused them. She said ' Harry ' was much better, and invited him and me to stay at Corrabach Hall till he was quite well : it would be less strain on your household, while he was still in bed and helpless. So the plan is, that he shall be brought down on Friday, if he is really fit for the journey, and we drive straight to Corrabach. I am packing his bags and mine, clearing up our traces : his trunks to go to Corrabach, mine to stay here and make up their minds. I am going to Flints Farm again to-morrow, dutifully, though I am no flower for the bedside. I do so want to know if Rico has already called her Fiorita : or perhaps Florecita. It reminds me of old William's joke : *Now yuh tell me, little Missy : which is the best posey that grow ?* And the hushed whisper in which he said the answer : *The Collyposy !* Oh dear, I am so tired of feeling spiteful, but how else is one to feel.

" You looked most prosaically romantic, setting off in a rubber cape, followed by Lewis. Hope the roads were not very slippery, and that you had a good time, à la *Mademoiselle de Maupin*. Do remember, dear, not to devour little Lewis before you have got half-way——"

" Dear Mother : I half expected word from you before I left, but nothing came. Forrester drove me up here just before lunch. Rico seems much better, almost himself, and a little more than that. He broached out staying at Corrabach very tactfully. I told him Flora had asked me, and it seemed a good plan. Then I told him about St. Mawr. He was a little piqued, and there was a pause of very disapproving silence. Then he said : *Very well, darling. If you wish to keep the animal, do so by all means. I make a present of him again.* Me : *That's so good of you, Rico. Because I know revenge is sweet.* Rico : *Revenge, Loulina ! I don't think I was selling him for vengeance ! Merely to get rid of him to Flora, who can keep better hold over him.* Me : *But you know, dear, she was going to geld him !* Rico : *I don't think anybody knew it. We only wondered if it were possible, to make him more amenable. Did she tell you ?* Me : *No—Phœnix did. He had it from a groom.* Rico : *Dear me ! A concatenation of grooms ! So your mother rode off with Lewis, and carried St. Mawr out of danger ! I understand ! Let us hope worse won't befall.* Me : *Whom ?* Rico : *Never mind, dear ! It's so lovely to see you. You are looking rested. I thought those Countess of Witton roses the most marvellous things in the world, till you came, now they're quite in the background.* He had some very lovely red roses, in a crystal bowl : the room smelled of roses. Me : *Where did they come from ?* Rico : *Oh, Flora brought them !* Me : *Bowl and all ?* Rico : *Bowl and all ! Wasn't it dear of her ?* Me : *Why, yes ! But then she's the goddess of flowers, isn't she ?* Poor darling, he was offended that I should twit him while he is ill, so I relented. He has had a couple of marvellous invalid's bed-jackets sent from London : one a pinkish yellow, with rose-arabesque facings : this one in fine cloth. But unfortunately he has already dropped soup on it. The other is a lovely silvery and blue and green soft brocade. He had that one on to receive me, and I at once complimented him on it. He has got a new ring too : sent by Aspasia Weingartner, a rather lovely intaglio of Priapus under an apple bough, at least, so he says it is. He made a naughty face, and said : *The Priapus stage is rather advanced for poor me.* I asked what the Priapus stage was, but he said, *Oh, nothing !* Then nurse said : *There's a big classical dictionary that Miss Manby*

brought up, if you wish to see it. So I have been studying the Classical
Gods. The world always was a queer place. It's a very queer one
when Rico is the god Priapus. He would go round the orchard
painting life-like apples on the trees, and inviting nymphs to come
and eat them. And the nymphs would pretend they were real :
Why, Sir Prippy, what stunningly naughty apples ! There's nothing so
artificial as sinning nowadays. I suppose it once was real.

" I'm bored here : wish I had my horse."

" Dear Mother : I'm so glad you are enjoying your ride. I'm
sure it is like riding into history, like the Yankee at the Court of
King Arthur, in those old bye-lanes and Roman roads. They still
fascinate me : at least, more before I get there than when I am
actually there. I begin to feel real American and to resent the past.
Why doesn't the past decently bury itself, instead of sitting waiting
to be admired by the present ?

" Phœnix brought Poppy. I am so fond of her : rode for five
hours yesterday. I was glad to get away from this farm. The doctor
came, and said Rico would be able to go down to Corrabach to-
morrow. Flora came to hear the bulletin, and sailed back full of
zest. Apparently Rico is going to do a portrait of her, sitting up in
bed. What a mercy the bedclothes won't be mine, when Priapus
wields his palette from the pillow.

" Phœnix thinks you intend to go to America with St. Mawr, and
that I am coming too, leaving Rico this side—I wonder. I feel so
unreal, nowadays, as if I too were nothing more than a painting by
Rico on a millboard. I feel almost too unreal even to make up my
mind to anything. It is terrible when the life-flow dies out of one,
and everything is like cardboard, and oneself is like cardboard. I'm
sure it is worse than being dead. I realized it yesterday when Phœnix
and I had a picnic lunch by a stream. You see I must imitate you
in all things. He found me some watercresses, and they tasted so
damp and *alive*, I knew how deadened I was. Phœnix wants us to
go and have a ranch in Arizona, and raise horses, with St. Mawr, if
willing, for Father Abraham. I wonder if it matters what one does :
if it isn't all the same thing over again ? Only Phœnix, his funny
blank face, makes my heart melt and go sad. But I believe he'd be
cruel too. I saw it in his face when he didn't know I was looking.
Anything though, rather than this deadness and this paint-Priapus
business. Au revoir, mother dear ! Keep on having a good
time——"

" Dear Mother : I had your letter from Merriton : am so glad
you arrived safe and sound in body and temper. There was such

a funny letter from Lewis, too : I enclose it. What makes him take this extraordinary line ? But I'm writing to tell him to take St. Mawr to London, and wait for me there. I have telegraphed Mrs. Squire to get the house ready for me. I shall go straight there.

" Things developed here, as they were bound to. I just couldn't bear it. No sooner was Rico put in the automobile than a self-conscious importance came over him, like when the wounded hero is carried into the middle of the stage. *Why so solemn, Rico dear ?* I asked him, trying to laugh him out of it. *Not solemn, dear, only feeling a little transient.* I don't think he knew himself what he meant. Flora was on the steps as the car drew up, dressed in severe white. She only needed an apron, to become a nurse : or a veil, to become a bride. Between the two, she had an unbearable air of a woman in seduced circumstances, as *The Times* said. She ordered two men-servants about in subdued, you would have said hushed, but competent tones. And then I saw there was a touch of the priestess about her as well : Cassandra preparing for her violation : Iphigenia, with Rico for Orestes, on a stretcher : he looking like Adonis, fully prepared to be an unconscionable time in dying. They had given him a lovely room, downstairs, with doors opening on to a little garden all of its own. I believe it was Flora's boudoir. I left nurse and the men to put him to bed. Flora was hovering anxiously in the passage outside. *Oh, what a marvellous room ! Oh, how colourful, how beautiful !* came Rico's tones, the hero behind the scenes. I must say, it was like a harvest festival, with roses and gaillardias in the shadow, and cornflowers in the light, and a bowl of grapes, and nectarines among leaves. *I'm so anxious that he should be happy*, Flora said to me in the passage. *You know him best. Is there anything else I could do for him ?* Me : *Why, if you went to the piano and sang, I'm sure he'd love it. Couldn't you sing : Oh, my love is like a rred, rred rrose !*— You know how Rico imitates Scotch !

" Thank goodness I have a bedroom upstairs : nurse sleeps in a little ante-chamber to Rico's room. The Edwards' are still here, the blond young man with some very futuristic plaster on his face. *Awfully good of you to come !* he said to me, looking at me out of one eye, and holding my hand fervently. How's that for cheek ? *It's awfully good of Miss Manby to let me come*, said I. He : *Ah, but Flora is always a sport, a topping good sport !*

" I don't know what's the matter, but it just all put me into a fiendish temper. I felt I couldn't sit there at luncheon with that bright, youthful company, and hear about their tennis and their polo and their hunting and have their flirtatiousness making me sick. So I asked for a tray in my room. Do as I might, I couldn't help being horrid.

"Oh, and Rico ! He really is too awful. Lying there in bed with every ear open, like Adonis waiting to be persuaded not to die. Seizing a hushed moment to take Flora's hand and press it to his lips, murmuring : *How awfully good you are to me, dear Flora !* And Flora : *I'd be better, if I knew how, Harry !* So cheerful with it all ! No, it's too much. My sense of humour is leaving me : which means, I'm getting into too bad a temper to be able to ridicule it all. I suppose I feel in the minority. It's an awful thought, to think that most all the young people in the world are like this : so bright and cheerful, and *sporting*, and so brimming with libido. How awful !

"I said to Rico : *You're very comfortable here, aren't you ?* He : *Comfortable ! It's comparative heaven.* Me : *Would you mind if I went away ?* A deadly pause. He is deadly afraid of being left alone with Flora. He feels safe so long as I am about, and he can take refuge in his marriage ties. He : *Where do you want to go, dear ?* Me : *To mother. To London. Mother is planning to go to America, and she wants me to go.* Rico : *But you don't want to go t—he—e—re—e !* You know, mother, how Rico can put a venomous emphasis on a word, till it suggests pure poison. It nettled me. *I'm not sure,* I said. Rico : *Oh, but you can't stand that awful America.* Me : *I want to try again.* Rico : *But Lou dear, it will be winter before you get there. And this is absolutely the wrong moment for me to go over there. I am only just making headway over here. When I am absolutely sure of a position in England, then we nip across the Atlantic and scoop in a few dollars, if you like. Just now, even when I am well, would be fatal. I've only just sketched in the outline of my success in London, and one ought to arrive in New York ready-made as a famous and important Artist.* Me : *But mother and I didn't think of going to New York. We thought we'd sail straight to New Orleans—if we could : or to Havana. And then go west to Arizona.* The poor boy looked at me in such distress. *But Loulina darling, do you mean you want to leave me in the lurch for the winter season ? You can't mean it. We're just getting on so splendidly, really !* I was surprised at the depth of feeling in his voice : how tremendously his career as an artist—a popular artist—matters to him. I can never believe it. You know, mother, you and I feel alike about daubing paint on canvas : every possible daub that can be daubed has already been done, so people ought to leave off. Rico is so shrewd. I always think he's got his tongue in his cheek, and I'm always staggered once more to find that he takes it absolutely seriously. His career ! The Modern British Society of Painters : perhaps even the Royal Academy ! Those people we see in London, and those portraits Rico does ! He may even be a second Laszlo, or a thirteenth Orpen, and die happy ! Oh ! mother ! How can it really matter to *anybody* !

" But I was really rather upset, when I realized how his heart was fixed on his career, and that I might be spoiling everything for him. So I went away to think about it. And then I realized how unpopular you are, and how unpopular I shall be myself, in a little while. A sort of hatred for people has come over me. I hate their ways and their bunk, and I feel like kicking them in the face, as St. Mawr did that young man. Not that I should ever do it. And I don't think I should ever have made my final announcement to Rico, if he hadn't been such a beautiful pig in clover, here at Corrabach Hall. He has known the Manbys all his life ; they and he are sections of one engine. He would be far happier with Flora : or I won't say happier, because there is something in him which rebels : but he would on the whole fit much better. I myself am at the end of my limit, and beyond it. I can't ' mix ' any more, and I refuse to. I feel like a bit of eggshell in the mayonnaise : the only thing is to take it out, you can't beat it in. I *know* I shall cause a fiasco, even in Rico's career, if I stay. I shall go on being rude and hateful to people as I am at Corrabach, and Rico will lose all his nerve.

" So I have told him. I said this evening, when no one was about : *Rico dear, listen to me seriously. I can't stand these people. If you ask me to endure another week of them, I shall either become ill, or insult them, as mother does. And I don't want to do either.* Rico : *But darling, isn't everybody perfect to you !* Me : *I tell you, I shall just make a break, like St. Mawr, if I don't get out. I simply can't stand people.* The poor darling, his face goes so blank and anxious. He knows what I mean, because, except that they tickle his vanity all the time, he hates them as much as I do. But his vanity is the chief thing to him. He : *Lou darling, can't you wait till I get up, and we can go away to the Tyrol or somewhere for a spell ?* Me : *Won't you come with me to America, to the South-West ? I believe it's marvellous country.* I saw his face switch into hostility ; quite vicious. He : *Are you so keen on spoiling everything for me ? Is that what I married you for ? Do you do it deliberately ?* Me : *Everything is already spoilt for me. I tell you I can't stand people, your Floras and your Aspasias, and your forthcoming young Englishmen. After all, I am an American, like mother, and I've got to go back.* He : *Really ! And am I to come along as part of the luggage ? Labelled cabin !* Me : *You do as you wish, Rico.* He : *I wish to God you did as you wished, Lou dear. I'm afraid you do as Mrs. Witt wishes. I always heard that the holiest thing in the world was a mother.* Me : *No dear, it's just that I can't*

stand people. He (with a snarl) : *And I suppose I'm lumped in as* PEOPLE !
And when he'd said it, it was true. We neither of us said anything for
a time. Then he said, calculating : *Very well, dear ! You take a trip
to the land of stars and stripes, and I'll stay here and go on with my work.
And when you've seen enough of their stars and tasted enough of their stripes,
you can come back and take your place again with me.* We left it at that.

" You and I are supposed to have important business connected
with our estates in Texas—it sounds so well—so we are making a
hurried trip to the States, as they call them. I shall leave for London
early next week——"

Mrs. Witt read this long letter with satisfaction. She herself had
one strange craving : to get back to America. It was not that she
idealized her native country : she was a tartar of restlessness there,
quite as much as in Europe. It was not that she expected to
arrive at any blessed abiding-place. No, in America she would go
on fuming and chafing the same. But at least she would be in
America, in her own country. And that was what she wanted.

She picked up the sheet of poor paper, that had been folded in
Lou's letter. It was the letter from Lewis, quite nicely written.
" Lady Carrington, I write to tell you and Sir Henry that I think
I had better quit your service, as it would be more comfortable all
round. If you will write and tell me what you want me to do with
St. Mawr, I will do whatever you tell me. With kind regards to
Lady Carrington and Sir Henry, I remain, Your obedient servant,
Morgan Lewis."

Mrs. Witt put the letter aside, and sat looking out of the window.
She felt, strangely, as if already her soul had gone away from her
actual surroundings. She was there, in Oxfordshire, in the body, but
her spirit had departed elsewhere. A listlessness was upon her. It
was with an effort she roused herself, to write to her lawyer in
London, to get her release from her English obligations. Then she
wrote to the London hotel.

For the first time in her life she wished she had a maid, to do little
things for her. All her life, she had had too much energy to endure
any one hanging round her, personally. Now she gave up. Her
wrists seemed numb, as if the power in her were switched off.

When she went down they said Lewis had asked to speak to her.
She had hardly seen him since they had arrived at Merriton.

" I've had a letter from Lady Carrington, Mam. She says will
I take St. Mawr to London and wait for her there. But she says I am
to come to you, Mam, for definite orders."

" Very well, Lewis. I shall be going to London in a few days time.

You arrange for St. Mawr to go up one day this week, and you will take him to the Mews. Come to me for anything you want. And don't talk of leaving my daughter. We want you to go with St. Mawr to America, with us and Phœnix."

" And your horse, Mam ? "

" I shall leave him here at Merriton. I shall give him to Miss Atherton."

" Very good, Mam ! "

" Dear Daughter : I shall be in my old quarters in Mayfair next Saturday, calling the same day at your house to see if everything is ready for you. Lewis has fixed up with the railway : he goes to town to-morrow. The reason of his letter was that I had asked him if he would care to marry me, and he turned me down with emphasis. But I will tell you about it. You and I are the scribe and the Pharisee ; I never could write a letter, and you could never leave off——"

" Dearest Mother : I smelt something rash, but I know it's no use saying : How *could* you ? I only wonder, though, that you should think of marriage. You know, dear, I ache in every fibre to be left alone, from all that sort of thing. I feel all bruises, like one who has been assassinated. I do so understand why Jesus said : *Noli me tangere.* Touch me not, I am not yet ascended unto the Father. Everything had hurt him so much, wearied him so beyond endurance, he felt he could not bear one little human touch on his body. I am like that. I can hardly bear even Elena to hand me a dress. As for a man—and marriage—ah, no ! *Noli me tangere, homine !* I am not yet ascended unto the Father. Oh, leave me alone, leave me alone ! That is all my cry to all the world.

" Curiously, I feel that Phœnix understands what I feel. He leaves me so understandingly alone, he almost gives me my sheath of aloneness : or at least, he protects me in my sheath. I am grateful for him.

" Whereas Rico feels my aloneness as a sort of shame to himself. He wants at least a blinding *pretence* of intimacy. Ah, intimacy ! The thought of it fills me with aches, and the pretence of it exhausts me beyond myself.

" Yes, I long to go away to the west, to be away from the world like one dead and in another life, in a valley that life has not yet entered.

" Rico asked me : What are you doing with St. Mawr ? When I said we were taking him with us, he said : *Oh, the Corpus delicti !* Whether that means anything I don't know. But he has grown sarcastic beyond my depth.

" I shall see you to-morrow——"

Lou arrived in town, at the dead end of August, with her maid and
Phœnix. How wonderful it seemed to have London empty of all
her set : her own little house to herself, with just the housekeeper
and her own maid. The fact of being alone in those surroundings
was so wonderful. It made the surroundings themselves seem all
the more ghastly. Everything that had been actual to her was
turning ghostly : even her little drawing-room was the ghost of
a room, belonging to the dead people who had known it, or to all
the dead generations that had brought such a room into being,
evolved it out of their quaint domestic desires. And now, in herself,
those desires were suddenly spent : gone out like a lamp that suddenly dies. And then she saw her pale, delicate room with its little
green agate bowl and its two little porcelain birds and its soft,
roundish chairs, turned into something ghostly, like a room set out
in a museum. She felt like fastening little labels on the furniture :
Lady Louise Carrington, Lounge Chair. Last used August 1923. Not for
the benefit of posterity : but to remove her own self into another
world, another realm of existence.

"My house, my house, my house, how can I ever have taken so
much pains about it !" she kept saying to herself. It was like one of
her old hats, suddenly discovered neatly put away in an old hatbox.
And what a horror : an old "fashionable" hat.

Lewis came to see her, and he sat there in one of her delicate
mauve chairs, with his feet on a delicate old carpet from Turkestan,
and she just wondered. He wore his leather gaiters and khaki
breeches as usual, and a faded blue shirt. But his beard and hair
were trimmed, he was tidy. There was a certain fineness of contour
about him, a certain subtle gleam, which made him seem, apart from
his rough boots, not at all gross, or coarse, in that setting of rather
silky, oriental furnishings. Rather he made the Asiatic, sensuous
exquisiteness of her old rugs and her old white Chinese figures seem
a weariness. Beauty ! What was beauty, she asked herself ? The
oriental exquisiteness seemed to her all like dead flowers whose hour
had come, to be thrown away.

Lou could understand her mother's wanting, for a moment, to
marry him. His detachedness and his acceptance of something in
destiny which people cannot accept. Right in the middle of him he
accepted something from destiny, that gave him a quality of eternity.
He did not care about persons, people, even events. In his own odd
way he was an aristocrat, inaccessible in his aristocracy. But it was
the aristocracy of the invisible powers, the greater influences,
nothing to do with human society.

"You don't really want to leave St. Mawr, do you?" Lou asked him. "You don't really want to quit, as you said?"

He looked at her steadily, from his pale grey eyes, without answering, not knowing what to say.

"Mother told me what she said to you. But she doesn't mind, she says you are entirely within your rights. She has a real regard for you. But we mustn't let our regards run us into actions which are beyond our scope, must we? That makes everything unreal. But you will come with us to America with St. Mawr, won't you? We depend on you."

"I don't want to be uncomfortable," he said.

"Don't be," she smiled. "I myself hate unreal situations—I feel I can't stand them any more. And most marriages are unreal situations. But apart from anything exaggerated, you like being with mother and me, don't you?"

"Yes, I do. I like Mrs. Witt as well. But not——"

"I know. There won't be any more of that——"

"You see, Lady Carrington," he said, with a little heat, "I'm not by nature a marrying man. And I'd feel I was selling myself."

"Quite! Why do you think you are not a marrying man, though?"

"Me! I don't feel myself after I've been with women." He spoke in a low tone, looking down at his hands. "I feel messed up. I'm better to keep to myself. Because——" and here he looked up with a flare in his eyes: "women—they only want to make you give in to them, so that they feel almighty, and you feel small."

"Don't you like feeling small?" Lou smiled. "And don't you want to make them give in to you?"

"Not me," he said. "I don't want nothing. Nothing, I want."

"Poor mother!" said Lou. "She thinks if she feels moved by a man, it must result in marriage—or that kind of thing. Surely she makes a mistake. I think you and Phœnix and mother and I might live somewhere in a far-away wild place, and make a good life: so long as we didn't begin to mix up marriage, or love, or that sort of thing into it. It seems to me men and women have really hurt one another so much, nowadays, that they had better stay apart till they have learned to be gentle with one another again. Not all this forced passion and destructive philandering. Men and women should stay apart, till their hearts grow gentle towards one another again. Now, it's only each one fighting for his own—or her own—underneath the cover of tenderness."

" *Dear !—darling !—Yes, my love !* " mocked Lewis, with a faint smile of amused contempt.

" Exactly. People always say *dearest !* when they hate each other most."

Lewis nodded, looking at her with a sudden sombre gloom in his eyes. A queer bitterness showed on his mouth. But even then he was so still and remote.

The housekeeper came and announced The Honourable Laura Ridley. This was like a blow in the face to Lou. She rose hurriedly —and Lewis rose, moving to the door.

" Don't go, please, Lewis," said Lou—and then Laura Ridley appeared in the doorway. She was a woman a few years older than Lou, but she looked younger. She might have been a shy girl of twenty-two, with her fresh complexion, her hesitant manner, her round, startled brown eyes, her bobbed hair.

" Hello ! " said the newcomer. " Imagine your being back ! I saw you in Paddington."

Those sharp eyes would see everything.

" I thought every one was out of town," said Lou. " This is Mr. Lewis."

Laura gave him a little nod, then sat on the edge of her chair.

" No," she said. " I did go to Ireland to my people, but I came back. I prefer London when I can be more or less alone in it. I thought I'd just run in for a moment, before you're gone again. Scotland, isn't it ? "

" No, mother and I are going to America."

" America ! Oh, I thought it was Scotland."

" It was. But we have suddenly to go to America."

" I see ! And what about Rico ? "

" He is staying on in Shropshire. Didn't you hear of his accident ? " Lou told about it briefly.

" But how awful ! " said Laura. " But there ! I knew it ! I had a premonition when I saw that horse. We had a horse that killed a man. Then my father got rid of it. But ours was a mare, that one. Yours is a boy."

" A full-grown man, I'm afraid."

" Yes, of course, I remember. But how awful ! I suppose you won't ride in the Row. The awful people that ride there nowadays, anyhow ! Oh, aren't they awful ! Aren't people monstrous, really ! My word, when I see the horses crossing Hyde Park Corner, on a wet day, and coming down smash on those slippery stones, giving their riders a fractured skull ! No joke ! "

She inquired details of Rico.

"Oh, I suppose I shall see him when he gets back," she said. "But I'm sorry you are going. I shall miss you, I'm afraid. Though you won't be staying long in America. No one stays there longer than they can help."

"I think the winter through, at least," said Lou.

"Oh, all the winter ! So long ? I'm sorry to hear *that*. You're one of the few, very few people one can talk *really* simply with. Extraordinary, isn't it, how few really simple people there are ! And they get fewer and fewer. I stayed a fortnight with my people, and a week of that I was in bed. It was really horrible. They really try to take the life out of one, *really* ! Just because one won't be as they are, and play their game. I simply refused, and came away."

"But you can't cut yourself off altogether," said Lou.

"No, I suppose not. One has to see somebody. Luckily one has a few artists for friends. They're the only real people, anyhow——" She glanced round inquisitively at Lewis, and said, with a slight, impertinent elvish smile on her virgin face :

"Are you an artist ? "

"No, Mam ! " he said. " I'm a groom."

"Oh, I see ! " She looked him up and down.

"Lewis is St. Mawr's master," said Lou.

"Oh, the horse ! The terrible horse ! " She paused a moment. Then again she turned to Lewis with that faint smile, slightly condescending, slightly impertinent, slightly flirtatious.

"Aren't you afraid of him ? " she asked.

"No, Mam."

"Aren't you *really* ! And can you always master him ? "

"Mostly. He knows me."

"Yes ! I suppose that's it." She looked him up and down again, then turned away to Lou.

"What have you been painting lately ? " said Lou. Laura was not a bad painter.

"Oh, hardly anything. I haven't been able to get on at all. This is one of my bad intervals."

Here Lewis rose, and looked at Lou.

"All right," she said. " Come in after lunch, and we'll finish those arrangements."

Laura gazed after the man, as he dived out of the room, as if her eyes were gimlets that could bore into his secret.

In the course of the conversation she said :

"What a curious little man that was ! "

" Which ? "

" The groom who was here just now. *Very* curious ! Such peculiar eyes. I shouldn't wonder if he had psychic powers."

" What sort of psychic powers ? " said Lou.

" Could *see* things. And hypnotic too. He might have hypnotic powers."

" What makes you think so ? "

" He gives me that sort of feeling. Very curious ! Probably he hypnotizes the horse. Are you leaving the horse here, by the way, in stable ? "

" No, taking him to America."

" Taking him to America ! How extraordinary ! "

" It's mother's idea. She thinks he might be valuable as a stock horse on a ranch. You know we still have interest in a ranch in Texas."

" Oh, I see ! Yes, probably he'd be very valuable, to improve the breed of the horses over there. My father has some very lovely hunters. Isn't it disgraceful, he would never let me ride ! "

" Why ? "

" Because we girls weren't important, in his opinion. So you're taking the horse to America ! With the little man ? "

" Yes, St. Mawr will hardly behave without him."

" I see !—I see—ee—ee ! Just you and Mrs. Witt and the little man. I'm sure you'll find he has psychic powers."

" I'm afraid I'm not so good at finding things out," said Lou.

" Aren't you ? No, I suppose not. I am. I have a flair. I sort of *smell* things. Then the horse is already here, is he ? When do you think you'll sail ? "

" Mother is finding a merchant boat that will go to Galveston, Texas, and take us along with the horse. She knows people who will find the right thing. But it takes time."

" What a much nicer way to travel, than on one of those great liners ! Oh, how awful they are ! So vulgar ! Floating palaces they call them ! My word, the people inside the palaces ! Yes, I should say that would be a much pleasanter way of travelling : on a cargo boat."

Laura wanted to go down to the Mews to see St. Mawr. The two women went together.

St. Mawr stood in his box, bright and tense as usual.

" Yes ! " said Laura Ridley, with a slight hiss. " Yes ! Isn't he beautiful. Such very perfect legs ! " She eyed him round with those gimlet, sharp eyes of hers. " Almost a pity to let him go out of

England. We need some of his perfect *bone*, I feel. But his eye ! Hasn't he got a look in it, my word ! "

" I can never see that he looks wicked," said Lou.

" Can't you ! " Laura had a slight hiss in her speech, a sort of aristocratic decision in her enunciation, that got on Lou's nerves. " He looks wicked to me ! "

" He's not *mean*," said Lou. " He'd never do anything mean to you."

" Oh, mean ! I daresay not. No ! I'll grant him that, he gives fair warning. His eye says *Beware* ! But isn't he a beauty, *isn't* he ! " Lou could feel the peculiar reverence for St. Mawr's breeding, his show qualities. Herself, all she cared about was the horse himself, his real nature. " Isn't it extraordinary," Laura continued, " that you never get a *really* perfectly satisfactory animal ! There's always something wrong. And in men too. Isn't it curious ? There's always something—something wrong—or something missing. Why is it ? "

" I don't know," said Lou. She felt unable to cope with any more. And she was glad when Laura left her.

The days passed slowly, quietly, London almost empty of Lou's acquaintances. Mrs. Witt was busy getting all sorts of papers and permits : such a fuss ! The battle light was still in her eye. But about her nose was a dusky, pinched look that made Lou wonder.

Both women wanted to be gone : they felt they had already flown in spirit, and it was weary, having the body left behind.

At last all was ready : they only awaited the telegram to say when their cargo-boat would sail. Trunks stood there packed, like great stones locked for ever. The Westminster house seemed already a shell. Rico wrote and telegraphed, tenderly, but there was a sense of relentless effort in it all, rather than of any real tenderness. He had taken his position.

Then the telegram came, the boat was ready to sail.

" There now ! " said Mrs. Witt, as if it had been a sentence of death.

" Why do you look like that, mother ? "

" I feel I haven't an ounce of energy left in my body."

" But how queer, for you, mother. Do you think you are ill ? "

" No, Louise. I just feel that way : as if I hadn't an ounce of energy left in my body."

" You'll feel yourself again, once you are away."

" Maybe I shall."

After all, it was only a matter of telephoning. The hotel and the railway porters and taxi-men would do the rest.

It was a grey, cloudy day, cold even. Mother and daughter sat in a cold first-class carriage and watched the little Hampshire countryside go past : little, old, unreal it seemed to them both, and passing away like a dream whose edges only are in consciousness. Autumn ! Was this autumn ? Were these trees, fields, villages ? It seemed but the dim, dissolving edges of a dream, without inward substance.

At Southampton it was raining : and just a chaos, till they stepped on to a clean boat, and were received by a clean young captain, quite sympathetic, and quite a gentleman. Mrs. Witt, however, hardly looked at him, but went down to her cabin and lay down in her bunk.

There, lying concealed, she felt the engines start, she knew the voyage had begun. But she lay still. She saw the clouds and the rain, and refused to be disturbed.

Lou had lunch with the young captain, and she felt she ought to be flirty. The young man was so polite and attentive ! And she wished so much she were alone.

Afterwards, she sat on deck and saw the Isle of Wight pass shadowy, in a misty rain. She didn't know it was the Isle of Wight. To her, it was just the lowest bit of the British Isles. She saw it fading away : and with it, her life, going like a clot of shadow in a mist of nothingness. She had no feelings about it, none : neither about Rico, nor her London house, nor anything. All passing in a grey curtain of rainy drizzle, like a death, and she, with not a feeling left.

They entered the Channel, and felt the slow heave of the sea. And soon, the clouds broke in a little wind. The sky began to clear. By mid-afternoon it was blue summer, on the blue, running waters of the Channel. And soon, the ship steering for Santander, there was the coast of France, the rocks twinkling like some magic world.

The magic world ! And back of it, that post-war Paris, which Lou knew only too well, and which depressed her so thoroughly. Or that post-war Monte Carlo, the Riviera still more depressing even than Paris. No, no one must land, even on magic coasts. Else you found yourself in a railway station and a " centre of civilization " in five minutes.

Mrs. Witt hated the sea, and stayed, as a rule, practically the whole time of the crossing, in her bunk. There she was now, silent, shut up like a steel trap, as in her tomb. She did not even read. Just lay and stared at the passing sky. And the only thing to do was to leave her alone.

Lewis and Phœnix hung on the rail, and watched everything. Or they went down to see St. Mawr. Or they stood talking in the doorway of the wireless operator's cabin. Lou begged the Captain to give them jobs to do.

The queer, transitory, unreal feeling, as the ship crossed the great heavy Atlantic. It was rather bad weather. And Lou felt, as she had felt before, that this grey, wolf-like, cold-blooded Ocean hated men and their ships and their smoky passage. Heavy grey waves, a low-sagging sky : rain : yellow, weird evenings with snatches of sun : so it went on. Till they got way South, into the westward-running stream. Then they began to get blue weather and blue water.

To go South ! Always to go South, away from the arctic horror as far as possible ! This was Lou's instinct. To go out of the clutch of greyness and low skies, of sweeping rain, and of slow, blanketting snow. Never again to see the mud and rain and snow of a northern winter, nor to feel the idealistic, Christianized tension of the now irreligious North.

As they neared Havana, and the water sparkled at night with phosphorus, and the flying-fishes came like drops of bright water, sailing out of the massive-slippery waves, Mrs. Witt emerged once more. She still had that shut-up, deathly look on her face. But she prowled round the deck, and manifested at least a little interest in affairs not her own. Here at sea, she hardly remembered the existence of St. Mawr or Lewis or Phœnix. She was not very deeply aware even of Lou's existence—but, of course, it would all come back, once they were on land.

They sailed in hot sunshine out of a blue, blue sea, past the castle into the harbour at Havana. There was a lot of shipping : and this was already America. Mrs. Witt had herself and Lou put ashore immediately. They took a motor-car and drove at once to the great boulevard that is the centre of Havana. Here they saw a long rank of motor-cars, all drawn up ready to take a couple of hundred American tourists for one more tour. There were the tourists, all with badges in their coats, lest they should get lost.

" They get so drunk by night," said the driver in Spanish, " that the policemen find them lying in the road—turn them over, see the badge—and, hup !—carry them to their hotel." He grinned sardonically.

Lou and her mother lunched at the Hôtel d'Angleterre, and Mrs. Witt watched transfixed while a couple of her countrymen, a stout successful man and his wife, lunched abroad. They had cocktails-

then lobster—and a bottle of hock—then a bottle of champagne—
then a half-bottle of port.   And Mrs. Witt rose in haste as the liqueurs
came.   For that successful man and his wife had gone on imbibing
with a sort of fixed and deliberate will, apparently tasting nothing,
but saying to themselves : " Now we're drinking Rhine wine ! Now
we're drinking 1912 champagne. Yah, Prohibition ! Thou canst
not put it over me."   Their complexions became more and more
lurid. Mrs. Witt fled, fearing a Havana débâcle. But she said
nothing.

In the afternoon, they motored into the country, to see the great
brewery gardens, the new villa suburb, and through the lanes past
the old, decaying plantations with palm-trees. In one lane they met
the fifty motor-cars with the two hundred tourists all with badges
on their chests and self-satisfaction on their faces. Mrs. Witt watched
in grim silence.

" Plus ça change, plus c'est la même chose," said Lou, with a
wicked little smile.   " On n'est pas mieux ici, mother."

" I know it," said Mrs. Witt.

The hotels by the sea were all shut up : it was not yet the " season."
Not till November. And then ! Why, then Havana would be an
American city, in full leaf of green dollar bills. The green leaf of
American prosperity shedding itself recklessly, from every roaming
sprig of a tourist, over this city of sunshine and alcohol. Green leaves
unfolded in Pittsburg and Chicago, showering in winter downfall
in Havana.

Mother and daughter drank tea in a corner of the Hôtel d'Angleterre once more, and returned to the ferry.

The Gulf of Mexico was blue and rippling, with the phantom of
islands on the south. Great porpoises rolled and leaped, running in
front of the ship in the clear water, diving, travelling in perfect
motion, straight, with the tip of the ship touching the tip of their
tails, then rolling over, cork-screwing, and showing their bellies as
they went. Marvellous ! The marvellous beauty and fascination
of natural wild things ! The horror of man's unnatural life, his
heaped-up civilization !

The flying fishes burst out of the sea in clouds of silvery, transparent motion. Blue above and below, the Gulf seemed a silent,
empty, timeless place where man did not really reach. And Lou
was again fascinated by the glamour of the universe.

But bump ! She and her mother were in a first-class hotel again,
calling down the telephone for the bell-boy and ice-water. And soon
they were in a Pullman, off towards San Antonio.

It was America, it was Texas. They were at their ranch, on the great level of yellow autumn, with the vast sky above. And after all, from the hot wide sky, and the hot, wide, red earth, there *did* come something new, something not used-up. Lou *did* feel exhilarated.

The Texans were there, tall blond people, ingenuously cheerful, ingenuously, childishly intimate, as if the fact that you had never seen them before was as nothing compared to the fact that you'd all been living in one room together all your lives, so that nothing was hidden from either of you. The one room being the mere shanty of the world in which we all live. Strange, uninspired cheerfulness, filling, as it were, the blank of complete incomprehension.

And off they set in their motor-cars, chiefly high-legged Fords, rattling away down the red trails between yellow sunflowers or sere grass or dry cotton, away, away into great distances, cheerfully raising the dust of haste. It left Lou in a sort of blank amazement. But it left her amused, not depressed. The old screws of emotion and intimacy that had been screwed down so tightly upon her fell out of their holes, here. The Texan intimacy weighed no more on her than a postage stamp, even if, for the moment, it stuck as close. And there was a certain underneath recklessness, even a stoicism in all the apparently childish people, which left one free. They might appear childish : but they stoically depended on themselves alone, in reality. Not as in England, where every man waited to pour the burden of himself upon you.

St. Mawr arrived safely, a bit bewildered. The Texans eyed him closely, struck silent, as ever, by anything pure-bred and beautiful. He was somehow too beautiful, too perfected, in this great open country. The long-legged Texan horses, with their elaborate saddles, seemed somehow more natural.

Even St. Mawr felt himself strange, as it were naked and singled out, in this rough place. Like a jewel among stones, a pearl before swine, maybe. But the swine were no fools. They knew a pearl from a grain of maize, and a grain of maize from a pearl. And they knew what they wanted. When it was pearls, it was pearls ; though chiefly, it was maize. Which shows good sense. They could see St. Mawr's points. Only he needn't draw the point too fine, or it would just not pierce the tough skin of this country.

The ranch-man mounted him—just threw a soft skin over his back, jumped on, and away down the red trail, raising the dust among the tall wild yellow of sunflowers, in the hot wild sun. Then back again in a fume, and the man slipped off.

" He's got the stuff in him, he sure has," said the man.

And the horse seemed pleased with this rough handling. Lewis looked on in wonder, and a little envy.

Lou and her mother stayed a fortnight on the ranch. It was all so queer : so crude, so rough, so easy, so artificially civilized, and so meaningless. Lou could not get over the feeling that it all meant nothing. There were no roots of reality at all. No consciousness below the surface, no meaning in anything save the obvious, the blatantly obvious. It was like life enacted in a mirror. Visually, it was wildly vital. But there was nothing behind it. Or like a cinematograph : flat shapes, exactly like men, but without any substance of reality, rapidly rattling away with talk, emotions, activity, all in the flat, nothing behind it. No deeper consciousness at all. So it seemed to her.

One moved from dream to dream, from phantasm to phantasm.

But at least, this Texan life, if it had no bowels, no vitals, at least it could not prey on one's own vitals. It was this much better than Europe.

Lewis was silent, and rather piqued. St. Mawr had already made advances to the boss' long-legged, arched-necked, glossy-maned Texan mare. And the boss was pleased.

What a world !

Mrs. Witt eyed it all shrewdly. But she failed to participate. Lou was a bit scared at the emptiness of it all, and the queer phantasmal self-consciousness. Cowboys just as self-conscious as Rico, far more sentimental, inwardly vague and unreal. Cowboys that went after their cows in black Ford motor-cars : and who self-consciously saw Lady Carrington falling to them, as elegant young ladies from the East fall to the noble cowboy of the films, or in Zane Grey. It was all film-psychology.

And at the same time, these boys led a hard, hard life, often dangerous and gruesome. Nevertheless, inwardly they were self-conscious film-heroes. The boss himself, a man over forty, long and lean and with a great deal of stringy energy, showed off before her in a strong silent manner, existing for the time being purely in his imagination of the sort of picture he made of her, the sort of impression he made on her.

So they all were, coloured up like a Zane Grey book-jacket, all of them living in the mirror. The kind of picture they made to somebody else.

And at the same time, with energy, courage, and a stoical grit getting their work done, and putting through what they had to put through.

It left Lou blank with wonder. And in the face of this strange, cheerful living in the mirror—a rather cheap mirror at that—England began to seem real to her again.

Then she had to remember herself back in England. And no, oh God, England was not real either, except poisonously.

What was real? What under heaven was real?

Her mother had gone dumb and, as it were, out of range. Phœnix was a bit assured and bouncy, back more or less in his own conditions. Lewis was a bit impressed by the emptiness of everything, the *lack* of concentration. And St. Mawr followed at the heels of the boss' long-legged Texan mare, almost slavishly.

What, in heaven's name, was one to make of it all?

Soon, she could not stand this sort of living in a film-setting, with the mechanical energy of " making good," that is, making money, to keep the show going. The mystic duty to " make good," meaning to make the ranch pay a laudable interest on the " owners'" investment. Lou herself being one of the owners. And the interest that came to her, from her father's will, being the money she spent to buy St. Mawr and to fit up that house in Westminster. Then also the mystic duty to " feel good." Everybody had to *feel good, fine !* " How are you this morning, Mr. Latham ? "—" *Fine !* Eh ! don't you feel good out here, eh ? Lady Carrington ? "—" *Fine !* "—Lou pronounced it with the same ringing conviction. It was Coué all the time !

" Shall we stay here long, mother ? " she asked.

" Not a day longer than you want to, Louise. I stay entirely for your sake."

" Then let us go, mother."

They left St. Mawr and Lewis. But Phœnix wanted to come along. So they motored to San Antonio, got into the Pullman, and travelled as far as El Paso. Then they changed to go north. Santa Fé would be at least " easy." And Mrs. Witt had acquaintances there.

They found the fiesta over in Santa Fé : Indians, Mexicans, artists had finished their great effort to amuse and attract the tourists. *Welcome, Mr. Tourist,* said a great board on one side of the high-road. And on the other side, a little nearer to town : *Thank You, Mr. Tourist.*

" Plus ça change——" Lou began.

" Ça ne change jamais—except for the worse ! " said Mrs. Witt,

like a pistol going off.   And Lou held her peace, after she had sighed
to herself, and said in her own mind : " *Welcome also Mrs. and Miss
Tourist !* "

There was no getting a word out of Mrs. Witt, these days.   Whereas
Phœnix was becoming almost loquacious.

They stayed a while in Santa Fé, in the clean, comfortable,
" homely " hotel, where " every room had its bath " : a spotless
white bath, with very hot water night and day.   The tourists and
commercial travellers sat in the big hall down below, everybody
living in the mirror !   And of course, they knew Lady Carrington
down to her shoe-soles.   And they all expected her to know them
down to their shoe-soles.   For the only object of the mirror is to
reflect images.

For two days mother and daughter ate in the mayonnaise intimacy
of the dining-room.   Then Mrs. Witt struck, and telephoned down
every meal-time, for her meal in her room.   She got to staying in bed
later and later, as on the ship.   Lou became uneasy.   This was worse
than Europe.

Phœnix was still there, as a sort of half-friend, half-servant
retainer.   He was perfectly happy, roving round among the Mexicans
and Indians, talking Spanish all day, and telling about England and
his two mistresses, rolling the ball of his own importance.

" I'm afraid we've got Phœnix for life," said Lou.

" Not unless we wish," said Mrs. Witt indifferently.   And she
picked up a novel which she didn't want to read, but which she was
going to read.

" What shall we do next, mother ? " Lou asked.

" As far as I am concerned, there is no next," said Mrs. Witt.

" Come, mother !   Let's go back to Italy or somewhere, if it's as
bad as that."

" Never again, Louise, shall I cross that water.   I have come home
to die."

" I don't see much home about it—the Gonsalez Hotel in Santa Fé."

" Indeed not !   But as good as anywhere else, to die in."

" Oh, mother, don't be silly !   Shall we look for somewhere where
we can be by ourselves ? "

" I leave it to you, Louise.   I have made my last decision."

" What is that, mother."

" Never, never to make another decision."

" Not even to decide to die ? "

" No, not even that."

" Or *not* to die ? "

" Not that either."

Mrs. Witt shut up like a trap. She refused to rise from her bed that day.

Lou went to consult Phœnix. The result was, the two set out to look at a little ranch that was for sale.

It was autumn, and the loveliest time in the south-west, where there is no spring, snow blowing into the hot lap of summer ; and no real summer, hail falling in thick ice, from the thunderstorms : and even no very definite winter, hot sun melting the snow and giving an impression of spring at any time. But autumn there is, when the winds of the desert are almost still, and the mountains fume no clouds. But morning comes cold and delicate, upon the wild sun-flowers and the puffing, yellow-flowered greasewood. For the desert blooms in autumn. In spring it is grey ash all the time, and only the strong breath of the summer sun, and the heavy splashing of thunder rain succeeds at last, by September, in blowing it into soft, puffy yellow fire.

It was such a delicate morning when Lou drove out with Phœnix towards the mountains, to look at this ranch that a Mexican wanted to sell. For the brief moment the high mountains had lost their snow : it would be back again in a fortnight : and stood dim and delicate with autumn haze. The desert stretched away pale, as pale as the sky, but silvery and sere, with hummock-mounds of shadow, and long wings of shadow, like the reflection of some great bird. The same eagle-shadows came like rude paintings of the out-stretched bird, upon the mountains, where the aspens were turning yellow. For the moment, the brief moment, the great desert-and-mountain landscape had lost its certain cruelty, and looked tender, dreamy. And many, many birds were flickering around.

Lou and Phœnix bumped and hesitated over a long trail : then wound down into a deep canyon : and then the car began to climb, climb, climb, in steep rushes, and in long, heart-breaking, uneven pulls. The road was bad, and driving was no joke. But it was the sort of road Phœnix was used to. He sat impassive and watchful, and kept on, till his engine boiled. He was *himself* in this country : impassive, detached, self-satisfied, and silently assertive. Guarding himself at every moment, but, on his guard, sure of himself. Seeing no difference at all between Lou or Mrs. Witt and himself, except that they had money and he had none, while he had a native import-ance which they lacked. He depended on them for money, they on him for the power to live out here in the West. Intimately, he was as good as they. Money was their only advantage.

As Lou sat beside him in the front seat of the car, where it bumped less than behind, she felt this. She felt a peculiar tough-necked arrogance in him, as if he were asserting himself to put something over her. He wanted her to allow him to make advances to her, to allow him to suggest that he should be her lover. And then, finally, she would marry him, and he would be on the same footing as she and her mother.

In return, he would look after her, and give her his support and countenance, as a man, and stand between her and the world. In this sense, he would be faithful to her, and loyal. But as far as other women went, Mexican women or Indian women : why, that was none of her business. His marrying her would be a pact between two aliens, on behalf of one another, and he would keep his part of it all right. But himself, as a private man and a predative alien-blooded male, this had nothing to do with her. It didn't enter her scope and count. She was one of these nervous white women with lots of money. She was very nice too. But as a *squaw*—as a real woman in a shawl whom a man went after for the pleasure of the night—why, she hardly counted. One of these white women who talk clever and know things like a man. She could hardly expect a half-savage male to acknowledge her as his female counterpart.—No ! She had the bucks ! And she had all the paraphernalia of the white man's civilization, which a savage can play with and so escape his own hollow boredom. But his own real female counterpart ? Phœnix would just have shrugged his shoulders, and thought the question not worth answering. How could there be any answer in *her*, to the phallic male in him ? Couldn't ! Yet it would flatter his vanity and his self-esteem immensely, to possess her. That would be possessing the very clue to the white man's overwhelming world. And if she would let him possess her, he would be absolutely loyal to her, as far as affairs and appearances went. Only, the aboriginal phallic male in him simply couldn't recognize her as a woman at all. In this respect, she didn't exist. It needed the shawled Indian or Mexican woman, with their squeaky, plaintive voices, their shuffling, watery humility, and the dark glances of their big, knowing eyes. When an Indian woman looked at him from under her black fringe, with dark, half-secretive suggestion in her big eyes : and when she stood before him hugged in her shawl, in such apparently complete quiescent humility : and when she spoke to him in her mousey squeak of a high, plaintive voice, as if it were difficult for her female bashfulness even to emit so much sound : and when she shuffled away with her legs wide apart, because of her wide-topped, white, high buckskin boots with tiny white feet, and her dark-knotted hair so full of hard, yet subtle lure : and when he remembered the almost watery softness of the Indian woman's dark, warm flesh : then he was a male, an old, secretive, rat-like male. But before Lou's straightforwardness and utter sexual incompetence, he just stood in contempt. And to him, even a French cocotte was utterly devoid of the right sort of sex. She couldn't really move him. She couldn't satisfy the furtiveness in him. He needed this plaintive, squeaky, dark-fringed Indian quality. Something furtive and soft and rat-like, really to rouse him.

Nevertheless he was ready to trade his sex, which, in his opinion, every white woman was secretly pining for, for the white woman's money and social privileges. In the daytime, all the thrill and excitement of the white man's motor-cars and moving pictures and ice-cream sodas and so forth. In the night, the soft, watery-soft warmth of an Indian or half-Indian woman. This was Phœnix's idea of life for himself.

Meanwhile, if a white woman gave him the privileges of the white man's world, he would do his duty by her as far as all that went.

Lou, sitting very, very still beside him as he drove the car—he was not a very good driver, not quick and marvellous as some white men are, particularly some French chauffeurs she had known, but usually a little behindhand in his movements—she knew more or less all that he felt. More or less she divined as a woman does. Even from a certain rather assured stupidity of his shoulders, and a certain rather stupid assertiveness of his knees, she knew him.

But she did not judge him too harshly. Somewhere deep, deep in herself she knew she too was at fault. And this made her sometimes inclined to humble herself, as a woman, before the furtive assertiveness of this underground, " knowing " savage. He was so different from Rico.

Yet, after all, *was* he ? In his rootlessness, his drifting, his real meaninglessness, was he different from Rico ? And his childish, spellbound absorption in the motor-car, or in the moving-pictures or in an ice-cream soda—was it very different from Rico ? Anyhow, was it really any better ? Pleasanter, perhaps, to a woman, because of the childishness of it.

The same with his opinion of himself as a sexual male ! So childish, really, it was almost thrilling to a woman. But then, so stupid also, with that furtive lurking in holes and imagining it could not be detected. He imagined he kept himself dark, in his sexual rat-holes. He imagined he was not detected !

No, no, Lou was not such a fool as she looked, in his eyes anyhow.

She knew what she wanted. She wanted relief from the nervous tension and irritation of her life, she wanted to escape from the friction which is the whole stimulus in modern social life. She wanted to be still : only that, to be very, very still, and recover her own soul.

When Phœnix presumed she was looking for some secretly sexual male such as himself, he was ridiculously mistaken. Even the illusion of the beautiful St. Mawr was gone. And Phœnix, roaming round like a sexual rat in promiscuous back-yards !—*Merci, mon cher !* For that was all he was : a sexual rat in the great barn-yard of man's habitat, looking for female rats !

Merci, mon cher ! You are had.

Nevertheless, in his very mistakenness, he was a relief to her. His mistake was amusing rather than impressive. And the fact that one-half of his intelligence was a complete dark blank, that too was a relief.

Strictly, and perhaps in the best sense, he was a servant. His very unconsciousness and his very limitation served as a shelter, as one shelters within the limitations of four walls. The very decided limits to his intelligence were a shelter to her. They made her feel safe.

But that feeling of safety did not deceive her. It was the feeling one derived from having a *true* servant attached to one, a man whose psychic limitations left him incapable of anything but service, and whose strong flow of natural life, at the same time, made him need to serve.

And Lou, sitting there so very still and frail, yet self-contained, had not lived for nothing. She no longer wanted to fool herself. She had no desire at all to fool herself into thinking that a Phœnix might be a husband and a mate. No desire that way at all. His obtuseness was a servant's obtuseness. She was grateful to him for serving, and she paid him a wage. Moreover, she provided him with something to do, to occupy his life. In a sense, she gave him his life, and rescued him from his own boredom. It was a balance.

He did not know what she was thinking. There was a certain physical sympathy between them. His obtuseness made him think it was also a sexual sympathy.

" It's a nice trip, you and me," he said suddenly, turning and looking her in the eyes with an excited look, and ending on a foolish little laugh.

She realized that she should have sat in the back seat.

" But it's a bad road," she said. " Hadn't you better stop and put the sides of the hood up ? Your engine is boiling."

He looked away with a quick switch of interest to the red thermometer in front of his machine.

" She's boiling," he said, stopping, and getting out with a quick alacrity to go to look at the engine.

Lou got out also, and went to the back seat, shutting the door decisively.

" I think I'll ride at the back," she said, " it gets so frightfully hot in front, when the engine heats up. Do you think she needs some water ? Have you got some in the canteen ? "

" She's full," he said, peering into the steaming valve.

" You can run a bit out, if you think there's any need. I wonder if it's much further ! "

" *Quién sabe ?* " said he, slightly impertinent.

She relapsed into her own stillness. She realized how careful, how very careful she must be of relaxing into sympathy, and reposing, as it were, on Phœnix. He would read it as a sexual appeal. Perhaps he couldn't help it. She had only herself to blame. He was obtuse, as a man and a savage. He had only one interpretation, sex, for any woman's approach to him.

And she knew, with the last clear knowledge of weary disillusion, that she did not want to be mixed up in Phœnix's sexual promiscuities. The very thought was an insult to her. The crude, clumsy servant-male : no, no, not that. He was a good fellow, a very good fellow, as far as he went. But he fell far short of physical intimacy.

" No, no," she said to herself, " I was wrong to ride in the front seat with him. I must sit alone, just alone. Because sex, mere sex, is repellent to me. I will never prostitute myself again. Unless something touches my very spirit, the very quick of me, I will stay alone, just alone. Alone, and give myself only to the unseen presences, serve only the other, unseen presences."

She understood now the meaning of the Vestal Virgins, the Virgins of the holy fire in the old temples. They were symbolic of herself, of woman weary of the embrace of incompetent men, weary, weary, weary of all that, turning to unseen gods, the unseen spirits, the hidden fire, and devoting herself to that, and that alone. Receiving thence her pacification and her fulfilment.

Not these little, incompetent, childish self-opinionated men ! Not these to touch her. She watched Phœnix's rather stupid shoulders, as he drove the car on between the piñon trees and the cedars of the narrow mesa ridge, to the mountain foot. He was a good fellow. But let him run among women of his own sort. Something was beyond him. And this something must remain beyond him, never allow itself to come within his reach. Otherwise he would paw it and mess it up, and be as miserable as a child that has broken its father's watch.

No, no ! She had loved an American, and lived with him for a fortnight. She had had a long, intimate friendship with an Italian. Perhaps it was love on his part. And she had yielded to him. Then her love and marriage to Rico.

And what of it all ? Nothing. It was almost nothing. It was as if only the outside of herself, her top layers, were human. This inveigled her into intimacies. As soon as the intimacy penetrated, or attempted to penetrate inside her, it was a disaster. Just a humiliation and a breaking-down.

Within these outer layers of herself lay the successive inner sanctuaries of herself. And these were inviolable. She accepted it.

" I am not a marrying woman," she said to herself. " I am not a lover nor a mistress nor a wife. It is no good. Love can't really come into me from the outside, and I can never, never mate with any man, since the mystic new man will never come to me. No, no, let me know myself and my rôle. I am one of the eternal Virgins, serving the eternal fire. My dealings with men have only broken my stillness and messed up my doorways. It has been my own fault. I ought to stay virgin, and still, very, very still, and serve the most perfect service. I want my temple and my loneliness and my Apollo mystery of the inner fire. And with men, only the delicate, subtler, more remote relations. No coming near. A coming near only breaks the delicate veils, and broken veils, like broken flowers, only lead to rottenness."

She felt a great peace inside herself as she made this realization. And a thankfulness. Because, after all, it seemed to her that the hidden fire was alive and burning in this sky, over the desert, in the mountains. She felt a certain latent holiness in the very atmosphere, a young, spring-fire of latent holiness, such as she had never felt in Europe, or in the East. " For me," she said, as she looked away at the mountains in shadow and the pale-warm desert beneath, with wings of shadow upon it : " For me, this place is sacred. It is blessed."

But as she watched Phœnix : as she remembered the motor-cars and tourists, and the rather dreary Mexicans of Santa Fé, and the lurking, invidious Indians, with something of a rat-like secretiveness and defeatedness in their bearing, she realized that the latent fire of the vast landscape struggled under a great weight of dirt-like inertia. She had to mind the dirt, most carefully and vividly avoid

it and keep it away from her, here in this place that at last seemed
sacred to her.

The motor-car climbed up, past the tall pine-trees, to the foot of
the mountains, and came at last to a wire gate, where nothing was to
be expected. Phœnix opened the gate, and they drove on, through
more trees, into a clearing where dried up bean-plants were yellow.

" This man got no water for his beans," said Phœnix. " Not got
much beans this year."

They climbed slowly up the incline, through more pine trees, and
out into another clearing, where a couple of horses were grazing.
And there they saw the ranch itself, little low cabins with patched
roofs, under a few pine-trees, and facing the long twelve-acre
clearing, or field, where the Michaelmas daisies were purple mist,
and spangled with clumps of yellow flowers.

" Not got no alfalfa here neither ! " said Phœnix, as the car waded
past the flowers. " Must be a dry place up here. Got no water,
sure they haven't."

Yet it was the place Lou wanted. In an instant, her heart sprang
to it. The instant the car stopped, and she saw the two cabins
inside the rickety fence, the rather broken corral beyond, and behind
all, tall, blue balsam pines, the round hills, the solid uprise of the
mountain flank : and getting down, she looked across the purple
and gold of the clearing, downwards at the ring of pine-trees standing
so still, so crude and untameable, the motionless desert beyond the
bristles of the pine crests, a thousand feet below : and beyond the
desert, blue mountains, and far, far-off blue mountains in Arizona :
" *This is the place*," she said to herself.

This little tumble-down ranch, only a homestead of a hundred-
and-sixty acres, was, as it were, man's last effort towards the wild
heart of the Rockies, at this point. Sixty years before, a restless
schoolmaster had wandered out from the East, looking for gold
among the mountains. He found a very little, then no more. But
the mountains had got hold of him, he could not go back.

There was a little trickling spring of pure water, a thread of treasure perhaps better than gold. So the schoolmaster took up a homestead on the lot where this little spring arose. He struggled, and got
himself his log cabin erected, his fence put up, sloping at the
mountain-side through the pine-trees and dropping into the hollows
where the ghost-white mariposa lilies stood leafless and naked in
flower, in spring, on tall invisible stems. He made the long clearing
for alfalfa.

And fell so into debt, that he had to trade his homestead away, to

clear his debt.　Then he made a tiny living teaching the children of
the few American prospectors who had squatted in the valleys,
beside the Mexicans.

The trader who got the ranch tackled it with a will.　He built
another log cabin, and a big corral, and brought water from the
canyon two miles and more across the mountain slope, in a little
runnel ditch, and more water, piped a mile or more down the little
canyon immediately above the cabins.　He got a flow of water for
his houses : for being a true American, he felt he could not *really* say
he had conquered his environment till he had got running water,
taps, and wash-hand basins inside his house.

Taps, running water and wash-hand basins he accomplished.
And, undaunted through the years, he prepared the basin for a
fountain in the little fenced-in enclosure, and he built a little bath-
house.　After a number of years, he sent up the enamelled bath-tub
to be put in the little log bath-house on the little wild ranch hung
right against the savage Rockies, above the desert.

But here the mountains finished him.　He was a trader down
below, in the Mexican village.　This little ranch was, as it were, his
hobby, his ideal.　He and his New England wife spent their summers
there : and turned on the taps in the cabins and turned them off
again, and felt really that civilization had conquered.

All this plumbing from the savage ravines of the canyons—one of
them nameless to this day—cost, however, money.　In fact, the
ranch cost a great deal of money.　But it was all to be got back.
The big clearing was to be irrigated for alfalfa, the little clearing for
beans, and the third clearing, under the corral, for potatoes.　All these
things the trader could trade to the Mexicans, very advantageously.

And moreover, since somebody had started a praise of the famous
goats' cheese made by Mexican peasants in New Mexico, goats
there should be.

Goats there were : five hundred of them, eventually.　And they
fed chiefly in the wild mountain hollows, the no-man's-land.　The
Mexicans call them fire-mouths, because everything they nibble
dies.　Not because of their flaming mouths, really, but because they
nibble a live plant down, down to the quick, till it can put forth
no more.

So, the energetic trader, in the course of five or six years, had got
the ranch ready.　The long three-roomed cabin was for him and his
New England wife.　In the two-roomed cabin lived the Mexican
family who really had charge of the ranch.　For the trader was mostly
fixed to his store, seventeen miles away, down in the Mexican village.

The ranch lay over eight thousand feet up, the snows of winter came deep and the white goats, looking dirty yellow, swam in snow with their poor curved horns poking out like dead sticks. But the corral had a long, cosy, shut-in goat-shed all down one side, and into this crowded the five hundred, their acrid goat-smell rising like hot acid over the snow. And the thin, pock-marked Mexican threw them alfalfa out of the log barn. Until the hot sun sank the snow again, and froze the surface, when patter-patter went the two thousand little goat-hoofs, over the silver-frozen snow, up at the mountain. Nibble, nibble, nibble, the fire-mouths, at every tender twig. And the goat-bell climbed, and the baa-ing came from among the dense and shaggy pine-trees. And sometimes, in a soft drift under the trees, a goat, or several goats, went through, into the white depths, and some were lost thus, to reappear dead and frozen at the thaw.

By evening, they were driven down again, like a dirty yellowish-white stream carrying dark sticks on its yeasty surface, tripping and bleating over the frozen snow, past the bustling dark green pine-trees, down to the trampled mess of the corral. And everywhere, everywhere over the snow, yellow stains and dark pills of goat-droppings melting into the surface crystal. On still, glittering nights, when the frost was hard, the smell of goats came up like some uncanny acid fire, and great stars sitting on the mountain's edge seemed to be watching like the eyes of a mountain lion, brought by the scent. Then the coyotes in the near canyon howled and sobbed, and ran like shadows over the snow. But the goat corral had been built tight.

In the course of years the goat-herd had grown from fifty to five hundred, and surely that was increase. The goat-milk cheeses sat drying on their little racks. In spring, there was a great flowing and skipping of kids. In summer and early autumn, there was a pest of flies, rising from all that goat-smell and that cast-out whey of goats'-milk after the cheese-making. The rats came, and the pack-rats, swarming.

And after all, it was difficult to sell or trade the cheeses, and little profit to be made. And in dry summers, no water came down in the narrow ditch-channel, that straddled in wooden runnels over the deep clefts in the mountain-side. No water meant no alfalfa. In winter the goats scarcely drank at all. In summer they could be watered at the little spring. But the thirsty land was not so easy to accommodate.

Five hundred fine white Angora goats, with their massive hand-

some padres ! They were beautiful enough. And the trader made
all he could of them. Come summer, they were run down into the
narrow tank filled with the fiery dipping fluid. Then their lovely
white wool was clipped. It was beautiful, and valuable, but
comparatively little of it.

And it all cost, cost, cost. And a man was always let down. At
one time no water. At another a poison-weed. Then a sickness.
Always some mysterious malevolence fighting, fighting against the
will of man. A strange invisible influence coming out of the livid
rock-fastnesses in the bowels of those uncreated Rocky Mountains,
preying upon the will of man, and slowly wearing down his resistance, his onward-pushing spirit. The curious, subtle thing, like a
mountain fever, got into the blood, so that the men at the ranch, and
the animals with them, had bursts of queer, violent, half-frenzied
energy, in which, however, they were wont to lose their wariness.
And then, damage of some sort. The horses ripped and cut themselves, or they were struck by lightning, the men had great hurts,
or sickness. A curious disintegration working all the time, a sort of
malevolent breath, like a stupefying, irritant gas, coming out of the
unfathomed mountains.

The pack-rats with their bushy tails and big ears came down out
of the hills, and were jumping and bouncing about : symbols of
the curious debasing malevolence that was in the spirit of the place.
The Mexicans in charge, good honest men, worked all they could.
But they were like most of the Mexicans in the south-west, as if they
had been pithed, to use one of Kipling's words. As if the invidious
malevolence of the country itself had slowly taken all the pith of
manhood from them, leaving a hopeless sort of corpus of a man.

And the same happened to the white men, exposed to the open
country. Slowly, they were pithed. The energy went out of them.
And more than that, the interest. An inertia of indifference invading
the soul, leaving the body healthy and active, but wasting the soul,
the living interest, quite away.

It was the New England wife of the trader who put most energy
into the ranch. She looked on it as her home. She had a little white
fence put all round the two cabins : the bright brass water-taps she
kept shining in the two kitchens : outside the kitchen door she had
a little kitchen garden and nasturtiums, after a great fight with
invading animals, that nibbled everything away. And she got so
far as the preparation of the round concrete basin which was to be
a little pool, under the few enclosed pine-trees between the two
cabins, a pool with a tiny fountain jet.

But this, with the bath-tub, was her limit, as the five hundred goats were her man's limit. Out of the mountains came two breaths of influence : the breath of the curious, frenzied energy, that took away one's intelligence as alcohol or any other stimulus does : and then the most strange invidiousness that ate away the soul. The woman loved her ranch, almost with passion. It was she who felt the stimulus, more than the men. It seemed to enter her like a sort of sex passion, intensifying her ego, making her full of violence and of blind female energy. The energy, and the blindness of it ! A strange blind frenzy, like an intoxication while it lasted. And the sense of beauty that thrilled her New England woman's soul.

Her cabin faced the slow downslope of the clearing, the alfalfa field : her long, low cabin, crouching under the great pine-tree that threw up its trunk sheer in front of the house, in the yard. That pine-tree was the guardian of the place. But a bristling, almost demonish guardian, from the far-off crude ages of the world. Its great pillar of pale, flakey-ribbed copper rose there in strange callous indifference, and the grim permanence, which is in pine-trees. A passionless, non-phallic column, rising in the shadows of the pre-sexual world, before the hot-blooded ithyphallic column ever erected itself. A cold, blossomless, resinous sap surging and oozing gum, from that pallid brownish bark. And the wind hissing in the needles, like a vast nest of serpents. And the pine cones falling plumb as the hail hit them. Then lying all over the yard, open in the sun like wooden roses, but hard, sexless, rigid with a blind will.

Past the column of that pine-tree, the alfalfa field sloped gently down, to the circling guard of pine-trees, from which silent, living barrier isolated pines rose to ragged heights at intervals, in blind assertiveness. Strange, those pine-trees ! In some lights all their needles glistened like polished steel, all subtly glittering with a whitish glitter among darkness, like real needles. Then again, at evening, the trunks would flare up orange-red, and the tufts would be dark, alert tufts like a wolf's tail touching the air. Again, in the morning sunlight they would be soft and still, hardly noticeable. But all the same, present, and watchful. Never sympathetic, always watchfully on their guard, and resistant, they hedged one in with the aroma and the power and the slight horror of the pre-sexual primeval world. The world where each creature was crudely limited to its own ego, crude and bristling and cold, and then crowding in packs like pine-trees and wolves.

But beyond the pine-trees, ah, there beyond, there was beauty for the spirit to soar in. The circle of pines, with the loose trees rising high and ragged at intervals, this was the barrier, the fence to the foreground. Beyond was only distance, the desert a thousand feet below, and beyond.

The desert swept its great fawn-coloured circle around, away beyond and below like a beach, with a long mountain-side of pure blue shadow closing in the near corner, and strange bluish hummocks of mountains rising like wet rock from a vast strand, away in the middle distance, and beyond, in the farthest distance, pale blue crests of mountains looking over the horizon, from the west, as if peering in from another world altogether.

Ah, that was beauty !—perhaps the most beautiful thing in the world. It was pure beauty, *absolute* beauty ! There ! That was it. To the little woman from New England, with her tense, fierce soul and her egoistic passion of service, this beauty was absolute, a *ne plus ultra*. From her doorway, from her porch, she could watch the vast, eagle-like wheeling of the daylight, that turned as the eagles which lived in the near rocks turned overhead in the blue, turning their luminous, dark-edged-patterned bellies and underwings upon the pure air, like winged orbs. So the daylight made the vast turn upon the desert, brushing the farthest outwatching mountains. And sometimes, the vast strand of the desert would float with curious undulations and exhalations amid the blue fragility of mountains, whose upper edges were harder than the floating bases. And sometimes she would see the little brown adobe houses of the village Mexicans, twenty miles away, like little cube crystals of insect-houses dotting upon the desert, very distinct, with a cotton-wood tree or two rising near. And sometimes she would see the far-off rocks, thirty miles away, where the canyon made a gateway between the mountains. Quite clear, like an open gateway out of a vast yard, she would see the cut-out bit of the canyon-passage. And on the desert itself, curious puckered folds of mesa-sides. And a blackish crack which in places revealed the otherwise invisible canyon of the Rio Grande. And beyond everything, the mountains like icebergs showing up from an outer sea. Then later, the sun would go down blazing above the shallow cauldron of simmering darkness, and the round mountain of Colorado would lump up into uncanny significance, northwards. That was always rather frightening. But morning came again, with the sun peeping over the mountain slopes and lighting the desert away in the distance long, long before it lighted on her yard. And then she would see another valley, like magic and very lovely, with green fields and long tufts of cotton-wood trees, and a few long-cubical adobe houses, lying floating in shallow light below, like a vision.

Ah ! It was beauty, beauty absolute, at any hour of the day : whether the perfect clarity of morning, or the mountains beyond the simmering desert at noon, or the purple lumping of northern mounds under a red sun at night. Or whether the dust whirled in tall columns, travelling across the desert far away, like pillars of cloud by day, tall, leaning pillars of dust hastening with ghostly haste : or whether, in the early part of the year, suddenly in the morning a whole sea of solid white would rise rolling below, a solid mist from melted snow, ghost-white under the mountain sun, the world below blotted out : or whether the black rain and cloud streaked down, far across the desert, and lightning stung down with sharp white stings on the horizon : or the cloud travelled and burst overhead, with rivers of fluid blue fire running out of heaven and exploding on earth, and hail coming down like a world of ice shattered above : or the hot sun rode in again : or snow fell in heavy silence : or the world was blinding white under a blue sky, and one must hurry under the pine-trees for shelter against that vast, white, back-beating light which rushed up at one and made one almost unconscious, amid the snow.

It was always beauty, *always* ! It was always great, and splendid, and, for some reason, natural. It was never grandiose or theatrical. Always, for some reason, perfect. And quite simple, in spite of it all.

So it was, when you watched the vast and living landscape. The landscape lived, and lived as the world of the gods, unsullied and unconcerned. The great circling landscape lived its own life, sumptuous and uncaring. Man did not exist for it.

And if it had been a question simply of living through the eyes, into the *distance*, then this would have been Paradise, and the little New England woman on her ranch would have found what she was always looking for, the earthly paradise of the spirit.

But even a woman cannot live only into the distance, the beyond. Willy-nilly she finds herself juxtaposed to the near things, the thing in itself. And willy-nilly she is caught up into the fight with the immediate object.

The New England woman had fought to make the nearness as perfect as the distance : for the distance was absolute beauty. She had been confident of success. She had felt quite assured, when the water came running out of her bright brass taps, the wild water of the hills caught, tricked into the narrow iron pipes, and led tamely to her kitchen, to jump out over her sink, into her wash-basin, at her service. *There !* she said. I have tamed the waters of the mountain to my service.

So she had, for the moment.

At the same time, the invisible attack was being made upon her. While she revelled in the beauty of the luminous world that wheeled around and below her, the grey, rat-like spirit of the inner mountains was attacking her from behind. She could not keep her attention. And, curiously, she could not keep even her speech. When she was saying something, suddenly the next word would be gone out of her, as if a pack-rat had carried it off. And she sat blank, stuttering, staring in the empty cupboard of her mind, like Mother Hubbard, and seeing the cupboard bare. And this irritated her husband intensely.

Her chickens, of which she was so proud, were carried away. Or they strayed. Or they fell sick. At first she could cope with her circumstances. But after a while, she couldn't. She couldn't care. A drug-like numbness possessed her spirit, and at the very middle of her, she couldn't care what happened to her chickens.

The same when a couple of horses were struck by lightning. It frightened her. The rivers of fluid fire that suddenly fell out of the sky and exploded on the earth nearby, as if the whole earth had burst like a bomb, frightened her from the very core of her, and made her know, secretly and with cynical certainty, *that there was no merciful God in the heavens.* A very tall, elegant pine-tree just above her cabin took the lightning, and stood tall and elegant as before, but with a white seam spiralling from its crest, all down its tall trunk, to earth. The perfect scar, white and long as lightning itself. And every time she looked at it, she said to herself, in spite of herself : *There is no Almighty loving God. The God there is shaggy as the pine-trees, and horrible as the lightning.* Outwardly, she never confessed this. Openly, she thought of her dear New England Church as usual. But in the violent undercurrent of her woman's soul, after the storms, she would look at that living seamed tree, and the voice would say in her, almost savagely : *What nonsense about Jesus and a God of Love, in a place like this ! This is more awful and more splendid. I like it better.* The very chipmunks, in their jerky helter-skelter, the blue jays wrangling in the pine-tree in the dawn, the grey squirrel undulating to the tree-trunk, then pausing to chatter at her and scold her, with a shrewd fearlessness, as if she were the alien, the outsider, the creature that should not be permitted among the trees, all destroyed the illusion she cherished, of love, universal love. There was no love on this ranch. There was life, intense, bristling life, full of energy, but also, with an undertone of savage sordidness.

The black ants in her cupboard, the pack-rats bouncing on her ceiling like hippopotamuses in the night, the two sick goats : there was a peculiar undercurrent of squalor, flowing under the curious *tussle* of wild life. That was it. The wild life, even the life of the trees and flowers, seemed one bristling, hair-raising tussle. The very flowers came up bristly, and many of them were fang-mouthed, like the dead-nettle : and none had any real scent. But they were very fascinating, too, in their very fierceness. In May, the curious columbines of the stream-beds, columbines scarlet outside and yellow in, like the red and yellow of a herald's uniform—farther from the dove nothing could be : then the beautiful rosy-blue of the great tufts of the flower they called blue-bell, but which was really a flower of the snap-dragon family : these grew in powerful beauty in the little clearing of the pine-trees, followed by the flower the settlers had mysteriously called herb honeysuckle : a tangle of long drops of pure fire-red, hanging from slim invisible stalks of smoke colour. The purest, most perfect vermilion scarlet, cleanest fire-colour, hanging in long drops like a shower of fire-rain that is just going to strike the earth. A little later, more in the open, there came another sheer fire-red flower, sparking, fierce red stars running up a bristly grey ladder, as if the earth's fire-centre had blown out some red sparks, white-speckled and deadly inside, puffing for a moment in the day air.

So it was ! The alfalfa field was one raging, seething conflict of plants trying to get hold. One dry year, and the bristly wild things had got hold : the spiky, blue-leaved thistle-poppy with its moon-white flowers, the low clumps of blue nettle-flower, the later rush, after the sereness of June and July, the rush of red sparks and Michaelmas daisies, and the tough wild sunflowers, strangling and choking the dark, tender green of the clover-like alfalfa ! A battle, a battle, with banners of bright scarlet and yellow.

When a really defenceless flower did issue, like the moth-still, ghost-centred mariposa lily, with its inner moth-dust of yellow, it came invisible. There was nothing to be seen, but a hair of greyish grass near the oak-scrub. Behold, this invisible long stalk was balancing a white, ghostly, three-petalled flower, naked out of nothingness. A mariposa lily !

Only the pink wild roses smelled sweet, like the old world. They were sweet-briar roses. And the dark blue hare-bells among the oak-scrub, like the ice-dark bubbles of the mountain flowers in the Alps, the Alpenglocken.

The roses of the desert are the cactus flowers, crystal of translucent yellow or of rose-colour. But set among spines the devil himself must have conceived in a moment of sheer ecstasy.

Nay, it was a world before and after the God of Love. Even the very humming-birds hanging about the flowering squaw-berry bushes, when the snow had gone, in May, they were before and after the God of Love. And the blue jays were crested dark with challenge, and the yellow-and-dark woodpecker was fearless like a warrior in war-paint, as he struck the wood. While on the fence the hawks sat motionless, like dark fists clenched under heaven, ignoring man and his ways.

Summer, it was true, unfolded the tender cotton-wood leaves, and the tender aspen. But what a tangle and ghostly aloofness in the aspen thickets high up on the mountains, the coldness that is in the eyes and the long cornelian talons of the bear.

Summer brought the little wild strawberries, with their savage aroma, and the late summer brought the rose-jewel raspberries in the valley cleft. But how lonely, how harsh-lonely and menacing it was, to be alone in that shadowy, steep cleft of a canyon just above the cabins, picking raspberries, while the thunder gathered thick and blue-purple at the mountain tops. The many wild raspberries hanging rose-red in the thickets. But the stream bed below all silent, waterless. And the trees all bristling in silence, and waiting like warriors at an outpost. And the berries waiting for the sharp-eyed, cold, long-snouted bear to come rambling and shaking his heavy sharp fur. The berries grew for the bears, and the little New England woman, with her uncanny sensitiveness to underlying influences, felt all the time she was stealing. Stealing the wild raspberries in the secret little canyon behind her home. And when she had made them into jam, she could almost taste the theft in her preserves.

She confessed nothing of this. She tried even to confess nothing of her dread. But she was afraid. Especially she was conscious of the prowling, intense aerial electricity all the summer, after June. The air was thick with wandering currents of fierce electric fluid, waiting to discharge themselves. And almost every day there was the rage and battle of thunder. But the air was never cleared. There was no relief. However the thunder raged, and spent itself, yet, afterwards, among the sunshine was the strange lurking and wandering of the electric currents, moving invisible, with strange menace, between the atoms of the air. She knew. Oh, she knew !

And her love for her ranch turned sometimes into a certain repulsion. The underlying rat-dirt, the everlasting bristling tussle of the wild life, with the tangle and the bones strewing. Bones of horses struck by lightning, bones of dead cattle, skulls of goats with little horns : bleached, unburied bones. Then the cruel electricity of the mountains. And then, most mysterious but worst of all, the animosity of the spirit of place : the crude, half-created spirit of place, like some serpent-bird forever attacking man, in a hatred of man's onward-struggle towards further creation.

The seething cauldron of lower life, seething on the very tissue of the higher life, seething the soul away, seething at the marrow. The vast and unrelenting will of the swarming lower life, working forever against man's attempt at a higher life, a further created being.

At last, after many years, the little woman admitted to herself that she was glad to go down from the ranch, when November came with snows. She was glad to come to a more human home, her house in the village. And as winter passed by, and spring came again, she knew she did not want to go up to the ranch again. It had broken something in her. It had hurt her terribly. It had maimed her for ever in her hope, her belief in paradise on earth. Now, she hid from herself her own corpse, the corpse of her New England belief in a world ultimately all for love. The belief, and herself with it, was a corpse. The gods of those inner mountains were grim and invidious and relentless, huger than man, and lower than man. Yet man could never master them.

The little woman in her flower-garden away below, by the stream-irrigated village, hid away from the thought of it all. She would not go to the ranch any more.

The Mexicans stayed in charge, looking after the goats. But the place didn't pay. It didn't pay, not quite. It had paid. It might pay. But the effort, the effort ! And as the marrow is eaten out of a man's bones and the soul out of his belly, contending with the strange rapacity of savage life, the lower stage of creation, he cannot make the effort any more.

Then also, the war came, making many men give up their enterprises at civilization.

Every new stroke of civilization has cost the lives of countless brave men, who have fallen defeated by the " dragon," in their efforts to win the apples of the Hesperides, or the fleece of gold. Fallen in their efforts to overcome the old, half-sordid savagery of the lower stages of creation, and win to the next stage.

For all savagery is half-sordid. And man is only himself when he is fighting on and on, to overcome the sordidness.

And every civilization, when it loses its inward vision and its cleaner energy, falls into a new sort of sordidness, more vast and

more stupendous than the old savage sort. An Augean stables of
metallic filth.

And all the time, man has to rouse himself afresh, to cleanse the
new accumulations of refuse. To win from the crude wild nature
the victory and the power to make another start, and to cleanse
behind him the century-deep deposits of layer upon layer of refuse :
even of tin cans.

The ranch dwindled. The flock of goats declined. The water
ceased to flow. And at length the trader gave it up.

He rented the place to a Mexican, who lived on the handful of
beans he raised, and who was being slowly driven out by the vermin.

And now arrived Lou, new blood to the attack. She went back to
Santa Fé, saw the trader and a lawyer, and bought the ranch for
twelve hundred dollars. She was so pleased with herself.

She went upstairs to tell her mother.

" Mother, I've bought a ranch."

" It is just as well, for I can't stand the noise of automobiles outside
here another week."

" It is quiet on my ranch, mother : the stillness simply speaks."

" I had rather it held its tongue. I am simply drugged with all
the bad novels I have read. I feel as if the sky was a big cracked bell
and a million clappers were hammering human speech out of it."

" Aren't you interested in my ranch, mother ? "

" I hope I may be, by and by."

Mrs. Witt actually got up the next morning, and accompanied her
daughter in the hired motor-car, driven by Phœnix, to the ranch :
which was called Las Chivas. She sat like a pillar of salt, her face
looking what the Indians call a False Face, meaning a mask. She
seemed to have crystallized into neutrality. She watched the desert
with its tufts of yellow greasewood go lurching past : she saw the
fallen apples on the ground in the orchards near the adobe cottages :
she looked down into the deep arroyo, and at the stream they forded
in the car, and at the mountains blocking up the sky ahead, all with
indifference. High on the mountains was snow : lower, blue-grey
livid rock : and below the livid rock the aspens were expiring their
daffodil yellow, this year, and the oak-scrub was dark and reddish,
like gore. She saw it all with a sort of stony indifference.

" Don't you think it's lovely ? " said Lou.

" I can *see* it is lovely," replied her mother.

The Michaelmas daisies in the clearing as they drove up to the
ranch were sharp-rayed with purple, like a coming night.

Mrs. Witt eyed the two log cabins, one of which was dilapidated and practically abandoned. She looked at the rather rickety corral, whose long planks had silvered and warped in the fierce sun. On one of the roof-planks a pack-rat was sitting erect like an old Indian keeping watch on a pueblo roof. He showed his white belly, and folded his hands and lifted his big ears, for all the world like an old immobile Indian.

" Isn't it for all the world as if *he* were the real boss of the place, Louise ? " she said cynically.

And turning to the Mexican, who was a rag of a man, but a pleasant, courteous fellow, she asked him why he didn't shoot the rat.

" Not worth a shell ! " said the Mexican, with a faint hopeless smile.

Mrs. Witt paced round and saw everything : it did not take long. She gazed in silence at the water of the spring, trickling out of an iron pipe into a barrel, under the cottonwood tree in an arroyo.

" Well, Louise," she said. " I am glad you feel competent to cope with so much hopelessness and so many rats."

" But, mother, you must admit it is beautiful."

" Yes, I suppose it is. But to use one of your Henry's phrases, beauty is a cold egg, as far as I am concerned."

" Rico never would have said that beauty was a cold egg to him."

" No, he wouldn't. He sits on it like a broody old hen on a china imitation. Are you going to bring him here ? "

" *Bring* him ! No. But he can come if he likes," stammered Lou.

" *Oh—h!* Won't it be beau—ti—ful ! " cried Mrs. Witt, rolling her head and lifting her shoulders in savage imitation of her son-in-law.

" Perhaps he won't come, mother," said Lou, hurt.

" He will most certainly come, Louise, to see what's doing : unless you tell him you don't want him."

" Anyhow, I needn't think about it till spring," said Lou, anxiously pushing the matter aside.

Mrs. Witt climbed the steep slope above the cabins, to the mouth of the little canyon. There she sat on a fallen tree, and surveyed the world beyond : a world not of men. She could not fail to be roused.

" What is your idea in coming here, daughter ? " she asked.

" I love it here, mother."

" But what do you expect to achieve by it ? "

" I was rather hoping, mother, to escape achievement. I'll tell you—and you mustn't get cross if it sounds silly. As far as people go, my heart is quite broken. As far as people go, I don't want any more. I can't stand any more. What heart I ever

had for it—for life with people—is quite broken. I want to be
alone, mother : with you here, and Phœnix perhaps to look after
horses and drive a car. But I want to be by myself, really."

" With Phœnix in the background ! Are you sure he won't be
coming into the foreground before long ? "

" No, mother, no more of that. If I've got to say it, Phœnix is
a servant : he's really placed, as far as I can see. Always the same,
playing about in the old back-yard. I can't take those men seriously.
I can't fool round with them, or fool myself about them. I can't
and I won't fool myself any more, mother, especially about men.
They don't count. So why should you want them to pay me out ? "

For the moment, this silenced Mrs. Witt. Then she said :

" Why, *I* don't want it. Why should I ! But after all you've got
to live. You've never *lived* yet : not in my opinion."

" Neither, mother, in my opinion, have you," said Lou drily.

And this silenced Mrs. Witt altogether. She had to be silent, or
angrily on the defensive. And the latter she wouldn't be. She
couldn't, really, in honesty.

" What do you call life ? " Lou continued. " Wriggling half-
naked at a public show, and going off in a taxi to sleep with some
half-drunken fool who thinks he's a man because—Oh, mother, I
don't even want to think of it. I know you have a lurking idea that
that is life. Let it be so then. But leave me out. Men in that
aspect simply nauseate me : so grovelling and ratty. Life in that
aspect simply drains all my life away. I tell you, for all that sort
of thing, I'm broken, absolutely broken : if I wasn't broken to start
with."

" Well, Louise," said Mrs. Witt after a pause, " I'm convinced
that ever since men and women were men and women, people who
took things seriously, and had time for it, got their hearts broken.
Haven't I had mine broken ! It's as sure as having your virginity
broken : and it amounts to about as much. It's a beginning rather
than an end."

" So it is, mother. It's the beginning of something else, and the
end of something that's done with. I *know*, and there's no altering
it, that I've got to live differently. It sounds silly, but I don't know
how else to put it. I've got to live for something that matters, way,
way down in me. And I think sex would matter, to my very soul,
if it was really sacred. But cheap sex kills me."

" You have had a fancy for rather cheap men, perhaps."

" Perhaps I have. Perhaps I should always be a fool, where
people are concerned. Now I want to leave off that kind of foolery.

There's something else, mother, that I want to give myself to. I know it. I know it absolutely. Why should I let myself be shouted down any more? "

Mrs. Witt sat staring at the distance, her face a cynical mask.

" What is the something bigger? And *pray*, what is it bigger than? " she asked, in that tone of honied suavity which was her deadliest poison. " I want to learn. I am out to know. I'm terribly intrigued by it. Something bigger! Girls in my generation occasionally entered convents, for *something bigger*. I always wondered if they found it. They seemed to me inclined in the imbecile direction, but perhaps that was because I was *something less*——"

There was a definite pause between the mother and daughter, a silence that was a pure breach. Then Lou said :

" You know quite well I'm not conventy, mother, whatever else I am—even a bit of an imbecile. But that kind of religion seems to me the other half of men. Instead of running after them you run away from them, and get the thrill that way. I don't hate men *because* they're men, as nuns do. I dislike them because they're not men enough : babies, and playboys, and poor things showing off all the time, even to themselves. I don't say I'm any better. I only wish, with all my soul, that some men *were* bigger and stronger and *deeper* than I am. . . ."

" How do you know they're not? " asked Mrs. Witt.

" How *do* I know? " said Lou mockingly.

And the pause that was a breach resumed itself. Mrs. Witt was teasing with a little stick the bewildered black ants among the fir-needles.

" And no doubt you are right about men," she said at length. " But at your age, the only sensible thing is to try and keep up the illusion. After all, as you say, you may be no better."

" I may be no better. But keeping up the illusion means fooling myself. And I won't do it. When I see a man who is even a bit attractive to me—even as much as Phœnix—I say to myself : *Would you care for him afterwards? Does he really mean anything to you, except just a sensation?* And I know he doesn't. No, mother, of this I am convinced : either my taking a man shall have a meaning and a mystery that penetrates my very soul, or I will keep to myself. And what I *know* is, that the time has come for me to keep to myself. No more messing about."

" Very well, daughter. You will probably spend your life keeping to yourself."

" Do you think I mind! There's something else for me, mother.

There's something else even that loves me and wants me. I can't tell you what it is. It's a spirit. And it's here, on this ranch. It's here, in this landscape. It's something more real to me than men are, and it soothes me, and it holds me up. I don't know what it is, definitely. It's something wild, that will hurt me sometimes and will wear me down sometimes. I know it. But it's something big, bigger than men, bigger than people, bigger than religion. It's something to do with wild America. And it's something to do with me. It's a mission, if you like. I am imbecile enough for that ! But it's my mission to keep myself for the spirit that is wild, and has waited so long here : even waited for such as me. Now I've come ! Now I'm here. Now I am where I want to be : with the spirit that wants me. And that's how it is. And neither Rico nor Phœnix nor anybody else really matters to me. They are in the world's back-yard. And I am here, right deep in America, where there's a wild spirit wants me, a wild spirit more than men. And it doesn't want to save me either. It needs me. It craves for me. And to it, my sex is deep and sacred, deeper than I am, with a deep nature aware deep down of my sex. It saves me from cheapness, mother. And even you could never do that for me."

Mrs. Witt rose to her feet, and stood looking far, far away, at the turquoise ridge of mountains half sunk under the horizon.

" How much did you say you paid for Las Chivas ? " she asked.

" Twelve hundred dollars," said Lou, surprised.

" Then I call it cheap, considering all there is to it : even the name."

To her father, she was The Princess. To her Boston aunts and uncles she was just *Dollie Urquhart, poor little thing*.

Colin Urquhart was just a bit mad. He was of an old Scottish family, and he claimed royal blood. The blood of Scottish kings flowed in his veins. On this point, his American relatives said, he was just a bit " off." They could not bear any more to be told *which* royal blood of Scotland blued his veins. The whole thing was rather ridiculous, and a sore point. The only fact they remembered was that it was not Stuart.

He was a handsome man, with a wide-open blue eye that seemed sometimes to be looking at nothing, soft black hair brushed rather low on his low, broad brow, and a very attractive body. Add to this a most beautiful speaking voice, usually rather hushed and diffident, but sometimes resonant and powerful like bronze, and you have the sum of his charms. He looked like some old Celtic hero. He looked as if he should have worn a greyish kilt and a sporran, and shown his knees. His voice came direct out of the hushed Ossianic past.

For the rest, he was one of those gentlemen of sufficient but not excessive means who fifty years ago wandered vaguely about, never arriving anywhere, never doing anything, and never definitely being anything, yet well received and familiar in the good society of more than one country.

He did not marry till he was nearly forty, and then it was a wealthy Miss Prescott, from New England. Hannah Prescott at twenty-two was fascinated by the man with the soft black hair not yet touched by grey, and the wide, rather vague, blue eyes. Many women had been fascinated before her. But Colin Urquhart, by his very vagueness, had avoided any decisive connection.

Mrs. Urquhart lived three years in the mist and glamour of her husband's presence. And then it broke her. It was like living with a fascinating spectre. About most things he was completely, even ghostly oblivious. He was always charming, courteous, perfectly gracious in that hushed, musical voice of his. But absent. When all came to all, he just wasn't there. "Not all there," as the vulgar say.

He was the father of the little girl she bore at the end of the first year. But this did not substantiate him the more. His very beauty and his haunting musical quality became dreadful to her after the first few months. The strange echo : he was like a living echo ! His very flesh, when you touched it, did not seem quite the flesh of a real man.

Perhaps it was that he was a little bit mad. She thought it definitely the night her baby was born.

" Ah, so my little princess has come at last ! " he said, in his throaty, singing Celtic voice, like a glad chant, swaying absorbed.

It was a tiny, frail baby, with wide, amazed blue eyes. They christened it Mary Henrietta. She called the little thing *My Dollie*. He called it always *My Princess*.

It was useless to fly at him. He just opened his wide blue eyes wider, and took a childlike, silent dignity there was no getting past.

Hannah Prescott had never been robust. She had no great desire to live. So when the baby was two years old she suddenly died.

The Prescotts felt a deep but unadmitted resentment against Colin Urquhart. They said he was selfish. Therefore they discontinued Hannah's income, a month after her burial in Florence, after they had urged the father to give the child over to them, and he had courteously, musically, but quite finally refused. He treated the Prescotts as if they were not of his world, not realities to him : just casual phenomena, or gramophones, talking-machines that had to be answered. He answered them. But of their actual existence he was never once aware.

They debated having him certified unsuitable to be guardian of his own child. But that would have created a scandal. So they did the simplest thing, after all—washed their hands of him. But they wrote scrupulously to the child, and sent her modest presents of money at Christmas, and on the anniversary of the death of her mother.

To The Princess her Boston relatives were for many years just a nominal reality. She lived with her father, and he travelled continually, though in a modest way, living on his moderate income. And never going to America. The child changed nurses all the time. In Italy it was a contadina ; in India she had an ayah ; in Germany she had a yellow-haired peasant girl.

Father and child were inseparable. He was not a recluse. Wherever he went he was to be seen paying formal calls, going out to luncheon or to tea, rarely to dinner. And always with the child. People called her Princess Urquhart, as if that were her christened name.

She was a quick, dainty little thing with dark gold hair that went a soft brown, and wide, slightly prominent blue eyes that were at once so candid and so knowing. She was always grown up ; she never really grew up. Always strangely wise, and always childish.

It was her father's fault.

" My little Princess must never take too much notice of people and the things they say and do," he repeated to her. " People don't know what they are doing and saying. They chatter-chatter, and they hurt one another, and they hurt themselves very often, till they cry. But don't take any notice, my little Princess. Because it is all nothing. Inside everybody there is another creature, a demon which doesn't care at all. You peel away all the things they say and do and feel, as cook peels away the outside of the onions. And in the middle of everybody there is a green demon which you can't peel away. And this green demon never changes, and it doesn't care at all about all the things that happen to the outside leaves of the person, all the chatter-chatter, and all the husbands and wives and children, and troubles and fusses. You peel everything away from people, and there is a green, upright demon in every man and woman ; and this demon is a man's real self, and a woman's real self. It doesn't really care about anybody, it belongs to the demons and the primitive fairies, who never care. But, even so, there are big demons and mean demons, and splendid demonish fairies, and vulgar ones. But there are no royal fairy women left. Only you, my little Princess. You are the last of the royal race of the old people ; the last, my Princess. There are no others. You and I are the last. When I am dead there will be only you. And that is why, darling, you will never care for any of the people in the world very much. Because their demons are all dwindled and vulgar. They are not royal. Only you are royal, after me. Always remember that. And always remember, it is a *great secret*. If you tell people, they will try to kill you, because they will envy you for being a Princess. It is our great secret, darling. I am a prince, and you a princess, of the old, old blood. And we keep our secret between us, all alone. And so, darling, you must treat all people very politely, because *noblesse oblige*. But you must never forget that you alone are the last of Princesses, and that all others are less than you are, less noble, more vulgar. Treat them politely and gently and kindly, darling. But you are the Princess, and they are commoners. Never try to think of them as if they were like you. They are not. You will find, always, that they are lacking, lacking in the royal touch, which only you have——"

The Princess learned her lesson early—the first lesson, of absolute reticence, the impossibility of intimacy with any other than her father ; the second lesson, of naïve, slightly benevolent politeness. As a small child, something crystallized in her character, making her clear and finished, and as impervious as crystal.

" Dear child ! " her hostesses said of her. " She is so quaint and old-fashioned ; such a lady, poor little mite ! "

She was erect, and very dainty. Always small, nearly tiny in physique, she seemed like a changeling beside her big, handsome, slightly mad father. She dressed very simply, usually in blues or delicate greys, with little collars of old Milan point, or very finely-worked linen. She had exquisite little hands, that made the piano sound like a spinet when she played. She was rather given to wearing cloaks and capes, instead of coats, out of doors, and little eighteenth-century sort of hats. Her complexion was pure apple-blossom.

She looked as if she had stepped out of a picture. But no one, to her dying day, ever knew exactly the strange picture her father had framed her in, and from which she never stepped.

Her grandfather and grandmother and her Aunt Maud demanded twice to see her, once in Rome and once in Paris. Each time they were charmed, piqued, and annoyed. She was so exquisite and such a little virgin. At the same time so knowing and so oddly assured. That odd, assured touch of condescension, and the inward coldness, infuriated her American relations.

Only she really fascinated her grandfather. He was spellbound ; in a way, in love with the little faultless thing. His wife would catch him brooding, musing over his grandchild, long months after the meeting, and craving to see her again. He cherished to the end the fond hope that she might come to live with him and her grandmother.

" Thank you so much, grandfather. You are so very kind. But Papa and I are such an old couple, you see, such a crochety old couple, living in a world of our own."

Her father let her see the world—from the outside. And he let her read. When she was in her teens she read Zola and Maupassant, and with the eyes of Zola and Maupassant she looked on Paris. A little later she read Tolstoi and Dostoevsky. The latter confused her. The others, she seemed to understand with a very shrewd, canny understanding, just as she understood the Decameron stories as she read them in their old Italian, or the Nibelung poems. Strange and *uncanny*, she seemed to understand things in a cold light perfectly,

with all the flush of fire absent. She was something like a changeling,
not quite human.

This earned her, also, strange antipathies. Cabmen and railway-
porters, especially in Paris and Rome, would suddenly treat her with
brutal rudeness, when she was alone. They seemed to look on her
with sudden violent antipathy. They sensed in her curious impertinence, an easy, sterile impertinence towards the things *they* felt most.
She was so assured, and her flower of maidenhood was so scentless.
She could look at a lusty, sensual Roman cabman as if he were a sort
of grotesque, to make her smile. She knew all about him, in Zola.
And the peculiar condescension with which she would give him her
order, as if she, frail, beautiful thing, were the only reality, and he,
coarse monster, were a sort of Caliban floundering in the mud on
the margin of the pool of the perfect lotus, would suddenly enrage
the fellow, the real Mediterranean who prided himself on his *beauté
male*, and to whom the phallic mystery was still the only mystery.
And he would turn a terrible face on her, bully her in a brutal,
coarse fashion—hideous. For to him she had only the blasphemous
impertinence of her own sterility.

Encounters like these made her tremble, and made her know she
must have support from the outside. The power of her spirit did not
extend to these low people, and they had all the physical power.
She realized an implacability of hatred in their turning on her. But she
did not lose her head. She quietly paid out money and turned away.

Those were dangerous moments, though, and she learned to be
prepared for them. The Princess she was, and the fairy from the
North, and could never understand the volcanic phallic rage with
which coarse people could turn on her in a paroxysm of hatred.
They never turned on her father like that. And quite early she
decided it was the New England mother in her whom they hated.
Never for one minute could she see with the old Roman eyes, see
herself as sterility, the barren flower taking on airs and an intolerable
impertinence. This was what the Roman cabman saw in her. And
he longed to crush the barren blossom. Its sexless beauty and its
authority put him in a passion of brutal revolt.

When she was nineteen her grandfather died, leaving her a considerable fortune in the safe hands of responsible trustees. They
would deliver her her income, but only on condition that she resided
for six months in the year in the United States.

" Why should they make me conditions ? " she said to her father.
" I refuse to be imprisoned six months in the year in the United
States. We will tell them to keep their money."

" Let us be wise, my little Princess, let us be wise. No, we are almost poor, and we are never safe from rudeness. I cannot allow anybody to be rude to me. I hate it, I hate it ! " His eyes flamed as he said it. " I could kill any man or woman who is rude to me. But we are in exile in the world. We are powerless. If we were really poor, we should be quite powerless, and then I should die. No, my Princess. Let us take their money, then they will not dare to be rude to us. Let us take it, as we put on clothes, to cover ourselves from their aggressions."

There began a new phase, when the father and daughter spent their summers on the Great Lakes or in California, or in the South-West. The father was something of a poet, the daughter something of a painter. He wrote poems about the lakes or the red-wood trees, and she made dainty drawings. He was physically a strong man, and he loved the out-of-doors. He would go off with her for days, paddling in a canoe and sleeping by a camp-fire. Frail little Princess, she was always undaunted, always undaunted. She would ride with him on horseback over the mountain trails till she was so tired she was nothing but a bodiless consciousness sitting astride her pony. But she never gave in. And at night he folded her in her blankets on a bed of balsam-pine twigs, and she lay and looked at the stars unmurmuring. She was fulfilling her rôle.

People said to her as the years passed, and she was a woman of twenty-five, then a woman of thirty, and always the same virgin dainty Princess, " knowing " in a dispassionate way, like an old woman, and utterly intact ·

" Don't you ever think what you will do when your father is no longer with you ? "

She looked at her interlocutor with that cold, elfin detachment of hers :

" No, I never think of it," she said.

She had a tiny, but exquisite little house in London, and another small, perfect house in Connecticut, each with a faithful housekeeper. Two homes, if she chose. And she knew many interesting literary and artistic people. What more ?

So the years passed imperceptibly. And she had that quality of the sexless fairies, she did not change. At thirty-three she looked twenty-three.

Her father, however, was ageing, and becoming more and more queer. It was now her task to be his guardian in his private madness. He spent the last three years of life in the house in Connecticut. He was very much estranged, sometimes had fits of violence which almost killed the little Princess. Physical violence was horrible to her ; it seemed to shatter her heart. But she found a woman a few years younger than herself, well-educated and sensitive, to be a sort of nurse-companion to the mad old man. So the fact of madness was never openly admitted. Miss Cummins, the companion, had a passionate loyalty to the Princess, and a curious affection, tinged with love, for the handsome, white-haired, courteous old man, who was never at all aware of his fits of violence once they had passed.

The Princess was thirty-eight years old when her father died. And quite unchanged. She was still tiny, and like a dignified, scentless flower. Her soft brownish hair, almost the colour of beaver fur, was bobbed, and fluffed softly round her apple-blossom face, that was modelled with an arched nose like a proud old Florentine portrait. In her voice, manner and bearing she was exceedingly still, like a flower that has blossomed in a shadowy place. And from her blue eyes looked out the Princess's eternal laconic challenge, that grew almost sardonic as the years passed. She was the Princess, and sardonically she looked out on a princeless world.

She was relieved when her father died, and at the same time, it was as if everything had evaporated around her. She had lived in a sort of hot-house, in the aura of her father's madness. Suddenly the hot-house had been removed from around her, and she was in the raw, vast, vulgar open air.

Quoi faire ? What was she to do ? She seemed faced with absolute nothingness. Only she had Miss Cummins, who shared with her the secret, and almost the passion for her father. In fact the Princess felt that her passion for her mad father had in some curious way transferred itself largely to Charlotte Cummins during the last years. And now Miss Cummins was the vessel that held the passion for the dead man. She herself, the Princess, was an empty vessel.

An empty vessel in the enormous warehouse of the world.

Quoi faire ? What was she to do ? She felt that, since she could not evaporate into nothingness, like alcohol from an unstoppered bottle, she must *do* something. Never before in her life had she felt the incumbency. Never, never had she felt she must *do* anything. That was left to the vulgar.

Now her father was dead, she found herself on the *fringe* of the vulgar crowd, sharing their necessity to *do* something. It was a little humiliating. She felt herself becoming vulgarized. At the same time she found herself looking at men with a shrewder eye : an eye to marriage. Not that she felt any sudden interest in men, or attraction towards them. No. She was still neither interested nor attracted towards men vitally. But *marriage*, that peculiar abstraction, had imposed a sort of spell on her. She thought that *marriage*, in the blank abstract, was the thing she ought to *do*. That *marriage* implied a man she also knew. She knew all the facts. But the man seemed a property of her own mind rather than a thing in himself, another being.

His father died in the summer, the month after her thirty-eighth birthday. When all was over, the obvious thing to do, of course, was to travel. With Miss Cummins. The two women knew each other intimately, but they were always Miss Urquhart and Miss Cummins to one another, and a certain distance was instinctively maintained. Miss Cummins, from Philadelphia, of scholastic stock, and intelligent but untravelled, four years younger than the Princess, felt herself immensely the junior of her " lady." She had a sort of passionate veneration for the Princess, who seemed to her ageless, timeless. She could not see the rows of tiny, dainty, exquisite shoes in the Princess's cupboard without feeling a stab at the heart, a stab of tenderness and reverence, almost of awe.

Miss Cummins also was virginal, but with a look of puzzled surprise in her brown eyes. Her skin was pale and clear, her features well modelled, but there was a certain blankness in her expression, where the Princess had an odd touch of Renaissance grandeur. Miss Cummins' voice was also hushed almost to a whisper ; it was the inevitable effect of Colin Urquhart's room. But the hushedness had a hoarse quality.

The Princess did not want to go to Europe. Her face seemed turned west. Now her father was gone, she felt she would go west, westwards, as if for ever. Following, no doubt, the March of Empire, which is brought up rather short on the Pacific coast, among swarms of wallowing bathers.

No, not the Pacific coast. She would stop short of that. The South-West was less vulgar. She would go to New Mexico.

She and Miss Cummins arrived at the Rancho del Cerro Gordo towards the end of August, when the crowd was beginning to drift back east. The ranch lay by a stream on the desert some four miles from the foot of the mountains, a mile away from the Indian pueblo of San Cristobal. It was a ranch for the rich ; the Princess paid thirty dollars a day for herself and Miss Cummins. But then she had a little cottage to herself, among the apple-trees of the orchard, with an excellent cook. She and Miss Cummins, however, took dinner at evening in the large guest-house. For the Princess still entertained the idea of *marriage*.

The guests at the Rancho del Cerro Gordo were of all sorts, except the poor sort. They were practically all rich, and many were romantic. Some were charming, others were vulgar, some were movie people, quite quaint and not unattractive in their vulgarity, and many were Jews. The Princess did not care for Jews, though they were usually the most interesting to *talk* to. So she talked a good deal with the Jews, and painted with the artists, and rode with the young men from college, and had altogether quite a good time. And yet she felt something of a fish out of water, or a bird in the wrong forest. And *marriage* remained still completely in the abstract. No connecting it with any of these young men, even the nice ones.

The Princess looked just twenty-five. The freshness of her mouth, the hushed, delicate-complexioned virginity of her face gave her not a day more. Only a certain laconic look in her eyes was disconcerting. When she was *forced* to write her age, she put twenty-eight, making the figure *two* rather badly, so that it just avoided being a three.

Men hinted marriage at her. Especially boys from college suggested it from a distance. But they all failed before the look of sardonic ridicule in the Princess's eyes. It always seemed to her rather preposterous, quite ridiculous, and a tiny bit impertinent on their part.

The only man that intrigued her at all was one of the guides, a man called Romero—Domingo Romero. It was he who had sold the ranch itself to the Wilkiesons, ten years before, for two thousand dollars. He had gone away, then reappeared at the old place. For he was the son of the old Romero, the last of the Spanish family that had owned miles of land around San Cristobal. But the coming of the white man and the failure of the vast flocks of sheep, and the fatal inertia which overcomes all men, at last, on the desert near the mountains, had finished the Romero family. The last descendants were just Mexican peasants.

Domingo, the heir, had spent his two thousand dollars, and was working for white people. He was now about thirty years old, a tall, silent fellow, with a heavy closed mouth and black eyes that looked across at one almost sullenly. From behind he was handsome, with a strong, natural body, and the back of his neck very dark and well-shapen, strong with life. But his dark face was long and heavy, almost sinister, with that peculiar heavy meaningless in it, characteristic of the Mexicans of his own locality. They are strong, they seem healthy. They laugh and joke with one another. But their physique and their natures seem static, as if there were nowhere, nowhere at all for their energies to go, and their faces, degenerating to misshapen heaviness, seem to have no *raison d'être*, no radical meaning. Waiting either to die or to be aroused into passion and hope. In some of the black eyes a queer, haunting mystic quality, sombre and a bit gruesome, the skull-and-cross-bones look of the Penitentes. They had found their *raison d'être* in self-torture and death-worship. Unable to wrest a *positive* significance for themselves from the vast, beautiful, but vindictive landscape they were born into, they turned on their own selves, and worshipped death through self-torture. The mystic gloom of this showed in their eyes.

But as a rule the dark eyes of the Mexicans were heavy and half-alive, sometimes hostile, sometimes kindly, often with the fatal Indian glaze on them, or the fatal Indian glint.

Domingo Romero was *almost* a typical Mexican to look at, with the typical heavy, dark, long face, clean-shaven, with an almost brutally heavy mouth. His eyes were black and Indian-looking. Only, at the centre of their hopelessness was a spark of pride, or self-confidence, or dauntlessness. Just a spark in the midst of the blackness of static despair.

But this spark was the difference between him and the mass of men. It gave a certain alert sensitiveness to his bearing and a certain beauty to his appearance. He wore a low-crowned black hat, instead of the ponderous headgear of the usual Mexican, and his clothes were thinnish and graceful. Silent, aloof, almost imperceptible in the landscape, he was an admirable guide, with a startling quick intelligence that anticipated difficulties about to arise. He could cook, too, crouching over the camp-fire and moving his lean deft brown hands. The only fault he had was that he was not forthcoming, he wasn't chatty and cosy.

"Oh, don't send Romero with us," the Jews would say. "One can't get any response from him."

Tourists come and go, but they rarely *see* anything, inwardly. None of them ever saw the spark at the middle of Romero's eye; they were not alive enough to see it.

The Princess caught it one day, when she had him for a guide. She was fishing for trout in the canyon, Miss Cummins was reading a book, the horses were tied under the trees, Romero was fixing a proper fly on her line. He fixed the fly and handed her the line, looking up at her. And at that moment she caught the spark in his eye. And instantly she knew that he was a gentleman, that his "demon," as her father would have said, was a fine demon. And instantly her manner towards him changed.

He had perched her on a rock over a quiet pool, beyond the cotton-wood trees. It was early September, and the canyon already cool, but the leaves of the cotton-woods were still green. The Princess stood on her rock, a small but perfectly-formed figure, wearing a soft, close grey sweater and neatly-cut grey riding breeches, with tall black boots, her fluffy brown hair straggling from under a little grey felt hat. A woman ? Not quite. A changeling of some sort, perched in outline there on the rock, in the bristling wild canyon. She knew perfectly well how to handle a line. Her father had made a fisher-man of her.

Romero, in a black shirt and with loose black trousers pushed into wide black riding boots, was fishing a little further down. He had put his hat on a rock behind him ; his dark head was bent a little forward, watching the water. He had caught three trout. From time to time he glanced upstream at the Princess, perched there so daintily. He saw she had caught nothing.

Soon he quietly drew in his line and came up to her. His keen eye watched her line, watched her position. Then, quietly, he suggested certain changes to her, putting his sensitive brown hand before her. And he withdrew a little, and stood in silence, leaning against a tree, watching her. He was helping her across the distance. She knew it, and thrilled. And in a moment she had a bite. In two minutes she landed a good trout. She looked round at him quickly, her eyes sparkling, the colour heightened in her cheeks. And as she met his eyes a smile of greeting went over his dark face, very sudden, with an odd sweetness.

She knew he was helping her. And she felt in his presence a subtle, insidious male *kindliness* she had never known before waiting upon her. Her cheek flushed, and her blue eyes darkened.

After this, she always looked for him, and for that curious dark beam of a man's kindliness which he could give her, as it were, from his chest, from his heart. It was something she had never known before.

A vague, unspoken intimacy grew up between them. She liked his voice, his appearance, his presence. His natural language was Spanish ; he spoke English like a foreign language, rather slow, with a slight hesitation, but with a sad, plangent sonority lingering over from his Spanish. There was a certain subtle correctness in his appearance ; he was always perfectly shaved ; his hair was thick and rather long on top, but always carefully groomed behind. And his fine black cashmere shirt, his wide leather belt, his well-cut, wide black trousers going into the embroidered cowboy boots had a

certain inextinguishable elegance. He wore no silver rings or buckles.
Only his boots were embroidered and decorated at the top with an
inlay of white *suède*. He seemed elegant, slender, yet he was very
strong.

And at the same time, curiously, he gave her the feeling that death
was not far from him. Perhaps he too was half in love with death.
However that may be, the sense she had that death was not far from
him made him " possible " to her.

Small as she was, she was quite a good horsewoman. They gave
her at the ranch a sorrel mare, very lovely in colour, and well-made,
with a powerful broad neck and the hollow back that betokens a
swift runner. Tansy, she was called. Her only fault was the usual
mare's failing, she was inclined to be hysterical.

So that every day the Princess set off with Miss Cummins and
Romero, on horseback, riding into the mountains. Once they went
camping for several days, with two more friends in the party.

" I think I like it better," the Princess said to Romero, " when
we three go alone."

And he gave her one of his quick, transfiguring smiles.

It was curious no white man had ever showed her this capacity for
subtle gentleness, this power to *help* her in silence across a distance,
if she were fishing without success, or tired of her horse, or if Tansy
suddenly got scared. It was as if Romero could send her *from his
heart* a dark beam of succour and sustaining. She had never known
this before, and it was very thrilling.

Then the smile that suddenly creased his dark face, showing the
strong white teeth. It creased his face almost into a savage grotesque.
And at the same time there was in it something so warm, such a dark
flame of kindliness for her, she was elated into her true Princess self.

Then that vivid, latent spark in his eye, which she had seen, and
which she knew he was aware she had seen. It made an inter-
recognition between them, silent and delicate. Here he was delicate
as a woman in this subtle inter-recognition.

And yet his presence only put to flight in her the *idée fixe* of
" marriage." For some reason, in her strange little brain, the idea
of *marrying* him could not enter. Not for any definite reason. He
was in himself a gentleman, and she had plenty of money for two.
There was no actual obstacle. Nor was she conventional.

No, now she came down to it, it was as if their two " dæmons "
could marry, were perhaps married. Only their two *selves*, Miss
Urquhart and Señor Domingo Romero, were for some reason
incompatible. There was a peculiar subtle intimacy of inter-

recognition between them. But she did not see in the least how it would lead to marriage. Almost she could more easily marry one of the nice boys from Harvard or Yale.

The time passed, and she let it pass. The end of September came, with aspens going yellow on the mountain heights, and oak-scrub going red. But as yet the cotton-woods in the valley and canyons had not changed.

" When will you go away ? " Romero asked her, looking at her fixedly, with a blank black eye.

" By the end of October," she said. " I have promised to be in Santa Barbara at the beginning of November."

He was hiding the spark in his eye from her. But she saw the peculiar sullen thickening of his heavy mouth.

She had complained to him many times that one never saw any wild animals, except chipmunks and squirrels, and perhaps a skunk and a porcupine. Never a deer, or a bear, or a mountain lion.

" Are there no bigger animals in these mountains ? " she asked, dissatisfied.

" Yes," he said. " There are deer—I see their tracks. And I saw the tracks of a bear."

" But why can one never see the animals themselves ? " She looked dissatisfied and wistful like a child.

" Why, it's pretty hard for you to see them. They won't let you come close. You have to keep still, in a place where they come. Or else you have to follow their tracks a long way."

" I can't bear to go away till I've seen them : a bear, or a deer——"

The smile came suddenly on his face, indulgent.

" Well, what do you want ? Do you want to go up into the mountains to some place, to wait till they come ? "

" Yes," she said, looking up at him with a sudden naïve impulse of recklessness.

And immediately his face became sombre again, responsible.

" Well," he said, with slight irony, a touch of mockery of her. " You will have to find a house. It's very cold at night now. You would have to stay all night in a house."

" And there are no houses up there ? " she said.

" Yes," he replied. " There is a little shack that belongs to me, that a miner built a long time ago, looking for gold. You can go there and stay one night, and maybe you see something. Maybe ! I don't know. Maybe nothing come."

" How much chance is there ? "

"Well, I don't know. Last time when I was there I see three deer come down to drink at the water, and I shot two raccoons. But maybe this time we don't see anything."

"Is there water there?" she asked.

"Yes, there is a little round pond, you know, below the spruce trees. And the water from the snow runs into it."

"Is it far away?" she asked.

"Yes, pretty far. You see that ridge there"—and turning to the mountains he lifted his arm in the gesture which is somehow so moving, out in the West, pointing to the distance—"that ridge where there are no trees, only rock"—his black eyes were focussed on the distance, his face impassive, but as if in pain—"you go round that ridge, and along, then you come down through the spruce trees to where that cabin is. My father bought that placer claim from a miner who was broke, but nobody ever found any gold or anything, and nobody ever goes there. Too lonesome!"

The Princess watched the massive, heavy-sitting, beautiful bulk of the Rocky Mountains. It was early in October, and the aspens were already losing their gold leaves; high up, the spruce and pine seemed to be growing darker; the great flat patches of oak-scrub on the heights were red like gore.

"Can I go over there?" she asked, turning to him and meeting the spark in his eye.

His face was heavy with responsibility.

"Yes," he said, "you can go. But there'll be snow over the ridge, and it's awful cold, and awful lonesome."

"I should like to go," she said, persistent.

"All right," he said. "You can go if you want to."

She doubted, though, if the Wilkiesons would let her go; at least alone with Romero and Miss Cummins.

Yet an obstinacy characteristic of her nature, an obstinacy tinged perhaps with madness, had taken hold of her. She wanted to look over the mountains into their secret heart. She wanted to descend to the cabin below the spruce trees, near the tarn of bright green water. She wanted to see the wild animals move about in their wild unconsciousness.

"Let us say to the Wilkiesons that we want to make the trip round the Frijoles canyon," she said.

The trip round the Frijoles canyon was a usual thing. It would not be strenuous, nor cold, nor lonely: they could sleep in the log house that was called an hotel.

Romero looked at her quickly.

" If you want to say that," he replied, " you can tell Mrs. Wilkie-son. Only I know she'll be mad with me if I take you up in the mountains to that place. And I've got to go there first with a pack-horse, to take lots of blankets and some bread. Maybe Miss Cummins can't stand it. Maybe not. It's a hard trip."

He was speaking, and thinking, in the heavy, disconnected Mexican fashion.

" Never mind ! " The Princess was suddenly very decisive and stiff with authority. " I want to do it. I will arrange with Mrs. Wilkieson. And we'll go on Saturday."

He shook his head slowly.

" I've got to go up on Sunday with a pack-horse and blankets," he said. " Can't do it before."

" Very well ! " she said, rather piqued. " Then we'll start on Monday."

She hated being thwarted even the tiniest bit.

He knew that if he started with the pack on Sunday at dawn he would not be back until late at night. But he consented that they should start on Monday morning at seven. The obedient Miss Cummins was told to prepare for the Frijoles trip. On Sunday Romero had his day off. He had not put in an appearance when the Princess retired on Sunday night, but on Monday morning, as she was dressing, she saw him bringing in the three horses from the corral. She was in high spirits.

The night had been cold. There was ice at the edges of the irriga-tion ditch, and the chipmunks crawled into the sun and lay with wide, dumb, anxious eyes, almost too numb to run.

" We may be away two or three days," said the Princess.

" Very well. We won't begin to be anxious about you before Thursday, then," said Mrs. Wilkieson, who was young and capable : from Chicago. " Anyway," she added, " Romero will see you through. He's so trustworthy."

The sun was already on the desert as they set off towards the mountains, making the greasewood and the sage pale as pale-grey sands, luminous the great level around them. To the right glinted the shadows of the adobe pueblo, flat and almost invisible on the plain, earth of its earth. Behind lay the ranch and the tufts of tall, plumy cottonwoods, whose summits were yellowing under the perfect blue sky.

Autumn breaking into colour in the great spaces of the South-West.

But the three trotted gently along the trail, towards the sun that sparkled yellow just above the dark bulk of the ponderous mountains. Side-slopes were already gleaming yellow, flaming with a second light, under the coldish blue of the pale sky. The front slopes were in shadow, with submerged lustre of red oak-scrub and dull-gold aspens, blue-black pines and grey-blue rock. While the canyon was full of a deep blueness.

They rode single file, Romero first, on a black horse. Himself in black, he made a flickering black spot in the delicate pallor of the great landscape, where even pine-trees at a distance take a film of blue paler than their green. Romero rode on in silence past the tufts of furry greasewood. The Princess came next, on her sorrel mare. And Miss Cummins, who was not quite happy on horseback, came last, in the pale dust that the others kicked up. Sometimes her horse sneezed, and she started.

But on they went, at a gentle trot. Romero never looked round. He could hear the sound of the hoofs following, and that was all he wanted.

For the rest, he held ahead. And the Princess, with that black, unheeding figure always travelling away from her, felt strangely helpless, withal elated.

They neared the pale, round foot-hills, dotted with the round dark piñon and cedar shrubs. The horses clinked and clattered among stones. Occasionally a big round greasewood held out fleecy tufts of flowers, pure gold. They wound into blue shadow, then up a steep stony slope, with the world lying pallid away behind and below. Then they dropped into the shadow of the San Cristobal canyon.

The stream was running full and swift. Occasionally the horses snatched at a tuft of grass. The trail narrowed and became rocky ; the rocks closed in ; it was dark and cool as the horses climbed and climbed upwards, and the tree-trunks crowded in in the shadowy, silent tightness of the canyon. They were among cottonwood trees that ran straight up and smooth and round to an extraordinary height. Above, the tips were gold, and it was sun. But away below, where the horses struggled up the rocks and wound among the trunks, there was still blue shadow by the sound of waters and an occasional grey festoon of old man's beard, and here and there a pale, dipping crane's-bill flower among the tangle and the debris of the virgin place. And again the chill entered the Princess's heart as she realized what a tangle of decay and despair lay in the virgin forests.

They scrambled downwards, splashed across stream, up rocks and along the trail of the other side. Romero's black horse stopped, looked down quizzically at the fallen trees, then stepped over lightly. The Princess's sorrel followed, carefully. But Miss Cummins's buckskin made a fuss, and had to be got round.

In the same silence, save for the clinking of the horses and the splashing as the trail crossed stream, they worked their way upwards in the tight, tangled shadow of the canyon. Sometimes, crossing stream, the Princess would glance upwards, and then always her heart caught in her breast. For high up, away in heaven, the mountain heights shone yellow, dappled with dark spruce firs, clear almost as speckled daffodils against the pale turquoise blue lying high and serene above the dark-blue shadow where the Princess was. And she would snatch at the blood-red leaves of the oak as her horse crossed a more open slope, not knowing what she felt.

They were getting fairly high, occasionally lifted above the canyon itself, in the low groove below the speckled, gold-sparkling heights which towered beyond. Then again they dipped and crossed stream, the horses stepping gingerly across a tangle of fallen, frail aspen stems, then suddenly floundering in a mass of rocks. The black emerged ahead, his black tail waving. The Princess let her mare find her own footing; then she too emerged from the clatter. She rode on after the black. Then came a great frantic rattle of the buckskin behind. The Princess was aware of Romero's dark face looking round, with a strange, demon-like watchfulness, before she herself looked round, to see the buckskin scrambling rather lamely beyond the rocks, with one of his pale buff knees already red with blood.

"He almost went down!" called Miss Cummins.

But Romero was already out of the saddle and hastening down the path. He made quiet little noises to the buckskin, and began examining the cut knee.

"Is he hurt?" cried Miss Cummins anxiously, and she climbed hastily down.

"Oh, my goodness!" she cried, as she saw the blood running down the slender buff leg of the horse in a thin trickle. "Isn't that *awful?*" She spoke in a stricken voice, and her face was white.

Romero was still carefully feeling the knee of the buckskin. Then he made him walk a few paces. And at last he stood up straight and shook his head.

"Not very bad!" he said. "Nothing broken."

Again he bent and worked at the knee. Then he looked up at the Princess.

"He can go on," he said. "It's not bad."

The Princess looked down at the dark face in silence.

" What, go on right up here ? " cried Miss Cummins. " How many hours ? "

" About five," said Romero simply.

" Five hours ! " cried Miss Cummins. " A horse with a lame knee ! And a steep mountain ! Why-y ! "

" Yes, it's pretty steep up there," said Romero, pushing back his hat and staring fixedly at the bleeding knee. The buckskin stood in a stricken sort of dejection. " But I think he'll make it all right," the man added.

" Oh ! " cried Miss Cummins, her eyes bright with sudden passion of unshed tears. " I wouldn't think of it. I wouldn't ride him up there, not for any money."

" Why wouldn't you ? " asked Romero.

" It *hurts* him."

Romero bent down again to the horse's knee.

" Maybe it hurts him a little," he said. " But he can make it all right, and his leg won't get stiff."

" What ! Ride him five hours up the steep mountains ? " cried Miss Cummins. " I couldn't. I just couldn't do it. I'll lead him a little way and see if he can go. But I *couldn't* ride him again. I couldn't. Let me walk."

" But Miss Cummins, dear, if Romero says he'll be all right ? " said the Princess.

" I know it hurts him. Oh, I just couldn't bear it."

There was no doing anything with Miss Cummins. The thought of a hurt animal always put her into a sort of hysterics.

They walked forward a little, leading the buckskin. He limped rather badly. Miss Cummins sat on a rock.

" Why, it's agony to see him ! " she cried. " It's *cruel !* "

" He won't limp after a bit, if you take no notice of him," said Romero. " Now he plays up, and limps very much, because he wants to make you see."

" I don't think there can be much playing up," said Miss Cummins bitterly. " We can *see* how it must hurt him."

" It don't hurt much," said Romero.

But now Miss Cummins was silent with antipathy.

It was a deadlock. The party remained motionless on the trail, the Princess in the saddle, Miss Cummins seated on a rock, Romero standing black and remote near the drooping buckskin.

" Well ! " said the man suddenly at last. " I guess we go back, then."

And he looked up swiftly at his horse, which was cropping at the mountain herbage and treading on the trailing reins.

"No!" cried the Princess. "Oh no!" Her voice rang with a great wail of disappointment and anger. Then she checked herself.

Miss Cummins rose with energy.

"Let me lead the buckskin home," she said, with cold dignity, "and you two go on."

This was received in silence. The Princess was looking down at her with a sardonic, almost cruel gaze.

"We've only come about two hours," said Miss Cummins. "I don't mind a bit leading him home. But I *couldn't* ride him. I *couldn't* have him ridden with that knee."

This again was received in dead silence. Romero remained impassive, almost inert.

"Very well, then," said the Princess. "You lead him home. You'll be quite all right. Nothing can happen to you, possibly. And say to them that we have gone on and shall be home to-morrow —or the day after."

She spoke coldly and distinctly. For she could not bear to be thwarted.

"Better all go back, and come again another day," said Romero —non-committal.

"There will never *be* another day," cried the Princess. "I want to go on."

She looked at him square in the eyes, and met the spark in his eye.

He raised his shoulders slightly.

"If you want it," he said. "I'll go on with you. But Miss Cummins can ride my horse to the end of the canyon, and I lead the buckskin. Then I come back to you."

It was arranged so. Miss Cummins had her saddle put on Romero's black horse, Romero took the buckskin's bridle, and they started back. The Princess rode very slowly on, upwards, alone. She was at first so angry with Miss Cummins that she was blind to everything else. She just let her mare follow her own inclinations.

The peculiar spell of anger carried the Princess on, almost unconscious, for an hour or so. And by this time she was beginning to climb pretty high. Her horse walked steadily all the time. They emerged on a bare slope, and the trail wound through frail aspenstems. Here a wind swept, and some of the aspens were already bare. Others were fluttering their discs of pure, solid yellow leaves, so *nearly* like petals, while the slope ahead was one soft, glowing fleece of daffodil yellow ; fleecy like a golden foxskin, and yellow as daffodils alive in the wind and the high mountain sun.

She paused and looked back. The near great slopes were mottled with gold and the dark hue of spruce, like some unsinged eagle, and the light lay gleaming upon them. Away through the gap of the canyon she could see the pale blue of the egg-like desert, with the crumpled dark crack of the Rio Grande Canyon. And far, far off, the blue mountains like a fence of angels on the horizon.

And she thought of her adventure. She was going on alone with Romero. But then she was very sure of herself, and Romero was not the kind of man to do anything to her against her will. This was her first thought. And she just had a fixed desire to go over the brim of the mountains, to look into the inner chaos of the Rockies. And she wanted to go with Romero, because he had some peculiar kinship with her ; there was some peculiar link between the two of them. Miss Cummins anyhow would have been only a discordant note.

She rode on, and emerged at length in the lap of the summit. Beyond her was a great concave of stone and stark, dead-grey trees, where the mountain ended against the sky. But nearer was the dense black, bristling spruce, and at her feet was the lap of the summit, a flat little valley of sere grass and quiet-standing yellow aspens, the stream trickling like a thread across.

It was a little valley or shell from which the stream was gently poured into the lower rocks and trees of the canyon. Around her was a fairy-like gentleness, the delicate sere grass, the groves of delicate-stemmed aspens dropping their flakes of bright yellow. And the delicate, quick little stream threading through the wild, sere grass.

Here one might expect deer and fawns and wild things, as in a little paradise. Here she was to wait for Romero, and they were to have lunch.

She unfastened her saddle and pulled it to the ground with a crash, letting her horse wander with a long rope. How beautiful Tansy looked, sorrel, among the yellow leaves that lay like a patina on the sere ground. The Princess herself wore a fleecy sweater of a pale, sere buff, like the grass, and riding breeches of a pure orange-tawny colour. She felt quite in the picture.

From her saddle pouches she took the packages of lunch, spread a little cloth, and sat to wait for Romero. Then she made a little fire. Then she ate a devilled egg. Then she ran after Tansy, who was straying across-stream. Then she sat in the sun, in the stillness near the aspens, and waited.

The sky was blue. Her little alp was soft and delicate as fairy-land. But beyond and up jutted the great slopes, dark with the pointed feathers of spruce, bristling with grey dead trees among grey rock, or dappled with dark and gold. The beautiful, but fierce, heavy, cruel mountains, with their moments of tenderness.

She saw Tansy start, and begin to run. Two ghost-like figures on horseback emerged from the black of the spruce across the stream. It was two Indians on horseback, swathed like seated mummies in their pale-grey cotton blankets. Their guns jutted beyond the saddles. They rode straight towards her, to her thread of smoke.

As they came near, they unswathed themselves and greeted her, looking at her curiously from their dark eyes. Their black hair was somewhat untidy, the long rolled plaits on their shoulders were soiled. They looked tired.

They got down from their horses near her little fire—a camp was a camp—swathed their blankets round their hips, pulled the saddles from their ponies and turned them loose, then sat down. One was a young Indian whom she had met before, the other was an older man.

" You all alone ? " said the younger man.

"Romero will be here in a minute," she said, glancing back along the trail.

" Ah, Romero ! You with him ? Where are you going ? "

" Round the ridge," she said. " Where are you going ? "

" We going down to Pueblo."

" Been out hunting ? How long have you been out ? "

" Yes. Been out five days." The young Indian gave a little meaningless laugh.

" Got anything ? "

" No. We see tracks of two deer—but not got nothing."

The Princess noticed a suspicious-looking bulk under one of the saddles—surely a folded-up deer. But she said nothing.

" You must have been cold," she said.

" Yes, very cold in the night. And hungry. Got nothing to eat since yesterday. Eat it all up." And again he laughed his little meaningless laugh. Under their dark skins, the two men looked peaked and hungry. The Princess rummaged for food among the saddle-bags. There was a lump of bacon—the regular stand-back— and some bread. She gave them this, and they began toasting slices of it on long sticks at the fire. Such was the little camp Romero saw as he rode down the slope : the Princess in her orange breeches, her head tied in a blue-and-brown silk kerchief, sitting opposite the

two dark-headed Indians across the camp-fire, while one of the
Indians was leaning forward toasting bacon, his two plaits of braid-
swathed hair dangling as if wearily.

Romero rode up, his face expressionless. The Indians greeted him
in Spanish. He unsaddled his horse, took food from the bags, and
sat down at the camp to eat. The Princess went to the stream for
water, and to wash her hands.

" Got coffee ? " asked the Indians.

" No coffee this outfit," said Romero.

They lingered an hour or more in the warm midday sun. Then
Romero saddled the horses. The Indians still squatted by the fire.
Romero and the Princess rode away, calling *Adios !* to the Indians,
over the stream and into the dense spruce whence the two strange
figures had emerged.

When they were alone, Romero turned and looked at her curiously,
in a way she could not understand, with such a hard glint in his eyes.
And for the first time she wondered if she was rash.

" I hope you don't mind going alone with me," she said.

" If you want it," he replied.

They emerged at the foot of the great bare slope of rocky summit,
where dead spruce-trees stood sparse and bristling like bristles on
a grey dead hog. Romero said the Mexicans, twenty years back, had
fired the mountains, to drive out the whites. This grey concave
slope of summit was corpse-like.

The trail was almost invisible. Romero watched for the trees
which the Forest Service had blazed. And they climbed the stark
corpse slope, among dead spruce, fallen and ash-grey, into the wind.
The wind came rushing from the west, up the funnel of the canyon,
from the desert. And there was the desert, like a vast mirage tilting
slowly upwards towards the west, immense and pallid, away beyond
the funnel of the canyon. The Princess could hardly look.

For an hour their horses rushed the slope, hastening with a great
working of the haunches upwards, and halting to breathe, scrambling
again, and rowing their way up length by length, on the livid,
slanting wall. While the wind blew like some vast machine.

After an hour they were working their way on the incline, no
longer forcing straight up. All was grey and dead around them ;
the horses picked their way over the silver-grey corpses of the spruce.
But they were near the top, near the ridge.

Even the horses made a rush for the last bit. They had worked
round to a scrap of spruce forest near the very top. They hurried
in, out of the huge, monstrous, mechanical wind, that whistled

inhumanly and was palely cold. So, stepping through the dark screen of trees, they emerged over the crest.

In front now was nothing but mountains, ponderous, massive, down-sitting mountains, in a huge and intricate knot, empty of life or soul. Under the bristling black feathers of spruce nearby lay patches of white snow. The lifeless valleys were concaves of rock and spruce, the rounded summits and the hog-backed summits of grey rock crowded one behind the other like some monstrous herd in arrest.

It frightened the Princess, it was *so* inhuman. She had not thought it could be so inhuman, so, as it were, anti-life. And yet now one of her desires was fulfilled. She had seen it, the massive, gruesome, repellent core of the Rockies. She saw it there beneath her eyes, in its gigantic, heavy gruesomeness.

And she wanted to go back. At this moment she wanted to turn back. She had looked down into the intestinal knot of these mountains. She was frightened. She wanted to go back.

But Romero was riding on, on the lee side of the spruce forest, above the concaves of the inner mountains. He turned round to her and pointed at the slope with a dark hand.

" Here a miner has been trying for gold," he said. It was a grey, scratched-out heap near a hole—like a great badger hole. And it looked quite fresh.

" Quite lately ? " said the Princess.

" No, long ago—twenty, thirty years." He had reined in his horse and was looking at the mountains. "Look ! " he said. " There goes the Forest Service trail—along those ridges, on the top, way over there till it comes to Lucytown, where is the Government road. We go down there—no trail—see behind that mountain—you see the top, no trees, and some grass ? "

His arm was lifted, his brown hand pointing, his dark eyes piercing into the distance, as he sat on his black horse twisting round to her. Strange and ominous, only the demon of himself, he seemed to her. She was dazed and a little sick, at that height, and she could not see any more. Only she saw an eagle turning in the air beyond, and the light from the west showed the pattern on him underneath.

" Shall I ever be able to go so far ? " asked the Princess faintly, petulantly.

" Oh yes ! All easy now. No more hard places."

They worked along the ridge, up and down, keeping on the lee side, the inner side, in the dark shadow. It was cold. Then the trail laddered up again, and they emerged on a narrow ridge-track, with the mountain slipping away enormously on either side. The Princess was afraid. For one moment she looked out, and saw the desert, the desert ridges, more desert, more blue ridges, shining pale and very vast, far below, vastly palely tilting to the western horizon. It was ethereal and terrifying in its gleaming, pale, half-burnished immensity, tilted at the west. She could not bear it. To the left was the ponderous, involved mass of mountains all kneeling heavily.

She closed her eyes and let her consciousness evaporate away. The mare followed the trail. So on and on, in the wind again.

They turned their backs to the wind, facing inwards to the mountains. She thought they had left the trail; it was quite invisible.

" No," he said, lifting his hand and pointing. " Don't you see the blazed trees ? "

And making an effort of consciousness, she was able to perceive on a pale-grey dead spruce stem the old marks where an axe had chipped a piece away. But with the height, the cold, the wind, her brain was numb.

They turned again and began to descend ; he told her they had left the trail. The horses slithered in the loose stones, picking their way downward. It was afternoon, the sun stood obtrusive and gleaming in the lower heavens—about four o'clock. The horses went steadily, slowly, but obstinately onwards. The air was getting colder. They were in among the lumpish peaks and steep concave valleys. She was barely conscious at all of Romero.

He dismounted and came to help her from her saddle. She tottered, but would not betray her feebleness.

" We must slide down here," he said. " I can lead the horses."

They were on a ridge, and facing a steep bare slope of pallid, tawny mountain grass on which the western sun shone full. It was steep and concave. The Princess felt she might start slipping, and go down like a toboggan into the great hollow.

But she pulled herself together. Her eye blazed up again with excitement and determination. A wind rushed past her ; she could hear the shriek of spruce trees far below. Bright spots came on her cheeks as her hair blew across. She looked a wild, fairy-like little thing.

" No," she said. " I will take my horse."

" Then mind she doesn't slip down on top of you," said Romero. And away he went, nimbly dropping down the pale, steep incline, making from rock to rock, down the grass, and following any little slanting groove. His horse hopped and slithered after him, and sometimes stopped dead, with forefeet pressed back, refusing to go further. He, below his horse, looked up and pulled the reins gently, and encouraged the creature. Then the horse once more dropped his forefeet with a jerk, and the descent continued.

The Princess set off in blind, reckless pursuit, tottering and yet nimble. And Romero, looking constantly back to see how she was faring, saw her fluttering down like some queer little bird, her orange breeches twinkling like the legs of some duck, and her head, tied in the blue and buff kerchief, bound round and round like the head of some blue-topped bird. The sorrel mare rocked and slipped behind her. But down came the Princess in a reckless intensity, a tiny, vivid spot on the great hollow flank of the tawny mountain. So tiny! Tiny as a frail bird's egg. It made Romero's mind go blank with wonder.

But they had to get down, out of that cold and dragging wind. The spruce trees stood below, where a tiny stream emerged in stones. Away plunged Romero, zigzagging down. And away behind, up the slope, fluttered the tiny, bright-coloured Princess, holding the end of the long reins, and leading the lumbering, four-footed, sliding mare.

At last they were down. Romero sat in the sun, below the wind, beside some squaw-berry bushes. The Princess came near, the colour flaming in her cheeks, her eyes dark blue, much darker than the kerchief on her head, and glowing unnaturally.

"We make it," said Romero.

"Yes," said the Princess, dropping the reins and subsiding on to the grass, unable to speak, unable to think.

But, thank heaven, they were out of the wind and in the sun.

In a few minutes her consciousness and her control began to come back. She drank a little water. Romero was attending to the saddles. Then they set off again, leading the horses still a little further down the tiny stream-bed. Then they could mount.

They rode down a bank and into a valley grove dense with aspens. Winding through the thin, crowding, pale-smooth stems, the sun shone flickering beyond them, and the disc-like aspen leaves, waving queer mechanical signals, seemed to be splashing the gold light before her eyes. She rode on in a splashing dazzle of gold.

Then they entered shadow and the dark, resinous spruce trees. The fierce boughs always wanted to sweep her off her horse. She had to twist and squirm past.

But there was a semblance of an old trail. And all at once they emerged in the sun on the edge of the spruce-grove, and there was a little cabin, and the bottom of a small, naked valley with grey rock and heaps of stones, and a round pool of intense green water, dark green. The sun was just about to leave it.

Indeed, as she stood, the shadow came over the cabin and over herself; they were in the lower gloom, a twilight. Above, the heights still blazed.

It was a little hole of a cabin, near the spruce trees, with an earthen floor and an unhinged door. There was a wooden bed-bunk, three old sawn-off log-lengths to sit on as stools, and a sort of fire-place; no room for anything else. The little hole would hardly contain two people. The roof had gone—but Romero had laid on thick spruce-boughs.

The strange squalor of the primitive forest pervaded the place, the squalor of animals and their droppings, the squalor of the wild. The Princess knew the peculiar repulsiveness of it. She was tired and faint.

Romero hastily got a handful of twigs, set a little fire going in the stove grate, and went out to attend to the horses. The Princess vaguely, mechanically, put sticks on the fire, in a sort of stupor, watching the blaze, stupefied and fascinated. She could not make much fire—it would set the whole cabin alight. And smoke oozed out of the dilapidated mud-and-stone chimney.

When Romero came in with the saddle-pouches and saddles, hanging the saddles on the wall, there sat the little Princess on her stump of wood in front of the dilapidated fire-grate, warming her tiny hands at the blaze, while her orange breeches glowed almost like another fire. She was in a sort of stupor.

" You have some whisky now, or some tea? Or wait for some soup ? " he asked.

She rose and looked at him with bright, dazed eyes, half comprehending; the colour glowing hectic in her cheeks.

" Some tea," she said, " with a little whisky in it. Where's the kettle ? "

" Wait," he said. " I'll bring the things."

She took her cloak from the back of her saddle, and followed him into the open. It was a deep cup of shadow. But above the sky was still shining, and the heights of the mountains were blazing with aspen like fire blazing.

Their horses were cropping the grass among the stones. Romero clambered up a heap of grey stones and began lifting away logs and rocks, till he had opened the mouth of one of the miner's little old workings. This was his cache. He brought out bundles of blankets, pans for cooking, a little petrol camp-stove, an axe, the regular camp outfit. He seemed so quick and energetic and full of force. This quick force dismayed the Princess a little.

She took a saucepan and went down the stones to the water. It was very still and mysterious, and of a deep green colour, yet pure, transparent as glass. How cold the place was ! How mysterious and fearful.

She crouched in her dark cloak by the water, rinsing the saucepan, feeling the cold heavy above her, the shadow like a vast weight upon her, bowing her down. The sun was leaving the mountain tops, departing, leaving her under profound shadow. Soon it would crush her down completely.

Sparks ? Or eyes looking at her across the water ? She gazed, hypnotized. And with her sharp eyes she made out in the dusk the pale form of a bob-cat crouching by the water's edge, pale as the stones among which it crouched, opposite. And it was watching her with cold, electric eyes of strange intentness, a sort of cold, icy wonder and fearlessness. She saw its *museau* pushed forward, its tufted ears pricking intensely up. It was watching her with cold, animal curiosity, something demonish and conscienceless.

She made a swift movement, spilling her water. And in a flash the creature was gone, leaping like a cat that is escaping ; but strange and soft in its motion, with its little bob-tail. Rather fascinating. Yet that cold, intent, demonish watching ! She shivered with cold and fear. She knew well enough the dread and repulsiveness of the wild.

Romero carried in the bundles of bedding and the camp outfit. The windowless cabin was already dark inside. He lit a lantern, and then went out again with the axe. She heard him chopping wood as she fed sticks to the fire under her water. When he came in with an armful of oak-scrub faggots, she had just thrown the tea into the water.

" Sit down," she said, " and drink tea."

He poured a little bootleg whisky into the enamel cups, and in the silence the two sat on the log-ends, sipping the hot liquid and coughing occasionally from the smoke.

"We burn these oak sticks," he said. " They don't make hardly any smoke."

Curious and remote he was, saying nothing except what had to be said. And she, for her part, was as remote from him. They seemed far, far apart, worlds apart, now they were so near.

He unwrapped one bundle of bedding, and spread the blankets and the sheepskin in the wooden bunk.

" You lie down and rest," he said, " and I make the supper."

She decided to do so. Wrapping her cloak round her, she lay down in the bunk, turning her face to the wall. She could hear him preparing supper over the little petrol stove. Soon she could smell the soup he was heating ; and soon she heard the hissing of fried chicken in a pan.

" You eat your supper now ? " he said.

With a jerky, despairing movement, she sat up in the bunk, tossing back her hair. She felt cornered.

" Give it me here," she said.

He handed her first the cupful of soup. She sat among the blankets, eating it slowly. She was hungry. Then he gave her an enamel plate with pieces of fried chicken and currant jelly, butter and bread. It was very good. As they ate the chicken he made the coffee. She said never a word. A certain resentment filled her. She was cornered.

When supper was over he washed the dishes, dried them, and put everything away carefully, else there would have been no room to move in the hole of a cabin. The oak-wood gave out a good bright heat.

He stood for a few moments at a loss. Then he asked her :

" You want to go to bed soon ? "

" Soon," she said. " Where are you going to sleep ? "

" I make my bed here——" he pointed to the floor along the wall. " Too cold out of doors."

" Yes," she said. " I suppose it is."

She sat immobile, her cheeks hot, full of conflicting thoughts. And she watched him while he folded the blankets on the floor, a sheepskin underneath. Then she went out into the night.

The stars were big. Mars sat on the edge of a mountain, for all the world like the blazing eye of a crouching mountain lion. But she herself was deep, deep below in a pit of shadow. In the intense silence she seemed to hear the spruce forest crackling with electricity and cold. Strange, foreign stars floated on that unmoving water. The night was going to freeze. Over the hills came the far sobbing-singing howling of the coyotes. She wondered how the horses would be.

Shuddering a little, she turned to the cabin. Warm light showed through its chinks. She pushed at the rickety, half-opened door.

" What about the horses ? " she said.

" My black, he won't go away. And your mare will stay with him. You want to go to bed now ? "

" I think I do."

" All right. I feed the horses some oats."

And he went out into the night.

He did not come back for some time. She was lying wrapped up tight in the bunk.

He blew out the lantern, and sat down on his bedding to take off his clothes. She lay with her back turned. And soon, in the silence, she was asleep.

She dreamed it was snowing, and the snow was falling on her through the roof, softly, softly, helplessly, and she was going to be buried alive. She was growing colder and colder, the snow was weighing down on her. The snow was going to absorb her.

She awoke with a sudden convulsion, like pain. She was really very cold ; perhaps the heavy blankets had numbed her. Her heart seemed unable to beat, she felt she could not move.

With another convulsion she sat up. It was intensely dark. There was not even a spark of fire, the light wood had burned right away. She sat in thick oblivious darkness. Only through a chink she could see a star.

What did she want ? Oh, what did she want ? She sat in bed and rocked herself woefully. She could hear the steady breathing of the sleeping man. She was shivering with cold ; her heart seemed as if it could not beat. She wanted warmth, protection, she wanted to be taken away from herself. And at the same time, perhaps more deeply than anything, she wanted to keep herself intact, intact, untouched, that no one should have any power over her, or rights to her. It was a wild necessity in her that no one, particularly no man, should have any rights or power over her, that no one and nothing should possess her.

Yet that other thing ! And she was so cold, so shivering, and her heart could not beat. Oh, would not someone help her heart to beat ?

She tried to speak, and could not. Then she cleared her throat.

" Romero," she said strangely, " it is so cold."

Where did her voice come from, and whose voice was it, in the dark ?

She heard him at once sit up, and his voice, startled, with a resonance that seemed to vibrate against her, saying :

" You want me to make you warm ? "

" Yes."

As soon as he had lifted her in his arms, she wanted to scream to him not to touch her. She stiffened herself. Yet she was dumb.

And he was warm, but with a terrible animal warmth that seemed to annihilate her. He panted like an animal with desire. And she was given over to this thing.

She had never, never wanted to be given over to this. But she had *willed* that it should happen to her. And according to her will, she lay and let it happen. But she never wanted it. She never wanted to be thus assailed and handled, and mauled. She wanted to keep herself to herself.

However, she had willed it to happen, and it had happened. She panted with relief when it was over.

Yet even now she had to lie within the hard, powerful clasp of this other creature, this man. She dreaded to struggle to go away. She dreaded almost too much the icy cold of that other bunk.

" Do you want to go away from me ? " asked his strange voice. Oh, if it could only have been a thousand miles away from her ! Yet she had willed to have it thus close.

" No," she said.

And she could feel a curious joy and pride surging up again in him : at her expense. Because he had got her. She felt like a victim there. And he was exulting in his power over her, his possession, his pleasure.

When dawn came, he was fast asleep. She sat up suddenly.

" I want a fire," she said.

He opened his brown eyes wide, and smiled with a curious tender luxuriousness.

" I want you to make a fire," she said.

He glanced at the chinks of light. His brown face hardened to the day.

" All right," he said. " I'll make it."

She hid her face while he dressed. She could not bear to look at him. He was so suffused with pride and luxury. She hid her face almost in despair. But feeling the cold blast of air as he opened the door, she wriggled down into the warm place where he had been. How soon the warmth ebbed, when he had gone !

He made a fire and went out, returning after a while with water.

" You stay in bed till the sun comes," he said. " It very cold."

" Hand me my cloak."

She wrapped the cloak fast round her, and sat up among the blankets. The warmth was already spreading from the fire.

" I suppose we will start back as soon as we've had breakfast ? "

He was crouching at his camp-stove making scrambled eggs. He looked up suddenly, transfixed, and his brown eyes, so soft and luxuriously widened, looked straight at her.

" You want to ? " he said.

" We'd better get back as soon as possible," she said, turning aside from his eyes.

" You want to get away from me ? " he asked, repeating the question of the night in a sort of dread.

" I want to get away from here," she said decisively. And it was true. She wanted supremely to get away, back to the world of people.

He rose slowly to his feet, holding the aluminium frying-pan.

" Don't you like last night ? " he asked.

" Not really," she said. " Why ? Do you ? "

He put down the frying-pan and stood staring at the wall. She could see she had given him a cruel blow. But she did not relent. She was getting her own back. She wanted to regain possession of all herself, and in some mysterious way she felt that he possessed some part of her still.

He looked round at her slowly, his face greyish and heavy.

" You Americans," he said, " you always want to do a man down."

" I am not American," she said. " I am British. And I don't want to do any man down. I only want to go go back, now."

" And what will you say about me, down there ? "

" That you were very kind to me, and very good."

He crouched down again, and went on turning the eggs. He gave her her plate, and her coffee, and sat down to his own food.

But again he seemed not to be able to swallow. He looked up at her.

" You don't like last night ? " he asked.

" Not really," she said, though with some difficulty. " I don't care for that kind of thing."

A blank sort of wonder spread over his face, at these words, followed immediately by a black look of anger, and than a stony, sinister despair.

" You don't ? " he said, looking her in the eyes.

" Not really," she replied, looking back with steady hostility into his eyes.

Then a dark flame seemed to come from his face.

" I make you," he said, as if to himself.

He rose and reached her clothes, that hung on a peg : the fine linen underwear, the orange breeches, the fleecy jumper, the blue-

and-buff kerchief ; then he took up her riding boots and her bead
moccasins. Crushing everything in his arms, he opened the door.
Sitting up, she saw him stride down to the dark-green pool in the
frozen shadow of that deep cup of a valley. He tossed the clothing
and the boots out on the pool. Ice had formed. And on the pure,
dark green mirror, in the slaty shadow, the Princess saw her things
lying, the white linen, the orange breeches, the black boots, the blue
moccasins, a tangled heap of colour. Romero picked up rocks and
heaved them out at the ice, till the surface broke and the fluttering
clothing disappeared in the rattling water, while the valley echoed
and shouted again with the sound.

She sat in despair among the blankets, hugging tight her pale-
blue cloak. Romero strode straight back to the cabin.

" Now you stay here with me," he said.

She was furious. Her blue eyes met his. They were like two
demons watching one another. In his face, beyond a sort of
unrelieved gloom, was a demonish desire for death.

He saw her looking round the cabin, scheming. He saw her eyes
on his rifle. He took the gun and went out with it. Returning, he
pulled out her saddle, carried it to the tarn, and threw it in. Then
he fetched his own saddle, and did the same.

" Now will you go away ? " he said, looking at her with a
smile.

She debated within herself whether to coax him and wheedle him.
But she knew he was already beyond it. She sat among her blankets
in a frozen sort of despair, hard as hard ice with anger.

He did the chores, and disappeared with the gun. She got up in
her blue pyjamas, huddled in her cloak, and stood in the doorway.
The dark-green pool was motionless again, the stony slopes were
pallid and frozen. Shadow still lay, like an after-death, deep in this
valley. Always in the distance she saw the horses feeding. If she
could catch one ! The brilliant yellow sun was half-way down the
mountain. It was nine o'clock.

All day she was alone, and she was frightened. What she was
frightened of she didn't know. Perhaps the crackling in the dark
spruce wood. Perhaps just the savage, heartless wildness of the
mountains. But all day she sat in the sun in the doorway of the
cabin, watching, watching for hope. And all the time her bowels
were cramped with fear.

She saw a dark spot that probably was a bear, roving across the
pale grassy slope in the far distance, in the sun.

When, in the afternoon, she saw Romero approaching, with silent suddenness, carrying his gun and a dead deer, the cramp in her bowels relaxed, then became colder. She dreaded him with a cold dread.

"There is deer-meat," he said, throwing the dead doe at her feet.

"You don't want to go away from here," he said. "This is a nice place."

She shrank into the cabin.

"Come into the sun," he said, following her. She looked up at him with hostile, frightened eyes.

"Come into the sun," he repeated, taking her gently by the arm, in a powerful grasp.

She knew it was useless to rebel. Quietly he led her out, and seated himself in the doorway, holding her still by the arm.

"In the sun it is warm," he said. "Look, this is a nice place. You are such a pretty white woman, why do you want to act mean to me? Isn't this a nice place? Come! Come here! It is sure warm here."

He drew her to him, and in spite of her stony resistance, he took her cloak from her, holding her in her thin blue pyjamas.

"You sure are a pretty little white woman, small and pretty," he said. "You sure won't act mean to me—you don't want to, I know you don't."

She, stony and powerless, had to submit to him. The sun shone on her white, delicate skin.

"I sure don't mind hell fire," he said. "After this."

A queer, luxurious good-humour seemed to possess him again. But though outwardly she was powerless, inwardly she resisted him, absolutely and stonily.

When later he was leaving her again, she said to him suddenly:

"You think you can conquer me this way. But you can't. You can never conquer me."

He stood arrested, looking back at her, with many emotions conflicting in his face—wonder, surprise, a touch of horror, and an unconscious pain that crumpled his face till it was like a mask. Then he went out without saying a word, hung the dead deer on a bough, and started to flay it. While he was at this butcher's work, the sun sank and cold night came on again.

"You see," he said to her as he crouched, cooking the supper, "I ain't going to let you go. I reckon you called to me in the night, and I've some right. If you want to fix it up right now with me, and say you want to be with me, we'll fix it up now and go down to the ranch to-morrow and get married or whatever you want. But you've got to say you want to be with me. Else I shall stay right here, till something happens."

She waited a while before she answered :

" I don't want to be with anybody against my will. I don't dislike you ; at least, I didn't, till you tried to put your will over mine. I won't have anybody's will put over me. You can't succeed. Nobody could. You can never get me under your will. And you won't have long to try, because soon they will send someone to look for me."

He pondered this last, and she regretted having said it. Then, sombre, he bent to the cooking again.

He could not conquer her, however much he violated her. Because her spirit was hard and flawless as a diamond. But he could shatter her. This she knew. Much more, and she would be shattered.

In a sombre, violent excess he tried to expend his desire for her. And she was racked with agony, and felt each time she would die. Because, in some peculiar way, he had got hold of her, some unrealized part of her which she never wished to realize. Racked with a burning, tearing anguish, she felt that the thread of her being would break, and she would die. The burning heat that racked her inwardly.

If only, only she could be alone again, cool and intact ! If only she could recover herself again, cool and intact ! Would she ever, ever, ever be able to bear herself again ?

Even now she did not hate him. It was beyond that. Like some racking, hot doom. Personally he hardly existed.

The next day he would not let her have any fire, because of attracting attention with the smoke. It was a grey day, and she was cold. He stayed around, and heated soup on the petrol stove. She lay motionless in the blankets.

And in the afternoon she pulled the clothes over her head and broke into tears. She had never really cried in her life. He dragged the blankets away and looked to see what was shaking her. She sobbed in helpless hysterics. He covered her over again and went outside, looking at the mountains, where clouds were dragging and leaving a little snow. It was a violent, windy, horrible day, the evil of winter rushing down.

She cried for hours. And after this a great silence came between them. They were two people who had died. He did not touch her any more. In the night she lay and shivered like a dying dog. She felt that her very shivering would rupture something in her body, and she would die.

At last she had to speak.

" Could you make a fire ? I am so cold," she said, with chattering teeth.

" Want to come over here ? " came his voice.

" I would rather you made me a fire," she said, her teeth knocking together and chopping the words in two.

He got up and kindled a fire. At last the warmth spread, and she could sleep.

The next day was still chilly, with some wind. But the sun shone. He went about in silence, with a dead-looking face. It was now so dreary and so like death she wished he would do anything rather than continue in this negation. If now he asked her to go down with him to the world and marry him, she would do it. What did it matter ? Nothing mattered any more.

But he would not ask her. His desire was dead and heavy like ice within him. He kept watch around the house.

On the fourth day as she sat huddled in the doorway in the sun, hugged in a blanket, she saw two horsemen come over the crest of the grassy slope—small figures. She gave a cry. He looked up quickly and saw the figures. The men had dismounted. They were looking for the trail.

" They are looking for me," she said.

" Muy bien," he answered in Spanish.

He went and fetched his gun, and sat with it across his knees.

" Oh ! " she said. " Don't shoot ! "

He looked across at her.

" Why ? " he said. " You like staying with me ? "

" No," she said. " But don't shoot."

" I ain't going to Pen," he said.

" You won't have to go to Pen," she said. " Don't shoot ! "

" I'm going to shoot," he muttered.

And straightaway he kneeled and took very careful aim. The Princess sat on in an agony of helplessness and hopelessness.

The shot rang out. In an instant she saw one of the horses on the pale grassy slope rear and go rolling down. The man had dropped in the grass, and was invisible. The second man clambered on his horse, and on that precipitous place went at a gallop in a long swerve towards the nearest spruce-tree cover. Bang ! Bang ! went Romero's shots. But each time he missed, and the running horse leaped like a kangaroo towards cover.

It was hidden. Romero now got behind a rock ; tense silence, in the brilliant sunshine. The Princess sat on the bunk inside the cabin, crouching, paralysed. For hours, it seemed, Romero knelt behind this rock, in his black shirt, bare-headed, watching. He had a beautiful, alert figure. The Princess wondered why she did not feel sorry for him. But her spirit was hard and cold, her heart could not melt. Though now she would have called him to her, with love.

But no, she did not love him. She would never love any man. Never ! It was fixed and sealed in her, almost vindictively.

Suddenly she was so startled she almost fell from the bunk. A shot rang out quite close from behind the cabin. Romero leaped straight into the air, his arms fell outstretched, turning as he leaped. And even while he was in the air, a second shot rang out, and he fell with a crash, squirming, his hands clutching the earth towards the cabin door.

The Princess sat absolutely motionless, transfixed, staring at the prostrate figure. In a few moments the figure of a man in the Forest Service appeared close to the house ; a young man in a broad-brimmed Stetson hat, dark flannel shirt, and riding-boots, carrying a gun. He strode over to the prostrate figure.

" Got you, Romero ! " he said aloud. And he turned the dead man over. There was already a little pool of blood where Romero's breast had been.

" H'm ! " said the Forest Service man. " Guess I got you nearer than I thought."

And he squatted there, staring at the dead man.

The distant calling of his comrade aroused him. He stood up.

" Hullo, Bill ! " he shouted. " Yep ! Got him ! Yep ! Done him in, apparently."

The second man rode out of the forest on a grey horse. He had a ruddy, kind face, and round brown eyes, dilated with dismay.

" He's not passed out ? " he asked anxiously.

" Looks like it," said the first young man, coolly.

The second dismounted and bent over the body. Then he stood up again, and nodded.

" Yea-a ! " he said. " He's done in all right. It's him all right, boy ! It's Domingo Romero."

" Yep ! I know it ! " replied the other.

Then in perplexity he turned and looked into the cabin, where the Princess squatted, staring with big owl eyes from her red blanket.

" Hello ! " he said, coming towards the hut. And he took his hat off. Oh, the sense of ridicule she felt ! Though he did not mean any.

But she could not speak, no matter what she felt.

"What'd this man start firing for?" he asked.

She fumbled for words, with numb lips.

"He had gone out of his mind!" she said, with solemn, stammering conviction.

"Good Lord! You mean to say he'd gone out of his mind? Whew! That's pretty awful! That explains it then. H'm!"

He accepted the explanation without more ado.

With some difficulty they succeeded in getting the Princess down to the ranch. But she, too, was not a little mad.

"I'm not quite sure where I am," she said to Mrs. Wilkieson, as she lay in bed. "Do you mind explaining?"

Mrs. Wilkieson explained tactfully.

"Oh, yes!" said the Princess. "I remember. And I had an accident in the mountains, didn't I? Didn't we meet a man who'd gone mad, and who shot my horse from under me?"

"Yes, you met a man who had gone out of his mind."

The real affair was hushed up. The Princess departed east in a fortnight's time, in Miss Cummins's care. Apparently she had recovered herself entirely. She was the Princess, and a virgin intact.

But her bobbed hair was grey at the temples, and her eyes were a little mad. She was slightly crazy.

"Since my accident in the mountains, when a man went mad and shot my horse from under me, and my guide had to shoot him dead, I have never felt quite myself."

So she put it.

Later, she married an elderly man, and seemed pleased.

THERE was a woman who loved her husband, but she could not
live with him. The husband, on his side, was sincerely attached to
his wife, yet he could not live with her. They were both under forty,
both handsome and both attractive. They had the most sincere
regard for one another, and felt, in some odd way, eternally married
to one another. They knew one another more intimately than they
knew anybody else, they felt more known to one another than to
any other person.

Yet they could not live together. Usually, they kept a thousand
miles apart, geographically. But when he sat in the greyness of
England, at the back of his mind, with a certain grim fidelity, he
was aware of his wife, her strange yearning to be loyal and faithful,
having her gallant affairs away in the sun, in the south. And she,
as she drank her cocktail on the terrace over the sea, and turned
her grey, sardonic eyes on the heavy dark face of her admirer, whom
she really liked quite a lot, she was actually preoccupied with the
clear-cut features of her handsome young husband, thinking of how
he would be asking his secretary to do something for him, asking in
that good-natured, confident voice of a man who knows that his
request will be only too gladly fulfilled.

The secretary, of course, adored him. She was *very* competent,
quite young, and quite good-looking. She adored him. But then
all his servants always did, particularly his women-servants. His
men-servants were likely to swindle him.

When a man has an adoring secretary, and you are the man's
wife, what are you to do ? Not that there was anything " wrong "
—if you know what I mean !—between them. Nothing you could
call adultery, to come down to brass tacks. No, no ! They were
just the young master and his secretary. He dictated to her, she
slaved for him and adored him, and the whole thing went on
wheels.

He didn't " adore " her. A man doesn't need to adore his
secretary. But he depended on her. " I simply rely on Miss
Wrexall." Whereas he could never rely on his wife. The one

thing he knew finally about *her* was that she didn't intend to be relied on.

So they remained friends, in the awful unspoken intimacy of the once-married. Usually each year they went away together for a holiday, and, if they had not been man and wife, they would have found a great deal of fun and stimulation in one another. The fact that they were married, had been married for the last dozen years, and couldn't live together for the last three or four, spoilt them for one another. Each had a private feeling of bitterness about the other.

However, they were awfully kind. He was the soul of generosity, and held her in real tender esteem, no matter how many gallant affairs she had. Her gallant affairs were part of her modern necessity. "After all, I've got to *live*. I can't turn into a pillar of salt in five minutes just because you and I can't live together! It takes years for a woman like me to turn into a pillar of salt. At least I hope so!"

"Quite!" he replied. "Quite! By all means put them in pickle, make pickled cucumbers of them, before you crystallize out. That's my advice."

He was like that: so awfully clever and enigmatic. She could more or less fathom the idea of the pickled cucumbers, but the "crystallizing out"—what did that signify?

And did he mean to suggest that he himself had been well pickled and that further immersion was for him unnecessary, would spoil his flavour? Was that what he meant? And herself, was she the brine and the vale of tears?

You never knew how catty a man was being, when he was really clever and enigmatic, withal a bit whimsical. He was adorably whimsical, with a twist of his flexible, vain mouth, that had a long upper lip, so fraught with vanity! But then a handsome, clear-cut, histrionic young man like that, how could he help being vain? The women made him so.

Ah, the women! How nice men would be if there were no other women!

And how nice the women would be if there were no other men! That's the best of a secretary. She may have a husband, but a husband is the mere shred of a man, compared to a boss, a chief, a man who dictates to you and whose words you faithfully write down and then transcribe. Imagine a wife writing down anything her husband said to her! But a secretary! Every *and* and *but* of his she preserves for ever. What are candied violets in comparison!

Now it is all very well having gallant affairs under the southern sun, when you know there is a husband whom you adore dictating to a secretary whom you are too scornful to hate yet whom you rather despise, though you allow she has her good points, away north in the place you ought to regard as home. A gallant affair isn't much good when you've got a bit of grit in your eye. Or something at the back of your mind.

What's to be done? The husband, of course, did not send his wife away.

" You've got your secretary and your work," she said. " There's no room for me."

" There's a bedroom and a sitting-room exclusively for you," he replied. " And a garden and half a motor-car. But please yourself entirely. Do what gives you most pleasure."

" In that case," she said, " I'll just go south for the winter."

" Yes, do ! " he said. " You always enjoy it."

" I always do," she replied.

They parted with a certain relentlessness that had a touch of wistful sentiment behind it. Off she went to her gallant affairs, that were like the curate's egg, palatable in parts. And he settled down to work. He said he hated working, but he never did anything else. Ten or eleven hours a day. That's what it is to be your own master !

So the winter wore away, and it was spring, when the swallows homeward fly, or northward, in this case. This winter, one of a series similar, had been rather hard to get through. The bit of grit in the gallant lady's eye had worked deeper in the more she blinked. Dark faces might be dark, and icy cocktails might lend a glow ; she blinked her hardest to blink that bit of grit away, without success. Under the spicy balls of the mimosa she thought of that husband of hers in his library, and of that neat, competent but *common* little secretary of his, for ever taking down what he said !

" How a man can *stand* it ! How *she* can stand it, common little thing as she is, I don't know ! " the wife cried to herself.

She meant this dictating business, this ten hours a day intercourse, *à deux*, with nothing but a pencil between them, and a flow of words.

What was to be done? Matters, instead of improving, had grown worse. The little secretary had brought her mother and sister into the establishment. The mother was a sort of cook-housekeeper, the sister was a sort of upper maid—she did the fine laundry, and looked after " his " clothes, and valeted him beautifully. It was really an excellent arrangement. The old mother was a splendid plain cook, the sister was all that could be desired as a valet de chambre, a fine laundress, an upper parlour-maid, and a table-waiter. And all economical to a degree. They knew his affairs by heart. His secretary flew to town when a creditor became dangerous, and she *always* smoothed over the financial crisis.

" He," of course, had debts, and he was working to pay them off. And if he had been a fairy prince who could call the ants to help him, he would not have been more wonderful than in securing this secretary and her family. They took hardly any wages. And they seemed to perform the miracle of loaves and fishes daily.

" She," of course, was the wife who loved her husband, but helped him into debt, and she still was an expensive item. Yet when she appeared at her " home," the secretarial family received her with most elaborate attentions and deference. The knight returning from the Crusades didn't create a greater stir. She felt like Queen Elizabeth at Kenilworth, a sovereign paying a visit to her faithful subjects. But perhaps there lurked always this hair in her soup ! Won't they be glad to be rid of me again !

But they protested No ! No ! They had been waiting and hoping and praying she would come. They had been pining for her to be there, in charge : the mistress, " his " wife. Ah, " his " wife !

" His " wife ! His halo was like a bucket over her head.

The cook-mother was " of the people," so it was the upper-maid daughter who came for orders.

" What will you order for to-morrow's lunch and dinner, Mrs. Gee ? "

" Well, what do you usually have ? "

" Oh, we want *you* to say."

" No, what do you *usually* have ? "

" We don't have anything fixed. Mother goes out and chooses the best she can find, that is nice and fresh. But she thought you would tell her now what to get."

" Oh, I don't know ! I'm not very good at that sort of thing. Ask her to go on just the same ; I'm quite sure she knows best."

" Perhaps you'd like to suggest a sweet ? "

" No, I don't care for sweets—and you know Mr. Gee doesn't. So don't make one for me."

Could anything be more impossible ! They had the house spotless and running like a dream ; how could an incompetent and extravagant wife dare to interfere, when she saw their amazing and almost inspired economy ! But they ran the place on simply nothing !

Simply marvellous people ! And the way they strewed palm-branches under her feet !

But that only made her feel ridiculous.

" Don't you think the family manage very well ? " he asked her tentatively.

"Awfully well ! Almost romantically well ! " she replied. " But I suppose you're perfectly happy ? "

" I'm perfectly comfortable," he replied.

" I can see you are," she replied. " Amazingly so ! I never knew such comfort ! Are you sure it isn't bad for you ? "

She eyed him stealthily. He looked very well, and extremely handsome, in his histrionic way. He was shockingly well-dressed and valeted. And he had that air of easy *aplomb* and good humour which is so becoming to a man, and which he only acquires when he is cock of his own little walk, made much of by his own hens.

" No ! " he said, taking his pipe from his mouth and smiling whimsically round at her. " Do I look as if it were bad for me ? "

" No, you don't," she replied promptly : thinking, naturally, as a woman is supposed to think nowadays, of his health and comfort, the foundation, apparently, of all happiness.

Then, of course, away she went on the backwash.

" Perhaps for your work, though, it's not so good as it is for *you*," she said in a rather small voice. She knew he couldn't bear it if she mocked at his work for one moment. And he knew that rather small voice of hers.

" In what way ? " he said, bristles rising.

" Oh, I don't know," she answered indifferently. " Perhaps it's not good for a man's work if he is too comfortable."

" I don't know about *that* ! " he said, taking a dramatic turn round the library and drawing at his pipe. " Considering I work, actually, by the clock, for twelve hours a day, and for ten hours when it's a short day, I don't think you can say I am deteriorating from easy comfort."

" No, I suppose not," she admitted.

Yet she did think it, nevertheless. His comfortableness didn't consist so much in good food and a soft bed, as in having nobody, absolutely nobody and nothing to contradict him. " I do like to think he's got nothing to aggravate him," the secretary had said to the wife.

" Nothing to aggravate him ! " What a position for a man ! Fostered by women who would let nothing " aggravate " him. If anything would aggravate his wounded vanity, this would !

So thought the wife. But what was to be done about it? In the silence of midnight she heard his voice in the distance, dictating away, like the voice of God to Samuel, alone and monotonous, and she imagined the little figure of the secretary busily scribbling short-hand. Then in the sunny hours of morning, while he was still in bed—he never rose till noon—from another distance came that sharp insect-noise of the typewriter, like some immense grasshopper chirping and rattling. It was the secretary, poor thing, typing out his notes.

That girl—she was only twenty-eight—really slaved herself to skin and bone. She was small and neat, but she was actually worn out. She did far more work than he did, for she had not only to take down all those words he uttered, she had to type them out, make three copies, while he was still resting.

" What on earth she gets out of it," thought the wife, " I don't know. She's simply worn to the bone, for a very poor salary, and he's never kissed her, and never will, if I know anything about him."

Whether his never kissing her—the secretary, that is—made it worse or better, the wife did not decide. He never kissed anybody. Whether she herself—the wife, that is—wanted to be kissed by him, even that she was not clear about. She rather thought she didn't.

What on earth did she want then? She was his wife. What on earth did she want of him?

She certainly didn't want to take him down in shorthand, and type out again all those words. And she didn't really want him to kiss her ; she knew him too well. Yes, she knew him too well. If you know a man too well, you don't want him to kiss you.

What then? What did she want? Why had she such an extra-ordinary hang-over about him? Just because she was his wife? Why did she rather " enjoy " other men—and she was relentless about enjoyment—without ever taking them seriously? And why must she take him so damn seriously, when she never really " enjoyed " him?

Of course she *had* had good times with him, in the past, before—ah ! before a thousand things, all amounting really to nothing. But she enjoyed him no more. She never even enjoyed being with him. There was a silent, ceaseless tension between them, that never broke, even when they were a thousand miles apart.

Awful ! That's what you call being married ! What's to be done about it? Ridiculous, to know it all and not do anything about it !

She came back once more, and there she was, in her own house, a sort of super-guest, even to him. And the secretarial family devoting their lives to him.

Devoting their lives to him ! But actually ! Three women pouring out their lives for him day and night ! And what did they get in return ? Not one kiss ! Very little money, because they knew all about his debts, and had made it their life-business to get them paid off ! No expectations ! Twelve hours' work a day ! Comparative isolation, for he saw nobody !

And beyond that ? Nothing ! Perhaps a sense of uplift and importance because they saw his name and photograph in the newspapers sometimes. But would anybody believe that it was good enough ?

Yet they adored it ! They seemed to get a deep satisfaction out of it, like people with a mission. Extraordinary !

Well, if they did, let them. They were, of course, rather common, " of the people " ; there might be a sort of glamour in it for them.

But it was bad for him. No doubt about it. His work was getting diffuse and poor in quality—and what wonder ! His whole tone was going down—becoming commoner. Of course it was bad for him.

Being his wife, she felt she ought to do something to save him. But how could she ? That perfectly devoted, marvellous secretarial family, how could she make an attack on them ? Yet she'd love to sweep them into oblivion. Of course they were bad for him : ruining his work, ruining his reputation as a writer, ruining his life. Ruining him with their slavish service.

Of course she ought to make an onslaught on them ! But how *could* she ? Such devotion ! And what had she herself to offer in their place ? Certainly not slavish devotion to him, nor to his flow of words ! Certainly not !

She imagined him stripped once more naked of secretary and secretarial family, and she shuddered. It was like throwing the naked baby in the dust-bin. Couldn't do that !

Yet something must be done. She felt it. She was almost tempted to get into debt for another thousand pounds, and send in the bill, or have it sent in to him, as usual.

But no ! Something more drastic !

Something more drastic, or perhaps more gentle. She wavered between the two. And wavering, she first did nothing, came to no decision, dragged vacantly on from day to day, waiting for sufficient energy to take her departure once more.

It was spring ! What a fool she had been to come up in spring ! And she was forty ! What an idiot of a woman to go and be forty !

She went down the garden in the warm afternoon, when birds were whistling loudly from the cover, the sky being low and warm, and she had nothing to do. The garden was full of flowers : he loved them for their theatrical display. Lilac and snowball bushes, and laburnum and red may, tulips and anemones and coloured daisies. Lots of flowers ! Borders of forget-me-nots ! Bachelor's buttons ! What absurd names flowers had ! She would have called them blue dots and yellow blobs and white frills. Not so much sentiment, after all !

There is a certain nonsense, something showy and stagey about spring, with its pushing leaves and chorus-girl flowers, unless you have something corresponding inside you. Which she hadn't.

Oh, heaven ! Beyond the hedge she heard a voice, a steady rather theatrical voice. Oh, heaven ! He was dictating to his secretary. in the garden. Good God, was there nowhere to get away from it !

She looked around : there was indeed plenty of escape. But what was the good of escaping ? He would go on and on. She went quietly towards the hedge, and listened.

He was dictating a magazine article about the modern novel. "What the modern novel lacks is architecture." Good God ! Architecture ! He might just as well say : What the modern novel lacks is whalebone, or a teaspoon, or a tooth stopped.

Yet the secretary took it down, took it down, took it down ! No, this could not go on ! It was more than flesh and blood could bear.

She went quietly along the hedge, somewhat wolf-like in her prowl, a broad, strong woman in an expensive mustard-coloured silk jersey and cream-coloured pleated skirt. Her legs were long and shapely, and her shoes were expensive.

With a curious wolf-like stealth she turned the hedge and looked across at the small, shaded lawn where the daisies grew impertinently. " He " was reclining in a coloured hammock under the pink-flowering horse-chestnut tree, dressed in white serge with a fine yellow-coloured linen shirt. His elegant hand dropped over the side of the hammock and beat a sort of vague rhythm to his words. At a little wicker table the little secretary, in a green knitted frock, bent her dark head over her note-book, and diligently made those awful shorthand marks. He was not difficult to take down, as he dictated slowly, and kept a sort of rhythm, beating time with his dangling hand.

" In every novel there must be one outstanding character with which we always sympathize—with *whom* we always sympathize—even though we recognize its—even when we are most aware of the human frailties——"

Every man his own hero, thought the wife grimly, forgetting that every woman is intensely her own heroine.

But what did startle her was a blue bird dashing about near the feet of the absorbed, shorthand-scribbling little secretary. At least it was a blue-tit, blue with grey and some yellow. But to the wife it seemed blue, that juicy spring day, in the translucent afternoon. The blue bird, fluttering round the pretty but rather *common* little feet of the little secretary.

The blue bird ! The blue bird of happiness ! Well, I'm blest,—thought the wife. Well, I'm blest !

And as she was being blest, appeared another blue bird—that is, another blue-tit—and began to wrestle with the first blue-tit. A couple of blue birds of happiness, having a fight over it ! Well, I'm blest !

She was more or less out of sight of the human preoccupied pair. But " he " was disturbed by the fighting blue birds, whose little feathers began to float loose.

" Get out ! " he said to them mildly, waving a dark-yellow handkerchief at them. " Fight your little fight, and settle your private affairs elsewhere, my dear little gentlemen."

The little secretary looked up quickly, for she had already begun to write it down. He smiled at her his twisted whimsical smile.

" No, don't take that down," he said affectionately. " Did you see those two tits laying into one another ? "

" No ! " said the little secretary, gazing brightly round, her eyes half-blinded with work.

But she saw the queer, powerful, elegant, wolf-like figure of the wife, behind her, and terror came into her eyes.

" I did ! " said the wife, stepping forward with those curious, shapely, she-wolf legs of hers, under the very short skirt.

" Aren't they extraordinarily vicious little beasts ? " said he.

" Extraordinarily ! " she re-echoed, stooping and picking up a little breast-feather. " Extraordinarily ! See how the feathers fly ! "

And she got the feather on the tip of her finger, and looked at it. Then she looked at the secretary, then she looked at him. She had a queer, were-wolf expression between her brows.

" I think," he began, " these are the loveliest afternoons, when there's no direct sun, but all the sounds and the colours and the scents are sort of dissolved, don't you know, in the air, and the whole thing is steeped, steeped in spring. It's like being on the inside ; you know how I mean, like being inside the egg and just ready to chip the shell."

" Quite like that ! " she assented, without conviction.

There was a little pause. The secretary said nothing. They were waiting for the wife to depart again.

" I suppose," said the latter, " you're awfully busy, as usual ? "

" Just about the same," he said, pursing his mouth deprecatingly.

Again the blank pause, in which he waited for her to go away again.

" I know I'm interrupting you," she said.

" As a matter of fact," he said, " I was just watching those two blue-tits."

" Pair of little demons ! " said the wife, blowing away the yellow feather from her finger-tip.

" Absolutely ! " he said.

" Well, I'd better go, and let you get on with your work," she said.

" No hurry ! " he said, with benevolent nonchalance. " As a matter of fact, I don't think it's a great success, working out of doors."

" What made you try it ? " said the wife. " You know you never could do it."

" Miss Wrexall suggested it might make a change. But I don't think it altogether helps, do you, Miss Wrexall ? "

" I'm sorry," said the little secretary.

" Why should *you* be sorry ? " said the wife, looking down at her as a wolf might look down half-benignly at a little black-and-tan mongrel. " You only suggested it for his good, I'm sure ! "

" I thought the air might be good for him," the secretary admitted.

" Why do people like you never think about yourselves ? " the wife asked.

The secretary looked her in the eye.

" I suppose we do, in a different way," she said.

" A *very* different way ! " said the wife ironically. " Why don't you make *him* think about *you* ? " she added, slowly, with a sort of drawl. " On a soft spring afternoon like this, you ought to have him dictating poems to you, about the blue birds of happiness fluttering round your dainty little feet. I know *I* would, if I were his secretary."

There was a dead pause. The wife stood immobile and statuesque, in an attitude characteristic of her, half turning back to the little secretary, half averted. She half turned her back on everything.

The secretary looked at him.

"As a matter of fact," he said, "I was doing an article on the Future of the Novel."

"I know that," said the wife. "That's what's so awful! Why not something lively in the life of the novelist?"

There was a prolonged silence, in which he looked pained, and somewhat remote, statuesque. The little secretary hung her head. The wife sauntered slowly away.

"Just where were we, Miss Wrexall?" came the sound of his voice.

The little secretary started. She was feeling profoundly indignant. Their beautiful relationship, his and hers, to be so insulted!

But soon she was veering downstream on the flow of his words, too busy to have any feelings, except one of elation at being so busy.

Tea-time came; the sister brought out the tea-tray into the garden. And immediately, the wife appeared. She had changed, and was wearing a chicory-blue dress of fine cloth. The little secretary had gathered up her papers and was departing, on rather high heels.

"Don't go, Miss Wrexall," said the wife.

The little secretary stopped short, then hesitated.

"Mother will be expecting me," she said.

"Tell her you're not coming. And ask your sister to bring another cup. I want you to have tea with us."

Miss Wrexall looked at the man, who was reared on one elbow in the hammock, and was looking enigmatical, Hamletish.

He glanced at her quickly, then pursed his mouth in a boyish negligence.

"Yes, stay and have tea with us for once," he said. "I see strawberries, and I know you're the bird for them."

She glanced at him, smiled wanly, and hurried away to tell her mother. She even stayed long enough to slip on a silk dress.

"Why, how smart you are!" said the wife, when the little secretary reappeared on the lawn, in chicory-blue silk.

"Oh, don't look at my dress, compared to yours!" said Miss Wrexall. They were of the same colour, indeed!

"At least you earned yours, which is more than I did mine," said the wife, as she poured tea. "You like it strong?"

She looked with her heavy eyes at the smallish, birdy, blue-clad, overworked young woman, and her eyes seemed to speak many inexplicable dark volumes.

"Oh, as it comes, thank you," said Miss Wrexall, leaning nervously forward.

" It's coming pretty black, if you want to ruin your digestion,"
said the wife.

" Oh, I'll have some water in it, then."

" Better, I should say."

" How'd the work go—all right ? " asked the wife, as they drank
tea, and the two women looked at each other's blue dresses.

" Oh ! " he said. " As well as you can expect. It was a piece of
pure flummery. But it's what they want. Awful rot, wasn't it,
Miss Wrexall ? "

Miss Wrexall moved uneasily on her chair.

" It interested me," she said, " though not so much as the novel."

" The novel ? Which novel ? " said the wife. " Is there another
new one ? "

Miss Wrexall looked at him. Not for words would she give away
any of his literary activities.

" Oh, I was just sketching out an idea to Miss Wrexall," he
said.

" Tell us about it ! " said the wife. " Miss Wrexall, *you* tell us
what it's about."

She turned on her chair, and fixed the little secretary.

" I'm afraid "—Miss Wrexall squirmed—" I haven't got it very
clearly myself, yet."

" Oh, go along ! Tell us what you *have* got then ! "

Miss Wrexall sat dumb and very vexed. She felt she was being
baited. She looked at the blue pleatings of her skirt.

" I'm afraid I can't," she said.

" Why are you afraid you can't ? You're so *very* competent. I'm
sure you've got it all at your finger-ends. I expect you write a good
deal of Mr. Gee's books for him, really. He gives you the hint, and
you fill it all in. Isn't that how you do it ? " She spoke ironically,
and as if she were teasing a child. And then she glanced down at
the fine pleatings of her own blue skirt, very fine and expensive.

" Of course you're not speaking seriously ? " said Miss Wrexall,
rising on her mettle.

" Of course I am ! I've suspected for a long time—at least, for
some time—that you write a good deal of Mr. Gee's books for him,
from his hints."

It was said in a tone of raillery, but it was cruel.

" I should be terribly flattered," said Miss Wrexall, straightening
herself, " if I didn't know you were only trying to make me feel a
fool."

" Make you feel a fool ? My dear child !—why, nothing could be farther from me ! You're twice as clever, and a million times as competent as I am. Why, my dear child, I've the greatest admiration for you ! I wouldn't do what you do, not for all the pearls in India. I *couldn't*, anyhow——"

Miss Wrexall closed up and was silent.

" Do you mean to say my books read as if——" he began, rearing up and speaking in a harrowed voice.

" I do ! " said the wife. " *Just* as if Miss Wrexall had written them from your hints. I *honestly* thought she did—when you were too busy——"

" How very clever of you ! " he said.

" Very ! " she cried. " Especially if I was wrong ! "

" Which you were," he said.

" How very extraordinary ! " she cried. " Well, I am once more mistaken ! "

There was a complete pause.

It was broken by Miss Wrexall, who was nervously twisting her fingers.

" You want to spoil what there is between me and him, I can see that," she said bitterly.

" My dear, but what *is* there between you and him ? " asked the wife.

" I was *happy* working with him, working for him ! I was *happy* working for him ! " cried Miss Wrexall, tears of indignant anger and chagrin in her eyes.

" My dear child ! " cried the wife, with simulated excitement, " go *on* being happy working with him, go on being happy while you can ! If it makes you happy, why then, enjoy it ! Of course ! Do you think I'd be so cruel as to want to take it away from you ?— working with him ? *I* can't do shorthand and typewriting and double-entrance book-keeping, or whatever it's called. I tell you, I'm utterly incompetent. I never earn anything. I'm the parasite on the British oak, like the mistletoe. The blue bird doesn't flutter round my feet. Perhaps they're too big and trampling."

She looked down at her expensive shoes.

" If I *did* have a word of criticism to offer," she said, turning to her husband, " it would be to you, Cameron, for taking so much from her and giving her nothing."

" But he gives me everything, everything ! " cried Miss Wrexall. " He gives me everything ! "

" What do you mean by everything ? " said the wife, turning on her sternly.

Miss Wrexall pulled up short. There was a snap in the air, and a change of currents.

"I mean nothing that *you* need begrudge me," said the little secretary rather haughtily. "I've never made myself cheap."

There was a blank pause.

"My God!" said the wife. "You don't call that being cheap? Why, I should say you got nothing out of him at all, you only give! And if you don't call that making yourself cheap—my God!"

"You see, we see things different," said the secretary.

"I should say we do!—*thank God!*" rejoined the wife.

"On whose behalf are you thanking God?" he asked sarcastically.

"Everybody's, I suppose! Yours, because you get everything for nothing, and Miss Wrexall's, because she seems to like it, and mine because I'm well out of it all."

"You *needn't* be out of it all," cried Miss Wrexall magnanimously, "if you didn't *put* yourself out of it all."

"Thank you, my dear, for your offer," said the wife, rising. "But I'm afraid no man can expect *two* blue birds of happiness to flutter round his feet, tearing out their little feathers!"

With which she walked away.

After a tense and desperate interim, Miss Wrexall cried:

"And *really*, need any woman be jealous of *me*?"

"Quite!" he said.

And that was all he did say.

SUN

I

" Take her away, into the sun," the doctors said.

She herself was sceptical of the sun, but she permitted herself to be carried away, with her child, and a nurse, and her mother, over the sea.

The ship sailed at midnight. And for two hours her husband stayed with her, while the child was put to bed, and the passengers came on board. It was a black night, the Hudson swayed with heavy blackness, shaken over with spilled dribbles of light. She leaned on the rail, and looking down thought : This is the sea ; it is deeper than one imagines, and fuller of memories. At that moment the sea seemed to heave like the serpent of chaos that has lived for ever.

" These partings are no good, you know," her husband was saying, at her side. " They're no good. I don't like them."

His tone was full of apprehension, misgiving, and there was a certain note of clinging to the last straw of hope.

" No, neither do I," she responded in a flat voice.

She remembered how bitterly they had wanted to get away from one another, he and she. The emotion of parting gave a slight tug at her emotions, but only caused the iron that had gone into her soul to gore deeper.

So, they looked at their sleeping son, and the father's eyes were wet. But it is not the wetting of the eyes which counts, it is the deep iron rhythm of habit, the year-long, life-long habits ; the deep-set stroke of power.

And in their two lives the stroke of power was hostile, his and hers. Like two engines running at variance, they shattered one another.

" All ashore ! All ashore ! "

" Maurice, you must go ! "

And she thought to herself : For him it is *All ashore !* For me it is *Out to sea !*

Well, he waved his hanky on the midnight dreariness of the pier as the boat inched away ; one among a crowd. One among a crowd ! *C'est ça !*

The ferry-boats, like great dishes piled with rows of lights, were still slanting across the Hudson. That black mouth must be the Lackawanna Station.

The ship ebbed on, the Hudson seemed interminable. But at last they were round the bend, and there was the poor harvest of lights at the Battery. Liberty flung up her torch in a tantrum. There was the wash of the sea.

And though the Atlantic was grey as lava, she did come at last into the sun. Even she had a house above the bluest of seas, with a vast garden, or vineyard, all vines and olives dropping steeply, terrace after terrace, to the strip of coast-plain ; and the garden full of secret places, deep groves of lemon far down in the cleft of earth, and hidden, pure green reservoirs of water ; then a spring issuing out of a little cavern, where the old Sicules had drunk before the Greeks came ; and a grey goat bleating, stabled in an ancient tomb, with all the niches empty. There was the scent of mimosa, and beyond, the snow of the volcano.

She saw it all, and in a measure it was soothing. But it was all external. She didn't really care about it. She was herself, just the same, with all her anger and frustration inside her, and her incapacity to feel anything real. The child irritated her, and preyed on her peace of mind. She felt so horribly, ghastly responsible for him : as if she must be responsible for every breath he drew. And that was torture to her, to the child, and to everybody else concerned.

" You know, Juliet, the doctor told you to lie in the sun, without your clothes. Why don't you ? " said her mother.

" When I am fit to do so, I will. Do you want to kill me ? " Juliet flew at her.

" To kill you, no ! Only to do you good."

" For God's sake, leave off wanting to do me good."

The mother at last was so hurt and incensed, she departed.

The sea went white—and then invisible. Pouring rain fell. It was cold, in the house built for the sun.

Again a morning when the sun lifted himself naked and molten, sparkling over the sea's rim. The house faced south-west. Juliet lay in her bed and watched him rise. It was as if she had never seen the sun rise before. She had never seen the naked sun stand up pure upon the sea-line, shaking the night off himself.

So the desire sprang secretly in her to go naked in the sun. She cherished her desire like a secret.

But she wanted to go away from the house—away from people. And it is not easy, in a country where every olive tree has eyes, and every slope is seen from afar, to go hidden.

But she found a place : a rocky bluff, shoved out to the sea and sun and overgrown with large cactus, the flat-leaved cactus called prickly pear.   Out of this blue-grey knoll of cactus rose one cypress tree, with a pallid, thick trunk, and a tip that leaned over, flexible, up in the blue.   It stood like a guardian looking to sea ; or a low, silvery candle whose huge flame was darkness against light : earth sending up her proud tongue of gloom.

Juliet sat down by the cypress trees and took off her clothes.   The contorted cactus made a forest, hideous yet fascinating, about her. She sat and offered her bosom to the sun, sighing, even now, with a certain hard pain, against the cruelty of having to give herself.

But the sun marched in blue heaven and sent down his rays as he went.   She felt the soft air of the sea on her breasts, that seemed as if they would never ripen.   But she hardly felt the sun.   Fruits that would wither and not mature, her breasts.

Soon, however, she felt the sun inside them, warmer than ever love had been, warmer than milk or the hands of her baby.   At last, at last her breasts were like long white grapes in the hot sun.

She slid off all her clothes and lay naked in the sun, and as she lay she looked up through her fingers at the central sun, his blue pulsing roundness, whose outer edges streamed brilliance.   Pulsing with marvellous blue, and alive, and streaming white fire from his edges, the sun !   He faced down to her with his look of blue fire, and enveloped her breasts and her face, her throat, her tired belly, her knees, her thighs and her feet.

She lay with shut eyes, the colour of rosy flame through her lids. It was too much.   She reached and put leaves over her eyes.   Then she lay again, like a long white gourd in the sun, that must ripen to gold.

She could feel the sun penetrating even into her bones ; nay, further, even into her emotions and her thoughts.   The dark tensions of her emotion began to give way, the cold dark clots of her thoughts began to dissolve.   She was beginning to feel warm right through. Turning over, she let her shoulders dissolve in the sun, her loins, the backs of her thighs, even her heels.   And she lay half stunned with wonder at the thing that was happening to her.   Her weary, chilled heart was melting, and, in melting, evaporating.

When she was dressed again she lay once more and looked up at the cypress tree, whose crest, a flexible filament, fell this way and that in the breeze.   Meanwhile, she was conscious of the great sun roaming in heaven.

So, dazed, she went home, only half-seeing, sun-blinded and sun-dazed. And her blindness was like a richness to her, and her dim, warm, heavy half-consciousness was like wealth.

" Mummy ! Mummy ! " her child came running towards her, calling in that peculiar bird-like little anguish of want, always wanting her. She was surprised that her drowsed heart for once felt none of the anxious love-anguish in return. She caught the child up in her arms, but she thought : He should not be such a lump ! If he were in the sun, he would spring up.

She resented, rather, his little hands clutching at her, especially at her neck. She pulled her throat away. She did not want to be touched. She put the child gently down.

" Run ! " she said. " Run in the sun ! "

And there and then she took off his clothes and set him naked on the warm terrace.

" Play in the sun ! " she said.

He was frightened and wanted to cry. But she, in the warm indolence of her body, and the complete indifference of her heart, rolled him an orange across the red tiles, and with his soft, unformed little body he toddled after it. Then immediately he had it, he dropped it because it felt strange against his flesh. And he looked back at her, querulous, wrinkling his face to cry, frightened because he was stark.

" Bring me the orange," she said, amazed at her own deep indifference to his trepidation. " Bring Mummy the orange."

" He shall not grow up like his father," she said to herself. " Like a worm that the sun has never seen."

II

She had had the child so much on her mind, in a torment of responsibility, as if, having borne him, she had to answer for his whole existence. Even if his nose were running, it had been repulsive and a goad in her vitals, as if she must say to herself: Look at the thing you brought forth !

Now a change took place. She was no longer vitally interested in the child, she took the strain of her anxiety and her will from off him. And he thrived all the more for it.

She was thinking inside herself, of the sun in his splendour, and her mating with him. Her life was now a whole ritual. She lay always awake, before dawn, watching for the grey to colour to pale gold, to know if clouds lay on the sea's edge. Her joy was when he rose all molten in his nakedness, and threw off blue-white fire, into the tender heaven.

But sometimes he came ruddy, like a big, shy creature. And

sometimes slow and crimson red, with a look of anger, slowly pushing and shouldering. Sometimes again she could not see him, only the level cloud threw down gold and scarlet from above, as he moved behind the wall.

She was fortunate. Weeks went by, and though the dawn was sometimes clouded, and afternoon was sometimes grey, never a day passed sunless, and most days, winter though it was, streamed radiant. The thin little wild crocuses came up mauve and striped, the wild narcissi hung their winter stars.

Every day she went down to the cypress tree, among the cactus grove on the knoll with yellowish cliffs at the foot. She was wiser and subtler now, wearing only a dove-grey wrapper, and sandals. So that in an instant, in any hidden niche, she was naked to the sun. And the moment she was covered again she was grey and invisible.

Every day, in the morning towards noon, she lay at the foot of the powerful, silver-pawed cypress tree, while the sun rode jovial in heaven. By now she knew the sun in every thread of her body, there was not a cold shadow left. And her heart, that anxious, straining heart, had disappeared altogether, like a flower that falls in the sun, and leaves only a ripe seed-case.

She knew the sun in heaven, blue-molten with his white fire edges, throwing off fire. And though he shone on all the world, when she lay unclothed he focussed on her. It was one of the wonders of the sun, he could shine on a million people and still be the radiant, splendid, unique sun, focussed on her alone.

With her knowledge of the sun, and her conviction that the sun *knew* her, in the cosmic carnal sense of the word, came over her a feeling of detachment from people, and a certain contempt for human beings altogether. They were so un-elemental, so unsunned. They were so like graveyard worms.

Even the peasants passing up the rocky, ancient little road with their donkeys, sun-blackened as they were, were not sunned right through. There was a little soft white core of fear, like a snail in a shell, where the soul of the man cowered in fear of death, and in fear of the natural blaze of life. He dared not quite emerge : always innerly cowed. All men were like that.

Why admit men !

With her indifference to people, to men, she was not now so cautious about being unseen. She had told Marinina, who went shopping for her in the village, that the doctor had ordered sun-baths. Let that suffice.

Marinina was a woman over sixty, tall, thin, erect, with curling

dark grey hair, and dark grey eyes that had the shrewdness of
thousands of years in them, with the laugh that underlies all long
experience. Tragedy is lack of experience.

" It must be beautiful to go unclothed in the sun," said Marinina,
with a shrewd laugh in her eyes, as she looked keenly at the other
woman. Juliet's fair, bobbed hair curled in a little cloud at her
temple. Marinina was a woman of Magna Græcia, and had far
memories. She looked again at Juliet. " But you have to be beautiful yourself, if you're not going to give offence to the sun ? Isn't it
so ? " she added, with that queer, breathless little laugh of the women
of the past.

" Who knows if I am beautiful ! " said Juliet.

But beautiful or not, she felt that by the sun she was appreciated.
Which is the same.

When, out of the sun at noon, sometimes she stole down over the
rocks and past the cliff-edge, down to the deep gully where the
lemons hung in cool eternal shadow, and in the silence slipped off
her wrapper to wash herself quickly at one of the deep, clear green
basins, she would notice, in the bare green twilight under the lemon
leaves, that all her body was rosy, rosy and turning to gold. She
was like another person. She was another person.

So she remembered that the Greeks had said, a white, unsunned
body was fishy and unhealthy.

And she would rub a little olive oil in her skin, and wander a moment
in the dark underworld of the lemons, balancing a lemon flower in
her navel, laughing to herself. There was just a chance some
peasant might see her. But if he did he would be more afraid of
her than she of him. She knew the white core of fear in the clothed
bodies of men.

She knew it even in her little son. How he mistrusted her, now
that she laughed at him, with the sun in her face ! She insisted on
his toddling naked in the sunshine, every day. And now his little
body was pink, too, his blond hair was pushed thick from his brow,
his cheeks had a pomegranate scarlet, in the delicate gold of the
sunny skin. He was bonny and healthy, and the servants, loving
his red and gold and blue, called him an angel from heaven.

But he mistrusted his mother : she laughed at him. And she saw
in his wide blue eyes, under the little frown, that centre of fear, misgiving, which she believed was at the centre of all male eyes, now.
She called it fear of the sun.

" He fears the sun," she would say to herself, looking down into
the eyes of the child.

And as she watched him toddling, swaying, tumbling in the sunshine, making his little, bird-like noises, she saw that he held himself tight and hidden from the sun, inside himself. His spirit was like a snail in a shell, in a damp, cold crevice inside himself. It made her think of his father. She wished she could make him come forth, break out in a gesture of recklessness and salutation.

She determined to take him with her, down to the cypress tree among the cactus. She would have to watch him, because of the thorns. But surely in that place he would come forth from that little shell, deep inside him. That little civilized tension would disappear off his brow.

She spread a rug for him and sat him down. Then she slid off her wrapper and lay down herself, watching a hawk high in the blue, and the tip of the cypress hanging over.

The boy played with stones on the rug. When he got up to toddle away, she sat up too. He turned and looked at her. Almost, from his blue eyes, it was the challenging, warm look of the true male. And he was handsome, with the scarlet in the golden blond of his skin. He was not really white. His skin was gold-dusky.

" Mind the thorns, darling," she said.

" Thorns ! " re-echoed the child, in a birdy chirp, still looking at her over his shoulder, like some naked cherub in a picture, doubtful.

" Nasty prickly thorns."

" 'Ickly thorns ! "

He staggered in his little sandals over the stones, pulling at the dry wild mint. She was quick as a serpent, leaping to him, when he was going to fall against the prickles. It surprised even herself. " What a wild cat I am, really ! " she said to herself.

She brought him every day, when the sun shone, to the cypress tree.

" Come ! " she said. " Let us go to the cypress tree."

And if there was a cloudy day, with the tramontana blowing, so that she could not go down, the child would chirp incessantly :
" Cypress tree ! Cypress tree ! "

He missed it as much as she did.

It was not just taking sunbaths. It was much more than that. Something deep inside her unfolded and relaxed, and she was given. By some mysterious power inside her, deeper than her known consciousness and will, she was put into connection with the sun, and the stream flowed of itself, from her womb. She herself, her conscious self, was secondary, a secondary person, almost an onlooker. The true Juliet was this dark flow from her deep body to the sun.

She had always been mistress of herself, aware of what she was doing, and held tense for her own power. Now she felt inside her quite another sort of power, something greater than herself, flowing by itself. Now she was vague, but she had a power beyond herself.

III

The end of February was suddenly very hot. Almond blossom was falling like pink snow, in the touch of the smallest breeze. The mauve, silky little anemones were out, the asphodels tall in bud, and the sea was cornflower blue.

Juliet had ceased to trouble about anything. Now, most of the day, she and the child were naked in the sun, and it was all she wanted. Sometimes she went down to the sea to bathe : often she wandered in the gullies where the sun shone in, and she was out of sight. Sometimes she saw a peasant with an ass, and he saw her. But she went so simply and quietly with her child ; and the fame of the sun's healing power, for the soul as well as for the body, had already spread among the people ; so that there was no excitement.

The child and she were now both tanned with a rosy-golden tan, all over. " I am another being ! " she said to herself, as she looked at her red-gold breasts and thighs.

The child, too, was another creature, with a peculiar, quiet, sun-darkened absorption. Now he played by himself in silence, and she hardly need notice him. He seemed no longer to know when he was alone.

There was not a breeze, and the sea was ultramarine. She sat by the great silver paw of the cypress tree, drowsed in the sun, but her breasts alert, full of sap. She was becoming aware that an activity was rousing in her, an activity which would carry her into a new way of life. Still she did not want to be aware. She knew well enough the vast cold apparatus of civilization, so difficult to evade.

The child had gone a few yards down the rocky path, round the great sprawling of a cactus. She had seen him, a real gold-brown infant of the winds, with burnt gold hair and red cheeks, collecting the speckled pitcher-flowers and laying them in rows. He could balance now, and was quick for his own emergencies, like an absorbed young animal playing silent.

Suddenly she heard him speaking : " *Look, Mummy ! Mummy, look !* " A note in his bird-like voice made her lean forward sharply.

Her heart stood still. He was looking over his naked little shoulder at her, and pointing with a loose little hand at a snake which had reared itself up a yard away from him, and was opening its mouth so that its forked, soft tongue flickered black like a shadow, uttering a short hiss.

" Look, Mummy ! "

" Yes, darling, it's a snake ! " came the slow, deep voice.

He looked at her, his wide blue eyes uncertain whether to be afraid or not. Some stillness of the sun in her reassured him.

" Snake ! " he chirped.

" Yes, darling ! Don't touch it, it can bite."

The snake had sunk down, and was reaching away from the coils in which it had been basking asleep, and slowly was easing its long, gold-brown body into the rocks, with slow curves. The boy turned and watched it in silence. Then he said :

" Snake going ! "

" Yes ! Let it go. It likes to be alone."

He still watched the slow, easing length as the creature drew itself apathetic out of sight.

" Snake gone back," he said.

" Yes, it's gone back. Come to Mummy a moment."

He came and sat with his plump, naked little body on her naked lap, and she smoothed his burnt, bright hair. She said nothing, feeling that everything was passed. The curious soothing power of the sun filled her, filled the whole place like a charm, and the snake was part of the place, along with her and the child.

Another day, in the dry stone wall of one of the olive terraces, she saw a black snake horizontally creeping.

" Marinina," she said, " I saw a black snake. Are they harmful ? "

" Ah, the black snakes, no ! But the yellow ones, yes ! If the yellow ones bite you, you die. But they frighten me, they frighten me, even the black ones, when I see one."

Juliet still went to the cypress tree with the child. But she always looked carefully round before she sat down, examining everywhere where the child might go. Then she would lie and turn to the sun again, her tanned, pear-shaped breasts pointing up. She would take no thought for the morrow. She refused to think outside her garden, and she could not write letters. She would tell the nurse to write.

IV

It was March, and the sun was growing very powerful. In the hot hours she would lie in the shade of the trees, or she would even go down to the depths of the cool lemon grove. The child ran in the distance, like a young animal absorbed in life.

One day she was sitting in the sun on the steep slope of the gully, having bathed in one of the great tanks. Below, under the lemons, the child was wading among the yellow oxalis flowers of the shadow, gathering fallen lemons, passing with his tanned little body into flecks of light, moving all dappled.

Suddenly, high over the land's edge, against the full-lit pale blue sky, Marinina appeared, a black cloth tied round her head, calling quietly : "*Signora ! Signora Giulietta !*"

Juliet faced round, standing up. Marinina paused a moment, seeing the naked woman standing alert, her sun-faded fair hair in a little cloud. Then the swift old woman came on down the slant of the steep track.

She stood a few steps, erect, in front of the sun-coloured woman, and eyed her shrewdly.

"But how beautiful you are, you !" she said coolly, almost cynically. "There is your husband."

"My husband !" cried Juliet.

The old woman gave a shrewd bark of a little laugh, the mockery of the women of the past.

"Haven't you got one, a husband, you ?" she taunted.

"But where is he ?" cried Juliet.

The old woman glanced over her shoulder.

"He was following me," she said. "But he will not have found the path." And she gave another little bark of a laugh.

The paths were all grown high with grass and flowers and nepitella, till they were like bird-trails in an eternally wild place. Strange, the vivid wildness of the old places of civilization, a wildness that is not gaunt.

Juliet looked at her serving-woman with meditating eyes.

"Oh, very well !" she said at last. "Let him come."

"Let him come here ? Now ?" asked Marinina, her laughing, smoke-grey eyes looking with mockery into Juliet's. Then she gave a little jerk of her shoulders.

"All right, as you wish. But for him it is a rare one !"

She opened her mouth in a laugh of noiseless joy. Then she pointed down to the child, who was heaping lemons against his little chest. "Look how beautiful the child is ! That, certainly, will please him, poor thing. Then I'll bring him."

"Bring him," said Juliet.

The old woman scrambled rapidly up the track again. Maurice was standing grey-faced, in his grey felt hat and his dark grey suit, at a loss among the vine terraces. He looked pathetically out of place, in that resplendent sunshine and the grace of the old Greek world ; like a blot of ink on the pale, sun-glowing slope.

" Come ! " said Marinina to him. " She is down here."

And swiftly she led the way, striding with a rapid stride, making her way through the grasses. Suddenly she stopped on the brow of the slope. The tops of the lemon trees were dark, away below.

" You, you go down here," she said to him, and he thanked her, looking up at her swiftly.

He was a man of forty, clean-shaven, grey-faced, very quiet and really shy. He managed his own business carefully, without startling success, but efficiently. And he confided in nobody. The old woman of Magna Græcia saw him at a glance : he is good, she said to herself, but not a man, poor thing.

" Down there is the Signora ! " said Marinina, pointing like one of the Fates.

And again he said " Thank you ! Thank you ! " without a twinkle, and stepped carefully into the track. Marinina lifted her chin with a joyful wickedness. Then she strode off towards the house.

Maurice was watching his step through the tangle of Mediterranean herbage, so he did not catch sight of his wife till he came round a little bend, quite near her. She was standing erect and nude by the jutting rock, glistening with the sun and with warm life. Her breasts seemed to be lifting up, alert, to listen, her thighs looked brown and fleet. Her glance on him, as he came like ink on blotting-paper, was swift and nervous.

Maurice, poor fellow, hesitated, and glanced away from her. He turned his face aside.

" Hello, Julie ! " he said, with a little nervous cough—" Splendid ! Splendid ! "

He advanced with his face averted, shooting further glances at her, as she stood with the peculiar satiny gleam of the sun on her tanned skin. Somehow she did not seem so terribly naked. It was the golden-rose tan of the sun that clothed her.

" Hello, Maurice ! " she said, hanging back from him. " I wasn't expecting you so soon."

" No," he said. " No ! I managed to slip away a little earlier."

And again he coughed awkwardly.

They stood several yards away from one another, and there was silence.

" Well ! " he said, " er—this is splendid, splendid ! You are—er—splendid ! Where is the boy ? "

" There he is," she said, pointing down to where a naked urchin in the deep shade was piling fallen lemons together.

The father gave an odd little laugh.

" Ah, yes, there he is ! So there's the little man ! Fine ! " he said. He really was thrilled in his suppressed nervous soul. " Hello, Johnny ! " he called, and it sounded rather feeble. " Hello, Johnny ! "

The child looked up, spilling lemons from his chubby arms, but did not respond.

" I guess we'll go down to him," said Juliet, as she turned and went striding down the path. Her husband followed, watching the rosy, fleet-looking lifting and sinking of her quick hips, as she swayed a little in the socket of her waist. He was dazed with admiration, but also, at a deadly loss. What should he do with himself? He was utterly out of the picture, in his dark grey suit and pale grey hat, and his grey, monastic face of a shy business man.

" He looks all right, doesn't he," said Juliet, as they came through the deep sea of yellow-flowering oxalis, under the lemon trees.

" Ah !—yes ! yes ! Splendid ! Splendid ! Hello, Johnny ! Do you know Daddy ? Do you know Daddy, Johnny ? "

He crouched down and held out his hands.

" Lemons ! " said the child, birdily chirping. " Two lemons ! "

" Two lemons ! " replied the father. " Lots of lemons."

The infant came and put a lemon in each of his father's open hands. Then he stood back to look.

" Two lemons ! " repeated the father. " Come, Johnny ! Come and say ' Hello ' to Daddy."

" Daddy going back ? " said the child.

" Going back ? Well—well—not to-day."

And he gathered his son in his arms.

" Take a coat off ! Daddy take a coat off ! " said the boy, squirming debonair away from the cloth.

" All right, son ! Daddy take a coat off."

He took off his coat and laid it carefully aside, then again took his son in his arms. The naked woman looked down at the naked infant in the arms of the man in his shirt sleeves. The boy had pulled off the father's hat, and Juliet looked at the sleek, black-and-grey hair of her husband, not a hair out of place. And utterly, utterly indoors. She was silent for a long time, while the father talked to the child, who was fond of his Daddy.

"What are you going to do about it, Maurice?" she said, suddenly.

He looked at her swiftly, sideways.

" Er—about what, Julie ? "

" Oh, everything ! About this ! I can't go back into East Forty-Seventh."

" Er——" he hesitated, " no, I suppose not—not just now at least."

" Never," she said, and there was a silence.

" Well—er—I don't know," he said.

" Do you think you can come out here ? " she said.

" Yes, I can stay for a month. I think I can manage a month," he hesitated. Then he ventured a complicated, shy peep at her, and hid his face again.

She looked down at him, her alert breasts lifted with a sigh, as if a breeze of impatience shook them.

" I can't go back," she said slowly. " I can't go back on this sun. If you can't come here——"

She ended on an open note. He glanced at her again and again, furtively, but with growing admiration and lessening confusion.

" No ! " he said. " This kind of thing suits you. You are splendid ! No, I don't think you can go back."

He was thinking of her in the New York flat, pale, silent, oppressing him terribly. He was the soul of gentle timidity, in his human relations, and her silent, awful hostility after the baby was born, had frightened him deeply. Because he had realized she couldn't help it. Women were like that. Their feelings took a reverse direction, even against their own selves, and it was awful—awful ! Awful, awful to live in the house with a woman like that, whose feelings were reversed even against herself ! He had felt himself ground down under the millstone of her helpless enmity. She had ground even herself down to the quick, and the child as well. No, anything rather than that.

" But what about *you* ? " she asked.

" I ? Oh, I ! I can carry on the business, and—er—come over here for the holidays—as long as you like to stay. You stay as long as you wish." He looked a long time down at the earth, then glanced up at her with a touch of supplication in his uneasy eyes.

" Even for ever ? "

" Well—er—yes, if you like. For ever is a long time. One can't set a date."

" And I can do anything I like ? " She looked him straight in the eyes, challenging. And he was powerless against her rosy, wind-hardened nakedness.

" Er—yes ! I suppose so ! So long as you don't make yourself unhappy—or the boy."

Again he looked up at her with a complicated, uneasy appeal—thinking of the child, but hoping for himself.

" I won't," she said quickly.

" No ! " he said. " No ! I don't think you will."

There was a pause. The bells of the village were hastily clanging midday. That meant lunch.

She slipped into her grey crêpe kimono, and fastened a broad green sash round her waist. Then she slipped a little blue shirt over the boy's head, and they went up to the house.

At table she watched her husband, his grey city face, his fixed, black-grey hair, his very precise table manners, and his extreme moderation in eating and drinking. Sometimes he glanced at her, furtively, from under his black lashes. He had the gold-grey eyes of an animal that has been caught young, and reared completely in captivity.

They went on to the balcony for coffee. Below, beyond, on the next podere across the steep little gully, a peasant and his wife were sitting under an almond tree, near the green wheat, eating their midday meal from a little white cloth spread on the ground. There was a huge piece of bread, and glasses with dark wine.

Juliet put her husband with his back to this picture ; she sat facing. Because, the moment she and Maurice had come out on the balcony, the peasant had glanced up.

V

She knew him, in the distance, perfectly. He was a rather fat, very broad fellow of about thirty-five, and he chewed large mouthfuls of bread. His wife was stiff and dark-faced, handsome, sombre. They had no children. So much Juliet had learned.

The peasant worked a great deal alone, on the opposite podere. His clothes were always very clean and cared-for, white trousers and a coloured shirt, and an old straw hat. Both he and his wife had that air of quiet superiority which belongs to individuals, not to a class.

His attraction was in his vitality, the peculiar quick energy which gave a charm to his movements, stout and broad as he was. In the early days before she took to the sun, Juliet had met him suddenly, among the rocks, when she had scrambled over to the next podere. He had been aware of her before she saw him, so that when she did look up, he took off his hat, gazing at her with shyness and pride, from his big blue eyes. His face was broad, sunburnt, he had a cropped brown moustache, and thick brown eyebrows, nearly as thick as his moustache, meeting under his low, wide brow.

" Oh ! " she said. " Can I walk here ? "

" Surely ! " he replied, with that peculiar hot haste which characterized his movement. " My padrone would wish you to walk wherever you like on his land."

And he pressed back his head in the quick, vivid, shy generosity of his nature. She had gone on quickly. But instantly she had recognized the violent generosity of his blood, and the equally violent *farouche* shyness.

Since then she had seen him in the distance every day, and she came to realize that he was one who lived a good deal to himself, like a quick animal, and that his wife loved him intensely, with a jealousy that was almost hate ; because, probably, he wanted to give himself still, still further, beyond where she could take him.

One day, when a group of peasants sat under a tree, she had seen him dancing quick and gay with a child—his wife watching darkly.

Gradually Juliet and he had become intimate, across the distance. They were aware of one another. She knew, in the morning, the moment he arrived with his ass. And the moment she went out on the balcony he turned to look. But they never saluted. Yet she missed him when he did not come to work on the podere.

Once, in the hot morning when she had been walking naked, deep in the gully between the two estates, she had come upon him, as he was bending down, with his powerful shoulders, picking up wood to pile on his motionless, waiting donkey. He saw her as he lifted his flushed face, and she was backing away. A flame went over his eyes, and a flame flew over her body, melting her bones. But she backed away behind the bushes, silently, and retreated whence she had come. And she wondered a little resentfully over the silence in which he could work, hidden in the bushy places. He had that wild animal faculty.

Since then there had been a definite pain of consciousness in the body of each of them, though neither would admit it, and they gave no sign of recognition. But the man's wife was instinctively aware.

And Juliet had thought : Why shouldn't I meet this man for an hour, and bear his child ? Why should I have to identify my life with a man's life ? Why not meet him for an hour, as long as the desire lasts, and no more ? There is already the spark between us.

But she had never made any sign. And now she saw him looking up, from where he sat by the white cloth, opposite his black-clad wife, looking up at Maurice. The wife turned and looked, too, saturnine.

And Juliet felt a grudge come over her. She would have to bear Maurice's child again. She had seen it in her husband's eyes. And she knew it from his answer, when she spoke to him.

"Will you walk about in the sun, too, without your clothes?" she asked him.

"Why—er—yes! Yes, I should like to, while I'm here—I suppose it's quite private?"

There was a gleam in his eyes, a desperate kind of courage of his desire, and a glance at the alert lifting of her breasts in her wrapper. In his way, he was a man, too, he faced the world and was not entirely quenched in his male courage. He would dare to walk in the sun, even ridiculously.

But he smelled of the world, and all its fetters and its mongrel cowering. He was branded with the brand that is not a hall-mark.

Ripe now, and brown-rosy all over with the sun, and with a heart like a fallen rose, she had wanted to go down to the hot, shy peasant and bear his child. Her sentiments had fallen like petals. She had seen the flushed blood in the burnt face, and the flame in the southern blue eyes, and the answer in her had been a gush of fire. He would have been a procreative sun-bath to her, and she wanted it.

Nevertheless, her next child would be Maurice's. The fatal chain of continuity would cause it.

I

SHE had thought that this marriage, of all marriages, would be an adventure. Not that the man himself was exactly magical to her. A little, wiry, twisted fellow, twenty years older than herself, with brown eyes and greying hair, who had come to America a scrap of a wastrel, from Holland, years ago, as a tiny boy, and from the gold-mines of the west had been kicked south into Mexico, and now was more or less rich, owning silver-mines in the wilds of the Sierra Madre : it was obvious that the adventure lay in his circumstances, rather than his person. But he was still a little dynamo of energy, in spite of accidents survived, and what he had accomplished he had accomplished alone. One of those human oddments there is no accounting for.

When she actually *saw* what he had accomplished, her heart quailed. Great green-covered, unbroken mountain-hills, and in the midst of the lifeless isolation, the sharp pinkish mounds of the dried mud from the silver-works. Under the nakedness of the works, the walled-in, one-storey adobe house, with its garden inside, and its deep inner verandah with tropical climbers on the sides. And when you looked up from this shut-in flowered patio, you saw the huge pink cone of the silver-mud refuse, and the machinery of the extracting plant against heaven above. No more.

To be sure, the great wooden doors were often open. And then she could stand outside, in the vast open world. And see great, void, tree-clad hills piling behind one another, from nowhere into no-where. They were green in autumn time. For the rest, pinkish, stark dry and abstract.

And in his battered Ford car her husband would take her into the dead, thrice-dead little Spanish town forgotten among the mountains. The great, sun-dried dead church, the dead portales, the hopeless covered market-place, where, the first time she went, she saw a dead dog lying between the meat stalls and the vegetable array, stretched out as if for ever, nobody troubling to throw it away. Deadness within deadness.

Everybody feebly talking silver, and showing bits of ore. But silver was at a standstill. The great war came and went. Silver was a dead market. Her husband's mines were closed down. But she and he lived on in the adobe house under the works, among the flowers that were never very flowery to her.

She had two children, a boy and a girl. And her eldest, the boy, was nearly ten years old before she aroused from her stupor of subjected amazement. She was now thirty-three, a large, blue-eyed, dazed woman, beginning to grow stout. Her little, wiry, tough, twisted, brown-eyed husband was fifty-three, a man as tough as wire, tenacious as wire, still full of energy, but dimmed by the lapse of silver from the market, and by some curious inaccessibility on his wife's part.

He was a man of principles, and a good husband. In a way, he doted on her. He never quite got over his dazzled admiration of her. But essentially, he was still a bachelor. He had been thrown out on the world, a little bachelor, at the age of ten. When he married he was over forty, and had enough money to marry on. But his capital was all a bachelor's. He was boss of his own works, and marriage was the last and most intimate bit of his own works.

He admired his wife to extinction, he admired her body, all her points. And she was to him always the rather dazzling Californian girl from Berkeley, whom he had first known. Like any sheikh, he kept her guarded among those mountains of Chihuahua. He was jealous of her as he was of his silver-mine : and that is saying a lot.

At thirty-three she really was still the girl from Berkeley, in all but physique. Her conscious development had stopped mysteriously with her marriage, completely arrested. Her husband had never become real to her, neither mentally nor physically. In spite of his late sort of passion for her, he never meant anything to her, physically. Only morally he swayed her, downed her, kept her in an invincible slavery.

So the years went by, in the adobe house strung round the sunny patio, with the silver-works overhead. Her husband was never still. When the silver went dead, he ran a ranch lower down, some twenty miles away, and raised pure-bred hogs, splendid creatures. At the same time, he hated pigs. He was a squeamish waif of an idealist, and really hated the physical side of life. He loved work, work, work, and making things. His marriage, his children, were something he was making, part of his business, but with a sentimental income this time.

Gradually her nerves began to go wrong : she must get out. She must get out. So he took her to El Paso for three months. And at least it was the United States.

But he kept his spell over her. The three months ended : back she was, just the same, in her adobe house among those eternal green or pinky-brown hills, void as only the undiscovered is void. She taught her children, she supervised the Mexican boys who were her servants. And sometimes her husband brought visitors, Spaniards or Mexicans or occasionally white men.

He really loved to have white men staying on the place. Yet he had not a moment's peace when they were there. It was as if his wife were some peculiar secret vein of ore in his mines, which no one must be aware of except himself. And she was fascinated by the young gentlemen, mining engineers, who were his guests at times. He, too, was fascinated by a real gentleman. But he was an old-timer miner with a wife, and if a gentleman looked at his wife, he felt as if his mine were being looted, the secrets of it pryed out.

It was one of these young gentlemen who put the idea into her mind. They were all standing outside the great wooden doors of the patio, looking at the outer world. The eternal, motionless hills were all green, it was September, after the rains. There was no sign of anything, save the deserted mine, the deserted works, and a bunch of half-deserted miner's dwellings.

" I wonder," said the young man, " what there is behind those great blank hills."

" More hills," said Lederman. " If you go that way, Sonora and the coast. This way is the desert—you came from there—and the other way, hills and mountains."

" Yes, but what *lives* in the hills and the mountains ? *Surely* there is something wonderful ? It looks *so* like nowhere on earth : like being on the moon."

" There's plenty of game, if you want to shoot. And Indians, if you call *them* wonderful."

" Wild ones ? "

" Wild enough."

" But friendly ? "

" It depends. Some of them are quite wild, and they don't let anybody near. They kill a missionary at sight. And where a missionary can't get, nobody can."

" But what does the government say ? "

" They're so far from everywhere, the government leaves 'em alone. And they're wily ; if they think there'll be trouble, they send a delegation to Chihuahua and make a formal submission. The government is glad to leave it at that."

" And do they live quite wild, with their own savage customs and religion ? "

" Oh, yes. They use nothing but bows and arrows. I've seen them in town, in the Plaza, with funny sort of hats with flowers round them, and a bow in one hand, quite naked except for a sort of shirt, even in cold weather—striding round with their savage's bare legs."

" But don't you suppose it's wonderful, up there in their secret villages ? "

" No. What would there be wonderful about it ? Savages are savages, and all savages behave more or less alike : rather low-down and dirty, unsanitary, with a few cunning tricks, and struggling to get enough to eat."

" But surely they have old, old religions and mysteries—it *must* be wonderful, surely it must."

" I don't know about mysteries—howling and heathen practices, more or less indecent. No, I see nothing wonderful in that kind of stuff. And I wonder that you should, when you have lived in London or Paris or New York——"

" Ah, *everybody* lives in London or Paris or New York "—said the young man, as if this were an argument.

And this peculiar vague enthusiasm for unknown Indians found a full echo in the woman's heart. She was overcome by a foolish romanticism more unreal than a girl's. She felt it was her destiny to wander into the secret haunts of these timeless, mysterious, marvellous Indians of the mountains.

She kept her secret. The young man was departing, her husband was going with him down to Torreon, on business : would be away for some days. But before the departure, she made her husband talk about the Indians : about the wandering tribes, resembling the Navajo, who were still wandering free ; and the Yaquis of Sonora : and the different groups in the different valleys of Chihuahua State.

There was supposed to be one tribe, the Chilchuis, living in a high valley to the south, who were the sacred tribe of all the Indians. The descendants of Montezuma and the old Aztec or Totonac kings still lived among them, and the old priests still kept up the ancient religion, and offered human sacrifices—so it was said. Some scientists had been to the Chilchui country, and had come back gaunt and exhausted with hunger and bitter privation, bringing various curious, barbaric objects of worship, but having seen nothing extraordinary in the hungry, stark village of savages.

Though Lederman talked in this off-hand way, it was obvious he felt some of the vulgar excitement at the idea of ancient and mysterious savages.

" How far away are they ? " she asked.

" Oh—three days on horseback—past Cuchitee and a little lake there is up there."

Her husband and the young man departed. The woman made her crazy plans. Of late, to break the monotony of her life, she had harassed her husband into letting her go riding with him, occasionally, on horseback. She was never allowed to go out alone. The country truly was not safe, lawless and crude.

But she had her own horse, and she dreamed of being free as she had been as a girl, among the hills of California.

Her daughter, nine years old, was now in a tiny convent in the little half-deserted Spanish mining-town five miles away.

" Manuel," said the woman to her house-servant, " I'm going to ride to the convent to see Margarita, and take her a few things. Perhaps I shall stay the night in the convent. You look after Freddy and see everything is all right till I come back."

" Shall I ride with you on the master's horse, or shall Juan ? " asked the servant.

" Neither of you. I shall go alone."

The young man looked her in the eyes, in protest. Absolutely impossible that the woman should ride alone !

" I shall go alone," repeated the large, placid-seeming, fair-complexioned woman, with peculiar overbearing emphasis. And the man silently, unhappily yielded.

" Why are you going alone, mother ? " asked her son, as she made up parcels of food.

" Am I *never* to be let alone ? Not one moment of my life ? " she cried, with sudden explosion of energy. And the child, like the servant, shrank into silence.

She set off without a qualm, riding astride on her strong roan horse, and wearing a riding suit of coarse linen, a riding skirt over her linen breeches, a scarlet neck-tie over her white blouse, and a black felt hat on her head. She had food in her saddle-bags, an army canteen with water, and a large, native blanket tied on behind the saddle. Peering into the distance, she set off from her home. Manuel and the little boy stood in the gateway to watch her go. She did not even turn to wave them farewell.

But when she had ridden about a mile, she left the wild road and took a small trail to the right, that led into another valley, over steep places and past great trees, and through another deserted mining-settlement. It was September, the water was running freely in the little stream that had fed the now-abandoned mine. She got down to drink, and let the horse drink too.

She saw natives coming through the trees, away up the slope. They had seen her, and were watching her closely. She watched in turn. The three people, two women and a youth, were making a wide detour, so as not to come too close to her. She did not care. Mounting, she trotted ahead up the silent valley, beyond the silver-works, beyond any trace of mining. There was still a rough trail that led over rocks and loose stones into the valley beyond. This trail she had already ridden, with her husband. Beyond that she knew she must go south.

Curiously she was not afraid, although it was a frightening country, the silent, fatal-seeming mountain-slopes, the occasional distant, suspicious, elusive natives among the trees, the great carrion birds occasionally hovering, like great flies, in the distance, over some carrion or some ranch house or some group of huts.

As she climbed, the trees shrank and the trail ran through a thorny scrub, that was trailed over with blue convolvulus and an occasional pink creeper. Then these flowers lapsed. She was nearing the pine-trees.

She was over the crest, and before her another silent, void, green-clad valley. It was past midday. Her horse turned to a little runlet of water, so she got down to eat her midday meal. She sat in silence looking at the motionless unliving valley, and at the sharp-peaked hills, rising higher to rock and pine-trees, southwards. She rested two hours in the heat of the day, while the horse cropped around her.

Curious that she was neither afraid nor lonely. Indeed, the loneliness was like a drink of cold water to one who is very thirsty. And a strange elation sustained her from within.

She travelled on, and camped at night in a valley beside a stream, deep among the bushes. She had seen cattle and had crossed several trails. There must be a ranch not far off. She heard the strange wailing shriek of a mountain-lion, and the answer of dogs. But she sat by her small camp fire in a secret hollow place and was not really afraid. She was buoyed up always by the curious, bubbling elation within her.

It was very cold before dawn. She lay wrapped in her blanket looking at the stars, listening to her horse shivering, and feeling like a woman who has died and passed beyond. She was not sure that she had not heard, during the night, a great crash at the centre of herself, which was the crash of her own death. Or else it was a crash at the centre of the earth, and meant something big and mysterious.

With the first peep of light she got up, numb with cold, and made a fire. She ate hastily, gave her horse some pieces of oil-seed cake, and set off again. She avoided any meeting—and since she met nobody, it was evident that she in turn was avoided. She came at last in sight of the village of Cuchitee, with its black houses with their reddish roofs, a sombre, dreary little cluster below another silent, long-abandoned mine. And beyond, a long, great mountain-side, rising up green and light to the darker, shaggier green of pine-trees. And beyond the pine-trees stretches of naked rock against the sky, rock slashed already and brindled with white stripes of snow. High up, the new snow had already begun to fall.

And now, as she neared, more or less, her destination, she began to go vague and disheartened. She had passed the little lake among yellowing aspen trees whose white trunks were round and suave like the white round arms of some woman. What a lovely place ! In California she would have raved about it. But here she looked and saw that it was lovely, but she didn't care. She was weary and spent with her two nights in the open, and afraid of the coming night. She didn't know where she was going, or what she was going for. Her horse plodded dejectedly on, towards that immense and forbidding mountain-slope, following a stony little trail. And if she had had any will of her own left, she would have turned back, to the village, to be protected and sent home to her husband.

But she had no will of her own. Her horse splashed through a brook, and turned up a valley, under immense yellowing cotton-wood trees. She must have been near nine thousand feet above sea-level, and her head was light with the altitude and with weariness. Beyond the cotton-wood trees she could see, on each side, the steep sides of mountain-slopes hemming her in, sharp-plumaged with overlapping aspen, and, higher up, with sprouting, pointed spruce and pine-tree. Her horse went on automatically. In this tight valley, on this slight trail, there was nowhere to go but ahead, climbing.

Suddenly her horse jumped, and three men in dark blankets were on the trail before her.

" Adios ! " came the greeting, in the full, restrained Indian voice.

" Adios ! " she replied, in her assured, American woman's voice.

" Where are you going ? " came the quiet question, in Spanish.

The men in the dark sarapes had come closer, and were looking up at her.

" On ahead," she replied coolly, in her hard, Saxon Spanish.

These were just natives to her : dark-faced, strongly-built men in dark sarapes and straw hats. They would have been the same as the men who worked for her husband, except, strangely, for the long black hair that fell over their shoulders. She noted this long black hair with a certain distaste. These must be the wild Indians she had come to see.

" Where do you come from ? " the same man asked. It was always the one man who spoke. He was young, with quick, large, bright black eyes that glanced sideways at her. He had a soft black moustache on his dark face, and a sparse tuft of beard, loose hairs on his chin. His long black hair, full of life, hung unrestrained on his shoulders. Dark as he was, he did not look as if he had washed lately.

His two companions were the same, but older men, powerful and silent. One had a thin black line of moustache, but was beardless. The other had the smooth cheeks and the sparse dark hairs marking the lines of his chin with the beard characteristic of the Indians.

" I come from far away," she replied, with half-jocular evasion.

This was received in silence.

" But where do you live ? " asked the young man, with that same quiet insistence.

" In the north," she replied airily.

Again there was a moment's silence. The young man conversed quietly, in Indian, with his two companions.

" Where do you want to go, up this way ? " he asked suddenly, with challenge and authority, pointing briefly up the trail.

" To the Chilchui Indians," answered the woman laconically.

The young man looked at her. His eyes were quick and black, and inhuman. He saw, in the full evening light, the faint sub-smile of assurance on her rather large, calm, fresh-complexioned face ; the weary, bluish lines under her large blue eyes ; and in her eyes, as she looked down at him, a half-childish, half-arrogant confidence in her own female power. But in her eyes also, a curious look of trance.

" *Usted es Señora ?* You are a lady ? " the Indian asked her.

" Yes, I am a lady," she replied complacently.

" With a family ? "

" With a husband and two children, boy and girl," she said.

The Indian turned to his companions and translated, in the low, gurgling speech, like hidden water running. They were evidently at a loss.

"Where is your husband?" asked the young man.

"Who knows?" she replied airily. "He has gone away on business for a week."

The black eyes watched her shrewdly. She, for all her weariness, smiled faintly in the pride of her own adventure and the assurance of her own womanhood, and the spell of the madness that was on her.

"And what do *you* want to do?" the Indian asked her.

"I want to visit the Chilchui Indians—to see their houses and to know their gods," she replied.

The young man turned and translated quickly, and there was a silence almost of consternation. The grave elder men were glancing at her sideways, with strange looks, from under their decorated hats. And they said something to the young man, in deep chest voices.

The latter still hesitated. Then he turned to the woman.

"Good!" he said. "Let us go. But we cannot arrive until to-morrow. We shall have to make a camp to-night."

"Good!" she said. "I can make a camp."

Without more ado, they set off at a good speed up the stony trail. The young Indian ran alongside her horse's head, the other two ran behind. One of them had taken a thick stick, and occasionally he struck her horse a resounding blow on the haunch, to urge him forward. This made the horse jump, and threw her back in the saddle, which, tired as she was, made her angry.

"Don't do that!" she cried, looking round angrily at the fellow. She met his black, large, bright eyes, and for the first time her spirit really quailed. The man's eyes were not human to her, and they did not see her as a beautiful white woman. He looked at her with a black, bright inhuman look, and saw no woman in her at all. As if she were some strange, unaccountable *thing*, incomprehensible to him, but inimical. She sat in her saddle in wonder, feeling once more as if she had died. And again he struck her horse, and jerked her badly in the saddle.

All the passionate anger of the spoilt white woman rose in her. She pulled her horse to a standstill, and turned with blazing eyes to the man at her bridle.

"Tell that fellow not to touch my horse again," she cried.

She met the eyes of the young man, and in their bright black inscrutability she saw a fine spark, as in a snake's eye, of derision. He spoke to his companion in the rear, in the low tones of the Indian. The man with the stick listened without looking. Then, giving a strange low cry to the horse, he struck it again on the rear, so that it leaped forward spasmodically up the stony trail, scattering the stones, pitching the weary woman in her seat.

The anger flew like a madness into her eyes, she went white at the gills. Fiercely she reined in her horse. But before she could turn, the young Indian had caught the reins under the horse's throat, jerked them forward, and was trotting ahead rapidly, leading the horse.

The woman was powerless. And along with her supreme anger there came a slight thrill of exultation. She knew she was dead.

The sun was setting, a great yellow light flooded the last of the aspens, flared on the trunks of the pine-trees, the pine-needles bristled and stood out with dark lustre, the rocks glowed with unearthly glamour. And through this effulgence the Indian at her horse's head trotted unweariedly on, his dark blanket swinging, his bare legs glowing with a strange transfigured ruddiness in the powerful light, and his straw hat with its half-absurd decorations of flowers and feathers shining showily above his river of long black hair. At times he would utter a low call to the horse, and then the other Indian, behind, would fetch the beast a whack with the stick.

The wonder-light faded off the mountains, the world began to grow dark, a cold air breathed down. In the sky, half a moon was struggling against the glow in the west. Huge shadows came down from steep rocky slopes. Water was rushing. The woman was conscious only of her fatigue, her unspeakable fatigue, and the cold wind from the heights. She was not aware how moonlight replaced daylight. It happened while she travelled unconscious with weariness.

For some hours they travelled by moonlight. Then suddenly they came to a standstill. The men conversed in low tones for a moment.

" We camp here," said the young man.

She waited for him to help her down. He merely stood holding the horse's bridle. She almost fell from the saddle, so fatigued.

They had chosen a place at the foot of rocks that still gave off a little warmth of the sun. One man cut pine-boughs, another erected little screens of pine-boughs against the rock for shelter, and put boughs of balsam pine for beds. The third made a small fire, to heat tortillas. They worked in silence.

The woman drank water. She did not want to eat—only to lie down.

" Where do I sleep ? " she asked.

The young man pointed to one of the shelters. She crept in and lay inert. She did not care what happened to her, she was so weary, and so beyond everything. Through the twigs of spruce she could see the three men squatting round the fire on their hams, chewing the tortillas they picked from the ashes with their dark fingers, and drinking water from a gourd. They talked in low, muttering tones, with long intervals of silence. Her saddle and saddle-bags lay not far from the fire, unopened, untouched. The men were not interested in her nor her belongings. There they squatted with their hats on their heads, eating, eating mechanically, like animals, the dark sarape with its fringe falling to the ground before and behind, the powerful dark legs naked and squatting like an animal's, showing the dirty white shirt and the sort of loin-cloth which was the only other garment, underneath. And they showed no more sign of interest in her than if she had been a piece of venison they were bringing home from the hunt, and had hung inside a shelter.

After a while they carefully extinguished the fire, and went inside their own shelter. Watching through the screen of boughs, she had a moment's thrill of fear and anxiety, seeing the dark forms cross and pass silently in the moonlight. Would they attack her now?

But no! They were as if oblivious of her. Her horse was hobbled; she could hear it hopping wearily. All was silent, mountain-silent, cold, deathly. She slept and woke and slept in a semi-conscious numbness of cold and fatigue. A long, long night, icy and eternal, and she aware that she had died.

II

Yet when there was a stirring, and a clink of flint and steel, and the form of a man crouching like a dog over a bone, at a red splutter of fire, and she knew it was morning coming, it seemed to her the night had passed too soon.

When the fire was going, she came out of her shelter with one real desire left: for coffee. The men were warming more tortillas.

" Can we make coffee? " she asked.

The young man looked at her, and she imagined the same faint spark of derision in his eyes. He shook his head.

" We don't take it," he said. " There is no time."

And the elder men, squatting on their haunches, looked up at her in the terrible paling dawn, and there was not even derision in their eyes. Only that intense, yet remote, inhuman glitter which was terrible to her. They were inaccessible. They could not see her as a woman at all. As if she *were* not a woman. As if, perhaps, her whiteness took away all her womanhood, and left her as some giant, female white ant. That was all they could see in her.

Before the sun was up, she was in the saddle again, and they were climbing steeply, in the icy air. The sun came, and soon she was very hot, exposed to the glare in the bare places. It seemed to her they were climbing to the roof of the world. Beyond against heaven were slashes of snow.

During the course of the morning, they came to a place where the horse could not go farther. They rested for a time with a great slant of living rock in front of them, like the glossy breast of some earth-beast. Across this rock, along a wavering crack, they had to go. It seemed to her that for hours she went in torment, on her hands and knees, from crack to crevice, along the slanting face of this pure rock-mountain. An Indian in front and an Indian behind walked slowly erect, shod with sandals of braided leather. But she in her riding-boots dared not stand erect.

Yet what she wondered, all the time, was why she persisted in clinging and crawling along these mile-long sheets of rock. Why she did not hurl herself down, and have done ! The world was below her.

When they emerged at last on a stony slope, she looked back, and saw the third Indian coming carrying her saddle and saddle-bags on his back, the whole hung from a band across his forehead. And he had his hat in his hand, as he stepped slowly, with the slow, soft, heavy tread of the Indian, unwavering in the chinks of rock, as if along a scratch in the mountain's iron shield.

The stony slope led downwards. The Indians seemed to grow excited. One ran ahead at a slow trot, disappearing round the curve of stones. And the track curved round and down, till at last in the full blaze of the mid-morning sun, they could see a valley below them, between walls of rock, as in a great wide chasm let in the mountains. A green valley, with a river, and trees, and clusters of low flat sparkling houses. It was all tiny and perfect, three thousand feet below. Even the flat bridge over the stream, and the square with the houses around it, the bigger buildings piled up at opposite ends of the square, the tall cotton-wood trees, the pastures and stretches of yellow-sere maize, the patches of brown sheep or goats in the distance, on the slopes, the railed enclosures by the stream-side. There it was, all small and perfect, looking magical, as any place will look magical, seen from the mountains above. The unusual thing was that the low houses glittered white, whitewashed, looking like crystals of salt, or silver. This frightened her.

They began the long, winding descent at the head of the barranca, following the stream that rushed and fell. At first it was all rocks; then the pine-trees began, and soon, the silver-limbed aspens. The flowers of autumn, big pink daisy-like flowers, and white ones, and many yellow flowers, were in profusion. But she had to sit down and rest, she was so weary. And she saw the bright flowers shadowily, as pale shadows hovering, as one who is dead must see them.

At length came grass and pasture-slopes between mingled aspen and pine-trees. A shepherd, naked in the sun save for his hat and his cotton loin-cloth, was driving his brown sheep away. In a grove of trees they sat and waited, she and the young Indian. The one with the saddle had also gone forward.

They heard a sound of someone coming. It was three men, in fine sarapes of red and orange and yellow and black, and with brilliant feather head-dresses. The oldest had his grey hair braided with fur, and his red and orange-yellow sarape was covered with curious black markings, like a leopard-skin. The other two were not grey-haired, but they were elders too. Their blankets were in stripes, and their head-dresses not so elaborate.

The young Indian addressed the elders in a few quiet words. They listened without answering or looking at him or at the woman, keeping their faces averted and their eyes turned to the ground, only listening. And at length they turned and looked at the woman.

The old chief, or medicine-man, whatever he was, had a deeply wrinkled and lined face of dark bronze, with a few sparse grey hairs round the mouth. Two long braids of grey hair, braided with fur and coloured feathers, hung on his shoulders. And yet, it was only his eyes that mattered. They were black and of extraordinary piercing strength, without a qualm of misgiving in their demonish, dauntless power. He looked into the eyes of the white woman with a long, piercing look, seeking she knew not what. She summoned all her strength to meet his eyes and keep up her guard. But it was no good. He was not looking at her as one human being looks at another. He never even perceived her resistance or her challenge, but looked past them both, into she knew not what.

She could see it was hopeless to expect any human communication with this old being.

He turned and said a few words to the young Indian.

"He asks what do you seek here?" said the young man in Spanish.

"I? Nothing! I only came to see what it was like."

This was again translated, and the old man turned his eyes on her once more. Then he spoke again, in his low muttering tone, to the young Indian.

"He says, why does she leave her house with the white men? Does she want to bring the white man's God to the Chilchui?"

"No," she replied, foolhardy. "I came away from the white man's God myself. I came to look for the God of the Chilchui."

Profound silence followed, when this was translated. Then the old man spoke again, in a small voice almost of weariness.

"Does the white woman seek the gods of the Chilchui because she is weary of her own God?" came the question.

"Yes, she does. She is tired of the white man's God," she replied, thinking that was what they wanted her to say. She would like to serve the gods of the Chilchui.

She was aware of an extraordinary thrill of triumph and exultance passing through the Indians, in the tense silence that followed when this was translated. Then they all looked at her with piercing black eyes, in which a steely covetous intent glittered incomprehensible. She was the more puzzled, as there was nothing sensual or sexual in the look. It had a terrible glittering purity that was beyond her. She was afraid, she would have been paralysed with fear, had not something died within her, leaving her with a cold, watchful wonder only.

The elders talked a little while, then the two went away, leaving her with the young man and the oldest chief. The old man now looked at her with a certain solicitude.

"He says are you tired?" asked the young man.

"Very tired," she said.

"The men will bring you a carriage," said the young Indian.

The carriage, when it came, proved to be a litter consisting of a sort of hammock of dark woollen frieze, slung on to a pole which was borne on the shoulders of two long-haired Indians. The woollen hammock was spread on the ground, she sat down on it, and the two men raised the pole to their shoulders. Swinging rather as if she were in a sack, she was carried out of the grove of trees, following the old chief, whose leopard-spotted blanket moved curiously in the sunlight.

They had emerged in the valley-head. Just in front were the maize fields, with ripe ears of maize. The corn was not very tall, in this high altitude. The well-worn path went between it, and all she could see was the erect form of the old chief, in the flame and black sarape, stepping soft and heavy and swift, his head forward, looking

neither to right nor left. Her bearers followed, stepping rhythmically, the long blue-black hair glistening like a river down the
naked shoulders of the man in front.

They passed the maize, and came to a big wall or earthwork made
of earth and adobe bricks. The wooden doors were open. Passing
on, they were in a network of small gardens, full of flowers and herbs
and fruit trees, each garden watered by a tiny ditch of running water.
Among each cluster of trees and flowers was a small, glittering white
house, windowless, and with closed door. The place was a network
of little paths, small streams, and little bridges among square,
flowering gardens.

Following the broadest path—a soft narrow track between leaves
and grass, a path worn smooth by centuries of human feet, no hoof
of horse nor any wheel to disfigure it—they came to the little river of
swift bright water, and crossed on a log bridge. Everything was
silent—there was not a human being anywhere. The road went on
under magnificent cotton-wood trees. It emerged suddenly outside
the central plaza or square of the village.

This was a long oblong of low white houses with flat roofs, and two
bigger buildings, having as it were little square huts piled on top of
bigger long huts, stood at either end of the oblong, facing each other
rather askew. Every little house was a dazzling white, save for the
great round beam-ends which projected under the flat eaves, and for
the flat roofs. Round each of the bigger buildings, on the outside of
the square, was a stockyard fence, inside which was garden with
trees and flowers, and various small houses.

Not a soul was in sight. They passed silently between the houses
into the central square. This was quite bare and arid, the earth
trodden smooth by endless generations of passing feet, passing
across from door to door. All the doors of the windowless houses
gave on to this blank square, but all the doors were closed. The
firewood lay near the threshold, a clay oven was still smoking, but
there was no sign of moving life.

The old man walked straight across the square to the big house at
the end, where the two upper storeys, as in a house of toy bricks,
stood each one smaller than the lower one. A stone staircase, outside, led up to the roof of the first storey.

At the foot of this staircase the litter-bearers stood still, and
lowered the woman to the ground.

"You will come up," said the young Indian who spoke Spanish.

She mounted the stone stairs to the earthen roof of the first house,
which formed a platform round the wall of the second storey. She

followed around this platform to the back of the big house. There they descended again, into the garden at the rear.

So far they had seen no one. But now two men appeared, bareheaded, with long braided hair, and wearing a sort of white shirt gathered into a loin-cloth. These went along with the three newcomers, across the garden where red flowers and yellow flowers were blooming, to a long, low white house. There they entered without knocking.

It was dark inside. There was a low murmur of men's voices. Several men were present, their white shirts showing in the gloom, their dark faces invisible. They were sitting on a great log of smooth old wood, that lay along the far wall. And save for this log, the room seemed empty. But no, in the dark at one end was a couch, a sort of bed, and someone lying there, covered with furs.

The old Indian in the spotted sarape, who had accompanied the woman, now took off his hat and his blanket and his sandals. Laying them aside, he approached the couch, and spoke in a low voice. For some moments there was no answer. Then an old man with the snow-white hair hanging round his darkly-visible face, roused himself like a vision, and leaned on one elbow, looking vaguely at the company, in tense silence.

The grey-haired Indian spoke again, and then the young Indian, taking the woman's hand, led her forward. In her linen riding habit, and black boots and hat, and her pathetic bit of a red tie, she stood there beside the fur-covered bed of the old, old man, who sat reared up, leaning on one elbow, remote as a ghost, his white hair streaming in disorder, his face almost black, yet with a far-off intentness, not of this world, leaning forward to look at her.

His face was so old, it was like dark glass, and the few curling hairs that sprang white from his lips and chin were quite incredible. The long white locks fell unbraided and disorderly on either side of the glassy dark face. And under a faint powder of white eyebrows, the black eyes of the old chief looked at her as if from the far, far dead, seeing something that was never to be seen.

At last he spoke a few deep, hollow words, as if to the dark air.

" He says, do you bring your heart to the god of the Chilchui ? " translated the young Indian.

" Tell him yes," she said, automatically.

There was a pause. The old Indian spoke again, as if to the air. One of the men present went out. There was a silence as if of eternity in the dim room that was lighted only through the open door.

The woman looked round. Four old men with grey hair sat on the log by the wall facing the door. Two other men, powerful and impassive, stood near the door. They all had long hair, and wore white shirts gathered into a loin-cloth. Their powerful legs were naked and dark. There was a silence like eternity.

At length the man returned, with white and dark clothing on his arm. The young Indian took them, and holding them in front of the woman, said :

" You must take off your clothes, and put these on."

" If all you men will go out," she said.

" No one will hurt you," he said quietly.

" Not while you men are here," she said.

He looked at the two men by the door. They came quickly forward, and suddenly gripped her arms as she stood, without hurting her, but with great power. Then two of the old men came, and with curious skill slit her boots down with keen knives, and drew them off, and slit her clothing so that it came away from her. In a few moments she stood there white and uncovered. The old man on the bed spoke, and they turned her round for him to see. He spoke again, and the young Indian deftly took the pins and comb from her fair hair, so that it fell over her shoulders in a bunchy tangle.

Then the old man spoke again. The Indian led her to the bed-side. The white-haired, glassy-dark old man moistened his finger-tips at his mouth, and most delicately touched her on the breasts and on the body, then on the back. And she winced strangely each time, as the finger-tips drew along her skin, as if Death itself were touching her.

And she wondered, almost sadly, why she did not feel shamed in her nakedness. She only felt sad and lost. Because nobody felt ashamed. The elder men were all dark and tense with some other deep, gloomy, incomprehensible emotion, which suspended all her agitation, while the young Indian had a strange look of ecstasy on his face. And she, she was only utterly strange and beyond herself, as if her body were not her own.

They gave her the new clothing : a long white cotton shift, that came to her knees : then a tunic of thick blue woollen stuff, embroid-ered with scarlet and green flowers. It was fastened over one shoulder only, and belted with a braid sash of scarlet and black wool.

When she was thus dressed, they took her away, barefoot, to a little house in the stockaded garden. The young Indian told her she might have what she wanted. She asked for water to wash herself. He brought it in a jar, together with a long wooden bowl. Then he fastened the gate-door of her house, and left her a prisoner. She could see through the bars of the gate-door of her house, the red flowers of the garden, and a humming bird. Then from the roof of the big house she heard the long, heavy sound of a drum, unearthly to her in its summons, and an uplifted voice calling from the house-top in a strange language, with a far-away emotionless intonation, delivering some speech or message. And she listened as if from the dead.

But she was very tired. She lay down on a couch of skins, pulling over her the blanket of dark wool, and she slept, giving up everything.

When she woke it was late afternoon, and the young Indian was entering with a basket-tray containing food, tortillas, and corn-mush with bits of meat, probably mutton, and a drink made of honey, and some fresh plums. He brought her also a long garland of red and yellow flowers with knots of blue buds at the end. He sprinkled the garland with water from a jar, then offered it to her, with a smile. He seemed very gentle and thoughtful, and on his face and in his dark eyes was a curious look of triumph and ecstasy, that frightened her a little. The glitter had gone from the black eyes, with their curving dark lashes, and he would look at her with this strange soft glow of ecstasy that was not quite human, and terribly impersonal, and which made her uneasy.

" Is there anything you want ? " he said, in his low, slow, melodious voice, that always seemed withheld, as if he were speaking aside to somebody else, or as if he did not want to let the sound come out to her.

" Am I going to be kept a prisoner here ? " she asked.

" No, you can walk in the garden to-morrow," he said softly. Always this curious solicitude.

" Do you like that drink ? " he said, offering her a little earthen-ware cup. " It is very refreshing."

She sipped the liquor curiously. It was made with herbs and sweetened with honey, and had a strange, lingering flavour. The young man watched her with gratification.

" It has a peculiar taste," she said.

" It is very refreshing," he replied, his black eyes resting on her always with that look of gratified ecstasy. Then he went away. And presently she began to be sick, and to vomit violently, as if she had no control over herself.

Afterwards she felt a great soothing languor steal over her, her limbs felt strong and loose and full of languor, and she lay on her couch listening to the sounds of the village, watching the yellowing sky, smelling the scent of burning cedar-wood, or pine-wood. So distinctly she heard the yapping of tiny dogs, the shuffle of far-off feet, the murmur of voices, so keenly she detected the smell of smoke, and flowers, and evening falling, so vividly she saw the one bright star infinitely remote, stirring above the sunset, that she felt as if all her senses were diffused on the air, that she could distinguish the sound of evening flowers unfolding, and the actual crystal sound of the heavens, as the vast belts of the world-atmosphere slid past one another, and as if the moisture ascending and the moisture descending in the air resounded like some harp in the cosmos.

She was a prisoner in her house, and in the stockaded garden, but she scarcely minded. And it was days before she realized that she never saw another woman. Only the men, the elderly men of the big house, that she imagined must be some sort of temple, and the men priests of some sort. For they always had the same colours, red, orange, yellow, and black, and the same grave, abstracted demeanour.

Sometimes an old man would come and sit in her room with her, in absolute silence. None spoke any language but Indian, save the one younger man. The older men would smile at her, and sit with her for an hour at a time, sometimes smiling at her when she spoke in Spanish, but never answering save with this slow, benevolent-seeming smile. And they gave off a feeling of almost fatherly solicitude. Yet their dark eyes, brooding over her, had something away in their depths that was awesomely ferocious and relentless. They would cover it with a smile, at once, if they felt her looking. But she had seen it.

Always they treated her with this curious impersonal solicitude, this utterly impersonal gentleness, as an old man treats a child. But underneath it she felt there was something else, something terrible. When her old visitor had gone away, in his silent, insidious, fatherly fashion, a shock of fear would come over her; though of what she knew not.

The young Indian would sit and talk with her freely, as if with great candour. But with him, too, she felt that everything real was unsaid. Perhaps it was unspeakable. His big dark eyes would rest on her almost cherishingly, touched with ecstasy, and his beautiful, slow, languorous voice would trail out its simple, ungram-matical Spanish. He told her he was the grandson of the old, old man, son of the man in the spotted sarape : and they were caciques, kings from the old, old days, before even the Spaniards came. But he himself had been in Mexico City, and also in the United States.

He had worked as a labourer, building the roads in Los Angeles. He had travelled as far as Chicago.

" Don't you speak English, then ? " she asked.

His eyes rested on her with a curious look of duplicity and conflict, and he mutely shook his head.

" What did you do with your long hair, when you were in the United States ? " she asked. " Did you cut it off ? "

Again, with the look of torment in his eyes, he shook his head.

" No," he said, in a low, subdued voice, " I wore a hat, and a handkerchief tied round my head."

And he relapsed into silence, as if of tormented memories.

" Are you the only man of your people who has been to the United States ? " she asked him.

" Yes. I am the only one who has been away from here for a long time. The others come back soon, in one week. They don't stay away. The old men don't let them."

" And why did you go ? "

" The old men want me to go—because I shall be the cacique——"

He talked always with the same *naïveté*, an almost childish candour. But she felt that this was perhaps just the effect of his Spanish. Or perhaps speech altogether was unreal to him. Anyhow, she felt that all the real things were kept back.

He came and sat with her a good deal—sometimes more than she wished—as if he wanted to be near her. She asked him if he was married. He said he was—with two children.

" I should like to see your children," she said.

But he answered only with that smile, a sweet, almost ecstatic smile, above which the dark eyes hardly changed from their enigmatic abstraction.

It was curious, he would sit with her by the hour, without ever making her self-conscious, or sex-conscious. He seemed to have no sex, as he sat there so still and gentle and apparently submissive, with his head bent a little forward, and the river of glistening black hair streaming maidenly over his shoulders.

Yet when she looked again, she saw his shoulders broad and powerful, his eyebrows black and level, the short, curved, obstinate black lashes over his lowered eyes, the small, fur-like line of moustache above his blackish, heavy lips, and the strong chin, and she knew that in some other mysterious way he was darkly and powerfully male. And he, feeling her watching him, would glance up at her swiftly with a dark, lurking look in his eyes, which immediately he veiled with that half-sad smile.

The days and the weeks went by, in a vague kind of contentment. She was uneasy sometimes, feeling she had lost the power over herself. She was not in her own power, she was under the spell of some other control. And at times she had moments of terror and horror. But then these Indians would come and sit with her, casting their insidious spell over her by their very silent presence, their silent, sexless, powerful physical presence. As they sat they seemed to take her will away, leaving her will-less and victim to her own indifference. And the young man would bring her sweetened drink, often the same emetic drink, but sometimes other kinds. And after drinking, the languor filled her heavy limbs, her senses seemed to float in the air, listening, hearing. They had brought her a little female dog, which she called Flora. And once, in the trance of her senses, she felt she *heard* the little dog conceive, in her tiny womb, and begin to be complex, with young. And another day she could hear the vast sound of the earth going round, like some immense arrow-string booming.

But as the days grew shorter and colder, when she was cold, she would get a sudden revival of her will, and a desire to go out, to go away. And she insisted to the young man, she wanted to go out.

So one day, they let her climb to the topmost roof of the big house where she was, and look down the square. It was the day of the big dance, but not everybody was dancing. Women with babies in their arms stood in their doorways, watching. Opposite, at the other end of the square, there was a throng before the other big house, and a small, brilliant group on the terrace-roof of the first storey, in front of wide open doors of the upper storey. Through these wide open doors she could see fire glinting in darkness and priests in headdresses of black and yellow and scarlet feathers, wearing robe-like blankets of black and red and yellow, with long green fringes, were moving about. A big drum was beating slowly and regularly, in the dense, Indian silence. The crowd below waited.

Then a drum started on a high beat, and there came the deep, powerful burst of men singing a heavy, savage music, like a wind roaring in some timeless forest, many mature men singing in one breath, like the wind ; and long lines of dancers walked out from under the big house. Men with naked, golden-bronze bodies and streaming black hair, tufts of red and yellow feathers on their arms, and kilts of white frieze with a bar of heavy red and black and green embroidery round their waists, bending slightly forward and stamping the earth in their absorbed, monotonous stamp of the dance, a fox-fur, hung by the nose from their belt behind, swaying with the sumptuous swaying of a beautiful fox-fur, the tip of the tail writhing above the dancer's heels. And after each man, a woman with a strange elaborate headdress of feathers and sea-shells, and wearing a short black tunic, moving erect, holding up tufts of feathers in each hand, swaying her wrists rhythmically and subtly beating the earth with her bare feet.

So, the long line of the dance unfurling from the big house opposite. And from the big house beneath her, strange scent of incense, strange tense silence, then the answering burst of inhuman male singing, and the long line of the dance unfurling.

It went on all day, the insistence of the drum, the cavernous, roaring, storm-like sound of male singing, the incessant swinging of the fox-skins behind the powerful, gold-bronze, stamping legs of the men, the autumn sun from a perfect blue heaven pouring on the rivers of black hair, men's and women's, the valley all still, the walls of rock beyond, the awful huge bulking of the mountain against the pure sky, its snow seething with sheer whiteness.

For hours and hours she watched, spell-bound, and as if drugged. And in all the terrible persistence of the drumming and the primeval, rushing deep singing, and the endless stamping of the dance of fox-tailed men, the tread of heavy, bird-erect women in their black tunics, she seemed at last to feel her own death ; her own obliteration. As if she were to be obliterated from the field of life again. In the strange towering symbols on the heads of the changeless, absorbed women she seemed to read once more the *Mene Mene Tekel Upharsin*. Her kind of womanhood, intensely personal and individual, was to be obliterated again, and the great primeval symbols were to tower once more over the fallen individual independence of woman. The sharpness and the quivering nervous consciousness of the highly-bred white woman was to be destroyed again, womanhood was to be cast once more into the great stream of impersonal sex and impersonal passion. Strangely, as if clairvoyant, she saw the immense sacrifice prepared. And she went back to her little house in a trance of agony.

After this, there was always a certain agony when she heard the drums at evening, and the strange uplifted savage sound of men singing round the drum, like wild creatures howling to the invisible gods of the moon and the vanished sun. Something of the chuckling, sobbing cry of the coyote, something of the exultant bark of the fox, the far-off wild melancholy exultance of the howling wolf, the torment of the puma's scream, and the insistence of the ancient fierce human male, with his lapses of tenderness and his abiding ferocity.

Sometimes she would climb the high roof after nightfall, and listen to the dim cluster of young men round the drum on the bridge just beyond the square, singing by the hour. Sometimes there would be a fire, and in the fire-glow, men in their white shirts or naked save for a loin-cloth, would be dancing and stamping like spectres, hour after hour in the dark cold air, within the fire-glow, forever dancing and stamping like turkeys, or dropping squatting by the fire to rest, throwing their blankets round them.

" Why do you all have the same colours ? " she asked the young Indian. " Why do you all have red and yellow and black, over your white shirts ? And the women have black tunics ? "

He looked into her eyes, curiously, and the faint, evasive smile came on to his face. Behind the smile lay a soft, strange malignancy.

" Because our men are the fire and the daytime, and our women are the spaces between the stars at night," he said.

" Aren't the women even stars ? " she said.

" No. We say they are the spaces between the stars, that keep the stars apart."

He looked at her oddly, and again the touch of derision came into his eyes.

" White people," he said, " they know nothing. They are like children, always with toys. We know the sun, and we know the moon. And we say, when a white woman sacrifice herself to our gods, then our gods will begin to make the world again, and the white man's gods will fall to pieces."

" How sacrifice herself ? " she asked quickly.

And he, as quickly covered, covered himself with a subtle smile.

" She sacrifice her own gods and come to our gods, I mean that," he said, soothingly.

But she was not reassured. An icy pang of fear and certainty was at her heart.

" The sun he is alive at one end of the sky," he continued, " and the moon lives at the other end. And the man all the time have to keep the sun happy in his side of the sky, and the woman have to keep the moon quiet at her side of the sky. All the time she have to work at this. And the sun can't ever go into the house of the moon, and the moon can't ever go into the house of the sun, in the sky. So the woman, she asks the moon to come into her cave, inside her. And the man, he draws the sun down till he has the power of the sun. All the time he do this. Then when the man gets a woman, the sun goes into the cave of the moon, and that is how everything in the world starts."

She listened, watching him closely, as one enemy watches another who is speaking with double meaning.

" Then," she said, " why aren't you Indians masters of the white men ? "

" Because," he said, " the Indian got weak, and lost his power with the sun, so the white men stole the sun. But they can't keep him—they don't know how. They got him, but they don't know what to do with him, like a boy who catch a big grizzly bear, and can't kill him, and can't run away from him. The grizzly bear eats the boy that catch him, when he want to run away from him. White men don't know what they are doing with the sun, and white women don't know what they do with the moon. The moon she got angry with white women, like a puma when someone kills her little ones. The moon, she bites white women—here inside," and he pressed his side. " The moon, she is angry in a white woman's cave. The Indian can see it. And soon," he added, " the Indian women get the moon back and keep her quiet in their house. And the Indian men get the sun, and the power over all the world. White men don't know what the sun is. They never know."

He subsided into a curious exultant silence.

" But," she faltered, " why do you hate us so ? Why do you hate me ? "

He looked up suddenly with a light on his face, and a startling flame of a smile.

" No, we don't hate," he said softly, looking with a curious glitter into her face.

" You do," she said, forlorn and hopeless.

And after a moment's silence, he rose and went away.

III

Winter had now come, in the high valley, with snow that melted in the day's sun, and nights that were bitter cold. She lived on, in a kind of daze, feeling her power ebbing more and more away from her, as if her will were leaving her. She felt always in the same relaxed, confused, victimised state, unless the sweetened herb drink would numb her mind altogether, and release her senses into a sort of heightened, mystic acuteness and a feeling as if she were diffusing out deliciously into the harmony of things. This at length became the only state of consciousness she really recognized : this exquisite sense of bleeding out into the higher beauty and harmony of things. Then she could actually hear the great stars in heaven, which she saw through her door, speaking from their motion and brightness, saying things perfectly to the cosmos, as they trod in perfect ripples, like bells on the floor of heaven, passing one another and grouping in the timeless dance, with the spaces of dark between. And she could hear the snow on a cold, cloudy day twittering and faintly whistling in the sky, like birds that flock and fly away in autumn, suddenly calling farewell to the invisible moon, and slipping out of the plains of the air, releasing peaceful warmth. She herself would call to the arrested snow to fall from the upper air. She would call to the unseen moon to cease to be angry, to make peace again with the unseen sun like a woman who ceases to be angry in her house. And she would smell the sweetness of the moon relaxing to the sun in the wintry heaven, when the snow fell in a faint, cold-perfumed relaxation, as the peace of the sun mingled again in a sort of unison with the peace of the moon.

She was aware too of the sort of shadow that was on the Indians of the valley, a deep stoical disconsolation, almost religious in its depth.

" We have lost our power over the sun, and we are trying to get him back. But he is wild with us, and shy like a horse that has got away. We have to go through a lot." So the young Indian said to her, looking into her eyes with a strained meaning. And she, as if bewitched, replied :

" I hope you will get him back."

The smile of triumph flew over his face.

" Do you hope it ? " he said.

" I do," she answered fatally.

" Then all right," he said. " We shall get him."

And he went away in exultance.

She felt she was drifting on some consummation, which she had no will to avoid, yet which seemed heavy and finally terrible to her.

It must have been almost December, for the days were short when she was taken again before the aged man, and stripped of her clothing, and touched with the old finger-tips.

The aged cacique looked her in the eyes, with his eyes of lonely, far-off, black intentness, and murmured something to her.

" He wants you to make the sign of peace," the young man translated, showing her the gesture. " Peace and farewell to him."

She was fascinated by the black, glass-like, intent eyes of the old cacique, that watched her without blinking, like a basilisk's, over-powering her. In their depths also she saw a certain fatherly compassion, and pleading. She put her hand before her face, in the required manner, making the sign of peace and farewell. He made the sign of peace back again to her, then sank among his furs. She thought he was going to die, and that he knew it.

There followed a day of ceremonial, when she was brought out before all the people, in a blue blanket with white fringe, and holding blue feathers in her hands. Before an altar of one house she was perfumed with incense and sprinkled with ash. Before the altar of the opposite house she was fumigated again with incense by the gorgeous, terrifying priests in yellow and scarlet and black, their faces painted with scarlet paint. And then they threw water on her. Meanwhile she was faintly aware of the fire on the altar, the heavy, heavy sound of a drum, the heavy sound of men beginning powerfully, deeply, savagely to sing, the swaying of the crowd of faces in the plaza below, and the formation for a sacred dance.

But at this time her commonplace consciousness was numb, she was aware of her immediate surroundings as shadows, almost immaterial. With refined and heightened senses she could hear the sound of the earth winging on its journey, like a shot arrow, the ripple-rustling of the air, and the boom of the great arrow-string. And it seemed to her there were two great influences in the upper air, one golden towards the sun, and one invisible silver ; the first travelling like rain ascending to the gold presence sunwards, the second like rain silverily descending the ladders of space towards the hovering, lurking clouds over the snowy mountain-top. Then between them, another presence, waiting to shake himself free of moisture, of heavy white snow that had mysteriously collected about him. And in summer, like a scorched eagle, he would wait to shake himself clear of the weight of heavy sunbeams. And he was coloured like fire. And he was always shaking himself clear, of snow or of heavy heat, like an eagle rustling.

Then there was a still stranger presence, standing watching from the blue distance, always watching. Sometimes running in upon the wind, or shimmering in the heat-waves. The blue wind itself, rushing as it were out of the holes into the sky, rushing out of the sky down upon the earth. The blue wind, the go-between, the invisible ghost that belonged to two worlds, that played upon the ascending and the descending chords of the rains.

More and more her ordinary personal consciousness had left her, she had gone into that other state of passional cosmic consciousness, like one who is drugged. The Indians, with their heavily religious natures, had made her succumb to their vision.

Only one personal question she asked the young Indian :

" Why am I the only one that wears blue ? "

" It is the colour of the wind. It is the colour of what goes away and is never coming back, but which is always here, waiting like death among us. It is the colour of the dead. And it is the colour that stands away off, looking at us from the distance, that cannot come near to us. When we go near, it goes farther. It can't be near. We are all brown and yellow and black hair, and white teeth and red blood. We are the ones that are here. You with blue eyes, you are the messengers from the far-away, you cannot stay, and now it is time for you to go back."

" Where to ? " she asked.

" To the way-off things like the sun and the blue mother of rain, and tell them that we are the people on the world again, and we can bring the sun to the moon again, like a red horse to a blue mare ; we are the people. The white women have driven back the moon in the sky, won't let her come to the sun. So the sun is angry. And the Indian must give the moon to the sun."

" How ? " she said.

" The white woman got to die and go like a wind to the sun, tell him the Indians will open the gate to him. And the Indian women will open the gate to the moon. The white women don't let the moon come down out of the blue coral. The moon used to come down among the Indian women, like a white goat among the flowers. And the sun want to come down to the Indian men, like an eagle to the pine-trees. The sun, he is shut out behind the white man, and the moon she is shut out behind the white woman, and they can't get away. They are angry, everything in the world gets angrier. The Indian says, he will give the white woman to the sun, so the sun will leap over the white man and come to the Indian again. And the moon will be surprised, she will see the gate open, and she not know which way to go. But the Indian woman will call to the moon, *Come ! Come ! Come back into my grasslands. The wicked white woman can't harm you any more.* Then the sun will look over the heads of the white men, and see the moon in the pastures of our women, with the Red Men standing around like pine-trees. Then he will leap over the heads of the white men, and come running past to the Indians through the spruce trees. And we, who are red and black and yellow, we who stay, we shall have the sun on our right hand and the moon on our left. So we can bring the rain down out of the blue meadows, and up out of the black ; and we can call the wind that tells the corn to grow, when we ask him, and we shall make the clouds to break, and the sheep to have twin lambs. And we shall be full of power, like a spring day. But the white people will be a hard winter, without snow——"

" But," said the white woman, " I don't shut out the moon—how can I ? "

" Yes," he said, " you shut the gate, and then laugh, think you have it all your own way."

She could never quite understand the way he looked at her. He was always so curiously gentle, and his smile was so soft. Yet there was such a glitter in his eyes, and an unrelenting sort of hate came out of his words, a strange, profound, impersonal hate. Personally he liked her, she was sure. He was gentle with her, attracted by her in some strange, soft, passionless way. But impersonally he hated her with a mystic hatred. He would smile at her, winningly. Yet if, the next moment, she glanced round at him unawares, she would catch that gleam of pure after-hate in his eyes.

" Have I got to die and be given to the sun ? " she asked.

" Sometime," he said, laughing evasively. " Sometime we all die."

They were gentle with her, and very considerate with her. Strange men, the old priests and the young cacique alike, they watched over her and cared for her like women. In their soft, insidious understanding, there was something womanly. Yet their eyes, with that strange glitter, and their dark, shut mouths that would open to the broad jaw, the small, strong, white teeth, had something very primitively male and cruel.

One wintry day, when snow was falling, they took her to a great dark chamber in the big house. The fire was burning in a corner on a high raised dais under a sort of hood or canopy of adobe-work. She saw in the fire-glow the glowing bodies of the almost naked priests, and strange symbols on the roof and walls of the chamber. There was no door or window in the chamber, they had descended by a ladder from the roof. And the fire of pinewood danced continually, showing walls painted with strange devices, which she could not understand, and a ceiling of poles making a curious pattern of black and red and yellow, and alcoves or niches in which were curious objects she could not discern.

The older priests were going through some ceremony near the fire, in silence, intense Indian silence. She was seated on a low projection of the wall, opposite the fire, two men seated beside her. Presently they gave her a drink from a cup, which she took gladly, because of the semi-trance it would induce.

In the darkness and in the silence she was accurately aware of everything that happened to her : how they took off her clothes, and, standing her before a great, weird device on the wall, coloured blue and white and black, washed her all over with water and the amole infusion ; washed even her hair, softly, carefully, and dried it on white cloths, till it was soft and glistening. Then they laid her on a couch under another great indecipherable image of red and black and yellow, and now rubbed all her body with sweet-scented oil, and massaged all her limbs, and her back, and her sides, with a long, strange, hypnotic massage. Their dark hands were incredibly powerful, yet soft with a watery softness she could not understand. And the dark faces, leaning near her white body, she saw were darkened with red pigment, with lines of yellow round the cheeks. And the dark eyes glittered absorbed, as the hands worked upon the soft white body of the woman.

They were so impersonal, absorbed in something that was beyond her. They never saw her as a personal woman : she could tell that. She was some mystic object to them, some vehicle of passions too remote for her to grasp. Herself in a state of trance, she watched their faces bending over her, dark, strangely glistening with the transparent red paint, and lined with bars of yellow. And in this weird, luminous-dark mask of living face, the eyes were fixed with an unchanging steadfast gleam, and the purplish-pigmented lips were closed in a full, sinister, sad grimness. The immense fundamental sadness, the grimness of ultimate decision, the fixity of revenge, and the nascent exultance of those that are going to triumph —these things she could read in their faces, as she lay and was rubbed into a misty glow by their uncanny dark hands. Her limbs, her flesh, her very bones at last seemed to be diffusing into a roseate sort of mist, in which her consciousness hovered like some sungleam in a flushed cloud.

She knew the gleam would fade, the cloud would go grey. But at present she did not believe it. She knew she was a victim ; that all this elaborate work upon her was the work of victimising her. But she did not mind. She wanted it.

Later, they put a short blue tunic on her and took her to the upper terrace, and presented her to the people. She saw the plaza below her full of dark faces and of glittering eyes. There was no pity : only the curious hard exultance. The people gave a subdued cry when they saw her, and she shuddered. But she hardly cared.

Next day was the last. She slept in a chamber of the big house. At dawn they put on her a big blue blanket with a fringe, and led her out into the plaza, among the throng of silent, dark-blanketed

people. There was pure white snow on the ground, and the dark
people in their dark-brown blankets looked like inhabitants of
another world.

A large drum was slowly pounding, and an old priest was declaring
from a housetop. But it was not till noon that a litter came forth,
and the people gave that low, animal cry which was so moving. In
the sack-like litter sat the old, old cacique, his white hair braided
with black braid and large turquoise stones. His face was like a piece
of obsidian. He lifted his hand in token, and the litter stopped in
front of her. Fixing her with his old eyes, he spoke to her for a few
moments, in his hollow voice. No one translated.

Another litter came, and she was placed in it. Four priests moved
ahead, in their scarlet and yellow and black, with plumed head-
dresses. Then came the litter of the old cacique. Then the light
drums began, and two groups of singers burst simultaneously into
song, male and wild. And the golden-red, almost naked men,
adorned with ceremonial feathers and kilts, the rivers of black hair
down their backs, formed into two files and began to tread the
dance. So they threaded out of the snowy plaza, in two long, sumptuous lines of dark red-gold and black and fur, swaying with a faint
tinkle of bits of shell and flint, winding over the snow between the
two bee-clusters of men who sang around the drum.

Slowly they moved out, and her litter, with its attendance of
feathered, lurid, dancing priests, moved after. Everybody danced
the tread of the dance-step, even, subtly, the litter-bearers. And
out of the plaza they went, past smoking ovens, on the trail to the
great cotton-wood trees, that stood like grey-silver lace against the
blue sky, bare and exquisite above the snow. The river, diminished,
rushed among fangs of ice. The chequer-squares of gardens within
fences were all snowy, and the white houses now looked yellowish.

The whole valley glittered intolerably with pure snow, away to
the walls of the standing rock. And across the flat cradle of snow-
bed wound the long thread of the dance, shaking slowly and sumptuously in its orange and black motion. The high drums thudded
quickly, and on the crystalline frozen air the swell and roar of the
chant of savages was like an obsession.

She sat looking out of her litter with big, transfixed blue eyes,
under which were the wan markings of her drugged weariness.
She knew she was going to die, among the glisten of this snow, at the
hands of this savage, sumptuous people. And as she stared at
the blaze of the blue sky above the slashed and ponderous mountain,
she thought : " I am dead already. What difference does it make, the

transition from the dead I am to the dead I shall be, very soon ! "
Yet her soul sickened and felt wan.

The strange procession trailed on, in perpetual dance, slowly
across the plain of snow, and then entered the slopes between the
pine-trees. She saw the copper-dark men dancing the dance-tread,
onwards, between the copper-pale tree trunks. And at last she, too,
in her swaying litter, entered the pine-trees.

They were travelling on and on, upwards, across the snow under
the trees, past the superb shafts of pale, flaked copper, the rustle and
shake and tread of the threading dance, penetrating into the
forest, into the mountain. They were following a stream-bed : but
the stream was dry, like summer, dried up by the frozenness of the
head-waters. There were dark, red-bronze willow bushes with
wattles like wild hair, and pallid aspen-trees looking cold flesh
against the snow. Then jutting dark rocks.

At last she could tell that the dancers were moving forward no
more. Nearer and nearer she came upon the drums, as to a lair of
mysterious animals. Then through the bushes she emerged into a
strange amphitheatre. Facing was a great wall of hollow rock,
down the front of which hung a great, dripping, fang-like spoke of
ice. The ice came pouring over the rock from the precipice above,
and then stood arrested, dripping out of high heaven, almost down
to the hollow stones where the stream-pool should be below. But
the pool was dry.

On either side the dry pool the lines of dancers had formed, and
the dance was continuing without intermission, against a background of bushes.

But what she felt was that fanged inverted pinnacle of ice, hanging
from the lip of the dark precipice above. And behind the great rope
of ice she saw the leopard-like figures of priests climbing the hollow
cliff face, to the cave that like a dark socket bored a cavity, an orifice,
half-way up the crag.

Before she could realize, her litter-bearers were staggering in the
footholds, climbing the rock. She, too, was behind the ice. There it
hung, like a curtain that is not spread, but hangs like a great fang.
And near above her was the orifice of the cave sinking dark into the
rock. She watched it as she swayed upwards.

On the platform of the cave stood the priests, waiting in all their
gorgeousness of feathers and fringed robes, watching her ascent.
Two of them stooped to help her litter-bearer. And at length she
was on the platform of the cave, far in behind the shaft of ice, above
the hollow amphitheatre among the bushes below, where men were

dancing, and the whole populace of the village was clustered in silence.

The sun was sloping down the afternoon sky, on the left. She knew that this was the shortest day of the year, and the last day of her life. They stood her facing the iridescent column of ice, which fell down marvellously arrested, away in front of her.

Some signal was given, and the dance below stopped. There was now absolute silence. She was given a little to drink, then two priests took off her mantle and her tunic, and in her strange pallor she stood there, between the lurid robes of the priests, beyond the pillar of ice, beyond and above the dark-faced people. The throng below gave the low, wild cry. Then the priest turned her round, so she stood with her back to the open world, her long blond hair to the people below. And they cried again.

She was facing the cave, inwards. A fire was burning and flickering in the depths. Four priests had taken off their robes, and were almost as naked as she was. They were powerful men in the prime of life, and they kept their dark, painted faces lowered.

From the fire came the old, old priest, with an incense-pan. He was naked and in a state of barbaric ecstasy. He fumigated his victim, reciting at the same time in a hollow voice. Behind him came another robeless priest, with two flint knives.

When she was fumigated, they laid her on a large flat stone, the four powerful men holding her by the outstretched arms and legs. Behind stood the aged man, like a skeleton covered with dark glass, holding a knife and transfixedly watching the sun ; and behind him again was another naked priest, with a knife.

She felt little sensation, though she knew all that was happening. Turning to the sky, she looked at the yellow sun. It was sinking. The shaft of ice was like a shadow between her and it. And she realized that the yellow rays were filling half the cave, though they had not reached the altar where the fire was, at the far end of the funnel-shaped cavity.

Yes, the rays were creeping round slowly. As they grew ruddier, they penetrated farther. When the red sun was about to sink, he would shine full through the shaft of ice deep into the hollow of the cave, to the innermost.

She understood now that this was what the men were waiting for. Even those that held her down were bent and twisted round, their black eyes watching the sun with a glittering eagerness, and awe, and craving. The black eyes of the aged cacique were fixed like black mirrors on the sun, as if sightless, yet containing some terrible answer to the reddening winter planet. And all the eyes of the priests were fixed and glittering on the sinking orb, in the reddening, icy silence of the winter afternoon.

They were anxious, terribly anxious, and fierce. Their ferocity wanted something, and they were waiting the moment. And their ferocity was ready to leap out into a mystic exultance, of triumph. But still they were anxious.

Only the eyes of that oldest man were not anxious. Black, and fixed, and as if sightless, they watched the sun, seeing beyond the sun. And in their black, empty concentration there was power, power intensely abstract and remote, but deep, deep to the heart of the earth, and the heart of the sun. In absolute motionlessness he watched till the red sun should send his ray through the column of ice. Then the old man would strike, and strike home, accomplish the sacrifice and achieve the power.

The mastery that man must hold, and that passes from race to race.

He had decided to sit up all night, as a kind of penance. The telegram had simply said : " Ophelia's condition critical." He felt, under the circumstances, that to go to bed in the *wagon-lit* would be frivolous. So he sat wearily in the first-class compartment as night fell over France.

He ought, of course, to be sitting by Ophelia's bedside. But Ophelia didn't want him. So he sat up in the train.

Deep inside him was a black and ponderous weight : like some tumour filled with sheer gloom, weighing down his vitals. He had always taken life seriously. Seriousness now overwhelmed him. His dark, handsome, clean-shaven face would have done for Christ on the Cross, with the thick black eyebrows tilted in the dazed agony.

The night in the train was like an inferno : nothing was real. Two elderly Englishwomen opposite him had died long ago, perhaps even before he had. Because, of course, he was dead himself.

Slow, grey dawn came in the mountains of the frontier, and he watched it with unseeing eyes. But his mind repeated :—

> " And when the dawn came, dim and sad
> And chill with early showers,
> Her quiet eyelids closed : she had
> Another morn than ours."

And his monk's changeless, tormented face showed no trace of the contempt he felt, even self-contempt, for this bathos, as his critical mind judged it.

He was in Italy : he looked at the country with faint aversion. Not capable of much feeling any more, he had only a tinge of aversion as he saw the olives and the sea. A sort of poetic swindle.

It was night again when he reached the home of the Blue Sisters, where Ophelia had chosen to retreat. He was ushered into the Mother Superior's room, in the palace. She rose and bowed to him in silence, looking at him along her nose. Then she said in French :

" It pains me to tell you. She died this afternoon."

He stood stupefied, not feeling much, anyhow, but gazing at nothingness from his handsome, strong-featured monk's face.

The Mother Superior softly put her white, handsome hand on his arm and gazed up into his face, leaning to him.

" Courage ! " she said softly. " Courage, no ? "

He stepped back. He was always scared when a woman leaned at him like that. In her voluminous skirts, the Mother Superior was very womanly.

" Quite ! " he replied in English. " Can I see her ? "

The Mother Superior rang a bell, and a young sister appeared. She was rather pale, but there was something naïve and mischievous in her hazel eyes. The elder woman murmured an introduction, the young woman demurely made a slight reverence. But Matthew held out his hand, like a man reaching for the last straw. The young nun unfolded her white hands and shyly slid one into his, passive as a sleeping bird.

And out of the fathomless Hades of his gloom he thought : " What a nice hand ! "

They went along a handsome but cold corridor, and tapped at a door. Matthew, walking in far-off Hades, still was aware of the soft, fine voluminousness of the women's black skirts, moving with soft, fluttered haste in front of him.

He was terrified when the door opened, and he saw the candles burning round the white bed, in the lofty, noble room. A sister sat beside the candles, her face dark and primitive, in the white coif, as she looked up from her breviary. Then she rose, a sturdy woman, and made a little bow, and Matthew was aware of creamy-dusky hands twisting a black rosary, against the rich, blue silk on her bosom.

The three sisters flocked silent, yet fluttered and very feminine, in their volumes of silky black skirts, to the bed-head. The Mother Superior leaned, and with utmost delicacy lifted the veil of white lawn from the dead face.

Matthew saw the dead, beautiful·composure of his wife's face, and instantly, something leaped like laughter in the depths of him, he gave a little grunt, and an extraordinary smile came over his face.

The three nuns, in the candle glow that quivered warm and quick like a Christmas tree, were looking at him with heavily compassionate eyes, from under their coif-bands. They were like a mirror. Six eyes suddenly started with a little fear, then changed, puzzled, into wonder. And over the three nuns' faces, helplessly facing him in the candle-glow, a strange, involuntary smile began to come. In the three faces, the same smile growing so differently, like three subtle flowers opening. In the pale young nun, it was almost pain, with

a touch of mischievous ecstasy. But the dark Ligurian face of the
watching sister, a mature, level-browed woman, curled with a pagan
smile, slow, infinitely subtle in its archaic humour. It was the
Etruscan smile, subtle and unabashed, and unanswerable.

The Mother Superior, who had a large-featured face something
like Matthew's own, tried hard not to smile. But he kept his
humorous, malevolent chin uplifted at her, and she lowered her face
as the smile grew, grew and grew over her face.

The young, pale sister suddenly covered her face with her sleeve,
her body shaking. The Mother Superior put her arm over the girl's
shoulder, murmuring with Italian emotion : " Poor little thing !
Weep, then, poor little thing ! " But the chuckle was still there,
under the emotion. The sturdy dark sister stood unchanging,
clutching the black beads, but the noiseless smile immovable.

Matthew suddenly turned to the bed, to see if his dead wife had
observed him. It was a movement of fear.

Ophelia lay so pretty and so touching, with her peaked, dead little
nose sticking up, and her face of an obstinate child fixed in the final
obstinacy. The smile went away from Matthew, and the look of
super-martyrdom took its place. He did not weep : he just gazed
without meaning. Only, on his face deepened the look : I knew this
martyrdom was in store for me !

She was so pretty, so childlike, so clever, so obstinate, so worn—
and so dead ! He felt so blank about it all.

They had been married ten years. He himself had not been
perfect—no, no, not by any means ! But Ophelia had always wanted
her own will. She had loved him, and grown obstinate, and left him,
and grown wistful, or contemptuous, or angry, a dozen times, and
a dozen times come back to him.

They had no children. And he, sentimentally, had always
wanted children. He felt very largely sad.

Now she would never come back to him. This was the thirteenth
time, and she was gone for ever.

But was she ? Even as he thought it, he felt her nudging him
somewhere in the ribs, to make him smile. He writhed a little, and
an angry frown came on his brow. He was not *going* to smile ! He
set his square, naked jaw, and bared his big teeth, as he looked down
at the infinitely provoking dead woman. " At it again ! "—he
wanted to say to her, like the man in Dickens.

He himself had not been perfect. He was going to dwell on his
own imperfections.

He turned suddenly to the three women, who had faded back-

wards beyond the candles, and now hovered, in the white frames of
their coifs, between him and nowhere. His eyes glared, and he
bared his teeth.

"Mea culpa ! Mea culpa !" he snarled.

"Macchè !" exclaimed the daunted Mother Superior, and her
two hands flew apart, then together again, in the density of the
sleeves, like birds nesting in couples.

Matthew ducked his head and peered round, prepared to bolt.
The Mother Superior, in the background, softly intoned a Pater
Noster, and her beads dangled. The pale young sister faded farther
back. But the black eyes of the sturdy, black-avised sister twinkled
like eternally humorous stars upon him, and he felt the smile digging
him in the ribs again.

"Look here !" he said to the women, in expostulation, "I'm
awfully upset. I'd better go."

They hovered in fascinating bewilderment. He ducked for the
door. But even as he went, the smile began to come on his face,
caught by the tail of the sturdy sister's black eye, with its everlasting
twink. And, he was secretly thinking, he wished he could hold both
her creamy-dusky hands, that were folded like mating birds,
voluptuously.

But he insisted on dwelling upon his own imperfections. *Mea
culpa !* he howled at himself. And even as he howled it, he felt
something nudge him in the ribs, saying to him : *Smile !*

The three women left behind in the lofty room looked at one
another, and their hands flew up for a moment, like six birds flying
suddenly out of the foliage, then settling again.

"Poor thing !" said the Mother Superior, compassionately.

"Yes ! Yes ! Poor thing !" cried the young sister, with naïve,
shrill impulsiveness.

"Già !" said the dark-avised sister.

The Mother Superior noiselessly moved to the bed, and leaned over
the dead face.

"She seems to know, poor soul !" she murmured. "Don't you
think so ?"

The three coifed heads leaned together. And for the first time
they saw the faint ironical curl at the corners of Ophelia's mouth.
They looked in fluttering wonder.

"She has seen him !" whispered the thrilling young sister.

The Mother Superior delicately laid the fine-worked veil over the
cold face. Then they murmured a prayer for the anima, fingering
their beads. Then the Mother Superior set two of the candles

straight upon their spikes, clenching the thick candle with firm, soft grip, and pressing it down.

The dark-faced, sturdy sister sat down again with her little holy book. The other two rustled softly to the door, and out into the great white corridor. There softly, noiselessly sailing in all their dark drapery, like dark swans down a river, they suddenly hesitated. Together they had seen a forlorn man's figure, in a melancholy overcoat, loitering in the cold distance at the corridor's end. The Mother Superior suddenly pressed her pace into an appearance of speed.

Matthew saw them bearing down on him, these voluminous figures with framed faces and lost hands. The young sister trailed a little behind.

" Pardon, ma Mère ! " he said, as if in the street. " I left my hat somewhere. . . ."

He made a desperate, moving sweep with his arm, and never was man more utterly smileless.

KATHERINE FARQUHAR was a handsome women of forty, no longer slim, but attractive in her soft, full feminine way. The French porters ran round her, getting a voluptuous pleasure from merely carrying her bags. And she gave them ridiculously high tips, because, in the first place, she had never really known the value of money, and secondly, she had a morbid fear of underpaying anyone, but particularly a man who was eager to serve her.

It was really a joke to her, how eagerly these Frenchmen—all sorts of Frenchmen—ran round her, and *Madame'd* her. Their voluptuous obsequiousness. Because, after all, she was Boche. Fifteen years of marriage to an Englishman—or rather to two Englishmen—had not altered her racially. Daughter of a German Baron she was, and remained in her own mind and body, although England had become her life-home. And surely she looked German, with her fresh complexion and her strong, full figure. But, like most people in the world, she was a mixture, with Russian blood and French blood also in her veins. And she had lived in one country and another, till she was somewhat indifferent to her surroundings. So that perhaps the Parisian men might be excused for running round her so eagerly, and getting a voluptuous pleasure from calling a taxi for her, or giving up a place in the omnibus to her, or carrying her bags, or holding the menu card before her. Nevertheless, it amused her. And she had to confess she liked them, these Parisians. They had their own kind of manliness, even if it wasn't an English sort ; and if a woman looked pleasant and soft-fleshed, and a wee bit helpless, they were ardent and generous. Katherine understood so well that Frenchmen were rude to the dry, hard-seeming, competent English-woman or American. She sympathized with the Frenchman's point of view ; too much obvious capacity to help herself is a disagreeable trait in a woman.

At the Gare de l'Est, of course, everybody was expected to be Boche, and it was almost a convention, with the porters, to assume a certain small-boyish superciliousness. Nevertheless, there was the same voluptuous scramble to escort Katherine Farquhar to her seat in the first-class carriage. *Madame* was travelling alone.

She was going to Germany via Strasburg, meeting her sister in Baden-Baden. Philip, her husband, was in Germany, collecting some sort of evidence for his newspaper. Katherine felt a little weary of newspapers, and of the sort of " evidence " that is extracted out of nowhere to feed them. However, Philip was quite clever, he was a little somebody in the world.

Her world, she had realized, consisted almost entirely of little somebodies. She was outside the sphere of the nobodies, always had been. And the Somebodies with a capital " S " were all safely dead. She knew enough of the world to-day to know that it is not going to put up with any great Somebody ; but many little nobodies and a sufficient number of little somebodies. Which, after all, is as it should be, she felt.

Sometimes she had vague misgivings.

Paris, for example, with its Louvre and its Luxembourg and its cathedral, seemed intended for Somebody. In a ghostly way it called for some supreme Somebody. But all its little men, nobodies and somebodies, were as sparrows twittering for crumbs, and dropping their little droppings on the palace cornices.

To Katherine, Paris brought back again her first husband, Alan Anstruther, that red-haired fighting Celt, father of her two grown-up children. Alan had had a weird innate conviction that he was beyond ordinary judgment. Katherine could never quite see where it came in. Son of a Scottish baronet, and captain in a Highland regiment did not seem to her stupendous. As for Alan himself, he was handsome in uniform, with his kilt swinging and his blue eye glaring. Even stark naked and without any trimmings, he had a bony, dauntless, overbearing manliness of his own. The one thing Katherine could *not quite* appreciate was his silent, indomitable assumption that he was actually first-born, a born lord. He was a clever man, too, ready to assume that General This or Colonel That might really be his superior. Until he actually came into contact with General This or Colonel That. Whereupon his over-weening blue eye arched in his bony face, and a faint tinge of contempt infused itself into his homage.

Lordly, or not, he wasn't much of a success in the worldly sense. Katherine had loved him, and he had loved her : that was indisputable. But when it came to innate conviction of lordliness, it was a question which of them was worse. For she, in her amiable, queen-bee self thought that ultimately hers was the right to the last homage.

Alan had been too unyielding and haughty to say much. But sometimes he would stand and look at her in silent rage, wonder, and indignation. The wondering indignation had been *almost* too much for her. What did the man think he was ?

He was one of the hard, clever Scotsmen, with a philosophic tendency, but without sentimentality. His contempt of Nietzsche, whom she adored, was intolerable. Alan just asserted himself like a pillar of rock, and expected the tides of the modern world to recede around him. They didn't.

So he concerned himself with astronomy, gazing through a telescope and watching the worlds beyond worlds. Which seemed to give him relief.

After ten years they had ceased to live together, passionate as they both were. They were too proud and unforgiving to yield to one another, and much too haughty to yield to any outsider.

Alan had a friend, Philip, also a Scotsman, and a university friend. Philip, trained for the bar, had gone into journalism, and had made himself a name. He was a little black Highlander of the insidious sort, clever and *knowing*. This look of knowing in his dark eyes, and the feeling of secrecy that went with his dark little body, made him interesting to women. Another thing he could do was to give off a great sense of warmth and offering, like a dog when it loves you. He seemed to be able to do this at will. And Katherine, after feeling cool about him and rather despising him for years, at last fell under the spell of the dark, insidious fellow.

" You ! " she said to Alan, whose overweening masterfulness drove her wild. " You don't even know that a woman exists. And that's where Philip Farquhar is more than you are. He *does* know something of what a woman *is*."

" Bah ! the little——" said Alan, using an obscene word of contempt.

Nevertheless, the friendship endured, kept up by Philip, who had an almost uncanny love for Alan. Alan was mostly indifferent. But he was used to Philip, and habit meant a great deal to him.

" Alan really is an amazing man ! " Philip would say to Katherine. " He is the only real man, what I call a real man, that I have ever met."

" But why is he the only real man ? " she asked. " Don't you call yourself a real man ? "

" Oh, *I*—I'm different ! My strength lies in giving in—and then recovering myself. I do let myself be swept away. But, so far, I've always managed to get myself back again. Alan——" and Philip even had a half-reverential, half-envious way of uttering the word— " Alan *never* lets himself be swept away. And he's the only man I know who doesn't."

" Yah ! " she said. " He is fooled by plenty of things. You can fool him through his vanity."

" No," said Philip. " Never altogether. You *can't* deceive him right through. When a thing really touches Alan, it is tested once and for all. You know if it's false or not. He's the only man I ever met who *can't help* being real."

" Ha ! You overrate his reality," said Katherine, rather scornfully.

And later, when Alan shrugged his shoulders with that mere indifferent tolerance, at the mention of Philip, she got angry.

" You are a poor friend," she said.

" Friend ! " he answered. " I never was Farquhar's friend ! If he asserts that he's mine, that's his side of the question. I never positively cared for the man. He's too much over the wrong side of the border for me."

" Then," she answered, " you've no business to let him *consider* he is your friend. You've no right to let him think so much of you. You should tell him you don't like him."

" I've told him a dozen times. He seems to enjoy it. It seems part of his game."

And he went away to his astronomy.

Came the war, and the departure of Alan's regiment for France.

" There ! " he said. " Now you have to pay the penalty of having married a soldier. You find him fighting your own people. So it is."

She was too much struck by this blow even to weep.

" Good-bye ! " he said, kissing her gently, lingeringly. After all, he had been a husband to her.

And as he looked back at her, with the gentle, protective husband-knowledge in his blue eyes, and at the same time that other quiet realization of destiny, her consciousness fluttered into incoherence. She only wanted to alter everything, to alter the past, to alter all the flow of history—the terrible flow of history. Secretly somewhere inside herself she felt that with her queen-bee love, and queen-bee will, she *could* divert the whole flow of history—nay, even reverse it.

But in the remote, realizing look that lay at the back of his eyes, back of all his changeless husband-care, she saw that it could never be so. That the whole of her womanly, motherly concentration could never put back the great flow of human destiny. That, as he said, only the cold strength of a man, accepting the destiny of destruction, could see the human flow through the chaos and beyond to a new outlet. But the chaos first, and the long rage of destruction.

For an instant her will broke. Almost her soul seemed broken. And then he was gone. And as soon as he was gone she recovered the core of her assurance.

Philip was a great consolation to her. He asserted that the war was monstrous, that it should never have been, and that men should refuse to consider it as anything but a colossal, disgraceful accident.

She, in her German soul, knew that it was no accident. It was inevitable, and even necessary. But Philip's attitude soothed her enormously, restored her to herself.

Alan never came back. In the spring of 1915 he was missing. She had never mourned for him. She had never really considered him dead. In a certain sense she had triumphed. The queen-bee had recovered her sway, as queen of the earth ; the woman, the mother, the female with the ear of corn in her hand, as against the man with the sword.

Philip had gone through the war as a journalist, always throwing his weight on the side of humanity, and human truth and peace. He had been an inexpressible consolation. And in 1921 she had married him.

The thread of fate might be spun, it might even be measured out, but the hand of Lachesis had been stayed from cutting it through.

At first it was wonderfully pleasant and restful and voluptuous, especially for a woman of thirty-eight, to be married to Philip. Katherine felt he caressed her senses, and soothed her, and gave her what she wanted.

Then, gradually, a curious sense of degradation started in her spirit. She felt unsure, uncertain. It was almost like having a disease. Life became dull and unreal to her, as it had never been before. She did not even struggle and suffer. In the numbness of her flesh she could feel no reactions. Everything was turning into mud.

Then again, she would recover, and *enjoy* herself wonderfully. And after a while, the suffocating sense of nullity and degradation once more. Why, why, why did she feel degraded, in her secret soul ? *Never*, of course, outwardly.

The memory of Alan came back into her. She still thought of him and his relentlessness with an arrested heart, but without the angry hostility she used to feel. A little awe of him, of his memory, stole back into her spirit. She resisted it. She was not used to feeling awe.

She realized, however, the difference between being married to a soldier, a ceaseless born fighter, a sword not to be sheathed, and this other man, this cunning civilian, this subtle equivocator, this adjuster of the scales of truth.

Philip was cleverer than she was. He set her up, the queen-bee, the mother, the woman, the female judgment, and he served her with subtle, cunning homage. He put the scales, the balance in her hand. But also, cunningly, he blindfolded her, and manipulated the scales when she was sightless.

Dimly she had realized all this. But only dimly, confusedly, because she was blindfolded. Philip had the subtle, fawning power that could keep her always blindfolded.

Sometimes she gasped and gasped from her oppressed lungs. And sometimes the bony, hard, masterful, but honest face of Alan would come back, and suddenly it would seem to her that she was all right again, that the strange, voluptuous suffocation, which left her soul in mud, was gone, and she could breathe the air of the open heavens once more. Even fighting air.

It came to her on the boat crossing the Channel. Suddenly she seemed to feel Alan at her side again, as if Philip had never existed. As if Philip had never meant anything more to her than the shop-assistant measuring off her orders. And escaping, as it were, by herself across the cold, wintry Channel, she suddenly deluded herself into feeling as if Philip had never existed, only Alan had ever been her husband. He was her husband still. And she was going to meet him.

This gave her her blitheness in Paris, and made the Frenchmen so nice to her. For the Latins love to feel a woman is really enveloped in the spell of some man. Beyond all race is the problem of man and woman.

Katherine now sat dimly, vaguely excited and almost happy in the railway carriage on the East railroad. It was like the old days when she was going home to Germany. Or even more like the old days when she was coming back to Alan. Because, in the past, when he was her husband, feel as she might towards him, she could never get over the sensation that the wheels of the railway carriage had wings, when they were taking her back to him. Even when she knew that he was going to be awful to her, hard and relentless and destructive, still the motion went on wings.

Whereas towards Philip she moved with a strange, disintegrating reluctance. She decided not to think of him.

As she looked unseeing out of the carriage window, suddenly, with a jolt, the wintry landscape realized itself in her consciousness. The flat, grey, wintry landscape, ploughed fields of greyish earth that looked as if they were compounded of the clay of dead men. Pallid, stark, thin trees stood like wire beside straight, abstract roads. A ruined farm between a few more trees. And a dismal village filed past, with smashed houses like rotten teeth between the straight rows of the village street.

With sudden horror she realized that she must be in the Marne country, the ghastly Marne country, century after century digging the corpses of frustrated men into its soil. The border country, where the Latin races and the Germanic neutralize one another into horrid ash.

Perhaps even the corpse of her own man among that grey clay.

It was too much for her. She sat ashy herself with horror, wanting to escape.

" If I had only known," she said. " If only I had known, I would have gone by Basle."

The train drew up at Soissons ; name ghastly to her. She simply tried to make herself unreceptive to everything. And mercifully luncheon was served. She went down to the restaurant car, and sat opposite to a little French officer in horizon-blue uniform, who suggested anything but war. He looked so naïve, rather child-like and nice, with the certain innocence that so many French people preserve under their so-called wickedness, that she felt really relieved. He bowed to her with an odd, shy little bow when she returned him his half-bottle of red wine, which had slowly jigged its way the length of the table, owing to the motion of the train. How nice he was ! And how he would give himself to a woman, if she would only find real pleasure in the male that he was.

Nevertheless, she herself felt very remote from this business of male and female, and giving and taking.

After luncheon, in the heat of the train and the flush of her half-bottle of white wine, she went to sleep again, her feet grilling uncomfortably on the iron plate of the carriage floor. And as she slept, life, as she had known it, seemed all to turn artificial to her, the sunshine of the world an artificial light, with smoke above, like the light of torches, and things artificially growing, in a night that was lit up artificially with such intensity that it gave the illusion of day. It had been an illusion, her life-day, as a ballroom evening is an illusion. Her love and her emotions, her very panic of love, had been an illusion. She realized how love had become panic-stricken inside her, during the war.

And now even this panic of love was an illusion. She had run to Philip to be saved. And now, both her panic-love and Philip's salvation were an illusion.

What remained then ? Even panic-stricken love, the intensest thing, perhaps, she had ever felt, was only an illusion. What was left? The grey shadows of death?

When she looked out again it was growing dark, and they were at Nancy. She used to know this country as a girl. At half-past seven she was in Strasburg, where she must stay the night as there was no train over the Rhine till morning.

The porter, a blond, hefty fellow, addressed her at once in Alsatian German. He insisted on escorting her safely to her hotel—a German hotel—keeping guard over her like an appointed sentinel, very faithful and competent, so different from Frenchmen.

It was a cold, wintry night, but she wanted to go out after dinner to see the minster. She remembered it all so well, in that other life.

The wind blew icily in the street. The town seemed empty, as if its spirit had left it. The few squat, hefty foot-passengers were all talking the harsh Alsatian German. Shop-signs were in French, often with a little concession to German underneath. And the shops were full of goods, glutted with goods from the once-German factories of Mulhausen and other cities.

She crossed the night-dark river, where the wash-houses of the washerwomen were anchored along the stream, a few odd women still kneeling over the water's edge, in the dim electric light, rinsing their clothes in the grim, cold water. In the big square the icy wind was blowing, and the place seemed a desert. A city once more conquered.

After all she could not remember her way to the cathedral. She saw a French policeman in his blue cape and peaked cap, looking a lonely, vulnerable, silky specimen in this harsh Alsatian city. Crossing over to him she asked him in French where was the cathedral.

He pointed out to her, the first turning on the left. He did not seem hostile; nobody seemed really hostile. Only the great frozen weariness of winter in a conquered city, on a weary everlasting border-line.

And the Frenchmen seemed far more weary, and also more sensitive, than the crude Alsatians.

She remembered the little street, the old, overhanging houses with black timbers and high gables. And like a great ghost, a reddish flush in its darkness, the uncanny cathedral breasting the oncomer, standing gigantic, looking down in darkness out of darkness, on the pigmy humanness of the city. It was built of reddish stone, that had a flush in the night, like dark flesh. And vast, an incomprehensibly tall, strange thing, it looked down out of the night. The great rose window, poised high, seemed like a breast of the vast Thing, and prisms and needles of stone shot up, as if it were plumage, dimly, half-visible in heaven.

There it was, in the upper darkness of the ponderous winter night, like a menace. She remembered, her spirit used in the past to soar aloft with it. But now, looming with a faint rust of blood out of the upper black heavens, the Thing stood suspended, looking down with vast, demonish menace, calm and implacable.

Mystery and dim, ancient fear came over the woman's soul. The cathedral looked so strange and demonish-heathen. And an ancient, indomitable blood seemed to stir in it. It stood there like some vast silent beast with teeth of stone, waiting, and wondering when to stoop against this pallid humanity.

And dimly she realized that behind all the ashy pallor and sulphur of our civilization, lurks the great blood-creature waiting, implacable and eternal, ready at last to crush our white brittleness and let the shadowy blood move erect once more, in a new implacable pride and strength. Even out of the lower heavens looms the great blood-dusky Thing, blotting out the Cross it was supposed to exalt.

The scroll of the night sky seemed to roll back, showing a huge, blood-dusky presence looming enormous, stooping, looking down, awaiting its moment.

As she turned to go away, to move away from the closed wings of the minster, she noticed a man standing on the pavement, in the direction of the post-office which functions obscurely in the Cathedral Square. Immediately, she knew that that man, standing dark and motionless, was Alan. He was alone, motionless, remote.

He did not move towards her. She hesitated, then went in his direction, as if going to the post-office. He stood perfectly motionless, and her heart died as she drew near. Then, as she passed, he turned suddenly, looking down on her.

It was he, though she could hardly see his face, it was so dark, with a dusky glow in the shadow.

"Alan!" she said.

He did not speak, but laid his hand detainingly on her arm, as he used in the early days, with strange silent authority. And turning her with a faint pressure on her arm, he went along with her, leisurely, through the main street of the city, under the arcade where the shops were still lighted up.

She glanced at his face ; it seemed much more dusky, and duskily ruddy, than she had known him. He was a stranger : and yet it was he, no other. He said nothing at all. But that was also in keeping.

His mouth was closed, his watchful eyes seemed changeless, and there was a shadow of silence around him, impenetrable, but not cold. Rather aloof and gentle, like the silence that surrounds a wild animal.

She knew that she was walking with his spirit. But that even did not trouble her. It seemed natural. And there came over her again the feeling she had forgotten, the restful, thoughtless pleasure of a woman who moves in the aura of the man to whom she belongs. As a young woman she had had this unremarkable, yet very precious feeling, when she was with her husband. It had been a full content-ment ; and perhaps the fullness of it had made her unconscious of it. Later, it seemed to her she had almost wilfully destroyed it, this soft flow of contentment which she, a woman, had from him as a man.

Now, afterwards, she realized it. And as she walked at his side through the conquered city, she realized that it was the one enduring thing a woman can have, the intangible soft flood of contentment that carries her along at the side of the man she is married to. It is her perfection and her highest attainment.

Now, in the afterwards, she knew it. Now the strife was gone. And dimly she wondered why, why, why she had ever fought against it. No matter what the man does or is, as a person, if a woman can move at his side in this dim, full flood of contentment, she has the highest of him, and her scratching efforts at getting more than this, are her ignominious efforts at self-nullity.

Now, she knew it, and she submitted. Now that she was walking with a man who came from the halls of death, to her, for her relief. The strong, silent kindliness of him towards her, even now, was able to wipe out the ashy, nervous horror of the world from her body. She went at his side, still and released, like one newly unbound, walking in the dimness of her own contentment.

At the bridge-head he came to a standstill, and drew his hand from her arm. She knew he was going to leave her. But he looked at her from under his peaked cap, darkly but kindly, and he waved his hand with a slight, kindly gesture of farewell, and of promise, as if in farewell he promised never to leave her, never to let the kindliness go out in his heart, to let it stay here always.

She hurried over the bridge with tears running down her cheeks, and on to her hotel. Hastily she climbed to her room. And as she undressed, she avoided the sight of her own face in the mirror. She must not rupture the spell of his presence.

Now, in the afterwards she realized *how* careful she must be, not to break the mystery that enveloped her. Now that she knew he had come back to her from the dead, she was aware how precious and how fragile the coming was. He had come back with his heart dark and kind, wanting her even in the afterwards. And not in any sense must she go against him. The warm, powerful, silent ghost had come back to her. It was he. She must not even try to think about him definitely, not to realize him or to understand. Only in her own woman's soul could she silently ponder him, darkly, and know him present in her, without ever staring at him or trying to find him out. Once she tried to lay hands on him, to *have* him, to *realize* him, he would be gone for ever, and gone for ever this last precious flood of her woman's peace.

" Ah, no ! " she said to herself. " If he leaves his peace with me, I must ask no questions whatsoever."

And she repented, silently, of the way she had questioned and demanded answers, in the past. What were the answers, when she had got them ? Terrible ash in the mouth.

She now knew the supreme modern terror, of a world all ashy and nerve-dead. If a man could come back out of death to save her from this, she would not ask questions of him, but be humble, and beyond tears grateful.

In the morning, she went out into the icy wind, under the grey sky, to see if he would be there again. Not that she *needed* him : his presence was still about her. But he might be waiting.

The town was stony and cold. The people looked pale, chilled through, and doomed in some way. Very far from her they were. She felt a sort of pity for them, but knew she could do nothing, nothing in time or eternity. And they looked at her, and looked quickly away again, as if they were uneasy in themselves.

The cathedral reared its great reddish-grey façade in the stark light ; but it did not loom as in the night. The cathedral square was hard and cold. Inside, the church was cold and repellent, in spite of the glow of stained glass. And he was nowhere to be found.

So she hastened away to her hotel and to the station, to catch the 10.30 train into Germany.

It was a lonely, dismal train, with a few forlorn souls waiting to cross the Rhine. Her Alsatian porter looked after her with the same dogged care as before. She got into the first-class carriage that was going through to Prague—she was the only passenger travelling first. A real French porter, in blouse and moustache, and swagger, tried to say something a bit jeering to her, in his few words of German. But she only looked at him, and he subsided. He didn't really want to be rude. There was a certain hopelessness even about that.

The train crept slowly, disheartened, out of town. She saw the

weird humped-up creature of the cathedral in the distance, pointing
its one finger above the city. Why, oh, why, had the old Germanic
races put it there, like that !

Slowly the country disintegrated into the Rhine flats and marshes,
the canals, the willow trees, the overflow streams, the wet places
frozen but not flooded. Weary the place all seemed. And old
Father Rhine flowing in greenish volume, implacable, separating
the races now weary of race struggle, but locked in the toils as in the
coils of a great snake, unable to escape. Cold, full, green, and
utterly disheartening the river came along under the wintry sky,
passing beneath the bridge of iron.

There was a long wait in Kehl, where the German officials and the
French observed a numb, dreary kind of neutrality. Passport and
customs examination was soon over. But the train waited and
waited, as if unable to get away from that point of pure negation,
where the two races neutralized one another, and no polarity was
felt, no life—no principle dominated.

Katherine Farquhar just sat still, in the suspended silence of her
husband's return. She heeded neither French nor German, spoke
one language or the other at need, hardly knowing. She waited,
while the hot train steamed and hissed, arrested at the perfect neutral
point of the new border line, just across the Rhine.

And at last a little sun came out, and the train silently drew away,
nervously, from the neutrality.

In the great flat field of the Rhine plain, the shallow flood water
was frozen, the furrows ran straight towards nowhere, the air seemed
frozen, too, but the earth felt strong and barbaric, it seemed to
vibrate, with its straight furrows, in a deep, savage undertone.
There was the frozen, savage thrill in the air also, something wild
and unsubdued, pre-Roman.

This part of the Rhine valley, even on the right bank in Germany,
was occupied by the French ; hence the curious vacancy, the
suspense, as if no men lived there, but some spirit was watching,
watching over the vast, empty, straight-furrowed fields and the
water-meadows. Stillness, emptiness, suspense, and a sense of
something still impending.

A long wait in the station of Appenweier, on the main line of the
Right-bank railway. The station was empty. Katherine remembered its excited, thrilling bustle in pre-war days.

" Yes," said the German guard to the stationmaster, " what do
they hurry us out of Strasburg for, if they are only going to keep us
so long here ? "

The heavy Badisch German ! The sense of resentful impotence in the Germans ! Katherine smiled to herself. She realized that here the train left the occupied territory.

At last they set off, northwards, free for the moment, in Germany. It was the land beyond the Rhine, Germany of the pine forests. The very earth seemed strong and unsubdued, bristling with a few reeds and bushes, like savage hair. There was the same silence, and waiting, and the old barbaric undertone of the white-skinned north, under the waning civilization. The audible overtone of our civilization seemed to be wearing thin, the old, low, pine-forest hum and roar of the ancient north seemed to be sounding through. At least, in Katherine's inner ear.

And there were the ponderous hills of the Black Forest, heaped and waiting sullenly, as if guarding the inner Germany. Black round hills, black with forest, save where white snow-patches of field had been cut out. Black and white, waiting there in the near distance, in sullen guard.

She knew the country so well. But not in this present mood, the emptiness, the sullenness, the heavy, recoiled waiting.

Steinbach ! Then she was nearly there ! She would have to change in Oos, for Baden-Baden, her destination. Probably Philip would be there to meet her, in Oos ; he would have come down from Heidelberg.

Yes, there he was ! And at once she thought he looked ill, yellowish. His figure hollow and defeated.

" Aren't you well ? " she asked, as she stepped out of the train on to the empty station.

" I'm so frightfully cold," he said. " I can't get warm."

" And the train was so hot," she said.

At last a porter came to carry her bags across to the little connecting train.

" How are you ? " he said, looking at her with a certain pinched look in his face, and fear in his eyes.

" All right ! It all feels very queer," she said.

" I don't know how it is," he said, " but Germany freezes my inside, and does something to my chest."

" We needn't stay long," she said easily.

He was watching the bright look in her face. And she was thinking how queer and *chétif* he looked ! Extraordinary ! As she looked at him she felt for the first time, with curious clarity, that it was humiliating to be married to him, even in name. She was humiliated even by the fact that her name was Katherine Farquhar. Yet she used to think it a nice name !

" Just think of me married to that little man ! " she thought to herself. " Think of my having his name ! "

It didn't fit. She thought of her own name : Katherine von Todtnau ; or of her married name : Katherine Anstruther. The first seemed most fitting. But the second was her second nature. The third, Katherine Farquhar, wasn't her at all.

" Have you seen Marianne ? " she asked.

" Oh, yes ! "

He was very brief. What was the matter with him ?

" You'll have to be careful, with your cold," she said politely.

" I *am* careful ! " he cried petulantly.

Marianne, her sister, was at the station, and in two minutes they were rattling away in German, and laughing and crying and exploding with laughter again. Philip quite ignored. In these days of frozen economy, there was no taxi. A porter would wheel up the luggage on a trolley, the new arrivals walked to their little hotel, through the half-deserted town.

" But the little one is quite nice ! " said Marianne deprecatingly.

" Isn't he ! " cried Katherine in the same tone.

And both sisters stood still and laughed in the middle of the street. " The little one " was Philip.

" The other was more a man," said Marianne. " But I'm sure this one is easier. *The little one !* Yes, he *should* be easier," and she laughed in her mocking way.

" The stand-up-mannikin ! " said Katherine, referring to those little toy men weighted at the base with lead, that always stand up again.

Philip was very unhappy in this atmosphere. His strength was in his weakness, his appeal, his clinging dependence. He quite cunningly got his own way, almost every time : but always by seeming to give in. In every emergency he bowed as low as need be and let the storm pass over him. Then he rose again, the same as ever, sentimental, on the side of the angels, offering defiance to nobody. The defiant men had been killed off during the war. He had seen it and secretly smiled. When the lion is shot, the dog gets the spoil. So he had come in for Katherine, Alan's lioness. A live dog is better than a dead lion. And so the little semi-angelic journalist exulted in the triumph of his weakness.

But in Germany, in weird post-war Germany, he seemed snuffed out again. The air was so cold and vacant, all feeling seemed to have gone out of the country. Emotion, even sentiment, was numbed quite dead, as in a frost-bitten limb. And if the sentiment were numbed out of him, he was truly dead.

" I'm most frightfully glad you've come, Kathy," he said. " I could hardly have held out another day here, without you. I feel you're the only thing on earth that remains real."

" You don't seem very real to me," she said.

" I'm not real ! I'm *not !*—not when I'm alone. But when I'm with you I'm the most real man alive. I know it ! "

This was the sort of thing that had fetched her in the past, thrilled her through and through in her womanly conceit, even made her fall in love with the little creature who could so generously admit such pertinent truths. So different from the lordly Alan, who expected a woman to bow down to him !

Now, however, some of the coldness of numbed Germany seemed to have got into her breast too. She felt a cruel derision of the whimpering little beast who claimed reality only through a woman. She did not answer him, but looked out at the snow falling between her and the dark trees. Another world ! When the snow left off, how bristling and ghostly the cold fir-trees looked, tall, conical creatures crowding darkly and half-whitened with snow ! So tall, so wolfish !

Philip shivered and looked yellower. There was shortage of fuel, shortage of food, shortage of everything. He wanted Katherine to go to Paris with him. But she would stay at least two weeks near her people. The shortage she would put up with. She saw at evening the string of decent townsfolk waiting in the dark—the town was not half-lighted—to fill their hot-water bottles at the hot spring outside the Kurhaus, silent, spectral, unable to afford fire to heat their own water. And she felt quite cold about Philip's shivering. Let him shiver.

The snow was crisp and dry, she walked out in the forest, up the steep slopes. The world was curiously vacant, gone wild again. She realized how very quickly the world would go wild, if catastrophes overtook mankind. Philip, yellow and hollow, would trudge stumbling and reeling beside her : ludicrous. He was a man who never would walk firm on his legs. Now he just flopped. She could feel Alan among the trees, the thrill and vibration of him. And sometimes she would glance with beating heart at a great round fir-trunk that stood so alive and potent, so physical, bristling all its vast drooping greenness above the snow. She could feel him, Alan, in the trees' potent presence. She wanted to go and press herself against the trunk. But Philip would sit down on the snow, saying :

" Look here, Kathy, I can't go any farther. I've simply got no strength left ! "

She stood on the path, proud, contemptuous, but silent, looking away towards where the dull, reddish rocks cropped out. And there, among the rocks, she was sure, Alan was waiting for her. She felt fierce and overbearing. Yet she took the stumbling Philip home.

He was really ill. She put him to bed, and he stayed in bed. The doctor came. But Philip was in a state of panic, afraid of everything. Katherine would walk out by herself, into the forest. She was expecting Alan, and was tingling to meet him. Then Philip would lie in bed half-conscious, and when she came back he would say, his big eyes glowing :

" You must have been *very far !* " And on the last two words he would show his large front teeth in a kind of snarl.

" Not very far," she said.

One day Alan came to her from out of the dull reddish rocks in the forest. He was wearing a kilt that suited him so : but a khaki tunic. And he had no cap on. He came walking towards her, his knees throwing the kilt in the way she knew so well. He came triumphantly, rather splendid, and she waited trembling. He was always utterly silent. But he led her away with his arm round her, and she yielded in a complete yielding she had never known before. And among the rocks he made love to her, and took her in the silent passion of a husband, took a complete possession of her.

Afterwards she walked home in a muse, to find Philip seriously ill. She could see, he really might die. And she didn't care a bit. But she tended him, and stayed with him, and he seemed to be better.

The next day, however, she wanted to go out in the afternoon, she *must !* She could feel her husband waiting, and the call was imperative. She must go. But Philip became almost hysterical when she wanted to leave him.

" I assure you I shall die while you are out ! I assure you I shall die if you leave me now ! " He rolled his eyes wildly, and looked so queer, she felt it was true. So she stayed, sullen and full of resentment, her consciousness away among the rocks.

The afternoon grew colder and colder. Philip shivered in bed, under the great bolster.

" But it's a murderous cold ! It's murdering me ! " he said.

She did not mind it. She sat abstracted, remote from him, her spirit going out into the frozen evening. A very powerful flow seemed to envelop her in another reality. It was Alan calling to her, holding her. And the hold seemed to grow stronger every hour.

She slept in the same room as Philip. But she had decided not to go to bed. He was really very weak. She would sit up with him. Towards midnight he roused, and said faintly :

" Katherine, I can't bear it ! "—and his eyes rolled up showing only the whites.

" What ? What can't you bear ? " she said, bending over him.

" I can't bear it ! I can't bear it ! Hold me in your arms. Hold me ! Hold me ! " he whispered in pure terror of death.

Curiously reluctant, she began to push her hands under his shoulders, to raise him. As she did so, the door opened, and Alan came in, bareheaded, and a frown on his face. Philip lifted feeble hands, and put them round Katherine's neck, moaning faintly. Silent, bareheaded, Alan came over to the bed and loosened the sick man's hands from his wife's neck, and put them down on the sick man's own breast.

Philip unfurled his lips and showed his big teeth in a ghastly grin of death. Katherine felt his body convulse in strange throes under the hands, then go inert. He was dead. And on his face was a sickly grin of a thief caught in the very act.

But Alan drew her away, drew her to the other bed, in the silent passion of a husband come back from a very long journey.

" HE is very fine and strong somewhere, but he does need a level-headed woman to look after him."

That was the *friendly* feminine verdict upon him. It flattered him, it pleased him, it galled him.

Having divorced a very charming and clever wife, who had held this opinion for ten years, and at last had got tired of the level-headed protective game, his gall was uppermost.

" I want to throw Jimmy out on the world, but I know the poor little man will go and fall on some woman's bosom. That's the worst of him. If he could only stand alone for ten minutes. But he can't. At the same time, there *is* something fine about him, something rare."

This had been Clarissa's summing-up as she floated away in the arms of the rich young American. The rich young American got rather angry when Jimmy's name was mentioned. Clarissa was now *his* wife. But she did sometimes talk as if she were still married to Jimmy.

Not in Jimmy's estimation, however. That worm had turned. Gall was uppermost. Gall and wormwood. He knew exactly what Clarissa thought—and said—about him. And the " something fine, something rare, something strong " which he was supposed to have " about him " was utterly outbalanced, in his feelings at least, by the " poor little man " nestled upon " some woman's bosom," which he was supposed to *be*.

" I am *not*," he said to himself, " a poor little man nestled upon some woman's bosom. If I could only find the right sort of woman, she should nestle on mine."

Jimmy was now thirty-five, and this point, to nestle or to be nestled, was the emotional crux and turning-point.

He imagined to himself some really *womanly* woman, to whom he should be *only* " fine and strong," and not for one moment " the poor little man." Why not some simple uneducated girl, some Tess of the D'Urbervilles, some wistful Gretchen, some humble Ruth gleaning an aftermath? Why not? Surely the world was full of such !

The trouble was he never met them.   He only met sophisticated women.   He really never had a chance of meeting " real " people. So few of us ever do.   Only the people we *don't* meet are the " real " people, the simple, genuine, direct, spontaneous, unspoilt souls.   Ah, the simple, genuine, unspoilt people we *don't* meet !   What a tragedy it is !

Because, of course, they must be there !   Somewhere !   Only we never come across them.

Jimmy was terribly handicapped by his position.   It brought him into contact with so many people.   Only never the right sort.   Never the " real " people : the simple, genuine, unspoilt, etc. etc.

He was editor of a high-class, rather high-brow, rather successful magazine, and his rather personal, very candid editorials brought him shoals, swarms, hosts of admiring acquaintances.   Realize that he was handsome, and could be extraordinarily " nice," when he liked, and was really very clever, in his own critical way, and you see how many chances he had of being adored and protected.

In the first place his good looks : the fine, clean lines of his face, like the face of the laughing faun in one of the faun's unlaughing, moody moments.   The long, clean lines of the cheeks, the strong chin and the slightly arched, full nose, the beautiful dark-grey eyes with long lashes, and the thick black brows. In his mocking moments, when he seemed most himself, it was a pure Pan face, with thick black eyebrows cocked up, and grey eyes with a sardonic goaty gleam, and nose and mouth curling with satire.   A good-looking, smooth-skinned satyr.   That was Jimmy at his best.   In the opinion of his men friends.

In his own opinion, he was a sort of Martyred Saint Sebastian, at whom the wicked world shot arrow after arrow—Mater Dolorosa nothing to him—and he counted the drops of blood as they fell : when he could keep count.   Sometimes—as for instance when Clarissa said she was really departing with the rich young American, and should she divorce Jimmy, or was Jimmy going to divorce her ?—then the arrows assailed him like a flight of starlings, flying straight at him, jabbing at him, and the drops of martyred blood simple spattered down, he couldn't keep count.

So, naturally, he divorced Clarissa.

In the opinion of his men friends, he was, or should be, a consistently grinning faun, satyr, or Pan-person.   In his own opinion, he was a Martyred Saint Sebastian with the mind of a Plato.   In the opinion of his woman friends, he was a fascinating little man with a profound understanding of life and the capacity really to understand a woman and to make a woman feel a queen ; which of course was to make a woman feel her *real* self. . . .

He might, naturally, have made rich and resounding marriages, especially after the divorce. He didn't. The reason was, secretly, his resolve never to make any woman feel a queen any more. It was the turn of the women to make him feel a king.

Some unspoilt, unsophisticated, wild-blooded woman, to whom he would be a sort of Solomon of wisdom, beauty, and wealth. She would need to be in reduced circumstances to appreciate his wealth, which amounted to the noble sum of three thousand pounds and a little week-ending cottage in Hampshire. And to be unsophisticated she would have to be a woman of the people. Absolutely.

At the same time, not just the " obscure vulgar simplican."

He received many letters, many, many, many, enclosing poems, stories, articles, or more personal unbosomings. He read them all : like a solemn rook pecking and scratching among the litter.

And one—not one letter, but one correspondent—might be *the* one —Mrs. Emilia Pinnegar, who wrote from a mining village in Yorkshire. She was, of course, unhappily married.

Now Jimmy had always had a mysterious feeling about these dark and rather dreadful mining villages in the north. He himself had scarcely set foot north of Oxford. He felt that these miners up there must be the real stuff. And Pinnegar was a name, surely ! And Emilia !

She wrote a poem, with a brief little note, that, if the editor of the *Commentator* thought the verses of no value, would he simply destroy them. Jimmy, as editor of the *Commentator*, thought the verses quite good and admired the brevity of the note. But he wasn't sure about printing the poem. He wrote back, Had Mrs. Pinnegar nothing else to submit ?

Then followed a correspondence. And at length, upon request, this from Mrs. Pinnegar :

" You ask me about myself, but what shall I say ? I am a woman of thirty-one, with one child, a girl of eight, and I am married to a man who lives in the same house with me, but goes to another woman. I try to write poetry, if it is poetry, because I have no other way of expressing myself at all, and even if it doesn't matter to anybody besides myself, I feel I must and will express myself, if only to save myself from developing cancer or some disease that women have. I was a school-teacher before I was married, and I got my certificates at Rotherham College. If I could, I would teach again, and live alone.   But married women teachers can't get jobs any more, they aren't allowed——"

THE COAL-MINER

By His Wife

The donkey-engine's beating noise
And the rattle, rattle of the sorting screens
Come down on me like the beat of his heart,
And mean the same as his breathing means.

The burning big pit-hill with fumes
Fills the air like the presence of that fair-haired man.
And the burning fire burning deeper and deeper
Is his will insisting since time began.

As he breathes the chair goes up and down
In the pit-shaft ; he lusts as the wheel-fans spin
The sucking air : he lives in the coal
Underground : and his soul is a strange engine.

That is the manner of man he is.
I married him and I should know.
The mother earth from bowels of coal
Brought him forth for the overhead woe.

This was the poem that the editor of the *Commentator* hesitated about.   He reflected, also, that Mrs. Pinnegar didn't sound like one of the nestling, unsophisticated rustic type.   It was something else that still attracted him : something desperate in a woman, something tragic.

THE NEXT EVENT

If at evening, when the twilight comes,
    You ask me what the day has been,
I shall not know.   The distant drums
    Of some new-comer intervene

Between me and the day that's been.
    Some strange man leading long columns
Of unseen soldiers through the green
    Sad twilight of these smoky slums.

And as the darkness slowly numbs
    My senses, everything I've seen
Or heard the daylight through, becomes
    Rubbish behind an opaque screen.

> Instead, the sound of muffled drums
>   Inside myself : I have to lean
> And listen as my strength succumbs,
>   To hear what these oncomings mean.
>
> Perhaps the Death-God striking his thumbs
>   On the drums in a deadly rat-ta-ta-plan.
> Or a strange man marching slow as he strums
>   The tune of a new weird hope in Man.
>
> What does it matter ! The day that began
>   In coal-dust is ending the same, in crumbs
> Of darkness like coal. I live if I can ;
>   If I can't, then I welcome whatever comes.

This poem sounded so splendidly desperate, the editor of the *Commentator* decided to print it, and, moreover, to see the authoress. He wrote, Would she care to see him, if he happened to be in her neighbourhood ? He was going to lecture in Sheffield. She replied, Certainly.

He gave his afternoon lecture, on *Men in Books and Men in Life*. Naturally, men in books came first. Then he caught a train to reach the mining village where the Pinnegars lived.

It was February, with gruesome patches of snow. It was dark when he arrived at Mill Valley, a sort of thick, turgid darkness full of menace, where men speaking in a weird accent went past like ghosts, dragging their heavy feet and emitting the weird scent of the coal-mine underworld. Weird and a bit gruesome it was.

He knew he had to walk uphill to the little market-place. As he went, he looked back and saw the black valleys with bunches of light, like camps of demons it seemed to him. And the demonish smell of sulphur and coal in the air, in the heavy, pregnant, clammy darkness.

They directed him to New London Lane, and down he went down another hill. His skin crept a little. The place felt uncanny and hostile, hard, as if iron and minerals breathed into the black air. Thank goodness he couldn't see much, or be seen. When he had to ask his way the people treated him in a " heave-half-a-brick-at-him " fashion.

After much weary walking and asking, he entered a lane between trees, in the cold slushy mud of the unfrozen February. The mines, apparently, were on the outskirts of the town, in some mud-sunk country. He could see the red, sore fires of the burning pit-hill through the trees, and he smelt the sulphur. He felt like some modern Ulysses wandering in the realms of Hecate. How much more dismal and horrible, a modern Odyssey among mines and factories, than any Sirens, Scyllas or Charybdises.

So he mused to himself as he waded through icy black mud, in a black lane, under black trees that moaned an accompaniment to the sound of the coal-mine's occasional hissing and chuffing, under a black sky that quenched even the electric sparkle of the colliery. And the place seemed unhabited like a cold black jungle.

At last he came in sight of a glimmer. Apparently, there were dwellings. Yes, a new little street, with one street-lamp, and the houses all apparently dark. He paused. Absolute desertion. Then three children.

They told him the house, and he stumbled up a dark passage. There was light on the little back-yard. He knocked, in some trepidation. A rather tall woman, looking down at him with a "Who are you?" look, from the step above.

"Mrs. Pinnegar?"

"Oh, is it you, Mr. Frith? Come in."

He stumbled up the step into the glaring light of the kitchen. There stood Mrs. Pinnegar, a tall woman with a face like a mask of passive anger, looking at him coldly. Immediately he felt his own shabbiness and smallness. In utter confusion, he stuck out his hand.

"I had an awful time getting here," he said. "I'm afraid I shall make a frightful mess of your house." He looked down at his boots.

"That's all right," she said. "Have you had your tea?"

"No—but don't you bother about me."

There was a little girl with fair hair in a fringe over her forehead, troubled blue eyes under the fringe, and two dolls. He felt easier.

"Is this your little girl?" he asked. "She's awfully nice. What is her name?"

"Jane."

"How are you, Jane?" he said. But the child only stared at him with the baffled, bewildered, pained eyes of a child who lives with hostile parents.

Mrs. Pinnegar set his tea, bread, and butter, jam, and buns. Then she sat opposite him. She was handsome, dark straight brows and grey eyes with yellow grains in them, and a way of looking straight at you as if she were used to holding her own. Her eyes were the nicest part of her. They had a certain kindliness, mingled, like the yellow grains among the grey, with a relentless, unyielding feminine will. Her nose and mouth were straight, like a Greek mask, and the expression was fixed. She gave him at once the impression of a woman who has made a mistake, who knows it, but who will not change : who cannot now change.

He felt very uneasy. Being a rather small, shambling man, she made him aware of his physical inconspicuousness. And she said not a word, only looked down on him, as he drank his tea, with that changeless look of a woman who is holding her own against Man and Fate. While, from the corner across the kitchen, the little girl with her fair hair and her dolls, watched him also in absolute silence, from her hot blue eyes.

" This seems a pretty awful place," he said to her.

" It is. It's absolutely awful," the woman said.

" You ought to get away from it," he said.

But she received this in dead silence.

It was exceedingly difficult to make any headway. He asked about Mr. Pinnegar. She glanced at the clock.

" He comes up at nine," she said.

" Is he down the mine ? "

" Yes. He's on the afternoon shift."

There was never a sound from the little girl.

" Doesn't Jane ever talk ? " he asked.

" Not much," said the mother, glancing round.

He talked a little about his lectures, about Sheffield, about London. But she was not really interested. She sat there rather distant, very laconic, looking at him with those curious unyielding eyes. She looked to him like a woman who has had her revenge, and is left stranded on the reefs where she wrecked her opponent. Still unrelenting, unregretting, unyielding, she seemed rather undecided as to what her revenge had been, and what it had all been about.

" You ought to get away from here," he said to her.

" Where to ? " she asked.

" Oh "—he made a vague gesture—" anywhere, so long as it is *quite* away."

She seemed to ponder this, under her portentous brow.

" I don't see what difference it would make," she said. Then glancing round at her child : " I don't see what difference anything would make, except getting out of the world altogether. But there's *her* to consider." And she jerked her head in the direction of the child.

Jimmy felt definitely frightened. He wasn't used to this sort of grimness. At the same time he was excited. This handsome, laconic woman, with her soft brown hair and her unflinching eyes with their gold flecks, seemed to be challenging him to something. There was a touch of challenge in her remaining gold-flecked kindness. Somewhere, she had a heart. But what had happened to it? And why?

What had gone wrong with her? In some way, she must have gone against herself.

" Why don't you come and live with me? " he said, like the little gambler he was.

The queer, conflicting smile was on his face. He had taken up her challenge, like a gambler. The very sense of a gamble, in which he could not lose desperately, excited him. At the same time, he was scared of her, and determined to get beyond his scare.

She sat and watched him, with the faintest touch of a grim smile on her handsome mouth.

" How do you mean, live with you? " she said.

" Oh—I mean what it usually means," he said, with a little puff of self-conscious laughter.

" You're evidently not happy here. You're evidently in the wrong circumstances altogether. You're obviously *not* just an ordinary woman. Well, then, break away. When I say, Come and live with me, I mean just what I say. Come to London and live with me as my wife, if you like, and then if we want to marry, when you get a divorce, why, we can do it."

Jimmy made this speech more to himself than to the woman. That was how he was. He worked out all his things inside himself, as if it were all merely an interior problem of his own. And while he did so, he had an odd way of squinting his left eye and wagging his head loosely, like a man talking absolutely to himself, and turning his eyes inwards.

The woman watched him in a sort of wonder. This was something she was *not* used to. His extraordinary manner, and his extraordinary bald proposition, roused her from her own tense apathy.

" Well! " she said. " That's got to be thought about. What about *her?* "—and again she jerked her head towards the round-eyed child in the corner. Jane sat with a completely expressionless face, her little red mouth fallen a little open. She seemed in a sort of trance : as if she understood like a grown-up person, but, as a child, sat in a trance, unconscious.

The mother wheeled round in her chair and stared at her child. The little girl stared back at her mother, with hot, troubled, almost guilty blue eyes. And neither said a word. Yet they seemed to exchange worlds of meaning.

"Why, of course," said Jimmy, twisting his head again; "she'd come, too."

The woman gave a last look at her child, then turned to him, and started watching *him* with that slow, straight stare.

"It's not"—he began, stuttering—"it's not anything *sudden* and unconsidered on my part. I've been considering it for quite a long time—ever since I had the first poem, and your letter."

He spoke still with his eyes turned inwards, talking to himself. And the woman watched him unflinchingly.

"Before you ever saw me?" she asked, with a queer irony.

"Oh, of course. Of course before I ever saw you. Or else I never *should* have seen you. From the very first, I had a definite feeling——"

He made odd, sharp gestures, like a drunken man, and he spoke like a drunken man, his eyes turned inward, talking to himself. The woman was no more than a ghost moving inside his own consciousness, and he was addressing her there.

The actual woman sat outside looking on in a sort of wonder. This was really something new to her.

"And now you see me, do you want me, really, to come to London?"

She spoke in a dull tone of incredulity. The thing was just a little preposterous to her. But why not? It would have to be something a little preposterous, to get her out of the tomb she was in.

"Of course I do!" he cried, with another scoop of his head and scoop of his hand. "*Now* I do *actually* want you, now I actually see you." He never looked at her. His eyes were still turned in. He was still talking to himself, in a sort of drunkenness with himself.

To her, it was something extraordinary. But it roused her from apathy.

He became aware of the hot blue eyes of the hot-cheeked little girl fixed upon him from the distant corner. And he gave a queer little giggle.

"Why, it's more than I could ever have hoped for," he said, "to have you and Jane to live with me! Why, it will mean *life* to me." He spoke in an odd, strained voice, slightly delirious. And for the first time he looked up at the woman and, apparently, *straight* at her. But, even as he seemed to look straight at her, the curious cast was in his eye, and he was only looking at himself, inside himself, at the shadows inside his own consciousness.

"And when would you like me to come?" she asked, rather coldly.

"Why, as soon as possible. Come back with me to-morrow, if

you will. I've got a little house in St. John's Wood, *waiting* for you
Come with me to-morrow. That's the simplest."

She watched him for some time, as he sat with ducked head. He
looked like a man who is drunk—drunk with himself. He was
going bald at the crown, his rather curly black hair was thin.

"I couldn't come to-morrow, I should need a few days," she said.

She wanted to see his face again. It was as if she could not
remember what his face was like, this strange man who had appeared
out of nowhere, with such a strange proposition.

He lifted his face, his eyes still cast in that inturned, blind look.
He looked now like a Mephistopheles who has gone blind. With his
black brows cocked up, Mephistopheles, Mephistopheles blind and
begging in the street.

"Why, of course it's wonderful that it's happened like this for me, "
he said, with odd pouting emphasis, pushing out his lips. "I was
finished, absolutely finished. I was finished while Clarissa was with
me. But after she'd gone, I was *absolutely* finished. And I thought
there was no chance for me in the world again. It seems to me perfectly marvellous that this has happened—that I've come across
you——" he lifted his face sightlessly—"and Jane—Jane—why she's
really too good to be true." He gave a slight hysterical laugh. "She
really is."

The woman, and Jane, watched him with some embarrassment.

"I shall have to settle up here, with Mr. Pinnegar," she said,
rather coldly musing. "Do you want to see him?"

"Oh, I——" he said, with a deprecating gesture, "I don't *care*.
But if you think I'd better—why, certainly——"

"I do think you'd better," she said.

"Very well, then, I *will*. I'll see him whenever you like."

"He comes in soon after nine," she said.

"All right, I'll see him then. Much better. But I suppose I'd
better see about finding a place to sleep first. Better not leave it too
late."

"I'll come with you and ask for you."

"Oh, you'd better not, really. If you tell me where to go——"

He had taken on a protective tone : he was protecting her against
herself and against scandal. It was his manner, his rather Oxfordy
manner, more than anything else, that went beyond her. She
wasn't used to it.

Jimmy plunged out into the gulfing blackness of the Northern
night, feeling how horrible it was, but pressing his hat on his brow
in a sense of strong adventure. He was going through with it.

At the baker's shop, where she had suggested he should ask for a bed, they would have none of him. Absolutely they didn't like the looks of him. At the Pub, too, they shook their heads : didn't want to have anything to do with him. But, in a voice more expostulatingly Oxford than ever, he said :

" But look here—you can't ask a man to sleep under one of these hedges. Can't I see the landlady ? "

He persuaded the landlady to promise to let him sleep on the big, soft settee in the parlour, where the fire was burning brightly. Then, saying he would be back about ten, he returned through mud and drizzle up New London Lane.

The child was in bed, a saucepan was boiling by the fire. Already the lines had softened a little in the woman's face.

She spread a cloth on the table. Jimmy sat in silence, feeling that she was hardly aware of his presence. She was absorbed, no doubt, in the coming of her husband. The stranger merely sat on the sofa, and waited. He felt himself wound up tight. And once he was really wound up, he could go through with anything.

They heard the nine o'clock whistle at the mine. The woman then took the saucepan from the fire and went into the scullery. Jimmy could smell the smell of potatoes being strained. He sat quite still. There was nothing for him to do or to say. He was wearing his big black-rimmed spectacles, and his face, blank and expressionless in the suspense of waiting, looked like the death-mask of some sceptical philosopher, who could wait through the ages, and who could hardly distinguish life from death at any time.

Came the heavy-shod tread up the house entry, and the man entered, rather like a blast of wind. The fair moustache stuck out from the blackish, mottled face, and the fierce blue eyes rolled their whites in the coal-blackened sockets.

" This gentleman is Mr. Frith," said Emily Pinnegar.

Jimmy got up, with a bit of an Oxford wriggle, and held out his hand, saying : " How do you do ? "

His grey eyes, behind the spectacles, had an uncanny whitish gleam.

" My hand's not fit to shake hands," said the miner. " Take a seat."

" Oh, nobody minds coal-dust," said Jimmy, subsiding on to the sofa. " It's clean dirt."

" They say so," said Pinnegar.

He was a man of medium height, thin, but energetic in build

Mrs. Pinnegar was running hot water into a pail from the bright brass tap of the stove, which had a boiler to balance the oven. Pinnegar dropped heavily into a wooden arm-chair, and stooped to pull off his ponderous grey pit-boots. He smelled of the strange, stale underground. In silence he pulled on his slippers, then rose, taking his boots into the scullery. His wife followed with the pail of hot water. She returned and spread a coarse roller-towel on the steel fender. The man could be heard washing in the scullery, in the semi-dark. Nobody said anything. Mrs. Pinnegar attended to her husband's dinner.

After a while, Pinnegar came running in, naked to the waist, and squatted plumb in front of the big red fire, on his heels. His head and face and the front part of his body were all wet. His back was grey and unwashed. He seized the towel from the fender and began to rub his face and head with a sort of brutal vigour, while his wife brought a bowl, and with a soapy flannel silently washed his back, right down to the loins, where the trousers were rolled back. The man was entirely oblivious of the stranger—this washing was part of the collier's ritual, and nobody existed for the moment. The woman, washing her husband's back, stooping there as he kneeled with knees wide apart, squatting on his heels on the rag hearthrug, had a peculiar look on her strong, handsome face, a look sinister and derisive. She was deriding something or somebody ; but Jimmy could not make out whom or what.

It was a new experience for him to sit completely and brutally excluded, from a personal ritual. The collier vigorously rubbed his own fair short hair, till it all stood on end, then he stared into the red-hot fire, oblivious, while the red colour burned in his cheeks. Then again he rubbed his breast and his body with the rough towel, brutally, as if his body were some machine he was cleaning, while his wife, with a peculiar slow movement, dried his back with another towel.

She took away the towel and bowl. The man was dry. He still squatted with his hands on his knees, gazing abstractedly, blankly into the fire. That, too, seemed part of his daily ritual. The colour flushed in his cheeks, his fair moustache was rubbed on end. But his hot blue eyes stared hot and vague into the red coals, while the red glare of the coal fell on his breast and naked body.

He was a man of about thirty-five, in his prime, with a pure smooth skin and no fat on his body. His muscles were not large, but quick, alive with energy. And as he squatted bathing abstractedly in the glow of the fire, he seemed like some pure-moulded engine that sleeps between its motions, with incomprehensible eyes of dark iron-blue.

He looked round, always averting his face from the stranger on the sofa, shutting him out of consciousness. The wife took out a bundle from the dresser-cupboard, and handed it to the outstretched, work-scarred hand of the man on the hearth. Curious, that big, horny, work-battered clean hand, at the end of the suave, thin, naked arm.

Pinnegar unrolled his shirt and undervest in front of the fire, warmed them for a moment in the glow, vaguely, sleepily, then, pulled them over his head. And then at last he rose, with his shirt hanging over his trousers, and in the same abstract, sleepy way, shutting the world out of his consciousness, he went out again to the scullery, pausing at the same dresser-cupboard to take out his rolled-up day trousers.

Mrs. Pinnegar took away the towels and set the dinner on the table —rich, oniony stew out of a hissing brown stew-jar, boiled potatoes, and a cup of tea. The man returned from the scullery, in his clean flannelette shirt and black trousers, his fair hair neatly brushed. He planked his wooden arm-chair beside the table, and sat heavily down, to eat.

Then he looked at Jimmy, as one wary, probably hostile man looks at another.

" You're a stranger in these parts, I gather ? " he said. There was something slightly formal, even a bit pompous, in his speech.

" An absolute stranger," replied Jimmy, with a slight aside grin.

The man dabbed some mustard on his plate, and glanced at his food to see if he would like it.

" Come from a distance, do you ? " he asked, as he began to eat. As he ate, he seemed to become oblivious again of Jimmy, bent his head over his plate, and ate. But probably he was ruminating something all the time, with barbaric wariness.

" From London," said Jimmy, warily.

" London ! " said Pinnegar, without looking from his plate.

Mrs. Pinnegar came and sat, in ritualistic silence, in her tall-backed rocking-chair under the light.

" What brings you this way, then ? " asked Pinnegar, stirring his tea.

" Oh ! " Jimmy writhed a little on the sofa. " I came to see Mrs. Pinnegar."

The miner took a hasty gulp of tea.

" You're acquainted then, are you ? " he said, still without looking round. He sat with his side-face to Jimmy.

" Yes, we are *now*," explained Jimmy. " I didn't know Mrs. Pinnegar till this evening. As a matter of fact, she sent me some poems for the *Commentator*—I'm the editor—and I thought they were good, so I wrote and told her so. Then I felt I wanted to come and see her, and she was willing, so I came."

The man reached out, cut himself a piece of bread, and swallowed a large mouthful.

" You thought her poetry was good ? " he said, turning at last to Jimmy and looking straight at him, with a stare something like the child's, but aggressive. " Are you going to put it in your magazine ? "

" Yes, I think I am," said Jimmy.

" I never read but one of her poems—something about a collier she knew all about, because she'd married him," he said, in his peculiar harsh voice, that had a certain jeering clang in it, and a certain indomitableness.

Jimmy was silent. The other man's harsh fighting-voice made him shrink.

" I could never get on with the *Commentator* myself," said Pinnegar, looking round for his pudding, pushing his meat-plate aside. " Seems to me to go a long way round to get nowhere."

" Well, probably it *does*," said Jimmy, squirming a little. " But so long as the *way* is interesting ! I don't see that anything gets anywhere at present—certainly no periodical."

" I don't know," said Pinnegar. " There's some facts in the *Liberator*—and there's some ideas in the *Janus*. I can't see the use myself, of all these feelings folk say they have. They get you nowhere."

" But," said Jimmy, with a slight pouf of laughter, " where do you *want* to get ? It's all very well talking about getting somewhere, but where, where in the world to-day do you *want* to get ? In general, I mean. If you want a better job in the mine—all right, go ahead and get it. But when you begin to talk about getting somewhere, in *life*—why, you've got to know what you're talking about."

" I'm a man, aren't I ? " said the miner, going very still and hard.

" But what do you *mean*, when you say you're a man ? " snarled Jimmy, really exasperated. " What do you mean ? Yes, you *are* a man. But what about it ? "

" Haven't I the right to say I won't be made use of ? " said the collier, slow, harsh, and heavy.

" You've got a right to *say* it," retorted Jimmy, with a pouf of laughter. " But it doesn't *mean* anything. We're all made use of, from King George downwards. We have to be. When you eat your pudding you're making use of hundreds of·people—including your wife."

" I know it. I know it. It makes no difference, though. I'm not going to be made use of."

Jimmy shrugged his shoulders.

" Oh, all right ! " he said. " That's just a phrase, like any other."

The miner sat very still in his chair, his face going hard and remote. He was evidently thinking over something that was stuck like a barb in his consciousness, something he was trying to harden over, as the skin sometimes hardens over a steel splinter in the flesh.

" I'm nothing but made use of," he said, now talking hard and final, to himself, and staring out into space. " Down the pit, I'm made use of, and they give me a wage, such as it is. At the house, I'm made use of, and my wife sets the dinner on the table as if I was a customer in a shop."

" But what do you *expect ?* " cried Jimmy, writhing in his chair.

" Me ? What do I expect ? I expect nothing. But I tell you what——" he turned, and looked straight and hard into Jimmy's eyes—" I'm not going to put up with anything, either."

Jimmy saw the hard finality in the other man's eyes, and squirmed away from it.

" If you *know* what you're not going to put up with——" he said.

" I don't want my wife writing poetry ! And sending it to a parcel of men she's never seen. *I* don't want my wife sitting like Queen Boadicea, when I come home, and a face like a stone wall with holes in it. I don't know what's wrong with her. She doesn't know herself. But she does as she likes. Only, mark you, I do the same."

" Of course ! " cried Jimmy, though there was no of course about it.

" She's told you I've got another woman ? "

" Yes."

" And I'll tell you for why. If I give in to the coal face, and go down the mine every day to eight hours' slavery, more or less, somebody's got to give in to me."

" Then," said Jimmy, after a pause, " if you mean you want your wife to submit to you—well, that's the problem. You have to marry the woman who *will* submit."

It was amazing, this from Jimmy. He sat there and lectured the collier like a Puritan Father, completely forgetting the disintegrating flutter of Clarissa, in his own background.

" I want a wife who'll please me, who'll want to please me," said the collier.

" Why should *you* be pleased, any more than anybody else ? " asked the wife coldly.

" My child, my little girl wants to please me—if her mother would let her. But the women hang together. I tell you "—and here he turned to Jimmy, with a blaze in his dark blue eyes—" I want a woman to please me, a woman who's anxious to please me. And if I can't find her in my own home, I'll find her out of it."

" I hope she pleases you," said the wife, rocking slightly.

" Well," said the man, " she does."

" Then why don't you go and live with her altogether ? " she said. He turned and looked at her.

" Why don't I ? " he said. " Because I've got my home. I've got my house, I've got my wife, let her be what she may, as a woman to live with. And I've got my child. Why should I break it all up ? "

" And what about me ? " she asked, coldly and fiercely.

" You ? You've got a home. You've got a child. You've got a man who works for you. You've got what you want. You do as you like——"

" Do I ? " she asked, with intolerable sarcasm.

" Yes. Apart from the bit of work in the house, you do as you like. If you want to go, you can go. But while you live in my house, you must respect it. You bring no men here, you see."

" Do *you* respect your home ? " she said.

" Yes ! I do ! If I get another woman—who pleases me—I deprive you of nothing. All I ask of you is to do your duty as a housewife."

" Down to washing your back ! " she said, heavily sarcastic ; and, Jimmy thought, a trifle vulgar.

" Down to washing my back, since it's got to be washed," he said. " What about the other woman ? Let her do it."

" This is my home."

The wife gave a strange movement, like a mad woman.

Jimmy sat rather pale and frightened. Behind the collier's quietness he felt the concentration of almost cold anger and an unchanging will. In the man's lean face he could see the bones, the fixity of the male bones, and it was as if the human soul, or spirit, had gone into the living skull and skeleton, almost invulnerable.

Jimmy, for some strange reason, felt a wild anger against this bony and logical man. It was the hard-driven coldness, fixity, that he could not bear.

" Look here ! " he cried, in a resonant Oxford voice, his eyes glaring and casting inwards behind his spectacles. " You say Mrs. Pinnegar is *free*—free to do as she pleases. In that case, you have no objection if she comes with me right away from here."

The collier looked at the pale, strange face of the editor in wonder.

Jimmy kept his face slightly averted, and sightless, seeing nobody. There was a Mephistophelian tilt about the eyebrows, and a Martyred Sebastian straightness about the mouth.

" Does she *want* to ? " asked Pinnegar, with devastating incredulity. The wife smiled faintly, grimly. She could see the vanity of her husband in his utter inability to believe that she could prefer the other man to him.

" That," said Jimmy, " you must ask her yourself. But it's what I came here for : to ask her to come and live with me, and bring the child."

" You came without having seen her, to ask her that ? " said the husband, in growing wonder.

" Yes," said Jimmy, vehemently, nodding his head with drunken emphasis. " Yes ! Without ever having seen her ! "

" You've caught a funny fish this time, with your poetry," he said turning with curious husband-familiarity to his wife. She hated this off-hand husband-familiarity.

" What sort of fish have *you* caught ? " she retorted. " And what did you catch *her* with ? "

" Bird-lime ! " he said, with a faint, quick grin.

Jimmy was sitting in suspense. They all three sat in suspense, for some time.

" And what are you saying to him ? " said the collier at length.

Jimmy looked up, and the malevolent half-smile on his face made him look rather handsome again, a mixture of faun and Mephisto. He glanced curiously, invitingly, at the woman who was watching him from afar.

" I say yes ! " she replied, in a cool voice.

The husband became very still, sitting erect in his wooden arm-chair and staring into space. It was as if he were fixedly watching something fly away from him, out of his own soul. But he was not going to yield at all, to any emotion.

He could not now believe that this woman should *want* to leave him. Yet she did.

" I'm sure it's all for the best," said Jimmy, in his Puritan Father voice. " You don't mind, really "—he drawled uneasily—" if she brings the child. I give you my word I'll do my very best for it."

The collier looked at him as if he were very far away. Jimmy quailed under the look. He could see that the other man was relentlessly killing the emotion in himself, stripping himself, as it were, of his own flesh, stripping himself to the hard unemotional bone of the human male.

"I give her a blank cheque," said Pinnegar, with numb lips. "She does as she pleases."

"So much for fatherly love, compared with selfishness," she said.

He turned and looked at her with that curious power of remote anger. And immediately she became still, quenched.

"I give you a blank cheque, as far as I'm concerned," he repeated abstractedly.

"It *is* blank indeed!" she said, with her first touch of bitterness.

Jimmy looked at the clock. It was growing late : he might be shut out of the public-house. He rose to go, saying he would return in the morning. He was leaving the next day, at noon, for London.

He plunged into the darkness and mud of that black, night-ridden country. There was a curious elation in his spirits, mingled with fear. But then he always needed an element of fear, really, to elate him. He thought with terror of those two human beings left in that house together. The frightening state of tension ! He himself could never bear an extreme tension. He always had to compromise, to become apologetic and pathetic. He would be able to manage Mrs. Pinnegar that way. Emily ! He must get used to saying it. Emily ! The Emilia was absurd. He had never known an Emily.

He felt really scared, and really elated. He was doing something big. It was not that he was in *love* with the woman. But, my God, he wanted to take her away from that man. And he wanted the adventure of her. Absolutely the adventure of her. He felt really elated, really himself, really manly.

But in the morning he returned rather sheepishly to the collier's house. It was another dark, drizzling day, with black trees, black road, black hedges, blackish brick houses, and the smell and the sound of collieries under a skyless day. Like living in some weird underground.

Unwillingly he went up that passage-entry again, and knocked at the back door, glancing at the miserable little back garden with its cabbage-stalks and its ugly sanitary arrangements.

The child opened the door to him : with her fair hair, flushed cheeks, and hot, dark-blue eyes.

"Hello, Jane!" he said.

The mother stood tall and square, by the table, watching him with portentous eyes, as he entered. She was handsome, but her skin was not very good : as if the battle had been too much for her health. Jimmy glanced up at her smiling his slow, ingratiating smile, that always brought a glow of success into a woman's spirit. And as he saw her gold-flecked eyes searching in his eyes, without a bit of kindliness, he thought to himself : " My God, however am I going to sleep with that woman ! " His will was ready, however, and he would manage it somehow.

And when he glanced at the motionless, bony head and lean figure of the collier seated in the wooden arm-chair by the fire, he was the more ready. He must triumph over that man.

" What train are you going by ? " asked Mrs. Pinnegar.

" By the 12-30." He looked up at her as he spoke, with the wide, shining, childlike, almost coy eyes that were his peculiar asset. She looked down at him in a sort of interested wonder. She seemed almost fascinated by his childlike, shining, inviting dark-grey eyes, with their long lashes : such an absolute change from that resentful unyielding that looked out always from the back of her husband's blue eyes. Her husband always seemed like a menace to her, in his thinness, his concentration, his eternal unyielding. And this man looked at one with the wide, shining, fascinating eyes of a young Persian kitten, something at once bold and shy and coy and strangely inviting. She fell at once under their spell.

" You'll have dinner before you go," she said.

" No ! " he cried in panic, unwilling indeed to eat before that other man. " No, I ate a fabulous breakfast. I will get a sandwich when I change in Sheffield : *really !* "

She had to go out shopping. She said she would go out to the station with him when she got back. It was just after eleven.

" But look here," he said, addressing also the thin abstracted man who sat unnoticing, with a newspaper, " we've got to get this thing settled. I *want* Mrs. Pinnegar to come and live with me, her and the child. And she's coming ! So don't you think, now, it would be better if she came right along with me to-day ! Just put a few things in a bag and come along. Why drag the thing out ? "

" I tell you," replied the husband, " she has a blank cheque from me to do as she likes."

" All right, then ! Won't you do that ? Won't you come along with me now ? " said Jimmy, looking up at her exposedly, but casting his eyes a bit inwards. Throwing himself with deliberate impulsiveness on her mercy.

" I can't ! " she said decisively. " I can't come to-day."

" But why not—really ? Why not, while I'm here ? You have that blank cheque, you can do as you please——"

" The blank cheque won't get me far," she said rudely : " I can't come to-day, anyhow."

" When can you come, then ? " he said, with that queer, petulant pleading. " The sooner the better, surely."

" I can come on Monday," she said abruptly.

" Monday ! " He gazed up at her in a kind of panic, through his spectacles. Then he set his teeth again, and nodded his head up and down. " All right, then ! To-day is Saturday. Then Monday ! "

" If you'll excuse me," she said, " I've got to go out for a few things. I'll walk to the station with you when I get back."

She bundled Jane into a little sky-blue coat and bonnet, put on a heavy black coat and black hat herself, and went out.

Jimmy sat very uneasily opposite the collier, who also wore spectacles to read. Pinnegar put down the newspaper and pulled the spectacles off his nose, saying something about a Labour Government.

" Yes," said Jimmy. " After all, best be logical. If you *are* democratic, the only logical thing is a Labour Government. Though, personally, one Government is as good as another, to me."

" Maybe so ! " said the collier. " But *something's* got to come to an end, sooner or later."

" Oh, a great deal ! " said Jimmy, and they lapsed into silence.

" Have you been married before ? " asked Pinnegar, at length.

" Yes. My wife and I are divorced."

" I suppose you want me to divorce *my* wife ? " said the collier.

" Why—yes !—that would be best——"

" It's the same to me," said Pinnegar ; " divorce or no divorce. I'll *live* with another woman, but I'll never *marry* another. Enough is as good as a feast. But if she wants a divorce, she can have it."

" It would certainly be best," said Jimmy.

There was a long pause. Jimmy wished the woman would come back.

" I look on you as an instrument," said the miner. " Something had to break. You are the instrument that breaks it."

It was strange to sit in the room with this thin, remote, wilful man. Jimmy was a bit fascinated by him. But, at the same time, he hated him because he could not be in the same room with him without being under his spell. He felt himself dominated. And he hated it.

" My wife," said Pinnegar, looking up at Jimmy with a peculiar, almost humourous, teasing grin, " expects to see me go to the dogs when she leaves me. It is her last hope."

Jimmy ducked his head and was silent, not knowing what to say. The other man sat still in his chair, like a sort of infinitely patient prisoner, looking away out of the window and waiting.

" She thinks," he said again, " that she has some wonderful future awaiting her somewhere, and you're going to open the door."

And again the same amused grin was in his eyes.

And again Jimmy was fascinated by the man. And again he hated the spell of this fascination. For Jimmy wanted to be, in his own mind, the strongest man among men, but particularly among women. And this thin, peculiar man could dominate him. He knew it. The very silent unconsciousness of Pinnegar dominated the room, wherever he was.

Jimmy hated this.

At last Mrs. Pinnegar came back, and Jimmy set off with her. He shook hands with the collier.

" Good-bye ! " he said.

" Good-bye ! " said Pinnegar, looking down at him with those amused blue eyes, which Jimmy knew he would never be able to get beyond.

And the walk to the station was almost a walk of conspiracy against the man left behind, between the man in spectacles and the tall woman. They arranged the details for Monday. Emily was to come by the nine o'clock train : Jimmy would meet her at Marylebone, and install her in his house in St. John's Wood. Then, with the child, they would begin a new life. Pinnegar would divorce his wife, or she would divorce him : and then, another marriage.

Jimmy got a tremendous kick out of it all on the journey home. He felt he had really done something desperate and adventurous. But he was in too wild a flutter to analyse any results. Only, as he drew near London, a sinking feeling came over him. He was desperately tired after it all, almost too tired to keep up.

Nevertheless, he went after dinner and sprang it all on Severn.

" You damn fool ! " said Severn, in consternation. " What did you do it for ? "

" Well," said Jimmy, writhing. " Because I *wanted* to."

" Good God ! The woman sounds like the head of Medusa. You're a hero of some stomach, I must say ! Remember Clarissa ? "

" Oh," writhed Jimmy. " But this is different."

" Ay, her name's Emma, or something of that sort, isn't it ? "

" Emily ! " said Jimmy briefly.

" Well, you're a fool, anyway, so you may as well keep on acting in character. I've no doubt, by playing weeping-willow, you'll outlive all the female storms you ever prepare for yourself. I never yet did see a weeping-willow uprooted by a gale, so keep on hanging your harp on it, and you'll be all right. Here's luck ! But for a man who was looking for a little Gretchen to adore him, you're a corker!"

Which was all that Severn had to say. But Jimmy went home with his knees shaking. On Sunday morning he wrote an anxious letter. He didn't know how to begin it : *Dear Mrs. Pinnegar* and *Dear Emily* seemed either too late in the day or too early. So he just plunged in, without dear anything.

" I want you to have this before you come. Perhaps we have been precipitate. I only beg you to decide *finally*, for yourself, before you come. Don't come, please, unless you are absolutely sure of yourself. If you are *in the least* unsure, wait a while, wait till you are quite certain, one way or the other.

" For myself, if you don't come I shall understand. But please send me a telegram. If you do come, I shall welcome both you and the child. Yours ever—J. F."

He paid a man his return fare, and three pounds extra, to go on the Sunday and deliver this letter.

The man came back in the evening. He had delivered the letter. There was no answer.

Awful Sunday night : tense Monday morning !

A telegram : "*Arrive Marylebone* 12.50 *with Jane. Yours ever. Emily.*"

Jimmy set his teeth and went to the station. But when he felt her looking at him, and so met her eyes : and after that saw her coming slowly down the platform, holding the child by the hand, her slow cat's eyes smouldering under her straight brows, smouldering at him : he almost swooned. A sickly grin came over him as he held out his hand. Nevertheless he said :

" I'm *awfully* glad you came."

And as he sat in the taxi, a perverse but intense desire for her came over him, making him almost helpless. He could feel, so strongly, the presence of that other man about her, and this went to his head like neat spirits. That other man ! In some subtle, inexplicable way, he was actually bodily present, the husband. The woman moved in his aura. She was hopelessly married to him.

And this went to Jimmy's head like neat whisky. Which of the two would fall before him with a greater fall—the woman, or the man, her husband ?

THERE was a little snow on the ground, and the church clock had just struck midnight. Hampstead in the night of winter for once was looking pretty, with clean white earth and lamps for moon, and dark sky above the lamps.

A confused little sound of voices, a gleam of hidden yellow light. And then the garden door of a tall, dark Georgian house suddenly opened, and three people confusedly emerged. A girl in a dark blue coat and fur turban, very erect : a fellow with a little dispatch-case, slouching : a thin man with a red beard, bareheaded, peering out of the gateway down the hill that swung in a curve downwards towards London.

" Look at it ! A new world ! " cried the man in the beard, ironic- ally, as he stood on the step and peered out.

" No, Lorenzo ! It's only whitewash ! " cried the young man in the overcoat. His voice was handsome, resonant, plangent, with a weary sardonic touch. As he turned back his face was dark in shadow.

The girl with the erect, alert head, like a bird, turned back to the two men.

" What was that ? " she asked, in her quick, quiet voice.

" Lorenzo says it's a new world. I say it's only whitewash," cried the man in the street.

She stood still and lifted her woolly, gloved finger. She was deaf and was taking it in.

Yes, she had got it. She gave a quick, chuckling laugh, glanced very quickly at the man in the bowler hat, then back at the man in the stucco gateway, who was grinning like a satyr and waving good- bye.

" Good-bye, Lorenzo ! " came the resonant, weary cry of the man in the bowler hat.

" Good-bye ! " came the sharp, night-bird call of the girl.

The green gate slammed, then the inner door. The two were alone in the street, save for the policeman at the corner. The road curved steeply downhill.

" You'd better mind how you *step* ! " shouted the man in the bowler hat, leaning near the erect, sharp girl, and slouching in his walk. She paused a moment, to make sure what he had said.

" Don't mind me, I'm quite all right. Mind yourself ! " she said quickly. At that very moment he gave a wild lurch on the slippery snow, but managed to save himself from falling. She watched him, on tiptoes of alertness. His bowler hat bounced away in the thin snow. They were under a lamp near the curve. As he ducked for his hat he showed a bald spot, just like a tonsure, among his dark, thin, rather curly hair. And when he looked up at her, with his thick black brows sardonically arched, and his rather hooked nose self-derisive, jamming his hat on again, he seemed like a satanic young priest. His face had beautiful lines, like a faun, and a doubtful martyred expression. A sort of faun on the Cross, with all the malice of the complication.

" Did you hurt yourself ? " she asked, in her quick, cool, unemotional way.

" No ! " he shouted derisively.

" Give me the machine, won't you ? " she said, holding out her woolly hand. " I believe I'm safer."

" Do you *want* it ? " he shouted.

" Yes, I'm sure I'm safer."

He handed her the little brown dispatch-case, which was really a Marconi listening machine for her deafness. She marched erect as ever. He shoved his hands deep in his overcoat pockets and slouched along beside her, as if he wouldn't make his legs firm. The road curved down in front of them, clean and pale with snow under the lamps. A motor-car came churning up. A few dark figures slipped away into the dark recesses of the houses, like fishes among rocks above a sea-bed of white sand. On the left was a tuft of trees sloping upwards into the dark.

He kept looking around, pushing out his finely shaped chin and his hooked nose as if he were listening for something. He could still hear the motor-car climbing on to the Heath. Below was the yellow, foul-smelling glare of the Hampstead Tube station. On the right the trees.

The girl, with her alert pink-and-white face looked at him sharply, inquisitively. She had an odd nymph-like inquisitiveness, sometimes like a bird, sometimes a squirrel, sometimes a rabbit : never quite like a woman. At last he stood still, as if he would go no farther. There was a curious, baffled grin on his smooth, cream-coloured face.

" James," he said loudly to her, leaning towards her ear. " Do you hear somebody *laughing* ? "

" Laughing ? " she retorted quickly. " Who's laughing ? "

" I don't know. *Somebody !* " he shouted, showing his teeth at her in a very odd way.

" No, I hear nobody," she announced.

" But it's most *extraordinary !* " he cried, his voice slurring up and down. " Put on your machine."

" Put it on ? " she retorted. " What for ? "

" To see if you can *hear* it," he cried.

" Hear what ? "

" The *laughing*. Somebody laughing. It's most *extraordinary*."

She gave her odd little chuckle and handed him her machine. He held it while she opened the lid and attached the wires, putting the band over her head and the receivers at her ears, like a wireless operator. Crumbs of snow fell down the cold darkness. She switched on : little yellow lights in glass tubes shone in the machine. She was connected, she was listening. He stood with his head ducked, his hands shoved down in his overcoat pockets.

Suddenly he lifted his face and gave the weirdest, slightly neighing laugh, uncovering his strong, spaced teeth, and arching his black brows, and watching her with queer, gleaming, goat-like eyes.

She seemed a little dismayed.

" There ! " he said. " Didn't you hear it ? "

" I heard *you !* " she said, in a tone which conveyed that *that* was enough.

" But didn't you hear *it !* " he cried, unfurling his lips oddly again.

" No ! " she said.

He looked at her vindictively, and stood again with ducked head. She remained erect, her fur hat in her hand, her fine bobbed hair banded with the machine-band and catching crumbs of snow, her odd, bright-eyed, deaf nymph's face lifted with blank listening.

" There ! " he cried, suddenly jerking up his gleaming face. " You mean to tell me you can't——" He was looking at her almost diabolically. But something else was too strong for him. His face wreathed with a startling, peculiar smile, seeming to gleam, and suddenly the most extraordinary laugh came bursting out of him, like an animal laughing. It was a strange, neighing sound, amazing in her ears. She was startled, and switched her machine quieter.

A large form loomed up : a tall, clean-shaven young policeman.

" A radio ? " he asked laconically.

" No, it's my machine. I'm deaf ! " said Miss James quickly and distinctly. She was not the daughter of a peer for nothing.

The man in the bowler hat lifted his face and glared at the fresh-faced young policeman with a peculiar white glare in his eyes.

" Look here ! " he said distinctly. " Did you hear someone laughing ? "

" Laughing ? I heard you, sir."

" No, *not* me." He gave an impatient jerk of his arm, and lifted his face again. His smooth, creamy face seemed to gleam, there were subtle curves of derisive triumph in all its lines. He was careful not to look directly at the young policeman. " The most extraordinary laughter I ever heard," he added, and the same touch of derisive exultation sounded in his tones.

The policeman looked down on him cogitatingly.

" It's perfectly all right," said Miss James coolly. " He's not drunk. He just hears something that we don't hear."

" Drunk ! " echoed the man in the bowler hat, in profoundly amused derision. " If I were merely drunk——" And off he went again in the wild, neighing, animal laughter, while his averted face seemed to flash.

At the sound of the laughter something roused in the blood of the girl and of the policeman. They stood nearer to one another, so that their sleeves touched and they looked wonderingly across at the man in the bowler hat. He lifted his black brows at them.

" Do you mean to say you heard nothing ? " he asked.

" Only you," said Miss James.

" Only you, sir ! " echoed the policeman.

" What was it like ? " asked Miss James.

" Ask me to *describe* it ! " retorted the young man, in extreme contempt. " It's the most marvellous sound in the world."

And truly he seemed wrapped up in a new mystery.

" Where does it come from ? " asked Miss James, very practical.

" *Apparently*," it answered in contempt, " from over there." And he pointed to the trees and bushes inside the railings over the road.

" Well, let's go and see ! " she said. " I can carry my machine and go on listening."

The man seemed relieved to get rid of the burden. He shoved his hands in his pockets again and sloped off across the road. The police-man, a queer look flickering on his fresh young face, put his hand round the girl's arm carefully and subtly, to help her. She did not lean at all on the support of the big hand, but she was interested, so she did not resent it. Having held herself all her life intensely aloof from physical contact, and never having let any man touch her, she now, with a certain nymph-like voluptuousness, allowed the large hand of the young policeman to support her as they followed the quick wolf-like figure of the other man across the road uphill. And she could feel the presence of the young policeman, through all the thickness of his dark-blue uniform, as something young and alert and bright.

When they came up to the man in the bowler hat, he was standing with his head ducked, his ears pricked, listening beside the iron rail inside which grew big black holly-trees tufted with snow, and old, ribbed, silent English elms.

The policeman and the girl stood waiting. She was peering into the bushes with the sharp eyes of a deaf nymph, deaf to the world's noises. The man in the bowler hat listened intensely. A lorry rolled downhill, making the earth tremble.

"There!" cried the girl, as the lorry rumbled darkly past. And she glanced round with flashing eyes at her policeman, her fresh soft face gleaming with startled life. She glanced straight into the puzzled, amused eyes of the young policeman. He was just enjoying himself.

"Don't you see?" she said, rather imperiously.

"What is it, Miss?" answered the policeman.

"I mustn't point," she said. "Look where I look."

And she looked away with brilliant eyes, into the dark holly bushes. She must see something, for she smiled faintly, with subtle satisfaction, and she tossed her erect head in all the pride of vindication. The policeman looked at her instead of into the bushes. There was a certain brilliance of triumph and vindication in all the poise of her slim body.

"I always knew I should see him," she said triumphantly to herself.

"Whom do you see?" shouted the man in the bowler hat.

"Don't you see him too?" she asked, turning round her soft, arch, nymph-like face anxiously. She was anxious for the little man to see.

"No, I see nothing. What do you see, James?" cried the man in the bowler hat, insisting.

"A man."

"Where?"

"There. Among the holly bushes."

"Is he there now?"

"No! He's gone."

" What sort of a man ? "

" I don't know."

" What did he look like ? "

" I can't tell you."

But at that instant the man in the bowler hat turned suddenly, and the arch, triumphant look flew to his face.

" Why, he must be *there* ! " he cried, pointing up the grove. " Don't you hear him laughing ? He must be behind those trees."

And his voice, with curious delight, broke into a laugh again, as he stood and stamped his feet on the snow, and danced to his own laughter, ducking his head. Then he turned away and ran swiftly up the avenue lined with old trees.

He slowed down as a door at the end of a garden path, white with untouched snow, suddenly opened, and a woman in a long-fringed black shawl stood in the light. She peered out into the night. Then she came down to the low garden gate. Crumbs of snow still fell. She had dark hair and a tall dark comb.

" Did you knock at my door ? " she asked of the man in the bowler hat.

" I ? No ! "

" Somebody knocked at my door."

" Did they ? Are you sure ? They can't have done. There are no footmarks in the snow."

" Nor are there ! " she said. " But somebody knocked and called something."

" That's very curious," said the man. " Were you expecting someone ? "

" No. Not exactly expecting any one. Except that one is always expecting Somebody, you know." In the dimness of the snow-lit night he could see her making big, dark eyes at him.

" Was it someone laughing ? " he said.

" No. It was no one laughing, exactly. Someone knocked, and I ran to open, hoping as one always hopes, you know——"

" What ? "

" Oh—that something wonderful is going to happen."

He was standing close to the low gate. She stood on the opposite side. Her hair was dark, her face seemed dusky, as she looked up at him with her dark, meaningful eyes.

" Did you wish someone would come ? " he asked.

" Very much," she replied, in her plangent Jewish voice. She must be a Jewess.

" No matter who ? " he said, laughing.

"So long as it was a man I could like," she said, in a low, meaningful, falsely shy voice.

"Really!" he said. "Perhaps after all it was I who knocked—without knowing."

"I think it was," she said. "It must have been."

"Shall I come in?" he asked, putting his hand on the little gate.

"Don't you think you'd better?" she replied.

He bent down, unlatching the gate. As he did so the woman in the black shawl turned, and, glancing over her shoulder, hurried back to the house, walking unevenly in the snow, on her high-heeled shoes. The man hurried after her, hastening like a hound to catch up.

Meanwhile the girl and the policeman had come up. The girl stood still when she saw the man in the bowler hat going up the garden walk after the woman in the black shawl with the fringe.

"Is he going in?" she asked quickly.

"Looks like it, doesn't it?" said the policeman.

"Does he know that woman?"

"I can't say. I should say he soon will," replied the policeman.

"But who is she?"

"I couldn't say who she is."

The two dark, confused figures entered the lighted doorway, then the door closed on them.

"He's gone," said the girl outside on the snow. She hastily began to pull off the band of her telephone-receiver, and switched off her machine. The tubes of secret light disappeared, she packed up the little leather case. Then, pulling on her soft fur cap, she stood once more ready.

The slightly martial look which her long, dark-blue, military-seeming coat gave her was intensified, while the slightly anxious, bewildered look of her face had gone. She seemed to stretch herself, to stretch her limbs free. And the inert look had left her full soft cheeks. Her cheeks were alive with the glimmer of pride and a new dangerous surety.

She looked quickly at the tall young policeman. He was clean-shaven, fresh-faced, smiling oddly under his helmet, waiting in subtle patience a few yards away. She saw that he was a decent young man, one of the waiting sort.

The second of ancient fear was followed at once in her by a blithe, unaccustomed sense of power.

"Well!" she said. "I should say it's no use waiting." She spoke decisively.

" You don't have to wait for him, do you ? " asked the policeman.

" Not at all. He's much better where he is." She laughed an odd, brief laugh. Then glancing over her shoulder, she set off down the hill, carrying her little case. Her feet felt light, her legs felt long and strong. She glanced over her shoulder again. The young policeman was following her, and she laughed to herself. Her limbs felt so lithe and so strong, if she wished she could easily run faster than he. If she wished she could easily kill him, even with her hands.

So it seemed to her. But why kill him ? He was a decent young fellow. She had in front of her eyes the dark face among the holly bushes, with the brilliant, mocking eyes. Her breast felt full of power, and her legs felt long and strong and wild. She was surprised herself at the strong, bright, throbbing sensation beneath her breasts, a sensation of triumph and of rosy anger. Her hands felt keen on her wrists. She who had always declared she had not a muscle in her body ! Even now, it was not muscle, it was a sort of flame.

Suddenly it began to snow heavily, with fierce frozen puffs of wind. The snow was small, in frozen grains, and hit sharp on her face. It seemed to whirl round her as if she herself were whirling in a cloud. But she did not mind. There was a flame in her, her limbs felt flamey and strong, amid the whirl.

And the whirling, snowy air seemed full of presences, full of strange unheard voices. She was used to the sensation of noises taking place which she could not hear. This sensation became very strong. She felt something was happening in the wild air.

The London air was no longer heavy and clammy, saturated with ghosts of the unwilling dead. A new, clean tempest swept down from the Pole, and there were noises.

Voices were calling. In spite of her deafness she could hear someone, several voices, calling and whistling, as if many people were hallooing through the air :

" He's come back ! Aha ! He's come back ! "

There was a wild, whistling, jubilant sound of voices in the storm of snow. Then obscured lightning winked through the snow in the air.

" Is that thunder and lightning ? " she asked of the young policeman, as she stood still, waiting for his form to emerge through the veil of whirling snow.

" Seems like it to me," he said.

And at that very moment the lightning blinked again, and the dark, laughing face was near her face, it almost touched her cheek.

She started back, but a flame of delight went over her.

" There ! " she said. " Did you see that ? "

" It lightened," said the policeman.

She was looking at him almost angrily. But then the clean, fresh animal look of his skin, and the tame-animal look in his frightened eyes amused her, she laughed her low, triumphant laugh. He was obviously afraid, like a frightened dog that sees something uncanny.

The storm suddenly whistled louder, more violently, and, with a strange noise like castanets, she seemed to hear voices clapping and crying :

" He is here ! He's come back ! "

She nodded her head gravely.

The policeman and she moved on side by side. She lived alone in a little stucco house in a side street down the hill. There was a church and a grove of trees and then the little old row of houses. The wind blew fiercely, thick with snow. Now and again a taxi went by, with its lights showing weirdly. But the world seemed empty, uninhabited save by snow and voices.

As the girl and the policeman turned past the grove of trees near the church, a great whirl of wind and snow made them stand still, and in the wild confusion they heard a whirling of sharp, delighted voices, something like seagulls, crying :

" He's here ! He's here ! "

" Well, I'm jolly glad he's back," said the girl calmly.

" What's that ? " said the nervous policeman, hovering near the girl.

The wind let them move forward. As they passed along the railings it seemed to them the doors of the church were open, and the windows were out, and the snow and the voices were blowing in a wild career all through the church.

" How extraordinary that they left the church open ! " said the girl.

The policeman stood still. He could not reply.

And as they stood they listened to the wind and the church full of whirling voices all calling confusedly.

" *Now* I hear the laughing," she said suddenly.

It came from the church : a sound of low, subtle, endless laughter, a strange, naked sound.

" Now I hear it ! " she said.

But the policeman did not speak. He stood cowed, with his tail between his legs, listening to the strange noises in the church.

The wind must have blown out one of the windows, for they could see the snow whirling in volleys through the black gap, and whirling inside the church like a dim light. There came a sudden crash, followed by a burst of chuckling, naked laughter. The snow seemed to make a queer light inside the building, like ghosts moving, big and tall.

There was more laughter, and a tearing sound. On the wind, pieces of paper, leaves of books, came whirling among the snow through the dark window. Then a white thing, soaring like a crazy bird, rose up on the wind as if it had wings, and lodged on a black tree outside, struggling. It was the altar-cloth.

There came a bit of gay, trilling music. The wind was running over the organ-pipes like pan-pipes, quickly up and down. Snatches of wild, gay, trilling music, and bursts of the naked low laughter.

"Really!" said the girl. "This is most extraordinary. Do you hear the music and the people laughing?"

"Yes, I hear somebody on the organ!" said the policeman.

"And do you get the puff of warm wind? Smelling of spring. Almond blossom, that's what it is! A most marvellous scent of almond blossom. *Isn't* it an extraordinary thing!"

She went on triumphantly past the church, and came to the row of little old houses. She entered her own gate in the little railed entrance.

"Here I am!" she said finally. "I'm home now. Thank you very much for coming with me."

She looked at the young policeman. His whole body was white as a wall with snow, and in the vague light of the arc-lamp from the street his face was humble and frightened.

"Can I come in and warm myself a bit?" he asked humbly. She knew it was fear rather than cold that froze him. He was in mortal fear.

"Well!" she said. "Stay down in the sitting-room if you like. But don't come upstairs, because I am alone in the house. You can make up the fire in the sitting-room, and you can go when you are warm."

She left him on the big, low couch before the fire, his face bluish and blank with fear. He rolled his blue eyes after her as she left the room. But she went up to her bedroom, and fastened her door.

In the morning she was in her studio upstairs in her little house, looking at her own paintings and laughing to herself. Her canaries were talking and shrilly whistling in the sunshine that followed the storm. The cold snow outside was still clean, and the white glare in the air gave the effect of much stronger sunshine than actually existed.

She was looking at her own paintings, and chuckling to herself over their comicalness. Suddenly they struck her as absolutely absurd. She quite enjoyed looking at them, they seemed to her so grotesque. Especially her self-portrait, with its nice brown hair and its slightly opened rabbit-mouth and its baffled, uncertain rabbit-eyes. She looked at the painted face and laughed in a long, rippling laugh, till the yellow canaries like faded daffodils almost went mad in an effort to sing louder. The girl's long, rippling laugh sounded through the house uncannily.

The housekeeper, a rather sad-faced young woman of a superior sort—nearly all people in England are of the superior sort, superiority being an English ailment—came in with an inquiring and rather disapproving look.

" Did you call, Miss James ? " she asked loudly.

" No. No, I didn't call. Don't shout, I can hear quite well," replied the girl.

The housekeeper looked at her again.

" You knew there was a young man in the sitting-room ? " she said.

" No. Really ! " cried the girl. " What, the young policeman ? I'd forgotten all about him. He came in in the storm to warm himself. Hasn't he gone ? "

" No, Miss James."

" How extraordinary of him ! What time is it ? Quarter to nine ! Why didn't he go when he was warm ? I must go and see him, I suppose."

" He says he's lame," said the housekeeper censoriously and loudly.

" Lame ! That's extraordinary. He certainly wasn't last night. But don't shout. I can hear quite well."

" Is Mr. Marchbanks coming in to breakfast, Miss James ? " said the housekeeper, more and more censorious.

" I couldn't say. But I'll come down as soon as mine is ready. I'll be down in a minute, anyhow, to see the policeman. Extraordinary that he is still here."

She sat down before her window, in the sun, to think a while. She could see the snow outside, the bare, purplish trees. The air all seemed rare and different. Suddenly the world had become quite different : as if some skin or integument had broken, as if the old, mouldering London sky had crackled and rolled back, like an old skin, shrivelled, leaving an absolutely new blue heaven.

" It really is extraordinary ! " she said to herself. " I certainly saw that man's face. What a wonderful face it was ! I shall never forget it. Such laughter ! He laughs longest who laughs last. He certainly will have the last laugh. I like him for that : he will laugh last. Must be someone really extraordinary ! How very nice to be the one to laugh last. He certainly will. What a wonderful being ! I suppose I must call him a being. He's not a person exactly.

"But how wonderful of him to come back and alter all the world immediately ! *Isn't* that extraordinary. I wonder if he'll have altered Marchbanks. Of course Marchbanks never *saw* him. But he heard him. Wouldn't that do as well, I wonder !—I *wonder !* "

She went off into a muse about Marchbanks. She and he were *such* friends. They had been friends like that for almost two years. Never lovers. Never that at all. But *friends*.

And after all, she had been in love with him : in her head. This seemed now so funny to her : that she had been, in her head, so much in love with him. After all, life was too absurd.

Because now she saw herself and him as such a funny pair. He so funnily taking life terribly seriously, especially his own life. And she so ridiculously *determined* to save him from himself. Oh, how absurd ! *Determined* to save him from himself, and wildly in love with him in the effort. The determination to save him from himself.

Absurd ! Absurd ! Absurd ! Since she had seen the man laughing among the holly-bushes—*such* extraordinary, wonderful laughter—she had seen her own ridiculousness. Really, what fantastic silliness, saving a man from himself ! Saving anybody. What fantastic silliness ! How much more amusing and lively to let a man go to perdition in his own way. Perdition was more amusing than salvation anyhow, and a much better place for most men to go to.

She had never been in love with any man, and only spuriously in love with Marchbanks. She saw it quite plainly now. After all, what nonsense it all was, this being-in-love business. Thank goodness she had never made the humiliating mistake.

No, the man among the holly-bushes had made her see it all so plainly : the ridiculousness of being in love, the *infra dig.* business of chasing a man or being chased by a man.

"Is love *really* so absurd and *infra dig.* ? " she said aloud to herself.

"Why, of course ! " came a deep, laughing voice.

She started round, but nobody was to be seen.

"I expect it's that man again ! " she said to herself. "It really *is* remarkable, you know. I consider it's a remarkable thing that

I never really wanted a man, *any* man. And there I am over thirty.
It *is* curious. Whether it's something wrong with me, or right with
me, I can't say. I don't know till I've proved it. But I believe, if
that man kept on laughing something would happen to me."

She smelt the curious smell of almond blossom in the room, and
heard the distant laugh again.

" I do wonder why Marchbanks went with that woman last night
—that Jewish-looking woman. Whatever could he want of her ?—
or she him ? So strange, as if they both had made up their minds to
something ! How extraordinarily puzzling life is ! So messy, it all
seems.

" Why does nobody ever laugh in life like that man ? He *did* seem
so wonderful. So scornful ! And so proud ! And so real ! With
those laughing, scornful, amazing eyes, just laughing and disappearing again. I can't imagine him chasing a Jewish-looking woman.
Or chasing any woman, thank goodness. It's all *so* messy. My
policeman would be messy if one would let him : like a dog. I do
dislike dogs, really I do. And men do seem so doggy !——"

But even while she mused, she began to laugh again to herself with
a long, low chuckle. How wonderful of that man to come and
laugh like that and make the sky crack and shrivel like an old skin !
Wasn't he wonderful ! Wouldn't it be wonderful if he just touched
her. Even touched her. She felt, if he touched her, she herself
would emerge new and tender out of an old, hard skin. She was
gazing abstractedly out of the window.

" There he comes, just now," she said abruptly. But she meant
Marchbanks, not the laughing man.

There he came, his hands still shoved down in his overcoat
pockets, his head still rather furtively ducked, in the bowler hat, and
his legs still rather shambling. He came hurrying across the road,
not looking up, deep in thought, no doubt. Thinking profoundly,
with agonies of agitation, no doubt about his last night's experience.
It made her laugh.

She, watching from the window above, burst into a long laugh,
and the canaries went off their heads again.

He was in the hall below. His resonant voice was calling, rather
imperiously :

" James ! Are you coming down ? "

" No," she called. " You come up."

He came up two at a time, as if his feet were a bit savage with the
stairs for obstructing him.

In the doorway he stood staring at her with a vacant, sardonic look, his grey eyes moving with a queer light. And she looked back at him with a curious, rather haughty carelessness.

" Don't you want your breakfast ? " she asked. It was his custom to come and take breakfast with her each morning.

" No," he answered loudly. " I went to a tea-shop."

" Don't shout," she said. " I can hear you quite well."

He looked at her with mockery and a touch of malice.

" I believe you always could," he said, still loudly.

" Well, anyway, I can now, so you needn't shout," she replied.

And again his grey eyes, with the queer, greyish phosphorescent gleam in them, lingered malignantly on her face.

" Don't look at me," she said calmly. " I know all about everything."

He burst into a pouf of malicious laughter.

" Who taught you—the policeman ? " he cried.

" Oh, by the way, he must be downstairs ! No, he was only incidental. So, I suppose, was the woman in the shawl. Did you stay all night ? "

" Not entirely. I came away before dawn. What did you do ? "

" Don't shout. I came home long before dawn." And she seemed to hear the long, low laughter.

" Why, what's the matter ! " he said curiously. " What have you been doing ? "

" I don't quite know. Why ?—are you going to call me to account ? "

" Did you hear that laughing ? "

" Oh, yes. And many more things. And saw things too."

" Have you seen the paper ? "

" No. Don't shout, I can hear."

" There's been a great storm, blew out the windows and doors of the church outside here, and pretty well wrecked the place."

" I saw it. A leaf of the church Bible blew right in my face : from the Book of Job——" She gave a low laugh.

" But what else did you see ? " he cried loudly.

" I saw *him*."

" Who ? "

" Ah, that I can't say."

" But what was he like ? "

" That I can't tell you. I don't really know."

" But you must know. Did your policeman see him too ? "

" No, I don't suppose he did. My policeman ! " And she went off into a long ripple of laughter. " He is by no means mine. But I *must* go downstairs and see him."

"It's certainly made you very strange," Marchbanks said. "You've got no *soul*, you know."

"Oh, thank goodness for that!" she cried. "My policeman has one, I'm sure. *My policeman!*" And she went off again into a long peal of laughter, the canaries pealing shrill accompaniment.

"What's the matter with you?" he said.

"Having no soul. I never had one really. It was always fobbed off on me. Soul was the only thing there was between you and me. Thank goodness it's gone. Haven't you lost yours? The one that seemed to worry you, like a decayed tooth?"

"But what are you *talking* about?" he cried.

"I don't know," she said. "It's all so extraordinary. But look here, I *must* go down and see my policeman. He's downstairs in the sitting-room. You'd better come with me."

They went down together. The policeman, in his waistcoat and shirt-sleeves, was lying on the sofa, with a very long face.

"Look here!" said Miss James to him. "Is it true you're lame?"

"It is true. That's why I'm here. I can't walk," said the fair-haired young man as tears came to his eyes.

"But how did it happen? You weren't lame last night," she said.

"I don't know how it happened—but when I woke up and tried to stand up, I couldn't do it." The tears ran down his distressed face.

"How very extraordinary!" she said. "What can we do about it?"

"Which foot is it?" asked Marchbanks. "Let us have a look at it."

"I don't like to," said the poor devil.

"You'd better," said Miss James.

He slowly pulled off his stocking, and showed his white left foot curiously clubbed, like the weird paw of some animal. When he looked at it himself, he sobbed.

And as he sobbed, the girl heard again the low, exulting laughter. But she paid no heed to it, gazing curiously at the weeping young policeman.

"Does it hurt?" she asked.

"It does if I try to walk on it," wept the young man.

"I'll tell you what," she said. "We'll telephone for a doctor, and he can take you home in a taxi."

The young fellow shamefacedly wiped his eyes.

"But have you no idea how it happened?" asked Marchbanks anxiously.

"I haven't myself," said the young fellow.

At that moment the girl heard the low, eternal laugh right in her ear. She started, but could see nothing.

She started round again as Marchbanks gave a strange, yelping cry, like a shot animal. His white face was drawn, distorted in a curious grin, that was chiefly agony but partly wild recognition. He was staring with fixed eyes at something. And in the rolling agony of his eyes was the horrible grin of a man who realizes he has made a final, and this time fatal, fool of himself.

" Why," he yelped in a high voice, " I knew it was he ! " And with a queer shuddering laugh he pitched forward on the carpet and lay writhing for a moment on the floor. Then he lay still, in a weird, distorted position, like a man struck by lightning.

Miss James stared with round, staring brown eyes.

" Is he dead ? " she asked quickly.

The young policeman was trembling so that he could hardly speak. She could hear his teeth chattering.

" Seems like it," he stammered.

There was a faint smell of almond blossom in the air.

"WELL, my dear!" said Henrietta. "If I had such a worried look on my face, when I was going down to spend the week-end with the man I was engaged to—and going to be married to in a month— well! I should either try and change my face, or hide my feelings, or something."

"You shut up!" said Hester curtly. "Don't look at my face, if it doesn't please you."

"Now, my dear Hester, don't go into one of your tempers! Just look in the mirror, and you'll see what I mean."

"Who cares what you mean! You're not responsible for my face," said Hester desperately, showing no intention of looking in the mirror, or of otherwise following her sister's kind advice.

Henrietta, being the younger sister, and mercifully unengaged, hummed a tune lightly. She was only twenty-one, and had not the faintest intention of jeopardizing her peace of mind by accepting any sort of fatal ring. Nevertheless, it *was* nice to see Hester "getting off", as they say; for Hester was nearly twenty-five, which is serious.

The worst of it was, lately Hester had had her famous "worried" look on her face, when it was a question of the faithful Joe: dark shadows under the eyes, drawn lines down the cheeks. And when Hester looked like that, Henrietta couldn't help feeling the most horrid jangled echo of worry and apprehension in her own heart, and she hated it. She simply couldn't stand that sudden feeling of fear.

"What I mean to say," she continued, "*is*—that it's jolly unfair to Joe, if you go down looking like that. Either put a better face on it, or——" But she checked herself. She was going to say "don't go". But really, she did hope that Hester would go through with this marriage. Such a weight off her, Henrietta's, mind.

"Oh hang!" cried Hester. "Shut up!" And her dark eyes flashed a spark of fury and misgiving at the young Henrietta.

Henrietta sat down on the bed, lifted her chin, and composed her face like a meditating angel. She really was intensely fond of Hester, and the worried look was such a terribly bad sign.

" Look here, Hester ! " she said. " Shall I come down to Mark-bury with you ? *I* don't mind, if you'd like me to."

" My dear girl," cried Hester in desperation, " what earthly use do you think that would be ? "

" Well, I thought it might take the edge off the intimacy, if that's what worries you."

Hester re-echoed with a hollow, mocking laugh.

" Don't be such a *child*, Henrietta, really ! " she said.

And Hester set off alone, down to Wiltshire, where her Joe had just started a little farm, to get married on. After being in the artillery, he had got sick and tired of business : besides, Hester would never have gone into a little surburban villa. Every woman sees her home through a wedding ring. Hester had only taken a squint through her engagement ring, so far. But Ye Gods ! not Golders Green, not even Harrow !

So Joe had built a little brown wooden bungalow—largely with his own hands : and at the back was a small stream with two willows, old ones. At the sides were brown sheds, and chicken runs. There were pigs in a hog-proof wire fence, and two cows in a field, and a horse. Joe had thirty-odd acres, with only a youth to help him. But of course, there would be Hester.

It all looked very new and tidy. Joe was a worker. He too looked rather new and tidy, very healthy and pleased with himself. He didn't even see the " worried look ". Or if he did, he only said :

" You're looking a big fagged, Hester. Going up to the City takes it out of you, more than you know. You'll be another girl down here."

" Shan't I just ! " cried Hester.

She did like it, too !—the lots of white and yellow hens, and the pigs so full of pep ! And the yellow thin blades of willow leaves showering softly down at the back of her house, from the leaning old trees. She liked it awfully : especially the yellow leaves on the earth.

She told Joe she thought it was all lovely, topping, fine ! And he was awfully pleased. Certainly *he* looked fit enough.

The mother of the helping youth gave them dinner at half-past twelve. The afternoon was all sunshine and little jobs to do, after she had dried the dishes for the mother of the youth.

" Not long now, Miss, before you'll be cooking at this range : and a good little range it is."

" Not long now, no ! " echoed Hester, in the hot little wooden kitchen, that was overheated from the range.

The woman departed. After tea, the youth also departed and Joe and Hester shut up the chickens and the pigs. It was nightfall. Hester went in and made the supper, feeling somehow a bit of a fool, and Joe made a fire in the living-room, he feeling rather important and luscious.

He and Hester would be alone in the bungalow, till the youth appeared next morning. Six months ago, Hester would have enjoyed it. They were so perfectly comfortable together, he and she. They had been friends, and his family and hers had been friends for years, donkey's years. He was a perfectly decent boy, and there would never have been anything messy to fear from him. Nor from herself. Ye Gods, no !

But now, alas, since she had promised to marry him, he had made the wretched mistake of falling " in love " with her. He had never been that way before. And if she had known he would get this way now, she would have said decidedly : Let us remain friends, Joe, for this sort of thing is a come-down. Once he started cuddling and petting, she couldn't stand him. Yet she felt she ought to. She imagined she even ought to like it. Though where the *ought* came from, she could not see.

" I'm afraid, Hester," he said sadly, " you're not in love with me as I am with you."

" Hang it all ! " she cried. " If I'm not, you ought to be jolly well thankful, that's all I've got to say."

Which double-barrelled remark he heard, but did not register. He never liked looking anything in the very pin-point middle of the eye. He just left it, and left all her feelings comfortably in the dark. Comfortably for him, that is.

He was extremely competent at motor-cars and farming and all that sort of thing. And surely she, Hester, was as complicated as a motor-car ! Surely she had as many subtle little valves and magnetos and accelerators and all the rest of it, to her make-up ! If only he would try to handle *her* as carefully as he handled his car ! She needed starting, as badly as ever any automobile did. Even if a car had a self-starter, the man had to give it the right twist. Hester felt she would need a lot of cranking up, if ever she was to start off on the matrimonial road with Joe. And he, the fool, just sat in a motionless car and pretended he was making heaven knows how many miles an hour.

This evening she felt really desperate. She had been quite all right doing things with him, during the afternoon, about the place. Then she liked being with him. But now that it was evening and they were alone, the stupid little room, the cosy fire, Joe, Joe's pipe, and Joe's smug sort of hypocritical face, all was just too much for her.

"Come and sit here, dear," said Joe persuasively, patting the sofa at his side. And she, because she believed a *nice* girl would have been only too delighted to go and sit " there ", went and sat beside him. But she was boiling. What cheek ! What cheek of him even to have a sofa ! She loathed the vulgarity of sofas.

She endured his arm round her waist, and a certain pressure of his biceps which she presumed was cuddling. He had carefully knocked his pipe out. But she thought how smug and silly his face looked, all its natural frankness and straightforwardness had gone. How ridiculous of him to stroke the back of her neck ! How idiotic he was, trying to be lovey-dovey ! She wondered what sort of sweet nothings Lord Byron, for example, had murmured to his various ladies. Surely not so blithering, not so incompetent ! And how monstrous of him, to kiss her like that.

"I'd infinitely rather you'd play to me, Joe," she snapped.

"You don't want me to play to you to-night, do you, dear ? " he said.

"Why not to-night ? I'd love to hear some Tchaikowsky, something to stir me up a bit."

He rose obediently, and went to the piano. He played quite well. She listened. And Tchaikowsky might have stirred her up all right. The music itself, that is. If she hadn't been so desperately aware that Joe's love-making, if you can call it such, became more absolutely impossible after the sound of the music.

"That was fine ! " she said. "Now do me my favourite nocturne."

While he concentrated on the fingering, she slipped out of the house.

Oh ! she gasped a sigh of relief to be in the cool October air. The darkness was dim, in the west was a half moon freshly shining, and all the air was motionless, dimness lay like a haze on the earth.

Hester shook her hair, and strode away from the bungalow, which was a perfect little drum, re-echoing to her favourite nocturne. She simply rushed to get out of earshot.

Ah ! the lovely night ! She tossed her short hair again, and felt like Mazeppa's horse, about to dash away into the infinite. Though the infinite was only a field belonging to the next farm. But Hester felt herself seething in the soft moonlight. Oh ! to rush away over the edge of the beyond ! if the beyond, like Joe's breadknife, did

have an edge to it. "I know I'm an idiot," she said to herself.
But that didn't take away the wild surge of her limbs. Oh! If
there were only some other solution, instead of Joe and his spooning.
Yes, SPOONING! The word made her lose the last shred of her self-
respect, but she said it aloud.

There was, however, a bunch of strange horses in this field, so
she made her way cautiously back through Joe's fence. It was just
like him, to have such a little place that you couldn't get away from
the sound of his piano, without trespassing on somebody else's ground.

As she drew near the bungalow, however, the drumming of Joe's
piano suddenly ceased. Oh Heaven! she looked wildly round. An
old willow leaned over the stream. She stretched, crouching, and
with the quickness of a long cat, climbed up into the net of cool-
bladed foliage.

She had scarcely shuffled and settled into a tolerable position,
when he came round the corner of the house and into the moonlight,
looking for her. How dare he look for her! She kept as still as a bat
among the leaves, watching him as he sauntered with erect, tire-
somely manly figure and lifted head, staring round in the darkness.
He looked for once very ineffectual, insignificant, and at a loss.
Where was his supposed male magic? Why was he so slow and
unequal to the situation?

There! He was calling softly and self-consciously: "Hester!
Hester! Where have you put yourself?"

He was angry really. Hester kept still in her tree, trying not to
fidget. She had not the faintest intention of answering him. He
might as well have been on another planet. He sauntered vaguely
and unhappily out of sight.

Then she had a qualm. "Really, my girl, it's a bit thick, the
way you treat him! Poor old Joe!"

Immediately something began to hum inside her: "I hear those
tender voices calling Poor Old Joe!"

Nevertheless, she didn't want to go indoors to spend the evening
tête à tête—my word!—with him.

"Of course it's absurd to think I could possibly fall in love like
that. I would rather fall into one of his pig-troughs. It's so frightfully common. As a matter of fact, it's just a proof that he doesn't
love me."

This thought went through her like a bullet. "The very fact of
his being in love with me proves that he doesn't love me. No man
that loved a woman could be in love with her like that. It's so
insulting to her."

She immediately began to cry, and fumbling in her sleeve for her hanky, she nearly fell out of the tree. Which brought her to her senses.

In the obscure distance she saw him returning to the house, and she felt bitter. "Why did he start all this mess? I never wanted to marry anybody, and I certainly never bargained for anybody falling in love with me. Now I'm miserable, and I feel abnormal. Because the majority of girls must like this in-love business, or men wouldn't do it. And the majority must be normal. So I'm abnormal, and I'm up a tree. I loathe myself. As for Joe, he's spoilt all there was between us, and he expects me to marry him on the strength of it. It's perfectly sickening! What a mess life is. How I loathe messes!"

She immediately shed a few more tears, in the course of which she heard the door of the bungalow shut with something of a bang. He had gone indoors, and he was going to be righteously offended. A new misgiving came over her.

The willow tree was uncomfortable. The air was cold and damp. If she caught another chill she'd probably snuffle all winter long. She saw the lamplight coming warm from the window of the bungalow, and she said "Damn!" which meant, in her case, that she was feeling bad.

She slid down out of the tree, and scratched her arm and probably damaged one of her nicest pair of stockings. "Oh hang!" she said with emphasis, preparing to go into the bungalow and have it out with poor old Joe. "I will *not* call him Poor Old Joe!"

At that moment she heard a motor-car slow down in the lane, and there came a low, cautious toot from a hooter. Headlights shone at a standstill near Joe's new iron gate.

"The cheek of it! The unbearable cheek of it! There's that young Henrietta come down on me!"

She flew along Joe's cinder-drive like a Mænad.

"Hello, Hester!" came Henrietta's young voice, coolly floating from the obscurity of the car. "How's everything?"

"What cheek!" cried Hester. "What amazing cheek!" She leaned on Joe's iron gate, and panted.

"How's everything?" repeated Henrietta's voice blandly.

"What do you mean by it?" demanded Hester, still panting.

"Now, my girl, don't go off at a tangent! We weren't coming in unless you came out. You needn't think we want to put our noses in your affairs. We're going down to camp on Bonamy. Isn't the weather too divine!"

Bonamy was Joe's pal, also an old artillery man, who had set up a " farm " about a mile further along the land. Joe was by no means a Robinson Crusoe in his bungalow.

" Who are you, anyway ? " demanded Hester.

" Same old birds," said Donald, from the driver's seat. Donald was Joe's brother. Henrietta was sitting in front, next to him.

" Same as ever," said Teddy, poking his head out of the car. Teddy was a second cousin.

" Well," said Hester, sort of climbing down. " I suppose you may as well come in, now you *are* here. Have you eaten ? "

" Eaten, yes," said Donald. " But we aren't coming in this trip, Hester ; don't you fret."

" Why not ? " flashed Hester, up in arms.

" 'Fraid of brother Joe," said Donald.

" Besides, Hester," said Henrietta anxiously, " you know you don't want us."

" Henrietta, don't be a fool ! " flashed Hester.

" *Well*, Hester—— ! " remonstrated the pained Henrietta.

" Come on in, and no more nonsense ! " said Hester.

" Not this trip, Hester," said Donny.

" No sir ! " said Teddy.

" But what idiots you all are ! Why not ? " cried Hester.

" 'Fraid of our elder brother," said Donald.

" All right," said Hester. " Then I'll come along with you."

She hastily opened the gate.

" Shall I just have a peep ? I'm pining to see the house," said Henrietta, climbing with a long leg over the door of the car.

The night was now dark, the moon had sunk. The two girls crunched in silence along the cinder track to the house.

" You'd say, if you'd rather I didn't come in—or if Joe'd rather," said Henrietta anxiously. She was very much disturbed in her young mind, and hoped for a clue. Hester walked on without answering. Henrietta laid her hand on her sister's arm. Hester shook it off, saying :

" My dear Henrietta, do be normal ! "

And she rushed up the three steps to the door, which she flung open, displaying the lamplit living-room, Joe in an arm-chair by the low fire, his back to the door. He did not turn round.

" Here's Henrietta ! " cried Hester, in a tone which meant : " *How's that ?* "

He got up and faced round, his brown eyes in his stiff face very angry.

" How did *you* get here ? " he asked rudely.

" Came in a car," said young Henrietta, from her Age of Innocence.

" With Donald and Teddy—they're there just outside the gate," said Hester. " The old gang ! "

" Coming in ? " asked Joe, with greater anger in his voice.

" I suppose you'll go out and invite them," said Hester.

Joe said nothing, just stood like a block.

" I expect you'll think it's awful of me to come intruding," said Henrietta meekly. " We're just going on to Bonamy's." She gazed innocently round the room. " But it's an adorable little place, awfully good taste in a cottagey sort of way. I like it awfully. Can I warm my hands ? "

Joe moved from in front of the fire. He was in his slippers. Henrietta dangled her long red hands, red from the night air, before the grate.

" I'll rush right away again," she said.

" Oh-h," drawled Hester curiously. " Don't do that ! "

" Yes, I must. Donald and Teddy are waiting."

The door stood wide open, the headlights of the car could be seen in the lane.

" Oh-h ! " Again that curious drawl from Hester. " I'll tell them you're staying the night with me. I can do with a bit of company."

Joe looked at her.

" What's the game ? " he said.

" No game at all ! Only now Tatty's come, she may as well stay."

" Tatty " was the rather infrequent abbreviation of " Henrietta ".

" Oh, but Hester ! " said Henrietta. " I'm going on to Bonamy's with Donald and Teddy."

" Not if I want you to stay here ! " said Hester.

Henrietta looked all surprised, resigned helplessness.

" What's the game ? " repeated Joe. " Had you fixed up to come down here to-night ? "

" No Joe, really ! " said Henrietta, with earnest innocence. " I hadn't the faintest idea of such a thing, till Donald suggested it, at four o'clock this afternoon. Only the weather was too perfectly divine, we had to go out somewhere, so we thought we'd descend on Bonamy. I hope *he* won't be frightfully put out, as well."

" And if we had arranged it, it wouldn't have been a crime," struck in Hester. " And anyway, now you're here you might as well all camp here."

" Oh no, Hester ! I know Donald will never come inside the gate. He was angry with me for making him stop, and it was I who tooted. It wasn't him, it was me. The curiosity of Eve, I suppose. Anyhow I've put my foot in it, as usual. So now I'd better clear out as fast as I can. Good night ! "

She gathered her coat round her with one arm and moved vaguely to the door.

" In that case, I'll come along with you," said Hester.

" But Hester ! " cried Henrietta. And she looked inquiringly at Joe.

" I know as little as you do," he said, " what's going on."

His face was wooden and angry, Henrietta could make nothing of him.

" Hester ! " cried Henrietta. " Do be sensible ! What's gone wrong ! Why don't you at least *explain*, and give everybody a chance ! Talk about being normal !—you're always flinging it at *me !* "

There was a dramatic silence.

" What's happened ? " Henrietta insisted, her eyes very bright and distressed, her manner showing that she was determined to be sensible.

" Nothing, of course ! " mocked Hester.

" Do *you* know, Joe ? " said Henrietta, like another Portia, turning very sympathetically to the man.

For a moment Joe thought how much nicer Henrietta was than her sister.

" I only know she asked me to play the piano, and then she dodged out of the house. Since then, her steering gear's been out or order."

" Ha-ha-ha ! " laughed Hester falsely and melodramatically. " I like that. I like my dodging out of the house ! I went out for a breath of fresh air. I should like to know whose steering gear is out of order, talking about my dodging out of the house ! "

" You dodged out of the house," said Joe.

" Oh, did I ? And why should I, pray ? "

" I suppose you have your own reasons."

" I have too. And very good reasons."

There was a moment of stupefied amazement . . . Joe and Hester had known each other so well, for such a long time. And now look at them !

" But why did you, Hester ? " asked Henrietta, in her most breathless naïve fashion.

" Why did I what ? "

There was a low toot from the motor-car in the lane.

" They're calling me ! Good-bye ! " cried Henrietta, wrapping her coat round her and turning decisively to the door.

" If you go, my girl, I'm coming with you," said Hester.

" But why ? " cried Henrietta in amazement. The horn tooted again. She opened the door, and called into the night :

" Half a minute ! " Then she closed the door again, softly, and turned once more in her amazement to Hester.

" But why, Hester ? "

Hester's eyes almost squinted with exasperation. She could hardly bear even to glance at the wooden and angry Joe.

" Why ? "

" Why ? " came the soft reiteration of Henrietta's question.

All the attention focused on Hester, but Hester was a sealed book.

" Why ? "

" She doesn't know herself," said Joe, seeing a loophole.

Out rang Hester's crazy and melodramatic laugh.

" Oh, doesn't she ! " Her face flew into sudden strange fury. " Well, if you want to know, I absolutely *can't stand* your making love to me, if that's what you call the business."

Henrietta let go the door handle, and sank weakly into a chair.

The worst had come to the worst. Joe's face became purple, then slowly paled to yellow.

" Then," said Henrietta in a hollow voice, " you can't marry him."

" I couldn't possibly marry him if he kept on being *in love* with me." She spoke the two words with almost snarling emphasis.

" And you couldn't possibly marry him if he *wasn't*," said the guardian angel, Henrietta.

" Why not," cried Hester. " I could stand him all right till he started being in love with me. Now, he's simply out of the question."

There was a pause, out of which came Henrietta's :

" After all, Hester, a man's *supposed* to be in love with the woman he wants to marry."

" Then he'd better keep it to himself, that's all I've got to say."

There was a pause. Joe, silent as ever, looked more wooden and sheepishly angry.

" But Hester ! Hasn't a man *got* to be in love with you——— ? "

" Not with me ! You've not had it to put up with, my girl."

Henrietta sighed helplessly.

" Then you can't marry him, that's obvious. What an awful pity ! "

A pause.

" Nothing can be so perfectly humiliating as a man making love to you," said Hester. " I *loathe* it."

" Perhaps it's because it's the wrong man," said Henrietta sadly, with a glance at the wooden and sheepish Joe.

" I don't believe I could stand that sort of thing, with *any* man. Henrietta, do you know what it is, being stroked and cuddled? It's too perfectly awful and ridiculous."

" Yes ! " said Henrietta, musing sadly. " As if one were a perfectly priceless meat-pie, and the dog licked it tenderly before he gobbled it up. It *is* rather sickening, I agree."

" And what's so awful, a perfectly decent man will go and get that way. Nothing is so awful as a man who has fallen in love," said Hester.

" I know what you mean, Hester. So doggy ! " said Henrietta sadly.

The motor horn tooted exasperatedly. Henrietta rose like a Portia who has been a failure. She opened the door, and suddenly yelled fiercely into the night :

" Go on without me. I'll walk. Don't wait."

" How long will you be ? " came a voice.

" I don't know. If I want to come, I'll walk," she yelled.

" Come back for you in an hour."

" Right," she shrieked, and slammed the door in their distant faces. Then she sat down dejectedly, in the silence. She was going to stand by Hester. That *fool*, Joe, standing there like a mutton-head !

They heard the car start, and retreat down the lane.

" Men are awful ! " said Henrietta dejectedly.

" Anyhow, you're mistaken," said Joe with sudden venom, to Hester. " I'm not in love with you, Miss Clever."

The two women looked at him as if he were Lazarus risen.

" And I never was in love with you, that way," he added, his brown eyes burning with a strange fire of self-conscious shame and anger, and naked passion.

" Well, what a liar you must be then. That's all I can say ! " replied Hester coldly.

" Do you mean," said young Henrietta acidly, " that you put it all on ? "

" I thought she expected it of me," he said, with a nasty little smile that simply paralysed the two young women. If he had turned into a boa-constrictor, they would not have been more amazed. That sneering little smile ! Their good-natured Joe !

" I thought it was expected of me," he repeated, jeering.

Hester was horrified.

" Oh, but how beastly of you to do it ! " cried Henrietta to him.

" And what a lie ! " cried Hester. " He liked it."

" Do you think he did, Hester ? " said Henrietta.

" I liked it in a way," he said impudently. " But I shouldn't have liked it, if I thought she didn't."

Hester flung out her arms.

" Henrietta," she cried, " why can't we kill him ? "

" I wish we could," said Henrietta.

" What are you to do, when you know a girl's rather strict, and you like her for it—and you're not going to be married for a month —and—and you—and you've got to get over the interval somehow— and what else does Rudolf Valentino do for you ?—you like *him*——"

" He's dead, poor dear. But I loathed him, *really*," said Hester.

" You didn't seem to," said he.

" Well, anyhow, you aren't Rudolf Valentino, and I loathe *you* in the rôle."

" You won't get a chance again. I loathe *you* altogether."

" And I'm extremely relieved to hear it, my boy."

There was a lengthy pause, after which Henrietta said with decision :

" Well, that's that ! Will you come along to Bonamy's with me, Hester, or shall I stay here with you ? "

" *I* don't care, my girl," said Hester with bravado.

" Neither do I care what you do," said he. " But I call it pretty rotten of you, not to tell me right out, at first."

" I thought it was real with you then, and I didn't want to hurt you," said Hester.

" You look as if you didn't want to hurt me," he said.

" Oh, *now*," she said, " since it was all pretence, it doesn't matter."

" I should say it doesn't," he retorted.

There was a silence. The clock, which was intended to be their family clock, ticked rather hastily.

" Anyway," he said, " I consider you've let me down."

" I like that ! " she cried, " considering what you've played off on me ! "

He looked her straight in the eye. They knew each other so well. Why had he tried that silly love-making game on her ? It was a betrayal of their simple intimacy. He saw it plainly, and repented.

And she saw the honest, patient love for her in his eyes, and the queer, quiet central desire. It was the first time she had seen it, that quiet, patient, central desire of a young man who has suffered during his youth, and seeks now almost with the slowness of age. A hot flush went over her heart. She felt herself responding to him.

"What have you decided, Hester?" said Henrietta.

"I'll stay with Joe, after all," said Hester.

"Very well," said Henrietta. "And I'll go along to Bonamy's." She opened the door quietly, and was gone.

Joe and Hester looked at one another from a distance.

"I'm sorry, Hester," said he.

"You know, Joe," she said, "I don't mind what you do, if you love me *really*."

I KNEW Carlotta Fell in the early days before the war. Then she was escaping into art, and was just "Fell." That was at our famous but uninspired school of art, the Thwaite, where I myself was diligently murdering my talent. At the Thwaite they always gave Carlotta the Still-life prizes. She accepted them calmly, as one of our conquerors, but the rest of the students felt vicious about it. They called it buttering the laurels, because Carlotta was Hon., and her father a well-known peer.

She was by way of being a beauty, too. Her family was not rich, yet she had come into five hundred a year of her own, when she was eighteen; and that, to us, was an enormity. Then she appeared in the fashionable papers, affecting to be wistful, with pearls, slanting her eyes. Then she went and did another of her beastly still-lives, a cactus-in-a-pot.

At the Thwaite, being snobs, we were proud of her too. She showed off a bit, it is true, playing bird of paradise among the pigeons. At the same time, she *was* thrilled to be with us, and out of her own set. Her wistfulness and yearning "for something else" was absolutely genuine. Yet she was not going to hobnob with us either, at least not indiscriminately.

She was ambitious, in a vague way. She wanted to coruscate, somehow or other. She had a family of clever and "distinguished" uncles, who had flattered her. What then?

Her cactuses-in-a-pot were admirable. But even she didn't expect them to start a revolution. Perhaps she would rather glow in the wide if dirty skies of life, than in the somewhat remote and unsatisfactory ether of Art.

She and I were "friends" in a bare, stark, but real sense. I was poor, but I didn't really care. She didn't really care either. Whereas I did care about some passionate vision which, I could feel, lay embedded in the half-dead body of this life. The quick body within the dead. I could *feel* it. And I wanted to get at it, if only for myself.

She didn't know what I was after. Yet she could feel that I was It, and, being an aristocrat of the Kingdom of It, as well as the realm of Great Britain, she was loyal—loyal to me because of It, the quick body which I imagined within the dead.

Still, we never had much to do with one another. .I had no money. She never wanted to introduce me to her own people. I didn't want it either. Sometimes we had lunch together, sometimes we went to a theatre, or we drove in the country, in some car that belonged to neither of us. We never flirted or talked love. I don't think she wanted it, any more than I did. She wanted to marry into her own surroundings, and I knew she was of too frail a paste to face my future.

Now I come to think of it, she was always a bit sad when we were together. Perhaps she looked over seas she would never cross. She belonged finally, fatally, to her own class. Yet I think she hated them. When she was in a group of people who talked " smart," titles and *beau monde* and all that, her rather short nose would turn up, her wide mouth press into discontent, and a languor of bored irritation come even over her broad shoulders. Bored irritation, and a loathing of climbers, a loathing of the ladder altogether. She hated her own class : yet it was also sacrosanct to her. She disliked, even to me, mentioning the titles of her friends. Yet the very hurried resentment with which she said, when I asked her, Who is it ?—

" Lady Nithsdale, Lord Staines—old friends of my mother," proved that the coronet was wedged into her brow, like a ring of iron grown into a tree.

She had another kind of reverence for a true artist : perhaps more genuine, perhaps not ; anyhow, more free and easy.

She and I had a curious understanding in common : an inkling, perhaps, of the unborn body of life hidden within the body of this half-death which we call life : and hence a tacit hostility to the commonplace world, its inert laws. We were rather like two soldiers on a secret mission in an enemy country. Life, and people, was an enemy country to us both. But she would never declare herself.

She always came to me to find out what I thought, particularly in a moral issue. Profoundly, fretfully discontented with the conventional moral standards, she didn't know how to take a stand of her own. So she came to me. She had to try to get her own feelings straightened out. In that she showed her old British fibre. I told her what, as a young man, I thought : and usually she was resentful. She did so want to be conventional. She would even act quite perversely, in her determination to be conventional. But she always had to

come back to me, to ask me again.   She depended on me morally.
Even when she disagreed with me, it soothed her, and restored her
to know my point of view.   Yet she disagreed with me.

We had then a curious abstract intimacy, that went very deep,
yet showed no obvious contact.   Perhaps I was the only person in
the world with whom she felt, in her uneasy self, at home, at peace.
And to me, she was always of my own *intrinsic* sort, of my own
species.   Most people are just another species to me.   They might
as well be turkeys.

But she would always *act* according to the conventions of her class,
even perversely.   And I knew it.

So, just before the war she married Lord Lathkill.   She was
twenty-one.   I did not see her till war was declared ; then she asked
me to lunch with her and her husband, in town.   He was an officer
in a Guards regiment, and happened to be in uniform, looking very
handsome and well set-up, as if he expected to find the best of life
served up to him for ever.   He was very dark, with dark eyes and fine
black hair, and a very beautiful, diffident voice, almost womanish
in its slow, delicate inflections.   He seemed pleased and flattered at
having Carlotta for a wife.

To me he was beautifully attentive, almost deferential, because
I was poor, and of the other world, those poor devils of outsiders.
I laughed at him a little, and laughed at Carlotta, who was a bit
irritated by the gentle delicacy with which he treated me.

She was elated too.   I remember her saying :

" We need war, don't you think ?   Don't you think men need the
fight, to keep life chivalrous and put martial glamour into
it ? "

And I remember saying, " I think we need some sort of fight ;
but my sort isn't the war sort."   It was August, we could take it
lightly.

" What's your sort ? " she asked quickly.

" I don't know : single-handed, anyhow," I said, with a grin.
Lord Lathkill made me feel like a lonely sansculotte, he was so
completely unostentatious, so very willing to pay all the attention
to me, and yet so subtly complacent, so unquestionably sure of his
position.   Whereas I was not a very sound earthenware pitcher
which had already gone many times to the well.

He was not conceited, not half as *conceited* as I was.   He was willing
to leave me all the front of the stage, even with Carlotta.   He felt
so sure of some things, like a tortoise in a glittering, polished tortoiseshell that mirrors eternity.   Yet he was not quite easy with me.

" You are Derbyshire ? " I said to him, looking into his face. " So am I ! I was born in Derbyshire."

He asked me with a gentle, uneasy sort of politeness, where ? But he was a bit taken aback. And his dark eyes, brooding over me, had a sort of fear in them. At the centre they were hollow with a certain misgiving. He was so sure of *circumstances*, and not by any means sure of the man in the middle of the circumstances. Himself ! Himself ! That was already a ghost.

I felt that he saw in me something crude but real, and saw himself as something in its own way perfect, but quite unreal. Even his love for Carlotta, and his marriage, was a circumstance that was inwardly unreal to him. One could tell by the curious way in which he waited, before he spoke. And by the hollow look, almost a touch of madness, in his dark eyes, and in his soft, melancholy voice.

I could understand that she was fascinated by him. But God help him if ever circumstances went against him !

She had to see me again, a week later, to talk about him. So she asked me to the opera. She had a box, and we were alone, and the notorious Lady Perth was two boxes away. But this was one of Carlotta's conventional perverse little acts, with her husband in France. She only wanted to talk to me about him.

So she sat in the front of her box, leaning a little to the audience and talking sideways to me. Any one would have known at once there was a *liaison* between us, how *dangereuse* they would never have guessed. For there, in the full view of the world—her world at least, not mine—she was talking sideways to me, saying in a hurried, yet stony voice :

" What do you think of Luke ? "

She looked up at me heavily, with her sea-coloured eyes, waiting for my answer.

" He's tremendously charming," I said, above the theatreful of faces.

" Yes, he's that ! " she replied, in the flat, plangent voice she had when she was serious, like metal ringing flat, with a strange far-reaching vibration. " Do you think he'll be happy ? "

" *Be* happy ! " I ejaculated. " When, *be* happy ? "

" With me," she said, giving a sudden little snirt of laughter, like a schoolgirl, and looking up at me shyly, mischievously, anxiously.

" If you make him," I said, still casual.

" How can I make him ? "

She said it with flat plangent earnestness. She was always like that, pushing me deeper in than I wanted to go.

" Be happy yourself, I suppose : and quite sure about it. And then *tell* him you're happy, and tell him he is, too, and he'll be it."

" Must I do all that ? " she said rapidly. " Not otherwise ? "

I knew I was frowning at her, and she was watching my frown.

" Probably not," I said roughly. " He'll never make up his mind about it himself."

" How did you know ? " she asked, as if it had been a mystery.

" I didn't. It only seems to me like that."

" Seems to you like that," she re-echoed, in that sad, clean monotone of finality, always like metal. I appreciate it in her, that she does not murmur or whisper. But I wished she left me alone, in that beastly theatre.

She was wearing emeralds, on her snow-white skin, and leaning forward gazing fixedly down into the auditorium, as a crystal-gazer into a crystal. Heaven knows if she saw all those little facets of faces and plastrons. As for me, I knew that, like a sansculotte, I should never be king till breeches were off.

" I had terrible work to make him marry me," she said, in her swift, clear, low tones.

" Why ? "

" He was frightfully in love with me. *He is !* But he thinks he's unlucky. . . ."

" Unlucky, how ? In cards or in love ? " I mocked.

" In both," she said briefly, with sudden cold resentment at my flippancy. There was over her eyes a glaze of fear. " It's in their family."

" What did you say to him ? " I asked, rather laboured, feeling the dead weight.

" I promised to have luck for two," she said. " And war was declared a fortnight later."

" Ah, well ! " I said. " That's the world's luck, not yours."

" Quite ! " she said.

There was a pause.

" Is his family supposed to be unlucky ? " I asked.

" The Worths ? Terribly ! They really are ! "

It was interval, and the box door had opened. Carlotta always had her eye, a good half of it at least, on the external happenings. She rose, like a reigning beauty—which she wasn't, and never became—to speak to Lady Perth, and, out of spite, did not introduce me.

Carlotta and Lord Lathkill came, perhaps a year later, to visit us when we were in a cottage in Derbyshire, and he was home on leave.

She was going to have a child, and was slow, and seemed depressed. He was vague, charming, talking about the country and the history of the lead mines. But the two of them seemed vague, as if they never got anywhere.

The last time I saw them was when the war was over, and I was leaving England. They were alone at dinner, save for me. He was still haggard, with a wound in the throat. But he said he would soon be well. His slow, beautiful voice was a bit husky now. And his velvety eyes were hardened, haggard, but there was weariness, emptiness in the hardness.

I was poorer than ever, and felt a little weary myself. Carlotta was struggling with his silent emptiness. Since the war, the melancholy fixity of his eyes was more noticeable, the fear at the centre was almost monomania. She was wilting and losing her beauty.

There were twins in the house. After dinner, we went straight up to look at them, to the night nursery. They were two boys, with their father's fine dark hair, both of them.

He had put out his cigar, and leaned over the cots, gazing in silence. The nurse, dark-faced and faithful, drew back. Carlotta glanced at her children; but more helplessly, she gazed at him.

"Bonny children! Bonny boys, aren't they, nurse?" I said softly.

"Yes, sir!" she said quickly. "They are!"

"Ever think I'd have twins, roistering twins?" said Carlotta, looking at me.

"I never did," said I.

"Ask Luke whether it's bad luck or bad management," she said, with that schoolgirl's snirt of laughter, looking up apprehensively at her husband.

"Oh, I!" he said, turning suddenly and speaking loud, in his wounded voice. "I call it amazing good luck, myself! Don't know what other people think about it." Yet he had the fine, wincing fear in his body, of an injured dog.

After that, for years I did not see her again. I heard she had a baby girl. Then a catastrophe happened: both the twins were killed in a motor-car accident in America, motoring with their aunt.

I learned the news late, and did not write to Carlotta. What could I say?

A few months later, crowning disaster, the baby girl died of some sudden illness. The Lathkill ill-luck seemed to be working surely.

Poor Carlotta! I had no further news of her, only I heard that she and Lord Lathkill were both living in seclusion, with his mother, at the place in Derbyshire.

When circumstances brought me to England, I debated within myself, whether I should write or not to Carlotta. At last I sent a note to the London address.

I had a reply from the country : " So glad you are within reach again ! When will you come and see us ? "

I was not very keen on going to Riddings. After all, it was Lord Lathkill's place, and Lady Lathkill, his mother, was old and of the old school. And I always something of a sansculotte, who will only be king when breeches are off."

" Come to town," I wrote, " and let us have lunch together."

She came. She looked older, and pain had drawn horizontal lines across her face.

" You're not a bit different," she said to me.

" And you're only a little bit," I said.

" Am I ! " she replied, in a deadened, melancholic voice. " Perhaps ! I suppose while we live we've got to live. What do you think ? "

" Yes, I think it. To be the living dead, that's awful."

" Quite ! " she said, with terrible finality.

" How is Lord Lathkill ? " I asked.

" Oh," she said. " It's finished him, as far as living is concerned. But he's very willing for *me* to live."

" And you, are you willing ? " I said.

She looked up into my eyes, strangely.

" I'm not sure," she said. " I need help. What do you think about it ? "

" Oh, God, live if you can ! "

" Even take help ? " she said, with her strange involved simplicity.

" Ah, certainly."

" Would you recommend it ? "

" Why, yes ! You are a young thing——" I began.

" Won't you come down to Riddings ? " she said quickly.

" And Lord Lathkill—and his mother ? " I asked.

" They want you."

" Do you want me to come ? "

" I want you to, yes ! Will you ? "

" Why, yes, if you want me."

" When, then ? "

" When you wish."

" Do you mean it ? "

" Why, of course."

" You're not afraid of the Lathkill ill-luck ? "

" *I!* " I exclaimed in amazement; such amazement, that she gave her schoolgirl snirt of laughter.

"Very well, then," she said. "Monday? Does that suit you?"

We made arrangements, and I saw her off at the station.

I knew Riddings, Lord Lathkill's place, from the outside. It was an old Derbyshire stone house, at the end of the village of Middleton: a house with three sharp gables, set back not very far from the high road, but with a gloomy moor for a park behind.

Monday was a dark day over the Derbyshire hills. The green hills were dark, dark green, the stone fences seemed almost black. Even the little railway station, deep in the green, cleft hollow, was of stone, and dark and cold, and seemed in the underworld.

Lord Lathkill was at the station. He was wearing spectacles, and his brown eyes stared strangely. His black hair fell lank over his forehead.

"I'm so awfully glad you've come," he said. "It is cheering Carlotta up immensely."

Me, as a man myself, he hardly seemed to notice. I was something which had arrived, and was expected. Otherwise he had an odd, unnatural briskness of manner.

"I hope I shan't disturb your mother, Lady Lathkill," I said as he tucked me up in the car.

"On the contrary," he sang, in his slow voice, "she is looking forward to your coming as much as we both are. Oh, no, don't look on Mother as too old-fashioned, she's not so at all. She's tremendously up to date in art and literature and that kind of thing. She has her leaning towards the uncanny—spiritualism, and that kind of thing—nowadays, but Carlotta and I think that if it gives her an interest, all well and good."

He tucked me up most carefully in the rugs, and the servant put a footwarmer at my feet.

"Derbyshire, you know, is a cold county," continued Lord Lathkill, "especially among the hills."

"It's a very dark county," I said.

"Yes, I suppose it is, to one coming from the tropics. We, of course, don't notice it; we rather like it."

He seemed curiously smaller, shrunken, and his rather long cheeks were sallow. His manner, however, was much more cheerful, almost communicative. But he talked, as it were, to the faceless air, not really to me. I wasn't really there at all. He was talking to himself. And when once he looked at me, his brown eyes had a hollow look, like gaps with nothing in them except a haggard, hollow fear. He was gazing through the windows of nothingness, to see if I were really there.

It was dark when we got to Riddings. The house had no door in the front, and only two windows upstairs were lit. It did not seem very hospitable. We entered at the side, and a very silent man-servant took my things.

We went upstairs in silence, in the dead-seeming house. Carlotta had heard us, and was at the top of the stairs. She was already dressed ; her long white arms were bare ; she had something glittering on a dull green dress.

" I was so afraid you wouldn't come," she said, in a dulled voice, as she gave me her hand. She seemed as if she would begin to cry. But of course she wouldn't. The corridor, dark-panelled and with blue carpet on the floor, receded dimly, with a certain dreary gloom. A servant was diminishing in the distance, with my bags, silently. There was a curious, unpleasant sense of the fixity of the materials of the house, the obscene triumph of dead matter. Yet the place was warm, central-heated.

Carlotta pulled herself together, and said, dulled :

" Would you care to speak to my mother-in-law before you go to your room ? She would like it."

We entered a small drawing-room, abruptly. I saw the water-colours on the walls and a white-haired lady in black bending round to look at the door as she rose, cautiously.

" This is Mr. Morier, Mother-in-law," said Carlotta, in her dull, rather quick way, " on his way to his room."

The dowager Lady Lathkill came a few steps forward, leaning from heavy hips, and gave me her hand. Her crest of hair was snow white, and she had curious blue eyes, fixed, with a tiny dot of a pupil, peering from her pink, soft-skinned face of an old and well-preserved woman. She wore a lace fichu. The upper part of her body was moderately slim, leaning forward slightly from her heavy black-silk hips.

She murmured something to me, staring at me fixedly for a long time, but as a bird does, with shrewd, cold, far-distant sight. As a hawk, perhaps, looks shrewdly far down, in his search. Then, muttering, she presented to me the other two people in the room : a tall, short-faced, swarthy young woman with the hint of a black moustache ; and a plump man in a dinner-jacket, rather bald and ruddy, with a little grey moustache, but yellow under the eyes. He was Colonel Hale.

They all seemed awkward, as if I had interrupted them at a séance. I didn't know what to say : they were utter strangers to me.

" Better come and choose your room, then," said Carlotta, and I bowed dumbly, following her out of the room. The old Lady Lathkill still stood planted on her heavy hips, looking half round after us with her ferret's blue eyes. She had hardly any eyebrows, but they were arched high up on her pink, soft forehead, under the crest of icily white hair. She had never emerged for a second from the remote place where she unyieldingly kept herself.

Carlotta, Lord Lathkill and I tramped in silence down the corridor and round a bend. We could none of us get a word out. As he suddenly, rather violently flung open a door at the end of the wing, he said, turning round to me with a resentful, hangdog air :

" We did you the honour of offering you our ghost room. It doesn't look much, but it's our equivalent for a royal apartment."

It was a good-sized room with faded, red-painted panelling show-ing remains of gilt, and the usual big, old mahogany furniture, and a big pinky-faded carpet with big, whitish, faded roses. A bright fire was burning in the stone fire-place.

" Why ? " said I, looking at the stretches of the faded, once hand-some carpet.

" Why what ? " said Lord Lathkill. " Why did we offer you this room ? "

" Yes ! No ! Why is it your equivalent for a royal apartment ? "

" Oh, because our ghost is as rare as sovereignty in her visits, and twice as welcome. Her gifts are infinitely more worth having."

" What sort of gifts ? "

" The family fortune. She invariably restores the family fortune. That's why we put you here, to tempt her."

" What temptation should *I* be ?—especially to restoring your family fortunes. I didn't think they needed it, anyhow."

" Well ! " he hesitated. " Not exactly in money : we can manage modestly that way ; but in everything else but money——"

There was a pause. I was thinking of Carlotta's " luck for two." Poor Carlotta ! She looked worn now. Especially her chin looked worn, showing the edge of the jaw. She had sat herself down in a chair by the fire, and put her feet on the stone fender, and was leaning forward, screening her face with her hand, still careful of her com-plexion. I could see her broad, white shoulders, showing the shoulder-blades, as she leaned forward, beneath her dress. But it was as if some bitterness, had soaked all the life out of her, and she was only weary, or inert, drained of her feelings. It grieved me, and the thought passed through my mind that a man should take her in his arms and cherish her body, and start her flame again. If she would let him, which was doubtful.

Her courage was fallen, in her body ; only her spirit fought on. She would have to restore the body of her life, and only a living body could do it.

" What *about* your ghost ? " I said to him. " Is she really ghastly ? "

" Not at all ! " he said. " She's supposed to be lovely. But I have no experience, and I don't know anybody who has. We hoped you'd come, though, and tempt her. Mother had a message about you, you know."

" No, I didn't know."

" Oh, yes ! When you were still in Africa. The medium said : ' There is a man in Africa. I can only see M, a double M. He is thinking of your family. It would be good if he entered your family.' Mother was awfully puzzled, but Carlotta said ' Mark Morier ' at once."

" That's not why I asked you down," said Carlotta quickly, look-ing round, shading her eyes with her hand as she looked at me.

I laughed, saying nothing.

" But, of course," continued Lord Lathkill, " you *needn't* have this room. We have another one ready as well. Would you like to see it ? "

" How does your ghost manifest herself ? " I said, parrying.

" Well, I hardly knew. She seems to be a very grateful *presence*, and that's about all I do know. She was apparently quite *persona grata* to every one she visited. *Gratissima*, apparently ! "

" *Benissimo !* " said I.

A servant appeared in the doorway, murmuring something I could not hear. Everybody in the house, except Carlotta and Lord Lath-kill, seemed to murmur under their breath.

" What's she say ? " I asked.

" If you will stay in this room ? I told her you might like a room on the front. And if you'll take a bath ? " said Carlotta.

" Yes ! " said I. And Carlotta repeated to the maid-servant.

" And for heaven's sake speak to me loudly," said I to that elderly correct female in her starched collar, in the doorway.

" Very good, sir ! " she piped up. " And shall I make the bath hot, or medium ? "

" Hot ! " said I, like a cannon-shot.

" Very good, sir ! " she piped up again, and her elderly eyes twinkled as she turned and disappeared.

Carlotta laughed, and I sighed.

We were six at table. The pink Colonel with the yellow creases under his blue eyes sat opposite me, like an old boy with a liver. Next him sat Lady Lathkill, watching from her distance. Her pink, soft old face, naked-seeming, with its pin-point blue eyes, was a real modern witch-face.

Next me, on my left, was the dark young woman, whose slim, swarthy arms had an indiscernible down on them. She had a blackish neck, and her expressionless yellow-brown eyes said nothing, under level black brows. She was inaccessible. I made some remarks, without result. Then I said :

"I didn't hear your name when Lady Lathkill introduced me to you."

Her yellow-brown eyes stared into mine for some moments before she said :

"Mrs. Hale !" Then she glanced across the table. "Colonel Hale is my husband."

My face must have signalled my surprise. She stared into my eyes very curiously, with a significance I could not grasp, a long, hard stare. I looked at the bald, pink head of the Colonel bent over his soup, and I returned to my own soup.

"Did you have a good time in London ? " said Carlotta.

"No," said I. "It was dismal."

"Not a good word to say for it ? "

"Not one."

"No nice people ? "

"Not my sort of nice."

"What's your sort of nice ? " she asked, with a little laugh.

The other people were stone. It was like talking into a chasm.

"Ah ! If I knew myself, I'd look for them ! But not sentimental, with a lot of soppy emotions on top, and nasty ones underneath."

"Who are you thinking of ? " Carlotta looked up at me as the man brought the fish. She had a crushed sort of roguishness. The other diners were images.

"I ? Nobody. Just everybody. No, I think I was thinking of the Obelisk Memorial Service."

"Did you go to it ? "

"No, but I fell into it."

"Wasn't it moving ? "

"Rhubarb, senna, that kind of moving ! "

She gave a little laugh, looking up into my face, from the fish.

"What was wrong with it ? "

I noticed that the Colonel and Lady Lathkill each had a little dish of rice, no fish, and that they were served second—oh, humility !— and that neither took the white wine. No, they had no wine-glasses. The remoteness gathered about them, like the snows on Everest. The dowager peered across at me occasionally, like a white ermine out of the snow, and she had that cold air about her, of being good, and containing a secret of goodness : remotely, ponderously, fixedly knowing better. And I, with my chatter, was one of those fabulous fleas that are said to hop upon glaciers.

" Wrong with it ? *It* was wrong, all wrong. In the rain, a soppy crowd, with soppy bare heads, soppy emotions, soppy chrysanthemums and prickly laurestinus ! A steam of wet mob-emotions ! Ah, no, it shouldn't be allowed."

Carlotta's face had fallen. She again could feel death in her bowels, the kind of death the war signifies.

" Wouldn't you have us honour the dead ? " came Lady Lathkill's secretive voice across at me, as if a white ermine had barked.

" Honour the dead ! " My mind opened in amazement. " Do you think they'd be honoured ? "

I put the question in all sincerity.

" They would understand the *intention* was to honour them," came her reply.

I felt astounded.

" If I were dead, would I be honoured if a great, steamy wet crowd came after me with soppy chrysanthemums and prickly laurestinus ? Ugh ! I'd run to the nethermost ends of Hades. Lord, how I'd run from them ! "

The manservant gave us roast mutton, and Lady Lathkill and the Colonel chestnuts in sauce. Then he poured the burgundy. It was good wine. The pseudo-conversation was interrupted.

Lady Lathkill ate in silence, like an ermine in the snow, feeding on his prey. Sometimes she looked round the table, her blue eyes peering fixedly, completely uncommunicative. She was very watchful to see that we were all properly attended to ; " The currant jelly for Mr. Morier," she would murmur, as if it were her table. Lord Lathkill, next her, ate in complete absence. Sometimes she murmured to him, and he murmured back, but I never could hear what they said. The Colonel swallowed the chestnuts in dejection, as if all were weary duty to him now. I put it down to his liver.

It was an awful dinner-party. I never could hear a word anybody said, except Carlotta. They all let their words die in their throats, as if the larynx were the coffin of sound.

Carlotta tried to keep her end up, the cheerful hostess sort of thing. But Lady Lathkill somehow, in silence and apparent humility, had stolen the authority that goes with the hostess, and she hung on to it grimly, like a white ermine sucking a rabbit. Carlotta kept glancing miserably at me, to see what I thought. I didn't think anything. I just felt frozen within the tomb. And I drank the good, good warm burgundy.

"Mr. Morier's glass!" murmured Lady Lathkill, and her blue eyes with their black pin-points rested on mine a moment.

"Awfully nice to drink good burgundy!" said I pleasantly.

She bowed her head slightly, and murmured something inaudible.

"I beg your pardon?"

"Very glad you like it!" she repeated, with distaste at having to say it again, out loud.

"Yes, I do. It's good."

Mrs. Hale, who had sat tall and erect and alert, like a black she-fox, never making a sound, looked round at me to see what sort of specimen I was. She was just a bit intrigued.

"Yes, thanks," came a musical murmur from Lord Lathkill. "I think I *will* take some more."

The man, who had hesitated, filled his glass.

"I'm awfully sorry I can't drink wine," said Carlotta, absently. "It has the wrong effect on me."

"I should say it has the wrong effect on everybody," said the Colonel, with an uneasy attempt to be there. "But some people like the effect, and some don't."

I looked at him in wonder. Why was he chipping in? He looked as if he'd liked the effect well enough, in his day.

"Oh, no!" retorted Carlotta coldly. "The effect on different people is quite different."

She closed with finality, and a further frost fell on the table.

"Quite so," began the Colonel, trying, since he'd gone off the deep end, to keep afloat.

But Carlotta turned abruptly to me.

"Why is it, do you think, that the effect is so different on different people?"

"And on different occasions," said I, grinning through my burgundy. "Do you know what they say? They say that alcohol, if it has an effect on your psyche, takes you back to old states of consciousness, and old reactions. But some people it doesn't stimulate at all, there is only a nervous reaction of repulsion."

"There's certainly a nervous reaction of repulsion in me," said Carlotta.

" As there is in all higher natures," murmured Lady Lathkill.

" Dogs hate whisky," said I.

" That's quite right," said the Colonel. " Scared of it ! "

" I've often thought," said I, "about those old states of consciousness. It's supposed to be an awful retrogression, reverting back to
them. Myself, my desire to go onwards takes me back a little."

" Where to ? " said Carlotta.

" Oh, I don't know ! To where you feel a bit warm, and like
smashing the glasses, don't you know ?

> " J'avons bien bu et nous boirons !
>   Cassons les verres nous les payerons !
>   Compagnons ! Voyez vous bien !
>   Voyez vous bien !
>   Voyez ! voyez ! voyez vous bien
>   Que les d'moiselles sont belles
>   Où nous allons ! "

I had the effrontery to sing this verse of an old soldier's song while
Lady Lathkill was finishing her celery and nut salad. I sang it
quite nicely, in a natty, well-balanced little voice, smiling all over
my face meanwhile. The servant, as he went round for Lady Lathkill's plate, furtively fetched a look at me. *Look !* thought I.
You chicken that's come untrussed !

The partridges had gone, we had swallowed the *flan,* and were at
dessert. They had accepted my song in complete silence. Even
Carlotta ! My *flan* had gone down in one gulp, like an oyster.

" You're quite right ! " said Lord Lathkill, amid the squashing of
walnuts. " I mean the state of mind of a Viking, shall we say, or of
a Cataline conspirator, might be frightfully good for us, if we could
recapture it."

" A Viking ! " said I, stupefied. And Carlotta gave a wild snirt
of laughter.

" Why not a Viking ? " he asked in all innocence.

" A Viking ! " I repeated, and swallowed my port. Then I
looked round at my black-browed neighbour.

" Why do you never say anything ? " I asked.

" What should I say ? " she replied, frightened at the thought.

I was finished. I gazed into my port as if expecting the ultimate
revelation.

Lady Lathkill rustled her finger-tips in the finger-bowl, and laid
down her napkin decisively. The Colonel, old buck, rose at once
to draw back her chair. *Place aux hommes !* I bowed to my neigh-

bour, Mrs. Hale, a most disconcerting bow, and she made a circuit to get by me.

" You won't be awfully long ? " said Carlotta, looking at me with her slow, hazel-green eyes, between mischief and wistfulness and utter depression.

Lady Lathkill steered heavily past me as if I didn't exist, perching rather forward, with her crest of white hair, from her big hips. She seemed abstracted, concentrated on something, as she went.

I closed the door, and turned to the men.

> " Dans la première auberge
> *J'eus b'en bu !* "

sang I in a little voice.

" Quite right," said Lord Lathkill. " You're quite right."

And we sent the port round.

" This house," I said, " needs a sort of spring cleaning."

" You're quite right," said Lord Lathkill.

" There's a bit of a dead smell ! " said I. " We need Bacchus, and Eros, to sweeten it up, to freshen it."

" You think Bacchus and Eros ? " said Lord Lathkill, with complete seriousness ; as if one might have telephoned for them.

" In the best sense," said I. As if we were going to get them from Fortnum and Mason's, at least.

" What exactly is the best sense ? " asked Lord Lathkill.

" Ah ! The flame of life ! There's a dead smell here."

The Colonel fingered his glass with thick, inert fingers, uneasily.

" Do you think so ? " he said, looking up at me heavily.

" Don't you ? "

He gazed at me with blank, glazed blue eyes, that had deathly yellow stains underneath. Something was wrong with him, some sort of breakdown. He should have been a fat, healthy, jolly old boy. Not very old either : probably not quite sixty. But with this collapse on him, he seemed, somehow, to smell.

" You know," he said, staring at me with a sort of gruesome challenge, then looking down at his wine, " there's more things than we're aware of, happening to us ! " He looked up at me again, shutting his full lips under his little grey moustache, and gazing with a glazed defiance.

" Quite ! " said I.

He continued to gaze at me with glazed, gruesome defiance.

" Ha ! " He made a sudden movement, and seemed to break up, collapse and become brokenly natural. " There, you've said it. I married my wife when I was a kid of twenty."

"Mrs. Hale?" I exclaimed.

"Not this one"—he jerked his head towards the door—"my first wife." There was a pause; he looked at me with shamed eyes, then turned his wineglass round and his head dropped. Staring at his twisting glass, he continued: "I married her when I was twenty, and she was twenty-eight. You might say, she married me. Well, there it was! We had three children—I've got three married daughters—and we got on all right. I suppose she mothered me, in a way. And I never thought a thing. I was content enough, wasn't tied to her apron strings, and she never asked questions. She was always fond of me, and I took it for granted. I took it for granted. Even when she died—I was away in Salonika—I took it for granted, if you understand me. It was part of the rest of things—war—life—death. I knew I should feel lonely when I got back. Well, then I got buried—shell dropped, and the dug-out caved in—and that queered me. They sent me home. And the minute I saw the Lizard light—it was evening when we got up out of the Bay—I realized that Lucy had been waiting for me. I could feel her there, at my side, more plainly than I feel you now. And do you know, at that moment I woke up to her, and she made an awful impression on me. She seemed, if you get me, tremendously powerful, important; everything else dwindled away. There was the Lizard light blinking a long way off, and that meant home. And all the rest was my wife, Lucy: as if her skirts filled all the darkness. In a way, I was frightened; but that was because I couldn't quite get myself into line. I felt: *Good God! I never knew her!* And she was this tremendous thing! I felt like a child, and as weak as a kitten. And, believe me or not, from that day to this she's never left me. I know quite well she can hear what I'm saying. But she'll let me tell you. I knew that at dinner-time."

"But what made you marry again?" I said.

"She made me!" He went a trifle yellow on his cheek-bones. "I could feel her telling me, '*Marry! Marry!*' Lady Lathkill had messages from her too; she was her great friend in life. I didn't think of marrying. But Lady Lathkill had the same message, that I must marry. Then a medium described the girl, in detail: my present wife. I knew her at once, friend of my daughters. After that the messages became more insistent, waking me three and four times in the night. Lady Lathkill urged me to propose, and I did it, and was accepted. My present wife was just twenty-eight, the age Lucy had been——"

"How long ago did you marry the present Mrs. Hale?"

" A little over a year ago. Well, I thought I had done what was required of me. But directly after the wedding, such a state of terror came over me—perfectly unreasonable—I became almost unconscious. My present wife asked me if I was ill, and I said I was. We got to Paris. I felt I was dying. But I said I was going out to see a doctor, and I found myself kneeling in a church. Then I found peace—and Lucy. She had her arms round me, and I was like a child at peace. I must have knelt there for a couple of hours in Lucy's arms. I *never* felt like that when I was alive : why, I couldn't stand that sort of thing ! It's all come on after—after—— And now, I daren't offend Lucy's spirit. If I do, I suffer tortures till I've made peace again, till she folds me in her arms. Then I can live. But she won't let me go near the present Mrs. Hale. I—I— I daren't go near her."

He looked up at me with fear, and shame, and shameful secrecy, and a sort of gloating showing in his unmanned blue eyes. He had been talking as if in his sleep.

" Why did your dead wife urge you to marry again ? " I said.

" I don't know," he replied. " I don't know. She was older than I was, and all the cleverness was on her side. She was a very clever woman, and I was never much in the intellectual line, myself. I just took it for granted she liked me. She never showed jealousy, but I think now, perhaps she was jealous all the time, and kept it under. I don't know. I think she never felt quite straight about having married me. It seems like that. As if she had something on her mind. Do you know, while she was alive, I never gave it a thought. And now I'm aware of nothing else but her. It's as if her spirit wanted to live in my body, or at any rate—I don't know——"

His blue eyes were glazed, almost fishy, with fear and gloating shame. He had a short nose, and full, self-indulgent lips, and a once-comely chin. Eternally a careless boy of thirteen. But now, care had got him in decay.

" And what does your present wife say ? " I asked.

He poured himself some more wine.

" Why," he replied, " except for her, I shouldn't mind so much. She says nothing. Lady Lathkill has explained everything to her, and she agrees that—that—a spirit from the other side is more important than mere pleasure—you know what I mean. Lady Lath-kill says that this is a preparation for my next incarnation, when I am going to serve Woman, and help Her to take Her place."

He looked up again, trying to be proud in his shame.

" Well, what a damned curious story ! " exclaimed Lord Lathkill.

" Mother's idea for herself—she had it in a message too—is that she is coming on earth the next time to save the animals from the cruelty of man. That's why she hates meat at table, or anything that has to be killed."

" And does Lady Lathkill encourage you in this business with your dead wife ? " said I.

" Yes. She helps me. When I get as you might say at cross purposes with Lucy—with Lucy's spirit, that is—Lady Lathkill helps to put it right between us. Then I'm all right, when I know I'm loved."

He looked at me stealthily, cunningly.

" Then you're all wrong," said I, " surely."

" And do you mean to say," put in Lord Lathkill, " that you don't live with the present Mrs. Hale at all ? Do you mean to say you never *have* lived with her ? "

" I've got a higher claim on me," said the unhappy Colonel.

" My God ! " said Lord Lathkill.

I looked in amazement : the sort of chap who picks up a woman and has a good time with her for a week, then goes home as nice as pie, and now look at him ! It was obvious that he had a terror of his black-browed new wife, as well as of Lucy's spirit. A devil and a deep sea with a vengeance !

" A damned curious story ! " mused Lord Lathkill. " I'm not so sure I like it. Something's wrong somewhere. We shall have to go upstairs."

" Wrong ! " said I. " Why, Colonel, don't you turn round and quarrel with the spirit of your first wife, fatally and finally, and get rid of her ? "

The Colonel looked at me, still diminished and afraid, but perking up a bit, as we rose from table.

" How would you go about it ? " he said.

" I'd just face her, wherever she seemed to be, and say : ' *Lucy, go to blazes !* ' "

Lord Lathkill burst into a loud laugh, then was suddenly silent as the door noiselessly opened, and the dowager's white hair and pointed uncanny eyes peered in, then entered.

" I think I left my papers in here, Luke," she murmured.

" Yes, mother. There they are. We're just coming up."

" Take your time."

He held the door, and ducking forward, she went out again, clutching some papers. The Colonel had blenched yellow on his cheek-bones.

We went upstairs to the small drawing-room.

"You were a long time," said Carlotta, looking in all our faces.
"Hope the coffee's not cold. We'll have fresh if it is."

She poured out, and Mrs. Hale carried the cups. The dark young
woman thrust out her straight, dusky arm, offering me sugar, and
gazing at me with her unchanging, yellow-brown eyes. I looked
back at her, and being clairvoyant in this house, was conscious of
the curves of her erect body, the sparse black hairs there would
be on her strong-skinned dusky thighs. She was a woman of thirty,
and she had had a great dread lest she should never marry. Now
she was as if mesmerized.

"What do you do usually in the evenings?" I said.

She turned to me as if startled, as she nearly always did when
addressed.

"We do nothing," she replied. "Talk; and sometimes Lady
Lathkill reads."

"What does she read?"

"About spiritualism."

"Sounds pretty dull."

She looked at me again, but she did not answer. It was difficult
to get anything out of her. She put up no fight, only remained in the
same swarthy, passive, negative resistance. For a moment I wondered that no men made love to her: it was obvious they didn't.
But then, modern young men are accustomed to being attracted,
flattered, impressed: they expect an effort to please. And Mrs.
Hale made none: didn't know how. Which for me was her mystery.
She was passive, static, locked up in a resistant passivity that had
fire beneath it.

Lord Lathkill came and sat by us. The Colonel's confession had
had an effect on him.

"I'm afraid," he said to Mrs. Hale, "you have a thin time here."

"Why?" she asked.

"Oh, there is so little to amuse you. Do you like to dance?"

"Yes," she said.

"Well, then," he said, "let us go downstairs and dance to the
Victrola. There are four of us. You'll come, of course?" he said to me.

Then he turned to his mother.

"Mother, we shall go down to the morning-room and dance.
Will you come too? Will you, Colonel?"

The dowager gazed at her son.

"I will come and look on," she said.

"And I will play the pianola, if you like," volunteered the Colonel.

We went down, and pushed aside the chintz chairs and the rugs.

Lady Lathkill sat in a chair, the Colonel worked away at the pianola. I danced with Carlotta, Lord Lathkill with Mrs. Hale.

A quiet soothing came over me, dancing with Carlotta. She was very still and remote, and she hardly looked at me. Yet the touch of her was wonderful, like a flower that yields itself to the morning. Her warm, silken shoulder was soft and grateful under my hand, as if it knew me with that second knowledge which is part of one's childhood, and which so rarely blossoms again in manhood and womanhood. It was as if we had known each other perfectly, as children, and now, as man and woman met in the full, further sympathy. Perhaps, in modern people, only after long suffering and defeat, can the naked intuition break free between woman and man.

She, I knew, let the strain and the tension of all her life depart from her then, leaving her nakedly still, within my arm. And I only wanted to be with her, to have her in my touch.

Yet after the second dance she looked at me, and suggested that she should dance with her husband. So I found myself with the strong, passive shoulder of Mrs. Hale under my hand, and her inert hand in mine, as I looked down at her dusky, dirty-looking neck— she wisely avoided powder. The duskiness of her mesmerized body made me see the faint dark sheen of her thighs, with intermittent black hairs. It was as if they shone through the silk of her mauve dress, like the limbs of a half-wild animal, that is locked up in its own helpless dumb winter, a prisoner.

She knew, with the heavy intuition of her sort, that I glimpsed her crude among the bushes, and felt her attraction. But she kept looking away over my shoulder, with her yellow eyes, towards Lord Lathkill.

Myself or him, it was a question of which got there first. But she preferred him. Only for some things she would rather it were me.

Luke had changed curiously. His body seemed to have come alive, in the dark cloth of his evening suit ; his eyes had a devil-may-care light in them, his long cheeks at ouch of scarlet, and his black hair felt loose over his forehead. He had again some of that Guardsman's sense of well-being and claim to the best in life, which I had noticed the first time I saw him. But now it was a little more florid, defiant, with a touch of madness.

He looked down at Carlotta with uncanny kindness and affection. Yet he was glad to hand her over to me. He, too, was afraid of her : as if with her his bad luck had worked. Whereas, in a throb of crude brutality, he felt it would not work with the dark young woman. So, he handed Carlotta over to me with relief, as if, with me, she would be safe from the doom of his bad luck. And he, with the other woman, would be safe from it too. For the other woman was outside the circle.

I was glad to have Carlotta again : to have that inexpressible delicate and complete quiet of the two of us, resting my heart in a balance now at last physical as well as spiritual. Till now, it had always been a fragmentary thing. Now, for this hour at least, it was whole, a soft, complete, physical flow, and a unison deeper even than childhood.

As she danced she shivered slightly, and I seemed to smell frost in the air. The Colonel, too, was not keeping the rhythm.

" Has it turned colder ? " I said.

" I wonder ? " she answered, looking up at me with a slow beseeching. Why, and for what was she beseeching me ? I pressed my hand a little closer, and her small breasts seemed to speak to me. The Colonel recovered the rhythm again.

But at the end of the dance she shivered again, and it seemed to me I too was chilled.

" Has it suddenly turned colder ? " I said, going to the radiator. It was quite hot.

" It seems to me it has," said Lord Lathkill, in a queer voice.

The Colonel was sitting abjectly on the music stool, as if broken.

" Shall we have another ? Shall we try a tango ? " said Lord Lathkill. " As much of it as we can manage ? "

" I—I——" the Colonel began, turning round on the seat, his face yellow. " I'm not sure——"

Carlotta shivered. The frost seemed to touch my vitals. Mrs. Hale stood stiff, like a pillar of brown rock-salt, staring at her husband.

" We had better leave off," murmured Lady Lathkill, rising.

Then she did an extraordinary thing. She lifted her face, staring to the other side, and said suddenly, in a clear, cruel sort of voice :

" Are you here, Lucy ? "

She was speaking across to the spirits. Deep inside me leaped a jump of laughter. I wanted to howl with laughter. Then instantly, I went inert again. The chill gloom seemed to deepen suddenly in the room, everybody was overcome. On the piano-seat the Colonel sat yellow and huddled, with a terrible hang-dog look of guilt on his face. There was a silence, in which the cold seemed to creak. Then came again the peculiar bell-like ringing of Lady Lathkill's voice :

" Are you here ? What do you wish us to do ? "

A dead and ghastly silence, in which we all remained transfixed.

Then from somewhere came two slow thuds, and a sound of drapery moving. The Colonel, with mad fear in his eyes, looked round at the uncurtained windows, and crouched on his seat.

" We must leave this room," said Lady Lathkill.

" I'll tell you what, mother," said Lord Lathkill curiously ; " you and the Colonel go up, and we'll just turn on the Victrola."

That was almost uncanny of him. For myself, the cold effluence of these people had paralysed me. Now I began to rally. I felt that Lord Lathkill was sane, it was these other people who were mad.

Again from somewhere indefinite came two slow thuds.

" We must leave this room," repeated Lady Lathkill in monotony.

" All right, mother. You go. I'll just turn on the Victrola."

And Lord Lathkill strode across the room. In another moment the monstrous barking howl of the opening of a jazz tune, an event far more extraordinary than thuds, poured from the unmoving bit of furniture called a Victrola.

Lady Lathkill silently departed. The Colonel got to his feet.

" I wouldn't go if I were you, Colonel," said I. " Why not dance ? I'll look on this time."

I felt as if I were resisting a rushing, cold dark current.

Lord Lathkill was already dancing with Mrs. Hale, skating delicately along, with a certain smile of obstinacy, secrecy, and excitement kindled on his face. Carlotta went up quietly to the Colonel, and put her hand on his broad shoulder. He let himself be moved into the dance, but he had no heart in it.

There came a heavy crash, out of the distance. The Colonel stopped as if shot : in another moment he would go down on his knees. And his face was terrible. It was obvious he really felt another presence, other than ours, blotting us out. The room seemed dree and cold. It was heavy work, bearing up.

The Colonel's lips were moving, but no sound came forth. Then, absolutely oblivious of us, he went out of the room.

The Victrola had run down. Lord Lathkill went to wind it up again, saying :

" I suppose mother knocked over a piece of furniture."

But we were all of us depressed, in abject depression.

" Isn't it awful ! " Carlotta said to me, looking up beseechingly.

" Abominable ! " said I.

" What do you think there is in it ? "

" God knows. The only thing is to stop it, as one does hysteria. It's on a par with hysteria."

" Quite," she said.

Lord Lathkill was dancing, and smiling very curiously down into his partner's face. The Victrola was at its loudest.

Carlotta and I looked at one another, with hardly the heart to start again. The house felt hollow and gruesome. One wanted to get out, to get away from the cold, uncanny blight which filled the air.

" Oh, I say, keep the ball rolling," called Lord Lathkill.

" Come," I said to Carlotta.

Even then she hung back a little. If she had not suffered, and lost so much, she would have gone upstairs at once to struggle in the silent wrestling of wills with her mother-in-law. Even now, *that* particular fight drew her, almost the strongest. But I took her hand.

" Come," I said. " Let us dance it down. We'll roll the ball the opposite way."

She danced with me, but she was absent, unwilling. The empty gloom of the house, the sense of cold, and of deadening opposition, pressed us down. I was looking back over my life, and thinking how the cold weight of an unliving spirit was slowly crushing all warmth and vitality out of everything. Even Carlotta herself had gone numb again, cold and resistant even to me. The thing seemed to happen wholesale in her.

" One has to choose to live," I said, dancing on.

But I was powerless. With a woman, when her spirit goes inert in opposition, a man can do nothing. I felt my life-flow sinking in my body.

" This house is awfully depressing," I said to her, as we mechanically danced. " Why don't you *do* something? Why don't you get out of this tangle? Why don't you break it? "

" How ? " she said.

I looked down at her, wondering why she was suddenly hostile.

" You needn't fight," I said. " You needn't fight it. Don't get tangled up in it. Just side-step, on to another ground."

She made a pause of impatience before she replied :

" I don't see where I am to side-step to, precisely."

" You do," said I. " A little while ago, you were warm and unfolded and good. Now you are shut up and prickly, in the cold. You needn't be. Why not stay warm ? "

" It's nothing I do," she said coldly.

" It is. Stay warm to me. I am here. Why clutch in a tug-of-war with Lady Lathkill ? "

" Do I clutch in a tug-of-war with my mother-in-law ? "

" You know you do."

She looked up at me, with a faint little shadow of guilt and beseeching, but with a *moue* of cold obstinacy dominant.

" Let's have done," said I.

And in cold silence we sat side by side on the lounge.

The other two danced on. They at any rate were in unison. One could see from the swing of their limbs. Mrs. Hale's yellow-brown eyes looked at me every time she came round.

" Why does she look at me ? " I said.

" I can't imagine," said Carlotta, with a cold grimace.

" I'd better go upstairs and see what's happening," she said, suddenly rising and disappearing in a breath.

Why should she go ? Why should she rush off to the battle of wills with her mother-in-law ? In such a battle, while one has any life to lose, one can only lose it. There is nothing positively to be done, but to withdraw out of the hateful tension.

The music ran down. Lord Lathkill stopped the Victrola.

" Carlotta gone ? " he said.

" Apparently."

" Why didn't you stop her ? "

" Wild horses wouldn't stop her."

He lifted his hand with a mocking gesture of helplessness.

" The lady loves her will," he said. " Would you like to dance ? "

I looked at Mrs. Hale.

" No," I said. " I won't butt in. I'll play the pianola. The Victrola's a brute."

I hardly noticed the passage of time. Whether the others danced or not, I played, and was unconscious of almost everything. In the midst of one rattling piece, Lord Lathkill touched my arm.

" Listen to Carlotta. She says closing time," he said, in his old musical voice, but with the sardonic ring of war in it now.

Carlotta stood with her arms dangling, looking like a penitent schoolgirl.

" The Colonel has gone to bed. He hasn't been able to manage a reconciliation with Lucy," she said. " My mother-in-law thinks we ought to let him try to sleep."

Carlotta's slow eyes rested on mine, questioning, penitent—or so I imagined—and somewhat sphinx-like.

" Why, of course," said Lord Lathkill. " I wish him all the sleep in the world."

Mrs. Hale said never a word.

" Is mother retiring too ? " asked Luke.

" I think so."

" Ah ! then supposing we up and look at the supper-tray."

We found Lady Lathkill mixing herself some nightcap brew over a spirit-lamp : something milky and excessively harmless. She stood at the sideboard stirring her potations, and hardly noticed us. When she had finished she sat down with her steaming cup.

"Colonel Hale all right, mother ? " said Luke, looking across at her.

The dowager, under her uplift of white hair, stared back at her son. There was an eye-battle for some moments, during which he maintained his arch, debonair ease, just a bit crazy.

" No," said Lady Lathkill, " he is in great trouble."

" Ah ! " replied her son. " Awful pity we can't do anything for him. But if flesh and blood can't help him, I'm afraid I'm a dud. Suppose he didn't mind our dancing ? Frightfully good for *us !* We've been forgetting that we're flesh and blood, mother."

He took another whisky and soda, and gave me one. And in a paralysing silence Lady Lathkill sipped her hot brew, Luke and I sipped our whiskies, the young woman ate a little sandwich. We all preserved an extraordinary aplomb, and an obstinate silence.

It was Lady Lathkill who broke it. She seemed to be sinking downwards, crouching into herself like a skulking animal.

" I suppose," she said, " we shall all go to bed ? "

" You go, mother. We'll come along in a moment."

She went, and for some time we four sat silent. The room seemed to become pleasanter, the air was more grateful.

" Look here," said Lord Lathkill at last. " What do you think of this ghost business ? "

" I ? " said I. " I don't like the atmosphere it produces. There may be ghosts, and spirits, and all that. The dead must be some-where ; there's no such place as nowhere. But they don't affect me particularly. Do they you ? "

" Well," he said, " no, not directly. Indirectly I suppose it does."

" I think it makes a horribly depressing atmosphere, spiritualism," said I. " I want to kick."

" Exactly ! And ought one ? " he asked in his terribly sane-seeming way.

This made me laugh. I knew what he was up to.

" I don't know what you mean by *ought*," said I. " If I really want to kick, if I know I can't stand a thing, I kick. Who's going to authorize me, if my own genuine feeling doesn't ? "

" Quite," he said, staring at me like an owl, with a fixed, medita-tive stare.

"Do you know," he said, " I suddenly thought at dinner-time, what corpses we all were, sitting eating our dinners. I thought it when I saw you look at those little Jerusalem artichoke things in a white sauce. Suddenly it struck me, you were alive and twinkling, and we were all bodily dead. Bodily dead, if you understand. Quite alive in other directions, but bodily dead. And whether we ate vegetarian or meat made no difference. We were bodily dead."

"Ah, with a slap in the face," said I, "we come to life! You or I or anybody."

"I *do* understand poor Lucy," said Luke. "Don't you? She forgot to be flesh and blood while she was alive, and now she can't forgive herself, nor the Colonel. That must be pretty rough, you know, not to realize it till you're dead, and you haven't, so to speak, anything left to go on. I mean, it's awfully important to be flesh and blood."

He looked so solemnly at us, we three broke simultaneously into an uneasy laugh.

"Oh, but I *do* mean it," he said. "I've only realized how very extraordinary it is to be a man of flesh and blood, alive. It seems so ordinary, in comparison, to be dead, and merely spirit. That seems so commonplace. But fancy having a living face, and arms, and thighs. Oh, my God, I'm glad I've realized in time!"

He caught Mrs. Hale's hand, and pressed her dusky arm against his body.

"Oh, but if one had died without realizing it!" he cried. "Think how ghastly for Jesus, when he was risen and wasn't touchable! How very awful, to have to say *Noli me tangere!* Ah, touch me, touch me *alive!*"

He pressed Mrs. Hale's hand convulsively against his breast. The tears had already slowly gathered in Carlotta's eyes and were dropping on to her hands in her lap.

"Don't cry, Carlotta," he said. "Really, don't. We haven't killed one another. We're too decent, after all. We've almost become two spirits side by side. We've almost become two ghosts to one another, wrestling. Oh, but I want you to get back your body, even if I can't give it you. I want my flesh and blood, Carlotta, and I want you to have yours. We've suffered so much the other way. And the children, it is as well they are dead. They were born of our will and our disembodiment. Oh, I feel like the Bible. Clothe me with flesh again, and wrap my bones with sinew, and let the fountain of blood cover me. My spirit is like a naked nerve on the air."

Carlotta had ceased to weep. She sat with her head dropped, as if asleep. The rise and fall of her small, slack breasts was still heavy, but they were lifting on a heaving sea of rest. It was as if a slow, restful dawn were rising in her body, while she slept. So slack, so broken she sat, it occurred to me that in this crucifixion business the crucified does not put himself alone on the cross. The woman is nailed even more inexorably up, and crucified in the body even more cruelly.

It is a monstrous thought. But the deed is even more monstrous. Oh, Jesus, didn't you know that you couldn't be crucified alone?— that the two thieves crucified along with you were the two women, your wife and your mother! You called them two thieves. But what would they call you, who had their women's bodies on the cross? The abominable trinity on Calvary!

I felt an infinite tenderness for my dear Carlotta. She could not yet be touched. But my soul streamed to her like warm blood. So she sat slack and drooped, as if broken. But she was not broken. It was only the great release.

Luke sat with the hand of the dark young woman pressed against his breast. His face was warm and fresh, but he too breathed heavily, and stared unseeing. Mrs. Hale sat at his side erect and mute. But she loved him, with erect, black-faced, remote power.

" Morier ! " said Luke to me. " If you can help Carlotta, you will, won't you ? I can't do any more for her now. We are in mortal fear of each other."

" As much as she'll let me," said I, looking at her drooping figure, that was built on such a strong frame.

The fire rustled on the hearth as we sat in complete silence. How long it lasted I cannot say. Yet we were none of us startled when the door opened.

It was the Colonel, in a handsome brocade dressing-gown, looking worried.

Luke still held the dark young woman's hand clasped against his thigh. Mrs. Hale did not move.

" I thought you fellows might help me," said the Colonel, in a worried voice, as he closed the door.

" What is wrong, Colonel ? " said Luke.

The Colonel looked at him, looked at the clasped hands of Luke and the dark young woman, looked at me, looked at Carlotta, without changing his expression of anxiety, fear, and misery. He didn't care about us.

" I can't sleep," he said. " It's gone wrong again. My head feels as if there was a cold vacuum in it, and my heart beats, and something screws up inside me. I know it's Lucy. She hates me again. I can't stand it."

He looked at us with eyes half-glazed, obsessed. His face seemed as if the flesh were breaking under the skin, decomposing.

" Perhaps, poor thing," said Luke, whose madness seemed really sane this night, " perhaps you hate *her*."

Luke's strange concentration instantly made us feel a tension, as of hate, in the Colonel's body.

" I ? " The Colonel looked up sharply, like a culprit. " I ! I wouldn't say that, if I were you."

" Perhaps that's what's the matter," said Luke, with mad, beautiful calm. " Why can't you feel kindly towards her, poor thing ! She must have been done out of a lot while she lived."

It was as if he had one foot in life and one in death, and knew both sides. To us it was like madness.

" I—I ! " stammered the Colonel ; and his face was a study. Expression after expression moved across it : of fear, repudiation, dismay, anger, repulsion, bewilderment, guilt. " I was good to her."

" Ah, yes," said Luke. " Perhaps *you* were good to her. But was your body good to poor Lucy's body, poor dead thing ! "

He seemed to be better acquainted with the ghost than with us.

The Colonel gazed blankly at Luke, and his eyes went up and down, up and down, up and down, up and down.

" My body !." he said blankly.

And he looked down amazedly at his little round stomach, under the silk gown, and his stout knee, in its blue-and-white pyjama.

" My body ! " he repeated blankly.

" Yes," said Luke. " Don't you see, you may have been awfully good to her. But her poor woman's body, were you ever good to that? "

" She had everything she wanted. She had three of my children," said the Colonel dazedly.

" Ah yes, that may easily be. But your body of a man, was it ever good to her body of a woman ? That's the point. If you understand the marriage service : with my body I thee worship. That's the point. No getting away from it."

The queerest of all accusing angels did Lord Lathkill make, as he sat there with the hand of the other man's wife clasped against his thigh. His face was fresh and naïve, and the dark eyes were bright with a clairvoyant candour, that was like madness, and perhaps was supreme sanity.

The Colonel was thinking back, and over his face a slow understanding was coming.

" It may be," he said. " It may be. Perhaps, that way, I despised her. It may be, it may be."

" I know," said Luke. " As if she weren't worth noticing, what you did to her. Haven't I done it myself? And don't I know now, it's a horrible thing to do, to oneself as much as to her? Her poor ghost, that ached, and never had a real body! It's not so easy to worship with the body. Ah, if the Church taught us *that* sacrament : *with my body I thee worship!* that would easily make up for any honouring and obeying the woman might do. But that's why she haunts you. You ignored and disliked her body, and she was only a living ghost. Now she wails in the afterworld, like a still-wincing nerve."

The Colonel hung his head, slowly pondering. Pondering with all his body. His young wife watched the sunken, bald head in a kind of stupor. His day seemed so far from her day. Carlotta had lifted her face ; she was beautiful again, with the tender before-dawn freshness of a new understanding.

She was watching Luke, and it was obvious he was another man to her. The man she knew, the Luke who was her husband, was gone, and this other strange, uncanny creature had taken his place. She was filled with wonder. Could one so change, as to become another creature entirely ? Ah, if it were so ! If she herself, as she knew herself, could cease to be ! If that woman who was married to Luke, married to him in an intimacy of misfortune that was like a horror, could only cease to be, and let a new, delicately-wild Carlotta take her place !

" It may be," said the Colonel, lifting his head. " It may be." There seemed to come a relief over his soul, as he realized. " I didn't worship her with my body. I think maybe I worshipped other women that way ; but maybe I never did. But I thought I was good to her. And I thought she didn't want it."

" It's no good thinking. We all want it," asserted Luke. " And before we die, we know it. I say, before we die. It may be after. But everybody wants it, let them say and do what they will. Don't you agree, Morier ? "

I was startled when he spoke to me. I had been thinking of Carlotta : how she was looking like a girl again, as she used to look at the Thwaite, when she painted cactuses-in-a-pot. Only now, a certain rigidity of the will had left her, so that she looked even younger than when I first knew her, having now a virginal, flower-like *stillness* which she had not had then. I had always believed that people could be born again : if they would only let themselves.

" I'm sure they do," I said to Luke.

But I was thinking, if people were born again, the old circumstances would not fit the new body.

" What about yourself, Luke ? " said Carlotta abruptly.

" I ! " he exclaimed, and the scarlet showed in his cheek. " I !
I'm not fit to be spoken about. I've been moaning like the ghost of
disembodiment myself, ever since I became a man."

The Colonel said never a word. He hardly listened. He was
pondering, pondering. In this way, he, too, was a brave man.

" I have an idea what you mean," he said. " There's no denying
it, I didn't like her body. And now, I suppose it's too late."

He looked up bleakly : in a way, willing to be condemned, since
he knew vaguely that something was wrong. Anything better
than the blind torture.

" Oh, I don't know," said Luke. " Why don't you, even now,
love her a little with your real heart ? Poor disembodied thing !
Why don't you take her to your warm heart, even now, and comfort
her inside there ? Why don't you be kind to her poor ghost, bodily ? "

The Colonel did not answer. He was gazing fixedly at Luke.
Then he turned, and dropped his head, alone in a deep silence.
Then, deliberately, but not lifting his head, he pulled open his
dressing-gown at the breast, unbuttoned the top of his pyjama jacket,
and sat perfectly still, his breast showing white and very pure, so
much younger and purer than his averted face. He breathed with
difficulty, his white breast rising irregularly. But in the deep
isolation where he was, slowly a gentleness of compassion came over
him, moulding his elderly features with strange freshness, and
softening his blue eye with a look it had never had before. Something of the tremulous gentleness of a young bridegroom had come
upon him, in spite of his baldness, his silvery little moustache, the
weary marks of his face.

The passionate, compassionate soul stirred in him and was pure,
his youth flowered over his face and eyes.

We sat very still, moved also in the spirit of compassion. There
seemed a presence in the air, almost a smell of blossom, as if time
had opened and gave off the perfume of spring. The Colonel gazed
in silence into space, his smooth white chest, with the few dark
hairs, open and rising and sinking with life.

Meanwhile his dark-faced young wife watched as if from afar.
The youngness that was on him was not for her.

I knew that Lady Lathkill would come. I could feel her far off
in her room, stirring and sending forth her rays. Swiftly I steeled
myself to be in readiness. When the door opened, I rose and walked
across the room.

She entered with characteristic noiselessness, peering in round the door, with her crest of white hair, before she ventured bodily in. The Colonel looked at her swiftly, and swiftly covered his breast, holding his hand at his bosom, clutching the silk of his robe.

" I was afraid," she murmured, " that Colonel Hale might be in trouble."

" No," said I. " We are all sitting very peacefully. There is no trouble."

Lord Lathkill also rose.

" No trouble at all, I assure you, mother ! " he said.

Lady Lathkill glanced at us both, then turned heavily to the Colonel.

" She is unhappy to-night ? " she asked.

The Colonel winced.

" No," he said hurriedly. " No, I don't think so." He looked up at her with shy, wincing eyes.

" Tell me what I can do," she said in a very low tone, bending towards him.

" Our ghost is walking to-night, mother," said Lord Lathkill. " Haven't you felt the air of spring, and smelt the plum-blossom ? Don't you feel us all young ? Our ghost is walking, to bring Lucy home. The Colonel's breast is quite extraordinary, white as plum-blossom, mother, younger-looking than mine, and he's already taken Lucy into his bosom, in his breast, where he breathes like the wind among trees. The Colonel's breast is white and extraordinarily beautiful, mother, I don't wonder poor Lucy yearned for it, to go home into it at last. It's like going into an orchard of plum-blossom, for a ghost."

His mother looked round at him, then back at the Colonel, who was still clutching his hand over his chest, as if protecting something.

" You see, I didn't understand where I'd been wrong," he said, looking up at her imploringly. " I never realized that it was my body which had not been good to her."

Lady Lathkill curved sideways to watch him. But her power was gone. His face had come smooth with the tender glow of compassionate life, that flowers again. She could not get at him.

" It's no good, mother. You know our ghost is walking. She's supposed to be absolutely like a crocus, if you know what I mean : harbinger of spring in the earth. So it says in my great-grandfather's diary : for she rises with silence like a crocus at the feet, and violets in the hollows of the heart come out. For she is of the feet and the hands, the thighs and breast, the face and the all-concealing belly, and her name is silent, but her odour is of spring, and her contact is the all-in-all." He was quoting from his great-grandfather's diary, which only the sons of the family read. And as he quoted he rose curiously on his toes, and spread his fingers, bringing his hands together till the finger-tips touched. His father had done that before him, when he was deeply moved.

Lady Lathkill sat down heavily in the chair next the Colonel.

" How do you feel ? " she asked him, in a secretive mutter.

He looked round at her, with the large blue eyes of candour.

" I never knew what was wrong," he said, a little nervously. " She only wanted to be looked after a bit, not to be a homeless, houseless ghost. It's all right ! She's all right here." He pressed his clutched hand on his breast. " It's all right ; it's all right. She'll be all right now."

He rose, a little fantastic in his brocade gown, but once more manly, candid and sober.

" With your permission," he said, " I will retire."—He made a little bow.—" I am glad you helped me. I didn't know—didn't know."

But the change in him, and his secret wondering were so strong in him, he went out of the room scarcely being aware of us.

Lord Lathkill threw up his arms, and stretched quivering.

" Oh, pardon, pardon," he said, seeming, as he stretched, quivering, to grow bigger and almost splendid, sending out rays of fire to the dark young woman. " Oh, mother, thank you for my limbs, and my body ! Oh, mother, thank you for my' knees and my shoulders at this moment ! Oh, mother, thank you that my body is straight and alive ! Oh, mother, torrents of spring, torrents of spring, whoever said that ? "

" Don't you forget yourself, my boy ? " said his mother.

" Oh no, dear no ! Oh, mother dear, a man has to be in love in his thighs, the way you ride a horse. Why don't we stay in love that way all our lives ? Why do we turn into corpses with consciousness ? Oh, mother of my body, thank you for my body, you strange woman with white hair ! I don't know much about you, but my body came from you, so thank you, my dear. I shall think of you to-night ! "

" Hadn't we better go ? " she said, beginning to tremble.

" Why, yes," he said, turning and looking strangely at the dark young woman. " Yes, let us go ; let us go ! "

Carlotta gazed at him, then, with strange, heavy, searching look, at me. I smiled to her, and she looked away. The dark young woman looked over her shoulder as she went out. Lady Lathkill hurried past her son, with head ducked. But still he laid his hand on her shoulder, and she stopped dead.

"Good night, mother ; mother of my face and my thighs. Thank you for the night to come, dear mother of my body."

She glanced up at him rapidly, nervously, then hurried away. He stared after her, then switched off the light.

"Funny old mother ! " he said. "I never realized before that she was the mother of my shoulders and my hips, as well as my brain. Mother of my thighs ! "

He switched off some of the lights as we went, accompanying me to my room.

"You know," he said, "I can understand that the Colonel is happy, now the forlorn ghost of Lucy is comforted in his heart. After all, he married her ! And she must be content at last : he has a beautiful chest, don't you think ? Together they will sleep well. And then he will begin to live the life of the living again. How friendly the house feels to-night ! But, after all, it is my old home. And the smell of plum-blossom—don't you notice it ? It is our ghost, in silence like a crocus. There, your fire has died down ! But it's a nice room ! I hope our ghost will come to you. I think she will. Don't speak to her. It makes her go away. She, too, is a ghost of silence. We talk far too much. But now I am going to be silent, too, and a ghost of silence. Good night ! "

He closed the door softly and was gone. And softly, in silence, I took off my things. I was thinking of Carlotta, and a little sadly, perhaps, because of the power of circumstance over us. This night I could have worshipped her with my body, and she, perhaps, was stripped in the body to be worshipped. But it was not for me, at this hour, to fight against circumstances.

I had fought too much, even against the most imposing circumstances, to use any more violence for love. Desire is a sacred thing, and should not be violated.

"Hush ! " I said to myself. "I will sleep, and the ghost of my silence can go forth, in the subtle body of desire, to meet that which is coming to meet it. Let my ghost go forth, and let me not interfere. There are many intangible meetings, and unknown fulfilments of desire."

So I went softly to sleep, as I wished to, without interfering with the warm, crocus-like ghost of my body.

And I must have gone far, far down the intricate galleries of sleep, to the very heart of the world. For I know I passed on beyond the strata of images and words, beyond the iron veins of memory, and even the jewels of rest, to sink in the final dark like a fish, dumb, soundless, and imageless, yet alive and swimming.

And at the very core of the deep night the ghost came to me, at the heart of the ocean of oblivion, which is also the heart of life. Beyond hearing, or even knowledge of contact, I met her and knew her. How I know it I don't know. Yet I know it with eyeless, wingless knowledge.

For man in the body is formed through countless ages, and at the centre is the speck, or spark, upon which all his formation has taken place. It is even not himself, deep beyond his many depths. Deep from him calls to deep. And according as deep answers deep, man glistens and surpasses himself.

Beyond all the pearly mufflings of consciousness, of age upon age of consciousness, deep calls yet to deep, and sometimes is answered. It is calling and answering, new-awakened God calling within the deep of man, and new God calling answer from the other deep. And sometimes the other deep is a woman, as it was with me, when my ghost came.

Women were not unknown to me. But never before had woman come, in the depths of night, to answer my deep with her deep. As the ghost came, came as a ghost of silence, still in the depth of sleep.

I know she came. I know she came even as a woman, to my man. But the knowledge is darkly naked as the event. I only know, it was so. In the deep of sleep a call was called from the deeps of me, and answered in the deeps, by a woman among women. Breasts or thighs or face, I remember not a touch, no, nor a movement of my own. It is all complete in the profundity of darkness. Yet I know it was so.

I awoke towards dawn, from far, far away. I was vaguely conscious of drawing nearer and nearer, as the sun must have been drawing towards the horizon, from the complete beyond. Till at last the faint pallor of mental consciousness coloured my waking.

And then I was aware of a pervading scent, as of plum-blossom, and a sense of extraordinary silkiness—though where, and in what contact, I could not say. It was as the first blemish of dawn.

And even with so slight a conscious registering, *it* seemed to disappear. Like a whale that has sounded to the bottomless seas. That knowledge of *it*, which was the mating of the ghost and me, disappeared from me, in its rich weight of certainty, as the scent of the plum-blossom moved down the lanes of my consciousness, and my limbs stirred in a silkiness for which I have no comparison.

As I became aware, I also became uncertain. I wanted to be certain of *it*, to have definite evidence. And as I sought for evidence, *it* disappeared, my perfect knowledge was gone. I no longer knew in full.

Now as the daylight slowly amassed, in the windows from which I had put back the shutters, I sought in myself for evidence, and in the room.

But I shall never know. I shall never know if it was a ghost, some sweet spirit from the innermost of the ever-deepening cosmos ; or a woman, a very woman, as the silkiness of my limbs seems to attest ; or a dream, a hallucination ! I shall never know. Because I went away from Riddings in the morning, on account of the sudden illness of Lady Lathkill.

" You will come again," Luke said to me. " And in any case, you will never really go away from us."

" Good-bye," she said to me. " At last it was perfect ! "

She seemed so beautiful, when I left her, as if it were the ghost again, and I was far down the deeps of consciousness.

The following autumn, when I was overseas once more, I had a letter from Lord Lathkill. He wrote very rarely.

" Carlotta has a son," he said, " and I an heir. He has yellow hair, like a little crocus, and one of the young plum-trees in the orchard has come out of all season into blossom. To me he is flesh and blood of our ghost itself. Even mother doesn't look over the wall, to the other side, any more. It's all this side for her now.

" So our family refuses to die out, by the grace of our ghost. We are calling him Gabriel.

" Dorothy Hale also is a mother, three days before Carlotta. She has a black lamb of a daughter, called Gabrielle. By the bleat of the little thing, I know its father. Our own is a blue-eyed one, with the dangerous repose of a pugilist. I have no fears of our family misfortune for him, ghost-begotten and ready-fisted.

" The Colonel is very well, quiet, and self-possessed. He is farming in Wiltshire, raising pigs. It is a passion with him, the *crême de la crême* of swine. I admit, he has golden sows as elegant as a young Diane de Poictiers, and young hogs like Perseus in the first red-gold flush of youth. He looks me in the eye, and I look him back, and we understand. He is quiet, and proud now, and very hale and hearty, raising swine *ad maiorem gloriam Dei*. A good sport !

" I am in love with this house and its inmates, including the plum-blossom-scented one, she who visited you, in all the peace. I cannot understand why you wander in uneasy and distant parts of the earth. For me, when I am at home, I am there. I have peace upon my bones, and if the world is going to come to a violent and untimely end, as prophets aver, I feel the house of Lathkill will survive, built upon our ghost. So come back, and you'll find we shall not have gone away. . . ."

I met Luis Colmenares in Venice, not having seen him for years. He is a Mexican exile living on the scanty remains of what was once wealth, and eking out a poor and lonely existence by being a painter. But his art is only a sedative to him. He wanders about like a lost soul, mostly in Paris or in Italy, where he can live cheaply. He is rather short, rather fat, pale, with black eyes, which are always looking the other way, and a spirit the same, always averted.

"Do you know who is in Venice?" he said to me. "Cuesta! He is in the Hôtel Romano. I saw him bathing yesterday on the Lido."

There was a world of gloomy mockery in this last sentence.

"Do you mean Cuesta, the bull-fighter?" I asked.

"Yes. Don't you know, he retired? Do you remember? An American woman left him a lot of money. Did you ever see him?"

"Once," said I.

"Was it before the revolution? Do you remember, he retired and bought a hacienda very cheap from one of Madero's generals, up in Chihuahua? It was after the Carranzista, and I was already in Europe."

"How does he look now?" I said.

"Enormously fat, like a yellow, round, small whale in the sea. You saw him? You know he was rather short and rather fat always. I think his mother was a Mixtec Indian woman. Did you ever know him?"

"No," said I. "Did you?"

"Yes. I knew him in the old days, when I was rich, and thought I should be rich for ever."

He was silent, and I was afraid he had shut up for good. It was unusual for him to be even as communicative as he had been. But it was evident that having seen Cuesta, the toreador whose fame once rang through Spain and through Latin America, had moved him deeply. He was in a ferment, and could not quite contain himself.

"But he wasn't interesting, was he?" I said. "Wasn't he just a—a bull-fighter—a brute?"

Colmenares looked at me out of his own blackness. He didn't want to talk. Yet he had to.

" He was a brute, yes," he admitted grudgingly. " But not just a brute. Have you seen him when he was at his best ? Where did you see him ? I never liked him in Spain, he was too vain. But in Mexico he was very good. Have you seen him play with the bull, and play with death ? He was marvellous. Do you remember him, what he looked like ? "

" Not very well," said I.

" Short, and broad, and rather fat, with rather a yellow colour, and a pressed-in nose. But his eyes, they were marvellous, also rather small, and yellow, and when he looked at you, so strange and cool, you felt your inside melting. Do you know that feeling ? He looked into the last little place of you, where you keep your courage. Do you understand ? And so you felt yourself melting. Do you know what I mean ? "

" More or less, perhaps," said I.

Colmenares' black eyes were fixed on my face, dilated and gleaming, but not really seeing me at all. He was seeing the past. Yet a curious force streamed out of his face ; one understood him by the telepathy of passion, inverted passion.

" And in the bull-ring, he was marvellous. He would stand with his back to the bull, and pretend to be adjusting his stocking, while the bull came charging on him. And with a little glance over his shoulder, he would make a small movement, and the bull had passed him without getting him. Then he would smile a little, and walk after it. It is marvellous that he was not killed hundreds of times, but I saw him bathing on the Lido to-day, like a fat, yellow, small whale. It is extraordinary ! But I did not see his eyes. . . ."

A queer look of abstracted passion was on Colmenares' fat, pale, clean-shaven face. Perhaps the toreador had cast a spell over him, as over so many people in the old and the new world.

" It is strange that I have never seen eyes anywhere else like his. Did I tell you, they were yellow, and not like human eyes at all ? They didn't look at you. I don't think they ever looked at anybody. He only looked at the little bit inside your body where you keep your courage. I don't think he could see people, any more than an animal can : I mean see them personally, as I see you and you see me. He was an animal, a marvellous animal. I have often thought, if human beings had not developed minds and speech, they would have become marvellous animals like Cuesta, with those marvellous eyes, much more marvellous than a lion's or a tiger's. Have you noticed a lion or a tiger never sees you personally ? It never really looks at you. But also it is afraid to look at the last little bit of you, where your courage lives inside you. But Cuesta was not afraid. He looked straight at it, and it melted."

" And what was he like, in ordinary life ? " said I.

" He did not talk, was very silent. He was not clever at all. He was not even clever enough to be a general. And he could be very brutal and disgusting. But usually he was quiet. But he was always *something*. If you were in the room with him, you always noticed him more than anybody, more than women or men, even very clever people. He was stupid, but he made you physically. aware of him ; like a cat in the room. I tell you, that little bit of you where you keep your courage was enchanted by him ; he put over you an enchantment."

" Did he do it on purpose ? "

" Well ! It is hard to say. But he knew he could do it. To some people, perhaps, he could not do it. But he never saw such people. He only saw people who were in his enchantment. And of course, in the bull-ring, he mesmerized everybody. He could draw the natural magnetism of everybody to him—everybody. And then he was marvellous, he played with death as if it were a kitten, so quick, quick as a star, and calm as a flower, and all the time, laughing at death. It is marvellous he was never killed. But he retired very young. And then suddenly it was he who killed the bull, with one hand, one stroke. He was very strong. And the bull sank down at his feet, heavy with death. The people went mad ! And he just glanced at them, with his yellow eyes, in a cool, beautiful contempt, as if he were an animal that wrapped the skin of death round him. Ah, he was wonderful ! And to-day I saw him bathing on the Lido, in an American bathing-suit, with a woman. His bathing-suit was just a little more yellow than he is. I have held the towel when he was being rubbed down and massaged, often. He had the body of an Indian, very smooth, with hardly any hair, and creamy-yellow. I always thought it had something childish about it, so soft. But also, it had the same mystery as his eyes, as if you could never touch it, as if, when you touched it, still it was not he. When he had no clothes on, he was naked. But it seemed he would have many, many more nakednesses before you really came to *him*. Do you under-stand me at all ? Or does it seem to you foolish ? "

" It interests me," I said. " And women, of course, fell for him by the thousand ? "

" By the million ! And they were mad because of him. Women

went mad, once they felt him. It was not like Rudolf Valentino, sentimental. It was madness, like cats in the night which howl, no longer knowing whether they are on earth or in hell or in paradise. So were the women. He could have had forty beautiful women every night, and different ones each night, from the beginning of the year to the end."

"But he didn't, naturally?"

"Oh, no! At first, I think, he took many women. But later, when I knew him, he took none of those that besieged him. He had two Mexican women whom he lived with, humble women, Indians. And all the others he spat at, and spoke of them with terrible, obscene language. I think he would have liked to whip them, or kill them, for pursuing him."

"Only he must enchant them when he was in the bull-ring," said I.

"Yes. But that was like sharpening his knife on them."

"And when he retired—he had plenty of money—how did he amuse himself?"

"He was rich, he had a big *hacienda*, and many people like slaves to work for him. He raised cattle. I think he was very proud to be *hacendado* and *padròn* of so many people, with a little army of his own. I think he was proud, living like a king. I had not heard of him for years. Now, suddenly, he is in Venice with a Frenchwoman, a Frenchwoman who talks bad Spanish——"

"How old is he?"

"How old? He is about fifty, or a little less."

"So young! And will you speak to him?"

"I don't know. I can't make up my mind. If I speak to him, he will think I want money."

There was a certain note of hatred now in Colmenares' voice.

"Well, why shouldn't he give you money? He is still rich, I suppose?"

"Rich, yes! He must always be rich. He has got American money. An American woman left him half a million dollars. Did you never hear of it?"

"No. Then why shouldn't he give you money? I suppose you often gave him some, in the past?"

"Oh, that—that is *quite* the past. He will never give me anything —or a hundred francs, something like that! Because he is mean. Did you never hear of the American woman who left him half a million dollars, and committed suicide?"

"No. When was it?"

" It was a long time ago—about 1914, or 1913. I had already lost all my money. Her name was Ethel Cane. Did you never hear of her ? "

" I don't think I did," I said, feeling it remiss not to have heard of the lady.

" Ah ! You should have known her. She was extraordinary. I had known her in Paris, even before I came back to Mexico and knew Cuesta well. She was almost as extraordinary as Cuesta : one of those American women, born rich, but what we should call provincial. She didn't come from New York or Boston, but somewhere else. Omaha or something. She was blonde, with thick, straight, blonde hair, and she was one of the very first to wear it short, like a Florentine page-boy. Her skin was white, and her eyes very blue, and she was not thin. At first, there seemed something childish about her—do you know that look, rather round cheeks and clear eyes, so false-innocent ? Her eyes especially were warm and naïve and false-innocent, but full of light. Only sometimes they were bloodshot. Oh, she was extraordinary ! It was only when I knew her better I noticed how her blonde eyebrows gathered together above her nose, in a diabolic manner. She was much too much a personality to be a lady, and she had all that terrible American energy ! Ah, energy ! She was a dynamo. In Paris she was married to a dapper little pink-faced American who got yellow at the gills, bilious, running after her when she would not have him. He painted pictures and wanted to be modern. She knew all the people, and had all sorts come to her, as if she kept a human menagerie. And she bought old furniture and brocades ; she would go mad if she saw someone get a piece of velvet brocade with the misty bloom of years on it, that she coveted. She coveted such things, with lust, and would go into a strange sensual trance, looking at some old worm-eaten chair. And she would go mad if someone else got it, and not she : that nasty old wormy chair of the quat-trocento ! Things ! She was mad about ' things.' But it was only for a time. She always got tired, especially of her own enthusiasms.

" That was when I knew her in Paris. Then I think she divorced that husband, and, when the revolutions in Mexico became quieter, she came to Mexico. I think she was fascinated by the idea of Carranza. If ever she heard of a man who seemed to have a dramatic sort of power in him, she must know that man. It was like her lust for brocade and old chairs and a perfect æsthetic setting. Now it was to know the most dangerous man, especially if he looked like a prophet or a reformer. She was a socialist also, at this time. She no longer was in love with chairs.

" She found me again in Mexico : she knew thousands of people, and whenever one of them might be useful to her, she remembered him. So she remembered me, and it was nothing to her that I was now poor. I know she thought of me as ' that little Luis Something,' but she had a certain use for me, and found, perhaps, a certain little flavour in me. At least she asked me often to dinner, or to drive with her. She was curious, quite reckless and a dare-devil, yet shy and awkward out of her own *milieu*. It was only in intimacy that she was unscrupulous and dauntless as a devil incarnate. In public, and in strange places, she was very uneasy, like one who has a bad conscience towards society, and is afraid of it. And for that reason she could never go out without a man to stand between her and all the others.

" While she was in Mexico, I was that man. She soon discovered that I was satisfactory. I would perform all the duties of a husband without demanding any of the rights. Which was what she wanted. I think she was looking round for a remarkable and epoch-making husband. But, of course, it would have to be a husband who would be a fitting instrument for her remarkable and epoch-making energy and character. She was extraordinary, but she could only work through individuals, through others. By herself she could accomplish nothing. She lay on a sofa and mused and schemed, with the energy boiling inside her. Only when she had a group, or a few real individuals, or just one man, then she could start something, and make them all dance in a tragi-comedy, like marionettes.

" But in Mexico, men do not care for women who will make them dance like puppets. In Mexico, women must run in the dust like the Indian women, with meek little heads. American women are not very popular. Their energy, and their power to make other people do things, are not in request. The men would rather go to the devil in their own way, than be sent there by the women, with a little basket in which to bring home the goods.

" So Ethel found not a cold shoulder, but a number of square, fat backs turned to her. They didn't want her. The revolutionaries would not take any notice of her at all. They wanted no woman interfering. General Isidor Garabay danced with her, and expected her immediately to become his mistress. But, as she said, she was having *none of that*. She had a terrible way of saying ' I'm having none of that ! '—like hitting a mirror with a hammer. And as nobody wanted to get into trouble over her, they were having none of her.

" At first, of course, when the generals saw her white shoulders and blonde hair and innocent face, they thought at once : 'Here is a *type* for us !' They were not deceived by her innocent look. But they were deceived by what looked like her helplessness. The blood would come swelling into her neck and face, her eyes would go hot, her whole figure would swell with repellent energy, and she would say something very American and very crushing, in French, or in American. None of *that !* Stop *that !*

"She, too, had a lot of power. She could send out of her body a repelling energy, to compel people to submit to her will. Men in Europe or the United States nearly always crumpled up before her. But in Mexico she had come to the wrong shop. The men were a law to themselves. While she was winning and rather lovely, with her blue eyes so full of light and her white skin glistening with energetic health, they expected her to become at once their mistress. And when they saw, very quickly, that she was having *none of that*, they turned on their heels and showed her their fat backs. Because she was clever, and remarkable, and had wonderful energy and a wonderful power for making people dance while she pulled the strings, they didn't care a bit. They, too, wanted *none of that*. They would, perhaps, have carried her off and shared her as a mistress, except for the fear of trouble with the American Government.

"So, soon, she began to be bored, and to think of returning to New York. She said that Mexico was a place without a soul and without a culture, and it had not even brain enough to be mechanically efficient. It was a city and a land of naughty little boys doing obscene little things, and one day it would learn its lesson. I told her that history is the account of a lesson which nobody ever learns, and she told me the world certainly *had* progressed. Only not in Mexico, she supposed. I asked her why she had come, then, to Mexico. And she said she had thought there was something doing, and she would like to be in it. But she found it was only naughty and mostly cowardly little boys letting off guns and doing mediocre obscenities, so she would leave them to it. I told her I supposed it was life. And she replied that since it was not good enough for her, it was not life to her.

"She said all she wanted was to live the life of the imagination and get it acted on. At the time, I thought this ridiculous. I thought she was just trying to find somebody to fall in love with. Later, I saw she was right. She had an imaginary picture of herself as an extraordinary and potent woman who would make a stupendous change in the history of man. Like Catherine of Russia, only cosmopolitan, not merely Russian. And it is true, she *was* an extraordinary woman, with tremendous power of will, and truly amazing energy, even for an American woman. She was like a locomotive-engine stoked up inside and bursting with steam, which it has to let off by rolling a lot of trucks about. But I did not see how this was to cause a change in the tide of mortal affairs. It was only a part of the hubbub of traffic. She sent the trucks bouncing against one another with a clash of buffers, and sometimes she derailed some unfortunate item of the rolling-stock. But I did not see how this was to change the history of mankind. She seemed to have arrived just a little late, as some heroes, and heroines also, to-day, always do.

" I wondered always, why she did not take a lover. She was a woman between thirty and forty, very healthy and full of this extra-ordinary energy. She saw many men, and was always drawing them out, always on the *qui vive* to start them rolling down some incline. She attracted men, in a certain way. Yet she had no lover.

" I wondered even with regard to myself. We were friends, and a great deal together. Certainly I was under her spell. I came running as soon as I thought she wanted me. I did the things she suggested I should do. Even among my own acquaintances, when I found everybody laughing at me and disliking me for being at the service of an American woman, and I tried to rebel against her, and put her in her place, as the Mexicans say—which means, to them, in bed with no clothes on—still, the moment I saw her, with a look and a word she won me round. She was very clever. She flattered me, of course. She made me feel intelligent. She drew me out. There was her cleverness. She made *me* clever. I told her all about Mexico : all my life : all my ideas of history, philosophy. I sounded awfully clever and original, to myself. And she listened with such attention, which I thought was deep interest in what I was saying. But she was waiting for something she could fasten on, so that she could 'start something.' That was her constant craving, to 'start something.' But, of course, I thought she was interested in *me*.

" She would lie on a large couch that was covered with old sarapes—she began to buy them as soon as she came to Mexico—herself wrapped in a wonderful black shawl that glittered all over with brilliant birds and flowers in vivid colour, a very fine specimen of the embroidered shawls our Mexican ladies used to wear at a bull-fight or in an open-air *fiesta* : and there, with her white arms glisten-ing through the long fringe of the shawl, the old Italian jewellery rising on her white, dauntless breast, and her short, thick, blonde hair falling like yellow metal, she would draw me out, draw me out. I never talked so much in my life before or since. Always talk ! And I believe I talked very well, really, really very clever. But nothing besides talk ! Sometimes I stayed till after midnight. And sometimes she would snort with impatience or boredom, rather like a horse, flinging back her head and shaking that heavy blonde hair. And I think some part of her wanted me to make love to her.

" But I didn't. I couldn't. I was there, under her influence, in her power. She could draw me out in talk, marvellously. I'm sure I was very clever indeed. But any other part of me was stiff, petrified. I couldn't even touch her. I couldn't even take her hand in mine. It was a physical impossibility. When I was away from her, I could think of her white, healthy body with a voluptuous shiver. I could even run to her apartment, intending to kiss her, and make her my mistress that very might. But the moment I was in her presence, it left me. I could not touch her. I was averse from touching her. Physically, for some reason, I hated her.

" And I felt within myself, it was because she was repelling me and because she was always hating men, hating all active maleness in a man. She only wanted passive maleness, and then this ' talk,' this life of the imagination, as she called it. Inside herself she seethed, and she thought it was because she wanted to be made love to, very much made love to. But it wasn't so. She seethed against all men, with repulsion. She was cruel to the body of a man. But she excited his mind, his spirit. She loved to do that. She loved to have a man hanging round, like a servant. She loved to stimulate him, especially his mind. And she, too, when the man was not there, she thought she wanted him to be her lover. But when he was there, and he wanted to gather for himself that mysterious fruit of her body, she revolted against him with a fearful hate. A man must be *absolutely* her servant, and only that. That was what she meant by the life of the imagination.

" And I was her servant. Everybody jeered at me. But I said to myself, I would make her my mistress. I almost set my teeth to do it. That was when I was away from her. When I came to her, I could not even touch her. When I tried to make myself touch her, something inside me began to shudder. It was impossible. And I knew it was because, with her inner body, she was repelling me, always really repelling me.

" Yet she wanted me too. She was lonely : lonesome, she said. She was lonesome, and she would have liked to get me making love to her external self. She would even, I think, have become my mistress, and allowed me to take her sometimes for a little, miserable, humiliating moment, then quickly have got rid of me again. But I couldn't do it. Her inner body *never* wanted me. And I couldn't just be her prostitute. Because, immediately she would have despised me, and insulted me if I had persisted in trying to get some satisfaction of her. I knew it. She had already had two husbands, and she was a woman who always ached to tell *all*, everything. She had told me too much. I had seen one of her American husbands. I did not choose to see myself in a similar light : or plight.

" No, she wanted to live the life of the imagination. She said, the imagination could master everything ; so long, of course, as one was not shot in the head, or had an eye put out. Talking of the Mexican atrocities, and of the famous case of raped nuns, she said it was all nonsense that a woman was broken because she had been raped. She could rise above it. The imagination could rise above *anything*, that was not real organic damage. If one lived the life of the imagination, one could rise above any experience that ever happened to one. One could even commit murder, and rise above that. By using the imagination, and by using cunning, a woman can justify herself in anything, even the meanest and most bad things. A woman uses her imagination on her own behalf, and she becomes more innocent to herself than an innocent child, no matter what bad things she has done."

" Men do that, too," I interrupted. " It's the modern dodge. That's why everybody to-day is innocent. To the imagination all things are pure, if you did them yourself."

Colmenares looked at me with quick, black eyes, to see if I were mocking him. He did not care about me and my interruptions. He was utterly absorbed in his recollections of that woman, who had made him so clever, and who had made him her servant, and from whom he had never had any satisfaction.

" And then what ? " I asked him. " Then did she try her hand on Cuesta ? "

" Ah ! " said Colmenares, rousing, and glancing at me suspiciously again. " Yes ! That was what she did. And I was jealous. Though I couldn't bring myself to touch her, yet I was excruciated with jealousy, because she was interested in someone else. She was interested in someone besides myself, and my vanity suffered tortures of jealousy. Why was I such a fool ? Why, even now, could I kill that fat, yellow pig Cuesta ? A man is always a fool."

" How did she meet the bull-fighter ? " I asked. " Did you introduce him to her ? "

" She went once to the bull-fight, because every one was talking about Cuesta. She did not care for such things as the bull-ring ; she preferred the modern theatre, Duse and Reinhardt, and ' things of the imagination.' But now she was going back to New York, and she had never seen a bull-fight, so she must see one. I got seats in the shade—high up, you know—and went with her.

" At first she was very disgusted, and very contemptuous, and a little bit frightened, you know, because a Mexican crowd in a bull-ring is not very charming. She was afraid of people. But she sat stubborn and sulky, like a sulky child, saying : Can't they do any-thing more subtle than this, to get a thrill ? It's on such a low level !

" But when Cuesta at last began to play with a bull, she began to get excited. He was in pink and silver, very gorgeous, and looking very ridiculous, as usual. Till he began to play ; and then there really was something marvellous in him, you know, so quick and so light and so playful—do you know ? When he was playing with a bull and playing with death in the ring, he was the most playful thing I have ever seen : more playful than kittens or leopard cubs : and you know how they play ; do you? Oh, marvellous ! More gay and light than if they had lots of wings all over them, all wings of playing ! Well, he was like that, playing with death in the ring, as if he had all kinds of gay little wings to spin him with the quickest, tiniest, most beautiful little movements, quite unexpected, like a soft leopard cub. And then at the end, when he killed the bull and the blood squirted past him, ugh ! it was as if all his body laughed, and still the same soft, surprised laughter like a young thing, but more cruel than anything you can imagine. He fascinated me, but I always hated him. I would have liked to stick him as he stuck the bulls.

" I could see that Ethel was trying not to be caught by his spell. He had the most curious charm, quick and unexpected like play, you know, like leopard kittens, or slow sometimes, like tiny little bears. And yet the perfect cruelty. It was the joy in cruelty ! She hated the blood and messiness and dead animals. Ethel hated all that. It was not the life of the imagination. She was very pale, and very silent. She leaned forward and hardly moved, looking white and obstinate and subdued. And Cuesta had killed three bulls before she made any sign of any sort. I did not speak to her. The fourth bull was a beauty, full of life, curling and prancing like a narcissus-flower in January. He was a very special bull, brought from Spain, and not so stupid as the others. He pawed the ground and blew the breath on the ground, lowering his head. And Cuesta opened his arms to him with a little smile, but endearing, lovingly endearing, as a man might open his arms to a little maiden he really loves, but, really, for her to come to his body, his warm, open body, to come softly. So he held his arms out to the bull, with love. And that was what fascinated the women. They screamed and they fainted, longing to go into the arms of Cuesta, against his soft, round body, that was more yearning than a fico. But the bull, of course, rushed past him, and only got two darts sticking in his shoulder. That was the love.

" Then Ethel shouted, *Bravo! Bravo!* and I saw that she, too, had gone mad. Even Cuesta heard her, and he stopped a moment and looked at her. He saw her leaning forward, with her short, thick hair hanging like yellow metal, and her face dead-white, and her eyes glaring to his, like a challenge. They looked at one another, for a second, and he gave a little bow, then turned away. But he was changed. He didn't play so unconsciously any more : he seemed to be thinking of something, and forgetting himself. I was afraid he would be killed ; but so afraid ! He seemed absent-minded, and taking risks too great. When the bull came after him over the gangway barrier, he even put his hand on its head as he vaulted back, and one horn caught his sleeve and tore it just a little. Then he seemed to be absent-mindedly looking at the tear, while the bull was almost touching him again. And the bull was mad. Cuesta was a dead man it seemed, for sure : yet he seemed to wake up and *waked* himself just out of reach. It was like an awful dream, and it seemed to last for hours. I think it must have been a long time, before the bull was killed. He killed him at last, as a man takes his mistress at last because he is almost tired of playing with her. But he liked to kill his own bull.

" Ethel was looking like death, with beads of perspiration on her face. And she called to him : ' That's enough ! That's enough now ! *Ya es bastante! Basta!* ' He looked at her, and heard what she said. They were both alike there, they heard and saw in a flash. And he lifted his face, with the rather squashed nose and the yellow eyes, and he looked at her, and though he was so far away, he seemed quite near. And he was smiling like a small boy. But I could see he was looking at the little place in her body, where she kept her courage. And she was trying to catch his look on her imagination, not on her naked inside body. And they both found it difficult. When he tried to look at her, she set her imagination in front of him, like a mirror they put in front of a wild dog. And when she tried to catch him in her imagination, he seemed to melt away, and was gone. So neither really had caught the other.

" But he played with two more bulls, and killed them, without ever looking at her. And she went away when the people were applaud-

ing him, and did not look at him. Neither did she speak to me of
him. Neither did she go to any more bull-fights.

"It was Cuesta who spoke to me of her, when I met him at
Clavel's house. He said to me, in his very coarse Spanish : And
what about your American skirt ? I told him, there was nothing
to say about her. She was leaving for New York. So he told me to
ask her if she would like to come and say good-bye to Cuesta, before
she went. I said to him : But why should I mention your name to
her ? She has never mentioned yours to me. He made an obscene
joke to me.

"And it must have been because I was thinking of him that she
said that evening : Do you know Cuesta ? I told her I did, and
she asked me what I thought of him. I told her I thought he was
a marvellous beast, but he wasn't really a man. 'But he is a beast
with imagination,' she said to me. 'Couldn't one get a response out
of him ? ' I told her I didn't know, but I didn't want to try. I
would leave Cuesta to the bull-ring. I would never dream of trying
my imagination on him. She said, always ready with an answer :
'But wasn't there a marvellous *thing* in him, something quite exceptional ? ' I said, maybe ! But so has a rattlesnake a marvellous
thing in him : two things, one in his mouth, one in his tail. But I
didn't want to try to get response out of a rattlesnake. She wasn't
satisfied, though. She was tortured. I said to her : 'Anyhow, you
are leaving on Thursday.' 'No, I've put it off,' she said. 'Till
when ? ' 'Indefinite,' she said.

"I could tell she was tormented. She had been tormented ever
since she had been to the bull-fight, because she couldn't get past
Cuesta. She couldn't get past him, as the Americans say. He
seemed like a fat, squat, yellow-eyed demon just smiling at her, and
dancing ahead of her. 'Why don't you bring him here ? ' she said
at last, though she didn't want to say it.—' But why ? What is the
good of bringing him here ? Would you bring a criminal here, or
a yellow scorpion ? '—' I would if I wanted to find out about it.'—
' But what is there to find out about Cuesta ? He is just a sort of
beast. He is less than a man.'—' Maybe he's a *schwarze Bestie*,' she
said, ' and I'm a *blonde Bestie*. Anyway, bring him.'

"I always did what she wanted me, though I never wanted to
myself. So it was now. I went to a place where I knew Cuesta
would be, and he asked me : ' How is the blonde skirt ? Has she
gone yet ? ' I said, ' No. Would you like to see her ? ' He looked
at me with his yellow eyes, and that pleasant look which was really
hate undreaming. ' Did she tell you to ask me ? ' he said. ' No,'

I said. ' We were talking of you, and she said, bring the fabulous animal along and let us see what he really is.'—' He is the animal for her meat, this one,' he said, in his vulgar way. Then he pretended he wouldn't come. But I knew he would. So I said I would call for him.

" We were going in the evening, after tea, and he was dressed to kill, in a light French suit. We went in his car. But he didn't take flowers or anything. Ethel was nervous and awkward, offering us cocktails and cigarettes, and speaking French, though Cuesta didn't understand any French at all. There was another old American woman there, for chaperon.

" Cuesta just sat on a chair, with his knees apart and his hands between his thighs, like an Indian. Only his hair, which was done up in his little pigtail, and taken back from his forehead, made him look like a woman, or a Chinaman ; and his flat nose and little yellow eyes made him look like a Chinese idol, maybe a god or a demon, as you please. He just sat and said nothing, and had that look on his face which wasn't a smile, and wasn't a grimace, it was nothing. But to me it meant rhapsodic hate.

" She asked him in French if he liked his profession, and how long he had been doing it, and if he got a great kick out of it, and was he a pure-blood Indian ?—all that kind of thing. I translated to him as short as possible, Ethel flushing with embarrassment. He replied just as short, to me, in his coarse, flat sort of voice, as if he knew it was mere pretence. But he looked at her, straight into her face, with that strange, far-off sort of stare, yet very vivid, taking no notice of her, yet staring right into her : as if all that she was putting forward to him was merely window-dressing, and he was just looking way in, to the marshes and the jungle in her, where she didn't even look herself. It made one feel as if there was a mountain behind her, Popocatepetl, that he was staring at, expecting a mountain-lion to spring down off a tree on the slopes of the mountain, or a snake to lean down from a bough. But the mountain was all she stood for, and the mountain-lion or the snake was her own animal self, that he was watching for, like a hunter.

" We didn't stay long, but when we left she asked him to come in whenever he liked. He wasn't really the person to have calling on one : and he knew it, as she did. But he thanked her, and hoped he would one day be able to receive her at her—meaning his— humble house in the Guadalupe Road, where everything was her own. She said : ' Why, sure, I'll come one day. I should love to.' Which he understood, and bowed himself out like some quick but lurking animal : quick as a scorpion, with silence of venom the same.

" After that he would call fairly often, at about five o'clock, but never alone, always with some other man. And he never said anything, always responded to her questions in the same short way, and always looked at her when he was speaking to the other man. He never once *spoke* to her—always spoke to his interpreter, in his flat, coarse Spanish. And he always looked at *her* when he was speaking to someone else.

" She tried every possible manner in which to touch his imagination : but never with any success. She tried the Indians, the Aztecs, the history of Mexico, politics, Don Porfirio, the bull-ring, love, women, Europe, America—and all in vain. All she got out of him was *Verdad!* He was utterly uninterested. He actually *had* no mental imagination. Talk was just a noise to him. The only spark she roused was when she talked of money. Then the queer half-smile deepened on his face, and he asked his interpreter if the Señora was very rich. To which Ethel replied she didn't really know what he meant by rich : he must be rich himself. At which, he asked the interpreter friend if she had more than a million American dollars. To which she replied that perhaps she had—but she wasn't sure. And he looked at her so strangely, even more like a yellow scorpion about to sting.

" I asked him later, what made him put such a crude question ? Did he think of offering to marry her ? ' Marry a —— ? ' he replied, using an obscene expression. But I didn't know even then what he really intended. Yet I saw he had her on his mind.

" Ethel was gradually getting into a state of tension. It was as if something tortured her. She seemed like a woman who would go insane. I asked her : ' Why, whatever's wrong with you ? ' ' I'll tell you, Luis,' she said, ' but don't you say anything to anybody, mind. It's Cuesta ! I don't know whether I want him or not.'—' You don't know whether he wants *you* or not,' said I.—' I can handle that,' she said, ' if I know about myself : if I know my own mind. But I don't. My mind says he's a nada-nada, a dumb-bell, no brain, no imagination, no anything. But my body says he's marvellous, and he's got something I haven't got, and he's stronger than I am, and he's more an angel or a devil than a man, and I'm too merely human to get him—and all that, till I feel I shall just go crazy, and take an overdose of drugs. What am I to *do* with my body, I tell you ? What am I to *do* with it ? I've got to master it. I've got to be *more* than that man. I've got to get all round him, and past him. I've *got* to.'—' Then just take the train to New York to-night, and forget him,' I said.—' I can't ! That's side-tracking. I *won't* side-track my body. I've got to get the best of it. I've got to.'—' Well,' I said, ' you're a point or two beyond me. If it's a question of getting all round Cuesta, and getting past him, why, take the train, and you'll forget him in a fortnight. Don't fool yourself you're in love with the fellow.'—' I'm afraid he's stronger than I am,' she cried out.—' And what then ? He's stronger than I am, but that doesn't prevent me sleeping. A jaguar even is stronger than I am, and an anaconda could swallow me whole. I tell you, it's all in a day's march. There's a kind of animal called Cuesta. Well, what of it ? '

" She looked at me, and I could tell I made no impression on her. She despised me. She sort of wanted to go off the deep end about something. I said to her : ' God's love, Ethel, cut out the Cuesta caprice ! It's not even good acting.' But I might just as well have mewed, for all the notice she took of me.

" It was as if some dormant Popocatepetl inside her had begun to erupt. She didn't love the fellow. Yet she was in a blind kill-me-quick sort of state, neither here nor there, nor hot nor cold, nor desirous nor undesirous, but just simply *insane*. In a certain kind of way, she seemed to want him. And in a very definite kind of way, she seemed *not* to want him. She was in a kind of hysterics, lost her feet altogether. I tried might and main to get her away to the United States. She'd have come sane enough, once she was there. But I thought she'd kill me, when she found I'd been trying to interfere. Oh, she was not quite in her mind, that's sure.

" ' If my body is stronger than my imagination, I shall kill myself,' she said.—' Ethel,' I said, ' people who talk of killing themselves always call a doctor if they cut their finger. What's the quarrel between your body and your imagination ? Aren't they the same thing ? '—' No ! ' she said. ' If the imagination has the body under control, you can do anything, it doesn't matter what you do, physically. If my body was under the control of my imagination, I could take Cuesta for my lover, and it would be an imaginative act. But if my body acted without my imagination, I—I'd kill myself.—' But what do you mean by your body acting without your imagination ? ' I said. ' You are not a child. You've been married twice. You know what it means. You even have two children. You must have had at least several lovers. If Cuesta is to be another of your lovers, I think it is deplorable, but I think it only shows you are very much like all the other women who fall in love with him. If you've fallen in love with him, your imagination has nothing to do but to accept the fact and put as many roses on the ass's head as you like.' She looked at me very solemnly, and seemed to think about it. Then she said : ' But my imagination has not fallen in love with him. He wouldn't meet me imaginatively. He's a brute. And once I start, where's it going to end ? I'm afraid my body has fallen— not fallen in love with him, but fallen *for* him. It's abject ! And if I can't get my body on its feet again, and either forget him or else get him to make it an imaginative act with me—I—I shall kill myself.'—' All right,' said I. ' I don't know what you are talking about, imaginative acts and unimaginative acts. The act is always the same.'—' It isn't ! ' she cried, furious with me. ' It is either imaginative or else it's *impossible*—to me.' Well, I just spread my hands. What could I say, or do ? I simply hated her way of putting it. Imaginative act ! Why, I would hate performing an imaginative act with a woman. Damn it, the act is either real, or let it alone. But now I knew why I had never even touched her, or kissed her, not once : because I couldn't stand that imaginative sort of bullying from her. It is death to a man.

" I said to Cuesta : ' Why do you go to Ethel ? Why don't you stay away, and make her go back to the United States ? Are you in love with her ? ' He was obscene, as usual. ' Am I in love with a cuttle-fish, that is all arms and eyes, and no legs or tail ! That blonde is a cuttlefish. She is an octopus, all arms and eyes and beak, and a lump of jelly.'—' Then why don't you leave her alone ? '— ' Even cuttlefish is good when it's cooked in sauce,' he said. ' You had much better leave her alone,' I said.—' Leave her alone yourself, my esteemed Señor,' he said to me. And I knew I had better go no further.

" She said to him one evening, when only I was there—and she said it in Spanish, direct to him : ' Why do you never come alone to see me ? Why do you always come with another person ? Are you afraid ? ' He looked at her, and his eyes never changed. But he said, in his usual flat, meaningless voice : ' It is because I cannot speak, except Spanish.'—' But we could understand one another,' she said, giving one of her little violent snorts of impatience and embarrassed rage. ' Who knows ! ' he replied, imperturbably.

" Afterwards, he said to me : ' What does she want ? She hates a man as she hates a red-hot iron. A white devil, as sacred as the communion wafer ! '—' Then why don't you leave her alone ? ' I said.—' She is so rich,' he smiled. ' She has all the world in her thousand arms. She is as rich as God. The Archangels are poor

beside her, she is so rich and so white-skinned and white-souled.'—
' Then all the more, why don't you leave her alone? ' But he did not
answer me.

" He went alone, however, to see her. But always in the early
evening. And he never stayed more than half an hour. His car,
well-known everywhere, waited outside : till he came out in his
French-grey suit and glistening brown shoes, his hat rather on the
back of his head.

" What they said to one another, I don't know. But she became
always more distraught and absorbed, as if she were brooding over
a single idea. I said to her : ' Why take it so seriously ? Dozens
of women have slept with Cuesta, and think no more of it. Why take
him seriously ? '—' I don't,' she said. ' I take myself seriously,
that's the point.'—' Let it be the point. Go on taking yourself
seriously, and leave him out of the question altogether.'

" But she was tired of my playing the wise uncle, and I was tired of
her taking herself seriously. She took herself so seriously, it seemed to
me she would deserve what she got, playing the fool with Cuesta.
Of course she did not love him at all. She only wanted to see if she
could make an impression on him, make him yield to her will.
But all the impression she made on him was to make him call her
a squid and an octopus and other nice things. And I could see their
' love ' did not go forward at all.

" ' Have you made love to her ? ' I asked him.—' I have not
touched the zopilote,' he said. ' I hate her bare white neck.'

" But still he went to see her : always, for a very brief call, before
sundown. She asked him to come to dinner, with me. He said he
could never come to dinner, nor after dinner, as he was always
engaged from eight o'clock in the evening onwards. She looked at
him as much as to tell him she knew it was a lie and a subterfuge,
but he never turned a hair. He was, she put it, utterly unimaginative : an impervious animal.

" ' You, however, come one day to your poor house in the Guadalupe Road,' he said—meaning his house. He had said it, sugges-
tively, several times.

" ' But you are always engaged in the evening,' she said.

" ' Come, then, at night—come at eleven, when I am free,' he
said, with supreme animal impudence, looking into her eyes.

" ' Do you receive calls so late ? ' she said, flushing with anger and
embarrassment and obstinacy.

" ' At times,' he said. ' When it is very special.'

" A few days later, when I called to see her as usual, I was told she was ill, and could see no one. The next day, she was still not to be seen. She had had a dangerous nervous collapse. The third day, a friend rang me up to say Ethel was dead.

"The thing was hushed up. But it was known she had poisoned herself. She left a note to me, in which she merely said : ' It is as I told you. Good-bye. But my testament holds good.'

"In her will, she had left half her fortune to Cuesta. The will had been made some ten days before her death—and it was allowed to stand. He took the money——"

Colmenares' voice tailed off into silence.

"Her body had got the better of her imagination, after all," I said.

"It was worse than that," he said.

"How ? "

He was a long time before he answered. Then he said :

"She actually went to Cuesta's house that night, way down there beyond the Volador market. She went by appointment. And there in his bedroom he handed her over to half a dozen of his bull-ring gang, with orders not to bruise her. Yet at the inquest there were a few deep, strange bruises, and the doctors made reports. Then apparently the visit to Cuesta's house came to light, but no details were ever told. Then there was another revolution, and in the hubbub this affair was dropped. It was too shady, anyhow. Ethel had certainly encouraged Cuesta at her apartment."

"But how do you know he handed her over like that ? "

"One of the men told me himself. He was shot afterwards."

I

THERE was a man who loved islands. He was born on one, but it didn't suit him, as there were too many other people on it, besides himself. He wanted an island all of his own : not necessarily to be alone on it, but to make it a world of his own.

An island, if it is big enough, is no better than a continent. It has to be really quite small, before it *feels* like an island ; and this story will show how tiny it has to be, before you can presume to fill it with your own personality.

Now circumstances so worked out, that this lover of islands, by the time he was thirty-five, actually acquired an island of his own. He didn't own it as freehold property, but he had a ninety-nine years' lease of it, which, as far as a man and an island are concerned, is as good as everlasting. Since, if you are like Abraham, and want your offspring to be numberless as the sands of the sea-shore, you don't choose an island to start breeding on. Too soon there would be overpopulation, overcrowding, and slum conditions. Which is a horrid thought, for one who loves an island for its insulation. No, an island is a nest which holds one egg, and one only. This egg is the islander himself.

The island acquired by our potential islander was not in the remote oceans. It was quite near at home, no palm trees nor boom of surf on the reef, nor any of that kind of thing ; but a good solid dwelling-house, rather gloomy, above the landing-place, and beyond, a small farmhouse with sheds, and a few outlying fields. Down on the little landing-bay were three cottages in a row, like coastguards' cottages, all neat and whitewashed.

What could be more cosy and home-like ? It was four miles if you walked all round your island, through the gorse and the black-thorn bushes, above the steep rocks of the sea and down in the little glades where the primroses grew. If you walked straight over the two humps of hills, the length of it, through the rocky fields where the cows lay chewing, and through the rather sparse oats, on into the gorse again, and so to the low cliffs' edge, it took you only twenty minutes. And when you came to the edge, you could see another, bigger island lying beyond. But the sea was between you and it. And as you returned over the turf where the short, downland cowslips nodded, you saw to the east still another island, a tiny one this time, like the calf of the cow. This tiny island also belonged to the islander.

Thus it seems that even islands like to keep each other company.

Our islander loved his island very much. In early spring, the little ways and glades were a snow of blackthorn, a vivid white among the Celtic stillness of close green and grey rock, blackbirds calling out in the whiteness their first long, triumphant calls. After the blackthorn and the nestling primroses came the blue apparition of hyacinths, like elfin lakes and slipping sheets of blue, among the bushes and under the glade of trees. And many birds with nests you could peep into, on the island all your own. Wonderful what a great world it was !

Followed summer, and the cowslips gone, the wild roses faintly fragrant through the haze. There was a field of hay, the foxgloves stood looking down. In a little cove, the sun was on the pale granite where you bathed, and the shadow was in the rocks. Before the mist came stealing, and you went home through the ripening oats, the glare of the sea fading from the high air as the fog-horn started to moo on the other island. And then the sea-fog went, it was autumn, the oat-sheaves lying prone, the great moon, another island, rose golden out of the sea, and rising higher, the world of the sea was white.

So autumn ended with rain, and winter came, dark skies and dampness and rain, but rarely frost. The island, your island, cowered dark, holding away from you. You could feel, down in the wet, sombre hollows, the resentful spirit coiled upon itself, like a wet dog coiled in gloom, or a snake that is neither asleep nor awake. Then in the night, when the wind left off blowing in great gusts and volleys, as at sea, you felt that your island was a universe, infinite and old as the darkness ; not an island at all, but an infinite dark world where all the souls from all the other bygone nights lived on, and the infinite distance was near.

Strangely, from your little island in space, you were gone forth into the dark, great realms of time, where all the souls that never die veer and swoop on their vast, strange errands. The little earthly island has dwindled, like a jumping-off place, into nothingness, for you have jumped off, you know not how, into the dark wide mystery of time, where the past is vastly alive, and the future is not separated off.

This is the danger of becoming an islander. When, in the city, you wear your white spats and dodge the traffic with the fear of death down your spine, then you are quite safe from the terrors of infinite time. The moment is your little islet in time, it is the spatial universe that careers round you.

But once isolate yourself on a little island in the sea of space, and the moment begins to heave and expand in great circles, the solid earth is gone, and your slippery, naked dark soul finds herself out in the timeless world, where the chariots of the so-called dead dash down the old streets of centuries, and souls crowd on the foot-ways that we, in the moment, call bygone years. The souls of all the dead are alive again, and pulsating actively around you. You are out in the other infinity.

Something of this happened to our islander. Mysterious " feel-ings " came upon him, that he wasn't used to ; strange awarenesses of old, far-gone men, and other influences ; men of Gaul, with big moustaches, who had been on his island, and had vanished from the face of it, but not out of the air of night. They were there still, hurtling their big, violent, unseen bodies through the night. And there were priests, with golden knives and mistletoe ; then other priests with a crucifix ; then pirates with murder on the sea.

Our islander was uneasy. He didn't believe, in the daytime, in any of this nonsense. But at night it just was so. He had reduced himself to a single point in space, and, a point being that which has neither length nor breadth, he had to step off it into somewhere else. Just as you must step into the sea, if the waters wash your foothold away, so he had, at night, to step off into the other worlds of undying time.

He was uncannily aware, as he lay in the dark, that the blackthorn grove that seemed a bit uncanny even in the realm of space and day, at night was crying with old men of an invisible race, around the altar stone. What was a ruin under the hornbeam trees by day, was a moaning of blood-stained priests with crucifixes, on the ineffable night. What was a cave and a hidden beach between coarse rocks, became in the invisible dark the purple-lipped imprecation of pirates.

To escape any more of this sort of awareness, our islander daily concentrated upon his material island. Why should it not be the Happy Isle at last ? Why not the last small isle of the Hesperides, the perfect place, all filled with his own gracious, blossom-like spirit ? A minute world of pure perfection, made by man, himself.

He began, as we begin all our attempts to regain Paradise, by spending money. The old, semi-feudal dwelling-house he restored, let in more light, put clear lovely carpets on the floor, clear, flower-petal curtains at the sullen windows, and wines in the cellars of rock. He brought over a buxom housekeeper from the world, and a soft-spoken, much-experienced butler. These two were to be islanders.

In the farmhouse he put a bailiff, with two farm-hands. There were Jersey cows, tinkling a slow bell, among the gorse. There was a call to meals at midday, and the peaceful smoking of chimneys at evening, when rest descended.

A jaunty sailing-boat with a motor accessory rode in the shelter in the bay, just below the row of three white cottages. There was also a little yawl, and two row-boats drawn up on the sand. A fishing-net was drying on its supports, a boat-load of new white planks stood criss-cross, a woman was going to the well with a bucket.

In the end cottage lived the skipper of the yacht, and his wife and son. He was a man from the other, large island, at home on this sea. Every fine day he went out fishing, with his son, every fair day there was fresh fish in the island.

In the middle cottage lived an old man and wife, a very faithful couple. The old man was a carpenter, and man of many jobs. He was always working, always the sound of his plane or his saw ; lost in his work, he was another kind of islander.

In the third cottage was a mason, a widower with a son and two daughters. With the help of his boy, this man dug ditches and built fences, raised buttresses and erected a new outbuilding, and hewed stone from the little quarry. One daughter worked at the big house.

It was a quiet, busy little world. When the islander brought you over as his guest, you met first the dark-bearded, thin, smiling skipper, Arnold, then his boy Charles. At the house, the smooth-lipped butler who had lived all over the world valeted you, and created that curious creamy-smooth, disarming sense of luxury around you which only a perfect and rather untrustworthy servant can create. He disarmed you and had you at his mercy. The buxom housekeeper smiled and treated you with the subtly respectful familiarity that is only dealt out to the true gentry. And the rosy maid threw a glance at you, as if you were very wonderful, coming from the great outer world. Then you met the smiling but watchful bailiff, who came from Cornwall, and the shy farm-hand from Berkshire, with his clean wife and two little children ; then the rather sulky farm-hand from Suffolk. The mason, a Kent man, would talk to you by the yard, if you let him. Only the old carpenter was gruff and elsewhere absorbed.

Well then, it was a little world to itself, and everybody feeling very safe, and being very nice to you, as if you were really something special. But it was the islander's world, not yours. He was the Master. The special smile, the special attention was to the Master. They all knew how well off they were. So the islander was no longer Mr. So-and-so. To everyone on the island, even to you yourself, he was " the Master."

Well, it was ideal. The Master was no tyrant. Ah, no ! He was a delicate, sensitive, handsome Master, who wanted everything perfect and everybody happy. Himself, of course, to be the fount of this happiness and perfection.

But in his way, he was a poet. He treated his guests royally, his servants liberally. Yet he was shrewd, and very wise. He never came the boss over his people. Yet he kept his eye on everything, like a shrewd, blue-eyed young Hermes. And it was amazing what a lot of knowledge he had at hand. Amazing what he knew about Jersey cows, and cheese-making, ditching and fencing, flowers and gardening, ships and the sailing of ships. He was a fount of knowledge about everything, and this knowledge he imparted to his people in an odd, half-ironical, half-portentous fashion, as if he really belonged to the quaint, half-real world of the gods.

They listened to him with their hats in their hands. He loved white clothes ; or creamy white ; and cloaks, and broad hats. So, in fine weather, the bailiff would see the elegant tall figure in creamy-white serge coming like some bird over the fallow, to look at the weeding of the turnips. Then there would be a doffing of hats, and a few minutes of whimsical, shrewd, wise talk, to which the bailiff answered admiringly, and the farm-hands listened in silent wonder, leaning on their hoes. The bailiff was almost tender, to the Master.

Or, on a windy morning, he would stand with his cloak blowing in the sticky sea-wind, on the edge of the ditch that was being dug to drain a little swamp, talking in the teeth of the wind to the man below, who looked up at him with steady and inscrutable eyes.

Or at evening in the rain he would be seen hurrying across the yard, the broad hat turned against the rain. And the farm-wife would hurriedly exclaim : " The Master ! Get up, John, and clear him a place on the sofa." And then the door opened, and it was a cry of : " Why, of all things, if it isn't the Master ! Why, have ye turned out then, of a night like this, to come across to the like of we ? " And the bailiff took his cloak, and the farm-wife his hat, the two farm-hands drew their chairs to the back, he sat on the sofa and took a child up near him. He was wonderful with children, talked to them simply wonderful, made you think of Our Saviour Himself, said the woman.

He was always greeted with smiles, and the same peculiar deference, as if he were a higher, but also frailer being. They handled him almost tenderly, and almost with adulation. But when he left, or when they spoke of him, they had often a subtle, mocking smile on their faces. There was no need to be afraid of " the Master." Just let him have his own way. Only the old carpenter was sometimes sincerely rude to him ; so he didn't care for the old man.

It is doubtful whether any of them really liked him, man to man, or even woman to man. But then it is doubtful if he really liked any of them, as man to man, or man to woman. He wanted them to be happy, and the little world to be perfect. But anyone who wants the world to be perfect must be careful not to have real likes or dislikes. A general goodwill is all you can afford.

The sad fact is, alas, that general goodwill is always felt as something of an insult, by the mere object of it ; and so it breeds a quite special brand of malice. Surely general goodwill is a form of egoism, that it should have such a result !

Our islander, however, had his own resources. He spent long hours in his library, for he was compiling a book of reference to all the flowers mentioned in the Greek and Latin authors. He was not a great classical scholar ; the usual public-school equipment. But there are such excellent translations nowadays. And it was so lovely, tracing flower after flower as it blossomed in the ancient world.

So the first year on the island passed by. A great deal had been done. Now the bills flooded in, and the Master, conscientious in all things, began to study them. The study left him pale and breathless. He was not a rich man. He knew he had been making a hole in his capital, to get the island into running order. When he came to look, however, there was hardly anything left but hole. Thousands and thousands of pounds had the island swallowed into nothingness.

But surely the bulk of the spending was over ! Surely the island would now begin to be self-supporting, even if it made no profit ! Surely he was safe. He paid a good many of the bills, and took a little heart. But he had had a shock, and the next year, the coming year, there must be economy, frugality. He told his people so, in simple and touching language. And they said : " Why, surely ! Surely ! "

So, while the wind blew and the rain lashed outside, he would sit in his library with the bailiff over a pipe and pot of beer, discussing farm projects. He lifted his narrow handsome face, and his blue eye became dreamy. " *What* a wind ! " It blew like cannon shots. He thought of his island, lashed with foam, and inaccessible, and he exulted. . . . No, he must not lose it. He turned back to the farm projects with the zest of genius, and his hands flicked white emphasis, while the bailiff intoned : " Yes, sir ! Yes, sir ! You're right, Master ! "

But the man was hardly listening. He was looking at the Master's blue lawn shirt and curious pink tie with the fiery red stone, at the enamel sleeve-links, and at the ring with the peculiar scarab. The brown searching eyes of the man of the soil glanced repeatedly over the fine, immaculate figure of the Master, with a sort of slow, calculating wonder. But if he happened to catch the Master's bright, exalted glance, his own eye lit up with a careful cordiality and deference, as he bowed his head slightly.

Thus between them they decided what crops should be sown, what fertilizers should be used in different places, which breed of pigs should be imported, and which line of turkeys. That is to say, the bailiff, by continually cautiously agreeing with the Master, kept out of it, and let the young man have his own way.

The Master knew what he was talking about. He was brilliant at grasping the gist of a book, and knowing how to apply his knowledge. On the whole, his ideas were sound. The bailiff even knew it. But in the man of the soil there was no answering enthusiasm. The brown eyes smiled their cordial deference, but the thin lips never changed. The Master pursed his own flexible mouth in a boyish versatility, as he cleverly sketched in his ideas to the other man, and the bailiff made eyes of admiration, but in his heart he was not attending, he was only watching the Master as he would have watched a queer, caged animal, quite without sympathy, not implicated.

So, it was settled, and the Master rang for Elvery, the butler, to bring a sandwich. He, the Master, was pleased. The butler saw it, and came back with anchovy and ham sandwiches, and a newly opened bottle of vermouth. There was always a newly opened bottle of something.

It was the same with the mason. The Master and he discussed

the drainage of a bit of land, and more pipes were ordered, more
special bricks, more this, more that.

Fine weather came at last ; there was a little lull in the hard
work on the island. The Master went for a short cruise in his
yacht. It was not really a yacht, just a little bit of a thing. They
sailed along the coast of the mainland, and put in at the ports.
At every port some friend turned up, the butler made elegant little
meals in the cabin. Then the Master was invited to villas and
hotels, his people disembarked him as if he were a prince.

And oh, how expensive it turned out ! He had to telegraph to
the bank for money. And he went home again, to economize.

The marsh-marigolds were blazing in the little swamp where the
ditches were being dug for drainage. He almost regretted, now, the
work in hand. The yellow beauties would not blaze again.

Harvest came, and a bumper crop. There must be a harvest-
home supper. The long barn was now completely restored and
added to. The carpenter had made long tables. Lanterns hung
from the beams of the high-pitched roof. All the people of the
island were assembled. The bailiff presided. It was a gay scene.

Towards the end of the supper the Master, in a velvet jacket,
appeared with his guests. Then the bailiff rose and proposed " The
Master ! Long life and health to the Master ! " All the people
drank the health with great enthusiasm and cheering. The Master
replied with a little speech : They were on an island in a little
world of their own. It depended on them all to make this world
a world of true happiness and content. Each must do his part. He
hoped he himself did what he could, for his heart was in his island,
and with the people of his island.

The butler responded : As long as the island had such a Master,
it could not help but be a little heaven for all the people on it.
This was seconded with virile warmth by the bailiff and the mason,
the skipper was beside himself. Then there was dancing, the old
carpenter was fiddler.

But under all this, things were not well. The very next morning
came the farm-boy to say that a cow had fallen over the cliff. The
Master went to look. He peered over the not very high declivity,
and saw her lying dead, on a green ledge under a bit of late-flowering
broom. A beautiful, expensive creature, already looking swollen.
But what a fool, to fall so unnecessarily !

It was a question of getting several men to haul her up the bank,
and then of skinning and burying her. No one would eat the meat.
How repulsive it all was !

This was symbolic of the island. As sure as the spirits rose in the human breast, with a movement of joy, an invisible hand struck malevolently out of the silence. There must not be any joy, nor even any quiet peace. A man broke a leg, another was crippled with rheumatic fever. The pigs had some strange disease. A storm drove the yacht on a rock. The mason hated the butler, and refused to let his daughter serve at the house.

Out of the very air came a stony, heavy malevolence. The island itself seemed malicious. It would go on being hurtful and evil for weeks at a time. Then suddenly again one morning it would be fair, lovely as a morning in Paradise, everything beautiful and flowing. And everybody would begin to feel a great relief, and a hope for happiness.

Then as soon as the Master was opened out in spirit like an open flower, some ugly blow would fall. Somebody would send him an anonymous note, accusing some other person on the island. Somebody else would come hinting things against one of his servants.

"Some folks think they've got an easy job out here, with all the pickings they make !" the mason's daughter screamed at the suave butler, in the Master's hearing. He pretended not to hear.

"My man says this island is surely one of the lean kine of Egypt, it would swallow a sight of money, and you'd never get anything back out of it," confided the farm-hand's wife to one of the Master's visitors.

The people were not contented. They were not islanders. "We feel we're not doing right by the children," said those who had children. "We feel we're not doing right by ourselves," said those who had no children. And the various families fairly came to hate one another.

Yet the island was so lovely. When there was a scent of honey-suckle and the moon brightly flickering down on the sea, then even the grumblers felt a strange nostalgia for it. It set you yearning, with a wild yearning ; perhaps for the past, to be far back in the mysterious past of the island, when the blood had a different throb. Strange floods of passion came over you, strange violent lusts and imaginations of cruelty. The blood and the passion and the lust which the island had known. Uncanny dreams, half-dreams, half-evocated yearnings.

The Master himself began to be a little afraid of his island. He felt here strange violent feelings he had never felt before, and lustful desires that he had been quite free from. He knew quite well now that his people didn't love him at all. He knew that their spirits were secretly against him, malicious, jeering, envious, and lurking to down him. He became just as wary and secretive with regard to them.

But it was too much. At the end of the second year, several departures took place. The housekeeper went. The Master always blamed self-important women most. The mason said he wasn't going to be monkeyed about any more, so he took his departure, with his family. The rheumatic farm-hand left.

And then the year's bills came in, the Master made up his accounts. In spite of good crops, the assets were ridiculous, against the spending. The island had again lost, not hundreds but thousands of pounds. It was incredible. But you simply couldn't believe it ! Where had it all gone·?

The Master spent gloomy nights and days going through accounts in the library. He was thorough. It became evident, now the housekeeper had gone, that she had swindled him. Probably everybody was swindling him. But he hated to think it, so he put the thought away.

He emerged, however, pale and hollow-eyed from his balancing of unbalanceable accounts, looking as if something had kicked him in the stomach. It was pitiable. But the money had gone, and there was an end of it. Another great hole in his capital. How could people be so heartless ?

It couldn't go on, that was evident. He would soon be bankrupt. He had to give regretful notice to his butler. He was afraid to find out how much his butler had swindled him. Because the man was such a wonderful butler, after all. And the farm-bailiff had to go. The Master had no regrets in that quarter. The losses on the farm had almost embittered him.

The third year was spent in rigid cutting down of expenses. The island was still mysterious and fascinating. But it was also treacherous and cruel, secretly, fathomlessly malevolent. In spite of all its fair show of white blossom and bluebells, and the lovely dignity of foxgloves bending their rose-red bells, it was your implacable enemy.

With reduced staff, reduced wages, reduced splendour, the third year went by. But it was fighting against hope. The farm still lost a good deal. And once more, there was a hole in that remnant of capital. Another hole in that which was already a mere remnant round the old holes. The island was mysterious in this also : it seemed to pick the very money out of your pocket, as if it were an octopus with invisible arms stealing from you in every direction.

Yet the Master still loved it. But with a touch of rancour now.

He spent, however, the second half of the fourth year intensely working on the mainland, to be rid of it. And it was amazing how difficult he found it, to dispose of an island. He had thought that everybody was pining for such an island as his ; but not at all. Nobody would pay any price for it. And he wanted now to get rid of it, as a man who wants a divorce at any cost.

It was not till the middle of the fifth year that he transferred it, at a considerable loss to himself, to an hotel company who were willing to speculate in it. They were to turn it into a handy honeymoon-and-golf island.

There, take that, island which didn't know when it was well off. Now be a honeymoon-and-golf island !

II

THE SECOND ISLAND

The islander had to move. But he was not going to the mainland. Oh, no ! He moved to the smaller island, which still belonged to him. And he took with him the faithful old carpenter and wife, the couple he never really cared for ; also a widow and daughter, who had kept house for him the last year ; also an orphan lad, to help the old man.

The small island was very small ; but being a hump of rock in the sea, it was bigger than it looked. There was a little track among the rocks and bushes, winding and scrambling up and down around the islet, so that it took you twenty minutes to do the circuit. It was more than you would have expected.

Still, it was an island. The islander moved himself, with all his books, into the commonplace six-roomed house up to which you had to scramble from the rocky landing-place. There were also two joined-together cottages. The old carpenter lived in one, with his wife and the lad, the widow and daughter lived in the other.

At last all was in order. The Master's books filled two rooms. It was already autumn, Orion lifting out of the sea. And in the dark nights, the Master could see the lights on his late island, where the hotel company were entertaining guests who would advertise the new resort for honeymoon-golfers.

On his lump of rock, however, the Master was still master. He explored the crannies, the odd handbreadths of grassy level, the steep little cliffs where the last harebells hung, and the seeds of summer were brown above the sea, lonely and untouched. He peered down the old well. He examined the stone pen where the pig had been kept. Himself, he had a goat.

Yes, it was an island. Always, always, underneath among the rocks the Celtic sea sucked and washed and smote its feathery greyness. How many different noises of the sea ! Deep explosions, rumblings, strange long sighs and whistling noises ; then voices, real voices of people clamouring as if they were in a market, under the waters : and again, the far-off ringing of a bell, surely an actual bell ! Then a tremendous trilling noise, very long and alarming, and an undertone of hoarse gasping.

On this island there were no human ghosts, no ghosts of any ancient race. The sea, and the spume and the weather, had washed them all out, washed them out so there was only the sound of the sea itself, its own ghost, myriad-voiced, communing and plotting and shouting all winter long. And only the smell of the sea, with a few bristly bushes of gorse and coarse tufts of heather, among the grey, pellucid rocks, in the grey, more-pellucid air. The coldness, the greyness, even the soft, creeping fog of the sea, and the islet of rock humped up in it all, like the last point in space.

Green star Sirius stood over the sea's rim. The island was a shadow. Out at sea a ship showed small lights. Below, in the rocky cove, the row-boat and the motor-boat were safe. A light shone in the carpenter's kitchen. That was all.

Save, of course, that the lamp was lit in the house, where the widow was preparing supper, her daughter helping. The islander went in to his meal. Here he was no longer the Master, he was an islander again and he had peace. The old carpenter, the widow and daughter were all faithfulness itself. The old man worked while ever there was light to see, because he had a passion for work. The widow and her quiet, rather delicate daughter of thirty-three worked for the Master, because they loved looking after him, and they were infinitely grateful for the haven he provided them. But they didn't call him " the Master." They gave him his name : " Mr. Cathcart, sir ! " softly, and reverently. And he spoke back to them also softly, gently, like people far from the world, afraid to make a noise.

The island was no longer a " world." It was a sort of refuge. The islander no longer struggled for anything. He had no need. It was as if he and his few dependents were a small flock of sea-birds alighted on this rock, as they travelled through space, and keeping together without a word. The silent mystery of travelling birds.

He spent most of his day in his study. His book was coming

along. The widow's daughter could type out his manuscript for
him, she was not uneducated. It was the one strange sound on the
island, the typewriter. But soon even its spattering fitted in with
the sea's noises, and the wind's.

The months went by. The islander worked away in his study, the
people of the island went quietly about their concerns. The goat
had a little black kid with yellow eyes. There were mackerel in the
sea. The old man went fishing in the row-boat with the lad, when
the weather was calm enough ; they went off in the motor-boat
to the biggest island for the post. And they brought supplies, never
a penny wasted. And the days went by, and the nights, without
desire, without ennui.

The strange stillness from all desire was a kind of wonder to the
islander. He didn't want anything. His soul at last was still in
him, his spirit was like a dim-lit cave under water, where strange
sea-foliage expands upon the watery atmosphere, and scarcely
sways, and a mute fish shadowily slips in and slips away again. All
still and soft and uncrying, yet alive as rooted seaweed is alive.

The islander said to himself : " Is this happiness ? " He said
to himself : " I am turned into a dream. I feel nothing, or I
don't know what I feel. Yet it seems to me I am happy."

Only he had to have something upon which his mental activity
could work. So he spent long, silent hours in his study, working
not very fast, nor very importantly, letting the writing spin softly
from him as if it were drowsy gossamer. He no longer fretted
whether it were good or not, what he produced. He slowly, softly
spun it like gossamer, and if it were to melt away as gossamer in
autumn melts, he would not mind. It was only the soft evanescence
of gossamy things which now seemed to him permanent. The very
mist of eternity was in them. Whereas stone buildings, cathedrals
for example, seemed to him to howl with temporary resistance,
knowing they must fall at last ; the tension of their long endurance
seemed to howl forth from them all the time.

Sometimes he went to the mainland and to the city. Then he
went elegantly, dressed in the latest style, to his club. He sat in a
stall at the theatre, he shopped in Bond Street. He discussed terms
for publishing his book. But over his face was that gossamy look of
having dropped out of the race of progress, which made the vulgar
city people feel they had won it over him, and made him glad to
go back to his island.

He didn't mind if he never published his book. The years were
blending into a soft mist, from which nothing obtruded. Spring

came. There was never a primrose on his island, but he found a winter-aconite. There were two little sprayed bushes of blackthorn, and some wind-flowers. He began to make a list of the flowers of his islet, and that was absorbing. He noted a wild currant bush and watched for the elder flowers on a stunted little tree, then for the first yellow rags of the broom, and wild roses. Bladder campion, orchids, stitchwort, celandine, he was prouder of them than if they had been people on his island. When he came across the golden saxifrage, so inconspicuous in a damp corner, he crouched over it in a trance, he knew not for how long, looking at it. Yet it was nothing to look at. As the widow's daughter found, when he showed it her.

He had said to her, in real triumph :

" I found the golden saxifrage this morning."

The name sounded splendid. She looked at him with fascinated brown eyes, in which was a hollow ache that frightened him a little.

" Did you, sir ? Is it a nice flower ? "

He pursed his lips and tilted his brows.

" Well—not showy exactly. I'll show it you if you like."

" I should like to see it."

She was so quiet, so wistful. But he sensed in her a persistency which made him uneasy. She said she was so happy : really happy. She followed him quietly, like a shadow, on the rocky track where there was never room for two people to walk side by side. He went first, and could feel her there, immediately behind him, following so submissively, gloating on him from behind.

It was a kind of pity for her which made him become her lover : though he never realized the extent of the power she had gained over him, and how *she* willed it. But the moment he had fallen, a jangling feeling came upon him, that it was all wrong. He felt a nervous dislike of her. He had not wanted it. And it seemed to him, as far as her physical self went, she had not wanted it either. It was just her will. He went away, and climbed at the risk of his neck down to a ledge near the sea. There he sat for hours, gazing all jangled at the sea, and saying miserably to himself : " We didn't want it. We didn't really want it."

It was the automatism of sex that had caught him again. Not that he hated sex. He deemed it, as the Chinese do, one of the great life-mysteries. But it had become mechanical, automatic, and he wanted to escape that. Automatic sex shattered him, and filled him with a sort of death. He thought he had come through, to a new stillness of desirelessness. Perhaps beyond that, there was a new fresh delicacy of desire, an unentered frail communion of two people meeting on untrodden ground.

Be that as it might, this was not it. This was nothing new or fresh. It was automatic, and driven from the will. Even she, in her true self, hadn't wanted it. It was automatic in her.

When he came home, very late, and saw her face white with fear and apprehension of his feeling against her, he pitied her, and spoke to her delicately, reassuringly. But he kept himself remote from her.

She gave no sign. She served him with the same silence, the same hidden hunger to serve him, to be near where he was. He felt her love following him with strange, awful persistency. She claimed nothing. Yet now, when he met her bright, brown, curiously vacant eyes, he saw in them the mute question. The question came direct at him, with a force and a power of will he never realized.

So he succumbed, and asked her again.

" Not," she said, " if it will make you hate me."

" Why should it ? " he replied, nettled. " Of course not."

" You know I would do anything on earth for you."

It was only afterwards, in his exasperation, he remembered what she had said, and was more exasperated. Why should she pretend to do this *for him ?* Why not for herself ? But in his exasperation, he drove himself deeper in. In order to achieve some sort of satisfaction, which he never did achieve, he abandoned himself to her. Everybody on the island knew. But he did not care.

Then even what desire he had left him, and he felt only shattered. He felt that only with her will had she wanted him. Now he was shattered and full of self-contempt. His island was smirched and spoiled. He had lost his place in the rare, desireless levels of Time to which he had at last arrived, and he had fallen right back. If only it had been true, delicate desire between them, and a delicate meeting on the third rare place where a man might meet a woman, when they were both true to the frail, sensitive, crocus-flame of desire in them. But it had been no such thing : automatic, an act of will, not of true desire, it left him feeling humiliated.

He went away from the islet, in spite of her mute reproach. And he wandered about the continent, vainly seeking a place where he could stay. He was out of key ; he did not fit in the world any more.

There came a letter from Flora—her name was Flora—to say she was afraid she was going to have a child. He sat down as if he were shot, and he remained sitting. But he replied to her :

"Why be afraid? If it is so, it is so, and we should rather be pleased than afraid."

At this very moment, it happened there was an auction of islands. He got the maps, and studied them. And at the auction he bought, for very little money, another island. It was just a few acres of rock away in the north, on the outer fringe of the isles. It was low, it rose low out of the great ocean. There was not a building, not even a tree on it. Only northern sea-turf, a pool of rain-water, a bit of sedge, rock, and sea-birds. Nothing else. Under the weeping wet western sky.

He made a trip to visit his new possession. For several days, owing to the seas, he could not approach it. Then, in a light sea-mist, he landed, and saw it hazy, low, stretching apparently a long way. But it was illusion. He walked over the wet, springy turf, and dark-grey sheep tossed away from him, spectral, bleating hoarsely. And he came to the dark pool, with the sedge. Then on in the dampness, to the grey sea sucking angrily among the rocks.

This was indeed an island.

So he went home to Flora. She looked at him with guilty fear, but also with a triumphant brightness in her uncanny eyes. And again he was gentle, he reassured her, even he wanted her again, with that curious desire that was almost like toothache. So he took her to the mainland, and they were married, since she was going to have his child.

They returned to the island. She still brought in his meals, her own along with them. She sat and ate with him. He would have it so. The widowed mother preferred to stay in the kitchen. And Flora slept in the guest-room of his house, mistress of his house.

His desire, whatever it was, died in him with nauseous finality. The child would still be months coming. His island was hateful to him, vulgar, a suburb. He himself had lost all his finer distinction. The weeks passed in a sort of prison, in humiliation. Yet he stuck it out, till the child was born. But he was meditating escape. Flora did not even know.

A nurse appeared, and ate at table with them. The doctor came sometimes, and, if the sea were rough, he too had to stay. He was cheery over his whisky.

They might have been a young couple in Golders Green.

The daughter was born at last. The father looked at the baby, and felt depressed, almost more than he could bear. The millstone was tied round his neck. But he tried not to show what he felt. And Flora did not know. She still smiled with a kind of half-witted triumph in her joy, as she got well again. Then she began again to look at him with those aching, suggestive, somehow impudent eyes. She adored him so.

This he could not stand. He told her that he had to go away for a time. She wept, but she thought she had got him. He told her he had settled the best part of his property on her, and wrote down for her what income it would produce. She hardly listened, only looked at him with those heavy, adoring, impudent eyes. He gave her a cheque-book, with the amount of her credit duly entered. This did arouse her interest. And he told her, if she got tired of the island, she could choose her home wherever she wished.

She followed him with those aching, persistent brown eyes, when he left, and he never even saw her weep.

He went straight north, to prepare his third island.

III

THE THIRD ISLAND

The third island was soon made habitable. With cement and the big pebbles from the shingle beach, two men built him a hut, and roofed it with corrugated iron. A boat brought over a bed and table, and three chairs, with a good cupboard, and a few books. He laid in a supply of coal and paraffin and food—he wanted so little.

The house stood near the flat shingle bay where he landed, and where he pulled up his light boat. On a sunny day in August the men sailed away and left him. The sea was still and pale blue. On the horizon he saw the small mail-steamer slowly passing north-wards, as if she were walking. She served the outer isles twice a week. He could row out to her if need be, in calm weather, and he could signal her from a flagstaff behind his cottage.

Half-a-dozen sheep still remained on the island, as company ; and he had a cat to rub against his legs. While the sweet, sunny days of the northern autumn lasted, he would walk among the rocks, and over the springy turf of his small domain, always coming to the ceaseless, restless sea. He looked at every leaf, that might be different from another, and he watched the endless expansion and contraction of the water-tossed sea-weed. He had never a tree, not even a bit of heather to guard. Only the turf, and tiny turf-plants, and the sedge by the pool, the seaweed in the ocean. He was glad. He didn't want trees or bushes. They stood up like people, too

assertive. His bare, low-pitched island in the pale blue sea was all
he wanted.

He no longer worked at his book. The interest had gone. He
liked to sit on the low elevation of his island, and see the sea ;
nothing but the pale, quiet sea. And to feel his mind turn soft and
hazy, like the hazy ocean. Sometimes, like a mirage, he would
see the shadow of land rise hovering to northwards. It was a big
island beyond. But quite without substance.

He was soon almost startled when he perceived the steamer on
the near horizon, and his heart contracted with fear, lest it were
going to pause and molest him. Anxiously he watched it go, and
not till it was out of sight did he feel truly relieved, himself again.
The tension of waiting for human approach was cruel. He did not
want to be approached. He did not want to hear voices. He was
shocked by the sound of his own voice, if he inadvertently spoke to
his cat. He rebuked himself for having broken the great silence.
And he was irritated when his cat would look up at him and mew
faintly, plaintively. He frowned at her. And she knew. She was
becoming wild, lurking in the rocks, perhaps fishing.

But what he disliked most was when one of the lumps of sheep
opened its mouth and baa-ed its hoarse, raucous baa. He watched
it, and it looked to him hideous and gross. He came to dislike the
sheep very much.

He wanted only to hear the whispering sound of the sea, and the
sharp cries of the gulls, cries that came out of another world to
him. And best of all, the great silence.

He decided to get rid of the sheep when the boat came. They
were accustomed to him now, and stood and stared at him with
yellow or colourless eyes, in an insolence that was almost cold
ridicule. There was a suggestion of cold indecency about them.
He disliked them very much. And when they jumped with staccato
jumps off the rocks, and their hoofs made the dry, sharp hit, and the
fleece flopped on their square backs, he found them repulsive,
degrading.

The fine weather passed, and it rained all day. He lay a great
deal on his bed, listening to the water trickling from his roof into
the zinc water-butt, looking through the open door at the rain, the
dark rocks, the hidden sea. Many gulls were on the island now :
many sea-birds of all sorts. It was another world of life. Many of
the birds he had never seen before. His old impulse came over
him, to send for a book, to know their names. In a flicker of the
old passion, to know the name of everything he saw, he even decided

to row out to the steamer. The names of these birds ! He must know their names, otherwise he had not got them, they were not quite alive to him.

But the desire left him, and he merely watched the birds as they wheeled or walked around him, watched them vaguely, without discrimination. All interest had left him. Only there was one gull, a big, handsome fellow, who would walk back and forth, back and forth in front of the open door of the cabin, as if he had some mission there. He was big, and pearl-grey, and his roundnesses were as smooth and lovely as a pearl. Only the folded wings had shut black pinions, and on the closed black feathers were three very distinct white dots, making a pattern. The islander wondered very much, why this bit of trimming on the bird out of the far, cold seas. And as the gull walked back and forth, back and forth in front of the cabin, strutting on pale-dusky gold feet, holding up his pale yellow beak, that was curved at the tip, with curious alien import-ance, the man wondered over him. He was portentous, he had a meaning.

Then the bird came no more. The island, which had been full of sea-birds, the flash of wings, the sound and cut of wings and sharp eerie cries in the air, began to be deserted again. No longer they sat like living eggs on the rocks and turf, moving their heads, but scarcely rising into flight round his feet. No longer they ran across the turf among the sheep, and lifted themselves upon low wings. The host had gone. But some remained, always.

The days shortened, and the world grew eerie. One day the boat came : as if suddenly, swooping down. The islander found it a violation. It was torture to talk to those two men, in their homely clumsy clothes. The air of familiarity around them was very repugnant to him. Himself, he was neatly dressed, his cabin was neat and tidy. He resented any intrusion, the clumsy homeliness, the heavy-footedness of the two fishermen was really repulsive to him.

The letters they had brought he left lying unopened in a little box. In one of them was his money. But he could not bear to open even that one. Any kind of contact was repulsive to him. Even to read his name on an envelope. He hid the letters away.

And the hustle and horror of getting the sheep caught and tied and put in the ship made him loathe with profound repulsion the whole of the animal creation. What repulsive god invented animals and evil-smelling men ? To his nostrils, the fishermen and the sheep alike smelled foul ; an uncleanness on the fresh earth.

He was still nerve-racked and tortured when the ship at last lifted sail and was drawing away, over the still sea. And sometimes days after, he would start with repulsion, thinking he heard the munching of sheep.

The dark days of winter drew on. Sometimes there was no real day at all. He felt ill, as if he were dissolving, as if dissolution had already set in inside him. Everything was twilight, outside, and in his mind and soul. Once, when he went to the door, he saw black heads of men swimming in his bay. For some moments he swooned unconscious. It was the shock, the horror of unexpected human approach. The horror in the twilight ! And not till the shock had undermined him and left him disembodied, did he realize that the black heads were the heads of seals swimming in. A sick relief came over him. But he was barely conscious, after the shock. Later on, he sat and wept with gratitude, because they were not men. But he never realized that he wept. He was too dim. Like some strange, ethereal animal, he no longer realized what he was doing.

Only he still derived his single satisfaction from being alone, absolutely alone, with the space soaking into him. The grey sea alone, and the footing of his sea-washed island. No other contact. Nothing human to bring its horror into contact with him. Only space, damp, twilit, sea-washed space ! This was the bread of his soul.

For this reason, he was most glad when there was a storm, or when the sea was high. Then nothing could get at him. Nothing could come through to him from the outer world. True, the terrific violence of the wind made him suffer badly. At the same time, it swept the world utterly out of existence for him. He always liked the sea to be heavily rolling and tearing. Then no boat could get at him. It was like eternal ramparts round his island.

He kept no track of time, and no longer thought of opening a book. The print, the printed letters, so like the depravity of speech, looked obscene. He tore the brass label from his paraffin stove. He obliterated any bit of lettering in his cabin.

His cat had disappeared. He was rather glad. He shivered at her thin, obtrusive call. She had lived in the coal-shed. And each morning he had put her a dish of porridge, the same as he ate. He washed her saucer with repulsion. He did not like her writhing about. But he fed her scrupulously. Then one day she did not come for her porridge ; she always mewed for it. She did not come again.

He prowled about his island in the rain, in a big oilskin coat, not knowing what he was looking at, nor what he went out to see. Time had ceased to pass. He stood for long spaces, gazing from a white, sharp face, with those keen, far-off blue eyes of his, gazing fiercely and almost cruelly at the dark sea under the dark sky. And if he saw the labouring sail of a fishing-boat away on the cold waters, a strange malevolent anger passed over his features.

Sometimes he was ill. He knew he was ill, because he staggered as he walked, and easily fell down. Then he paused to think what it was. And he went to his stores and took out dried milk and malt, and ate that. Then he forgot again. He ceased to register his own feelings.

The days were beginning to lengthen. All winter the weather had been comparatively mild, but with much rain, much rain. He had forgotten the sun. Suddenly, however, the air was very cold, and he began to shiver. A fear came over him. The sky was level and grey, and never a star appeared at night. It was very cold. More birds began to arrive. The island was freezing. With trembling hands he made a fire in his grate. The cold frightened him.

And now it continued, day after day, a dull, deathly cold. Occasional crumblings of snow were in the air. The days were greyly longer, but no change in the cold. Frozen grey daylight. The birds passed away, flying away. Some he saw lying frozen. It was as if all life were drawing away, contracting away from the north, contracting southwards. " Soon," he said to himself, " it will all be gone, and in all these regions nothing will be alive." He felt a cruel satisfaction in the thought.

Then one night there seemed to be a relief; he slept better, did not tremble half-awake, and writhe so much, half-conscious. He had become so used to the quaking and writhing of his body, he hardly noticed it. But when for once it slept deep, he noticed that.

He woke in the morning to a curious whiteness. His window was muffled. It had snowed. He got up and opened his door, and shuddered. Ugh ! how cold ! All white, with a dark leaden sea, and black rocks curiously speckled with white. The foam was no longer pure. It seemed dirty. And the sea ate at the whiteness of the corpse-like land. Crumbles of snow were silting down the dead air.

On the ground the snow was a foot deep, white and smooth and soft, windless. He took a shovel to clear round his house and shed. The pallor of morning darkened. There was a strange rumbling of far-off thunder, in the frozen air, and through the newly-falling snow, a dim flash of lightning. Snow now fell steadily down, in the motionless obscurity.

He went out for a few minutes. But it was difficult. He stumbled and fell in the snow, which burned his face. Weak, faint, he toiled home. And when he recovered, took the trouble to make hot milk.

It snowed all the time. In the afternoon again there was a muffled rumbling of thunder, and flashes of lightning blinking reddish through the falling snow. Uneasy, he went to bed and lay staring fixedly at nothingness.

Morning seemed never to come. An eternity long he lay and waited for one alleviating pallor on the night. And at last it seemed the air was paler. His house was a cell faintly illuminated with white light. He realized the snow was walled outside his window. He got up, in the dead cold. When he opened his door, the motionless snow stopped him in a wall as high as his breast. Looking over the top of it, he felt the dead wind slowly driving, saw the snow-powder lift and travel like a funeral train. The blackish sea churned and champed, seeming to bite at the snow, impotent. The sky was grey, but luminous.

He began to work in a frenzy, to get at his boat. If he was to be shut in, it must be by his own choice, not by the mechanical power of the elements. He must get to the sea. He must be able to get at his boat.

But he was weak, and at times the snow overcame him. It fell on him, and he lay buried and lifeless. Yet every time, he struggled alive before it was too late, and fell upon the snow with the energy of fever. Exhausted, he would not give in. He crept indoors and made coffee and bacon. Long since he had cooked so much. Then he went at the snow once more. He must conquer the snow, this new, white brute force which had accumulated against him.

He worked in the awful, dead wind, pushing the snow aside, pressing it with his shovel. It was cold, freezing hard in the wind, even when the sun came out for a while, and showed him his white, lifeless surroundings, the black sea rolling sullen, flecked with dull spume, away to the horizons. Yet the sun had power on his face. It was March.

He reached the boat. He pushed the snow away, then sat down under the lee of the boat, looking at the sea, which nearly swirled to his feet, in the high tide. Curiously natural the pebbles looked, in a world gone all uncanny. The sun shone no more. Snow was falling in hard crumbs, that vanished as if by a miracle as they touched the hard blackness of the sea. Hoarse waves rang in the shingle, rushing up at the snow. The wet rocks were brutally black. And all the time the myriad swooping crumbs of snow, demonish, touched the dark sea and disappeared.

During the night there was a great storm. It seemed to him he could hear the vast mass of snow striking all the world with a ceaseless thud ; and over it all, the wind roared in strange hollow volleys, in between which came a jump of blindfold lightning, then the low roll of thunder heavier than the wind. When at last the dawn faintly discoloured the dark, the storm had more or less subsided, but a steady wind drove on. The snow was up to the top of his door.

Sullenly, he worked to dig himself out. And he managed through sheer persistency, to get out. He was in the tail of a great drift, many feet high. When he got through, the frozen snow was not more than two feet deep. But his island was gone. Its shape was all changed, great heaping white hills rose where no hills had been, inaccessible, and they fumed like volcanoes, but with snow powder. He was sickened and overcome.

His boat was in another, smaller drift. But he had not the strength to clear it. He looked at it helplessly. The shovel slipped from his hands, and he sank in the snow, to forget. In the snow itself, the sea resounded.

Something brought him to. He crept to his house. He was almost without feeling. Yet he managed to warm himself, just that part of him which leaned in snow-sleep over the coal fire. Then again, he made hot milk. After which, carefully, he built up the fire.

The wind dropped. Was it night again ? In the silence, it seemed he could hear the panther-like dropping of infinite snow. Thunder rumbled nearer, crackled quick after the bleared reddened lightning. He lay in bed in a kind of stupor. The elements ! The elements ! His mind repeated the word dumbly. You can't win against the elements.

How long it went on, he never knew. Once, like a wraith, he got out, and climbed to the top of a white hill on his unrecognizable island. The sun was hot. " It is summer," he said to himself, " and the time of leaves." He looked stupidly over the whiteness of his foreign island, over the waste of the lifeless sea. He pretended to imagine he saw the wink of a sail. Because he knew too well there would never again be a sail on that stark sea.

As he looked, the sky mysteriously darkened and chilled. From far off came the mutter of the unsatisfied thunder, and he knew it was the signal of the snow rolling over the sea. He turned, and felt its breath on him.

At seventy-two, Pauline Attenborough could still sometimes be mistaken, in the half-light, for thirty. She really was a wonderfully preserved woman, of perfect *chic*. Of course, it helps a great deal to have the right frame. She would be an exquisite skeleton, and her skull would be an exquisite skull, like that of some Etruscan woman, with feminine charm still in the swerve of the bone and the pretty naïve teeth.

Mrs. Attenborough's face was of the perfect oval, and slightly flat type that wears best. There is no flesh to sag. Her nose rode serenely, in its finely bridged curve. Only her big grey eyes were a tiny bit prominent on the surface of her face, and they gave her away most. The bluish lids were heavy, as if they ached sometimes with the strain of keeping the eyes beneath them arch and bright ; and at the corners of the eyes were fine little wrinkles which would slacken with haggardness, then be pulled up tense again, to that bright, gay look like a Leonardo woman who really could laugh outright.

Her niece Cecilia was perhaps the only person in the world who was aware of the invisible little wire which connected Pauline's eye-wrinkles with Pauline's will-power. Only Cecilia *consciously* watched the eyes go haggard and old and tired, and remain so, for hours ; until Robert came home. Then ping !—the mysterious little wire that worked between Pauline's will and her face went taut, the weary, haggard, prominent eyes suddenly began to gleam, the eyelids arched, the queer curved eyebrows which floated in such frail arches on Pauline's forehead began to gather a mocking significance, and you had the *real* lovely lady, in all her charm.

She really had the secret of everlasting youth ; that is to say, she could don her youth again like an eagle. But she was sparing of it. She was wise enough not to try being young for too many people. Her son Robert, in the evenings, and Sir Wilfred Knipe sometimes in the afternoon to tea : then occasional visitors on Sunday, when Robert was home : for these she was her lovely and changeless self, that age could not wither, nor custom stale : so bright and kindly and yet subtly mocking, like Mona Lisa who knew a thing or two. But Pauline knew more, so she needn't be smug at all, she could laugh that lovely mocking Bacchante laugh of hers, which was at the same time never malicious, always good-naturedly tolerant, both of virtues and vices. The former, of course, taking much more tolerating. So she suggested, roguishly.

Only with her niece Cecilia she did not trouble to keep up the glamour. Ciss was not very observant, anyhow : and more than that, she was plain : more still, she was in love with Robert : and most of all, she was thirty, and dependent on her Aunt Pauline. Oh, Cecilia ! Why make music for her !

Cecilia, called by her aunt and by her cousin Robert just Ciss, like a cat spitting, was a big dark-complexioned pug-faced young woman who very rarely spoke, and when she did, couldn't get it out. She was the daughter of a poor Congregational minister who had been, while he lived, brother to Ronald, Aunt Pauline's husband. Ronald and the Congregational minister were both well dead, and Aunt Pauline had had charge of Ciss for the last five years.

They lived all together in a quite exquisite though rather small Queen Anne house some twenty-five miles out of town, secluded in a little dale, and surrounded by small but very quaint and pleasant grounds. It was an ideal place and an ideal life for Aunt Pauline, at the age of seventy-two. When the kingfishers flashed up the little stream in the garden, going under the alders, something still flashed in her heart. She was that kind of woman.

Robert, who was two years older than Ciss, went every day to town, to his chambers in one of the Inns. He was a barrister, and, to his secret but very deep mortification, he earned about a hundred pounds a year. He simply *couldn't* get above that figure, though it was rather easy to get below it. Of course, it didn't matter. Pauline had money. But then what was Pauline's was Pauline's, and though she could give almost lavishly, still, one was always aware of having a *lovely* and *undeserved* present made to one : presents are so much nicer when they are undeserved, Aunt Pauline would say.

Robert too was plain, and almost speechless. He was medium-sized, rather broad and stout, though not fat. Only his creamy, clean-shaven face was rather fat, and sometimes suggestive of an Italian priest, in its silence and its secrecy. But he had grey eyes like his mother, but very shy and uneasy, not bold like hers. Perhaps Ciss was the only person who fathomed his awful shyness and *malaise*, his habitual feeling that he was in the wrong place : almost like a soul that has got into the wrong body. But he never did

anything about it. He went up to his chambers, and read law. It
was, however, all the weird old processes that interested him.   He
had, unknown to everybody but his mother, a quite extraordinary
collection of old Mexican legal documents, reports of processes and
trials, pleas, accusations, the weird and awful mixture of ecclesias-
tical law and common law in seventeenth-century Mexico. He had
started a study in this direction through coming across a report of
a trial of two English sailors, for murder, in Mexico in 1620, and
he had gone on, when the next document was an accusation against
a Don Miguel Estrada for seducing one of the nuns of the Sacred
Heart Convent in Oaxaca in 1680.

Pauline and her son Robert had wonderful evenings with these
old papers. The lovely lady knew a little Spanish. She even looked
a trifle Spanish herself, with a high comb and a marvellous dark
brown shawl embroidered in thick silvery silk embroidery. So she
would sit at the perfect old table, soft as velvet in its deep brown
surface, a high comb in her hair, ear-rings with dropping pendants
in her ears, her arms bare and still beautiful, a few strings of pearls
round her throat, a puce velvet dress on and this or another beautiful
shawl, and by candlelight she looked, yes, a Spanish high-bred beauty
of thirty-two or three. She set the candles to give her face just the
chiaroscuro she knew suited her ; her high chair that rose behind
her face was done in old green brocade, against which her face
emerged like a Christmas rose.

They were always three at table ; and they always drank a bottle
of champagne : Pauline two glasses, Ciss two glasses, Robert the rest.
The lovely lady sparkled and was radiant. Ciss, her black hair
bobbed, her broad shoulders in a very nice and becoming dress that
Aunt Pauline had helped her to make, stared from her aunt to her
cousin and back again, with rather confused, mute, hazel eyes, and
played the part of an audience suitably impressed. She *was* impressed, somewhere, all the time. And even rendered speechless by
Pauline's brilliancy, even after five years. But at the bottom of her
consciousness were the data of as weird a document as Robert ever
studied : all the things she knew about her aunt and cousin.

Robert was always a gentleman, with an old-fashioned punctilious
courtesy that covered his shyness quite completely. He was, and
Ciss knew it, more confused than shy. He was worse than she was.
Cecilia's own confusion dated from only five years back—Robert's
must have started before he was born. In the lovely lady's womb
he must have felt *very* confused.

He paid all his attention to his mother, drawn to her as a humble flower to the sun. And yet, priest-like, he was all the time aware, with the tail of his consciousness, that Ciss was there, and that she was a bit shut out of it, and that something wasn't right. He was aware of the third consciousness in the room. Whereas to Pauline, her niece Cecilia was an appropriate part of her own setting, rather than a distinct consciousness.

Robert took coffee with his mother and Ciss in the warm drawing-room, where all the furniture was so lovely, all collectors' pieces—Mrs. Attenborough had made her own money, dealing privately in pictures and furniture and rare things from barbaric countries—and the three talked desultorily till about eight or half-past. It was very pleasant, very cosy, very homely even : Pauline made a real home cosiness out of so much elegant material. The chat was simple, and nearly always bright. Pauline was her *real* self, emanating a friendly mockery and an odd, ironic gaiety. Till there came a little pause.

At which Ciss always rose and said good night and carried out the coffee tray, to prevent Burnett from intruding any more.

And then ! Oh, then, the lovely glowing intimacy of the evening, between mother and son, when they deciphered manuscripts and discussed points, Pauline with that eagerness of a girl, for which she was famous. And it was quite genuine. In some mysterious way she had *saved up* her power for being thrilled, in connection with a man. Robert, solid, rather quiet and subdued, seemed like the elder of the two : almost like a priest with a young girl pupil. And that was rather how he felt.

Ciss had a flat for herself just across the courtyard, over the old coachhouse and stables. There were no horses. Robert kept his car in the coachhouse. Ciss had three very nice rooms up there, stretching along in a row one after another, and she had got used to the ticking of the stable clock.

But sometimes she did not go up to her rooms. In the summer she would sit on the lawn, and from the open window of the drawing-room upstairs she would hear Pauline's wonderful heart-searching laugh. And in the winter the young woman would put on a thick coat and walk slowly to the little balustraded bridge over the stream, and then look back at the three lighted windows of that drawing-room where mother and son were so happy together.

Ciss loved Robert, and she believed that Pauline intended the two of them to marry : when she was dead. But poor Robert, he was so convulsed with shyness already, with man or woman. What would he be when his mother was dead—in a dozen more years ? He would be just a shell, the shell of a man who had never lived.

The strange unspoken sympathy of the young with one another, when they are overshadowed by the old, was one of the bonds between Robert and Ciss. But another bond, which Ciss did not know how to draw tight, was the bond of passion. Poor Robert was by nature a passionate man. His silence and his agonized, though hidden, shyness were both the result of a secret physical passionateness. And how Pauline could play on this ! Ah, Ciss was not blind to the eyes which he fixed on his mother, eyes fascinated yet humiliated, full of shame. He was ashamed that he was not a man. And he did not love his mother. He was fascinated by her. Completely fascinated. And for the rest, paralysed in a life-long confusion.

Ciss stayed in the garden till the lights leapt up in Pauline's bedroom—about ten o'clock. The lovely lady had retired. Robert would now stay another hour or so, alone. Then he too would retire. Ciss, in the dark outside, sometimes wished she could creep up to him and say : " Oh, Robert ! It's all wrong ! " But Aunt Pauline would hear. And anyhow, Ciss couldn't do it. She went off to her own rooms, once more, and so for ever.

In the morning coffee was brought up on a tray to each of the three relatives. Ciss had to be at Sir Wilfred Knipe's at nine o'clock, to give two hours' lessons to his little granddaughter. It was her sole serious occupation, except that she played the piano for the love of it. Robert set off to town about nine. And, as a rule, Aunt Pauline appeared to lunch, though sometimes not until tea-time. When she appeared, she looked fresh and young. But she was inclined to fade rather quickly, like a flower without water, in the day-time. Her hour was the candle hour.

So she always rested in the afternoon. When the sun shone, if possible she took a sun bath. This was one of her secrets. Her lunch was very light, she could take her sun-and-air-bath before noon or after, as it pleased her. Often it was in the afternoon, when the sun shone very warmly into a queer little yew-walled square just behind the stables. Here Ciss stretched out the lying-chair and rugs, and put the light parasol handy in the silent little enclosure of thick dark yew-hedges beyond the red walls of the unused stables. And hither came the lovely lady with her book. Ciss then had to be on guard in one of her own rooms, should her aunt, who was very keen-eared, hear a footstep.

One afternoon it occurred to Cecilia that she herself might while away this rather long afternoon by taking a sun bath. She was growing restive. The thought of the flat roof of the stable buildings, to which she could climb from a loft at the end, started her on a new adventure. She often went on to the roof : she had to, to wind up the stable clock, which was a job she had assumed to herself. Now she took a rug, climbed out under the heavens, looked at the sky and the great elm-tops, looked at the sun, then took off her things and lay down perfectly serenely, in a corner of the roof under the parapet, full in the sun.

It was rather lovely, to bask all one's length like this in warm sun and air. Yes, it was very lovely ! It even seemed to melt some of the hard bitterness of her heart, some of that core of unspoken resentment which never dissolved. Luxuriously, she spread herself, so that the sun should touch her limbs fully, fully. If she had no other lover, she should have the sun ! She rolled voluptuously. And suddenly, her heart stood still in her body, and her hair almost rose on end as a voice said very softly, musingly in her ear :

" No, Henry dear ! It was not my fault you died instead of marrying that Claudia. No, darling. I was quite, quite willing for you to marry her, unsuitable though she was."

Cecilia sank down on her rug powerless and perspiring with dread. That awful voice, so soft, so musing, yet so unatural. Not a human voice at all. Yet there must, there must be someone on the roof ! Oh ! how unspeakably awful !

She lifted her weak head and peeped across the sloping leads. Nobody ! The chimneys were far too narrow to shelter anybody. There was nobody on the roof. Then it must be someone in the trees, in the elms. Either that, or terror unspeakable, a bodiless voice ! She reared her head a little higher.

And as she did so, came the voice again :

" No, darling ! I told you you would tire of her in six months. And you see, it was true, dear. It was true, true, true ! I wanted to spare you that. So it wasn't I who made you feel weak and disabled, wanting that very silly Claudia ; poor thing, she looked so woebegone afterwards ! Wanting her and not wanting her, you got *yourself* into that perplexity, my dear. I only warned you. What else could I do ? And you lost your spirit and died without ever knowing me again. It was bitter, bitter——"

The voice faded away. Cecilia subsided weakly on to her rug, after the anguished tension of listening. Oh, it was awful. The sun shone, the sky was blue, all seemed so lovely and afternoony and summery. And yet, oh, horror !—she was going to be forced to believe in the supernatural ! And she loathed the supernatural, ghosts and voices and rappings and all the rest.

But that awful creepy bodiless voice, with its rusty sort of whisper of an overtone ! It had something so fearfully familiar in it too ! and yet was so utterly uncanny. Poor Cecilia could only lie there unclothed, and so all the more agonizingly helpless, inert, collapsed in sheer dread.

And then she heard the thing sigh ! A deep sigh that seemed weirdly familiar, yet was not human. " Ah, well ; ah, well, the heart must bleed ! Better it should bleed than break. It is grief, grief ! But it wasn't my fault, dear. And Robert could marry our poor dull Ciss to-morrow, if he wanted her. But he doesn't care about it, so why force him into anything ! " The sounds were very uneven, sometimes only a husky sort of whisper. Listen ! Listen !

Cecilia was about to give vent to loud and piercing screams of hysteria, when the last two sentences arrested her. All her caution and her cunning sprang alert. It was Aunt Pauline ! It must be Aunt Pauline, practising ventriloquism or something like that ! What a devil she was !

Where was she ? She must be lying down there, right below where Cecilia herself was lying. And it was either some fiend's trick of ventriloquism, or else thought transference that conveyed itself like sound. The sounds were very uneven. Sometimes quite inaudible, sometimes only a brushing sort of noise. Ciss listened intently. No, it could not be ventriloquism. It was worse, some form of thought transference. Some horror of that sort. Cecilia still lay weak and inert, terrified to move, but she was growing calmer with suspicion. It was some diabolic trick of that unnatural woman.

But *what a devil* of a woman ! She even knew that she, Cecilia, had mentally accused her of killing her son Henry. Poor Henry was Robert's elder brother, twelve years older than Robert. He had died suddenly when he was twenty-two, after an awful struggle with himself, because he was passionately in love with a young and very good-looking actress, and his mother had humorously despised him for the attachment. So he had caught some sudden ordinary disease, but the poison had gone to his brain and killed him, before he ever regained consciousness. Ciss knew the few facts from her own father. And lately, she had been thinking that Pauline was going to kill Robert as she had killed Henry. It was clear murder : a mother murdering her sensitive sons, who were fascinated by her : the Circe !

" I suppose I may as well get up," murmured the dim unbreaking voice. " Too much sun is as bad as too little. Enough sun, enough love thrill, enough proper food, and not too much of any of them, and a woman might live for ever. I verily believe for ever. If she absorbs as much vitality as she expends! Or perhaps a trifle more!"

It was certainly Aunt Pauline! How, how horrible! She, Ciss, was hearing Aunt Pauline's thoughts. Oh, how ghastly! Aunt Pauline was sending out her thoughts in a sort of radio, and she, Ciss, had to *hear* what her aunt was thinking. How ghastly! How insufferable! One of them would surely have to die.

She twisted and she lay inert and crumpled, staring vacantly in front of her. Vacantly! Vacantly! And her eyes were staring almost into a hole. She was staring into it unseeing, a hole going down in the corner from the lead gutter. It meant nothing to her. Only it frightened her a little more.

When suddenly out of the hole came a sigh and a last whisper. "Ah, well! Pauline! Get up, it's enough for to-day!" Good God! Out of the hole of the rain-pipe! The rain-pipe was acting as a speaking-tube! Impossible! No, quite possible. She had read of it even in some book. And Aunt Pauline, like the old and guilty woman she was, talked aloud to herself. That was it!

A sullen exultance sprang into Ciss's breast. *That* was why she would never have anybody, not even Robert, in her bedroom. That was why she never dozed in a chair, never sat absent-minded anywhere, but went to her room, and kept to her room, except when she roused herself to be alert. When she slackened off, she talked to herself! She talked in a soft little crazy voice, to herself. But she was not crazy. It was only her thoughts murmuring themselves aloud.

So she had qualms about poor Henry! Well she might have! Ciss believed that Aunt Pauline had loved her big, handsome, brilliant first-born much more than she loved Robert, and that his death had been a terrible blow and a chagrin to her. Poor Robert had been only ten years old when Henry died. Since then he had been the substitute.

Ah, how awful!

But Aunt Pauline was a strange woman. She had left her husband when Henry was a small child, some years even before Robert was born. There was no quarrel. Sometimes she saw her husband again, quite amicably, but a little mockingly. And she even gave him money.

For Pauline earned all her own. Her father had been a Consul in the East and in Naples: and a devoted collector of beautiful and exotic things. When he died, soon after his grandson Henry was born, he left his collection of treasures to his daughter. And Pauline, who had really a passion and a genius for loveliness, whether in texture or form or colour, had laid the basis of her fortune on her father's collection. She had gone on collecting, buying where she could, and selling to collectors and to museums. She was one of the first to sell old, weird African wooden figures to the museums, and ivory carvings from New Guinea. She bought Renoir as soon as she saw his pictures. But not Rousseau. And all by herself, she made a fortune.

After her husband died, she had not married again. She was not even *known* to have had lovers. If she did have lovers, it was not among the men who admired her most and paid her devout and open attendance. To these she was a " friend."

Cecilia slipped on her clothes and caught up her rug, hastened carefully down the ladder to the loft. As she descended she heard the ringing musical call : " All right, Ciss ! " which meant that the lovely lady was finished, and returning to the house. Even her voice was marvellously young and sonorous, beautifully balanced and self-possessed. So different from the little voice in which she talked to herself. *That* was much more the voice of an old woman.

Ciss hastened round to the yew enclosure, where lay the comfortable chaise-longue with the various delicate rugs. Everything Pauline had was choice, to the fine straw mat on the floor. The great yew walls were beginning to cast long shadows. Only in the corner, where the rugs tumbled their delicate colours, was there hot, still sunshine.

The rugs folded up, the chair lifted away, Cecilia stooped to look at the mouth of the rain-pipe. There it was, in the corner, under a little hood of masonry and just projecting from the thick leaves of the creeper on the wall. If Pauline, lying there, turned her face towards the wall, she would speak into the very mouth of the hole. Cecilia was reassured. She had heard her aunt's thoughts indeed, but by no uncanny agency.

That evening, as if aware of something, Pauline was a little quicker than usual, though she looked her own serene, rather mysterious self. And after coffee she said to Robert and Ciss : " I'm so sleepy. The sun has made me so sleepy. I feel full of sunshine like a bee. I shall go to bed, if you don't mind. You two sit and have a talk."

Cecilia looked quickly at her cousin.

" Perhaps you would rather be alone," she said to him.

"No, no," he replied. "Do keep me company for a while, if it doesn't bore you."

The windows were open, the scent of the honeysuckle wafted in, with the sound of an owl. Robert smoked in silence. There was a sort of despair in the motionless, rather squat body. He looked like a caryatid bearing a weight.

"Do you remember Cousin Henry?" Cecilia asked him suddenly. He looked up in surprise.

"Yes, very well," he said.

"What did he look like?" she said, glancing into her cousin's big secret-troubled eyes, in which there was so much frustration.

"Oh, he was handsome: tall and fresh-coloured, with mother's soft brown hair." As a matter of fact, Pauline's hair was grey. "The ladies admired him very much; he was at all the dances."

"And what kind of character had he?"

"Oh, very good-natured and jolly. He liked to be amused. He was rather quick and clever, like mother, and very good company."

"And did he love your mother?"

"Very much. She loved him too—better than she does me, as a matter of fact. He was so much more nearly her idea of a man."

"Why was he more her idea of a man?"

"Tall—handsome—attractive, and very good company—and would, I believe, have been very successful at law. I'm afraid I am merely negative in all those respects."

Ciss looked at him attentively, with her slow-thinking hazel eyes. Under his impassive mask, she knew he suffered.

"Do you think you are so much more negative than he?" she said.

He did not lift his face. But after a few moments he replied:

"My life, certainly, is a negative affair."

She hesitated before she dared ask him:

"And do you mind?"

He did not answer her at all. Her heart sank.

"You see, I am afraid my life is as negative as yours is," she said. "And I'm beginning to mind bitterly. I'm thirty."

She saw his creamy, well-bred hand tremble.

"I suppose," he said, without looking at her, "'one will rebel when it is too late.'"

That was queer, from him.

"Robert," she said, "do you like me at all?"

She saw his dusky, creamy face, so changeless in its folds, go pale.

"I am very fond of you," he murmured.

" Won't you kiss me ? Nobody ever kisses me," she said pathetically.

He looked at her, his eyes strange with fear and a certain haughtiness. Then he rose and came softly over to her, and kissed her
gently on the cheek.

" It's an awful shame, Ciss ! " he said softly.

She caught his hand and pressed it to her breast.

" And sit with me sometime in the garden," she said, murmuring
with difficulty. " Won't you ? "

He looked at her anxiously and searchingly.

" What about mother ? " he said.

Ciss smiled a funny little smile, and looked into his eyes. He
suddenly flushed crimson, turning aside his face. It was a painful
sight.

" I know," he said, " I am no lover of women."

He spoke with sarcastic stoicism against himself, but even she
did not know the shame it was to him.

" You never try to be ! " she said.

Again his eyes changed uncannily.

" Does one have to try ? " he said.

" Why, yes ! One never does anything if one doesn't try."

He went pale again.

" Perhaps you are right," he said.

In a few minutes she left him, and went to her rooms. At least,
she had tried to take off the everlasting lid from things.

The weather continued sunny, Pauline continued her sun-baths,
and Ciss lay on the roof eavesdropping in the literal sense of the word.
But Pauline was not to be heard. No sound came up the pipe.
She must be lying with her face away into the open. Ciss listened
with all her might. She could just detect the faintest, faintest murmur away below, but no audible syllable.

And at night, under the stars, Cecilia sat and waited in silence,
on the seat which kept in view the drawing-room windows and the
side-door into the garden. She saw the light go up in her aunt's
room. She saw the lights at last go out in the drawing-room. And
she waited. But he did not come. She stayed on in the darkness
half the night, while the owl hooted. But she stayed alone.

Two days she heard nothing, her aunt's thoughts were not
revealed and at evening nothing happened. Then the second night,
as she sat with heavy, helpless persistence in the garden, suddenly
she started. He had come out. She rose and went softly over the
grass to him.

" Don't speak," he murmured.

And in silence, in the dark, they walked down the garden and over the little bridge to the paddock, where the hay, cut very late, was in cock. There they stood disconsolate under the stars.

" You see," he said, " how can I ask for love, if I don't feel any love in myself. You know I have a real regard for you——"

" How can you feel any love, when you never feel anything ? " she said.

" That is true," he replied.

And she waited for what next.

" And how can I marry ? " he said. " I am a failure even at making money. I can't ask my mother for money."

She sighed deeply.

" Then don't bother yet about marrying," she said. " Only love me a little. Won't you ? "

He gave a short laugh.

" It sounds so atrocious, to say it is hard to begin," he said.

She sighed again. He was so stiff to move.

" Shall we sit down a minute," she said. And then as they sat on the hay, she added : " May I touch you ? Do you mind ? "

" Yes, I mind ! But do as you wish," he replied, with that mixture of shyness and queer candour which made him a little ridiculous, as he knew quite well. But in his heart there was almost murder.

She touched his black, always tidy hair with her fingers.

" I suppose I shall rebel one day," he said again, suddenly.

They sat some time, till it grew chilly. And he held her hand fast, but he never put his arms round her. At last she rose and went indoors, saying good night.

The next day, as Cecilia lay stunned and angry on the roof, taking her sun-bath, and becoming hot and fierce with sunshine, suddenly she started. A terror seized her in spite of herself. It was the voice.

" *Caro, caro, tu non l'hai visto !* " it was murmuring away, in a language Cecilia did not understand. She lay and writhed her limbs in the sun, listening intently to words she could not follow. Softly, whisperingly, with infinite caressiveness and yet with that subtle, insidious arrogance under its velvet, came the voice, murmuring in Italian : " *Bravo, si molto bravo, poverino, ma uomo come te non lo sara mai, mai, mai !* " Oh, especially in Italian Cecilia heard the poisonous charm of the voice, so caressive, so soft and flexible, yet so utterly egoistic. She hated it with intensity as it sighed and whispered out of nowhere. Why, why should it be so delicate, so subtle and flexible and beautifully controlled, while she herself was so clumsy ! Oh, poor Cecilia, she writhed in the afternoon sun, knowing her own clownish clumsiness and lack of suavity, in comparison.

" No, Robert dear, you will never be the man your father was, though you have some of his looks. He was a marvellous lover, soft as a flower yet piercing as a humming-bird. No, Robert dear, you will never know how to serve a woman as Monsignor Mauro did. *Cara, cara mia bellissima, ti ho aspettato come l'agonizzante aspetta la morte, morte deliziosa, quasi quasi troppo deliziosa per un' anima humana*—Soft as a flower, yet probing like a humming-bird. He gave himself to a woman as he gave himself to God. Mauro ! Mauro ! How you loved me ! "

The voice ceased in reverie, and Cecilia knew what she had guessed before, that Robert was not the son of her Uncle Ronald, but of some Italian.

" I am disappointed in you, Robert. There is no poignancy in you. Your father was a Jesuit, but he was the most perfect and poignant lover in the world. You are a Jesuit like a fish in a tank. And that Ciss of yours is the cat fishing for you. It is less edifying even than poor Henry."

Cecilia suddenly bent her mouth down to the tube, and said in a deep voice :

" Leave Robert alone ! Don't kill him as well."

There was a dead silence, in the hot July afternoon that was lowering for thunder. Cecilia lay prostrate, her heart beating in great thumps. She was listening as if her whole soul were an ear. At last she caught the whisper :

" Did someone speak ? "

She leaned again to the mouth of the tube.

" Don't kill Robert as you killed me," she said with slow enunciation, and a deep but small voice.

" Ah ! " came the sharp little cry. " Who is that speaking ? "

" Henry ! " said the deep voice.

There was a dead silence. Poor Cecilia lay with all the use gone out of her. And there was dead silence. Till at last came the whisper :

" I didn't kill Henry. No, NO ! Henry, surely you can't blame me ! I loved you, dearest. I only wanted to help you."

" You killed me ! " came the deep, artificial, accusing voice. " Now, let Robert live. Let him go ! Let him marry ! "

There was a pause.

" How very, very awful ! " mused the whispering voice. " Is it possible, Henry, you are a spirit, and you condemn me ? "

" Yes ! I condemn you ! "

Cecilia felt all her pent-up rage going down that rain-pipe. At the same time, she almost laughed. It was awful.

She lay and listened and listened. No sound ! As if time had ceased, she lay inert in the weakening sun. The sky was yellowing. Quickly she dressed herself, went down, and out to the corner of the stables.

" Aunt Pauline ! " she called discreetly. " Did you hear thunder ? "

" Yes ! I am going in. Don't wait," came a feeble voice.

Cecilia retired, and from the loft watched, spying, as the figure of the lovely lady, wrapped in a lovely wrap of old blue silk, went rather totteringly to the house.

The sky gradually darkened, Cecilia hastened in with the rugs. Then the storm broke. Aunt Pauline did not appear to tea. She found the thunder trying. Robert also did not arrive till after tea, in the pouring rain. Cecilia went down the covered passage to her own house, and dressed carefully for dinner, putting some white columbines at her breast.

The drawing-room was lit with a softly-shaded lamp. Robert, dressed, was waiting, listening to the rain. He too seemed strangely crackling and on edge. Cecilia came in, with the white flowers nodding at her breast. Robert was watching her curiously, a new look on his face. Cecilia went to the bookshelves near the door, and was peering for something, listening acutely. She heard a rustle, then the door softly opening. And as it opened, Ciss suddenly switched on the strong electric light by the door.

Her aunt, in a dress of black lace over ivory colour, stood in the doorway. Her face was made up, but haggard with a look of unspeakable irritability, as if years of suppressed exasperation and dislike of her fellow-men had suddenly crumpled her into an old witch.

" Oh, aunt ! " cried Cecilia.

" Why, mother, you're a little old lady ! " came the astounded voice of Robert : like an astonished boy : as if it were a joke.

" Have you only just found it out ? " snapped the old woman venomously.

" Yes ! Why, I thought——" his voice tailed out in misgiving.

The haggard, old Pauline, in a frenzy of exasperation, said :

" Aren't we going down ? "

She had never even noticed the excess of light, a thing she shunned. And she went downstairs almost tottering.

At table she sat with her face like a crumpled mask of unspeakable irritability. She looked old, very old, and like a witch. Robert and Cecilia fetched furtive glances at her. And Ciss, watching Robert, saw that he was so astonished and repelled by his mother's looks, that he was another man.

" What kind of a drive home did you have ? " snapped Pauline, with an almost gibbering irritability.

" It rained, of course," he said.

" How clever of you to have found that out ! " said his mother, with the grisly grin of malice that had succeeded her arch smirk.

" I don't understand," he said with quiet suavity.

" It's apparent," said his mother, rapidly and sloppily eating her food.

She rushed through the meal like a crazy dog, to the utter consternation of the servant. And the moment it was over, she darted in a queer, crab-like way upstairs. Robert and Cecilia followed her, thunderstruck, like two conspirators.

" You pour the coffee. I loathe it ! I'm going ! Good night ! " said the old woman, in a succession of sharp shots. And she scrambled out of the room.

There was a dead silence. At last he said :

" I'm afraid mother isn't well. I must persuade her to see a doctor."

" Yes ! " said Cecilia.

The evening passed in silence. Robert and Ciss stayed on in the drawing-room, having lit a fire. Outside was cold rain. Each pretended to read. They did not want to separate. The evening passed with ominous mysteriousness, yet quickly.

At about ten o'clock, the door suddenly opened, and Pauline appeared, in a blue wrap. She shut the door behind her, and came to the fire. Then she looked at the two young people in hate, real hate.

" You two had better get married quickly," she said in an ugly voice. " It would look more decent ; such a passionate pair of lovers ! "

Robert looked up at her quietly.

" I thought you believed that cousins should not marry, mother," he said.

" I do ! But you're not cousins. Your father was an Italian priest." Pauline held her daintily-slippered foot to the fire, in an old coquettish gesture. Her body tried to repeat all the old graceful gestures. But the nerve had snapped, so it was a rather dreadful caricature.

" Is that really true, mother ? " he asked.

" True ! What do you think ? He was a distinguished man, or he wouldn't have been my lover. He was far too distinguished a man to have had you for a son. But that joy fell to me."

" How unfortunate all round," he said slowly.

" Unfortunate for you ? *You* were lucky. It was *my* misfortune," she said acidly to him.

She was really a dreadful sight, like a piece of lovely Venetian glass that has been dropped, and gathered up again in horrible, sharp-edged fragments.

Suddenly she left the room again.

For a week it went on. She did not recover. It was as if every nerve in her body had suddenly started screaming in an insanity of discordance. The doctor came, and gave her sedatives, for she never slept. Without drugs, she never slept at all, only paced back and forth in her room, looking hideous and evil, reeking with male-volence. She could not bear to see either her son or her niece. Only when either of them came, she asked in pure malice :

" Well ! When's the wedding ! Have you celebrated the nup-tials yet ? "

At first Cecilia was stunned by what she had done. She realized vaguely that her aunt, once a definite thrust of condemnation had penetrated her beautiful armour, had just collapsed squirming inside her shell. It was too terrible. Ciss was almost terrified into repen-tance. Then she thought : This is what she always was. Now let her live the rest of her days in her true colours.

But Pauline would not live long. She was literally shrivelling away. She kept her room, and saw no one. She had her mirrors taken away.

Robert and Cecilia sat a good deal together. The jeering of the mad Pauline had not driven them apart, as she had hoped. But Cecilia dared not confess to him what she had done.

" Do you think your mother ever loved anybody ? " Ciss asked him tentatively, rather wistfully, one evening.

He looked at her fixedly.

" Herself ! " he said at last.

" She didn't even *love* herself," said Ciss. " It was something else—what was it ? " She lifted a troubled, utterly puzzled face to him.

" Power ! " he said curtly.

" But what power ? " she asked.   " I don't understand."

" Power to feed on other lives," he said bitterly.   " She was beautiful, and she fed on life.   She has fed on me as she fed on Henry.   She put a sucker into one's soul, and sucked up one's essential life."

" And don't you forgive her ? "

" No."

" Poor Aunt Pauline ! "

But even Ciss did not mean it.   She was only aghast.

" I *know* I've got a heart," he said, passionately striking his breast. " But it's almost sucked dry.   I *know* people who want power over others."

Ciss was silent ;   what was there to say ?

And two days later, Pauline was found dead in her bed, having taken too much veronal, for her heart was weakened.   From the grave even she hit back at her son and her niece.   She left Robert the noble sum of one thousand pounds ;   and Ciss one hundred. All the rest, with the nucleus of her valuable antiques, went to form the " Pauline Attenborough Museum."

RAWDON was the sort of man who said, privately, to his men friends, over a glass of wine after dinner : " No woman shall sleep again under my roof ! "

He said it with pride, rather vaunting, pursing his lips. " Even my housekeeper goes home to sleep."

But the housekeeper was a gentle old thing of about sixty, so it seemed a little fantastic. Moreover the man had a wife, of whom he was secretly rather proud, as a piece of fine property, and with whom he kept up a very witty correspondence, epistolary, and whom he treated with humorous gallantry when they occasionally met for half an hour. Also he had a love affair going on. At least, if it wasn't a love affair, what was it ? However !

" No, I've come to the determination that no woman shall ever sleep under my roof again—not even a female cat ! "

One looked at the roof, and wondered what it had done amiss. Besides, it wasn't his roof. He only rented the house. What does a man mean, anyhow, when he says " my roof " ? *My* roof ! The only roof I am conscious of having, myself, is the top of my head. However, he hardly can have meant that no woman should sleep under the elegant dome of his skull. Though there's no telling. You see the top of a sleek head through a window, and you say, " By Jove, what a pretty girl's head ! " And after all, when the individual comes out, it's in trousers.

The point, however, is that Rawdon said so emphatically—no, not emphatically, succinctly : " No woman shall ever again sleep under my roof." It was a case of futurity. No doubt he had had his ceilings whitewashed, and their memories put out. Or rather, repainted, for it was a handsome wooden ceiling. Anyhow, if ceilings have eyes, as walls have ears, then Rawdon had given his ceilings a new outlook, with a new coat of paint, and all memory of any woman's having slept under them—for after all, in decent circumstances we sleep under ceilings, not under roofs—was wiped out for ever.

" And will you neither sleep under any woman's roof ? "

That pulled him up rather short. He was not prepared to sauce his gander as he had sauced his goose. Even I could see the thought flitting through his mind, that some of his pleasantest holidays depended on the charm of his hostess. Even some of the nicest hotels were run by women.

" Ah ! Well ! That's not quite the same thing, you know. When one leaves one's own house one gives up the keys of circumstance, so to speak. But, as far as possible, I make it a rule not to sleep under a roof that is openly, and obviously, and obtrusively a woman's roof ! "

" Quite ! " said I with a shudder. " So do I ! "

Now I understood his mysterious love affair less than ever. He was never known to speak of this love affair : he did not even write about it to his wife. The lady—for she was a lady—lived only five minutes' walk from Rawdon. She had a husband, but he was in diplomatic service or something like that, which kept him occupied in the sufficiently-far distance. Yes, far enough. And, as a husband, he was a complete diplomat. A balance of power. If he was entitled to occupy the wide field of the world, she, the other and contrasting power, might concentrate and consolidate her position at home.

She was a charming woman, too, and even a beautiful woman. She had two charming children, long-legged, stalky, clove-pink-half-opened sort of children. But really charming. And she was a woman with a certain mystery. She never talked. She never said anything about herself. Perhaps she suffered ; perhaps she was frightfully happy, and made *that* her cause for silence. Perhaps she was wise enough even to be beautifully silent about her happiness. Certainly she never mentioned her sufferings, or even her trials : and certainly she must have a fair handful of the latter, for Alec Drummond sometimes fled home in the teeth of a gale of debts. He simply got through his own money and through hers, and, third and fatal stride, through other people's as well. Then something had to be done about it. And Janet, dear soul, had to put her hat on and take journeys. But she never said anything of it. At least, she did just hint that Alec didn't *quite* make enough money to meet expenses. But after all, we don't go about with our eyes shut, and Alec Drummond, whatever else he did, didn't hide his prowess under a bushel.

Rawdon and he were quite friendly, but really ! None of them ever talked. Drummond didn't talk, he just went off and behaved in his own way. And though Rawdon would chat away till the small hours, *he* never "talked." Not to his nearest male friend did he ever mention Janet save as a very pleasant woman and his neighbour : he admitted he adored her children. They often came to see him.

And one felt about Rawdon, he was making a mystery of something. And that was rather irritating. He went every day to see Janet, and of course we saw him going : going or coming. How can one help but see ? But he always went in the morning, at about eleven, and did not stay for lunch : or he went in the afternoon, and came home to dinner. Apparently he was never there in the evening. Poor Janet, she lived like a widow.

Very well, if Rawdon wanted to make it so blatantly obvious that it was only platonic, purely platonic, why wasn't he natural ? Why didn't he say simply : " I'm very fond of Janet Drummond, she is my very dear friend ? " Why did he sort of curl up at the very mention of her name, and curdle into silence : or else say rather forcedly : " Yes, she is a charming woman. I see a good deal of her, but chiefly for the children's sake. I'm devoted to the children ! " Then he would look at one in such a curious way, as if he were hiding something. And after all, what was there to hide ? If he was the woman's friend, why not ? It could be a charming friendship. And if he were her lover, why, heaven bless me, he ought to have been proud of it, and showed just a glint, just an honest man's glint.

But no, never a glint of pride or pleasure in the relation either way. Instead of that, this rather theatrical reserve. Janet, it is true, was just as reserved. If she could, she avoided mentioning his name. Yet one knew, sure as houses, she felt something. One suspected her of being more in love with Rawdon than ever she had been with Alec. And one felt that there was a hush put upon it all. She had had a hush put upon her. By whom ? By both the men ? Or by Rawdon only ? Or by Drummond ? Was it for her husband's sake ? Impossible ! For her children's ? But why ! Her children were devoted to Rawdon.

It now had become the custom for them to go to him three times a week, for music. I don't mean he taught them the piano. Rawdon was a very refined musical amateur. He had them sing, in their delicate girlish voices, delicate little songs, and really he succeeded wonderfully with them ; he made them so true, which children rarely are, musically, and so pure and effortless, like little flamelets of sound. It really was rather beautiful, and sweet of him. And he taught them *music*, the delicacy of the feel of it. They had a regular teacher for the practice.

Even the little girls, in their young little ways, were in love with Rawdon! So if their mother were in love too, in her ripened womanhood, why not?

Poor Janet! She was so still, and so elusive: the hush upon her! She was·rather like a half-opened rose that somebody had tied a string round, so that it couldn't open any more. But why? Why? In her there was a real touch of mystery. One could never *ask* her, because one knew her heart was too keenly involved: or her pride.

Whereas there was, really, no mystery about Rawdon, refined and handsome and subtle as he was. He *had* no mystery: at least, to a man. What *he* wrapped himself up in was a certain amount of mystification.

Who wouldn't be irritated to hear a fellow saying, when for months and months he has been paying a daily visit to a lonely and very attractive woman—nay, lately even a twice-daily visit, even if always before sundown—to hear him say, pursing his lips after a sip of his own very moderate port: " I've taken a vow that no woman shall sleep under my roof again! "

I almost snapped out: " Oh, what the hell! And what about your Janet? " But I remembered in time, it was not *my* affair, and if he wanted to have his mystifications, let him have them.

If he meant he wouldn't have his wife sleep under his roof again, that one could understand. They were really very witty with one another, he and she, but fatally and damnably married.

Yet neither wanted a divorce. And neither put the slightest claim to any control over the other's behaviour. He said: " Women live on the moon, men on the earth." And she said: " I don't mind in the least if he loves Janet Drummond, poor thing. It would be a change for him, from loving himself. And a change for her, if somebody loved her—— "

Poor Janet! But he wouldn't have her sleep under his roof, no, not for any money. And apparently he never slept under hers—if she could be said to have one. So what the deuce?

Of course, if they were friends, just friends, all right! But then in that case, why start talking about not having a woman sleep under your roof? Pure mystification!

The cat never came out of the bag. But one evening I distinctly heard it mewing inside its sack, and I even believe I saw a claw through the canvas.

It was in November—everything much as usual—myself pricking my ears to hear if the rain had stopped, and I could go home, because I was just a little bored about "cornemuse" music. I had been having dinner with Rawdon, and listening to him ever since on his favourite topic : not, of course, women, and why they shouldn't sleep under his roof, but fourteenth-century melody and windbag accompaniment.

It was not late—not yet ten o'clock—but I was restless, and wanted to go home. There was no longer any sound of rain. And Rawdon was perhaps going to make a pause in his monologue.

Suddenly there was a tap at the door, and Rawdon's man, Hawken, edged in. Rawdon, who had been a major in some fantastic capacity during the war, had brought Hawken back with him. This fresh-faced man of about thirty-five appeared in the doorway with an intensely blank and bewildered look on his face. He was really an extraordinarily good actor.

"A lady, sir ! " he said, with a look of utter blankness.

"A what ? " snapped Rawdon.

"A lady ! "—then with a most discreet drop in his voice : " Mrs. Drummond, sir ! " He looked modestly down at his feet.

Rawdon went deathly white, and his lips quivered.

"Mrs. Drummond ! Where ? "

Hawken lifted his eyes to his master in a fleeting glance.

"I showed her into the dining-room, there being no fire in the drawing-room."

Rawdon got to his feet, and took two or three agitated strides. He could not make up his mind. At last he said, his lips working with agitation :

"Bring her in here."

Then he turned with a theatrical gesture to me.

"What this is all about, I *don't* know," he said.

"Let me clear out," said I, making for the door.

He caught me by the arm :

"No, for God's sake ! For God's sake, stop and see me through ! "

He gripped my arm till it really hurt, and his eyes were quite wild. I did not know my Olympic Rawdon.

Hastily I backed away to the side of the fire—we were in Rawdon's room, where the books and piano were—and Mrs. Drummond appeared in the doorway. She was much paler than usual, being a rather warm-coloured woman, and she glanced at me with big reproachful eyes, as much as to say : You intruder ! You interloper ! For my part, I could do nothing but stare. She wore a black wrap, which I knew quite well, over her black dinner-dress.

"Rawdon ! " she said, turning to him, and blotting out my

existence from her consciousness. Hawken softly closed the door, and I could *feel* him standing on the threshold outside, listening keen as a hawk.

"Sit down, Janet," said Rawdon, with a grimace of a sour smile, which he could not get rid of once he had started it, so that his face looked very odd indeed, like a mask which he was unable either to fit on or take off. He had several conflicting expressions all at once, and they had all stuck.

She let her wrap slip back on her shoulders, and knitted her white fingers again her skirt, pressing down her arms, and gazing at him with a terrible gaze. I began to creep to the door.

Rawdon started after me.

"No, don't go! Don't go! I specially want you not to go," he said in extreme agitation.

I looked at her. She was looking at him with a heavy, sombre kind of stare. Me she absolutely ignored. Not for a second could she forgive me for existing on the earth. I slunk back to my post behind the leather arm-chair, as if hiding.

"Do sit down, Janet," he said to her again. "And have a smoke. What will you drink?"

"No, thanks!" she said, as if it were one word slurred out. "No thanks."

And she proceeded again to fix him with that heavy, portentous stare.

He offered her a cigarette, his hand trembling as he held out the silver box.

"Nothanks!" she slurred out again, not even looking at the box, but keeping him fixed with that dark and heavy stare.

He turned away, making a great delay lighting a cigarette, with his back to her, to get out of the stream of that stare. He carefully went for an ash-tray, and put it carefully within reach—all the time trying not to be swept away on that stare. And she stood with her fingers locked, her straight, plump, handsome arms pressed downwards against her skirt, and she gazed at him.

He leaned his elbow on the mantelpiece abstractedly for a moment —then he started suddenly, and rang the bell. She turned her eyes from him for a moment, to watch his middle finger pressing the bell-button. Then there was a tension of waiting, an interruption in the previous tension. We waited. Nobody came. Rawdon rang again.

"That's very curious!" he murmured to himself. Hawken was usually so prompt. Hawken, not being a woman, slept under the roof, so there was no excuse for his not answering the bell. The tension in the room had now changed quality, owing to this new suspense. Poor Janet's sombre stare became gradually loosened, so to speak. Attention was divided. Where was Hawken? Rawdon rang the bell a third time, a long peal. And now Janet was no longer the centre of suspense. Where was Hawken? The question loomed large over every other.

" I'll just look in the kitchen," said I, making for the door.

" No, no. I'll go," said Rawdon.

But I was in the passage—and Rawdon was on my heels.

The kitchen was very tidy and cheerful, but empty ; only a bottle of beer and two glasses stood on the table. To Rawdon the kitchen was as strange a world as to me—he never entered the servants' quarters. But to me it was curious that the bottle of beer was empty, and both the glasses had been used. I knew Rawdon wouldn't notice.

" That's very curious ! " said Rawdon : meaning the absence of his man.

At that moment we heard a step on the servants' stairs, and Rawdon opened the door, to reveal Hawken descending with an armful of sheets and things.

" What are you doing ? "

" Why !——" and a pause. " I was airing the clean laundry, like—not to waste the fire last thing."

Hawken descended into the kitchen with a very flushed face and very bright eyes and rather ruffled hair, and proceeded to spread the linen on chairs before the fire.

" I hope I've not done wrong, sir," he said in his most winning manner. " Was you ringing ? "

" Three times ! Leave that linen, and bring a bottle of the fizz."

" I'm sorry, sir. You can't hear the bell from the front, sir."

It was perfectly true. The house was small, but it had been built for a very nervous author, and the servants' quarters were shut off, padded off from the rest of the house.

Rawdon said no more about the sheets and things, but he looked more peaked than ever.

We went back to the music-room. Janet had gone to the hearth, and stood with her hand on the mantel. She looked round at us, baffled.

" We're having a bottle of fizz," said Rawdon. " Do let me take your wrap."

" And where was Hawken ? " she asked satirically.

" Oh, busy somewhere upstairs."

" He's a busy young man, that ! " she said sardonically. And she sat uncomfortably on the edge of the chair where I had been sitting.

When Hawken came with the tray, she said :

" I'm not going to drink."

Rawdon appealed to me, so I took a glass. She looked inquiringly at the flushed and bright-eyed Hawken, as if she understood something.

The man-servant left the room. We drank our wine, and the awkwardness returned.

" Rawdon ! " she said suddenly, as if she were firing a revolver at him. " Alec came home to-night in a bigger mess than ever, and wanted to make love to me to get it off his mind. I can't stand it any more. I'm in love with you, and I simply can't stand Alec getting too near to me. He's dangerous when he's crossed—and when he's worked up. So I just came here. I didn't see what else I could do."

She left off as suddenly as a machine-gun leaves off firing. We were just dazed.

" You are quite right," Rawdon began, in a vague and neutral tone. . . .

" I am, am I not ? " she said eagerly.

" I'll tell you what I'll do," he said. " I'll go round to the hotel to-night, and you can stay here."

" Under the kindly protection of Hawken, you mean ! " she said, with quiet sarcasm.

" Why !—I could send Mrs. Betts, I suppose," he said.

Mrs. Betts was his housekeeper.

" You couldn't stay and protect me yourself ? " she said quietly.

" I ! I ! Why, I've made a vow—haven't I, Joe ? "—he turned to me—" not to have any woman sleep under my roof again."— He got the mixed sour smile on his face.

She looked up at the ceiling for a moment, then lapsed into silence. Then she said :

" Sort of monastery, so to speak ! "

And she rose and reached for her wrap, adding :

" I'd better go, then."

" Joe will see you home," he said.

She faced round on me.

" Do you mind *not* seeing me home, Mr. Bradley ? " she said, gazing at me.

" Not if you don't want me," said I.

" Hawken will drive you," said Rawdon.

" Oh, no, he won't ! " she said. " I'll walk. Good night."

" I'll get my hat," stammered Rawdon, in an agony. " Wait !
Wait ! The gate will be locked."

" It was open when I came," she said.

He rang for Hawken to unlock the iron doors at the end of the
short drive, whilst he himself huddled into a great-coat and scarf,
fumbling for a flashlight.

" You won't go till I come back, will you ? " he pleaded to me.
" I'd be awfully glad if you'd stay the night. The sheets *will* be
aired."

I had to promise—and he set off with an umbrella, in the rain,
at the same time asking Hawken to take a flashlight and go in front.
So that was how they went, in single file along the path over the
fields to Mrs. Drummond's house, Hawken in front, with flashlight
and umbrella, curving round to light up in front of Mrs. Drummond,
who, with umbrella only, walked isolated between two lights,
Rawdon shining his flashlight on her from the rear from under his
umbrella. I turned indoors.

So that was over ! At least, for the moment !

I thought I would go upstairs and see how damp the bed in the
guest-chamber was, before I actually stayed the night with Rawdon.
He never had guests—preferred to go away himself.

The guest-chamber was a good room across a passage and round
a corner from Rawdon's room—its door just opposite the padded
service-door. This latter service-door stood open, and a light shone
through. I went into the spare bedroom, switching on the light.

To my surprise, the bed looked as if it had just been left—the
sheets tumbled, the pillows pressed. I put in my hands under the
bedclothes, and it was warm. Very curious !

As I stood looking round in mild wonder, I heard a voice call
softly : " Joe ! "

" Yes ! " said I instinctively, and, though startled, strode at once
out of the room and through the servants' door, towards the voice.
Light shone from the open doorway of one of the servants' rooms.

There was a muffled little shriek, and I was standing looking into
what was probably Hawken's bedroom, and seeing a soft and pretty
white leg and a very pretty feminine posterior very thinly dimmed in
a rather short night-dress, just in the act of climbing into a narrow
little bed, and, then arrested, the owner of the pretty posterior burying her face in the bedclothes, to be invisible, like the ostrich in the
sand.

I discreetly withdrew, went downstairs and poured myself a glass of wine. And very shortly Rawdon returned looking like Hamlet in the last Act.

He said nothing, neither did I. We sat and merely smoked. Only as he was seeing me upstairs to bed, in the now immaculate bedroom, he said pathetically :

" Why aren't women content to be what a man wants them to be ? "

" Why aren't they ! " said I wearily.

" I thought I had made everything clear," he said.

" You start at the wrong end," said I.

And as I said it, the picture came into my mind of the pretty feminine butt-end in Hawken's bedroom. Yes, Hawken made better starts, wherever he ended.

When he brought me my cup of tea in the morning, he was very soft and catlike. I asked him what sort of day it was, and he asked me if I'd had a good night, and was I comfortable.

" Very comfortable ! " said I. " But I turned you out, I'm afraid."

" Me, sir ? " He turned on me a face of utter bewilderment.

But I looked him in the eye.

" Is your name Joe ? " I asked him.

" You're right, sir."

" So is mine," said I. " However, I didn't see her face, so it's all right. I suppose you *were* a bit tight, in that little bed ! "

" Well, sir ! " and he flashed me a smile of amazing impudence, and lowered his tone to utter confidence. " This is the best bed in the house, this is." And he touched it softly.

" You've not tried them all, surely ? "

A look of indignant horror on his face !

" No, sir, indeed I haven't."

That day, Rawdon left for London, on his way to Tunis, and Hawken was to follow him. The roof of his house looked just the same.

The Drummonds moved too—went away somewhere, and left a lot of unsatisfied tradespeople behind.

THERE was a woman who was beautiful, who started with all the advantages, yet she had no luck. She married for love, and the love turned to dust. She had bonny children, yet she felt they had been thrust upon her, and she could not love them. They looked at her coldly, as if they were finding fault with her. And hurriedly she felt she must cover up some fault in herself. Yet what it was that she must cover up she never knew. Nevertheless, when her children were present, she always felt the centre of her heart go hard. This troubled her, and in her manner she was all the more gentle and anxious for her children, as if she loved them very much. Only she herself knew that at the centre of her heart was a hard little place that could not feel love, no, not for anybody. Everybody else said of her : " She is such a good mother. She adores her children." Only she herself, and her children themselves, knew it was not so. They read it in each other's eyes.

There were a boy and two little girls. They lived in a pleasant house, with a garden, and they had discreet servants, and felt themselves superior to anyone in the neighbourhood.

Although they lived in style, they felt always an anxiety in the house. There was never enough money. The mother had a small income, and the father had a small income, but not nearly enough for the social position which they had to keep up. The father went in to town to some office. But though he had good prospects, these prospects never materialized. There was always the grinding sense of the shortage of money, though the style was always kept up.

At last the mother said, " I will see if *I* can't make something." But she did not know where to begin. She racked her brains, and tried this thing and the other, but could not find anything successful. The failure made deep lines come into her face. Her children were growing up, they would have to go to school. There must be more money, there must be more money. The father, who was always very handsome and expensive in his tastes, seemed as if he never *would* be able to do anything worth doing. And the mother, who had a great belief in herself, did not succeed any better, and her tastes were just as expensive.

And so the house came to be haunted by the unspoken phrase : *There must be more money !   There must be more money !* The children could hear it all the time, though nobody said it aloud. They heard it at Christmas, when the expensive and splendid toys filled the nursery.   Behind the shining modern rocking-horse, behind the smart doll's-house, a voice would start whispering : "There *must* be more money !   There *must* be more money !" And the children would stop playing, to listen for a moment. They would look into each other's eyes, to see if they had all heard. And each one saw in the eyes of the other two that they too had heard. "There *must* be more money !   There *must* be more money !"

It came whispering from the springs of the still-swaying rocking-horse, and even the horse, bending his wooden, champing head, heard it. The big doll, sitting so pink and smirking in her new pram, could hear it quite plainly, and seemed to be smirking all the more self-consciously because of it. The foolish puppy, too, that took the place of the teddy-bear, he was looking so extraordinarily foolish for no other reason but that he heard the secret whisper all over the house : "There *must* be more money !"

Yet nobody ever said it aloud. The whisper was everywhere, and therefore no one spoke it. Just as no one ever says : "We are breathing !" in spite of the fact that breath is coming and going all the time.

"Mother," said the boy Paul one day, "why don't we keep a car of our own ? Why do we always use uncle's, or else a taxi ?"

"Because we're the poor members of the family," said the mother.

"But why *are* we, mother ?"

"Well—I suppose," she said slowly and bitterly, "it's because your father has no luck."

The boy was silent for some time.

"Is luck money, mother ?" he asked, rather timidly.

"No, Paul. Not quite. It's what causes you to have money."

"Oh !" said Paul vaguely. "I thought when Uncle Oscar said *filthy lucker*, it meant money."

"*Filthy lucre* does mean money," said the mother. "But it's lucre, not luck."

"Oh !" said the boy. "Then what *is* luck, mother ?"

"It's what causes you to have money. If you're lucky you have money. That's why it's better to be born lucky than rich. If you're rich, you may lose your money. But if you're lucky, you will always get more money."

" Oh ! Will you ? And is father not lucky ? "

" Very unlucky, I should say," she said bitterly.

The boy watched her with unsure eyes.

" Why ? " he asked.

" I don't know. Nobody ever knows why one person is lucky and another unlucky."

" Don't they ? Nobody at all ? Does *nobody* know ? "

" Perhaps God. But He never tells."

" He ought to, then. And aren't you lucky either, mother ? "

" I can't be, if I married an unlucky husband."

" But by yourself, aren't you ? "

" I used to think I was, before I married. Now I think I am very unlucky indeed."

" Why ? "

" Well—never mind ! Perhaps I'm not really," she said.

The child looked at her, to see if she meant it. But he saw, by the lines of her mouth, that she was only trying to hide something from him.

" Well, anyhow," he said stoutly, " I'm a lucky person."

" Why ? " said his mother, with a sudden laugh.

He stared at her. He didn't even know why he had said it.

" God told me," he asserted, brazening it out.

" I hope He did, dear ! " she said, again with a laugh, but rather bitter.

" He did, mother ! "

" Excellent ! " said the mother, using one of her husband's exclamations.

The boy saw she did not believe him ; or rather, that she paid no attention to his assertion. This angered him somewhere, and made him want to compel her attention.

He went off by himself, vaguely, in a childish way, seeking for the clue to " luck." Absorbed, taking no heed of other people, he went about with a sort of stealth, seeking inwardly for luck. He wanted luck, he wanted it, he wanted it. When the two girls were playing dolls in the nursery, he would sit on his big rocking-horse, charging madly into space, with a frenzy that made the little girls peer at him uneasily. Wildly the horse careered, the waving dark hair of the boy tossed, his eyes had a strange glare in them. The little girls dared not speak to him.

When he had ridden to the end of his mad little journey, he

climbed down and stood in front of his rocking-horse, staring fixedly into its lowered face. Its red mouth was slightly open, its big eye was wide and glassy-bright.

" Now ! " he would silently command the snorting steed. " Now, take me to where there is luck ! Now take me ! "

And he would slash the horse on the neck with the little whip he had asked Uncle Oscar for. He *knew* the horse could take him to where there was luck, if only he forced it. So he would mount again, and start on his furious ride, hoping at last to get there. He knew he could get there.

" You'll break your horse, Paul ! " said the nurse.

" He's always riding like that ! I wish he'd leave off ! " said his elder sister Joan.

But he only glared down on them in silence. Nurse gave him up. She could make nothing of him. Anyhow he was growing beyond her.

One day his mother and his Uncle Oscar came in when he was on one of his furious rides. He did not speak to them.

" Hallo, you young jockey ! Riding a winner ? " said his uncle.

" Aren't you growing too big for a rocking-horse ? You're not a very little boy any longer, you know," said his mother.

But Paul only gave a blue glare from his big, rather close-set eyes. He would speak to nobody when he was in full tilt. His mother watched him with an anxious expression on her face.

At last he suddenly stopped forcing his horse into the mechanical gallop, and slid down.

" Well, I got there ! " he announced fiercely, his blue eyes still flaring, and his sturdy long legs straddling apart.

" Where did you get to ? " asked his mother.

" Where I wanted to go," he flared back at her.

" That's right, son ! " said Uncle Oscar. " Don't you stop till you get there. What's the horse's name ? "

" He doesn't have a name," said the boy.

" Gets on without all right ? " asked the uncle.

" Well, he has different names. He was called Sansovino last week."

" Sansovino, eh ? Won the Ascot. How did you know his name ? "

" He always talks about horse-races with Bassett," said Joan.

The uncle was delighted to find that his small nephew was posted with all the racing news. Bassett, the young gardener, who had been wounded in the left foot in the war and had got his present job through Oscar Cresswell, whose batman he had been, was a perfect blade of the " turf." He lived in the racing events, and the small boy lived with him.

Oscar Cresswell got it all from Bassett.

" Master Paul comes and asks me, so I can't do more than tell him, sir," said Bassett, his face terribly serious, as if he were speaking of religious matters.

" And does he ever put anything on a horse he fancies ? "

" Well—I don't want to give him away—he's a young sport, a fine sport, sir. Would you mind asking him himself ? He sort of takes a pleasure in it, and perhaps he'd feel I was giving him away, sir, if you don't mind."

Bassett was serious as a church.

The uncle went back to his nephew, and took him off for a ride in the car.

" Say, Paul, old man, do you ever put anything on a horse ? " the uncle asked.

The boy watched the handsome man closely.

" Why, do you think I oughtn't to ? " he parried.

" Not a bit of it ! I thought perhaps you might give me a tip for the Lincoln."

The car sped on into the country, going down to Uncle Oscar's place in Hampshire.

" Honour bright ? " said the nephew.

" Honour bright, son ! " said the uncle.

" Well, then, Daffodil."

" Daffodil ! I doubt it, sonny. What about Mirza ? "

" I only know the winner," said the boy. " That's Daffodil."

" Daffodil, eh ? "

There was a pause. Daffodil was an obscure horse comparatively.

" Uncle ! "

" Yes, son ? "

" You won't let it go any further, will you ? I promised Bassett."

" Bassett be damned, old man ! What's he got to do with it ? "

" We're partners. We've been partners from the first. Uncle, he lent me my first five shillings, which I lost. I promised him, honour bright, it was only between me and him ; only you gave me that ten-shilling note I started winning with, so I thought you were lucky. You won't let it go any further, will you ? "

The boy gazed at his uncle from those big, hot, blue eyes, set rather close together. The uncle stirred and laughed uneasily.

"Right you are, son! I'll keep your tip private. Daffodil, eh? How much are you putting on him?"

"All except twenty pounds," said the boy. "I keep that in reserve."

The uncle thought it a good joke.

"You keep twenty pounds in reserve, do you, you young romancer? What are you betting, then?"

"I'm betting three hundred," said the boy gravely. "But it's between you and me, Uncle Oscar! Honour bright?"

The uncle burst into a roar of laughter.

"It's between you and me all right, you young Nat Gould," he said, laughing. "But where's your three hundred?"

"Bassett keeps it for me. We're partners."

"You are, are you! And what is Bassett putting on Daffodil?"

"He won't go quite as high as I do, I expect. Perhaps he'll go a hundred and fifty."

"What, pennies?" laughed the uncle.

"Pounds," said the child, with a surprised look at his uncle. "Bassett keeps a bigger reserve than I do."

Between wonder and amusement Uncle Oscar was silent. He pursued the matter no further, but he determined to take his nephew with him to the Lincoln races.

"Now, son," he said, "I'm putting twenty on Mirza, and I'll put five for you on any horse you fancy. What's your pick?"

"Daffodil, uncle."

"No, not the fiver on Daffodil!"

"I should if it was my own fiver," said the child.

"Good! Good! Right you are! A fiver for me and a fiver for you on Daffodil."

The child had never been to a race-meeting before, and his eyes were blue fire. He pursed his mouth tight, and watched. A Frenchman just in front had put his money on Lancelot. Wild with excitement, he flayed his arms up and down, yelling "*Lancelot! Lancelot!*" in his French accent.

Daffodil came in first, Lancelot second, Mirza third. The child, flushed and with eyes blazing, was curiously serene. His uncle brought him four five-pound notes, four to one.

"What am I to do with these?" he cried, waving them before the boy's eyes.

"I suppose we'll talk to Bassett," said the boy. "I expect I have fifteen hundred now; and twenty in reserve; and this twenty."

His uncle studied him for some moments.

" Look here, son ! " he said. " You're not serious about Bassett and that fifteen hundred, are you ? "

" Yes, I am. But it's between you and me, uncle. Honour bright ! "

" Honour bright all right, son ! But I must talk to Bassett."

" If you'd like to be a partner, uncle, with Bassett and me, we could all be partners. Only, you'd have to promise, honour bright, uncle, not to let it go beyond us three. Bassett and I are lucky, and you must be lucky, because it was your ten shillings I started winning with. . . ."

Uncle Oscar took both Bassett and Paul into Richmond Park for an afternoon, and there they talked.

" It's like this, you see, sir," Bassett said. " Master Paul would get me talking about racing events, spinning yarns, you know, sir. And he was always keen on knowing if I'd made or if I'd lost. It's about a year since, now, that I put five shillings on Blush of Dawn for him : and we lost. Then the luck turned, with that ten shillings he had from you : that we put on Singhalese. And since that time, it's been pretty steady, all things considering. What do you say, Master Paul ? "

" We're all right when we're sure," said Paul. " It's when we're not quite sure that we go down."

" Oh, but we're careful then," said Bassett.

" But when are you *sure ?* " smiled Uncle Oscar.

" It's Master Paul, sir," said Basset, in a secret, religious voice. " It's as if he had it from heaven. Like Daffodil, now, for the Lincoln. That was as sure as eggs."

" Did you put anything on Daffodil ? " asked Oscar Cresswell.

" Yes, sir. I made my bit."

" And my nephew ? "

Bassett was obstinately silent, looking at Paul.

" I made twelve hundred, didn't I, Bassett ? I told uncle I was putting three hundred on Daffodil."

" That's right," said Bassett, nodding.

" But where's the money ? " asked the uncle.

" I keep it safe locked up, sir. Master Paul he can have it any minute he likes to ask for it."

" What, fifteen hundred pounds ? "

" And twenty ! And *forty*, that is, with the twenty he made on the course.

" It's amazing ! " said the uncle.

"If Master Paul offers you to be partners, sir, I would, if I were you : if you'll excuse me," said Bassett.

Oscar Cresswell thought about it.

"I'll see the money," he said.

They drove home again, and, sure enough, Bassett came round to the garden-house with fifteen hundred pounds in notes. The twenty pounds reserve was left with Joe Glee, in the Turf Commission deposit.

"You see, it's all right, uncle, when I'm *sure !* Then we go strong, for all we're worth. Don't we, Bassett ? "

"We do that, Master Paul."

"And when are you sure ? " said the uncle, laughing.

"Oh, well, sometimes I'm *absolutely* sure, like about Daffodil," said the boy ; "and sometimes I have an idea ; and sometimes I haven't even an idea, have I, Bassett ? Then we're careful, because we mostly go down."

"You do, do you ! And when you're sure, like about Daffodil, what makes you sure, sonny ? "

"Oh, well, I don't know," said the boy uneasily. "I'm sure, you know, uncle ; that's all."

"It's as if he had it from heaven, sir," Bassett reiterated.

"I should say so ! " said the uncle.

But he became a partner. And when the Leger was coming on Paul was " sure " about Lively Spark, which was a quite inconsiderable horse. The boy insisted on putting a thousand on the horse, Bassett went for five hundred, and Oscar Cresswell two hundred. Lively Spark came in first, and the betting had been ten to one against him. Paul had made ten thousand.

"You see," he said, " I was absolutely sure of him."

Even Oscar Cresswell had cleared two thousand.

"Look here, son," he said, " this sort of thing makes me nervous."

"It needn't, uncle ! Perhaps I shan't be sure again for a long time."

"But what are you going to do with your money?" asked the uncle.

"Of course," said the boy, " I started it for mother. She said she had no luck, because father is unlucky, so I thought if *I* was lucky, it might stop whispering."

"What might stop whispering ? "

"Our house. I *hate* our house for whispering."

"What does it whisper ? "

"Why—why "—the boy fidgeted—" why, I don't know. But it's always short of money, you know, uncle. "

" I know it, son, I know it."

" You know people send mother writs, don't you, uncle ? "

" I'm afraid I do," said the uncle.

" And then the house whispers, like people laughing at you behind your back. It's awful, that is ! I thought if I was lucky——"

" You might stop it," added the uncle.

The boy watched him with big blue eyes, that had an uncanny cold fire in them, and he said never a word.

" Well, then ! " said the uncle. " What are we doing ? "

" I shouldn't like mother to know I was lucky," said the boy.

" Why not, son ? "

" She'd stop me."

" I don't think she would."

" Oh ! "—and the boy writhed in an odd way—" I *don't* want her to know, uncle."

" All right, son ! We'll manage it without her knowing."

They managed it very easily. Paul, at the other's suggestion, handed over five thousand pounds to his uncle, who deposited it with the family lawyer, who was then to inform Paul's mother that a relative had put five thousand pounds into his hands, which sum was to be paid out a thousand pounds at a time, on the mother's birthday, for the next five years.

" So she'll have a birthday present of a thousand pounds for five successive years," said Uncle Oscar. " I hope it won't make it all the harder for her later."

Paul's mother had her birthday in November. The house had been " whispering " worse than ever lately, and, even in spite of his luck, Paul could not bear up against it. He was very anxious to see the effect of the birthday letter, telling his mother about the thousand pounds.

When there were no visitors, Paul now took his meals with his parents, as he was beyond the nursery control. His mother went into town nearly every day. She had discovered that she had an odd knack of sketching furs and dress materials, so she worked secretly in the studio of a friend who was the chief " artist " for the leading drapers. She drew the figures of ladies in furs and ladies in silk and sequins for the newspaper advertisements. This young woman artist earned several thousand pounds a year, but Paul's mother only made several hundreds, and she was again dissatisfied. She so wanted to be first in something, and she did not succeed, even in making sketches for drapery advertisements.

She was down to breakfast on the morning of her birthday. Paul

watched her face as she read her letters. He knew the lawyer's
letter. As his mother read it, her face hardened and became more
expressionless. Then a cold, determined look came on her mouth.
She hid the letter under the pile of others, and said not a word
about it.

"Didn't you have anything nice in the post for your birthday,
mother?" said Paul.

"Quite moderately nice," she said, her voice cold and absent.
She went away to town without saying more.

But in the afternoon Uncle Oscar appeared. He said Paul's
mother had had a long interview with the lawyer, asking if the
whole five thousand could not be advanced at once, as she was in
debt.

"What do you think, uncle?" said the boy.

"I leave it to you, son."

"Oh, let her have it, then! We can get some more with the
other," said the boy.

"A bird in the hand is worth two in the bush, laddie!" said
Uncle Oscar.

"But I'm sure to *know* for the Grand National; or the Lincoln-
shire; or else the Derby. I'm sure to know for *one* of them," said
Paul.

So Uncle Oscar signed the agreement, and Paul's mother touched
the whole five thousand. Then something very curious happened.
The voices in the house suddenly went mad, like a chorus of frogs
on a spring evening. There were certain new furnishings, and Paul
had a tutor. He was *really* going to Eton, his father's school, in the
following autumn. There were flowers in the winter, and a blossoming of the luxury Paul's mother had been used to. And yet the voices
in the house, behind the sprays of mimosa and almond-blossom, and
from under the piles of iridescent cushions, simply trilled and
screamed in a sort of ecstasy: "There *must* be more money!
Oh-h-h; there *must* be more money. Oh, now, now-w! Now-w-w
—there *must* be more money!—more than ever! More than
ever!"

It frightened Paul terribly. He studied away at his Latin and
Greek with his tutors. But his intense hours were spent with Bassett. The Grand National had gone by: he had not "known,"
and had lost a hundred pounds. Summer was at hand. He was
in agony for the Lincoln. But even for the Lincoln he didn't
"know," and he lost fifty pounds. He became wild-eyed and
strange, as if something were going to explode in him.

"Let it alone, son ! Don't you bother about it ! " urged Uncle Oscar. But it was as if the boy couldn't really hear what his uncle was saying.

"I've got to know for the Derby ! I've got to know for the Derby ! " the child reiterated, his big blue eyes blazing with a sort of madness.

His mother noticed how overwrought he was.

"You'd better go to the seaside. Wouldn't you like to go now to the seaside, instead of waiting ? I think you'd better," she said, looking down at him anxiously, her heart curiously heavy because of him.

But the child lifted his uncanny blue eyes.

"I couldn't possibly go before the Derby, mother ! " he said. "I couldn't possibly ! "

"Why not ? " she said, her voice becoming heavy when she was opposed. "Why not ? You can still go from the seaside to see the Derby with your Uncle Oscar, if that's what you wish. No need for you to wait here. Besides, I think you care too much about these races. It's a bad sign. My family has been a gambling family, and you won't know till you grow up how much damage it has done. But it has done damage. I shall have to send Bassett away, and ask Uncle Oscar not to talk racing to you, unless you promise to be reasonable about it : go away to the seaside and forget it. You're all nerves ! "

"I'll do what you like, mother, so long as you don't send me away till after the Derby," the boy said.

"Send you away from where ? Just from this house ? "

"Yes," he said, gazing at her.

"Why, you curious child, what makes you care about this house so much, suddenly ? I never knew you loved it."

He gazed at her without speaking. He had a secret within a secret, something he had not divulged, even to Bassett or to his Uncle Oscar.

But his mother, after standing undecided and a little bit sullen for some moments, said :

"Very well, then ! Don't go to the seaside till after the Derby, if you don't wish it. But promise me you won't let your nerves go to pieces. Promise you won't think so much about horse-racing and *events*, as you call them ! "

"Oh, no," said the boy casually. "I won't think much about them, mother. You needn't worry. I wouldn't worry, mother, if I were you."

" If you were me and I were you," said his mother, " I wonder what we *should* do ! "

" But you know you needn't worry, mother, don't you ? " the boy repeated.

" I should be awfully glad to know it," she said wearily.

" Oh, well, you *can*, you know. I mean, you *ought* to know you needn't worry," he insisted.

" Ought I ? Then I'll see about it," she said.

Paul's secret of secrets was his wooden horse, that which had no name. Since he was emancipated from a nurse and a nursery-governess, he had had his rocking-horse removed to his own bedroom at the top of the house.

" Surely, you're too big for a rocking-horse ! " his mother had remonstrated.

" Well, you see, mother, till I can have a *real* horse, I like to have *some* sort of animal about," had been his quaint answer.

" Do you feel he keeps you company ? " she laughed.

" Oh, yes ! He's very good, he always keeps me company, when I'm there," said Paul.

So the horse, rather shabby, stood in an arrested prance in the boy's bedroom.

The Derby was drawing near, and the boy grew more and more tense. He hardly heard what was spoken to him, he was very frail, and his eyes were really uncanny. His mother had sudden strange seizures of uneasiness about him. Sometimes, for half an hour, she would feel a sudden anxiety about him that was almost anguish. She wanted to rush to him at once, and know he was safe.

Two nights before the Derby, she was at a big party in town, when one of her rushes of anxiety about her boy, her first-born, gripped her heart till she could hardly speak. She fought with the feeling, might and main, for she believed in common sense. But it was too strong. She had to leave the dance and go downstairs to telephone to the country. The children's nursery-governess was terribly surprised and startled at being rung up in the night.

" Are the children all right, Miss Wilmot ? "

" Oh, yes, they are quite all right."

" Master Paul ? Is he all right ? "

" He went to bed as right as a trivet. Shall I run up and look at him ? "

" No," said Paul's mother reluctantly. " No ! Don't trouble. It's all right. Don't sit up. We shall be home fairly soon." She did not want her son's privacy intruded upon.

" Very good," said the governess.

It was about one o'clock when Paul's mother and father drove up to their house. All was still. Paul's mother went to her room and slipped off her white fur cloak. She had told her maid not to wait up for her. She heard her husband downstairs, mixing a whisky and soda.

And then, because of the strange anxiety at her heart, she stole upstairs to her son's room. Noiselessly she went along the upper corridor. Was there a faint noise ? What was it ?

She stood, with arrested muscles, outside his door, listening. There was a strange, heavy, and yet not loud noise. Her heart stood still. It was a soundless noise, yet rushing and powerful. Something huge, in violet, hushed motion. What was it ? What in God's name was it ? She ought to know. She felt that she knew the noise. She knew what it was.

Yet she could not place it. She couldn't say what it was. And on and on it went, like a madness.

Softly, frozen with anxiety and fear, she turned the door-handle.

The room was dark. Yet in the space near the window, she heard and saw something plunging to and fro. She gazed in fear and amazement.

Then suddenly she switched on the light, and saw her son, in his green pyjamas, madly surging on the rocking-horse. The blaze of light suddenly lit him up, as he urged the wooden horse, and lit her up, as she stood, blonde, in her dress of pale green and crystal, in the doorway.

" Paul ! " she cried. " Whatever are you doing ? "

" It's Malabar ! " he screamed, in a powerful, strange voice. " It's Malabar ! "

His eyes blazed at her for one strange and senseless second, as he ceased urging his wooden horse. Then he fell with a crash to the ground, and she, all her tormented motherhood flooding upon her, rushed to gather him up.

But he was unconscious, and unconscious he remained, with some brain-fever. He talked and tossed, and his mother sat stonily by his side.

" Malabar ! It's Malabar ! Bassett, Bassett, I *know* ! It's Malabar ! "

So the child cried, trying to get up and urge the rocking-horse that gave him his inspiration.

" What does he mean by Malabar ? " asked the heart-frozen mother.

"I don't know," said the father stonily.

"What does he mean by Malabar?" she asked her brother Oscar.

"It's one of the horses running for the Derby," was the answer.

And, in spite of himself, Oscar Cresswell spoke to Bassett, and himself put a thousand on Malabar : at fourteen to one.

The third day of the illness was critical : they were waiting for a change. The boy, with his rather long, curly hair, was tossing ceaselessly on the pillow. He neither slept nor regained consciousness, and his eyes were like blue stones. His mother sat, feeling her heart had gone, turned actually into a stone.

In the evening, Oscar Cresswell did not come, but Bassett sent a message, saying could he come up for one moment, just one moment? Paul's mother was very angry at the intrusion, but on second thoughts she agreed. The boy was the same. Perhaps Bassett might bring him to consciousness.

The gardener, a shortish fellow with a little brown moustache, and sharp little brown eyes, tiptoed into the room, touched his imaginary cap to Paul's mother, and stole to the bedside, staring with glittering, smallish eyes at the tossing, dying child.

"Master Paul!" he whispered. "Master Paul! Malabar came in first all right, a clean win. I did as you told me. You've made over seventy thousand pounds, you have ; you've got over eighty thousand. Malabar came in all right, Master Paul."

"Malabar! Malabar! Did I say Malabar, mother? Did I say Malabar? Do you think I'm lucky, mother? I knew Malabar, didn't I? Over eighty thousand pounds! I call that lucky, don't you, mother? Over eighty thousand pounds! I knew, didn't I know I knew? Malabar came in all right. If I ride my horse till I'm sure, then I tell you, Bassett, you can go as high as you like. Did you go for all you were worth, Bassett?"

"I went a thousand on it, Master Paul."

"I never told you, mother, that if I can ride my horse, and *get there*, then I'm absolutely sure—oh, absolutely! Mother, did I ever tell you? I *am* lucky!"

"No, you never did," said the mother.

But the boy died in the night.

And even as he lay dead, his mother heard her brother's voice saying to her : "My God, Hester, you're eighty-odd thousand to the good, and a poor devil of a son to the bad. But, poor devil, poor devil, he's best gone out of a life where he rides his rocking-horse to find a winner."

VIRGINIA BODOIN had a good job : she was head of a department in a certain government office, held a responsible position, and earned, to imitate Balzac and be precise about it, seven hundred and fifty pounds a year. That is already something. Rachel Bodoin, her mother, had an income of about six hundred a year, on which she had lived in the capitals of Europe since the effacement of a never very important husband.

Now, after some years of virtual separation and " freedom," mother and daughter once more thought of settling down. They had become, in course of time, more like a married couple than mother and daughter. They knew one another very well indeed, and each was a little " nervous " of the other. They had lived together and parted several times. Virginia was now thirty, and she didn't look like marrying. For four years she had been as good as married to Henry Lubbock, a rather spoilt young man who was musical. Then Henry let her down : for two reasons. He couldn't stand her mother. Her mother couldn't stand him. And anybody whom Mrs. Bodoin could not stand she managed to sit on, disastrously. So Henry had writhed horribly, feeling his mother-in-law sitting on him tight, and Virginia, after all, in a helpless sort of family loyalty, sitting alongside her mother. Virginia didn't really want to sit on Henry. But when her mother egged her on, she couldn't help it. For ultimately, her mother had power over her ; a strange *female* power, nothing to do with parental authority. Virginia had long thrown parental authority to the winds. But her mother had another, much subtler form of domination, female and thrilling, so that when Rachel said : " Let's squash him ! " Virginia had to rush wickedly and gleefully to the sport. And Henry knew quite well when he was being squashed. So that was one of his reasons for going back on Vinny. He called her Vinny, to the superlative disgust of Mrs. Bodoin, who always corrected him : " My daughter *Virginia*—— "

The second reason was, again to be Balzacian, that Virginia hadn't a sou of her own. Henry had a sorry two hundred and fifty.

Virginia, at the age of twenty-four, was already earning four hundred and fifty. But she was earning them. Whereas Henry managed to earn about twelve pounds per annum, by his precious music. He had realized that he would find it hard to earn more. So that marrying, except with a wife who could keep him, was rather out of the question. Vinny would inherit her mother's money. But then Mrs. Bodoin had the health and muscular equipment of the Sphinx. She would live for ever, seeking whom she might devour, and devouring him. Henry lived with Vinny for two years, in the married sense of the words : and Vinny felt they *were* married, minus a mere ceremony. But Vinny had her mother always in the background ; often as far back as Paris or Biarritz, but still, within letter reach. And she never realized the funny little grin that came on her own elvish face when her mother, even in a letter, spread her skirts and calmly sat on Henry. She never realized that in spirit she promptly and mischievously sat on him too : she could no more have helped it than the tide can help turning to the moon. And she did not dream that he felt it, and was utterly mortified in his masculine vanity. Women, very often, hypnotize one another, and then, hypnotized, they proceed gently to wring the neck of the man they think they are loving with all their hearts. Then they call it utter perversity on his part, that he doesn't like having his neck wrung. They think he is repudiating a heart-felt love. For they are hypnotized. Women hypnotize one another, without knowing it.

In the end, Henry backed out. He saw himself being simply reduced to nothingness by two women, an old witch with muscles like the Sphinx, and a young, spell-bound witch, lavish, elvish and weak, who utterly spoilt him but who ate his marrow.

Rachel would write from Paris : " My Dear Virginia, as I had a windfall in the way of an investment, I am sharing it with you. You will find enclosed my cheque for twenty pounds. No doubt you will be needing it to buy Henry a suit of clothes, since the spring is apparently come, and the sunlight may be tempted to show him up for what he is worth. I don't want my daughter going around with what is presumably a street-corner musician, but please pay the tailor's bill yourself, or you may have to do it over again later." Henry got a suit of clothes, but it was as good as a shirt of Nessus, eating him away with subtle poison.

So he backed out. He didn't jump out, or bolt, or carve his way out at the sword's point. He sort of faded out, distributing his departure over a year or more. He was fond of Vinny, and he could hardly do without her, and he was sorry for her. But at length he couldn't see her apart from her mother. She was a young, weak, spendthrift witch, accomplice of her tough-clawed witch of a mother.

Henry made other alliances, got a good hold on elsewhere, and gradually extricated himself. He saved his life, but he had lost, he felt, a good deal of his youth and marrow. He tended now to go fat, a little puffy, somewhat insignificant. And he had been handsome and striking-looking.

The two witches howled when he was lost to them. Poor Virginia was really half crazy, she didn't know what to do with herself. She had a violent recoil from her mother. Mrs. Bodoin was filled with furious contempt for her daughter : that she should let such a hooked fish slip out of her hands ! That she should allow such a person to turn her down ! " I don't quite see my daughter seduced and thrown over by a sponging individual such as Henry Lubbock," she wrote. " But if it has happened, I suppose it is somebody's fault——"

There was a mutual recoil, which lasted nearly five years. But the spell was not broken. Mrs. Bodoin's mind never left her daughter, and Virginia was ceaselessly aware of her mother, somewhere in the universe. They wrote, and met at intervals, but they kept apart in recoil.

The spell, however, was between them, and gradually it worked. They felt more friendly. Mrs. Bodoin came to London. She stayed in the same quiet hotel with her daughter : Virginia had had two rooms in an hotel for the past three years. And, at last, they thought of taking an apartment together.

Virginia was now over thirty. She was still thin and odd and elvish, with a very slight and piquant cast in one of her brown eyes, and she still had her odd, twisted smile, and her slow, rather deep-toned voice, that caressed a man like the stroking of subtle finger-tips. Her hair was still a natural tangle of curls, a bit dishevelled. She still dressed with a natural elegance which tended to go wrong and a tiny bit sluttish. She still might have a hole in her expensive and perfectly new stockings, and still she might have to take off her shoes in the drawing-room, if she came to tea, and sit there in her stockinged-feet. True, she had elegant feet : she was altogether elegantly shaped. But it wasn't that. It was neither coquetry nor vanity. It was simply that, after having gone to a good shoemaker and paid five guineas for a pair of perfectly simple and natural shoes, made to her feet, the said shoes would hurt her excruciatingly, when she had walked half a mile in them, and she would simply have to take them off, even if she sat on the kerb to do it. It was a fatality. There was a touch of the *gamin* in her very feet, a certain sluttishness that wouldn't let them stay properly in nice proper shoes. She practically always wore her mother's old shoes. " Of course I go through life in mother's old shoes. If she died and left me without a supply, I suppose I should have to go in a bath-chair," she would say, with her odd twisted little grin. She was so elegant, and yet a slut. It was her charm, really.

Just the opposite of her mother. They could wear each other's shoes and each other's clothes, which seemed remarkable, for Mrs. Bodoin seemed so much the bigger of the two. But Virginia's shoulders were broad ; if she was thin, she had a strong frame, even when she looked a frail rag.

Mrs. Bodoin was one of those women of sixty or so, with a terrible inward energy and a violent sort of vitality. But she managed to hide it. She sat with perfect repose, and folded hands. One thought : What a calm woman ! Just as one may look at the snowy summit of a quiescent volcano, in the evening light, and think : What peace !

It was a strange *muscular* energy which possessed Mrs. Bodoin, as it possesses, curiously enough, many women over fifty, and is usually distasteful in its manifestations. Perhaps it accounts for the lassitude of the young.

But Mrs. Bodoin recognized the bad taste in her energetic coevals, so she cultivated repose. Her very way of pronouncing the word, in two syllables : re-pòse, making the second syllable run on into the twilight, showed how much suppressed energy she had. Faced with the problem of iron-grey hair and black eyebrows, she was too clever to try dyeing herself back into youth. She studied her face, her whole figure, and decided that it was *positive*. There was no denying it. There was no wispiness, no hollowness, no limp frail blossom-on-a-bending-stalk about her. Her figure, though not stout, was full, strong, and *cambré*. Her face had an aristocratic arched nose, aristocratic, who-the-devil-are-you grey eyes, and cheeks rather long but also rather full. Nothing appealing or youthfully skittish here.

Like an independent woman, she used her wits, and decided most emphatically not to be either youthful or skittish or appealing. She would keep her dignity, for she was fond of it. She was positive. She liked to be positive. She was used to her positivity. So she would just *be* positive.

She turned to the positive period ; to the eighteenth century, to

Voltaire, to Ninon de l'Enclos and the Pompadour, to Madame la
Duchesse and Monsieur le Marquis. She decided that she was not
much in the line of la Pompadour or la Duchesse, but almost exactly
in the line of Monsieur le Marquis. And she was right. With hair
silvering to white, brushed back clean from her positive brow and
temples, cut short, but sticking out a little behind, with her rather
full, pink face and thin black eyebrows plucked to two fine, superficial crescents, her arching nose and her rather full insolent eyes she
was perfectly eighteenth century, the early half. That she was
Monsieur le Marquis rather than Madame la Marquise made her
really modern.

Her appearance was perfect. She wore delicate combinations of
grey and pink, maybe with a darkening iron-grey touch, and her
jewels were of soft old coloured paste. Her bearing was a sort of alert
repose, very calm, but very assured. There was, to use a vulgarism,
no getting past her.

She had a couple of thousand pounds she could lay hands on.
Virginia, of course, was always in debt. But, after all, Virginia was
not to be sniffed at. She made seven hundred and fifty a year.

Virginia was oddly clever, and not clever. She didn't *really* know
anything, because anything and everything was interesting to her
for the moment, and she picked it up at once. She picked up languages with extraordinary ease, she was fluent in a fortnight. This
helped her enormously with her job. She could prattle away with
heads of industry, let them come from where they liked. But she
didn't *know* any language, not even her own. She picked things up
in her sleep, so to speak, without knowing anything about them.

And this made her popular with men. With all her curious
facility, they didn't feel small in front of her, because she was like
an instrument. She had to be prompted. Some man had to set
her in motion, and then she worked, really cleverly. She could
collect the most valuable information. She was very useful. She
worked with men, spent most of her time with men, her friends were
practically all men. She didn't feel easy with women.

Yet she had no lover, nobody seemed eager to marry her, nobody
seemed eager to come close to her at all. Mrs. Bodoin said : " I'm
afraid Virginia is a one-man woman. I am a one-man woman.
So was my mother, and so was my grandmother. Virginia's father
was the only man in my life, the only one. And I'm afraid Virginia
is the same, tenacious. Unfortunately, the man was what he was,
and her life is just left there."

Henry had said, in the past, that Mrs. Bodoin wasn't a one-man woman, she was a no-man woman, and that if she could have had her way, everything male would have been wiped off the face of the earth, and only the female element left.

However, Mrs. Bodoin thought that it was now time to make a move. So she and Virginia took a quite handsome apartment in one of the old Bloomsbury Squares, fitted it up and furnished it with extreme care, and with some quite lovely things, got in a very good man, an Austrian, to cook, and they set up married life together, mother and daughter.

At first it was rather thrilling. The two reception-rooms, looking down on the dirty old trees of the Square garden, were of splendid proportions, and each with three great windows coming down low, almost to the level of the knees. The chimney-piece was late eighteenth century. Mrs. Bodoin furnished the rooms with a gentle suggestion of Louis-Seize merged with Empire, without keeping to any particular style. But she had, saved from her own home, a really remarkable Aubusson carpet. It looked almost new, as if it had been woven two years ago, and was startling, yet somehow rather splendid, as it spread its rose-red borders and wonderful florid array of silver-grey and gold-grey roses, lilies and gorgeous swans and trumpeting volutes away over the floor. Very æsthetic people found it rather loud, they preferred the worn, dim yellowish Aubusson in the big bedroom. But Mrs. Bodoin loved her drawing-room carpet. It was positive, but it was not vulgar. It had a certain grand air in its floridity. She felt it gave her a proper footing. And it behaved very well with her painted cabinets and grey-and-gold brocade chairs and big Chinese vases, which she liked to fill with big flowers : single Chinese peonies, big roses, great tulips, orange lilies. The dim room of London, with all its atmospheric colour, would stand the big, free, fisticuffing flowers.

Virginia, for the first time in her life, had the pleasure of making a home. She was again entirely under her mother's spell, and swept away, thrilled to her marrow. She had had no idea that her mother had got such treasures as the carpets and painted cabinets and brocade chairs up her sleeve : many of them the débris of the Fitzpatrick home in Ireland, Mrs. Bodoin being a Fitzpatrick. Almost like a child, like a bride, Virginia threw herself into the business of fixing up the rooms. " Of course, Virginia, I consider this is *your* apartment," said Mrs. Bodoin. " I am nothing but your *dame de compagnie*, and shall carry out your wishes entirely, if you will only express them."

Of course Virginia expressed a iew, but not many. She introduced some wild pictures bought from impecunious artists whom she patronized. Mrs. Bodoin thought the pictures positive about the wrong things, but as far as possible, she let them stay : looking on them as the necessary element of modern ugliness. But by that element of modern ugliness, wilfully so, it was easy to see the things that Virginia had introduced into the apartment.

Perhaps nothing goes to the head like setting up house. You can get drunk on it. You feel you are creating something. Nowadays it is no longer the " home," the domestic nest. It is " my rooms," or " my house," the great garment which reveals and clothes " my personality." Mrs. Bodoin, deliberately scheming for Virginia, kept moderately cool over it, but even she was thrilled to the marrow, and of an intensity and ferocity with the decorators and furnishers, astonishing. But Virginia was just all the time tipsy with it, as if she had touched some magic button on the grey wall of life, and with an Open Sesame ! her lovely and coloured rooms had begun to assemble out of fairyland. It was far more vivid and wonderful to her than if she had inherited a duchy.

The mother and daughter, the mother in a sort of faded russet crimson and the daughter in silver, began to entertain. They had, of course, mostly men. It filled Mrs. Bodoin with a sort of savage impatience to entertain women. Besides, most of Virginia's acquaintances were men. So there were dinners and well-arranged evenings.

It went well, but something was missing. Mrs. Bodoin wanted to be gracious, so she held herself rather back. She stayed a little distant, was calm, reposed, eighteenth century, and determined to be a foil to the clever and slightly-elvish Virginia. It was a pose, and alas, it stopped something. She was very nice with the men, no matter what her contempt of them. But the men were uneasy with her : afraid.

What they all felt, all the men guests, was that *for them*, nothing really happened. Everything that happened was between mother and daughter. All the flow was between mother and daughter. A subtle, hypnotic spell encompassed the two women, and, try as they might, the men were shut out. More than one young man, a little dazzled, *began* to fall in love with Virginia. But it was impossible. Not only was he shut out, he was, in some way, annihilated. The spontaneity was killed in his bosom. While the two women sat, brilliant and rather wonderful, in magnetic connection at opposite ends of the table, like two witches, a double Circe turning the men not into swine—the men would have liked that well enough—but into lumps.

It was tragic. Because Mrs. Bodoin wanted Virginia to fall in love and marry. She really wanted it, and she attributed Virginia's lack of forthcoming to the delinquent Henry. She never realized the hypnotic spell, which of course encompassed her as well as Virginia, and made men just an impossibility to both women, mother and daughter alike.

At this time, Mrs. Bodoin hid her humour. She had a really marvellous faculty of humorous imitation. She could imitate the Irish servants from her old home, or the American women who called on her, or the modern ladylike young men, the asphodels, as she called them : " Of course you know the asphodel is a kind of onion ! Oh, yes, just an over-bred onion " : who wanted, with their murmuring voices and peeping under their brows, to make her feel very small and very bourgeois. She could imitate them all with a humour that was really touched with genius. But it was devastating. It demolished the objects of her humour so absolutely, smashed them to bits with a ruthless hammer, pounded them to nothing so terribly, that it frightened people, particularly men. It frightened men off.

So she hid it. She hid it. But there it was, up her sleeve, her merciless, hammer-like humour, which just smashed its object on the head and left him brained. She tried to disown it. She tried to pretend, even to Virginia, that she had the gift no more. But in vain ; the hammer hidden up her sleeve hovered over the head of every guest, and every guest felt his scalp creep, and Virginia felt her inside creep with a little, mischievous, slightly idiotic grin, as still another fool male was mystically knocked on the head. It was a sort of uncanny sport.

No, the plan was not going to work : the plan of having Virginia fall in love and marry. Of course the men *were* such lumps, such *œufs farcies*. There was one, at least, that Mrs. Bodoin had real hopes of. He was a healthy and normal and very good-looking boy of good family, with no money, alas, but clerking to the House of Lords and very hopeful, and not very clever, but simply in love with Virginia's cleverness. He was just the one Mrs. Bodoin would have married for herself. True, he was only twenty-six, to Virginia's thirty-one. But he had rowed in the Oxford eight, and adored horses, talked horses adorably, and was simply infatuated by Virginia's cleverness. To him Virginia had the finest mind on earth. She was as wonderful as Plato, but infinitely more attractive, because she was a woman, and winsome with it. Imagine a winsome Plato with untidy curls and the tiniest little brown-eyed squint and just a hint of woman's pathetic need for a protector, and you may imagine Adrian's feeling for Virginia. He adored her on his knees, but he felt he could protect her.

" Of course, he's just a very nice *boy !* " said Mrs. Bodoin. " He's a boy, and that's all you can say. And he always will be a boy. But that's the very nicest kind of man, the only kind you can live with : the eternal boy. Virginia, aren't you attracted to him ? "

" Yes, mother ! I think he's an awfully nice *boy*, as you say," replied Virginia, in her rather slow, musical, whimsical voice. But the mocking little curl in the intonation put the lid on Adrian. Virginia was not marrying a nice *boy !* She could be malicious too, against her mother's taste. And Mrs. Bodoin let escape her a faint gesture of impatience.

For she had been planning her own retreat, planning to give Virginia the apartment outright, and half of her own income, if she would marry Adrian. Yes, the mother was already scheming how best she could live with dignity on three hundred a year, once Virginia was happily married to that most attractive if slightly brainless *boy*.

A year later, when Virginia was thirty-two, Adrian, who had married a wealthy American girl and been transferred to a job in the legation at Washington in the meantime, faithfully came to see Virginia as soon as he was in London, faithfully kneeled at her feet, faithfully thought her the most wonderful spiritual being, and faithfully felt that she, Virginia, could have done wonders with him, which wonders would now never be done, for he had married in the meantime.

Virginia was looking haggard and worn. The scheme of a *ménage à deux* with her mother had not succeeded. And now, work was telling on the younger woman. It is true, she was amazingly facile. But facility wouldn't get her all the way. She had to earn her money, and earn it hard. She had to slog, and she had to concentrate. While she could work by quick intuition and without much responsibility, work thrilled her. But as soon as she had to get down to it, as they say, grip and slog and concentrate, in a really responsible position, it wore her out terribly. She had to do it all off her nerves. She hadn't the same sort of fighting power as a man. Where a man can summon his old Adam in him to fight through his work, a woman has to draw on her nerves, and on her nerves alone. For the old Eve in her will have nothing to do with such work. So that mental responsibility, mental concentration, mental slogging wear out a woman terribly, especially if she is head of a department, and not working *for* somebody.

So poor Virginia was worn out. She was thin as a rail. Her nerves were frayed to bits. And she could never forget her beastly work. She would come home at tea-time speechless and done for. Her mother, tortured by the sight of her, longed to say : " Has anything gone wrong, Virginia ? Have you had anything particularly trying at the office to-day ? " But she learned to hold her tongue, and say nothing. The question would be the last straw to Virginia's poor overwrought nerves, and there would be a little scene which, despite Mrs. Bodoin's calm and forbearance, offended the elder woman to the quick. She had learned, by bitter experience, to leave her child alone, as one would leave a frail tube of vitriol alone. But of course, she could not keep her *mind* off Virginia. That was impossible. And poor Virginia, under the strain of work and the strain of her mother's awful ceaseless mind, was at the very end of her strength and resources.

Mrs. Bodoin had always disliked the fact of Virginia's doing a job. But now she hated it. She hated the whole government office with violent and virulent hate. Not only was it undignified for Virginia to be tied up there, but it was turning her, Mrs. Bodoin's daughter, into a thin, nagging, fearsome old maid. Could anything be more utterly English and humiliating to a well-born Irishwoman ?

After a long day attending to the apartment, skilfully darning one of the brocade chairs, polishing the Venetian mirrors to her satisfaction, selecting flowers, doing certain shopping and housekeeping, attending perfectly to everything, then receiving callers in the afternoon, with never-ending energy, Mrs. Bodoin would go up from the drawing-room after tea and write a few letters, take her bath, dress with great care—she enjoyed attending to her person—and come down to dinner as fresh as a daisy, but far more energetic than that quiet flower. She was ready now for a full evening.

She was conscious, with gnawing anxiety, of Virginia's presence in the house, but she did not see her daughter till dinner was announced. Virginia slipped in, and away to her room unseen, never going into the drawing-room to tea. If Mrs. Bodoin heard her daughter's key in the latch, she quickly retired into one of the rooms till Virginia was safely through. It was too much for poor Virginia's nerves even to catch sight of anybody in the house, when she came in from the office. Bad enough to hear the murmur of visitors' voices behind the drawing-room door.

And Mrs. Bodoin would wonder : How is she ? How is she to-night ? I wonder what sort of a day she's had ? And this thought would roam prowling through the house, to where Virginia was lying on her back in her room. But the mother would have to consume her anxiety till dinner-time. And then Virginia would appear, with black lines under her eyes, thin, tense, a young woman out of an office, the stigma upon her : badly dressed, a little acid in humour, with an impaired digestion, not interested in anything, blighted by her work. And Mrs. Bodoin, humiliated at the very sight of her, would control herself perfectly, say nothing but the mere smooth nothings of casual speech, and sit in perfect form presiding at a carefully-cooked dinner thought out entirely to please Virginia. Then Virginia hardly noticed what she ate.

Mrs. Bodoin was pining for an evening with life in it. But Virginia would lie on the couch and put on the loud-speaker. Or she would put a humorous record on the gramophone, and be amused, and hear it again, and be amused, and hear it again, six times, and six times be amused by a mildly funny record that Mrs. Bodoin now knew off by heart. " Why, Virginia, I could repeat that record over to you, if you wished it, without your troubling to wind up that gramophone." And Virginia, after a pause in which she seemed not to have heard what her mother said, would reply, " I'm sure you could, mother." And that simple speech would convey such volumes of contempt for all that Rachel Bodoin was or ever could be or ever had been, contempt for her energy, her vitality, her mind, her body, her very existence, that the elder woman would curl. It seemed as if the ghost of Robert Bodoin spoke out of the mouth of the daughter, in deadly venom. Then Virginia would put on the record for the seventh time.

During the second ghastly year, Mrs. Bodoin realized that the game was up. She was a beaten woman, a woman without object or meaning any more. The hammer of her awful female humour, which had knocked so many people on the head, all the people, in fact, that she had come into contact with, had at last flown backwards and hit herself on the head. For her daughter was her other self, her *alter ego*. The secret and the meaning and the power of Mrs. Bodoin's whole life lay in the hammer, that hammer of her living humour which knocked everything on the head. That had been her lust and her passion, knocking everybody and everything humorously on the head. She had felt inspired in it : it was a sort of mission. And she had hoped to hand on the hammer to Virginia, her clever, unsolid but still actual daughter, Virginia. Virginia was the continuation of Rachel's own self. Virginia was Rachel's *alter ego*, her other self.

But, alas, it was a half-truth. Virginia had had a father. This fact, which had been utterly ignored by the mother, was gradually brought home to her by the curious recoil of the hammer. Virginia was her father's daughter. Could anything be more unseemly, horrid, more perverse in the natural scheme of things? For Robert Bodoin had been fully and deservedly knocked on the head by Rachel's hammer. Could anything, then, be more disgusting than that he should resurrect again in the person of Mrs. Bodoin's own daughter, her own *alter ego* Virginia, and start hitting back with a little spiteful hammer that was David's pebble against Goliath's battle-axe!

But the little pebble was mortal. Mrs. Bodoin felt it sink into her brow, her temple, and she was finished. The hammer fell nerveless from her hand.

The two women were now mostly alone. Virginia was too tired to have company in the evening. So there was the gramophone or loud-speaker, or else silence. Both women had come to loathe the apartment. Virginia felt it was the last grand act of bullying on her mother's part, she felt bullied by the assertive Aubusson carpet, by the beastly Venetian mirrors, by the big overcultured flowers. She even felt bullied by the excellent food, and longed again for a Soho restaurant and her two poky, shabby rooms in the hotel. She loathed the apartment : she loathed everything. But she had not the energy to move. She had not the energy to do anything. She crawled to her work, and for the rest, she lay flat, gone.

It was Virginia's worn-out inertia that really finished Mrs. Bodoin. That was the pebble that broke the bone of her temple : " To have to attend my daughter's funeral, and accept the sympathy of all her fellow-clerks in her office, no, that is a final humiliation which I must spare myself. No ! If Virginia must be a lady-clerk, she must be it henceforth on her own responsibility. I will retire from her existence."

Mrs. Bodoin had tried hard to persuade Virginia to give up her work and come and live with her. She had offered her half her income. In vain. Virginia stuck to her office.

Very well ! So be it ! The apartment was a fiasco, Mrs. Bodoin was longing, longing to tear it to pieces again. One last and final blow of the hammer ! " Virginia, don't you think we'd better get rid of this apartment, and live around as we used to ? Don't you think we'll do that ? "—" But all the money you've put into it ? and the lease for ten years ! " cried Virginia, in a kind of inertia.— " Never mind ! We had the pleasure of making it. And we've had

as much pleasure out of living in it as we shall ever have.   Now we'd
better get rid of it—quickly—don't you think ? "

Mrs. Bodoin's arms were twitching to snatch the pictures off the
walls, roll up the Aubusson carpet, take the china out of the ivory-
inlaid cabinet there and then, at that very moment.

" Let us wait till Sunday before we decide," said Virginia.

" Till Sunday ! Four days ! As long as that ?   Haven't we
already decided in our own minds ? " said Mrs. Bodoin.

" We'll wait till Sunday, anyhow," said Virginia.

The next evening, the Armenian came to dinner.   Virginia called
him Arnold, with the French pronunciation, Arnault.   Mrs. Bodoin,
who barely tolerated him, and could never get his name, which
seemed to have a lot of bouyoums in it, called him either the Armenian, or the Rahat Lakoum, after the name of the sweetmeat, or
simply the Turkish Delight.

" Arnault is coming to dinner to-night, mother."

" Really ! The Turkish Delight is coming here to dinner ?   Shall
I provide anything special ? "   Her voice sounded as if she would
suggest snails in aspic.

" I don't think so."

Virginia had seen a good deal of the Armenian at the office when
she had to negotiate with him on behalf of the Board of Trade.   He
was a man of about sixty, a merchant, had been a millionaire, was
ruined during the war, but was now coming on again, and represented trade in Bulgaria.   He wanted to negotiate with the British
Government, and the British Government sensibly negotiated with
him : at first through the medium of Virginia.   Now things were
going satisfactorily between Monsieur Arnault, as Virginia called
him, and the Board of Trade, so that a sort of friendship had followed
the official relations.

The Turkish Delight was sixty, grey-haired and fat.   He had
numerous grandchildren growing up in Bulgaria, but he was a
widower.   He had a grey moustache cut like a brush, and glazed
brown eyes over which hung heavy lids with white lashes.   His
manner was humble, but in his bearing there was a certain dogged
conceit.   One notices the combination sometimes in Jews.   He had
been very wealthy and kow-towed to, he had been ruined and humiliated, terribly humiliated, and now, doggedly, he was rising up
again, his sons backing him, away in Bulgaria.   One felt he was
not alone.   He had his sons, his family, his tribe behind him, away
in the Near East.

He spoke bad English, but fairly fluent guttural French.   He did not speak much, but he sat. He sat, with his short, fat thighs, as if for eternity, *there*. There was a strange potency in his fat immobile sitting, as if his posterior were connected with the very centre of the earth. And his brain, spinning away at the one point in question, business, was very agile. Business absorbed him. But not in a nervous, personal way. Somehow the family, the tribe was always felt behind him. It was business for the family, the tribe.

With the English he was humble, for the English like such aliens to be humble, and he had had a long schooling from the Turks. And he was always an outsider. Nobody would ever take any notice of him in society. He would just be an outsider, *sitting*.

" I hope, Virginia, you won't ask that Turkish-carpet gentleman when we have other people. *I* can bear it," said Mrs. Bodoin. " Some people might mind."

" Isn't it hard when you can't choose your own company in your own house," mocked Virginia.

" No ! *I* don't care. I can meet anything ; and I'm sure, in the way of selling Turkish carpets, your acquaintance is very good. But I don't suppose you look on him as a personal friend—— ? "

" I do. I like him quite a lot."

" Well——! As you will. But consider your *other* friends."

Mrs. Bodoin was really mortified this time. She looked on the Armenian as one looks on the fat Levantine in a fez who tries to sell one hideous tapestries at Port Said, or on the sea-front at Nice, as being outside the class of human beings, and in the class of insects. That he had been a millionaire, and might be a millionaire again, only added venom to her feeling of disgust at being forced into contact with such scum. She could not even squash him, or annihilate him. In scum, there is nothing to squash, for scum is only the unpleasant residue of that which was never anything but squashed.

However, she was not quite just. True, he was fat, and he sat, with short thighs, like a toad, as if seated for a toad's eternity. His colour was of a dirty sort of paste, his black eyes were glazed under heavy lids. And he never spoke until spoken to, waiting in his toad's silence, like a slave.

But his thick, fine white hair, which stood up on his head like a soft brush, was curiously virile. And his curious small hands, of the same soft dull paste, had a peculiar, fat, soft masculine breeding of their own. And his dull brown eye could glint with the subtlety of serpents, under the white brush of eyelash. He was tired, but he was not defeated. He had fought, and won, and lost, and was fighting again, always at a disadvantage. He belonged to a defeated race which accepts defeat, but which gets its own back by cunning. He was the father of sons, the head of a family, one of the heads of a defeated but indestructible tribe. He was not alone, and so you could not lay your finger on him. His whole consciousness was patriarchal and tribal. And somehow, he was humble, but he was indestructible.

At dinner he sat half-effaced, humble, yet with the conceit of the humble. His manners were perfectly good, rather French. Virginia chattered to him in French, and he replied with that peculiar non-chalance of the boulevards, which was the only manner he could command when speaking French. Mrs. Bodoin understood, but she was what one would call a heavy-footed linguist, so when she said anything, it was intensely in English. And the Turkish Delight replied in his clumsy English, hastily. It was not his fault that French was being spoken. It was Virginia's.

He was very humble, conciliatory, with Mrs. Bodoin. But he cast at her sometimes that rapid glint of a reptilian glance as if to say : " Yes ! I see you ! You are a handsome figure. As an *objet de vertu* you are almost perfect." Thus his connoisseur's, antique-dealer's eye would appraise her. But then his thick white eyebrows would seem to add : " But what, under holy Heaven, are you as a woman ? You are neither wife nor mother nor mistress, you have no perfume of sex, you are more dreadful than a Turkish soldier or an English official. No man on earth could embrace you. You are a ghoul, you are a strange genie from the underworld ! " And he would secretly invoke the holy names, to shield him.

Yet he was in love with Virginia. He saw, first and foremost, the child in her, as if she were a lost child in the gutter, a waif with a faint, fascinating cast in her brown eyes, waiting till someone would pick her up. A fatherless waif ! And he was tribal father, father through all the ages.

Then, on the other hand, he knew her peculiar disinterested cleverness in affairs. That, too, fascinated him : that odd, almost second-sight cleverness about business, and entirely impersonal, entirely in the air. It seemed to him very strange. But it would be an immense help to him in his schemes. He did not really under-stand the English. He was at sea with them. But with her, he would have a clue to everything. For she was, finally, quite a somebody among these English, these English officials.

He was about sixty. His family was established, in the East, his grandsons were growing up. It was necessary for him to live in

London, for some years. This girl would be useful. She had no money, save what she would inherit from her mother. But he would risk that : she would be an investment in his business. And then the apartment. He liked the apartment extremely. He recognized the. *cachet*, and the lilies and swans of the Aubusson carpet really did something to him. Virginia said to him : " Mother gave me the apartment." So he looked on that as safe. And finally, Virginia was almost a virgin, probably quite a virgin, and, as far as the paternal oriental male like himself was concerned, entirely virgin. He had a very small idea of the silly puppy-sexuality of the English, so different from the prolonged male voluptuousness of his own pleasures. And last of all, he was physically lonely, getting old, and tired.

Virginia of course did not know why she liked being with Arnault. Her cleverness was amazingly stupid when it came to life, to living. She said he was " quaint." She said his nonchalant French of the boulevards was " amusing." She found his business cunning " intriguing," and the glint in his dark glazed eyes, under the white, thick lashes, " sheiky." She saw him quite often, had tea with him in his hotel, and motored with him one day down to the sea.

When he took her hand in his own soft still hands, there was something so caressing, so possessive in his touch, so strange and positive in his leaning towards her, that though she trembled with fear, she was helpless.—" But you are so thin, dear little thin thing, you need repose, repose, for the blossom to open, poor little blossom, to become a little fat ! " he said in his French.

She quivered, and was helpless. It certainly was quaint ! He was so strange and positive, he seemed to have all the power. The moment he realized that she would succumb into his power, he took full charge of the situation, he lost all his hesitation and his humility. He did not want just to make love to her : he wanted to marry her, for all his multifarious reasons. And he must make himself master of her.

He put her hand to his lips, and seemed to draw her life to his in kissing her thin hand. " The poor child is tired, she needs repose, she needs to be caressed and cared for," he said in his French. And he drew nearer to her.

She looked up in dread at his glinting, tired dark eyes under the white lashes. But he used all his will, looking back at her heavily and calculating that she must submit. And he brought his body quite near to her, and put his hand softly on her face, and made her lay her face against his breast, as he soothingly stroked her arm with his other hand. " Dear little thing ! Dear little thing ! Arnault loves her so dearly ! Arnault loves her ! Perhaps she will marry her Arnault. Dear little girl, Arnault will put flowers in her life, and make her life perfumed with sweetness and content."

She leaned against his breast and let him caress her. She gave a fleeting, half poignant, half vindictive thought to her mother. Then she felt in the air the sense of destiny, destiny. Oh, so nice, not to have to struggle. To give way to destiny.

" Will she marry her old Arnault ? Eh ? Will she marry him ? " he asked in a soothing, caressing voice, at the same time compulsive.

She lifted her head and looked at him : the thick white brows, the glinting, tired dark eyes. How queer and comic ! How comic to be in his power ! And he was looking a little baffled.

" Shall I ? " she said, with her mischievous twist of a grin.

" *Mais oui !* " he said, with all the sang-froid of his old eyes. " *Mais oui ! Je te contenterai, tu le verras.*"

" *Tu me contenteras !* " she said, with a flickering smile of real amusement at his assurance. " Will you really content me ? "

" But surely ! I assure it you. And you will marry me ? "

" You must tell mother," she said, and hid wickedly against his waistcoat again, while the male pride triumphed in him.

Mrs. Bodoin had no idea that Virginia was intimate with the Turkish Delight : she did not inquire into her daughter's movements. During the famous dinner, she was calm and a little aloof, but entirely self-possessed. When, after coffee, Virginia left her alone with the Turkish Delight, she made no effort at conversation, only glanced at the rather short, stout man in correct dinner-jacket, and thought how his sort of fatness called for a fez and the full muslin breeches of a bazaar merchant in *The Thief of Baghdad*.

" Do you really prefer to smoke a hookah ? " she asked him, with a slow drawl.

" What is a hookah, please ? "

" One of those water-pipes. Don't you all smoke them, in the East ? "

He only looked mystified and humble, and silence resumed. She little knew what was simmering inside his stillness.

" Madame," he said, " I want to ask you something."

" You do ? Then why not ask it ? " came her slightly melancholy drawl.

" Yes ! It is this. I wish I may have the honour to marry your daughter. She is willing."

There was a moment's blank pause. Then Mrs. Bodoin leaned towards him from her distance, with curious portentousness.

" What was that you said ? " she asked. " Repeat it ! "

" I wish I may have the honour to marry your daughter. She is willing to take me."

His dark, glazed eyes looked at her, then glanced away again. Still leaning forward, she gazed fixedly on him, as if spellbound, turned to stone. She was wearing pink topaz ornaments, but he judged they were paste, moderately good.

" Did I hear you say she is willing to take you ? " came the slow, melancholy, remote voice.

" Madame, I think so," he said, with a bow.

" I think we'll wait till she comes," she said, leaning back.

There was silence. She stared at the ceiling. He looked closely round the room, at the furniture, at the china in the ivory-inlaid cabinet.

" I can settle five thousand pounds on Mademoiselle Virginia, Madame," came his voice. " Am I correct to assume that she will bring this apartment and its appointments into the marriage settlement ? "

Absolute silence. He might as well have been on the moon. But he was a good sitter. He just sat until Virginia came in.

Mrs. Bodoin was still staring at the ceiling. The iron had entered her soul finally and fully. Virginia glanced at her, but said :

" Have a whisky-and-soda, Arnault ? "

He rose and came towards the decanters, and stood beside her : a rather squat, stout man with white head, silent with misgiving. There was the fizz of the syphon : then they came to their chairs.

" Arnault has spoken to you, mother ? " said Virginia.

Mrs. Bodoin sat up straight, and gazed at Virginia with big, owlish eyes, haggard. Virginia was terrified, yet a little thrilled. Her mother was beaten.

" Is it true, Virginia, that you are *willing* to marry this—oriental gentleman ? " asked Mrs. Bodoin slowly.

" Yes, mother, quite true," said Virginia, in her teasing soft voice.

Mrs. Bodoin looked owlish and dazed.

" May I be excused from having any part in it, or from having anything to do with your future *husband*—I mean having any business to transact with him ? " she asked dazedly, in her slow, distinct voice.

" Why, of course ! " said Virginia, frightened, smiling oddly.

There was a pause. Then Mrs. Bodoin, feeling old and haggard, pulled herself together again.

" Am I to understand that your future husband would like to possess this apartment ? " came her voice.

Virginia smiled quickly and crookedly. Arnault just sat, planted on his posterior, and heard. She reposed on him.

"Well—perhaps!" said Virginia. "Perhaps he would like to know that I possessed it." She looked at him.

Arnault nodded gravely.

"And do you *wish* to possess it?" came Mrs. Bodoin's slow voice. "Is it your intention to *inhabit* it, with your *husband*?" She put eternities into her long, stressed words.

"Yes, I think it is," said Virginia. "You know you *said* the apartment was mine, mother."

"Very well! It shall be so. I shall send my lawyer to this—oriental gentleman, if you will leave written instructions on my writing-table. May I ask when you think of getting—*married*?"

"When do you think, Arnault?" said Virginia.

"Shall it be, in two weeks?" he said, sitting erect, with his fists on his knees.

"In about a fortnight, mother," said Virginia.

"I have heard? In two weeks! Very well! In two weeks everything shall be at your disposal. And now, please excuse me." She rose, made a slight general bow, and moved calmly and dimly from the room. It was killing her, that she could not shriek aloud and beat that Levantine out of the house. But she couldn't. She had imposed the restraint on herself.

Arnault stood and looked with glistening eyes round the room. It would be his. When his sons came to England, here he would receive them.

He looked at Virginia. She too was white and haggard, now. And she flung away from him, as if in resentment. She resented the defeat of her mother. She was still capable of dismissing him for ever, and going back to her mother.

"Your mother is a wonderful lady," he said, going to Virginia and taking her hand. "But she has no husband to shelter her, she is unfortunate. I am sorry she will be alone. I should be happy if she would like to stay here with us."

The sly old fox knew what he was about.

"I'm afraid there's no hope of that," said Virginia, with a return to her old irony.

She sat on the couch, and he caressed her softly and paternally, and the very incongruity of it, there in her mother's drawing-room, amused her. And because he saw that the things in the drawing-room were handsome and valuable, and now they were his, his blood flushed and he caressed the thin girl at his side with passion, because she represented these valuable surroundings, and brought them to his possession. And he said : "And with me you will be very comfortable, very content, oh, I shall make you content, not like madame your mother. And you will get fatter, and bloom like the rose. I shall make you bloom like the rose. And shall we say next week, hein ? Shall it be next week, next Wednesday, that we marry ? Wednesday is a good day. Shall it be then ? "

" Very well ! " said Virginia, caressed again into a luxurious sense of destiny, reposing on fate, having to make no effort, no more effort, all her life.

Mrs. Bodoin moved into an hotel next day, and came into the apartment to pack up and extricate herself and her immediate personal belongings only when Virginia was necessarily absent. She and her daughter communicated by letter, as far as was necessary.

And in five days' time Mrs. Bodoin was clear. All business that could be settled was settled, all her trunks were removed. She had five trunks, and that was all. Denuded and outcast, she would depart to Paris, to live out the rest of her days.

The last day, she waited in the drawing-room till Virginia should come home. She sat there in her hat and street things, like a stranger.

" I just waited to say good-bye," she said. " I leave in the morning for Paris. This is my address. I think everything is settled ; if not, let me know and I'll attend to it. Well, good-bye ! —and I hope you'll be *very happy !* "

She dragged out the last words sinisterly ; which restored Virginia, who was beginning to lose her head.

" Why, I think I may be," said Virginia, with the twist of a smile.

" I shouldn't wonder," said Mrs. Bodoin pointedly and grimly. " I think the Armenian grandpapa knows very well what he's about. You're just the harem type, after all." The words came slowly, dropping, each with a plop ! of deep contempt.

" I suppose I am ! Rather fun ! " said Virginia. " But I wonder where I got it ? Not from you, mother——" she drawled mischievously.

" I should say *not*."

" Perhaps daughters go by contraries, like dreams," mused Virginia wickedly. " All the harem was left out of you, so perhaps it all had to be put back into me."

Mrs. Bodoin flashed a look at her.

" You have *all* my *pity !* " she said.

" Thank you, dear. You have just a bit of mine."

THE fashion in women changes nowadays even faster than women's fashions. At twenty, Lina M'Leod was almost painfully modern. At sixty, almost obsolete !

She started off in life to be really independent. In that remote day, forty years ago, when a woman said she was going to be independent, it meant she was having no nonsense with men. She was kicking over the masculine traces, and living her own life, manless.

To-day, when a girl says she is going to be independent, it means she is going to devote her attentions almost exclusively to men ; though not necessarily to " a man."

Miss M'Leod had an income from her mother. Therefore, at the age of twenty, she turned her back on that image of tyranny, her father, and went to Paris to study art. Art having been studied, she turned her attention to the globe of earth. Being terribly independent, she soon made Africa look small : she dallied energetically with vast hinterlands of China : and she knew the Rocky Mountains and the deserts of Arizona, as if she had been married to them. All this, to escape mere man.

It was in New Mexico she purchased the blue moccasins, blue bead moccasins, from an Indian who was her guide and her subordinate. In her independence she made use of men, of course, but merely as servants, subordinates.

When the war broke out she came home. She was then forty-five, and already going grey. Her brother, two years older than herself, but a bachelor, went off to the war ; she stayed at home in the small family mansion in the country, and did what she could. She was small and erect and brief in her speech, her face was like pale ivory, her skin like a very delicate parchment, and her eyes were very blue. There was no nonsense about her, though she did paint pictures. She never even touched her delicately parchment face with pigment. She was good enough as she was, honest-to-God, and the country town had a tremendous respect for her.

In her various activities she came pretty often into contact with

Percy Barlow, the clerk at the bank. He was only twenty-two when she first set eyes on him, in 1914, and she immediately liked him. He was a stranger in the town, his father being a poor country vicar in Yorkshire. But he was of the confiding sort. He soon confided in Miss M'Leod, for whom he had a towering respect, how he disliked his stepmother, how he feared his father was but as wax in the hands of that downright woman, and how, in consequence, he was homeless. Wrath shone in his pleasant features, but somehow it was an amusing wrath ; at least to Miss M'Leod.

He was distinctly a good-looking boy, with stiff dark hair and odd, twinkling grey eyes under thick dark brows, and a rather full mouth and a queer, deep voice that had a caressing touch of hoarseness. It was his voice that somehow got behind Miss M'Leod's reserve. Not that he had the faintest intention of so doing. He looked up to her immensely : " she's miles above me."

When she watched him playing tennis, letting himself go a bit too much, hitting too hard, running too fast, being too nice to his partner, her heart yearned over him. The orphan in him ! Why should he go and be shot ? She kept him at home as long as possible, working with her at all kinds of war-work. He was so absolutely willing to do everything she wanted : devoted to her.

But at last the time came when he must go. He was now twenty-four, and she forty-seven. He came to say good-bye, in his awkward fashion. She suddenly turned away, leaned her forehead against the wall, and burst into bitter tears. He was frightened out of his wits. Before he knew what was happening he had his arm in front of his face and was sobbing too.

She came to comfort him. " Don't cry, dear, don't ! It will all be all right."

At last he wiped his face on his sleeve and looked at her sheepishly. " It was you crying as did me in," he said. Her blue eyes were brilliant with tears. She suddenly kissed him.

" You are such a dear ! " she said wistfully. Then she added, flushing suddenly vivid pink under her transparent parchment skin : " It wouldn't be right for you to marry an old thing like me, would it ? "

He looked at her dumbfounded.

" No, I'm too old," she added hastily.

" Don't talk about old ! You're not old ! " he said hotly.

" At least I'm too old for *that*," she said sadly.

" Not as far as I'm concerned," he said. " You're younger than me, in most ways, I'm hanged if you're not ! "

" Are you hanged if I'm not ? " she teased wistfully.

" I am," he said.   "And if I thought you wanted me, I'd be jolly proud if you married me.   I would, I assure you."

" Would you ? " she said, still teasing him.

Nevertheless, the next time he was home on leave she married him, very quietly, but very definitely.   He was a young lieutenant. They stayed in her family home, Twybit Hall, for the honeymoon. It was her house now, her brother being dead.   And they had a strangely happy month.   She had made a strange discovery :   a man.

He went off to Gallipoli, and became a captain.   He came home in 1919, still green with malaria, but otherwise sound.   She was in her fiftieth year.   And she was almost white-haired ;   long, thick, white hair, done perfectly, and perfectly creamy, colourless face, with very blue eyes.

He had been true to her, not being very forward with women. But he was a bit startled by her white hair.   However, he shut his eyes to it, and loved her.   And she, though frightened and somewhat bewildered, was happy.   But she was bewildered.   It always seemed awkward to her, that he should come wandering into her room in his pyjamas when she was half dressed, and brushing her hair. And he would sit there silent, watching her brush the long swinging river of silver, of her white hair, the bare, ivory-white slender arm working with a strange mechanical motion, sharp and forcible, brushing down the long silvery stream of hair.   He would sit as if mesmerized, just gazing.   And she would at last glance round sharply, and he would rise, saying some little casual thing to her and smiling to her oddly with his eyes.   Then he would go out, his thin cotton pyjamas hitching up over his hips, for he was a rather big-built fellow.   And she would feel dazed, as if she did not quite know her own self any more.   And the queer, ducking motion of his silently going out of her door impressed her ominously, his curious cat head, his big hips and limbs.

They were alone in the house, save for the servants.   He had no work.   They lived modestly, for a good deal of her money had been lost during the war.   But she still painted pictures.   Marriage had only stimulated her to this.   She painted canvases of flowers, beautiful flowers that thrilled her soul.   And he would sit, pipe in fist, silent, and watch her.   He had nothing to do.   He just sat and watched her small, neat figure and her concentrated movements, as she painted.   Then he knocked out his pipe, and filled it again.

She said that at last she was perfectly happy.   And he said that he was perfectly happy. They were always together. He hardly went out, save riding in the lanes. And practically nobody came to the house.

But still, they were very silent with one another. The old chatter had died out. And he did not read much. He just sat still, and smoked, and was silent. It got on her nerves sometimes, and she would think as she had thought in the past, that the highest bliss a human being can experience is perhaps the bliss of being quite alone, quite, quite alone.

His bank firm offered to make him manager of the local branch, and, at her advice, he accepted. Now he went out of the house every morning and came home every evening, which was much more agreeable. The rector begged him to sing again in the church choir : and again she advised him to accept. These were the old grooves in which his bachelor life had run. He felt more like himself.

He was popular : a nice, harmless fellow, everyone said of him. Some of the men secretly pitied him. They made rather much of him, took him home to luncheon, and let him loose with their daughters. He was popular among the daughters too : naturally, for if a girl expressed a wish, he would instinctively say : " What ! Would you like it ? I'll get it for you." And if he were not in a position to satisfy the desire, he would say : " I only wish I could do it for you. I'd do it like a shot." All of which he meant.

At the same time, though he got on so well with the maidens of the town, there was no coming forward about him. He was, in some way, not wakened up. Good-looking, and big, and service-able, he was inwardly remote, without self-confidence, almost without a self at all.

The rector's daughter took upon herself to wake him up. She was exactly as old as he was, a smallish, rather sharp-faced young woman who had lost her husband in the war, and it had been a grief to her. But she took the stoic attitude of the young : " You've got to live, so you may as well do it ! She was a kindly soul, in spite of her sharpness. And she had a very perky little red-brown pomeranian dog that she had bought in Florence in the street, but which had turned out a handsome little fellow. Miss M'Leod looked down a bit on Alice Howells and her pom, so Mrs. Howells felt no special love for Miss M'Leod—" Mrs. Barlow, that is ! " she would add sharply. " For it's quite impossible to think of her as anything but Miss M'Leod ! "

Percy was really more at ease at the rectory, where the pom

yapped and Mrs. Howells changed her dress three or four times a day and looked it, than in the semi-cloisteral atmosphere of Twybit Hall, where Miss M'Leod wore tweeds and a natural knitted jumper, her skirts rather long, her hair done up pure silver, and painted her wonderful flower pictures in the deepening silence of the daytime. At evening she would go up to change, after he came home. And though it thrilled her to have a man coming into her room as he dressed, snapping his collar-stud, to tell her something trivial as she stood bare-armed in her silk slip, rapidly coiling up the rope of silver hair behind her head, still, it worried her. When he was there, he couldn't keep away from her. And he would watch her, watch her, watch her as if she was the ultimate revelation. Sometimes it made her irritable. She was so absolutely used to her own privacy. What was he looking at? She never watched *him*. Rather she looked the other way. His watching tried her nerves. She was turned fifty. And his great silent body loomed almost dreadful.

He was quite happy playing tennis or croquet with Alice Howells and the rest. Alice was choir-mistress, a bossy little person outwardly, inwardly rather forlorn and affectionate, and not very sure that life hadn't let her down for good. She was now over thirty —and had no one but the pom and her father and the parish— nothing in her really intimate life. But she was very cheerful, busy, even gay, with her choir and school work, her dancing, and flirting, and dressmaking.

She was intrigued by Percy Barlow. "How *can* a man be so nice to *everybody*?" she asked him, a little exasperated. "Well, why not?" he replied, with the odd smile of his eyes. "It's not why he shouldn't, but how he manages to do it! How can you have so much good-nature? I *have* to be catty to some people, but you're nice to *everybody*."

"Oh, am I!" he said ominously.

He was like a man in a dream, or in a cloud. He was quite a good bank-manager, in fact very intelligent. Even in appearance, his great charm was his beautifully-shaped head. He had plenty of brains, really. But in his will, in his body, he was asleep. And sometimes this lethargy, or coma, made him look haggard. And sometimes it made his body seem inert and despicable, meaningless.

Alice Howells longed to ask him about his wife. "*Do* you love her? *Can* you really care for her?" But she daren't. She daren't ask him one word about his wife. Another thing she couldn't do, she couldn't persuade him to dance. Never, not once. But in everything else he was pliable as wax.

Mrs. Barlow—Miss M'Leod—stayed out at Twybit all the time. She did not even come in to church on Sunday. She had shaken off church, among other things. And she watched Percy depart, and felt just a little humiliated. He was going to sing in the choir ! Yes, marriage was also a humiliation to her. She had distinctly married beneath her.

The years had gone by : she was now fifty-seven, Percy was thirty-four. He was still, in many ways, a boy. But in his curious silence, he was ageless. She managed him with perfect ease. If she expressed a wish, he acquiesced at once. So now it was agreed he should not come to her room any more. And he never did. But sometimes she went to him in his room, and was winsome in a pathetic, heart-breaking way.

She twisted him round her little finger, as the saying goes. And yet secretly she was afraid of him. In the early years he had displayed a clumsy but violent sort of passion, from which she had shrunk away. She felt it had nothing to do with her. It was just his indiscriminating desire for Woman, and for his own satisfaction. Whereas she was not just unidentified Woman, to give him his general satisfaction. So she had recoiled, and withdrawn herself. She had put him off. She had regained the absolute privacy of her room.

He was perfectly sweet about it. Yet she was uneasy with him now. She was afraid of him ; or rather, not of him, but of a mysterious something in him. She was not a bit afraid of *him*, oh no ! And when she went to him now, to be nice to him, in her pathetic winsomeness ʼof an unused woman of fifty-seven, she found him sweet-natured as ever, but really indifferent. He saw her pathos and her winsomeness. In some way, the mystery of her, her thick white hair, her vivid blue eyes, her ladylike refinement still fascinated him. But his bodily desire for her had gone, utterly gone. And secretly, she was rather glad. But as he looked at her, looked at her, as he lay there so silent, she was afraid, as if some finger were pointed at her. Yet she knew, the moment she spoke to him, he would twist his eyes to that good-natured and " kindly " smile of his.

It was in the late, dark months of this year that she missed the blue moccasins. She had hung them on a nail in his room. Not that he ever wore them : they were too small. Nor did she : they were too big. Moccasins are male footwear, among the Indians, not female. But they were of a lovely turquoise-blue colour, made all of little turquoise beads, with little forked flames of dead-white and dark-green. When, at the beginning of their marriage, he had exclaimed over them, she had said : " Yes ! Aren't they a lovely colour ! So blue ! " And he had replied : " Not as blue as your eyes, even then."

So naturally, she had hung them up on the wall in his room, and there they had stayed. Till, one November day, when there were no flowers, and she was pining to paint a still-life with something blue in it—oh, so blue, like delphiniums !—she had gone to his room for the moccasins. And they were not there. And though she hunted, she could not find them. Nor did the maids know anything of them.

So she asked him : " Percy, do you know where those blue moccasins are, which hung in your room ? " There was a moment's dead silence. Then he looked at her with his good-naturedly twinkling eyes, and said : " No, _I_ know nothing of them." There was another dead pause. She did not believe him. But being a perfect lady, she only said, as she turned away : " Well then, how curious it is ! " And there was another dead pause. Out of which he asked her what she wanted them for, and she told him. Whereon the matter lapsed.

It was November, and Percy was out in the evening fairly often now. He was rehearsing for a " play " which was to be given in the church schoolroom at Christmas. He had asked her about it. " Do you think it's a bit _infra dig._ if I play one of the characters ? " She had looked at him mildly, disguising her real feeling. " If you don't feel _personally_ humiliated," she said, " then there's nothing else to consider." And he had answered : " Oh, it doesn't upset _me_ at all." So she mildly said : " Then do it, by all means." Adding at the back of her mind : If it amuses you, child !—but she thought, a change had indeed come over the world, when the master of Twybit Hall, or even, for that matter, the manager of the dignified Stubbs' Bank, should perform in public on a schoolroom stage in amateur theatricals. And she kept calmly aloof, preferring not to know any details. She had a world of her own.

When he had said to Alice Howells : " You don't think other folk'll mind—clients of the bank and so forth—think it beneath my dignity ? " she had cried, looking up into his twinkling eyes : " Oh, you don't have to keep _your_ dignity on ice, Percy—any more than I do mine."

The play was to be performed for the first time on Christmas Eve : and after the play, there was the midnight service in church. Percy therefore told his wife not to expect him home till the small hours, at least. So he drove himself off in the car.

As night fell, and rain, Miss M'Leod felt a little forlorn. She was left out of everything. Life was slipping past her. It was Christmas Eve, and she was more alone than she had ever been. Percy only seemed to intensify her aloneness, leaving her in this fashion.

She decided not to be left out. She would go to the play too. It was past six o'clock, and she had worked herself into a highly nervous state. Outside was darkness and rain : inside was silence, forlornness. She went to the telephone and rang up the garage in Shewbury. It was with great difficulty she got them to promise to send a car for her : Mr. Slater would have to fetch her himself in the two-seater runabout : everything else was out.

She dressed nervously, in a dark-green dress with a few modest jewels. Looking at herself in the mirror, she still thought herself slim, young looking and distinguished. She did not see how old-fashioned she was, with her uncompromising erectness, her glistening knob of silver hair sticking out behind, and her long dress.

It was a three-miles drive in the rain, to the small country town. She sat next to old Slater, who was used to driving horses and was nervous and clumsy with a car, without saying a word. He thankfully deposited her at the gate of St. Barnabas' School.

It was almost half-past seven. The schoolroom was packed and buzzing with excitement. " I'm afraid we haven't a seat left, Mrs. Barlow ! " said Jackson, one of the church sidesmen, who was standing guard in the school porch, where people were still fighting to get in. He faced her in consternation. She faced him in consternation. " Well, I shall have to stay somewhere, till Mr. Barlow can drive me home," she said. " Couldn't you put me a chair somewhere ? "

Worried and flustered, he went worrying and flustering the other people in charge. The schoolroom was simply packed solid. But Mr. Simmons, the leading grocer, gave up his chair in the front row to Mrs. Barlow, whilst he sat in a chair right under the stage, where he couldn't see a thing. But he could see Mrs. Barlow seated between his wife and daughter, speaking a word or two to them occasionally, and that was enough.

The lights went down : *The Shoes of Shagput* was about to begin. The amateur curtains were drawn back, disclosing the little amateur stage with a white amateur back-cloth daubed to represent a Moorish courtyard. In stalked Percy, dressed as a Moor, his face darkened. He looked quite handsome, his pale grey eyes queer and startling in his dark face. But he was afraid of the audience—he spoke away from them, stalking around clumsily. After a certain amount of would-be funny dialogue, in tripped the heroine, Alice

Howells, of course. She was an Eastern houri, in white gauze Turkish trousers, silver veil, and—the blue moccasins. The whole stage was white, save for her blue moccasins, Percy's dark-green sash, and a negro boy's red fez.

When Mrs. Barlow saw the blue moccasins, a little bomb of rage exploded in her. This, of all places! The blue moccasins that she had bought in the western deserts! The blue moccasins that were not so blue as her own eyes! *Her* blue moccasins! On the feet of that creature, Mrs. Howells.

Alice Howells was not afraid of the audience. She looked full at them, lifting her silver veil. And of course she saw Mrs. Barlow, sitting there like the Ancient of Days in judgment, in the front row. And a bomb of rage exploded in *her* breast too.

In the play, Alice was the wife of the grey-bearded old Caliph, but she captured the love of the young Ali, otherwise Percy, and the whole business was the attempt of these two to evade Caliph and negro-eunuchs and ancient crones, and get into each other's arms. The blue shoes were very important: for while the sweet Leila wore them, the gallant Ali was to know there was danger. But when she took them off, he might approach her.

It was all quite childish, and everybody loved it, and Miss M'Leod might have been quite complacent about it all, had not Alice Howells got her monkey up, so to speak. Alice, with a lot of make-up, looked boldly handsome. And suddenly bold she was, bold as the devil. All these years the poor young widow had been " good," slaving in the parish, and only even flirting just to cheer things up, never going very far and knowing she could never get anything out of it, but determined never to mope.

Now the sight of Miss M'Leod sitting there so erect, so coolly " higher plane," and calmly superior, suddenly let loose a devil in Alice Howells. All her limbs went suave and molten, as her young sex, long pent up, flooded even to her finger-tips. Her voice was strange, even to herself, with its long, plaintive notes. She felt all her movements soft and fluid, she felt herself like living liquid. And it was lovely. Underneath it all was the sting of malice against Miss M'Leod, sitting there so erect, with her great knob of white hair.

Alice's business, as the lovely Leila, was to be seductive to the rather heavy Percy. And seductive she was. In two minutes, she had him spell-bound. He saw nothing of the audience. A faint, fascinated grin came on to his face, as he acted up to the young woman in the Turkish trousers. His rather full, hoarse voice changed and became clear, with a new, naked clang in it. When the two sang together, in the simple banal duets of the play, it was with a most fascinating intimacy. And when, at the end of Act One, the lovely Leila kicked off the blue moccasins, saying : " Away, shoes of bondage, shoes of sorrow ! " and danced a little dance all alone, barefoot, in her Turkish trousers, in front of her fascinated hero, his smile was so spell-bound that everybody else was spell-bound too.

Miss M'Leod's indignation knew no bounds. When the blue moccasins were kicked across the stage by the brazen Alice, with the words : " Away, shoes of bondage, shoes of sorrow ! " the elder woman grew pink with fury, and it was all she could do not to rise and snatch the moccasins from the stage, and bear them away. She sat in speechless indignation during the brief curtain between Act One and Act Two. Her moccasins ! Her blue moccasins ! Of the sacred blue colour, the turquoise of heaven.

But there they were, in Act Two, on the feet of the bold Alice. It was becoming too much. And the love-scenes between Percy and the young woman were becoming nakedly shameful. Alice grew worse and worse. She was worked up now, caught in her own spell, and unconscious of everything save of him, and the sting of that other woman, who presumed to own him. Own him ? Ha-ha ! For he was fascinated. The queer smile on his face, the concentrated gleam of his eyes, the queer way he leaned forward from his loins towards her, the new, reckless, throaty twang in his voice —the audience had before their eyes a man spell-bound and lost in passion.

Miss M'Leod sat in shame and torment, as if her chair was red-hot. She too was fast losing her normal consciousness, in the spell of rage. She was outraged. The second Act was working to its climax. The climax came. The lovely Leila kicked off the blue shoes : " Away, shoes of bondage, away ! " and flew barefoot to the enraptured Ali, flinging herself into his arms. And if ever a man was gone in sheer desire, it was Percy, as he pressed the woman's lithe form against his body, and seemed unconsciously to envelop her, unaware of everything else. While she, blissful in his spell, but still aware of the audience and of the superior Miss M'Leod, let herself be wrapped closer and closer.

Miss M'Leod rose to her feet and looked towards the door. But the way out was packed with people standing holding their breath as the two on the stage remained wrapped in each other's arms, and the three fiddles and the flute softly woke up. Miss M'Leod could not bear it. She was on her feet, and beside herself. She could not get out. She could not sit down again.

" Percy ! " she said, in a low clear voice. " Will you hand me my moccasins ? "

He lifted his face like a man startled in a dream, lifted his face from the shoulder of his Leila. His gold-grey eyes were like softly-startled flames. He looked in sheer horrified wonder at the little white-haired woman standing below.

" Eh ! " he said, purely dazed.

" Will you please hand me my moccasins ! "—and she pointed to where they lay on the stage.

Alice had stepped away from him, and was gazing at the risen viper of the little elderly woman on the tip of the audience. Then she watched him move across the stage, bending forward from the loins in his queer mesmerized way, pick up the blue moccasins, and stoop down to hand them over the edge of the stage to his wife, who reached up for them.

" Thank you ! " said Miss M'Leod, seating herself, with the blue moccasins in her lap.

Alice recovered her composure, gave a sign to the little orchestra, and began to sing at once, strong and assured, to sing her part in the duet that closed the Act. She knew she could command public opinion in her favour.

He too recovered at once, the little smile came back on his face, he calmly forgot his wife again as he sang his share in the duet. It was finished. The curtains were pulled to. There was immense cheering. The curtains opened, and Alice and Percy bowed to the audience, smiling both of them their peculiar secret smile, while Miss M'Leod sat with the blue moccasins on her lap.

The curtains were closed, it was the long interval. After a few moments of hesitation, Mrs. Barlow rose with dignity, gathered her wrap over her arm, and with the blue moccasins in her hand, moved towards the door. Way was respectfully made for her.

" I should like to speak to Mr. Barlow," she said to Jackson, who had anxiously ushered her in, and now would anxiously usher her out.

" Yes, Mrs. Barlow."

He led her round to the smaller class-room at the back, that acted as dressing-room. The amateur actors were drinking lemonade, and chattering freely. Mrs. Howells came forward, and Jackson whispered the news to her. She turned to Percy.

" Percy, Mrs. Barlow wants to speak to you. Shall I come with you ? "

" Speak to me ? Aye, come on with me."

The two followed the anxious Jackson into the other half-lighted class-room, where Mrs. Barlow stood in her wrap, holding the moccasins. She was very pale, and she watched the two butter-muslin Turkish figures enter, as if they could not possibly be real. She ignored Mrs. Howells entirely.

" Percy," she said, " I want you to drive me home."

" Drive you home ! " he echoed.

" Yes, please ! "

" Why—when ? " he said, with vague bluntness.

" Now,—if you don't mind——"

" What—in this get-up ? " He looked at himself.

" I could wait while you changed."

There was a pause. He turned and looked at Alice Howells, and Alice Howells looked at him. The two women saw each other out of the corners of their eyes : but it was beneath notice. He turned to his wife, his black face ludicrously blank, his eyebrows cocked.

" Well, you see," he said, " it's rather awkward. I can hardly hold up the third Act while I've taken you home and got back here again, can I ? "

" So you intend to play in the third Act ? " she asked with cold ferocity.

" Why, I must, mustn't I ? " he said blankly.

" Do you *wish* to ? " she said, in all her intensity.

" I do, naturally. I want to finish the thing up properly," he replied, in the utter innocence of his head ; about his heart he knew nothing.

She turned sharply away.

" Very well ! " she said. And she called to Jackson, who was standing dejectedly by the door : " Mr. Jackson, will you please find some car or conveyance to take me home ? "

" Aye ! I say, Mr. Jackson," called Percy in his strong, demo-cratic voice, going forward to the man. " Ask Tom Lomas if he'll do me a good turn and get my car out of the rectory garage, to drive Mrs. Barlow home. Aye, ask Tom Lomas ! And if not him, ask Mr. Pilkington—Leonard. The key's there. You don't mind, do you ? I'm ever so much obliged——"

The three were left awkwardly alone again.

" I expect you've had enough with two acts," said Percy soothingly to his wife. " These things aren't up to your mark. I know it. They're only child's play. But, you see, they please the people. We've got a packed house, haven't we ? "

His wife had nothing to answer. He looked so ludicrous, with his dark-brown face and butter-muslin bloomers. And his mind was so ludicrously innocent. His body, however, was not so ridiculously innocent as his mind, as she knew when he turned to the other woman.

"You and I, we're more on the nonsense level, aren't we?" he said, with the new, throaty clang of naked intimacy in his voice. His wife shivered.

"Absolutely on the nonsense level," said Alice, with easy assurance.

She looked into his eyes, then she looked at the blue moccasins in the hand of the other woman. He gave a little start, as if realizing something for himself.

At that moment Tom Lomas looked in, saying heartily: "Right you are, Percy! I'll have my car here in half a tick. I'm more handy with it than yours."

"Thanks, old man! You're a Christian."

"Try to be—especially when you turn Turk! Well——" He disappeared.

"I say, Lina," said Percy in his most amiable democratic way, "would you mind leaving the moccasins for the next act? We s'll be in a bit of a hole without them."

Miss M'Leod faced him and stared at him with the full blast of her forget-me-not blue eyes, from her white face.

"Will you pardon me if I don't?" she said.

"What!" he exclaimed. "Why? Why not? It's nothing but play, to amuse the people. I can't see how it can hurt the *moccasins*. I understand you don't quite like seeing me make a fool of myself. But anyhow, I'm a bit of a born fool. What?"—and his blackened face laughed with a Turkish laugh. "Oh, yes, you have to realize I rather enjoy playing the fool," he resumed. "And, after all, it doesn't really hurt *you*, now does it? Shan't you leave us those moccasins for the last act?"

She looked at him, then at the moccasins in her hand. No, it was useless to yield to so ludicrous a person. The vulgarity of his wheedling, the commonness of the whole performance! It was useless to yield even the moccasins. It would be treachery to herself.

"I'm sorry," she said. "But I'd so much rather they weren't used for this kind of thing. I never intended them to be." She stood with her face averted from the ridiculous couple.

He changed as if she had slapped his face. He sat down on top of the low pupils' desk, and gazed with glazed interest round the class-room. Alice sat beside him, in her white gauze and her bedizened face. They were like two rebuked sparrows on one twig, he with his great, easy, intimate limbs, she so light and alert. And as he sat he sank into an unconscious physical sympathy with her. Miss M'Leod walked towards the door.

" You'll have to think of something as'll do instead," he muttered to Alice in a low voice, meaning the blue moccasins. And leaning down, he drew off one of the grey shoes she had on, caressing her foot with the slip of his hand over its slim bare shape. She hastily put the bare foot behind her other, shod foot.

Tom Lomas poked in his head, his overcoat collar turned up to his ears.

" Car's here," he said.

" Right-o ! Tom ! I'll chalk it up to thee, lad ! " said Percy with heavy breeziness. Then, making a great effort with himself, he rose heavily and went across to the door, to his wife, saying to her, in the same stiff voice of false heartiness :

" You'll be as right as rain with Tom. You won't mind if I don't come out ? No ! I'd better not show myself to the audience. Well—I'm glad you came, if only for a while. Good-bye then ! I'll be home after the service—but I shan't disturb you. Good-bye ! Don't get wet now——" And his voice, falsely cheerful, stiff with anger, ended in a clang of indignation.

Alice Howells sat on the infants' bench in silence. She was ignored. And she was unhappy, uneasy, because of the scene.

Percy closed the door after his wife. Then he turned with a looming slowness to Alice, and said in a hoarse whisper : " Think o' that, now ! "

She looked up at him anxiously. His face, in its dark pigment, was transfigured with indignant anger. His yellow-grey eyes blazed, and a great rush of anger seemed to be surging up volcanic in him. For a second his eyes rested on her upturned, troubled dark-blue eyes, then glanced away, as if he didn't want to look at her in his anger. Even so, she felt a touch of tenderness in his glance.

" And that's all she's ever cared about—her own things and her own way," he said, in the same hoarse whisper, hoarse with suddenly-released rage. Alice Howells hung her head in silence.

" Not another damned thing, but what's her own, her own—and her own holy way—damned holy-holy-holy, all to herself." His voice shook with hoarse, whispering rage, burst out at last.

Alice Howells looked up at him in distress.

" Oh, don't say it ! " she said. " I'm sure she's fond of you."

" *Fond* of me ! Fond of *me* ! " he blazed, with a grin of transcendent irony. " It makes her sick to look at me. I am a hairy brute, I own it. Why, she's never once touched me to be fond of me—never once—though she pretends sometimes. But a man knows——" and he made a grimace of contempt. " He knows when a woman's just stroking him, good doggie !—and when she's really a bit woman-fond of him. That woman's never been real fond of anybody or anything, all her life—she couldn't, for all her show of kindness. She's limited to herself, that woman is ; and I've looked up to her as if she was God. More fool me ! If God's not good-natured and good-hearted, then what is He——? "

Alice sat with her head dropped, realizing once more that men aren't really fooled. She was upset, shaken by his rage, and frightened, as if she too were guilty. He had sat down blankly beside her. She glanced up at him.

" Never mind ! " she said soothingly. " You'll like her again to-morrow."

He looked down at her with a grin, a grey sort of grin. " Are you going to stroke me good doggie ! as well ? " he said.

" Why ? " she asked, blank.

But he did not answer. Then after a while he resumed : " Wouldn't even leave the moccasins ! And she'd hung them up in my room, left them there for years—any man'd consider they were his. And I did want this show to-night to be a success ! What are you going to do about it ? "

" I've sent over for a pair of pale-blue satin bed-slippers of mine —they'll do just as well," she replied.

" Aye ! For all that, it's done me in."

" You'll get over it."

" Happen so ! She's curdled my inside, for all that. I don't know how I'm going to be civil to her."

" Perhaps you'd better stay at the rectory to-night," she said softly.

He looked into her eyes. And in that look, he transferred his allegiance.

" *You* don't want to be drawn in, do you ? " he asked, with troubled tenderness.

But she only gazed with wide, darkened eyes into his eyes, so she was like an open, dark doorway to him. His heart beat thick, and the faint, breathless smile of passion came into his eyes again.

" You'll have to go on, Mrs. Howells. We can't keep them waiting any longer."

It was Jim Stokes, who was directing the show. They heard the clapping and stamping of the impatient audience.

" Goodness ! " cried Alice Howells, darting to the door.

THEY were true idealists, from New England. But that is some time ago : before the war. Several years before the war, they met and married ; he a tall, keen-eyed young man from Connecticut, she a smallish, demure, Puritan-looking young woman from Massachusetts. They both had a little money. Not much, however. Even added together, it didn't make three thousand dollars a year. Still —they were free. Free !

‘Ah ! Freedom ! To be free to live one's own life ! To be twenty-five and twenty-seven, a pair of true idealists with a mutual love of beauty, and an inclination towards " Indian thought "—meaning, alas, Mrs. Besant—and an income a little under three thousand dollars a year ! But what is money ? All one wishes to do is to live a full and beautiful life. In Europe, of course, right at the fountain-head of tradition. It might possibly be done in America : in New England, for example. But at a forfeiture of a certain amount of " beauty." True beauty takes a long time to mature. The baroque is only half-beautiful, half-matured. No, the real silver bloom, the real golden-sweet bouquet of beauty had its roots in the Renaissance, not in any later or shallower period.

Therefore the two idealists, who were married in New Haven, sailed at once to Paris : Paris of the old days. They had a studio apartment on the Boulevard Montparnasse, and they became real Parisians, in the old, delightful sense, not in the modern, vulgar. It was the shimmer of the pure impressionists, Monet and his followers, the world seen in terms of pure light, light broken and unbroken. How lovely ! How lovely the nights, the river, the mornings in the old streets and by the flower-stalls and the book-stalls, the afternoons up on Montmartre or in the Tuileries, the evenings on the boulevards !

They both painted, but not desperately. Art had not taken them by the throat, and they did not take Art by the throat. They painted : that's all. They knew people—nice people, if possible, though one had to take them mixed. And they were happy.

Yet it seems as if human beings must set their claws in *something*.

To be " free," to be " living a full and beautiful life," you must, alas, be attached to something. A " full and beautiful life " means a tight attachment to *something*—at least, it is so for all idealists—or else a certain boredom supervenes ; there is a certain waving of loose ends upon the air, like the waving, yearning tendrils of the vine that spread and rotate, seeking something to clutch, something up which to climb towards the necessary sun. Finding nothing, the vine can only trail, half-fulfilled, upon the ground. Such is free-dom !—a clutching of the right pole. And human beings are all vines. But especially the idealist. He is a vine, and he needs to clutch and climb. And he despises the man who is a mere *potato*, or turnip, or lump of wood.

Our idealists were frightfully happy, but they were all the time reaching out for something to cotton on to. At first, Paris was enough. They explored Paris *thoroughly*. And they learned French till they almost felt like French people, they could speak it so glibly.

Still, you know, you never talk French with your *soul*. It can't be done. And though it's very thrilling, at first, talking in French to clever Frenchmen—they seem *so* much cleverer than oneself—still, in the long run, it is not satisfying. The endlessly clever *materialism* of the French leaves you cold, in the end, gives a sense of barrenness and incompatibility with true New England depth. So our two idealists felt.

They turned away from France—but ever so gently. France had disappointed them. " We've loved it, and we've got a great deal out of it. But after a while, after a considerable while, several years, in fact, Paris leaves one feeling disappointed. It hasn't quite got what one wants."

" But Paris isn't France."

" No, perhaps not. France is quite different from Paris. And France is lovely—quite lovely. But *to us*, though we love it, it doesn't say a great deal."

So, when the war came, the idealists moved to Italy. And they loved Italy. They found it beautiful, and more poignant than France. It seemed much nearer to the New England conception of beauty : something pure, and full of sympathy, without the *materialism* and the *cynicism* of the French. The two idealists seemed to breathe their own true air in Italy.

And in Italy, much more than in Paris, they felt they could thrill to the teachings of the Buddha. They entered the swelling stream of modern Buddhistic emotion, and they read the books, and they practised meditation, and they deliberately set themselves to

eliminate from their own souls greed, pain, and sorrow. They did
not realize—yet—that Buddha's very eagerness to free himself from
pain and sorrow is in itself a sort of greed. No, they dreamed of a
perfect world, from which all greed, and nearly all pain, and a great
deal of sorrow, were eliminated.

But America entered the war, so the two idealists had to help.
They did hospital work. And though their experience made them
realize more than ever that greed, pain, and sorrow *should* be
eliminated from the world, nevertheless the Buddhism, or the
theosophy, didn't emerge very triumphant from the long crisis.
Somehow, somewhere, in some part of themselves, they felt that
greed, pain, and sorrow would never be eliminated, because most
people don't care about eliminating them, and never will care. Our
idealists were far too western to think of abandoning all the world
to damnation, while they saved their two selves. They were far too
unselfish to sit tight under a bho-tree and reach Nirvana in a mere
couple.

It was more than that, though. They simply hadn't enough
Seitzfleisch to squat under a bho-tree and get to Nirvana by contem-
plating anything, least of all their own navel. If the whole wide
world was not going to be saved, they, personally, were not so very
keen on being saved just by themselves. No, it would be so lonesome. They were New Englanders, so it must be all or nothing.
Greed, pain, and sorrow must either be eliminated from *all the
world*, or else, what was the use of eliminating them from oneself?
No use at all ! One was just a victim.

And so,. although they still *loved* " Indian thought," and felt
very tender about it : well, to go back to our metaphor, the pole
up which the green and anxious vines had clambered so far now
proved dry-rotten. It snapped, and the vines came slowly subsiding
to earth again. There was no crack and crash. The vines held
themselves up by their own foliage, for a while. But they subsided.
The beanstalk of " Indian thought " had given way before Jack and
Jill had climbed off the tip of it to a further world.

They subsided with a slow rustle back to earth again. But they
made no outcry. They were again " disappointed." But they never
admitted it. " Indian thought " had let them down. But they
never complained. Even to one another, they never said a word.
They were disappointed, faintly but deeply disillusioned, and they
both knew it. But the knowledge was tacit.

And they still had so much in their lives. They still had Italy—
dear Italy. And they still had freedom, the priceless treasure. And

they still had so much " beauty." About the fulness of their lives they were not quite so sure. They had one little boy, whom they loved as parents should love their children, but whom they wisely refrained from fastening upon, to build their lives on him. No, no, they must live their own lives ! They still had strength of mind to know that.

But they were now no longer so very young. Twenty-five and twenty-seven had become thirty-five and thirty-seven. And though they had had a very wonderful time in Europe, and though they still loved Italy—dear Italy !—yet : they were disappointed. They had got a lot out of it : oh, a very great deal indeed ! Still, it hadn't given them quite, not *quite*, what they had expected. Europe was lovely, but it was dead. Living in Europe, you were living on the past. And Europeans, with all their superficial charm, were not *really* charming. They were materialistic, they had no *real* soul. They just did not understand the inner urge of the spirit, because the inner urge was dead in them, they were all survivals. There, that was the truth about Europeans : they were survivals, with no more getting ahead in them.

It was another bean-pole, another vine-support crumbled under the green life of the vine. And very bitter it was, this time. For up the old tree-trunk of Europe the green vine had been clambering silently for more than ten years, ten hugely important years, the years of real living. The two idealists had *lived* in Europe, lived on Europe and on European life and European things as vines in an everlasting vineyard.

They had made their home here : a home such as you could never make in America. Their watchword had been " beauty." They had rented, the last four years, the second floor of an old Palazzo on the Arno, and here they had all their " things." And they derived a profound, profound satisfaction from their apartment : the lofty, silent, ancient rooms with windows on the river, with glistening, dark-red floors, and the beautiful furniture that the idealists had " picked up."

Yes, unknown to themselves, the lives of the idealists had been running with a fierce swiftness horizontally, all the time. They had become tense, fierce hunters of " things " for their home. While their souls were climbing up to the sun of old European culture or old Indian thought, their passions were running horizontally, clutching at " things." Of course they did not buy the things for the things' sakes, but for the sake of " beauty." They looked upon their home as a place entirely furnished by loveliness, not by

" things " at all. Valerie had some very lovely curtains at the
windows of the long *salotto*, looking on the river : curtains of queer
ancient material that looked like finely-knitted silk, most beautifully
faded down from vermilion and orange, and gold, and black, down
to a sheer soft glow. Valerie hardly ever came into the *salotto*
without mentally falling on her knees before the curtains. " Chartres ! " she said. " To me they are Chartres ! " And Melville never
turned and looked at his sixteenth-century Venetian bookcase, with
its two or three dozen of choice books, without feeling his marrow
stir in his bones. The holy of holies !

The child silently, almost sinisterly, avoided any rude contact
with these ancient monuments of furniture, as if they had been nests
of sleeping cobras, or that " thing " most perilous to the touch, the
Ark of the Covenant. His childish awe was silent and cold, but final.

Still, a couple of New England idealists cannot live merely on
the bygone glory of their furniture. At least, one couple could not.
They got used to the marvellous Bologna cupboard, they got used
to the wonderful Venetian bookcase, and the books, and the Siena
curtains and bronzes, and the lovely sofas and side-tables and chairs
they had " picked up " in Paris. Oh, they had been picking things
up since the first day they landed in Europe. And they were still
at it. It is the last interest Europe can offer to an outsider : or to
an insider either.

When people came, and were thrilled by the Melville interior,
then Valerie and Erasmus felt they had not lived in vain : that
they still were living. But in the long mornings, when Erasmus was
desultorily working at Renaissance Florentine literature, and Valerie
was attending to the apartment : and in the long hours after lunch ;
and in the long, usually very cold and oppressive evenings in the
ancient palazzo : then the halo died from around the furniture,
and the things became things, lumps of matter that just stood there
or hung there, *ad infinitum*, and said nothing ; and Valerie and
Erasmus almost hated them. The glow of beauty, like every other
glow, dies down unless it is fed. The idealists still dearly loved their
things. But they had got them. And the sad fact is, things that
glow vividly while you're getting them, go almost quite cold after a
year or two. Unless, of course, people envy them very much, and
the museums are pining for them. And the Melvilles' " things,"
though very good, were not quite so good as that.

So, the glow gradually went out of everything, out of Europe, out
of Italy—" the Italians are *dears* "—even out of that marvellous
apartment on the Arno. " Why, if I had this apartment, I'd never,

never even want to go out of doors ! It's too lovely and perfect."
That was something, of course—to hear that.

And yet Valerie and Erasmus went out of doors : they even
went out to get away from its ancient, cold-floored, stone-heavy
silence and dead dignity. " We're living on the past, you know,
Dick," said Valerie to her husband. She called him Dick.

They were grimly hanging on. They did not like to give in.
They did not like to own up that they were through. For twelve
years, now, they had been " free " people living a " full and beautiful life." And America for twelve years had been their anathema,
the Sodom and Gomorrah of industrial materialism.

It wasn't easy to own that you were " through." They hated to
admit that they wanted to go back. But at last, reluctantly, they
decided to go, " for the boy's sake."—" We can't *bear* to leave
Europe. But Peter is an American, so he had better look at America
while he's young." The Melvilles had an entirely English accent
and manner ; almost ; a little Italian and French here and there.

They left Europe behind, but they took as much of it along with
them as possible. Several van-loads, as a matter of fact. All those
adorable and irreplaceable " things." And all arrived in New York,
idealists, child, and the huge bulk of Europe they had lugged along.

Valerie had dreamed of a pleasant apartment, perhaps on River-
side Drive, where it was not so expensive as east of Fifth Avenue,
and where all their wonderful things would look marvellous. She
and Erasmus house-hunted. But alas ! their income was quite under
three thousand dollars a year. They found—well, everybody knows
what they found. Two small rooms and a kitchenette, and don't
let us unpack a *thing !*

The chunk of Europe which they had bitten off went into a
warehouse, at fifty dollars a month. And they sat in two small
rooms and a kitchenette, and wondered why they'd done it.

Erasmus, of course, ought to get a job. This was what was
written on the wall, and what they both pretended not to see. But
it had been the strange, vague threat that the Statue of Liberty
had always held over them : " Thou shalt get a job ! " Erasmus
had the tickets, as they say. A scholastic career was still possible for
him. He had taken his exams brilliantly at Yale, and had kept up
his " researches," all the time he had been in Europe.

But both he and Valerie shuddered. A scholastic career ! The
scholastic world ! The *American* scholastic world ! Shudder upon
shudder ! Give up their freedom, their full and beautiful life ?
Never ! Never ! Erasmus would be forty next birthday.

The " things " remained in warehouse. Valerie went to look at them. It cost her a dollar an hour, and horrid pangs. The " things " poor things, looked a bit shabby and wretched, in that warehouse.

However, New York was not all America. There was the great clean West. So the Melvilles went West, with Peter, but without the things. They tried living the simple life, in the mountains. But doing their own chores became almost a nightmare. " Things " are all very well to look at, but it's awful handling them, even when they're beautiful. To be the slave of hideous things, to keep a stove going, cook meals, wash dishes, carry water and clean floors : pure horror of sordid anti-life !

In the cabin on the mountains, Valerie dreamed of Florence, the lost apartment ; and her Bologna cupboard and Louis-Quinze chairs, above all, her " Chartres " curtains, stood in New York and costing fifty dollars a month.

A millionaire friend came to the rescue, offering them a cottage on the Californian coast—California ! Where the new soul is to be born in man. With joy the idealists moved a little farther west, catching at new vine-props of hope.

And finding them straws ! The millionaire cottage was perfectly equipped. It was perhaps as labour-savingly perfect as is possible : electric heating and cooking, a white-and-pearl-enamelled kitchen, nothing to make dirt except the human being himself. In an hour or so the idealists had got through their chores. They were " free " —free to hear the great Pacific pounding the coast, and to feel a new soul filling their bodies.

Alas ! the Pacific pounded the coast with hideous brutality, brute force itself ! And the new soul, instead of sweetly stealing into their bodies, seemed only meanly to gnaw the old soul out of their bodies. To feel you are under the fist of the most blind and crunching brute force : to feel that your cherished idealist's soul is being gnawed out of you, and only irritation left in place of it : well, it isn't good enough.

After about nine months, the idealists departed from the Californian west. It had been a great experience, they were glad to have had it. But, in the long run, the West was not the place for them, and they knew it. No, the people who wanted new souls had better get them. They, Valerie and Erasmus Melville, would like to develop the old soul a little further. Anyway, they had not felt any influx of new soul, on the Californian coast. On the contrary.

So, with a slight hole in their material capital, they returned to Massachusetts and paid a visit to Valerie's parents, taking the boy along. The grandparents welcomed the child—poor expatriated

boy—and were rather cold to Valerie, but really cold to Erasmus.
Valerie's mother definitely said to Valerie, one day, that Erasmus
ought to take a job, so that Valerie could live decently. Valerie
haughtily reminded her mother of the beautiful apartment on the
Arno, and the " wonderful " things in store in New York, and of the
" marvellous and satisfying life " she and Erasmus had led. Valerie's
mother said that she didn't think her daughter's life looked so very
marvellous at present : homeless, with a husband idle at the age
of forty, a child to educate, and a dwindling capital : looked the
reverse of marvellous to *her*. Let Erasmus take some post in one of
the universities.

" What post ? What university ? " interrupted Valerie.

" That could be found, considering your father's connections and
Erasmus's qualifications," replied Valerie's mother. " And you
could get all your valuable things out of store, and have a really
lovely home, which everybody in America would be proud to visit.
As it is, your furniture is eating up your income, and you are living
like rats in a hole, with nowhere to go to."

This was very true. Valerie was beginning to pine for a home,
with her " things." Of course she could have sold her furniture for
a substantial sum. But nothing would have induced her to. Whatever else passed away, religions, cultures, continents, and hopes,
Valerie would *never* part from the " things " which she and Erasmus
had collected with such passion. To these she was nailed.

But she and Erasmus still would not give up that freedom, that
full and beautiful life they had so believed in. Erasmus cursed
America. He did not *want* to earn a living. He panted for Europe.

Leaving the boy in charge of Valerie's parents, the two idealists
once more set off for Europe. In New York they paid two dollars
and looked for a brief, bitter hour at their " things." They sailed
" student class "—that is, third. Their income now was less than
two thousand dollars, instead of three. And they made straight for
Paris—cheap Paris.

They found Europe, this time, a complete failure. " We have
returned like dogs to our vomit," said Erasmus ; " but the vomit
has staled in the meantime." He found he couldn't stand Europe.
It irritated every nerve in his body. He hated America too. But
America at least was a darn sight better than this miserable, dirt-
eating continent ; which was by no means cheap any more, either.

Valerie, with her heart on her things—she had really burned to
get them out of that warehouse, where they had stood now for three
years, eating up two thousand dollars—wrote to her mother she

thought Erasmus would come back if he could get some suitable work in America. Erasmus, in a state of frustration bordering on rage and insanity, just went round Italy in a poverty-stricken fashion, his coat-cuffs frayed, hating everything with intensity. And when a post was found for him in Cleveland University, to teach French, Italian, and Spanish literature, his eyes grew more beady, and his long, queer face grew sharper and more rat-like, with utter baffled fury. He was forty, and the job was upon him.

" I think you'd better accept, dear. You don't care for Europe any longer. As you say, it's dead and finished. They offer us a house on the college lot, and mother says there's room in it for all our things. I think we'd better cable ' Accept '."

He glowered at her like a cornered rat. One almost expected to see rat's whiskers twitching at the sides of the sharp nose.

" Shall I send the cablegram ? " she asked.

" Send it ! " he blurted.

And she went out and sent it.

He was a changed man, quieter, much less irritable. A load was off him. He was inside the cage.

But when he looked at the furnaces of Cleveland, vast and like the greatest of black forests, with red and white-hot cascades of gushing metal, and tiny gnomes of men, and terrific noises, gigantic, he said to Valerie :

" Say what you like, Valerie, this is the biggest thing the modern world has to show."

And when they were in their up-to-date little house on the college lot of Cleveland University, and that woebegone débris of Europe, Bologna cupboard, Venice book-shelves, Ravenna bishop's chair, Louis-Quinze side-tables, " Chartres " curtains, Siena bronze lamps, all were arrayed, and all looked perfectly out of keeping, and therefore very impressive ; and when the idealists had had a bunch of gaping people in, and Erasmus had showed off in his best European manner, but still quite cordial and American ; and Valerie had been most ladylike, but for all that, " we prefer America " ; then Erasmus said, looking at her with queer sharp eyes of a rat :

" Europe's the mayonnaise all right, but America supplies the good old lobster—what ? "

" Every time ! " she said, with satisfaction.

And he peered at her. He was in the cage : but it was safe inside. And she, evidently, was her real self at last. She had got the goods. Yet round his nose was a queer, evil, scholastic look, of pure scepticism. But he liked lobster.

I

WHEN the vicar's wife went off with a young and penniless man the scandal knew no bounds. Her two little girls were only seven and nine years old respectively. And the vicar was such a good husband. True, his hair was grey. But his moustache was dark, he was handsome, and still full of furtive passion for his unrestrained and beautiful wife.

Why did she go? Why did she burst away with such an *éclat* of revulsion, like a touch of madness?

Nobody gave any answer. Only the pious said she was a bad woman. While some of the good women kept silent. They knew.

The two little girls never knew. Wounded, they decided that it was because their mother found them negligible.

The ill wind that blows nobody any good swept away the vicarage family on its blast. Then lo and behold! the vicar, who was somewhat distinguished as an essayist and a controversialist, and whose case had aroused sympathy among the bookish men, received the living of Papplewick. The Lord had tempered the wind of misfortune with a rectorate in the north country.

The rectory was a rather ugly stone house down by the river Papple, before you come into the village. Further on, beyond where the road crosses the stream, were the big old stone cotton-mills, once driven by water. The road curved up-hill, into the bleak stone streets of the village.

The vicarage family received decided modification, upon its transference into the rectory. The vicar, now the rector, fetched up his old mother and his sister, and a brother from the city. The two little girls had a very different *milieu* from the old home.

The rector was now forty-seven years old; he had displayed an intense and not very dignified grief after the flight of his wife. Sympathetic ladies had stayed him from suicide. His hair was almost white, and he had a wild-eyed, tragic look. You had only to look at him, to know how dreadful it all was, and how he had been wronged.

Yet somewhere there was a false note. And some of the ladies, who had sympathized most profoundly with the vicar, secretly rather disliked the rector. There was a certain furtive self-righteousness about him, when all was said and done.

The little girls, of course, in the vague way of children, accepted the family verdict. Granny, who was over seventy and whose sight was failing, became the central figure in the house. Aunt Cissie, who was over forty, pale, pious, and gnawed by an inward worm, kept house. Uncle Fred, a stingy and grey-faced man of forty, who just lived dingily for himself, went into town every day. And the rector, of course, was the most important person, after Granny.

They called her the Mater. She was one of those physically vulgar, clever old bodies who had got her own way all her life by buttering the weaknesses of her menfolk. Very quickly she took her cue. The rector still "loved" his delinquent wife, and would " love her " till he died. Therefore hush! The rector's feeling was sacred. In his heart was enshrined the pure girl he had wedded and worshipped.

Out in the evil world, at the same time, there wandered a disreputable woman who had betrayed the rector and abandoned his little children. She was now yoked to a young and despicable man, who no doubt would bring her the degradation she deserved. Let this be clearly understood, and then hush! For in the pure loftiness of the rector's heart still bloomed the pure white snow-flower of his young bride. This white snow-flower did not wither. That other creature, who had gone off with that despicable young man, was none of his affair.

The Mater, who had been somewhat diminished and insignificant as a widow in a small house, now climbed into the chief arm-chair in the rectory, and planted her old bulk firmly again. She was not going to be dethroned. Astutely she gave a sigh of homage to the rector's fidelity to the pure white snow-flower, while she pretended to disapprove. In sly reverence for her son's great love, she spoke no word against that nettle which flourished in the evil world, and which had once been called Mrs. Arthur Saywell. Now, thank heaven, having married again, she was no more Mrs. Arthur Saywell. No woman bore the rector's name. The pure white snow-flower bloomed *in perpetuum*, without nomenclature. The family even thought of her as She-who-was-Cynthia.

All this was water on the Mater's mill. It secured her against Arthur's ever marrying again. She had him by his feeblest weakness, his skulking self-love. He had married an imperishable white snow-flower. Lucky man ! He had been injured. Unhappy man ! He had suffered. Ah, what a heart of love ! And he had—forgiven ! Yes, the white snow-flower was forgiven. He even had made provision in his will for her, when that other scoundrel—but hush ! Don't even *think* too near to that horrid nettle in the rank outer world ! She-who-was-Cynthia. Let the white snow-flower bloom inaccessible on the heights of the past. The present is another story.

The children were brought up in this atmosphere of cunning self-sanctification and of unmentionability. They too, saw the snow-flower on inaccessible heights. They too knew that it was throned in lone splendour aloft their lives, never to be touched.

At the same time, out of the squalid world sometimes would come a rank, evil smell of selfishness and degraded lust, the smell of that awful nettle, She-who-was-Cynthia. This nettle actually contrived at intervals, to get a little note through to the girls, her children. And at this the silver-haired Mater shook inwardly with hate. For if She-who-was-Cynthia ever came back, there wouldn't be much left of the Mater. A secret gust of hate went from the old granny to the girls, children of that foul nettle of lust, that Cynthia who had had such an affectionate contempt for the Mater.

Mingled with all this, was the children's perfectly distinct recollection of their real home, the vicarage in the south, and their glamorous but not very dependable mother, Cynthia. She had made a great glow, a flow of life, like a swift and dangerous sun in the home, forever coming and going. They always associated her presence with brightness, but also with danger ; with glamour, but with fearful selfishness.

Now the glamour was gone, and the white snow-flower, like a porcelain wreath, froze on its grave. The danger of instability, the peculiarly *dangerous* sort of selfishness, like lions and tigers, was also gone. There was now a complete stability, in which one could perish safely.

But they were growing up. And as they grew, they became more definitely confused, more actively puzzled. The Mater, as she grew older, grew blinder. Somebody had to lead her about. She did not get up till towards midday. Yet blind or bed-ridden, she held the house.

Besides, she wasn't bed-ridden. Whenever the *men* were present, the Mater was in her throne. She was too cunning to court neglect. Especially as she had rivals.

Her great rival was the younger girl, Yvette. Yvette had some of the vague, careless blitheness of She-who-was-Cynthia. But this one was more docile. Granny perhaps had caught her in time. Perhaps !

The rector adored Yvette, and spoiled her with a doting fondness ; as much as to say : am I not a soft-hearted, indulgent old boy ! He liked to have this opinion of himself, and the Mater knew his weaknesses to a hair's-breadth. She knew them, and she traded on them by turning them into decorations for him, for his character. He wanted, in his own eyes, to have a fascinating character, as women want to have fascinating dresses. And the Mater cunningly put beauty-spots over his defects and deficiencies. Her mother-love gave her the clue to his weaknesses, and she hid them for him with decorations. Whereas She-who-was-Cynthia— ! But don't mention *her*, in this connection. In her eyes, the rector was almost hump-backed and an idiot.

The funny thing was, Granny secretly hated Lucille, the elder girl, more than the pampered Yvette. Lucille, the uneasy and irritable, was more conscious of being under Granny's power, than was the spoilt and vague Yvette.

On the other hand, Aunt Cissie hated Yvette. She hated her very name. Aunt Cissie's life had been sacrificed to the Mater, and Aunt Cissie knew it, and the Mater knew she knew it. Yet as the years went on, it became a convention. The convention of Aunt Cissie's sacrifice was accepted by everybody, including the self-same Cissie. She prayed a good deal about it. Which also showed that she had her own private feelings somewhere, poor thing. She had ceased to be Cissie, she had lost her life and her sex. And now, she was creeping towards fifty, strange green flares of rage would come up in her, and at such times, she was insane.

But Granny held her in her power. And Aunt Cissie's one object in life was to look after the Mater.

Aunt Cissie's green flares of hellish hate would go up against all young things, sometimes. Poor thing, she prayed and tried to obtain forgiveness from heaven. But what had been done to her, *she* could not forgive, and the vitriol would spurt in her veins sometimes.

It was not as if the Mater were a warm, kindly soul. She wasn't. She only seemed it, cunningly. And the fact dawned gradually on the girls. Under her old-fashioned lace cap, under her silver hair, under the black silk of her stout, short, forward-bulging body, this old woman had a cunning heart, seeking forever her own female power. And through the weakness of the unfresh, stagnant men she had bred, she kept her power, as her years rolled on, from seventy to eighty, and from eighty on the new lap, towards ninety.

For in the family there was a whole tradition of " loyalty " ; loyalty to one another, and especially to the Mater. The Mater, of course, was the pivot of the family. The family was her own extended ego. Naturally she covered it with her power. And her sons and daughters, being weak and disintegrated, naturally were loyal. Outside the family, what was there for them but danger and insult and ignominy ? Had not the rector experienced it, in his marriage ? So now, caution ! Caution and loyalty, fronting the world ! Let there be as much hate and friction *inside* the family, as you like. To the outer world, a stubborn fence of unison.

II

BUT it was not until the girls finally came home from school that they felt the full weight of Granny's dead old hand on their lives. Lucille was now nearly twenty-one, and Yvette nineteen. They had been to a good girls' school, and had had a finishing year in Lausanne, and were quite the usual thing, tall young creatures with fresh, sensitive faces and bobbed hair and young-manly, deuce-take-it manners.

" What's so awfully *boring* about Papplewick," said Yvette, as they stood on the Channel boat watching the grey, grey cliffs of Dover draw near, " is that there are no *men* about. Why doesn't Daddy have some good old sports for friends ? As for Uncle Fred, he's the limit ! "

" Oh, you never know what will turn up," said Lucille, more philosophic.

" You jolly well know what to expect," said Yvette. " Choir on Sundays, and I hate mixed choirs. Boys' voices are *lovely*, when there are no women. And Sunday School and Girls' Friendly, and socials, all the dear old souls that inquire after Granny ! Not a decent young fellow for miles."

" Oh, I don't know ! " said Lucille. " There's always the Framleys. And you know Gerry Somercotes *adores* you."

" Oh, but I *hate* fellows who adore me ! " cried Yvette, turning up her sensitive nose. " They *bore* me. They hang on like lead."

" Well, what *do* you want, if you can't stand being adored ? *I* think it's perfectly all right to be adored. You know you'll never marry them, so why not let them go on adoring, if it amuses them."

" Oh, but I *want* to get married," cried Yvette.

" Well, in that case, let them go on adoring you till you find one that you can *possibly* marry."

"I never should, that way. Nothing puts me off like an adoring fellow. They *bore* me so! They make me feel beastly."

"Oh, so they do me, if they get pressing. But at a distance, I think they're rather nice."

"I should like to fall *violently* in love."

"Oh, very likely! I shouldn't! I should hate it. Probably so would you, if it actually happened. After all, we've got to settle down a bit, before we know what we want."

"But don't you *hate* going back to Papplewick?" cried Yvette, turning up her young, sensitive nose.

"No, not particularly. I suppose we shall be rather bored. I wish Daddy would get a car. I suppose we shall have to drag the old bikes out. Wouldn't you like to get up to Tansy Moor?"

"Oh, *love* it! Though it's an awful *strain*, shoving an old push-bike up those hills."

The ship was nearing the grey cliffs. It was summer, but a grey day. The two girls wore their coats with fur collars turned up, and little *chic* hats pulled down over their ears. Tall, slender, fresh-faced, naive, yet confident, too confident, in their school-girlish arrogance, they were so terribly English. They seemed so free, and were as a matter of fact so tangled and tied up, inside themselves. They seemed so dashing and unconventional, and were really so conventional, so, as it were, shut up indoors inside themselves. They looked like bold, tall young sloops, just slipping from the harbour into the wide seas of life. And they were, as a matter of fact, two poor young rudderless lives, moving from one chain anchorage to another.

The rectory struck a chill into their hearts as they entered. It seemed ugly, and almost sordid, with the dank air of that middle-class, degenerated comfort which has ceased to be comfortable and has turned stuffy, unclean. The hard, stone house struck the girls as being unclean, they could not have said why. The shabby furniture seemed somehow sordid, nothing was fresh. Even the food at meals had that awful dreary sordidness which is so repulsive to a young thing coming from abroad. Roast beef and wet cabbage, cold mutton and mashed potatoes, sour pickles, inexcusable puddings.

Granny, who "loved a bit of pork," also had special dishes, beef-tea and rusks, or a small savoury custard. The grey-faced Aunt Cissie ate nothing at all. She would sit at table, and take a single lonely and naked boiled potato on to her plate. She never ate meat. So she sat in sordid durance, while the meal went on, and Granny quickly slobbered her portion—lucky if she spilled nothing on her protuberant stomach. The food was not appetizing in itself : how could it be, when Aunt Cissie hated food herself, hated the fact of eating, and never could keep a maid-servant for three months? The girls ate with repulsion, Lucille bravely bearing up, Yvette's tender nose showing her disgust. Only the rector, white-haired, wiped his long grey moustache with his serviette, and cracked jokes. He too was getting heavy and inert, sitting in his study all day, never taking exercise. But he cracked sarcastic little jokes all the time, sitting there under the shelter of the Mater.

The country, with its steep hills and its deep, narrow valleys, was dark and gloomy, yet had a certain powerful strength of its own. Twenty miles away was the black industrialism of the north. Yet the village of Papplewick was comparatively lonely, almost lost, the life in it stony and dour. Everything was stone, with a hardness that was almost poetic, it was so unrelenting.

It was as the girls had known : they went back into the choir, they helped in the parish. But Yvette struck absolutely against Sunday School, the Band of Hope, the Girls' Friendlies—indeed against all those functions that were conducted by determined old maids and obstinate, stupid, elderly men. She avoided church duties as much as possible, and got away from the rectory whenever she could. The Framleys, a big, untidy, jolly family up at the Grange, were an enormous stand-by. And if anybody asked her out to a meal, even if a woman in one of the workmen's houses asked her to stay to tea, she accepted at once. In fact, she was rather thrilled. She liked talking to the working men, they had often such fine, hard heads. But of course they were in another world.

So the months went by. Gerry Somercotes was still an adorer. There were others, too, sons of farmers or mill-owners. Yvette really ought to have had a good time. She was always out to parties and dances, friends came for her in their motor-cars, and off she went to the city, to the afternoon dance in the chief hotel, or in the gorgeous new Palais de Danse, called the Pally.

Yet she always seemed like a creature mesmerized. She was never free to be quite jolly. Deep inside her worked an intolerable irritation, which she thought she *ought* not to feel, and which she hated feeling, thereby making it worse. She never understood at all whence it arose.

At home, she truly was irritable, and outrageously rude to Aunt Cissie. In fact, Yvette's awful temper became one of the family by-words.

Lucille, always more practical, got a job in the city as private secretary to a man who needed somebody with fluent French and shorthand. She went back and forth every day, by the same train as Uncle Fred. But she never travelled with him, and wet or fine, bicycled to the station, while he went on foot.

The two girls were both determined that what they wanted was a really jolly social life. And they resented with fury that the rectory was, for their friends, impossible. There were only four rooms downstairs : the kitchen, where lived the two discontented maid-servants : the dark dining-room : the rector's study : and the big, "homely," dreary living-room or drawing-room. In the dining-room there was a gas fire. Only in the living-room was a good hot fire kept going. Because, of course, here Granny reigned.

In this room the family was assembled. At evening, after dinner, Uncle Fred and the rector invariably played cross-word puzzles with Granny.

"Now, Mater, are you ready ? N blank blank blank blank W : a Siamese functionary."

"Eh ? Eh ? M blank blank blank blank W ? "

Granny was hard of hearing.

"No, Mater. Not M ! N blank blank blank blank W : a Siamese functionary."

"N blank blank blank blank W : a Chinese functionary."

"SIAMESE."

"Eh ? "

"SIAMESE ! SIAM ! "

"A Siamese functionary ! Now what can that be ? " said the old lady profoundly, folding her hands on her round stomach. Her two sons proceeded to make suggestions, at which she said Ah ! Ah ! The rector was amazingly clever at cross-word puzzles. But Fred had a certain technical vocabulary.

"This certainly is a hard nut to crack," said the old lady, when they were all stuck.

Meanwhile Lucille sat in a corner with her hands over her ears, pretending to read, and Yvette irritably made drawings, or hummed loud and exasperating tunes, to add to the family concert. Aunt Cissie continually reached for a chocolate, and her jaws worked ceaselessly. She literally lived on chocolates. Sitting in the distance, she put another into her mouth, then looked again at the parish magazine. Then she lifted her head, and saw it was time to fetch Granny's cup of Horlick's.

While she was gone, in nervous exasperation Yvette would open the window. The room was never fresh, she imagined it smelt :

smelt of Granny. And Granny, who was hard of hearing, heard like a weasel when she wasn't wanted to.

"Did you open the window, Yvette? I think you might remember there are older people than yourself in the room," she said.

"It's stifling! It's unbearable! No wonder we've all of us always got colds."

"I'm sure the room is large enough, and a good fire burning." The old lady gave a little shudder. "A draught to give us all our death."

"Not a draught at all," roared Yvette. "A breath of fresh air."

The old lady shuddered again, and said:

"Indeed!"

The rector, in silence, marched to the window and firmly closed it. He did not look at his daughter meanwhile. He hated thwarting her. But she must know what's what!

The cross-word puzzles, invented by Satan himself, continued till Granny had had her Horlick's, and was to go to bed. Then came the ceremony of Good night! Everybody stood up. The girls went to be kissed by the blind old woman, the rector gave his arm, and Aunt Cissie followed with a candle.

But this was already nine o'clock, although Granny was really getting old, and should have been in bed sooner. But when she was in bed, she could not sleep, till Aunt Cissie came.

"You see," said Granny, "I have *never* slept alone. For fifty-four years I never slept a night without the Pater's arm round me. And when he was gone I tried to sleep alone. But as sure as my eyes closed to sleep, my heart nearly jumped out of my body, and I lay in a palpitation. Oh, you may think what you will, but it was a fearful experience, after fifty-four years of perfect married life! I would have prayed to be taken first, but the Pater, well, no I don't think he would have been able to bear up."

So Aunt Cissie slept with Granny. And she hated it. She said *she* could never sleep. And she grew greyer and greyer, and the food in the house got worse, and Aunt Cissie had to have an operation.

But the Mater rose as ever, towards noon, and at the midday meal, she presided from her arm-chair, with her stomach protruding; her reddish, pendulous face, that had a sort of horrible majesty, dropping soft under the wall of her high brow, and her blue eyes peering unseeing. Her white hair was getting scanty, it was altogether a little indecent. But the rector jovially cracked his jokes to her, and she pretended to disapprove. But she was perfectly complacent, sitting in her ancient obesity, and after meals, getting the wind from her stomach, pressing her bosom with her hand as she " rifted " in gross physical complacency.

What the girls minded most was that, when they brought their young friends to the house, Granny always was there, like some awful idol of old flesh, consuming all the attention. There was only the one room for everybody. And there sat the old lady, with Aunt Cissie keeping an acrid guard over her. Everybody must be presented first to Granny : she was ready to be genial, she liked company. She had to know who everybody was, where they came from, every circumstance of their lives. And then, when she was *au fait*, she could get hold of the conversation.

Nothing could be more exasperating to the girls. " Isn't old Mrs. Saywell wonderful ! She takes *such* an interest in life, at nearly ninety ! "

" She does take an interest in people's affairs, if that's life," said Yvette.

Then she would immediately feel guilty. After all, it *was* wonderful to be nearly ninety, and have such a clear mind ! And Granny never *actually* did anybody any harm. It was more that she was in the way. And perhaps it was rather awful to hate somebody because they were old and in the way.

Yvette immediately repented, and was nice. Granny blossomed forth into reminiscences of when she was a girl, in the little town in Buckinghamshire. She talked and talked away, and was *so* entertaining. She really *was* rather wonderful.

Then in the afternoon Lottie and Ella and Bob Framley came, with Leo Wetherell.

" Oh, come in ! "—and in they all trooped to the sitting-room, where Granny, in her white cap, sat by the fire.

" Granny, this is Mr. Wetherell."

" Mr. What-did-you-say ? You must excuse me, I'm a little deaf ! "

Granny gave her hand to the uncomfortable young man, and gazed silently at him, sightlessly.

" You are not from our parish ? " she asked him.

" Dinnington ! " he shouted.

" We want to go a picnic to-morrow, to Bonsall Head, in Leo's car. We can all squeeze in," said Ella, in a low voice.

" Did you say Bonsall Head ? " asked Granny.

" Yes ! "

There was a blank silence.

" Did you say you were going in a car ? "

" Yes ! In Mr. Wetherell's."

" I hope he's a good driver.   It's a very dangerous road."

" He's a *very* good driver."

" Not a very good driver ? "

" Yes ! He *is* a very good driver."

" If you go to Bonsall Head, I think I must send a message to Lady Louth."

Granny always dragged in this miserable Lady Louth, when there was company.

" Oh, we shan't go that way," cried Yvette.

" Which way ? " said Granny.   " You must go by Heanor."

The whole party sat, as Bob expressed it, like stuffed ducks, fidgeting on their chairs.

Aunt Cissie came in—and then the maid with the tea.   There was the eternal and everlasting piece of bought cake.   Then appeared a plate of little fresh cakes.   Aunt Cissie had actually sent to the baker's.

" Tea, Mater ! "

The old lady gripped the arms of her chair.   Everybody rose and stood, while she waded slowly across, on Aunt Cissie's arm, to her place at table.

During tea Lucille came in from town, from her job.   She was simply worn out, with black marks under her eyes.   She gave a cry, seeing all the company.

As soon as the noise had subsided, and the awkwardness was resumed, Granny said :

" You have never mentioned Mr. Wetherell to me, have you, Lucille ? "

" I don't remember," said Lucille.

" You can't have done.   The name is strange to me."

Yvette absently grabbed another cake, from the now almost empty plate.   Aunt Cissie, who was driven almost crazy by Yvette's vague and inconsiderate ways, felt the green rage fuse in her heart. She picked up her own plate, on which was the one cake she allowed herself, and said with vitriolic politeness, offering it to Yvette :

" Won't you have mine ? "

" Oh, thanks ! " said Yvette, starting in her angry vagueness. And with an appearance of the same insouciance, she helped herself to Aunt Cissie's cake also, adding as an afterthought : " If you're sure you don't want it."

She now had two cakes on her plate.   Lucille had gone white as

a ghost, bending to her tea.   Aunt Cissie sat with a green
look of poisonous resignation.   The awkwardness was an
agony.

But Granny, bulkily enthroned and unaware, only said, in the
centre of the cyclone :

" If you are motoring to Bonsall Head to-morrow, Lucille, I wish
you would take a message from me to Lady Louth."

" Oh ! " said Lucille, giving a queer look across the table at the
sightless old woman.   Lady Louth was the King Charles' Head of
the family, invariably produced by Granny for the benefit of
visitors.   " Very well ! "

" She was so very kind last week.   She sent her chauffeur over
with a Cross-word Puzzle book for me."

" But you thanked her then," cried Yvette.

" I should like to send her a note."

" We can post it," cried Lucille.

" Oh no ! I should like you to take it.   When Lady Louth called
last time. . . ."

The young ones sat like a shoal of young fishes dumbly mouthing
at the surface of the water, while Granny went on about Lady
Louth.   Aunt Cissie, the two girls knew, was still helpless, almost
unconscious in a paroxysm of rage about the cake.   Perhaps, poor
thing, she was praying.

It was a mercy when the friends departed.   But by that time
the two girls were both haggard-eyed.   And it was then that Yvette,
looking round, suddenly saw the stony, implacable will-to-power in
the old and motherly-seeming Granny.   She sat there bulging
backwards in her chair, impassive, her reddish, pendulous old face
rather mottled, almost unconscious, but implacable, her face like a
mask that hid something stony, relentless.   It was the static inertia
of her unsavoury power.   Yet in a minute she would open her
ancient mouth to find out every detail about Leo Wetherell.   For
the moment she was hibernating in her oldness, her agedness.   But
in a minute her mouth would open, her mind would flicker awake
and with her insatiable greed for life, other people's life, she would
start on her quest for every detail.   She was like the old toad which
Yvette had watched, fascinated, as it sat on the ledge of the beehive,
immediately in front of the little entrance by which the bees emerged,
and which, with a demonish lightning-like snap of its pursed jaws,
caught every bee as it came out to launch into the air, swallowed
them one after the other, as if it could consume the whole hive-
full, into its aged, bulging, purse-like wrinkledness.   It had been

swallowing bees as they launched into the air of spring, year after
year, year after year, for generations.

But the gardener, called by Yvette, was in a rage, and killed the
creature with a stone.

" 'Appen tha *art* good for th' snails," he said, as he came down
with the stone. " But tha 'rt none goin' ter emp'y th' bee-'ive into
thy guts."

III

The next day was dull and low, and the roads were awful, for it
had been raining for weeks, yet the young ones set off on their trip,
without taking Granny's message either. They just slipped out
while she was making her slow trip upstairs after lunch. Not for
anything would they have called at Lady Louth's house. That
widow of a knighted doctor, a harmless person indeed, had become
an obnoxity in their lives.

Six young rebels, they sat very perkily in the car as they swished
through the mud. Yet they had a peaked look too. After all, they
had nothing really to rebel against, any of them. They were left
so very free in their movements. Their parents let them do almost
entirely as they liked. There wasn't really a fetter to break, nor a
prison-bar to file through, nor a bolt to shatter. The keys of their
lives were in their own hands. And there they dangled inert.

It is very much easier to shatter prison bars than to open undiscovered doors to life. As the younger generation finds out somewhat
to its chagrin. True, there was Granny. But poor old Granny, you
couldn't actually say to her : " Lie down and die, you old woman ! "
She might be an old nuisance, but she never really *did* anything.
It wasn't fair to hate her.

So the young people set off on their jaunt, trying to be very full
of beans. They could really do as they liked. And so, of course,
there was nothing to do but sit in the car and talk a lot of criticism
of other people, and silly flirty gallantry that was really rather a bore.
If there had only been a few " strict orders " to be disobeyed ! But
nothing : beyond the refusal to carry the message to Lady Louth,
of which the rector would approve because he didn't encourage
King Charles' Head either.

They sang, rather scrappily, the latest would-be comic songs, as
they went through the grim villages. In the great park the deer
were in groups near the road, roe deer and fallow, nestling in the
gloom of the afternoon under the oaks by the road, as if for the
stimulus of human company.

Yvette insisted on stopping and getting out to talk to them. The girls, in their Russian boots, tramped through the damp grass, while the deer watched them with big, unfrightened eyes. The hart trotted away mildly, holding back his head, because of the weight of the horns. But the doe, balancing her big ears, did not rise from under the tree, with her half-grown young ones, till the girls were almost in touch. Then she walked light-foot away, lifting her tail from her spotted flanks, while the young ones nimbly trotted.

" Aren't they awfully dainty and nice ! " cried Yvette. " You'd wonder they could lie so cosily in this horrid wet grass."

" Well, I suppose they've got to lie down *sometime*," said Lucille. " And it's *fairly* dry under the tree." She looked at the crushed grass, where the deer had lain.

Yvette went and put her hand down, to feel how it felt.

" Yes ! " she said doubtfully, " I believe it's a bit warm."

The deer had bunched again a few yards away, and were standing motionless in the gloom of the afternoon. Away below the slopes of grass and trees, beyond the swift river with its balustraded bridge, sat the huge ducal house, one or two chimneys smoking bluely. Behind it rose purplish woods.

The girls, pushing their fur collars up to their ears, dangling one long arm, stood watching in silence, their wide Russian boots protecting them from the wet grass. The great house squatted square and creamy-grey below. The deer, in little groups, were scattered under the old trees close by. It all seemed so still, so unpretentious, and so sad.

" I wonder where the Duke is now," said Ella.

" Not here, wherever he is," said Lucille. " I expect he's abroad where the sun shines."

The motor horn called from the road, and they heard Leo's voice :

" Come on, boys ! If we're going to get to the Head and down to Amberdale for tea, we'd better move."

They crowded into the car again, with chilled feet, and set off through the park, past the silent spire of the church, out through the great gates and over the bridge, on into the wide, damp, stony village of Woodlinkin, where the river ran. And thence, for a long time, they stayed in the mud and dark and dampness of the valley, often with sheer rock above them ; the water brawling on one hand, the steep rock or dark trees on the other.

Till, through the darkness of overhanging trees, they began to climb, and Leo changed the gear. Slowly the car toiled up through

the whitey-grey mud, into the stony village of Bolehill, that hung
on the slope, round the old cross, with its steps, that stood where
the road branched, on past the cottages whence came a wonderful
smell of hot tea-cakes, and beyond, still upwards, under dripping
trees and past broken slopes of bracken, always climbing. Until
the cleft became shallower, and the trees finished, and the slopes
on either side were bare, gloomy grass, with low dry-stone walls.
They were emerging on to the Head.

The party had been silent for some time. On either side the road
was grass, then a low stone fence, and the swelling curve of the hill-
summit, traced with the low, dry stone walls. Above this, the low sky.

The car ran out, under the low, grey sky, on the naked tops.

" Shall we stay a moment ? " called Leo.

" Oh yes ! " cried the girls.

And they scrambled out once more, to look around. They knew
the place quite well. But still, if one came to the Head, one got out
to look.

The hills were like the knuckles of a hand, the dales were below,
between the fingers, narrow, steep, and dark. In the deeps a train
was steaming, slowly pulling north : a small thing of the underworld. The noise of the engine re-echoed curiously upwards. Then
came the dull, familiar sound of blasting in a quarry.

Leo, always on the go, moved quickly.

" Shall we be going ? " he said. " Do we *want* to get down to
Amberdale for tea ? Or shall we try somewhere nearer ? "

They all voted for Amberdale, for the Marquis of Grantham.

" Well, which way shall we go back ? Shall we go by Codnor and
over Crosshill, or shall we go by Ashbourne ? "

There was the usual dilemma. Then they finally decided on the
Codnor top road. Off went the car, gallantly.

They were on the top of the world, now, on the back of the fist.
It was naked, too, as the back of your fist, high under heaven, and
dull, heavy green. Only it was veined with a network of old stone
walls, dividing the fields, and broken here and there with ruins of
old lead-mines and works. A sparse stone farm bristled with six
naked sharp trees. In the distance was a patch of smoky grey stone,
a hamlet. In some fields grey, dark sheep fed silently, sombrely.
But there was not a sound nor a movement. It was the roof of
England, stony and arid as any roof. Beyond, below, were the
shires.

" ' And see the coloured counties,' " said Yvette to herself. Here
anyhow they were not coloured. A stream of rooks trailed out from

nowhere. They had been walking, pecking, on a naked field that had been manured. The car ran on between the grass and the stone walls of the upland lane, and the young people were silent, looking out over the far network of stone fences, under the sky, looking for the curves downward that indicated a drop to one of the underneath, hidden dales.

Ahead was a light cart, driven by a man, and trudging along at the side was a woman, sturdy and elderly, with a pack on her back. The man in the cart had caught her up, and now was keeping pace.

The road was narrow. Leo sounded the horn sharply. The man on the cart looked round, but the woman on foot only trudged steadily, rapidly forward, without turning her head.

Yvette's heart gave a jump. The man on the cart was a gipsy, one of the black, loose-bodied, handsome sort. He remained seated on his cart, turning round and gazing at the occupants of the motor-car, from under the brim of his cap. And his pose was loose, his gaze insolent in its indifference. He had a thin black moustache under his thin, straight nose, and a big silk handkerchief of red and yellow tied round his neck. He spoke a word to the woman. She stood a second, solid, to turn round and look at the occupants of the car, which had now drawn quite close. Leo honked the horn again, imperiously. The woman, who had a grey-and-white kerchief tied round her head, turned sharply, to keep pace with the cart, whose driver also had settled back, and was lifting the reins, moving his loose, light shoulders. But still he did not pull aside.

Leo made the horn scream, as he put the brakes on and the car slowed up near the back of the cart. The gipsy turned round at the din, laughing in his dark face under his dark-green cap, and said something which they did not hear, showing white teeth under the line of black moustache, and making a gesture with his dark, loose hand.

" Get out o' the way then ! " yelled Leo.

For answer, the man delicately pulled the horse to a standstill, as it curved to the side of the road. It was a good roan horse and a good, natty, dark-green cart.

Leo, in a rage, had to jam on the brake and pull up too.

" Don't the pretty young ladies want to hear their fortunes ? " said the gipsy on the cart, laughing except for his dark, watchful eyes, which went from face to face, and lingered on Yvette's young, tender face.

She met his dark eyes for a second, their level search, their insolence, their complete indifference to people like Bob and Leo, and something took fire in her breast. She thought : " He is stronger than I am ! He doesn't care ! "

" Oh yes, let's ! " cried Lucille at once.

" Oh yes ! " chorused the girls.

" I say ! What about the time ? " cried Leo.

" Oh, bother the old time ! Somebody's always dragging in time by the forelock," cried Lucille.

" Well, if you don't mind *when* we get back, *I* don't," said Leo heroically.

The gipsy man had been sitting loosely on the side of his cart, watching the faces. He now jumped softly down from the shaft, his knees a bit stiff. He was apparently a man something over thirty, and a beau in his way. He wore a sort of shooting-jacket, double-breasted, coming only to the hips, of dark green-and-black frieze ; rather tight black trousers, black boots, and a dark-green cap ; with the big yellow-and-red bandanna handkerchief round his neck. His appearance was curiously elegant, and quite expensive in its gipsy style. He was handsome, too, pressing in his chin with the old, gipsy conceit, and now apparently not heeding the strangers any more, as he led his good roan horse off the road, preparing to back his cart.

The girls saw for the first time a deep recess in the side of the road, and two caravans smoking. Yvette got quickly down. They had suddenly come upon a disused quarry, cut into the slope of the roadside, and in this sudden lair, almost like a cave, were three caravans, dismantled for the winter. There was also deep at the back, a shelter built of boughs, as a stable for the horse. The grey, crude rock rose high above the caravans, and curved round towards the road. The floor was heaped chips of stone, with grasses growing among. It was a hidden, snug winter camp.

The elderly woman with the pack had gone into one of the caravans, leaving the door open. Two children were peeping out, shewing black heads. The gipsy man gave a little call, as he backed his cart into the quarry, and an elderly man came out to help him untackle.

The gipsy himself went up the steps into the newest caravan, that had its door closed. Underneath, a tied-up dog ranged forth. It was a white hound, spotted liver-coloured. It gave a low growl as Leo and Bob approached.

At the same moment, a dark-faced gipsy-woman with a pink shawl or kerchief round her head and big gold ear-rings in her ears, came down the steps of the newest caravan, swinging her flounced, voluminous green skirt. She was handsome in a bold, dark, long-faced way, just a bit wolfish. She looked like one of the bold, loping Spanish gipsies.

"Good morning, my ladies and gentlemen," she said, eyeing the girls from her bold, predative eyes. She spoke with a certain foreign stiffness.

"Good afternoon!" said the girls.

"Which beautiful little lady like to hear her fortune? Give me her little hand?"

She was a tall woman, with a frightening way of reaching forward her neck like a menace. Her eyes went from face to face, very active, heartlessly searching out what she wanted. Meanwhile the man, apparently her husband, appeared at the top of the caravan steps smoking a pipe, and with a small, black-haired child in his arms. He stood on his limber legs, casually looking down on the group, as if from a distance, his long black lashes lifted from his full, conceited, impudent black eyes. There was something peculiarly transfusing in his stare. Yvette felt it, felt it in her knees. She pretended to be interested in the white-and-liver-coloured hound.

"How much do you want, if we all have our fortunes told?" asked Lottie Framley, as the six fresh-faced young Christians hung back rather reluctantly from this pagan pariah woman.

"All of you? Ladies and gentlemen, all?" said the woman shrewdly.

"I don't want mine told! You go ahead!" cried Leo.

"Neither do I," said Bob. "You four girls."

"The four ladies?" said the gipsy woman, eyeing them shrewdly, after having looked at the boys. And she fixed her price. "Each one give me a sheeling, and a little bit more for luck? A little bit!" She smiled in a way that was more wolfish than cajoling, and the force of her will was felt, heavy as iron beneath the velvet of her words.

"All right," said Leo. "Make it a shilling a head. Don't spin it out too long."

"Oh, you!" cried Lucille at him. "We want to hear it all."

The woman took two wooden stools, from under a caravan, and placed them near the wheel. Then she took the tall, dark Lottie Framley by the hand, and bade her sit down.

"You don't care if everybody hear?" she said, looking up curiously into Lottie's face.

Lottie blushed dark with nervousness, as the gipsy woman held her hand, and stroked her palm with hard, cruel-seeming fingers.

"Oh, I don't mind," she said.

The gipsy woman peered into the palm tracing the lines of the hand with a hard, dark forefinger. But she seemed clean.

And slowly she told the fortune, while the others, standing listening, kept on crying out : "Oh, that's Jim Baggaley ! Oh, I, I don't believe it ! Oh, that's not true ! A fair woman who lives beneath a tree ! Why, whoever's that ?" until Leo stopped them with a manly warning :

"Oh, hold on, girls ! You give everything away."

Lottie retired blushing and confused, and it was Ella's turn. She was much more calm and shrewd, trying to read the oracular words. Lucille kept breaking out with : "Oh, I say !" The gipsy man at the top of the steps stood imperturbable, without any expression at all. But his bold eyes kept staring at Yvette, she could feel them on her cheek, on her neck, and she dared not look up. But Framley would sometimes look up at him, and got a level stare back from the handsome face of the male gipsy, from the dark conceited proud eyes. It was a peculiar look, in the eyes that belonged to the tribe of the humble : the pride of the pariah, the half-sneering challenge of the outcast, who sneered at law-abiding men, and went his own way. All the time, the gipsy man stood there, holding his child in his arms, looking on without being concerned.

Lucille was having her hand read—"You have been across the sea, and there you met a man—a brown-haired man—but he was too old——"

"Oh, I *say* !" cried Lucille, looking round at Yvette.

But Yvette was abstracted, agitated, hardly heeding : in one of her mesmerized states.

"You will marry in a few years—not now, but a few years— perhaps four—and you will not be rich, but you will have plenty —enough—and you will go away, a long journey."

"With my husband, or without ?" cried Lucille.

"With him——"

When it came to Yvette's turn, and the woman looked up boldly, cruelly, searching for a long time in her face; Yvette said nervously :

"I don't think I want mine told. No, I won't have mine told ! No, I won't, really !"

"You are afraid of something ?" said the gipsy woman cruelly.

"No, it's not that——" Yvette fidgeted.

"You have some secret ? You are afraid I shall say it ? Come, would you like to go in the caravan, where nobody hears ?"

The woman was curiously insinuating ; while Yvette was always wayward, perverse. The look of perversity was on her soft, frail young face now, giving her a queer hardness.

" Yes ! " she said suddenly. " Yes ! I might do that ! "

" Oh, I say ! " cried the others. " Be a sport ! "

" I don't think you'd *better !* " cried Lucille.

" Yes ! " said Yvette, with that hard little way of hers. " I'll do that. I'll go in the caravan."

The gipsy woman called something to the man on the steps. He went into the caravan for a moment or two, then reappeared, and came down the steps, setting the small child on its uncertain feet, and holding it by the hand. A dandy, in his polished black boots, tight black trousers and tight dark-green jersey, he walked slowly across with the toddling child to where the elderly gipsy was giving the roan horse a feed of oats, in the bough shelter between pits of grey rock, with dry bracken upon the stone chip floor. He looked at Yvette as he passed, staring her full in the eyes, with his pariah's bold yet dishonest stare. Something hard inside her met his stare. But the surface of her body seemed to turn to water. Nevertheless, something hard in her registered the peculiar pure lines of his face, of his straight, pure nose, of his cheeks and temples. The curious dark, suave purity of all his body, outlined in the green jersey : a purity like a living sneer.

And as he loped slowly past her, on his flexible hips, it seemed to her still that he was stronger than she was. Of all the men she had ever seen, this one was the only one who was stronger than she was, in her own kind of strength, her own kind of understanding.

So, with curiosity, she followed the woman up the steps of the caravan, the skirts of her well-cut tan coat swinging and almost showing her knees, under the pale-green cloth dress. She had long, long-striding, fine legs, too slim rather than too thick, and she wore curiously-patterned pale-and-fawn stockings of fine wool, suggesting the legs of some delicate animal.

At the top of the steps she paused and turned, debonair, to the others, saying in her naive, lordly way, so off-hand :

" I won't let her be long."

Her grey fur collar was open, showing her soft throat and pale green dress, her little plaited tan-coloured hat came down to her ears, round her soft, fresh face. There was something soft and yet overbearing, unscrupulous, about her. She knew the gipsy man had turned to look at her. She was aware of the pure dark nape of his neck, the black hair groomed away. He watched as she entered his house.

What the gipsy told her, no one ever knew. It was a long time to wait, the others felt. Twilight was deepening on the gloom, and it was turning raw and cold. From the chimney on the second caravan came smoke and a smell of rich food. The horse was fed, a yellow blanket strapped round him, and two gipsy men talked together in the distance, in low tones. There was a peculiar feeling of silence and secrecy in that lonely, hidden quarry.

At last the caravan door opened, and Yvette emerged, bending forward and stepping with long, witch-like slim legs down the steps. There was a stooping, witch-like silence about her as she emerged on the twilight.

" Did it seem long ? " she said vaguely, not looking at anybody and keeping her own counsel hard within her soft, vague waywardness. " I hope you weren't bored ! Wouldn't tea be nice ! Shall we go ? "

" You get in ! " said Bob. " I'll pay."

The gipsy-woman's full, metallic skirts of jade-green alpaca came swinging down the steps. She rose to her height, a big, triumphant-looking woman with a dark wolf face. The pink cashmere kerchief stamped with red roses, was slipping to one side over her black and crimped hair. She gazed at the young people in the twilight with bold arrogance.

Bob put two half-crowns in her hand.

" A little bit more, for luck, for your young lady's luck," she wheedled, like a wheedling wolf. "Another bit of silver, to bring you luck."

" You've got a shilling for luck, that's enough," said Bob calmly and quietly, as they moved away to the car.

" A little bit of silver ! Just a little bit, for your luck in love ! "

Yvette, with the sudden long, startling gestures of her long limbs, swung round as she was entering the car, and with long arm out-stretched, strode and put something into the gipsy's hand, then stepped, bending her height, into the car.

" Prosperity to the beautiful young lady, and the gipsy's blessing on her," came the suggestive, half-sneering voice of the woman.

The engine *birred !* then *birred !* again more fiercely, and started. Leo switched on the lights, and immediately the quarry with the gipsies fell back into the blackness of night.

" Good night ! " called Yvette's voice, as the car started. But hers was the only voice that piped up, chirpy and impudent in its nonchalance. The headlights glared down the stone lane.

" Yvette, you've got to tell us what she said to you," cried Lucille, in the teeth of Yvette's silent will *not* to be asked.

" Oh, nothing at *all* thrilling," said Yvette, with false warmth. " Just the usual old thing : a dark man who means good luck, and a fair one who means bad : and a death in the family, which if it means Granny, won't be so *very* awful : and I shall marry when I'm twenty-three, and have heaps of money and heaps of love, and two children. All sounds very nice, but it's a bit too much of a good thing, you know."

" Oh, but why did you give her more money ? "

" Oh well, I wanted to ! You *have* to be a bit lordly with people like that——"

IV

THERE was a terrific rumpus down at the rectory, on account of Yvette and the Window Fund. After the war, Aunt Cissie had set her heart on a stained glass window in the church, as a memorial for the men of the parish who had fallen. But the bulk of the fallen had been nonconformists, so the memorial took the form of an ugly little monument in front of the Wesleyan chapel.

This did not vanquish Aunt Cissie. She canvassed, she had bazaars, she made the girls get up amateur theatrical shows, for her precious window. Yvette, who quite liked the acting and showing-off part of it, took charge of the farce called *Mary in the Mirror*, and gathered in the proceeds, which were to be paid to the Window Fund when accounts were settled. Each of the girls was supposed to have a money-box for the Fund.

Aunt Cissie, feeling that the united sums must now almost suffice, suddenly called in Yvette's box. It contained fifteen shillings. There was a moment of green horror.

" Where is all the rest ? "

" Oh ! " said Yvette casually. " I just borrowed it. It wasn't so awfully much."

" What about the three pounds thirteen for *Mary in the Mirror* ? " asked Aunt Cissie, as if the jaws of Hell were yawning.

" Oh quite ! I just borrowed it. I can pay it back."

Poor Aunt Cissie ! The green tumour of hate burst inside her, and there was a ghastly, abnormal scene, which left Yvette shivering with fear and nervous loathing.

Even the rector was rather severe.

" If you needed money, why didn't you tell me ? " he said coldly. " Have you ever been refused anything in reason ? "

" I—I thought it didn't matter," stammered Yvette.

" And what have you done with the money ? "

" I suppose I've spent it," said Yvette, with wide distraught eyes and a peaked face.

" Spent it, on what ? "

" I can't remember everything : stockings and things, and I gave some of it away."

Poor Yvette ! Her lordly airs and ways were already hitting back at her, on the reflex. The rector was angry : his face had a snarling, doggish look, a sort of sneer. He was afraid his daughter was developing some of the rank, tainted qualities of She-who-was-Cynthia.

" You *would* do the large with somebody else's money, wouldn't you ? " he said, with a cold, mongrel sort of sneer, which showed what an utter unbeliever he was, at the heart. The inferiority of a heart which has no core of warm belief in it, no pride in life. He had utterly no belief in her.

Yvette went pale, and very distant. Her pride, that frail, precious flame which everybody tried to quench, recoiled like a flame blown far away, on a cold wind, as if blown out, and her face, white now and still like a snowdrop, the white snow-flower of his conceit, seemed to have no life in it, only this pure, strange abstraction.

" He has no belief in me ! " she thought in her soul. " I am really nothing to him. I am nothing, only a shameful thing. Everything is shameful, everything is shameful ! "

A flame of passion or rage, while it might have overwhelmed or infuriated her, would not have degraded her as did her father's unbelief, his final attitude of a sneer against her.

He became a little afraid, in the silence of sterile thought. After all, he needed the *appearance* of love and belief and bright life, he would never dare to face the fat worm of his own unbelief that stirred in his heart.

" What have you to say for yourself ? " he asked.

She only looked at him from that senseless snowdrop face which haunted him with fear, and gave him a helpless sense of guilt. That other one, She-who-was-Cynthia, she had looked back at him with the same numb, white fear, the fear of his degrading unbelief, the worm which was his heart's core. He *knew* his heart's core was a fat, awful worm. His dread was lest any one else should know. His anguish of hate was against any one who knew, and recoiled.

He saw Yvette recoiling, and immediately his manner changed to the worldly old good-humoured cynic which he affected.

" Ah well ! " he said. " You have to pay it back, my girl, that's all. I will advance you the money out of your allowance. But I shall charge you four per cent a month's interest. Even the devil himself must pay a percentage on his debts. Another time, if you can't trust yourself, don't handle money which isn't your own. Dishonesty isn't pretty."

Yvette remained crushed, and deflowered and humiliated. She crept about, trailing the rays of her pride. She had a revulsion even from herself. Oh, why had she ever touched the leprous money! Her whole flesh shrank as if it were defiled. Why was that? Why, why was that?

She admitted herself wrong in having spent the money. " Of course I shouldn't have done it. They are quite right to be angry," she said to herself.

But where did the horrible wincing of her flesh come from? Why did she feel she had caught some physical contagion?

" Where you're so *silly*, Yvette," Lucille lectured her : poor Lucille was in great distress—" is that you give yourself away to them all. You might *know* they'd find out. I could have raised the money for you, and saved all this bother. It's perfectly awful! But you never will think beforehand where your actions are going to land you! Fancy Aunt Cissie saying all those things to you! How *awful!* Whatever would Mamma have said, if she'd heard it?"

When things went very wrong, they thought of their mother, and despised their father and all the low brood of the Saywells. Their mother, of course, had belonged to a higher, if more dangerous and " immoral " world. More selfish, decidedly. But with a showier gesture. More unscrupulous and more easily moved to contempt : but not so humiliating.

Yvette always considered that she got her fine, delicate flesh from her mother. The Saywells were all a bit leathery, and grubby somewhere inside. But then the Saywells never let you down. Whereas the fine She-who-was-Cynthia had let the rector down with a bang, and his little children along with him. Her little children! They could not quite forgive her.

Only dimly, after the row, Yvette began to realize the other sanctity of herself, the sanctity of her sensitive, clean flesh and blood, which the Saywells with their so-called morality succeeded in defiling. They always wanted to defile it. They were the life unbelievers. Whereas, perhaps She-who-was-Cynthia had only been a moral unbeliever.

Yvette went about dazed and peaked and confused. The rector paid in the money to Aunt Cissie, much to that lady's rage. The helpless tumour of her rage was still running. She would have liked to announce her niece's delinquency in the parish magazine. It was anguish to the destroyed woman that she could not publish the news to all the world. The selfishness! The selfishness! The selfishness!

Then the rector handed his daughter a little account with himself: her debt to him, interest thereon, the amount deducted from her small allowance. But to her credit he had placed a guinea, which was the fee he had to pay for complicity.

"As father of the culprit," he said humorously, "I am fined one guinea. And with that I wash the ashes out of my hair."

He was always generous about money. But somehow, he seemed to think that by being free about money he could absolutely call himself a generous man. Whereas he used money, even generosity, as a hold over her.

But he let the affair drop entirely. He was by this time more amused than anything, to judge from appearances. He thought still he was safe.

Aunt Cissie, however, could not get over her convulsion. One night when Yvette had gone rather early, miserably, to bed, when Lucille was away at a party, and she was lying with soft, peaked limbs aching with a sort of numbness and defilement, the door softly opened, and there stood Aunt Cissie, pushing her grey-green face through the opening of the door. Yvette started up in terror.

"Liar! Thief! Selfish little beast!" hissed the maniacal face of Aunt Cissie. "You little hypocrite! You liar! You selfish beast! You greedy little beast!"

There was such extraordinary impersonal hatred in that grey-green mask, and those frantic words, that Yvette opened her mouth to scream with hysterics. But Aunt Cissie shut the door as suddenly as she had opened it, and disappeared. Yvette leaped from her bed and turned the key. Then she crept back, half demented with fear of the squalid abnormal, half numbed with paralysis of damaged pride. And amid it all, up came a bubble of distracted laughter. It *was* so filthily ridiculous!

Aunt Cissie's behaviour did not hurt the girl so very much. It was after all somewhat fantastic. Yet hurt she was: in her limbs, in her body, in her sex, hurt. Hurt, numbed, and half destroyed, with only her nerves vibrating and jangled. And still so young, she could not conceive what was happening.

Only she lay and wished she were a gipsy. To live in a camp, in a caravan, and never set foot in a house, not know the existence

of a parish, never look at a church. Her heart was hard with
repugnance against the rectory. She loathed these houses with
their indoor sanitation and their bathrooms, and their extraordinary repulsiveness. She hated the rectory, and everything it
implied. The whole stagnant, sewerage sort of life, where sewerage
is never mentioned, but where it seems to smell from the centre to
every two-legged inmate, from Granny to the servants, was foul.
If gipsies had no bathrooms, at least they had no sewerage. There
was fresh air. In the rectory there was *never* fresh air. And in the
souls of the people, the air was stale till it stank.

Hate kindled her heart, as she lay with numbed limbs. And she
thought of the words of the gipsy woman : " There is a dark man
who never lived in a house. He loves you. The other people are
treading on your heart. They will tread on your heart till you
think it is dead. But the dark man will blow the one spark up into
fire again, good fire. You will see what good fire."

Even as the woman was saying it, Yvette felt there was some
duplicity somewhere. But she didn't mind. She hated with the
cold, acrid hatred of a child the rectory interior, the sort of putridity
in the life. She liked that big, swarthy, wolf-like gipsy-woman, with
the big gold rings in her ears, the pink scarf over her wavy black
hair, the tight bodice of brown velvet, the green, fan-like skirt.
She liked her dusky, strong, relentless hands, that had pressed so
firm, like wolf's paws, in Yvette's own soft palm. She liked her.
She liked the danger and the covert fearlessness of her. She liked
her covert, unyielding sex, that was immoral, but with a hard,
defiant pride of its own. Nothing would ever get that woman under.
She would despise the rectory and the rectory morality, utterly !
She would strangle Granny with one hand. And she would have
the same contempt for Daddy and for Uncle Fred, as men, as she
would have for fat old slobbery Rover, the Newfoundland dog. A
great, sardonic female contempt, for such domesticated dogs, calling
themselves men.

And the gipsy man himself ! Yvette quivered suddenly, as if she
had seen his big, bold eyes upon her, with the naked insinuation of
desire in them. The absolutely naked insinuation of desire made
her lie prone and powerless in the bed, as if a drug had cast her in
a new, molten mould.

She never confessed to anybody that two of the ill-starred Window
Fund pounds had gone to the gipsy woman. What if Daddy and
Aunt Cissie knew *that* ! Yvette stirred luxuriously in the bed. The
thought of the gipsy had released the life of her limbs, and crystal-

lized in her heart the hate of the rectory : so that now she felt potent, instead of impotent.

When, later, Yvette told Lucille about Aunt Cissie's dramatic interlude in the bedroom doorway, Lucille was indignant.

" Oh, hang it all ! " cried she. " She might let it drop now. I should think we've heard enough about it by now ! Good heavens, you'd think Aunt Cissie was a perfect bird of paradise ! Daddy's dropped it, and after all, it's his business if it's anybody's. Let Aunt Cissie shut up ! "

It was the very fact that the rector had dropped it, and that he again treated the vague and inconsiderate Yvette as if she were some specially-licensed being, that kept Aunt Cissie's bile flowing. The fact that Yvette really was most of the time unaware of other people's feelings, and being unaware, couldn't care about them, nearly sent Aunt Cissie mad. Why should that young creature, with a delinquent mother, go through life as a privileged being, even unaware of other people's existence, though they were under her nose ?

Lucille at this time was very irritable. She seemed as if she simply went a little unbalanced, when she entered the rectory. Poor Lucille, she was so thoughtful and responsible. She did all the extra troubling, thought about doctors, medicines, servants, and all that sort of thing. She slaved conscientiously at her job all day in town, working in a room with artificial light from ten till five. And she came home to have her nerves rubbed almost to frenzy by Granny's horrible and persistent inquisitiveness and parasitic agedness.

The affair of the Window Fund had apparently blown over, but there remained a stuffy tension in the atmosphere. The weather continued bad. Lucille stayed at home on the afternoon of her half holiday, and did herself no good by it. The rector was in his study, she and Yvette were making a dress for the latter young woman, Granny was resting on the couch.

The dress was of blue silk velours, French material, and was going to be very becoming. Lucille made Yvette try it on again : she was nervously uneasy about the hang, under the arms.

" Oh, bother ! " cried Yvette, stretching her long, tender, childish arms, that tended to go bluish with the cold. " Don't be so frightfully *fussy*, Lucille ! It's quite all right."

" If that's all the thanks I get, slaving my half-day away making dresses for you, I might as well do something for myself ! "

" Well, Lucille ! You know I never *asked* you ! You know you can't bear it unless you *do* supervise," said Yvette, with that irritating blandness of hers, as she raised her naked elbows and peered over her shoulder into the long mirror.

" Oh yes ! you never *asked* me ! " cried Lucille. " As if I didn't know what you meant, when you started sighing and flouncing about."

" I ! " said Yvette, with vague surprise. " Why, when did I start sighing and flouncing about ? "

" Of course you know you did."

" Did I ? No, I didn't know ! When was it ? " Yvette could put a peculiar annoyance into her mild, straying questions.

" I shan't do another thing to this frock, if you don't stand still and *stop* it," said Lucille, in her rather sonorous, burning voice.

" You know you are most awfully nagging and irritable, Lucille," said Yvette, standing as if on hot bricks.

" Now, Yvette ! " cried Lucille, her eyes suddenly flashing in her sister's face, with wild flashes. " Stop it at once ! Why should everybody put up with your abominable and overbearing temper ? "

" Well, I don't know about *my* temper," said Yvette, writhing slowly out of the half-made frock, and slipping into her dress again.

Then, with an obstinate little look on her face, she sat down again at the table, in the gloomy afternoon, and began to sew at the blue stuff. The room was littered with blue clippings, the scissors were lying on the floor, the workbasket was spilled in chaos all over the table, and a second mirror was perched perilously on the piano.

Granny, who had been in a semi-coma, called a doze, roused herself on the big, soft couch and put her cap straight.

" I don't get much peace for my nap," she said, slowly feeling her thin white hair, to see that it was in order. She had heard vague noises.

Aunt Cissie came in, fumbling in a bag for a chocolate.

" I never saw such a mess ! " she said. " You'd better clear some of that litter away, Yvette."

" All right," said Yvette. " I will in a minute."

" Which means never ! " sneered Aunt Cissie, suddenly darting and picking up the scissors.

There was silence for a few moments, and Lucille slowly pushed her hands in her hair, as she read a book.

" You'd better clear away, Yvette," persisted Aunt Cissie.

" I will, before tea," replied Yvette, rising once more and pulling the blue dress over her head, flourishing her long, naked arms through the sleeveless armholes. Then she went between the mirrors, to look at herself once more.

As she did so, she sent the second mirror, that she had perched carelessly on the piano, sliding with a rattle to the floor. Luckily it did not break. But everybody started badly.

"She's smashed the mirror!" cried Aunt Cissie.

"Smashed a mirror! Which mirror! Who's smashed it?" came Granny's sharp voice.

"I haven't smashed anything," came the calm voice of Yvette. "It's quite all right."

"You'd better not perch it up there again," said Lucille.

Yvette, with a little impatient shrug at all the fuss, tried making the mirror stand in another place. She was not successful.

"If one had a fire in one's own room," she said crossly, "one needn't have a lot of people fussing when one wants to sew."

"Which mirror are you moving about?" asked Granny.

"One of our own that came from the vicarage," said Yvette rudely.

"Don't break it in *this* house, wherever it came from," said Granny.

There was a sort of family dislike for the furniture that had belonged to She-who-was-Cynthia. It was most of it shoved into the kitchen, and the servants' bedrooms.

"Oh, *I'm* not superstitious," said Yvette, "about mirrors or any of that sort of thing."

"Perhaps you're not," said Granny. "People who never take the responsibility for their own actions usually don't care what happens."

"After all," said Yvette, "I may say it's my own looking-glass, even if I did break it."

"And I say," said Granny, "that there shall be no mirrors broken in *this* house, if we can help it; no matter who they belong to, or did belong to. Cissie, have I got my cap straight?"

Aunt Cissie went over and straightened the old lady. Yvette loudly and irritatingly trilled a tuneless tune.

"And now, Yvette, will you please clear away?" said Aunt Cissie.

"Oh, bother!" cried Yvette angrily. "It's simply *awful* to live with a lot of people who are always nagging and fussing over trifles."

"What people, may I ask?" said Aunt Cissie ominously.

Another row was imminent. Lucille looked up with a queer cast in her eyes. In the two girls, the blood of She-who-was-Cynthia was roused.

" Of course you may ask ! You know quite well I mean the people in this beastly house," said the outrageous Yvette.

" At least," said Granny, " we don't come of half-depraved stock."

There was a second's electric pause. Then Lucille sprang from her low seat, with sparks flying from her.

" You shut up ! " she shouted, in a blast full upon the mottled majesty of the old lady.

The old woman's breast began to heave with heaven knows what emotions. The pause this time, as after the thunderbolt, was icy.

Then Aunt Cissie, livid, sprang upon Lucille, pushing her like a fury.

" Go to your room ! " she cried hoarsely. " Go to your room ! "

And she proceeded to push the white but fiery-eyed Lucille from the room. Lucille let herself be pushed, while Aunt Cissie vociferated :

" Stay in your room till you've apologized for this—till you've apologized to the Mater for this ! "

" I shan't apologize ! " came the clear voice of Lucille, from the passage, while Aunt Cissie shoved her.

Aunt Cissie drove her more wildly upstairs.

Yvette stood tall and bemused in the sitting-room, with the air of offended dignity, at the same time bemused, which was so odd on her. She still was bare-armed, in the half-made blue dress. And even *she* was half-aghast at Lucille's attack on the majesty of age. But also, she was coldly indignant against Granny's aspersion of the maternal blood in their veins.

" Of course I meant no offence," said Granny.

" Didn't you ? " said Yvette coolly.

" Of course not. I only said we're not depraved, just because we happen to be superstitious about breaking mirrors."

Yvette could hardly believe her ears. Had she heard right ? Was it possible ! Or was Granny, at her age, just telling a barefaced lie ?

Yvette knew that the old woman was telling a cool, barefaced lie. But already, so quickly, Granny believed her own statement.

The rector appeared, having left time for a lull.

" What's wrong ? " he asked cautiously, genially.

" Oh, nothing ! " drawled Yvette. " Lucille told Granny to shut up, when she was saying something. And Aunt Cissie drove her up to her room. *Tant de bruit pour une omelette !* Though Lucille *was* a bit over the mark, that time."

The old lady couldn't quite catch what Yvette said.

" Lucille really will have to learn to control her nerves," said the old woman. " The mirror fell down, and it worried me. I said so to Yvette, and she said something about superstitions and the people in the beastly house. I told her the people in the house were not depraved, if they happened to mind when a mirror was broken. And at that Lucille flew at me and told me to shut up. It really is disgraceful how these children give way to their nerves. I know it's nothing but nerves."

Aunt Cissie had come in during this speech. At first even she was dumb. Then it seemed to her, it was as Granny had said.

" I have forbidden her to come down until she comes to apologize to the Mater," she said.

" I doubt if she'll apologize," said the calm, queenly Yvette, holding her bare arms.

" And I don't want any apology," said the old lady. " It is merely nerves. I don't know what they'll come to, if they have nerves like that, at their age ! She must take Vibrofat. I am sure Arthur would like his tea, Cissie."

Yvette swept her sewing together, to go upstairs. And again she trilled her tune, rather shrill and tuneless. She was trembling inwardly.

" More glad rags ! " said her father to her, genially.

" More glad rags ! " she reiterated sagely, as she sauntered upstairs, with her day dress over one arm. She wanted to console Lucille, and ask her how the blue stuff hung now.

At the first landing she stood as she nearly always did, to gaze through the window that looked to the road and the bridge. Like the Lady of Shalott, she seemed always to imagine that someone would come along singing *Tirra-lirra !* or something equally intelligent, by the river.

V

IT was nearly tea-time. The snowdrops were out by the short drive going to the gate from the side of the house, and the gardener was pottering at the round, damp flower-beds, on the wet grass that sloped to the stream. Past the gate went the whitish muddy road, crossing the stone bridge almost immediately, and winding in a curve up to the steep, clustering, stony, smoking northern village, that perched over the grim stone mills which Yvette could see ahead down the narrow valley, their tall chimneys long and erect.

The rectory was on one side the Papple, in the rather steep valley, the village was beyond and above, further down, on the other side the swift stream. At the back of the rectory the hill went up steep, with a grove of dark, bare larches, through which the road disappeared. And immediately across stream from the rectory, facing the house, the river-bank rose steep and bushy, up to the sloping, dreary meadows, that sloped up again to dark hillsides of trees, with grey rock cropping out.

But from the end of the house, Yvette could only see the road curving round past the wall with its laurel hedge, down to the bridge, then up again round the shoulder to that first hard cluster of houses in Papplewick village, beyond the dry-stone walls of the steep fields.

She always expected *something* to come down the slant of the road from Papplewick, and she always lingered at the landing window. Often a cart came, or a motor-car, or a lorry with stone, or a labourer, or one of the servants. But never anybody who sang *Tirra-lirra!* by the river. The tirra-lirra-ing days seem to have gone by.

This day, however, round the corner on the white-grey road, between the grass and the low stone walls, a roan horse came stepping bravely and briskly downhill, driven by a man in a cap, perched on the front of his light cart. The man swayed loosely to the swing of the cart, as the horse stepped downhill, in the silent sombreness of the afternoon. At the back of the cart, long duster-brooms of reed and feather stuck out, nodding on their stalks of cane.

Yvette stood close to the window, and put the casement-cloth curtains behind her, clutching her bare upper arms with her hands.

At the foot of the slope the horse started into a brisk trot to the bridge. The cart rattled on the stone bridge, the brooms bobbed and flustered, the driver sat as if in a kind of dream, swinging along. It was like something seen in a sleep.

But as he crossed the end of the bridge, and was passing along the rectory wall, he looked up at the grim stone house that seemed to have backed away from the gate, under the hill. Yvette moved her hands quickly on her arms. And as quickly, from under the peak of his cap, he had seen her, his swarthy predative face was alert.

He pulled up suddenly at the white gate, still gazing upwards at the landing window ; while Yvette, always clasping her cold and mottled arms, still gazed abstractedly down at him, from the window.

His head gave a little, quick jerk of signal, and he led his horse

well aside, on to the grass. Then, limber and alert, he turned back
the tarpaulin of the cart, fetched out various articles, pulled forth
two or three of the long brooms of reed or turkey-feathers, covered
the cart, and turned towards the house, looking up at Yvette as
he opened the white gate.

She nodded to him, and flew to the bathroom to put on her
dress, hoping she had disguised her nod so that he wouldn't be
sure she had nodded. Meanwhile she heard the hoarse deep roaring
of that old fool, Rover, punctuated by the yapping of that young
idiot, Trixie.

She and the housemaid arrived at the same moment at the sitting-
room door.

" Was it the man selling brooms ? " said Yvette to the maid.
" All right ! " and she opened the door. " Aunt Cissie, there's a
man selling brooms. Shall I go ? "

" What sort of a man ? " said Aunt Cissie, who was sitting at
tea with the rector and the Mater : the girls having been excluded
for once from the meal.

" A man with a cart," said Yvette.

" A gipsy," said the maid.

Of course Aunt Cissie rose at once. She had to look at him.

The gipsy stood at the back door, under the steep dark bank
where the larches grew. The long brooms flourished from one
hand, and from the other hung various objects of shining copper
and brass : a saucepan, a candlestick, plates of beaten copper.
The man himself was neat and dapper, almost rakish, in his dark
green cap and double-breasted green check coat. But his manner
was subdued, very quiet : and at the same time proud, with a
touch of condescension and aloofness.

" Anything to-day, lady ? " he said, looking at Aunt Cissie with
dark, shrewd, searching eyes, but putting a very quiet tenderness
into his voice.

Aunt Cissie saw how handsome he was, saw the flexible curve of
his lips under the line of black moustache, and she was fluttered.
The merest hint of roughness or aggression on the man's part would
have made her shut the door contemptuously in his face. But he
managed to insinuate such a subtle suggestion of submission into
his male bearing, that she began to hesitate.

" The candlestick is lovely ! " said Yvette. " Did you make it ? "

And she looked up at the man with her naive, childlike eyes,
that were as capable of double meanings as his own.

" Yes, lady ! " He looked back into her eyes for a second, with that naked suggestion of desire which acted on her like a spell, and robbed her of her will. Her tender face seemed to go into a sleep.

"It's awfully nice!" she murmured vaguely.

Aunt Cissie began to bargain for the candlestick : which was a low, thick stem of copper, rising from a double bowl. With patient aloofness the man attended to her, without ever looking at Yvette, who leaned against the doorway and watched in a muse.

"How is your wife?" she asked him suddenly, when Aunt Cissie had gone indoors to show the candlestick to the rector, and ask him if he thought it was worth it.

The man looked fully at Yvette, and a scarcely discernible smile curled his lips. His eyes did not smile : the insinuation in them only hardened to a glare.

"She's all right. When are you coming that way again?" he murmured, in a low, caressive, intimate voice.

"Oh, I don't know," said Yvette vaguely.

"You come Fridays, when I'm there," he said.

Yvette gazed over his shoulder as if she had not heard him. Aunt Cissie returned, with the candlestick and the money to pay for it. Yvette turned nonchalant away, trilling one of her broken tunes, abandoning the whole affair with a certain rudeness.

Nevertheless, hiding this time at the landing window, she stood to watch the man go. What she wanted to know, was whether he really had any power over her. She did not intend him to see her this time.

She saw him go down to the gate, with his brooms and pans, and out to the cart. He carefully stowed away his pans and his brooms, and fixed down the tarpaulin over the cart. Then with a slow, effortless spring of his flexible loins, he was on the cart again, and touching the horse with the reins. The roan horse was away at once, the cart-wheels grinding uphill, and soon the man was gone, without looking round. Gone like a dream which was only a dream, yet which she could not shake off.

"No, he hasn't any power over me!" she said to herself : rather disappointed really, because she wanted somebody, or something, to have power over her.

She went up to reason with the pale and overwrought Lucille, scolding her for getting into a state over nothing.

"What does it *matter*," she expostulated, "if you told Granny to shut up! Why, everybody ought to be told to shut up, when they're being beastly. But she didn't mean it, you know. No, she didn't mean it. And she's quite sorry she said it. There's absolutely no reason to make a fuss. Come on, let's dress ourselves up and sail down to dinner like duchesses. Let's have our own back that way. Come on, Lucille ! "

There was something strange and mazy, like having cobwebs over one's face, about Yvette's vague blitheness ; her queer, misty side-stepping from an unpleasantness. It was cheering too. But it was like walking in one of those autumn mists, when gossamer strands blow over your face. You don't quite know where you are.

She succeeded, however, in persuading Lucille, and the girls got out their best party frocks : Lucille in green and silver, Yvette in a pale lilac colour with turquoise chenille threading. A little rouge and powder, and their best slippers, and the gardens of paradise began to blossom. Yvette hummed and looked at herself, and put on her most *dégagé* airs of one of the young marchionesses. She had an odd way of slanting her eyebrows and pursing her lips, and to all appearances detaching herself from every earthly consideration, and floating through the cloud of her own pearl-coloured reserves. It was amusing, and not quite convincing.

" Of course I am beautiful, Lucille," she said blandly. " And you're perfectly lovely, now you look a bit reproachful. Of course you're the most aristocratic of the two of us, with your nose ! And now your eyes look reproachful, that adds an appealing look, and you're perfect, perfectly lovely. But I'm more *winning*, in a way. Don't you agree ? " She turned with arch, complicated simplicity to Lucille.

She was truly simple in what she said. It was just what she thought. But it gave no hint of the very different *feeling* that also preoccupied her : the feeling that she had been looked upon, not from the outside, but from the inside, from her secret female self. She was dressing herself up and looking her most dazzling, just to counteract the effect that the gipsy had had on her, when he had looked at her, and seen none of her pretty face and her pretty ways, but just the dark, tremulous potent secret of her virginity.

The two girls started downstairs in state when the dinner-gong rang : but they waited till they heard the voices of the men. Then they sailed down and into the sitting-room, Yvette preening herself in her vague, debonair way, always a little bit absent ; and Lucille shy, ready to burst into tears.

" My goodness gracious ! " exclaimed Aunt Cissie, who was still wearing her dark-brown knitted sports coat. " What an apparition ! Wherever do you think you're going ? "

" We're dining with the family," said Yvette naively, " and we've put on our best gewgaws in honour of the occasion."

The rector laughed aloud, and Uncle Fred said :

" The family feels itself highly honoured."

Both the elderly men were quite gallant, which was what Yvette wanted.

" Come and let me feel your dresses, do ! " said Granny. " Are they your best ? It *is* a shame I can't see them."

" To-night, Mater," said Uncle Fred, " we shall have to take the young ladies in to dinner, and live up to the honour. Will you go with Cissie ? "

" I certainly will," said Granny. " Youth and beauty must come first."

" Well, to-night, Mater ! " said the rector, pleased.

And he offered his arm to Lucille, while Uncle Fred escorted Yvette.

But it was a draggled, dull meal, all the same. Lucille tried to be bright and sociable, and Yvette really was most amiable, in her vague, cobwebby way. Dimly, at the back of her mind, she was thinking : Why are we all only like mortal pieces of furniture ? Why is nothing *important ?*

That was her constant refrain to herself : Why is nothing important ? Whether she was in church, or at a party of young people, or dancing in the hotel in the city, the same little bubble of a question rose repeatedly on her consciousness : Why is nothing important ?

There were plenty of young men to make love to her : even devotedly. But with impatience she had to shake them off. Why were they so unimportant ?—so irritating !

She never even thought of the gipsy. He was a perfectly negligible incident. Yet the approach of Friday loomed strangely significant. " What are we doing on Friday ? " she said to Lucille. To which Lucille replied that they were doing nothing. And Yvette was vexed.

Friday came, and in spite of herself she thought all day of the quarry off the road up high Bonsall Head. She wanted to be there. That was all she was conscious of. She wanted to be there. She had not even a dawning idea of going there. Besides, it was raining again. But as she sewed the blue dress, finishing it for the party up at Lambley Close to-morrow, she just felt that her soul was up there, at the quarry, among the caravans, with the gipsies. Like one lost, or whose soul was stolen, she was not present in her body, the shell of her body. Her intrinsic body was away at the quarry, among the caravans.

The next day, at the party, she had no idea that she was being sweet to Leo. She had no idea that she was snatching him away from the tortured Ella Framley. Not until, when she was eating her pistachio ice, he said to her :

" Why don't you and me get engaged, Yvette ? I'm absolutely sure it's the right thing for us both."

Leo was a bit common, but good-natured and well-off. Yvette quite liked him. But engaged ! How perfectly silly ! She felt like offering him a set of her silk underwear, to get engaged to.

" But I thought it was Ella ! " she said, in wonder.

" Well ! It might ha' been, but for you. It's your doings, you know ! Ever since those gipsies told your fortune, I felt it was me or nobody, for you, and you or nobody, for me."

" Really ! " said Yvette, simply lost in amazement. " Really ! "

" Didn't you feel a bit the same ? " he asked.

" Really ! " Yvette kept on gasping softly, like a fish.

" You felt a bit the same, didn't you ? " he said.

" What ? About what ? " she asked, coming to.

" About me, as I feel about you."

" Why ? What ? Getting engaged, you mean ? I ? No ! Why how *could* I ? I could never have dreamed of such an impossible thing."

She spoke with her usual heedless candour, utterly unoccupied with his feelings.

" What was to prevent you ? " he said, a bit nettled. " I thought you did."

" Did you *really now* ? " she breathed in amazement, with that soft, virgin, heedless candour which made her her admirers and her enemies.

She was so completely amazed, there was nothing for him to do but twiddle his thumbs in annoyance.

The music began, and he looked at her.

" No ! I won't dance any more," she said, drawing herself up and gazing away rather loftily over the assembly, as if he did not exist. There was a touch of puzzled wonder on her brow, and her soft, dim virgin face did indeed suggest the snowdrop of her father's pathetic imagery.

" But of course *you* will dance," she said, turning to him with young condescension. " Do ask somebody to have this with you."

He rose, angry, and went down the room.

She remained soft and remote in her amazement. Expect Leo to propose to her ! She might as well have expected old Rover the

Newfoundland dog to propose to her. Get engaged, to any man on earth ? No, good heavens, nothing more ridiculous could be imagined !

It was then, in a fleeting side-thought, that she realized that the gipsy existed. Instantly, she was indignant. Him, of all things ! Him ! Never !

" Now why ? " she asked herself, again in hushed amazement. " Why ? It's *absolutely* impossible : absolutely ! So why is it ? "

This was a nut to crack. She looked at the young men dancing, elbows out, hips prominent, waists elegantly in. They gave her no clue to her problem. Yet she did particularly dislike the forced elegance of the waists and the prominent hips, over which the well-tailored coats hung with such effeminate discretion.

" There is something about me which they don't see and never would see," she said angrily to herself. And at the same time, she was relieved that they didn't and couldn't. It made life so very much simpler.

And again, since she was one of the people who are conscious in visual images, she saw the dark-green jersey rolled on the black trousers of the gipsy, his fine, quick hips, alert as eyes. They were elegant. The elegance of these dancers seemed so stuffed, hips merely wadded with flesh. Leo the same, thinking himself such a fine dancer, and a fine figure of a fellow !

Then she saw the gipsy's face ; the straight nose, the slender mobile lips, and the level, significant stare of the black eyes, which seemed to shoot her in some vital, undiscovered place, unerring.

She drew herself up angrily. How dared he look at her like that ? So she gazed glaringly at the insipid beaux on the dancing floor. And she despised them. Just as the raggle-taggle gipsy women despise men who are not gipsies, despise their dog-like walk down the streets, she found herself despising this crowd. Where among them was the subtle, lonely, insinuating challenge that could reach her ?

She did not want to mate with a housedog.

Her sensitive nose turned up, her soft brown hair fell like a soft sheath round her tender, flower-like face, as she sat musing. She seemed so virginal. At the same time, there was a touch of the tall young virgin *witch* about her, that made the housedog men shy off. She might metamorphose into something uncanny before you knew where you were.

This made her lonely, in spite of all the courting. Perhaps the courting only made her lonelier.

Leo, who was a sort of mastiff among the housedogs, returned after his dance, with fresh cheery-o! courage.

"You've had a little think about it, haven't you?" he said, sitting down beside her: a comfortable, well-nourished, determined sort of fellow. She did not know why it irritated her so unreasonably, when he hitched up his trousers at the knee, over his good-sized but not very distinguished legs, and lowered himself assuredly on to a chair.

"Have I?" she said vaguely. "About what?"

"You know what about," he said. "Did you make up your mind?"

"Make up my mind about what?" she asked, innocently.

In her upper consciousness, she truly had forgotten.

"Oh!" said Leo, settling his trousers again. "About me and you getting engaged, you know." He was almost as off-hand as she.

"Oh, that's *absolutely* impossible," she said, with mild amiability, as if it were some stray question among the rest. "Why, I never even thought of it again. Oh, don't talk about that sort of nonsense! That sort of thing is *absolutely* impossible," she reiterated like a child.

"That sort of thing is, is it?" he said, with an odd smile at her calm, distant assertion. "Well, what sort of thing *is* possible, then? You don't want to die an old maid, do you?"

"Oh, I don't mind," she said absently.

"I do," he said.

She turned round and looked at him in wonder.

"Why?" she said. "Why should you mind if I was an old maid?"

"Every reason in the world," he said, looking up at her with a bold, meaningful smile, that wanted to make its meaning blatant, if not patent.

But instead of penetrating into some deep, secret place, and shooting her there, Leo's bold and patent smile only hit her on the outside of the body, like a tennis ball, and caused the same kind of sudden irritated reaction.

"I think this sort of thing is awfully silly," she said, with minx-like spite. "Why, you're practically engaged to—to——" she pulled herself up in time—"probably half a dozen other girls. I'm not flattered by what you've said. I should hate it if anybody knew! Hate it! I shan't breathe a word of it, and I hope you'll have the sense not to. There's Ella!"

And keeping her face averted from him, she sailed away like a tall, soft flower, to join poor Ella Framley.

Leo flapped his white gloves.

" Catty little bitch ! " he said to himself. But he was of the mastiff type, he rather liked the kitten to fly in his face. He began definitely to single her out.

VI

THE next week it poured again with rain. And this irritated Yvette with strange anger. She had intended it should be fine. Especially she insisted it should be fine towards the week-end. Why, she did not ask herself.

Thursday, the half-holiday, came with a hard frost, and sun. Leo arrived with his car, the usual bunch. Yvette disagreeably and unaccountably refused to go.

" No thanks, I don't feel like it," she said.

She rather enjoyed being Mary-Mary-quite-contrary.

Then she went for a walk by herself, up the frozen hills, to the Black Rocks.

The next day also came sunny and frosty. It was February, but in the north country the ground did not thaw in the sun. Yvette announced that she was going for a ride on her bicycle, and taking her lunch as she might not be back till afternoon.

She set off, not hurrying. In spite of the frost, the sun had a touch of spring. In the park, the deer were standing in the distance, in the sunlight, to be warm. One doe, white-spotted, walked slowly across the motionless landscape.

Cycling, Yvette found it difficult to keep her hands warm, even when bodily she was quite hot. Only when she had to walk up the long hill, to the top, and there was no wind.

The upland was very bare and clear, like another world. She had climbed on to another level. She cycled slowly, a little afraid of taking the wrong lane, in the vast maze of stone fences. As she passed along the lane she thought was the right one, she heard a faint tapping noise, with a slight metallic resonance.

The gipsy man was seated on the ground with his back to the cart-shaft, hammering a copper bowl. He was in the sun, bare-headed, but wearing his green jersey. Three small children were moving quietly round, playing in the horse's shelter : the horse and cart were gone. An old woman, bent, with a kerchief round her head, was cooking over a fire of sticks. The only sound was the rapid, ringing tap-tap-tap ! of the small hammer on the dull copper.

The man looked up at once, as Yvette stepped from her bicycle, but he did not move, though he ceased hammering. A delicate, barely discernible smile of triumph was on his face. The old woman looked round, keenly, from under her dirty grey hair. The man spoke a half-audible word to her, and she turned again to her fire. He looked up at Yvette.

"How are you all getting on?" she asked politely.

"All right, eh! You sit down a minute?" He turned as he sat, and pulled a stool from under the caravan for Yvette. Then, as she wheeled her bicycle to the side of the quarry, he started hammering again, with that bird-like, rapid light stroke.

Yvette went to the fire to warm her hands.

"Is this the dinner cooking?" she asked childishly, of the old gipsy, as she spread her long tender hands, mottled red with the cold, to the embers.

"Dinner, yes!" said the old woman. "For him! And for the children."

She pointed with the long fork at the three black-eyed, staring children, who were staring at her from under their black fringes. But they were clean. Only the old woman was not clean. The quarry itself they had kept perfectly clean.

Yvette crouched in silence, warming her hands. The man rapidly hammered away with intervals of silence. The old hag slowly climbed the steps to the third, oldest caravan. The children began to play again, like little wild animals, quiet and busy.

"Are they your children?" asked Yvette, rising from the fire and turning to the man.

He looked her in the eyes, and nodded.

"But where's your wife?"

"She's gone out with the basket. They've all gone out, cart and all, selling things. I don't go selling things. I make them, but I don't go selling them. Not often. I don't often."

"You make all the copper and brass things?" she said.

He nodded, and again offered her the stool. She sat down.

"You said you'd be here on Fridays," she said. "So I came this way, as it was so fine."

"Very fine day!" said the gipsy, looking at her cheek, that was still a bit blanched by the cold, and the soft hair over her reddened ear, and the long, still mottled hands on her knee.

"You get cold, riding a bicycle?" he asked.

"My hands!" she said, clasping them nervously.

"You didn't wear gloves?"

"I did, but they weren't much good."

"Cold comes through," he said.

"Yes!" she replied.

The old woman came slowly, grotesquely down the steps of the caravan, with some enamel plates.

"The dinner cooked, eh?" he called softly.

The old woman muttered something, as she spread the plates near the fire. Two pots hung from a long iron horizontal bar, over the embers of the fire. A little pan seethed on a small iron tripod. In the sunshine, heat and vapour wavered together.

He put down his tools and the pot, and rose from the ground.

"You eat something along of us?" he asked Yvette, not looking at her.

"Oh, I brought my lunch," said Yvette.

"You eat some stew?" he said. And again he called quietly, secretly to the old woman, who muttered in answer, as she slid the iron pot towards the end of the bar.

"Some beans, and some mutton in it," he said.

"Oh thanks awfully!" said Yvette. Then, suddenly taking courage, added: "Well yes, just a very little, if I may."

She went across to untie her lunch from her bicycle, and he went up the steps to his own caravan. After a minute, he emerged, wiping his hands on a towel.

"You want to come up and wash your hands?" he said.

"No, I think not," she said. "They are clean."

He threw away his wash-water, and set off down the road with a high brass jug, to fetch clean water from the spring that trickled into a small pool, taking a cup to dip it with.

When he returned, he set the jug and the cup by the fire, and fetched himself a short log, to sit on. The children sat on the floor by the fire, in a cluster, eating beans and bits of meat with spoon or fingers. The man on the log ate in silence, absorbedly. The woman made coffee in the black pot on the tripod, hobbling upstairs for the cups. There was silence in the camp. Yvette sat on her stool, having taken off her hat and shaken her hair in the sun.

"How many children have you?" Yvette asked suddenly.

"Say five," he replied slowly, as he looked up into her eyes.

And again the bird of her heart sank down and seemed to die. Vaguely, as in a dream, she received from him the cup of coffee. She was aware only of his silent figure, sitting like a shadow there on the log, with an enamel cup in his hand, drinking his coffee in silence. Her will had departed from her limbs, he had power over her: his shadow was on her.

And he, as he blew his hot coffee, was aware of one thing only, the mysterious fruit of her virginity, her perfect tenderness in the body.

At length he put down his coffee-cup by the fire, then looked round at her. Her hair fell across her face, as she tried to sip from the hot cup. On her face was that tender look of sleep, which a nodding flower has when it is full out. Like a mysterious early flower, she was full out, like a snowdrop which spreads its three white wings in a flight into the waking sleep of its brief blossoming. The waking sleep of her full-opened virginity, entranced like a snowdrop in the sunshine, was upon her.

The gipsy, supremely aware of her, waited for her like the substance of shadow, as shadow waits and is there.

At length his voice said, without breaking the spell :

" You want to go in my caravan now, and wash your hands ? "

The childlike, sleep-waking eyes of her moment of perfect virginity looked into his, unseeing. She was only aware of the dark strange effluence of him bathing her limbs, washing her at last purely will-less. She was aware of *him*, as a dark, complete power.

" I think I might," she said.

He rose silently, then turned to speak, in a low command, to the old woman. And then again he looked at Yvette, and putting his power over her, so that she had no burden of herself, or of action.

" Come ! " he said.

She followed simply, followed the silent, secret, overpowering motion of his body in front of her. It cost her nothing. She was gone in his will.

He was at the top of the steps, and she at the foot, when she become aware of an intruding sound. She stood still, at the foot of the steps. A motor-car was coming. He stood at the top of the steps, looking round strangely. The old woman harshly called something, as with rapidly increasing sound, a car rushed near. It was passing.

Then they heard the cry of a woman's voice, and the brakes on the car. It had pulled up, just beyond the quarry.

The gipsy came down the steps, having closed the door of the caravan.

" You want to put your hat on," he said to her.

Obediently she went to the stool by the fire, and took up her hat. He sat down by the cart-wheel, darkly, and took up his tools. The rapid tap-tap-tap of his hammer, rapid and angry now like the sound of a tiny machine-gun, broke out just as the voice of the woman was heard crying :

" May we warm our hands at the camp fire ? "

She advanced, dressed in a sleek but bulky coat of sable fur.
A man followed, in a blue great-coat ; pulling off his fur gloves
and pulling out a pipe.

" It looked so tempting," said the woman in the coat of many
dead little animals, smiling a broad, half-condescending, half-
hesitant simper, around the company.

No one said a word.

She advanced to the fire, shuddering a little inside her coat, with
the cold. They had been driving in an open car.

She was a very small woman, with a rather large nose : probably
a Jewess. Tiny almost as a child, in that sable coat she looked
much more bulky than she should, and her wide, rather resentful
brown eyes of a spoilt Jewess gazed oddly out of her expensive get-up.

She crouched over the low fire, spreading her little hands, on
which diamonds and emeralds glittered.

" Ugh ! " she shuddered. " Of course we ought not to have
come in an open car ! But my husband won't even let me say
I'm cold ! " She looked round at him with her large, childish,
reproachful eyes, that had still the canny shrewdness of a bourgeois
Jewess : a rich one, probably.

Apparently she was in love, in a Jewess's curious way, with the
big, blond man. He looked back at her with his abstracted blue
eyes, that seemed to have no lashes, and a small smile creased his
smooth, curiously naked cheeks. The smile didn't mean anything
at all.

He was a man one connects instantly with winter sports, ski-ing
and skating. Athletic, unconnected with life, he slowly filled his
pipe, pressing in the tobacco with long, powerful, reddened finger.

The Jewess looked at him to see if she got any response from
him. Nothing at all, but that odd, blank smile. She turned again
to the fire, tilting her eyebrows and looking at her small, white,
spread hands.

He slipped off his heavily-lined coat, and appeared in one of
the handsome, sharp-patterned knitted jerseys, in yellow and grey
and black, over well-cut trousers, rather wide. Yes, they were
both expensive ! And he had a magnificent figure, an athletic,
prominent chest. Like an experienced camper, he began building
the fire together, quietly : like a soldier on campaign.

" D'you think they'd mind if we put some fir-cones on, to make
a blaze ? " he asked of Yvette, with a silent glance at the hammering
gipsy.

" Love it, I should think," said Yvette, in a daze, as the spell of the gipsy slowly left her, feeling stranded and blank.

The man went to the car, and returned with a little sack of cones, from which he drew a handful.

" Mind if we make a blaze ? " he called to the gipsy.

" Eh ? "

" Mind if we make a blaze with a few cones ! "

" You go ahead ! " said the gipsy.

The man began placing the cones lightly, carefully on the red embers. And soon, one by one, they caught fire, and burned like roses of flame, with a sweet scent.

" Ah, lovely, lovely ! " cried the little Jewess, looking up at her man again. He looked down at her quite kindly, like the sun on ice. " Don't you love fire ? Oh, I love it ! " the little Jewess cried to Yvette, across the hammering.

The hammering annoyed her. She looked round with a slight frown on her fine little brows, as if she would bid the man stop. Yvette looked round too. The gipsy was bent over his copper bowl, legs apart, head down, lithe arm lifted. Already he seemed so far from her.

The man who accompanied the little Jewess strolled over to the gipsy, and stood in silence looking down on him, holding his pipe to his mouth. Now they were two men, like two strange male dogs, having to sniff one another.

" We're on our honeymoon," said the little Jewess, with an arch, resentful look at Yvette. She spoke in a rather high, defiant voice, like some bird, a jay, or a rook, calling.

" Are you really ? " said Yvette.

" Yes ! Before we're married ! Have you heard of Simon Fawcett ? "—she named a wealthy and well-known engineer of the north country. " Well, I'm Mrs. Fawcett, and he's just divorcing me ! " She looked at Yvette with curious defiance and wistfulness.

" Are you really ! " said Yvette.

She understood now the look of resentment and defiance in the little Jewess's big, childlike brown eyes. She was an honest little thing, but perhaps her honesty was *too* rational. Perhaps it partly explained the notorious unscrupulousness of the well-known Simon Fawcett.

" Yes ! As soon as we get the divorce, I'm going to marry Major Eastwood."

Her cards were now all on the table. She was not going to deceive anybody.

Behind her, the two men were talking briefly. She glanced round, and fixed the gipsy with her big brown eyes.

He was looking up, as if shyly, at the big fellow in the sparkling jersey, who was standing pipe in mouth, man to man, looking down.

"With the horses back of Arras," said the gipsy, in a low voice.

They were talking war. The gipsy had served with the artillery teams, in the Major's own regiment.

"*Ein schöner Mensch!*" said the Jewess. "A handsome man, eh?"

For her, too, the gipsy was one of the common men, the Tommies.

"Quite handsome!" said Yvette.

"You are cycling?" asked the Jewess in a tone of surprise.

"Yes! Down to Papplewick. My father is rector of Papplewick: Mr. Saywell!"

"Oh!" said the Jewess. "I know! A clever writer! Very clever! I have read him."

The fir-cones were all consumed already, the fire was a tall pile now of crumbling, shattering fire-roses. The sky was clouding over for afternoon. Perhaps towards evening it would snow.

The Major came back, and slung himself into his coat.

"I thought I remembered his face!" he said. "One of our grooms, A1 man with horses."

"Look!" cried the Jewess to Yvette. "Why don't you let us motor you down to Normanton. We live in Scoresby. We can tie the bicycle on behind."

"I think I will," said Yvette.

"Come!" called the Jewess to the peeping children, as the blond man wheeled away the bicycle. "Come! Come here!" and taking out her little purse, she held out a shilling.

"Come!" she cried. "Come and take it!"

The gipsy had laid down his work, and gone into his caravan. The old woman called hoarsely to the children, from her enclosure. The two elder children came stealing forward. The Jewess gave them the two bits of silver, a shilling and a florin, which she had in her purse, and again the hoarse voice of the unseen old woman was heard.

The gipsy descended from his caravan and strolled to the fire. The Jewess searched his face with the peculiar bourgeois boldness of her race.

"You were in the war, in Major Eastwood's regiment?" she said.

"Yes, lady!"

"Imagine you both being here now! It's going to snow." She looked up at the sky.

" Later on," said the man, looking at the sky.

He too had gone inaccessible. His race was very old, in its peculiar battle with established society, and had no conception of winning. Only now and then it could score.

But since the war, even the old sporting chance of scoring now and then, was pretty well quenched. There was no question of yielding. The gipsy's eyes still had their bold look : but it was hardened and directed far away, the touch of insolent intimacy was gone. He had been through the war.

He looked at Yvette.

" You're going back in the motor-car ? " he said.

" Yes ! " she replied, with a rather mincing mannerism. " The weather is so treacherous ! "

" Treacherous weather ! " he repeated, looking at the sky.

She could not tell in the least what his feelings were. In truth, she wasn't very much interested. She was rather fascinated, now, by the little Jewess, mother of two children, who was taking her wealth away from the well-known engineer and transferring it to the penniless, sporting young Major Eastwood, who must be five or six years younger than she. Rather intriguing !

The blond man returned.

" A cigarette, Charles ! " cried the little Jewess, plaintively.

He took out his case, slowly, with his slow, athletic movement. Something sensitive in him made him slow, cautious, as if he had hurt himself against people. He gave a cigarette to his wife, then one to Yvette, then offered the case, quite simply, to the gipsy. The gipsy took one.

" Thank you, sir ! "

And he went quietly to the fire, and stooping, lit it at the red embers. Both women watched him.

" Well, good-bye ! " said the Jewess, with her old bourgeois free-masonry. " Thank you for the warm fire."

" Fire is everybody's," said the gipsy.

The young child came toddling to him.

" Good-bye ! " said Yvette. " I hope it won't snow for you."

" We don't mind a bit of snow," said the gipsy.

" Don't you ? " said Yvette. " I should have thought you would ! "

" No ! " said the gipsy.

She flung her scarf royally over her shoulder, and followed the fur coat of the Jewess, which seemed to walk on little legs of its own.

VII

Yvette was rather thrilled by the Eastwoods, as she called them. The little Jewess had only to wait three months now, for the final decree. She had boldly rented a small summer cottage, by the moors up at Scoresby, not far from the hills. Now it was dead winter, and she and the Major lived in comparative isolation, without any maid-servant. He had already resigned his commission in the regular army, and called himself Mr. Eastwood. In fact, they were already Mr. and Mrs. Eastwood, to the common world.

The little Jewess was thirty-six, and her two children were both over twelve years of age. The husband had agreed that she should have the custody, as soon as she was married to Eastwood.

So there they were, this queer couple, the tiny, finely-formed little Jewess with her big, resentful, reproachful eyes, and her mop of carefully-barbered black, curly hair, an elegant little thing in her way ; and the big, pale-eyed young man, powerful and wintry, the remnant, surely, of some old uncanny Danish stock : living together in a small modern house near the moors and the hills, and doing their own housework.

It was a funny household. The cottage was hired furnished, but the little Jewess had brought along her dearest pieces of furniture. She had an odd little taste for the rococo, strange curving cupboards inlaid with mother-of-pearl, tortoiseshell, ebony, heaven knows what ; strange tall flamboyant chairs from Italy, with sea-green brocade : astonishing saints with wind-blown, richly-coloured carven garments and pink faces : shelves of weird old Saxe and Capo di Monte figurines : and finally, a strange assortment of astonishing pictures painted on the back of glass, done probably in the early years of the nineteenth century, or in the late eighteenth.

In this crowded and extraordinary interior she received Yvette, when the latter made a stolen visit. A whole system of stoves had been installed into the cottage, every corner was warm, almost hot. And there was the tiny rococo figurine of the Jewess herself, in a perfect little frock, and an apron, putting slices of ham on the dish, while the great snow-bird of a major, in a white sweater and grey trousers, cut bread, mixed mustard, prepared coffee, and did all the rest. He had even made the dish of jugged hare which followed the cold meats and caviare.

The silver and the china were really valuable, part of the bride's trousseau. The Major drank beer from a silver mug, the little Jewess and Yvette had champagne in lovely glasses, the Major brought in coffee. They talked away. The little Jewess had a burning indignation against her first husband. She was intensely moral, so moral, that she was a divorcée. The Major too, strange wintry bird, so powerful, handsome, too, in his way, but pale round the eyes as if he had no eyelashes, like a bird, he too had a curious indignation against life, because of the false morality. That powerful, athletic chest hid a strange, snowy sort of anger. And his tenderness for the little Jewess was based on his sense of outraged justice, the abstract morality of the north blowing him, like a strange wind, into isolation.

As the afternoon drew on, they went to the kitchen, the Major pushed back his sleeves, showing his powerful athletic white arms, and carefully, deftly washed the dishes, while the women wiped. It was not for nothing his muscles were trained. Then he went round attending to the stoves of the small house, which only needed a moment or two of care each day. And after this, he brought out a small, closed car and drove Yvette home, in the rain, depositing her at the back gate, a little wicket among the larches, through which the earthen steps sloped downwards to the house.

She was really amazed by this couple.

"Really, Lucille!" she said. "I do meet the most extra-ordinary people!" And she gave a detailed description.

"I think they sound rather nice!" said Lucille. "I like the Major doing the housework, and looking so frightfully Bond-streety with it all. I should think *when they're married*, it would be rather fun knowing them."

"Yes!" said Yvette vaguely. "Yes! Yes, it would!"

The very strangeness of the connection between the tiny Jewess and that pale-eyed, athletic young officer made her think again of her gipsy, who had been utterly absent from her consciousness, but who now returned with sudden painful force.

"What is it, Lucille," she asked, "that brings people together? People like the Eastwoods, for instance? And Daddy and Mamma, so frightfully unsuitable? And that gipsy woman who told my fortune, like a great horse, and the gipsy man, so fine and delicately cut? What is it?"

"I suppose it's sex, whatever that is," said Lucille.

"Yes, what is it? It's not really anything *common*, like common sensuality, you know, Lucille. It really isn't."

"No, I suppose not," said Lucille. "Anyhow, I suppose it needn't be."

"Because, you see, the *common* fellows, you know, who make a girl feel *low* : nobody cares much about them. Nobody feels any connection with them. Yet they're supposed to be the sexual sort."

" I suppose," said Lucille, " there's the low sort of sex, and there's the other sort, that isn't low. It's frightfully complicated, really ! I *loathe* common fellows. And I never feel anything *sexual* "—she laid a rather disgusted stress on the word—" for fellows who aren't common. Perhaps I haven't got any sex."

" That's just it ! " said Yvette. " Perhaps neither of us has. Perhaps we haven't really *got* any sex, to connect us with men."

" How horrible it sounds : *connect us with men !* " cried Lucille, with revulsion. " Wouldn't you hate to be connected with men that way ? Oh I think it's an awful pity there has to *be* sex ! It would be so much better if we could still be men and women, without that sort of thing."

Yvette pondered. Far in the background was the image of the gipsy as he had looked round at her, when she had said : " The weather is so treacherous." She felt rather like Peter when the cock crew, as she denied him. Or rather, she did not deny the gipsy ; she didn't care about his part in the show, anyhow. It was some hidden part of herself which she denied : that part which mysteriously and unconfessedly responded to him. And it was a strange, lustrous black cock which crew in mockery of her.

" Yes ! " she said vaguely. " Yes ! Sex is an awful bore, you know, Lucille. When you haven't got it, you feel you *ought* to have it, somehow. And when you've got it—or *if* you have it—" she lifted her head and wrinkled her nose disdainfully—" you hate it."

" Oh, I don't know ! " cried Lucille. " I think I should *like* to be awfully in love with a man."

" You think so ! " said Yvette, again wrinkling her nose. " But if you were you wouldn't."

" How do you know ? " asked Lucille.

" Well, I don't really," said Yvette. " But I think so ! Yes, I think so ! "

" Oh, it's very likely ! " said Lucille disgustedly. " And anyhow one would be sure to get out of love again, and it would be merely disgusting."

" Yes," said Yvette. " It's a problem." She hummed a little tune.

" Oh, hang it all, it's not a problem for us two yet. We're neither of us really in love, and we probably never shall be, so the problem is settled that way."

" I'm not so sure ! " said Yvette sagely. " I'm not so sure. I believe, one day, I shall fall *awfully* in love."

" Probably you never will," said Lucille brutally. " That's what most old maids are thinking all the time."

Yvette looked at her sister from pensive but apparently insouciant eyes.

" Is it ? " she said. " Do you really think so, Lucille ? How perfectly awful for them, poor things ! Why ever do they *care ?* "

" Why do they ? " said Lucille. " Perhaps they don't, really— Probably it's all because people say : *Poor old girl, she couldn't catch a man.*"

" I suppose it is ! " said Yvette. " They get to mind the beastly things people always do say about old maids. What a shame ! "

" Anyhow we have a good time, and we do have lots of boys who make a fuss of us," said Lucille.

" Yes ! " said Yvette. " Yes ! But I couldn't possibly marry any of them."

" Neither could I," said Lucille. " But why should we ? Why should we bother about marrying, when we have a perfectly good time with the boys, who are awfully good sorts, and you must say, Yvette, awfully sporting and *decent* to us."

" Oh, they are ! " said Yvette absently.

" I think it's time to think of marrying somebody," said Lucille, " when you feel you're *not* having a good time any more. Then marry, and just settle down."

" Quite ! " said Yvette.

But now, under all her bland, soft amiability, she was annoyed with Lucille. Suddenly she wanted to turn her back on Lucille.

Besides, look at the shadows under poor Lucille's eyes, and the wistfulness in the beautiful eyes themselves. Oh, if some awfully nice, kind, protective sort of man would but marry her ! And if the sporting Lucille would let him !

Yvette did not tell the rector, nor Granny, about the Eastwoods. It would only have started a lot of talk which she detested. The rector wouldn't have minded, for himself, privately. But he too knew the necessity of keeping as clear as possible from that poisonous, many-headed serpent, the tongue of the people.

" But I don't *want* you to come if your father doesn't know," cried the little Jewess.

" I suppose I'll have to tell him," said Yvette. " I'm sure he doesn't mind, really. But if he knew, he'd have to, I suppose.'"

The young officer looked at her with an odd amusement, bird-like and unemotional, in his keen eyes.　He too was by way of falling in love with Yvette.　It was her peculiar virgin tenderness, and her straying, absent-minded detachment from things, which attracted him.

She was aware of what was happening, and she rather preened herself.　Eastwood piqued her fancy.　Such a smart young officer, awfully good class, so calm and amazing with a motor-car, and quite a champion swimmer, it was intriguing to see him quietly, calmly washing dishes, smoking his pipe, doing his job so alert and skilful. Or, with the same interested care with which he made his investigation into the mysterious inside of an automobile, concocting jugged hare in the cottage kitchen.　Then going out in the icy weather and cleaning his car till it looked like a live thing, like a cat when she has licked herself.　Then coming in to talk so unassumingly and responsively, if briefly, with the little Jewess.　And apparently, never bored.　Sitting at the window with his pipe in bad weather, silent for hours, abstracted, musing, yet with his athletic body alert in its stillness.

Yvette did not flirt with him.　But she *did* like him.

" But what about your future ? " she asked him.

" What about it ? " he said, taking his pipe from his mouth, the unemotional point of a smile in his bird's eyes.

" A career !　Doesn't every man have to carve out a career ? —like some huge goose with gravy ? "　She gazed with odd naiveté into his eyes.

" I'm perfectly all right to-day, and I shall be all right to-morrow," he said, with a cold, decided look.　" Why shouldn't my future be continuous to-days and to-morrows ? "

He looked at her with unmoved searching.

" Quite ! " she said.　" I hate jobs, and all that side of life." But she was thinking of the Jewess's money.

To which he did not answer.　His anger was of the soft, snowy sort, which comfortably muffles the soul.

They had come to the point of talking philosophically together. The little Jewess looked a bit wan.　She was curiously naive, and not possessive in her attitude to the man.　Nor was she at all catty with Yvette.　Only rather wan, and dumb.

Yvette, on a sudden impulse, thought she had better clear herself.

" I think life's *awfully* difficult," she said.

" Life is ! " cried the Jewess.

" What's so beastly, is that one is supposed to *fall in love*, and get married ! " said Yvette, curling up her nose.

" Don't you *want* to fall in love and get married ? " cried the Jewess, with great glaring eyes of astounded reproach.

" No, not particularly ! " said Yvette.   " Especially as one feels there's nothing else to do.   It's an awful chicken-coop one has to run into."

" But you don't know what love is ! " cried the Jewess.

" No ! " said Yvette.   " Do you ? "

" I ! " bawled the tiny Jewess.   " I !   My goodness, don't I ! " She looked with reflective gloom at Eastwood, who was smoking his pipe, the dimples of his disconnected amusement showing on his smooth, scrupulous face.   He had a very fine, smooth skin, which yet did not suffer from the weather, so that his face looked naked as a baby's.   But it was not a round face : it was characteristic enough, and took queer ironical dimples, like a mask which is comic but frozen.

" Do you mean to say you don't know what love is ? " insisted the Jewess.

" No ! " said Yvette, with insouciant candour.   " I don't believe I do !   Is it awful of me, at my age ? "

" Is there never any man that makes you feel quite, quite different ? " said the Jewess, with another big-eyed look at Eastwood. He smoked, utterly unimplicated.

" I don't think there is," said Yvette.   " Unless—yes !—unless it is that gipsy "—she had put her head pensively sideways.

" Which gipsy ? " bawled the little Jewess.

" The one who was a Tommy and looked after horses in Major Eastwood's regiment in the war," said Yvette coolly.

The little Jewess gazed at Yvette with great eyes of stupor.

" You're not in love with that *gipsy* ! " she said.

" Well ! " said Yvette.   " I don't know.   He's the only one that makes me feel—different !   He really is ! "

" But how ?   How ?   Has he ever *said* anything to you ? "

" No !   No ! "

" Then how ?   What has he done ? "

" Oh, just looked at me ! "

" How ? "

" Well, you see, I don't know.   But different !   Yes, different ! Different, quite different from the way any man ever looked at me."

" But *how* did he look at you ? " insisted the Jewess.

" Why—as if he really, but *really*, *desired* me," said Yvette, her meditative face looking like the bud of a flower.

" What a vile fellow ! What *right* had he to look at you like that ? " cried the indignant Jewess.

" A cat may look at a king," calmly interposed the Major, and now his face had the smiles of a cat's face.

" You think he oughtn't to ? " asked Yvette, turning to him.

" Certainly not ! A gipsy fellow, with half a dozen dirty women trailing after him ! Certainly not ! " cried the tiny Jewess.

" I wondered ! " said Yvette. " Because it *was* rather wonderful, really ! And it *was* something quite different in my life."

" I think," said the Major, taking his pipe from his mouth, " that desire is the most wonderful thing in life. Anybody who can really feel it, is a king, and I envy nobody else ! " He put back his pipe.

The Jewess looked at him stupefied.

" But, Charles ! " she cried. " Every common low man in Halifax feels nothing else ! "

He again took his pipe from his mouth.

" That's merely appetite," he said.

And he put back his pipe.

" You think the gipsy is the real thing ? " Yvette asked him.

He lifted his shoulders.

" It's not for me to say," he replied. " If I were you, I should know, I shouldn't be asking other people."

" Yes—but——" Yvette trailed out.

" Charles ! You're wrong ! How *could* it be the real thing ! As if she could possibly marry him and go round in a caravan ! "

" I didn't say marry him," said Charles.

" Or a love affair ! Why, it's monstrous ! What would she think of herself ! That's not love ! That's—that's prostitution ! "

Charles smoked for some moments.

" That gipsy was the best man we had, with horses. Nearly died of pneumonia. I thought he *was* dead. He's a resurrected man to me. I'm a resurrected man myself, as far as that goes." He looked at Yvette. " I was buried for twenty hours under snow," he said. " And not much the worse for it, when they dug me out."

There was a frozen pause in the conversation.

" Life's awful ! " said Yvette.

" They dug me out by accident," he said.

" Oh !——" Yvette trailed slowly. " It might be destiny, you know."

To which he did not answer.

THE rector heard about Yvette's intimacy with the Eastwoods, and she was somewhat startled by the result. She had thought he wouldn't care. Verbally, in his would-be humorous fashion, he was so entirely unconventional, such a frightfully good sport. As he said himself, he was a conservative anarchist ; which meant, he was like a great many more people, a mere unbeliever. The anarchy extended to his humorous talk, and his secret thinking. The conservatism, based on a mongrel fear of the anarchy, controlled every action. His thoughts, secretly, were something to be scared of. Therefore, in his life, he was fanatically afraid of the unconventional.

When his conservatism and his abject sort of fear were uppermost, he always lifted his lip and bared his teeth a little, in a dog-like sneer.

" I hear your latest friends are the half-divorced Mrs. Fawcett and the *maquereau* Eastwood," he said to Yvette.

She didn't know what a *maquereau* was, but she felt the poison in the rector's fangs.

" I just know them," she said. " They're awfully nice, really. And they'll be married in about a month's time."

The rector looked at her insouciant face with hatred. Somewhere inside him, he was cowed, he had been born cowed. And those who are born cowed are natural slaves, and deep instinct makes them fear with poisonous fear those who might suddenly snap the slave's collar round their necks.

It was for this reason the rector had so abjectly curled up, still so abjectly curled up before She-who-was-Cynthia : because of his slave's fear of her contempt, the contempt of a born-free nature for a base-born nature.

Yvette too had a free-born quality. She too, one day, would know him, and clap the slave's collar of her contempt round his neck.

But should she ? He would fight to the death, this time, first. The slave in him was cornered this time, like a cornered rat, and with the courage of a cornered rat.

" I suppose they're your sort ! " he sneered.

" Well, they are, really," she said, with that blithe vagueness. " I do like them awfully. They seem so solid, you know, so honest."

" You've got a peculiar notion of honesty ! " he sneered. " A young sponge going off with a woman older than himself, so that he can live on her money ! The woman leaving her home and her children ! I don't know where you get your idea of honesty. Not from me, I hope. And you seem to be very well acquainted with them, considering you say you just know them.   Where did you meet them ? ''

" When I was out bicycling.   They came along in their car, and we happened to talk.   She told me at once who she was, so that I shouldn't make a mistake.   She *is* honest."

Poor Yvette was struggling to bear up.

" And how often have you seen them since ? "

" Oh, I've just been over twice."

" Over where ? "

" To their cottage in Scoresby."

He looked at her in hate, as if he could kill her.   And he backed away from her, against the window-curtains of his study, like a rat at bay.   Somewhere in his mind he was thinking unspeakable depravities about his daughter, as he had thought them of She-who-was-Cynthia.   He was powerless against the lowest insinuations of his own mind.   And these depravities which he attributed to the still-uncowed but frightened girl in front of him, made him recoil, showing all his fangs in his handsome face.

" So you just know them, do you ? " he said.   " Lying is in your blood, I see.   I don't believe you get it from me."

Yvette half averted her mute face, and thought of Granny's bare-faced prevarication.   She did not answer.

" What takes you creeping round such couples ? " he sneered. " Aren't there enough decent people in the world for you to know ? Any one would think you were a stray dog, having to run round indecent couples, because the decent ones wouldn't have you. Have you got something worse than lying in your blood ? "

" What have I got worse than lying in my blood? " she asked.   A cold deadness was coming over her.   Was she abnormal, one of the semi-criminal abnormals ?   It made her feel cold and dead.

In his eyes, she was just brazening out the depravity that underlay her virgin, tender, bird-like face.   She-who-was-Cynthia had been like this : a snow-flower.   And he had convulsions of sadistic horror, thinking what might be the *actual* depravity of She-who-was-Cynthia.   Even his *own* love for her, which had been the lust-love of the born cowed, had been a depravity, in secret, to him.   So what must an illegal love be ?

" You know best yourself, what you have got," he sneered. " But it is something you had best curb, and quickly, if you don't intend to finish in a criminal-lunacy asylum."

" Why ? " she said, pale and muted, numbed with frozen fear. " Why criminal lunacy ?   What have I done ? "

"That is between you and your Maker," he jeered. "I shall never ask. But certain tendencies end in criminal lunacy,. unless they are curbed in time."

"Do you mean like knowing the Eastwoods?" asked Yvette, after a pause of numb fear.

"Do I mean like nosing round such people as Mrs. Fawcett, a Jewess, and ex-Major Eastwood, a man who goes off with an older woman for the sake of her money? Why yes, I do!"

"But you *can't* say that," cried Yvette. "He's an awfully simple, straightforward man."

"He is apparently one of your sort."

"Well in a way I thought he was. I thought you'd like him too," she said simply, hardly knowing what she said.

The rector backed into the curtains, as if the girl menaced him with something fearful.

"Don't say any more," he snarled, abject. "Don't say any more. You've said too much, to implicate you. I don't want to learn any more horrors."

"But what horrors?" she persisted.

The very naïveté of her unscrupulous innocence repelled him, cowed him still more.

"Say no more!" he said, in a low, hissing voice. "But I will kill you before you shall go the way of your mother."

She looked at him, as he stood there backed against the velvet curtains of his study, his face yellow, his eyes distraught like a rat's with fear and rage and hate, and a numb, frozen loneliness came over her. For her too, the meaning had gone out of everything.

It was hard to break the frozen, sterile silence that ensued. At last, however, she looked at him. And in spite of herself, beyond her own knowledge, the contempt for him was in her young, clear, baffled eyes. It fell like the slave's collar over his neck, finally.

"Do you mean I mustn't know the Eastwoods?" she said.

"You can know them if you wish," he sneered. "But you must not expect to associate with your Granny and your Aunt Cissie, and Lucille, if you do. I cannot have *them* contaminated. Your Granny was a faithful wife and a faithful mother, if ever one existed. She has already had one shock of shame and abomination to endure. She shall never be exposed to another."

Yvette heard it all dimly, half hearing.

"I can send a note and say you disapprove," she said dimly.

"You follow your own course of action. But remember, you have to choose between clean people, and reverence for your

Granny's blameless old age, and people who are unclean in their minds and their bodies."

Again there was a silence. Then she looked at him, and her face was more puzzled than anything. But somewhere at the back of her perplexity was that peculiar calm, virgin contempt of the free-born for the base-born. He, and all the Saywells, were base-born.

"All right," she said. "I'll write and say you disapprove."

He did not answer. He was partly flattered, secretly triumphant, but abjectly.

"I have tried to keep this from your Granny and Aunt Cissie," he said. "It need not be public property, since you choose to make your friendship clandestine."

There was a dreary silence.

"All right," she said. "I'll go and write."

And she crept out of the room.

She addressed her little note to Mrs. Eastwood. "Dear Mrs. Eastwood, Daddy doesn't approve of my coming to see you. So you will understand if we have to break it off. I'm awfully sorry ——" That was all.

Yet she felt a dreary blank when she had posted her letter. She was now even afraid of her own thoughts. She wanted, now, to be held against the slender, fine-shaped breast of the gipsy. She wanted him to hold her in his arms, if only for once, for once, and comfort and confirm her. She wanted to be confirmed by him, against her father, who had only a repulsive fear of her.

And at the same time she cringed and winced, so that she could hardly walk, for fear the thought was obscene, a criminal lunacy. It seemed to wound her heels as she walked, the fear. The fear, the great cold fear of the base-born, her father, everything human and swarming. Like a great bog humanity swamped her, and she sank in, weak at the knees, filled with repulsion and fear of every person she met.

She adjusted herself, however, quite rapidly to her new conception of people. She had to live. It is useless to quarrel with one's bread and butter. And to expect a great deal out of life is puerile. So, with the rapid adaptability of the post-war generation, she adjusted herself to the new facts. Her father was what he was. He would always play up to appearances. She would do the same. She too would play up to appearances.

So, underneath the blithe, gossamer-straying insouciance, a certain hardness formed, like rock crystallizing in her heart. She lost her illusions in the collapse of her sympathies. Outwardly, she seemed the same. Inwardly she was hard and detached, and, unknown to herself, revengeful.

Outwardly she remained the same. It was part of her game. While circumstances remained as they were, she must remain, at least in appearance, true to what was expected of her.

But the revengefulness came out in her new vision of people. Under the rector's apparently gallant handsomeness, she saw the weak, feeble nullity. And she despised him. Yet still, in a way, she liked him too. Feelings are so complicated.

It was Granny whom she came to detest with all her soul. That obese old woman, sitting there in her blindness like some great red-blotched fungus, her neck swallowed between her heaped-up shoulders and her rolling, ancient chins, so that she was neckless as a double potato, her Yvette really hated, with that pure, sheer hatred which is almost a joy. Her hate was so clear, that while she was feeling strong, she enjoyed it.

The old woman sat with her big, reddened face pressed a little back, her lace cap perched on her thin white hair, her stub nose still assertive, and her old mouth shut like a trap. This motherly old soul, her mouth gave her away. It always had been one of the compressed sort. But in her great age, it had gone like a toad's, lipless, the jaw pressing up like the lower jaw of a trap. The look Yvette most hated was the look of that lower jaw pressing relentlessly up, with an ancient prognathous thrust, so that the snub nose in turn was forced to press upwards, and the whole face was pressed a little back, beneath the big, wall-like forehead. The will, the ancient, toad-like, obscene *will* in the old woman, was fearful, once you saw it : a toad-like self-will that was godless, and less than human ! It belonged to the old, enduring race of toads, or tortoises. And it made one feel that Granny would never die. She would live on like these higher reptiles, in a state of semi-coma, for ever.

Yvette dared not even suggest to her father that Granny was not perfect. He would have threatened his daughter with the lunatic asylum. That was the threat he always seemed to have up his sleeve : the lunatic asylum. Exactly as if a distaste for Granny and for that horrible house of relatives was in itself a proof of lunacy, dangerous lunacy.

Yet in one of her moods of irritable depression, she did once fling out :

" How perfectly beastly this house is ! Aunt Lucy comes, and Aunt Nell, and Aunt Alice, and they make a ring like a ring of crows, with Granny and Aunt Cissie, all lifting their skirts up and warming their legs at the fire, and shutting Lucille and me out. We're nothing but outsiders in this beastly house ! "

Her father glanced at her curiously. But she managed to put a petulance into her speech, and a mere cross rudeness into her look, so that he could laugh, as at a childish tantrum. Somewhere, though, he knew that she coldly, venomously meant what she said, and he was wary of her.

Her life seemed now nothing but an irritable friction against the unsavoury household of the Saywells, in which she was immersed. She loathed the rectory with a loathing that consumed her life, a loathing so strong that she could not really go away from the place. While it endured, she was spellbound to it, in revulsion.

She forgot the Eastwoods again. After all, what was the revolt of the little Jewess, compared to Granny and the Saywell bunch ! A husband was never more than a semi-casual thing ! But a family !—an awful, smelly family that would never disperse, stuck half dead round the base of a fungoid old woman ! How was one to cope with that ?

She did not forget the gipsy entirely. But she had no time for him. She, who was bored almost to agony, and who had nothing at all to do, she had not time to think even, seriously, of anything. Time being, after all, only the current of the soul in its flow.

She saw the gipsy twice. Once he came to the house, with things to sell. And she, watching him from the landing window, refused to go down. He saw her too, as he was putting his things back into his cart. But he too gave no sign. Being a race that exists only to be harrying the outskirts of our society, forever hostile and living only by spoil, he was too much master of himself, and too wary, to expose himself openly to the vast and gruesome clutch of our law. He had been through the war. He had been enslaved against his will, that time.

So now, he showed himself at the rectory, and slowly, quietly busied himself at his cart outside the white gate, with that air of silent and forever-unyielding outsideness which gave him his lonely, predative grace. He knew she saw him. And she should see him unyielding, quietly hawking his copper vessels, on an old, old warpath against such as herself.

Such as herself ? Perhaps he was mistaken. Her heart, in its stroke, now rang hard as his hammer upon his copper, beating against circumstances. But he struck stealthily on the outside, and she still more secretly on the inside of the establishment. She liked him. She liked the quiet, noiseless clean-cut presence of him. She liked that mysterious endurance in him, which endures in opposition, without any idea of victory. And she liked that peculiar added relentlessness, the disillusion in hostility, which belongs to after the war. Yes, if she belonged to any side, and to any clan, it was to his. Almost she could have found it in her heart to go with him, and be a pariah gipsy-woman.

But she was born inside the pale. And she liked comfort, and a certain prestige. Even as a mere rector's daughter, one did have a certain prestige. And she liked that. Also she liked to chip against the pillars of the temple, from the inside. She wanted to be safe under the temple roof. Yet she enjoyed chipping fragments off the supporting pillars. Doubtless many fragments had been whittled away from the pillars of the Philistine, before Samson pulled the temple down.

" I'm not sure one shouldn't have one's fling till one is twenty-six, and then give in, and marry ! "

This was Lucille's philosophy, learned from older women. Yvette was twenty-one. It meant she had five more years in which to have this precious fling. And the fling meant, at the moment, the gipsy. The marriage, at the age of twenty-six, meant Leo or Gerry.

So, a woman could eat her cake and have her bread and butter.

Yvette, pitched in gruesome, deadlocked hostility to the Saywell household, was very old and very wise : with the agedness and the wisdom of the young, which always overleaps the agedness and the wisdom of the old, or the elderly.

The second time she met the gipsy by accident. It was March, and sunny weather, after unheard-of rains. Celandines were yellow in the hedges, and primroses among the rocks. But still there came a smell of sulphur from far-away steel-works, out of the steel-blue sky.

And yet it was spring !

Yvette was cycling slowly along by Codnor Gate, past the lime quarries, when she saw the gipsy coming away from the door of a stone cottage. His cart stood there in the road. He was returning with his brooms and copper things, to the cart.

She got down from her bicycle. As she saw him, she loved with curious tenderness the slim lines of his body in the green jersey, the turn of his silent face. She felt she knew him better than she knew anybody on earth, even Lucille, and belonged to him, in some way, for ever.

" Have you made anything new and nice ? " she asked innocently, looking at his copper things.

" I don't think," he said, glancing back at her.

The desire was still there, still curious and naked, in his eyes. But it was more remote, the boldness was diminished. There was a tiny glint, as if he might dislike her. But this dissolved again, as he saw her looking among his bits of copper and brass-work. She searched them diligently.

There was a little oval brass plate, with a queer figure like a palm-tree beaten upon it.

" I like that," she said. " How much is it ? "

" What you like," he said.

This made her nervous : he seemed off-hand, almost mocking.

" I'd rather you said," she told him, looking up at him.

" You give me what you like," he said.

" No ! " she said, suddenly. " If you won't tell me I won't have it."

" All right," he said. " Two shilling."

She found half-a-crown, and he drew from his pocket a handful of silver, from which he gave her her sixpence.

" The old gipsy dreamed something about you," he said, looking at her with curious, searching eyes.

" Did she ! " cried Yvette, at once interested. " What was it ? "

" She said : ' Be braver in your heart, or you lose your game.' She said it this way : ' Be braver in your body, or your luck will leave you.' And she said as well : ' Listen for the voice of water.' "

Yvette was very much impressed.

" And what does it mean ? " she asked.

" I asked her," he said. " She says she don't know."

" Tell me again what it was," said Yvette.

" 'Be braver in your body, or your luck will go.' And : ' Listen for the voice of water.' "

He looked in silence at her soft, pondering face. Something almost like a perfume seemed to flow from her young bosom direct to him, in a grateful connection.

" I'm to be braver in my body, and I'm to listen for the voice of water ! All right ! " she said. " I don't understand, but perhaps I shall."

She looked at him with clear eyes. Man or woman is made up of many selves. With one self, she loved this gipsy man. With many selves, she ignored him or had a distaste for him.

" You're not coming up to the Head no more ? " he asked.

Again she looked at him absently.

" Perhaps I will," she said, " some time. Some time."

"Spring weather!" he said, smiling faintly and glancing round at the sun. "We're going to break camp soon, and go away."

"When?" she said.

"Perhaps next week."

"Where to?"

Again he made a move with his head.

"Perhaps up north," he said.

She looked at him.

"All right!" she said. "Perhaps I *will* come up before you go, and say good-bye to your wife and to the old woman who sent me the message."

IX

YVETTE did not keep her promise. The few March days were lovely, and she let them slip. She had a curious reluctance, always, towards taking action, or making any real move of her own. She always wanted someone else to make a move for her, as if she did not want to play her own game of life.

She lived as usual, went out to her friends, to parties, and danced with the undiminished Leo. She wanted to go up and say good-bye to the gipsies. She wanted to. And nothing prevented her.

On the Friday afternoon especially she wanted to go. It was sunny, and the last yellow crocuses down the drive were in full blaze, wide open, the first bees rolling in them. The Papple rushed under the stone bridge, uncannily full, nearly filling the arches. There was the scent of a mezereon tree.

And she felt too lazy, too lazy, too lazy. She strayed in the garden by the river, half dreamy, expecting something. While the gleam of spring sun lasted, she would be out of doors. Indoors Granny, sitting back like some awful old prelate, in her bulk of black silk and her white lace cap, was warming her feet by the fire, and hearing everything that Aunt Nell had to say. Friday was Aunt Nell's day. She usually came for lunch, and left after an early tea. So the mother and the large, rather common daughter, who was a widow at the age of forty, sat gossiping by the fire, while Aunt Cissie prowled in and out. Friday was the rector's day for going to town : it was also the housemaid's half day.

Yvette sat on a wooden seat in the garden, only a few feet above the bank of the swollen river, which rolled a strange, uncanny mass of water. The crocuses were passing in the ornamental beds, the grass was dark green where it was mown, the laurels looked a little brighter. Aunt Cissie appeared at the top of the porch steps, and called to ask if Yvette wanted that early cup of tea. Because of the river just below, Yvette could not hear what Aunt Cissie said, but she guessed, and shook her head. An early cup of tea, indoors, when the sun actually shone ? No thanks !

She was conscious of her gipsy, as she sat there musing in the sun. Her soul had the half painful, half easing knack of leaving her, and straying away to some place, to somebody that had caught her imagination. Some days she would be at the Framleys', even though she did not go near them. Some days, she was all the time in spirit with the Eastwoods. And to-day it was the gipsies. She was up at their encampment in the quarry. She saw the man hammering his copper, lifting his head to look at the road ; and the children playing in the horse-shelter : and the women, the gipsy's wife and the strong, elderly woman, coming home with their packs, along with the elderly man. For this afternoon, she felt intensely that *that* was home for her : the gipsy camp, the fire, the stool, the man with the hammer, the old crone.

It was part of her nature, to get these fits of yearning for some place she knew ; to be in a certain place ; with somebody who meant home to her. This afternoon it was the gipsy camp. And the man in the green jersey made it home to her. Just to be where he was, that was to be at home. The caravans, the brats, the other women : everything was natural to her, her home, as if she had been born there. She wondered if the gipsy was aware of her : if he could see her sitting on the stool by the fire ; if he would lift his head and see her as she rose, looking at him slowly and significantly, turning towards the steps of his caravan. Did he know? Did he know?

Vaguely she looked up the steep of dark larch trees north of the house, where unseen the road climbed, going towards the Head. There was nothing, and her glance strayed down again. At the foot of the slope the river turned, thrown back harshly, ominously, against the low rocks across stream, then pouring past the garden to the bridge. It was unnaturally full, and whitey-muddy, and ponderous. " Listen for the voice of water," she said to herself. " No need to listen for it, if the voice means the noise ! "

And again she looked at the swollen river breaking angrily as it came round the bend. Above it the black-looking kitchen garden hung, and the hard-natured fruit trees. Everything was on the tilt, facing south and south-west, for the sun. Behind, above the house and the kitchen garden hung the steep little wood of withered-seeming larches. The gardener was working in the kitchen garden, high up there, by the edge of the larch-wood.

She heard a call. It was Aunt Cissie and Aunt Nell. They

were on the drive, waving Good-bye! Yvette waved back. Then Aunt Cissie, pitching her voice against the waters, called:

"I shan't be long. Don't forget Granny is alone!"

"All right!" screamed Yvette rather ineffectually.

And she sat on her bench and watched the two undignified, long-coated women walk slowly over the bridge and begin the curving climb on the opposite slope, Aunt Nell carrying a sort of suit-case in which she brought a few goods for Granny and took back vegetables or whatever the rectory garden or cupboard was yielding. Slowly the two figures diminished, on the whitish, up-curving road, labouring slowly up towards Papplewick village. Aunt Cissie was going as far as the village for something.

The sun was yellowing to decline. What a pity! Oh, what a pity the sunny day was going, and she would have to turn indoors, to those hateful rooms, and Granny! Aunt Cissie would be back directly: it was past five. And all the others would be arriving from town, rather irritable and tired, soon after six.

As she looked uneasily round, she heard, across the running of water, the sharp noise of a horse and cart rattling on the road hidden in the larch trees. The gardener was looking up too. Yvette turned away again, lingering, strolling by the full river a few paces, unwilling to go in; glancing up the road to see if Aunt Cissie were coming. If she saw her, she would go indoors.

She heard somebody shouting, and looked round. Down the path through the larch trees the gipsy was bounding. The gardener, away beyond, was also running. Simultaneously she became aware of a great roar, which, before she could move, accumulated to a vast deafening snarl. The gipsy was gesticulating. She looked round, behind her.

And to her horror and amazement, round the bend of the river she saw a shaggy, tawny wave-front of water advancing like a wall of lions. The roaring sound wiped out everything. She was powerless, too amazed and wonder-struck, she wanted to see it.

Before she could think twice, it was near, a roaring cliff of water. She almost fainted with horror. She heard the scream of the gipsy, and looked up to see him bounding upon her, his black eyes starting out of his head.

"Run!" he screamed, seizing her arm.

And in the instant the first wave was washing her feet from under her, swirling, in the insane noise, which suddenly for some reason seemed like stillness, with a devouring flood over the garden. The horrible mowing of water!

The gipsy dragged her heavily, lurching, plunging, but still keeping foot-hold both of them, towards the house. She was barely conscious : as if the flood was in her soul.

There was one grass-banked terrace of the garden, near the path round the house. The gipsy clawed his way up this terrace to the dry level of the path, dragging her after him, and sprang with her past the windows to the porch steps. Before they got there, a new great surge of water came mowing, mowing trees down even, and mowed them down too.

Yvette felt herself gone in an agonizing mill-race of icy water, whirled, with only the fearful grip of the gipsy's hand on her wrist. They were both down and gone. She felt a dull but stunning bruise somewhere.

Then he pulled her up. He was up, streaming forth water, clinging to the stem of the great wistaria that grew against the wall, crushed against the wall by the water. Her head was above water, he held her arm till it seemed dislocated : but she could not get her footing. With a ghastly sickness like a dream, she struggled and struggled, and could not get her feet. Only his hand was locked on her wrist.

He dragged her nearer till her one hand caught his leg. He nearly went down again. But the wistaria held him, and he pulled her up to him. She clawed at him, horribly ; and got to her feet, he hanging on like a man torn in two, to the wistaria trunk.

The water was above her knees. The man and she looked into each other's ghastly streaming faces.

" Get to the steps ! " he screamed.

It was only just round the corner : four strides ! She looked at him : she could not go. His eyes glared on her like a tiger's, and he pushed her from him. She clung to the wall, and the water seemed to abate a little. Round the corner she staggered, but staggering, reeled and was pitched up against the cornice of the balustrade of the porch steps, the man after her.

They got on to the steps, when another roar was heard amid the roar, and the wall of the house shook. Up heaved the water round their legs again, but the gipsy had opened the hall door. In they poured with the water, reeling to the stairs. And as they did so, they saw the short but strange bulk of Granny emerge in the hall, away down from the dining-room door. She had her hands lifted and clawing, as the first water swirled round her legs, and her coffin-like mouth was opened in a hoarse scream.

Yvette was blind to everything but the stairs. Blind, unconscious of everything save the steps rising beyond the water, she clambered up like a wet, shuddering cat, in a state of unconsciousness. It was not till she was on the landing, dripping and shuddering till she could not stand erect, clinging to the banisters, while the house shook and the water raved below, that she was aware of the sodden gipsy, in paroxysms of coughing at the head of the stairs, his cap gone, his black hair over his eyes, peering between his washed-down hair at the sickening heave of water below, in the hall. Yvette, fainting, looked too and saw Granny bob up, like a strange float, her face purple, her blind blue eyes bolting, spume hissing from her mouth. One old purple hand clawed at a banister rail, and held for a moment, showing the glint of a wedding ring.

The gipsy, who had coughed himself free and pushed back his hair, said to that awful float-like face below :

" Not good enough ! Not good enough ! "

With a low thud like thunder, the house was struck again, and shuddered, and a strange cracking, rattling, spitting noise began. Up heaved the water like a sea. The hand was gone, all sign of anything was gone, but upheaving water.

Yvette turned in blind unconscious frenzy, staggering like a wet cat to the upper staircase, and climbing swiftly. It was not till she was at the door of her room that she stopped, paralysed by the sound of a sickening, tearing crash, while the house swayed.

" The house is coming down ! " yelled the green-white face of the gipsy, in her face.

He glared into her crazed face.

" Where is the chimney ? The back chimney—which room ? The chimney will stand—— "

He glared with strange ferocity into her face, forcing her to understand. And she nodded with a strange, crazed poise, nodded quite serenely, saying :

" In here ! In here ! It's all right."

They entered her room, which had a narrow fire-place. It was a back room with two windows, one on each side the great chimney-flue. The gipsy, coughing bitterly and trembling in every limb, went to the window to look out.

Below, between the house and the steep rise of the hill, was a wild mill-race of water rushing with refuse, including Rover's green dog-kennel. The gipsy coughed and coughed, and gazed down blankly. Tree after tree went down, mown by the water, which must have been ten feet deep.

Shuddering and pressing his sodden arms on his sodden breast, a look of resignation on his livid face, he turned to Yvette. A fearful tearing noise tore the house, then there was a deep, watery explosion. Something had gone down, some part of the house, the floor heaved and wavered beneath them. For some moments both were suspended, stupefied. Then he roused.

" Not good enough ! Not good enough ! This will stand. This here still stand. See, that chimney ! Like a tower. Yes ! All right ! All right ! You take your clothes off and go to bed. You'll die of the cold."

" It's all right ! It's quite all right ! " she said to him, sitting on a chair and looking up into his face with her white, insane little face, round which the hair was plastered.

" No ! " he cried. " No ! Take your things off and I'll rub you with this towel. I rub myself. If the house falls then die warm. If it don't fall, then live, not die of pneumonia."

Coughing, shuddering violently, he pulled up his jersey hem and wrestled with all his shuddering, cold-racked might, to get off his wet, tight jersey.

" Help me ! " he cried, his face muffled.

She seized the edge of the jersey, obediently, and pulled with all her might. The garment came over his head, and he stood in his braces.

" Take your things off ! Rub with this towel ! " he commanded ferociously, the savageness of the war on him. And like a thing obsessed, he pushed himself out of his trousers, and got out of his wet, clinging shirt, emerging slim and livid, shuddering in every fibre with cold and shock.

He seized a towel, and began quickly to rub his body, his teeth chattering like plates rattling together. Yvette dimly saw it was wise. She tried to get out of her dress. He pulled the horrible wet death-gripping thing off her, then, resuming his rubbing, went to the door, tip-toeing on the wet floor.

There he stood, naked, towel in hand, petrified. He looked west, towards where the upper landing window had been, and was looking into the sunset, over an insane sea of waters, bristling with uptorn trees and refuse. The end corner of the house where the porch had been, and the stairs, had gone. The wall had fallen, leaving the floors sticking out. The stairs had gone.

Motionless, he watched the water. A cold wind blew in upon him. He clenched his rattling teeth with a great effort of will, and turned into the room again, closing the door.

Yvette, naked, shuddering so much that she was sick, was trying to wipe herself dry.

"All right!" he cried. "All right! The water don't rise no more! All right!"

With his towel he began to rub her, himself shaking all over, but holding her gripped by the shoulder, and slowly, numbedly rubbing her tender body, even trying to rub up into some dryness the pitiful hair of her small head.

Suddenly he left off.

"Better lie in the bed," he commanded, "I want to rub myself."

His teeth went snap-snap-snap-snap, in great snaps, cutting off his words. Yvette crept shaking and semi-conscious into her bed. He, making strained efforts to hold himself still and rub himself warm, went again to the north window, to look out.

The water had risen a little. The sun had gone down, and there was a reddish glow. He rubbed his hair into a black, wet tangle, then paused for breath, in a sudden access of shuddering, then looked out again, then rubbed again on his breast, and began to cough afresh, because of the water he had swallowed. His towel was red : he had hurt himself somewhere : but he felt nothing.

There was still the strange huge noise of water, and the horrible bump of things bumping against the walls. The wind was rising with sundown, cold and hard. The house shook with explosive thuds, and weird, weird frightening noises came up.

A terror creeping over his soul, he went again to the door. The wind, roaring with the waters, blew in as he opened it. Through the awesome gap in the house he saw the world, the waters, the chaos of horrible waters, the twilight, the perfect new moon high above the sunset, a faint thing, and clouds pushing dark into the sky, on the cold, blustery wind.

Clenching his teeth again, fear mingling with resignation, or fatalism, in his soul, he went into the room and closed the door, picking up her towel to see if it were drier than his own, and less blood-stained, again rubbing his head, and going to the window.

He turned away, unable to control his spasms of shivering. Yvette had disappeared right under the bedcolthes, and nothing of her was visible but a shivering mound under the white quilt. He laid his hand on this shivering mound, as if for company. It did not stop shivering.

"All right!" he said. "All right! Water's going down!"

She suddenly uncovered her head and peered out at him from a white face. She peered into his greenish, curiously calm face, semi-conscious. His teeth were chattering unheeded, as he gazed down at her, his black eyes still full of the fire of life and a certain vagabond calm of fatalistic resignation.

" Warm me ! " she moaned, with chattering teeth. " Warm me ! I shall die of shivering."

A terrible convulsion went through her curled-up white body, enough indeed to rupture her and cause her to die.

The gipsy nodded, and took her in his arms, and held her in a clasp like a vice, to still his own shuddering. He himself was shuddering fearfully, and only semi-conscious. It was the shock.

The vice-like grip of his arms round her seemed to her the only stable point in her consciousness. It was a fearful relief to her heart, which was strained to bursting. And though his body, wrapped round her strange and lithe and powerful, like tentacles, rippled with shuddering as an electric current, still the rigid tension of the muscles that held her clenched steadied them both, and gradually the sickening violence of the shuddering, caused by shock, abated, in his body first, then in hers, and the warmth revived between them. And as it roused, their tortured, semi-conscious minds became unconscious, they passed away into sleep.

X

The sun was shining in heaven before men were able to get across the Papple with ladders. The bridge was gone. But the flood had abated, and the house, that leaned forwards as if it were making a stiff bow to the stream, stood now in mud and wreckage, with a great heap of fallen masonry and debris at the south-west corner. Awful were the gaping mouths of rooms !

Inside, there was no sign of life. But across-stream the gardener had come to reconnoitre, and the cook appeared, thrilled with curiosity. She had escaped from the back door and up through the larches to the high-road, when she saw the gipsy bound past the house : thinking he was coming to murder somebody. At the little top gate she had found his cart standing. The gardener had led the horse away to the Red Lion up at Darley, when night had fallen.

This the men from Papplewick learned when at last they got across the stream with ladders, and to the back of the house. They were nervous, fearing a collapse of the building, whose front was all undermined and whose back was choked up. They gazed with horror at the silent shelves of the rector's rows of books, in his torn-open study ; at the big brass bedstead of Granny's room, the bed so deep and comfortably made, but one brass leg of the bedstead perching tentatively over the torn void ; at the wreckage of the maid's room upstairs. The housemaid and the cook wept. Then a man climbed in cautiously through a smashed kitchen window, into the jungle and morass of the ground floor. He found the body of the old woman : or at least he saw her foot, in its flat black slipper, muddily protruding from a mud-heap of debris. And he fled.

The gardener said he was sure that Miss Yvette was not in the house. He had seen her and the gipsy swept away. But the policeman insisted on a search, and the Framley boys rushing up at last, the ladders were roped together. Then the whole party set up a loud yell. But without result. No answer from within.

A ladder was up, Bob Framley climbed, smashed a window, and clambered into Aunt Cissie's room. The perfect homely familiarity of everything terrified him like ghosts. The house might go down any minute.

They had just got the ladder up to the top floor, when men came running from Darley, saying the old gipsy had been to the Red Lion for the horse and cart, leaving word that his son had seen Yvette at the top of the house. But by that time the policeman was smashing the window of Yvette's room.

Yvette, fast asleep, started from under the bedclothes with a scream, as the glass flew. She clutched the sheets round her nakedness. The policeman uttered a startled yell, which he converted into a cry of : " Miss Yvette ! Miss Yvette ! "

He turned round on the ladder and shouted to the faces below : " Miss Yvette's in bed !—in bed ! "

And he perched there on the ladder, an unmarried man, clutching the window in peril, not knowing what to do.

Yvette sat up in bed, her hair in a matted tangle, and stared with wild eyes, clutching up the sheets at her naked breast. She had been so very fast asleep, that she was still not there.

The policeman, terrified at the flabby ladder, climbed into the room, saying :

" Don't be frightened, Miss ! Don't you worry any more about it. You're safe now."

And Yvette, so dazed, thought he meant the gipsy. Where was the gipsy ? This was the first thing in her mind. Where was her gipsy of this world's-end night ?

He was gone ! He was gone ! And a policeman was in the room ! A policeman !

She rubbed her hand over her dazed brow.

" If you'll get dressed, Miss, we can get you down to safe ground. The house is likely to fall. I suppose there's nobody in the other rooms ? "

He stepped gingerly into the passage and gazed in terror through the torn-out end of the house, and far off saw the rector coming down in a motor-car, on the sunlit hill.

Yvette, her face gone numb and disappointed, got up quickly, closing the bedclothes, and looked at herself a moment, then opened her drawers for clothing. She dressed herself, then looked in a mirror, and saw her matted hair with horror. Yet she did not care. The gipsy was gone, anyhow.

Her own clothes lay in a sodden heap. There was a great sodden place on the carpet where his had been, and two blood-stained filthy towels. Otherwise there was no sign of him.

She was tugging at her hair when the policeman tapped at her door. She called him to come in. He saw with relief that she was dressed and in her right senses.

" We'd better get out of the house as soon as possible, Miss," he reiterated. " It might fall any minute."

" Really ! " said Yvette calmly. " Is it as bad as that ? "

There were great shouts. She had to go to the window. There, below, was the rector, his arms wide open, tears streaming down his face.

" I'm perfectly all right, Daddy ! " she said, with the calmness of her contradictory feelings. She would keep the gipsy a secret from him. At the same time, tears ran down her face.

" Don't you cry, Miss, don't you cry ! The rector's lost his mother, but he's thanking his stars to have his daughter. We all thought you were gone as well, we did that ! "

" Is Granny drowned ? " said Yvette.

" I'm afraid she is, poor lady ! " said the policeman, with a grave face.

Yvette wept away into her hanky, which she had had to fetch from a drawer.

" Dare you go down that ladder, Miss ? " said the policeman.

Yvette looked at the sagging depth of it, and said promptly to herself : " No ! Not for anything ! " But then she remembered the gipsy's saying : " Be braver in the body."

" Have you been in all the other rooms ? " she said, in her weeping, turning to the policeman.

" Yes, Miss ! But you was the only person in the house, you know, save the old lady. Cook got away in time, and Lizzie was up at her mother's. It was only you and the poor old lady we was fretting about. Do you think you dare go down that ladder ? "

" Oh, yes ! " said Yvette, with indifference. The gipsy was gone anyway.

And now the rector in torment watched his tall, slender daughter slowly stepping backwards down the sagging ladder, the policeman, peering heroically from the smashed window, holding the ladder's top end.

At the foot of the ladder Yvette appropriately fainted in her father's arms, and was borne away with him, in the car, by Bob, to the Framley home. There the poor Lucille, a ghost of ghosts, wept with relief till she had hysterics, and even Aunt Cissie cried out among her tears : " Let the old be taken and the young spared ! Oh I *can't* cry for the Mater, now Yvette is spared ! "

And she wept gallons.

The flood was caused by the sudden bursting of the great reservoir, up in Papple Highdale, five miles from the rectory. It was found out later that an ancient, perhaps even a Roman mine tunnel, unsuspected, undreamed of, beneath the reservoir dam, had collapsed, undermining the whole dam. That was why the Papple had been, for that last day, so uncannily full. And then the dam had burst.

The rector and the two girls stayed on at the Framleys', till a new home could be found. Yvette did not attend Granny's funeral. She stayed in bed.

Telling her tale, she only told how the gipsy had got her inside the porch, and she had crawled to the stairs out of the water. It was known that he had escaped : the old gipsy had said so, when he fetched the horse and cart from the Red Lion.

Yvette could tell little. She was vague, confused, she seemed hardly to remember anything. But that was just like her.

It was Bob Framley who said :

" You know, I think that gipsy deserves a medal."

The whole family suddenly was struck.

" Oh, we *ought* to thank him ! " cried Lucille.

The rector himself went with Bob in the car. But the quarry was deserted. The gipsies had lifted camp and gone, no one knew whither.

And Yvette, lying in bed, moaned in her heart : " Oh, I love him ! I love him ! I love him ! " The grief over him kept her prostrate. Yet practically, she too was acquiescent in the fact of his disappearance. Her young soul knew the wisdom of it.

But after Granny's funeral, she received a little letter, dated from some unknown place.

" Dear Miss, I see in the paper you are all right after your ducking, as is the same with me. I hope I see you again one day, maybe at Tideswell cattle-fair, or maybe we come that way again. I come that day to say good-bye ! and I never said it, well, the water give no time, but I live in hopes. Your obdt. servant Joe Boswell."

And only then she realized that he had a name.

THE MAN WHO DIED

PART I

THERE was a peasant near Jerusalem who acquired a young game-cock which looked a shabby little thing, but which put on brave feathers as spring advanced, and was resplendent with arched and orange neck by the time the fig-trees were letting out leaves from their end-tips.

This peasant was poor, he lived in a cottage of mud-brick, and had only a dirty little inner courtyard with a tough fig-tree for all his territory. He worked hard among the vines and olives and wheat of his master, then came home to sleep in the mud-brick cottage by the path. But he was proud of his young rooster. In the shut-in yard were three shabby hens which laid small eggs, shed the few feathers they had, and made a disproportionate amount of dirt. There was also, in a corner under a straw roof, a dull donkey that often went out with the peasant to work, but sometimes stayed at home. And there was the peasant's wife, a black-browed youngish woman who did not work too hard. She threw a little grain, or the remains of the porridge mess, to the fowls, and she cut green fodder with a sickle, for the ass.

The young cock grew to a certain splendour. By some freak of destiny, he was a dandy rooster, in that dirty little yard with three patchy hens. He learned to crane his neck and give shrill answers to the crowing of other cocks, beyond the walls, in a world he knew nothing of. But there was a special fiery colour to his crow, and the distant calling of the other cocks roused him to unexpected outbursts.

"How he sings," said the peasant, as he got up and pulled his day-shirt over his head.

"He is good for twenty hens," said the wife.

The peasant went out and looked with pride at his young rooster. A saucy, flamboyant bird, that has already made the final acquaintance of the three tattered hens. But the cockerel was tipping his head, listening to the challenge of far-off unseen cocks, in the unknown world. Ghost voices, crowing at him mysteriously out of limbo. He answered with a ringing defiance, never to be daunted.

" He will surely fly away one of these days," said the peasant's wife.

So they lured him with grain, caught him, though he fought with all his wings and feet, and they tied a cord round his shank, fastening it against the spur ; and they tied the other end of the cord to the post that held up the donkey's straw pent-roof.

The young cock, freed, marched with a prancing stride of indignation away from the humans, came to the end of his string, gave a tug and a hitch of his tied leg, fell over for a moment, scuffled frantically on the unclean earthen floor, to the horror of the shabby hens, then with a sickening lurch, regained his feet, and stood to think. The peasant and the peasant's wife laughed heartily, and the young cock heard them. And he knew, with a gloomy, foreboding kind of knowledge, that he was tied by the leg.

He no longer pranced and ruffled and forged his feathers. He walked within the limits of his tether sombrely. Still he gobbled up the best bits of food. Still, sometimes, he saved an extra-best bit for his favourite hen of the moment. Still he pranced with quivering, rocking fierceness upon such of his harem as came nonchalantly within range, and gave off the invisible lure. And still he crowed defiance to the cock-crows that showered up out of limbo, in the dawn.

But there was now a grim voracity in the way he gobbled his food, and a pinched triumph in the way he seized upon the shabby hens. His voice, above all, had lost the full gold of its clangour. He was tied by the leg and he knew it. Body, soul and spirit were tied by that string.

Underneath, however, the life in him was grimly unbroken. It was the cord that should break. So one morning, just before the light of dawn, rousing from his slumbers with a sudden wave of strength, he leaped forward on his wings, and the string snapped. He gave a wild strange squawk, rose in one lift to the top of the wall, and there he crowed a loud and splitting crow. So loud, it woke the peasant.

At the same time, at the same hour before dawn, on the same morning, a man awoke from a long sleep in which he was tied up. He woke numb and cold, inside a carved hole in the rock. Through all the long sleep his body had been full of hurt, and it was still full of hurt. He did not open his eyes. Yet he knew that he was awake, and numb, and cold, and rigid, and full of hurt, and tied up. His face was banded with cold bands, his legs were bandaged together. Only his hands were loose.

He could move if he wanted : he knew that. But he had no want. Who would want to come back from the dead ? A deep, deep nausea stirred in him, at the premonition of movement. He resented already the fact of the strange, incalculable moving that had already taken place in him : the moving back into consciousness. He had not wished it. He had wanted to stay outside, in the place where even memory is stone dead.

But now, something had returned to him, like a returned letter, and in that return he lay overcome with a sense of nausea. Yet suddenly his hands moved. They lifted up, cold, heavy and sore. Yet they lifted up, to drag away the cloth from his face, and push at the shoulder bands. Then they fell again, cold, heavy, numb, and sick with having moved even so much, unspeakably unwilling to move further.

With his face cleared, and his shoulders free, he lapsed again, and lay dead, resting on the cold nullity of being dead. It was the most desirable. And almost, he had it complete : the utter cold nullity of being outside.

Yet when he was most nearly gone, suddenly, driven by an ache at the wrists, his hands rose and began pushing at the bandages of his knees, his feet began to stir, even while his breast lay cold and dead still.

And at last, the eyes opened. On to the dark. The same dark ! yet perhaps there was a pale chink, of the all-disturbing night, prizing open the pure dark. He could not lift his head. The eyes closed. And again it was finished.

Then suddenly he leaned up, and the great world reeled. Bandages fell away. And narrow walls of rock closed upon him, and gave the new anguish of imprisonment. There were chinks of light. With a wave of strength that came from revulsion, he leaned forward, in that narrow well of rock, and leaned frail hands on the rock near the chinks of light.

Strength came from somewhere, from revulsion ; there was a crash and a wave of light, and the dead man was crouching in his lair, facing the animal onrush of light. Yet it was hardly dawn, and the strange, piercing keenness of daybreak's sharp breath was on him. It meant full awakening.

Slowly, slowly he crept down from the cell of rock, with the caution of the bitterly wounded. Bandages and linen and perfume fell away, and he crouched on the ground against the wall of rock, to recover oblivion. But he saw his hurt feet touching the earth again, with unspeakable pain, the earth they had meant to touch no more, and he saw his thin legs that had died, and pain unknowable, pain like utter bodily disillusion, filled him so full that he stood up, with one torn hand on the ledge of the tomb.

To be back! To be back again, after all that! He saw the linen swathing-bands fallen round his dead feet, and stooping, he picked them up, folded them, and laid them back in the rocky cavity from which he had emerged. Then he took the perfumed linen sheet, wrapped it round him as a mantle, and turned away, to the wanness of the chill dawn.

He was alone; and having died, was even beyond loneliness.

Filled still with the sickness of unspeakable disillusion, the man stepped with wincing feet down the rocky slope, past the sleeping soldiers, who lay wrapped in their woollen mantles under the wild laurels. Silent, on naked, scarred feet, wrapped in a white linen shroud, he glanced down for a moment on the inert, heap-like bodies of the soldiers. They were repulsive, a slow squalor of limbs, yet he felt a certain compassion. He passed on towards the road, lest they should wake.

Having nowhere to go, he turned from the city that stood on her hills. He slowly followed the road away from the town, past the olives, under which purple anemones were drooping in the chill of dawn, and rich-green herbage was pressing thick. The world, the same as ever, the natural world, thronging with greenness, a nightingale winsomely, wistfully, coaxingly calling from the bushes beside a runnel of water, in the world, the natural world of morning and evening, forever undying, from which he had died.

He went on, on scarred feet, neither of this world nor of the next. Neither here nor there, neither seeing nor yet sightless, he passed dimly on, away from the city and its precincts, wondering why he should be travelling, yet driven by a dim, deep nausea of disillusion, and a resolution of which he was not even aware.

Advancing in a kind of half-consciousness under the dry stone wall of the olive orchard, he was roused by the shrill wild crowing of a cock just near him, a sound which made him shiver as if electricity had touched him. He saw a black and orange cock on a bough above the road, then running through the olives of the upper level, a peasant in a grey woollen shirt-tunic. Leaping out of greenness, came the black and orange cock with the red comb, his tail-feathers streaming lustrous.

"O stop him, Master!" called the peasant. "My escaped cock!"

The man addressed, with a sudden flicker of a smile, opened his great white wings of a shroud in front of the leaping bird. The cock fell back with a squawk and a flutter, the peasant jumped forward, there was a terrific beating of wings, and whirring of feathers, then the peasant had the escaped cock safely under his arm, its wings shut down, its face crazily craning forward, its round eyes goggling from its white chops.

" It's my escaped cock ! " said the peasant, soothing the bird with his left hand, as he looked perspiringly up into the face of the man wrapped in white linen.

The peasant changed countenance, and stood transfixed, as he looked into the dead-white face of the man who had died. That dead-white face, so still, with the black beard growing on it as if in death ; and those wide-open black sombre eyes, that had died, and those washed scars on the waxy forehead ! The slow-blooded man of the field let his jaw drop, in childish inability to meet the situation.

" Don't be afraid," said the man in the shroud. " I am not dead. They took me down too soon. So I have risen up. Yet if they discover me, they will do it all over again. . . ."

He spoke in a voice of old disgust. Humanity ! Especially humanity in authority ! There was only one thing it could do. He looked with black, indifferent eyes into the quick, shifty eyes of the peasant. The peasant quailed, and was powerless under the look of deathly indifference, and strange cold resoluteness. He could only say the one thing he was afraid to say :

" Will you hide in my house, Master ? "

" I will rest there. But if you tell any one, you know what will happen. You will have to go before a judge."

" Me ! I shan't speak. Let us be quick ! "

The peasant looked round in fear, wondering sulkily why he had let himself in for this doom. The man with scarred feet climbed painfully up to the level of the olive garden, and followed the sullen, hurrying peasant across the green wheat among the olive trees. He felt the cool silkiness of the young wheat under his feet that had been dead, and the roughishness of its separate life was apparent to him. At the edges of rocks, he saw the silky, silvery-haired buds of the scarlet anemone bending downwards. And they too were in another world. In his own world he was alone, utterly alone. These things around him were in a world that had never died. But he himself had died, or had been killed from out of it, and all that remained now was the great void nausea of utter disillusion.

They came to a clay cottage, and the peasant waited dejectedly for the other man to pass.

"Pass!" he said. "Pass! We have not been seen."

The man in white linen entered the earthen room, taking with him the aroma of strange perfumes. The peasant closed the door, and passed through the inner doorway into the yard, where the ass stood within the high walls, safe from being stolen. There the peasant, in great disquietude, tied up the cock. The man with the waxen face sat down on a mat near the hearth, for he was spent and barely conscious. Yet he heard outside the whispering of the peasant to his wife, for the woman had been watching from the roof.

Presently they came in, and the woman hid her face. She poured water, and put bread and dried figs on a wooden platter. "Eat, Master!" said the peasant. "Eat! No one has seen."

But the stranger had no desire for food. Yet he moistened a little bread in the water, and ate it, since life must be. But desire was dead in him, even for food and drink. He had risen without desire, without even the desire to live, empty save for the all-overwhelming disillusion that lay like nausea where his life had been. Yet perhaps, deeper even than disillusion, was a desireless resoluteness, deeper even than consciousness.

The peasant and his wife stood near the door, watching. They saw with terror the livid wounds on the thin waxy hands and the thin feet of the stranger, and the small lacerations in the still dead forehead. They smelled with terror the scent of rich perfumes that came from him, from his body. And they looked at the fine, snowy, costly linen. Perhaps really he was a dead king, from the region of terrors. And he was still cold and remote in the region of death, with perfumes coming from his transparent body as if from some strange flower.

Having with difficulty swallowed some of the moistened bread, he lifted his eyes to them. He saw them as they were: limited, meagre in their life, without any splendour of gesture and of courage. But they were what they were, slow inevitable parts of the natural world. They had no nobility, but fear made them compassionate.

And the stranger had compassion on them again, for he knew that they would respond best to gentleness, giving back a clumsy gentleness again.

"Do not be afraid," he said to them gently. "Let me stay a little while with you. I shall not stay long. And then I shall go away forever. But do not be afraid. No harm will come to you through me."

They believed him at once, yet the fear did not leave them. And they said:

" Stay, Master, while ever you will. Rest ! Rest quietly ! ''
But they were afraid.

So he let them be, and the peasant went away with the ass. The
sun had risen bright, and in the dark house with the door shut,
the man was again as if in the tomb. So he said to the woman,
" I would lie in the yard.''

And she swept the yard for him, and laid him a mat, and he
lay down under the wall in the morning sun. There he saw the
first green leaves spurting like flames from the ends of the enclosed
fig-tree, out of the bareness to the sky of spring above. But the
man who had died could not look, he only lay quite still in the sun,
which was not yet too hot, and had no desire in him, not even to
move. But he lay with his thin legs in the sun, his black perfumed
hair falling into the hollows of his neck, and his thin colourless arms
utterly inert. As he lay there, the hens clucked and scratched, and
the escaped cock, caught and tied by the leg again, cowered in a
corner.

The peasant woman was frightened. She came peeping, and,
seeing him never move, feared to have a dead man in the yard.
But the sun had grown stronger, he opened his eyes and looked at
her. And now she was frightened of the man who was alive, but
spoke nothing.

He opened his eyes, and saw the world again bright as glass. It
was life, in which he had no share any more. But it shone outside
him, blue sky, and a bare fig-tree with little jets of green leaf.
Bright as glass, and he was not of it, for desire had failed.

Yet he was there, and not extinguished. The day passed in a
kind of coma, and at evening he went into the house. The peasant
man came home, but he was frightened, and had nothing to say.
The stranger too ate of the mess of beans, a little. Then he washed
his hands and turned to the wall, and was silent. The peasants
were silent too. They watched their guest sleep. Sleep was so near
death he could still sleep.   ·

Yet when the sun came up, he went again to lie in the yard. The
sun was the one thing that drew him and swayed him, and he still
wanted to feel the cool air of the morning in his nostrils, see the
pale sky overhead. He still hated to be shut up.

As he came out, the young cock crowed. It was a diminished,
pinched cry, but there was that in the voice of the bird stronger
than chagrin. It was the necessity to live, and even to cry out the
triumph of life. The man who had died stood and watched the
cock who had escaped and been caught, ruffling himself up, rising

forward on his toes, throwing up his head, and parting his beak in another challenge from life to death. The brave sounds rang out, and though they were diminished by the cord round the bird's leg, they were not cut off. The man who had died looked nakedly on life, and saw a vast resoluteness everywhere flinging itself up in stormy or subtle wave-crests, foam-tips emerging out of the blue invisible, a black and orange cock or the green flame-tongues out of the extremes of the fig-tree. They came forth, these things and creatures of spring, glowing with desire and with assertion. They came like crests of foam, out of the blue flood of the invisible desire, out of the vast invisible sea of strength, and they came coloured and tangible, evanescent, yet deathless in their coming. The man who had died looked on the great swing into existence of things that had not died, but he saw no longer their tremulous desire to exist and to be. He heard instead their ringing, ringing, defiant challenge to all other things existing.

The man lay still, with eyes that had died now wide open and darkly still, seeing the everlasting resoluteness of life. And the cock, with the flat, brilliant glance, glanced back at him, with a bird's half-seeing look. And always the man who had died saw not the bird alone, but the short, sharp wave of life of which the bird was the crest. He watched the queer, beaky motion of the creature as it gobbled into itself the scraps of food ; its glancing of the eye of life, ever alert and watchful, overweening and cautious, and the voice of its life, crowing triumph and assertion, yet strangled by a cord of circumstance. He seemed to hear the queer speech of very life, as the cock triumphantly imitated the clucking of the favourite hen, when she had laid an egg, a clucking which still had, in the male bird the hollow chagrin of the cord round his leg. And when the man threw a bit of bread to the cock, it called with an extraordinary cooing tenderness, tousling and saving the morsel for the hens. The hens ran up greedily, and carried the morsel away beyond the reach of the string.

Then, walking complacently after them, suddenly the male bird's leg would hitch at the end of his tether, and he would yield with a kind of collapse. His flag fell, he seemed to diminish, he would huddle in the shade. And he was young, his tail-feathers, glossy as they were, were not fully grown. It was not till evening again that the tide of life in him made him forget. Then when his favourite hen came strolling unconcernedly near him, emitting the lure, he pounced on her with all his feathers vibrating. And the man who had died watched the unsteady, rocking vibration of the bent bird, and it was not the bird he saw, but one wave-tip of life overlapping for a minute another, in the tide of the swaying ocean of life. And the destiny of life seemed more fierce and compulsive to him even than the destiny of death. The doom of death was a shadow compared to the raging destiny of life, the determined surge of life.

At twilight the peasant came home with the ass, and he said : " Master ! It is said that the body was stolen from the garden, and the tomb is empty, and the soldiers are taken away, accursed Romans ! And the women are there to weep."

The man who had died looked at the man who had not died.

" It is well," he said. " Say nothing, and we are safe."

And the peasant was relieved. He looked rather dirty and stupid, and even as much flaminess as that of the young cock, which he had tied by the leg, would never glow in him. He was without fire. But the man who had died thought to himself :

" Why, then, should he be lifted up ? Clods of earth are turned over for refreshment, they are not to be lifted up. Let the earth remain earthy, and hold its own against the sky. I was wrong to seek to lift it up. I was wrong to try to interfere. The ploughshare of devastation will be set in the soil of Judea, and the life of this peasant will be overturned like the sods of the field. No man can save the earth from tillage. It is tillage, not salvation. . . ."

So he saw the man, the peasant, with compassion ; but the man who had died no longer wished to interfere in the soul of the man who had not died, and who could never die, save to return to earth. Let him return to earth in his own good hour, and let no one try to interfere when the earth claims her own.

So the man with scars let the peasant go from him, for the peasant had no birth in him. Yet the man who had died said to himself : " He is my host."

And at dawn, when he was better, the man who had died rose up, and on slow, sore feet retraced his way to the garden. For he had been betrayed in a garden, and buried in a garden. And as he turned round the screen of laurels, near the rock-face, he saw a woman hovering by the tomb, a woman in blue and yellow. She peeped again into the mouth of the hole, that was like a deep cupboard. But still there was nothing. And she wrung her hands and wept. And as she turned away, she saw the man in white, standing by the laurels, and she gave a cry, thinking it might be a spy, and she said :

" They have taken him away ! "

So he said to her :

" Madeleine ! "

Then she reeled as if she would fall, for she knew him. And he said to her :

" Madeleine ! Do not be afraid. I am alive. They took me down too soon, so I came back to life. Then I was sheltered in a house."

She did not know what to say, but fell at his feet to kiss them.

" Don't touch me, Madeleine," he said. " Not yet ! I am not yet healed and in touch with men."

So she wept because she did not know what to do. And he said :

" Let us go aside, among the bushes, where we can speak unseen."

So in her blue mantle and her yellow robe, she followed him among the trees, and he sat down under a myrtle bush. And he said :

" I am not yet quite come to. Madeleine, what is to be done next ? "

" Master ! " she said. " Oh, we have wept for you ! And will you come back to us ? "

" What is finished is finished, and for me the end is past," he said. " The stream will run till no more rains fill it, then it will dry up. For me, that life is over."

" And will you give up your triumph ? " she said sadly.

" My triumph," he said, " is that I am not dead. I have outlived my mission, and know no more of it. It is my triumph. I have survived the day and the death of my interference, and am still a man. I am young still, Madeleine, not even come to middle age. I am glad all that is over. It had to be. But now I am glad it is over, and the day of my interference is done. The teacher and the saviour are dead in me ; now I can go about my business, into my own single life."

She heard him, and did not fully understand. But what he said made her feel disappointed.

" But you will come back to us ? " she said, insisting.

" I don't know what I shall do," he said. " When I am healed, I shall know better. But my mission is over, and my teaching is finished, and death has saved me from my own salvation. Oh, Madeleine, I want to take my single way in life, which is my portion. My public life is over, the life of my self-importance. Now I can wait on life, and say nothing, and have no one betray me. I wanted to be greater than the limits of my hands and feet, so I brought betrayal on myself. And I know I wronged Judas, my poor Judas. For I have died, and now I know my own limits. Now I can live without striving to sway others any more. For my reach ends in my finger-tips, and my stride is no longer than the ends of my toes. Yet I would embrace multitudes, I who have never truly embraced even one. But Judas and the high priests saved me from my own salvation, and soon I can turn to my destiny like a bather in the sea at dawn, who has just come down to the shore alone."

"Do you want to be alone henceforward?" she asked. "And was your mission nothing? Was it all untrue?"

"Nay!" he said. "Neither were your lovers in the past nothing. They were much to you, but you took more than you gave. Then you came to me for salvation from your own excess. And I, in my mission, I too ran to excess. I gave more than I took, and that also is woe and vanity. So Pilate and the high priests saved me from my own excessive salvation. Don't run to excess now in living, Madeleine. It only means another death."

She pondered bitterly, for the need for excessive giving was in her, and she could not bear to be denied.

"And will you not come back to us?" she said. "Have you risen for yourself alone?"

He heard the sarcasm in her voice, and looked at her beautiful face which still was dense with excessive need for salvation from the woman she had been, the female who had caught men at her will. The cloud of necessity was on her, to be saved from the old, wilful Eve, who had embraced many men and taken more than she gave. Now the other doom was on her. She wanted to give without taking. And that too, is hard, and cruel to the warm body.

"I have not risen from the dead in order to seek death again," he said.

She glanced up at him, and saw the weariness settling again on his waxy face, and the vast disillusion in his dark eyes, and the underlying indifference. He felt her glance, and said to himself:

"Now my own followers will want to do me to death again, for having risen up different from their expectation."

"But you will come to us, to see us, us who love you?" she said.

He laughed a little and said:

"Ah, yes." Then he added, "Have you a little money? Will you give me a little money? I owe it."

She had not much, but it pleased her to give it to him.

"Do you think," he said to her, "that I might come and live with you in your house?"

She looked up at him with large blue eyes, that gleamed strangely.

"Now?" she said with peculiar triumph.

And he, who shrank now from triumph of any sort, his own or another's, said :

" Not now ! Later, when I am healed, and . . . and I am in touch with the flesh."

The words faltered in him. And in his heart he knew he would never go to live in her house. For the flicker of triumph had gleamed in her eyes ; the greed of giving. But she murmured in a humming rapture :

" Ah, you know I would give up everything to you."

" Nay ! " he said. " I didn't ask that."

A revulsion from all the life he had known came over him again, the great nausea of disillusion, and the spear-thrust through his bowels. He crouched under the myrtle bushes, without strength. Yet his eyes were open. And she looked at him again, and she saw that it was not the Messiah. The Messiah had not risen. The enthusiasm and the burning purity were gone, and the rapt youth. His youth was dead. This man was middle-aged and disillusioned, with a certain terrible indifference, and a resoluteness which love would never conquer. This was not the Master she had so adored, the young, flamy, unphysical exalter of her soul. This was nearer to the lovers she had known of old, but with a greater indifference to the personal issue, and a lesser susceptibility.

She was thrown out of the balance of her rapturous, anguished adoration. This risen man was the death of her dream.

" You should go now," he said to her. " Do not touch me, I am in death. I shall come again here, on the third day. Come if you will, at dawn. And we will speak again."

She went away, perturbed and shattered. Yet as she went, her mind discarded the bitterness of the reality, and she conjured up rapture and wonder, that the Master was risen and was not dead. He was risen, the Saviour, the exalter, the wonder-worker ! He was risen, but not as man ; as pure God, who should not be touched by flesh, and who should be rapt away into Heaven. It was the most glorious and most ghostly of the miracles.

Meanwhile the man who had died gathered himself together at last, and slowly made his way to the peasant's house. He was glad to go back to them, and away from Madeleine and his own associates. For the peasants had the inertia of earth and would let him rest, and as yet, would put no compulsion on him.

The woman was on the roof, looking for him. She was afraid that he had gone away. His presence in the house had become like gentle wine to her. She hastened to the door, to him.

" Where have you been ? " she said. " Why did you go away ? "

" I have been to walk in a garden, and I have seen a friend, who gave me a little money. It is for you."

He held out his thin hand, with the small amount of money, all that Madeleine could give him. The peasant's wife's eyes glistened, for money was scarce, and she said :

" Oh, Master ! And is it truly mine ? "

" Take it ! " he said. " It buys bread, and bread brings life."

So he lay down in the yard again, sick with relief at being alone again. For with the peasants he could be alone, but his own friends would never let him be alone. And in the safety of the yard, the young cock was dear to him, as it shouted in the helpless zest of life, and finished in the helpless humiliation of being tied by the leg. This day the ass stood swishing her tail under the shed. The man who had died lay down and turned utterly away from life, in the sickness of death in life.

But the woman brought wine and water, and sweetened cakes, and roused him, so that he ate a little, to please her. The day was hot, and as she crouched to serve him, he saw her breasts sway from her humble body, under her smock. He knew she wished he would desire her, and she was youngish, and not unpleasant. And he, who had never known a woman, would have desired her if he could. But he could not want her, though he felt gently towards her soft, crouching, humble body. But it was her thoughts, her conscious-ness, he could not mingle with. She was pleased with the money, and now she wanted to take more from him. She wanted the embrace of his body. But her little soul was hard, and short-sighted, and grasping, her body had its little greed, and no gentle reverence of the return gift. So he spoke a quiet, pleasant word to her, and turned away. He could not touch the little, personal body, the little, personal life of this woman, nor in any other. He turned away from it without hesitation.

Risen from the dead, he had realized at last that the body, too, has its little life, and beyond that, the greater life. He was virgin, in recoil from the little, greedy life of the body. But now he knew that virginity is a form of greed ; and that the body rises again to give and to take, to take and to give, ungreedily. Now he knew that he had risen for the woman, or women, who knew the greater life of the body, not greedy to give, not greedy to take, and with whom he could mingle his body. But having died, he was patient, knowing there was time, an eternity of time. And he was driven by no greedy desire, either to give himself to others, or to grasp anything for himself. For he had died.

The peasant came home from work, and said :

" Master, I thank you for the money. But we did not want it. And all I have is yours."

But the man who had died was sad, because the peasant stood there in the little, personal body, and his eyes were cunning and sparkling with the hope of greater rewards in money, later on. True, the peasant had taken him in free, and had risked getting no reward. But the hope was cunning in him. Yet even this was as men are made. So when the peasant would have helped him to rise, for night had fallen, the man who had died said :

" Don't touch me, brother. I am not yet risen to the Father."

The sun burned with greater splendour, and burnished the young cock brighter. But the peasant kept the string renewed, and the bird was a prisoner. Yet the flame of life burned up to a sharp point in the cock, so that it eyed askance and haughtily the man who had died. And the man smiled and held the bird dear, and he said to it :

" Surely thou art risen to the Father, among birds."

And the young cock, answering, crowed.

When at dawn on the third morning the man went to the garden, he was absorbed, thinking of the greater life of the body, beyond the little, narrow, personal life. So he came through the thick screen of laurel and myrtle bushes, near the rock, suddenly, and he saw three women near the tomb. One was Madeleine, and one was the woman who had been his mother, and the third was a woman he knew, called Joan. He looked up, and saw them all, and they saw him, and they were all afraid.

He stood arrested in the distance, knowing they were there to claim him back, bodily. But he would in no wise return to them. Pallid, in the shadow of a grey morning that was blowing to rain, he saw them, and turned away. But Madeleine hastened towards him.

" I did not bring them," she said. " They have come of themselves. See, I have brought you money ! . . . Will you not speak to them ? "

She offered him some gold pieces, and he took them, saying :

" May I have this money ? I shall need it. I cannot speak to them, for I am not yet ascended to the Father. And I must leave you now."

" Ah ! Where will you go ? " she cried.

He looked at her, and saw she was clutching for the man in him who had died and was dead, the man of his youth and his mission, of his chastity and his fear, of his little life, his giving without taking.

" I must go to my Father ! " he said.

" And you will leave us ? There is your mother ! " she cried, turning round with the old anguish, which yet was sweet to her.

" But now I must ascend to my Father," he said, and he drew back into the bushes, and so turned quickly, and went away, saying to himself :

" Now I belong to no one and have no connection, and mission or gospel is gone from me. Lo ! I cannot make even my own life, and what have I to save ? . . . I can learn to be alone."

So he went back to the peasants' house, to the yard where the young cock was tied by the leg, with a string. And he wanted no one, for it was best to be alone ; for the presence of people made him lonely. The sun and the subtle salve of spring healed his wounds, even the gaping wound of disillusion through his bowels was closing up. And his need of men and women, his fever to have them and to be saved by them, this too was healing in him. Whatever came of touch between himself and the race of men, henceforth, should come without trespass or compulsion. For he said to himself :

" I tried to compel them to live, so they compelled me to die. It is always so, with compulsion. The recoil kills the advance. Now is my time to be alone."

Therefore he went no more to the garden, but lay still and saw the sun, or walked at dusk across the olive slopes, among the green wheat, that rose a palm-breadth higher every sunny day. And always he thought to himself :

" How good it is to have fulfilled my mission, and to be beyond it. Now I can be alone, and leave all things to themselves, and the fig-tree may be barren if it will, and the rich may be rich. My way is my own alone."

So the green jets of leaves unspread on the fig-tree, with the bright, translucent, green blood of the tree. And the young cock grew brighter, more lustrous with the sun's burnishing ; yet always tied by the leg with a string. And the sun went down more and more in pomp, out of the gold and red-flushed air. The man who had died was aware of it all, and he thought :

" The Word is but the midge that bites at evening. Man is tormented with words like midges, and they follow him right into the tomb. But beyond the tomb they cannot go. Now I have passed the place where words can bite no more and the air is clear, and there is nothing to say, and I am alone within my own skin, which is the walls of all my domain."

So he healed of his wounds, and enjoyed his immortality of being alive without fret. For in the tomb he had slipped that noose which we call care. For in the tomb he had left his striving self, which cares and asserts itself. Now his uncaring self healed and became whole within his skin, and he smiled to himself with pure aloneness, which is one sort of immortality.

Then he said to himself: "I will wander the earth, and say nothing. For nothing is so marvellous as to be alone in the phenomenal world, which is raging, and yet apart. And I have not seen it, I was too much blinded by my confusion within it. Now I will wander among the stirring of the phenomenal world, for it is the stirring of all things among themselves which leaves me purely alone."

So he communed with himself, and decided to be a physician. Because the power was still in him to heal any man or child who touched his compassion. Therefore he cut his hair and his beard after the right fashion, and smiled to himself. And he bought himself shoes, and the right mantle, and put the right cloth over his head, hiding all the little scars. And the peasant said:

" Master, will you go forth from us ? "

" Yes, for the time is come for me to return to men."

So he gave the peasant a piece of money, and said to him :

" Give me the cock that escaped and is now tied by the leg. For he shall go forth with me."

So for a piece of money the peasant gave the cock to the man who had died, and at dawn the man who had died set out into the phenomenal world, to be fulfilled in his own loneliness in the midst of it. For previously he had been too much mixed up in it. Then he had died. Now he must come back, to be alone in the midst. Yet even now he did not go quite alone, for under his arm, as he went, he carried the cock, whose tail fluttered gaily behind, and who craned his head excitedly, for he too was adventuring out for the first time into the wider phenomenal world, which is the stirring of the body of cocks also. And the peasant woman shed a few tears, but then went indoors, being a peasant, to look again at the pieces of money. And it seemed to her, a gleam came out of the pieces of money, wonderful.

The man who had died wandered on, and it was a sunny day. He looked around as he went, and stood aside as the pack-train passed by, towards the city. And he said to himself :

" Strange is the phenomenal world, dirty and clean together !
And I am the same. Yet I am apart ! And life bubbles variously.
Why should I have wanted it to bubble all alike ? What a pity I
preached to them ! A sermon is so much more likely to cake into
mud, and to close the fountains, than is a psalm or a song. I made
a mistake. I understand that they executed me for preaching to
them. Yet they could not finally execute me, for now I am risen
in my own aloneness, and inherit the earth, since I lay no claim
on it. And I will be alone in the seethe of all things ; first and
foremost, forever, I shall be alone. But I must toss this bird into
the seethe of phenomena, for he must ride his wave. How hot he
is with life ! Soon, in some place, I shall leave him among the
hens. And perhaps one evening, I shall meet a woman who can
lure my risen body, yet leave me my aloneness. For the body of
my desire has died, and I am not in touch anywhere. Yet how do
I know ! All at least is life. And this cock gleams with bright
aloneness, though he answers the lure of hens. And I shall hasten
on to that village on the hill ahead of me ; already I am tired and
weak, and want to close my eyes to everything."

Hastening a little with the desire to have finished going, he
overtook two men going slowly, and talking. And being soft-footed
he heard they were speaking of himself. And he remembered
them, for he had known them in his life, the life of his mission.
So he greeted them, but did not disclose himself in the dusk, and
they did not know him. He said to them :

" What then of him who would be king, and was put to death
for it ? "

They answered suspiciously : " Why ask you of him ? "

" I have known him, and thought much about him," he said.
So they replied : " He has risen."

" Yea ! And where is he, and how does he live ? "

" We know not, for it is not revealed. Yet he is risen, and in a
little while will ascend unto the Father."

" Yea ! And where then is his Father ? "

" Know ye not ? You are then of the Gentiles ! The Father is
in Heaven, above the cloud and the firmament."

" Truly ? Then how will he ascend ? "

" As Elijah the Prophet, he shall go up in a glory."

" Even into the sky."

" Into the sky."

" Then is he not risen in the flesh ? "

" He is risen in the flesh."

" And will he take flesh up into the sky ? "

" The Father in Heaven will take him up."

The man who had died said no more, for his say was over, and words beget words, even as gnats. But the man asked him : " Why do you carry a cock ? "

" I am a healer," he said, " and the bird hath virtue."

" You are not a believer ? "

" Yea ! I believe the bird is full of life and virtue."

They walked on in silence after this, and he felt they disliked his answer. So he smiled to himself, for a dangerous phenomenon in the world is a man of narrow belief, who denies the right of his neighbour to be alone. And as they came to the outskirts of the village, the man who had died stood still in the gloaming and said in his old voice :

" Know ye me not ? "

And they cried in fear : " Master ! "

" Yea ! " he said, laughing softly. And he turned suddenly away, down a side lane, and was gone under the wall before they knew.

So he came to an inn where the asses stood in the yard. And he called for fritters, and they were made for him. So he slept under a shed. But in the morning he was wakened by a loud crowing, and his cock's voice ringing in his ears. So he saw the rooster of the inn walking forth to battle, with his hens, a goodly number, behind him. Then the cock of the man who had died sprang forth, and a battle began between the birds. The man of the inn ran to save his rooster, but the man who had died said :

" If my bird wins I will give him thee. And if he lose, thou shalt eat him."

So the birds fought savagely, and the cock of the man who had died killed the common cock of the yard. Then the man who had died said to his young cock :

" Thou at least hast found thy kingdom, and the females to thy body. Thy aloneness can take on splendour, polished by the lure of thy hens."

And he left his bird there, and went on deeper into the phenomenal world, which is a vast complexity of entanglements and allurements. And he asked himself a last question :

" From what, and to what, could this infinite whirl be saved ? "

So he went his way, and was alone. But the way of the world was past belief, as he saw the strange entanglement of passions and circumstance and compulsion everywhere, but always the dread insomnia of compulsion. It was fear, the ultimate fear of death, that made men mad. So always he must move on, for if he stayed, his neighbours wound the strangling of their fear and bullying round him. There was nothing he could touch, for all, in a mad assertion of the ego, wanted to put a compulsion on him, and violate his intrinsic solitude. It was the mania of cities and societies and hosts, to lay a compulsion upon a man, upon all men. For men and women alike were mad with the egoistic fear of their own nothingness. And he thought of his own mission, how he had tried to lay the compulsion of love on all men. And the old nausea came back on him. For there was no contact without a subtle attempt to inflict a compulsion. And already he had been compelled even into death. The nausea of the old wound broke out afresh, and he looked again on the world with repulsion, dreading its mean contacts.

PART II

THE wind came cold and strong from inland, from the invisible snows of Lebanon. But the temple, facing south and west, towards Egypt, faced the splendid sun of winter as he curved down towards the sea, the warmth and radiance flooded in between the pillars of painted wood. But the sea was invisible, because of the trees, though its dashing sounded among the hum of pines. The air was turning golden to afternoon. The woman who served Isis stood in her yellow robe, and looked up at the steep slopes coming down to the sea, where the olive-trees silvered under the wind like water splashing. She was alone save for the goddess. And in the winter afternoon the light stood erect and magnificent off the invisible sea, filling the hills of the coast. She went towards the sun, through the grove of Mediterranean pine-trees and ever-green oaks, in the midst of which the temple stood, on a little, tree-covered tongue of land between two bays.

It was only a very little way, and then she stood among the dry trunks of the outermost pines, on the rocks under which the sea smote and sucked, facing the open where the bright sun gloried in winter. The sea was dark, almost indigo, running away from the land, and crested with white. The hand of the wind brushed it strangely with shadow, as it brushed the olives of the slopes with silver. And there was no boat out. The three boats were drawn high upon the steep shingle of the little bay, by the small grey tower. Along the edge of the shingle ran a high wall, inside which was a garden occupying the brief flat of the bay, then rising in terraces up the steep slope of the coast. And there, some little way up, within another wall, stood the low white villa, white and alone as the coast, overlooking the sea. But higher, much higher up, where the olives had given way to pine-trees again, ran the coast road, keeping to the height to be above the gullies that came down to the bays.

Upon it all poured the royal sunshine of the January afternoon. Or rather, all was part of the great sun, glow and substance and immaculate loneliness of the sea, and pure brightness.

Crouching in the rocks above the dark water, which only swung up and down, two slaves, half naked, were dressing pigeons for the evening meal. They pierced the throat of a blue, live bird, and let the drops of blood fall into the heaving sea, with curious concentration. They were performing some sacrifice, or working some incantation. The woman of the temple, yellow and white and alone like a winter narcissus, stood between the pines of the small, humped peninsula where the temple secretly hid, and watched.

A black-and-white pigeon, vividly white, like a ghost escaped over the low dark sea, sped out, caught the wind, tilted, rode, soared, and swept over the pine-trees, and wheeled away, a speck, inland. It had escaped. The priestess heard the cry of the boy slave, a garden slave of about seventeen. He raised his arms to heaven in anger as the pigeon wheeled away, naked and angry and young he held out his arms. Then he turned and seized the girl in an access of rage, and beat her with his fist that was stained with pigeon's blood. And she lay down with her face hidden, passive and quivering. The woman who owned them watched. And as she watched, she saw another onlooker, a stranger, in a low, broad hat, and a cloak of grey homespun, a dark bearded man standing on the little causeway of a rock that was the neck of her temple peninsula. By the blowing of his dark-grey cloak she saw him. And he saw her, on the rocks like a white-and-yellow narcissus, because of the flutter of her white linen tunic, below the yellow mantle of wool. And both of them watched the two slaves.

The boy suddenly left off beating the girl. He crouched over her, touching her, trying to make her speak. But she lay quite inert, face down on the smoothed rock. And he put his arms round her and lifted her, but she slipped back to earth like one dead, yet far too quickly for anything dead. The boy, desperate, caught her by the hips and hugged her to him, turning her over there. There she seemed inert, all her fight was in her shoulders. He twisted her over, intent and unconscious, and pushed his hands between her thighs, to push them apart. And in an instant he was covering her in the blind, frightened frenzy of a boy's first passion. Quick and frenzied his young body quivered naked on hers, blind, for a minute. Then it lay quite still, as if dead.

And then, in terror, he peeped up. He peeped round, and drew slowly to his feet, adjusting his loin-rag. He saw the stranger, and then he saw, on the rocks beyond, the lady of Isis, his mistress. And as he saw her, his whole body shrank and cowed, and with a strange cringing motion he scuttled lamely towards the door in the wall.

The girl sat up and looked after him. When she had seen him disappear, she too looked round. And she saw the stranger and the priestess. Then with a sullen movement she turned away, as if she had seen nothing, to the four dead pigeons and the knife, which lay there on the rock. And she began to strip the small feathers, so that they rose on the wind like dust.

The priestess turned away. Slaves ! Let the overseer watch them. She was not interested. She went slowly through the pines again, back to the temple, which stood in the sun in a small clearing at the centre of the tongue of land. It was a small temple of wood, painted all pink and white and blue, having at the front four wooden pillars rising like stems to the swollen lotus-bud of Egypt at the top, supporting the roof and open, spiky lotus-flowers of the outer frieze, which went round under the eaves. Two low steps of stone led up to the platform before the pillars, and the chamber behind the pillars was open. There a low stone altar stood, with a few embers in its hollow, and the dark stain of blood in its end groove.

She knew her temple so well, for she had built it at her own expense, and tended it for seven years. There it stood, pink and white, like a flower in the little clearing, backed by blackish ever-green oaks ; and the shadow of afternoon was already washing over its pillar-bases.

She entered slowly, passing through to the dark inner chamber, lighted by a perfumed oil-flame. And once more she pushed shut the door, and once more she threw a few grains of incense on a brazier before the goddess, and once more she sat down before her goddess, in the almost-darkness, to muse, to go away into the dreams of the goddess.

It was Isis ; but not Isis, Mother of Horus. It was Isis Bereaved, Isis in Search. The goddess, in painted marble, lifted her face and strode, one thigh forward through the frail fluting of her robe, in the anguish of bereavement and of search. She was looking for the fragments of the dead Osiris, dead and scattered asunder, dead, torn apart, and thrown in fragments over the wide world. And she must find his hands and his feet, his heart, his thighs, his head, his belly, she must gather him together and fold her arms round the re-assembled body till it became warm again, and roused to life, and could embrace her, and could fecundate her womb. And the strange rapture and anguish of search went on through the years, as she lifted her throat and her hollowed eyes looked inward, in the tormented ecstasy of seeking, and the delicate navel of her bud-like belly showed through the frail, girdled robe with the eternal asking, asking, of her search. And through the years she found him bit by bit, heart and head and limbs and body. And yet she had not found the last reality, the final clue to him, that alone could bring him really back to her. For she was Isis of the subtle lotus, the womb which waits submerged and in bud, waits for the touch of that other inward sun that streams its rays from the loins of the male Osiris.

This was the mystery the woman had served alone for seven years, since she was twenty, till now she was twenty-seven. Before, when she was young, she had lived in the world, in Rome, in Ephesus, in Egypt. For her father had been one of Anthony's captains and comrades, had fought with Anthony and had stood with him when Cæsar was murdered, and through to the days of shame. Then he had come again across to Asia, out of favour with Rome, and had been killed in the mountains beyond Lebanon. The widow, having no favour to hope for from Octavius, had retired to her small property on the coast under Lebanon, taking her daughter from the world, a girl of nineteen, beautiful but unmarried.

When she was young the girl had known Cæsar, and had shrunk from his eagle-like rapacity. The golden Anthony had sat with her many a half-hour, in the splendour of his great limbs and glowing manhood, and talked with her of the philosophies and the gods. For he was fascinated as a child by the gods, though he mocked at them, and forgot them in his own vanity. But he said to her :

" I have sacrificed two doves for you, to Venus, for I am afraid you make no offering to the sweet goddess. Beware you will offend her. Come, why is the flower of you so cool within ? Does never a ray nor a glance find its way through ? Ah, come, a maid should open to the sun, when the sun leans towards her to caress her."

And the big, bright eyes of Anthony laughed down on her, bathing her in his glow. And she felt the lovely glow of his male beauty and his amorousness bathe all her limbs and her body. But it was as he said : the very flower of her womb was cool, was almost cold, like a bud in shadow of frost, for all the flooding of his sunshine. So Anthony, respecting her father, who loved her, had left her.

And it had always been the same. She saw many men, young and old. And on the whole, she liked the old ones best, for they talked to her still and sincere, and did not expect her to open like a flower to the sun of their maleness. Once she asked a philosopher : " Are all women born to be given to men ? " To which the old man answered slowly :

" Rare women wait for the re-born man. For the lotus, as you know, will not answer to all the bright heat of the sun. But she curves her dark, hidden head in the depths, and stirs not. Till, in the night, one of these rare, invisible suns that have been killed and shine no more, rises among the stars in unseen purple, and like the violet, sends its rare, purple rays out into the night. To these the lotus stirs as to a caress, and rises upwards through the flood, and lifts up her bent head, and opens with an expansion such as no other flower knows, and spreads her sharp rays of bliss, and offers her soft, gold depths such as no other flower possesses, to the penetration of the flooding, violet-dark sun that has died and risen and makes no show. But for the golden brief day-suns of show such as Anthony, and for the hard winter suns of power, such as Cæsar, the lotus stirs not, nor will ever stir. Those will only tear open the bud. Ah, I tell you, wait for the re-born and wait for the bud to stir."

So she had waited. For all the men were soldiers or politicians in the Roman spell, assertive, manly, splendid apparently, but of an inward meanness, an inadequacy. And Rome and Egypt alike, had left her alone, unroused. And she was a woman to herself, she would not give herself for a surface glow, nor marry for reasons. She would wait for the lotus to stir.

And then, in Egypt, she had found Isis, in whom she spelled her mystery. She had brought Isis to the shores of Sidon, and lived with her in the mystery of search ; whilst her mother, who loved affairs, controlled the small estate and the slaves with a free hand.

When the woman had roused from her muse and risen to perform the last brief ritual to Isis, she replenished the lamp and left the sanctuary, locking the door. In the outer world, the sun had already set, and twilight was chill among the humming trees, which hummed still, though the wind was abating.

A stranger in a dark, broad hat rose from the corner of the temple steps, holding his hat in the wind. He was dark-faced, with a black pointed beard. " O Madam, whose shelter may I implore ? " he said to the woman, who stood in her yellow mantle on a step above him, beside a pink-and-white painted pillar. Her face was rather long and pale, her dusky blonde hair was held under a thin gold net. She looked down on the vagabond with indifference. It was the same she had seen watching the slaves.

" Why come you down from the road ? " she asked.

" I saw the temple like a pale flower on the coast, and would rest among the trees of the precincts, if the lady of the goddess permits."

" It is Isis in Search," she said, answering his first question.

" The goddess is great," he replied.

She looked at him still with mistrust. There was a faint remote smile in the dark eyes lifted to her, though the face was hollow with suffering. The vagabond divined her hesitation, and was mocking her.

" Stay here upon the steps," she said. " A slave will show you the shelter."

" The lady of Egypt is gracious."

She went down the rocky path of the humped peninsula, in her gilded sandals. Beautiful were her ivory feet, beneath the white tunic, and above the saffron mantle her dusky-blonde head bent as with endless musings. A woman entangled in her own dream. The man smiled a little, half-bitterly, and sat again on the step to wait, drawing his mantle round him, in the cold twilight.

At length a slave appeared, also in hodden grey.

" Seek ye the shelter of our lady ? " he said insolently.

" Even so."

" Then come."

With the brusque insolence of a slave waiting on a vagabond, the young fellow led through the trees and down into a little gully in the rock, where, almost in darkness, was a small cave, with a litter of the tall heaths that grew on the waste places of the coast, under the stone-pines. The place was dark, but absolutely silent from the wind. There was still a faint odour of goats.

" Here sleep ! " said the slave. " For the goats come no more on this half-island. And there is water ! " He pointed to a little basin of rock where the maidenhair fern fringed a dripping mouthful of water.

Having scornfully bestowed his patronage, the slave departed. The man who had died climbed out to the tip of the peninsula, where the wave thrashed. It was rapidly getting dark, and the stars were coming out. The wind was abating for the night. Inland, the steep grooved upslope was dark to the long wavering outline of the crest against the translucent sky. Only now and then, a lantern flickered towards the villa.

The man who had died went back to the shelter. There he took bread from his leather pouch, dipped it in the water of the tiny spring, and slowly ate. Having eaten and washed his mouth, he looked once more at the bright stars in the pure windy sky, then settled the heath for his bed. Having laid his hat and his sandals aside, and put his pouch under his cheek for a pillow, he slept, for he was very tired. Yet during the night the cold woke him, pinching wearily through his weariness. Outside was brilliantly starry, and still windy. He sat and hugged himself in a sort of coma, and towards dawn went to sleep again.

In the morning the coast was still chill in shadow, though the sun was up behind the hills, when the woman came down from the villa towards the goddess. The sea was fair and pale blue, lovely in newness, and at last the wind was still. Yet the waves broke white in the many rocks, and tore in the shingle of the little bay. The woman came slowly, towards her dream. Yet she was aware of an interruption.

As she followed the little neck of rock on to her peninsula, and climbed the slope between the trees to the temple, a slave came down and stood, making his obeisance. There was a faint insolence in his humility. " Speak ! " she said.

" Lady, the man is there, he still sleeps. Lady, may I speak ? "

" Speak ! " she said, repelled by the fellow.

" Lady, the man is an escaped malefactor."

The slave seemed to triumph in imparting the unpleasant news.

" By what sign ? "

" Behold his hands and feet ! Will the lady look on him ? "

" Lead on ! "

The slave led quickly over the mound of the hill down to the tiny ravine. There he stood aside, and the woman went into the crack towards the cave. Her heart beat a little. Above all she must preserve her temple inviolate.

The vagabond was asleep with his cheek on his scrip, his mantle wrapped round him, but his bare, soiled feet curling side by side, to keep each other warm, and his hand lying loosely clenched in sleep. And in the pale skin of his feet usually covered by sandal-straps, she saw the scars, and in the palm of the loose hand.

She had no interest in men, particularly in the servile class. Yet she looked at the sleeping face. It was worn, hollow, and rather ugly. But, a true priestess, she saw the other kind of beauty in it, the sheer stillness of the deeper life. There was even a sort of majesty in the dark brows, over the still, hollow cheeks. She saw that his black hair, left long, in contrast to the Roman fashion, was touched with gray at the temples, and the black pointed beard had threads of gray. But that must be suffering or misfortune, for the man was young. His dusky skin had the silvery glisten of youth still.

There was a beauty of much suffering, and the strange calm candour of finer life in the whole delicate ugliness of the face. For the first time she was touched on the quick at the sight of a man, as if the tip of a fine flame of living had touched her. It was the first time. Men had roused all kinds of feeling in her, but never had touched her with the flame-tip of life.

She went back under the rock to where the slave waited.

" Know ! " she said. " This is no malefactor, but a free citizen of the east. Do not disturb him. But when he comes forth, bring him to me ; tell him I would speak with him."

She spoke coldly, for she found slaves invariably repellent, a little repulsive. They were so embedded in the lesser life, and their appetites and their small consciousness were a little disgusting. So she wrapped her dream round her, and went to the temple, where a slave-girl brought winter roses and jasmine, for the altar. But to-day, even in her ministrations, she was disturbed.

The sun rose over the hill, sparkling, the light fell triumphantly on the little pine-covered peninsula of the coast, and on the pink temple, in the pristine newness. The man who had died woke up, and put on his sandals. He put on his hat too, slung his scrip under his mantle, and went out, to see the morning in all its blue and its new gold. He glanced at the little yellow-and-white narcissus sparkling gaily in the rocks. And he saw the slave waiting for him like a menace.

" Master ! " said the slave. " Our lady would speak with you at the house of Isis."

" It is well," said the wanderer.

He went slowly, staying to look at the pale blue sea like a flower in unruffled bloom, and the white fringes among the rocks, like white rock-flowers, the hollow slopes sheering up high from the shore, grey with olive-trees and green with bright young wheat, and set with the white small villa. All fair and pure in the January morning.

The sun fell on the corner of the temple, he sat down on the step in the sunshine, in the infinite patience of waiting. He had come back to life, but not the same life that he had left, the life of little people and the little day. Re-born, he was in the other life, the greater day of the human consciousness. And he was alone and apart from the little day, and out of contact with the daily people. Not yet had he accepted the irrevocable *noli me tangere* which separates the re-born from the vulgar. The separation was absolute, as yet here at the temple he felt peace, the hard, bright pagan peace with hostility of slaves beneath.

The woman came into the dark inner doorway of the temple, from the shrine, and stood there, hesitating. She could see the dark figure of the man, sitting in that terrible stillness that was portentous to her, had something almost menacing in its patience.

She advanced across the outer chamber of the temple, and the man, becoming aware of her, stood up. She addressed him in Greek, but he said :

" Madam, my Greek is limited. Allow me to speak vulgar Syrian."

" Whence come you ? Whither go you ? " she asked, with a hurried preoccupation of a priestess.

" From the east beyond Damascus—and I go west as the road goes," he replied slowly.

She glanced at him with sudden anxiety and shyness.

" But why do you have the marks of a malefactor ? " she asked abruptly.

" Did the Lady of Isis spy upon me in my sleep ? " he asked, with a gray weariness.

" The slave warned me—your hands and feet——" she said.

He looked at her. Then he said :

" Will the Lady of Isis allow me to bid her farewell, and go up to the road ? "

The wind came in a sudden puff, lifting his mantle and his hat. He put up his hand to hold the brim, and she saw again the thin brown hand with its scar.

" See ! The scar ! " she said, pointing.

" Even so ! " he said. " But farewell, and to Isis my homage and my thanks for sleep."

He was going. But she looked up at him with her wondering blue eyes.

" Will you not look at Isis ? " she said, with sudden impulse. And something stirred in him, like pain.

" Where then ? " he said.

" Come ! "

He followed her into the inner shrine, into the almost-darkness.

When his eyes got used to the faint glow of the lamp, he saw the goddess striding like a ship, eager in the swirl of her gown, and he made his obeisance.

"Great is Isis!" he said. "In her search she is greater than death. Wonderful is such walking in a woman, wonderful the goal. All men praise thee, Isis, thou greater than the mother unto man."

The woman of Isis heard, and threw incense on the brazier. Then she looked at the man.

"Is it well with thee here?" she asked him. "Has Isis brought thee home to herself?"

He looked at the priestess in wonder and trouble.

"I know not," he said.

But the woman was pondering that this was the lost Osiris. She felt it in the quick of her soul. And her agitation was intense.

He would not stay in the close, dark, perfumed shrine. He went out again to the morning, to the cold air. He felt something approaching to touch him, and all his flesh was still woven with pain and the wild commandment: *Noli me tangere!* Touch me not! Oh, don't touch me!

The woman followed into the open with timid eagerness. He was moving away.

"O stranger, do not go! O stay awhile with Isis!"

He looked at her, at her face open like a flower, as if a sun had risen in her soul. And again his loins stirred.

"Would you detain me, girl of Isis?" he said.

"Stay! I am sure you are Osiris!" she said.

He laughed suddenly. "Not yet!" he said. Then he looked at her wistful face. "But I will sleep another night in the cave of the goats, if Isis wills it," he added.

She put her hands together with a priestess's childish happiness.

"Ah! Isis will be glad!" she said.

So he went down to the shore, in great trouble, saying to himself: "Shall I give myself into this touch? Shall I give myself into this touch? Men have tortured me to death with their touch. Yet this girl of Isis is a tender flame of healing. I am a physician, yet I have no healing like the flame of this tender girl. The flame of this tender girl! Like the first pale crocus of the spring. How could I have been blind to the healing and the bliss in the crocus-like body of a tender woman! Ah, tenderness! More terrible and lovely than the death I died——"

He pried small shell-fish from the rocks, and ate them with relish and wonder for the simple taste of the sea. And inwardly, he was tremulous, thinking: " Dare I come into touch? For this is further than death. I have dared to let them lay hands on me and put me to death. But dare I come into this tender touch of life? Oh, this is harder——"

But the woman went into the shrine again, and sat rapt in pure muse, through the long hours, watching the swirling stride of the yearning goddess, and the navel of the bud-like belly, like a seal on the virgin urge of the search. And she gave herself to the woman-flow and to the urge of Isis in Search.

Towards sundown she went on the peninsula to look for him. And she found him gone towards the sun, as she had gone the day before, and sitting on the pine-needles at the foot of the tree, where she had stood when first she saw him. Now she approached tremulously and slowly, afraid lest he did not want her. She stood near him unseen, till suddenly he glanced up at her from under his broad hat, and saw the westering sun in her netted hair. He was startled, yet he expected her.

" Is that your home? " he said, pointing to the white low villa on the slope of olives.

" It is my mother's house. She is a widow, and I am her only child."

" And are these all her slaves? "

" Except those that are mine."

Their eyes met for a moment.

" Will you too sit to see the sun go down? " he said.

He had not risen to speak to her. He had known too much pain. So she sat on the dry brown pine-needles, gathering her saffron mantle round her knees. A boat was coming in, out of the open glow into the shadow of the bay, and slaves were lifting small nets, their babble coming off the surface of the water.

" And this is home to you," he said.

" But I serve Isis in Search," she replied.

He looked at her. She was like a soft, musing cloud, somehow remote. His soul smote him with passion and compassion.

" Mayst thou find thy desire, maiden," he said, with sudden earnestness.

" And art thou not Osiris? " she asked.

He flushed suddenly.

" Yes, if thou wilt heal me ! " he said. " For the death aloofness is still upon me, and I cannot escape it."

She looked at him for a moment in fear, from the soft blue sun of her eyes. Then she lowered her head, and they sat in silence in the warmth and glow of the western sun : the man who had died, and the woman of the pure search.

The sun was curving down to the sea, in grand winter splendour. It fell on the twinkling, naked bodies of the slaves, with their ruddy broad hams and their small black heads, as they ran spreading the nets on the pebble beach. The all-tolerant Pan watched over them. All-tolerant Pan should be their god for ever.

The woman rose as the sun's rim dipped, saying :

" If you will stay, I shall send down victual and covering."

" The lady your mother, what will she say ? "

The woman of Isis looked at him strangely, but with a tinge of misgiving.

" It is my own," she said.

" It is good," he said, smiling faintly, and foreseeing difficulties.

He watched her go, with her absorbed, strange motion of the self-dedicate. Her dun head was a little bent, the white linen swung about her ivory ankles. And he saw the naked slaves stand to look at her, with a certain wonder, and even a certain mischief. But she passed intent through the door in the wall, on the bay.

The man who had died sat on at the foot of the tree overlooking the strand, for on the little shore everything happened. At the small stream which ran in round the corner of the property wall, women slaves were still washing linen, and now and again came the hollow chock ! chock ! chock ! as they beat it against the smooth stones, in the dark little hollow of the pool. There was a smell of olive-refuse on the air ; and sometimes still the faint rumble of the grindstone that was milling the olives, inside the garden, and the sound of the slave calling to the ass at the mill. Then through the doorway a woman stepped, a gray-haired woman in a mantle of whitish wool, and there followed her a bare-headed man in a toga, a Roman : probably her steward or overseer. They stood on the high shingle above the sea, and cast round a rapid glance. The broad-hammed, ruddy-bodied slaves bent absorbed and abject over the nets, picking them clean, the women washing linen thrust their palms with energy down on the wash, the old slave bent absorbed at the water's edge, washing the fish and the polyps of the catch. And the woman and the overseer saw it all, in one glance. They also saw, seated at the foot of the tree on the rocks of the peninsula, the strange man silent and alone. And the man who had died saw that they spoke of him. Out of the little sacred world of the peninsula he looked on the common world, and saw it still hostile.

The sun was touching the sea, across the tiny bay stretched the shadow of the opposite humped headland. Over the shingle, now blue and cold in shadow, the elderly woman trod heavily, in shadow too, to look at the fish spread in the flat basket of the old man crouching at the water's edge : a naked old slave with fat hips and shoulders, on whose soft, fairish-orange body the last sun twinkled, then died. The old slave continued cleaning the fish absorbedly, not looking up : as if the lady were the shadow of twilight falling on him.

Then from the gateway stepped two slave-girls with flat baskets on their heads, and from one basket the terra-cotta wine-jar and the oil-jar poked up, leaning slightly. Over the massive shingle, under the wall, came the girls, and the woman of Isis in her saffron mantle stepped in twilight after them. Out at sea, the sun still shone. Here was shadow. The mother with gray head stood at the sea's edge and watched the daughter, all yellow and white, with dun blonde head, swinging unseeing and unheeding after the slave-girls, towards the neck of rock of the peninsula ; the daughter, travelling in her absorbed other-world. And not moving from her place, the elderly mother watched that procession of three file up the rise of the headland, between the trees, and disappear, shut in by trees. No slave had lifted a head to look. The gray-haired woman still watched the trees where her daughter had disappeared. Then she glanced again at the foot of the tree, where the man who had died was still sitting, inconspicuous now, for the sun had left him ; and only the far blade of the sea shone bright. It was evening. Patience ! Let destiny move !

The mother plodded with a stamping stride up the shingle : not long and swinging and rapt, like the daughter, but short and determined. Then down the rocks opposite came two naked slaves trotting with huge bundles of dark green on their shoulders, so that their broad, naked legs twinkled underneath like insects' legs, and their heads were hidden. They came trotting across the shingle, heedless and intent on their way, when suddenly the man, the Roman-looking overseer, addressed them, and they stopped dead. They stood invisible under their loads, as if they might disappear altogether, now they were arrested. Then a hand came out and pointed to the peninsula. Then the two green-heaped slaves trotted on, towards the temple precincts. The gray-haired woman joined the man, and slowly the two passed through the door again, from the shingle of the sea to the property of the villa. Then the old, fat-shouldered slave rose, pallid in the shadow, with his tray of fish from the sea, and the woman rose from the pool, dusky and alive, piling the wet linen in a heap on to the flat baskets, and the slaves who had cleaned the net gathered its whitish folds together. And the old slave with the fish basket on his shoulder, and the women slaves with the heaped baskets of wet linen on their heads, and the two slaves with the folded net, and the slave with oars on his shoulders, and the boy with the folded sail on his arm, gathered in a naked group near the door, and the man who had died heard the low buzz of their chatter. Then as the wind wafted cold, they began to pass through the door.

It was the life of the little day, the life of little people. And the man who had died said to himself : " Unless we encompass it in the greater day, and set the little life in the circle of the greater life, all is disaster."

Even the tops of the hills were in shadow. Only the sky was still upwardly radiant. The sea was a vast milky shadow. The man who had died rose a little stiffly, and turned into the grove.

There was no one at the temple. He went on to his lair in the rock. There, the slave-men had carried out the old heath of the bedding, swept the rock floor, and were spreading with nice art the myrtle, then the rougher heath, then the soft, bushy heath-tips on top, for a bed. Over it all they put a well-tanned white ox-skin. The maids had laid folded woollen covers at the head of the cave, and the wine-jar, the oil-jar, a terra-cotta drinking-cup, and a basket containing bread, salt, cheese, dried figs and eggs, stood neatly arranged. There was also a little brazier of charcoal. The cave was suddenly full, and a dwelling-place.

The woman of Isis stood in the hollow by the tiny spring.

Only one slave at a time could pass. The girl-slaves waited at the entrance to the narrow place. When the man who had died appeared, the woman sent the girls away. The men-slaves still arranged the bed, making the job as long as possible. But the woman of Isis dismissed them too. And the man who had died came to look at his house.

" Is it well ? " the woman asked him.

" It is very well," the man replied. " But the lady, your mother, and he who is no doubt the steward, watched while the slaves brought the goods. Will they not oppose you ? "

" I have my own portion ! Can I not give of my own ? Who is going to oppose me and the gods ? " she said, with a certain soft fury, touched with exasperation. So that he knew that her mother would oppose her, and that the spirit of the little life would fight against the spirit of the greater. And he thought : " Why did the woman of Isis relinquish her portion in the daily world ? She should have kept her goods fiercely ! "

" Will you eat and drink ? " she said. " On the ashes are warm eggs. And I will go up to the meal at the villa. But in the second hour of the night I shall come down to the temple. O, then, will you come too to Isis ? " She looked at him, and a queer glow dilated her eyes. This was her dream, and it was greater than herself. He could not bear to thwart her or hurt her in the least thing now. She was in the full glow of her woman's mystery.

" Shall I wait at the temple ? " he said.

" O, wait at the second hour and I shall come." He heard the humming supplication in her voice and his fibres quivered.

" But the lady, your mother ? " he said gently.

The woman looked at him, startled.

" She will not thwart me ! " she said.

So he knew that the mother would thwart the daughter, for the daughter had left her goods in the hands of her mother, who would hold fast to this power.

But she went, and the man who had died lay reclining on his couch, and ate the eggs from the ashes, and dipped his bread in oil, and ate it, for his flesh was dry : and he mixed wine and water, and drank. And so he lay still, and the lamp made a small bud of light.

He was absorbed and enmeshed in new sensations. The woman of Isis was lovely to him, not so much in form, as in the wonderful womanly glow of her. Suns beyond suns had dipped her in mysterious fire, the mysterious fire of a potent woman, and to touch her was like touching the sun. Best of all was her tender desire for him, like sunshine, so soft and still.

" She is like sunshine upon me," he said to himself, stretching his limbs. " I have never before stretched my limbs in such sunshine, as her desire for me. The greatest of all gods granted me this."

At the same time he was haunted by the fear of the outer world. " If they can, they will kill us," he said to himself. " But there is a law of the sun which protects us."

And again he said to himself : " I have risen naked and branded. But if I am naked enough for this contact, I have not died in vain. Before I was clogged."

He rose and went out. The night was chill and starry, and of a great wintry splendour. "There are destinies of splendour," he said to the night, " after all our doom of littleness and meanness and pain."

So he went up silently to the temple, and waited in darkness against the inner wall, looking out on a gray darkness, stars, and rims of trees. And he said again to himself : " There are destinies of splendour, and there is a greater power."

So at last he saw the light of her silk lanthorn swinging, coming intermittent between the trees, yet coming swiftly. She was alone, and near, the light softly swishing on her mantle-hem. And he trembled with fear and with joy, saying to himself : " I am almost more afraid of this touch than I was of death. For I am more nakedly exposed to it."

" I am here, Lady of Isis," he said softly out of the dark.

" Ah ! " she cried, in fear also, yet in rapture. For she was given to her dream.

She unlocked the door of the shrine, and he followed after her. Then she latched the door shut again. The air inside was warm and close and perfumed. The man who had died stood by the closed door, and watched the woman. She had come first to the goddess. And dim-lit, the goddess-statue stood surging forward, a little fearsome like a great woman-presence urging.

The priestess did not look at him. She took off her saffron mantle and laid it on a low couch. In the dim light she was bare armed, in her girdled white tunic. But she was still hiding herself away from him. He stood back in shadow, and watched her softly fan the brazier and fling on incense. Faint clouds of sweet aroma arose on the air. She turned to the statue in the ritual of approach, softly swaying forward with a slight lurch, liked a moored boat, tipping towards the goddess.

He watched the strange rapt woman, and he said to himself : " I must leave her alone in her rapture, her female mysteries." So she tipped in her strange forward-swaying rhythm before the goddess. Then she broke into a murmur of Greek, which he could not understand. And, as she murmured, her swaying softly subsided, like a boat on a sea that grows still. And as he watched her, he saw her soul in its aloneness, and its female difference. He said to himself : How different she is from me, how strangely different ! She is afraid of me, and my male difference. She is getting herself naked and clear of her fear. How sensitive and softly alive she is, with a life so different from mine ! How beautiful with a soft strange courage of life, so different from my courage of death ! What a beautiful thing, like the heart of a rose, like the core of a flame. She is making herself completely penetrable. Ah ! how terrible to fail her, or to trespass on her !

She turned to him, her face glowing from the goddess.

" You are Osiris, aren't you ? " she said naively.

" If you will," he said.

" Will you let Isis discover you ?   Will you not take off your things ? "

He looked at the woman, and lost his breath.   And his wounds, and especially the death-wound through his belly, began to cry again.

" It has hurt so much ! " he said.   " You must forgive me if I am still held back."

But he took off his cloak and his tunic, and went naked towards the idol, his breast panting with the sudden terror of overwhelming pain, memory of overwhelming pain, and grief too bitter.

" They did me to death ! " he said in excuse of himself, turning his face to her for a moment.

And she saw the ghost of the death in him, as he stood there thin and stark before her, and suddenly she was terrified, and she felt robbed.   She felt the shadow of the gray, grisly wing of death triumphant.

" Ah, Goddess," he said to the idol, in the vernacular.   " I would be so glad to live, if you would give me my clue again."

For here again he felt desperate, faced by the demand of life, and burdened still by his death.

" Let me anoint you ! " the woman said to him softly.   " Let me anoint the scars !   Show me, and let me anoint them ! "

He forgot his nakedness in this re-evoked old pain.   He sat on the edge of the couch, and she poured a little ointment into the palm of his hand.   And as she chafed his hand, it all came back, the nails, the holes, the cruelty, the unjust cruelty against him who had offered only kindness.   The agony of injustice and cruelty came over him again, as in his death-hour.   But she chafed the palm, murmuring : " What was torn becomes a new flesh, what was a wound is full of fresh life ; this scar is the eye of the violet."

And he could not help smiling at her, in her naive priestess's absorption.   This was her dream, and he was only a dream-object to her.   She would never know or understand what he was.   Especially she would never know the death that was gone before in him.   But what did it matter ?   She was different.   She was woman : her life and her death were different from his.   Only she was good to him.

When she chafed his feet with oil and tender, tender healing, he could not refrain from saying to her :

" Once a woman washed my feet with tears, and wiped them with her hair, and poured on precious ointment."

The woman of Isis looked up at him from her earnest work, interrupted again.

" Were they hurt then ? " she said. " Your feet ? "

" No, no ! It was while they were whole."

" And did you love her ? "

" Love had passed in her. She only wanted to serve," he replied. " She had been a prostitute."

" And did you let her serve you ? " she asked.

" Yea."

" Did you let her serve you with the corpse of her love ? "

" Ay ! "

Suddenly it dawned on him : I asked them all to serve me with the corpse of their love. And in the end I offered them only the corpse of my love. This is my body—take and eat—my corpse——

A vivid shame went through him. " After all," he thought, " I wanted them to love with dead bodies. If I had kissed Judas with live love, perhaps he would never have kissed me with death. Perhaps he loved me in the flesh, and I willed that he should love me bodylessly, with the corpse of love——"

There dawned on him the reality of the soft warm love which is in touch, and which is full of delight. " And I told them, blessed are they that mourn," he said to himself. " Alas, if I mourned even this woman here, now I am in death, I should have to remain dead, and I want so much to live. Life has brought me to this woman with warm hands. And her touch is more to me now than all my words. For I want to live——"

" Go then to the goddess ! " she said softly, gently pushing him towards Isis. And as he stood there dazed and naked as an unborn thing, he heard the woman murmuring to the goddess, murmuring, murmuring with a plaintive appeal. She was stooping now, looking at the scar in the soft flesh of the socket of his side, a scar deep and like an eye sore with endless weeping, just in the soft socket above the hip. It was here that his blood had left him, and his essential seed. The woman was trembling softly and murmuring in Greek. And he in the recurring dismay of having died, and in the anguished perplexity of having tried to force life, felt his wounds crying aloud, and the deep places of the body howling again : " I have been murdered, and I lent myself to murder. They murdered me, but I lent myself to murder——"

The woman, silent now, but quivering, laid oil in her hand and put her palm over the wound in his right side. He winced, and the wound absorbed his life again, as thousands of times before. And in the dark, wild pain and panic of his consciousness rang only one cry : " Oh, how can she take this death out of me ? How can she take from me this death ? She can never know ! She can never understand ! She can never equal it ! . . ."

In silence, she softly rhythmically chafed the scar with oil. Absorbed now in her priestess's task, softly, softly gathering power, while the vitals of the man howled in panic. But as she gradually gathered power, and passed in a girdle round him to the opposite scar, gradually warmth began to take the place of the cold terror, and he felt : " I am going to be warm again, and I am going to be whole ! I shall be warm like the morning. I shall be a man. It doesn't need understanding. It needs newness. She brings me newness——"

And he listened to the faint, ceaseless wail of distress of his wounds, sounding as if for ever under the horizons of his consciousness. But the wail was growing dim, more dim.

He thought of the woman toiling over him : " She does not know ! She does not realize the death in me. But she has another consciousness. She comes to me from the opposite end of the night."

Having chafed all his lower body with oil, having worked with her slow intensity of a priestess, so that the sound of his wounds grew dimmer and dimmer, suddenly she put her breast against the wound in his left side, and her arms round him, folding over the wound in his right side, and she pressed him to her, in a power of living warmth, like the folds of a river. And the wailing died out altogether, and there was a stillness, and darkness in his soul, un-broken dark stillness, wholeness.

Then slowly, slowly, in the perfect darkness of his inner man, he felt the stir of something coming. A dawn, a new sun. A new sun was coming up in him, in the perfect inner darkness of himself. He waited for it breathless, quivering with a fearful hope. . . . " Now I am not myself. I am something new. . . ."

And as it rose, he felt, with a cold breath of disappointment, the girdle of the living woman slip down from him, the warmth and the glow slipped from him, leaving him stark. She crouched, spent, at the feet of the goddess, hiding her face.

Stooping, he laid his hand softly on her warm, bright shoulder, and the shock of desire went through him, shock after shock, so that he wondered if it were another sort of death : but full of magnificence.

Now all his consciousness was there in the crouching, hidden woman. He stooped beside her and caressed her softly, blindly, murmuring inarticulate things. And his death and his passion of sacrifice were all as nothing to him now, he knew only the crouching fulness of the woman there, the soft white rock of life. . . . " On this rock I built my life." The deep-folded, penetrable rock of the living woman ! The woman, hiding her face. Himself bending over, powerful and new like dawn.

He crouched to her, and he felt the blaze of his manhood and his power rise up in his loins, magnificent.

" I am risen ! "

Magnificent, blazing indomitable in the depths of his loins, his own sun dawned, and sent its fire running along his limbs, so that his face shone unconsciously.

He untied the string on the linen tunic, and slipped the garment down, till he saw the white glow of her white-gold breasts. And he touched them, and he felt his life go molten. " Father ! " he said, " why did you hide this from me ? " And he touched her with the poignancy of wonder, and the marvellous piercing transcendence of desire. " Lo ! " he said, " this is beyond prayer." It was the deep, interfolded warmth, warmth living and penetrable, the woman, the heart of the rose ! My mansion is the intricate warm rose, my joy is this blossom !

She looked up at him suddenly, her face like a lifted light, wistful, tender, her eyes like many wet flowers. And he drew her to his breast with a passion of tenderness and consuming desire, and the last thought : " My hour is upon me, I am taken unawares——"

So he knew her, and was one with her.

Afterwards, with a dim wonder, she touched the great scars in his sides with her finger-tips, and said :

" But they no longer hurt ? "

" They are suns ! " he said. " They shine from your touch. They are my atonement with you."

And when they left the temple, it was the coldness before dawn. As he closed the door, he looked again at the goddess, and he said : " Lo, Isis is a kindly goddess ; and full of tenderness. Great gods are warm-hearted, and have tender goddesses."

The woman wrapped herself in her mantle and went home in silence, sightless, brooding like the lotus softly shutting again, with its gold core full of fresh life. She saw nothing, for her own petals were a sheath to her. Only she thought : " I am full of Osiris. I am full of the risen Osiris ! . . ."

But the man looked at the vivid stars before dawn, as they rained down to the sea, and the dogstar green towards the sea's rim. And he thought : " How plastic it is, how full of curves and folds like an invisible rose of dark-petalled openness that shows where the dew touches its darkness ! How full it is, and great beyond all gods. How it leans around me, and I am part of it, the great rose of Space. I am like a grain of its perfume, and the woman is a grain of its beauty. Now the world is one flower of many petalled darknesses, and I am in its perfume as in a touch."

So, in the absolute stillness and fulness of touch, he slept in his cave while the dawn came. And after the dawn, the wind rose and brought a storm, with cold rain. So he stayed in his cave in the peace and the delight of being in touch, delighting to hear the sea, and the rain on the earth, and to see one white-and-gold narcissus bowing wet, and still wet. And he said : " This is the great atonement, the being in touch. The gray sea and the rain, the wet narcissus and the woman I wait for, the invisible Isis and the unseen sun are all in touch, and at one."

He waited at the temple for the woman, and she came in the rain. But she said to him :

" Let me sit awhile with Isis. And come to me, will you come to me, in the second hour of night ? "

So he went back to the cave and lay in stillness and in the joy of being in touch, waiting for the woman who would come with the night, and consummate again the contact. Then when night came the woman came, and came gladly, for her great yearning too was upon her, to be in touch, to be in touch with him, nearer.

So the days came, and the nights came, and days came again, and the contact was perfected and fulfilled. And he said : " I will ask her nothing, not even her name, for a name would set her apart."

And she said to herself : " He is Osiris. I wish to know no more."

Plum-blossom blew from the trees, the time of the narcissus was past, anemones lit up the ground and were gone, the perfume of bean-field was in the air. All changed, the blossom of the universe changed its petals and swung round to look another way. The spring was fulfilled, a contact was established, the man and the woman were fulfilled of one another, and departure was in the air.

One day he met her under the trees, when the morning sun was hot, and the pines smelled sweet, and on the hills the last pear-bloom was scattering. She came slowly towards him, and in her gentle lingering, her tender hanging back from him, he knew a change in her.

" Hast thou conceived ? " he asked her.

" Why ? " she said.

" Thou art like a tree whose green leaves follow the blossom, full of sap. And there is a withdrawing about thee."

" It is so," she said. " I am with young by thee. Is it good ? "

" Yea ! " he said. " How should it not be good ? So the nightingale calls no more from the valley-bed. But where wilt thou bear the child, for I am naked of all but life."

" We will stay here," she said.

" But the lady, your mother ? "

A shadow crossed her brow. She did not answer.

" What when she knows ? " he said.

" She begins to know."

" And would she hurt you ? "

" Ah, not me ! What I have is all my own. And I shall be big with Osiris. . . . But thou, do you watch her slaves."

She looked at him, and the peace of her maternity was troubled by anxiety.

" Let not your heart be troubled ! " he said. " I have died the death once."

So he knew the time was come again for him to depart. He would go alone, with his destiny. Yet not alone, for the touch would be upon him, even as he left his touch on her. And invisible suns would go with him.

Yet he must go. For here on the bay the little life of jealousy and property was resuming sway again, as the suns of passionate fecundity relaxed their sway. In the name of property, the widow and her slaves would seek to be revenged on him for the bread he had eaten, and the living touch he had established, the woman he had delighted in. But he said : " Not twice ! They shall not now profane the touch in me. My wits against theirs."

So he watched. And he knew they plotted. So he moved from the little cave, and found another shelter, a tiny cove of sand by the sea, dry and secret under the rocks.

He said to the woman :

" I must go now soon. Trouble is coming to me from the slaves. But I am a man, and the world is open. But what is between us is good, and is established. Be at peace. And when the nightingale calls again from your valley-bed, I shall come again, sure as Spring."

She said : " O don't go ! Stay with me on half the island, and

I will build a house for you and me under the pine-trees by the temple, where we can live apart."

Yet she knew that he would go. And even she wanted the coolness of her own air around her, and the release from anxiety.

"If I stay," he said, "they will betray me to the Romans and to their justice. But I will never be betrayed again. So when I am gone, live in peace with the growing child. And I shall come again : all is good between us, near or apart. The suns come back in their seasons : and I shall come again."

"Do not go yet," she said. "I have set a slave to watch at the neck of the peninsula. Do not go yet, till the harm shows."

But as he lay in his little cove, on a calm, still night, he heard the soft knock of oars, and the bump of a boat against the rock. So he crept out to listen. And he heard the Roman overseer say :

"Lead softly to the goat's den. And Lysippus shall throw the net over the malefactor while he sleeps, and we will bring him before justice, and the Lady of Isis shall know nothing of it. . . ."

The man who had died caught a whiff of flesh from the oiled and naked slaves as they crept up, then the faint perfume of the Roman. He crept nearer to the sea. The slave who sat in the boat sat motionless, holding the oars, for the sea was quite still. And the man who had died knew him.

So out of the deep cleft of a rock he said, in a clear voice :

"Art thou not that slave who possessed the maiden under the eyes of Isis ? Art thou not the youth ? Speak !"

The youth stood up in the boat in terror. His movement sent the boat bumping against the rock. The slave sprang out in wild fear, and fled up the rocks. The man who had died quickly seized the boat and stepped in, and pushed off. The oars were yet warm with the unpleasant warmth of the hands of the slaves. But the man pulled slowly out, to get into the current which set down the coast, and would carry him in silence. The high coast was utterly dark against the starry night. There was no glimmer from the peninsula : the priestess came no more at night. The man who had died rowed slowly on, with the current, and laughed to himself : "I have sowed the seed of my life and my resurrection, and put my touch forever upon the choice woman of this day, and I carry her perfume in my flesh like essence of roses. She is dear to me in the middle of my being. But the gold and flowing serpent is coiling up again, to sleep at the root of my tree."

"So let the boat carry me. To-morrow is another day."